VICTORIA HOLT VICTORIA

VICTORIA HOLT

Bride of Pendorric

The Shadow
of the Lynx

King of the Castle

Mistress of Mellyn

Octopus / Heinemann

Bride of Pendorric was first published in the United States
by Doubleday & Company, Inc in 1963;
in Great Britain by William Collins Sons & Co. Ltd in 1963.
The Shadow of the Lynx was first published in the United States
by Doubleday & Company, Inc in 1971;
in Great Britain by William Collins Sons & Co. Ltd in 1971.
King of the Castle was first published in the United States
by Doubleday & Company, Inc in 1967;
in Great Britain by William Collins Sons & Co. Ltd in 1967.
Mistress of Mellyn was first published in the United States
by Doubleday & Company, Inc in 1960;
in Great Britain by William Collins Sons & Co. Ltd in 1961.

This edition first published in the United States of America
by arrangement with Doubleday & Company, Inc
in 1980 jointly by

William Heinemann Inc
450 Park Avenue,
New York, NY 10022

and

Octopus Books Inc
747 Third Avenue,
New York, NY 10017

ISBN 0 905712 51 X

Printed in the United States of America
by R. R. Donnelley and Sons Company.

CONTENTS

BRIDE OF PENDORRIC

Chapter One

I often marvelled after I went to Pendorric that one's existence could change so swiftly, so devastatingly. I had heard life compared with a kaleidoscope and this is how it appeared to me, for there was the pleasant scene full of peace and contentment when the pattern began to change, first here, then there, until the picture which confronted me was no longer calm and peaceful but filled with menace. I had married a man who seemed to me all that I wanted in a husband – solicitous, loving, passionately devoted; then suddenly it was as though I were married to a stranger.

I first saw Roc Pendorric when I came up from the beach one morning to find him sitting in the studio with my father; in his hands he held a terracotta statue for which I had been the original, a slim child of about seven. I remembered when my father had made it more than eleven years before; he had always said it was not for sale.

The blinds had not yet been drawn and the two men made a striking contrast sitting there in the strong sunlight: my father so fair, the stranger so dark. On the island my father was often called Angelo because of the fairness of his hair and skin and his almost guileless expression, for he was a very sweet-tempered man. It might have been because of this that I fancied there was something saturnine about his companion.

'Ah, here is my daughter Favel,' said my father as though they had been speaking of me.

They both stood up, the stranger towering above my father, who was of medium height. He took my hand and his long dark eyes studied me with something rather calculating in the intentness of his scrutiny. He was lean, which accentuated his height, and his hair was almost black; there was an expression in his alert eyes which made me feel he was seeking something which amused him, and it occurred to me that there might be a streak of malice in his amusement. He had rather pointed ears which gave him the look of a satyr. His was a face of contrasts; there was a gentleness about the full lips as well as sensuality; there was no doubt of the firmness of the jaw; there was arrogance in the long straight nose; and mingling with the undoubted humour in the quick eyes was a suggestion of mischief. I came to believe later that he fascinated me so quickly because I could not be sure of him; and it took me a very long time to discover the sort of man he was.

At that moment I wished that I had dressed before coming up from the beach.

'Mr. Pendorric has been looking round the studio,' said my father. 'He has bought the Bay of Naples water-colour.'

'I'm glad,' I answered. 'It's beautiful.'

He held out the little statue. 'And so is this.'

'I don't think that's for sale,' I told him.

'It's much too precious, I'm sure.'

He seemed to be comparing me with the figure and I guessed my father had told him – as he did everyone who admired it: 'That's my daughter when she was seven.'

'But,' he went on, 'I've been trying to persuade the artist to sell. After all, *he* still has the original.'

Father laughed in the rather hearty way he did when he was with customers who were ready to spend money, forced laughter. Father had always been happier creating his works of art than selling them. When my mother was alive she had done most of the selling; since I had left school, only a few months before this, I found myself taking it over. Father would give his work away to anyone who he thought appreciated it, and he needed a strong-minded woman to look after business transactions; that was why, after my mother had died, we became very poor. But since I had been at home, I flattered myself that we were beginning to pay our way.

'Favel, could you get us a drink?' my father asked.

I said I would if they would wait while I changed, and leaving them together went into my bedroom which led off the studio as did both our bedrooms. In a few minutes I had put on a blue linen dress, after which I went to our tiny kitchen to see about drinks; when I went back to the studio Father was showing the man a bronze Venus – one of our most expensive pieces.

If he buys that, I thought, I'll be able to settle a few bills. I would seize on the money and do it too, before Father had a chance of gambling it away at cards or roulette.

Roc Pendorric's eyes met mine over the bronze and, as I caught the flicker of amusement there, I guessed I must have shown rather clearly how anxious I was for him to buy it. He put it down and turned to me as though the statue couldn't hold his interest while I was there, and I felt annoyed with myself for interrupting them. Then I caught the gleam in his eyes and I wondered whether that was what he had expected me to feel.

He started to talk about the island then; he had arrived only yesterday, and had not even visited the villas of Tiberius and San Michele yet. But he had heard of Angelo's studio and the wonderful works of art to be picked up there; and so this had been his first excursion.

Father was flushed with pleasure; but I wasn't quite sure whether to believe him or not.

'And when I came and found that Angelo was Mr. Frederick Farington who spoke English like the native he is, I was even more delighted. My Italian is appalling, and the boasts of "English spoken here" are often . . . well, a little boastful. Please, Miss Farington, do tell me what I ought to see while I stay here.'

I started to tell him about the villas, the grottoes and the other well-known attractions. 'But,' I added, 'it always seems to me after coming back from

England that the scenery and the blue of the sea are the island's real beauties.'

'It would be nice to have a companion to share in my sight-seeing,' he said.

'Are you travelling alone?' I asked.

'Quite alone.'

'There are so many visitors to the island,' I said consolingly. 'You're sure to find someone who is eager to do the tours as you are.'

'It would be necessary, of course, to find the right companion . . . someone who really knows the island.'

'The guides do, of course.'

His eyes twinkled. 'I wasn't thinking of a guide.'

'The rest of the natives would no doubt be too busy.'

'I'll find what I want,' he assured me; and I had a feeling that he would.

He went over to the bronze Venus and began fingering it again.

'That attracts you,' I commented.

He turned to me and studied me as intently as he had the bronze. 'I'm enormously attracted,' he told me. 'I can't make up my mind. May I come back later?'

'But of course,' said Father and I simultaneously.

He did come back. He came back and back again. In my innocence I thought at first that he was hesitating about the bronze Venus; then I wondered whether it was the studio that attracted him because it probably seemed very bohemian to him, full of local colour and totally unlike the place he came from. One couldn't expect people to buy every time they came. It was a feature of our studio and others like it that people dropped in casually, stopped for a chat and a drink, browsed about the place and bought when something pleased them.

What disturbed me was that I was beginning to look forward to his visits. There were times when I was sure he came to see me, and there were others when I told myself that I was imagining this, and the thought depressed me.

Three days after his first visit I went down to one of the little beaches on the Marina Piccola to bathe, and he was there. We swam together and lay on the beach in the sun afterwards.

I asked if he was enjoying his stay.

'Beyond expectations,' he answered.

'You've been sightseeing, I expect.'

'Not much. I'd like to, but I still think it's dull alone.'

'Really? People usually complain of the awful crowds, not of being alone.'

'Mind you,' he pointed out, 'I wouldn't want *any* companion.' There was a suggestion in those long eyes which slightly tilted at the corners. I was sure, in that moment, that he was the type whom most women would find irresistible, and that he knew it. This knowledge disturbed me; I myself was becoming too conscious of that rather blatant masculinity and I wondered whether I had betrayed this to him.

I said rather coolly: 'Someone was asking about the bronze Venus this morning.'

His eyes shone with amusement. 'Oh well, if I miss it, I'll only have *myself* to blame.' His meaning was perfectly clear and I felt annoyed with him. Why did he think we kept a studio and entertained people there if not in the hope of selling things? How did he think we lived?

'We'd hate you to have it unless you were really keen about it.'

'But I never have anything that I'm not keen about,' he replied. 'Actually though, I prefer the figure of the younger Venus.'

'Oh . . . that!'

He put his hand on my arm and said: 'It's charming. Yes, I prefer her.'

'I simply must be getting back,' I told him.

He leaned on his elbow and smiled at me, and I had a feeling that he knew far too much of what was going on in my mind and was fully aware that I found his company extremely stimulating and wanted more of it – that he was something more to me than a prospective buyer.

He said lightly: 'Your father tells me that you're the commercial brains behind the enterprise. I bet he's right.'

'Artists need someone practical to look after them,' I replied. 'And now that my mother is dead . . .'

I knew that my voice changed when I spoke of her. It still happened, although she had been dead three years. Annoyed with myself as I always was when I betrayed emotion I said quickly: 'She died of T.B. They came here in the hope that it would be good for her. She was a wonderful manager.'

'And so you take after her.' His eyes were full of sympathy now and I was pleased out of all proportion that he should understand how I felt. I thought then that I had imagined that streak of mischief in him. Perhaps mischief was not the right description; but the fact was that while I was becoming more and more attracted by this man, I was often conscious of something within him that I could not understand, some quality, something which he was determined to keep hidden from me. This often made me uneasy, while it in no way decreased my growing interest in him, but rather added to it. Now I saw only his sympathy which was undoubtedly genuine.

'I hope so,' I answered. 'I think I do.'

'She must have been an excellent business woman.'

'She was.' I still could not control the pain in my voice as I remembered, and pictures of the past flashed in and out of my mind. I saw her – small and dainty, with the brilliant colour in her cheeks which was so becoming and a sign of her illness; that tremendous energy which was like a fire consuming her – until the last months. The island had seemed a different place when she was in it. In the beginning she had taught me to read and write and to be quick with figures. I remembered long lazy days when I lay on one of the little beaches or swam in the blue water or lay on my back and drifted; all the beauty of the place, all the echoes of ancient history were the background for one of the happiest existences a child could know. I had run wild, it was true. Sometimes I talked to the tourists; sometimes I joined the boatmen who took visitors to the grottoes or on tours of the island; sometimes I climbed the path to the villa of Tiberius and sat looking over the sea to Naples. Then I would come back to the studio and listen to the talk going on there; I shared my father's pride in his work, my mother's joy when she had succeeded in making a good sale.

They were so important to each other; and there were times when they seemed to me like two brilliant butterflies dancing in the sunshine, intoxicated with the joy of being alive because they knew that the sun of their happiness must go down quickly and finally.

I had been indignant when they told me I must go away to school in England. It was a necessity, my mother pointed out, for she had reached the limit of her capabilities, and although I was a tolerable linguist (we spoke English at home, Italian to our neighbours and, as there were many French and German visitors to our studio, I soon had a smattering of these languages) I had had no real education. My mother was anxious that I should go to her old school which was small and in the heart of Sussex. Her old headmistress was still in charge and I suspected that it was all very much as it had been in my mother's day. After a term or two I became reconciled, partly because I quickly made friends with Esther McBane, partly because I returned to the island for Christmas, Easter and summer holidays; and as I was a normal uncomplicated person I enjoyed both worlds.

But then my mother died and nothing was the same again. I found out that I had been educated on the jewellery which had once been hers; she had planned for me to go to a university, but the jewellery had realized less than she had hoped (for one quality she shared with my father was optimism) and the cost of my schooling was more than she had bargained for. So when she died I went back to school for two more years because that was her wish. Esther was a great comfort at that time; she was an orphan who was being brought up by an aunt, so she had a good deal of sympathy to offer. She came to stay with us during summer holidays and it helped both Father and me not to fret so much with a visitor in the studio. We said that she must come every summer, and she assured us she would. We left school at the same time and she came home with me at the end of our final term. During that holiday we would discuss what we were going to do with our lives. Esther planned to take up art seriously. As for myself, I had my father to consider, so I was going to try to take my mother's place in the studio although I feared that was something I should never be able to do entirely.

I smiled, remembering that long letter I had had from Esther, which in itself was unusual for Esther abhorred letter-writing and avoided it whenever possible. On the way back to Scotland she had met a man; he was growing tobacco in Rhodesia and was home for a few months. That letter had been full of this adventure. There had been one more letter two months later. Esther was getting married and going out to Rhodesia.

It was exciting and she was wonderfully happy; but I knew it was the end of our friendship because the only bond between us now could be through letters which Esther would have neither time nor inclination to write. I did have one to say that she had arrived, but marriage had made a different person of Esther; she had grown far from the long-legged untidy-haired girl who used to walk in the grounds of the little school with me and talk about dedicating herself to Art.

I was brought out of the past by the sight of Roc Pendorric's face close to mine, and now there was nothing but sympathy in his eyes. 'I've stirred up sad memories.'

'I was thinking about my mother and the past.'

He nodded and was silent for a few seconds. Then he said: 'You don't ever think of going back to her people . . . or your father's people?'

'People?' I murmured.

'Didn't she ever talk to you about her home in England?'

I was suddenly very surprised. 'No, she never mentioned it.'

'Perhaps the memory was unhappy.'

'I never realized it before, but neither of them ever talked about . . . before they married. As a matter of fact I think they felt that all that happened before was insignificant.'

'It must have been a completely happy marriage.'

'It was.'

We were silent again. Then he said: 'Favel! It's an unusual name.'

'No more unusual than yours. I always thought a roc was a legendary bird.'

'Fabulous, of immense size and strength, able to lift an elephant . . . if it wanted to.'

He spoke rather smugly and I retorted: 'I'm sure even you would be incapable of lifting an elephant. Is it a nick-name?'

'I've been Roc for as long as I can remember. But it's short for Petroc.'

'Still unusual.'

'Not in the part of the world I come from. I've had a lot of ancestors who had to put up with it. The original one was a sixth-century saint who founded a monastery. I think Roc is a modern version that's all my own. Do you think it suits me?'

'Yes,' I answered. 'I think it does.'

Rather to my embarrassment he leaned forward and kissed the tip of my nose. I stood up hastily. 'It really is time I was getting back to the studio,' I said.

Our friendship grew quickly and to me was wholly exciting. I did not realize then how inexperienced I was, and imagined that I was capable of dealing with any situation. I forgot then that my existence had been bounded by school in England with its regulations and restrictions, our casual unconventional studio on an island whose main preoccupation was with passing visitors, and my life with my father who still thought of me as a child. I had imagined myself to be a woman of the world, whereas no one who could lay a true claim to such a description would have fallen in love with the first man who seemed different from anyone else she had met.

But there was a magnetism about Roc Pendorric when he set himself out to charm, and he certainly was determined to charm me.

Roc came to the studio every day. He always took the statuette in his hands and caressed it lovingly.

'I'm determined to have it, you know,' he said one day.

'Father will never sell.'

'I never give up hope.' And as I looked at the strong line of his jaw, the brilliance of his dark eyes, I believed him. He was a man who would take what he wanted from life; and it occurred to me that there would be few to deny him. That was why he was so anxious to possess the statue. He hated to be frustrated.

He bought the bronze Venus then.

'Don't think,' he told me, 'that this means I've given up trying for the other. It'll be mine yet; you see.'

There was an acquisitive gleam in his eyes when he said that and a certain mischief too. I knew what he meant, of course.

We swam together. We explored the whole island and we usually chose the less well-known places to avoid the crowds. He hired two Neapolitan boatmen to take us on sea trips and there were wonderful days when we lay back in the boat letting our hands trail in the turquoise and emerald water while Guiseppe and Umberto, watching us with the indulgent looks Latins bestow on lovers, sang arias from Italian opera for our entertainment.

In spite of his dark looks there must have been something essentially English about Roc, because Guiseppe and Umberto were immediately aware of his nationality. This ability to decide a person's nationality often surprised me but it never seemed to fail. As for myself, there was little difficulty in placing me. My hair was dark blonde and there was a platinum-coloured streak in it which had been there when I was born; it had the effect of making me look even fairer than I was. My eyes were the shade of water, and borrowed their colour from what I was wearing. Sometimes they were green, at others quite blue. I had a short pert nose, a wide mouth and good teeth. I was by no means a beauty, but I had always looked more like a visitor to the island than a native.

During those weeks I was never quite sure of Roc. There were times when I was perfectly happy to enjoy each moment as it came along and not concern myself with the future; but when I was alone – at night, for instance – I wondered what I should do when he went home.

In those early days I knew the beginning of that frustration which later was to bring such fear and terror into my life. His gaiety often seemed to be a cloak for deeper feelings; even during his most tender moments I would imagine I saw speculation in his eyes. He intrigued me in a hundred ways. I knew that given any encouragement I could love him completely, but I was never sure of him, and perhaps that was one of the reasons why every moment I was with him held the maximum excitement.

One day soon after we met we climbed to the villa of Tiberius, and never had that wonderful view seemed so superb as it did on that day. It was all there for our delight as I had seen it many times before – Capri and Monte Solaro, the Gulf of Salerno from Amalfi to Paestum, the Gulf of Naples from Sorrento to Cape Misena. I knew it well, and yet because I was sharing it with Roc it had a new magic.

'Have you ever seen anything so enchanting?' I asked.

He seemed to consider. Then he said: 'I live in a place which seems to me as beautiful.'

'Where?'

'Cornwall. Our bay is beautiful – more so I think because it changes more often. Don't you get weary of sapphire seas? Now, I've seen ours as blue – or almost; I've seen it green under the beating rain and brown after a storm and pink in the dawn; I've seen it mad with fury pounding the rocks and sending the spray high, and I've seen it as silky as this sea. This is very beautiful, I grant you, and I don't think Roman emperors ever honoured us in Cornwall with their villas and legends of their dancing boys and girls, but we have a history of our own which is just as enthralling.'

'I've never been to Cornwall.'

He suddenly turned to me and I was caught in an embrace which made me gasp. He said, with his face pressed against mine: 'But you will . . . soon.'

I was conscious of the rose-red ruins, the greenish statue of the Madonna, the deep blue of the sea, and life seemed suddenly too wonderful to be true.

He had lifted me off my feet and held me above him, laughing at me.

I said primly: 'Someone will see us.'

'Do you care?'

'Well, I object to being literally swept off my feet.'

He released me and to my disappointment he did not say any more about Cornwall. That incident was typical of our relationship.

I realized that my father was taking a great interest in our friendship. He was always delighted to see Roc, and he would sometimes come to the door of the studio to meet us after we'd been out on one of our excursions, looking like a conspirator, I thought. He was not a subtle man and it did not take me long to discover that some plan was forming in his mind and that it concerned Roc and me.

Did he think that Roc would propose to me? Was Roc's feeling for me more marked than I dared hope, and had my father noticed this? And suppose I married Roc, what of the studio? How would my father get along without me? – because if I married Roc I should have to go away with him.

I felt unsettled. I knew I wanted to marry Roc – but I was not sure about his feelings for me. How could I leave my father? But I had when I was at school, I reminded myself. Yes, and look at the result. Right from the beginning, being in love with Roc was an experience that kept me poised between ecstasy and anxiety.

But Roc had not talked of marriage.

Father often asked him to a meal; invitations Roc always accepted on condition that he should provide the wine. I cooked omelettes, fish, pasta and even roast beef with Yorkshire pudding; the meals were well cooked because one of the things my mother had taught me was how to cook, and there had always been a certain amount of English dishes served in the studio.

Roc seemed to enjoy those meals thoroughly and would sit long over them talking and drinking. He began to talk a great deal about himself and his home in Cornwall; but he had a way of making Father talk, and he quickly learned about how we lived, the difficulties of making enough money during the tourist season to keep us during the lean months. I noticed that Father never discussed the time before his marriage, and Roc only made one or two attempts to persuade him. Then he gave it up, which was strange, because he was usually persistent – but it was characteristic of Roc simply because it was unexpected.

I remember one day coming in and finding them playing cards together. Father had that look on his face which always frightened me – that intent expression which made his eyes glow like blue fires; there was a faint pink colour in his cheeks, and as I came in he scarcely looked up.

Roc got up from his chair, but I could see that he shared my father's feeling for the game. I felt very uneasy as I thought: So he's a gambler too.

'Favel won't want to interrupt the game,' said my father.

I looked into Roc's eyes and said coldly: 'I hope you aren't playing for high stakes.'

'Don't worry your head about that, my dear,' said Father.

'He's determined to lure the lire from my pockets,' added Roc, his eyes sparkling.

'I'll go and get something to eat,' I told them, and went into the kitchen.

I shall have to make him understand Father can't afford to gamble, I told myself.

When we sat over the meal my father was jubilant, so I guessed he had won.

I spoke to Roc about it the next day at the beach.

'Please don't encourage my father to gamble. He simply can't afford it.'

'But he gets so much pleasure from it,' he replied.

'Lots of people get pleasure from things that aren't good for them.'

He laughed. 'You know, you're a bit of a martinet.'

'Please listen to me. We're not rich enough to risk losing money that has been so hard to come by. We live here very cheaply, but it's not easy. Is that impossible for you to understand?'

'Please don't worry, Favel,' he said, putting his hand over mine.

'Then you won't play for money with him any more?'

'Suppose he asks me? Shall I say, I decline the invitation because your strong-minded daughter forbids us?'

'You could do better than that.'

He looked pious. 'But it wouldn't be true.'

I shrugged my shoulders impatiently. 'Surely you can find other people to gamble with. Why do you have to choose him?'

He looked thoughtful and said: 'I suppose it's because I like the atmosphere of his studio.' We were lying on the beach and he reached out and turned me towards him. Looking into my face he went on: 'I like the treasures he has there.'

It was in moments like this when I believed his feelings matched my own. I was elated and at the same time afraid I should betray too much. So I stood up quickly and walked into the sea; he was close behind me.

'Don't you know, Favel,' he said, putting an arm round my bare shoulder, 'that I want very much to please you?'

I had to turn and smile at him then. Surely, I thought, the look he gave me was one of love.

We were happy and carefree when we swam, and later, as we lay in the sun on the beach, I felt once more that supreme happiness which is being in love.

Yet two days later I came in from the market and found them sitting at the card table. The game was finished but I could see by my father's face that he had lost and by Roc's that he had won.

I felt my cheeks aflame and my eyes were hard as I looked into Roc's face. I said nothing but went straight into the kitchen with my basket. I set it down angrily and to my dismay found my eyes full of tears. Tears of fury, I told myself, because he had made a fool of me. He was not to be trusted. This was a clear indication of it; he promised one thing and did another.

I wanted to rush out of the studio, to find some quiet spot away from everyone where I could stay until I was calm enough to face him again.

I heard a voice behind me: 'What can I do to help?'

I turned and faced him. I was grateful that the tears had not fallen. They were merely making my eyes look more brilliant, and he should not guess how wretched I was.

I said shortly: 'Nothing. I can manage, thank you.'

I turned back to the table and then I felt him standing close to me; he had gripped my shoulders and was laughing.

He put his face close to my ear and whispered: 'I kept my promise, you know. We didn't play for money.'

I shook him off and went to a drawer of the table which I opened and rummaged in without knowing for what.

'Nonsense,' I retorted. 'The game wouldn't have meant a thing to either of you if there'd been no stakes. It isn't that you enjoy playing cards. It's win or lose. And of course you both think that you're going to win every time. It seems absurdly childish to me. One of you has to lose.'

'But you must understand that I kept my promise.'

'Please don't bother to explain. I can trust my eyes you know.'

'We were gambling . . . certainly. You're right when you said it wouldn't interest us if we were not. Who do you think won this time?'

'I have a meal to prepare.'

'I won this.' He put his hand in his pocket and drew out the statuette.

Then he laughed. 'I determined to get it by fair means or foul. Fortunately it turned out to be fair. So you see I kept my promise to you, I had my gamble, and I own this delightful creature.'

'Take the knives and forks for me, will you please?' I said.

He slipped the statue into his pocket and grinned at me. 'With the greatest pleasure.'

The next day he asked me to marry him. At his suggestion we had climbed the steep path to the Grotto of Matromania. I had always thought it the least exciting of the grottoes and the Blue, Green, Yellow and Red or the Grotto of the Saints were all more worth a visit, but Roc said he had not seen it and wanted me to take him there.

'A very appropriate spot,' he commented when we reached it.

I turned to look at him and he caught my arm and held it tightly.

'Why?' I asked.

'You know,' he replied.

But I was never sure of him – not even at this moment when he regarded me with so much tenderness.

'Matromania,' he murmured.

'I'd heard that this was dedicated to Mithromania known as Mithras,' I said quickly because I was afraid of betraying my feelings.

'Nonsense,' he replied. 'This is where Tiberius held his revels for young men and maidens. I read it in the guidebook. It means matrimony because they married here.'

'There seem to be two opinions then.'

'Then we'd better give it another reason for its importance. It's the spot where Petroc Pendorric asked Favel Farington to marry him and where she said ...'

He turned to me and in that moment I was certain he loved me as passionately as I loved him.

There was no need for me to answer.

We went back to the studio; he was elated and I was happier than I had ever been before.

Father was so delighted when we told him the news that it was almost as though he wished to get rid of me. He refused to discuss what he would do when I had gone, and I was terribly worried until Roc told me that he would insist on his accepting an allowance. Why shouldn't he from his own son-in-law? He'd commission some pictures if that would make it easier. Perhaps that would be a good idea. 'We've lots of bare wall space at Pendorric,' he added.

And for the first time I began to think seriously about the place which would be my home; but although Roc was always ready to talk of it in general, he said he wanted me to see it and judge for myself. If he talked to me too much I might imagine something entirely different and perhaps be disappointed – though I couldn't believe I could be disappointed in a home I shared with him.

We were very much in love. Roc seemed no longer a stranger. I felt I understood him. There was a streak of mischief in him and he loved to tease me. 'Because,' he told me once, 'you're too serious, too old-fashioned in many ways to be true.'

I pondered on that and supposed I was different from girls he had known, because of my upbringing – the intimate family circle, the school which was run on the same lines as it had been twenty or thirty years before. Also, of course, I had felt my responsibilities deeply when my mother had died. I must learn to be more lighthearted, gay, up-to-date, I told myself.

Our wedding was going to be very quiet; there would be a few guests from the English colony, and Roc and I were going to stay at the studio for a week afterwards; then we were to go to England.

I asked him what his family would think of his returning with a bride they had never met.

'I've written and told them we'll soon be home. They're not so surprised as you imagine. One thing they have learned to expect from me is the unexpected,' he replied cheerfully. 'They're wild with delight. You see they think it's the duty of all Pendorrics to marry, and they believe I've waited long enough.'

I wanted to hear more about them. I wanted to be prepared, but he always put me off.

'I'm not very good at describing things,' he answered. 'You'll be there soon enough.'

'But this Pendorric . . . I gather it is something of a mansion.'

'It's the family home. I suppose you could call it that.'

'And . . . who is the family?'

'My sister, her husband, their twin daughters. You don't have to worry, you know. They won't be in our wing. It's a family custom that all who can, remain at home, and bring their families to live there.'

'And it's near the sea.'

'Right on the coast. You're going to love it. All Pendorrics do, and you'll be one of them very soon.'

I think it was about a week before my wedding day that I noticed the change in my father.

I came in quietly one day and found him sitting at the table staring ahead of him, and because he had not seen me for a few moments I caught him in repose; he looked suddenly old; and more than that . . . frightened.

'Father,' I cried, 'what's the matter?'

He started up and he smiled but his heart wasn't in it.

'The matter? Why, nothing's the matter.'

'But you were sitting there . . .'

'Why shouldn't I? I've been working on that bust of Tiberius. It tired me.'

I accepted his excuse temporarily and forgot about it.

But not for long. My father had never been able to keep things to himself and I began to believe that he was hiding something from me, something which caused him the utmost anxiety.

One early morning, about two days before the wedding, I awoke to find someone moving about in the studio. The illuminated dial of my bedside clock said three o'clock.

I hastily put on a dressing-gown, quietly opened the door of my room and, peeping out, saw a dark shadow seated at the table.

'Father!' I cried.

He started up. 'My dear child, I've disturbed you. It's all right. Do go back to bed.'

I went to him and made him sit down. I drew up a chair. 'Look here,' I insisted, 'you'd better tell me what's wrong.'

He hesitated and then said: 'But it's nothing. I couldn't sleep, so I thought it would do me good to come and sit out here for a while.'

'But why couldn't you sleep? There's something on your mind, isn't there?'

'I'm perfectly all right.'

'It's no use saying that when it obviously isn't true. Are you worried about me . . . about my marrying?'

Again that slight pause. Of course that's it, I thought. Naturally he's worried. He's beginning to realize how he'll miss me.

He said: 'My dear child, you're very much in love with Roc, aren't you?'

'Yes, Father.'

'Favel . . . you're sure, aren't you?'

'Are you worried because we've known each other such a short while?'

He did not answer that but murmured: 'You'll go right away from here . . . to his place in Cornwall . . . to Pendorric.'

'But we'll come to see you! And you'll come to stay with us.'

'I think,' he went on, and it was as though he were talking to himself, 'that if something prevented your marriage it would break my heart.'

He stood up suddenly. 'I'm cold. Let's get back to bed. I'm sorry I disturbed you, Favel.'

'Father, we really ought to have a talk. I wish you would tell me everything that's on your mind.'

'You go along to bed, Favel. I'm sorry I disturbed you.'

He kissed me and we went to our rooms. How often later I was to reproach myself for allowing him to evade me like that. I ought to have insisted on knowing.

There came the day when Roc and I were married and I was so overwhelmed by new and exciting experiences that I did not give a thought to what was happening to my father. I couldn't think of anyone but myself and Roc during those days.

It was wonderful to be together every hour of the days and nights. We would laugh over trifles; it was really the laughter of happiness which comes so easily, I discovered. Guiseppe and Umberto were delighted with us; their arias were more fervent than they used to be, and after we had left them Roc and I would imitate them, gesticulating wildly, setting our faces into tragic or comic masks, whatever the songs demanded, and because we sang out of tune we laughed the more. He would come into the kitchen when I was cooking, to help me he said; and he would sit on the table getting in my way until with mock exasperation I would attempt to turn him out, which always ended up by my being in his arms.

The memories of those days were to stay with me during the difficult times ahead; they sustained me when I needed to be sustained.

Roc was, as I had known he would be, a passionate and demanding lover; he carried me along with him, but I often felt bemused by the rich experiences which were mine. Yet I was certain then that everything was going to be wonderful. I was content to live in the moment; I had even stopped wondering what my new home would be like; I assured myself that my father would have nothing to worry about. Roc would take care of his future as he would take care of mine.

Then one day I went down to the market alone and came back sooner than I had expected.

The door of the studio was open and I saw them there – my father and my husband. The expression on both their faces shocked me. Roc's was grim; my father's tortured. I had the impression that my father had been saying something to Roc which he did not like, and I could not tell whether Roc was angry or shocked. I imagined my father seemed bewildered.

Then they saw me and Roc said quickly: 'Here's Favel.'

It was as though they had both drawn masks over their faces.

'Is anything the matter?' I demanded.

'Only that we're hungry,' answered Roc, coming over to me and taking my basket from me.

He smiled and, putting his arm round me, gave me a hug. 'It seems a long time since I've seen you.'

I looked beyond him to my father; he too was smiling but I thought there was a greyish tinge in his face.

'Father,' I insisted, 'what is it?'

'You're imagining things, my dear,' he assured me.

I could not throw off my uneasiness but I let them persuade me that all was well, because I could not bear that anything should disturb my new and wonderful happiness.

The sun was brilliant. It had been a busy morning in the studio. My father always went down to swim while I got our midday meal, and on that day I told Roc to go with him.

'Why don't you come too?'

'Because I have the lunch to get. I'll do it more quickly if you two go off.'

So they went off together.

Ten minutes later Roc came back. He came into the kitchen and sat on the table. His back was to the window and I noticed the sunlight through the prominent tips of his ears.

'At times,' I said, 'you look like a satyr.'

'That's what I am,' he told me.

'Why did you come back so soon?'

'I found I didn't want to be separated from you any longer, so I left your father on the beach and came back alone.'

I laughed at him. 'You *are* silly! Couldn't you bear to be away from me for another fifteen minutes?'

'Far too long,' he said.

I was delighted to have him with me pretending to help in the kitchen, but when we were ready to eat, my father had not come back.

'I do hope he's not got involved in some long conversation,' I said.

'He couldn't. You know how people desert the beach for food and siesta at this time of day.'

Five minutes later I began to get really anxious; and with good reason.

That morning my father went into the sea and he did not come back alive.

His body was recovered later that day. They said he must have been overcome by cramp and unable to save himself.

It seemed the only explanation then. My happiness was shattered, but how thankful I was that I had Roc. I told him that I did not know how I could have lived through that time if he had not been with me. My great and only consolation was that, although I had lost my father, Roc had come into my life.

It was only later that the terrible doubts began.

Chapter Two

All the joy had naturally gone out of our honeymoon, and I could not rid myself of the fear that I had failed my father in some way.

I remember lying in Roc's arms during the night that followed and crying out: 'There was something I could have done. I know it.'

Roc tried to comfort me. 'But what, my darling? How could you know that he was going to have cramp? It could happen to anybody, and, smooth as the sea was, if nobody heard his cry for help, that would be the end.'

'He never had cramp before.'

'There had to be a first time.'

'But Roc . . . there *was* something.'

He smoothed my hair back from my face. 'Darling, you mustn't upset yourself so. There's nothing we can do now.'

He was right. What could we do?

'He would be glad,' Roc told me, 'that I am here to take care of you.'

There was a note of relief in his voice when he said that which I could not understand, and I felt the first twinges of the fear which I was to come to know very well.

Roc took charge of everything. He said that we must get away from the island as quickly as possible because then I would begin to grow away from my tragedy. He would take me home and in time I should forget.

I left everything to him because I was too unhappy to make arrangements myself. Some of my father's treasures were packed up and sent to Pendorric to await our arrival; the rest were sold. Roc saw the landlord of our studio and arranged to get rid of the lease; and two weeks later we left Capri.

'Now we must try to put that tragedy out of our minds,' said Roc as we sailed to the mainland.

I looked at his profile and for one short moment I felt that I was looking at a stranger. I did not know why – except perhaps because I had begun to suspect, since my father's death, that there was a great deal I had to learn about my husband.

We spent two days in Naples, and while we were there he told me that he was not in any hurry to get home because I was still so shocked and dazed, and he wanted me to have time to recover before he took me to Pendorric.

'We'll finish our honeymoon, darling,' he said.

But my response was listless because I kept thinking of my father sitting at the studio table in the dark, and wondering what he had had on his mind.

'I ought to have found out,' I reiterated. 'How could I have been so thoughtless? I always knew when something worried him. He found it hard to hide anything from me. And he didn't hide that.'

'What do you mean?' demanded Roc almost fiercely.

'I think he was ill. Probably that was why he got this cramp. Roc, what happened on the beach that day? Did he look ill?'

'No. He looked the same as usual.'

'Oh Roc, if only you hadn't come back. If only you'd been with him.'

'It's no use saying If Only, Favel. I wasn't with him. We're going to leave Naples. It's too close. We're going to put all this behind us.' He took my hands and drew me to him, kissing me with tenderness and passion. 'You're my wife, Favel. Remember that. I'm going to make you forget how he died and remember only that we are together now. He wouldn't have you mourn for him.'

He was right. The shock did become modified as the weeks passed. I taught myself to accept the fact that my father's death was not so very unusual. I must remember that I had a husband to consider now and as he was so anxious for me to put the tragedy behind me and be happy, I must do my best to please him.

And it was easier as we went farther from the island.

Roc was charming to me during those days; and I felt that he was determined to make me forget all the sadness.

Once he said to me: 'We can do no good by brooding, Favel. Let's put it behind us. Let's remember that by a wonderful chance we met and fell in love.'

We stayed for two weeks in the south of France, and each day, it seemed, took me a step farther away from the tragedy. We hired a car and Roc took a particular delight in the hairpin bends, laughing at me as I held my breath while he skilfully controlled the car. The scenery delighted me, but as I gazed at terraces of orange stucco villas which seemed to cling to the cliff face, Roc would snap his fingers.

'Wait,' he would say, 'just wait till you see Pendorric!'

It was a joke between us that not all the beauty of the Maritime Alps nor the twists, turns and truly majestic gorges to be discovered on the Corniche road could compare with his native Cornwall.

Often I would say it for him while we sat under a multi-coloured umbrella in opulent Cannes or sunned ourselves on the beach of humbler Menton: 'But of course this is nothing compared with Cornwall.' Then we would laugh together and people passing would smile at us, knowing us for lovers.

At first I thought my gaiety was a little forced. I was so eager to please Roc and there was no doubt that nothing delighted him more than to see me happy. Then I found that I did not have to pretend. I was becoming so deeply in love with my husband that the fact that we were together could overwhelm me and all else seemed of little importance. Roc was eager to wean me from my sorrow; and because he was the sort of man who was determined to have his way he could not fail. I was conscious of his strength, of his dominating nature, and I was glad of it because I would not have wished him to be different. He was the perfect husband and I wondered how I could ever have had doubts about him.

But I grew suddenly uneasy one night in Nice. We had driven in from Villefranche, and as we did so, noticed the dark clouds which hung over the mountains – a contrast to the sparkling scene. Roc had suggested that we visit the Casino, and I as usual readily fell in with his suggestion. He took a turn at the tables and I was reminded then of the light in his eyes when he had sat with my father in the studio. There was the same burning excitement that used to alarm me when I saw it in my father's.

He won that night and was elated; but I couldn't hide my concern, and when in our hotel bedroom I betrayed this, he laughed at me.

'Don't worry,' he said, 'I'd never make the mistake of risking what I couldn't afford to lose.'

'You're a gambler,' I accused.

He took my face in his hands. 'Well, why not? he demanded. 'Life's supposed to be a gamble, isn't it, so perhaps it's the gamblers who come off best.'

He was teasing me as he used to before my father's death, and I assured myself it was only teasing; but that incident seemed to mark a change in our relationship. I was over the first shock; there was no need to treat me with such delicate care. I knew then that Roc would always be a gambler no matter how I tried to persuade him against it, and I experienced once more those faint twinges of apprehension.

Now that the results of the shock were diminishing, I began to think of the future, and there were occasions when I was uneasy. This happened first during the night when I awoke suddenly from a hazy dream in which I knew myself to be in some unspecified danger.

I lay in the darkness, aware of Roc beside me, sleeping deeply, and I thought: What is happening to me? Two months ago I did not know this man. My home was the studio on the island with my father, and now another artist works in the studio and I have no father.

I had a husband. But what did I know of him? – except that I was in love with him. Wasn't that enough? Ours was a deeply passionate relationship and I could at times become so completely absorbed in our need of each other that this seemed all I asked. But that was only a part of marriage. I considered the marriage of my parents and remembered how they had relied on each other and felt that all was well as long as the other was close by.

And here I was waking in the night after a nightmare which hung about me seeming like a vague warning.

That night I really looked the truth in the eye, which was that I knew very little of the man I had married or of the sort of life to which he was taking me.

I made up my mind that I must have a talk with him, and when we drove into the mountains next day I decided to do so. The fears of the night had departed and somehow seemed ridiculous by day, yet I told myself it was absurd that I should know so little of his background.

We found a small hotel where we stopped to have lunch.

I was thoughtful as we ate, and when Roc asked the reason, I blurted out: 'I want to know more about Pendorric and your family.'

'I'm ready for the barrage. Start firing.'

'First the place itself. Let me try to see it and then you fill it with the people.'

He leaned his elbows on the table and narrowed his eyes as though he were looking at something far away, which he could not see very clearly.

'The house first,' he said. 'It's about four hundred years old in some parts. Some of it has been restored. In fact there was a house there in the Dark Ages I believe – so the story goes. . . . We're built on the cliff rock some five hundred yards from the sea; I believe we were much farther from it in the beginning but the sea has a habit of encroaching, you know, and in hundreds of years it advances. We're built of grey Cornish granite calculated to stand against the south-west gales; as a matter of fact over the front archway – one of the oldest parts of the house – there's a motto in Cornish cut into the stone. Translated into English it is: 'When we build we believe we build for ever.' I remember my father's lifting me up to read that and telling me that we Pendorrics were as much a part of the house as that old archway and that Pendorrics would never rest in their graves if the time came when the family left the place.'

'How wonderful to belong to such a family!'

'You do now.'

'But as a kind of outsider . . . as all the people who married into the family must be.'

'You'll soon become one of us. It's always been so with Pendorric brides. In a short time they're upholding the family more enthusiastically than those who started life with the name Pendorric.'

'Are you a sort of squire in the neighbourhood?'

'Squires went out of fashion years ago. We own most of the farms in the district, and customs die harder in Cornwall than anywhere else in England. We cling to old traditions and superstitions. I'm sure that a practical young woman like yourself is going to be very impatient with some of the stories you hear; but bear with us – we're the fey Cornish, remember, and you married into us.'

'I'm sure I shan't complain. Tell me some more.'

'Well, there's the house – a solid rectangle facing north, south, east and west. Northwards we look over the hills to the farmlands – south we face straight out to sea, and east and west give you magnificent views of a coastline that is one of the most beautiful in England and the most treacherous. When the tide goes out you'll see the rocks like sharks' teeth, and you can imagine what happens to boats that find their way on to those. Oh, and I forgot to mention there's one view we don't much like from the east window. It's known to us in the family as Polhorgan's Folly. A house which looks like a replica of our own. We loathe it. We detest it. We nightly pray that it will be blown into the sea.'

'You don't mean that, of course.'

'Don't I?' His eyes flashed, but they were laughing at me.

'Of course you don't. You'd be horrified if it were.'

'There's actually no fear of it. It has stood there for fifty years – an absolute sham – trying to pretend to those visitors who stare up at it from the beach below that it is Pendorric of glorious fame.'

'But who built it?'

He was looking at me and there was something malicious in his gaze which alarmed me faintly because for a second it seemed as though it was directed at me; but then I realized that it was dislike of the owner of Polhorgan's Folly which inspired it.

'A certain Josiah Fleet, better known as Lord Polhorgan. He came there fifty years ago from the Midlands, where he had made a fortune from some commodity – I've forgotten what. He liked our coast, he liked our climate, and decided to build himself a mansion. He did, and spent a month or so there each year, until eventually he settled in altogether and took his name from the cove below him.'

'You certainly don't like him much. Or are you exaggerating?'

Roc shrugged his shoulders. 'Perhaps. It's really the natural enmity between the *nouveaux* poor and the *nouveaux* rich.'

'Are we very poor?'

'By the standards of my Lord Polhorgan . . . yes. I suppose what annoys us is that sixty years ago we were the lords of the manor and he was trudging the streets of Birmingham, Leeds or Manchester – I can never remember which – bare-footed. Industry and natural cunning made him a millionaire. Sloth and natural indolence brought us to our genteel poverty, when we wonder from week to week whether we shall have to call in the National Trust to take over our home and allow us to live in it and show it at half-a-crown a time to the curious public who want to know how the aristocracy once lived.'

'I believe you're bitter.'

'And you're critical. You're on the side of industry and natural cunning. Oh, Favel, what a perfect union! You see, you're all that I'm not. You're going to keep me in order marvellously!'

'You're laughing at me again.'

He gripped my hand so hard that I winced. 'It's my nature, darling, to laugh at everything, and sometimes the more serious I am the more I laugh.'

'I don't think you would ever allow anyone to keep you in order.'

'Well, you chose me, darling, and if I was what you wanted when you made the choice you'd hardly want to change me, would you?'

'I hope,' I said seriously, 'that we shan't change, that we shall always be as happy as we have been up till now.'

For a moment there was the utmost tenderness in his expression, then he was laughing again.

'I told you,' he said, 'I've made a very good match.'

I was suddenly struck by the thought that perhaps his family, who I imagined loved Pendorric as much as he did, would be disappointed that he had married a girl with no money, but I was touched and very happy because he had married me who could bring him nothing. I felt my nightmare evaporating and I wondered on what it could possibly have been founded.

'Are you friendly with this Lord Polhorgan?' I asked quickly to hide my emotion.

'Nobody could be friendly with him. We're polite to each other. We don't see much of him. He's a sick man, well guarded by a nurse and a staff of servants.'

'And his family?'

'He quarrelled with them all. And now he lives alone in his glory. There are a hundred rooms at Polhorgan . . . all furnished in the most flamboyant manner. I believe, though, that dust-sheets perpetually cover the flamboyance. You see why we call it the Folly.'

'Poor old man!'

'I knew your soft heart would be touched. You may meet him. He'll probably consider that he should receive the new Bride of Pendorric.'

'Why do you always refer to me as the Bride of Pendorric – as though in capital letters?'

'Oh, it's a saying at Pendorric. There are lots of crazy things like that.'

'And your family?'

'Now things are very different at Pendorric. Some of our furniture has been standing where it does at this moment for four hundred years. We've got old Mrs. Penhalligan, who is a daughter of Jesse and Lizzie Pleydell, and the Pleydells have looked after the Pendorrics for generations. There's always a faithful member of that family to see that we're cared for. Old Mrs. Penhalligan is a fine housekeeper, and she mends the counterpanes and curtains which are constantly falling apart. She keeps the servants in order at the same time – as well as ourselves. She's sixty-five, but her daughter Maria, who never married, will follow in her footsteps.'

'And your sister?'

'My sister's married to Charles Chaston, who worked as an agent when my father travelled a good deal. He manages the home farm with me now. They live in the northern section of the house. We shall have the south. Don't be afraid that you're going to be hemmed in by relations. It isn't a bit like that at Pendorric. You need never see the rest of the family if you don't want to, except at meals. We all eat together – it's an old family custom – and anyway the servant problem makes it a necessity now. You'll be surprised at the family customs we preserve. Really, you'll think you've stepped back a hundred years. I do myself after I've been away for a while.'

'And your sister, what is her name?'

'Morwenna. Our parents believed in following the family traditions and giving us Cornish names wherever possible. Hence the Petrocs and Morwennas. The twins are Lowella and Hyson – Hyson was my mother's maiden name. Lowella refers to herself as Lo and her sister as Hy. I suspect she has a nickname for all of us. She's an incorrigible creature.'

'How old are the twins?'

'Twelve.'

'Are they at school?'

'No. They do go from time to time, but Lowella has an unfortunate habit of running away and dragging Hyson with her. She always says that they can't be happy anywhere but at Pendorric. We're compromised at the moment by having a governess – a trained schoolmistress. It was difficult getting the permission of the educational authorities. but Charles and Morwenna want to keep them at home for a year or so until the child becomes more stable. You'll have to beware of Lowella.'

'How?'

'It'll be all right if she likes you. But she gets up to tricks. Hyson is different. She's the quiet one. They look exactly alike, but their temperaments are completely different. Thank heaven for that. No household could tolerate two Lowellas.'

'What about your parents?'

'They're dead and I remember very little about them. My mother died when we were five, and an aunt looked after us. She still comes to stay quite often and keeps a suite of rooms at Pendorric. Our father lived abroad a great deal when Charles came in. Charles is fifteen years older than Morwenna.'

'You said your mother died when *we* were five. Who else besides you?'

'Didn't I mention that Morwenna and I were twins?'

'No. You said that Lowella and Hyson were.'

'Well, twins run in families, you know. Quite obviously they've started to run in ours.'

'Is Morwenna like you?'

'We're not identical like Lowella and Hyson; but people say they can see a resemblance.'

'Roc,' I said leaning forward, 'you know, I'm beginning to feel I can't wait to meet this family of yours.'

'That's settled it,' he replied. 'It's time we went home.'

So I was, in a measure, prepared for Pendorric.

We had left London after lunch and it was eight o'clock before we got off the train.

Roc had said that he wished we could have motored down, because he wanted to make my crossing of the Tamar something of a ceremony.

However, he had arranged that his car should be waiting at the station so that he could drive me home. Old Toms, the chauffeur-gardener and man-of-all-work at Pendorric, had driven it in that morning.

So I found myself sitting beside Roc in his rather shabby Daimler and feeling a mingling of longing and apprehension, which seemed natural enough in the circumstances.

I was very anxious to make a good impression, for in this new life to which I was going I knew no one except my husband; and I had suddenly realized what an odd position I was in.

I was in a strange country – for the island had been my home – and without friends. If Esther McBane had been in England I should not have felt quite so lonely. She would at least have been one friend. But Esther was far away in Rhodesia now, as deeply absorbed in her new life as I was becoming in mine. There had been other school friends, but none as close as Esther, and as we had never exchanged letters after we left school those friendships had lapsed.

But what foolish thoughts these were! I might not have old friends, but I had a husband.

Roc swung the car out of the station yard, and as we left the town, the quiet of the summer evening closed in about us. We were in a narrow winding lane with banks on either side which were dotted with wild roses, and there was the sweet smell of honeysuckle in the air.

'Is it far to Pendorric?' I asked.

'Eight miles or so. The sea is ahead of us, the moor's behind us. We'll do some walking on the moors . . . or riding. Can you ride?'

'I'm afraid not.'

'I'll teach you. You're going to make this place home, Favel. Some people never can, but I think you will.'

'I believe I shall.'

We were silent and I studied the landscape avidly. The houses which we passed were little more than cottages, not by any means beautiful – indeed they struck me as rather grim – all made of that grey Cornish stone. I fancied I caught a whiff of the sea as we slowly climbed a steep hill and went forward into wooded country. We were soon descending again on the other side of the hill. 'When you see the sea you'll know we're not far from home,' Roc told me, and almost immediately we began to climb again.

At the top of the hill he stopped the car, and putting his arm along the back of the seat, pointed towards the sea.

'Can you see the house there, right on the edge of the cliff? That's the Folly. You can't see Pendorric from here because there's a hill in the way; but it's a little to the right.'

The Folly looked almost like a medieval castle.

'I wonder he didn't supply a drawbridge and a moat,' murmured Roc. 'Though heaven knows it would have been difficult to have a moat up there. Still, all the more laudable that he should achieve it.'

He started up the car, and when he had gone half a mile I caught my first glimpse of Pendorric.

It was so like the other house that I was astonished.

'They look close together from here,' said Roc, 'but there's a good mile between them on the coast road – of course as the crow flies they're a little nearer – but you can understand the wrath of the Pendorrics, can't you, to find *that* set up where they just can't get it out of their sight.'

We had now reached a major road, and we sped along this until we came to a turning and began to plunge down one of the steepest hills we had come upon as yet. The banks were covered with the wild flowers which I had noticed before, and stubby fir trees with their resinous scent.

At the bottom of the hill we struck the cliff road, and then I saw the coast in all its glory. The water was quiet on that night and I could hear the gentle swish as it washed against the rocks. The cliffs were covered in grass and bracken, and dotted here and there were clumps of pink, red, and white valerian; the sweep of the bay was magnificent. The tide was out, and in the evening light I saw those malignant rocks jutting cruelly out of the shallow water.

And there half a mile ahead of us was Pendorric itself, and I caught my breath for it was awe-inspiring. It towered above the sea a massive rectangle of grey stone, with crenellated towers and an air of impregnability, noble and arrogant as though defying the sea and the weather and anyone who came against it.

'This is your home, my dear,' said Roc, and I could hear the pride in his voice.

'It's . . . superb.'

'So you're not unhappy? I'm glad you're seeing it for the first time. Otherwise I might have thought you married *it* rather than me.'

'I would never marry a house!'

'No, you're too honest – too full of common sense . . . in fact too wonderful. That's why I fell in love with you and determined to marry you.'

We were roaring uphill again, and now that we were closer the house certainly dominated the landscape. There were lights in some of the windows and I saw the arch leading to the north portico.

'The grounds,' Roc explained, 'are on the south side. We can approach the house from the south; there are four porticoes – north, south, east and west. But we'll go into the north to-night because Morwenna and Charlie will be waiting for us there. Why, look,' he went on, and following his gaze I saw a slight figure in riding breeches and scarlet blouse, black hair flying, running towards us. Roc slowed the car and she leapt on to the running-board. Her face was brown with sun and weather, her eyes were long and black and very like Roc's.

'I wanted to be the first to see the bride!' she shouted.

'And you always get your way,' answered Roc. 'Favel, this is Lowella, of whom beware.'

'Don't listen to him,' said the girl. 'I expect I'll be your friend.'

'Thank you,' I said. 'I hope you will.'

The black eyes studied me curiously. 'I said she'd be fair,' she went on. 'I was certain.'

'Well, you're impeding our progress,' Roc told her. 'Either hop in or get off.'

'I'll stay here,' she announced. 'Drive in.'

Roc obeyed and we went slowly towards the house.

'They're all waiting to meet you,' Lowella told me. 'We're very excited. We've all been trying to guess what you'll be like. In the village they're all waiting to see you too. Every time one of us goes down they say, "And when will the Bride be coming to Pendorric?" '

'I hope they'll be pleased with me.'

Lowella looked at her uncle mischievously and I thought again how remarkably like him she was. 'Oh, it was time he was married,' she said. 'We were getting worried.'

'You see I was right to warn you,' put in Roc. 'She's the *enfant terrible*.'

'And not such an infant,' insisted Lowella. 'I'm twelve now, you know.'

'You grow more terrible with the years. I tremble to think what you'll be like at twenty.'

We had now passed through the gates and I saw the great stone arch looming ahead. Behind it was a portico guarded on either side by two huge carved lions, battered by the years but still looking fierce as though warning any to be wary of entering.

And there was a woman – so like Roc that I knew she was his twin sister – and behind her a man, whom I guessed to be her husband and father of the twins.

Morwenna came towards the car. 'Roc! So you're here at last. And this is Favel. Welcome to Pendorric, Favel.'

I smiled up at her, and for those first moments I was glad that she looked so like Roc, because it made me feel that she was not quite a stranger. Her dark hair was thick with a slight natural wave and it grew to a widow's peak which in the half-light gave the impression that she was wearing a sixteenth-century cap. She wore a dress of emerald-green linen which became her dark hair and eyes, and there were gold rings in her ears.

'I'm so glad to meet you at last,' I said. 'I do hope this isn't a shock to you.'

'Nothing my brother does ever shocks us, really, because we're expecting surprises.'

'You see I've brought them up in the right way,' said Roc lightly. 'Oh and here's Charlie.'

My hand was gripped so firmly that I winced. I was hoping Charles Chaston didn't notice this as I looked up into his plump bronzed face.

'We've all been eagerly waiting to see you, ever since we heard you were coming,' he told me.

I saw that Lowella was dancing round us in a circle; with her flying hair, and as she was chanting something to herself which might have been an incantation, she reminded me of a witch.

'Oh Lowella, do stop,' cried her mother with a little laugh. 'Where's Hyson?'

Lowella lifted her arms in a gesture which implied she had no idea.

'Go and find her. She'll want to say hallo to her Aunt Favel.'

'We're not calling her aunt,' said Lowella. 'She's too young. She's just going to be Favel. You'll like that better, won't you, Favel?'

'Yes, it sounds more friendly.'

'There you see,' said Lowella, and she ran into the house.

Morwenna slipped her arm through mine, and Roc came up and took the other as he called: 'Where's Toms? Toms! Come and bring in our baggage.'

I heard a voice say: 'Ay sir. I be coming.'

But before he appeared Morwenna and Roc were leading me through the portico, and with Charles hovering behind we entered the house.

I was in an enormous hall at either end of which was a beautiful curved staircase leading to a gallery. On the panelled walls were swords and shields and at the foot of each staircase a suit of armour.

'This is our wing,' Morwenna told me. 'It's a most convenient house, really, being built round a quadrangle. It is almost like four houses in one and it was built with the intention of keeping Pendorrics together in the days of large families. I believe years ago the house was crowded. Only a few servants lived in the attics; the rest of them were in the cottages. There are six of them side by side, most picturesque and insanitary – until Roc and Charles did something about it. We still draw on them for help; and we only keep Toms and his wife and daughter Hetty, and Mrs. Penhalligan and her daughter Maria, living in. A change from the old days. I expect you're hungry.'

I told her we had had dinner on the train.

'Then we'll have a snack later. You'll want to see something of the house, but perhaps you'd like to go to your own part first.'

I said I should, and as I spoke, my eye was caught by a portrait which hung on the wall of the gallery. It was a picture of a fair-haired young woman in a clinging blue gown which showed her shapely shoulders; her hair was piled high above her head and one ringlet hung over her shoulder. She clearly belonged to the late eighteenth century, and I thought that her picture, placed as it was, dominated the gallery and hall.

'How charming!' I said.

'Ah yes, one of the Brides of Pendorric,' Morwenna told me.

There it was again – that phrase which I had heard so often.

'She looks beautiful . . . and so happy.'

'Yes, she's my great-great-great- . . . one loses count of the greats . . . grandmother,' Morwenna said. 'She was happy when that was painted, but she died young.'

I found it difficult to take my eyes from the picture because there was something so appealing about that young face.

'I thought, Roc,' went on Morwenna, 'that now you're married you'd want the big suite.'

'Thanks,' Roc replied. 'That's exactly what I did want.'

Morwenna turned to me. 'The wings of the house are all connected. You don't have to use the separate entrances unless you wish to. So if you come up to the gallery I'll take you through.'

'There must be hundreds of rooms.'

'Eighty. Twenty in each of the four parts. I think it's much larger than it was in the beginning. A lot of it has been restored, but because of that motto over the arch they've been very careful to make it seem that what was originally built has lasted.'

We went past the suit of armour and up the stairs to the gallery.

'One thing,' said Morwenna, 'when you know your own wing you know all the others; you just have to imagine the rooms facing different directions.'

She led the way, and with Roc's arm still in mine we followed. When we reached the gallery we went through a side door which led to another corridor in which were beautiful marble figures set in alcoves.

'Not the best time to see the house,' commented Morwenna. 'It's neither light nor dark.'

'She'll have to wait till the morning to explore,' added Roc.

I looked through one of the windows down on to a large quadrangle in which grew some of the most magnificent hydrangeas I had ever seen.

I remarked on them and we paused to look down.

'The colours are wonderful in sunlight,' Morwenna told me. 'They thrive here. It's because we're never short of rain and there's hardly ever a frost. Besides, they're well sheltered in the quadrangle.'

It looked a charming place, that quadrangle. There was a pond, in the centre of which was a dark statue which I later discovered was of Hermes; and there were two magnificent palm trees growing down there so that it looked rather like an oasis in a desert. In between the paving-stones clumps of flowering shrubs bloomed and there were several white seats with gilded decorations.

Then I noticed all the windows which looked down on it and it occurred to me that it was a pity because one would never be able to sit there without a feeling of being overlooked.

Roc explained to me that there were four doors all leading into it, one from each wing.

We moved along the corridor through another door and Roc said that we were now in the south wing – our own. We went up a staircase and Morwenna went ahead of us, and when she threw open a door we entered a large room with enormous windows facing the sea. The deep red velvet curtains had been drawn back, and when I saw the seascape stretched out before me I gave a cry of pleasure and at once went to the window. I stood there looking out across the bay; the cliffs looked stark and menacing in the twilight and I could just glimpse the rugged outline of the rocks. The smell and the gentle whispering of the sea seemed to fill the room.

Roc was behind me. 'It's what everyone does,' he said. 'They never glance at the room; they look at the view.'

'The views are just as lovely from the east and west side,' said Morwenna, 'and very much the same.'

She turned a switch and the light from a large chandelier hanging from the centre of the ceiling made the room dazzlingly bright. I turned from the window and saw the four-poster bed, with the long stool at its foot, the tallboy, the cabinets – all belonging to an earlier generation, a generation of exquisite grace and charm.

'But it's lovely!' I said.

'We flatter ourselves that we have the best of both worlds,' Morwenna told me. 'We made an old powder closet into a bathroom.' She opened a door which led from the bedroom and disclosed a modern bathroom. I looked at it longingly and Roc laughed.

'You have a bath,' he said. 'I'll go and see what Toms is doing about the baggage. Afterwards we'll have something to eat, and perhaps I'll take you for a walk in the moonlight – if there's any to be had.'

I said I thought it was an excellent idea, and they left me.

When I was alone I went once more to the windows to gaze out at that magnificent view. I stood for some minutes, my eyes on the horizon, as I watched the intermittent flashes of the lighthouse.

Then I went into the bathroom, where bath salts and talcum powder had all been laid out for me – my sister-in-law's thoughtfulness, I suspected. She was obviously anxious to make me welcome, and I felt it had been a very pleasant homecoming.

If only I could have thought of Father at work in his studio I could have been very happy. But I had to start a new life; I must stop fretting. I had to be gay. I owed that to Roc; and he was the type of man who would want his wife to be gay.

I went into the bathroom, ran a bath and spent about half an hour luxuriating in it. When I came out, Roc had not returned, but my bags had been put in the room. I unpacked a small one and changed from my suit to a silk dress; and I was doing my hair at the dressing-table, which had a three-sided mirror, when there was a knock at the door.

'Come in,' I called, and turning saw a young woman and a child. I thought at first that the child was Lowella and I smiled at her. She did not return the smile but regarded me gravely, while the young woman said: 'Mrs. Pendorric, I am Rachel Bective, the children's governess. Your husband asked me to show you the way down when you were ready.'

'How do you do?' I said, and I was astonished by the change in Lowella.

There was an air of efficiency about Rachel Bective, whom I guessed to be around about thirty, and I remembered what Roc had told me about a schoolmistress looking after the twins' education. Her hair was a sandy colour and her brows and lashes so fair that she looked surprised; her teeth were sharp and white. I did not warm towards her. She seemed to me to be obviously summing me up, and her manner was calculating and critical.

'This is Hyson,' she said. 'I believe you met her sister.'

'Oh I see.' I smiled at the child. 'I thought you were Lowella.'

'I knew you did.' She was almost sullen.

'You are so much like her.'

'I only *look* like her.'

'Are you ready to come down?' asked Rachel Bective. 'There's to be a light supper because I believe you had dinner on the train.'

'Yes, we did and I'm quite ready.'

For the first time since I had come into the house I felt uncomfortable, and was glad when Rachel Bective led the way along the corridor and down the staircase.

We came to a gallery and I did not realize that it was not the same one which I had seen from the north side until I noticed the picture there and I knew that I had never seen that before.

It was the picture of a woman in a riding jacket. The habit was black and she was very fair; she wore a hard black hat, and about it was a band of blue velvet which hung down forming a snood at the back. She was very beautiful, but her large blue eyes, which were the same colour as the velvet band and snood, were full of brooding sadness. Moreover the picture had been painted so that it was impossible to escape those eyes. They followed you wherever you went, and even in that first moment I thought they were trying to convey some message.

'What a magnificent picture!' I cried.

'It's Barbarina,' said Hyson, and for a moment her face was filled with vitality and she looked exactly as Lowella had when she had welcomed us.

'What an extraordinary name! And who was she?'

'She was my grandmother,' Hyson told me proudly.

'She died . . . tragically, I believe,' put in Rachel Bective.

'How dreadful! And she looks so beautiful.'

I remembered then that I had seen a picture of another beautiful woman in the north hall when I had arrived and had heard that she too had died young.

Hyson said in a voice which seemed to hold a note of hysteria: '*She* was one of the Brides of Pendorric.'

'Well, I suppose she was,' I said, 'since she married your grandfather.'

This Hyson was a strange child; she had seemed so lifeless a moment ago; now she was vital and excited.

'She died twenty-five years ago when my mother and Uncle Roc were five years old.'

'How very sad!'

'You'll have to have *your* picture painted, Mrs. Pendorric,' said Rachel Bective.

'I hadn't thought of it.'

'I'm sure Mr. Pendorric will want it done.'

'He hasn't said anything about it.'

'It's early days yet. Well, I think we should go. They'll be waiting.'

We went along the gallery and through a door and were walking round the corridor facing the quadrangle again. I noticed that Hyson kept taking covert glances at me. I thought she seemed rather a neurotic child, and there was a quality about the governess which I found distinctly disturbing.

I woke up in the night and for a few seconds wondered where I was. Then I saw the enormous windows, heard the murmuring of the sea, and it sounded like the echo of voices I had heard in my dream.

I could smell the tang of seaweed and the freshness of the ocean. The rhythm of the waves seemed to keep time with Roc's breathing.

I raised myself, and leaning on my elbow looked at him. There was enough moonlight to show me the contours of his face which looked as though it had been cut out of stone. He appeared different in repose, and, realizing how rarely I saw him thus, again I had that feeling that I was married to a stranger.

I shook off my fancies. I reminded myself that I had sustained a great shock. My thoughts were so often with my father, and I wondered again and again what he must have experienced in that dreadful moment when the cramp had overtaken him and he realized that he could not reach land and there was no one at hand to help him. He had come face to face with death, and that must have been a moment of intense horror; and what seemed so terrible was that at that moment Roc and I were laughing together in the kitchen of the studio.

If Roc had only stayed with him . . .

I wished I could stop thinking of my father, sitting in the lonely studio in the darkness, of the anxiety I had seen on his face when I had come upon him and Roc together.

I must have been dreaming about the island and my father, for what was disturbing me was the memory of relief I had fancied I saw in Roc's face at the time of the tragedy. It was almost as though he had believed it was the best possible thing that could have happened.

Surely I must have imagined that. But when had I started to imagine it? Was it that hangover from some dream?

I lay down quietly so as not to disturb him, and after a while I slept. But again I was troubled by dreams. I could hear a murmur like background music and it might have been the movement of the waves or Roc's breathing beside me; then I heard the shrill laughter of Lowella, or it might have been Hyson, as she cried out: 'Two Brides of Pendorric died young. . . . Now you are a Bride of Pendorric.'

I remembered that dream next morning, and what had seemed full of significance in my sleep now seemed the natural result of a day crammed with new experiences.

The next day the sun was shining brilliantly. I stood at a window watching the light on the water, and it was as though some giant had thrown down a handful of diamonds.

Roc came and stood behind me, putting his hands on my shoulders.

'I can see you are coming under the spell of *that* Pendorric as well as this one.'

I turned and smiled at him. He looked so concerned that I threw my arms about his neck. He waltzed round the room with me and said: 'It is good to have you here at Pendorric. This morning I'm going to take you for a drive and show you off to the locals. You're going to find them very inquisitive. This afternoon I'll have to go into things with old Charles. I've been away a long time – longer than I planned for – and there'll be a little catching up to do. You can go off and explore on your own then, or perhaps Lowella will join you.'

I said: 'The other child is quite different, isn't she?'

'Hyson? Thank heaven. We couldn't do with two like Lowella. There'd be no peace.'

'And yet they're so alike I couldn't tell which was which.'

'You get to know the slight difference after a while. Perhaps it's in the voices. I'm not sure, but we can usually tell. It's strange, but with identicals you sometimes get two entirely different temperaments. It's as though characteristics have been divided into two neat little piles – one for one, one for the other. However, Rachel takes good care of them.'

'Oh . . . the governess.'

'That makes her sound rather Victorian, and there's nothing Victorian about Rachel. Actually she's more a friend of the family. She was an old schoolfellow of Morwenna's. Ready?'

We went out of the room and I followed where Roc led, realizing that I must expect to be a little vague as yet about the geography of the house.

We were on the third floor and it seemed that there were linking doors to all wings on all floors. I looked down at the quadrangle as we passed the windows. It was true that it was quite charming in sunlight. I imagined

myself sitting under one of the palm trees with a book. It would be the
utmost peace. Then I looked up at the windows.

'A pity,' I murmured.

'What?' asked Roc.

'That you'd always have the feeling of not being alone down there.'

'Oh . . . you mean the windows. They're all corridor windows, not the
sort for sitting at.'

'I suppose that does make a difference.'

I had not noticed that we had come round to the north wing until Roc
paused at a door, knocked and went in.

The twins were sitting at a table, exercise books before them; and with
them sat Rachel Bective. She smiled rather lazily when she saw me,
reminding me of a tortoise-shell cat who was sleeping pleasantly and is
suddenly disturbed.

'Hello, Favel!' cried Lowella leaping up. '*And* Uncle Roc!'

Lowella flung her arms about Roc's neck, lifted her feet from the ground
and was swung round and round.

Rachel Bective looked faintly amused; Hyson's face was expressionless.

'Help!' cried Roc. 'Come along, Favel . . . Rachel . . . rescue me.'

'Any excuse to stop lessons,' murmured Rachel.

Lowella released her uncle. 'If I want to find excuses I always can,' she
said gravely. 'That was meant to say how glad I was to see him and the
Bride.'

'I want you to entertain her this afternoon,' said Roc, 'while I'll be
working. Will you?'

'Of course.' Lowella smiled at me. 'I've such lots to tell you.'

'I'm looking forward to hearing.' I included Hyson in my smile but she
quickly looked away.

'Now you're here,' said Roc, 'you must have a look at the old schoolroom.
It's a real relic from the past. Generations of Pendorrics sat at that table.
My grandfather carved his initials on it and was sternly punished by his
governess.'

'How was he punished?' Lowella wanted to know.

'Probably with a big stick . . . or made to fast on bread and water and
learn pages of *Paradise Lost*.'

'I'd rather the stick,' said Lowella.

'You wouldn't. You'd hate that,' put in Hyson surprisingly.

'No, I'd love it, because I'd take the stick and start beating whoever was
beating me.' Lowella's eyes shone at the prospect.

'There you are, Rachel, that's a warning,' said Roc.

He had gone to the cupboard and showed me books which must have
been there for years; some were exercise books filled with the unformed
writing of children; there were several slates and pencil boxes.

'You'll have to have a good look when it's not lesson time, Favel. I believe
Rachel's getting a little impatient with us.'

He flashed a smile at Rachel, and because I thought I saw intimacy in it
I felt a pang of jealousy. Until now it had not occurred to me that the easy
manner in which my friendship with Roc had progressed was due to his

easygoing friendly nature. Now it occurred to me that he was very friendly with Rachel – and she with him, for if his smile for her was warm, hers was a good deal warmer. I began to wonder then how deep a friendship it was.

I was glad to leave the schoolroom, the exuberant Lowella, the silent Hyson, and Rachel who was too friendly – towards Roc. There were lots of questions I wanted to ask him about Rachel Bective but I felt that I might betray my jealousy if I did, so I decided to shelve the subject for the time being.

When I was sitting in the car with Roc I felt happy again. He was right when he had suggested that an entirely new life would help me to put the past behind me. So many new impressions were being superimposed on those old ones that they now seemed to belong to another life.

Roc put his hand over mine and I would have said he was a very contented man that morning.

'I can see you've taken to Pendorric like a duck to water.'

'It's all so intriguing, so beautiful . . . and the family is interesting.'

He grimaced. 'We're flattered. I'm going to drive you past the Folly; then you can see what a sham it is.'

We drove down the steep road and up again and then we were on a level with Polhorgan. At first glance it appeared to be as old as Pendorric.

'They've deliberately tried to make the stone look old. The gargoyles over the front porch are crumbling artistically.'

'There's no sign of life.'

'There never is from this side. The master of the house has his apartments on the south side, facing the sea. He owns the beach below and he has magnificent flower gardens laid out on the cliffs. Much grander than ours. He bought the land from my grandfather.'

'He has a wonderful view.'

'That's as well because he spends most of the time in his room. His heart won't allow him to do otherwise.'

We had passed the house and Roc went on: 'I'm taking this road which will carry us back to Pendorric because I want you to see our little village. I know you're going to love it.'

We had turned back and were going steeply down again to the coast road which led past Pendorric. I gazed at the house in a happy proprietorial way as we passed. In a short time we were roaring up the steep hill to the main road and I could see the sea on our left.

'It's the twists of our coast that make you lose your sense of direction,' Roc explained. 'This was once an area of terrific volcanic upheaval, which means that the land was flung in all directions. We've been rounding a sort of promontory and we're now coming into the village of Pendorric.'

We swooped down again and there it lay – the most enchanting little village I had ever seen. There was the church, its ancient tower, about which the ivy clung, clearly of Norman architecture, and it was set in the midst of the graveyard. On one side the stones were dark with age and on the other they were white and new-looking. There was the vicarage, a grey house set in a hollow with its lawn and gardens on an incline. Beyond the church was the row of cottages which Morwenna had mentioned; they had thatched roofs and tiny windows and were all joined together – the whole six of them. I imagine they were of the same period as the church.

Not far from the cottages was a garage with living quarters above it. 'It was once the blacksmith's forge,' Roc explained. 'The Bonds who lived there have been blacksmiths for generations. It broke old Jim Bond's heart when there were no longer enough horses in the district to make the smithy worth while, but they have compromised. The old forge is still in existence and I often pull up here to have the horses shod.'

He slowed down and called: 'Jim! Hi, Jim!'

A window above was thrown open and a handsome woman appeared there. Her black hair fell loosely about her shoulders and her scarlet blouse seemed too tight for her. She had the look of a gipsy.

'Morning, Mr. Roc,' she said.

'Why hallo, Dinah.'

'Nice to see you back, Mr. Roc.'

Roc waved a hand and at that moment a man came out to us.

'Morning, Jim,' said Roc.

He was a man in his fifties, an enormous man, just as one would have imagined a blacksmith should look; his sleeves were rolled up to display his brawny muscles. Roc went on: 'I've brought my wife along to show her the old forge and get her acquainted with the village.'

'I'm glad to see you, ma'am,' said Jim. 'Would 'ee care to come in and have a drop of our old cider?'

I said I should be delighted, and we got out of the car and went into the blacksmith's shop, where a strawberry roan was actually being shod. The smell of burning hoof filled the air, and the young man who was working at the forge said good-morning to us. He seemed to be Jim too.

I was told that he was young Jim, the son of old Jim, and that there had been Jim Bonds at the forge for as long as anyone could remember.

'And us reckons there always will be,' said old Jim. 'Though ... times change.' He looked a little sad.

'You never know when your luck will turn,' Roc told him.

Old Jim went to a corner and came out with glasses on a tray. He filled the glasses from a great barrel with a tap at the side which stood in a corner of the shop.

'The Bonds have always been noted for their cider,' Roc explained.

'Oh yes, m'dear,' said old Jim. 'Me Granny used to keep a live toad in the barrel and 'twas said that hers was a cider as had to be tasted to be believed. Now don't 'ee look scared like. We don't use the old toad now. 'Tis just the juice of good old Cornish apples and the way we Bonds have with 'em.'

'It's as potent as ever,' said Roc.

'It's very good,' I commented.

'Sometimes a bit too much for the foreigners,' said old Jim, looking at me as though he hoped I was teetering on the verge of intoxication.

The younger man went on stolidly with his work and hardly looked at us.

Then a door opened and the woman who had looked from the window came in. Her black eyes were sparkling and she swayed her hips as she walked; she was wearing a short full skirt and her shapely legs were bare and brown; her feet, slightly grubby, were in scuffed sandals.

I noticed that all three men were intensely aware of her the moment she came in. Old Jim scowled at her and didn't seem very pleased to see her; young Jim couldn't take his eyes from her; but it was Roc's expression which was not easy to construe. I could see immediately the effect she had on the others, but not on Roc. It was my husband whom I could not understand.

She herself studied me intently, taking in each detail of my appearance. I felt she was a little scornful of my clean linen dress, as she smoothed her hands over her hips and smiled at Roc. It was a familiar and, I thought, even intimate gaze. I was a little ashamed of myself then. Was I over-jealous because I had a very attractive husband? I must stop myself wondering what his relationship had been with every young woman he had known before he met me. 'This is Dinah, young Mrs. Bond,' Roc was explaining to me.

'How do you do?' I said.

She smiled. 'I do very well,' she answered, 'and I'm terribly glad to see Mr. Roc has brought a bride to Pendorric.'

'Thank you,' said Roc. He drained his glass. 'We have a lot to do this morning,' he added.

'Can I fill up your car, sir?' asked old Mr. Bond.

'We're all right for a bit, Jim,' said Roc, and I had a feeling that he was anxious to get away.

I felt a little dizzy – it was the cider, I told myself – and I was rather glad to get out into the fresh air.

The old man and Dinah stood watching as we drove away. There was a slow smile on Dinah's face.

'Dinah rather broke up the happy party,' I said.

'The old fellow hates her, I'm afraid. Life doesn't go smoothly at the old forge since Dinah came to live there.'

'She's very attractive.'

'That seems to be the majority opinion – including Dinah's. I hope it works out, but I fancy young Jim doesn't have too good a life between the old man and the young woman. Old Jim would have liked to see him marry one of the Pascoe girls from the cottages; they'd have had a little Jim by now. But young Jim – always a docile lad till he fell in love with Dinah – married her, and that has not made for peace at the old forge. She's half gipsy and used to live in a caravan in the woods about a mile away.'

'Is she a good and faithful wife?'

Roc laughed, 'Did she give you the impression that she was?'

'Far from it.'

Roc nodded. 'Dinah wouldn't pretend to be what she isn't.'

He pulled up the car before a gate and a voice called to us: 'Why, Mr. Pendorric, how nice to see you back.'

A plump, rosy-cheeked woman who had a basket full of roses on her arm and cutters in her hand came to the gate and leaned over.

'This is Mrs. Dark,' said Roc. 'Our vicar's wife.'

'So nice of you to call so quickly. We've been so eager to meet Mrs. Pendorric.'

We got out of the car and Mrs. Dark opened the gate and took us into a garden which consisted of a lawn bounded by flower beds and enclosed by hedges of macrocarpas.

'The vicar will be very pleased to see you. He's in the study working on his sermon. I hope you'll have some coffee.'

We told her we had just had cider at the forge. 'And,' added Roc, 'I'd like to show my wife the old church. Please don't disturb your husband.'

'He'd be so sorry if he missed you.' She turned to me. 'We're so pleased to have you with us, Mrs. Pendorric, and we do hope you're going to enjoy living here and will be with us quite a lot. It's always so pleasant when the big house takes an interest in village things.'

'Favel is already enormously interested in Pendorric affairs,' said Roc. 'She's looking forward to seeing the church.'

'I'll go and tell Peter you're here.'

We walked through the garden with her, and passing through a hedge were on the lawn that sloped down to the vicarage. Opposite the house was the church, and we went towards it while Mrs. Dark hurried across the lawn to the house.

'We don't seem to be able to escape people this morning,' said Roc, taking my arm. 'They're all determined to have a look at you. I wanted to show you the church on my own, but Peter Dark will be on our trail soon.'

I was conscious of the quietness about us as we passed the yews, which had grown cumbersome with age, and crossed a part of the old graveyard and went into the church.

I immediately felt that I had stepped back in time. There was a thirteenth-century church looking little different, I imagined, from what it had in the days when it had been built. The light filtered through the stained-glass windows on to the altar with its beautiful embroidered cloth and exquisite carving. On the wall, carved in stone, were the names of the vicars from the year 1280.

'They were all local people,' Roc explained, 'until the Darks came. They come from the Midlands somewhere and they seem to know far more about the place than any of us. Dark is an expert on old Cornish customs. He's collecting them and writing a book on them.'

His voice sounded hollow, and as I looked up at him I was not thinking of the Darks, nor the church, but of the expression I had seen in Rachel Bective's eyes that morning and later in those of Dinah Bond.

He was extremely attractive; I had known that the moment I set eyes on him. I had fallen deep in physical love with him when I knew little about him. I knew little more now and I was more deeply in love than ever. I was so happy with him except when the doubts came. I was wondering now whether I had married a philanderer who was a perfect lover because he was so experienced; and it was not turning out to be such a happy morning as I had imagined it would.

'Anything wrong?' asked Roc.

'Should there be?'

He took me by the shoulders and held me against him so that I couldn't see his eyes. 'I've got you . . . here in Pendorric. How could anything be wrong with that?'

I was startled by the sound of a footstep, and breaking away I saw that a man in clerical clothes had come into the church.

'Hallo, Vicar,' said Roc easily.

'Susan told me you were here.' He advanced towards us, a pleasant-mannered man with a happy, alert expression which suggested he found his life one of absorbing interest. He took my hand. 'Welcome to Pendorric, Mrs. Pendorric. We're so pleased to have you with us. What do you think of the church? Isn't it fascinating?'

'It is indeed.'

'I'm having a wonderful time going through the records. It's always been an ambition of mine to have a living in Cornwall. It's the most intriguing of all the counties – don't you think, Mrs. Pendorric?'

'I can well believe it might be.'

'So individual. I always say to Susan that as soon as you cross the Tamar you notice the difference. It's like entering a different world – far away from prosaic England. Here in Cornwall one feels anything might happen. It's a fey country. It's due to the old superstitions and customs. There are still people here who really do leave bread and milk on their doorsteps for the Little People. And they swear it's disappeared by morning.'

'I warned you,' said Roc, 'that our vicar is enthusiastic about the customs of the place.'

'I'm afraid I am. Mrs. Pendorric, are you interested?'

'I hadn't thought much about it. But I believe I could be.'

'Good. We must have a talk some time.' We started to walk round the church and he went on: 'These are the Pendorric pews. Set apart from the rest, you see . . . at the side of the pulpit. I believe in the old days they used to be filled by the family and the retainers. Things have changed considerably.'

He pointed to one of the most beautiful of the stained-glass windows. 'That was put in in seventeen ninety-two in memory of Lowella Pendorric. I think the colouring of the glass is the most exquisite I've ever seen.'

'You've seen her picture in the north hall,' Roc reminded me.

'Oh yes . . . didn't she die young?'

'Yes,' said the vicar, 'in childbirth with her first child. She was only eighteen. They call her the First Bride. . . .'

'The first! But there must have been other brides. I understood there had been Pendorrics for centuries.'

The vicar stared blankly at the window. 'The sayings become attached and the origins are often steeped in legend. This is a memorial to another Pendorric. A great hero. A friend and supporter of Jonathan Trelawny who is himself buried at Pelynt, not so very far from here. The Trelawny, you know, who defied James II and of whom we sing:

"And shall Trelawny die?
Here's twenty thousand Cornishmen will know the reason why." '

He went on to point out other features of the church, and after renewing his wife's invitation to coffee, he left us, but not before saying that he looked forward to meeting me soon and that if I wanted any information about ancient Cornwall he would be pleased to give it to me.

I thought his kind face was a little anxious as he laid his hand on my arm and said: 'It doesn't do to take much notice of these old stories, Mrs. Pendorric. They're interesting just as curiosities, that's all.'

He left us outside the church and Roc gave a little sigh.

'He can be rather trying when he gets on to his favourite hobby. I began to think we were in for one of his longer lectures and we'd never get rid of him.' He looked at his watch. 'Now we'll have to hurry. But just a quick look round the old graveyard. Some of the inscriptions are amusing.'

We picked our way between the gravestones; some were so old that the words which had been engraved upon them were obliterated altogether; others leaned at grotesque angles.

We stopped before one which must have been more sheltered from the winds and weather than most, for although the date on it was 1779 the words were clearly visible.

Roc began to read them aloud:

> *'When you, my friends, behold*
> *Where now I lie,*
> *Remember 'tis appointed*
> *For all men once to die.*
> *For I myself in prime of life*
> *The Lord took me away*
> *And none that's on the Earth can tell*
> *How long they in't may stay.'*

He turned to me, smiling: 'Cheerful!' he said. 'Your turn. When Morwenna and I were children we used to come here and read them to each other, taking turns.'

I paused before another stone, slightly less ancient, the date being 1842.

> *'Though some of you perhaps may think*
> *From dangers to be free*
> *Yet in a moment may be sent*
> *Into the grave like me.'*

I stopped and said: 'The theme is similar.'

'What do you expect here among the dead? It's appropriate enough.'

'I'd rather find one that didn't harp so much on death.'

'Not so easy,' said Roc. 'But follow me.' He led the way through the long grass and eventually stopped and began to read:

> *'Though I was both deaf and dumb*
> *Much pleasure did I take*

With my fingers and my thumb
All my wants to relate.'

We smiled. 'That's more cheerful,' I agreed. 'I'm so glad he was able to find pleasure through his misfortune.'

I turned to look at a stone nearby, and as I did so I tripped over the edge of a curb which was hidden in the long grass and I went sprawling headlong over a grave.

Roc picked me up. 'All right, darling? Not hurt?'

'I'm all right, thanks.' I looked ruefully at my stocking. 'A run-ladder. That seems to be all the damage.'

'Sure?' The anxiety in his eyes made me feel very happy and I forgot my earlier vague misgivings. I assured him that I was all right and he said? 'Now some of our neighbours would say that was an omen.'

'What sort of an omen?'

'I couldn't tell you. But falling over a grave! I'm sure they'd see something very significant in that. *And* on your first visit to the churchyard too.'

'Life must be very difficult for some people,' I mused. 'If they're continually seeing omens it doesn't give them much chance of exercising their own free will.'

'And you believe in being the master of your fate and captain of your soul, and the fault not being in your stars and so on?'

'Yes, I think I do. And you, Roc?'

He took my hand suddenly and kissed it. 'As usual you and I are in unison.' He looked about him and said: 'And that's the family vault over there.'

'I must see that.'

I made my way to it, more cautiously this time, Roc following. It was an ornate mausoleum of iron and gilt, with three steps leading down to the door.

'Locked away there are numerous dead Pendorrics,' said Roc.

I turned away. 'I've thought enough about death for one bright summer's morning,' I told him.

He put his arms round me and kissed me. Then he released me and went down the three steps to examine the door. I stood back, where he had left me, and saw that on one of the gilded spikes of the railings a wreath of laurels had been put.

I went towards it and looked at it more closely. There was a card attached to it and on it was written: 'For Barbarina.'

I did not mention the wreath to Roc when he came up to me. He did not seem to have noticed it.

I felt a strong desire to get away from this place of death; away to the sun and the sea.

Lunch was a pleasant meal served in one of the small rooms leading off the north hall. I felt that during it I became better acquainted with Morwenna and Charles, who were determined to make me feel at home. The twins and Rachel Bective ate with us. Lowella was garrulous; Hyson said scarcely a word; and Rachel behaved as though she were indeed a friend of the family. She reproved Lowella for over-exuberance, and seemed determined to be friendly with me. I wondered whether I had made a hasty judgment when I had decided I did not like her.

After lunch Roc and Charles went off together and I went to my room to get a book. I had decided that I would do what I had wanted to ever since I had seen it – sit under one of the palm trees in the quadrangle.

I took my book and found my way out. It was delightfully cool under the tree, and as I sat gloating on the beauty of the place it occurred to me there was a look of a Spanish patio about it. The hydrangeas were pink, blue, and white, and multi-coloured masses of delightful blooms; the lavender scented the air about the water over which bronze Hermes was poised; I saw the flash of gold as the fish swam to and fro.

I tried to read, but I found it difficult to concentrate because of those windows which would not allow me to feel alone. I looked up at them. Who would want to peer out at me I asked myself. And if someone did, what would it matter? I knew I was being absurd.

I went back to my book, and as I sat reading there I heard a movement close behind me, and I was startled when a pair of hands were placed over my eyes and quite unable to repress a gasp as I said rather more sharply than I intended: 'Who is it?'

As I touched the hands, which were not very large, I heard a low chuckle and a voice said: 'You have to guess.'

'Lowella.'

The child danced before me. 'I can stand on my head,' she announced. 'I bet you can't.'

She proved her words, her long thin legs in navy-blue shorts waving perilously near the pond.

'All right,' I told her, 'you've proved it.'

She turned a somersault and landed on her feet, then stood smiling at me, her face pink with the effort.

'How did you guess Lowella?' she asked.

'I couldn't think of anyone else.'

'It might have been Hyson.'

'I was certain it was Lowella.'

'Hyson doesn't do things like that, does she?'

'I think Hyson's a little shy.'

She turned another somersault.

'Are you afraid?' she asked suddenly.

'Afraid of what?'

'Being one of the Brides.'

'What brides?'

'The Brides of Pendorric, of course.'

She stood very still, her eyes narrowed, as she surveyed me. 'You don't know, do you?' she said.

'That's why I'm asking you to tell me.'

She came towards me and, putting her hands on my knees, she looked searchingly into my face; she was so close that I could see the long dark eyes which slightly resembled.Roc's, and the clear unblemished skin. I was aware of another quality which reminded me of Roc. I thought I sensed a certain mischief in her look but I was not sure.

'Will you tell me?' I asked.

For answer she looked over her shoulder and up at the windows, and I went on: 'Why did you ask me if I was afraid?'

'Because you're one of the Brides, of course. My granny was one. Her picture's in the south hall. Have you seen it?'

'Barbarina,' I said.

'Yes. Granny Barbarina. She's dead. You see, she was one of the Brides too.'

'This is all very mysterious to me. I don't know why she should die simply because she was a bride.'

'There was another Bride too. She's in the north hall. She was called Lowella and she used to haunt Pendorric until Granny Barbarina died. Then she rested in her grave.'

'Oh, I see, it's a ghost story.'

'In a way, but it's a live person's story too.'

'I'd like to hear it.'

Again she turned to look at me and I wondered whether she had been warned not to tell me.

'All right.' She spoke in a whisper. 'When Lowella in the south hall was a bride there was a great banquet to celebrate her wedding. Her father was very rich and lived in North Cornwall and he and her mother and all her sisters and brothers and cousins and aunts came to dance at a ball here at Pendorric. There were violins on the dais and they were all eating and dancing when the woman came into the hall. She had a little girl with her; it was her little girl, you see, and she said it was Petroc Pendorric's too. Not Roc's – because this was years and years ago. It was another Pendorric with that name – only they didn't call him Roc. This Petroc Pendorric was Lowella's bridegroom, you see, and the woman with the little girl thought he ought to have been hers. This woman lived wild in the woods with her mother, and the mother was a witch so that makes it a curse that works. She cursed Pendorric and the Bride and all the fun stopped then.'

'And how long ago did this happen?' I asked.

'Nearly two hundred years.'

'It's a long time.'

'But it's a story that goes on and on. It doesn't have an ending, you see. It's not only Lowella's story and Barbarina's story . . . it's yours too.'

'How could that be?'

'You haven't heard what the curse was. The Bride was to die in the prime of her life and she wouldn't rest in her grave until another Bride had gone to her death . . . in the prime of *her* life, of course.'

I smiled. I was astonished that I could feel so relieved. That ominous phrase the Brides of Pendorric was now explained. It was only this old legend which, because we were in Cornwall, where superstitions prevailed, had lived on and provided the old house with a ghost.

'You don't seem very worried. I would if I were you.'

'You haven't finished the story. What happened to that bride?'

'She died having her son exactly a year after her wedding day. She was eighteen years old, which you must admit is very young to die.'

'I expect a great many women died in childbirth. Particularly in those days.'

'Yes, but they said she used to haunt the place waiting for a bride to take her place.'

'To do the haunting, you mean?'

'You're like Uncle Roc. He always laughs at it. I don't laugh though. I know better.'

'So you believe in this haunting business.'

She nodded. 'I've got the second sight. That's why I'm telling you you won't always laugh.'

She leaped away from me and turned another somersault, her long thin legs swaying before me. I had the impression that she was rather pleased because I was going to be shocked out of my scepticism.

She came to stand before me again and with a virtuous expression said: 'I think you ought to know. You see, the Bride Lowella used to haunt Pendorric till my Granny Barbarina died. Then she rested in her grave because she'd lured another bride to take her place and do the haunting. My Granny Barbarina's been doing it for twenty-five years. I reckon she's tired. She'd want to rest in her tomb, wouldn't she? You can bet your life she's looking out for another bride to do the job.'

'I see what you mean,' I said lightly. 'I'm the bride.'

'You're laughing, aren't you?' She stepped back and turned another somersault. 'But you'll see.'

Her face seen from upside down looked jaunty as her long dark pony-tail trailed on the grass.

'I'm sure you've never seen the ghost of your grandmother – have you?'

She did not answer but regarded me stolidly for a few seconds; then she turned a rapid somersault and did a few more handsprings on the grass, going farther and farther away from me until she reached the north door. She went through this and I was alone.

I returned to my book but I found that I kept looking up at the windows. I had been right when I had thought so many windows would be disconcerting; they really were like the eyes of the house.

It's all this talk of ghosts, I thought. Well, I had been warned of the superstitions of the Cornish, and I suspected that Lowella had mischievously tried to frighten me.

The north door opened with a crash and I saw the brown face, the dark pony-tail, the light blue blouse and dark blue shorts.

'Hallo! Uncle Roc said I was to look after you in case you were lonely.'

'Well, you've been doing that after your fashion,' I told her.

'I couldn't find you. I went up to your room and you weren't there. I hunted everywhere and then I thought of the quad. So I came here. What would you like to do?'

'But you were here a little while ago.'

She looked at me blankly.

'You told me the story of the brides,' I reminded her.

She clapped her hands over her mouth. 'She *didn't,* did she?'

'You're not . . . Hyson, are you?'

'Of course not. I'm Lowella.'

'But she said . . .' Had she said she was Lowella? I was not sure.

'Did Hy pretend she was me?' The child began to laugh.

'You are Lowella, aren't you?' I persisted. 'You really are.'

She licked a finger and held it out and said:

'See my finger's wet?'

She wiped it.

'See my finger's dry?'

She drew it across her throat.

'Cut my throat if I tell a lie.'

She looked so earnest that I believed her.

'But why did she pretend she was you?'

Lowella's brows puckered, then she said: I think she doesn't like being the quiet one. So when I'm not there she thinks she'll be me. People who don't know us much can't tell the difference. Would you like to come to the stables and see our ponies?'

I said I would; I felt that I wanted to escape from the quadrangle as I had from the graveyard that morning.

Dinner that night was a comfortable meal. The twins did not join us and there were the five of us. Morwenna said that when I was ready she'd show me the house and explain how it was run.

'Roc thinks that just at first, until you've settled in, you would like things to go on as they are.' Morwenna smiled at her brother affectionately. 'But it's to be as you want. He's very insistent on that.'

'And don't think,' put in Roc, returning his sister's look, 'that Wenna will mind in the least whatever you want to do in the house. Now if you should want to root up her magnolia tree or turn the rose garden into a rockery, that would be quite another matter.'

Morwenna smiled at me. 'I've never been much of a housekeeper. Who cares? It's not really necessary. Mrs. Penhalligan's a treasure. I do love the garden, but of course if you want anything changed . . .'

'So,' cried Roc, 'the battle of the trees is about to begin.'

'Don't take any notice of him,' Morwenna said. 'He loves to tease us. But then I expect you've discovered that by now.'

I said I had and that I knew nothing of gardening and had always lived in a tiny studio which was as different from a mansion as any place could be.

I felt very happy to hear this banter between Roc and his sister because the affection which lay beneath it was very obvious. I was certain that Roc was anxious that Morwenna should not feel put out because he had brought a wife into the midst of their household, which could easily bring a lot of change. I loved him for his consideration of his sister; and when they asked me questions about Capri and were very careful not to mention my father, I guessed that Roc had warned them of my grief.

How considerate he was of us all; I loved him all the more because he never made a show of his care for us, but he hid it under that teasing manner.

Morwenna and Charles were clearly trying to make me feel at home, because they were kindly and so fond of Roc. I was less certain of Rachel. She seemed absorbed in impressing on the servants that she was an honoured member of the family; she was a little on the defensive I thought, and, when her face was in repose, I fancied I caught a bitterness in her expression.

We sat in one of the small drawing-rooms drinking coffee which was served to us by Mrs. Penhalligan while Charles and Roc talked estate business, and Morwenna and Rachel, one on either side of me, launched into a description of local affairs. I found it all very interesting, particularly after the brief glimpse I had had that morning of the little village. Morwenna said she would drive me into Plymouth when I wanted to shop because it would be better for me to have someone who knew the shops the first time I went.

I thanked her, and Rachel said that if by any chance Morwenna wasn't available I could count on her.

'That's nice of you,' I replied.

'Only too pleased to do all I can for Roc's bride,' she murmured.

Bride! Bride! I thought impatiently. Why not wife, which would have sounded so much more natural? I think it was from that moment that the eeriness of the house seemed to close in on me and I was conscious of the darkness outside.

We went to bed early, and when Roc and I were walking along the corridor on our way to our rooms on the south side I looked out of the window to the quadrangle and remembered my conversation with the twins that afternoon.

Roc stood close to me as I looked down.

'You like the quadrangle garden, don't you?'

'Apart from the eyelike windows which are watching all the time.'

He laughed. 'You mentioned that before. Don't worry. We're all too busy to peep.'

As we went along to our bedroom Roc said: 'Something's on your mind, darling.'

'Oh . . . it's nothing really.'

'There is something then.'

I tried to laugh lightly, but I was aware of the silence of that great house and I could not stop thinking of all the tragedies and comedies which must have taken place within those walls over the hundreds of years they had been standing. I could not feel indifference to the past, which in such a place seemed so much closer than it possibly could in my father's studio.

I blurted out what had happened that afternoon.

'Oh, those terrible twins!' he groaned.

'This story about the Brides of Pendorric . . .'

'Such stories abound in Cornwall. You could probably go to a dozen places and hear a similar story. These people are not cold-blooded Anglo-Saxons, you know. They're Celtic – a different race from the phlegmatic

English. I know of course that they may have haunted houses in Huntingdon, Hereford and Oxfordshire – but they're merely houses. According to the Cornish, the whole of Cornwall is haunted. If it's not the piskies it's the knackers from the mines. There are the Little People in their scarlet jackets and sugar-loaf hats. There are footlings who are born feet first, which is supposed to be a sign of their magical powers. There are pillar families – those inheriting power from fishermen ancestors who rendered some service to a mermaid; there are witches, white and black. So of course there are a few common ghosts.'

'I gather Pendorric has that kind.'

'No big house in Cornwall could possibly be without at least one. It's a status symbol. I'll bet Lord Polhorgan would give a thousand or two for a ghost. But the Cornish won't have it. He's not one of us, so he's going to be denied the privilege of being haunted.

I felt comforted, though I scorned myself for needing reassurance; but that child this afternoon had really unnerved me, chiefly because I had believed I was talking to Lowella. I thought Hyson a very strange little person indeed and I did not like the streak of mischief, the almost gloating pleasure in my uneasiness which I had noticed.

'About the story,' I said. 'After all, it concerns the Brides of Pendorric of whom I am one.'

'It was very unfortunate that Lowella Pendorric died exactly a year to the day after her wedding. That probably gave rise to the whole thing. She brought the heir into the world and departed. A common enough occurrence in those days, but you have to remember that here in Cornwall people are always looking for something on which to hang a legend.'

'And she was supposed to haunt the place after that?'

He nodded. 'Brides came and went and they must have forgotten the legend although they'd tell you now that Lowella Pendorric continued to walk by night. Then my mother died when Morwenna and I were five years old. She was only twenty-five.'

'How did she die?'

'That's just what revived the legend, I imagine. She fell from the north gallery into the hall, when the balustrade gave way. The wood was worm-eaten and it was very frail. The shock and the fall combined killed her. It was an unfortunate accident, and because the picture of Lowella hangs in the gallery the story soon got round that it was Lowella's influence that caused her to fall. Lowella was tired of haunting the house, they said, so she decided Barbarina should take her place. I am certain that the part about having to haunt the house until another bride took her place started at that time. You'll hear now that the ghost of Pendorric is my mother Barbarina. Rather a young ghost for such an old house, but you see we haunt in relays.'

'I see,' I said slowly.

He put his hands on my shoulders and laughed; I laughed with him.

Everything seemed comfortingly normal that night.

The woman in the riding jacket and blue-banded hat had begun to haunt my thoughts and I found myself drawn towards the spot where her picture

hung, whenever I was alone in that part of the house. I was not anxious that
anyone should guess how much the picture attracted me, because I thought
it would appear that I was affected by this ridiculous legend.

It was so realistic that the eyes seemed as though they flickered as you
watched them, the lips as though they were about to speak. I wondered
what her feelings had been when she felt the balustrade giving way beneath
her weight; I wondered if she had felt an unhealthy interest in that other
bride . . . as I was beginning to feel in her.

No, I told myself. I was merely interested in the painting and I was
certainly not going to allow the legend to bother me.

All the same, I couldn't resist going to look at the picture.

Roc found me there two mornings later. He put his arm through mine
and said he had come to take me for a drive.

'We don't take after her, do we?' he said. 'Morwenna and I are both dark
as Spaniards. You mustn't feel morbid about her. She's only a picture, you
know.'

He drove me out to the moor that morning; and I was fascinated by that
stretch of wild country with its tors and boulders so strangely shaped that
they looked like grotesque parodies of human beings.

I thought that Roc was trying to make me understand Cornwall, because
he knew that I had been upset by the legend and he wanted to make me
laugh at it.

We drove for miles, through Callington and St. Cleer, little towns with
grey granite façades, and out on to the moor again. He showed me the
Trevethy Quoit, a Neolithic tomb made of blocks of stone; he pointed out
the burial grounds of men who had lived before history was recorded; he
wanted me to know that a country which could offer so much proof of its
past must necessarily be one of legend.

He stopped the car high on the moor, and in the distance I could see that
fantastic formation of rock known as the Cheesewring.

He put his arm round me and said: 'One day I'll take you farther west
and show you the Merry Maidens. Nineteen stones in a circle which you
will be asked to believe were once nineteen girls who, deciding to defy
tradition and go dancing in a sacred place, were turned to stone; and indeed
the stones lean this way and that as if they had been caught and petrified
in the midst of a dance.' His eyes were very tender as he turned to me.
'You'll get used to us in time,' he went on. 'Everywhere you look in this
place there's some legend. You don't take them seriously.'

I knew then that he was worried about me and I told him not to be because
I had always prided myself on my common sense.

'I know,' he said. 'But your father's death was a greater shock than you
realize. I'm going to take extra special care of you.'

'Then,' I replied, 'I shall begin to feel very precious indeed, because I
fancy you have been taking rather a lot of care of me ever since that awful
day.'

'Well, remember I do happen to be your husband.'

I turned to him then and said almost fiercely, 'It's something I couldn't
possibly forget for a minute . . . even if I wanted to.'

He turned my face up to his and his kiss was tender.

'And you don't want to?'

I threw myself against him, and as I clung to him, his grip on me tightened. It was as though we were both trying to make each other understand the immense depth of the love between us.

It was the comfort I needed.

Roc could always emerge from an emotional scene with more ease than I could, and in a short time he was his old teasing self. He began to tell me stories of Cornish legends, some so fantastic that I accused him of inventing them.

Then we both started inventing stories about the place we passed, trying to cap each other's absurdities. It all seemed tremendous fun, although anyone listening to us would have thought we were crazy.

As we drove back in these high spirits I marvelled at the way in which Roc could always comfort and delight me.

During the next few days I spent a great deal of time in Roc's company. He would take me with him when he went on his rounds of the farms and I was welcomed everywhere, usually with a glass of some home-made wine or cider; I was even expected to eat a Cornish pasty as they came hot from the oven.

The people were warm and friendly once I had overcome a certain initial suspicion which they felt towards 'foreigners' from the other side of the Tamar. I was English; they were Cornish; therefore to them I was a foreigner.

'Once a foreigner, always a foreigner,' Roc told me. 'But of course marriage makes a difference. When you've produced a little Cornish man or woman you'll be accepted. Otherwise it would take all of fifty years.'

Morwenna and I drove into Plymouth one afternoon and stopped and had tea near the Hoe.

'Charles and I are very pleased Roc's married,' she told me. 'We wanted to see him happily settled.'

'You're very fond of him, aren't you?'

'Well, he is my brother, and my twin at that. And Roc's a rather special person. I expect you'll agree with that.'

As I agreed so wholeheartedly I felt my affection for Morwenna increasing.

'You can always rely on Roc,' went on Morwenna, and as she stirred her tea thoughtfully her eyes were vague as though she were looking back over the past.

'Were you very surprised when he wrote and said he was married?'

'Just at first, perhaps. But he's always done the unexpected. Charles and I were beginning to be afraid he'd never settle down, so when we heard, we were really delighted.'

'Even though he'd married someone who was a stranger to you.'

Morwenna laughed. 'That state of affairs didn't last long, did it? You're one of us now.'

That was a very pleasant jaunt because I was always so happy to talk

about Roc and to see signs of the affection he inspired in those people who
had known him all his life.

Morwenna and I called on the Darks at the vicarage and I had an
interesting afternoon listening to the stories the vicar had to tell of Cornish
superstitions.

'I think they're so sure that certain things are going to happen that they
make them happen,' he told me.

We also talked of the people who lived on the Pendorric estate and I
learned of some of the benefits which had come to them since Roc had been
in control. I glowed with pride as I listened.

It was at the vicarage that I met Dr. Andrew Clement, a man in his late
twenties or early thirties. He was tall, fair and friendly and we liked each
other from the start.

He told me that he too was what was known as a foreigner, having come
from Kent, and been in Cornwall some eighteen months.

'I come past Pendorric several times a week,' he told me, 'when I visit
your neighbour, Lord Polhorgan.'

'He's seriously ill, isn't he?'

'Not so much seriously ill as in danger of becoming so. He has angina and
threatening coronary thrombosis. We have to watch him very carefully. He
has a nurse living there all the time. Have you met her yet?'

'No, I haven't.'

'She does occasionally come to Pendorric,' said Morwenna. 'You'll meet
her sooner or later.'

That was a very pleasant afternoon, and as Morwenna and I drove back
the conversation turned to the twins.

'Rachel seems to be very efficient,' I said.

'Very.'

'I suppose you're lucky to get her. A person with her qualifications must
be rather difficult to come by nowadays.'

'She's here . . . temporarily. The twins will have to go to school in a year
or so. They can't be at home like this for ever.'

Was it my imagination, or had Morwenna's manner changed when I
mentioned Rachel?

There was a short silence between us and I reproved myself because I
suspected I was becoming over-sensitive. I was beginning to look for things
which didn't exist, and I wondered whether I had changed since coming to
Cornwall.

I wanted to go on talking about Rachel because I was eager to know more
about her. I wanted to find out what the relationship between her and Roc
had been – if in fact there had been anything unusual in their relationship.

But Morwenna had dismissed the subject. She began to talk animatedly
about the Darks and the changes they had made at the vicarage.

That afternoon I went to the quadrangle. I was drawn there somewhat
unwillingly, for I would rather have taken a book into the garden which
was on the south side and which led down to the beach. There I could have
sat in one of the sheltered arbours among the hydrangeas, the buddleias and

the sweet-smelling lavender, the house behind me, the sea before me. It would have been very pleasant. Yet because of that faint revulsion I had experienced in the quadrangle – mainly on account of the windows which looked down on it – I was aware of a compulsion to go there. I was not the sort of person who enjoyed feeling even vaguely afraid, and I was sure that by facing whatever disconcerted me I should more quickly overcome it.

I sat under the palm tree with my book and tried to concentrate, but once more I found myself continually glancing up at the windows.

I had not been there very long when the twins came out of the north door.

When I saw them together I had no difficulty in distinguishing between them. Lowella was so vital, Hyson so subdued. I began to wonder then whether it really had been Hyson who had warned me to beware of Barbarina, or whether it had been a mischievous trick of Lowella's to try to frighten me and then pretend that it was Hyson who had done it.

'Hallo,' called Lowella.

They came and sat on the grass and gazed at me.

'Are we disturbing you?' asked Lowella politely.

'I wasn't very deep in my book.'

'You like it here?' went on Lowella.

'It's very peaceful.'

'You're shut right in. You've got Pendorric all around you. Hy likes it here too. Don't you, Hy?'

Hyson nodded.

'Well,' went on Lowella, 'what do you think of *us*?'

'I hadn't given the matter a great deal of thought.'

'I didn't mean the two of us. I mean all of us. What do you think of Pendorric and Uncle Roc, Mummy, Daddy, and Becky Sharp?'

'Becky Sharp?'

'Old Bective, of course.'

'Why do you call her that?'

'Hy said she was like a Becky Sharp she read about in a book. Hy's always reading.'

I looked at Hyson who nodded gravely.

'She told me about Becky Sharp and I said, "That's Rachel." So I called her Becky Sharp. I give people names. I'm Lo. She's Hy. Wasn't it clever of Mummy and Daddy to give us names like that. Though I'm not sure that I like being Lo. I'd rather be Hy ... only in my name I mean. I'd rather be myself than old Hy. She's always sitting about and thinking.'

'Not a bad occupation.' I smiled at Hyson, who continued to regard me gravely.

'I've got names for everybody – my own secret names – and Becky Sharp is one of them.'

'Have you got one for me?'

'You! Well, you're the Bride, aren't you! You couldn't be anything else.'

'Does Miss Bective like the name you've given her?' I asked.

'She doesn't know. It's a secret. But you see, she was at school with Mummy and she was always coming here and Hy said, "One day she'll come to stay because she never wants to go away." '

'Has she said so?'

'Of course not. As if she would. It's all secret. Other people never know what Becky Sharp is up to. But she wants to stay. We thought she was going to marry Uncle Roc.'

Hyson came and put her hands on my knees; she looked into my face and said: 'It was what she wanted. I don't suppose she likes it much because you did.'

'You're not supposed to say that, Hy,' Lowella warned.

'I'll say it if I want to.'

'You can't. You mustn't.'

Hyson was suddenly fierce. 'I can and I will.'

Lowella chanted: 'You can't. You can't.' And began to run round the pond. Hyson went in pursuit of her. I watched them running about the quadrangle until Lowella disappeared through the north door. Hyson made as though to follow her, hesitated, and turning stood looking at me for a few moments. Then she came back.

'Lowella's really very childish,' she told me. She knelt at my feet and looked at me, and feeling a little embarrassed by her scrutiny I said: 'You never talk very much when she's there. Why not?'

She shrugged her shoulders. 'I never talk unless I have something to say,' she murmured primly.

Now it seemed she had nothing to say for she continued to kneel at my feet in a silence which went on for several minutes, then she rose suddenly and stood looking up at the windows.

She lifted her hand and waved, and following her gaze I saw that the curtain at one of the windows was slightly pulled back and someone was standing about a foot from the window looking down. I could just make out a vague figure in a black hat with a band of blue about it.

'Who's that?' I asked sharply.

She rose to her feet and said slowly: 'That was Granny!'

Then she smiled at me and walked sedately to the north door and I was alone in the quadrangle. I looked up at the window. There was no one there and the curtain had fallen.

'Barbarina,' I murmured and I felt as though eyes were watching me, mocking me, and I did not want to stay in the courtyard any longer.

This was ridiculous, I told myself. It was a trick. Of course, Lowella had gone in and they had decided to amuse themselves at my expense.

But it had not been a child I had seen at the window. It has been a tall woman.

I hurried into the house through the south door and I paused before the picture of Barbarina. I fancied that the eyes were mocking me.

This is absurd, I said as I mounted the staircase. I was a normal, uncomplicated person who did not believe in ghosts.

Had I changed since I came to Pendorric? Was I still so self-sufficient since I had experienced emotions which had only been names to me before I met Roc Pendorric? Love, jealousy – and now fear?

Chapter Three

I went straight up to my room, and as I opened the door I gasped, for a woman was sitting in an arm-chair with her back to the light. After my experience in the courtyard I must really have been unnerved, because it seemed several seconds before I recognized Morwenna.

'I'm afraid I startled you,' she said. 'I'm so sorry. I came up to look for you . . . and sat down for a moment.'

'It was silly of me, but I didn't expect to see anyone here.'

'I came up because Deborah has arrived. I want you to meet her.'

'Who, did you say?'

'Deborah Hyson. She's my mother's sister. She spends a lot of time here. She has been away and only got back this afternoon. I think she's come back on your account. She can't bear things to be happening in the family and not take part in them.'

'Could I have seen her at one of the windows not long ago?'

'Very likely. Was it the west side?'

'Yes, I think it was.'

'Then I expect it was Deborah. She has her rooms there.'

'She was looking down on the quadrangle and Hyson waved to her, then ran off without explaining.'

'Hyson's very fond of her, and she of Hyson. I'm glad, because Lowella is usually so much more popular. Are you coming down now? We're having tea in the winter parlour, and Deborah's very anxious to meet you.'

'Let's go, then.'

We went down to the little room on the first floor of the north wing, where a tall woman rose to greet me; I was almost certain that she was the one I had seen at the window.

She was not wearing the hat now, but her abundant white hair was in a style which might have been fashionable thirty years or so ago; and I noticed too that there was an old-fashioned look about her clothes. Her eyes were very blue and her frilly *crêpe de Chine* blouse matched them perfectly. She was very tall and slender in her black tailored suit.

She took both my hands and looked earnestly into my face.

'My dear,' she said, 'how glad I am that you have come!' I was astonished by the fervour of her greeting; and I could only conjecture that, like most of the family, she was delighted to see Roc married, and therefore was prepared to accept me as a blessing. 'As soon as I heard the news I came.'

'That's very kind of you.'

She smiled almost wistfully while her eyes remained on me.

'Come and sit beside me,' she said. 'We'll have lots to talk about. Morwenna dear, is that tea coming soon?'

'Almost at once,' Morwenna replied.

We sat side by side and she went on: 'You must call me Deborah, dear. The children do. Oh, by the children I mean Petroc and Morwenna. The twins call me Granny. They always have. I don't mind in the least.'

'You don't look like a granny!'

She smiled. 'I expect I do to the twins. They think anyone of twenty somewhat aged, and after that of course quite ancient. I'm rather glad they do, though. They hadn't a granny. I supplied the need.'

Mrs. Penhalligan brought in the tea and Morwenna poured it.

'Charles and Roc won't be in for an hour or so,' she told Deborah.

'I'll see them at dinner. Oh, here *are* the twins.'

The door burst open and Lowella rushed in, followed sedately by Hyson.

"Lo, Granny,' said Lowella, and walking to Deborah's chair was embraced and kissed. Hyson followed; and I noticed that the hug she received was even more affectionate. There was no doubt that these two were very fond of each other.

Lowella went to the tea-trolly to see what there was for tea, while Hyson stood leaning against Deborah's chair.

'I must say it is pleasant to be back,' said Deborah, 'though I miss the moor.' She explained to me: 'I have a house on Dartmoor. I was brought up there and now that my parents are dead it belongs to me. You must come out and see it one day.'

'I'll come with you,' said Lowella.

'Dear Lowella!' murmured Deborah. 'She never likes to be left out of anything. And you'll come too, Hyson, won't you?'

'Yes, Granny.'

'That's a good girl. I hope you're looking after your Aunt Favel, and making her feel at home.'

'We don't call her Aunt. She's just Favel and of *course* we've been looking after her,' said Lowella. 'Uncle Roc told us we had to.'

'And Hyson?'

'Yes, Granny, I've been showing her what she ought to see and telling her what she ought to know.'

Deborah smiled and began gently pulling Hyson's pony-tail in a caressing way.

She smiled at me: 'I must show you pictures of the children. I have lots of them in my rooms.'

'On the walls,' cried Lowella, 'and in albums with writing underneath. It says "Petroc aged six." "Morwenna in the Quadrangle aged eight." And there are lots of Granny Barbarina and Granny Deborah when they were little girls – only they're in Devon.'

Deborah leaned towards me. 'There's usually a person like myself in all families: the one who did not marry but could be called in to look after the children. She keeps all the pictures and knows the dates of birthdays.'

'Granny Deborah never forgets,' Lowella told me.

'Did I see you when I was in the quadrangle?' I could not prevent myself asking, for foolish as it was, I had to satisfy myself on this point.

'Yes. I had only just arrived. I hadn't told Morwenna or Roc that I was coming to-day. I peeped out and saw you and Hyson. I didn't know you'd seen me or I should have opened the window and spoken to you.'

'Hyson waved and I looked up and saw you. I was astonished when she said you were her granny.'

'And didn't she explain? Oh Hyson, my dear child!' She went on caressing the pony-tail.

'I told her it was my granny, and it was,' Hyson defended herself.

'You're eating very little,' Morwenna scolded Deborah and me. 'Do try these splits. Maria will be hurt if we sent too many back.'

'I always say this Cornish cream isn't as good as ours in Devonshire,' said Deborah.

Morwenna laughed. 'That's sheer prejudice. It's exactly the same.'

Deborah asked me about my life in Capri and how Roc and I had met.

'How delightful!' she cried when I had answered her questions. 'A lightning romance! I think it's charming, don't you, Morwenna?'

'We're all very pleased, of course ... particularly now that we know Favel.'

'And we were longing for the new Bride of Pendorric,' said Hyson quietly.

Everyone laughed and conversation was general while we finished tea.

When the meal was over, Hyson asked if she could help her granny unpack. Deborah was very pleased and said of course she could. She added: 'And I don't suppose Favel has seen my rooms, has she? We'll invite her to come with us, shall we, Hyson?'

I thought Hyson rather grudgingly agreed, but I accepted quickly because I was anxious to know more of this new member of the household.

The three of us went off together and soon were in the west corridor passing that very window at which Deborah had appeared and so startled me.

She opened the door of a room which had windows very like those in Roc's and my bedroom and which gave a superb view of the coastline stretching out towards the west and Land's End. My eyes went immediately to the bed – a four-poster like ours – because on the rose-coloured counterpane lay the black hat with the blue band. It was not really like the one in the picture but the colouring was similar. I felt rather foolish as well as relieved, because it was comforting to solve the mystery of the apparition so quickly, but at the same time it was disconcerting to remember how shaken I had been at the sight of it.

I saw then that a part of one of the walls was covered with photographs of all sizes and types, some being studio portraits, others snapshots.

Deborah laughed and followed my gaze. 'I have always hoarded pictures of the family. It's the same in Devonshire, isn't it, Hyson?'

'Yes, but they're all pictures of you before ... these are after.'

'Yes, of course. Time seems rather divided like that – before Barby's marriage ... and after.'

'Barbarina,' I murmured involuntarily.

'Yes, Barbarina. She was Barby to me, and I was Deb. No one else ever called us by those versions of our names. Barbarina was the name of an ancestress of ours. It's unusual, isn't it? Until Barbarina's marriage she and I were always together.' The blue eyes clouded momentarily and I guessed that there had been great devotion between the sisters. 'Oh well,' she went on, 'it's all so long ago. Sometimes I find it hard to believe that she is dead . . . and in her grave. . . .'

'But . . .' began Hyson.

Deborah laid her hand on the child's head and went on: 'When she . . . died, I came to live here and I brought up Petroc and Morwenna. I tried to take her place, but can anyone take the place of a mother?'

'They're very fond of you, I'm sure.'

'I think they are. Do let me show you the photographs. I think some of them are very charming. You'll want to see your husband in the various stages of his development, I expect. It's always rather fun, don't you think, to see people as they were years and years ago.'

I smiled at the mischievous-eyed boy in the open shirt and cricket flannels; and the picture of him standing side by side with Morwenna – Morwenna smiling coyly at the camera, Roc scowling at it. There was a picture of them as babies; they lay side by side and a beautiful woman was bending over them.

'Barbarina and her twins,' murmured Deborah.

'How beautiful she is!'

'Yes.' There was a note of infinite sadness in her voice. So she still mourns her sister, I thought; and there came into my mind the memory of the family vault with the laurel hanging on the spike. I guessed who had put that there.

I turned my attention to a picture of a man and a woman; I had no difficulty in recognizing Barbarina, and the man who was with her was so like Roc that I guessed he was Barbarina's husband.

There it was, the almost challenging smile, the face of a man who knew how to get the best out of life, the reckless gambler, the indefinable charm. I noticed that the ears of the man in the picture were Roc's ears, that the eyes were slightly tilted at the corners. It was a handsome face, made even more attractive by that streak of mischief . . . wickedness . . . or whatever it was that I had sensed in Roc.

'Roc's parents,' I said.

'Taken a year before the tragedy,' Deborah told me.

'It is very sad. He looks so fond of her. He must have been heartbroken.'

Deborah smiled grimly, but she did not speak.

'Aren't you going to show Favel the albums?' Hyson asked.

'Not now, dear. I've my settling in to do, and stories of the past can be a little boring, I'm afraid, to those who haven't lived them.'

'I'm certainly not bored. I'm very eager to learn all I can about the family.'

'Of course . . . now that you are one of us. And I shall enjoy showing you the albums at another time.'

It was a kind of dismissal, and I said I too had things to do and would see her later. She came towards me and, taking my hands, smiled at me affectionately.

'I can't tell you how pleased I am that you are here,' she told me earnestly; and there could be no doubting her sincerity.

'Everyone has been so charming to me at Pendorric,' I told her. 'No bride could have been more enthusiastically welcomed, and considering how sudden our marriage had been and my coming must have been rather a shock to the family, I'm very grateful to everybody.'

'Of course we welcome you, my dear.'

Hyson said earnestly: 'We've been waiting for her for years . . . haven't we, Granny?'

Deborah laughed, and gently pulled Hyson's ear. 'You take in everything, child,' she said. And to me: 'We're delighted that Roc's married. The Pendorrics usually marry young.'

The door opened and a little woman came into the room. She was dressed in black, which was not becoming to her sallow skin; her hair was what is know as iron grey and must have been almost black once; her dark bushy brows met over small worried eyes; she had a long thin nose and thin lips.

She was about to speak, but seeing me hesitated. Deborah said: 'This is my dear Carrie, who was our nurse and has never left me. Now she looks after me . . . completely, and I just don't know what I should do without her. Carrie, this is the new Mrs. Pendorric.'

The worried-looking eyes were fixed on me. 'Oh,' she murmured, 'the new Mrs. Pendorric, eh.'

Deborah smiled at me. 'You'll get to know Carrie very quickly. She'll do anything for you, I'm sure. She's a wonder with her needle. She makes most of my things as she always did.'

'I made for the two of them,' said Carrie with pride. 'And I used to say there was no one better dressed in the whole of Devonshire than Miss Barbarina and Miss Deborah.'

I noticed then the slight burr in her speech and the tenderness in her voice when she spoke of those two.

'Carrie, there's some unpacking to do.'

Carrie's expression changed and she looked almost disgruntled.

'Carrie hates leaving her beloved moor!' said Deborah with a laugh. 'It takes her quite a time to settle down on this side of the Tamar.'

'I wish we'd never crossed the Tamar,' Carrie muttered.

Deborah smiled at me and, putting her arm through mine, walked into the corridor with me.

'We have to humour Carrie,' she whispered. 'She's a privileged servant. She's getting on now and her mind wanders a little.' She withdrew her arm. 'It'll be fun showing you the pictures some time, Favel,' she went on. 'I can't tell you how pleased I am that you're here.'

I left her, feeling grateful for several reasons; not only was she affectionate and eager to be friends, but she had made me feel myself again now I was sure that it was a person of living flesh and blood who had looked down on me from the window.

The mail at Pendorric was brought up to our bedrooms with early-morning tea; and it was a few days later when Roc, looking through his, came to a letter which made him laugh aloud.

'It's come,' he called to me in the bathroom, 'I knew it would.'

'What?' I asked, coming out wrapped in a bath towel.

'Lord Polhorgan requests the pleasure of Mr. and Mrs. Pendorric's company on Wednesday at three-thirty.'

'Wednesday. That's to-morrow. Are we going?'

'Of course. I'm so eager for you to see the Folly.'

I thought very little more about Lord Polhorgan's invitation because I was far more interested in Pendorric; and I could not feel the almost malicious delight the family seemed to take in deriding the Folly and its master. As I said to Roc, if the man from Manchester, Leeds or Birmingham wanted to build a house on the cliffs, why shouldn't he? And if he wanted it to look like a medieval castle, again why shouldn't he? The Pendorrics had apparently been glad to sell him the land. It was not for them to tell him how he must use it.

As Roc and I set out that Wednesday afternoon he seemed to be enjoying some secret joke.

'I can't wait to see what you think of the set-up,' he told me.

To my unpractised eye the house looked as old as Pendorric. 'Do you know,' I said to Roc, as we approached the stone unicorns which did the same service as our battered lions, 'I shouldn't know that this wasn't a genuine antique if you hadn't told me.'

'Ah, you wait till you've had a chance to examine it.'

We pulled the bell in the great portico and heard it clanging through the hall.

A dignified manservant opened the door and, bowing his head, said solemnly: 'Good afternoon, sir. Good afternoon, madam. His lordship is waiting for you, so I'll take you up immediately.'

It took quite a long time to reach the room where our host was waiting for us; and I noticed that although the furniture was antique the carpets and curtains were expensively modern.

We were finally led to a large room with windows overlooking the beautifully laid-out cliff garden which ran down to the sea; and resting on a chaise-longue was the old man.

'My lord,' the manservant announced, 'Mr. and Mrs. Pendorric.'

'Ah! Bring them in, Dawson. Bring them in.'

He turned his head, and the intentness of those grey eyes was rather disturbing, particularly as they were directed towards me.

'Good of you to come,' he said rather brusquely, as though he didn't mean this. 'You'll have to forgive my not rising.'

'Please don't,' I said quickly, and I went to his chaise-longue and took his hand.

He had a high colour with a faint purplish tinge, and I noticed how the veins stood out on his long thin hands.

'Sit down, Mrs. Pendorric,' he said, still in the same brusque manner. 'Give your wife a chair, Pendorric. And put it near me . . . that's right, facing the light.'

I had to suppress a slight resentment that I was being put under a shrewd scrutiny, and I experienced a certain nervousness which I hadn't expected I should.

'Tell me, how do you like Cornwall, Mrs. Pendorric?'

He spoke sharply, jerkily, as though he were barking orders on a barrack square.

'I'm enchanted,' I said.

'And it compares favourably with that island place of yours?'

'Oh yes.'

'All I see of it now is this view.' He nodded towards the window.

'I can't imagine you'd find a more beautiful one anywhere.'

He looked from me to Roc; and I was aware that my husband's expression had become rather sardonic. He didn't like the old man, that much was clear; and I felt annoyed with him because I was afraid he made it obvious.

Our host was frowning towards the door. 'Late with tea,' he said. He must give his servants a difficult time, I thought, for even if he had asked for tea to be served immediately we arrived it was not very late; we had not been in the room more than three or four minutes.

Then the door opened and a tea wagon was wheeled in. It was overladen with cakes of all descriptions besides bread and butter and splits with bowls of clotted cream and jam.

'Ah,' Lord Polhorgan grunted, 'at last! Where's Nurse Grey?'

'Here I am.' A woman came into the room. She was so beautiful that for a moment I was startled. The blue in her striped dress matched her eyes, her starched apron was snowy white, and her cap, set almost jauntily on her masses of golden hair, called attention to its beauty. I had never seen a nurse's uniform worn so becomingly; then I realized that this woman would look dazzling whatever she wore, simply because she was so very beautiful.

'Good afternoon, Mr. Pendorric,' she said.

Roc had risen to his feet as she entered and I could not see his face as he looked at her. He said: 'Good afternoon, Nurse.' Then he turned. 'Favel, this is Nurse Grey, who looks after Lord Polhorgan.'

'I'm so glad to meet you.' She had a wide mouth and perfectly shaped teeth.

'What about giving Mrs. Pendorric some tea?' growled Lord Polhorgan.

'Of course,' said Nurse Grey. 'It's all here, I see. Now, Mrs. Pendorric, you'd like to sit near Lord Polhorgan. I'll put this little table here for you.'

I thanked her and she went to the tea wagon and began to pour out while Roc brought over a plate of splits and cream and jam which he set on the table.

'I don't need a nurse all the time,' Lord Polhorgan told me. 'But I may need one at any moment. That's why she's here. Quite an efficient woman.'

'I am sure she is.'

'Easy job. Gets a lot of free time. Beautiful surroundings.'

'Ideal,' I murmured, wondering how Nurse Grey liked being referred to in the third person. I glanced at her. She was smiling at Roc.

I handed Lord Polhorgan the splits, and I noticed that he moved slowly and was rather breathless as he took one.

'Shall I spread the jam and cream for you?' I asked.

'H'm!' he barked, which meant assent. 'Thanks!' he added when I had done it. 'Good of you. Now help yourself.'

Nurse Grey asked if I preferred China or Indian, and I was given delicious Mandarin Pekoe with lemon.

She then sat down near Roc. I very much wanted to hear what they were saying, but Lord Polhorgan demanded my attention by firing questions at me. He appeared to be very interested in the way we had lived on the island, and I promised to show him some of my father's work which had been sent to Pendorric.

'Good,' he said. He made me talk about my childhood and in a short time I was living it all again.

'You're not happy,' said Lord Polhorgan suddenly, and I blurted out the story of my father's death, to which he listened gravely and then said: 'You were very fond of him. Was your mother fond of him too?'

I told him something of their life together then, how they had lived for each other, how ill she had become and how they had made me aware that they wanted to live every hour to the full because they knew that the time would come when they could not be together; and as I did so I marvelled that I could talk so intimately to such a gruff old man on such short acquaintance.

He laid his veined hand on my arm. 'Is that how it is with you?' he said sharply, and he looked towards Roc, who was laughing with Nurse Grey.

I hesitated just a second too long.

'Marry in haste . . .' he added. 'Seem to have heard that said somewhere.'

I flushed. 'I'm very happy at Pendorric,' I retorted.

'You rush into things,' he said. 'Bad habit. I never rushed. Made decisions, yes . . . and sometimes quick ones, but always gave them adequate thought. You coming to see me again?'

'If you ask me.'

'Then you are asked now.'

'Thank you.'

'You won't want to, though.'

'Yes, I shall.'

He shook his head. 'You'll make excuses. Too busy. Another engagement. What would a young woman like you want with visiting a sick old man?'

'But I'd love to come.'

'You've got a kind heart. But kindness doesn't always go very deep. Don't want to hurt the old man . . . go now and then. But a bore. What a nuisance!'

'It will be nothing of the sort. You're so interested in things. And I'm attracted by this house.'

'Pretty vulgar, eh? The old man of the people who wanted to build up a bit of background. Doesn't go down well with the aristocrats, I can tell you.'

'Why shouldn't people build backgrounds if they want them?'

'Listen, young woman. There's no reason why anyone shouldn't build anything. You get your just deserts in this world. I wanted to make money and I made it. I wanted to have a family mansion . . . well, I've got it. In this world you say, I want this and I want that. And if you've got any guts you go and get it. You get what you pay for, and if it doesn't turn out as you planned, well then you have to look for where you went wrong because, you can depend on it, you've gone wrong somewhere.'

'I expect you're right.'

'I'd like you to come again even if you are bored. Perhaps you'd be less bored after a while . . . when we got to know each other.'

'I haven't started to be bored yet.'

He clenched and unclenched his hand, frowning at it. 'I'm an old man . . . incapacitated by illness . . . brought on, they tell me, by the life I've led.' He patted his chest. 'I've put a big strain on this, it seems, and now I've got to pay for it. All right, I say, life's a matter of settling bills and drawing dividends. I'm ready.'

'I can see you have a philosophy.'

'Play chess?'

'My mother taught me.'

'Your mother, eh?'

'She also taught me reading, writing and arithmetic, before I came to school in England.'

'I reckon you were the apple of her eye.'

'I was her only child.'

'Yes,' he said soberly. 'Well, if you played a game of chess with me now and then, you wouldn't be so bored with the old man's efforts at conversation. When will you come?'

I considered. 'The day after to-morrow,' I said.

'Good. Tea-time?'

'Yes, but I mustn't eat so many of these splits or I shall put on too much weight.'

He looked at me and his eyes were suddenly soft. 'You're as slight as a sylph,' he said.

Nurse Grey came over with plates of cakes, but we did not seem in the mood for eating any more.

I noticed that Nurse Grey's eyes had grown more luminous and that there was a faint pink colour in her cheeks. I wondered uneasily whether Roc had had anything to do with that, and I was reminded of Rachel Bective and Dinah Bond, the young blacksmith's wife.

The conversation became general, and after an hour we left.

Roc was clearly amused as we walked home.

'Another conquest for you,' he commented. 'The old fellow certainly took to you. I've never known him so gracious before.'

'Poor old man, I don't think people try to understand him.'

'They don't need to,' retorted Roc. 'He's as easy to read as an A.B.C. He's the typical self-made man – a character off the shelf. There are some people who mould themselves on old clichés. They decide the sort of person they're going to be and start playing the part; after a while they're so good at it that it becomes second nature. That's why there are so many stock characters in the world.' He grinned at me. 'You don't believe me, do you? Well, look at Lord P. Started selling newspapers . . . perhaps not newspapers, but some such job. It's the pattern that matters, not the detail. Never goes in for any fun, piles up the little capital to start with, and by the time he's thirty, industry and skill have turned it into a big capital and he's on the way to becoming a millionaire. That's all very well, but he can't be *himself* ... he has to be one of the band of self-made men. He clings to his rough manners. "I came up from nothing and I'm proud of it!" Doesn't go in for the ordinary graces of conventional living. "Why should I change myself? I'm perfect as I am." Oh, I don't have to *try* to understand Lord P. If he were made of glass I shouldn't be able to see through him more clearly.'

'You don't forgive him for building his house.'

Roc shrugged his shoulders. 'Perhaps not. It's a fake and I hate fakes. Suppose all the self-made men made up their minds to build along our coast? What a sight! No, I'm against these pseudo-antiques; and to have put one on our doorstep is an imposition. Polhorgan's Folly is an outsider here on our coast with houses like Pendorric, Mount Mellyn, Mount Widden, Cotehele and the like ... just as its master is ... with his Midland manners calling himself Lord Polhorgan. As though Tre, Pol and Pen did not belong to Cornishmen.'

'How vehement you are!' I said, and trying to speak lightly added: 'And if *I* made a conquest, what of you?'

He was smiling as he turned to me. 'Thea, you mean?'

'You call her that?'

'That's her name, my dear. Althea Grey – Thea to her friends.'

'Of whom you are one.'

'Of course, and so will you be. As for my conquest,' he went on, 'that's one of long standing. She has been here eighteen months, you know.'

Then he put his arm about me and began to sing:

'Wherever you hear Tre, Pol and Pen
You'll know that you're with Cornishmen.'

He smiled at me and continued:

'Alas, I have to add a rider.
One can't ignore the rich outsider.'

'I think,' I said, 'that you prefer the nurse to the invalid.' I saw the teasing light in his eyes.

'With you it's exactly the reverse,' he commented. 'That's why it was such a successful visit. I took care of the nurse while you devoted yourself to your host.'

Two days later, as we had arranged, I went to play chess with Lord Polhorgan. I came back and told Roc rather defiantly that I liked the old man even more than on the first occasion; which seemed to amuse him very much. Nurse Grey was not present, and I poured out the tea. The old man was delighted when he beat me, then he looked at me shrewdly and said: 'Sure you're not humouring the old man – letting him win, eh?' I replied that I had done my best to beat him, and that satisfied him. Before I left I had promised to call again in a day or so in order to give him a return match.

I was settling into life at Pendorric. I did a little gardening with Morwenna, and it was pleasant to chat with her while we worked.

'It's a useful hobby,' she said, 'because we haven't the gardeners we once had. In my father's day there were four of them; now it's Bill Pascoe from the cottages three afternoons a week, with Toms working when he gets a chance. Both Roc and I were always fond of growing things.'

'Roc doesn't do much in the gardens now,' I put in.

'Well, there's the farm to take up his time. He and Charles work hard on that.' She sat back on her heels and smiled at the fork in her hands. 'I'm so pleased they get on well together – but then of course they're two wonderful people. I've often thought how lucky I am.'

'I know what you mean,' I answered soberly. 'We're both lucky.'

Charles was very friendly to me in a quiet and unassuming way, and I liked his chubby charm. When Roc took me round the farm for the first time I was immediately aware of the respect Charles had for Roc's judgment, and that made me like him all the more.

I even liked Rachel Bective a little better than I had in the beginning and reproached myself for a too-hasty judgment because I had fancied I detected something rather sly in her sandy looks.

On one occasion we went for a walk together and she volunteered a little information about herself, telling me how she had met Morwenna when they had been at school together and had come to spend a summer holiday at Pendorric. From then she had been there often. She had to earn her living and had decided to take up teaching, so she had agreed to come here for a year to supervise the twins' education because she knew what a trial they were to their mother.

The twins themselves had a habit of coming upon me at unexpected moments, and seemed to take a special pleasure in leaping out on me and startling me.

Lowella addressed me as Bride, which at first I thought amusing but later was not so sure; Hyson had a habit of fixing her silent gaze on me whenever she was in my company, which I also found disconcerting.

Deborah was as determined as the others to make me feel at home; she told me that she felt like a mother towards me because Roc had been like her own son. I was sitting in the quadrangle one afternoon when I suddenly had the eerie feeling that I was being watched. I shook off this feeling which was always ready to worry me when I was in the quadrangle, but it persisted, and when I looked up at the window on the west side where I had seen Deborah on the day she arrived I almost expected to see her there.

I stared for a few seconds at those curtained windows; then I turned and looked at the east side. I was certain then that I saw a movement.

I waved and continued to look, but there was no response.

Ten minutes later Deborah joined me in the quadrangle.

'How you love this spot!' she said, and she pulled up one of the white and gilded chairs to sit close to me.

'My feelings for the place are a little mixed,' I told her frankly. 'I am immensely attracted, and yet I never feel exactly comfortable here.'

'Why ever not?'

I looked over my shoulder. 'It's the windows I think.'

'I often say it's a pity that it is only corridor windows which look down on the quadrangle. It would make such a lovely view and a change from the great vistas of sea from south, west and east, and country from the north.'

'It's the windows themselves. They take away privacy.'

She laughed. 'I believe you're rather a fanciful person after all.'

'Oh no, I'm not really. Were you on the east side a little while ago?'

She shook her head.

'I'm sure someone was looking down.'

'I shouldn't think so, dear, not from the east side. Those rooms are rarely used now. The furniture's covered in dustsheets . . . except in her rooms.'

'Her rooms?'

'Barbarina's. She always liked the east side. She didn't mind Polhorgan in the least, like the others did. *They* couldn't bear to look at it. She had her music room there. She said it was ideal because she could practise there to her heart's content without disturbing anyone.'

'Perhaps it was one of the twins I saw up there.'

'That may be so. The servants don't go there very much. Carrie looks after Barbarina's room. She gets rather angry if anyone else attempts to. But you should see them. You ought to see all over the house. You are after all its new mistress.'

'I would love to see Barbarina's rooms.'

'We could go now.'

I rose eagerly and she took my arm as we walked across the quadrangle to the east door. She seemed excited at the prospect of taking me on a tour of that part of the house.

The door closed behind us and as we walked along a short corridor which led into the hall I was conscious of silence. I told myself that it had something to do with my mood, for naturally if there was no one in this wing why should the silence surprise me?

'The servants say this is now the haunted part of the house,' Deborah told me.

'And Barbarina is the ghost?' I asked.

'You know the story then? Lowella Pendorric was supposed to have haunted the house until Barbarina took her place. A typical Cornish situation, my dear. I'm glad I was born on the other side of the Tamar. I shouldn't want to be perpetually ingratiating myself with piskies and ghosties and things that go bump in the night.'

I looked about the hall, which was an exact replica of the others in its proportions. There were the steel weapons on the walls, the pewter utensils on the refectory table, the suits of armour at the foot of the staircases. The pictures in the gallery were different, of course, and I gazed casually at them as we mounted the stairs.

We reached the corridor and I glanced through the windows at the quadrangle, wondering at which one I had seen a movement.

'Barby's rooms were on the second floor,' Deborah told me. 'I used to come and stay when she married. You see we had scarcely been separated all our lives and Barby didn't see why we ever should be. This became a second home to me. I was here as much as I was in Devonshire.'

We had mounted to the second floor and Deborah opened several of the doors to show me rooms shrouded in dust-sheets. They looked ghostly, as all such rooms do in large and silent houses.

Deborah smiled at me and I guessed she was reading my thoughts and perhaps trying to prove to me that I was not as immune from Cornish superstition as I should have liked her to believe.

'Now,' she said, and threw open a door. 'This is the music room.'

There were no dust-sheets here. The huge windows gave me a view of the coast, with Polhorgan rising majestically on the cliff top; but it was not the view I looked at this time, but the room, and I think what struck me most was that it had the look of a room which was being lived in. There was a dais at one end of it and on this was a stand with a piece of music opened on it. Beside the stand, on a chair, was a violin, looking as though it had just been placed there; the case lay open on a nearby table.

Deborah was watching me gravely, and I said slowly: 'This is how it was on the day she died?'

Deborah nodded. 'A silly habit. But some people find comfort from it. At first none of us could bear to move anything. Carrie dusts and puts things down exactly where they were. Carrie feels really fierce about it and it's more for her sake than anything else that we leave it as it is. I can't tell you how devoted she was to Barbarina.'

'And to you too.'

Deborah smiled. 'To me too. But Barbarina was her favourite.'

'You were identical twins?'

'Yes. Like Lowella and Hyson. When we were young some people found difficulty in telling us apart, but as we grew older all that passed. She was gay and amusing; I was rather stolid and slow-witted. There's more to looks than features, isn't there? It's beginning to show in Hyson and Lowella. It's only when they're asleep that they seem so much alike. As I was saying, Barby was everybody's favourite, and because she was as she was ... I seemed more dull and less interesting than I should if she had not always been with me.'

'Did you resent it?'

'Resent it! I adored Barbarina with the rest. In fact she hadn't a more devoted admirer. When she was praised I was happy because in a way it seemed as though I was being praised. It's sometimes like that with twins; they can share each other's triumphs and disasters more fully than ordinary people do.'

'And did she feel the same about you?'

'Absolutely. I wish you could have known Barbarina. She was a wonderful person. She was all that I should have liked to be myself; and because she looked so like me and was my twin sister, when we were little I was quite happy that it should be so.'

'It must have been a blow to you when she married.'

'We didn't let that part us more than we could help. I had to be in Devonshire for a good part of the time because our father needed me to look after him. Our mother had died when we were fifteen and he had never really got over the shock. But whenever I could I would be at Pendorric. She was very glad to see me. In fact, I don't know what she would have done ...' She hesitated and I had the impression that she was on the verge of confiding in me. Then she shrugged her shoulders and seemed to change her mind.

But here in Barbarina's music room I was conscious of a great desire to learn more about her. I was – although I wouldn't admit it at this stage – becoming more and more absorbed in the story of this woman who had been my immediate predecessor as a Pendorric Bride.

'Was it a happy marriage?' I asked.

Deborah turned away from me and went to the window; I was embarrassed, realizing that I had asked an awkward question, so I went to her and, laying my hand gently on her arm, said: 'I'm sorry. I'm being too inquisitive.'

She turned to me and I noticed how brilliant her eyes had become. She shook her head and smiled. 'Of course not, and naturally you're interested. After all, you're one of us now, aren't you? There's no reason why we should try to keep family secrets from you. Come and sit down and I will tell you about it.'

We sat in the window looking along the coast towards Rame Head and Plymouth. The headland jutted out darkly in the grey water and one could imagine it was a supine giantess who lay there. The tide was out and the tops of the jagged rocks were visible. I gazed at Polhorgan whose grey walls were the colour of the sea to-day.

'There's a distant family connection between the Hysons and the Pendorrics,' said Deborah. 'Cousins, many times removed. So from our childhood we knew Petroc and his family. I don't mean your Roc, of course, but his father who was Barbarina's Petroc. When he was a boy he used to stay with us. He was a year older than we were.'

'He was like Roc, wasn't he?'

'So like him that sometimes when I see Roc now I get a little shock and for the moment I think he's Petroc come back.'

'In looks, you mean?'

'Oh ... in many ways. The voice ... the gestures ... his ways ... everything. There's a very strong resemblance that runs through most of the Pendorric men. I used to hear stories of Petroc's father – another Petroc – and all that I heard could have applied to his son. Barbarina fell in love with him when she was about seven. She remained in that state until she died.'

'She must have been happy when she married him.'

'A feverish sort of ecstasy. It used to frighten me. She cared for him so much.'

'And he for her?'

Deborah smiled a little wistfully. 'Petroc liked women in general too much to care very deeply for one in particular. That's what I always felt, and so

I saw how it would be. I warned Barbarina, but she wouldn't listen of course.'

There was silence, and after a while she went on: 'We used to ride on Dartmoor. Our place is on the moor, you know. You must come and see it. The view is wonderful – if you like that kind of view. You can step from our garden right on to the moor. Once we all went riding together and they lost me. The mist came up as it does on the moor, and however well you think you know the place you can easily be hopelessly lost. You are apt to wander round and round in circles. It was really rather frightening. I found my way back but they didn't come home until next day. They'd sheltered in some hut they'd discovered, and Petroc had had the foresight to load up with chocolate. Sometimes I think he arranged the whole thing.'

'Why? I mean, if she was in love with him, couldn't he have been with her ... more comfortably?'

Again that silence. Then she sighed and said: 'He was in love with some local girl whom he'd promised to marry. She was a farmer's daughter. But the family wanted this marriage with the Hysons because our father was well off and money was badly needed at Pendorric. Barbarina was very unhappy. She'd heard that Petroc was going to marry this girl, and she knew he must be very much in love with her because Pendorric meant a great deal to him, and it was possible that if he couldn't bring some money into the family something would have to be done about it. So she knew he must have been deeply in love with the girl to contemplate marrying someone who couldn't bring a penny into the place. He was fond of Barbarina. It wouldn't have been any hardship to marry her ... if he hadn't been so besottedly in love with this other woman. Petroc was the sort of man who would get along with any woman ... like ... Well, you know the type.'

I nodded uneasily.

'Were the Pendorrics very poor then?'

'Not exactly, but the great change had set in. Things weren't what they had been for their sort of people. The house needed expensive renovations. And Petroc had gambled rather rashly in the hope of recuperating the family fortunes.'

'So he was a gambler.'

She nodded. 'As his father was.'

'And what happened after that night on the moor?'

'I think Petroc had made up his mind that he would have to marry Barbarina. Pendorric was important, so he would fall in with the wishes of his family and Barbarina's. But he couldn't tell Barbarina that ... bluntly. So they got lost on the moors and Barbarina was seduced and ... that made it all easy.'

'She told you this?'

'My dear Favel, Barbarina didn't have to *tell* me things. We were as close as two people can be. Don't forget that during the months of our gestation we had been as one. I knew exactly what had happened and why.'

'And after that she married him and she was happy.'

'What do you expect? Petroc couldn't be faithful. It wasn't in his nature to be, any more than it had been in his father's. He took up with the farmer's daughter again. It was a notorious scandal. But she wasn't the only one. Like his father he couldn't resist a woman nor a chance to gamble. Women couldn't resist them either. I thought that when Roc and Morwenna were born she would cease to fret for him, and for a while she did. I hoped that she would have more children and make them her life.'

'And you were disappointed?'

'Barbarina was a good mother, don't mistake me; but she wasn't one of those women who can ignore her husband's infidelities and become completely absorbed in her children. Petroc meant too much to her for that.'

'So she was very unhappy?'

'You can imagine it, can't you. A sensitive woman . . . in a place like this . . . and an unfaithful husband who didn't make a secret of his infidelities; there was nothing secret about Petroc. He never tried to pretend he was other than he was – a reckless gambler and a philanderer. He seemed to take up the attitude: It's a family characteristic, so there's nothing *I* can do about it.'

'Poor Barbarina,' I murmured.

'I used to come down as often as I could, and then when my father died I almost lived here. It was through me that she became interested in her music again. I believe that in other circumstances she might have been a concert violinist. She was really very good. But she had never practised enough. However, she found great pleasure in it, particularly towards the end. In fact she was very gifted. I remember when we were at school . . . we must have been about fourteen then . . . she was in the school play. It was *Hamlet* and she was Ophelia, a part which suited her absolutely. I was the ghost. That was about the limit of my capabilities. I believe I was a very poor one. But Barbarina was the hit of the show.'

'I can imagine that – from her picture, I mean. Particularly the one in the gallery.'

'Oh, that's Barbarina as she really was. Sometimes when I look at it I almost imagine she will step out of the frame and speak to me.'

'Yes, there's a touch of reality about it. The artist must have been a very good one.'

'It was painted about a year before her death. She took great pleasure in riding. In fact I sometimes felt it was a feverish sort of pleasure she was taking in things . . . her music . . . riding, and so on. She was lovely in that particular ensemble, and that was why she was painted in it. It was sad that she – like Ophelia – should have died before her time. I wish you could have heard her sing that song from the play. She had a strange voice . . . a little off-key, which suited the song and Ophelia. I remember at the school show how silent the audience was when she came on the stage in a flowering gown of white and flowers in her hair and in her hands. I can't sing; but it's that one that goes something like this:

> "How should I your true love know
> From another one?
> By his cockle hat and staff,
> And his sandal shoon.

> *He is dead and gone, lady,*
> *He is dead and gone;*
> *At his head a grass-green turf,*
> *At his heels a stone."* '

She quoted the words in a low monotone; then she flashed her smile at me. 'I wish I could make you hear it as she sang it. There was something about it that made one shiver. Afterwards it became one of her favourite songs and there was a verse which she didn't sing at the school play but she used to sing that later.

> *"Then up he rose, and donn'd his clothes,*
> *And dup'ed the chamber door;*
> *Let in the maid, that out a maid*
> *Never departed more."*

'There would be an odd little smile about her lips as she sang that, and I always felt it had something to do with that night on the moor.'

'Poor Barbarina! I'm afraid she wasn't very happy.'

Deborah clenched her fists as though in sudden anger. 'And she was meant to be happy. I never knew anyone so capable of being happy. If Petroc had been all that she hoped he would be . . . if . . . But what is the good? When is life ever what you hope it will be; and in any case it is all so long ago.'

'I heard about it; the balustrade was faulty and she fell to the hall.'

'It was unfortunate that it happened in the gallery where Lowella Pendorric hung. That really gave rise to all the talk.'

'It must have revived the legend.'

'Oh, it didn't take all that reviving. The people round about had always said that Pendorric was haunted by Lowella Pendorric, the Bride of long ago.'

'And now they say that Barbarina has taken her place.'

Deborah laughed; then she looked over her shoulder. 'Although I've always laughed at such talk, sometimes when I'm in this house I feel a little more inclined to accept it.'

'It's the atmosphere of old houses. The furniture is often standing in exactly the same place it was in hundreds of years ago. You can't help thinking that this house looked almost exactly the same to that Lowella whom they call the First Bride.'

'I only wish that Barbarina *would* come back!' said Deborah vehemently. 'I can't tell you what I'd give to see her again.' She stood up. 'Let's go for a walk. We're getting morbid sitting here in Barbarina's room. We'll have to get mackintoshes. Look at those clouds. The wind's in the south-west and that means rain's not far off.'

I said I should enjoy that, and we left the east wing together. She came with me to my room while I put on my outdoor things; then I went with her to hers; and when we were ready she led me round to the north wing and we paused on the gallery before the picture of Lowella Pendorric.

'This is where she fell,' explained Deborah. 'Look, you can see where the balustrade has been mended. It was woodworm, I believe. It should have been noticed long before. Actually the place is riddled with worm. It's inevitable and it'll cost a fortune to put it right.'

I looked up into Lowella Pendorric's painted face and I thought exultantly: But Roc is not really like his father and his grandfather, and the gambling, philandering Pendorrics. If he had been in his father's place he would have married the farmer's daughter, as he married me – for what had I to bring him? In ten minutes we were strolling along the cliff path, the warm sea-scented wind caressing our faces.

I had no wish to lead an idle life. On the island there had always been so much to do. I had been my father's house-keeper as well as his saleswoman. I pointed out to Roc that I wanted to do something.

'You might go down to the kitchens and have a little chat with Mrs. Penhalligan. She'd appreciate it. After all, you're the mistress of the house.'

'I will,' I agreed, 'because Morwenna won't mind in the least if I do make suggestions.'

He put his arm round me and hugged me. 'Aren't you the mistress of the house, anyway?'

'Roc,' I told him, 'I'm so happy. I wouldn't have thought it possible so soon after . . .'

Roc's kiss prevented me from going on with that.

'Didn't I tell you? And talking of having something to do . . . as Mrs. Pendorric you should take an interest in village activities, you know. It's expected, as I guess you've gathered from the Darks. I tell you, Favel, in a few weeks' time you'll not be complaining of having too little to do, but too much.'

'I think I'll begin by getting to know more of Mrs. Penhalligan and perhaps I'll call on the Darks. This afternoon, by the way, I've promised to have tea with Lord Polhorgan.'

'What, again? You really do like that old man.'

'Yes,' I said almost defiantly, 'I do.'

'Then enjoy yourself.'

'I believe I shall.'

Roc studied me, smiling as he did so. 'You certainly seem to hit it off.'

'I feel that he's really rather a lonely old man, and he seems sort of paternal.'

Roc's smile faded and he nodded slowly. 'You're still grieving,' he said.

'It's so hard to forget, Roc. Oh, I'm so happy here. I love it all; the family are so kind to me, and you . . .'

He was laughing. 'And I'm kind to you too? What did you expect? A wife-beater?'

Then he put his arms about me and held me close to him. 'Listen, Favel,' he said. 'I want you to be happy. It's what I want more than anything. I understand what you feel about the old man. He's paternal. That's what you said; and in a way he makes up for something you miss. He's lonely.

You can bet your life *he's* missed a lot. So you like each other. It's understandable.'

'I wish you liked him more, Roc.'

'Don't take any notice of what I've said. It was mostly said jokingly. When you get to know me better you'll understand what a joker I am.'

'Don't you think I know you well then?'

'Not as well as you will twenty years hence, darling. We'll go on learning about each other; that's what makes it all so exciting. It's like a voyage of discovery.'

He spoke lightly, but I went on thinking of what he had said, and I was still remembering those words when I passed under the great archway on my way out that afternoon, until I heard footsteps behind me and turning saw Rachel Bective, a twin walking sedately on either side of her.

'Hallo,' called Rachel, 'going for a walk?'

'I'm going to tea at Polhorgan.'

They caught up with me and we walked along together.

'Hope you're prepared,' warned Rachel. 'It's going to rain.'

'I've brought my mac.'

'The wind's blowing in from the south-west, and once it starts to rain here you begin to wonder whether it's ever going to stop.'

Hyson came to the other side of me so that I was in between her and Rachel; Lowella skipped on ahead.

'Do you go round by the cliff path to Polhorgan? asked Rachel. 'It's at least five minutes shorter.'

'I've always kept to this road.'

'We'll show you the short cut if you like.'

'Don't let me take you out of your way.'

'But we're only going for a walk.'

'Well, thanks – if it really won't.'

'Lowella,' Rachel called. 'We're going down Smugglers' Lane to show your Aunt Favel the short cut to Polhorgan.'

Lowella wheeled sharply round. 'Good. It'll be lovely and squelchy down Smugglers' Lane.'

'It won't. There hasn't been that much rain.'

We turned aside from the road and took a steep narrow path on either side of which the hedges had run so wild that sometimes we had to go in single file.

Lowella found a broken-off branch and went ahead of us beating the overgrown hedges and shouting: ' "Beware the awful avalanche. Beware the pine-tree's withered branch. Excelsior!" '

'Oh Lowella, do be quiet,' begged Rachel.

'Of course if you don't want me to lead you to safety, say so.'

'Hyson reads to her when they're in bed at night,' Rachel told me, 'and she goes on repeating what appeals to her.'

'You like reading, don't you?' I said to Hyson.

She merely nodded. Then she said: 'Lowella's such a child. As if this is anything like the awful avalanche!'

The path ended abruptly and we stepped on to what looked like a ledge.

Beneath us – a long way beneath us – was the sea, and beside us towering above rose the shaley face of the cliff with here and there a bush of gorse or bracken clinging to the brown earth.

'It's perfectly safe,' said Rachel Bective. 'Unless of course you have a phobia about heights.'

I told her I hadn't and added that we were several feet lower than we had been on the coast road.

'Yes, but that's a proper road. This is just a path, and a little farther on it gets even narrower. There's a notice saying use it at your own risk, but that's for visitors. Local people all use it.'

Lowella went on ahead, pretending to pick her way. 'Wouldn't it be super if we had a rope attaching us all,' she cried. 'Then if the Bride fell over the cliff, we'd haul her up.'

'That's kind of you, but I don't intend to fall.'

' "She's still the youth who bore 'mid snow and ice the banner with the strange device," ' murmured Hyson.

'Excelsior!' cried Lowella. 'Isn't it a smashing word!' She ran on, shouting it.

Rachel looked at me and shrugged her shoulders.

In a few seconds I saw what they meant about the path's narrowing; for some two yards it was little more than a shelf; we walked rather gingerly in single file; then we rounded a part of the cliff which projected over the water, and as we did so I saw that we were almost at Polhorgan.

'It's certainly a short cut,' I said. 'Thanks for showing me.'

'Shall we go back the same way?' Rachel asked the twins.

Lowella turned and was already on her way back. I heard her shouting 'Excelsior' as I went on to Polhorgan.

Lord Polhorgan was delighted to see me. I fancied the manservant treated me with rather special deference, and it occurred to me that it must be rare for his master to become so friendly in such a short space of time.

When I went into his room Nurse Grey was with him, reading to him from *The Financial Times*.

'Please don't let me interrupt,' I said. 'I must be early. I'll go and have a walk in the garden. I've always wanted to explore it.'

Lord Polhorgan looked at his watch. 'You are punctual,' he said, and waved a hand at Nurse Grey, who promptly folded the paper and rose. 'Never could abide people who have no respect for time. Unpunctuality is a vice. Glad to see you, Mrs. Pendorric. And I'd like to show you the garden, but I can't manage it these days. Too steep for me to walk; too steep for me to be wheeled.'

'I'll enjoy it from the window to-day,' I answered.

Nurse Grey must show you, one day.'

'I'd be delighted to,' said Althea Grey.

'Tell them to bring in the tea. And Nurse, there's no need for you to stay. Mrs. Pendorric will do the honours, I'm sure.'

Nurse Grey bowed her head and murmured: 'I'll hurry on the tea then.'

Lord Polhorgan nodded and the nurse went out, leaving us together.

'Tea first,' he said, 'and we'll have our chess after. Sit down and talk to me for a while. You're settling in here now. Liking it?'

'Very much.'

'All well at Pendorric?' He shot a quick glance at me from under his shaggy brows.

'Yes.' I went on impulsively: 'Did you expect it to be otherwise?'

He evaded the question. 'It's never easy settling in to a new life. Must have been very gay – that island of yours. Find it quiet here?'

'I like this quiet.'

'Better than the island?'

'When my mother was alive I was completely happy. I didn't think there was anything in the world but happiness. I was sad when I went away to school, but after a while I was used to that and being back was more fun than ever.'

He gave me a look of approval. 'You're a sensible young woman. I'm glad. Can't stand the other sort.'

'Nurse Grey seems a sensible young woman.'

'H'm. Too sensible perhaps.'

'Can one be too sensible?'

'Sometimes I wonder why she stays here. I don't think it's out of love for her patient. I'm what's known as an old curmudgeon, Mrs. Pendorric.'

I laughed. 'You can't be such a bad one, since you admit it.'

'Can't I? You forget, when a man's made money, he's invariably surrounded by people who are anxious to relieve him of it – or some of it.'

'And you think Nurse Grey . . .?'

He looked at me shrewdly. 'Handsome young woman . . . fond of gaiety. Not so much to be had here.'

'But she seems contented.'

'Ay, she does and all.' He nodded shrewdly. 'Often wonder why. Perhaps she thinks she won't be forgotten . . . when the great day comes.'

I must have shown my embarrassment, for he said quickly: 'A fine host I am. Why, you'll be making excuses not to come and see me if I don't watch out. Shouldn't like that . . . shouldn't like it at all.'

'I wouldn't make excuses to you. You're forthright and say what you mean, so I would try to do the same.'

'We're alike in that,' he said, and chuckled.

The tea arrived and I poured. This had become a habit which was a further indication of the rate at which our friendship had developed. He seemed to take pleasure in watching me.

While I was serving tea I saw Althea Grey walking through the gardens down to the beach. She had changed her uniform for brown jeans and a blouse the colour of delphiniums, which was a perfect foil for her fair hair, and I guessed her eyes matched the blouse. She looked back suddenly and, seeing me, waved; I waved back.

'It's Nurse Grey,' I explained to my host. 'She's off duty for a few hours I suppose.'

He nodded. 'Was she on her way down to the beach?'

'Yes.'

'Polhorgan Cove belongs to me by rights but I was soon led to understand that the natives wouldn't think very kindly of me if I made it a private beach. There's a gate and hedges shutting off the garden; but you go through the gate right on to the beach.'

'It's rather like Pendorric.'

'The same arrangement. Pendorrics own their beach and I own mine, but I don't think half the people who scramble over the rocks at low tide know that.'

'If the beaches were fenced off it would mean people couldn't walk along for very far; they'd have to keep coming up and making a detour.'

'Always believed that what was mine was mine and I had a right to say what was to be done with it. I was very unpopular when I first came, I can tell you. I've grown mellow. You learn as you get older. Sometimes if you stand out for your rights you lose what might mean more to you.'

He was momentarily sad, and I fancied that he looked a little more tired than when I had last seen him.

'Yes, I think there's a lot in that,' I said.

'There you were, with your mother and father on that island . . . perfectly happy, and I don't suppose you owned the house you lived in, let alone the ground all round and a private beach.'

'It's true. We were very poor and very happy.'

He frowned, and I wondered if I had been tactless. He went on rather brusquely: 'Nurse Grey goes down to the beach a great deal. Do you use yours much?'

'Not so far. But I shall, of course. I've hardly settled in yet.'

'I'm taking up too much of your time.'

'But I like coming and I enjoy playing chess.'

He was silent for a while, and then again he led me back to the subject of my life on the island.

I was surprised that he could be such a good listener, but while I talked he remained attentive and fired so many questions at me in his rather brusque manner that I went on talking about myself.

When the tea had been cleared away I drew up the exquisite little table on which we played; it was a dainty piece of French origin with inlaid ivory and tortoise-shell squares; I put out the ivory chessmen, which were as beautiful as the table, and the game began.

When we had been playing for about fifteen minutes, to my surprise I had him at a disadvantage. I was delightedly pursuing my strategy when, looking up, I saw that he was in considerable discomfort.

'Sorry,' he muttered. 'Please forgive me.' He was groping in his pocket.

'You've lost something?'

'A little silver box. I always keep it near me.'

I stood up and looking about me saw a small silver box on the floor at his feet. I picked it up and gave it to him. His relief was apparent as he quickly opened it and took a small white tablet from it. This he placed under his tongue. For some seconds he sat back gripping his chair.

I was alarmed because I knew that he was ill, and I got up, going to the bell to call the manservant, but seeing what I was about to do, Lord

Polhorgan shook his head. I stood uncertainly. 'Better in a minute,' he muttered.

'But you're ill. Shouldn't I . . .?'

He continued to shake his head while I stood helplessly by. In about five minutes he began to look a little better and it was as though a tension had been eased.

He drew a deep breath and murmured: 'Better now. I'm sorry.'

'Please don't be so sorry. Just tell me what I can do.'

'Just sit down . . . quietly. In a few minutes I'll be all right.'

I obeyed, watching him anxiously. The gilded French clock over the ornate fireplace ticked loudly, and apart from that there was silence in the room. From far away I could hear the gentle swishing of the waves against the rocks.

A few more minutes passed and he gave a deep sigh. Then he smiled at me. 'I'm sorry that happened while you were here. Mislaid my tablets. Don't usually stir without them. They must have dropped out of my pocket.'

'Please don't apologize. I'm the one who is sorry. I'm afraid I didn't know what to do.'

'There's nothing much anyone can do. If I'd had my box I'd have slipped a tablet into my mouth while you were busy over the game and you wouldn't have noticed anything. As it was . . . I delayed a little too long.'

'I'm glad I found them.'

'You look sad. Shouldn't, you know. I'm an old man. And one of the disadvantages of being old is that one is too old to deal with the disadvantages. But I've had my day. Besides, there's a lot of life in me yet. Don't like mislaying my tablets though. Could be dangerous.'

'What wonderful tablets they must be!'

'Not always effective. They are, ninety-nine times out of a hundred, though. T.N.T. Expand the veins and arteries.'

'And if they're not?'

'Then it's a dose of morphia.'

'I'm terribly sorry.'

He patted my hand. 'The old engine's creaking,' he said. 'I need decarbonizing. Pity I can't ask you to run me into old Jim Bond's and have it done, eh?'

'Shouldn't you rest now?'

'Don't you worry. I'll phone my doctor and ask him to come in and see me. Haven't been feeling so well this last day or so.'

'Shouldn't we phone at once?'

'Nurse Grey will do it when she comes in. Can't imagine how those tablets came to be on the floor.'

'Perhaps there's a hole in your pocket.'

He felt, and shook his head.

'You know, I think you ought to rest. Shall I go now? Or better still, telephone the doctor?'

'All right, then. His number's in the little book by the telephone. Dr. Clement.'

I went at once to the book and dialled the number. I was fortunate, for

Dr. Clement happened to be in. I told him that I was speaking from Polhorgan and that Lord Polhorgan wanted him to look in soon.

'Right,' said Dr. Clement. 'I'll be along.'

I replaced the receiver and went back to the table. 'Can I do anything for you?' I asked.

'Yes, sit down and finish the game. I'm afraid I let you get the better of me. I was thinking about my silver box. Just to show you how quickly I can recover we'll continue the game and I'll beat you yet.'

I kept taking uneasy glances at him as we played, which made him chuckle, and before we had finished the game Dr. Clement arrived.

I rose to go, but Lord Polhorgan wouldn't hear of it.

'I'm all right now,' he said. 'I only let Mrs. Pendorric call you because she was anxious about me. Tell her there's nothing to be done for me. The trouble was, Doctor, I'd mislaid my T.N.T.s and it was some minutes before Mrs. Pendorric found them.'

'You should always keep them within reach,' said Dr. Clement.

'I know. I know. Can't think what happened. Must have pulled them out of my pocket. Have some tea. Perhaps Mrs. Pendorric would ring for Dawson. That's cold by now.'

The doctor declined the tea and I said I really should go. I was certain that he would want to be alone with his patient.

'The game's unfinished,' protested Lord Polhorgan.

'We can finish it next time.'

'I've frightened you away,' said Dr. Clement almost wistfully.

I was determined to go, and I left. As I came through the portico I glanced at my watch and saw that I was half an hour earlier than I had intended to be, so instead of making my way to the road, or the path which led to the short cut Rachel and the twins had shown me that afternoon, I thought I would like to go down to the beach by way of the cliff garden and scramble over the rocks to Pendorric Cove, and through our own garden up to the house.

The tide was out, so it would be possible. I walked round to the side of the house and saw one of the Polhorgan gardeners emerging from a greenhouse. I asked him how I could get to the beach from the garden and he offered to show me the way.

He led me along a path bounded on each side by a box hedge; at the end of this path was a small gate, and passing through it I came on the cliff garden. It was a wonderful sight, for in this semi-tropical climate plants grew in profusion. There was a palm tree in a sheltered alcove which reminded me of those in the quadrangle; and the hydrangea blooms were even bigger than those at Pendorric; they flaunted their brilliant blues and pinks, whites and multi-colours. There seemed to be hundreds of fuchsias with larger flowers than I had seen before; and great white arum lilies which filled the air with their slightly funereal scent.

The path I had taken wound in zigzag fashion towards the sea to eliminate the strain of walking down such a steep slope; first I faced east, then west, then turned again as I went past borders of flowers whose names I did not know, past seats which had been set under arches and in alcoves the trellis-work of which was ablaze with Paul Scarlett, American Pillar and Golden Dawn roses.

I thought that if the sun were shining and the sea blue it would be almost too dazzling. But to-day was a grey day and the cry of the gulls seemed melancholy as they swooped and soared.

I came at length to the little gate which opened on to the beach, and as I stood in Polhorgan Cove I looked back at that wonderful garden set out on the cliff-side to the stone walls of Polhorgan's Folly looming above.

Not such a Folly, I thought. A lovely house in a lovely spot.

The tide was well out. I knew that at high tide it came up almost as far as the gates of Pendorric garden, and, I imagined, those of Polhorgan too. It was only when the tide was really out that one could walk along the beach. Even as far as I could see, the place was deserted. Ahead of me the rocks jutted out almost to the water, shutting me in the little bay which was known as Polhorgan's Cove. I guessed it would take me longer to reach Pendorric this way than by the road, so I started westwards immediately. It was not easy rounding the jagged rocks; there were so many to be climbed, and interesting little pools to be leaped over. I came to a large rock which actually did jut into the sea. It was rather difficult getting over that one, but I managed it; and then I saw our own beach, our garden, far less grand than that of Polhorgan, but perhaps as beautiful in its wild state.

I leaped on to the soft sand, and as I did so I heard the sound of laughter.

Then I saw them. She was half lying on the sand, her face propped up by her hands, and he was stretched out beside her leaning on one elbow. He looked as dark as he had when I had first seen him sitting in the studio with my father.

They were talking animatedly, and I thought uneasily: They wouldn't have expected to see me here suddenly.

I wanted them to know quickly that I was close by. Perhaps I was afraid that if I did not make my presence known I might hear or see something which I did not want to. I called out: 'Hallo.'

Roc sprang to his feet and for a few seconds stared at me; then he came running towards me, taking both my hands in his.

'Look who's here! I thought you were still at the Folly.'

'I hope I didn't startle you.'

He put his arm round me and laughed. 'In the most pleasant way,' he said.

We walked over to Althea Grey, who remained where she was on the sand. Her blue eyes, fixed on me, seemed shrewd and alert.

'Is everything all right at Polhorgan?' she asked.

I told her what had happened, and she got up.

'I'd better get back,' she said.

'Come up to Pendorric,' said Roc, 'and I'll drive you there.'

She looked up at the steep garden to the grey walls of Pendorric and shook her head. 'I don't think it would be any quicker. I'll go over the rocks.' She turned to me. 'I've done it so often, I'm becoming like a mountain goat. See you later,' she added, and started to hurry across the sand.

'You look shaken,' said Roc. 'I believe the old man often has those attacks.

He's been having them for years. Pity it happened when you were alone with him.'

We opened the gate and started the climb through the garden to the house. 'What made you come the beach way?' asked Roc.

'I don't know. Perhaps because it was a way I hadn't been before and as I was leaving a little early I thought I'd try it. Is Althea Grey a great friend of . . . the family?'

'Not of the family.'

'Only of you?'

'You know what a friendly type I am!'

He caught me to him and hugged me. Questions were on my lips but I hesitated. I didn't want him to think I was going to be foolishly jealous every time he spoke to another woman. I had to remember I had married a Pendorric and they were noted for their gallantries.

'Do you often meet on the beach?'

'This is a small place. One is always running up against neighbours.'

'I wonder why she preferred our beach to Polhorgan.'

'Ah, from Pendorric beach you can look up at real antiquity; from Polhorgan you only get the fake.'

'It's a very beautiful fake.'

'I believe you're getting very fond of his lordship.' He regarded me ironically: 'Ought *I* to be jealous?'

I laughed, but I felt almost as uneasy as I had when I had come into the cove and seen them lying there together. Was he trying to turn the tables, as guilty people often did? Was he saying: You spend your afternoon with Lord Polhorgan, so why shouldn't I spend mine with his nurse?

It was an incongruous suggestion, but he went on: 'I should be very jealous, so you mustn't provoke me.'

'I hope you will remember to do unto others as you would they should do unto you.'

'But you would never be jealous without reason. You're far too sensible.'

'Yet I suppose it would be more reasonable to be jealous of a beautiful young woman than a sick old man.'

'Often in these matters there are other factors to be considered besides personal charms.'

'Such as?'

'You don't find millionaires lurking on every rock and patch of sand.'

'What a hideous suggestion!'

'Isn't it? And I'm a beast to mention such mundane matters as money; but then, as you once said, I am a satyr, which is a form of beast, I suppose. Actually I fancied you were not very pleased to come upon Thea and me together and I wanted to tell you how ridiculous you were to be . . . not very pleased.'

'You're not hinting that you'd rather I didn't visit Lord Polhorgan?'

'Good heavens, no! I'm delighted that you do. Poor old man, he's only just beginning to realize that his millions can't buy him all he wants. He's getting more pleasure out of having a beautiful young woman to pour his tea and hover over his ivory chessmen than he's had for years. And all without paying out a penny! It's a revelation to him. It reminds me of Little Lord Fauntleroy, the terror of my youth because I was forced to read of his adventures by a well-meaning nurse. I found him particularly nauseating – perhaps because he was the opposite of myself. I could never see myself in plum-coloured velvet with my golden curls falling over my lace collar going to soften the hard heart of dear old Lord Somebody, Fauntleroy, I believe . . . old Fauntleroy. That was one thing I could never do – bring warring relations together by my childish charm.'

'Stop it Roc. Do you really object to my visits to Polhorgan?'

He picked up one of the Mrs. Sinkins pinks that grew in rather untidy clumps, filling the air with their delicious scent, and gravely put it into the buttonhole of my short linen jacket.

'I've been talking a lot of nonsense because I'm garrulous by nature. Darling, I want you to feel absolutely free. As for visiting Lord Polhorgan, don't for heaven's sake stop. I'm glad you're able to give him so much pleasure. I know he ruined our east view with his monstrosity, but he's an old man and he's sick. Go as often as he asks you.'

He leaned forward to smell the pink; then he kissed my lips. He took my hand and we climbed to the house.

As usual he had the power to make me accept what he wanted to; it was only when I was alone that I asked myself; Does he want me to visit Lord Polhorgan so that Althea Grey is free to be with him?

I went down to the kitchen one morning to find Mrs. Penhalligan at the table kneading dough, and there was the delicious smell of baking bread in the air.

The kitchens at Pendorric were enormous, and in spite of electric cookers, refrigerators and other recently installed modern equipment, looked as though they belonged to another age. There were several rooms – a bakehouse, a buttery, a washhouse and another room called the dairy which had a floor of blue tiles and had once been a store-room for milk, butter, eggs and such. Across the ceiling were great oak beams supplied with hooks on which joints of meat, hams, sides of bacon and Christmas puddings had once hung.

The kitchen itself, though large, was a cosy room with its red-tiled floor and dressers, its refectory table at which generations of servants had had their meals and the wooden one scrubbed white at which, on this occasion, Mrs. Penhalligan was working. Through an open door I could see Maria preparing vegetables in the washhouse.

Mrs. Penhalligan bridled with pleasure when she saw me.

I said: 'Good morning, Mrs. Penhalligan. I thought it was about time I paid a visit to the kitchens.'

'It's good to see you, ma'am,' she answered.

'Is that bread baking? It smells delicious.'

She looked pleased. 'We've always baked our own bread at Pendorric. There's nothing like the home-baked, I always say. I bake for Father at the same time. It's always been understood.'

'How is your father?'

'Oh, fair to middling, ma'am. Don't get no younger but he be wonderful for his age. He'll be ninety next Candlemas.'

'Ninety! That's a great age.'

'And there bain't much wrong with him ... 'cept of course his great affliction.'

'Oh?'

'You didn't know, ma'am, and I reckon none as yet thought fit to tell you. Father went blind ... oh – it'll be nigh on thirty years ago. No. I bain't telling you the truth. It'll be twenty-eight years. It started ... twenty-eight years come harvest time.'

'I'm very sorry.'

'Oh, don't 'ee be. Father bain't sorry for himself. He's happy enough ... with his pipe and all he wants to eat. He likes to sit at the door on sunny days and it 'ud astonish you, ma'am, how good his hearing is. Sort of makes up for not having his sight, so it seems.'

'I expect I'll see him some time.'

'He'd be real pleased if you stopped and had a little chat with him. He's always asking about Mr. Roc's new bride.'

'I'll look for him.'

'You can't make no mistake. It's the second of the cottages down Pendorric Village. Lives all alone there. Independent since Mother went. But Maria and me, we're always in and out. And we pop over with a plate of hot something for his dinner regular as clockwork. He don't pay no rent, and he's got his bit of pension. Father's all right. He'd be wonderful ... if he had his sight.'

I was glad Mrs. Penhalligan was the loquacious type, because I had been wondering what I should say to her.

'I've been hearing about how your family have been at Pendorric for generations.'

'Oh yes ... always Pleydells at Pendorric. But then Father and Mother didn't have no son. I was their only daughter. Then I married Penhalligan, who was gardener here till he died. And we only had one too – my Maria. She'll be working here till the end ... and then that'll be the end of the Pleydells at Pendorric.'

'What a pity!'

'All things has to come to an end, ma'am. And did you want to give me some orders or something?'

'Not really. I thought I'd like to see how things were worked down here.'

'Right and proper that you should, ma'am. You be the mistress. Miss Morwenna, she was never one to take much interest. Now Miss Bective ...' Mrs. Penhalligan's face hardened ... 'she was up another street. When she first come here, it was, "Mrs. Penhalligan, we'll have this and we'll have that." But I know my place if some don't, and I take orders from the mistress of the house and none other.'

'I expect she was trying to be helpful.'

'Helpful! I don't need help in my kitchen, ma'am – no more than I've got. My Maria's been well trained and I'm not doing too bad with Hetty Toms.'

'Everything is very well organized, I'm sure.'

'And so it should be – the years I've been at it. I was in the kitchen when the other Mrs. Pendorric first come here.'

I felt excited as I always did at the mention of Barbarina. 'Was she interested in the kitchen?'

'She were like yourself, ma'am. Interested, I'd say but not one to want to change things. I remember the day she came into my kitchen, her lovely face all glowing with health; she'd come in from a ride and she was in her riding clothes . . . breeches and coat like a man's. But there was nothing of the man about her. There was a little blue flower in her buttonhole and she had one of them riding hats on with a band of yellow round it. She always wore them – like in the picture in the south hall, only she's in blue there.'

'Yes, I know the picture well.'

'A lovely lady, and it was a pleasure to serve her. It was terrible when . . . But my tongue runs away with me. Maria always says so and she's right.'

'It's pleasant to have a chat, though. That's really what I came down for.'

Mrs. Penhalligan's face shone with pleasure as her nimble fingers went on kneading the dough.

'She was like that too – always ready for a chat, particularly in the beginning. Afterwards she was . . .'

I waited, and Mrs. Penhalligan frowned down at her dough.

'She was less friendly later?' I prompted.

'Oh, not less friendly. Just sad, I think; and sometimes she wouldn't seem to see you. Reckon she was thinking of other things, poor lady.'

'Of her troubles?'

'She had those. She was very fond of him, you see. . . .' She seemed to recall to whom she was talking, and stopped. 'I suppose, ma'am, you have a preference for the wholemeal bread. I bake some white – but more wholemeal. Father, he likes white – done in the old-fashioned coburg style. Father's one to have what he wants. Though I must say now, though, that his mind wanders a bit. It's not being able to see, I think. That must make a difference.'

I said I personally preferred wholemeal, and that I thought the bread she made was the best I had ever tasted.

Nothing could have delighted her more; she was my ally from that moment. She relaxed, too; she had concluded that although I was the mistress of the house I was fond of a gossip.

'I'll certainly look out for your father when I next pass the cottages,' I told her.

'I'll tell him. He'll be that pleased. You must be prepared though for him to wander a bit. He's close on ninety and he gets a bit muddled. He's had it on his mind a bit lately. I reckon it's because there's a new bride here at Pendorric.'

'Had what on his mind?' I asked.

'Well, ma'am, you'll have heard of course how Mr. Roc's and Miss Morwenna's mother died.'

'Yes, I have heard.'

'Well, Father was there when it happened. It preyed on his mind a bit for a time. Then he seemed to forget like . . . but things are likely to bring it back, which is all natural. And when he heard there was a new bride at Pendorric, you see . . .'

'Yes, I see. He was there, you say.'

'He were there. In the hall when she, poor soul, did crash from the gallery. He weren't completely blind then neither – but almost he were. He couldn't see clear enough, but he knew her were up there, and it was him that gave the alarm. That's why it preyed on his mind like. That's why he remembers now and then, though it be twenty-five years since it happened.'

'Does he believe . . . the story about the ghost?'

Mrs. Penhalligan looked surprised. 'Father knows there be such things. I don't rightly know what he thinks about Mrs. Pendorric's fall. He don't talk much. He just sits brooding. Can't get him to talk much about it. Might be better if we could.'

'I shall certainly look out for him when I pass the cottages, Mrs. Penhalligan.'

'You'll see him . . . puffing away at his old pipe. He'll be that pleased. Maria'll just be taking the first batch out of the oven. I still use the old cloam oven for bread. Can't be beat. Would you like to come and see it, ma'am?'

I said I would; and as I went through the kitchens to the bakehouse and returned the greeting of Maria and Hetty Toms, I was not thinking of them nor the golden-brown loaves fresh from the oven; I kept seeing that beautiful young woman crashing from the gallery, the smiling painted face of Lowella Pendorric behind her; and in the hall, an almost sightless man, peering towards the falling figure, trying so hard to see what was happening.

After my talk with Mrs. Penhalligan I felt that I was truly mistress of the house. The faithful housekeeper, daughter of the Pleydells who had served the family for generations, had accepted me. My sister-in-law had no great desire to manage the house, and I felt delighted to have something to do.

I wanted to know every inch and corner of Pendorric. I was beginning to love it, and to understand that a house which had stood for hundreds of years must necessarily have a stronger appeal than one which had stood only a few years.

I told Roc how I felt and he was delighted.

'What did I tell you?' he cried. 'The Brides of Pendorric fall fiercely in love with the place.'

'It must be because they're so happy to have become Pendorrics.'

The remark delighted him. He put his arm about me and I felt suddenly secure . . . safe.

'There are lots of things I want to ask you about the place,' I told him. 'Is it true that wood-worm is slowly destroying parts of it?'

'The little beasts are the enemies of the stately homes of England, darling. They're almost as destructive as the Inland Revenue.'

'That's another thing: You did seem rather sorry because you weren't so rich as Lord Polhorgan. Do you really think it'll be necessary to hand over Pendorric to the National Trust?'

Roc took my face in his hands and kissed me lightly.

'Don't worry, sweetheart. We'll manage to keep the wolf from the ancestral home.'

'So we aren't living beyond our means?'

He laughed lightheartedly. 'I always knew I'd married a business woman. Listen, darling; when I've talked over this with Charles I'm going to show you how things work here. I'm going to make use of you, you see. I'm going to show you all the inner workings of an estate like ours. Then you'll see what it's all about.'

'Oh, Roc dear, I'll love that.'

'I thought you would. But first I've got to make up for my long absence from home. Then I've got to prepare old Charlie. He's a bit old-fashioned. Keep the women out of business and all that. He doesn't realize the sort of woman I've found for myself. You see, Morwenna's never been the least bit interested in anything except the gardens.'

'Do persuade him soon.'

'Trust me.' He was serious suddenly. 'I want us to be . . . together in everything. Understand?'

I nodded. 'No secrets,' I added.

He held me tightly for a moment. 'Quite close . . . for ever and ever until death us do part.'

'Oh, Roc, don't talk of death.'

'Only as something in the dim and distant future, my love. But you're happy now.'

'Wonderfully happy.'

'That's how I want you to stay. So no worries about the house. Don't I have you to help me? Then there's Charles. He'd die rather than see the old place go. Not that it does completely if you hand over to the National Trust. But you can't tell me your home's the same if you're going to have people wandering round from two till six-thirty every afternoon except Wednesdays.'

I felt completely happy after that talk; never had the tragedy of my father's death seemed so far behind me. My life was here at Pendorric; it was true I was a newcomer, but everyone accepted me as a member of the family and Roc had given me the comfort that only he could give.

Soon afterwards I decided I would make a tour of all the rooms and see if I could detect anything that was in need of urgent repair. I was sure it was something which should be done, for Charles was interested in the farm, Morwenna in the garden, and Roc had the entire estate to manage.

I would begin with the east wing because that was the one which was unoccupied; and after luncheon one day I came down to the quadrangle, sat by the pond for a few minutes and then entered the house by way of the east door.

As soon as that door closed behind me I began to think of Barbarina, who had loved this part of the house, and I longed to see her music room again.

I went straight to that floor, and as I mounted the stairs a sudden impulse came to me to turn back, but I quickly thrust this aside, for I was not going to feel afraid every time I came to this part of the house simply because of an old legend.

When I reached the door of the music-room, I quickly turned the handle and went in.

Everything was as it had been when I had last seen it: the violin lying across the chair, the music on the stand.

I shut the door behind me, reminding myself that I had come here for a practical purpose. Where, I wondered, would wood-worm most likely be found? In the woodwork about the windows? In the oak beams across the ceiling? In the floor perhaps, or the doors? If it did exist, the sooner it was dealt with the better.

My eyes kept straying to the music stand, and I was picturing her there, her eyes bright with inspiration, faint colour in her cheeks. I knew exactly what she looked like, and I wondered what her thoughts had been the last time she had stood there, her violin in her slim hands with their tapering fingers.

'Barbarina!' The name was spoken in a whisper.

I felt a prickly sensation in my spine. I was not alone in this room.

'Barbarina! Are you there, Barbarina?'

A movement behind me made me spin round hastily. My eyes went to the door and I saw that the handle was slowly being turned.

My hands had involuntarily placed themselves across my heart, which was beating painfully as the door was slowly opened.

'Carrie!' I cried reproachfully. 'You startled me.'

The little eyes beneath those heavy brows glinted as she looked at me.

'So it's Mr. Roc's bride,' she said. 'I thought for the moment . . .'

'You thought I was someone else?'

She nodded slowly and looked about the room as though she were seeking something.

I went on because I wanted to know what was in her mind: 'You said: "Barbarina." '

Again she nodded without speaking.

'She's dead, Carrie.'

'She don't rest,' was the low reply.

'So you believe that she haunts the house . . . haunts these rooms?'

'I know when she's getting ready to walk. There's a kind of stirring.' She came close to me and looked in my face. 'I can feel it now.'

'Well, I can't.' Then I was afraid that I had spoken rather sharply, and I remembered that she had been nurse to Barbarina and Deborah and had loved them dearly. When loved ones died, often those who had lost them made themselves believe that they could come back. I could see the devotion shining in Carrie's eyes, and I knew that when she had heard me in the music room she had really hoped it was Barbarina.

'You will,' said Carrie.

I smiled disbelievingly. 'I must get on,' I said. 'I'm rather busy.'

I walked out of the music room, but I didn't want to stay any longer in the east wing. I went back to the quadrangle and sat there; and every now and then I would find myself looking up involuntarily at those windows.

When I next called on Lord Polhorgan, Dr. Clement was there. He had tea with us and I found his company pleasant, as I was sure our host did.

I was very pleased to see that Lord Polhorgan had recovered from his recent attack and I was surprised that he could appear as well as he did.

We talked about the village and I discovered that Dr. Clement, like the Reverend Peter Dark, was very interested in the customs of the place.

He lived on the outskirts of Pendorric village in a house which he had taken over from the doctor who had retired on his arrival.

'It's called Tremethick – which is apt, because in Cornish it means the doctor's house. You must come and meet my sister sometime.'

I said I should be delighted to; and he talked of his sister Mabell, who was interested in pottery and made quite a number of the little pots and ashtrays which were for sale in some of the shops in the towns along the coast. She was something of an artist, too, and not only supplied pottery but her pictures 'on sale or return' to the shops.

'It keeps her busy – that and the house.'

She had turned the old stables into a workshop and had her oven there.

'She'll never make a fortune out of her pottery,' our host commented. 'Too much mass-production against her.'

'Not a fortune, but a lot of pleasure,' retorted the doctor. 'And it pleases her that there's a small profit in it.'

There was no chess that day, and when I got up to go, the doctor said he had his car outside and would drive me home.

I told him that there was no need, but he insisted that he went past Pendorric, so I accepted.

As we drove along he asked if I always made the journey from Pendorric to Polhorgan by the top road, and I said that there were three ways of getting there: by that road, by Smugglers' Lane and the short cut, and by way of the beach and the gardens.

'If I'm in a hurry,' I told him, 'I take the short cut.'

'Oh yes,' he said, 'you can save quite five minutes that way. Once there was a road there with houses on either side. I found an old map the other day. It gives you some idea how the sea is gradually encroaching on the land. It couldn't have been more than a hundred and fifty years old. Why not come along now and meet Mabell? She'd be delighted to see you, and I'd run you back.'

I looked at my watch, and thinking that Roc might already be home, said that I didn't really think I had time.

He dropped me at Pendorric. I thanked him and he gave me a friendly wave as his car roared away.

I turned to the house. There was no one in sight, and I stood for a while under the arch and looked up at the inscription in Cornish.

It was a grey day; there had been no sun lately; nor would there be, Roc had told me, until the wind changed. It was now blowing straight in from the south-west – soft and balmy, the sort of wind that made one's skin glow.

The gulls seemed even more mournful than usual to-day, but that may have been because of the greyness of the sea and the leaden sky.

I walked round the house to the south side and stood for a moment looking down on the garden, but even the colours of the flowers seemed subdued.

I went into the house, and as soon as I entered the hall my eyes fixed themselves on the portrait of Barbarina. I was afraid they were making a habit of doing that. The eyes in the picture followed me as I passed the suits of armour and started to go up the stairs. I went up to the gallery and stood right beneath the portrait looking up at it, and as Barbarina's eyes looked straight into mine I could almost imagine the lips curved into a smile – a warm, inviting smile.

I was really being rather silly, I told myself.

The hall was gloomy to-day because it was so grey outside. If the sun were shining through those big mullioned windows it would seem quite different.

Was Roc home, I wondered. There was a great deal to be done on the farm and about the estate, and that work was still very much in arrears, because he had been abroad so long.

I walked along the gallery to the corridor. Several of the windows were open and I could never seem to resist looking down at the quadrangle. And as I stood there I could distinctly hear the music of a violin.

I threw up the window and leaned out. Yes, there was no doubt about it; and one of the windows on the east side was opened. Was the sound coming from the east wing?

It might well be. I was sure it was. My eyes went to the second floor. If someone were playing in the music room could I hear from across the corridor and the quadrangle?

I was ashamed of feeling so frightened. I was not going to be taken in by my foolish imagination. I reminded myself of the day Carrie had come into the music room while I was there, and how scared I had been because she went creeping around calling Barbarina; as soon as I had seen that it was Carrie I had ceased to be scared; I was not the least bit taken in by her talk of 'stirring.'

I began to walk resolutely round the corridor to the east wing. As I went in I heard the violin again. I hurried up the stairs to the music room.

There was no sound of the violin now. I threw open the door. The violin lay on the chair; the music was on the stand.

There was no one in the room and I felt the stillness of the house close about me.

Then suddenly I heard the shriek of a gull outside the window.

It seemed to be laughing at me.

Because I was not anxious to stay in the house, I decided to go for a walk in the direction of the home farm, hoping to meet Roc.

As I walked I reasoned with myself: Someone in the house plays the violin, and you presumed it came from the east wing because you had seen the violin there. If you really are disturbed about it, the simplest thing is to find out who in the house plays the violin and casually mention that you heard it being played.

Out of doors everything seemed so much more rational than it did in the house. As I climbed on to the road and walked across the fields in a northerly direction I was quickly recovering my good spirits. I had not walked this way before and I was delighted to explore fresh ground. The countryside seemed restful after the rugged coast views, and I was charmed by the greenish-gold of the freshly mown fields and the scarlet of the poppies growing here and there. I particularly noticed the occasional tree, slightly bent by the south-west gales, but taller than those stunted and distorted ones which survived along the coast. I could smell the fragrance of meadow-sweet growing on the banks mingling with the harebells and scabious.

And while I was contemplating all this I heard the sound of a car, and to my delight saw it was Roc's.

He pulled up and put his head out of the window.

'This is a pleasant surprise.'

'I've never walked this way. I thought I'd come and meet you.'

'Get in,' he commanded.

When he hugged me I felt secure again and very glad I had come.

'I got back from Polhorgan to find no one around, so I decided I wouldn't stay in.'

Roc started the car. 'And how was the old man to-day?'

'He seemed to have quite recovered.'

'I believe that's how it is with his complaint. Poor old fellow, it must be a trial for him, yet he's cheerful enough . . . about his health.'

'I think he's very brave.'

Roc gave me a quick look. 'Relations still remain friendly?'

'Of course.'

'Not everyone gets along with him so well. I'm glad you do.'

'I'm still surprised that you should be when you so obviously don't like him.'

'The lady of the manor has always gone round visiting the sick. It's an old custom. You've started well.'

'Surely the custom was to visit the sickly poor and take them soup and blankets.'

Roc burst out laughing. 'Imagine your arriving at Polhorgan with a bowl of soup and a red flannel blanket, and handing them to Dawson for the deserving millionaire!'

'This is quite a different sort of visiting anyway.'

'Is it? He wants company; they wanted comforts. Same thing, but in a different form. No, really, darling, I'm delighted that you're able to bring sunshine into the old man's life. You've brought such lots into mine, I can spare him a little. What do you talk about all the time? Does he tell you about his wicked family who deserted him?'

'He hasn't mentioned his family.'

'He will. He's waiting for the opportunity.'

'By the way,' I said, 'I heard someone playing the violin this afternoon. Who would it have been?'

'The violin?' Roc screwed up his eyes as though puzzled. 'Where?'

'I wasn't sure where. I thought it was in the east wing.'

'Hardly anyone goes there except old Carrie. Can't believe she's turned virtuoso. In our youth, Morwenna and I had a few lessons. They soon discovered, in my case at least, that it was no use trying to cultivate stony ground. Morwenna wasn't bad. But she dropped all that when she married Charles. Charles is tone-deaf – wouldn't know a Beethoven concerto from "God Save the Queen"; and Morwenna is the devoted wife. Everything that Charles thinks, she thinks; you could take her as a model, darling.'

'So you're the only two who could play the violin?'

'Wait a minute. Rachel gave the twins lessons at one time, I believe. Lowella takes after me and is about as talented in that direction as a bull calf. Hyson, now . . . she's different. I think Hyson was quite good at it.'

'It could have been Hyson or Rachel I heard playing.'

'You seem very interested. Not thinking of taking it up yourself? Or are you a secret genius? There's a lot I don't know about you, Favel, even though you are my wife.'

'And there's a lot I don't know about you.'

'What a good thing we have the rest of our lives in which to discover one another.'

As we came on to the coast road we met Rachel, and Roc slowed down the car for her to get in.

'I've been looking for the twins,' she told us. 'They went shrimping this afternoon, down at Tregallic Cove.'

'I hope you took advantage of your respite,' Roc said.

'I did. I went for a long walk as far as Gorman's Bay. I had tea there and planned to pick them up on the way back. I expect they've already gone home.'

'Favel thought she heard you playing the violin this afternoon.'

I turned and looked at Rachel. Her expression seemed faintly scornful, her sandy eyes more sly than usual.

'You'd hardly have heard me on the road from Gorman's Bay.'

'It must have been Hyson, then.'

Rachel shrugged her shoulders. 'I don't think Hyson will qualify for the concert platform, and I'd be surprised if she deserted shrimps for music.'

As we were going to the house the twins arrived, with their shrimping nets and a pail in which Lowella carried their catch.

Rachel said: 'By the way, Hyson, you didn't come back and play your violin this afternoon?'

Hyson looked bewildered. 'Whatever for?' she said.

'Your Aunt Favel thought she heard you.'

'Oh,' said Hyson thoughtfully. 'She didn't hear *me* playing it.'

She turned away abruptly, and I was sure it was because she didn't want me to see that Rachel's remark had excited her.

The next day it rained without stopping and continued through the night.

'There's nothing unusual about that,' Roc told me. 'It's another old Cornish custom. You'll begin to understand why ours is the greenest grass in this green and pleasant land.'

The soft south-west wind was blowing, and everything one touched seemed damp.

The following day the rain was less constant, though the louring sky promised more to come. The sea was muddy brown about the shore, and farther out it was a dull greyish-green.

Roc was going off to the farm, and as I had decided that I would go along to Polhorgan to complete that unfinished game of chess, he drove me there on his way.

Lord Polhorgan was delighted to see me; we had tea as usual and played our game of chess, which he won.

He liked to have an inquest after it was over, and point out where I had given him the game. It put him in a good humour and I enjoyed it, because, after all, the purpose of my visits was to give him pleasure.

As I was leaving, Dr. Clement called. He was getting out of his car as I came out by the unicorns, and looked disappointed.

'Just leaving?' he said.

'Yes, I've stayed rather longer than I meant to.'

'Mabell is very much looking forward to meeting you.'

'Tell her I'm also looking forward to it.'

'I'll get her to telephone you.'

'Please do. How ill is Lord Polhorgan?'

Dr. Clement looked serious. 'One can never be sure with a patient in his condition. He can become seriously ill very quickly.'

'I'm glad Nurse Grey is always at hand.'

'It's rather essential that he should have someone in attendance. Mind you . . .'

He did not continue, and I guessed he was about to offer a criticism of Althea Grey and changed his mind.

I smiled. 'Well, I'll have to hurry. Good-bye.'

'Good-bye.'

He went into the house and I made my way towards the coast road. Then I changed my mind and decided to use the short cut.

I had not gone far when I realized I'd been rather foolish to come, for the path was a mass of reddish-brown mud and I guessed Smugglers' Lane would be even worse. I stood still wondering whether to turn back, but as I should have to plough through mud to do so I decided it couldn't be much worse if I went on. My shoes were filthy by now in any case.

I had not quite reached the narrow ledge when I heard Roc's voice.

'Favel! Stop where you are. Don't move till I get to you.'

I turned sharply and saw him coming towards me.

'What's wrong?'

He didn't answer, but coming close he put out an arm and held me tightly against him for some seconds. Then he said: 'This path is dangerous after a heavy rain. Look! Can you see the cracks in the ground? Part of the cliff has collapsed. It's unsafe even here.'

He took my arm and drew me back the way I had come, carefully picking his steps.

When we reached the beginning of the cliff path he stopped and sighed deeply. 'I was thoroughly scared,' he said. 'It suddenly occurred to me. I came hurrying over to Polhorgan and they told me you'd just left. Look back. Can you see where the cliff-side has crumbled? Look at that heap of shale and uprooted bracken half-way down the slope.'

I saw it and shuddered.

'The narrow part is absolutely unsafe,' went on Roc. 'I'm surprised you didn't see the notice. Come to think of it I didn't see it myself.'

'It always says "This path used at own risk." But I thought that was for visitors who aren't used to the cliffs.'

'After heavy rain they take that away and put up another notice: "Path unsafe." Can't understand why it wasn't done.' He was frowning, and then he gave a sudden cry. 'Good lord,' he said, 'I wonder who did this?' He stooped and picked up a board which was lying face down. There were two muddy prongs attached to it which clearly had recently been embedded in the ground. 'I don't see how it could have fallen. Thank heaven I came.'

'I was going very carefully.'

'You might have managed, but . . . oh, my God . . . the risk.'

He held me close to him and I was deeply touched because I knew he was anxious that I should not see how frightened he was. He stuck the notice-board into the ground and said gruffly:

'The car's not far off. Come on! Let's get home.'

When we drove up to the portico Morwenna was busy forking plantains from the stretch of lawn.

Roc slammed the door and shouted: 'Someone must have uprooted the danger board on the cliff path. I just stopped Favel going along it in time.'

Morwenna stood up looking startled. 'Who on earth . . .?' she began.

'Some kids, I expect. It ought to be reported. It suddenly occurred to me that she might go that way – and she did.'

'I've often been over it when the danger board's been up.'

'There was a bad landslide,' Roc said shortly. He turned to me. 'The path shouldn't be used until they've done something about it. I'm going to speak to Admiral Weston – the chairman of the local council.'

Charles had come round by the side of the house; I noticed that his boots were muddy.

'Anything wrong?'

Roc repeated the story of what he seemed to regard as my narrow escape.

'Visitors,' grumbled Charles. 'I bet it's visitors.'

'All's well that ends well,' said Morwenna, drawing off her gardening gloves. 'I've had enough for to-day. I could do with a drink. What about you, Favel? I expect Roc could do with one, and Charles never says no.'

We went into the house to a little parlour leading off the hall. Morwenna took drinks from a cabinet and while she was serving them Rachel Bective came in with Hyson. They were wearing slippers, and Morwenna's look of approval called my attention to them. I guessed they had changed at the side door where the gum-boots and house shoes were kept ready for occasions like this.

The subject of the notice-board was brought up again, and Rachel Bective did not look at me as she said: 'That could have been dangerous. It was a good thing you rememberd, Roc.' Hyson was staring at her slippers, and I fancied I saw a slight smile curve her lips.

'Where's Lowella?' asked Morwenna.

Neither Rachel nor Hyson had any idea.

It was five or ten minutes later when Lowella joined us, and she was immediately followed by Deborah. Lowella told us that she had been swimming; and Deborah had obviously just got up from her usual afternoon nap, she still looked sleepy; and no one mentioned the notice-board incident after that, but I could see that several of them hadn't forgotten it. Roc still looked worried; Rachel Bective almost rueful; and Hyson secretive, as though she knew something which she was determined not to tell.

I half wondered whether Hyson had removed the board. She knew where I had gone and that I'd probably come home by the short cut. She might even have watched me. But what reason could she possibly have for doing it? There might be more than a streak of mischief in her nature. But, I decided, Roc had made a great deal out of something not very important, simply because of his love for me.

I felt rather cosily content, until the following day, when the doubts began.

The weather had completely changed by next morning. The sky was a guileless blue, and the sea sparkled so brilliantly that it was almost too dazzling to contemplate. It was like a sheet of silk with scarcely a ripple in it. Roc took me with him to the forge, where one of his horses was being shod that morning. I was offered another glass of cider from the barrel in the corner; and while young Jim shod the horse, Dinah came into the forge to give me the benefit of her bold lustrous stare; I guessed that she was wondering about my relationship with Roc, and that made me suspect that he and she had been on intimate terms at some time and that she was trying to convey this to me.

'Maybe,' she said, 'I'll tell Mrs. Pendorric's fortune one day.'

Old Jim murmured that he doubted whether Mrs. Pendorric would be interested in such nonsense.

She ignored him. 'I'm good with the cards but it's your own hand and the crystal that's best. I could tell you a fine fortune, Mrs. Pendorric.'

She smiled, throwing back her dark head so that the gold-coloured rings in her ears danced.

'One day perhaps . . .' I murmured.

'Don't make it too long. Delay's dangerous.'

When we left the forge and passed the row of cottages I saw an old man sitting at the door of one of them.

'Morning, Jesse,' called Roc.

'Morning sir.'

'We must speak to Jesse Pleydell,' Roc whispered.

The gnarled hands were grasping the bony knees and they were trembling. I wondered why; then I saw how very old he was and thought this was the reason.

'Be that your lady as is with you, sir?' he asked gently.

'It is, Jesse; she's come to make your acquaintance.'

'How do you do,' I said. 'Your daughter was talking to me about you.'

'She be a good girl, my Bessie ... and Maria, she be good too. Don't know what I'd do without 'em ... now I be so old and infirm like. 'Tis a pleasure to think of her ... up at the House.'

'We wish that you could be there too, Jesse,' said Roc, and the gentleness of his voice delighted me and made me feel as happy as I had before Dinah Bond had put misgivings into my mind.

'Ay, sir, that's where my place be. But since my eyes was took from me, it's little use I be to God or man.'

'Nonsense, we're all proud of you, Jesse. You've only got to live another twenty years and you'll make Pendorric famous.'

'Always one for a joke, Master Roc ... like his father. Now he were one for a joke till ...' His hands began to pluck at the cloth of his trousers nervously.

'Like father, like son,' said Roc. 'Well, we must be moving on.'

On impulse I stepped closer to the old man and laid a hand on his shoulder. He was very still, and a smile touched his lips.

'I'll come and see you again,' I said.

He nodded, and his hands began to tremble again as they sought his bony knee-caps and rested there.

''Tis like old times ...' he murmured. ' Like old times, with a new bride up to Pendorric. I wish *you* all the best of luck, m'dear.'

When we were out of earshot I said: 'Mrs. Penhalligan told me he was in the hall at the time of your mother's accident.'

'She told you that, did she?' He was frowning. 'How they do go on about things that are past and over.' He glanced at me, and, perhaps because I looked surprised at his mild annoyance, he went on: 'I suppose so little happens in their lives that they remember every little thing that's out of the ordinary routine.'

'I should certainly hope someone's untimely death would be very much out of routine.'

He laughed and put his arm through mine. 'Remember that, when you feel tempted to go scrambling over dangerous paths,' he said.

Then we came to the Darks' house and the Reverend Peter invited us in; he was so eager to show us pictures he had taken of the Helston Furry Dancers the preceding May.

That afternoon I went to the quadrangle – not to sit, for, in spite of the warm sun of the morning, the seats had not yet dried out after the rain. Hyson followed me there and gravely walked round at my side. The hydrangeas looked fresher than ever and their colours more brilliant.

Hyson said suddenly: 'Did you feel frightened when Uncle Roc rescued you on the cliff path?'

'No. It didn't occur to me that there was any danger until he pointed it out.'

'You probably would have got through all right. It was just that there *might* have been an accident.'

'It was a good thing I was stopped from going on, then, wasn't it?'

Hyson nodded. 'It was meant,' she said, in a small hollow voice.
I looked at her sharply.

'Perhaps,' she went on, 'it was just a warning. Perhaps . . .'

She was staring at one of the windows on the east side as she had before.
I looked up; there was no one there. She saw my glance and smiled faintly.

'Good-bye,' she said, and went into the house through the north door.

I felt irritated. What was the child trying to imply? I had an idea that she
wanted to make an impression on me. What was she suggesting? That
certain matters which were obscure to ordinary people were revealed to her?
Really it was rather silly of her. But she was only a child. I must remember
that; and it was rather sad if she were jealous of her sister.

Then quite suddenly I heard the voice, and for a moment I had no idea
from where it was coming. It floated down to me, a strange voice singing
slightly out of tune. I heard the words distinctly.

> *'He is dead and gone, lady,*
> *He is dead and gone;*
> *At his head a grass-green turf,*
> *At his feet a stone.'*

I looked up at the windows on the east side. Several of them were open.

Then I went resolutely through the east door and up the stairs to the
gallery.

'Hyson,' I called. 'Are you there, Hyson?'

There was no answer; and I realized how very cool it seemed in the house
after coming in from the sunshine. I was angry, telling myself that someone
was trying to tease me. I was more angry than I should have been; and
there, in that silent part of the house, I understood that I was so angry
because I was beginning to be a little frightened.

Chapter Four

I had begun to think that someone was amusing himself – or herself – at my
expense.

I had heard the playing of a violin; I had heard the singing. Why should
I be the one singled out to hear these things? I was sure it was because of
the legend and because I was the new Bride. Somebody in this house was
trying to make me nervous.

I wondered why. Had my practical attitude, my determination not to be
affected by stories of ghosts and hauntings, irritated someone? Was my

scepticism a challenge? That seemed the most likely. Someone who believed in the ghost of Pendorric was determined to make me change my tune.

I wondered to whom I could talk about this subject which was beginning to take up too much of my thoughts.

If I mentioned it to Roc, he would laugh and tell me I was coming under the spell of Pendorric as all the Brides did. Morwenna was always friendly, but somehow remote; as for Charles, I saw less of him than of anyone in the household and I couldn't imagine myself chatting cosily with him. The twins? Impossible. Lowella was too much of a scatterbrain, and I could never be sure what Hyson was thinking. Indeed, if someone was trying to scare me I rather suspected it might be Hyson, for after all, there was an element of childishness in the method.

I had never liked Rachel Bective and it occurred to me that she might have sensed my dislike, returned it, and was trying to make me uncomfortable in my new home.

There seemed only one person in whom I could confide and that was Deborah. She was more affectionate than Morwenna, more inclined to share confidences; and I felt that, being a Devonshire woman, she was practical and looked on superstition much as I myself did.

There was an opportunity to talk to her when I went to her room to look at her albums, and we sat in the window-seat of her sitting-room with the books across our knees while she explained the pictures to me. They had been arranged with care, in chronological order, with a caption beneath each; and most of the early ones were of Barbarina and her husband. There were several of Barbarina and Deborah herself, and I couldn't distinguish which was which.

'That's because we're in repose,' explained Deborah. 'She was much more animated than I; she had all the charm. But you don't see that in a snapshot.'

There were many of Roc and Morwenna; and I found it absorbingly interesting to study his little face and discover there a hint of traits which were his to-day.

Then I turned a page and there were no more pictures.

'That last one was taken a week before Barbarina died,' Deborah told me. 'After that I didn't use this book. This was what I thought of as Barbarina's Book. It couldn't go on after she had gone.' She picked up another album and opened it. I looked at pictures of an older Roc and Morwenna. 'After a while,' went on Deborah, 'life started to go on in a new pattern, and I took my pictures again.'

I turned a page and stopped, for I was looking at what I thought was a group consisting of Roc, Morwenna and Barbarina.

'This one doesn't belong in this book.'

Deborah smiled. 'Oh yes it does. That isn't Barbarina. She died six months before that was taken.'

'So it's you. But you look so exactly like her.'

'Yes . . . when she was no longer there to be compared with me, people thought I was more like her than I had been before. But that was because she wasn't there, of course.' She turned the page as though she couldn't bear to look at it. 'Oh, and here's Morwenna and Charles. He's very young there.

He came to Pendorric when he was eighteen or so. Petroc's idea was to train him so that he could take over, and that was what he did. See how Morwenna gazes up at him. He was a god to her.' She laughed. 'It was rather amusing to see the effect he had on her. Every sentence she uttered began with "Charles says . . ." or "Charles does . . ." She adored him from the moment he came to Pendorric, and she's gone on doing so ever since.'

'They're very happy, aren't they?'

'Sometimes I used to think that there was too much devotion there. I remember one occasion when he went down to market and was involved in a smash-up. It was only a minor affair, and he was in hospital for less than a week, but Morwenna was . . . stricken. And I thought then: "You're not living a life of your own, my dear. You're living Charles's life. That's well enough if Charles goes on living and loving you. But what if he doesn't?" I think she'd die of a broken heart.'

'Charles seems quite devoted to her.'

'Charles would always be a faithful husband, but there are other things in his life than his marriage. He's devoted to the Church, you know. Peter Dark often says he doesn't know what he'd do without him. Charles's father was a parson, and he was very strictly brought up. He's deeply religious. In fact I wonder he didn't take holy orders. I think cultivating the land is a sort of religion with him. As a matter of fact he has moulded Morwenna to his ways. There was a time when she was as ready for mischief as her brother. I've never known her go against Charles in any way . . . except perhaps one thing.'

I waited expectantly and Deborah hesitated as though wondering whether to go on.

'I meant . . . her friendship with Rachel Bective.'

'Oh, doesn't Charles like Rachel?'

'I don't think he has any strong feelings of dislike, but at one time Morwenna used to bring her home from school for every holiday. I asked if she hadn't another friend who might come, or whether Rachel hadn't a home of her own to go to, and I remember how stubborn Morwenna was. "She *must* come here," she said. "She wants to come and she hates going to her own home." Charles didn't actually say he disapproved of her, but he never took the two of them riding or with him when he went round the farms, as he took Morwenna when she was alone. I thought that would be enough to make her stop inviting Rachel. But it wasn't.'

'And now she's living here!'

'Only until the children go away to school again. And then I expect she'll find some excuse to stay, although perhaps now you're mistress of the house . . .'

Deborah sighed, and I knew what she meant. Unprivileged Rachel had come from a poor home to Pendorric, had loved what she had seen and longed to make it her own. Had she believed that *she* might be the new Bride of Pendorric? Roc had evidently been friendly with her, and I could understand how easy it was to fall in love with him. Was Rachel in love with Roc? Or had she been at some time? Yes, I decided in that moment, Rachel Bective might have a very good reason for resenting me.

I said slowly: 'Do you remember telling me about Barbarina's playing Ophelia and singing a song from the play?'

Deborah was very still for a few seconds and I was aware that she did not look at me. She nodded.

'I thought I heard someone singing that song in the east wing. I wondered who it could be.'

The silence seemed to go on for a long time, but perhaps it was only for a few seconds. Then Deborah said: 'I suppose anyone might sing that song.'

'Yes, I suppose so.'

Deborah turned to get one of the albums which I had not yet seen; she sat beside me explaining the pictures. She evidently did not appear to think it strange that I should have heard someone singing the song.

A few days later, in response to an invitation, I called at the doctor's house. It was a charming place – early nineteenth-century – surrounded by a garden in which were beehives. Mabell Clement was a very busy person, tall and fair like her brother, and she wore her hair in a thick plait which hung half-way down her back – at least that was how it was when I first met her; on later occasions I saw it made into a knot in the nape of her neck that was always threatening to escape restriction; she wore smocks, sometimes caught in at the waist by girdles, with raffia sandals, amber beads and swinging earrings.

She was determined that everyone should recognize her as an artist, and this seemed to be her one foible, for she appeared to be good-natured, easy-going, and a good hostess. She was very proud of her brother; and he was affectionately tolerant towards her. I imagine that meals were served at odd times in that household, for Mabell admitted that when the urge to paint or pot or look after her garden came to her she simply had to obey it.

I was shown over Tremethick itself, the pottery shed, and what was called the studio, and I had an interesting afternoon.

Dr. Clement said that he would drive me back to Pendorric, but half an hour before I was due to leave, a call came through from one of his patients and he had to go off immediately.

Thus I walked back to Pendorric alone.

As I came to the village there was no sign of anyone. It was one of those still afternoons, very hot and sultry; I passed the row of cottages, and looked for Jesse Pleydell, but he was not at his door to-day. I wondered whether to call on him as I had promised to do, but decided against it. I wanted to find out from Mrs. Penhalligan or Maria what tobacco he smoked and take some along for him when I went.

The churchyard lay on my right. It looked cool and somehow inviting. I hesitated and then slipped through the lych gate. I have always been attracted by graveyards, particularly deserted ones. There seems to me to be a sense of utter peace within them, and I liked to think of all those people lying beneath the grey stones who had once lived and suffered and now were at peace.

I walked among the tombstones and read some of the inscriptions as Roc had, not very long ago; and eventually I saw ahead of me the Pendorric vault.

Irresistibly attracted I went to it. I wanted to see if the laurel wreath was still there.

It was gone, but in its place was a small wreath of roses, and as I went closer I recognized the Paul Scarlets which grew in the garden. There was no note on the flowers, but I was sure they were there in memory of Barbarina. It occurred to me then that Carrie was the one who put them there.

I heard a rustle in the grass behind me, and turning sharply saw Dinah Bond picking her way towards me. She looked even more vital here among the dead than she did in the old blacksmith's shop; she held herself erect and swung her hips as she walked, in a manner which was both graceful and provocative.

'Hallo there, Mrs. Pendorric,' she called jauntily.

'Hallo,' I answered.

'It be quiet in here . . . peaceful like.'

'I thought the village looked peaceful to-day.'

'But too hot to move about much. There's thunder in the air. Can't you feel it? All still and waiting like . . . for the storm to break.'

'I expect you're right.'

She smiled at me half insolently, and what was worse, with something which I felt might have been compassion.

'Having a look at the family vault? I often do. I bet 'ee haven't been inside, Mrs. Pendorric.'

'No.'

She laughed: 'Time enough for that, I reckon you think. It's cold as death inside . . . and all the coffins laid out on shelves. Sometimes I come and look at it . . . like this afternoon . . . just for the pleasure of knowing I'm outside and not locked in – like Morwenna once was.'

'Morwenna! Locked in! How did that happen?'

'It's years ago. I was only a kid then . . . about six, I think. When are you going to let me tell your fortune?'

'Sometime, I expect.'

'No time like the present.'

'Why are you so anxious?'

'I'm just taken that way.'

'I haven't any silver to cross your palm with.'

'That! It's just a way to get the money. I wouldn't do it for money – not for you, Mrs. Pendorric. Now I'm married to Jim Bond, I don't do it professional like. That went out when I gave up my gipsy ways.'

'Tell me about the time Morwenna was locked in the vault and who did it.'

She didn't answer, but sat down on the edge of a gravestone, and resting her chin in her hands stared broodingly at the vault.

'The key of the vault was always kept in a cupboard in Mr. Petroc's study. It was a big key. She'd come down for the holidays.'

'Who?'

'Rachel Bective.'

'How old was she then?'

'I'd say about as old as those twins are now ... perhaps a year or so younger. I was always trailing them. I think it was the colour of her hair. Mine was that black and hers was ginger colour. I wanted to keep looking at it. Not that I liked it, mind. I liked Morwenna, though. "Miss Morwenna" we were told to call her. I never did, though, and she didn't mind.

'She was like Roc – they never minded things like that. But *she* did, that ginger one. She'd say to me: "You'll call me Miss Rachel or I'll know the reason why." Miss Rachel! Who did she think she was?'

'Tell me how Morwenna came to be in the vault.'

'I was always in the churchyard. I used to come here to play among the tombstones; and one day I saw them together and I hid and listened to them talking. After that I just wanted to watch them and listen to them some more, so I was often where they were, when they didn't know it. I knew they'd be at the vault, because I'd heard about it the day before when they were in the graveyard reading the inscriptions. Morwenna told Rachel that's what she used to do with her brother, and that made Rachel want to do it, for she did always want to do everything they did. She wanted to be one of them and she couldn't ... she couldn't ever be ... no more than she can now. Oh, she be educated, I do know ... but I'd be as good as her if I'd had the schooling.'

'What has she done to you, that you hate her so much?'

''Tain't what she's done to me. Her wouldn't deign to give much thought to the likes of I, Mrs. Pendorric. It's what she'd do to others.'

'You were telling me.'

'So I were.' She held her hands in front of her, as though she were reading her own fortune. Then she went on: 'I heard 'em talking. She wanted Morwenna to get this key so that they could have a look at the vault, and Morwenna didn't want to. You see, it was in her father's study. He was away at the time – he were often away after the accident – and she said to Morwenna: "You'll be sorry if you don't." I was up in a tree and they couldn't see me, but I knew that Morwenna would get the key because she knew she would really be sorry if she didn't. Then I heard they were coming there next afternoon, so I were there too.'

'So Morwenna did get the key.'

Dinah nodded. 'I was here in the graveyard next day when they came, and they had the key. Rachel Bective opened the door of the vault and they went in, though Morwenna didn't want to much, but Rachel was saying: "You've got to. You'll be sorry if you don't," and Morwenna was saying: "I can't. Not again." Then all of a sudden Rachel laughed and ran out of the vault, slamming the door after her. Then she locked it and Morwenna was shut in.'

'It must have been a horrible experience. I hope she didn't stay there long.'

Dinah shook her head. 'No. There's a little grating in the vault and Rachel was soon at that. She kept calling out: "I won't let you out till you say you'll ask me for Christmas. I'll go back and I'll tell them I don't know where you are. Nobody'll think you're in here because I'll take the key back and put it where it belongs . . . and it'll be weeks before they find you, then you'll be a skeleton like the bride in 'The Mistletoe Bough'." So Morwenna said she would do what she wanted and Rachel opened the door. I never forgot that, and I don't never pass this spot without thinking on it and how poor Morwenna had to say she would do what it was Rachel wanted, and how pleased Rachel looked in her sly way.'

'She was only a child, I suppose, and she must have longed to come to Pendorric for holidays.'

'And you reckon that excuses her . . . doing a thing like that!'

'It was a childish trick . . .'

'Oh, no 'tweren't. She'd have left her there if Morwenna hadn't given way.'

'I'm sure she wouldn't.'

Dinah looked at me scornfully. 'I'm beginning to read your fortune, Mrs. Pendorric, without so much as a look at your hand. You're one of them that says: "Oh no, it bain't that way" . . . just when you don't want it to be. Your sort has to beware.'

'You're quite wrong. I assure you I face facts when I know they're there to be faced.'

'Ay, but it's knowing they're there that's important, don't 'ee think, Mrs. Pendorric? I'll tell 'ee this: There's people that don't change much all through their lives. You can't tell 'tis so till you've proved like . . . but it don't do no harm to be on your guard. Oh, I do know a lot about Pendorrics . . . living close you might say, all of me born natural life.'

'I expect there's always been a great deal of gossip about the family.'

'There was at the time, and though I was yet to be born, they were still talking of it when I were a little 'un. My mother was a sharp one. Nothing much she missed. I remember hearing her talk of Louisa Sellick, the one he were sweet on before he married Miss Barbarina.'

'Louisa Sellick?' I repeated, for I had never heard that name mentioned before.

'Oh, 'tis an old story and all happened long ago. Ain't no sense in reviving it like . . . 'cept of course, you be the next Bride.'

I went over to Dinah, and looking down at her said earnestly: 'I sometimes get the impression that you're trying to warn me about something.'

She threw back her hair and laughed up at me. 'That's because I want to tell your fortune. They say "The gipsy warned me," don't 'em? 'Tis a kind of joke.'

'What do you know of Louisa Sellick?'

'Only what my mother told me. Sometimes I've been out that way . . . where she do live now, and I've seen her. But that was after he were dead like . . . so it weren't the same. They say he used to go out to visit her and that Barbarina Pendorric killed herself because she couldn't endure it no more . . . him liking Louisa better than her. She'd thought when she first married that it was all over; that were when Louisa went out to live on the moor.'

'And is Louisa still living there?'

Dinah nodded. 'Well, least she were when I were last that way. 'Tis Bedivere House – a sizeable place. He bought it for her. 'Twas their love nest, you might say. And when he rode out on his business he'd land up at Bedivere. Perhaps there'd be mist on the moors or he was too busy to get back to Pendorric . . . see what I mean? But it was found out that she were there . . . and then things happened.'

'Do you often go out that way?'

'Not now. I got a home of me own now, remember. I married Jim Bond, didn't I? I sleep on a goose-feather bed and there's four walls all round me. But when I go out that way . . . Dozmary Pool and Jamaica Inn way . . . I see the house and I look for Louisa. She ain't so young and pretty now . . . but we none of us stay that way for ever, do us?'

I remembered suddenly that listening to Dinah's conversation I had stayed out longer than I had intended to. I looked at my watch.

'I'd no idea it was so late,' I said.

She smiled lazily. 'You'd better get back, Mrs. Pendorric. Time don't matter to me, but I know it does to the likes of you. Some folks rush about like they thought they hadn't got much time left. Perhaps they're right. Who's to say?'

She was smiling her mocking enigmatic smile.

'Good-bye,' I said, and started to pick my way through the gravestones to the lych gate.

My interest in Barbarina grew as each day passed. I went often to that room of hers and thought about her. I wondered if she had been of a passionate and jealous nature. She must have been terribly unhappy if, as Dinah had suggested, her husband had paid periodic visits to that woman on the moor.

I had heard no more violin-playing, nor singing in that strange off-key voice. Whoever had been responsible for that had evidently decided to give it a rest, and I was only faintly disconcerted because I had failed to discover who was playing the part of the ghostly musician. But I did want to know more of Barbarina.

Deborah was always willing to talk about her, and in fact obviously delighted in doing so. She was gradually building up the picture of her sister in my mind; sometimes she would even describe the dresses they had worn for certain parties, and so vividly did she talk that it was as though Barbarina materialized before my eyes.

Since my talk with Dinah the picture had become even clearer, and I knew that one day soon my curiosity would be too much for me and I should have to go out on the moor to see if I could catch a glimpse of Louisa Sellick for myself.

I had not made any excursions alone by car so far, and I couldn't very well ask Roc to take me there, nor Morwenna. I had an uneasy feeling that I'd do better to leave the past alone, and yet, because I could not suppress a feeling that I ought to know, I seemed unable to stop. Dinah's veiled warnings didn't help me to leave the subject alone, either.

There were three small cars in the garage besides Roc's Daimler and

Charles's Land-Rover; Morwenna used one of them and I had been told that the others were for general use.

I had often said that I wanted to go into Plymouth to do some shopping, and although I didn't exactly say I was going there on this occasion, I let Morwenna think so.

Roc had gone off on estate business that morning and I hadn't even told him I was going out, which, after all, did occur to me on the spur of the moment.

I had paused by the picture of Barbarina in the gallery and looked up into those sadly brooding eyes, wondering whether when she had discovered that her husband was visiting that house on the moor she had confronted him with her discovery. 'I should if I ever found that Roc was involved in such an affair,' I said to myself; and I remembered the sly looks of Rachel, the bold ones of Dinah Bond, and the beauty of Nurse Grey.

I did seem to be growing very jealous since I had arrived at Pendorric. Was I changing my nature or discovering characteristics which I had not known before that I possessed?

In any case, I assured myself, I was not the sort to suffer in silence. If I had a shred of evidence that Roc was being unfaithful to *me*, I should confront him with it and insist on the truth.

What had Barbarina done?

Was I identifying myself with Barbarina and reading things from her life into mine so that our stories were beginning to seem similar?

In any case my interest in her was becoming a little morbid.

Although this thought occurred to me it did not prevent my wanting to see the house where my father-in-law had installed her rival, but I did try to tell myself that it was really the moor that fascinated me, and it was the ideal morning for a drive.

I set out about half past ten, and branching off the road to Plymouth I was on the moor in a very short time.

It was a glorious morning. A fresh breeze ruffled the rough grass and I felt a sense of adventure as I looked ahead at the folds of moor and drove for miles without seeing any person or building.

Eventually I slowed down before a signpost, and saw that I was only a few miles from Dozmary Pool.

I drove on. I could see the hills with Brown Willy towering above them and Rough Tor in the distance. This was a very lonely spot, and looking about me I saw several mounds which earlier Roc had pointed out to me as the burial grounds of ancient Britons.

It was here that King Arthur was reputed to have fought his last battle. If it were really so, I thought, it would have looked exactly as it looked to-day.

And suddenly I saw the Pool; it was not large and I guessed that at its widest part it could not have been more than a quarter of a mile across. I stopped the car, and getting out walked to the water's edge. There was no sound but the murmur of the wind in the rough grass.

I thought of the legend as I remembered it and as I supposed thousands of visitors to this place must have done: of Bedivere standing at the edge of the water with the dying Arthur's sword in his hand, debating whether or not to throw it, as commanded, into the middle of the mere.

Finally he had done so and an arm had appeared from the centre of the Pool and grasped the sword Excalibur.

I smiled and turned away.

Bedivere, I murmured. Bedivere House. It must be fairly near; Dinah had said so.

I got back into the car and drove slowly for half a mile, and then found a narrow road which I decided to explore.

I had not gone very far when a boy came out of a narrow lane and started to walk in the direction I was going. Drawing up beside him I saw that he was about fourteen; he smiled, and right from the first moment I knew there was something familiar in that smile.

'Are you lost?' he asked.

'Not exactly. I'm just wandering round. I've come from Dozmary Pool.'

He grinned. 'Well, this is a second-class road. It doesn't lead anywhere much except to Bedivere House . . . and then back on to the main road. Only it gets a bit rougher. Your best plan, if you want to get on to the main road, is to turn back.'

'Thank you,' I said. 'But I'll go on for a bit and look at Bedivere House. What's it like?'

'Oh, you can't miss it. It's the grey house with the green shutters.'

'Sounds interesting – especially with a name like that.'

'Oh, I don't know,' he said with a grin. 'I live there, you see.'

He had his back to the light, and then I noticed that the tips of his rather prominent ears were faintly pink and pointed.

He had stepped back. 'Good-bye,' he said.

'Good-bye.'

As I started off a woman came into sight. She was tall and slim and she had a mass of white curly hair.

'Ennis,' she called. 'Oh, there you are.'

She glanced at me as I passed, and as I rounded the bend I saw the house at once. The boy had been right; there was no mistaking it. There were the green shutters. It was more than a cottage – a house of some seven or eight rooms, I imagined. There was a green gate opening on to a lawn with a flower border. Inside it were plants which looked like tomatoes; and both the doors of the glass porch and the house itself were open.

I drove a little way past, then got out of the car and, shading my eyes, looked round me at the view.

I was aware of the woman and the boy coming back; they were arm in arm; and together they went into Bevidere House.

I was certain then that I had seen Louisa Sellick; but I did wonder who the boy could be. Ennis. I believed there was a Cornish saint of that name; there was no doubt of whom he reminded me. Of some of the portraits I had seen at Pendorric – and, of course, of Roc.

I was changing for dinner when I next saw Roc, and still thinking of the boy to whom I had spoken near Dozmary. By now my imagination had made the resemblance between him and Roc more startling.

Roc must have looked exactly like that at thirteen or fourteen, I told myself. I could picture him playing in the graveyard with Rachel and Morwenna; riding his horse out to Jim Bond's when it cast a shoe; swimming, boating . . .

I was already dressed when he came into our room, and was sitting at the window watching the waves below us.

'Hallo,' he called. 'Had a good day?'

'Yes, Roc. And you?'

I stood up and found myself staring at the tips of his ears. Surely only Pendorrics had such ears.

'Very good.'

'I took the Morris on to the moors,' I told him.

'I wish I'd been with you.'

'So do I.'

He picked me up and swung me off my feet.

'It's good to have you to come home to,' he said. 'I've talked to Charlie about your looking into estate affairs with me. We'd be partners then. What do you say?'

'I'm so glad, Roc.'

'You were the brains behind that studio,' he said. 'We need brains in Pendorric.'

I had a sudden vision of my father at work in the studio, and, as whenever I thought of him I must think also of his death, I knew that a shadow passed across my face.

Roc went on quickly: 'We need brains, now that the days of the *grands seigneurs* are over. It's the farm workers who get the best end of the stick these days. They've got their unions to look after them. I've never heard of a union to protect the interest of the poor landowners. Rents must not be put up; repairs must be done. You see how we could use a business woman like you!'

'Oh Roc, I'm going to love it.'

He kissed me. 'Good. You're in business.'

'Roc, you're not worried, are you?'

'I'm not the worrying type . . . otherwise . . .'

'Otherwise you would be?'

'Oh, darling, what's the good of worrying? If we can't afford to go on in the old way, we've got to adjust ourselves to the new. Temper the wind to the shorn lamb, or is it the other way round? My God, we're shorn all right – fleeced in fact. Left, right, and centre.'

I had put my arms about his neck and my fingers almost involuntarily caught his ears – a habit they had. He was smiling and I was vividly reminded of the boy I had seen that afternoon.

'Roc,' I said, 'I saw a pair of ears exactly like yours to-day.'

He burst out laughing. Then he looked grave. 'I thought they were unique. You've always told me so.'

'They're Pendorric ears.' I touched them with my forefinger. 'And they match your eyes. They give you that satyr's look.'

'For which I have to be truly thankful, because it was that which made you fall in love with me.'

'He had the same sort of eyes . . . now I come to think of it.'

'Tell me where you found this paragon.'

'It was on the moor near Dozmary Pool. I asked him the way and he told me he lived at a place called Bedivere House and his name was Ennis.'

There was just a short pause, but during it I fancied – or did I think this afterwards? – that Roc's expression had become a little guarded.

'What a lot of information he gave! After all you only asked the way, didn't you?'

'It was all very naturally given. But the likeness was really astonishing. I wonder if he's related to you.'

'There's Pendorric blood all over the duchy,' said Roc. 'You see we were a roisterous riotous band. Not that we were the only ones. The old days were very different from these. In those days it was "God bless the Squire and his relations and make us mind our proper stations"; it was touching the forelock and thinking themselves lucky to have a place in the stables, the kitchens or the gardens. It was the *droit de seigneur*. Now of course it's "We're as good as you" and crippling taxation. Ah, the good old days have gone for ever. And talking of the rights of the squire . . . well, there's your answer. You walk round this countryside and you'll discover traces of Pendorric in half the natives. It was the order of things.'

'You sound regretful. I believe you're sighing for the old days.'

He put his hand on my shoulder and smiled at me. Did I fancy that there was a hint of relief in his face, as though he had come up to a dangerous corner and had rounded it satisfactorily?

'Since I met and married Favel Farrington,' he replied, 'I ask nothing more of life.'

And although he was smiling, I couldn't doubt that he meant what he said; and, as usual, he had the power to disperse all my doubts and fears with a look, a word and a smile.

Roc kept his promise and the next day took me with him to his study, and, as much as he could in a short time, explained certain matters about the estate. It did not take me very long to grasp the fact that although we were by no means verging on bankruptcy we were in a way fighting a losing battle against the times.

Roc smiled at me ruefully. 'It's like the tide slowly but surely creeping in. The end of the old way is not exactly imminent, but it's creeping towards us. Mind you, we've hung on longer than most. I'd be sorry if we fell to the National Trust in my time.'

'You think it's certain to happen, Roc?'

'Nothing in life is certain darling. Suppose I were to win a hundred thousand . . . I reckon that would put us on our feet for a few generations.'

'You're not thinking of gambling?' I asked in alarm.

He put his arm about me. 'Don't worry,' he said. 'I never risk what I can't afford to lose.'

'You told me that before.'

'It's only one of many things I've told you before. How much I love you, for one thing.'

'The conversation is wandering from the point,' I said with a laugh.

'That's right,' he retorted. 'I know you're going to be a good business woman. You'll keep me on the straight path, won't you? Things have been in a far worse state than they are now, I can assure you; and we've pulled through. Why, in my father's day ...'

'What happened then?'

'We were in much greater difficulties. Fortunately my mother brought enough to put us on our feet again.'

I stared at the open book before me, and instead of the columns of figures saw that sad sweet face under the blue-banded hat. There seemed no escape from Barbarina.

Roc, who was standing behind my chair, stooped suddenly and kissed the top of my head. 'Don't let it worry you. Something will turn up, you'll see. It always does for me. Did I ever tell you I was born lucky?'

Strangely enough that was a very happy day for me, and the fact that the finances at Pendorric were not as sound as they should have been gave me a feeling of deep comfort.

I had begun to think that Roc was too much like his father and that my story was turning out to be too similar to that of Barbarina. But this was the difference: Barbarina had been married for her money when Roc's father was in love with Louisa Sellick. Roc, needing money for Pendorric, as his father had, had met me, a penniless girl, and had married her.

Oh no, my story was very different from that of Barbarina.

Mrs. Penhalligan was making Cornish pasties when I went down to the kitchen.

She looked up flushed and bright-eyed when I entered; her pink cotton sleeves were rolled up above the elbow, her short fat fingers busy.

One of the twins was sitting under the table eating a pasty.

'Good afternoon, Mrs. Pendorric,' said Mrs. Penhalligan.

'Good afternoon, Mrs. Penhalligan.'

Mrs. Penhalligan went on rolling her pastry. 'Don't do to let it hang about too long, ma'am,' she murmured apologetically. 'The secret be to make it and pop it into the oven as quick as you can. This be for Father. He's terrible particular about his pasty and he do want one regular each night. So when I bake I do four or five for him. I keep them in a tin ... they be all nice and fresh that way, though the best is them as is eaten straight from the oven.'

'I've come to ask what tobacco your father smokes. I thought I'd go along to see him when I have the time and take him something to smoke.'

A head popped over the side of the table. 'Beware the Ides of March,' said a voice low with prophecy.

'Oh give over, Miss Lowella, do,' said Mrs. Penhalligan.

'She's been under my feet all day. Looking through the window, popping up here and there with her talk of Beware of this and that. Reckon she belongs to be in Bodmin Asylum.'

Lowella smiled and went into the bakehouse.

'I don't know,' grumbled Mrs. Penhalligan. 'That Miss Bective, she's supposed to be looking after they two. Well, where be she to, half the time, I'm wondering.'

'You were going to tell me what tobacco.'

'That I were, and right good it is of you, ma'am. 'Tis Three Nuns – the Empire, you do know. His one extravagance. But then it's only the two ounces a week he smokes and Maria and me like him to have his little treat.'

'I'll remember.'

Lowella had come back; she was holding a small pasty in her hand.

'Someone won't be wanting her supper like as not,' commented Mrs. Penhalligan.

Lowella regarded us both solemnly before crawling under the table.

'He'll be that pleased,' went on Mrs. Penhalligan. 'I reckon he'll be sitting out this afternoon. It'll make his day.'

'I'll be getting along,' I told her.

As I made for the door Lowella darted out from under the table and reached it before me.

'I say, Bride,' she said, 'I'll come with you if you like – to see old Jesse, I mean.'

'Don't bother,' I replied. 'I know the way.'

She shrugged her shoulders and went back into the kitchen, presumably to sit under the table and finish her pasty and now and then pop up to tell Mrs. Penhalligan or Maria or Hetty to beware the Ides of March.

Not far from the cottages was a house which had been turned into a general store. It was small, overcrowded, and run by a Mrs. Robinson who had come to Pendorric for a holiday twenty years before, realized that the nearest shop was two miles away, and had bought the house and made it into a shop. She sold among other things the brands of tobacco smoked by her neighbours, and kept stocks in readiness for them. So I had no difficulty in getting what I wanted.

As I came out of the shop I saw that the twins were waiting for me.

I was not pleased, for I had wanted to be alone with the old man, but there was nothing I could do but accept their company as graciously as possible.

They fell into step beside me without a word, as though we had arranged to meet.

'Where's Miss Bective?' I asked.

The twins exchanged glances as though each was waiting for the other to speak.

It was Lowella who answered. 'She's gone off in the little Morris. She said we were to pick her six different wild flowers. It's botany.'

'How many have you found so far?'

'We haven't looked yet. My dear Bride, how long do you think it's going to take *us* to find six different wild flowers? Becky won't say much if we don't find 'em anyway. She'd never say we were undisciplined, would she, because if she did they'd say we ought to go to school, and if we went to school there wouldn't be any excuse for Becky to be at Pendorric.'

'Don't you think you ought to obey her instructions? After all she is your governess.'

'You oughtn't to be worrying about *us*,' said Hyson.

Lowella leaped on ahead and ran up the bank to pick a wild rose. She stuck it in her hair and danced before us singing, 'Beware . . . beware . . . beware the Ides of March.'

Hyson said: 'Lowella is quite childish sometimes. She goes on repeating things.'

'She seems to like warning people,' I commented. 'I remember "Beware the awful avalanche!" '

'I like Ides better,' called Lowella. 'You can't have avalanches in Cornwall, but you can have Ides anywhere. Pity they're in March and this is July.'

'She doesn't *know* anything,' put in Hyson scornfully. She went on to quote:

' *"March, July, October, May,*
The Ides fall on the fifteenth day." '

Lowella had paused. 'But what *are* Ides?'

'Just a date, stupid. Instead of saying the fifteenth, the Romans said the Ides.'

'Only a date,' wailed Lowella. 'It sounds marvellous. I thought it was something like witches . . . or ghosts. Fancy having to beware of a *date*.'

'If something was going to happen on a certain date, if it were prophesied to happen . . . that would be more frightening or as frightening as witches or ghosts.'

'Yes,' said Lowella slowly, 'I suppose it would.'

We had reached the row of cottages and old Jesse was seated at his door. I went over to him and said: 'Good afternoon. I'm Mrs. Pendorric.'

I noticed that his hands, resting on his knees, started to shake. ''Tis good of 'ee, ma'am,' he said.

'I've brought you some tobacco. I found out from Mrs. Penhalligan what brand you smoke.'

His trembling hands closed over the tin and he smiled. 'Why, 'twas thoughtful of 'ee, ma'am. I mind how kind *she* always were . . .'

Hyson had gone into the cottage and brought out a stool which she set beside the old man's chair. She nodded to me to sit down while she squatted on the other side of him. Lowella had disappeared.

'Your daughter has been baking pasties this morning,' I told him.

'A wonderful cook, my Bessie. Don't rightly know what I'd do without her. I've got a lot to be thankful for. Mr. Roc – he's been good to me. Is the little 'un here?'

'Yes, I'm here,' Hyson answered.

He nodded and turned to me. 'I hope you find this place to your liking, ma'am.'

'I'm delighted with it.'

''Tis a long time since we've had a new Bride at Pendorric.'

'There was my mother,' said Hyson, 'and before that my Granny Barbarina.'

'A sweet lady, she were. I remember the day she come.'

'Tell us, Jesse,' urged Hyson. 'The new Bride wants to hear about it.'

'Well, we'd seen her many a time. 'Twasn't like her coming from nowheres. I remember her as a little 'un, her and her sister. Used to visit us . . . and master and mistress used to visit them. Hyson their name was. Such pretty names. Miss Barbarina and Miss Deborah.'

'I was named after them,' put in Hyson.

'So you were pleased when she became Mrs. Pendorric,' I said.

'I reckon I were, Mrs. Pendorric. We didn't rightly know what would happen. We knew something of how it were, and there was talk of giving up Pendorric. Pendorric as it were in the old days, that be. Us didn't know what would happen to we like. There was talk of Mr. Petroc marrying that Sellick girl and then . . .'

'But he didn't,' Hyson said. 'He married my Granny Barbarina.'

'I remember the wedding. 'Twas a wonderful summer's day. It was there in the church. The Reverend Trewin were parson then. Oh, it were a grand wedding. And Miss Barbarina was a picture with Miss Deborah her maid of honour, and Mr. Petroc looking that handsome . . . and it was so right and proper that it should be.'

'What about the other girl?' I asked.

'Oh, that were reckoned to be done with. She'd gone away . . . and all was merry . . .'

'Merry as a marriage bell,' murmured Hyson.

'A wonderful mistress she were. Kind and good . . . and gentle like. She used to ride a lot and play the violin. Often I've been working on the quadrangle gardens and heard her.'

I was aware of Hyson, looking at me intently. Hyson, I thought, was it you who tried to scare me? And if so, why?

'Then she had a way of singing to herself. I remember once, coming home, I heard her singing in the graveyard. It sounded so queer and yet beautiful and like something not quite natural. I went in and saw her. She'd been putting flowers on the grave of little Ellen Pascoe from the cottages. Little Ellen had died of the meningitis, and it was her way of saying she was thinking of 'un. We thought a terrible lot of her here in the cottages.'

'You remember her very well,' I said softly.

'It seems only yesterday she were talking to me, as you be now. I was working then. Right up to the time she died I was working. But she knew I couldn't go on. I told her what was happening to me and she did comfort me. She said: "Never be feared, Jesse. I'll see that you be all right.' And every time she saw me she'd ask after me. And I was getting blind, Mrs. Pendorric. I can't even see you now. But you remind me of her in a way. You've got a kindness which was hers. Then you be happy. I can tell that.

So were she . . . at first. But it changed for her, poor gentle lady. Then she weren't happy no more. My tongue be running away with me, I fear. Bessie says I be alone so much that when people come to see me I've got so much to make up for.'

'I'm glad you want to talk,' I said. 'It's very interesting.'

'She's the new Bride, so she naturally wants to hear about the other one,' said Hyson.

'Ay,' went on the old man. 'You're happy . . . as she were when she first come. 'Twas only after, poor body . . . I wish you all happiness, Mrs. Pendorric. I wish for you to stay as you be now for evermore.'

I thanked him and asked him about his cottage; he told me that if I cared to look over it, he would be pleased. It was kept clean and tidy by his daughter and granddaughter. He rose, and taking a stick from the side of his chair led the way into the cottage. The door opened straight into the living-room; it was certainly clean and tidy. There was his armchair with his pipe-rack and ash-tray on a table beside it with a small transistor radio. There was a framed photograph on the wall, of Jesse standing, his hand resting on the shoulder of a woman sitting, whom I presumed to be his wife; they were both looking into the camera as though they were only engaged in the unpleasant duty for the sake of posterity. There were photographs of Mrs. Penhalligan at her wedding.

Leading from this sitting-room was a kitchen with a door which opened into a garden. This, like the cottage, was trim and well kept, with wallflowers and cabbage roses bordering a small lawn; a water barrel leaned against the wall to catch the rain.

There were two rooms upstairs, he told me; and he managed the stairs well enough. There was nothing wrong with him except his affliction and the fact that his memory was not what it had been.

He settled in his arm-chair and bade me be seated while he told me about his meeting and marriage to Lizzie, and how she had been under-housemaid up at Pendorric in the days when he had worked in the gardens there.

This went on for some time, and during it Hyson, presumably becoming bored, slipped away.

The old man said suddenly: 'The child has gone?'

'Yes,' I told him. 'I expect she's gone to find her sister. They're supposed to be collecting flowers for a botany lesson.'

'The little one . . . she questions and cross-questions . . .'

'She's a strange child.'

He nodded. 'She wants to know about it. It's on her mind. 'Tain't good, I reckon. Her's young. 'T'as nought to do with her.'

'I think the story has caught her imagination. It's because it's a ghost story.'

'Mrs. Pendorric.' He almost whispered my name, and I went closer to him.

'Yes, Jesse?'

'There's something I don't talk of no more. I told Mr. Petroc and he said, "Don't talk of it, Jesse. 'Tis better not." So I didn't talk. But I want to tell you, Mrs. Pendorric.'

'Why do you want to tell me, Jesse?'

'I don't know . . . but you be the next bride, see . . . and there's something tells me 'tis right and proper you should know.'

'Tell me, then.'

'My eyes was bad and getting worse. Days was when I couldn't make out shapes and such-like. I'd think I saw someone and when I come close I'd find it to be a piece of furniture. That bad they'd got to be. But the more bad they got the more I seemed to hear, and sometimes I knew summat without seeing or hearing. They say 'tis the compensation of the blind, Mrs. Pendorric.'

'Yes, Jesse, I am sure there are compensations.'

'That day I come into the hall, Mrs. Pendorric. And she were in the gallery. I knew who 'twas because I heard her speak. Low like she spoke . . . and then 'twas as though there were two shadows up there . . . I don't rightly know . . . and 'tis a long time to look back. But I believe, Mrs. Pendorric, that there were two on 'em up on that gallery a minute or two afore Mrs. Pendorric fell.'

'And you didn't make this known before?'

'Mr. Pendorric said for me not to. You see, the picture were there . . . the picture of the other bride, and they did say she'd haunted the place for more than a hundred years trying to lure a bride to take her place. There were two on 'em up there. I swear it, Mrs. Pendorric . . . but Mr. Petroc he didn't want it said. I'd always obeyed the master, as my father had and his father afore him, so I said nothing . . . but I tell *you* this, Mrs. Pendorric.'

'It's so long ago. It's best forgotten, Jesse.'

'So I thought, Mrs. Pendorric. And have thought these twenty-five years. But you being here . . . and reminding me of her . . . in a way . . . and you being so good and friendly to me like, well, I thought I should tell 'ee. 'Tis a warning like. And there's a feeling in here . . .' He tapped his chest. 'There's a feeling that I shouldn't keep 'ee in the dark.'

I couldn't see why he should feel this, but I thanked him for his concern.

I changed the subject, which wasn't difficult, for now that he had told me he seemed more relaxed as though he had done his duty. He talked of the cottage and the old days when his Lizzie had been alive; and after a time, I left.

I did not see the twins as I walked back to Pendorric.

The next day Nurse Grey telephoned me.

'Oh, Mrs. Pendorric,' she said, 'Lord Polhorgan has asked me to ring. He was wondering if you could come over this afternoon. He rather particularly wants to see you.'

I hesitated and said that I thought I could manage it, and asked how he was.

'Not quite so well. He had an attack during the night. He's resting to-day, but he says that he hoped you would be able to come, if not to-day, to-morrow.'

I set out that afternoon, wondering whether to pick some flowers from the garden to take to him; but as he had so many more than we had that seemed rather unnecessary.

When I arrived he was in his usual chair, not dressed, but wearing a Paisley silk dressing-gown and slippers. He seemed delighted to see me.

'Good of you to come so promptly,' he said. 'I was afraid you wouldn't be able to manage it.'

'I'm sorry you haven't been so well.'

'It's all ups and downs, my dear. I'll get over this little bout as I have others. They're bringing in the tea. Will you pour as usual?'

I did so and noticed that he ate very little and seemed rather more silent than usual, yet in a way expectant.

And as soon as the tea was cleared away he told me what, he said, he had been longing to ever since we had first met.

'Favel . . .' he began, and it was the first time he had used my Christian name, 'come and sit near me. I'm afraid what I have to say is going to be a great shock to you. I told you when we first met that I was an old curmudgeon, didn't I?'

I nodded.

'An impossible person. In my young days I thought of nothing but making money. It was the only thing of importance to me. Even when I married, my chief thought was to have sons . . . sons to whom I would leave my fortune . . . sons who would carry on my business and add new fortunes to the one I made. I had a successful business life, but I was not so successful in my domestic affairs. My wife left me for another man – one of my own employees. He wasn't a success. I couldn't understand why she could leave a luxurious home for him . . . but she did. I divorced her and I got the custody of our daughter, which was something she hadn't bargained for. The child was six years old at the time. Twelve years later *she* left me.'

'Doesn't it distress you to talk of the past?'

'It's a distressing subject but I want you to understand. My daughter left me because I was trying to arrange a marriage for her. I wanted her to marry Petroc Pendorric, who was then a widower. His wife had died accidentally and I thought there was a good opportunity of joining up the families. I was an outsider here, and I thought that if mine was linked with one of the oldest Cornish families I should be so no longer. Pendorric needed money. I had it. It seemed to me ideal, but *she* didn't agree.'

There was silence during which he looked at me helplessly, and for the first time since I had known him he seemed at a loss for words.

'There are often such disagreements in families,' I said.

'My wife went . . . my daughter went. You'd think I'd learned my lesson, wouldn't you? Flattered myself that in the world of commerce I'd learned all the lessons as they came along. So I had . . . But this was something I was pretty backward in. Favel, I don't know how to explain. Open that drawer. There's something in there that will tell you what I'm trying to.'

I went to the drawer, and opening it took out a photograph in a silver frame. As I stared at it I heard his voice, hoarse as I had never heard it before, with the depth of his emotion. 'Come here to me, my child.'

I came to him, and he no longer seemed the same man to me. Sitting there in that very luxurious room he had become more frail, more pitiable: and at the same time infinitely closer to me.

I acted on impulse, and going to him I took his frail body in my arms and held him against me as though he were a child and I was assuring him that he could rely on me to protect him.

'Favel . . .' he whispered.

I drew back and looked at him. His eyes were wet, so I took the silk handkerchief from the pocket of his dressing-gown and wiped them.

'Why didn't you tell me before . . . Grandfather?' I asked.

He laughed suddenly and his stern features were relaxed as I had never seen them before. 'Afraid to,' he said. 'Lost wife and daughter. Was making a bid for the granddaughter.'

It had been such a shock to me that I was still feeling all this was unreal. My thoughts were muddled. It did not occur to me in that moment to ask myself the explanation of that extraordinary coincidence which had allowed me to marry a man who came into my life by chance and turned out to be a neighbour of my grandfather. That was to come later.

'Well,' he asked, 'what do you think of your old grandfather?'

'I don't know yet what to think. I'm so bewildered.'

'I'll tell you what I think of my granddaughter, then. If I could have chosen just how I wanted her to be, she wouldn't have been different in one detail. Do you know, Favel, you're so like your mother that when you've been sitting there playing chess with me I've often found my mind slipping back . . . and I'd be thinking she'd never gone away. You've got the same fair hair, though she didn't have that white streak in it; and your eyes are the same colour . . . sometimes blue, sometimes green. And you're like her in your ways . . . the kindest heart and the impetuosity. Rushing in before you've had time to consider. I often wondered how that marriage of hers would work out. Used to tell myself it couldn't last, but it seems it did. And she chose a Cornish name for you. That shows, doesn't it, that she didn't think of the past always with regret.'

'But why was I never told? She never spoke of the past, and you . . .'

'She never told you? Nor did your father? You'd have thought they'd have mentioned it now and then. And you never asked, Favel. How was that?'

I looked back to those sunlit days of my childhood. 'I think that they felt all that had happened before their marriage was unimportant. That's how it strikes me now. Their lives were so . . . entwined. They lived for each other. Perhaps they knew she hadn't long to live. I suppose that sort of thing makes a difference. As for myself, I never thought of things being other than they were. That was why, when she died, everything changed so much for us.'

'And you were fond of your father too?' he said wistfully.

I nodded.

'He came down here to paint one summer. Rented a little place a mile or so away along the coast . . . little more than a shack. When she told me she was going to marry him I thought it was a joke at first. Soon learned it wasn't. She could be obstinate. . . . I told her she was a fool. Never stopped to think. Told her I wouldn't leave her a penny if she married this man. Told her he was after her money anyway. So they just went away one day and I never heard from her again.'

He was thinking of all the years that had been lost to him. Here he sat in the midst of his opulence – the loneliest old man I had ever met. And it need never have been.

Now he had learned that he was the one who had been foolish – not my mother and father. And pitiably he was reaching out to me to give him, for the short time left to him, the affection which more than twenty years ago he had rashly thrown away.

I turned to him impulsively and said: 'Grandfather, I'm glad I came home to you.'

'My dear child,' he murmured. 'My dearest child.' Then he went on: 'Tell me about her. Did she suffer much?'

I shook my head. 'There were several months when she knew and we knew. . . . They were terrible months, particularly for my father, but it wasn't really long – though it seemed so.'

'I could have paid for the best attention for her,' he said angrily.

'Grandfather,' I replied, 'it's over. It doesn't do any good to reproach yourself – or them – or anyone. You've got to put that behind you. I'm here now. Your own granddaughter. I shall see you more often now. I shan't feel like waiting for a reasonable period before calling again. You're my very own grandfather and it's wonderful that my home is so close to yours. . . .' I stopped, picturing myself coming into the studio and seeing Roc there with my father. 'It seems so strange that Roc should have come to my father's studio . . . and that we should have married,' I said slowly. 'I mean, it seems too lucky to be true.'

My grandfather smiled. 'It wasn't just a matter of chance, my dear. Your mother never wrote to me. I had no idea where she was or what was happening to her. I had told her that if she married her artist I wanted nothing to do with her, and she took me at my word. But . . . your father wrote. It was a month or so before Roc went abroad. He told me that your mother was dead and that they had a daughter: Favel. He asked me if I would like to see you, and he gave me the address of that studio place of yours.'

'I see,' I said. 'I wonder why Father wrote.'

'I had my suspicions. I thought he was after something. People often say that men in my position are *comfortably* off. Having money isn't always comfortable, I can tell you. You're constantly watching in case you're going to lose something; you're for ever on the alert for ways of increasing what you have; and you're always suspecting that people are seeking your acquaintance because they want a little of what you've got. No. I'd say I'm *un*comfortably off. In any case I was wary of your father. I said: He wants to borrow something. Lilith wouldn't let him write when she was alive – too proud. But now she's dead he's after something. I put his letter on one side and didn't answer it. But the thought of my granddaughter kept bothering me. I wondered what she was like . . . how old she was. Your father hadn't said. And I wanted to know more about her.'

He paused and looked at me reflectively, and I said: 'So you asked Roc to . . . spy out the land?'

He nodded. 'I knew he was going to Italy, so I asked him to do me this favour. I couldn't go myself. I wanted him to find out what this studio place was like and what my granddaughter was like. My plan was that when he came back, providing I liked what he told me, I'd invite my granddaughter to Polhorgan . . . her father too, perhaps, if she wouldn't come without him.'

'So that was why Roc came to the studio.'

'That was it. But you're impetuous like your mother. You fell in love with him. So instead of his bringing back a report to me, he brought you back as his bride.'

'So Roc . . . knew . . . all the time?'

'He knew.'

'But he didn't give me a hint . . . in fact he never has.'

'Well, you see, I'd asked him not to. I didn't want you to come over to see your grandfather. I wanted us to meet as strangers. I wanted to know what you thought of me and I wanted to know what I thought of you. But the minute I saw you – you were so like your mother – I felt she'd come back to me. My dear child, I can't tell you what a difference this has made to me.'

I touched his hand, but I was thinking of Roc . . . Roc as he had come into the studio, Roc lying on the beach talking about Pendorric, about the Folly and the man who lived in it, who, he knew all the time, was my grandfather.

'So Roc was carrying out your wishes,' I said.

'He did even more than I asked. He brought you home.'

'I can understand his not telling me *that* in the beginning, but later . . .'

'I told him that I wanted to break the news to you yourself.'

I was silent. Then I said? 'You wanted my mother to marry Roc's father.'

'Ah, that was in the days when I thought I could manage people's lives better than they could themselves. I know different now.'

'So I've pleased you . . . by marrying a Pendorric.'

'Had you wanted to marry a fisherman, Granddaughter, I'd have made no objection. I learn my lessons . . . in time. All the lonely years need not have happened if I'd not tried to interfere. Fancy, if I'd raised no objections to their marrying, I'd have had them with me all those years. She might never have died. I shouldn't have had to wait till my granddaughter was a married woman before I knew her.'

'Grandfather,' I insisted, 'you wanted my mother to marry a Pendorric. Are you glad I've married Roc?'

He was silent for a few moments; then he said: 'Because you're in love with him . . . yes. I shouldn't have wanted it otherwise.'

'But you spoke of linking the families. My mother left home because you wanted her to marry Roc's father.'

'That was years ago. I suspect those Pendorrics wanted not so much my daughter as my money, and your father wanted her for herself . . . must have done, because she knew me well enough to understand that when I said there'd be nothing for her if she ran away, I meant it.'

I was silent and he lay back in his chair and closed his eyes though he had taken my hand and kept it in his. I could see how the veins stood out at his temples and that he was more flushed than usual. Such excitement was not good for him, I was sure.

My grandfather! I thought, watching him. So I had a relative after all. My eyes went round the room at the paintings on the wall. They were all of the old school. Grandfather would not buy modern paintings, which he loathed, but all the same he would have an eye for a bargain. I guessed that the pictures in this room alone were worth a fortune.

Then I thought of the studio, and my mother who had bargained so fiercely over my father's work; and it seemed to me that life was indeed ironical.

I was glad that I had a grandfather. I had liked him from the moment we met; but I wished – oh, how I wished that he were not such a rich man. I remembered what he had said about being *un*comfortably off.

Although it was less than an hour since I had discovered I was the granddaughter of a millionaire, I understood very well what he meant.

I sat with him for an hour after that; we talked of the past and the future. I told him incidents from those early days which I had not thought of telling before, because I now understood how vitally interested he was in every seemingly insignificant detail. And he told me that Polhorgan was now my home and that I must treat it thus.

I walked back to Pendorric in a state of bewilderment, and when I was midway between the two houses I looked from one to the other.

My homes, I murmured. And my pride in them was spoilt by an uneasy suspicion which was beginning to grow within me.

I was relieved, when I went up to our bedroom, to find that Roc had come in.

'Roc,' I called, and as he turned to look at me he said: 'So he's told you?'

'How did you guess?'

'My darling, you look just like a woman who has been told that she is the granddaughter of a millionaire.'

'And you knew all the time!'

He nodded, smiling.

'It seems extraordinary that you could keep such a secret.'

He was laughing as he took me by the shoulders. 'It's women who can't keep secrets, you know.'

He put his arm round me and held me against him; but I withdrew myself because I wanted to look into his face.

'I want to think about it all . . . as it happened,' I said. 'You came to the studio, looking for me. You were going to report on me to my grandfather.'

'Yes. I was going to take some pictures of you to show him. I was determined to do the job thoroughly.'

'You did it very thoroughly indeed.'

'I'm glad that you approve of my methods.'

'And my father . . .' I said. 'He knew too.'

'Of course he knew. He'd lived near Pendorric. That was how he first met your mother.'

'Father knew . . . and didn't tell me.'

'I'd explained to him my promise of secrecy.'

'I can't understand. It was so unlike him to have secrets from me.'

'This was a very important matter. I reckon he wanted you to please your grandfather. It's understandable.'

I looked at him sharply; he was smiling complacently.

'How I wish . . .' I began.

'What do you wish?'

'That you hadn't known.'

'Why? What difference does it make?'

I was silent. I felt I was going too far. I was almost on the point of asking Roc whether he had married me on account of my grandfather's money, when I didn't even know that I was his heiress. But everything was changed. When I had thought of Barbarina I had continually told myself that our positions were so different because she had been married for her money. The simple fact was that now I was beginning to wonder whether I too had been.

'What's on your mind?' persisted Roc.

'It's the shock,' I replied evasively. 'When you think you haven't any family and you suddenly find yourself confronted by a grandfather . . . it's a little bewildering. It takes time to adjust yourself.'

'You're a little aloof, you're weighing me up. I don't much like it.' He was looking at me intently, very seriously.

'Why?'

'I'm afraid of being weighed in the balance and found wanting.'

'Why should you be afraid?'

'Because you're hiding something from me – or trying to.'

'You are the one who hides things successfully.'

'Only one thing – and I had made a promise not to tell.' He laughed suddenly, and seizing me, lifted me and held me up so that I had to look down on him. 'Listen,' he said, 'and get this clear. I married you because I fell in love with you. It would have been the same if you were the granddaughter of old Bill the Beachcomber. Understand me?'

I put out my hands and touched his ears; he lowered me until my face was on a level with his. Then he kissed me; and as usual, while I was with him, I forgot my fears.

Now that the news was out, the whole of Pendorric village was agog with it. I knew that I had only to appear for the subject to be discussed. People looked at me as though they had discovered something different about me. I was the focus of attention in the neighbourhood. In the first place I had come out of the blue as the Bride of Pendorric; and now it turned out that I was the granddaughter of old Lord Polhorgan. Many of them could remember my mother's running away with the painter; and it seemed a fitting romantic sequel that I should return as a bride.

Mrs. Robinson at the general store whispered to me that my story was good enough for the television; Dinah Bond told me, when I met her one day in the village, that she knew there was something dramatic in my hand and she would have told me if only I'd let her; Morwenna and Charles appeared to be delighted; Lowella was vociferous, squealing her delight, and went about singing something about 'When Grandpappa asked Grandmamma for the second minuet,' which appeared to be quite irrelevant; Hyson regarded me with silent interest as though this new development was not entirely unexpected.

For several days everyone talked of it, but I guessed that it would turn out to be a nine days' wonder.

There were two conversations which stood out in my mind. One I had with Rachel Bective, the other I overheard.

I had gone down to Pendorric beach to swim one afternoon and as I came out of the water I saw Rachel emerge from the gardens and step on to the beach.

I looked about for the twins, but she was alone.

She came over and said: 'What's the sea like to-day?'

'Quite warm,' I answered, and lay down on the shingle.

She sat down beside me and started playing idly with the pebbles.

'What a surprise it must have been for you!' she said. 'Had you no idea?'

'None at all.'

'Well, it's not everyone who gets presented with a grandfather at your time of life. And a millionaire peer at that!'

I thought her expression a trifle unpleasant and I half rose, preparing to go up through the gardens.

'Roc knew of course,' she went on. Then she laughed. 'He must have been tickled to death.'

'You think it's an amusing situation when families are broken up?'

'I think it's amusing that Roc should go out to find you and bring you back – his bride. No wonder he has been looking so smug.'

'What do you mean?'

Her greenish eyes under the sandy brows glinted a little; her mouth was straight and grim. I thought: she is either very hurt or very angry. And suddenly I wasn't so annoyed with her as I had been a few minutes before.

She seemed to take a grip of herself. 'Roc always liked to know what other people didn't. He'd think it great fun having a secret like that, and the rest of us being in the dark. Besides . . .' I waited for her to go on, but she shrugged her shoulders. Then she gave a harsh laugh which seemed to hold a note of bitterness. 'Some people have all the luck,' she said. 'Mrs. Pendorric *and* granddaughter of Lord Polhorgan, who already dotes on her.'

'I think I'll be getting back,' I said. 'It's not so warm as I thought.'

She nodded, and as I crunched my way over the shingle she sat looking out at the sea; and I could imagine the expression on her face, for she had betrayed the fact that she was jealous of me. Jealous because I was the granddaughter of a rich man? Or jealous because I was Roc's wife?

I believed it might be for both these reasons.

The second conversation took place the following day and I heard the end of it unwittingly. I was in the quadrangle gardens and one of the windows on the ground floor of the north wing was wide open, so the voice came

floating through to me and I had caught the gist of the conversation before
I could get out of earshot.

It was Charles and Morwenna who were speaking, and at first I did not
realize they were talking of me.

'I thought he was looking pleased with himself.' That was Charles.

'I've never known him so contented.'

'She's a pleasant creature.'

'She has everything.'

'Well, it won't be before it's needed, I can tell you. I've had some anxious
moments wondering what the outcome could possibly be. Of course we're
taking things rather for granted.'

'Not a bit of it. That type never leave much outside the family. After all,
she's his granddaughter and he can't last much longer. . . .'

I got up and walked across to the south door, my cheeks flaming.

As I entered the house my eyes went at once to the picture of Barbarina.
I stook looking up at it. I could almost fancy the expression had changed;
that a pitying look was in those blue eyes, that she was saying to me: 'I
understand. Who could understand better than one to whom it has all
happened before?'

My grandfather wanted the whole neighbourhood to know how delighted
he was to welcome his granddaughter home.

He told me that it was years since there had been any entertaining at
Polhorgan and he proposed to give a ball to which he would invite all the
local gentry.

'You are not nearly well enough,' I told him; but he assured me that he
would come to no harm. He put his hand over mine. 'Don't try to dissuade
me. It'll give me the greatest pleasure. The ball will be for you and your
husband. I want you to arrange it all; I want it to be a setting for you, my
dear. Please say you will.'

He looked so pleased at the prospect that I could only agree, and when
I told Roc and Morwenna about it they were amused and, I could see,
delighted. I had ceased to be angry with Morwenna and Charles, telling
myself that loving this old house as they obviously did, it was only natural
that they should be pleased because a member of the family might very
possibly come into a great deal of money.

'Just fancy,' said Morwenna, 'Polhorgan is going to throw off its dust-
sheets.'

The twins were delighted, and when Lowella was told that balls were not
for twelve-year-olds, she boldly called on my grandfather and asked for an
invitation for herself and her sister. Such conduct, which he called initiative,
delighted him, and he immediately wrote to Morwenna asking her to allow
the twins to attend.

Lowella was wild with excitement when she heard this; Hyson's eyes
gleamed with secret pleasure. Lowella went about the house quoting in an
ominous voice:

' "There was a sound of revelry by night. . . ." '

Morwenna helped arrange the list of invitations, for, as a Pendorric, she knew everyone in the neighbourhood.

'They will all want to come and see Lord Polhorgan's granddaughter,' she told me. Roc, who was present, put in: 'Nonsense. It's Mrs. Pendorric they want to see, for she's a far more important person than his lordship's granddaughter.'

'They must think it all very extraordinary,' I suggested.

'Nine days' wonder, darling,' Roc assured me. 'You know there are a lot of skeletons locked away in cupboards in these parts.'

'It's true enough,' Morwenna assured me.

Deborah was as excited as the twins at the prospect of the ball, and invited me to her room to see some material which Carrie was going to make up for her. There was a choice of two colours and she wanted me to help her decide.

Laid out on a table were two rolls of *crêpe de Chine* – one delicate mauve, the other pale pink.

I was fingering the stuff. 'One hardly ever sees it now,' I commented.

'We've had it a few years, haven't we, Carrie,' said Deborah.

I had not noticed Carrie come silently into the room; she carried a tape-measure about her neck, and a pair of scissors and a pin-cushion were attached to her belt.

'I found it in Plymouth,' she said. 'I was afraid there wouldn't be enough for the two of you.'

Deborah looked at me, smiling gently; then she laid her hand on Carrie's shoulder. 'Carrie's a wonder with her needle. I'm sure she'll make me something worthy of the ball.'

'You remember the dresses I made for the engagement party?' whispered Carrie, her eyes ecstatic. 'Empire style. You had the pink then; she had the mauve.'

'Yes, we decided we had to be different then.'

'Before that it was always the same. What one had the other had.'

'I've brought Mrs. Pendorric up to help me decide which colour,' said Deborah.

'Mauve was her colour. She wore it a lot . . . after . . .'

'Perhaps I'd better decide on the pink,' murmured Deborah.

She took me into her sitting-room, and as we sat together looking over the sea she said: 'I rather dread Carrie's making new things for me. It always brings it home to her. You see, in Devon she used to make everything in twos. She can't forget.'

When I left Deborah I ran into Rachel Bective. She gave me a grudging smile and looked almost wistful.

'Everyone's talking about the ball your grandfather's giving,' she said. 'I feel like Cinderella. Still, I suppose the governess can't expect to be invited.'

'What nonsense,' I retorted. 'Of course you're invited.'

The smile which lighted her face made her almost pretty.

'Oh,' she muttered in an embarrassed way, 'thank you I . . . I'm honoured.'

As she turned and left me I thought: Her trouble is this complex about being employed here. If only she could forget that, she'd be so much happier and I should like her so much better.

During the next few days I spent a great deal of time at Polhorgan. My grandfather was anxious that I should make a thorough tour of the house, and this I did in the company of Dawson and his wife, who were very respectful to me now that they knew I was their master's granddaughter.

Polhorgan was not built in the same mould as Pendorric. This was one large house whereas ours at Pendorric was like four smaller ones. At Polhorgan there was an immense hall which was to serve as the ballroom, and Dawson and his wife had uncovered the furniture so that I could see it in all its glory.

It was a magnificently-proportioned room, with its high vaulted ceiling and panelled walls; and there was a dais at one end which would be ideal for our orchestra. Dawson suggested that some of the exotic plants should be brought in from the greenhouses and that I might like to talk to Trehay, the head gardener, about what I should like.

Leading from this hall were several rooms which would serve as supper rooms. I could see that Mrs. Dawson was a most efficient woman and delighted at the prospect of being able to show what a skilful housekeeper she was.

She showed me the kitchens, which were models of modernity.

'All this, madam,' sighed Mrs. Dawson, 'and no one to use it for! I could have cooked for his lordship with one little stove, for all he eats. Although the nurse wants a bit of waiting on, I do assure you!'

Mrs. Dawson's lips tightened at the mention of Nurse Grey, and I began to wonder whether the nurse was generally unpopular in the household.

It was while she was showing me round that Althea Grey herself appeared. She was looking as attractive as ever in her uniform, and she gave me a pleasant smile. I was struck afresh by the perfection of her features, and I remembered uneasily the occasion when I had found her on the beach with Roc.

'So you're showing Mrs. Pendorric the house,' she said.

'Well, it looks like it, Nurse.' Mrs. Dawson's voice was tart.

'If you like I'll take over. I expect you have work to do.'

'As housekeeper I reckon it to be my duty to show Mrs. Pendorric the house, Nurse.'

Nurse Grey smiled at me and shrugged her shoulders; but as though defying Mrs. Dawson to challenge her right to be there, she remained with us.

Mrs. Dawson was put out, and behaved as though she were unaware of the nurse's presence. I wondered what Althea Grey had done to make herself so disliked.

We walked up a beautiful staircase and inspected the rooms on the first floor of the mansion with their enormous windows and those superb views to which I had become accustomed at Pendorric.

Mrs. Dawson uncovered some of the furniture and showed me beautiful pieces, mostly antique, which I guessed must be worth a great deal.

'Jewelled in every hole,' murmured Althea Grey, her lovely blue eyes mischievous.

The obvious hostility between them made me a little uncomfortable.

'I hear we're to have about sixty guests, Mrs. Pendorric,' said Althea Grey. 'It's a good thing we have a sizeable ballroom, otherwise we should be treading on each other's toes.'

'Well, Nurse,' put in Mrs. Dawson with a twitch of her nose, 'that shouldn't worry *you*, should it?'

'Oh but it will, I hate having my toes trodden on.' She laughed. 'Oh, you're thinking that as I'm merely Lord Polhorgan's nurse I shan't be there. But you're wrong, Mrs. Dawson. Of course I shall be there. I couldn't let him go without me in attendance, could I?'

She was smiling at me as though inviting me to join in her victory over Mrs. Dawson, who looked extremely put out; and I supposed this was the usual tug-of-war between two servants each of whom thought herself in a higher position than the other. That must be the reason for the animosity.

'Of course not,' I said hastily; and Mrs. Dawson's face was grim.

'I reckon, madam,' she said, 'that Nurse Grey could show you the upper rooms.'

I thanked her and assured her that I should be pleased if she stayed with us, but she muttered something about having things to see to, and left us.

Althea Grey grinned when we were alone. 'She'd make life a trial if I'd let her. Jealous old witch.'

'You think she's jealous of you?'

'They always are, you know. I've come up against this sort of thing before, nursing in private houses. They don't like it because they have to wait on us. They're anxious all the time to tell us that they're as good as we are.'

'It must be awkward for you.'

'I don't let it bother me. I can manage the Mrs. Dawson characters, I can tell you.'

In spite of her delicate beauty I was sure she could.

We had come to my grandfather's room, and when I went in with her he gave me his warm and welcoming smile, and I felt my spirits rising when I realized what a difference my coming had made to him.

Nurse Grey ordered tea and the three of us had it together. Conversation was all about the ball, and before she left us Nurse Grey warned my grandfather that he was becoming far too excited.

'You have your pills handy?' she said.

For answer he took the little silver box from his pocket and showed her. 'That's good.'

She smiled at me and left us together.

I had had a busy morning, and after lunch, because the sun was shining and it was a long time since I had been in the quadrangle, I went there and sat in my favourite spot under the palm tree.

I had not been there more than five minutes when the north door opened and a twin came out.

I was always a little ashamed of my inability to distinguish which was which when they were not together, and tried to discover without exposing my ignorance.

She came and stood before me. 'Hallo. How you like this place! But you haven't been here lately, have you?'

'I've been too busy.'

She regarded me solemnly. 'I know. It is a busy business, suddenly finding you're Lord Polhorgan's granddaughter.' She stood on one foot and hopped a few paces nearer. 'Just fancy! You might have been here always . . . if your mother and father hadn't gone away. Then we should always have known you.'

'That could easily have happened,' I admitted.

'But it was more exciting the other way. There wouldn't have been this ball perhaps . . . if you'd always been here. There wouldn't be any sense in giving a fatted-calf sort of ball if you'd never been away, would there?'

'Would you say this was like the prodigal's return?'

She nodded vigorously. 'You're rich now, aren't you; and you must have been poor, though perhaps you didn't eat the husks that the swine did eat.'

I was sure it was Lowella now. She had started to hop all round my seat, and when she was immediately behind me she stood close, breathing down my neck. 'Everybody wasn't pleased when *he* came home, were they? There was the brother who'd stayed at home. He didn't see why the fatted calf should be killed for the brother who'd run away when he wanted to.'

'Don't worry. I haven't got a brother who'll be jealous of my having a welcome.'

'There doesn't have to be a *brother*. A parable's different, isn't it? It doesn't always mean exactly what it says. You have to work it out – Becky says so. Carrie's waiting for me to try on my dress for the ball.'

'She's making it for you, is she?'

'Yes, it's gold colour. She's making two – exactly alike. It'll be fun. They won't know which is Hy and which is Lo.'

'You'd better go if Carrie wants to fit on your dress, hadn't you?'

'You come with me and see it. It's very pretty.'

She started to hop towards the west door and I rose and followed her into the house, unsure again whether I had been speaking to Hyson or Lowella.

She started to hum as we went up the stairs, and the song she hummed was the tune that I had heard in that strange, off-key voice which had startled me so. This humming was quite different, though, rather monotonous and tuneless.

'What's that you're singing?' I asked.

She stopped, turned slowly and looked down on me, for she was standing several stairs above me. I knew then that she was Hyson.

'It's Ophelia's song in *Hamlet*.'

'Did you learn it at school?'

She shook her head.

'Did Miss Bective teach it to you?' I was becoming too anxious, I realized; and she guessed it and found it amusing.

Again she shook her head. She was waiting mischievously for the next question.

I merely continued: 'It's a haunting tune,' and started up the stairs.

She ran on ahead of me until she came to the door of Carrie's sewing room.

Carrie was seated at an old-fashioned sewing machine and I saw that she was working on a gold-coloured dress.

There were two dressmaker's dummies in the room, one a child's and the other an adult's. On the smaller one was another gold-coloured dress, on the larger a mauve evening dress.

'Ah, there you are, Miss Hyson,' said Carrie. 'I've been waiting for you. Come here, do. That neck don't please me.'

'Here's Mrs. Pendorric, too' said Hyson. 'She wanted to see the dresses so I brought her up.'

I went over to the dummy on which the other gold-coloured dress had been arranged.

'It's lovely,' I said. 'This is Lowella's, of course.'

'I fitted it on Miss Hyson,' mumbled Carrie. 'Miss Lowella can't stand still for more than a second or two.'

'It's true,' said Hyson primly. 'Her mind flitters and flutters like a butterfly. She can't concentrate on anything for any length of time. Becky says it's deplorable.'

'Come here, then,' said Carrie, snipping a cotton and withdrawing the dress from the machine.

Hyson stood meekly while Carrie slipped off her dress and put on the gold-coloured silk.

'It's delightful,' I said.

'The neck's wrong.' Carrie was breathing heavily as she purred and clicked over the neck of the dress. I went over to the mauve dress and examined it. It was beautifully made, but like all Deborah's clothes it had that slightly old-world look. The rows of flounces in the long skirt would have been fashionable many years ago, so would the lace fichu at the neck. It was like a charming period piece.

'I thought you were going to make up the pink,' I said.

'Ur,' grunted Carrie, her mouth full of pins.

'I suppose Deborah changed her mind, but when I was here I thought she said she would have the pink.'

Hyson nodded at me vigorously and inclined her head towards a dress hanging behind the door. I looked and saw an exact replica of the dress, this time in pink.

I stared in astonishment.

'Carrie made two, didn't you, Carrie?' said Hyson. 'She made two gold dresses . . . one for me, one for Lowella, and she made two like that – one pink and one mauve – because ever since they left Devon they never had the same colour. It was different after they left Devon, wasn't it, Carrie?'

Hyson was regarding me almost triumphantly and I felt impatient with her.

'What on earth are you talking about?' I demanded.

Hyson became engrossed in the tips of her shoes and would not answer me.

'Carrie,' I insisted, 'I suppose Miss Deborah has had the two dresses made up. Perhaps it's as well if you've had the material for a long time – which I believe you said you had.'

'The pink's for Miss Deborah,' said Carrie. 'I like her in pink.'

'And the mauve . . .?'

Hyson darted away from Carrie and ran to me; she laid a hand on my arm and smiled up at me.

'The pink was made for Granny Deborah,' she whispered, 'and the mauve for Granny Barbarina.'

Carrie was smiling at the mauve dress as though she saw more than a dress; she said quietly: 'Mauve were your colour, my dear; and I always say there weren't two prettier maidens in Devonshire than my Miss Deborah and Miss Barbarina.'

I was suddenly impatient with the stuffy sewing room. I said. 'I've things to do,' and went out.

But when I had shut the door I asked myself what motive lay behind Hyson's strange behaviour. I could understand that Carrie's mind wandered a little; she was old; and she had clearly been devoted to Barbarina. Deborah had said that she had never recovered from the shock of her death. But where did Hyson come into this? She was just a mischievous child, I suspected; could it be that for some reason she resented my coming to Pendorric? That talk about the fatted calf – what had been the meaning behind that?

I looked over my shoulder and restrained the impulse to go back into the room. Instead I went along the corridor until I came to the door of Deborah's sitting-room.

I hesitated for a moment, then I knocked.

'Come in,' said Deborah.

She was seated at a table reading.

'My dear, what a pleasant surprise. Why, is anything wrong?'

'Oh no . . . nothing. I'm just a little puzzled, that's all.'

'Come and sit down and tell me what's puzzling you.'

'Hyson's a queer child, isn't she? I'm afraid I don't understand her.'

She shrugged her shoulders. 'It's not always easy to understand what goes on in the mind of a child.'

'But Hyson is so very strange. Lowella is quite different.'

'It's the case of the extrovert and the introvert. They are twins of entirely different character. Tell me what Hyson's been doing to upset you.'

I told her about the dress I had seen on the stand in Carrie's sewing room.

Deborah sighed. 'I know,' she said. 'She'd done it before I could stop her. I'd decided on the pink and the pattern; then I found that she was making up not only the pink but the mauve.'

'Does she really think that Barbarina is still alive?'

'Not all the time. There are occasions when she's as lucid as you or I. And at others she thinks she is back in the past. It doesn't matter. The dresses are exactly alike, so that I can wear either of them. I never scold her.'

'But, what about Hyson?' I said. 'Does Carrie talk to her?'

'Hyson understands perfectly the state of affairs. I've explained to her. But I've told her that she must never hurt Carrie's feelings. Hyson's a good child. She does her best. You look disapproving, my dear.'

'I think it's a little . . . unhealthy,' I said.

'Oh, it does no harm, and it makes Carrie happy. While she can believe that Barbarina is still with us she's contented. It's when she faces up to what really happened that she is depressed and sad. It's easier in Devonshire. There, of course, she is often under the impression that Barbarina is in Cornwall, and that we shall shortly be visiting her. Here it's not so easy, because she thinks Barbarina should be here.'

I was silent and she laid her hand over mine.

'My dear,' she went on softly, 'you're young and bursting with sound common sense. It's difficult for you to understand the vagaries of people whose minds are not quite as normal as your own. Don't let Carrie upset you. She's been like this for so long. I couldn't bear to make her unhappy . . . that's why I humour her. So I let her say: Miss Deborah shall go to the ball in the pink dress and Miss Barbarina in the mauve. It's of little consequence. And talking of dresses – tell me, what are you going to wear?'

I told her that it was a green and gold dress which I had bought in Paris during my honeymoon. I had so far had no chance to wear it and the ball seemed the ideal occasion.

'I'm sure you'll look wonderful, my dear, quite wonderful; and your grandfather and your husband will be so proud of you. Oh Favel, what a fortunate woman you are to find a husband and a grandfather all in a few months!'

'Yes,' I said slowly, 'it's certainly very strange.'

She laughed merrily. 'You see, strange things are beginning to happen to *you* since you came to Pendorric.'

It was arranged that Roc and I should go to Polhorgan half an hour before the guests were due to arrive, so that we should be there, with Lord Polhorgan, to receive them.

I bathed and dressed in good time, and was rather pleased with my appearance when I put on my dress. It was a sheath of green silk chiffon billowing out from the knees into a frothy skirt; there was a narrow gold belt at the waist and a gold tracing showed through the chiffon from the satin underskirt.

I had piled my hair high on my head, and I was delighted with the Parisian effect.

Roc came in while I was standing before the mirror, and taking my hands held me at arms' length to examine me.

'I haven't a doubt who'll be the belle of the ball,' he said. 'And what could be more apt?' He drew me to him and kissed me as lightly as though I were a porcelain figure which he feared might break under rough handling.

'You'd better dress,' I warned. 'Remember we have to be early.'

'First I want to give you this,' he said, and took a case from his pocket.

I opened it and saw a glittering necklace of emeralds and diamonds.

'Known – rather grandiosely – as the Pendorric Emeralds,' he told me. 'Worn at her wedding by her whom they call the First Bride.'

'They're exquisite, Roc.'

'I had them in mind when I suggested you should buy that dress. I don't pretend to know anything about clothes, but being green it did seem they'd match.'

'So I'm to wear them to-night?'

'Of course.' He took them from the case and fastened them about my neck. I had looked *soigné* before, but now I was regal. The emeralds did that for me.

'Why didn't you tell me that you were giving me these?'

'But in all the best scenes the jewels are clasped about the lady's neck at the precise psychological moment!'

'You have an eye for drama. Oh Roc, they're quite lovely. I shall be afraid of losing them.'

'Why should you? There's a safety chain. Pendorric brides have been wearing them for nearly two hundred years and not lost them. Why should this bride?'

'Thank you, Roc.'

He lifted his shoulders and surveyed me sardonically. 'Don't thank me, darling. Thank that other Petroc who married Lowella. He bought them for her. They're your heritage anyway. It'll be nice to show that opulent grandfather of yours that you've a husband who can give you something worth having.'

'You've given me so much that's worth having. I don't want to disparage the necklace, but . . .'

'I know, darling. Kind hearts are more than emeralds. A sentiment with which I am in complete agreement. But it's getting late, so we'll develop that line of thought later.'

'Yes, you'd better hurry.'

He went into the bathroom and I looked at my watch. We should be leaving in fifteen minutes. Knowing his tendency to talk while dressing, and feeling this would delay him, I went out of the room into the corridor and stood at the window looking down at the quadrangle. I was thinking about my grandfather and all that had happened to me in the last weeks, and it seemed to me that my life, which until then had run along expected lines, had suddenly become dramatic. I did not think I should be very surprised whatever happened to me next.

Still, I was happy. I was more deeply in love with my husband every day; I was growing fonder of my grandfather, and I found great pleasure in being the one who could bring such happiness into his life. I knew that he had changed a great deal since I had come; and, since he had revealed his relationship to me, even more. He often reminded me of a boy in his enthusiasm for simple things, and I understood that this was because he had never had time to be really young.

Some impulse made me lift my eyes from the pond and the palms. That feeling which came to me often when I was in the quadrangle was strong at that moment. I had never analysed it, but it was a feeling of eerie discomfort, a notion that I was being watched intently and not casually or in a friendly way.

My eyes went at once to the east windows ... to that floor on which Barbarina had had her music room.

There was a movement there. Someone was standing at the corridor window – not close, but a little way back. Now the figure came nearer. I could not see the face, but I knew it was a woman because she was wearing a mauve dress.

It was the one I had seen on the dressmaker's dummy; the dress which Carrie had made for Barbarina.

'Barbarina ...' I whispered.

For a few seconds I saw the dress clearly, for a pale hand had drawn back the curtains. I could not see the face, though ... then the curtain fell back into place.

I stood staring at the window.

Of course, I said to myself, it was Deborah. She has decided to wear the mauve dress after all. That's the answer. But why did she not wave to me or let me see her?

It had been all over in a few seconds, hadn't it? She couldn't have seen me.

Roc came out of the room, shouting that he was ready.

I was about to tell him what I had seen, but somehow it had become unimportant. When I saw Deborah at the ball in the mauve dress I should be satisfied.

The ballroom at Polhorgan was magnificent. Trehay, eager to show off his more exotic blooms, had made a wonderful show, but it was the hydrangeas, indigenous to Cornwall, that in my opinion were the most dazzling.

My grandfather was already in the ballroom in his wheelchair with Althea Grey beside him, looking startlingly beautiful in her eggshell-blue off-the-shoulder dress, with a white camellia adorning it. Her hand was resting on my grandfather's chair in a proprietorial way.

'You look more like your mother than ever,' said my grandfather brusquely; and I knew he was moved as I stooped and kissed him.

'It's going to be wonderful,' I replied. 'I'm so looking forward to meeting all your friends.'

My grandfather laughed. 'Not *my* friends. Few of them have ever been here before. They've come to meet Mrs. Pendorric – and that's a fact. What do you think of the ballroom?'

'Quite magnificent.'

'Have you got anything like this at Pendorric, Roc?'

'I'm afraid we don't run to such glory. Our halls are tiny in comparison.'

'Like that panelling? I had that specially brought here from the Midlands. Some old mansion that was broken up. Used to say to myself, "One day that'll be mine." Well, so it was in a way.'

'There's a lesson in it,' said Roc. 'Take what you want and pay for it.'

'I paid for it all right.'

'Lord Polhorgan,' said Althea, 'you mustn't get over-excited. If you do I shall have to insist on your going back to your room.'

'You see how I'm treated?' said my grandfather. 'I might be a schoolboy. In fact I'm sure at times Nurse Grey thinks I am.'

'I'm here to look after you,' she reminded him. 'Have you your T.N.T.?'

He put his hand in his pocket and held up the silver box.

'Good. Keep them handy.'

'I shall be keeping my eye on him too,' I said.

'How fortunate you are, sir,' Roc murmured. 'The two most beautiful women at the ball to watch over you!'

My grandfather put his hand over mine and smiled at me. 'Aye,' he agreed, 'I'm lucky.'

'That sounds like the first of the guests,' said Althea.

It was. Dawson, spectacular in black livery with gold frogs and buttons, was announcing the first arrivals.

I felt very proud standing there between my grandfather and my husband as I greeted the guests. My grandfather was cold and formal; Roc quite the opposite. I was, naturally, the centre of a great deal of interest; I guessed that many of these people wanted to see what sort of woman Roc Pendorric had married. The fact that I was Lord Polhorgan's granddaughter meant that they were aware of our romantic meeting, for they all knew my mother had run away from home and had not communicated with her father again. It made a good story, and naturally there had been a certain amount of gossip about it.

Roc was told that he was lucky, and now and then I sensed the underlying significance of that remark. Polhorgan was an imposing structure, but a great many of these people possessed houses as grand. The difference was that they had been in their families for hundreds of years, while my grandfather had earned the money to build his. Moreover, it was unlikely that any of these people could match the opulence of the furnishings they now saw. It was well known that my grandfather was either a millionaire or something near it.

So when they told Roc he was lucky, I presumed my grandfather's wealth had something to do with it.

However, I was beginning to enjoy myself. The music had started and the guests were still arriving. They were not all young; indeed there were some very old people present, for the invitations had been issued to whole families. It was going to be a very mixed ball.

The party from Pendorric had arrived, and the twins came ahead, arm in arm, looking exactly alike in their gold-coloured dresses; behind them Charles and Morwenna, and then . . . Deborah.

Deborah was wearing the pink dress which Carrie had made for her, and looking as though she had stepped out of a twenty-five-year-old magazine.

But pink! Then who had been wearing the mauve?

I forced myself to smile at them; but I could not stop thinking of the vision I had seen at the window. Who could it have been?

Deborah had taken my hands. 'You look lovely, dear. Is everything all right?'

'Why yes . . . I think so.'

'I thought you looked a little startled when you saw me.'

'Oh no . . . not really.'

'It *was* something. You must tell me later. I'd better pass on now.'

More guests were approaching, and Roc was introducing me. I took the outstretched hands, still thinking of the vision I had seen in the mauve dress.

I danced with Roc and with many others that night. I was aware of my grandfather's eyes, which never seemed to leave me.

I think I was a successful hostess.

I was grateful to Deborah, who was determined to put me at my ease since I had shown her that I was disturbed.

She took the first opportunity of talking to me.

Roc was dancing with Althea Grey and I was standing by my grandfather's chair when she came up.

'While you have a moment, Favel,' she said, 'I'd like to chat. Tell me, why were you startled when you saw me?'

I hesitated, then I replied: 'I thought I'd seen you earlier in the evening at the east window – before we left Pendorric . . . in the mauve dress.'

There was silence for a few seconds and I went on: 'I was dressed and waiting for Roc when I looked out of the window and saw someone in the mauve dress.'

'And you didn't recognize who it was?'

'I couldn't see a face. I only saw the dress and that someone was wearing it.'

'What ever did you think?'

'I thought you'd decided to wear it.'

'And when I came in the pink surely you didn't think you'd seen . . . Barbarina?'

'Oh no, I didn't think that really. But I wondered who . . .'

She touched my hand. 'Of course you wouldn't think it. You're too sensible.' She paused and said: 'There's a simple explanation. I had a choice of two dresses. Why shouldn't I try on the mauve and finally decide on the pink?'

'So it *was* you.'

She did not answer; she was staring dreamily at the dancers. I realized that I didn't believe what she was hinting. She had not said that she had tried on the mauve dress, she had put it differently. 'Why shouldn't I try on the mauve . . .?' It was as though she did not want to tell a lie but at the same time was trying to set my mind at rest.

That was just a fleeting thought which came into my head as I looked at her kind, gentle face.

Almost immediately I said to myself: Of course, Deborah tried on the mauve first. It was natural. And moreover it was the only explanation.

But why should she go to the east wing to do it? Because Carrie would have put the dress there, was the obvious answer.

I dismissed the matter from my mind. Deborah saw this and seemed contented.

Grandfather said that I must not remain at his side, as he liked to see me among the dancers. I told him I was rather anxious about him, as he looked more flushed than usual.

'I'm enjoying it,' he said. 'I should have liked to have done more of this in the past. Perhaps we will now, eh, now you've come home? Where's your husband?'

He was dancing with Nurse Grey and I pointed him out. They were the most striking couple in the room, I thought; she with her fair looks, he so dark.

'He ought to be dancing with you,' said my grandfather.

'He did suggest it, but I told him I wanted to talk to you.'

'Now that won't do. Ah, here's the doctor. Nice to see you unprofessionally, Dr. Clement.'

Andrew Clement smiled at me. 'It was good of you and Mrs. Pendorric to ask me.'

'Why don't you ask my granddaughter to dance? Don't want her to be glued to the old man's chair all the evening.'

Andrew Clement smiled at me and we went on to the floor together.

'Do you think this is too much excitement for my grandfather?' I asked.

'I wouldn't say he was too excited. No, I think it's doing him good. I'll tell you something, Mrs. Pendorric; he's been much better since you've been here.'

'Has he?'

'Oh yes, you've given him a real interest in life. There were times when I was afraid he'd die of melancholia . . . sitting in that room day after day, staring out at the sea. Now he's no longer lonely. I think he's changed a great deal; he's got something to live for, and you know he's a man of immense energy. He's always gone all out for what he wants, and managed to get it. Well, now he wants to live.'

'That's excellent news.'

'Oh yes, he's told me how delighted he is with you. He wanted me to witness his signature on some important documents the other day, and I said to Nurse Grey afterwards that I hadn't found him so well for a very long time. She said it was all thanks to that granddaughter of his on whom he doted.'

'I can't tell you how happy I am if I can be of help to him. Is your sister here to-night?'

'Oh yes, though ballroom dancing isn't much in her line. Now if it were folk-dancing . . .'

He laughed, and at that moment he was tapped on the shoulder by a dark, handsome young man. Andrew Clement pretended to scowl, and said: 'Oh, is it that sort of dance?'

'Afraid so,' said the young man. 'I'm claiming Mrs. Pendorric.'

As I danced with this young man he told me he was John Poldree and that he lived a few miles inland.

'I'm home for a bit,' he went on. 'Actually I'm studying law in London.'

'I'm so glad you were home for the ball,' I told him.

'Yes, it's good fun. All very exciting too – your turning out to be Lord Polhorgan's granddaughter.'

'Most people seem to think so.'

'Your grandfather has a striking-looking nurse, Mrs. Pendorric.'

'Yes, she's certainly very beautiful.'

'Who is she? I've seen her somewhere before.'

'Her name is Althea Grey.'

He shook his head. 'Can't recall the name. The face is familiar, though. Seem to connect her with some law case or other . . . I thought I had a good memory for such things, but it seems I'm not so good as I thought.'

'I should think if you'd met her you'd remember her.'

'Yes. That's why I was so sure. Well, it'll come back I expect.'

'Why don't you ask her?'

'As a matter of fact I did. She absolutely froze me. She was certain she had never met *me* before.'

There was a tap on his shoulder, and there was Roc waiting to claim me.

I was very happy dancing with my husband. His eyes were amused and I could see that he was enjoying himself.

'It's fun,' he said, 'but I don't see half enough of the hostess. I expect she has her duties, though.'

'The same thing applies to you.'

'Well, haven't you seen me performing? I've had my eyes on every wallflower.'

'I've seen you on several occasions dancing with Althea Grey. Was she wilting for lack of attention?'

'At things of this sort, people like Althea and Rachel could be at a disadvantage. The nurse and the governess! There's a certain amount of snobbery still in existence, you know.'

'So that's why you've been looking after Althea. What about poor Rachel?'

'I'd better keep an eye on her too.'

'Then,' I said lightly, 'as you're going to be so busily engaged elsewhere I'd better make the most of the time that belongs to me.'

He squeezed my hand. 'Have you forgotten,' he asked, his lips touching my ear, 'that the rest of our lives belong together?'

Supper was very gay. We had arranged that it should be served in three of the larger rooms which adjoined the hall; they all faced south and the great french windows opened on to terraces which looked over the gardens to the sea. There was plenty of moonlight, and the view was enchanting.

Trehay's flower scheme was as beautiful in the supper rooms as it was in the ballroom; and no effort had been spared to achieve the utmost luxury. On the overladen table were fish, pies, meats and delicacies of all description. Dawson and his under-servants in their smart livery took charge of the bar while Mrs. Dawson looked after the food.

I shared a table with my grandfather, John Poldree and his brother, Deborah and the twins.

Lowella was as silent as Hyson on this occasion; she seemed to be quite overawed, and when I whispered to her that she was unusually subdued, Hyson answered that they had made a vow not to call attention to themselves, in case someone should remember that they weren't really old enough to go to balls and tell Rachel to take them home.

They had escaped Rachel, they told me, and their parents; and so would I please not call attention to them in case Granny Deborah noticed?

I promised.

While we were talking together, some of the guests strolled out on to the terraces and I saw Roc and Althea Grey walk by the window.

They stood for a while looking out over the sea and seemed to be talking earnestly, and the sight of them threw a small shadow over my enjoyment.

It was midnight when several of the guests started to leave, and finally only the Pendorric party remained.

Althea Grey hovered while we said good-bye and congratulated each other on the success of the evening. Then she wheeled my grandfather's chair to the lift which he had had installed some years before when he had first been aware of his illness, and he went up to his bedroom while we went to our cars.

It was half-past one by the time we reached Pendorric, and as we drove under the old archway to the north portico, Mrs. Penhalligan opened the front door.

'Oh, Mrs. Penhalligan,' I said, 'you shouldn't have stayed up.'

'Well, madam,' she said, 'I thought you'd like a little refreshment before settling down for the night. I've got some soup for you.'

'Soup! On a hot summer's night!' cried Roc.

'Soup! Soup! Glorious Soup!' sang Lowella.

'One of the old customs,' Morwenna whispered to me. 'We can't escape them if we want to.'

We went into the north hall and Mrs. Penhalligan led the way into the small winter parlour where soup plates had been set out; and at the sight of them Lowella danced round the room chanting: ' "There was a sound of revelry by night".'

'Oh Lowella, please,' sighed Morwenna. 'Aren't you tired? It's after one.'

'I'm not in the least tired,' insisted Lowella indignantly. 'Oh, isn't this a wonderful ball!'

'The ball's over,' Roc reminded her.

'It's not— not till we're all in our beds. There's soup to be had before that's over.'

'You'd better let them sleep late to-morrow, Rachel,' said their mother.

Mrs Penhalligan came in with a tureen of soup and began ladling it out into the plates.

'It was always like this in the old days,' said Roc. 'We used to hide in the gallery and watch them come in; do you remember, Morwenna?'

Morwenna nodded.

'Who?' asked Hyson.

'Our parents, of course. We couldn't have been more than . . .'

'Five,' said Hyson, 'You'd have to be, wouldn't you, Uncle Roc? You couldn't have been more, could you?'

'What memories these children have!' murmured Roc lightly. 'Have you been coaching them, Aunt Deborah?'

'What soup's this?' asked Lowella.

'Taste it and see,' Roc told her.

She obeyed and rolled her eyes ecstatically.

We all agreed that it was not such a bad custom after all, and that although we should not have thought of hot soup on a summer's night there was something reviving about it and it was pleasant to sit back and talk about the evening.

When we had finished the soup no one seemed in a hurry to go to bed, so we talked about Polhorgan and the people we had met there, while the twins sat back in their seats, desperately trying to keep awake, looking like daffodils which had been left too long out of water.

'It's time they were in bed,' said Charles.

'Oh Daddy,' wailed Lowella, 'don't be so old-fashioned!'

'If you're not tired,' Roc pointed out, 'others might be. Aunt Deborah looks half asleep and so do you, Morwenna.'

'I know,' said Morwenna, 'but it's so comfortable sitting here and it's been such a pleasant evening I don't want it to end. So go on talking, all of you.'

'Yes do, quick,' cried Lowella; and everyone laughed and seemed suddenly wide awake. 'Go on, Uncle Roc.'

'This reminds me of Christmas,' said Roc obligingly, and Lowella smiled at him with loving gratitude and affection.

'When,' went on Roc, 'we sit around the fire, longing for our beds and too lazy to go to them.'

'Telling ghost stories,' said Charles.

'Tell some now,' pleaded Lowella. Do, please. Daddy. Uncle Roc.'

Hyson sat forward, suddenly alert.

'Most unseasonable,' commented Roc. 'You'll have to wait a few months yet, Lo.'

'I can't. I can't. I want a ghost story – *now*!'

'It certainly is time you were in bed,' commented Morwenna.

Lowella regarded me with solemn eyes. 'It'll be the Bride's first Christmas with us,' she announced. 'She'll love Christmas at Pendorric, won't she? I remember last Christmas we sang songs as well as telling ghost stories. Real Christmas songs. I'll tell you the one I like best.'

' "The Mistletoe Bough",' said Hyson.

'You'd like that, Bride, because it's all about another bride.'

'I expect your Aunt Favel knows it,' said Morwenna. 'Everyone does.'

'No,' I told them, 'I've never heard it. You see, Christmas on the island wasn't quite like an English Christmas.'

'Fancy! She's never heard of "The Mistletoe Bough".' Lowella looked shocked.

'Think what she's missed,' mocked Roc.

'I'm going to be the one to tell her,' declared Lowella. 'Listen, Bride! This other bride played hide and seek in a place . . .'

'Minster Lovel,' supplied Hyson.

'Well, the place doesn't matter two hoots, silly.'

'Lowella,' Morwenna admonished; but Lowella was rushing on.

'They were playing hide and seek and this bride got into the old chest, and the lock clicked and fastened her down for ever.'

'And they didn't open the chest until twenty years later,' put in Hyson. 'Then they found her – nothing but a skeleton.'

'Her wedding dress and orange blossom were all right, though,' added Lowella cheerfully.

'I'm sure,' said Roc ironically, 'that must have been a comfort.'

'You shouldn't laugh, Uncle Roc. It's sad, really.'

' "A spring lock lay in ambush there",' she sang.

' "And fastened her down for ever".'

'And the moral of that,' Roc put in, grinning at me, 'is, don't go hiding in oak chests if you're a bride.'

'Ugh!' shivered Morwenna. 'I'm not keen on that story. It's morbid.'

'That's why it appeals to your daughters, Wenna,' Roc told her.

Charles said: 'Look. I'm going up. The twins ought to have been in bed hours ago.'

Deborah yawned. 'I must say I find it hard to keep awake.'

'I've an idea,' cried Lowella. 'Let's all sing Christmas songs for a bit. Everyone has to sing a different one.'

'I've a better idea,' said her father. 'Bed.'

Rachel stood up. 'Come along,' she said to the twins. 'It must be nearly two.'

Lowella looked disgusted with us because we all rose; but no one took any notice of her, and we said good night and went upstairs.

The next day I went over to Polhorgan to see how my grandfather was after all the excitement.

Mrs. Dawson met me in the hall and I congratulated her on all that she and her husband had done to make the ball a success.

'Well, madam,' she said, bridling, 'it's a pleasure to be appreciated, I must say. Not that Dawson and I want *thanks*. It was our duty and we did it.'

'You did it admirably,' I told her.

Dawson came into the hall at that moment, and when Mrs. Dawson told him what I had said, he was as pleased as his wife.

I asked how my grandfather was that morning.

'Very contented, madam, but sleeping. A little tired after all the excitement, I think.'

'I won't disturb him for a while,' I said. 'I'll go into the garden.'

'I'm sending up his coffee in half an hour, madam,' Mrs. Dawson told me.

'Very well then, I'll wait till then.'

Dawson followed me into the garden; there was something conspiratorial about his manner, I thought; and when I paused by one of the greenhouses he was still beside me.

'Everyone in the house is glad, madam, that you've come home,' he told me. 'With one exception, that is.'

I turned to look at him in astonishment, and he did not meet my eyes. I had the impression that he was determined to be the good and faithful servant, dealing with a delicate situation because this was something I ought to know.

'Thank you, Dawson,' I said. 'Who is the exception?'

'The nurse.'

'Oh?'

He stuck out his lower lip and shook his head. 'She had other notions.'

'Dawson, you don't like Nurse Grey, do you?'

'There's nobody in this house that likes her, madam . . . except the young men. She being that sort. There's some that don't look beyond a pretty face.'

I thought it was the usual story of a nurse in the house who was determined to establish the fact that she was superior to the servants. Probably Nurse Grey gave orders in the kitchen, which they did not like. It was not an unusual situation. And now that they knew I was Lord Polhorgan's grand-daughter, they regarded me as the mistress of the house. This was the Dawsons' way of telling me I was accepted as such.

'Mrs. Dawson and I have always felt ourselves to be in a privileged position, madam. We have been with his lordship for a very long time.'

'But of course, you *are*,' I assured him.

'We were here, begging your pardon, when Miss Lilith was at home.'

'So you knew my mother?'

'A lovely young lady, and, if you'll forgive the liberty, madam, you're very like her.'

'Thank you.'

'That's why . . . Mrs. Dawson and I . . . made up our minds that we could talk to you, madam.'

'Please say everything that's in your mind, Dawson.'

'Well, we're uneasy, madam. There was a time when we thought she would try to marry him. There was no doubt that was what she was after. Mrs. Dawson and I had made up our minds that the minute that was decided on we should be looking for another position.'

'Miss Grey . . . marry my grandfather?'

'Such things have happened, madam. Rich old gentlemen do marry young nurses now and then. They get a feeling they can't do without them and the nurses have their eyes on the money, you see.'

'I'm sure my grandfather would never be married for his money. He's far too shrewd.'

'That was what we said. She could never achieve that, and she didn't. But Mrs. Dawson and I reckon it wasn't for want of trying.' He came closer to me and whispered: 'The truth is, madam, we reckon she's what you might call . . . an adventuress.'

'I see.'

'There's something more. Our married daughter came to see us not so

long ago. . . . It was just before you came home, madam. Well, she happened
to see Nurse Grey and she said she was sure she'd seen her picture in the
paper somewhere. Only she didn't think the name was Grey.'

'Why was her picture in the paper?'

'It was some case or other. Maureen couldn't remember what. But she
thought it was something bad.'

'People get mixed up about these things. Perhaps she'd won a beauty
competition or something like that.'

'Oh no, it wasn't that or Maureen would have remembered. It was
something to do with the courts. And it was Nurse something. But Maureen
didn't think it was Grey. It was just the face. She has got the sort of face,
madam, that once seen is never forgotten.'

'Did you ask her?'

'Oh no, madam, it wasn't the sort of thing we could ask. She would be
offended, and unless we'd got proof, she could deny it, couldn't she? No,
there's nothing we can put a finger on. And now you've come home it doesn't
seem the same. His lordship's not so likely to get caught – that's how Mrs.
Dawson and I see it, madam. But we're keeping our eyes open.'

'Oh . . . it's Mrs. Pendorric.'

I turned sharply to see Althea Grey smiling at me, and I flushed rather
guiltily, feeling at a disadvantage to have been discovered discussing her with
the butler. I wondered if she had overheard anything. Voices carried in the
open air.

'*You* don't look as if you've been up half the night,' she went on. 'And I'm
sure you must have been. What an evening! Lord Polhorgan was absolutely
delighted with the way everything went off.'

Dawson slipped away and I was left alone with her. Her hair, piled high
beneath the snowy cap, was beautiful; but I wondered what it was that made
her face so distinctive. Was it the thick brows, several shades darker than
her hair; the eyes of that lovely deep blue shade that is almost violet and
doesn't need to take its colour from anything because it is always a more
vivid blue than anything else could possibly be? The straight nose was
almost Egyptian, and seemed odd with such Anglo-Saxon fairness. The wide
mouth was slightly mocking now. I felt sure that even if she had not
overheard our conversation, she knew that Dawson had been speaking of
her derogatively.

It was a face of mystery, I decided, a face that concealed secrets; the face
of a woman of the world, a woman who had lived perhaps recklessly and
had no desire for the past to prejudice the present, or future.

I remembered that the young man with whom I had danced had mentioned
something from the past too. So Dawson's suspicions were very likely not
without some foundation.

I felt wary of this woman as I walked with her towards the house.

'Lord Polhorgan was hoping you'd come this morning. I told him you
most certainly would.'

'I was wondering how he felt after last night.'

'It did him a world of good. He enjoyed fêting his beautiful granddaughter.'

I felt that she was secretly laughing at me, and I was glad when I was with my grandfather and she had left us alone together.

It was a week later that there was a call in the night.

The telephone beside our bed rang and I was answering it before Roc had opened his eyes.

'This is Nurse Grey. Could you come over at one? Lord Polhorgan is very ill, and asking for you.'

I leaped out of bed.

'What on earth's happened?' asked Roc.

When I told him he made me slip on some clothes, and, doing the same himself, said: 'We'll drive over right away.'

'What's the time?' I asked Roc, as we drove the short distance between Pendorric and Polhorgan.

'Just after one.'

'He must be bad for her to ring us,' I said.

Roc put his hand over mine, as though to reassure me that whatever was waiting for me, he would be there to share it.

As we drove up to the portico the door opened and Dawson let us in.

'He's very bad, I'm afraid, madam.'

'I'll go straight up.'

I ran up the stairs, Roc at my heels. Roc waited outside the bedroom while I went in.

Althea Grey came towards me. 'Thank God you've come,' she said. 'He's been asking for you. I phoned as soon as I knew.'

I went to the bed where my grandfather lay back on his pillows; he was quite exhausted and I could see that he was finding it difficult to get his breath.

'Grandfather,' I said.

His lips formed the name Favel; but he did not say it.

I knelt by the bed and took his hand in mine; I kissed it, feeling desolate. I had found him such a short time ago. Was I to lose him so soon?

'I'm here, Grandfather. I came as soon as I heard you wanted me.'

I knew by the slight movement of his head that he understood.

Althea Grey was at my side. She whispered: 'He's not in pain. I've given him morphia. He'll be feeling the effect of it now. Dr. Clement will be here at any moment.'

I turned to look at her and I saw from her expression that his condition was very grave. Then I saw Roc standing some little way from the bed. Althea Grey moved back to where he was and I turned my attention to my grandfather.

'Favel.' It was a whisper. His fingers moved in mine, and I knew that he was trying to say something to me so I brought my face nearer to his.

'Are you there . . . Favel?'

'Yes, Grandfather,' I whispered.

'It's . . . good-bye, Favel.'

'*No.*'

He smiled. 'Such a short time. ... But it was a happy time ... the happiest time ... Favel, you must be ...'

His face puckered and I bent nearer to him.

'Don't talk, Grandfather. It's too much of an effort.'

His brows puckered into a frown. 'Favel ... must be ... careful. ... It'll be yours now. Make sure ...'

I guessed what he was trying to tell me. Even when he was fighting for his breath he was preoccupied with his money.

'It's different ...' he went on, 'when you have it. ... Can't be sure ... can never be sure. ... Favel ... take care. ...'

'Grandfather, please don't worry about me. Don't think about anything but getting better. You will get better. You *must*. ...'

He shook his head. 'Couldn't find ...' he began; but his battle for breath was too much for him; his eyes were closing. 'Tired,' he murmured. 'So tired. Favel ... stay ... be careful. ... It's different with money. Perhaps I was wrong ... but I wanted ... be careful. ... I wish I could stay a while to ... look after you, Favel.'

His lips were moving now but no sound came. He lay back on his pillows, his face looking shrunken and grey.

He was very near the end by the time Dr. Clement arrived.

We sat in the room where I had played so many games of chess with him – Dr. Clement, Roc, Nurse Grey and myself.

Dr. Clement was saying: 'It's not entirely unexpected. It could have happened at any time. Did he ring the bell?'

'No. Or I should have heard him. My room is next to his. The bell is always by his bed for him to ring if he wanted anything in the night. It was Dawson who went in. He said he was locking up when he saw Lord Polhorgan's light on. He found him gasping and in great pain. He called me and I saw that it was necessary to give him morphia, which I did.'

Dr. Clement rose and went to the door.

'Dawson,' he called. 'Are you there, Dawson?'

Dawson came into the room.

'I've heard that you came in and found Lord Polhorgan in distress.'

'Yes, sir. He'd snapped on the light and seeing it I looked in to make sure he was all right. I saw he was trying to ask for something, but I didn't know what, for a while. Then I found out it was his pills. I couldn't find them then so I called Nurse and came back with her. That was when she gave him the morphia.'

'So it seems as though this attack developed into a major one because he had no chance of holding it off.'

'I'd always impressed on him the need to have his pills at hand,' said Althea Grey.

Dawson was looking at her scornfully. 'I found them after, sir. After his lordship had had the morphia, that was. The box was lying on the floor. It had come open and the pills was scattered, sir. The bell was on the floor also.'

'He must have knocked them over when he reached for the pills,' said Althea Grey.

I looked at Roc, who was staring straight ahead of him.

'A sad business,' murmured Dr. Clement. 'I think I ought to give you a sedative, Mrs. Pendorric. You're looking all in.'

'I'll take her home,' said Roc. 'There's no point in waiting here now. We can do nothing till the morning.'

Dr. Clement smiled at me sadly. 'There was nothing we could do to prevent it,' he told me.

'If he had had his pills,' I said, 'that might have prevented it.'

'It might have.'

'What an unfortunate accident . . .' I began; and my eyes met Dawson's and I saw that his were gleaming with speculation.

'It couldn't be helped,' Roc was saying. 'It's easy to see how it happened . . . reaching out . . . in a hurry . . . knocking over the box and the bell.'

I shivered, and Roc put his arm through mine.

I wanted to get out of that room; there was something in Dawson's expression which frightened me; there was something too in the calm, beautiful features of Althea Grey.

I felt as though I were outside looking in on all that had happened since Roc and I came into this house. I saw myself leaning over my dying grandfather; I heard his voice warning me of some danger which he sensed ahead of me. Roc and Althea were standing together in that room of death. What words did they exchange while my grandfather told me to take care? What had been the expressions in their eyes as they looked at each other?

Dawson had done this with his hatred of the nurse, with his groundless suspicions. But did I really know that they were groundless?

I felt the cool night air on my face and Roc's tender voice beside me.

'Come on, darling, you're quite worn out. Clement's right. It has been a terrible shock to you.'

Those were sad weeks which followed, for only when I had lost him did I realize how fond I had become of my grandfather. I missed him deeply; not only his company, I began to understand; not only the complacent joy I had felt because I had brought so much pleasure into his lonely life; but he had given me a sense of security, and that I had lost. I had subconsciously felt that he was there – a powerful man of the world to whom I could go if I were in trouble. My own flesh and blood. I could have trusted him to do anything in his power to help me . . . should I have needed his help.

It seemed strange that I should have felt this need. I had a husband who could surely give me any protection I wanted; but it was the loss of my grandfather which brought home to me the true relationship between myself and my husband. To have lost him would have been complete desolation; he could amuse and delight me too, but the truth remained that I was not sure of him; I did not know him. Yet, in spite of this uncertainty I loved him infinitely, and my entire happiness depended on him. I was wretched because I must be suspicious of his relationship with Althea Grey, Rachel Bective and even Dinah Bond. And I had begun to feel – since I had discovered that

I had a grandfather – that he was someone who had for me a deep and uncomplicated affection. Now I had lost him.

I was his heir and there were many visits from his solicitors. When I heard the extent of the fortune he had left I felt dizzy at the prospect of my riches. There were several bequests. The Dawsons had been left a comfortable pension; there was a thousand pounds for the nurse who was employed by him at the time of his death; all the servants had been remembered and rewarded according to their length of service; he had left a sizeable sum to be used for the benefit of orphans – he himself had been an orphan – and I was very touched that he had remembered this charity. Death duties, I was informed, would swallow up a large proportion, but I should still have a considerable fortune.

Polhorgan itself was mine with all its contents; and this in itself was worth a great deal.

My grandfather's death seemed to have changed my whole life. I was so much poorer in affection, so much richer in worldly goods; and I was beginning to be afraid that this last fact coloured people's attitude towards me.

I fancied people like the Darks and Dr. Clement were not quite so friendly; that the people in the village whispered about me when I had passed. I had become not merely Mrs. Pendorric, but the rich Mrs. Pendorric. But it was in Pendorric itself that I felt the change most, and this was indeed disturbing. I felt that Morwenna and Charles were secretly delighted, and that the twins watched me a little furtively as though they had overheard gossip which had made them see me in a different light.

Deborah was more outspoken than the others. She said: 'Barbarina was an heiress, but nothing of course to be compared with yourself.'

I hated this kind of talk. I wished that my grandfather had not been such a rich man. I wished that he had left his money elsewhere, for I was realizing now that one of the facts which had made me so happy at Pendorric was that, although the old house and estate needed money, Roc had married me, a girl without a penny. I could no longer say to myself: 'He could only have married me for love.'

It was with my grandfather's money that the canker had touched our relationship.

It was some weeks after my grandfather's death that I had an interview with his solicitor and he brought home to me the advisability of making a will.

So I did so, and, with the exception of one or two legacies, I left the residue of my fortune to Roc.

September had come. The evenings were short and the mornings misty; but the afternoons were as warm as they had been in July.

It was two months since my grandfather's death and I was still mourning him. I had done nothing about Polhorgan, and the Dawsons and all the servants remained there; Althea Grey had decided to have a long holiday before looking for a new post and had taken a little cottage about a mile from Pendorric, which during the months of June, July and August was let to holiday-makers.

I knew I should have to do something about Polhorgan, and an idea had come to me. It was to turn the house into a home for orphans – such as my grandfather must have been – the deprived and unwanted ones.

When I mentioned this to Roc, he was startled.

'What an undertaking!' he said.

'Somehow I think it would have appealed to my grandfather because he was an orphan himself.'

Roc walked away from me – we were in our bedroom – and going to the window stared out at the sea.

'Well, Roc, you don't like the idea?'

'Darling, it's not the sort of project you can rush into.'

'No, of course not. I'm just thinking about it.'

'Things aren't what they used to be, remember. There'd be all sorts of bureaucratic regulations to be got over . . . and have you thought of the cost of running a place like that?'

'I haven't thought about anything very much. It was just a faint idea. I'm brooding on it, though.'

'We'll have to do a lot of brooding,' he said.

I had a notion that he was not impressed with the idea, and I shelved it for the time being, but I was determined not to give it up easily.

I often called on Jesse Pleydell, who always seemed delighted to see me apart from the tobacco I took him. Mrs. Penhalligan said I kept him supplied and he was grateful, though my visits meant as much to him as the tobacco.

I shall never forget that September day, because it brought the beginning of the real terror which came into my life, and it was at this time that I began to understand how the pleasant picture had changed piece by piece until I was confronted with the cruellest of suspicions and horror.

The day began normally enough. In the morning I went down to Mrs. Robinson's and bought the tobacco. Knowing that I was going, Deborah asked me to buy some hairpins for her, and Morwenna asked me to bring some bass she needed for tying up plants. I met Rachel and the twins as I was setting out; they were going on a nature ramble, so they all three walked with me as far as the shop. When I came back I met Roc and Charles going off to the home farm together.

But I didn't leave for the cottages until after tea, and when I arrived Jesse was sitting at his door catching the last of the sun.

I sat beside him talking for a while, and because I thought it was getting a little chilly I went inside with him and he made me a cup of tea. It was something he enjoyed doing, and I knew better than to offer to help. While we sat drinking the thick brew, Jesse talked of the old days and how the Pendorric gardens had looked in his time.

'Ah, madam, you should have been here forty years ago . . . that was the time. I had four men working under me all the time, and the flowers in the cliff garden were a picture . . . a real picture.'

He would go on and on in this strain, and because he enjoyed it I encouraged him to do so. I learned a good deal about life at Pendorric forty or fifty years ago when Jesse was in his prime. It was a more leisurely life, but even so the beginning of change had set in.

'Now when I were a boy things were different.'

That would have been about eighty years ago. Very different indeed, I thought.

'There was no talk then of not being able to keep up like,' mused Jesse. 'There was no thought that things 'ud ever be different from what they always had been. Polhorgan House wasn't here then – nor thought of – and all Polhorgan meant to us was the little old cove down there.'

I listened dreamily, staying rather longer than I had intended, and it was six o'clock when I rose to go.

It was always gloomy in the cottage on account of the small latticed windows, so I hadn't noticed how dark it had grown. The sea mist had been lurking in the air all day, but now it had thickened. It was warm and sea-scented and not by any means unpleasant; it hung in patches and in some spots was really thick. It was especially so near the church; and as I paused at the lych gate to look at the gravestones with the mist swirling about them, thinking how strangely picturesque everything was, I heard it; it seemed to be coming from inside the graveyard – singing in that strange, high voice, which was slightly out of tune.

> *'How should I your true love know*
> *From another one?*
> *By his cockle hat and staff*
> *And his sandal shoon.'*

My heart began to beat fast; my hand on the lych gate trembled. I looked about me, but I seemed to be alone with the mist.

Someone was in there singing, and I had to find out who, so I opened the lych gate and went into the graveyard. I was determined to know who it was who sang in that strange voice, and because I was sure that it was someone from the house, instinctively I made my way to the Pendorric vault. I was almost certain now that it must be Carrie. She brought wreaths for her beloved Barbarina and she would have heard her sing that song; what more natural than that hearing it often she had learned it by heart?

It must be Carrie.

As I reached the Pendorric vault, I drew up short in astonishment because the door was open. I had never seen it open before, and was under the impression that it would never be opened except when it was prepared to receive those who had died.

I went closer and as I did so I heard the voice again.

> *'He is dead and gone, lady,*
> *He is dead and gone;*
> *At his head a grass-green turf,*
> *At his heels a stone.'*

And it appeared to be coming from *inside* the vault.

I went down the stone steps. 'Who's there?' I called. 'Carrie. Are you in there?'

My voice sounded strange at the entrance of that dark vault.

'Carrie,' I called. 'Carrie.' I put my head inside and saw that four or five stone steps led down. I descended, calling: 'Carrie! Carrie! Are you there?'

There was silence. Because of the light from the open door I could see the ledges with the coffins on them; I could smell the dampness of the earth. Then suddenly I was in darkness, and for a few seconds I was so shocked and bewildered that I could not move. I could not even cry out in protest. It took me several seconds to understand that the door had closed on me and I was shut in the vault.

I gave a gasp of horror.

'Who's there?' I cried. 'Who shut the door?'

Then I tried to find the steps, but my eyes were not yet adjusted to the darkness, and groping I stumbled and found myself sprawling up the cold stone stairs.

Frantically I picked myself up. I could make out the shape of the steps now, and I mounted them. I pushed the door but it was firmly shut and I could not move it.

For some moments, I'm afraid, I was hysterical. I hammered on the door with my fists. 'Let me out of here,' I screamed. 'Let me out of here.'

My voice sounded hollow and I knew that it would not be heard outside.

I lay against the door, trying to think. Someone had lured me into this dreadful place, someone who wanted to be rid of me. How long could I live here? But I should be missed. Roc would miss me. He would come to look for me.

'Roc!' I called. 'Oh . . . Roc . . . come quickly.'

I covered my face with my hands. I did not want to look about me. I was suddenly afraid of what I might see, shut in this vault with the Pendorric dead. How long before I became one of them?

Then I thought I heard a movement near me. I listened. Was that the sound of breathing?

The horror was deepening. I did not believe in ghosts, I tried to tell myself. But it is easy to say that when you are above ground in some sunny spot, some well-lighted room. Very different, buried alive . . . among the dead!

I had never known real fear until that moment. I was clammy with sweat, my hair was probably standing on end. I did not know, because there was no room in my mind for anything but fear, the knowledge that I was locked in with the dead.

But I was not alone. I knew it. Some breathing, living thing was in this tomb with me.

I had covered my face with my hands because I did not want to see it. I dared not see.

Then a cold hand touched mine. I screamed, and I heard myself cry: 'Barbarina!' because in that moment I *believed* the legend of Pendorric. I believed that Barbarina had lured me to my tomb so that I could haunt Pendorric and she might rest in peace.

'Favel!' It was a sharp whisper and the one who said it was as frightened as I was.

'Hyson!'

'Yes, Favel. It's Hyson.'

Floods of relief! I was not alone. There was someone to share this horrible place with me. I felt ashamed of myself, but I couldn't help it. I had never been so glad to hear a human voice in the whole of my life.

'Hyson . . . what are you doing here?'

She had come up the stairs and snuggled close beside me.

'It's . . . frightening . . . with the door shut,' she said.

'Did you do this, Hyson?'

'Do it . . . do what?'

'Lock me in.'

'But I'm locked in with you.'

'How did you come to be in here?'

'I knew something was going to happen.'

'What? How?'

'I knew. I came to meet you . . . to see if you were all right.'

'What do you mean? How could you know?'

'I do know things. Then I heard the singing . . . and the door was open . . . so I came in.'

'Before I did?'

'Only a minute before. I was hiding down at the bottom of the steps when you came in.'

'I don't understand what it means.'

'It means Barbarina's lured you in. She didn't know I was here too.'

'Barbarina's *dead*.'

'She can't rest, till you take her place.'

I was recovering my calm. It was amazing what the presence of one small human being could do.

'That's nonsense, Hyson,' I said. 'Barbarina is dead and this story of her haunting the place is just an old legend.'

'She's waiting for a new bride to die.'

'I don't intend to die.'

'We'll both die,' said Hyson, almost unconcernedly; and I thought: She knows nothing of death; she has never seen death. She had looked at the television and seen people drop to the ground. Bang! You're dead. In a child's mind death is quick and neat, without suffering. One forgot that she was only a child posing as a seer.

'That's absurd,' I said. 'We shan't. There must be a certain amount of air coming into this place. They'll miss us and there'll be search parties to find us.'

'Why should they think of looking in the vault?'

'They'll look everywhere.'

'They'll never look in the vault.'

I was silent for a while. I was trying to think who could have done this, who had been waiting for me to leave Jesse Pleydell's cottage and lure me to the vault with singing, like some cruel siren of the sea.

Someone who wanted me out of the way had done this. Someone who had waited for me to enter the vault and descend the stone steps, and then glided out from some hiding place and locked the door on me.

I was recovering rapidly from my fear and realizing that I was not afraid of human scheming; I felt myself equal to deal with that. As soon as I could rid myself of the notion that I was being lured to death by someone who was dead, I felt my natural resilience returning. I was ready to match my wits with those of another human being. I could fight the living.

I said: 'Someone locked the door. Who could it be?'

'It was Barbarina,' whispered Hyson.

'That's not reasonable. Barbarina's dead.'

'She's in here, Favel . . . in her coffin. It's on the ledge with my grandfather's beside it. She couldn't rest, and she wants to. . . . That's why she's locked you in here.'

'Who opened the door?'

'Barbarina.'

'Who locked the door?'

'Barbarina.'

'Hyson, you're getting hysterical.'

'Am I?'

'You mustn't. We've got to think of how we can get out of here.'

'We never shall. Why did she lock me in too? It's like Meddlesome Matty. Granny was always warning me. I shouldn't have come.'

'You mean that then I should have been the only victim.' My voice was grim. I was ashamed of myself. It was a terrible experience for the child; and yet it was doing me such a lot of good not to be alone.

'We shall stay here,' said Hyson, 'for ever. It'll be like "The Mistletoe Bough." When they next open the vault there'll only be our bones, for we shall be skeletons.'

'What nonsense!'

'Do you remember the night of the ball? We all talked about it.'

I was silent with a new horror, because the idea flashed into my mind that on that night when we had sat drinking soup after the ball, one member of our party may have thought of the vault as a good substitute for the old oak chest.

I shivered. Could there be any other explanation than that someone wanted *me* out of the way?

I gripped Hyson's shoulder. 'Listen,' I said. 'We've got to find a way out of this place. Perhaps the door isn't really locked. Who could have locked it anyway?'

'Bar . . .'

'Oh, nonsense.' I stood up cautiously. 'Hyson,' I said, 'we must see what we can do.'

'She won't let us.'

'Give me your hand and we'll see what it's like here.'

'We know. It's all dead people in coffins.'

'I wish I had a torch. Let's try the door again. It may have got jammed.'

We stood on the top step and beat against it. It did not budge.

'I wonder how long we've been in here,' I said.

'An hour.'

'I don't think five minutes. Time goes slowly on occasions like this. But they'll miss us at dinner. They'll start searching for us in the house and then they'll be out, searching for us. I want to look round. There might be a grating somewhere. We might shout through that.'

'There'll be nobody in the churchyard to hear us.'

'There might be. And if they come looking . . .'

I dragged her to her feet and she cowered close to me. Then together, keeping close, we cautiously descended the steps.

Hyson was shivering. 'It's so cold,' she said.

I put my arm round her and we stepped gingerly forward into the darkness. I could see vague shapes about me and I knew these to be the coffins of dead Pendorrics.

Then suddenly I saw a faint light, and feeling my way towards it discovered that there was a grating at the side of the vault. I peered through it and fancied I saw the side of a narrow trench. I knew then that a certain amount of air was coming into the vault and I felt my spirits rising. I put my face close to the grating and shouted: 'Help! We're in the vault. Help!'

My voice sounded muffled as though it were thrown back at me, and I realized that however loudly I shouted I should not be heard unless someone were standing very close to the vault.

Nevertheless I went on shouting until I was hoarse, while Hyson stood shivering beside me.

'Let's try the door again,' I said. And we made our way slowly back to the steps. Once again we forced our weights against it and still it remained fast shut. Hyson was sobbing and bitterly cold, so I took off my coat and wrapped it round us both. We sat side by side on that top step, our arms about each other. I tried to comfort her and tell her that we should soon be rescued, that this was quite different from the old oak chest. We had seen the grating, hadn't we? That meant that air was coming in. Perhaps we should hear their voices. Then we would shout together.

Eventually she stopped trembling, and I think she slept.

I could not sleep although I felt exhausted, bitterly cold, stiff and cramped; and I sat there holding the body of the child against me, peering into the darkness, asking myself over and over again: Who has done this?

There was no means of knowing the time, for I could not see my watch. Hyson stirred and whimpered; I held her closer and whispered assurances to her, while I tried to think of a plan to escape from this place.

I pictured the family coming down to dinner. How upset they would be! Where was Favel? Roc would want to know. He would be a little anxious at first and then frantic with worry. They would already have been searching for us for hours.

Hyson had awakened suddenly: 'Favel . . . where are we?'

'It's all right. I'm here. We're together. . . .'

'We're in that place. Are we still alive, Favel?'

'That's one thing I'm sure of.'

'We're not . . . just ghosts, then?'

I pressed her hand. 'There are no such things,' I told her.

'Favel, you *dare* say that . . . down here . . . among them.'

'If they existed they would surely make us aware of them, just to prove me wrong, wouldn't they?'

I could feel the child holding her breath as she peered into the darkness. After a while she said: 'Have we been here all night?'

'I don't know, Hyson.'

'Will it be dark like this all the time?'

'There might be a little light through the grating when the day comes. Shall we go and look?'

We were so stiff and cramped that we could not move our limbs for some seconds.

'Listen!' said Hyson fearfully. 'I heard something!'

I listened with her, but I could hear nothing.

I felt my way cautiously down the steps, holding Hyson's hand as we went.

'There!' she whispered. 'I heard it again!'

She clung to me and I put my arm about her.

'If only we had a lighter or a match,' I murmured as we picked our way to where I thought the grating had been, but there was no light coming from the wall, so I guessed it was still dark outside. Then I saw a sudden flash of light; I heard a voice call: 'Favel! Hyson!'

The light had shown me the grating and I ran stumbling towards it shouting: 'We're here . . . in the vault. Favel and Hyson are here in the vault!'

The light came again and stayed. I recognized Deborah's voice. 'Favel! Is that you, Favel?'

'Here,' I cried. 'Here!'

'Oh, Favel! . . . thank God! Hyson . . . ?'

'Hyson's here with me. We're locked in the vault.'

'Locked in . . .'

'Please get us out . . . quickly.'

'I'll be back . . . soon as I can.'

The light disappeared and Hyson and I stood still hugging each other.

It seemed hours before the door was opened and Roc came striding down the steps. We ran to him – Hyson and I – and he held us both against him.

'What the . . .' he began. 'You gave us a nice fright. . . .'

Morwenna was there with Charles, who picked Hyson up in his arms and held her as though she were a baby.

Their torches showed us the damp walls of the vault, the ledges with the coffins; but Hyson and I turned shuddering away and looked towards the door.

'Your hands are like ice,' said Roc, chafing them. 'We've got the cars by the lych gate. We'll be home in a few minutes.'

I lay against him in the car, too numb, too exhausted for speech.

I did manage to ask the time.

'Two o'clock,' Roc told me. 'We've been searching since soon after eight.'

I went straight to bed and Mrs. Penhalligan brought me hot soup. I said I shouldn't be able to sleep; in fact I should be afraid to, for fear I should dream I was back in that dreadful place.

But I did sleep – almost immediately; and I was untroubled by dreams.

It was nine o'clock that morning before the sun shining through the windows woke me. Roc was sitting in a chair near the bed watching me, and I felt very happy because I was alive.

'What happened?' asked Roc.

'I heard someone singing and the door of the vault was open.'

'You thought the Pendorrics had left their coffins and were having a little sing-song?'

'I didn't know who it was. I went down the steps and then ... the door was locked on me.'

'What did you do?'

'Hammered on the door – called out. Hyson and I both used all our strength against it. Oh Roc ... it was horrible.'

'Not the most pleasant spot to spend a night, I must say.'

'Roc, who could have done it? Who could have locked us in?'

'No one.'

'But someone *did*. Why, if Deborah hadn't come there looking for us we'd still be there. Heaven knows how long we should have been there.'

'We decided to search every inch of the land for miles around. Deborah and Morwenna did Pendorric village, and the Darks joined up with them.'

'It was wonderful when we heard Deborah's voice calling us. But it seemed ages before she came back.'

'She thought she needed the key, and there's only one I know of – to the vault. It's kept in the cupboard in my study, and the cupboard is locked; so she had to find me first.'

'That's why it took so long.'

'We didn't waste any time, I can tell you. I couldn't imagine who could have got at the key and unlocked the vault. The sexton borrowed it some weeks ago. He must have thought he locked it.'

'But someone locked us in.'

Roc said: 'No, darling. The door wasn't locked. I discovered that when I tried to unlock it.'

'Not locked! But ...'

'Who would have locked you in?'

'That's what I'm wondering.'

'No one has a key except me. There has only been one for years. The key was locked in my cupboard. It was hanging on the nail there when I went to get it.'

'But Roc, I don't understand how ...'

'I think it's simple enough. It was a misty evening, wasn't it? You passed the lych gate and went into the churchyard. The door of the vault was open because old Pengally hadn't locked it when he was there a few weeks ago and the door had blown open.'

'It was a very still evening. There was no wind.'

'There was a gale the night before. It had probably been open all day and no one had noticed it. Few people go to the old part of the graveyard. Well, you saw it open, and went inside. The door shut on you.'

'But if it wasn't locked why didn't it open when we pushed with all our strength?'

'I expect it jammed. Besides, you probably panicked to find yourself shut in. Perhaps if you'd not believed the door was locked you would have discovered it was only jammed.'

'I don't believe it.'

He looked at me in astonishment. 'What on earth's in your mind?'

'I don't quite know . . . but someone locked us in.'

'Who?'

'Someone did it.'

He smoothed the hair back from my forehead.

'There's only one person who could,' he said. 'Myself.'

'Oh Roc . . . *no!*'

He threw himself down beside me and took me into his arms.

'Let me tell you something darling,' he said. 'I'd far rather have you here with me than in that vault with Hyson.'

He was laughing; he did not understand the chill of fear which had taken possession of me.

Chapter Five

I could now no longer delude myself. I had to face up to all the fears which I had refused to look in the face during the last weeks.

Someone had deliberately lured me into the vault and locked me in, for I refused to believe Roc's theory that the door had jammed. In the first moments it was true that I may have panicked; but when I had discovered Hyson and sought to comfort her, I had regained my composure. We had both tried to open that door with all our strength and had failed. And the reason was that it had been locked.

This could mean only one thing. Someone wanted to harm me.

Suppose Deborah had not come by? Suppose she had not heard our call, how long could we have lived in the vault? There was a little air coming in, it was true; but we should have starved to death eventually, because it was a fact that few people came that way, and if they did we should not have heard them unless they had come close to the grating and called us.

It might have been one week . . . two weeks. We should have been dead by then.

I believed that that was what someone was trying to do: kill me, but in a way which, when my death was discovered, would appear accidental.

Who?

It would be the person who would benefit most from my death. Roc?

I couldn't believe that. I was perhaps illogical, as women in love are supposed to be; but I was not going to believe for one moment that Roc would kill me. He wouldn't kill anyone – least of all me. He was a gambler, I knew; he might even be unfaithful to me; but he could never in any circumstances commit murder.

If I died, he would be very rich. He had married me knowing that I was the granddaughter of a millionaire; he had brought me back to my grandfather, and it must have occurred to him that I would become his heir. He needed money for Pendorric, and Roc and I were partners so that my fortune would make certain that Pendorric remained entirely ours. This was all true; and whether I died or not, Pendorric was safe.

I refused to look beyond that; but I did believe that someone had locked me into the vault in the hope that I should not be discovered until I was dead.

That brought me back to the all-important question: Who?

I thought back over everything that had happened and my mind kept returning to the day when Roc had first come to the studio. My father must have known who he was as soon as he heard his name – there could not be many Pendorrics in the world – yet he had not told me. Why? Because my grandfather had not wanted me to know. Roc was to report on me first, take pictures of me. I smiled ruefully. That was typical of my grandfather's arrogance. As for Father, he had probably done everything he did for what he would believe to be my good.

And the day he died? Roc had seemed strange that day. Or had he? He had come back to the studio and left my father to bathe alone. And when he knew what had happened, had he seemed . . . relieved, or had I imagined it?

I must stop thinking of Roc in this way, because if I was going to find out who was seeking to harm me I must look elsewhere.

There had been an occasion when I had taken the dangerous cliff path after the rain, and the warning had been removed. I remembered how uneasy I had felt then. But it was Roc who had remembered the path and dashed after me. It was reassuring to remember that. But why should it be reassuring? Because it showed that Roc loved me and wanted to protect me; that he could not possibly have had a hand in this.

But of course I knew he hadn't.

Who, then?

My mind went at once to those women in whom, I believed, he had once been interested . . . perhaps still was. One could never be quite sure with Roc. Rachel? Althea? And what of Dinah Bond?

I remembered that she had once told me that Morwenna had been locked in the vault. What of the conversation I had heard between Morwenna and Charles? Oh, but it was natural that they should talk of my inheritance, that they should be pleased because Roc had married an heiress instead of a penniless girl. Why should Morwenna want to be rid of me? What difference could it make to her?

But if I were out of the way my fortune would go to Roc and he would be free to marry ... Rachel ... Althea?

Rachel had been there when we had talked about the bride in the oak chest; and if I could believe Dinah Bond, she had, long ago, locked Morwenna in the vault. She had known where to get the key; but there was only one key and Roc had that; it was an enormous key that hung in his cupboard, and the cupboard was kept locked. When they had unlocked the vault they had had to find Roc first because he had the only key.

Rachel had known this and she had managed somehow, all those years ago, to get the key from Roc's father's cupboard.

Rachel, I thought. I had never liked her from the moment I had first seen her.

I was going to watch Rachel.

Morwenna said that such an experience was bound to have shocked me, and I ought to take things easily for the next few days. She was going to see that Hyson did.

'I'd rather it had been Lowella who was locked in with you,' she told me one day when I came out of the house and saw her working on the flower-beds on one of the front lawns. 'Hyson's too sensitive as it is.'

'It was a horrible experience.'

Morwenna straightened up and looked at me. 'For both of you. You poor dear! I should have been terrified.'

A shadow passed across her face and I guessed she was remembering that occasion, so long ago, when Rachel had locked her in and refused to let her out until she made a promise.

Deborah came out of the house.

'It's a lovely day,' she said. 'I'm beginning to wonder what my own garden is looking like.'

'Getting homesick?' asked Morwenna. She smiled at me. 'Deborah's like that. When she's on Dartmoor she thinks of Pendorric, and when she's here she gets homesick for the moor.'

'Yes, I love both places so much. They both seem like home to me. I was thinking, Favel, this horrible affair ... it's been such a shock, and you're not looking so well. Is she, Morwenna?'

'An experience like that is bound to upset anyone. I expect she'll have fully recovered in a day or so.'

'I thought of going to the moor for a week or so. Why not come with me, Favel? I'd love to show you the place.'

'Oh ... how kind of you!'

Leave Roc? I was thinking. Leave him to Althea? To Rachel? And how could I rest until I had solved this matter? I must find out who had a grudge against me, who wanted me out of the way. No doubt it would be very restful to spend a week with Deborah, but all the time I should be longing to be back in Pendorric.

'As a matter of fact,' I went on, 'I've got such lots to do here . . . and there's Roc. . . .'

'Don't forget,' Morwenna reminded Deborah, 'they haven't been married so very long.'

Deborah's face fell. 'Well, perhaps some other time – but I thought that you needed a little rest and . . .'

'I do appreciate your thinking of it and I shall look forward to coming later on.'

'I wish you'd take Hyson,' said Morwenna. 'This business has upset her more than you think.'

'Well, I must take dear Hyson,' replied Deborah. 'But I did so want to show Favel our old home.'

I laid my hand on her arm. 'You are kind, and I do hope you'll ask me again soon.'

'Of course I shall. I shall positively pester you until you accept. Were you going for a walk?'

'I was just going over to Polhorgan. There are one or two things I have to see Mrs. Dawson about.'

'May I walk with you?'

'It would be a great pleasure.'

We left Morwenna to her flowers and took the road to Polhorgan. I felt rather guilty about refusing Deborah's invitation and was anxious that she should not think me churlish.

I tried to explain to her.

'Of course I understand, my dear. You don't want to leave your husband. As a matter of fact I'm sure Roc would protest if you suggested it. But one day perhaps later on you'll come for a week-end when he has to go away. He does sometimes, on business, you know. We'll choose our opportunity. It was just that I thought, after that . . .'

She shivered.

'If it hadn't been for you we might be there still.'

'I've never ceased to be thankful that I happened to go into the graveyard. It was just that I was determined to search every square inch. And when I think how chancey it was I shudder. I might have walked right round the vault and you might not have heard me, nor I you.'

'I don't like thinking of it . . . even in broad daylight. It's so extraordinary, too, that Roc says the door wasn't locked . . . only jammed. I must say I feel a little foolish about that.'

'Well, of course a door *could* get jammed.'

'But we were so desperate. We hammered with all our might. It seems incredible. And yet there's only the one key and that was locked in Roc's cupboard.'

'So,' she went on, 'the only one who could have locked you in would have been Roc.' She laughed at the ludicrous idea; and I laughed with her.

'There used to be two keys, I remember,' she went on. 'Roc's father kept one in the cupboard there where Roc keeps it now.'

'And who had the other?'

She paused for a few seconds, then she said: 'Barbarina.'

We were silent after that and scarcely spoke until we said good-bye at Polhorgan.

I had never enjoyed going to Polhorgan since my grandfather's death. The place seemed so empty and useless without him; it had an air of being unlived-in, which I always think is so depressing – like a woman whose life has never been fulfilled. Roc often laughed at me for my feeling about houses; as though, he said, they had a personality of their own. Well, at the moment Polhorgan's personality was a negative one. Of course, I thought, if I filled it with orphans who had never seen the sea, had never had any care and attention, what a different house it would be!

Idealistic dreams! I could hear Roc's voice. 'Wait until you see how the bureaucrats are going to punish you. This is the Robin Hood State, in which the rich are robbed to help the poor.'

I didn't care what difficulties I should encounter. I was going to have my orphans – if fewer than I had first dreamed of.

Mrs. Dawson came out to greet me.

'Good morning, madam. Dawson and I were wondering if you'd come; and as you have, would you be pleased to take a cup of coffee in our sitting-room? There's something on our minds. . . .'

I said I should be delighted to, and Mrs. Dawson told me she would make the coffee at once and send for Dawson.

Ten minutes later I was in the Dawsons' comfortable sitting-room, drinking a cup of Mrs. Dawson's coffee.

Dawson had some difficulty in getting to the point, which I quickly perceived was an elaboration of the suspicions which had occurred to him the night my grandfather died.

'You see, madam, it's not easy to put into words. A man's afraid of saying too much . . . then again he's afraid of not saying enough.'

Dawson was the typical butler. Dignified, and self-assured, he was the type of manservant my grandfather would have insisted on having, because he was what Roc would have called a *cliché* butler in the same way that my grandfather was the *cliché* self-made man.

'You can be perfectly frank with me, Dawson,' I told him. 'I'll not repeat anything you say unless you wish me to.'

Dawson looked relieved. 'I would not wish, madam, to be taken to the courts by the woman in question. Although if it should be true that she had been there before, that could well be counted in my favour.'

'You mean Nurse Grey?'

Dawson said that he meant no other. 'I am not satisfied, madam, about the nature of his lordship's death; and having talked together, Mrs. Dawson and I have come to the conclusion that it was brought about by a deliberate act.'

'You mean because the pills were discovered under the bed?'

'Yes, madam, his lordship had had one or two minor attacks during the day, and Mrs. Dawson and I had noticed that often attacks would follow closely on one another, so it seemed almost certain that he would have another attack some time during the night.'

'Wouldn't he call the nurse when he had these attacks during the night?'

'Only if the attack got so bad he needed morphia. Then he'd ring the bell on his side table. But first he'd take his pill. The bell was on the floor too, madam, with the pills.'

'Yes, and it looked as though he knocked them over when reaching for the pills.'

'That may have been how it was intended to look, madam.'

'You are suggesting that Nurse Grey deliberately put the pills and the bell out of his reach?'

'Only within these four walls, madam.'

'But why should she wish him dead? She has lost a good job.'

'She had a good legacy,' put in Mrs. Dawson. 'And what's to prevent her finding another job where she'll get another legacy?'

'But you're not suggesting that she kills off her patients for the sake of the leagacies they leave her?'

'It might be so, madam, and I feel impelled to explain my suspicions regarding this young woman, and they are that she is an adventuress who needs to be watched.'

'Dawson,' I said, 'my grandfather is dead and buried. Dr. Clement was satisfied that he died from natural causes.'

'Mrs. Dawson and I don't doubt Dr. Clement's word, madam; but what we think is that his lordship was hastened to his death.'

'This is a terrible accusation, Dawson.'

'I know, madam; and that is why I would not want it to go beyond these four walls; but I thought you should be warned of our suspicions, the young woman still being in the neighbourhood.'

Mrs. Dawson stared thoughtfully into her coffee cup. 'I was talking to Mrs. Greenock,' she said, 'who owns Cormorant Cottage.'

'That's where Nurse Grey is living now, isn't it?'

'Yes, having a little rest between posts, so she says. Well, Mrs. Greenock wasn't very keen on letting to her. She was really after a long let that would go on all through the winter, and Nurse Grey wanted it for what she called an indefinite period. But it seems Mr. Pendorric persuaded Mrs. Greenock to let Nurse Grey have it.'

I was beginning to understand why the Dawsons had wanted to talk to me. They were not only underlining their suspicions as to why my grandfather had died when he did, but were telling me that we had an adventuress in our midst, who was none too scrupulous, and was more friendly with my husband than they considered wise.

If they had wanted to make me feel uneasy they had certainly succeeded.

I changed the subject as inconspicuously as I could; we talked about the problems of Polhorgan, and I told them that I wanted them to go on as they were until I made up my mind what to do about the house. I assured them that I had no intention of selling and that I wanted them to remain there and hoped they always would.

They were delighted with me as their new employer. Mrs. Dawson told me so with tears in her eyes and Dawson implied, without sacrificing one part of his dignity, that it was a pleasure to serve me.

But I was very unhappy because I knew that they had spoken as they did out of a genuine concern for my welfare.

That afternoon I went to see the Clements because I wanted to talk to the doctor unprofessionally about my grandfather.

Mabell Clement was emerging triumphant from what she called the pot house when I arrived, her hair half up, half down, and she was dressed in a cotton blouse and bunchy yellow skirt.

'Nice surprise,' she declared breezily. 'Andrew will be pleased. Come in and I'll make you a cup of tea. It's been one of the most successful days I've had for a long time.'

Andrew came to the door of the house to meet me and told me that I'd come at a fortunate time because it was his afternoon off, and his partner, Dr. Lee, was on duty.

Mabell made the tea, and, because she couldn't find the cosy, put a woollen balaclava over the pot. There were toasted scones – a little burned – and a cake which had sagged in the middle.

'It tastes rather like a Christmas pudding,' Mabell warned.

'I like Christmas pudding,' I assured her.

I liked Mabell too; she was one of the few people who were unimpressed by my sudden wealth.

While we were having tea I told Dr. Clement that I was disturbed about my grandfather's death.

'Could he have lived much longer if he hadn't had that attack?' I asked.

'He could have, yes. But we had to expect such attacks, and their consequences could be fatal. I was not in the least surprised when I got the call.'

'No, but he might have been alive now if he had been able to reach his pills in time.'

'Has Dawson been talking to you again?'

'Dawson spoke to you about this, didn't he?' I countered.

'Yes, at the time your grandfather died. He found the pills and the bell on the floor.'

'If he had been able to reach his pills . . . or his bell . . .'

'It seemed perfectly clear that he had tried and had knocked them over. In the circumstances a major attack developed, and . . . that was the end.'

Mabell brought over the cake which was like a Christmas pudding and I took a piece.

'It's over now,' she said gently. 'It's only disturbing to go over something that's finished.'

'Yet I would like to know.'

'Actually I think the Dawsons didn't get on with the nurse,' Mabell went on. 'Nurses are notoriously bossy; butlers notoriously dignified; housekeepers tend to regard the house as their domain and resent anyone but their employers. I think it was just not very unusual domestic strife; and now the Dawsons see a chance of settling an old score.'

'You see,' said Andrew, 'Dawson could suggest she deliberately put the pills and bell out of reach; she would emphatically deny it. There could be no proof either way.'

'She looks like a piece of Dresden china but I reckon she's as sturdy as earthenware,' mused Mabell. 'It must have been a pleasant job she had with Lord Polhorgan. In any case she seemed to like it. How long had she been with him?'

'More than eighteen months,' said Andrew.

'Was she a good nurse?' I asked.

'Quite efficient.'

'She seemed . . . hard,' I suggested.

'She was a nurse, and as such had had some experience of suffering. Nurses . . . doctors . . . you know they can't feel the same as someone like yourself. We see too much of it.'

'I know I can trust you two,' I said, 'so I'll say this: Do you think that she discovered she would get a thousand pounds when my grandfather died and that made her hasten his death?'

There was silence. Mabell took a long amber cigarette holder, opened a silver box and offered me a cigarette.

'Because,' I said slowly, 'if she would do a thing like that, it's rather a sobering thought that she's going into other sickrooms, and the lives of other patients will be put into her hands.'

Dr. Clement watched me intently. Then he said: 'At the moment she's resting. She's taking a holiday before going to a new post, and I think it would be very unwise to talk of this matter beyond this room.'

Mabell changed the subject in her blunt way. 'I suppose you've quite recovered from that midnight adventure of yours.'

'Oh . . . yes.'

'An unpleasant experience,' commented Andrew.

'I shiver even now when I think of it.'

'The door was jammed, wasn't it?'

'I was certain that we were locked in.'

'All the rain we've been having might make the door jam,' said Andrew. 'Yet . . .'

Mabell thoughtfully knocked the ash from her cigarette. 'Who on earth would have locked you in?'

'That's what I've been wondering ever since.'

Andrew leaned forward. 'So you don't believe the door jammed?'

I hesitated. What impression was I giving them? First I was repeating Dawson's suggestions against Nurse Grey, and now I was hinting that someone had locked me in the vault. They were two intelligent, uninhibited people. They would think I had a persecution mania if I was not careful.

'The general opinion seemed to be that the door had jammed. There was only one key anyway, and that was locked in a cupboard in my husband's study. He brought it down to the vault and it was he who found the door wasn't locked at all.'

'Well, thank heaven they did discover you.'

'If Deborah hadn't happened to come that way – and it was really purest chance that she did – goodness knows how long we should have been there. Perhaps we should be there now.'

'Oh no!' protested Mabell.

'Why not? Such things have been known to happen.'

Andrew lifted his shoulders. 'It didn't happen.'

'In future,' Mabell put in, 'you must be very careful.'

Andrew leaned forward and there was a puzzled expression in his eyes.

'Yes,' he repeated, 'in future you must be very careful.'

Mabell laughed rather nervously and began to talk about a pot she had made which she thought was unusual. When it was fired she wanted my opinion.

I felt that when I was not there they would talk of my affairs. They would say it was surprising that the door of the vault had been jammed and not locked and, perhaps, that Roc had the only key. They would undoubtedly have heard that Roc had persuaded Mrs. Greenock to let Althea Grey have Cormorant Cottage; and they would ask themselves: What is happening at Pendorric?

My uneasiness was deepening.

I didn't want to talk any more about the disturbed thoughts which were turning over in my mind; I feared that I had already said too much to the Clements. I wished that I could have talked to Roc of my fears, but I imagined he would laugh at them – besides, he himself was so much involved.

I tried therefore to go on as normally as possible. So exactly a week after my unfortunate adventure I called on Jesse Pleydell again. He greeted me with more than his usual warmth and made it very clear that he was glad I had come. So he too had heard the story.

We no longer sat outside his cottage – the afternoon was too chilly. I was in his own arm-chair, which he insisted on giving up to me while he made me a cup of tea.

He did allow me to pour it out, and when we were sitting opposite each other he said: 'I was worried like when I heard 'em talking.'

'You mean about . . .'

''Twere the last time you did come and see me.'

'It was very unfortunate.'

He shook his head. 'I don't like it much.'

'I didn't either.'

'You see, it's like as though . . .'

'We decided the sexton left the door open when he was last there, and that it must have been open for some time. Nobody noticed because . . . nobody went near it.'

'Oh, I don't know,' murmured Jesse.

We were silent for some time, then he said: 'Well, me dear, I reckon you should take extra care like. I reckon you should.'

'Jesse, what are you thinking?'

'If only these old eyes hadn't been so blind I should have seen who was up there in the gallery with her.'

'Jesse, have you any idea who it was?'

Jesse screwed up his face and beat on his knee. 'I'm feared I do,' he whispered.

'You think it was Lowella Pendorric, who died all those years ago.'

'I couldn't see like. But I be feared, for she were the bride, and 'twas said after, that she was marked for death as soon as she was the Bride of Pendorric.'

'And you think that I . . .'

'I think you have to take care, Mrs. Pendorric. I think you haven't got to go where harm can come to 'ee.'

'Perhaps you're right, Jesse,' I said, and after a pause: 'Your Michaelmas daisies are looking a picture.'

'Aye, reckon so. The bees be that busy on 'em. I was always one for Michaelmas daisies, though 'tis sad to see them since it means the end of summer.'

I left him, and as I came past the cottages and saw the church ahead of me I stopped at the lych gate and looked into the graveyard.

'Hello, Mrs. Pendorric.'

There was Dinah Bond coming towards me. 'I heard about 'ee,' she said. 'Poor Mrs. Pendorric. I reckon you was scared in that place.' She was almost laughing at me. 'You should have let me read your hand,' she went on. 'I might have warned you.'

'You weren't anywhere around when it happened, I suppose?' I asked.

'Oh no. My Jim had taken me into market with him. We didn't get back till late. Heard about it next morning though. I was sorry because I can guess what it feels like to be in that dark place.' She came up to the lych gate and leaned on it. 'I've been thinking,' she went on, 'there's something strange about this. Has it struck you that things seem to be happening twice?'

'What do you mean?'

'Well, Morwenna was shut in the vault, wasn't her? And then you were, with Hyson. Looks as though someone remembered that and thought to try it again.'

'Do you think someone locked me in, then? The general belief is that the door jammed.'

'Who's to say?' She shrugged her shoulders. 'Then there was Barbarina being an heiress and marrying a Pendorric, and there was Louisa Sellick, who had to go and live near Dozmary because of it. Now there's you – awful rich, they tell me you be, Mrs. Pendorric – and you're the New Bride while . . .'

'Please go on.'

She laughed. 'You wouldn't let me read your hand, would you? You didn't believe I was any good. All right, you wouldn't believe what I could tell 'ee. But 'tis all of a piece and so seems as though it was meant, if you get what I mean.'

'I'm afraid I don't.'

She came through the lych gate and walked past me, smiling as she went.

'You be awful rich, Mrs. Pendorric,' she murmured, 'but you bain't very bright, I'd say.'

She looked over her shoulder at me; then she began to walk towards the forge, swinging her hips in the provocative way which was second nature to her.

All this did not comfort me. I was longing to have a talk with Roc and tell him what was in my mind, but something warned me not to. It was of course the fact that I was not at all sure where Roc fitted into this.

The house seemed quiet. Deborah had taken Hyson and Carrie with her to Devonshire; and Lowella had refused to do any lessons since her sister was having a holiday. 'It wouldn't be fair to Hyson,' she explained piously. 'I should go so far ahead of her that she'd never catch up.'

Morwenna, declaring that this was hardly likely, at the same time gave way, and Lowella, who had become suddenly attached to her father – her affections changed as frequently as the winds – insisted on spending a lot of time at the home farm with him.

I found myself constantly listening for the sound of singing or the playing of a violin, and I became aware that that adventure in the vault had upset me more than I cared to admit. I wanted to get away from the house to think, so I took the car one afternoon and went on to the moor.

In the first place I had no intention of going the way I had before. I merely wanted to be alone to think; and I wanted to do my thinking right away from the house, because I was beginning to suspect that the house had an effect on me, making me more fanciful than I should otherwise have been.

I drew up on a lonely stretch of moor, shut off the engine and, lighting a cigarette, sat back to brood. I went over every detail of what had happened from the first day I had seen Roc; and whichever way I looked, one thought kept hammering in my mind: He knew that I was an heiress when he married me.

Dinah Bond had marvelled how events repeated themselves. Barbarina had been married for her money when her husband would have preferred Louisa Sellick. Had I been married for mine when my husband would have preferred . . .?

It was something I refused to accept. He could never have been such a good actor as to deceive me so utterly. I thought of the passion between us; I thought of the ways in which he had made love to me. Surely that could not have been all lies. I could hear his voice coming back to me: 'I'm a gambler, darling, but I never risk losing what I can't do without.'

He had never pretended to be a saint. He had never told me that I was the first woman he had ever loved. He had not denied that he was a gambler.

What had happened that day when he went down to swim with my father? What was I thinking now! My father's death had nothing to do with all this. That had been an unfortunate accident.

I threw away my cigarette, started up the car and drove on for some miles without noticing the direction in which I was going; then suddenly I was aware that I was lost.

The moor looked so much the same whatever road one took. I could only drive on until I came to a signpost.

This I did, and when I saw Dozmary on it I discovered I was very eager to have another glimpse of the boy who looked so like Roc. After all, I told myself, Louisa Sellick had played a part in the story of Barbarina, and it seemed as though her story was very closely linked with my own.

When I reached the Pool I left the car and went down to the water's edge; it looked cold and grey and the place was deserted. Leaving the car I started to walk, until I found the road which led to the house.

I started up this, then it occurred to me that if I met the boy again he might recognize me and wonder why I had come back; and as there was another path branching from this one – nothing more than a cart track – I took this and found I was mounting a slight incline.

Now I had a good view of the front of the house, although there were several large clumps of bracken between me and the road in which it stood. I sat down beside one of these clumps and looked at the house, which I could now study at my leisure. I saw a stable, and I guessed that the boy had his own horse; there was also a garage, and the garden at the front and sides of the house was well kept. I caught a glimpse of green-houses. It was a comfortable house set in rather unusual surroundings, for it didn't appear to have any neighbours. It must be rather lonely for Louisa Sellick when the boy went away to school, which I supposed he must do. Who was the boy? Her son? But he would be too young. He couldn't be more than thirteen or fourteen; surely Petroc Pendorric had been dead longer than that.

Then who was the boy? That was another of those questions which I didn't want to think too much about. There was beginning to be quite a number of them.

Suddenly the door of the glass-roofed porch opened and someone came out. It was the boy again. I could see the resemblance to Roc even from where I was. He seemed to be talking to someone in the house; then she came out. I think I must have cowered into the bracken, for I was suddenly afraid of being recognized, because the woman who had come out of Bedivere House was Rachel Bective.

She and the boy walked towards a car, and I recognized it as the little grey Morris from the Pendorric garages.

She got into it, and the boy stood waving while she drove away.

In a moment of panic it occurred to me that she might pass my car and recognize it. I ran down the cart track, and as I came to the main road I was relieved because she had gone in a direction away from where my car was parked.

I walked slowly back and drove thoughtfully home.

Why, I asked myself, was Rachel Bective visiting the boy who was so obviously a Pendorric?

Deborah and Hyson and Carrie returned to Pendorric after a few days. I thought the child looked pale and that the holiday had not done her much good.

'She misses Lowella,' Morwenna told me. 'They're never completely happy apart although they quarrel almost all the time when they're together.'

Deborah smiled sadly. 'When you're a twin you understand these things,' she said. '*We* do, don't we, Morwenna?'

'Yes, I suppose so,' replied Morwenna. 'Roc and I were very close always, though we rarely quarrelled.'

'Roc would never take the trouble to quarrel with anyone,' murmured Deborah. She turned to me: 'My dear, you're not looking as well as I should like to see you. You should have come with us. My moorland air would have done you the world of good.'

'Oh come, it's not as good as our sea air surely,' laughed Morwenna.

'It's change that's good for everyone.'

'I'm so glad you've come back,' I told Deborah. 'I've missed you.'

She was very pleased. 'Come up with me. I've brought you a little present from home.'

'For me! How charming of you!'

'It's something I treasure.'

'Then I shouldn't take it.'

'You must, my dear. What point would there be in giving you something I want to get rid of?'

She slipped her arm through mine and I thought: Perhaps I can ask Deborah. Not outright, of course, but perhaps indirectly. After all, she would know what was happening better than most people.

We went up to her bedroom, where Carrie was unpacking.

'Carrie,' cried Deborah, 'where's the little gift I brought for Mrs. Pendorric?'

'Here,' said Carrie without looking at me.

'Carrie hates leaving her beloved moor,' Deborah whispered to me.

She was holding out a small object wrapped in tissue paper. I opened it, and although it was one of the most exquisite things I had ever seen, I was dismayed. For in a frame set with jade and topaz was a delicate miniature of a young girl, her hair falling about her shoulders, her eyes serene.

'Barbarina,' I whispered.

Deborah was smiling down at the lovely face. 'I know how interested you have always been in her and I thought you'd like to have it.'

'It's a beautiful thing. It must be very valuable.'

'I'm so glad you like it.'

'Is there one of *you*? I would rather have that.'

My words evidently pleased her, for she looked very beautiful suddenly. 'People always wanted to paint Barbarina,' she said. 'Father invited lots of artists to the house – he was interested in the arts – and they used to say: "We must paint the twins, and we'll begin with Barbarina." They sometimes did; and when it was my turn, they forgot. I told you, didn't I, that she had something that I lacked. It drew everyone to her – and because I was so like her, I seemed like a pale shadow . . . a carbon copy, you might say, a little blurred, much less attractive.'

'Do you know, Deborah,' I said, 'you underrate yourself. I'm sure you were every bit as attractive.'

'Oh Favel, what a dear child you are! I feel so grateful to Roc for finding you and bringing you to us.'

'It's I who should be grateful. Everyone's been so kind to me . . . particularly you.'

'I? Boring you with my old photographs and chatter about the past!'

'I've found it immensely interesting. I want to ask you lots of things.'

'What's stopping you? Come and sit in the window. Oh, it *is* good to be back. I love the moor, but the sea is more exciting, perhaps. It's so unpredictable.'

'You must have missed the moor when Roc and Morwenna were young and you were looking after them.'

'Sometimes, but when they went away to school I'd go to Devonshire.'

'Did they go to Devon for school holidays?'

'Almost always they were at Pendorric. Then of course Morwenna started bringing Rachel for holidays, and it seemed to be a natural thing that she should come to us every time. Morwenna was extraordinarily fond of her for some reason. And she wasn't really a pleasant child. She locked Morwenna in the vault, once. Just for fun! *You* can understand how terrified poor Morwenna was. She had a nightmare soon after it happened and told me about it when I went in to comfort her. But it didn't make any difference to the friendship, and when Roc and Morwenna went to France, Rachel went with them.'

'When was that?'

'It was when they were older. They would have been about eighteen then. I always hoped that Morwenna would drop her, but she never did. And at that time the three of them became very friendly.'

'When they were about eighteen . . .'

'Yes. Morwenna was anxious to go to France. She wanted to improve her accent; and she said she'd like to go for two months. She had finished at her English boarding school and I was thinking that she might go abroad to school; but she said it would be much better for her to stay in some *pension* where she would learn the language, by mixing with people, more easily than she ever would at school.'

'And Morwenna went to France for two months.'

'Rachel went with her. So did Roc for a while. I was a bit alarmed at that time. Roc was with them so much and I was beginning to be afraid that he and Rachel . . .'

'You wouldn't have welcomed . . . that?'

'My dear, I expect I'm being rather mean, but somehow I should not have liked to see Rachel mistress of Pendorric. She hasn't the . . . charm. Oh, she's an educated girl, but there's something I don't like about her . . . something I don't altogether trust. This is strictly between ourselves, of course! I wouldn't say it to anyone else.'

'I think I know what you mean.'

'She's too sharp. One gets the idea that she's watching for the main chance all the time. I expect it's my stupid imagination, but I can tell you I had some very deep qualms at that time, because Roc was so anxious to see the girls settled in their *pension* comfortably. And he actually stayed there for a while and went back and forth while they were there. Every time he returned I was terrified that he would announce his intentions. Fortunately it all fell through.'

'It was a long time ago,' I said.

Deborah nodded.

I was thinking. They were eighteen, and the boy could be about fourteen now. Roc is thirty-two.

I had often felt that Rachel had some hold on the Pendorrics. She gave that impression. She was like a person with a chip on her shoulder and yet at the same time there was a certain truculence about her. It was as though she was continually implying: Treat me as a member of the family or else. . .!

And she visited the boy who was living with Louisa Sellick!

I said: 'I suppose at that time their father was dead . . . I mean Roc's and Morwenna's.'

'They were about eleven when he died. It was six years after Barbarina. . .'

So the boy was not his, I thought. Oh Roc, why do you keep these secrets from me? There's no need.

My impulse was to talk to Roc at the earliest opportunity, to tell him what I had conjectured.

When I went to my room I put the miniature on the mantelshelf and stood for some minutes looking into the serene eyes depicted there.

Then I decided to wait a while, to try to find out more about the nature of this web in which I was becoming entangled.

In the midst of this uncertainty Mabell Clement gave a party. When Roc and I drove over, we were both a little subdued; I felt weighed down with thoughts of the boy who lived on the moors, and conjectures as to what part Roc had played in bringing him into the world. I longed to talk to Roc and yet I was afraid to do so. Actually I was afraid to face up to the fact that Roc might not tell me the truth. I was pathetically eager that he should not lie to me, and at the same time I was desperately trying to keep intact that wonderful happiness which I had known.

As for Roc, he was telling himself that my adventure in the vault had naturally upset me a good deal and that I should need time to recover.

He treated me gently, and reminded me of those days immediately following my father's death.

Mabell, ear-rings swinging, was a wonderful hostess and there was an informal atmosphere about the party. Several of the local artists were present, for our scenery had made the district an artists' colony; and I was gratified when one of them mentioned my father and spoke with reverence of his work.

From the other side of the room I heard Roc's laughter and saw that he was the centre of a group, mainly women. He seemed to be amusing them, and I wished that I was with them. And how I wished that there were no more doubts and that I could escape from my misgivings into that complete and unadulterated happiness which no one on earth but Roc could give to me.

'Here's someone who wants to meet you.' Mabell was at my elbow and with her was a young man. I looked at him for some seconds before I recognized him.

'John Poldree, you remember?' he said.

'Why yes. The ball ...'

Mabell gave him a little push towards me and then was gone.

'It was a wonderful ball,' he went on.

'I'm so glad you enjoyed it.'

'And very sad of course that ...'

I nodded.

'There was something I wanted to tell you, Mrs. Pendorric. Though I don't suppose it matters much now.'

'Yes?'

'It's about the nurse.'

'Nurse Grey?'

'M'm. Where I'd seen her before.'

'And you remember?'

'Yes. It was something in one of the papers. It came back to me. Then I remembered that I was in Genoa at the time and it wasn't all that easy to get English papers. Having fixed the date I went and looked up old copies. She's the one all right. Nurse Althea Stoner Grey, Nurse Stoner Grey, she was called. If I'd heard the double-barrelled name I'd have remembered. But I couldn't mistake the face. It's rarely that you find a face as perfect as that one.'

'What did you find out?'

'I'm afraid I misjudged her. I'd got it into my head that she'd committed some crime. Hope I didn't give you the wrong impression. All the same it wasn't very pleasant. She was lucky to have a name like Stoner Grey. She could drop the first part and seem like a different person. After all, Grey's a fairly common name. Coupled with Stoner, far from it. She lost the case.'

'What was the case, then?'

'She'd been nursing an old man and he'd left her money; his estranged wife contested the will. It was only a few paragraphs and you know how disjointed these newspaper reports can be.'

'When did all this happen?'

'About six years ago.'

'I expect she's had a case or two in between that and coming to my grandfather.'

'No doubt of it.'

'Well, she must have brought good references to my grandfather, I imagine. He was the sort who would make sure of that.'

'That wouldn't be difficult with a woman like that. She's got a way of getting round people. You can see that. She's pretty hard-boiled, I should think.'

'I should think so too.'

He laughed. 'I wanted to tell you ever since I solved the mystery. I expect she's far away by now.'

'No. She's still living fairly near us. She's taking a little holiday and renting a cottage for a time. My grandfather left her a small legacy, so she probably feels she can afford a rest.'

'Must be a lucrative job – private nursing – providing you have the foresight to choose rich patients.'

'Of course, you couldn't be sure that they would conveniently die and leave the legacy.'

He lifted his shoulders. 'Smart woman, that one. I think she'd be the sort who'd choose with care.' He had picked up one of the pieces of pottery which were lying about the studio. 'Good, this,' he said.

And for him the subject was closed; but not for me. I could not get Nurse Grey out of mind, and when I thought of her I thought of Roc.

I was very quiet during the drive back to Pendorric.

I had noticed a change in Morwenna; there were days when she gave me the impression that she was walking in her sleep; and her dreams seemed to be happy ones, for at times her expression was almost rapturous. She was absent-minded, too, and I had on one or two occasions spoken to her and received no answer.

She came up to our room one evening when we were changing for dinner. 'There's something I want to tell you two.'

'We're all ears,' Roc told her.

She sat down and did not speak for a few seconds. Roc looked at me, his eyebrows raised.

'I didn't want to say anything to any of you until I was absolutely sure.'

'The suspense is becoming unbearable,' commented Roc lightly.

'I've told Charles, of course, and I wanted to tell you two before it became generally known.'

'Are we soon to hear the patter of little feet in the Pendorric nurseries?' asked Roc.

She stood up. 'Oh . . . Roc!' she cried, and threw herself into his arms. He hugged her and then began waltzing round the room with her. He stopped abruptly with exaggerated concern. 'Ah, we have to take great care of you now.' He released her and putting his hand on her shoulder kissed her cheek solemnly. 'Wenna,' he said, reverting to his childhood's name for her, 'I'm delighted. It's wonderful. Bless you.'

There was real emotion in his voice, and I was touched to see the affection between them.

'I knew you'd be pleased.'

I felt as though I were shut out of their rejoicing; and it occurred to me how very close they were, because Morwenna seemed to have forgotten my existence and I knew that when she had said she wanted to tell us first she had meant she had wanted to tell Roc. Of course, they were twins, and how true it was that the bond between twins was strong!

They suddenly seemed to remember me, and Morwenna immediately brought me into the picture.

'You'll think we're crazy, Favel.'

'No, of course not. I think it's wonderful news. Congratulations!'

She clasped her hands together and murmured: 'If only you knew!'

'We'll pray for a boy,' said Roc.

'It must be a boy this time – it must.'

'And what does old Charles say?'

'What do you think! He's rapturous. He's already thinking up names.'

'Make sure it's a good old Cornish name, but we don't want any more Petrocs about the place for a while.'

Morwenna said to me: 'After all these years. It does seem marvellous. You see, we've always wanted a boy. . . .'

We all went down to dinner together, and after the meal Roc proposed the health of the mother-to-be, and we all became quite hilarious.

Next day I had a talk with Morwenna, who had become more friendly, I thought; I liked her new serenity.

She told me that she was three months pregnant and had started to plan the child's layette; and she was so certain that it was going to be a boy that I was a little afraid for her, because I realized how disappointed she would be if it should be a girl.

'You probably think that I'm behaving like a young girl about to have her first baby,' she said with a laugh. 'Well, that's how I feel. Charles wanted a boy so much . . . and so do I, and I always felt I was letting him down in some way by not producing one.'

'I'm sure he didn't feel that.'

'Charles is such a *good* man. He would never show resentment. But I know he longed for a son. I'll have to be careful nothing goes wrong. It did about five years ago. I had a miscarriage and was very ill, and Dr. Elgin, who was here before Andrew Clement, said I shouldn't make any more attempts . . . not for some time in any case. So you see how we feel.'

'Well, you must take the greatest care.'

'Of course one can take too much care. Some people think you should carry on as normally as possible for as long as possible.'

'I'm sure you'll be all right; but suppose it should be a girl?'

Her face fell.

'You'd love it just the same,' I assured her. 'People always do.'

'I should love her, but it wouldn't be the same. I long for a boy, Favel. I can't tell you how I long for a boy.'

'What name have you decided to give him?' I asked. 'Or haven't you thought of that?'

'Charles is insisting that if it's a boy we call him Ennis. It's a name that's been given to lots of Pendorrics. If you and Roc have a son you'll call him Petroc. That's the custom: the eldest son of the eldest son. But Ennis is as Cornish as Petroc. It's rather charming, don't you think?'

'Ennis,' I repeated.

She was smiling, and the intensity of her expression disturbed me.

'He's certain to be Ennis,' she went on.

I turned to the book of baby patterns which was lying on her lap and expressed more interest in it than I really felt.

So even Morwenna's news added to my uneasiness. Ennis was a family name; and the boy on the moor had the looks as well as the name; Morwenna had taken Rachel away and Roc had been at hand to help make arrangements;

he had visited them during their sojourn abroad, and Deborah had been afraid that Roc was going to marry Rachel.

I thought I was controlling my suspicions, but I couldn't hide them from Roc.

One day he announced that he was going to take me out for the day. I mustn't imagine I knew Cornwall just because I had seen our little corner; he was going to take me farther afield.

There was an autumnal mist in the air when we left Pendorric in the Daimler, but Roc assured me that it was only the pride of the morning; the sun would break through before long; and he was right.

We drove on to the moor, and then turned northward and stopped at a country hotel for lunch.

It was over this meal that I realized Roc had brought me out to talk seriously to me.

'Now,' he said, filling my glass with Chablis, 'let's have it.'

'Have what?'

'What's on your mind?'

'On my mind?'

'Darling, innocence, in this case, is unbecoming. You know perfectly well what I mean. You've been looking at me for the last week or so as though you're wondering whether I'm Bluebeard and you're my ninth wife.'

'Well, Roc,' I replied, 'although you're my husband and we've been married quite a few months, I don't always feel I know you very well.'

'Am I one of those people who don't improve on acquaintance?'

As usual he caught me up in his mood; and I was already beginning to feel gay and that my suspicions were rather foolish.

'You remain . . . mysterious,' I told him.

'And it's time you began to clear up the mysteries, you're thinking?'

'As you're my husband I don't think there should be secrets between us.'

He gave me that disarming smile which always touched me deeply. 'Nor do I. I know what's disturbing you. You discovered that I haven't lived the life of a monk before my marriage. You're right in that. But you don't want details of every little peccadillo, do you?'

'No,' I told him, 'not every one. Only the important ones.'

'But when I met you I realized that nothing that had happened to me before was of the slightest significance.'

'And you haven't taken up the old way of life since you married me?'

'I can assure you that I have been faithful to you in thought and deed. There! Satisfied?'

'Yes, but . . .'

'So you're not?'

'There are people who seem to regard you in a certain way and I wondered whether they realize that any relationship which existed between you is now . . . merely friendship.'

'I know. You're thinking of Althea.'

'Well?'

'When she first came here to look after your grandfather I thought her the most beautiful woman I had ever seen. We became friends. The family was always urging me to marry. Morwenna had been married for years and they all implied that it was my duty to marry, but I had never felt that I wanted to settle down with any woman.'

'Until you met Althea Grey?'

'I hadn't actually come to that conclusion. But shall we say the idea occurred to me as a possibility.'

'And then my grandfather asked you to come and have a look at me, and you thought I was the better proposition?'

'That sounds a little like your grandfather. There was no question of "propositions." I had already decided that I did not want to marry Althea Grey, *before* your grandfather suggested I should come and look at you. And when I did see you, it happened. Just like that. You were the only one from then on.'

'Althea couldn't have been very pleased.'

He lifted his shoulders. 'It takes two to make a marriage.'

'I begin to understand. You must have come very near to being engaged to Althea Grey before you changed your mind. And what about Dinah Bond?'

'What about Dinah? She assisted in the education of most young men in the district.'

'I see. Not serious?'

'Absolutely not.'

'And Rachel Bective?'

'Never!' he said almost fiercely. He filled my glass. 'Catechism over?' he asked. 'Favel, I'm beginning to wonder whether you aren't somewhat jealous.'

'I don't think I should be jealous . . . without reason.'

'Well, now you know there is no reason.'

'Roc . . .' I hesitated and he urged me to go on. 'That boy I saw at Bedivere House . . .'

'Well?'

'He's so like the Pendorrics.'

'I know; you told me before. You're not imagining that he's the living evidence of *my* sinful past, Favel!'

'Well, I did wonder who he was.'

'Do you know, darling, you haven't enough to do. At the week-end I want to go out to one of the properties on the north coast. Come with me. We'll be away a couple of nights.'

'That will be lovely.'

'Something else on your mind?' he asked.

'So many things are not clear. In fact when I go back to the first time I saw you . . . it seems to me that that was when everything began to change.'

'Well obviously things couldn't be the same for either of us after we'd met. We were swept off our feet.'

'No, Roc. I didn't mean that. Even my father seemed to change.'

He looked grave suddenly; and then he seemed to come to a decision.

'There are certain things you didn't know about your father, Favel.'

'Things *I* didn't know.'

'Things he kept from you.'

'But he didn't. He always confided in me. We were so close . . . my mother, he and I.'

Roc shook his head. 'For one thing, my dear, he didn't tell you that he had written to your grandfather.'

I had to agree that this was so.

'Why do you think he wrote to your grandfather?'

'Because he thought it was time we met, I suppose.'

'Why should he think that was the time when for nineteen years he hadn't considered it necessary? I didn't want to tell you, Favel. In fact, I'd made up my mind not to . . . for years. I was going to wait until you were fifty. A nice cosy grandmother with the little ones playing at your knee. Then it would have seemed too far away to be painful. But I've come to the conclusion – in the last half-hour that there shouldn't be secrets between us.'

'I'm certain there shouldn't be. Please tell me what you know about my father.'

'He wrote to your grandfather because he was ill.'

'Ill? In what way?'

'He had caught your mother's disease through being with her constantly. She wouldn't go away from him, or he from her; they wanted to pretend that there was nothing wrong. So they stayed together and he was her only nurse until she was so very ill. He told me that if she had gone away she might have lived a little longer. But she didn't want to live like that.'

'And he too. . . . But I was never told.'

'He didn't want you to know. He was very anxious about you. So he wrote to your grandfather telling him of your existence. He hoped that your grandfather would ask you to Cornwall. He himself would have stayed in Capri; and when he became really ill you wouldn't have been there.'

'But he could have had attention. He could have gone to a sanatorium.'

'That's what I told him. That's what I believed he would do.'

'He told you all this . . . and not his own daughter!'

'My darling, the circumstances were unusual. He knew of me, and as soon as I turned up at the studio he knew why I had come. It would have been too much of a coincidence for a Pendorric to arrive only a month or so after he had sent off his letter to Polhorgan. Besides, he knew your grandfather's methods. So he guessed at once I had been sent to look round.'

'You told him, I suppose.'

'I had been asked by Lord Polhorgan not to, but it was impossible to hide it from your father. However, we agreed that we would say nothing to you, and that I should write and tell him what I had seen; then he would presumably write to his granddaughter and invite her to England. That was what your father hoped. But, as you know, we met . . . and that was enough for us.'

'And all the time he was so ill . . .'

'He knew that he was on the point of becoming *very* ill. So he was delighted when we said we were going to get married.'

'You don't think that he was made a little uneasy by it?'

'Why should he be?'

'You knew that I was the granddaughter of a millionaire.'

Roc laughed. 'Don't forget he'd had some experience of your grandfather. The fact that you were his granddaughter didn't mean that you would inherit his fortune. He might have taken an acute dislike to you, and me as his son-in-law, in which case you would have been "cut off with a shilling." No, your father was delighted. He knew I'd take care of you; and I fancy he was happier to think of you in my care than in your grandfather's.'

'I thought he was worried about something . . . just before he died. I thought he was uneasy . . . about *us*. What really happened on the day when you went down to bathe?'

'Favel, I think I know why your father died.'

'Why . . . he died?'

'He died because he no longer wished to live.'

'You mean . . .?'

'I believe he wanted a quick way out, and found it. We went down to the beach together. It was getting late, you remember. There were few people about; they were all having lunch behind the sun blinds; soon they would be deep in the siesta. When we reached the beach he said to me: "You know you'd rather be with Favel." I couldn't deny it. "Go back," he said, "leave me. I would rather go in alone." Then he looked at me very solemnly and said: "I'm glad you married her. Take care of her." '

'You're suggesting that he deliberately swam out to sea and had no intention of coming back?'

Roc nodded. 'Looking back, I can see now that he had the look of a man who has written "The End" to his life. Everything was in order.'

I was too filled with emotion to trust myself to speak. I could see it all so clearly; that day when Roc had come back to the kitchen and sat on the table watching me, his legs swinging, the light making the tips of his ears pink. He didn't know then what had happened, because it was only afterwards that one realized the significance of certain words . . . certain actions.

'Favel,' said Roc, 'let's get out of here. We'll drive out to the moor and we'll stop then and talk and talk. He trusted me to care for you, to comfort you. You must trust me too, Favel.'

When I was with Roc I believed everything he said; it was only when I was alone that the doubts set in.

If only my father had confided in me, I would never have let him do what he did. I would have cared for him, brought him to England; he could have had the best possible attention. There was no need for him to die so soon.

But had it been like that?

When I was alone I faced the fact that the talk with Roc had not really eased my fears; it had only added to them.

I couldn't help feeling that some clue to the solution of my problem might lie in that house near Dozmary Pool, and I found myself thinking of it continually – and the boy and the woman who lived there.

Suppose I called on Louisa Sellick. Why shouldn't I? I could tell her who I was; and that I had heard of her connection with Pendorric. Or could I, considering the nature of that connection?

I had caught a glimpse of her and she had appeared to be a kindly and tolerant woman. Could I go to her and say that I was constantly being compared with Barbarina Pendorric and that I was interested in everyone who had known her?

Scarcely.

And yet the idea that I should go kept worrying me.

Suppose I pretended I had lost my way. No, I didn't want to pretend.

I would go and find a reason when I got there.

I took out the little blue Morris which I had made a habit of driving and which was now looked upon as mine, and I went out to the moor.

I knew the way now and was soon passing the Pool and taking the second-class road which led to the house.

When I pulled up I was still undecided as to what I should say. What I really wanted to ask was: 'Who is the boy who is so like the Pendorrics?' And how could I do that?

While I was looking at the house the door of the glass-roofed porch opened and a woman came out. She was elderly and very plump; she had evidently seen me from a window and had come out to inquire what I wanted.

I got out of the car and said 'Good morning' as she approached.

I began: 'My name is Pendorric. Mrs. Pendorric.'

She caught her breath and her rosy face was immediately a deeper shade of red.

'Oh,' she said. 'Mrs. Sellick bain't here to-day.'

'I see. You're . . ?'

'I'm Polly that does for her.'

'You've got a wonderful view here,' I said conversationally.

'Us don't notice it much. Been here too long, I reckon.'

'So . . . Mrs. Sellick is not at home to-day.'

'She's taking the boy back to school. She'll be away to-night, back to-morrow.'

I noticed that the woman was trembling slightly.

'Is anything wrong?' I asked.

She came closer to me and whispered: 'You ain't come for to take the boy away, have 'ee?'

I stared at her in astonishment.

'You'd better come in,' she said. 'We can't talk here.'

I followed her over the lawn to the porch, and into a hall; she threw open the door of a cosy sitting-room.

'Sit down, Mrs. Pendorric. Mrs. Sellick would want me to give you something, like. Would you have coffee or some of my elderberry wine?'

'Mrs. Sellick didn't know I was coming. Perhaps I shouldn't stay.'

'I'd like to be the one to talk to you, Mrs. Pendorric. Mrs. Sellick, she'd be too proud like. She'd say, 'Yes . . . you must do what you wish . . .' and then when you'd gone she'd break her heart. No, I've often thought I'd like the chance to do the talking if this day ever come, and it seems like Providence that it has come when her's off with the boy.'

'I think there's some misunderstanding. . . .'

'There's no misunderstanding, Mrs. Pendorric. You're from Pendorric and 'tis what she's always feared. She's often said: "I made no conditions

then, Polly, and I'll make none now." She talks to me about everything. I
knew her from the first . . . you see. I came with her when she first came
to Bedivere. That was when he married. So we've been through a lot
together.'

'Yes, I see.'

'Well, let me get you some coffee.'

'I'd rather not. Mrs. Sellick might not be very pleased if she knew I'd
come in like this.'

'Her's the sweetest, mildest creature I ever saw, and I don't mind telling
you I've often thought her too mild. The likes of her gets put upon. But I
couldn't bear it to happen, see. Not twice in one lifetime . . . first losing *him*
and then the boy. It 'ud be too much. Well, she's had him since he were
three weeks old. She were a changed woman when Mr. Roc brought him
here.'

'Mr. Roc . . .!'

She nodded. 'I remember the day well. It was getting dusk. I reckon they'd
waited till then. They'd come straight from abroad. . . . Mr. Roc was driving
the car and the young woman was with him . . . nothing more than a girl,
though I didn't see much of her. Wore a hat pulled down over her face
. . . didn't want to be seen. She carried the baby in and put him straight into
Mrs. Sellick's arms; then she went back to the car and left Mr. Roc to do
the talking.'

Rachel! I thought.

'You see, she felt guilty like. She'd loved Mr. Roc's father and had thought
he was going to marry her. So he would have done, it was said, but the
Pendorrics wanted money in the family so he married that Miss Hyson
instead. He never gave up Louisa, although there were others too, but she
were the one he really cared for, and when his wife died he begged her to
marry him. But she wouldn't – for some reason. She used to think that
because his wife had died as she did it wouldn't be right. Then he was away
a lot but he came back to see Louisa. No one could be to him what she were.
You're a Pendorric yourself now and you've heard tell of all this, so there's
no need for me to repeat it. When he died she were heartbroken, and she
always longed for a child of his . . . even though 'twould have been born out
of wedlock. She took an interest in those twins of his and they were a
mischievous pair. They'd heard about their father and this house and they
came out once to have a look at Louisa. That was after he was dead; and
she brought them in and gave them cakes and tea. And after that they came
now and then. She told them that if they were ever in trouble – and they
were the kind who might be . . . of course, they've sobered down now, but
'twas different when they were young – she'd help them if it were in her
power. Well then she got this letter from Mr. Roc. Here was trouble all
right. A baby on the way and could she help?'

'I see.'

'Of course she could help. She wanted to help. So she took little Ennis
and she's been as a mother to him ever since. It was a turning point like. She
began to be happy again when that little boy came into this house. But she
never stopped being afeared. You see, he grew up such a beautiful child and

he weren't hers. She'd take no money for what she did; she'd make no conditions. So you see, she was always afraid that one day Mr. Roc would come and claim that boy. When she heard he was married she was certain he'd want the boy. . . . She was terrible frit, I can tell 'ee. And I'm telling 'ee all this because I've got to make 'ee *see*.'

'Did he come to see the boy?'

'Yes. He comes every now and then. Terrible fond of him he be, and the boy of him.'

'I'm glad that he didn't desert him entirely.'

'No question of that. But it's puzzling. The Pendorrics were never ones to care much about scandal. There was his father coming to see Louisa. Didn't keep it as dark as some thought he should. But I reckon it was because Mr. Roc was so young. Not much more than seventeen and Louisa advised him not to let it be known . . . for the boy's sake. He's known as Ennis Sellick and thinks Louisa's his aunt.' She stopped and looked at me beseechingly. 'Please, Mrs. Pendorric, you look kind . . . please understand that he have been here nigh on fourteen years. You can't take him now.'

'You mustn't worry about that,' I told her. 'We have no intention of taking him.'

She relaxed and smiled happily. 'Why, when you said as who you were . . .'

'I'm sorry I frightened you. As a matter of fact it was very wrong of me to call. My visit was one of curiosity. I'd heard of Mrs. Sellick and wanted to meet her. That was all.'

'And you won't take the boy?'

'No, certainly not. It would be too cruel.'

'Too cruel,' she repeated. 'Oh thank 'ee, Mrs. Pendorric. It'll be a weight off our minds. Now won't you let me give you a cup of coffee? Mrs. Sellick wouldn't like you to leave without.'

I accepted the invitation. I felt I needed it. While Polly was in the kitchen I was thinking: How can I trust him again? If he could deceive me about the boy, he could about other things. Why hadn't he told me? It would have been so much easier.

Polly returned with the coffee; she was quite happy now; at least my visit had done much to restore her contentment. She told me how she and Louisa had grown to love the moor, and how difficult it was to cultivate the garden, which was so stony.

'Moorland country bain't the most fertile ground, Mrs. Pendorric, I do assure you,' she was saying, when we heard the sound of a car drawing up outside the house.

'Why, it can't be Mrs. Sellick back already,' said Polly, rising and going to the window.

Her next words sent the blood drumming in my ears. 'Why 'tis Mr. Pendorric,' she said. 'Oh dear, I reckon he thought they wasn't going till to-morrow.'

I stood up, and my knees were trembling so much that I thought they would give way as I heard Roc's voice. 'Polly, I saw the car outside. Who's here?'

'Oh, you've come to-day, Mr. Pendorric,' answered Polly blithely. 'Well, Mrs. Sellick thought it 'ud be better to take two days over the driving, seeing it's so far. They'm staying in London and then they'll go on to the school to-morrow. Reckon you thought they wouldn't be leaving till to-day.'

He was coming through the glass-roofed porch; striding into the sitting-room in the manner of someone who well knows the way.

He threw open the door and stared at me. 'You!' he said; then his expression darkened. I had never seen him so angry.

We stood staring at each other and I think he felt the same about me as I did about him; that we were both looking at a stranger.

Polly came into the room. 'Mrs. Pendorric's been telling me as you won't want to take the boy away. . . .'

'*Has* she?' he said; and his eyes took in the used coffee cups.

'I was that relieved. Not that I thought you'd do it, Mr. Roc. It was that pleasant meeting your bride.'

'I'm sure it was,' Roc answered. 'You should have waited, darling, until I drove you over.'

His voice sounded quite cold, as it had never been before when he spoke to me.

'And you came to-day unbeknownst to each other, and there's two cars outside. Well it *is* a day!'

'Yes,' echoed Roc almost viciously, 'it *is* a day.'

'I'll heat up this coffee, Mr. Roc.'

'Oh, no thanks, Polly. I came to see the boy before he went to school, but I'm too late. Never mind. I've met my wife instead.'

Polly laughed. 'I'm sorry Mrs. Sellick didn't warn you, but she doesn't care about telephoning the house, as you know.'

'I know,' said Roc. He turned to me. 'Are you ready to go?'

'Yes,' I said. 'Good-bye, Polly, and thank you for the coffee.'

'It's been a pleasure,' said Polly.

She stood at the door smiling as we went out to the cars. Roc got into his, I into mine. I drove off and he followed me.

Near that bridge where it was said Arthur fought his last fight against Sir Mordred, Roc drove ahead of me and pulled up. I heard the door of his car slam and he came to stand by mine.

'So you lied to me,' I said.

'And you saw fit to pry into matters which are no concern of yours.'

'Perhaps they are some concern of mine.'

'You are quite wrong if you think so.'

'Shouldn't I be interested in my husband's son?'

'I would never have believed you'd do anything so petty. I had no idea I'd married a . . . spy.'

'And I can't understand why you should have lied. I should have understood.'

'How good of you! You are of course extremely tolerant and forgiving, I'm sure.'

'Roc!'

He looked at me so coldly that I shrank from him. 'There's really nothing more to be said, is there?'

'I think there is. There are things I want to know.'

'You'll find out. Your spy system seems excellent.'

He went to his car, and drove on towards Pendorric; and I followed him home.

Back at Pendorric, Roc only spoke to me when necessary. I knew that he was planning his trip to the north coast, but there was now no question of my going with him.

It was impossible to hide from the household that we had quarrelled, because neither of us was good enough at hiding our feelings; and I was sure they were all rather curious.

The next few days seemed unbearably long and I had not felt so wretched since the death of my father. Two days after that disastrous visit to Bedivere I went into the quadrangle and sat under the palm tree thinking ruefully that the summer was nearly over, and with it the happiness I had believed was mine.

The sun was shining but I could see the spiders' webs on the bushes, and beautiful as the Michaelmas daisies and chrysanthemums were they did underline the fact that winter was on the way. But because this was Cornwall, the roses were still blooming; and although the hydrangeas did not flower in such profusion, there were still some to brighten the quadrangle.

One of the twins must have seen me for she came out and began to walk unconcernedly towards the pond, humming as she came.

'Hallo,' she said. 'Mummy says we're not to sit on the seats because they're damp. We'll catch our deaths if we do. So what about you?'

'I don't think it's really damp.'

'Everything's damp. You might get pneumonia and die.'

I knew this was Hyson, and it occurred to me that since our adventure in the vault her attitude towards me had changed; and perhaps not towards me only; it seemed that she herself had changed.

'It would be one way. . . .' she said thoughtfully.

'One way of dying, you mean?'

Her face puckered suddenly. 'Don't talk of dying,' she said. 'I don't like it . . . much.'

'You're becoming awfully sensitive, Hyson,' I commented.

She looked thoughtfully up at the east windows as though watching for something.

'Are you expecting someone?' I asked.

She did not answer.

After a while she said: 'You must have been very glad that I was in the vault with you, Favel.'

'It was rather selfish of me, but I was.'

She came nearer to me and putting her hands on my knees, looking into my face. 'I was glad I was there too,' she said.

'Why? It wasn't very pleasant and you were horribly scared.'

She smiled her odd little smile. 'Yes, but there were two of us. That made a difference.'

She stepped back and put her lips in the position to suggest whistling. 'Can you whistle, Favel?'

'Not very well.'

'Nor can I. Lowella can.'

She stopped, looking up at the east windows.

'There it is,' she said.

It was the sound of the violin.

I stood up and caught Hyson's wrist. 'Who is it?' I asked.

'You know, don't you?'

'No, I don't. But I'm going to find out.'

'It's Barbarina.'

'You know Barbarina's dead.'

'Oh Favel, don't go in there. You know what it means. . . .'

'Hyson! What do you know? Who is playing the violin? Who locked us in the vault? Do you know that?'

For the moment I thought I saw a madness in the child's eyes, and it was not a pleasant sight. 'It's Barbarina,' she whispered. 'Listen to her playing. She's telling us she's getting tired. She means she won't wait much longer.'

I shook her a little because I could see that she was near hysteria. 'I'm going to find out who's playing that violin. You come with me. We'll find this person together.'

She was unwilling but I dragged her to the east door. As I opened it I could distinctly hear the sound of a violin.

'Come on,' I said, and we started up the stairs. The violin had stopped playing, but we went on to Barbarina's room; I threw open the door. The violin was lying on the chair; the music was still on the stand. The room was just as it had been when I had last seen it.

I looked at Hyson, but she had lowered her eyes and was staring at the floor.

I was more frightened than I had ever been, because never before had I felt so utterly alone. First I had had my parents to care for me; then – as I thought – a husband; finally a grandfather.

I had lost them all, for now I could no longer rely on Roc to protect me from the danger which I felt was close.

Chapter Six

Roc left for his week-end trip.

Before he went he said to me, when we were in the bedroom together: 'I don't like this at all, Favel. We've got to get it sorted out. I wish you hadn't gone snooping. It's all at such an unfortunate time.'

He was almost his old self and I immediately swung round to meet him half-way. Eagerly I waited for what he would say next.

'There's a simple explanation to all this,' he said. 'But I can't tell you yet. Will you wait a while and trust me?'

'But Roc . . .'

'All right,' he said. 'You can't. But this isn't going on. I'll think about it while I'm away; but promise me this: You won't think too badly of me, will you? I'm really not quite such a scoundrel as you believe I am.'

'Oh Roc,' I said, 'it's all so unnecessary. There was no need to tell me lies. I just wish you hadn't.'

'And you can't trust someone who has once lied, can you?'

He looked at me wistfully and I had the impression that he was trying to charm me as he had so many times before.

'Roc, tell me about it,' I pleaded. 'Tell me now. Then we can start being happy again.'

He hesitated. 'Not now, Favel.'

'But why not now?'

'It isn't only my affair. I've got to discuss it with someone else.'

'Oh, I see.'

'But you don't see. Listen, Favel. I love you. And you've got to love me too. You've got to trust me. Damn it, can't you have a little faith in me?'

I couldn't make myself say yes.

'All right.' He put his hands on my shoulders and gave me a swift kiss on the lips with nothing warm or passionate about it. 'See you on Monday or Tuesday.'

Then he was gone, leaving me as baffled and unhappy as before – or almost.

But the fact that he was away did give me an opportunity to think; and several little incidents from the past kept recurring to me. I had been in danger of losing my life on two occasions since coming to Pendorric; which was strange because it was within a very short time, and it was something which had never happened to me before in the whole of my life. I was thinking of that time when someone had removed the danger signal on the cliffs. But then it had been Roc who had *saved* me. At that time I had not known I was Lord Polhorgan's granddaughter. But Roc had, and if I had died then, Roc would have inherited nothing.

A horrible thought came to me. Was it meant to shift suspicion? Was the idea that, when later I had a fatal accident, people would remember how Roc had saved me then?

No, that was a hideous thought. I was suggesting that Roc had deliberately locked me in the vault and planned to leave me there!

It was as though my personality had split into two; there was part of me which was determined to defend Roc and prove him innocent, and another equally as determined to prove him guilty.

Who else could have locked the door of the vault? Who else could have come along and unlocked it and then pretended that it was jammed? Who else had a motive for wanting to be rid of me? On my death Roc would inherit my grandfather's fortune and be free to marry whomsoever he wished. Who would that be? Althea Grey?

Then I thought of what Polly had said that morning in Bedivere House: when Barbarina was dead, Roc's father had wanted to marry Louisa.

While I was brooding on these things there came a knock on the door and Morwenna came in. For a moment I felt envious of her radiant happiness.

'Oh hallo, Favel. I hoped I'd find you here.' She looked at me anxiously. 'Roc seems to have gone off in a bit of a huff. Why don't you make it up?'

I was silent and she shrugged her shoulders. 'It's unlike him,' she went on. 'Usually with him it's a big flare-up and then everything's as it was before. Yet this thing of yours seems to have been going on for days.'

'You mustn't let it bother you,' I said.

'Oh, I don't. It'll work itself out, I expect. But an annoying thing has happened. I've had to leave my car at the garage and I was wondering if you were using the Morris this morning.'

'Please have it,' I said. 'I can go to Polhorgan – I've got to go some time, and I don't need a car to go there.'

'Are you sure? I want to go into Plymouth. Dr. Clement says I've got to rest every day. He's going to be a bit fussy about me, so I thought I'd do a bit of knitting. It'll be something to do while I put my feet up. I want to get wools and patterns and there's so little to choose from here.'

'Do take the Morris and don't worry about me.'

She came over to me and, unexpectedly, kissed me. 'Things will soon be all right between you and Roc, I know,' she said.

When she had gone I left at once for Polhorgan. There was no sense in sitting about and brooding; I went by way of the coast road and tried to stop thinking of Roc's duplicity by planning the orphans' home I might one day have at Polhorgan.

When I arrived, Mr. and Mrs. Dawson came out to greet me, and I could tell by their portentous manner that they had been eagerly looking forward to telling me something.

I was taken to the sitting-room and given coffee, and then it came out.

'We wouldn't mention this, madam, but for the fact that Mrs. Penhalligan has been having a word with Mrs. Dawson, and that has somewhat coloured our views in the matter. It is a delicate subject, madam, and Mrs. Dawson and I trust that you will understand that it is only in our endeavour to serve you . . .'

I was anxious to cut short the circumlocution so I said: 'Oh yes, of course, I understand, Dawson.'

'Then, madam, I will tell you. I did not care to mention this before because I feared it might reflect on . . . one whom it was not my place to mention. But since Mrs. Penhalligan has spoken to Mrs. Dawson . . .'

'Please tell me all about it, Dawson.'

'Well, madam, Dr. Clement was so certain that his lordship died from natural causes and discouraged us from bringing forward what actually happened. There was no inquest, the cause of death being considered natural. But there is a way of hastening death, madam, and Mrs. Dawson and I have long been of the opinion that his lordship was hurried to the grave.'

'Yes, I know the bell and the box were on the floor, but he might very well have knocked them over when he was reaching for them.'

'So he might, madam; and who is to say he didn't? One cannot make suppositions in a court of law. But Mrs. Dawson overheard a conversation between his lordship and the nurse on the morning of the night he died.'

'Oh! What conversation?'

'His lordship threatened to dismiss her if she continued to see Mr. er . . .' Dawson coughed apologetically. 'Mr. Pendorric.'

I wanted to protest, but my throat seemed to have closed up and would not let my voice come through. I had had enough. I could not bear any more revelations.

'And it seems, madam, rather coincidental that not many hours later his lordship should be unable to reach his pills. Mrs. Dawson and I do not forget, madam, that a legacy was mentioned in that will for the nurse who was in his lordship's employ at the time of his death. . . .'

I was scarcely listening to them. I was thinking: How many lies has he told me? He did admit that he was almost engaged to Althea Grey. Then he had heard of my existence. He had married me as his father had married Barbarina. How much was he influenced by the past? It was as though we were actors in some obscure drama, playing the same parts which had been played before.

Barbarina had been married to bring money into Pendorric when her husband had been in love with Louisa Sellick. Had I been married for the same reason when *my* husband was in love with Althea Grey? Who was the vague shadow sensed by Jesse Pleydell on that day when Barbarina fell to her death? Was it her husband, Petroc Pendorric?

I'm becoming hysterical, I thought. I'm letting my imagination run away with me.

I should never have believed this of Roc before that scene in Bedivere House.

Now my thoughts would not be controlled. Had Althea Grey deliberately removed the pills, hoping to hasten his death? For he had to die, before I could inherit his money; and now . . . I had to die before it was theirs.

I wondered what gossip was going on all around me. Mrs. Penhalligan had talked to Mrs. Dawson. Did they all know, then, of the trouble between Roc and me? Did they know the reason?

The Dawsons were looking at me with concern and compassion. Were they warning me that Roc and Althea Grey were lovers? Were they suggesting that, since the nurse had had no compunction in hastening my grandfather to his death, she and her accomplice might have none in hastening me to mine?

I said: 'It was very unfortunate that my grandfather should have imagined these things. I think perhaps being such an invalid he was apt to worry over non-existent troubles. I have heard that it is a symptom of the illness he had.'

The Dawsons looked at me sorrowfully. Mrs. Dawson would have continued to speak, but Dawson was too much of a diplomatist to allow it. He lifted a hand and she was silent.

On his face was the expression of a man who can be satisfied that he has done his duty.

When I left Polhorgan I was afraid I should not be able to keep up my façade of serenity. I was too restless. There were so many things I wanted to find out and I had to go into action; one thing I could not endure was inactivity.

I wanted to talk to someone and I believed if Morwenna had not gone to Plymouth I should have sought her out and confided everything in her. There was Deborah. I could talk to her.

I hurried back to the house and went to Deborah's room. She was not in. Uncertainly I came down to the hall again, telling myself that it would be easier to think out of doors, when the hall telephone began to ring.

When I answered it there was a low chuckle at the other end of the line.

'Ah, I was hoping I'd catch you. This is Althea Grey.'

I was startled because she was so much in my thoughts and I was growing more and more certain that she was playing a big part in the tangle.

'I was wondering if you'd come and see me before I go.'

'Before you go?'

'Yes, I'm leaving very soon. To-morrow.'

'You mean leaving altogether?'

'Come along and I'll tell you all about it. I've been wanting to have a talk with you for some time. When can you?'

'Why . . . now.'

'Suits me.' Again there was that low laugh and she rang off.

I hurried out of the house, out along the coast road; and in due course came to Cormorant Cottage.

It was aptly named; even now the gulls were swooping and soaring about the little cove which lay below, and I saw some cormorants. The cottage itself was perched on a rock which jutted out over the sea; it was small and painted blue and white, and there was a steep path which led up to it. It was the ideal summer cottage.

'Hallo!' One of the windows was thrown up. 'I've been watching for you. I'll come down.'

I started up the path which was almost overgrown with St. John's Wort, and by the time I reached the door Althea was standing there.

'I'm just packing.'

'You're leaving?'

'M'm. Do come in and sit down.'

I stepped straight into a room with casement windows which looked on to the sea. It had clearly been furnished for renting with only the essentials, and everything in drab colours which wouldn't show the dirt.

'Rather a change from Polhorgan,' she commented, and held out a cigarette case while she looked at me with what seemed like amusement.

'Nice of you to come and see *me*.'

'I might say it was nice of you to ask me.'

'I was lucky to catch you in.'

'I'd only just come in. Roc's away for a few days.'

'Yes, I know.'

I raised my eyebrows, and again that flicker of amusement crossed her face. 'Grape-vine,' she said. 'You can scarcely move in this place without everyone knowing all about it. Did anyone see you come in here?'

'No. Why . . . I don't think so.'

'Because if someone did there'd be speculation, you bet.'

'I had no idea you were leaving Cornwall so soon.'

She shrugged her shoulders. 'The season's over. It's lonely. You walk for miles along the cliffs without meeting anyone. You see, you didn't meet anyone coming here from Pendorric. Not my cup of tea. By the way, would you like one?'

'No, thanks.'

'Coffee?'

'No, thank you. I can't stay long.'

'A pity. We've never had a real cosy chat, have we? And it's so peaceful here. I've often thought you were rather suspicious of me. I'd like to put that right.'

'Suspicious? What do you mean?'

'Now you're playing innocent.'

'I should like to know why you asked me here. I thought you had something to tell me.'

'I have. And this is the time to tell. You see, I've got another job and I like to tidy everything up before I go.' She stretched out her long slim legs and regarded them with satisfaction. 'Rich old gentleman going on a world tour needs a nurse in constant attendance. Rich old gentlemen seem to be my speciality.'

'Don't rich young ones ever come your way?'

'The trouble with the young is that they don't need nurses.' She burst into laughter. 'Mrs. Pendorric, you *are* uneasy.'

'Uneasy?'

'Well, this is a lonely spot and I don't believe you have a very high opinion of my character. You're beginning to regret coming and are wondering how you can quietly slip away. Yet you came of your own free will, remember. In fact, you jumped at it when I asked you. It wasn't really very wise, was it? You're here and nobody knows you've come. You're rather rash, Mrs. Pendorric. You act on the spur of the moment. Do come and look at my view.'

She took my hand and pulled me to my feet. She was strong and I remembered in that moment that Mabell Clement had said she only *looked* as though she were made of Dresden china.

She drew me to the window, holding my arm in a firm grip, while with her free hand she threw open the casement window. I looked down at the sheer drop to the sea. A long way below, the waves were breaking on the jagged rocks.

'Imagine,' she said, her voice close to my ear, 'someone falling from this window! Not a chance. It wouldn't do to let this cottage to anyone with sleep-walking tendencies or to someone who was planning a little homicide.'

For a few seconds I really believed that she had lured me here to kill me. I thought: She has planned this . . . so that the way will be free to Roc and my grandfather's fortune.

That she read my thoughts was obvious; but what I saw in her face was amusement as she released my arm.

'I think,' she said slowly, 'that you would be more comfortable sitting down.'

'What was your object in asking me here?' I demanded.

'That's what I'm going to tell you.' She almost pushed me on to the dingy settee and sat in the arm-chair opposite me.

'Mrs. Pendorric,' she said, 'you can stop being scared. I only intend to talk. You really shouldn't worry about me, you know. In a few days I shall have gone right away from this place.'

'Are you sorry to be going?'

'It's a mistake to be sorry. Once a thing's over it's done with. You were always a little jealous of me, weren't you? There's no need to be. After all, you married him, didn't you? It's true he did think of marrying me once.'

'What about you?'

'Certainly. It would have been a good marriage. I don't know whether it would have suited me; though I like adventure. But it's true I'm just past thirty now, so perhaps it is time I began to think about settling down.'

'You seem to find life . . . amusing.'

'Don't you? You should. It's the only way to live it. I've made a decision, Mrs. Pendorric; I'm going to tell you all you came to hear.'

She was laughing at me, and strangely enough I was ready to believe whatever she told me: for although she seemed tough and extremely worldly, experienced and capable of almost anything, she did seem truthful – largely because she would find it more amusing to tell the truth than lies.

'What were you doing before you came to Polhorgan?' I asked.

'Nursing, of course.'

'As Nurse Stoner Grey?'

She shook her head. 'In my last case I was Grey. Stoner Grey before that.'

'Why did you drop Stoner?'

'Unpleasant publicity. Not that I minded, but it might not have been easy to get the kind of job I wanted. People have long memories. So you knew about the Stoner Grey incident. Those Dawsons told you, I bet.'

'They were a bit vague about it. It was . . . someone else.'

She nodded. 'If all had gone well I might never have had to take up nursing again. There was nothing wrong with it. The old gentleman made a will in my favour; but they found he was *non compos mentis* . . . and his wife won the case.'

'I suppose you persuaded him to make that will.'

'Well, what do you think?' She leaned forward. 'You're a nice woman, Mrs. Pendorric, and I'm . . . not so nice. You see I didn't have your advantages. No nice millionaire for a grandfather. I wasn't really the sort of girl to marry into Pendorric. I'm an adventuress because I like adventure. It adds a spice to life. I lived the early part of my life in a back street and I didn't like that much. I was determined to break away. . . . I was like your grandfather in my way. I hadn't got the business flair, though. I didn't know how to set about earning millions. But it wasn't long before I found out that I was beautiful, and that's one of the best assets a girl can have. I took up nursing, and I intended to go into private nursing, which was a way of getting what I wanted. And I saw that I got the right jobs, too. That's why I came to look after your grandfather.'

'You hoped that *he* would leave you his money?'

'One can always hope. Then there was Roc. Adventuresses always weigh up all the possibilities, you know.'

'Roc must have seemed the more hopeful of the two, surely . . . when you got to know my grandfather.'

She laughed again. 'He did. But then he's too shrewd. He saw through me. He liked me, yes. And I liked him. I'd have liked him if he'd been one of the fishermen here. But he always held back; he seemed to be aware of something in me which . . . well, how shall we say? . . . wasn't quite what a gentleman looks for in his wife – not Roc's kind anyway. So we were good friends and then he went away and when he came back he'd married you. He's got a kind heart. He wanted to be friends still, and didn't want me to feel snubbed. That was why he was extra nice to me. But I saw you were getting a little jealous.' She laughed. 'All clear now?'

'Not quite,' I said. 'How did my grandfather die?'

She looked at me very intently and seemed more serious than she had during the whole of our interview.

'I have admitted to you that I look out for chances to improve my lot,' she said firmly, 'but I'm not a murderess. I've always believed that other people's lives mean as much to them as mine does to me. If I can get the better of people . . . all well and good. But I do draw the line at murder.' Once again the smile was in her eyes. 'So that's why you were so alarmed when you came in! Then I'm doubly glad you came. I want to clear up *that* little point before I go away. Your grandfather often mislaid his little box. He did so once when you were with him. Don't you remember?'

I did remember. I had left Polhorgan early and found her with Roc on Pendorric beach.

'He dropped the pills; it agitated him that he could not find them when

he needed them; and in that agitation he knocked over the bell. That was
how he died, Mrs. Pendorric. I'd be ready to swear it. He was, it's true, in
rather an agitated state. He was worried about you. He knew that at one
time your husband and I had been friendly and he spoke to me about it. It
upset him, although I assured him that there was nothing beyond friendship
in our relationship. But to worry over imaginary details is a feature of his
complaint. But I do assure you that I did nothing intentionally to hasten his
death.'

'I believe you,' I said, because I did.

'I'm glad. I shouldn't have liked you to think me capable of *that*. Most
other things . . . yes. But not murder.' She yawned and stretched her arms.
'Just think, in a month's time I'll be heading for the sun . . . when the mists
swirl round Pendorric and the south-west gales batter the walls of Polhorgan.
I've got loads of packing to do.'

I rose. 'Then I'd better go.'

She came to the door of the cottage with me, and when I had walked
down the path we said good-bye. She stood at the door watching me.

My encounter with Althea Grey had been rather bewildering, for she had
been embarrassingly frank. I had believed her while I was sitting with her,
but now I wondered whether she had been amusing herself with my
gullibility.

Was she really going away? At least she was not with Roc, and there was
some measure of comfort in that.

The day seemed to stretch out endlessly before me. I did not want to go
back to Pendorric, but there seemed nothing else to do. I thought I would
go now and find Deborah and talk to her, not that I was really anxious to
confide, even in her.

As I came towards the house Mrs. Penhalligan, who must have seen me
approaching, came running out. She was very agitated and could scarcely
speak coherently.

'Oh, Mrs. Pendorric, there's been an accident. . . .'

My heart missed a beat and then began to gallop to make up for it. Roc!
I thought. I ought to have been with him. . . .

'It's Miss Morwenna, ma'am. She's had an accident in her car. It was the
hospital that phoned.'

'Morwenna . . .' I breathed.

'Yes, it happened on Ganter Hill. They've taken her to Treganter
Hospital.'

'She's . . .?'

'They say it's very serious. Mr. Chaston's already gone.'

'I see.'

I felt bewildered. I could not think what I should do for the best.

'The twins . . .?' I began.

'Miss Bective is with them. She's told them.'

Deborah drove up at that moment. She got out of her car and called to
us: 'Isn't it warm this morning? Hallo . . . is anything wrong?'

I said: 'There's been an accident. It's Morwenna. She was driving in to Plymouth.'

'Is it bad? Is she hurt?'

I nodded. 'Charles has gone to Treganter Hospital. It's rather serious, I think.'

'Oh my God,' murmured Deborah. 'And Hyson . . . and Lowella?'

'They're with Rachel. She'll look after them.'

Deborah put her hands over her eyes. 'This is terrible.' There was a sob in her throat. 'At such a time. I wonder how badly hurt she is. It'll be tragic if this has harmed the child.'

'Do you think we ought to go to the hospital?'

'Yes,' said Deborah. 'Let's go at once. Poor Charles! Get in, Favel. It isn't very far.'

Mrs. Penhalligan stood watching us as we drove away.

Deborah looked grim and I thought: She loves Morwenna like a mother; and indeed it was natural that she should, for she had brought up Roc and his sister after their mother had died.

'I expect she was thinking of the child,' murmured Deborah. 'We ought not to have let her drive. She's been so absent-minded lately.'

'I could have driven her into Plymouth,' I said.

'Or I. Why did she want to go, anyway?'

'For knitting-wool and patterns.'

'It's so ironical. She's longed for another child, and because of it . . .'

I had suddenly remembered, and the memory struck me like a blow.

'Deborah,' I said slowly, 'Morwenna wasn't driving her own car. She was using the little blue Morris which I usually drive!'

Deborah nodded. 'But she'd driven it before. Beside, she has always been such a good driver.'

I was silent. The coincidence did not seem to impress Deborah as it did me. I was almost afraid to examine my thoughts.

I shook them off. I was becoming unnerved. At least first of all I must wait to hear what had caused the accident.

And if by any chance something in the car had gone wrong, should I be foolish to imagine that it was due to tampering, that someone, believing I should use the car, had done something which made an accident inevitable? I was not such an experienced driver as Morwenna. What would have happened if I had been in that car this morning?

Deborah had laid a hand on mine.

'Favel, we mustn't anticipate trouble dear. Let us hope and pray that she'll come through.'

That was a strange day of brooding horror. Morwenna's life was in danger; I believed mine was too, for I was certain that what had happened to her that day had been part of a plan and no accident, and that someone not very far from me was angry because the wrong person had walked into the trap.

There had been a witness of the accident. It had happened on Ganter Hill – not a very steep hill as Cornish hills go, but rather a long one which sloped gradually into Treganter. One of the local people had seen the car; there was no other involved. Suddenly it had begun to roll about the road, the steering clearly out of control; a glimpse had been caught of the frightened woman at the wheel as the car wobbled downhill and crashed into a tree.

In the late afternoon the hospital rang up, and as a result Charles took the twins to see Morwenna. Deborah and I went with them, at Charles's request. Quite clearly he feared what he would find when we arrived there.

Deborah and I did not go in to see Morwenna, because she was very weak and only her immediate family were allowed to see her.

I shall never forget Hyson's face as she came out. It was so pale, and seemed shrivelled so that she looked like an old woman. Lowella was crying; but Hyson shed no tears.

Charles told us that Morwenna's condition was still very serious, that he was going to stay at the hospital and wanted us to take the twins home; so I drove, while Deborah sat at the back, a twin on either side of her, her arms about them holding the sobbing Lowella and the silent Hyson.

When we reached Pendorric, Rachel and Mrs. Penhalligan were waiting to hear the news.

We were all very silent and upset, and Mrs. Penhalligan said we should try to eat something. We went into the winter parlour, and when we were there Hyson suddenly cried out: 'Her head was all bandaged. She didn't know me. Mummy didn't know me! She's going to die . . . and death's horrible!'

Deborah put her arms about the child. 'There, my darling, hush. You're frightening Lowella.'

Hyson broke free. Her eyes were wild and I could see that she was on the verge of hysteria. 'She should be frightened. We all should. Because Mummy's going to die and I . . . I hate it.'

'Mummy will get better,' Deborah comforted.

Hyson gazed straight before her for a few seconds and then suddenly her eyes were on me. She continued to stare at me, and Deborah, noticing this, took the child's head and held it against her breast.

'I'm going to take Hyson up to my room,' she said. 'She'll stay with me to-night. This has been terrible . . . terrible.'

She went out of the room, her arms about Hyson; but Hyson had turned once more to stare at me.

'I hate it . . . I hate it . . .' she cried.

Deborah gently led her away.

Roc came home at once, his business uncompleted, and when I saw him I realized again the depth of his affection for his sister. He was stunned by what had happened, and seemed to have forgotten all about our strained relationship.

The next days were spent in going to the hospital, although only Charles and Roc were allowed to see Morwenna. Deborah was wonderful with the twins, and I felt that Hyson needed a good deal of care during those days. I had not guessed how deep was her feeling for her mother.

It was three days after the accident when we heard that Morwenna would probably recover; but she had lost her baby; and she had not yet been told this.

I remember driving Charles home from the hospital after he had been given that information; he was very upset and talked to me more intimately than he ever had before.

'You see, Favel,' he said, 'it meant so much to her. I wanted a son, naturally; but she seemed to have a sort of obsession about it. And now there won't be any more children . . . ever. That much they can tell me.'

'As long as she recovers . . .' I whispered.

'Yes, as long as she recovers there mustn't be any more regrets.'

When we knew that Morwenna was out of danger Roc went away again. There was nothing he could do at home, he said; either he or Charles had to attend to business, and in the circumstances it was for Charles to remain at Pendorric, close to Treganter.

During the last days I had been so immersed in the tragedy of Morwenna's accident that I had not thought very much about my own position, but as soon as Roc had gone my fears began to return, especially as it seemed firmly established that it was some unusual fault in the steering that had been responsible for the accident; and I knew very well that there had been nothing wrong with the car when I had used it the day before.

I spent a sleepless night after Roc had gone, and the next morning Mabell Clement telephoned me and asked if I would come over and have morning coffee with her. She had sounded rather agitated, and when I arrived at Tremethick, Mabell took both my hands in a firm grip and said: 'Thank heaven you've come.'

'What's wrong?' I wanted to know.

'I've scarcely slept all night thinking of you. Andrew's very worried. We were talking about you nearly all last night. We don't like it, Favel.'

'I don't understand. What don't you like?'

'You know, or perhaps you don't . . . but I assure you he is, I mean Andrew. He's the most level-headed person I've ever known. And he's not satisfied. He thinks this is too much of a coincidence to be ignored.'

'You mean . . .'

'Sit down. I've got the coffee made. Andrew will be in at any moment. At least he's going to try to be. But young Mrs. Pengally's baby's due, so it's possible he'll be detained. If he is, *I've* got to make you see.'

'I've never seen you so agitated, Mabell.'

'I don't think I've ever *felt* so agitated. I've never before known anyone who's in danger of being murdered.'

I stared at her in horror, because I knew what she meant; and the fact that the thought was in her mind as well as mine gave it substance.

'We've got to be logical, Favel. We've got to look this thing right in the face. It's no use saying 'This sort of thing couldn't happen here . . . or to me.' That's what everybody says. But we know such things do occur. And you happen to be very rich. People envy money more than anything. They're ready to kill for it.'

'Yes, I think you're right, Mabell.'

'Now listen, Favel. Someone locked you in that vault and intended to keep you there, where your cries wouldn't be heard, and you would have died of fright or starvation or something. That was the plan.'

I nodded.

'If Miss Hyson hadn't happened to come that way and hear you call, you might still have been there . . . at least your body might . . . with that of the little girl.'

'I think you're right.'

'Well, suppose there was an explanation of that. Suppose the door did jam as they said it did . . .'

She paused, and I thought: As Roc said it did. Oh Roc . . . not you. That would be more than I could bear.

'. . . well, I suppose that's possible,' she continued. 'But what is so strange is that, not so long after, the car which you were expected to be driving should be involved in this accident. When Andrew and I heard what had happened we were quite stunned. You see the same idea occurred to us both.'

I tried to speak steadily. 'You think that the . . . person who locked me in the vault, tampered with the car?'

'I think two accidents like that can't be merely chance.'

'There was another.' I told her about the notice on the cliffs. 'Roc happened to remember, and came after me.'

I knew what was in her thoughts, because her mouth hardened and she said: 'It wasn't all that dangerous. It wasn't like the vault . . . and the car.'

'Still, someone did move the board. It might have been someone who knew I was at Polhorgan. And then of course there's this violin-playing and singing, and the story of the Brides.'

'As I said, we don't like it. We're very fond of you, Favel – myself and . . . Andrew. I think that someone is trying to harm you and it's someone at Pendorric.'

'It's a ghastly thought, and now that Roc's away . . .'

'Oh, so he's away?'

'Yes, he went last week-end on business and he came back when he heard about the accident. He's had to go back now.'

Mabell stood up. That hard expression was in her face again, and I knew whom she suspected.

'That nurse has left Cormorant Cottage,' she said.

'I knew she was going.'

'I wonder where she is now?'

We were silent for a few minutes, then Mabell burst out: 'I just don't like the thought of your being at Pendorric.'

'But it's my home.'

'I think you ought to get away for a bit . . . to sort things out. Why don't you come and stay here for a night or two? We could talk, and you'd feel safe here.'

I looked round the room with the pictures (which Mabell has been unable to sell) on the walls and examples of her handiwork in evidence over the brick fireplace.

It certainly seemed like a haven. I should feel perfectly at peace here. I should have time to think about what had happened, to talk about it with Mabell and Andrew; but there was no real reason why I should stay with them.

'It would seem so odd,' I began.

'Suppose I was going to paint your portrait. Would that give us an excuse?'

'Hardly. People would say I could easily come over for sittings.'

'But we hate the thought of your being there. We're afraid of what's going to happen next.'

I thought of Roc, going away on business; this time he had not suggested that I should go with him. So why shouldn't I stay with friends?

'Look,' said Mabell, 'I'll drive you back and you can pack a bag. Just your night things.'

She was so determined and I felt so uncertain that I allowed her to get out the car and drive me back to Pendorric.

When we reached the house I said: 'I'll have to explain to Mrs. Penhalligan that I shan't be home for a night or so. I'll tell her about the picture . . . only I must say it seems rather strange in the midst of all this trouble.'

'Stranger things have been happening,' said Mabell firmly.

I went up to my room and put a few things into a bag. The house seemed very quiet. I felt dazed, as I had since I had talked to Mabell. I was certain now that someone was determined to kill me; and that it could happen while I was in Pendorric. The playing of the violin, the singing – they had been the warning signs; someone had tried to unnerve me, to make me believe this story of the woman who was trying to lure me into the tomb to take her place.

But ghosts did not have keys to vaults; they did not tamper with cars.

My bag was packed. I would go down to the kitchen and tell Mrs. Penhalligan. If Morwenna had been here I should have explained to her that I was staying with the Clements for a while. I didn't want to disturb Charles. Of course I could tell Deborah.

I went along to her rooms. She was there reading when I entered, and as she looked at me the serenity faded from her face. She sprang to her feet. 'Favel, you're upset.'

'Well everything's been so upsetting.'

'My dear child.' She took my hand and led me to the window-seat. 'Sit down and tell me all about it.'

'I've just come to tell you that I'm spending a night or two with the Clements.'

She looked surprised. 'You mean the doctor and his sister?'

'Yes. Mabell's going to paint my portrait.' Even as I said the words I thought how puerile they sounded. She would know that I was making an excuse to leave Pendorric. She had always been so kind to me and I was sure she would understand if I explained to her. It was insulting to her intelligence not to tell her the truth, I felt. So I blurted out: 'As a matter of fact, Deborah, I want to get away. If it's only for a day or so I want to get away.'

She nodded. 'I understand. Things haven't been going quite smoothly between you and Roc and you're upset. And coming on top of all this . . .'

I was silent and relieved when she went on: 'It's perfectly understandable. It'll do you good, dear, to get away for a while. I feel the same myself. This anxiety about Morwenna has been . . . terrible. And now we know that she'll be all right we realize how tensed-up we've been, and we begin to feel the effects of the shock. So you're going to the Clements.'

'Yes. Mabell suggested it. I've just packed a bag.'

Deborah frowned. 'My dear, I suppose it's wise.'

'Wise?'

'Well, it's not as though Mabell's there alone, is it? You see, this is a small place and there's a lot of gossip. Quite absurd, of course, but there it is . . . and I've noticed . . . and I expect other people have too . . . that the doctor is rather interested in you.'

I felt myself flushing hotly. 'Dr. Clement!'

'He's quite young and people are so ready to talk. You might say there's always gossip about Pendorrics, and so there is. The men I mean. It's different with the women. Unfair of course, but that's the way of the world. The women have to be beyond reproach. Because of the children, my dear. This is ridiculous. It's really quite absurd, but so is the gossip and the scandal that goes on in this place. You must please yourself, Favel, but I don't really think that . . . in the circumstances . . . it would be wise for you to go to Tremethick.'

I was amazed; then I remembered the eager friendship of the Clements. Andrew Clement had always shown pleasure in my company; Mabell knew this. Was that why she had been so friendly with me?

'I'm sure Mabell Clement would understand if it were put to her,' said Deborah. 'Let's go to her and bring her in and explain.'

We did. Mabell looked surprised when we asked her in, but Deborah put the case very tactfully and, although Mabell quite clearly didn't agree, she made no attempt to persuade me.

'It's this place.' said Deborah, waving a hand. 'All small places are the same, I suppose. So little happens that people look for drama.'

'I shouldn't have said so *little* happens at Pendorric,' put in Mabell. 'Favel was shut in the vault and Morwenna has a crash that is almost fatal.'

'Such happenings give people a taste for more drama,' said Deborah. 'No, I'm certain it would be wrong. You see, my dears, suppose Favel is going to have her portrait painted, why shouldn't she come over every day?' She turned to me. 'Now if you do want to get away, dear, I'll take you to Devon for a week-end. Why not? You've always wanted to see my house. We could leave to-morrow if you liked. How would that be?'

'I'd like that,' I said.

Mabell seemed satisfied although disappointed that I was not going back with her.

'What more natural than that we should get away for a night or two,' said Deborah smiling. 'Then you'll be back by the time your husband returns.'

'It would be a . . . respite,' I said.

And Mabell agreed.

When Mabell had gone, Deborah told Charles what we planned. He thought it was an excellent idea. Rachel Bective was there to look after the twins; and he thought that by the time we returned we should know when Morwenna was leaving the hospital.

'My dear,' said Deborah, 'I don't see why we shouldn't leave to-day. Why wait till to-morrow? If you're ready to go, I am.'

I was very eager to get away from Pendorric because it was firmly in my mind that the menace which I felt close to me was somewhere in that house.

I collected together the things which I should need and Deborah went off to ask Carrie to do the same for her. Then Deborah brought her car round to the west porch, and Carrie came down with the bags.

As we drove round the side of the houe the twins came out of the north door.

They ran up to the car.

'Hallo, Granny Deb,' said Lowella. 'Hallo, Bride. We're going to see Mummy this afternoon. Daddy's taking us to the hospital.'

'That's wonderful, darling,' said Deborah, stopping to smile at them. 'Mummy will soon be home.'

'Where are you going?' demanded Lowella.

'I'm taking Favel to show her my house.'

Hyson had gripped the side of the car. 'Let me come with you.'

'Not this time, darling. You stay with Miss Bective. We'll be back soon.'

'I want to come. I want to be there. I don't want to stay here . . . alone,' said Hyson on a shrill note.

'Not this time, dear,' said Deborah. 'Take your hands away.' She touched them gently. Hyson dropped them and Deborah drove on. I turned and saw Rachel Bective come out of the house; then Hyson started to run after the car.

But Deborah had accelerated. We turned out of the drive.

We crossed the Tamar at Gunislake, and it seemed to me that as the distance between us and Pendorric grew greater, the higher Deborah's spirits rose. There was no doubt that recent events had depressed her considerably.

She talked a great deal about Morwenna, and what a relief it was to know that she was going to get well.

'When she recovers,' she said, 'I shall bring her over to the moor. I'm certain it would do her the world of good.'

I was beginning to see that she thought her moorland air the cure for all sickness, whether of the body or mind.

After passing through Tavistock we were soon on the moor. It reminded me very much of our own Cornish moors, but there was a subtle difference, Deborah told me; and you discovered it when you got to know them well. There was no moor like Dartmoor, she assured me, and insisted that Carrie corroborate this statement – which she readily did.

Carrie was excited too, and I caught their excitement and felt more at ease than I had since my quarrel with Roc.

Laranton Manor House stood alone about a mile from the village of

Laranton. It was an impressive building – Queen Anne in style – with massive iron gates at the entrance.

In the grounds was a cottage, and in this, Deborah told me, lived Mr. and Mrs. Hanson and their unmarried son, all of whom worked for her and kept the house in readiness for her return at any time.

She took out a key and opened the front door of the house about which clematis climbed. It must have been a lovely sight in season.

'Ah, it's good to be home,' she cried. 'Come along, my dear. Come in and see the old house which will always be home to me.'

I met Mrs. Hanson, who expressed no surprise to see her mistress home, and Deborah gave orders in her gentle but competent way.

'Mrs. Hanson, this is my nephew's bride. She's going to stay for a night or two. I want Carrie to get the blue room ready for her.'

'The blue room?' repeated Mrs. Hanson.

'Yes, please. I said the blue room. Carrie, put two hot-water bottles in the bed. You know how the first night in a strange bed always seems. And we should like something to eat, Mrs. Hanson. It's a fair journey from Pendorric.'

She made me sit down, for I was tired, she was sure.

'I'm going to cosset you,' she told me. 'Oh, it is fun to have you here. I've always wanted to bring you.'

I sat down in a chair near the big window which gave me a view of a neat lawn and flower-beds. 'Hanson's a good gardener, but it's not so easy to grow things on the moor as it is at Pendorric. The ground here is stony and it can be very cold in winter. Snow's a bit of a rarity at Pendorric; you should see it here in winter. There were times when Barbarina and I were kept in for a whole week – absolutely snowed up.'

I looked round the large room with its ingle-nook and pleasant furniture, and the large bowl of chrysanthemums on a gilt and marble console table.

'I've told Mrs. Hanson always to keep flowers in the house,' she told me, following my gaze. 'Barbarina used to look after the flowers, until she married. Then I took over. I didn't arrange them as artistically as she did.' She lifted her shoulders and smiled. 'I'm longing to show you your room. They should have it ready very soon. But first I'm hungry. Aren't you? It's our moorland air. Oh, it's good to be home.'

'I wonder you spend so much time at Pendorric,' I said, 'when you so clearly prefer it here.'

'Oh, it's because of the family . . . Morwenna, Roc, Hyson and Lowella! Pendorric's their home and if I want to be with them I have to be at Pendorric. I've brought Hyson here quite a lot. Lowella prefers the sea, but Hyson certainly has a taste for the moor.'

'She was very eager to come with us this time.'

'I know, dear child. But I did feel you needed a thorough rest. And with her mother in the hospital she should be there. When I'm here I feel young again. There's so much to remind me. I can almost imagine that Father is still alive and that at any moment Barbarina will come in through that door.'

'Did Barbarina come here often after her marriage?'

'Yes. She felt the same as I do about this place. After all it was home to her. She had spent the greater part of her life here. How I do harp on the past. It's a failing of the aged. Do forgive me, Favel. I want you to be happy here.'

'You're very kind.'

'My dear, I'm so fond of you.'

We were silent for a few moments and I thought that if I were with Deborah in some small country hotel I could have felt at ease. It was a pity that to escape from Pendorric I had to come to the house where Barbarina had spent the greater part of her life.

Mrs. Hanson came in to tell us that the meal was ready.

'An omelette, madam,' she said. 'If I'd had more time . . .'

'It'll be delicious, I'm sure,' smiled Deborah. 'Mrs. Hanson is one of the best cooks in Devon.'

The omelette was certainly delicious, and there was apple pie with clotted cream to follow.

'The real Devonshire cream,' Deborah told me gleefully. 'Now don't you agree it's better than the Cornish?'

I really couldn't tell the difference, so I said it was very good indeed.

'They copied it from us,' said Deborah; 'but they say we copied it from them!'

We were both growing more light-hearted, and I was sure it was a good thing that Deborah had brought me here! I could see quite clearly now that it would have been most unwise for me to have gone to the Clements'.

When the meal was over we went back to the drawing-room for coffee, and when we had finished, Deborah took me up and showed me my room.

It was right at the top of the house, very large and an odd shape. There were two windows, and the ceiling sloped slightly in a way which was charming and told me that we were immediately under the roof. The single bed at the opposite end of the room was partly in an alcove; and there was a desk, wardrobe, bedside table and dressing-table; on the bed was a blue coverlet, and the carpet was blue.

'This is delightful,' I said.

'And right at the top of the house. It's so light and airy, isn't it. Come and look out.'

We went to one of the windows, and because there was a half-moon I could see the moor stretched out beyond the gardens.

'You should see it in daylight,' Deborah told me. 'Miles and miles of moor. The gorse can be a picture, and the heather too. You can pick out the little streams. They look like flashes of silver in the sunlight.'

'I shall enjoy a good walk to-morrow.'

She didn't answer. She gazed, enraptured, at the moor.

She turned to me. 'Shall I help you unpack?'

'There's no need. I've brought very little.'

'There's plenty of room for your things.' She opened the door of the wardrobe.

I took out my night things and the two dresses I had brought with me, and she hung them on hangers.

'I'll show you the rest of the house,' she said.

I enjoyed my tour of the house. I saw the nursery where she told me she and Barbarina had played, the music room where Barbarina had learned the violin, the big drawing-room with its grand piano, and I had peered through the window at the walled garden outside.

'We used to grow lovely peaches on that wall. Our gardener saved all the best for Barbarina.'

'Weren't you a little jealous of her?' I asked.

'Jealous of Barbarina – never! Why, she and I were . . . close, as only twins can be. I could never really be jealous.'

'I think Barbarina was lucky to have you for a sister.'

'Yes, she was the lucky one . . . until the end, of course.'

'What really happened?' I felt compelled to ask. 'It was an accident, wasn't it?'

Her face crumpled suddenly and she turned away.

'It's so long ago,' she said almost piteously.

'And you still feel . . .?'

She seemed to pull herself together. 'There was a suggestion that someone was with her in the gallery at the time.'

'Did you believe it?'

'Yes.'

'Then who . . .?"

'It was never said, but lots of people had the idea that it was . . .'

'Her husband?'

'There was scandal about that woman. He was still seeing her. He never gave her up when he married Barbarina. He'd married Barbarina because of the money. He needed money. Houses like Pendorric are great monsters . . . they need continual feeding.'

'You think he killed her because he wanted to have Barbarina's fortune and marry Louisa Sellick?'

'It entered the minds of some people.'

'Yet he didn't marry her.'

'Perhaps he dared not.' She smiled at me bravely. 'I don't think we ought to be talking like this. It isn't fair to . . . Petroc.'

'I'm sorry. It's being here in her old home that reminded me.'

'Let's change the subject, shall we? Tell me what you would like to do while you're here.'

'See as much of the country as possible. I intend to be up early to-morrow. After all, I shall be here such a short time. I want to make the most of it.'

'Then I hope you get a good night's sleep. It's not always easy in a new bed, is it? I'll send Mrs. Hanson up with a nightcap. What do you like? Horlicks? Milo? Cocoa? Or just plain milk?'

I said I should prefer plain milk.

We sat talking a little while and then she said she would order the milk and take me up.

We mounted the lovely staircase right to the top of the house.

'One thing,' she told me, 'you'll be very quiet up here.'

'I'm sure I shall.'

'Barbarina always used to say that this was the room she liked best in the whole of the house. It was her room until she went to Pendorric.'

'Barbarina's room?' I said.

'The most charming of the bedrooms. That's why I gave it to you.'

'It was kind of you.'

'You . . . like it, don't you? If you don't I'll give you another.'

'I like it. . . .'

She laughed suddenly. 'It's Pendorric she's supposed to haunt. Not the old Manor.'

She drew the curtains across the windows and the room looked even more charming. Then she switched on the lamp which stood on the hexagonal bedside table.

'There! That should be comfortable. I hope you'll be warm enough. They should have put two bottles in the bed.' She prodded it. 'Yes, they have.'

She stood smiling at me. 'Good night, dear. Sleep well.'

Then she took my face in her hands and kissed it.

'The milk will be coming up. When would you like it – in five or ten minutes?'

'Five, please,' I said.

'All right. Good night, dear.'

She went out and left me. I undressed and, drawing back the curtains, stood for some seconds looking out over the moor. Peace, I thought. Here I shall be able to think about all the strange things which have been happening to me. I shall be able to make up my mind what I have to do.

There was a knock on my door and I was surprised to see Deborah, who came in carrying a glass of milk on a small tray.

She put this down on the hexagonal table.

'There you are, my dear. I thought I'd bring it myself.'

'Thank you.'

'You won't let it get cold, will you? Sleep well.'

She kissed me and went out.

I sat on the edge of the bed and, picking up the glass, sipped the milk, which was very hot.

I got into bed, but I was not in the least sleepy. I wished that I had brought something to read, but I had left Pendorric in such a hurry that I had forgotten to do so.

I looked around the room to see if I could find a book; then I noticed the drawer of the hexagonal table. Absently I opened it, and lying inside was a book with a leather cover. I took it out and saw written in a round childish hand on the fly-leaf: '*The dairy of Deborah and Barbarina Hyson.* This must be the only diary that ever has been written by two people, but of course we are not really two people in the same way that other people are. That is because we are twins. Signed: *Deborah Hyson. Barbarina Hyson.*'

I looked at those two signatures; they might have been written by the same hand.

So Deborah and Barbarina had kept a diary between them.

I was excited by my discovery; then I remembered that I was prying into

something private. I shut the book firmly and drank some more milk. But
I could not put the diary back into the drawer.

Barbarina had written in it. If I read what she had written I might learn
something about her and she had roused my curiosity from the moment I
had heard of her; now of course that curiosity was great because I had
always felt that Barbarina was in some way connected with the things which
were happening to me, and as I sat there in that strange bed it occurred to
me that my position was not less dangerous because I had left Pendorric for
a temporary respite. When I returned, more attempts might be made on my
life.

I remembered that strange singing I had heard in the graveyard before
I had been locked in the vault. If it was indeed true that someone was
planning to murder me, then that someone was going to make it appear that
my death was connected with the legend of Barbarina. And there was no
doubting the fact that, if the superstitious people who lived round Pendorric
were determined that the death of the Brides of Pendorric was due to some
metaphysical law, they would be less likely to report any strange incident
they might witness.

And as I held that book in my hand I became convinced that I should be
foolish to put aside something which might help me in my need. There might
be something in this book, some hint as to how Barbarina had met her death.
Had she been in a position similar to mine before that fatal fall? Had she
felt, as I was feeling now, that danger was creeping closer and closer, until
it eventually caught up with her? If she had felt that, might she not have
put it into her diary?

But this was her childhood diary; the one she shared with Deborah. There
would scarcely be anything in it about her life at Pendorric.

But I was determined to see, and I opened the book.

It had probably not been intended for a diary in the first place, for there
were no printed dates on the pages; but dates had been written in.

The first was September 6th. No year was given, and the entry read:
'Petroc came to-day. We think he is the best boy we have ever met. He
boasts a bit, but then all boys do. We think he likes us because we are asked
to his birthday party at Pendorric.'

The next entry was September 12th. 'Carrie is making our new dresses.
She didn't know which of us was which. She is going to put name tabs on
our clothes: Barbarina. Deborah. As if we cared. We always wear each
other's things, we told her. Barbarina's are Deborah's and Deborah's
Barbarina's; but she said we should have our own.'

It seemed just a childish account of their lives here in this house on the
moor, of the parties they went to. I had no idea who was writing because
the first person singular was never used; it was all in the first person plural.
I went on reading until I came to a blank page and thought for a moment
that was the end; but a few pages on there was more writing, yet it was not
the same. It had matured and I presumed that the diary had been forgotten
for some time and taken up again. There was more than a change in the
handwriting, for I read:

'*August 13th.* I was lost on the moor. It was wonderful.' I was excited because now I could say: That was actually written by Barbarina.

Barbarina seemed to have taken on the diary from that point.

'*August 16th.* Petroc has asked Father and of course Father is delighted. He pretended to be surprised. As if it isn't what they've all wanted for so long! I'm so happy. I'm longing to be at Pendorric. Then I shall escape from Deborah. Fancy wanting to escape from Deborah who up till now has always seemed a part of me. She is in a way a part of me. That was why she had to feel as I do about Petroc. There were always two of us to go places, to get ourselves out of trouble – silly little troubles, of course, which you think are so important when you're children. But that's all changed now. I want to get away – away from Deborah. I can't stand the way she looks at me when I've been with Petroc – as though she's trying to read my mind and can't, like she used to – as though she hates me. Am I beginning to hate her?

'*September 1st.* Yesterday Father, Deborah and I arrived at Pendorric for a visit. We're going ahead fast with arrangements for the wedding and I'm so excited. I saw Louisa Sellick to-day while I was out riding with Petroc. I suppose she's what people would call beautiful. She looks sad. That's because she knows now she has lost Petroc for ever. I asked Petroc about her. Perhaps I should have said nothing. But I was never one to stay calm. Deborah was the calm one. Petroc said it was all over. Is it? If it isn't I feel I could kill her. I won't share Petroc. Sometimes I wish I'd fallen in love with some of the others. George Fanshawe would have been a good husband and he was very much in love with me. So was Tom Kellerway. But it had to be Petroc. If Tom or George would fall in love with Deborah – Why is it they don't? We look so much alike that people can't tell us apart and yet they don't fall in love with Deborah. It's the same as it was when we were young. When we were at parties she'd keep in the background. I never did. She always said: "People don't want me. I get in on your ticket." And because she believed it and acted that way, it came to be true. Now Deborah doesn't know I'm going on with our diary I can write exactly what I feel. It's such a relief.

'*September 3rd.* Pendorric! What a wonderful old house. I love it. And Petroc! What is it about him that's different from everyone else in the world! Some magic! He's so gay, but sometimes I'm frightened. He doesn't seem to be entirely with me.'

I had come to several blank pages in the book, but after that the writing went on.

'*July 3rd.* I found this old diary to-day. It's ages since I wrote in it. The last time was just before I married. I see I've only put the months and days and left out the years. How like me! Still, it doesn't matter. I don't know why I want to write in it again. For comfort, I suppose. Since the twins were born I haven't thought of it. It's only now. I woke up last night and he wasn't there. I thought of that woman, Louisa Sellick. I hate her. There are rumours about her. I suppose he's still seeing her – and others. Could anyone be all that attractive and not take advantage of it? If I'd wanted a faithful husband I ought not to have married such an attractive man as

Petroc. I notice things. I've seen people at parties talking. They brightly change the subject when I come up. I know they're talking about Petroc and me – and some woman. Louisa Sellick probably. The servants look at me – pityingly. Mrs. Penhalligan for one – even old Jesse. What are they saying? Sometimes I feel I'll go mad if I let things drift like this. When I try to talk to Petroc he'll never be serious. He says, "Well, of course I love you." And I snap back: "And how many others too?" "Mine's a loving nature," he answers. He can never be serious. Life's so amusing to him. I want to shout at him that it's not so amusing to me. When I think of the old days in Father's house I remember how I used to love parties. Everyone made a fuss of me. And Deborah was there – she used to be as pleased as I was with my popularity. Once she said: "I enjoy it just as though it were mine." And I answered "It *is* yours, Deb. Don't you remember we always used to say that we weren't two people – but one." In those days that satisfied her.'

I had been so excited by what I read that I hadn't noticed what was happening to myself. I had actually yawned several times during the reading, and my lids now seemed so heavy that I couldn't keep my eyes open.

If I had been less enthralled I should not have been surprised, but the contents of this diary should surely have kept me wide awake.

I was determined to go on reading.

'*August 8th.* Deborah has been here for the last fortnight. She seems to come more often now. There is a change in Deb. She's become more *alive*. She laughs more easily. Something has changed her. Other people may not notice – but then they don't know her like I do. She borrowed my riding hat the other day – the black one with the band of blue round it. She stood before the looking-glass and said: "I don't believe anyone would know I wasn't you – not *anyone*." And actually she has grown more like me since she became more lovely. I know on several occasions the servants called her by my name. It amused her very much. I had an idea that she longed to be in my place. If only she knew. But that's something I wouldn't tell even her. It's too humiliating. No, I couldn't even tell Deborah about all the times when I wake up and find Petroc not with me, how I get up and walk about the room imagining what he's doing. If she knew what I had to suffer she wouldn't want to be in my place. She sees Petroc as so many others see him – just about the most fascinating man anyone could meet anywhere. It's different being his wife. Sometimes I hate him.

'*August 20th.* There was another scene yesterday. Petroc says I've got to be calm. He says he doesn't know what'll happen if I don't control myself more. Control myself! When he treats me like this! He says I'm too possessive. He says, "Don't pry into my life and I won't pry into yours." What sort of a marriage is this?

'*August 27th.* He has not been near me for more than a week. Sometimes I think everything is over between us. He can't stand scenes, he says. Of course he can't, because he's in the wrong. He just wants to go on living his own way – which is more or less the same as before he was married; but everything must seem all right on the surface. There mustn't be scandal. Petroc hates scandal. The fact is he's lazy. That's why he married me.

Pendorric needed money. I had it. It was simple. Marry money and there's no need to worry. Why does he have to be so amusing, so charming on the surface – so feckless and cruel underneath? If only I could be as light-hearted as he is! If only I could say "Oh – that's just Petroc. I must take him as I find him." But I can't. I love him too much. I don't want to share him. Sometimes I think I'll go mad. Petroc thinks so too. That's why he stays away. He hates it when I lose control. Father used to hate it too. But Father was kind and gentle with me. He used to say, "Barbarina my dear, you must be quiet. Look at Deborah. How calm she is. Be more like your sister, Barbarina." And that used to help. I'd remember that Deborah and I were like one. She had all the calmness in our nature. I was the volatile one. Father might deplore my wildness; but it was what made me attractive and Deborah a little dull. Deborah ought to comfort me now but even she has changed.

'*August 29th*. From my window I saw Deborah come back from a ride to-day. She was wearing a hat with a blue band. Not mine this time. She's got one exactly like it. As she came round from the stables the children were just going out with their nurse. They called to her. "Hallo, Mummy," they said. Deborah stooped and kissed first Morwenna, then Roc. The nurse said: "Morwenna's knee is healing up nicely, Mrs. Pendorric." Mrs. Pendorric! So the nurse and the children had mistaken her for me. I felt angry. I hated Deborah in that moment and it was like hating myself. I did hate myself. It was some minutes later when I said to myself, "But why didn't Deborah explain?" But she didn't. She just let them think she was the children's mother – the mistress of the house.

'*September 2nd*. If this goes on I think I shall kill myself. I've been thinking about it more and more. A quiet sleep for ever and ever. No more Petroc. No more jealousy. Sometimes I long for that. I often remember the Bride story. Some of the servants are sure Lowella Pendorric haunts the place. They won't go in the gallery where she hangs, after dark. This Lowella died after a year of marriage, having a son; she was cursed by her husband's mistress. The Pendorric men haven't changed much. When I think of my life at Pendorric, I'm ready to believe there might be a curse on the women of the house.

'*September 3rd*. Petroc says I'm getting more and more hysterical. How can I help that? All I ask is that he should be with me more, should love me as I love him. Surely that's not asking too much. All *he* cares about is that he should miss none of his pleasures, which means women – women all the time. Though I believe he's kept on with this Louisa Sellick. So he's faithful to her – after his fashion. There's one other thing that he cares about: Pendorric. What a fuss the other day when they discovered woodworm in the gallery. The wood's particularly bad in the balustrade – near Lowella Pendorric's picture – the one who was supposed to have died because of the curse, and haunt the place. That's what's made me think of her so much.

'*September 12th*. Deborah is still with us. She doesn't seem to want to go back to the moor. She certainly has changed. Sometimes I think she's growing more like I used to be, and I'm becoming more like she was. She's inclined to use my things as though they were hers. We did this in the old days but it was different then. She comes into my bedroom and talks. It's odd but I fancy she's trying to get me to talk about Petroc, and when I do she seems to shy away. The other day when we were talking she picked up a jacket of mine – a casual sort of thing in mustard colour. "You hardly wear it," she said. "I always like it." She slipped it on and as I looked at her I had a strange feeling that I *am* Deborah and that she's so longing to be in my place that she is Barbarina. I felt it was myself I was looking at. Is Petroc right? Is all that I'm suffering driving me crazy? Deborah took off the jacket but when she went out she slung it over her arm and I haven't seen it since.

'*September 14th.* I cry a lot. I'm so wretched. No wonder Petroc hardly ever comes near me. For some weeks he's been sleeping in the dressing-room. I try to tell myself it's better that way. Then I don't know whether he's there or not, so I don't have to wonder whom he's with. But of course I do.

'*September 20th.* I can't believe it. I must write it down. I think I'll go mad if I don't. I could bear the others; but not this. I know about Louisa Sellick and I can understand it – and up to a point forgive it. After all he wanted to marry her. It was because of Pendorric that he married me. But this. It's all so unnatural. I hate Deborah now. There isn't room for the two of us in this world. Perhaps there never was. We should have been one person. No wonder she's going about deceiving people – not correcting them when they call her Mrs. Pendorric. Petroc and Deborah! It's incredible. But of course it's not. It's inevitable in a way. After all, so much of me is Deborah and so much of her me. We are one – so why shouldn't we share Petroc as we have shared so many other things? Gradually she's been taking what's mine – not only my husband but my personality. The way she laughs now – the way she sings. That's not Deborah; it's Barbarina. I go about the house outwardly calm letting the servants think that I don't care. I stand there smiling when they talk to me and pretend to be interested as I did to-day when old Jesse talked about bringing something into the hall – some plant or other. It's getting too cold out of doors or something and he doesn't think the hothouse is quite right for it. Yes, yes, yes, I said, not listening. Poor old Jesse! He's almost blind now. I told him not to worry; we'd see he was all right. And Petroc will, of course. That's one thing about him – he's good to the servants. I'm writing trivialities to prevent myself thinking. Deborah and Petroc – I've seen them together. I know. It's her room he goes to. It leads from the gallery not far from that spot where the picture of Lowella Pendorric hangs. I lay listening last night and heard the door close. Deborah who is getting like I used to be – and Petroc. How I hate them – both! There shouldn't be two of us. I've tolerated others but I won't tolerate this. But how can I stop it?

'*September 21st.* I've decided to kill myself. I can't go on. I keep wondering how. Perhaps I'll walk into the sea. They say that after the first moment of struggle, it's an easy death. You don't feel it much. My body would be washed in and Petroc would see it. He'd never forget. I'd haunt him for the rest of his life. It would be his punishment and he deserves to be punished. It would be the legend coming true. The Bride of Pendorric would haunt the place, and I, Barbarina, would be that bride. It seems somehow right – inevitable. I think it is the only way.'

The rest of that page was blank and I thought I had come to the end of the diary. I yawned, I was very tired.

But as I turned the page I came to more writing, and what I read startled me so much that I was almost wide awake.

'*October 19th.* They think I am dead. Yet I am still here and they don't know it. Petroc doesn't know. It's a good thing that he can't bear to be near me, because he might discover the truth. He's away most of the time. He goes to Louisa Sellick for comfort. Let him. I don't care now. Everything is different. It's – exciting. There's no other word for it. I shouldn't write in this book. It's all so dangerous, but I like to go over it again and again. It's funny – really funny because it makes me laugh sometimes – but only when I'm alone. When I'm with anyone I'm calm – terribly calm. I have to be. I feel more alive now than I have for a long time – now that they think I'm dead. I must write it down. I'm afraid I'll forget if I don't. I had made up my mind how I would die. I was going to walk into the sea. Perhaps I'd leave a note for Petroc, telling him that he'd driven me to it. Then I'd be sure that I'd haunt him for the rest of his life. It all happened so suddenly. I hadn't planned it that way at all. Then suddenly I saw how it could be done. How a new bride could take the place of Lowella Pendorric, for it was time she rested in her grave, poor thing. Deborah came into my room. She was wearing my mustard-coloured jacket, and her eyes were bright; she looked sleek and contented, and I knew, as well as if she'd told me, that he'd been with her the previous night. "You're looking tired, Barby," she said. Tired! So would she, had she lain awake as I had. She'd be punished too. She would never forgive herself. I doubted whether she and Petroc would be lovers after I had gone. "Petroc's really concerned about the gallery," she said, "It'll probably mean replacing the whole thing." How dared she tell me how Petroc felt! How dared she talk in that proprietorial way about Petroc and Pendorric! She used to be so sensitive to my moods; but now her mind was full of Petroc. She picked up a scarf of mine – Petroc himself had bought it for me when we were in Italy – a lovely thing of emerald-coloured silk. She put it absently about her neck. The mustard-coloured jacket set it off perfectly. Something happened when she took that scarf. It seemed tremendously important. My husband – my scarf. I felt I hadn't a life of my own any more. I wonder now why I didn't snatch it away from her, but I didn't. "Come and look at the gallery," she said. "It's really quite dangerous. The workmen will be coming in to-morrow." I allowed myself to follow her out to the gallery; we stood beneath the picture of Lowella. "Here," she said, "Look, Barby." Then it happened. It suddenly seemed clear to me. I was going to die because there was no longer any reason to go on living. I had thought of walking into the sea. Deborah was standing close to the worm-eaten rail. It was a long drop down to the hall. I felt Lowella Pendorric was watching us from her canvas, saying: "A Bride must die that I may rest in peace." It was the old legend and there's a lot of truth in these old legends. That's why they persist. Deborah was, in a sense, a Bride of Pendorric. Petroc treated her as such – and she was part of me. There were times when

I was not sure which of us I was. I'm glad I wrote this down, although it's dangerous. This book must never be seen by anyone. It's safe enough. Only Carrie has ever seen it and she knows what happened as well as I do. When I read it, I can remember it clearly. It's the only way I can come back to what really happened on that day. I can live again that moment when she was standing there, perilously close, and I leaned forward and pushed her with all my might. I can hear her catch her breath in amazement – and horror. I can hear her voice, or did I imagine that? But I hear it all the same. "No, Barbarina!" Then I know of course that I am Barbarina and that it is Deborah who lies in the Pendorric vault. Then I can laugh and say: How clever I am. They think me dead and I am alive all these years. But it's only when I read this book that I am absolutely sure who I am.'

I felt limp with horror.

But there was more to be read and I went on reading.

'*October 20th*. I shouldn't write in the book any more. But I can't resist it. I want to write it down while I remember, because it's fading fast and I am not sure. There was someone in the hall. I was frightened. But it was only old Jesse and he couldn't see. I stood in the gallery, looking at the splintered wood. I wouldn't look down on to the hall. I didn't stay long. Old Jesse had run for help. He might not see me but he knew something was wrong. I ran into the nearest room because I had to get out of the gallery before I was seen. It was Deborah's. I threw myself on to her bed and I lay there, my heart thundering. I don't know how long I lay there but it seemed like hours. It was a few minutes actually. Voices, cries of horror. What was happening in the hall? I longed to see but I knew I must stay where I was. After a while there was a knock on the door. I was still lying on the bed when Mrs. Penhalligan came in. She said: "Miss Hyson, there's been a terrible accident." I raised myself and stared at her. "It's the gallery rail. 'Twas worse than we thought. Mrs. Pendorric—' I just went on staring at her. She went out and I heard her voice outside the door. "Miss Hyson, she be terrible shocked, poor dear. 'Tis not to be wondered at – they being so close – so near like. I for one couldn't tell one from the other."

'I went down to the sea and looked at it. It was grey and cold. I couldn't do it. It's easy to talk of dying; but when you face it – you're frightened. You're terribly frightened. I'd been so stunned by the news that they'd made me stay in bed until it was all over. I didn't see Petroc unless others were there too. That was as well. He was the one I feared. Surely he would know his own wife. But even so there was something I knew about Petroc. He wasn't the same. The gaiety had gone, the light-heartedness. He blamed himself. The servants were talking. They said it was *meant*. And it happened right under the picture of that other bride. It was no good going against what was meant. Barbarina was meant, to die, so that Lowella Pendorric could rest from the haunting. They wouldn't go near the gallery after dark. They believed Barbarina was haunting Pendorric. So she is. She haunted Petroc till the day he died. So the story was true. The Bride of Pendorric had died just as the story said she should and she couldn't rest in her grave.

'I couldn't go. I couldn't leave the children. They call me Aunt Deborah now. I *am* Deborah. I'm calm and serene. Carrie knows, though. Sometimes she calls me Miss Barbarina. I'm afraid of Carrie. But she'd never hurt me; she loves me too well. I was always her favourite. I was everybody's favourite. It's different now, though. People are different towards me. They call me Deborah and what is happening is that Deborah still lives and it is Barbarina who is dead.

'*January 1st.* I shall not write any more. There is nothing to write. Barbarina is dead. She had a fatal accident. Petroc hardly spoke to me again. I believe he thought that I was jealous of her, and that I did it hoping he'd marry me; he doesn't want to know too much about it in case it's true. I don't care about Petroc any more. I'm devoted to the children. It doesn't matter now that Petroc is never here. I'm not his wife any more; I'm his sister-in-law, taking care of his motherless children. I'm happier than I ever was since my marriage; though sometimes I think of my sister and it's as though she's with me. She comes to me at night when I'm alone and her eyes are mournful and accusing. She can't rest. She haunts me and she haunts Petroc. It's in the legend; and she'll continue to haunt Pendorric until another young bride takes her place; then she will rest for evermore.

'*March 20th.* I have been reading this book. I shall not read it any more. I shall not write in it any more. I shall hide it away. It worries me. Barbarina is dead and I am Deborah; I am calm and serene and I have devoted myself to Roc and Morwenna. Barbarina haunts me; that's because it's in the story that she should – until another bride takes her place. But reading this book upsets me. I shall not do it any more.'

There was one last entry. It stated simply:

'One day, there'll be a new bride at Pendorric and then Barbarina shall have her rest.'

So it was Barbarina who had brought me to this house, who had lured me to the vault, who had sought to kill me.

I did not know what to do. What could I do to-night? I was alone in this house with Barbarina and Carrie, for the Hansons would be in their cottage in the grounds.

I must lock my door. I attempted to get out of bed but my legs seemed unable to move, and even in my agitated state I could not fight the drowsiness which had taken possession of me. A thought came into my head that I was asleep and dreaming: and in that moment the book had slipped from my fingers and falling asleep was like entering a deep dark cave.

I awoke with a start. For a few seconds I was still in that deep, dark cave of oblivion; then objects started to take shape. Where was I? There was the hexagonal table. I remembered the diary, and then where I was.

I knew too that something had awakened me, and the knowledge quickly followed that I was not alone. Someone was in this room.

I had fallen asleep so suddenly that I was lying on my back. I had been aware of the hexagonal table by turning my eyes towards it without moving my head. The heavy sleepiness was still upon me and the deep darkness of the cave was threatening to close about me once more.

I was so tired . . . too tired to be afraid . . . too tired to care that I was not alone in the room.

I'm dreaming, I thought. Of course I'm dreaming. For from out of the shadows came a figure. It was a woman dressed in a blue house-coat. As the moonlight touched her face I knew who she was.

My heavy lids were pressing down over my eyes; vaguely I heard her voice.

'This time, little bride, there shall be no way out. They will no longer talk of Barbarina's ghost . . . but yours.'

I wanted to call out; but some waking instinct warned me not to, and I began to wonder whether after all I was in a dream.

Never before in my life had I been so frightened. Yet never had I been so sleepy, and terror was trying to ward off my sleepiness. What was happening to me? I longed to be in my bedroom at Pendorric with Roc beside me. That was safety. This was danger.

'This is a nightmare,' I told myself. 'In a moment you will wake up.'

She was standing at the foot of my bed looking at me while I watched her through half-closed eyes, waiting for what she would do next.

An impulse came to me to speak to her, but something warned me that I must first find out what she intended to do. This had never happened to me before. I was asleep; yet I was awake. I was terrified; and yet it was as though I stood outside this scene, a watcher in the shadows. I was looking on at the frightened woman in the bed and the other whose purpose was evil.

An idea hit me. I am drugged. The milk was drugged. The milk Deborah brought me. No . . . not *Deborah*. I didn't drink it all. If I had I should now be in a deep, drugged sleep.

She was smiling. Then I saw her hands move in a gesture as though she were sprinkling something over my bed. She went to the window and stooped for a few seconds; and then she stood upright and without giving another glance at my bed, ran from the room.

I was aware of thinking: It is a dream. Then suddenly it seemed I was wide awake. I was looking at a wall of flame. The curtains were on fire. For one second, two seconds, I stared at them, while it was as though I emerged from that black cave to reality.

I smelt petrol and in terrible understanding leaped out of bed and made for the door. I was not a second too soon, for as I did so my bed was aflame.

It is difficult to recall what happened next. I was aware of the blazing bed as I pulled at the door-handle and for one hideous second believed that I was locked in this room as I had been locked in the vault. But that was only due to my anxiety to get out quickly. The door was not locked.

I pulled it open and had the sense to shut it behind me. I saw her then. She was running along the corridor, and I went after her shouting: 'Fire!' as I did so. She turned to look at me.

I cried: 'Quick! My room's on fire. We must give the alarm.'

She looked at me in bewilderment. I knew then that she was mad, and for those few dramatic seconds I even forgot the danger we were in.

'You tried to kill me . . . *Barbarina!*' I said.

Horror dawned in her face. I heard her whisper as though to herself: 'The diary . . . Oh, my God, she's read the diary.'

I caught her arm. 'You've set my room on fire,' I said urgently. 'It'll spread . . . quickly. Where's Carrie? On this floor? Carrie! Carrie! Come quickly.'

Barbarina's lips were moving; she went on muttering to herself: 'It's there . . . in the diary . . . She's seen the diary. . . .'

Carrie came into the corridor, wrapping an old dressing-gown about her, her hair in a plait tied with a red tape.

'Carrie,' I shouted. 'My room's on fire. Phone the fire brigade quickly.'

'Carrie! Carrie! She . . . *knows* . . .' moaned Barbarina

I gripped Carrie's arm. 'Show me where the phone is. There's no time to lose. We must all get out of the house. Don't you understand?'

Still gripping Carrie I pulled her downstairs. I did not look back, being certain that Barbarina, knowing how deadly was the fire she had started, would follow us.

I never saw Barbarina again. By the time we had phoned for the brigade, the top floor was a mass of flame. All I knew was that Barbarina did not follow us downstairs. I have always believed that, rudely shaken out of her dream-world, she had had no thought of anything but the incriminating diary. To her it represented the only way of remembering what had actually happened; and to have lost it would have been to have lost touch with the past. Unbalanced as she was, she had made a futile attempt to save it. I do not like to think what happened to Barbarina when she burst into that room which by then must have been a roaring furnace.

It was nearly an hour before the fire brigade reached the isolated manor house, and by that time it was too late to save it. It was not until we had telephoned for the brigade and the Hansons had arrived that we missed Barbarina. Hanson bravely went up to try to rescue her. We had to prevent Carrie from dashing into the flames to bring out her mistress, for we knew it was hopeless.

Looking back it is hard to remember the sequence of events. But I do remember sitting in the Hansons' cottage drinking tea which Mrs. Hanson brought to me, when suddenly I heard a familiar voice.

'Roc!' I cried, and ran to him; we just stood together clinging.

And this was a Roc I had never known before because I had never seen him clearly through the fog of suspicion which surrounded him – strong in his power to protect, weak in his anxiety over my safety, ready to do battle with the powers of darkness for my sake, yet terrified for fear some harm had come to me.

Chapter Seven

It is a year since that night and yet the memory of it is with me as vividly as when it happened. Perhaps, if one has come near to violent death, as I did, it is an experience which is never far from the surface of the mind.

I often say to Roc: 'If it hadn't been that I was so absorbed in the diary I should have drunk all the milk; I should have been unconscious when Barbarina came into my room and that would have been the end of me.' To that Roc answers: 'All life is chance. If your father had never come to our coast, you would not have been here at all.'

And it is so.

It is difficult to understand everything that went on in Barbarina's mind; I am sure that for much of the time she believed she was Deborah. She could never have played the part so well if she had not; and her character must have changed after Deborah died so that she really did take on the personality of her twin. The more she behaved like Deborah, the more like her she grew, just as Deborah, when Petroc became her lover, began to be like Barbarina. The curse laid on the Brides of Pendorric became an obsession with her. It may have been that she believed Deborah's spirit had actually entered her body, and that she had become Deborah; and because she constantly thought of the sister whom she had sent to her death, she believed she was haunted by her and it was for this reason that she was anxious for another bride to take over the role of ghost at Pendorric.

But how can one follow the tortuous meandering of a sick mind?

My conjectures must have an element of truth in them, though, because there was no doubt that I had been in danger from the moment I had come to Pendorric.

Poor simple-minded Carrie, who had always been dominated by her charges, was easily caught up in this morbid dream-life of her mistress; Barbarina and Deborah were one and the same; and Carrie believed it, while she alone knew that the twin who had fallen to her death in the hall at Pendorric was Deborah. At times she could not understand Barbarina's interpretation of this strange phenomenon; namely that Deborah's mind and soul were now with Barbarina. Carrie could only accept this by telling herself that the two of them were really alive.

It was from Carrie that we gleaned a little understanding of Barbarina's madness; but the years during which she had devoted herself to Barbarina and her crazy conception of life had undermined her own sanity and Roc was anxious that she should not be upset. He sent her away in the care of an old nanny of his who had a cottage on the Devon coast, and there she is now.

It was not so easy with Hyson, for Barbarina had tried to draw the child into her orbit. She saw in Lowella and Hyson a repetition of herself and Deborah; and because for most of the time she believed she *was* Deborah, she had great sympathy for the less attractive twin. Barbarina's affection for the child was deep and possessive and Hyson was fascinated by the strangeness of Barbarina, who revealed herself more to the child than to anyone else. Hyson did not understand but she was aware of the strangeness and, like Barbarina, learned to project herself into that make-believe world; Barbarina had hinted that she still lived and Hyson believed her; she believed that Barbarina would lure me to my death, so that she might rest in her grave according to the legend.

It was from Carrie we learned that Barbarina had sometimes gone to the music room and played the violin, and that she sang Ophelia's song; and that it was she who had waited for me to leave Polhorgan and had removed the sign on the cliffs in the hope that I, less sure-footed than those accustomed to the path, would have a fatal accident. She it was who had locked me in the vault, for the only other key to the vault had been in her possession; she had often paid secret visits to the vault as, according to Carrie, she told her she wanted to be with Barbarina. She would never have come to the vault had not Hyson been missing and she, guessing where she was, had decided to abandon that method of disposing of me, for the sake of the child. She had quietly unlocked the door before going to find Roc. Then she had tampered with the car and chance again had stepped in so that it was Morwenna who had had an accident.

Often I reflect how easily the legend of the Brides might have gone on and on; for few people can have come as near to death as I did, and escape. If Barbarina had been a cold-blooded murderess I should never have escaped; but she was not that; if she had been, she would have planned more carefully; but she was caught in her world of make-believe; she was living on two levels and she could not see where reality and the dream-world merged. I discovered that she had trunks of Deborah's clothes and often wore them when she was in Devon. The Hansons were not aware of this, never having known Deborah, and when Carrie called her Barbarina they merely thought that Carrie was a little weak in the head. And Barbarina could lightly step back into the character of Deborah to assure them that this was so.

I often wondered what damage she would have done to Hyson if I had not come to Pendorric when I did. The child was neurotic, her head full of strange notions. She was already beginning to believe that she stood in the same relationship to Lowella as Deborah had to Barbarina. Barbarina had won her devotion by preferring her to her gayer sister; and that was when the damage began to be done.

But there again events worked against her. Hyson had endured the terrifying experience of being locked in the vault with me. She had known, because of the hints Barbarina loved to give the child, that something was going to happen that day. She believed that the figure she saw in the graveyard when she had hidden herself there was the ghost of Barbarina. Barbarina had been unwise to involve the child, but, because she was already identifying Hyson with Deborah, could not stop doing so. And when

Barbarina opened the door of the vault and sang the song which was to lure me inside, Hyson slipped in. Thus we were locked in together, and from that moment Hyson began to understand the horror of death, that it did not come lightly, that there must be suffering before oblivion was reached.

Then she saw her mother in the hospital and she must have known that Morwenna was lying where I was intended to be.

Death was hateful; it was frightening; and it touched those she loved. Her own mother. And even for me she had some affection.

She was frightened; and when she saw me going off with Barbarina in the car, guessing for what purpose, she broke into hysteria which so alarmed her father that he sent for Dr. Clement, but it was some time before they could understand the meaning of her incoherent words. Dr. Clement's first action was to telephone Roc; and Roc immediately drove to the manor.

Yet although I lived so dangerously up to that night when Roc came to me in Devon, it was during the following months that I learned so much more of life than I ever had before; the months of safety and serenity.

For one thing, I learned the story of the boy who lived in Louisa Sellick's house on the moor. Morwenna must have grown up too, because she confessed to Charles that he was hers. She had been afraid to do so before because the boy was the result of a brief passionate love affair which had occurred when she was seventeen.

Rachel Bective, who as a child had so longed to be asked to Pendorric that she had locked Morwenna in the vault in order to blackmail her into giving her an invitation, had proved a good friend. She had looked after Morwenna during her troubles, and of course Roc had been at hand. It had been his idea to ask Louisa's help, and he and Rachel took the child to her; Louisa had been only too glad to do what she could for Petroc's children.

As Roc said to me: 'I couldn't tell you the truth when I'd sworn to keep Morwenna's secret. But I did intend to persuade her that you should be brought in. The trouble was she was so afraid of Charles's knowing.'

There had been fear and drama in Pendorric before I arrived.

During the last year we have gone a long way towards turning Polhorgan into a home for orphans. I am going to be very busy keeping an eye on this particular project as I shall be starting my own family. Rachel Bective is going to be a nursery governess to the orphans, and Dr. Clement will be at hand to advise when we need him. The Dawsons will stay on and although there may be a little friction now and then between them and Rachel, that is inevitable, I suppose. I don't like Rachel – I doubt whether I ever shall – but I have wronged her in my thoughts so much that I try very hard to change my opinion. She was merely enamoured of a way of life which was not hers. The romantic big house must have been very appealing to an orphan, brought up by an aunt who had children of her own and didn't really want her. She saw her main opportunity in life when she was sent to a good school paid for with the money her parents had left with instructions that all of it be spent on their daughter's education. She had attached herself to Morwenna and clung; but she had been a good friend in Morwenna's trouble and often visited Bedivere House – as Roc did – to bring Morwenna news of the son she dared not see until she had confessed to Charles.

The twins have now gone to school – separate schools. Hyson had a holiday, a holiday at Bournemouth alone with her mother after Morwenna's recovery. They both needed to recuperate; and we feel that in time Hyson will grow away from that sinister influence which Barbarina cast about her. We shall have to be very careful in our treatment of Hyson.

This, then, has been an illuminating year.

We all seem to have grown up, become wise; but then I suppose it is experiences such as these which make us learn our lessons quickly.

Morwenna has cast off the burden which, like Christian in *Pilgrim's Progress*, she has carried for fourteen years, and Charles, she discovered, was less self-righteous than she had believed him to be. Indeed he was a little sad and reproachful that she had not trusted him all those years.

As a result, Ennis and Louisa are often at Pendorric. Morwenna would not take the boy from Louisa, but she does want to share him, and I have an idea that in time he will be to Charles as the son he did not have.

It may well be that one day we shall have to give up Pendorric as we know it. We shall probably have to throw it open to the public and have strangers walking through our rooms. We shall have our own apartments of course, but it will not be the same.

Roc is reconciled. 'You can't fight the times,' he says. 'It would be like trying to fight the sea.'

All the money I have will be used on Polhorgan, and that is how Roc wishes it to be.

He often teases me, reminding me that I once thought he schemed to marry an heiress and then planned to murder her.

'And yet,' he said, 'you loved me . . . after your fashion.'

He is right. During those months of danger I was deep in physical love with Roc; I knew only what I saw, what I heard, what I sensed.

But there are many facets of love, and of these I am learning more every day; and so is he. And that is why when we walk down the cliff gardens to Pendorric Cove and look towards Polhorgan, high on the cliff, or to Cormorant Cottage where Althea Grey once lived, we remember those doubts which, while they did not diminish our passion, yet were a sign that we had just begun that voyage of discovery which our life together will be.

THE SHADOW OF THE LYNX

NORA

Chapter One

Even as I stood on the deck and the *Carron Star* slipped away from the dockside I had to keep assuring myself that I was really leaving England, that I was making a clean break with the old life, and was in fact sailing away into the unknown. There I stood in my tartan cape, which flapped open in the breeze to show a serviceable skirt of the same material, my straw hat tied on with a long grey chiffon scarf, seventeen years old, travelling to the other side of the world with a man whom, a month ago, I had never seen and of whose existence I had been unaware.

On the wharf people were waving handkerchiefs, many of them surreptitiously wiping their eyes as they smiled bravely. There was no one to wave goodbye to me.

A middle-aged man with bold eyes and mutton-chop whiskers sidled close – too close.

'Any friends over there?' He was surveying me speculatively.

'No,' I replied.

He was smiling in a familiar fashion. 'Travelling alone?'

A voice behind me said: 'My ward is travelling with me.' And there was Stirling, his greenish eyes glinting derisively, his voice with the faint Australian accent clearly demanding to know why a stranger should dare to address *his* ward.

The man moved away awkwardly. Stirling did not speak to me. He merely stood beside me, leaning on the rail, and I was aware of a warm, happy feeling of security: I knew in that moment that I had taken a step away from the all-enveloping misery in which I had been living during the past weeks. I had lost the one I loved beyond everyone and everything; but here was Stirling and he was beside me – 'my guardian' as he called himself. It was not strictly true; but I liked it.

I think it was at that moment that I began to feel that Stirling and I were meant for each other.

But that is not the beginning. I should perhaps start when I was born, since that is where all stories start; but they really begin even before that. I often wondered about the prelude to my birth. I tried to picture my parents together – which was difficult because I never saw my mother. It was not a fact which worried me particularly, because there was my father, Thomas Tamasin – and possessing such a father, why should I fret because I had no mother?

She had 'gone away' as he put it when I was a year old. It was not until I was six years old that I understood what that meant.

Life was amusing lived with Thomas Tamasin. I believed that the two of us were enough. Why should we have wanted a third person? Even a mother would have been an intruder.

We had a series of housekeepers whose duty was to look after me; and it was not until I was six that I heard the word 'abandoned'. It was used by the housekeeper to a friend who had called to see her at our house which was then in north London. (We were constantly moving about to suit my father's enterprises, which were numerous.) I was sitting beneath the kitchen window, which was wide open, watching ants purposefully marching back and forth on the crazy paving.

'Poor mite!' said the housekeeper. 'What she misses is a mother.'

'And him?'

'Oh . . . him!' Laughter followed.

Then: 'She left him, didn't she?'

'So I've heard. She was a fast piece of goods. On the stage or something.'

'Oh . . . an actress!'

'No good anyway. Young Nora was not much more than twelve months old when she went off. There's something wrong with a woman who'll abandon a child at that age. He ought to have married again.'

'That what you tell him?'

'Go on with you?'

Abandon! I thought. And the child who had been abandoned was myself.

'What's abandoned?' I asked my father when he came home.

'Left. Run away from.'

'It's not a nice thing to be, is it?'

He agreed it wasn't.

'People would only abandon what they didn't like,' I commented.

He admitted this was probably so, and I didn't tell him that I knew I had been abandoned because it would have hurt him. I was always careful not to hurt him, just as he was not to hurt me. In any case, having him, what did I care that I was abandoned?

We never talked about my mother. There were so many other things to talk about. There were his plans for making a fortune – though not so much making it as spending it. There was always some project afoot. At one time he was going to put an invention on the market which would revolutionize the daily life of millions of people. I liked invention times because then he stayed at home working in the room at the top of the house and it was comforting to have him near. I would sit close to his work bench and we would talk for hours of what we would do when his genius was recognized and the world was profiting from it. 'Ourselves included,' he would say with that laugh of his which was like water running down a drainpipe and which always made me laugh too. He made a spring lock which didn't work as it was intended to; he made mechanical toys which never quite achieved their purpose, except one which was a boy on a seat which swung over the top of a rail, but even he used to get stuck up there sometimes. He sold a few of these and we had a saying: 'Remember the boy on the swing?' It was his great success; but it was not the fortune he was after. He tried market gardening, and for a period we lived in the country; but he wanted to experiment all the time, to produce something different; an ordinary living was not good enough for him.

'When my ship comes home . . .' he would say, and that was the prelude to our favourite game. We sailed round the world in our imaginations; we found places on the map and said, 'We'll go there.' We were always together in these imaginary journeys; we had adventures in which we met sea monsters more awe-inspiring than anything encountered by Sinbad. Sometimes he wrote them down and he sold one or two to a magazine. Our fortunes were made, he declared. Why hadn't he realized that he was a literary man? But that didn't work either. He wanted to get rich quickly.

He had inherited a little money and this he set aside for my education. That was an indication of his care for me. However improvident he might be in all else, he was determined that I should be secure. He wanted me to go to the best schools, he told me. I said I wanted only to be with him. So I should, he assured me, but while he was making our fortune I had to go to school. I went to several and learned quickly – the sooner to get away from it all.

It was just after my fifteenth birthday that he decided to go after gold. This was the greatest opportunity, this was the miracle. His life had been strewn with great chances which so far had proved to be mirages, but this was different. This would in truth make our fortunes.

'Gold!' he said, his eyes smouldering. 'We'll be millionaires, Nora. How would you like to be a millionaire?'

I thought I should like it very much, but where did we get this gold?

'It's there in the earth, waiting to be picked up. All you have to do is take it.'

'Then why isn't everyone a millionaire?'

'There speaks my practical daughter. It's a good question and there's a simple answer. It's because they're not as wise as we are going to be. We're going out to get it.'

'Where is it?'

'It's in Australia. They're finding it all over the place.'

'When do we start?'

'Well, Nora, just at first I'll have to go alone. It's no place for a girl who has to get educated.'

That was the moment of fear and the blank despair in my face must have frightened him.

'You have to learn the three Rs; you have to talk and act like a lady if you're going to be a millionaire.'

I reminded him that I was already acquainted with the three Rs. I also knew how to talk and act like a lady and did so except when I lost my temper.

'Well, you see Nora, you're too young just as yet. You stay behind for a while. I've found a good school where they'll look after you and in next to no time I'll be back. We'll be millionaires and start enjoying life. What would you like to do? Where would you like to go? There's no limit. We can start making plans without delay. The fortune is as good as in our pockets.'

He convinced me as he always could and he persuaded me to go to Danesworth House. 'Only a few months, Nora. Then . . . all the money in the world. Everything you can wish for. Now what will you have to start with?'

I said: 'There are lots of people looking for this gold. Suppose it takes years for you to find it?'

'I tell you, Nora, I have the Midas touch.'

'I could be your housekeeper. I could cook for you, look after you.'

'What! My millionaire daughter! No. We're going to have someone to look after us . . . for ever more. No more partings. No more intruders. That'll be the day. And all you have to do is wait awhile at Danesworth House while I go and get the gold.'

That was how he talked, forcefully, persuasively and so vividly that we were able to live in our imaginations through all the extravaganza he planned for us.

So I went to school and he sailed across the world; and every day I waited for the letter which would tell me that he had found his fortune and that we were millionaires.

School was just a tiresome bore. I was less in awe of Miss Emily and Miss Grainger than most of their pupils. I was good at my work; I avoided trouble; I was not interested in school-girl mischief. I only lived for the summons. I used to picture how it would come. In a letter perhaps: 'Come to Australia at once.' Or perhaps he, who loved surprises, would come to the school to take me away. There would be a summons to the study; and there in that cold arid room he would be standing; he would catch me up in his arms to the astonished disapproval of Miss Emily or Miss Grainger – for which he would care nothing – and he would shout: 'Pack your bags, Nora. You're leaving. We're millionaires.'

The letters came regularly. I knew that tired as he was with the day's work he always remembered how I would be waiting and watching for the posts.

There were letters from the ship posted at various ports of call. He described his fellow passengers amusingly for my benefit. I was terrified that his ship would run into a storm which would be dangerous and I was very uneasy until he wrote telling me that he had arrived.

He wrote vividly and I had a clear picture of those early days, and although he wrote with the utmost optimism, I understood the hardships he had to endure. I pictured his setting out with the tools he would need: pickaxes; the cradle he used for puddling; his billy-can; his rations. I pictured the field on which he worked – a desolate place it must have been with the trees chopped down and the tents pitched there. I imagined their sitting round the fire at night exchanging stories of their finds and most of all their hopes. He would be in the centre; he would have more colourful tales than anyone; and of course there was his charm and his way with words. Somehow he made me see those unkempt men, their backs aching as they bent over their cradles watching the water run through the soil that could reveal the longed-for golden streaks. I could see their grim faces and on all was the lust for gold – the longing, the yearning – for they would all see in the yellow dust the gateway to fortune.

He loved the life, I sensed that. If I could have been with him he would have been perfectly happy. I believe now that had he made his fortune he could not have enjoyed life half as much as he did when he was endeavouring to find it. I should have been there with him. I could have cooked the food while they worked on the diggings; I saw myself as the little mother of the colony. Had I been there I was sure I should never have wanted them to find gold in any quantity. I should have wanted them to go on forever seaching for it.

The months passed; he had moved to another field. He had found nothing but a little dust. Never mind. The new field was rich, he was sure; and one must have experience.

His optimism never flagged; he was always on the verge of great discovery. As to myself I must have seemed strange to my fellow pupils. I was aloof; I was not interested in school affairs but I managed to satisfy my teachers and I was left a good deal to myself. I was that 'odd Nora Tamasin whose father was a gold miner in Australia'. They had wormed that much out of me.

Then the tone of the letters changed. He met the Lynx.

'The Lynx is the most unusual man I have ever met. We were drawn to each other from the first. I have decided to join him. He knows the country inside out. He's been here for thirty-four years. If you could see him you'd know why they call him Lynx. He's got a pair of eyes that see everything. They're blue – not azure blue, not like the tropical seas, oh no! They're like steel or ice. I never knew a man who could so quell with a look. He's the big man round here. His name is Charles Herrick. He came out as a convict and now owns most of the place I'm in. He's a man in a million. It's going to be different from now on. I'm going into business in a big way. No more working overworked plots. It's all different and all because of Lynx.'

I thought a great deal about the Lynx. I was a little jealous of him because my father's letters were full of him. He admired him so much. And now, through those letters, I understood what hardships he had suffered. The stories of camp-fire gaiety, the songs they sang by firelight, the comradeship of the diggings were only half the story. I now sensed the apprehension, the careful rationing of food, the preservation of the precious water, the terrible despair when day after day the cradles revealed nothing but the worthless dust.

'Lynx is going to strike gold in a big way, Nora, and when he does I'll be with him. He's a man of experience. Besides a sizeable property he owns the local store and a hotel in Melbourne. He has hundreds of men working for him and he knows all there is to know about gold. He can't fail. I've told Lynx about you. He thinks that you should come out when you're educated. But I'll be home before then.'

I pictured Lynx – a pair of piercing eyes, a convict! Thirty-four years ago

people had been sent out to Australia when they had been found guilty of
some misdemeanour. Of what had Lynx been guilty? I wondered. Something
political perhaps. I was sure he was not a thief or a murderer. I wanted to
hear more of him.

'Lynx is a sort of king, magistrate, employer, dictator . . . the head of
things. He is just, but he'll have his own way. I've never felt such
friendship as I do for him. It was a lucky day when I met him. I've
thrown in all I have with him. He's certain that we'll find a rich vein
of gold. We're going to work as secretly as possible. If we don't keep it
dark we'll have diggers here from all over the place. The rumour only
has to get round and they come in their thousands. Lynx is wily and
we're in this together.'

Letters had been coming more or less regularly. Sometimes I would get
several together. My father would explain that there had been floods which
had made it impossible to get letters down to Melbourne, or an expected
ship had not arrived on time. There was always an explanation for delays
and he never failed to give it. The message which came to me through all
the letters was that however hard he was working, whatever was happening,
he never forgot me and the ultimate goal, which was for us to be together.

And then no letters came. At first, though disappointed, I was not unduly
alarmed. It was the floods or a delayed ship and there would be several
when they did come. But they did not come and the weeks went on and
there was still no news.

Two months passed. I was frantic with anxiety; and one day Miss Emily
sent for me to come to the study. It was an arid place with its polished floor,
its reverent silence broken only by the ticking of the ormolu clock on the
macramé-draped mantelpiece. Miss Emily was seated at the desk, her
expression one of pain which suggested, erroneously, that what was to follow
hurt her more than it hurt me. Parents thought Miss Emily very kind and
gratefully entrusted their children to her; they felt she would protect their
darlings from the harsher rule of Miss Grainger. In fact it was mild-seeming
Miss Emily who was really in charge, but she liked it to be believed that the
unpopular rules and regulations were made by her sister.

'I am sure,' she said, her elbows resting on the desk, the tips of her fingers
pressed together while she regarded me with some severity, 'I am *quite* sure
that you would not wish for charity. It is now two months since we heard
from your father and while Miss Grainger is always prepared to be
reasonable, she cannot be expected to feed and clothe you, at the same time
giving you an education fit for the daughter of a gentleman.'

'I am convinced that a letter from my father is on the way.'

Miss Emily coughed. 'It is a long time coming.'

'He is in Australia, Miss Emily. Posts are delayed.'

'Those were exactly Miss Grainger's words in the beginning. Now three
months' school bills are outstanding.'

'But I am sure it will be all right. Something has delayed the letters. I am
certain of it.'

'I wish I could be . . . for your sake. Miss Grainger is distressed but she has decided she can wait no longer. She cannot continue to support you – feed you, clothe you, educate you. . . .' She made each item sound like a labour of Hercules. 'But, however, she does not wish to turn you out.'

'Perhaps,' I said haughtily, 'it would be better if I left.'

'That is a rather foolish statement, I fear. Where would you go, pray?'

When Miss Emily 'prayed' it meant that she was really annoyed; but I was too apprehensive for caution. My fears for my father's safety – because I knew that only if something dreadful had happened to him could those letters have failed to arrive – made the wrath of Miss Emily comparatively unimportant to me.

'I could do something, I suppose,' I said spiritedly.

'You have no knowledge of the world. You, a girl of what is it? Sixteen?'

'Seventeen next month, Miss Emily.'

'Well, Miss Grainger is going to be very generous. She is not going to turn you adrift. She has a proposition and of course you will wish to accept it. Indeed you can do nothing else when you consider the alternative.'

Miss Emily's smile was pious; the palms of her hands were now pressed together and she turned her eyes up to the ceiling. 'You may stay at the school as one of our pupil teachers. That will go a *little* way towards earning your keep.'

So I became a pupil teacher and knew utter despair. It was not because of my position in the school but because with every passing day, when no letter came, my fears increased. I had never been so miserable in the whole of my life. Every day I would tell myself that a letter must come; and every night when I lay in my little attic bed – for I had moved from the dormitory – I asked myself whether it ever would. Should I live the rest of my life at Danesworth House waiting for news? I should grow old and fusty like Miss Graeme whose hair resembled a bird's nest made of grey-brown fluff; I should become pale and wan like Miss Carter; I should peer myopically like Mademoiselle and worry because I could not control the girls.

In the meantime I was less important than they were. I joined Mary Farrow in the attic bedroom with its bare boards and rush mats. Mary had been an orphan in the care of her grandmother and when Mary was sixteen the grandmother had died and Mary was left penniless. Miss Grainger had been magnanimous as with me, and Mary had become a pupil teacher. She was as colourless in her character as in her complexion, and was resigned to her future as I never could be.

We fared worse than the servants. They at least were not constantly reminded that they owed their position to Miss Grainger's charity. They were more useful than we were, too. We were apprentices and our board and lodgings were our only payment. We must not only give the younger children their lessons but act as nursemaids to them; we must keep our attic clean and be prepared to perform any task that might be imposed on us by Miss Emily or Miss Grainger – and they saw that there were plenty.

The mistresses despised us – as did the servants; even the children realized that they might take liberties in our classes which they dared take in no others. Miss Emily had a way of coming silently into a classroom – always when it was most unruly – and standing and listening with her gentle smile before she delivered a reproof in front of the children which made them more certain than ever that they could plague us. Poor Mary suffered more from them than I did. She was meek; I had a fiery temper and I think they were just a little in awe of me.

Sometimes I would lie in the narrow bed at one end of the attic waiting for the ghostly touch of the chestnut tree as the wind moved gently through its branches, and I would say to myself. 'Abandoned! This is the second time in your life. Why is it that people abandon you? There must be a reason for it. Twice in one lifetime.'

But my father would never abandon me. He would come back. I could not face a world without him. I had known such contentment merely to be with him and, until recently, the greatest gift to childhood – security. Not monetary security, but the only kind which is important to the child – the security of being loved.

I had been a pupil teacher for barely a month – though it seemed more like a year – when the news came.

I was reading to my class that morning, but I was not really attending. It was a warm spring day. A bee was now crawling up the window, now flying off in exasperation to return and fling itself against the glass in a desperate effort to free itself. It was trapped. There was no way out; but the window on the other side of the room was open and the foolish creature would not go there. He continued to buzz frantically up and down. Caught! Like myself.

The door opened suddenly and there was Miss Graeme looking at me oddly. I noticed that the breeze from the open door sent the bee in the opposite direction. He found the open window and flew out.

'You are wanted in the study,' said Miss Graeme.

My first thought was: There is news of him. Perhaps when I reach the study he will be there.

I turned to the door.

'You should leave your class some work,' reproved Miss Graeme.

I told them to go on reading; then I fled past Miss Graeme, up the stairs to the study. I knocked at the door and waited for the response. Miss Emily was seated at the desk, a letter before her.

'You may sit down, Nora. I have a letter here. There has been some delay in the posts owing to the floods in Australia.' I sat, keeping my eyes on her face. 'You will have to be brave, my dear,' she went on gently.

I felt sick with apprehension. It must be very bad news since she called me 'my dear'. It was. There could be nothing more terrible.

'The reason we have not heard from your father is that he is dead.'

I stumbled up to my attic and lay on my bed. The leaves of the chestnut tree lightly touched the window; the breeze made a soft moaning noise and the sunshine threw dancing patterns on the wall.

I should never see him again. There would be no fortune, no travels, no being together – only utter desolation. He was buried on the other side of the world, and all the time I had been waiting for a letter from him he had been lying in a coffin with the earth on top of him. Even Miss Emily was sorry for me.

'Go to your room,' she had said. 'You will need to recover from the shock of this.'

I had come blindly up to my room. I had not listened to what she was saying. Words came back to me as I lay there. 'It has settled your future.' I did not care for the future; I was only concerned with the misery of the present. I kept seeing him, remembering his laughing eyes, hearing his booming voice. 'When my ship comes home . . .'

And the terrible truth was that his ship would never come home. It had foundered on the rocks of death.

He had written to me as he was dying. How like him! The letter had come by way of his solicitors with the news of his death. Miss Emily had withheld it for a few hours to give me, as she said, a little time to recover from the initial shock.

'Don't grieve for me. We had a happy time together. Don't let any sadness touch your memories of me, Nora. I'd rather you forgot me altogether than thinking of me should make you sad. It was an accident . . . and it's finished me, but you're going to be all right, Nora. My good friend has promised me that. Lynx is a man of his word, and he has given me that word so that I can die happy. He is going to take care of you, Nora, and he'll do it better than I could. When you read this I'll be gone, but you'll not be alone. . . .'

The writing was scarcely legible. The last words were: 'Be happy' and they were only just decipherable. I pictured the pen falling from his hands as he wrote them. To the end all his love and concern had been for me.

I read the letter again and again. I would carry it with me always.

And I lay numbly on my bed, unable to think of what the future held, unable to think of anything but that he had gone.

Miss Emily sent for me. Miss Grainger was with her in the study and with them was a man in black with a white cravat and a very solemn expression. I thought he was my new guardian, but he could never be the man my father had described as Lynx.

'This is Nora Tamasin,' said Miss Emily. 'Nora, this is Mr. Marlin of Marlin Sons and Barlow – your father's solicitors.'

I sat down and listened without taking everything in; I was still numb with misery. But I gathered that everything had been legally arranged and I was to be given into the care of Mr. Charles Herrick, the man whom my father had appointed as my guardian.

'Mr. Herrick naturally wishes to take you into his home and you are to join him there as soon as possible. This is in Australia and your father's last wish was that you should do this. Mr. Herrick is unable to come to England but a member of his family will come to escort you to your new home. Mr. Herrick is anxious that you should not travel alone.'

I nodded, thinking: My father would have wanted that. He must have asked the Lynx – it was difficult to think of him with such a mild name as Mr. Herrick – to take great care of me.

It was expected that in a few weeks' time my guardian's emissary would arrive in England. I should in the meantime prepare myself to depart.

Mr. Marlin took his leave and Miss Emily said that everything was now most satisfactorily settled, by which I knew she meant that outstanding bills had been paid. The next few weeks I could utilize in preparation for my departure. There might be one or two things I needed to buy. I might do this – within reason – and Miss Emily would graciously allow one of the teachers to accompany me to the town and advise me on my purchases. Perhaps I would like to work at my books. Indeed I might feel that work was the best antidote to sorrow and might wish to continue to act as a pupil teacher for which work – although this had not been mentioned before – I seemed to have an aptitude.

'No, thank you, Miss Emily,' I said. 'I will prepare myself to meet whoever is coming for me and do what shopping I consider necessary.'

Miss Emily bowed her head.

I stayed in my attic quarters. Poor Mary was envious. She only saw that a new and exciting life stretched out before me; she did not realize what grief had led me to it. I shopped. I bought the tartan cape and skirt and strong boots which I thought would be needed where I was going. I had little interest in these purchases, nor in anything. I could think of nothing but the fact that my father was dead.

And at last I was once more summoned to the study.

'You will travel in the company of Miss Herrick, who is I gather your guardian's daughter – a lady of responsible years. You are to meet her at the Falcon Inn which is some five or six miles from the town of Canterbury. For some reason the lady is there. There is a mention of business which has to be performed. It seems a little inconvenient as I suppose you will be sailing from Gravesend or Tilbury. However, those are the instructions. At Canterbury a fly will be waiting to conduct you to the Falcon Inn. Miss Graeme will accompany you to London and see you safely on to the Canterbury train. You will be all right from there on.'

'Of course, Miss Emily.'

'After Miss Graeme has left you, you must on no account speak to strangers,' said Miss Grainger.

'I certainly should not, Miss Grainger.'

'So there is no difficulty. On Thursday morning at nine o'clock you will leave Danesworth House. The fly will take you to the station. The train leaves at nine-thirty. Cook will pack a sandwich for you.'

'I am sure there is no need for Miss Graeme to accompany me. I could easily change trains when I get to London.'

'That is quite out of the question,' said Miss Emily. 'You would have to get across London by yourself. Unthinkable! Why Canterbury should have been chosen, I can't imagine. But that is the case; and we have been requested by your guardian – through the solicitors – that you should be accompanied until you are safely on the Canterbury train. Therefore it is unthinkable that it could be otherwise.'

So Lynx's despotic rule could touch even Miss Emily.

I packed my bags; I waited; the girls and mistresses gave me their respectful interest. I was the sort of person to whom strange things happened. I might have enjoyed my new importance if I could have forgotten my father's death.

At last the day came and Miss Graeme and I left Danesworth House. We boarded the London train and sat side by side looking out at the green fields and the wheat which was turning to gold. Gold! I thought angrily. If he had never gone to look for gold he would be here now.

My eyes filled with angry tears. Why had he not been content to be an ordinary person! But then he would not have been himself. Miss Graeme touched my arm lightly and I saw that there were tears in her eyes. She started to tell me that sorrow came to us all and we had to 'bear up' and go on with our lives. There was 'someone' who had 'never spoken' but who had intended to and would have done so if he had come home from the war, but he died unnecessarily and cruelly on the battlefield. In the Crimea, I supposed; and so, instead of being a buxom and happy mother, she was a wizened grey-brown mouse of a school teacher.

I listened and tried to show my sympathy; then we ate our sandwiches and in due course arrived at the London station. Flustered and aware of her responsibilities, Miss Graeme hailed a cab and we went to Charing Cross station where finally I was put into the train.

The last I saw of Miss Graeme was her spare figure in the brown coat and skirt and the hat with the brown veil, looking forlorn and wistful as the train carried me away.

Now I began to feel apprehensive. The new life had begun and I was on my own. I could run away now if I liked. I had a little money – very little; I could take a post as governess. I had my teacher's experience. But my father had wanted me to go to the Lynx, so I was given no choice. Suppose I arrived in Australia and hated it. Suppose they did not want me. I knew so little of what lay before me. I had not asked enough questions. I had been submerged by my misery; and now suddenly, here I was, speeding along to Canterbury, looking out at the orchards of apples and pears which would not be ready for picking for almost another two months and then I should be far away. We went past the hop fields which in another month would be alive with the activities of the pickers; cowled tops of oast houses dominated the scene. I wanted to cry to the train driver: Stop. I am rushing towards the unknown. I want a little time to think.

Perhaps in that moment my grief had receded a little since I could feel this misgiving for the future when previously I had felt nothing but the tragedy of the present. But the train rushed on relentlessly. We were at the station. I alighted and the porter took my bags. The fly which was to take me to the Falcon Inn was waiting for me.

We drove away from the station, past the ancient walls of the town and out into the country.

'Is it far to the Falcon Inn?' I asked the driver.

'Well, it's some little way out, miss. Most people stay in the town.'

I wondered why Miss Herrick who had come to England to collect me should have arranged for the meeting to take place at this spot. It was as Miss Emily had remarked 'unusual'. Perhaps the Lynx had ordained it.

The countryside was lusciously green, we passed through several villages clustered round the church – village greens and ancient inns; and at length we came to the village of Widegates with its old church and row of houses, most of them Tudor, some earlier still. I caught a glimpse in the distance of grey towers and asked what they were.

'That would be Whiteladies, miss. It's the big house round here.'

'Whiteladies. Why is it called that?'

'It was a convent once and the nuns wore white habits, so the saying goes. Some of it still stands. The family built the house there keeping what was left of the convent.'

'Who are the family?'

'Their name is Cardew. The family's been there for three hundred years or more.'

We had pulled up at the Falcon Inn. The stone steps which led to the door were worn away in the middle; the sign on which was depicted a falcon was freshly painted and over the door was the date 1418.

The driver brought in my bags. 'Everything's settled, miss,' he said. So I went to the reception desk and told them who I was.

'Ah yes,' said the receptionist. 'I'll have you shown to your room. There is a message for you. Will you go down to the parlour when you are ready.'

I went to my room which was large but rather dark because of the leaded windows; the floor sloped slightly and the wooden beams proclaimed its age. There was water in the ewer so I hastily washed and combed my thick dark hair.

When I was ready I went down to the inn parlour to which I was directed by a maid. There was no woman there but a man rose as I entered. He put his hands behind his back and watched me. I remembered Miss Emily's injunctions not to speak to strangers. I certainly should not speak to this one if I could help it for his look struck me as being a trifle insolent.

But he spoke to me. 'You are looking for someone?' His accent was faintly unusual; he himself was tall and lean; his face was weathered brown as far as I could see, for he was standing with his back to the light and there was not much of it in any case as the windows were similar to those in my bedroom.

I nodded coolly.

'Perhaps I can help you.'

'Thank you. I don't need any help.'

'Oh, I can see you are very self-sufficient.'

I turned away. Perhaps I should go to the desk and ask for Miss Herrick. I felt Miss Emily would not approve of my waiting in this room with a rather forward stranger; and although I did not intend to allow Miss Emily's judgments to rule my life, in this instance I was in agreement with her.

'I am sure I *can* help you,' he said.

'I don't see how.'

'Then I will enlighten you. You are looking for a Miss Herrick.'

I looked startled and he laughed. It was very irritating laughter. He was truculent, very sure of himself.

'That's happens to be so,' I said primly.

'Well, you won't find Miss Herrick here.'

'What do you mean?'

'What I say. I always say what I mean.'

'Are you mistaking me for someone else?'

'You know very well I'm not. You are Nora Tamasin. Right.'

I was annoyed by the manner in which he answered his own question. Also I was bewildered. How could he know so much about me?

'And you have come here to meet Miss Herrick. She is not here.'

'How do you know?'

'Because I know where she is.'

'Where is she?'

'About forty miles north of Melbourne.'

'You are mistaken. The Miss Herrick I have come to meet is here in this inn. She sent a fly to meet me at the station.'

'I sent that fly.'

'You!'

'I reckon I should have introduced myself a little earlier. I just liked teasing you a bit because you looked so haughty. Adelaide, my sister, hasn't come. There was too much for her to do at home so my father thought I should be the one to come for you. Besides he wanted me to see a bit of England. So I'm here to take you back. Stirling Herrick, named after the Stirling River, just as Adelaide, my sister, is named after the town. It was my father's tribute to the country of his adoption.'

'Your father is Charles Herrick?'

'You've hit the nail right on the head, as they say. I've come to take you back. You're looking doubtful. You want to see my credentials? Right. Now here's a letter from that firm of solicitors, Marlin something . . . and I can prove to you over and over again that I am who I am.'

'This is all very strange.'

'It's all very simple. My father has promised to look after you so you're coming home with me. I'm a sort of brother. You're not looking very pleased about that.'

I said: 'I can't understand why he should have sent you.'

'Perfectly simple. He wanted me to come to England. I've been having talks about marketing our wool.'

'Here in Canterbury?'

'Oh yes. My business takes me all over the country. I had to ask you to come here so that we could have a day to get to know each other before you were rushed on to the ship. Now I am going to suggest we send for tea and over that we'll talk.'

He pulled the bell and when the maid came ordered tea. When I saw the thin bread and butter and scones with cream and strawberry jam, I realized I was hungry. He watched me while I poured out and there was amusement in his eyes, which were an unusual shade of green; they almost disappeared when he laughed and he looked as though he were accustomed to screwing them up against the strong light – which was very likely. I guessed he was in his twenties – about eight years my senior perhaps – and I thought it very unconventional that a young man should have been sent to be my travelling companion. Very different from the Miss Herrick I was expecting. I was sure Miss Emily would disapprove and that pleased me. I felt better than I had since I had received the news of my father's death.

'Why was I told that *Miss* Herrick would be waiting for me?' I demanded.

'It was arranged that she should come at the start, but Lynx decided that the house could not be run without Adelaide. He could spare me better.'

Lynx! The magic name. It was the first time he had used it so I said interrogatively: 'Lynx?' wanting to hear more of that strange man.

'That's my father. People often call him that. It means he has sharp eyes.'

'I gathered that.'

'You are really smart, I can see.' His smile was ironical.

I said: 'Does he really want me ... this Lynx?'

'He's promised your father to look after you so of course he wants you.'

'He might feel he must do it from a sense of duty because his conscience would worry him if he didn't.'

'He doesn't have any sense of duty ... nor conscience either. He does what he wants, and he wants you to live with us.'

'Why?'

'No one ever questions his motives. He knows what he wants and that's about all there is to say.'

'He sounds an impossible sort of person.'

'Lynx *is* possible, although you might doubt it until you know him.'

'You talk of him as though he's some sort of god.'

'Well, I reckon that's not a bad description.'

'Does everyone have to be as reverent as his son?'

That made him laugh. 'You have a sharp tongue, Nora Tamasin.'

'Do you think it will help to protect me against this Lynx?'

'You've got it wrong. He's the one who is going to protect you.'

'If I don't want to stay I shall come back here.'

He bowed his head.

'There would be ways and means, I am sure,' I added.

'And you'd find them, I reckon.'

I had eaten one scone; he finished the entire plateful. He folded his arms and smiled at me as though he found me amusing. I was not sure what to make of him. Of one thing I was certain. Messrs Marlin Sons and Barlow could not have known that he had come alone to take me back with him for they, like Miss Emily, would surely consider this rather improper.

'But,' I said, speaking my thoughts aloud, 'I suppose you are a sort of brother.'

He laughed. 'I reckon so, Sister Nora. And that makes everything all right. You don't think so.'

'You have a habit of attempting to read people's thoughts ... not always correctly.'

'But you are pleased.'

'It's too soon to answer that question. I hardly know you.'

'We're pleased to have a new sister.'

I was silent for a while; then I said, 'How did my father die?'

'Haven't they told you?'

'They merely said it was an accident.'

'An accident? He should have handed over the gold, then they wouldn't have shot him.'

'*They* shot him! Who?'

'No one knows who. He'd been out to the mine and was on his way back on the dray, bringing gold with him. There was a hold-up. They were waylaid. It often happens. Those fellows have a nose for gold. They know when it's being carried. So they held up the dray five miles out of Cradle Creek. Your father wouldn't give it up so they shot him.'

I felt bewildered. I had imagined his falling from a tree or being thrown from his horse. I had never thought of murder.

'So,' I said slowly, 'someone killed him.'

Stirling nodded. 'It happens now and then. It's a wild country and life's cheaper there than it is over here.'

'That was my *father*!' I felt furiously angry because someone had come along with a gun and wantonly taken that precious life. There was a new emotion to supersede my grief – anger against my father's murderer.

'If he had given up the gold he wouldn't have died,' said Stirling.

'Gold!' I said angrily.

'That's what they are all after. It's what they all want.'

'And this ... Lynx ... he does too?'

Stirling smiled. 'He wants it. He's determined to find it one day – so he will.'

'How I wish my father had never got this idea into his head! If he hadn't he would be here now.'

It was too much to contemplate. I turned away, determined that he should not see my intense emotion.

'It's like a fever,' he said. 'It gets into your brain. You think of everything you want in life and if you find gold ... real gold ... thousands of nuggets ... you can have it.'

'Everything?' I said.

'Everything you can think of.'

'My father found gold, it seems, and lost his life preserving it, and I lost him.'

'You're upset. You wait till you get out there. You'll understand then. It's a great life. You never know when you'll make a strike. It's a constant challenge, a constant hope.'

'And when you do someone kills you for it.'

'That's the life out there. Your father had bad luck.'

'It's ... hateful.'

'It's life. I've upset you. I should have broken it gently. The only thing that matters is that it happened.'

He stood up. 'You go back to your room. You rest awhile; and then we'll have some dinner together and talk some more. It's the best thing.'

I went up to my room, leaving him in the inn parlour. Was there to be no end to the shocks I was receiving, I asked myself. So he had been murdered. Killed in cold blood. It was fantastic. I pictured the dray lumbering along the road, the masked figure hiding under the trees and then 'Stand and deliver. Forfeit your gold or your life.' In my imagination I could see him clearly, the gold in bags about his waist perhaps. And he would say to himself: 'No, this is my gold . . . mine and Nora's.' Perhaps he was planning to bring me out to him so that I could share in the fortune, if fortune it was. So when the gun was pointing at him he refused to give up his gold, and so he gave up his life.

'I hate gold,' I said aloud. 'I wish it had never been discovered.' I thought in fury of the glittering eyes behind the mask, of a trigger that was coolly pulled, and a report that had put an end to all my happiness. Oh, how I hated my father's murderer!

He had not died immediately. They were able to take him to Lynx and he wrote his last letter to me. But he was dying then. And it need never have happened.

Stirling was right. I needed to be alone. This was almost as great a shock as the news of my father's death had been. It had not been an accident. It was deliberate murder.

I went to the window and looked out. Below me was the street with its ancient houses. I could see the spire of the church and the towers of the house they called Whiteladies. It had once been a convent, I remembered; the nuns had worn white habits; and this inn would have been there at the time. The pilgrims on their way to Canterbury would have stopped here – the last halt before they reached their goal. Looking down on the street I could so easily picture them, weary and footsore, yet relieved because the host of the Falcon Inn was waiting to welcome them and offer them food and shelter before they went on to Canterbury.

As I stood at the window I saw Stirling come out of the inn. I watched him walk purposefully down the street taking long strides, and looking as though he knew exactly where he was going.

So stunned had I been by first finding that he had come instead of Miss Herrrick to take me to Australia and then by his revelations about my father's death that I had not had time to consider him. So . . . he was the son of that man Lynx who was fast becoming a symbol in my mind. The all-powerful Lynx of whom people spoke with awe and the utmost respect. Why had Lynx not sent his daughter? Perhaps he did not care that she should travel alone. I had imagined her to be a middle-aged lady. But why had they said Miss Herrick would come and then sent a young man? It was all very strange.

Stirling had turned off the main street. I wondered where he had gone. His appearing like that had disturbed my train of thought. The sunlit street looked inviting. I could think better out of doors, I assured myself; so I put on my cape and went out. There were few people about. A lady with a parasol strolled by on the other side; a dog lay sleeping in a doorway. I walked down the street, glancing as I passed at the shop window where behind bottle glass wools, ribbons, hats and dresses were displayed. There was nothing there to interest me, so I went on and came to the turning which Stirling had taken. It led up a hill and there was a signpost which said: 'To Whiteladies'.

As I mounted the hill the grey walls came into sight; and when I reached the top I could look down and see the house in all its splendour. I knew that I could never forget it. I told myself afterwards that I knew even then what an important part it was to play in my life. I was spell-bound, bewitched, and in that moment forgot everything else but the magic of those towers, the ambience of monastic seclusion, the mullioned windows, the curved arches, the turrets and the tower, the sun shining on flinty grey walls. One almost expected to hear the sound of bells calling the nuns to prayer and to see white-clad figures emerging from the cloister.

I had an overwhelming desire to see more. I started to run downhill and I did not stop until I stood before the tall wrought-iron gate. This gate in itself was fascinating. I studied the intricate scrolls and mouldings; some white metal had been inlaid on the iron work on either side. I looked closer and saw that the decoration represented nuns. White Ladies, I thought; and I wondered whether it was the original gate which had stood there when there was a convent beyond it, long before the present house had been built. The grey stone wall stretched out on either side of the gates. Moss and lichen grew on it. How I should have loved to open the gate and walk into those magic precincts. This was more than a passing fancy; it was an urge which I had great difficulty in restraining. But how could one walk into someone's private house simply because it seemed the most fascinating place one had ever seen! I looked about me. There was a deep stillness everywhere. I felt completely alone. I remembered that Stirling had come this way. He would probably have passed this house without noticing it. I had decided that he would be lacking in imagination, and to him this would merely be a grey stone building; he would not think it exciting because centuries ago nuns in white robes had lived here. I wondered what it felt like to be shut away from the world; and I was suddenly interested and relieved to find that my thoughts had turned temporarily from my personal tragedy.

The wall was frustratingly high and as I walked along beside it I could only see the tower projecting above it. The view from the hilltop was much more revealing – only from that vantage point there was a sense of remoteness. Here one might be closer but the wall shut one out.

It seemed strange that when I was on the verge of going to a new country I should be so intrigued by an old house which I had never seen before and it seemed unlikely I should ever see again. Perhaps it was because I had been indifferent to everything for so long that I seized on this and believed I was more interested than I actually was.

As I walked beside the wall I heard voices.

'Ellen has brought out the tea, Lucie.' It was a clear high voice, very pleasant and I longed to see its owner.

'I will see if Lady Cardew is ready,' said another voice, deeper, slightly husky.

They went on talking but their voices were lowered and I could not hear what they were saying. What sort of people, I wondered, lived in this house? I *must* discover. I was in such a strange mood that I had almost convinced myself that if I could see on the other side of the wall I would find two white-robed nuns – ghosts from the past.

An enormous oak tree spread its branches over the walls. Its acorns would surely fall on Whiteladies' land. I studied the tree speculatively. I had not climbed a tree for some time. Such activities had not been encouraged at Danesworth House; but there was a fork which would make an adequate if not comfortable seat. I could not climb a tree. It was too undignified. Besides, what bad manners to spy on people. I fingered the soft silk scarf which my father had given me before he went to Australia; it was a soft shade of green and I loved it for itself in addition to the fact that it was one of his last gifts. I am sure he would have climbed the tree. Miss Emily would be horrified. That decided me – particularly as I heard the voices again.

'Are you feeling better, Mamma?' That was the clear young voice.

So I climbed to the fork of the tree which was just high enough to permit me to see over.

It was a beautiful scene. The grass was like green velvet, soft and smooth with an air of having been well tended through the centuries; there were flower beds containing roses and lavender; a fountain was throwing its silver spray over a white statue; the green shrubs had been cut into the shape of birds; a peacock strutted across the lawn displaying his magnificent tail while a plain little peahen followed in his glorious wake. It was a scene of utter peace. Close to the pond was a table laid for tea over which a big blue and white sunshade had been set; and seated at the table was a girl of about my age. She looked as though she were tall; she was certainly slender; a dainty Dresden figure. Her honey-coloured hair hung in long ringlets down her back; her gown was of pale blue with white lace collar and cuffs. She fitted the scene perfectly. There was another woman; she must be Lucie, I decided. She was about ten years older than the girl; and in a bath chair was a woman whom I guessed to be 'Mamma', fair-haired like the girl, delicate and fragile-looking with the same Dresden quality.

'It's pleasant in the shade, Mamma,' said the girl.

'I do hope so.' The voice was a little peevish. 'You know how the heat upsets me. Lucie, where are my smelling salts?'

I watched them talking together. Lucie had brought the chair closer to the girl who rose to make sure that the cushion behind Mamma's head was in the best place. Lucie went across the lawn presumably to fetch the smelling salts. I imagined her to be a companion, a higher servant, perhaps a poor relation. Poor Lucie!

They were talking but I only heard their voices when the breeze carried them to me. This breeze, which could be strong when it blew, was intermittent. What happened next was due to it. The scarf about my neck had become loosened during my climb. I had not noticed this and as I leaned forward to see and hear better, it caught in a branch and was dragged from my neck. It hung lightly suspended on the tree but as I was about to take it a stronger gust of wind caught it and, snatching it from me, carried it over the wall mischievously as though to punish me for eavesdropping. It fluttered across the grass and came to rest close to the group at the tea table but they did not seem to see it.

I was dismayed, thinking of the occasion when my father had given it to me. I either had to call to them and ask them to give it to me or to lose it.

I made up my mind that I could not shout to them from the tree. I would call at the house and concoct some story about its blowing over my head – which it had done – and I certainly would not tell them that inquisitiveness had made me climb a tree to spy on them.

I slid down to the foot of the tree and in my haste grazed my hand which started to bleed a little. While I was staring at it ruefully Stirling came towards me.

'Oak trees have their uses,' he said.

'What do you mean?'

'You know very well. You were spying on the tea party.'

'How could you know that unless you were spying too?'

'It's less shocking for me to climb trees than girls, you know.'

'So you were spying on them.'

'No. Like you I was merely taking a polite look.'

'You were interested enough to climb a tree and look over the wall!'

'Let's say my motives were similar to yours. But we have to retrieve the scarf. Come on. I'll go with you. As your deputy-guardian I can't allow you to enter a strange house alone.'

'How can we go in there?'

'Simple. You ask to see Lady Cardew and tell her that your scarf is lying on her beautiful lawn.'

'Do you think we should ask to see her? Perhaps we could tell one of the servants.'

'You are too retiring. No. We'll go in boldly and ask for Lady Cardew.'

We had reached the gates. Stirling opened them and we went into a cobbled courtyard at the end of which was an archway. Stirling went through this; I followed. We were on the lawn.

I felt uneasy. This was most unconventional, but Stirling was unconventional and unused to our formal manners; and as we crossed the grass towards the party at the tea table and they looked up in blank astonishment, I realized how very extraordinary our intrusion must seem.

'Good afternoon,' said Stirling. 'I hope we don't disturb you. We have come to retrieve my ward's scarf.'

The girl looked bewildered. 'Scarf?' she repeated.

'Oddly enough,' I said, trying to bring some normality into the scene, 'it blew from my neck over your wall.'

They still looked startled but they couldn't deny it because there was the scarf. Stirling picked it up and gave it to me; and as he did so he said: 'What have you done to your hand?'

'Oh dear,' said the girl, 'it's bleeding.'

'I grazed it against a tree when I was trying to catch my scarf,' I stammered. Stirling was looking at me with amusement and I thought for a moment that he was going to tell them I had climbed a tree to look at them.

The girl appeared concerned. She had a sweet expression. 'Are you staying here?' asked the one named Lucie. 'I feel sure you don't live here or we should know.'

'We're at the Falcon Inn,' I said.

'Nora,' cut in Stirling quickly, 'you are feeling faint.' He turned to the girl. 'Perhaps she should sit down for a moment.'

'Certainly,' said the girl. 'Certainly. Your hand should be attended to. Lucie could bandage it for you, couldn't you, Lucie?'

'But of course,' said Lucie meekly.

'You should take her into the house and bathe it. Take her to Mrs. Glee's room. She is certain to have water on the boil, and I do think it should be washed.'

'Come with me,' said Lucie. I wanted to protest because I was interested in the girl and would have preferred to stay and talk with her.

Stirling had sat down and was being offered a cup of tea.

I followed Lucie across the lawn towards the house. We went through a heavy iron studded door and were in a stone walled corridor. Facing us was a flight of stairs.

Lucie led the way up these stairs to a landing. 'The housekeeper's room is along here. This corridor leads to the servants' hall.'

We went up a spiral staircase to a landing on which there were several doors. Lucie knocked at one of them and we were told to enter. On a spirit stove was a kettle of hot water, and a middle-aged woman in a black bombazine dress with a white cap on her thick greying hair was sitting in an armchair dozing. I guessed this to be Mrs. Glee and I was right. Lucie explained about the scarf and I showed my hand.

'It's nothing but a light graze,' said Mrs. Glee.

'Miss Minta thinks it should be washed and dressed.'

Mrs. Glee grunted. 'Miss Minta and her bandages! There's always something. Last week it was that bird. Couldn't fly so Miss Minta took charge. Then there was that dog which was caught in a trap.'

I didn't much care to be compared with a bird and a dog, so I said: 'Really there's no need.' But Mrs. Glee ignored me and poured some water from the kettle into a basin. My hand was deftly washed and bandaged while I told them we were staying at the Falcon Inn and shortly leaving for Australia. When this was done I thanked Mrs. Glee and Lucie conducted me back to the lawn. I apologized as we went. I was afraid I was being rather a trouble, I said. It was no trouble, she informed me in such a way as to suggest in fact it was; but perhaps that was her manner.

'Miss Minta is very kindhearted,' I said.

'Very,' she agreed.

There were many questions I should have liked to ask but that would have been difficult even if she were communicative which she decidedly was not.

On the lawn Stirling was talking to Minta, and Lady Cardew was looking on languidly. I felt irritated by his complacent manner. It was due to me that we were here and he was getting the best of the adventure. I wondered what they had been talking about while I was away.

'You must have a cup of tea before you go,' said Minta, and as she poured the tea and brought it to me I was again struck by her grace – and kindness too. She really did seem concerned.

'Miss Cardew was telling me about the house,' said Stirling. 'It's the finest I ever saw.'

'And the most ancient,' laughed Minta. 'He tells me he has recently come from Australia and that he is taking you back with him because his father has become your guardian. Sugar?'

The egg-shell china cup was handed to me. I noticed her long white delicate fingers and the opal ring which she was wearing.

'How exciting it must be to be going to Australia,' she said.

'It must be exciting to live in a house like this,' I replied.

'Having lived all my life in it I think I have become somewhat blasé. It would only be if we lost it that we should realize what it means to us.'

'But you will never lose it,' I replied. 'Who could possibly part with such a place?'

'Oh never, of course,' she answered lightly.

Lucie was busy at the table. Lady Cardew's eyes were fixed on me but she did not appear to see me; she had scarcely spoken and seemed half asleep. I wondered if she were ill; she did not seem very old, but she certainly behaved like an old woman.

I asked Minta about the house, telling her that the cab driver had pointed it out to me. Yes, she said, it was true that it had been built on the site of the old nunnery. In fact quite a lot of the original building remained.

'Some of the rooms really are like cells, aren't they, Lucie?'

Lucie agreed that they were.

'It's been in the family for years now and of course I've disappointed them because I'm a girl. There are often girls in this family. But we've been here . . . how long is it, Lucie? 1550? Yes that's right. Henry VIII dissolved the monasteries and Whiteladies was partially destroyed then. My ancestor did something to please him and was given the place to build on, which he did in due course. There were lots of the stones left, so they were used; and, as I said, a good deal of the place remained.'

'Mr. Wakefield is here,' said Lucie. A man was coming across the lawn – the most exquisite man I had ever seen. His clothes were impeccably tailored and I discovered that his manners matched them.

Minta jumped up and ran towards him. He took her hand and kissed it. Charming! I thought. I knew Stirling would be amused. Then he went to Lady Cardew and did the same. He bowed to Lucie. Oh yes, Lucie was not quite one of the family.

Minta had turned to us. 'I'm afraid I don't know your names. You see, Franklyn, a scarf blew over and it belongs to Miss . . .'

'Tamasin,' I said. 'Nora Tamasin.' He bowed beautifully. I added: 'And this is Mr. Stirling Herrick.'

'From Australia,' added Minta.

'How interesting!' Mr. Franklyn Wakefield's face expressed polite interest in my scarf and us and I liked him for it.

'You're just in time for a cup of tea,' said Minta.

I realized of course that there was no reason why we should stay and unless we took our departure immediately we should become ungracious intruders. Stirling however made no attempt to move. He had settled back in his chair and was watching the scene and in particular Minta with an intentness which could only be described as eager.

I said, rising: 'You have been most kind. We must go. It only remains to say thank you for being so good to strangers.'

I sensed Stirling's annoyance with me. He wanted to stay; he seemed to have no idea that we were intruding on their privacy, or if he had he did not care. But I was determined.

Minta smiled at Lucie who immediately rose to conduct us to the gates.

'I do apologize for intruding on your tea-party,' I said.

'It was quite a diversion,' replied Lucie. There was that in her manner which I found disconcerting. She was aloof, yet somehow vulnerable. She seemed over-anxious to maintain a dignity which was perhaps due to the fact that she was a poor relation.

'Miss Minta is charming,' I said.

'I'll endorse that,' added Stirling.

'She *is* a delightful person,' agreed Lucie.

'And I am grateful to you for bandaging my hand, Miss . . .'

'Maryan,' she supplied. 'Lucie Maryan.'

'A poor relation certainly,' I thought.

Stirling, who, I was to discover, snapped his fingers at the conventional rules of polite society, asked bluntly, 'Are you a relation of the Cardews?'

She hesitated and for a moment I thought she was going to reprove him for his inquisitiveness. Then she said: 'I am nurse-companion to Lady Cardew.'

And then we had reached the gate. 'I trust,' she said coldly, 'that the hand soon heals. Goodbye.'

When we had passed through the iron gates Lucie shut them firmly behind us. We walked in silence for a few moments then Stirling laughed.

'Quite an adventure,' I said.

'Well, you certainly wanted to know what was going on behind that wall.'

'And so it seems did you.'

'It's a pretty scarf. We should both be grateful to it. It was our ticket of entrance, you might say.'

'It's an odd household.'

'Odd! How do you mean . . . odd?'

'On the surface there are the mother and daughter and nurse-companion. Very ordinary probably. But I felt there was something different there. The mother was quiet. I believe she was half asleep most of the time.'

'Well, she's an invalid.'

We were both silent after that. I glanced sideways at him and I knew he shared my mood. We were both bemused in some strange way.

I said, 'Do you know, when I stepped through that gate I felt as though I had walked into a new world . . . something quite different from anything I had known before. I felt that something tremendously dramatic was happening and because it was all so quiet and in a way ordinary that made it rather sinister.'

Stirling laughed. He was definitely not the fanciful type. It was no use trying to explain my feelings to him. Yet I did feel that I knew him better since this adventure in Whiteladies. I had forgotten that this time yesterday I was not aware of his existence. And for the first time since my father had died I felt excited – it was all the more intriguing because I was not quite sure why.

The next morning we left the Falcon Inn for London and the day after that we boarded the *Carron Star* at Tilbury.

My journey to the other side of the world had begun.

Chapter Two

I quickly realized that life on the *Carron Star* was going to be a little spartan, even though we travelled first class. I shared a cabin with a young clergyman's daughter who was going to Melbourne to be married. She was both elated and apprehensive; her fiancé had left England two years before to make a home for her in the New World and now had a small property there. She was worried about her trunks of clothes and the linen she was taking out. 'One has to be prepared,' she told me. Fortunately she wanted to talk about herself so much that she did not ask questions about me, for which I was glad.

She told me that the fare was £50 and I felt a glow of satisfaction because my new guardian was paying so much to have me conveyed to him.

We were lucky, she explained, in the first class, because passengers in the other two classes must bring their own cutlery, drinking mugs, cups and saucers, besides a water bottle. Her fiancé had been most insistent that she travel first class. It was really a great adventure for a young girl to travel across the world by herself; but her aunt had seen her safely aboard and her fiancé would be waiting to greet her. She wanted me to know that she was a very cherished young lady with her trunks of clothes and fine linen.

She did ask if I were travelling alone, so I told her I was with my guardian. She opened her eyes very wide when she saw Stirling who, she commented, seemed somewhat young for the role of guardian; and I am sure she thought there was something very odd about me from that moment.

In the dining-room I sat with Stirling. At first most people thought we were brother and sister, and when it became known that I was his ward there was some raising of eyebrows, but the wonder of this soon passed. The weather was rough to begin with and that meant that many were confined to their cabins; and when they emerged the unconventionality of our position seemed to have been accepted by most.

During the gale Stirling and I sat on deck and he talked to me about Australia. Lynx was never long out of the conversation and I was more impatient to see him than I was to see the new country. Every day seemed to bring me closer to Stirling. I began to understand him. His manner could be brusque, but this did not mean that he was angry or indifferent; he prided himself on his frankness and if he was blunt with me he expected me to be the same with him. He despised artificiality in any form. I learned this through his attitude to our fellow passengers. I thought often of those people whom we had met at Whiteladies and it seemed to me that Stirling was the complete antithesis of Franklyn Wakefield as I was to Minta. It was strange that these people whom I had seen so briefly should have impressed themselves so much on my mind that I compared them with everyone I met.

Life at sea might have been monotonous to some passengers who longed for their journey's end; not to me. I was interested in everything and most of all in Stirling. He undoubtedly chafed over the tediousness and was longing to be home. We breakfasted about nine and dined at twelve; and between that time Stirling and I would pace the decks for exercise while most people wrote their letters home so that they could be dispatched at the next port of call. But I had no one to write to – except a note to poor Mary. I often thought of her in the dreary attic, confined to life at Danesworth House and was sorry for her.

I remember sitting on deck with Stirling when most of the people were confined to their cabins because of the weather and feeling pleased because he admired me for being a good sailor. He was apt to be impatient with people's failings, I had learned. I wondered how I should match up to his expectations. I gathered that he spent a good deal of time on horseback. My father had taught me to ride when were in the country, but I imagined that hacking through the English country lanes might be different from galloping across the bush.

I mentioned this to Stirling and he hastened to reassure me.

'You'll be all right,' he told me. 'I'll find a horse for you. A gentleman of a horse at first, with as fine manners as that Mr. Wakefield you were so taken with. And after that . . .'

'A manly horse,' I suggested. 'As manly as Stirling Herrick.'

We laughed a great deal together. We argued, because there were so many things about which we did not agree. Stirling was often at variance with our fellow passengers; he would allow himself to be drawn into discussions with them and during these never minced his words. He was not very popular with some of the pompous gentlemen, but I noticed that many of the women had a ready smile for him.

Later I realized how good this voyage was for me. It took me completely away from those wretched months when I had first waited anxiously for news of my father and then staggered under the terrible blow when it came.

The pattern of life on board was breakfast in the saloon, the long mornings, luncheon at twelve, the slow afternoons, dinner at four for which passengers put on their more elaborate clothes and during which the band played light music, and then strolling about the decks until tea at seven.

We went ashore at Gibraltar and spent a pleasant morning there. It was wonderful to ride in a carriage with Stirling and see the sights of the place: the shops, the apes, and the rock itself.

'Sometimes,' I said, 'I wish this trip could go on for ever.'

Stirling grimaced.

'Suppose we missed the ship,' I suggested. 'Suppose we built a ship of our own and went on sailing round the world wherever the fancy took us.'

'What crazy things you think of!' He was derisive. How different from my father who would have gone on with the wild, impossible story of how we built our ship and the exotic places we sailed to.

'I remember him,' he said. 'He would talk in the most fantastic way, pretending that what he knew was impossible would happen.'

'It was a lovely way to live.'

'It was crazy. What sense is there in pretending something will happen when you know it won't?'

I would not allow any criticism of my father.

'It made life gay and exciting,' I protested.

'It was false. I think it's a waste of time to pretend you believe in the impossible.'

'You are very matter-of-fact and . . .'

'Dull?'

I was silent and he urged: 'Come on. Tell the truth.'

'I like to think wonderful things can happen.'

'Even when you know they can't?'

'Who says they can't?'

'Like coming ashore for a few hours and building a ship and sailing off round the world without a navigator, a captain or a pilot, taking no account of harbour dues and navigation. You'll have to grow up, Nora, when you're in Australia.'

I was annoyed, seeing in this an attack on my father.

'Perhaps I shouldn't have come.'

'It's too early to comment on that.'

'If you're going to think I'm childish . . .'

'We certainly shall if you indulge in childish fantasy as –'

'As my father did. Did you think him childish?'

'We thought him not very practical. His end showed that, didn't it? If he had handed over the gold he would be alive today. What sense is there in deluding yourself into thinking that you can hold something and giving your life to prove you're wrong?'

I was hurt and angry and yet not able to discuss my father logically. I grew silent and was angry with Stirling for spoiling a perfect day. But this was typical of my relationship with him. He made no concessions to polite conversation; he stated what he believed and nothing would make him diverge from it. I knew that what he said was right but I could not bear that my father should be subjected to censure.

Although at times I disliked his overbearance, when he showed – as he often did – that he was taking care of me, I felt a warm, comfortable emotion.

The weather had grown warm and I loved the tropical evenings. After the seven o'clock meal he would sit on deck and talk. Those were the occasions to which I most looked forward, even more than the sunlit days when we would walk up and down the deck or lean over the rail and he would point out a frolicking porpoise or a flying fish.

One evening as we sat on deck looking out into the warm darkness of the tropical waters I said to Stirling. 'What if Lynx doesn't like me?'

'He'd still look after you. He's given his word.'

'He sounds difficult to please.'

Stirling nodded. This was true. Lynx might be all-powerful but he was not always benevolent.

'He sounds like one of the Roman gods whom people were always placating.'

Stirling grinned at the comparison. 'People do try to please him naturally,' he said.

'And if they don't?'

'He lets them know.'

'Sometimes I think I should have done better to stay at Danesworth House.'

'You'll have to learn to be truthful if you want to please Lynx.'

'I'm not sure that I want to. I should hate to be his meek little slave.'

'You wait and see. You'll want to please him. Everybody does.'

'You're brutally frank about *my* father. Why shouldn't I be about yours?'

'You should always say what's in your mind, of course.'

'Well, I think your Lynx sounds like a conceited, power-crazy megalomaniac.'

'Let's consider that. He has a high opinion of himself – he shares that with everyone else. He likes to be in command and there is no one like him. So, slightly modified, your description might not be completely inaccurate.'

'Tell me more about him.'

So he talked of his father as we sat there and I made many pictures in my mind of this powerful man who had so impressed my father that he had left me in his care.

'He was sent out of England as a prisoner thirty-five years ago,' said Stirling. 'It had its effect on him. He's going back one day ... when he's ready.'

'When will he be ready?'

'He told me once that he will know when the time comes.'

'He does talk to you sometimes like an ordinary human being then?'

Stirling smiled. 'I believe you have made up your mind to dislike him. That is very unwise. Yes, he is human, very human.'

'And I've been thinking of him as a god!'

'He's like that too.'

'Half-god, half-man,' I mocked because I remembered how Stirling had talked of my father, and I knew that he compared the two of them; and as, in Stirling's opinion no one on earth could shine beside his father, mine suffered miserably in the comparison.

'Yes,' he went on, 'Lynx is human. He's a man . . . a real man, but much grander in every way than other men.'

'You tell me so much of your father. What of your mother? Does she subscribe to the general view of your father's greatness?'

'My mother is dead. She died when I was born.' His face had darkened almost imperceptibly with some emotion.

'I'm sorry. I know you have a sister because she was coming to meet me. Have you any other sisters and brothers?'

'There are only two of us. Adelaide, my sister, is eight years older than I am.'

I wondered about Adelaide. I asked questions, but a very colourless picture emerged. He only glowed when he talked of Lynx. I thought of my own mother who had 'gone away'; and I wondered about the sort of woman whom Lynx had married.

'What of your mother?' I asked. 'Did she go out as a prisoner, too?'

'No. My father was sent to work for hers. Imagine the Lynx being *sent* to work for anyone!'

'Well, he was a prisoner then, not the great Lynx he is today.' I reminded him.

'He was always a proud man. I suppose my grandfather realized that.'

'Your grandfather?'

'The man my father was sent to work for. Very soon my father had married his daughter – my mother.'

'That was clever of him,' I said ironically.

'It happened,' he replied laconically, unsure, I believed, whether to applaud his father's cleverness or deny his calculation.

'So he married out of bondage, one might say.'

'You have a sharp tongue, Nora.'

'I thought I was speaking my mind.'

'Certainly. But it's a pity you must believe the worst of people.'

'I was thinking how clever he was. He was sent as a servant to work out his term of imprisonment, so he made his master his father-in-law. I consider that clever and just the sort of thing I should expect from Lynx.'

'How can you expect anything of him when you don't know him?'

'I've spent quite a long time in your company and to do that is to know quite a bit about this wonderful man, for you talk of nothing else.'

'Very well, I'll not speak of him. You asked questions and I replied to them. That's all.'

'Of course I want to hear about this wonderful god-like creature. But tell me more about your mother.'

'How can I when I never knew her?'

'There must have been some stories.'

He frowned and was silent. There *were* stories, I decided, and he did not want to tell them. Why? Because I imagined they were not very flattering to Lynx.

'And did he never marry again?' I went on.

'He did not marry again.'

'All those years without a wife! I should have thought Lynx would have wanted a wife.'

'You should not judge him until you know him,' said Stirling rather sourly. Then he changed the subject quickly and talked about the country. It would be the end of winter when we arrived for I must not forget that winter in Australia was summer at home. The wattle would be in bloom and I should see the fine brave eucalypts – red stringybarks and grey ghost gums; and we should have to travel north from Melbourne through parts of the bush. I was not listening very intently. I kept thinking of Lynx's marrying and becoming his master's son-in-law. Perhaps, I thought, Fox would have been a better name for him. The more I heard of the perfection of this man the more I set my mind against him because I imagined that in every account of his prowess was some implied criticism of my father.

We sat gazing over the water while Stirling talked of my new home and at last I said: 'It's getting late. I must go in.'

Stirling conducted me to my cabin and said good-night. When I entered, my companion, who was already in her bunk, remarked that I seemed to find the company of Mr. Herrick very intriguing.

'Naturally we have a great deal to talk about since he is taking me to his country which will be my new home.'

'Mrs. Mullens was saying how *odd* it was for a young girl to have such a *young* guardian.'

'There is no law laid down that a guardian should be of a stipulated age. A guardian can be of any age. No one can prevent his being a guardian because he is not middle-aged, nor can people be prevented from gossiping. Nor again is there any law to prevent one listening to gossip – only that of good breeding, of course.'

That silenced her and I chuckled to myself. Stirling was right. I had a quick tongue. I must make of it a defensive weapon. Perhaps I should have an opportunity of trying it on Lynx. The thought amused me.

I should not let him command me, I assured myself, though he was my guardian and appointed as such by my own father. I would never be dominated by anyone as this man appeared to dominate people – even Stirling. I would ask no more questions about him. I would shut him out of my mind.

I fell asleep then, but my dreams were haunted by a tall man with the eyes of a lynx and the face of a fox.

We were three days out of Cape Town when we discovered Jemmy. We had had our usual meal at seven and gone out on to the deck to sit side by side while Stirling talked about his country. I was beginning to build up a clear picture. I saw the bush with its yellow wattle and enormous trees. Stirling was not one to offer glowing descriptions; his conversation was in fact inclined to be terse; but he did make me guess at the beauty of the jarrah tree blossom and the red flowering gum. I could image the red and yellow glory of the flowers they called kangaroo paws; I could see the yellow swamp daisies and the many coloured orchids. He mentioned casually the gay rosellas; and I longed to see the green lorikeets and red-winged parrots. Each day I was learning a little more about the country which would soon be mine.

Suddenly we heard the sound of violent sneezing. We were startled, believing ourselves to be alone on deck.

'Who was that?' said Stirling, looking about him.

There was a paroxysm of coughing which could only have come from someone close by. It was clear that the sufferer was desperately attempting to stifle his cough. Stirling and I looked at each other in amazement for we could see no one.

We took a few steps along the deck suspended from which were the lifeboats and as we passed one of these the coughing started again.

'Who's there?' called Stirling.

There was no answer – but the cough had started again, and this time there was no doubt that it came from the suspended lifeboat.

Stirling was agile. It did not take him long to hoist himself up to the boat. I heard his exclamation.

'It's a boy,' he said.

I saw the boy's head – tousled and dirty; his frightened eyes were enormous in his white, scared face.

Stirling had him by the arm and lowered him on to the deck. In a second the three of us were standing there together.

'A . . . stowaway!' I cried.

'Don't you tell them,' whimpered the boy.

I could see that he was in a poor state of health when that terrible racking cough started again.

'Don't be frightened.' I said. 'It's all right now.'

I must have sounded convincing because as the cough subsided he looked at me trustingly.

'You've no right be on the ship, have you?' I said gently. 'You stowed away.'

'Yes, miss.'

'How long have you been on?'

'Since London.'

Stirling cried: 'You young rogue! What do you thing you're doing?'

The boy cowered towards me, and I was determined to protect him as much as I could. 'He's ill,' I said.

'Serve him right.'

'You're hungry, I daresay,' I said to the boy. 'And you have a bad cough. Why, you're shivering. It's time you came out of hiding.'

'No!' he cried fearfully, and looked about him so wildly that I was afraid he was contemplating jumping overboard. I was filled with a deep pity for him.

'You've run away from home,' I said.

'Of course he has,' said Stirling.

'I haven't got a home.'

'Your father . . .'

'No father. No mother,' he said; and my heart was deeply touched. After all, hadn't I known what it meant to be without a mother and father, without a home? The misery of Danesworth House came back to me – not so much the bleak attic, the shivering draughts and the stuffy heat, but the memory of what it felt like to be abandoned, alone and unwanted.

'What's your name?' I asked.

'Jemmy,' he said.

'Well, Jemmy,' I assured him, 'you are not to worry. I'm going to see that everything is right.'

Stirling had raised his eyebrows, but I went on: 'You'll have to confess what you've done, but I'll explain; and the first thing is to get some hot food and a bed. You haven't slept in a bed since you left London, have you?'

He shook his head.

'And you have had no proper food. Only that which you have managed to steal.'

He nodded.

'That's going to be changed. You can trust me, Jemmy.'

'I don't want to go back.'

'You're not going back.'

That satisfied him.

One of the officers came on deck just then and seeing us with the boy hurried towards us. We explained what had happened and he took charge of Jemmy. The look the child gave me as he was taken away haunted me.

'You certainly played the lady bountiful,' said Stirling. 'Making everything right for stowaways – even rewarding them for their sins.'

'I think you are rather hard-hearted.'

'At least I haven't made promises I can't fulfil.'

'What do they do to stowaways?'

'I don't know, but I feel sure they receive the punishment they richly deserve.'

'That poor child was ill and hungry.'

'Naturally. What did he expect? To be received on board as a passenger? He must have had some idea of what would happen when he stowed away.'

'He wouldn't have thought of that. He would have seen a big ship as an escape from an intolerable existence. He would have dreamed of sailing away into the sunshine, starting a new life.'

'Another of those dreamers, it seems.'

That angered me. He was referring, of course, to my father. I said firmly. 'I don't want that child to suffer. How will they punish him? They'll be harsh, I suppose.'

'He'll probably have to work on board and when we get to Australia he'll be punished and sent back to England to be punished there.'

'It's cruel.'

'It's justice. Why should he evade it?'

'He's young and some people manage to evade punishment . . . by marrying their master's daughter, for instance.'

It was unfair, but he had criticized my father and I couldn't resist retaliating by attacking him. He merely laughed.

'People have to be clever to get the best out of life.'

'Some are helped,' I said. 'And if I can help that boy I will.'

'You should, shouldn't you? You've promised. Rashly, of course, but you have given your word.'

He was right. I was determined to do what I could for poor little Jemmy.

Everyone on board was talking about the stowaway. They had taken him to the sick bay and for days it was doubted whether he would survive the hardships he had suffered. He had spent a great deal of time in the lifeboat, cleverly ascertaining when there was to be lifeboat drill and then hiding himself in one of the cupboards where spare life-jackets were stored. He had prowled about the ship at night looking for food and had found a little now and then. He had almost died of exposure and hunger. So at least for a time he was comfortable, well cared for and too sick to contemplate what trouble might be awaiting him when he was well enough to be judged.

I thought of him constantly, and was troubled to think of the punishment in store for him.

I spoke to Stirling as we sat on deck. 'I want to do something about that boy.'

'What?' he asked.

'I want to save him. He is very young. All he has done is run away. It must have been something terrible he ran from. I'm going to help him. I must.'

'How? Will you build a ship and make him your captain?'

'Be serious. You must help me.'

'I? This has nothing to do with me.'

'It has to do with me and I'm your sister . . . or rather your father is my guardian. Surely that makes some sort of relationship between us?'

'It doesn't mean I have to take part in your crazy schemes.'

'If his fare was paid, if you employed him as your servant, if you took him with us, I am sure your all-powerful father could find some employment for him. You'll help, of course.'

'I can't think why you should assume that for one moment.'

'I don't believe you're as hard-hearted as you would like me to believe.'

'I hope I'm a practical man.'

'Of course you are. That's why you'll help this boy.'

'Because *you* have made a rash promise you can't keep?'

'No. But because the boy will be grateful to you forever, and in your father's many concerns he must find it not always easy to discover good servants. The boy can be given work on your father's property, in his hotel, or in some place in the Lynx Empire. So you see it is to your benefit to rescue him from his present dilemma.'

He laughed so much that he could not speak. I was uneasy. There was a hardness about him which I am sure he had inherited from his father. I was very worried about my poor little stowaway for whom no one but myself seemed to have any sympathy.

'Well,' said my cabin companion, 'Mr. Mullens says that this is an encouragement for people to hide themselves on ships. He said he never heard the like. We shall have half the riff-raff stowing away if they are going to be rewarded for doing so.'

'One can hardly say the poor boy has been rewarded,' I retorted, 'simply because he has been put to bed and nursed back to health. What did Mr. Mullens expect? He would be invited to walk the plank? Or perhaps be clapped into irons? These are not the days of the press gang, you know.'

She tossed her head. I was very odd, in her opinion. I suppose she discussed me with the Mullenses.

'Mr. Herrick has rescued him they say,' she smirked. 'So the boy is to become his servant.'

'Servant!' I cried.

'Doesn't he confide in you? *I* heard Mr. Herrick is paying his fare, so all is well and our young rascal has been turned into an honest boy overnight.'

I smiled happily. I went to Stirling's cabin and knocked on the door. He was alone and I threw my arms about his neck and kissed him. Embarrassed, he took my hands and removed them but I was too excited to feel rebuffed.

'You've done it, Stirling,' I cried. 'You've done it.'

'What are you talking about?' he demanded. But he knew.

Then he tried to excuse himself. 'He's travelling third. It may be rough but it's all he deserves. The fare was only seventeen guineas but naturally they don't need that since he's been sleeping in the lifeboat and hasn't been fed. I've paid seven pounds for him and he'll have quarters in the third class until Melbourne.'

'And then you'll find work for him?'

'He can act as my servant until we find something for him to do.'

'Oh, Stirling, it's wonderful! You've got a heart after all. I'm glad.'

'Now don't you go endowing me with anything like that. You'll be bitterly disappointed.'

'I know,' I replied. 'You're hard-hearted. You wouldn't help anyone. But you think the boy will be useful. That's it, eh?'

'That's it,' he agreed.

'All right. Have it the way you want it. It's the result that counts. Poor little Jemmy! He'll be a happy boy tonight.'

I felt close to Stirling after that. I even liked his way of pretending that he had acted from practical rather than sentimental reasons.

The rest of the journey was uneventful; and it was forty-five days after we had left Tilbury that we came to Melbourne.

It was late afternoon when we arrived and by the time we had disembarked, dusk was upon us.

I shall never forget standing there on the wharf with our bags around and Jemmy beside us in the ragged clothes which were all he had. This was my new home. I wondered what Jemmy was thinking. His dark eyes were enormous in his pale tragic young face. I reassured him and in comforting him, comforted myself.

A woman was coming towards us and I knew immediately that she was Adelaide – the one who should have come to England to fetch me. Adelaide was plainly dressed in a cape and a hat without trimming, which was tied under her chin with a ribbon for the wind was high. I was a little disappointed; she had none of the unusual looks of Stirling and was hardly as I would have expected the Lynx's daughter to be. The fact was she looked like a rather plain, staid countrywoman. I knew immediately that I was wrong to be disappointed because what I saw in her face was undoubtedly kindness.

'Adelaide, here's Nora,' said Stirling.

She took my hand and kissed me coolly. 'Welcome to Melbourne, Nora,' she said. 'I hope you had a good journey.'

'Interesting,' commented Stirling. 'All things considered.'

'We're staying at the Lynx,' she said, 'and catching the Cobb coach tomorrow morning.'

'Goodo,' said Stirling.

'The Lynx?' I queried.

'Our father's hotel in Collins Street,' Adelaide explained. 'I expect you'd like to be getting along. Is all the baggage here?' Her eyes had come to rest on Jemmy.

'He's part of the baggage,' said Stirling. I frowned at him, fearing that Jemmy might be hurt to hear himself so described; but he was unaware of the slight. 'We picked him up on the ship,' went on Stirling. 'Nora thinks he should be given some work to do.'

'Have you written to our father about him?'

'No, I am leaving it to Nora to explain to him.'

Adelaide looked a little startled but I pretended to be not in the least disturbed at the prospect of explaining Jemmy to their formidable parent.

'I have a buggy waiting,' she said. 'We'll get all this stuff sent to the hotel.' She turned to me. 'We're some forty miles out of Melbourne, but Cobb's are good. You can rely on Cobb's. So we come in frequently. The men ride in but I like Cobb's. I hope you will settle down here.'

'I hope so too,' I said.

'She will if she makes up her mind to,' said Stirling. 'She's a very determined person.'

I walked off with Adelaide and Stirling – Jemmy following. I was only vaguely aware of the bustle all around me, and the carts drawn by horses or bullocks and loaded with wool hides and meat.

'It's a busy town,' said Adelaide. 'It's grown quickly in the last few years. Gold has made it rich.'

'Gold!' I said a little bitterly; and she must have known that I was thinking of my father. There was something very sympathetic about this woman.

'It's pleasant to have the town not too far away,' she said. 'I hope you won't find us too isolated. Have you ever lived in a big city?'

'I did for a time, but I have lived in the country, too; and I felt very isolated in the place where I was first a pupil, then a teacher.'

She nodded. 'We'll do our best to make you feel at home. Ah, here's the buggy. I'll tell John to see about the baggage.'

'Jemmy will help,' said Stirling. 'Let him be worth his salt. He can come along later with John and the baggage.'

So it was arranged and I rode beside Stirling and Adelaide – my new brother and sister – into the town of Melbourne, just as the lamplighters, riding on horseback, were lighting the street-lamps with their long torches. They sang as they worked – the old songs which I had heard so often at home. I remember particularly 'Early One Morning' and 'Strawberry Fair'; and I felt that although I had journeyed thousands of miles, I was not far from home.

The hotel was full of graziers who had come in from the outback to Melbourne in order to negotiate their wool. They talked loudly of prices and the state of the market; but I was more interested in another type – those men with bronzed faces and calloused hands and an avid look in their eyes. They were the diggers who had found a little gold, I imagined, and came in to spend it.

We ate dinner at six o'clock in the dining-room. I sat between Adelaide and Stirling, and it was Stirling who talked of these men and pointed out those who had struck lucky and those who hoped to.

I said, 'Perhaps it would have been better if gold had not been discovered here.'

'Many of the good citizens of Melbourne would agree with you,' conceded Stirling. 'People are leaving their workaday jobs to go and look for a fortune. Mind you, many of them come back disillusioned before long. They dream of the nuggets they are going to pick up and a few grains of gold dust as is all they find.'

I shivered and thought of my father and wondered if he had ever come to this place and talked as these men were talking now.

'It's a life of hardship they lead at the diggings,' said Adelaide. 'They'd be much better off doing a useful job.'

'But some of them make their fortunes,' Stirling reminded her.

'Money is the root of all evil,' said Adelaide.

'The love of it,' Stirling corrected her. 'But don't we all love it?'

'Not it,' I put in. 'The things it can buy.'

'It's the same thing,' Stirling replied.

'Not necessarily. Some people might want it for the sake of others.'

Both he and Adelaide knew that I was thinking of my father and Adelaide hastily changed the subject. She told me once more that the homestead was some forty miles north of Melbourne. Their father had built it ten years before; he had designed it himself and it was a fine house – as houses in this part went. It was not exactly like an English mansion of course; but that would be absurd in such a place.

I asked what I should be expected to do there and Adelaide replied that I could help in the house. She supposed that in all the activities that went on I would be sure to find something which would appeal to me.

'Lynx doesn't like idle folk,' said Stirling.

'Don't call him by that ridiculous name,' reproved Adelaide. She turned to me. 'I'm sure you'll find plenty to do.'

She talked a little about the country until Stirling said: 'Let her find out for herself.'

Then Adelaide asked me questions about England and I told her of Danesworth House and how I had become a pupil teacher there.

'You must have been most unhappy there,' she said and seemed rather pleased about this. I understood. She felt I should fit more happily into my new life since the old had not been very good.

And so we talked until dinner was over; then I returned to my room and when I had been there a short time there was a knock on the door and Adelaide came in. She looked so anxious that I immediately asked her if anything was wrong.

'Oh no. I just thought we should have a little talk about everything. I'd like you to be prepared.' Then I knew that she was anxious on my behalf and that I had been right when I had thought her kind.

She sat down on the armchair and I took my place on the bed.

'This must be very strange to you.'

'Strange things have happened since my father died.'

'It is terrible to lose a father. I know what it is to lose a mother. I lost mine when I was eight years old. It's a long time ago, but it's something I shall never forget.'

'She died when Stirling was born. He told me.'

She nodded. 'Don't be afraid of my father,' she said.

'Why should I be?'

'Most people are.'

'Perhaps that is because they are dependent on him. I shall not feel that. If he wants to be rid of me I shall go away. I suppose it would be possible to find a post here – perhaps with a family who need a governess and are going to England. Perhaps ...' I was making situations to fit my needs, Stirling would say – just as my father had.

'Please don't talk of leaving us just as you have come. You'll give it a fair trial, won't you?'

'Of course. I was only thinking of what I should do if your father decided he didn't want me here.'

'But he has promised to look after you and he will. Your father was insistent that he should.'

'My father seemed to fall under his spell.'

'They were drawn to each other from the start. Yet they were so different. Your father dreamed of what he would do; my father did it. In a short time they had become great friends; your father had come into the mine and managed it with an enthusiasm which we had never known before. My father used to say: "Now Tom Tamasin is here we'll strike rich. He believes it so earnestly that it will come to pass." And then he died bringing gold from the mine.'

'So they have found gold.'

'Not in any quantity. There is a lot of hard work; a lot of men to be employed; and the yield is hardly worth the effort and expense. It's strange. In everything else my father has prospered. The property which came through my mother is worth ten times what it was when he took it over. This hotel which was just a primitive inn is now flourishing. As Melbourne grows so does the hotel with it. But I believe he loses money on the mine.

He won't give up, though. In his way he is as obsessed by the desire to find gold as those men you saw downstairs tonight.'

'Why do men feel this urge for gold?'

She shrugged her shoulders. 'As we were saying tonight, it is the thought of being rich, fabulously rich.'

'And your father . . . is he not rich?'

'Not in the way he wishes to be. He started years ago to search for gold. He'll never give up the search until he makes a fortune.'

'I wonder people can't be content if they have enough to make them secure, and then enjoy living.'

'You have a wise head on your shoulders. But you would never get some men to see it your way.'

'I thought your father was a wise man. Stirling talks of him as though he is Socrates, Plato, Hercules and Julius Caesar all rolled into one.'

'Stirling has talked too much. My father is just an unusual human being. He is autocratic because he is the centre of our world – but it is only a little world. Stand up to him. He'll respect you for it. I understand you, I think. There is a little of your father in you, and you are proud and not going to bow to anyone's will. I think you will be well equipped for your new country. I hope you will get along with Jessica.'

'Jessica? Stirling did not mention Jessica. Who is she?'

'A cousin of my mother's. She was orphaned early and lived with my mother since their childhood. They were like sisters and when my mother died she was nearly demented. I had to comfort her and that helped me to get over my own grief. She can be rather difficult and she is a little strange. The fact is she never quite got over my mother's death. She takes sudden likes and dislikes to people.'

'And you think she will dislike me?'

'One never knows. But whatever she does, always remember that she may at any time act a little strangely.'

'Do you mean that she is mad?'

'Oh dear me no. A little unbalanced. She will be quite placid for days. Then she helps in the house and is very good in the kitchen. She cooks very well when she is in the mood. We had a very good cook and her husband was a handyman – very useful about the place. They had a little cottage in the grounds. Then they caught the gold fever. They just walked out. Heaven knows where they are now. Probably regretting it in some tent town, sleeping rough and thinking of their comfortable bed in the cottage.'

'Perhaps they found gold.'

'If they had we should have heard. No. They'll come creeping back but my father won't have them. He was very angry when they left. It was one of the reasons I couldn't come to England as was first planned.'

'Everyone there thought it was Miss Herrick who was coming for me.'

'And so it would have been, but my father couldn't be left to the mercy of Jessica . . . so I stayed behind and Stirling came alone. Don't imagine that we haven't servants. There are plenty of them but none of the calibre of the Lambs. Some of them are aboriginals. They don't live in the house and we can't rely on them. They're nomads by nature and suddenly they'll wander off. One thing – you will never be lonely. There are so many people involved in my father's affairs. There's Jacob Jagger who manages the property; William Gardner who is in charge of the mine; and Jack Bell who runs the hotel. You will probably meet him before we leave. They often come to see my father. Then there are people who are employed in these various places.'

'And your father governs them all.'

'He divides his attention between them, but it's the mine that claims most of his attention.'

And there we were back to gold. She seemed to realize this, for she was very sensitive.

'You're tired,' she said. 'I'll leave you now. We have to be up early in the morning.'

She came towards me as though to kiss me; then she seemed to change her mind. They were not, I had already learned, a demonstrative family. My feelings towards her were warm, and I believed she would be a great comfort to me in the new life.

Early next morning we boarded the coach, which seated nine passengers and was drawn by four horses. It appeared to be strong though light and well sprung, with a canopy over the top to afford some protection against the sun and weather. This was one of the well-known coaches of Cobb and Co. who had made travel so much easier over the unmade roads of the outback.

I sat between Adelaide and Stirling and we were very soon on our way. Jack Bell, to whom I had been introduced before we left, stood at the door of the hotel to wave goodbye. He was a tall thin man who had failed in his search for gold and was clearly relieved to find himself in his present position. He was slightly obsequious to Stirling and Adelaide and curious about me; but I had seen too many of his kind the previous night to be specially interested in him.

Besides, the city demanded all my attention. I was delighted with it now that I could see it in daylight. I liked the long straight streets and the little trams drawn by horses; I caught a glimpse of greenery as we passed a park and for a time rode along by the Yarra Yarra river. But soon we had left the town behind. The roads were rough but the scenery magnificent. Above us towered the great eucalyptus reaching to the heavens, majestic and indifferent to those who walked below. Stirling talked to me enthusiastically of the country and it was easy to see that he loved it. He pointed out the red stringybarks, the ash and native beech; he directed my attention to the tall grey trunks of the ghostly-looking gums. There were some, he told me, who really believed that the souls of departed men and women occupied the trunks of those trees and turned them grey-white. Some of the aboriginals wouldn't pass a grove of ghost gums after dark. They believed that if they did they might disappear and that in the morning if anyone counted they would find another tree turned ghost. I was fascinated by those great trees which must have stood there for a hundred years or more – perhaps before Captain Cook sailed into Botany Bay or before the arrival of the First Fleet.

The wattle was in bloom and the haunting fragrance filled the air as its feather flowers swayed a little in the light breeze. Tree ferns were dwarfed by the giant eucalypts and the sun touched the smoke trees with its golden light. A flock of galahs had settled on a mound and they rose in a grey and pink cloud as the coach approached. Rosellas gave their whistling call as we passed; and the beauty of the scene moved me so deeply that I felt elated by it. I could not feel apprehensive of what lay before me; I could only enjoy the beautiful morning.

It was the proud boast of the Cobb Coaching Company that horses were changed every ten miles, which ensured the earliest possible arrival. But the roads were rough and clouds of dust enveloped us. I thought it was an adventurous drive but no one else seemed to share my opinion and it was taken for granted that there would be mishaps. Over hills and dales we went; over creeks with the water splashing the sides of the coach, over rocky and sandy surfaces, over deep potholes which more than once nearly over-turned the coach. All the time our driver talked to the horses; he seemed to love them dearly for he used the most affectionate terms when addressing them, urging them to 'Pull on faster, Bess me darling!' and 'Steady, Buttercup, there's a lady!' He was cheerful and courageous and laughed heartily when, having rocked over a hole in the narrow path with a sizeable drop the other side, we found ourselves still going.

Stirling was watching me intently as though almost hoping for some sign of dismay which I was determined not to show; and I gave no indication that travelling over the unmade roads of Australia seemed to me very different from sitting in a first-class carriage compartment going from Canterbury to London.

There was an occasion when one of the horses reared and the coach turned into the scrub. Then we had to get out and all the men worked together to get the coach back on to the road. But I could see that this was accepted as a normal occurrence.

We were delayed by this and spent the night at an inn which was very primitive. Adelaide and I shared a room with another traveller and there was no intimate conversation that night.

In the morning there was some difficulty about the harness and we were late starting. However, our spirits rose as we came out into the beautiful country and once more I smelt the wattle and watched the flight of brilliantly plumaged birds.

We were coming nearer and nearer to what I thought of as Lynx Territory and it was here that I had my first glimpse of what was called a tent town. To me there was something horribly depressing about it. The beautiful trees had been cut down and in their place was a collection of tents made of canvas and calico. I saw the smouldering fires on which the inhabitants boiled their billycans and cooked their dampers. There were unkempt men and women, tanned to a dirty brown by sun and weather. I saw women, their hair tangled, helping with the panning or cradling, and turning the handles to bring up the buckets full of earth which might contain the precious gold; along the road were open-fronted shacks displaying flour, meat and the implements which would be needed by those concerned in the search for gold.

'Now you're seeing a typical canvas town,' commented Stirling. 'There are many hereabouts. Lynx supplies the shops with their goods. It's another trade of his.'

'So we are coming into the Lynx Empire.'

That amused Stirling. He liked to think of it as such.

The diggers' children had run out to watch the coach as we galloped past. Some tried to run after it. I watched them as they fell behind and my heart was filled with pity for the children of the obsessed.

I was relieved when they were out of sight and I could feast my eyes on the dignified trees and watch for sleepy koalas nibbling the leaves which were the only ones they cared for, and now and then cry out with pleasure as a crimson-breasted rosella fluttered overhead.

It was dusk when we arrived.

The driver had gone a mile or so out of his way to drop us at the house. After all, we belonged to the Lynx household, which meant we must have special treatment. And as we stood there in the road before the house the grey towers of which made it look like a miniature mansion, I had the strange feeling that I had been there before. It was ridiculous. How could I have been? And yet the feeling persisted.

Two servants came running out. We had been long expected. One of them was dark-skinned; the other was named Jim.

'Take in all the baggage,' commanded Stirling. 'We'll sort it out later. This is Miss Nora who has come to live with us.'

'Here we are,' said Stirling. 'Home.'

'I walked with them to gates which were of wrought iron. Then I saw the name on them in white letters. It was 'Whiteladies'.

Chapter Three

Whiteladies! The same name as that other house. How very strange! And stranger still that Stirling had not mentioned this. I turned to him and said: 'But that was the name of the house near Canterbury.'

'Oh?' He pretended to look puzzled but I did not believe that he had forgotten.

'You remember,' I prompted. 'We climbed trees to look over the wall. Don't pretend you've forgotten.'

'That place,' he said. 'Oh, yes.'

'But it's the same *name*!'

'Well, I daresay there have been other houses called by that name.'

'That one was so called because of the nuns. There were no nuns here.'

'I expect my father just liked the name.'

I thought it was rather mysterious. 'You might have mentioned the coincidence,' I said.

'Oh come, we're home. Don't waste time on unimportant details.'

Adelaide joined us. 'This way, Nora.'

We went under an arch and through a stone-flagged passage into a cobbled courtyard. There was a door in a wall and over this hung a lantern. The place in the dim light of evening could have been built centuries ago. I knew it hadn't been, but whoever had built it had tried to make it seem so.

Adelaide pushed open the door and we went through a lobby into a large rectangular hall in which a refectory table stood. There were some straight-backed carved chairs which were either antiques or very good imitation.

'It's like one of the old mansions at home,' I said.

Adelaide looked pleased. 'My father likes everything to look as English as possible,' she explained. 'We grow English flowers in the garden whenever possible. Do you like gardening, Nora? If so, you can help me. I have my own little flower garden and I grow all my father's favourites there – or try to.'

I said I hadn't done much gardening so I wasn't sure whether I should be a good gardener.

'You can try and see,' said Adelaide cheerfully.

There was a staircase leading from the hall and we mounted this and were in a gallery. There were several rooms leading from this and a corridor at each end. Adelaide led the way down one of these and we mounted another staircase at the top of which was a landing.

She opened the door and said: 'This is your room. I'm sure you'd like to wash. Your baggage will arive soon. Dinner will be served in half an hour.'

She left me and I found a can of hot water so I washed my hands and face. I was combing my hair when there was a knock at the door and Adelaide looked in. She appeared to be somewhat harassed.

'My father is asking to see you.'

'Now?'

'Yes. He's in the library and he doesn't like waiting.'

I looked in the mirror. My eyes were brilliant. I was about to meet the man of whom I had heard so much. Already there was a defiant tilt to my head. I had made myself dislike him. If my father had never met him, I told myself illogically, he would be alive today.

My heart was beating faster. Suppose he disliked me? Suppose he decided to send me back? I felt afraid. I didn't want to go back. I had grown fond of Stirling. I could grow fond of Adelaide. They had made me feel already that I belonged; and it is better to belong to anyone than to no one at all. Yet a deep resentment burned in me towards that man who had governed their lives and was now preparing to govern mine.

'He will be getting impatient,' Adelaide warned me.

Let him! I thought defiantly. I would not allow him to dominate me. I would rather be sent back to England. It was only because Adelaide was anxious that I would hurry, so I put down my comb and followed her.

As soon as I set eyes on him I knew they were right. He *was* different from other men. There had never been anyone quite like him. He stood by the fireplace in which a few logs burned, his back to it, his hands in the pockets of buckskin breeches. He wore highly polished riding boots, I noticed, and wondered why I should think of his clothes at such a time when it was his personality which dominated everything in the room. His entire being expressed Power. He was very tall – six feet four at least – his fair hair was very faintly touched with white at the temples and he had a golden Vandyke beard. I could not see his lips because they were hidden by his moustache but I guessed they were thin and could be cruel. His nose was aquiline and arrogant; but of course the most startling feature was those eyes. They were like those of a jungle animal – predatory, alert, proud, cruel, implying that he would have little mercy on any who offended him; yet there was laughter in them as though they mocked those who could not match up to him. They were a dazzling blue, and they were on me now though he did not greet me. He said over my head: 'So this is the girl.'

'Yes, Father,' said Adelaide.

'She has a look of her father, eh, Adelaide?'

'Yes there is a resemblance.'

'Nora. Is that her name?'

I disliked being discussed as though I weren't there. My heart had started to thump uncomfortably because in spite of my determination not to be overawed, I was. I said in a voice which sounded both imperious and pert: '*I* can answer all questions concerning myself.' He raised his bushy golden eyebrows and the fierce blue fire was turned on me. I went on: 'I am indeed the girl and my name *is* Nora.'

For a second his expression changed. I thought he might be angry with what he considered my impertinence, but I was not sure.

'Well,' he said, 'it's been doubly confirmed so we can be sure of it. Do you think she'll like it here, Adelaide?'

I replied before Adelaide could speak: 'It's too early as yet to say.'

'She'd better like it because she has to stay.' He half closed his eyes and said: 'Send Jagger in and put dinner forward ten minutes. She'll be hungry. We don't want her to think we are going to starve her.'

This was dismissal. I turned, glad to escape. As we went out of the room we passed a man who was waiting to go into the library.

'This is Miss Nora Tamasin, Mr. Jagger,' said Adelaide. 'Nora, Mr. Jagger, who runs the property.'

Mr. Jagger was shortish and plump. I thought him most undistinguished; but perhaps that was because I had just left what I had sardonically christened 'the presence'. He had a very florid complexion and rather bold dark eyes; and I did not like the way they regarded me. But I scarcely noticed this; I was still burning with resentment against the Lynx. I realized that I had no idea what his library looked like; from the moment the door had opened I had seen only him.

Adelaide took me back to my room.

'I think you surprised him,' she said.

'And that didn't please him,' I added.

'I'm not sure. In any case, don't be late for dinner. You'll have to come as you are. There's not time to change. He said it was to be put forward ten minutes. I'll come and collect you so that you will be on time. He hates people to be late.'

As soon as she had left me I went to my looking-glass. My cheeks were scarlet and my eyes brilliant. He had had that effect on me. He had talked over me as though I did not exist and he had done it deliberately in order to disconcert me. Why had my father so admired him? Why had he given me into the care of a man like this? I was seventeen and it was therefore four years before I would be of age. And then what should I do? Become a pupil teacher? Oh, poor Miss Graeme with birds' nest hair and dreams of what might have been! But I would rather that than become a chattel of his. The term amused me and I began to laugh. I was actually excited – yes, I was! I was looking forward to seeing him again because I wanted to show him that although he might dominate the rest of his household, this should not be the case with me.

Almost immediately it seemed Adelaide was back to take me to dinner.

To my astonishment the table was laid in the big hall on the refectory table which I had noticed when we had entered. It was laid for about twelve people. Adelaide was obviously relieved because her father had not yet arrived.

'We are a very big party,' I said.

'We are never sure how many there will be,' she told me. 'Sometimes the managers are here. The family, now that you are here, are five in number. Tonight Mr. Jagger is here, and I believe William Gardner too. They often are. My father likes to discuss business affairs with them over the dinner table.'

Stirling came hurrying in – also relieved that his father had not yet put in an appearance. They were all apparently afraid of the man.

'So you have met,' he said. He wanted to hear me say how wonderful I thought his father was. 'You've spoken to him now.'

'Yes,' I admitted. 'Though he hasn't exactly spoken to me – rather *at* me. I replied on behalf of myself – if you can call that speaking to a person.'

'How did it go, Adelaide? Did he like her?'

'It was as Nora said; and it is early days yet.'

I could see that he thought the interview had not gone well and was disappointed and a little anxious. I liked his concern for me while I deplored his subservience to that man.

He came in then with his managers and I was angry with myself because I shared that awe which the others clearly felt. On one side of him was Jacob Jagger and on the other the man whom I discovered to be William Gardner. He looked round the room and nodded. Then he said: 'Where is Jessica? Not here yet. Well, we'll start without her.'

Stirling sat on his right hand. I thought there was some ritual significance in this. I, to my surprise, was placed on his left. Adelaide sat next to Stirling and there was an empty place beside me which I presumed was for the unpunctual Jessica. As the two men took their places farther down the table, servants came in and served the soup. It was hot and savoury but I was too excited to enjoy it.

The Lynx – I could not think of him by any other name – led the conversation. I had the impression that we were expected to speak only when spoken to. He talked to Stirling about the trip and asked what he thought of England. He listened with interest to his son's replies. Stirling was the only one present who did not appear to be afraid of him, but he implied a complete respect and behaved, I thought, as though he were in the presence of a deity.

'And what sort of sea trip, eh?' he asked.

'Rough at times. We had some rocky moments along the African coast. Some of the passengers did not care for it.'

'And what about Nora? How did she like it?'

He was still looking at Stirling, but I put in quickly: 'Tell your father, Stirling, that the rocking of the ship did not disturb me unduly.'

I fancied there was a glint of amusement in his eyes. 'So she was a good sailor, eh?'

'I would say she was.'

'Well, perhaps she'll settle in to our rough ways, then. Do you think she will?'

'Oh, I think so,' said Stirling, smiling at me.

'Can she ride? She'll need to here.'

'I have ridden at home,' I said, 'So I daresay I can here.'

He turned his gaze on me then. 'It's rough riding here,' he said, 'in more ways than one. You'll notice a difference.' He had a way of lifting one eyebrow which I fancied was meant to intimidate, but I felt a small triumph because I had made him stop this slighting way of talking over me. He had at last addressed a remark to me.

'I shall have to adjust myself to it,' I said.

'You are right; you will. You shouldn't give her a mount that's too frisky, Stirling.'

'Certainly I won't.'

She's come out here to live in Australia, not to meet an untimely end.'

'You are unduly concerned,' I said. 'I am able to take care of myself.'

'Well, that's going to make everything a lot easier for us.'

He turned his attention then to the men and there was a great deal of animated conversation about the mine. William Gardner was mainly concerned with this; I listened to the answers and questions and was aware of Lynx's avid interest in everything connected with gold.

While this conversation was going on the door opened and a woman came in; she glided to the chair beside me where she sat down.

'We wondered what had happened to you, Jessica,' said Adelaide. 'This is Nora.'

'Welcome to Whiteladies.' Her voice was quiet yet rough; she was very thin and gave the impression that she had dressed hurriedly. The fichu of lace at her neck was grubby and I noticed that a button on her dress was hanging by a thread. Her grey hair was abundant but not well dressed. What struck me most was the strange lost expression in her eyes; which might have been those of a sleep-walker.

'Didn't you hear the gong?' asked Adelaide.

Jessica shook her head; she was still looking at me intently. I smiled at her – reassuringly, I hoped, for I felt she was in need of reassurance.

'I hope you'll find it not too difficult to settle in,' said Jessica.

'I don't think I shall.'

'Have you brought clothes from England? There's not much here.'

I said I had brought a little.

'Your bags are in your room,' she told me. 'They've just been taken up.'

Lynx, impatient of this trivial conversation, talked loudly of the mine and the property and the talk was dominated by the men. I had noticed the mildly indifferent and faintly contemptuous glance Lynx had given to Jessica. She was aware of it too and her response baffled me. I wasn't quite sure what it meant – fear, dread, awe, dislike – even hatred? Of one thing I was certain. No one in this house was indifferent to Lynx. Stirling was more animated than I had ever seen him before; his attitude was little short of idolatry; and there was a strong feeling between father and son. I could see that if the Lynx cared for anyone beyond himself that one was Stirling; and I fancied that he wanted to make his son another such as himself – a worthy heir to his empire. He listened to Stirling's views, applauding them now and then with a certain parental pride of which I should not have thought him capable, or demolishing them with a devastating attack which nevertheless held a flavour of indulgence. So he was capable of loving someone other than himself. His feelings towards his daughter were less strong. She was calm and intelligent – a good woman, and she was useful to him. So he showed a certain affectionate tolerance towards her. But these were his own children; to others he was the stern master; and towards me he had no feelings at all; I represented a duty to him.

But there was a flicker of interest in his eyes as he turned to me.

'About her mount, Stirling,' he said. 'I had thought Tansy for her, but perhaps that wouldn't be wise.'

'It's very good of you to concern yourself,' I replied.

The blue eyes were on me now. 'You'll have to go carefully at first. This isn't riding in Rotten Row, you know.'

'I have never ridden in Rotten Row, so I couldn't know how different this may be.'

'No, certainly not Tansy,' he went on. 'Blundell. You'll ride Blundell. Her mouth's been toughened by beginners. She'll do till you're used to the land around here. Stirling, you might take her out tomorrow. Show her the property. Not that she'll ride round that in a day, eh Jagger?'

Jagger laughed sycophantically. 'I'd say it was an impossibility, sir, even for you.'

'Distances are different here from where you come from. You think fifty miles is a long way, I don't doubt. You'll have to get used to the wide open spaces. And don't go off by yourself. You could get lost in the bush for days and that wouldn't be pleasant. We don't want to have to send out search parties. We're too busy for that.'

'I shall try not to inconvenience you in any way.'

He was smiling again. I was glad that he had dropped that irritating habit of talking at me.

'I think we shall find Nora very self-sufficient,' said Adelaide.

'That's what we have to be out here,' he replied. 'Self-sufficient. If you are, you'll get on. If not . . . then it's better to get out.'

'Nora will be all right,' said Stirling, smiling at me reassuringly.

The conversation turned to England, and I was waiting for Stirling to mention to his father that we had seen a house called Whiteladies; but he said nothing of this. He talked of London and his father asked many questions, so the conversation flowed easily. Then he asked me about Danesworth House and I found myself talking freely. One quality he had: he seemed to be deeply interested in many things. This surprised me; I should have thought that, seeing himself as the centre of his world, the affairs of others would have seemed trivial to him. He regarded us all as lesser than himself; he was the ruler of us all, the arbiter of our lives and fates – but I was to learn that he was acutely interested in every detail of our lives. Even during that meal I became aware of the many facets of the affection between Stirling and his father and the milder emotion he felt for his daughter. I was aware of the silent Jessica beside me who contributed little to the conversation yet made me aware of her, perhaps because I had heard that she was strange. And there was William Gardner with the fanatical gleam in his eyes when he talked of the mine where my father had worked with him. There was Jacob Hagger – and whenever I looked his way I met a bold glance of approval. Dominating that table, of course, was the man of whom I had heard so much and whose reputation I had already begun to feel was not exaggerated.

The next morning I awakened early and lay in bed thinking of the previous night until a maid – whose name I discovered to be Mary – brought in my hot water. Adelaide had told me that breakfast was between seven-thirty and nine and that I could go down at any time during that period. I rose from my bed and looked out of the window. I was looking out on a lawn, in the centre of which was a pond and in this pond was a statue; water-lilies floated there. I caught my breath in amazement. If I could have put a table there and set up a blue-and-white sunshade over it, this could be that other Whiteladies on the summer afternoon when I had seen it.

I am imagining this, I told myself. Lots of gardens have lawns and a pond with water-lilies. After all, hadn't Adelaide told me that her father was anxious to recreate an English atmosphere? What had startled me was the coincidence of the names being the same, and the odd thing really was Stirling's not mentioning it when we went to that other house.

I looked at my watch. I must not be late for breakfast. I thought of quiet Jessica's gliding into the dining-room and the displeasure of Lynx, and Jessica's indifference – or was it indifference? She had some strong feeling for Lynx. She seemed as though she hated him and was deliberately late to show her defiance. I could understand that defiance. Hadn't I felt a little of it myself?

I found my way down to the hall, which was not used for breakfast. It was evidently not the ceremonial occasion that dinner seemed to be. At dinner, I thought, *he* likes to place himself at the head of the table like some baron of old while his fiefs sit in order of precedence and his serfs wait on him. At least I was above the salt. The thought amused me and I was smiling as I went into the small dining-room to which I was directed by Mary the maid.

Adelaide was already there. She smiled a good morning and asked if I had slept well. She said Stirling had already breakfasted and would come along very soon to take me out and show me round.

I replied that I was looking forward to seeing the neighbourhood and that I was deeply interested in the house. I had seen a house near Canterbury which it resembled.

'That doesn't surprise me,' said Adelaide. 'My father designed this place. He built it ten years ago.'

'He is an architect then?'

'He is an artist, which may surprise you. When I say he designed the place, I mean that he supervised the architect and told him exactly what he wanted.'

'Your father seems remarkably endowed.'

'Unusually so. He saw houses like this when he lived in England and was determined to create a little bit of England here. He had the gates brought from England. They are really old and were in fact taken from an English country house.'

'What a lot of trouble he went to!'

'He'll go to any amount of trouble to get what he wants.'

And here we were talking of him again. I changed the subject and asked about the garden. She was eager to show me and said that perhaps later in the day she would do so. I could probably give her advice as I was so recently from England.

Stirling came in, dressed in riding breeches and polished boots. He looked somewhat like his father – not quite so tall nor so commanding, and his greenish eyes lacked that hypnotic blue dazzle; but there could be no doubt that he was his father's son. I felt a sudden happiness to be with him. He made me feel secure here as he had on the ship; and although I put on a bold show and was determined that no one should think I was afraid of the man my father had appointed to be my guardian, the fact remained that I was. I found him completely unpredictable and I was not at all sure of the impression I had made on him.

'Are you ready?' Stirling wanted to know.

I said that I must change into my riding habit as I had not known we were to start immediately.

As soon as I had finished breakfast I went to my room and put on the riding clothes I had bought before leaving England. I remembered how shocked poor Miss Graeme had been because I had chosen green and my black riding hat had a narrow matching green ribbon about it.

When I went down to the stables Stirling looked at me with approval.

'Very elegant,' he commented. 'But it's your skill with the horse that counts.'

I was delighted to see Jemmy in the stables, dressed in breeches and coat which were a little too large for him; but he looked very different from the shivering scrap we had found on board ship; and he had a very special smile for me, which was gratifying.

I don't know what possessed me that morning. I knew I was wrong; but there was something in the fresh morning air and the bright sunshine which made me reckless. They were saddling Blundell, the horse *he* had thought fit for me to ride.

'It's little more than a pony,' I said scornfully. 'I thought I was to have a horse. I stopped having riding lessons years ago.'

Stirling grinned and said: 'You'd better have a look at Tansy.'

So I looked at Tansy – a lovely chestnut mare; and I was determined to ride her if just to show him that I was not one of the minions who accepted his word as law.

'She's frisky,' said Stirling.

'She's a mare, not an old nag.'

'Are you sure you can manage her?'

'My father taught me to ride when we lived in the country. I know how to manage a horse.'

'The country's rough here. Wouldn't you rather feel your way?'

'I'm not going to ride Blundell. I'd rather not ride at all.'

So they saddled Tansy and we set off. She *was* frisky and I knew I was going to need all my skill to control her; but, as I said, on that day I was reckless. For the first time since my father had died I felt a great uplifting of my spirits. I had not forgotten him; I should never do that; but it was almost as though he were beside me, rejoicing because at last I was delivered into safe hands. But it was not my guardian who gave me comfort; it was Stirling, riding beside me, so much more at home here than he had been in England, who made me feel secure. I knew then that I loved Stirling, and although he did not dominate my thoughts as his father did, my relationship with him brought me a deep contentment which I felt sure I could not feel with any other person. Instinctively I was aware that the affection I had for him would grow stronger every day.

'Does the sun always shine here?' I asked.

'Always.'

'Really always.'

'Almost always.'

'You're boastful about your country.'

'Put it down to national pride. You'll feel it after a while.'

'Do you think I shall come to accept this as my home?'

'You will. I'm certain of it.'

'I'm not. Your father didn't, did he?'

'What do you mean?'

'Why should he have to build a house like that one we saw near Canterbury? Why should Adelaide have to make an English garden for him. He must be homesick ... sometimes. Stirling, why didn't you tell me that this house had the same name as that other? It must have struck you forcefully.'

'It struck me, yes.'

'Then why didn't you *say*?'

'You'd never seen this. Then I thought it would be a nice surprise.'

'You think the most absurd things. Anyway, I'm glad. Going to that place seemed significant in some way. I don't think I shall ever forget it. Those people on the lawn for instance. Minta! Wasn't she lovely? And Mamma . . .'

'Not forgetting the exquisite Mr. Wakefield.'

'You mean *you* can't forget him.'

'Come now, you were the one who admired him. Such a perfect gentleman with his bows and hand-kissing.'

'Well, it *was* charming. And what of poor Lucie, the companion?'

'Poor Lucie! A pity she can't marry Mr. Wakefield and live graciously ever after.'

'He is obviously for Minta.'

'I believe you envy her.'

'What nonsense!'

'I hope so. If you're going to settle in here it won't do to hanker after fancy gentlemen.'

'I'm going to be perfectly happy here, thank you, in spite of the obvious lack of well-mannered gentlemen.'

That pleased him. He really was concerned for me.

'What a heavenly morning!' I cried.

'Careful!' he warned as Tansy caught her foot in a hole and nearly threw me. His hand was stretched out to grasp my reins but we were all right, I assured him.

The grounds of the house were, in my English eyes, very extensive. There were flower and kitchen gardens where men were working and large orchards where there were orange and lemon trees, with figs to give their fruit in the appropriate seasons. I saw that we could live off the land.

We left the estate behind us and rode for miles over rough country; Stirling pointed out land on the horizon which was part of the property managed by Jacob Jagger.

'It is indeed a vast Empire,' I said. 'Your father is the monarch of all he surveys, and you are the crown prince. How does it feel to be heir to all this and your father's son?'

'It feels good,' he said, and I understood that.

We rode in silence for a while and then he said: 'I think you have made a good impression on him.'

I was pleased but shrugged my shoulders to feign indifference.

'*I* think he expected me to bow three times and walk out backwards.'

'He doesn't like subservience all the time.'

'Only some of the time?'

'Only from those he considers should show it.'

'He's a bit of a tyrant, a bit of a brigand – but I can understand your feelings for him a little more, now that I've seen him.'

'I knew you would. I knew you'd feel the same. I want you to, Nora.'

'It will depend on the way he treats me.'

That made him laugh. As we cantered over the ground and I felt the wind on my face I experienced again that feeling of happiness. He felt it too, I think, for he said: 'Nora, I'm going to make you love this country. I'll take you into the bush; we'll camp out. It's the only way if you want to see the country beyond where a coach can take you. I'll show you how to boil a billycan for tea and how to make dampers and johnny cakes on a camp fire.'

'It sound good. I should like it, I'm sure.'

He was glowing with pleasure.

'What did your father say about Jemmy?'

'He said if he's prepared to work he can stay. If not, he'll be sent packing.'

'Did you tell him I persuaded you?'

'No. I let him think it was my idea.'

'Why? Because you thought it was rather weak of you to be persuaded by me?'

'I didn't know how he was going to feel about your making such a decision.'

'I suppose, had he known it was my idea, he might have said he wouldn't take in the boy.'

'He wouldn't have turned him away.'

'Well then, you wanted him to like me and you didn't want him to start off thinking I was domineering.'

'Perhaps. But I shall tell him later. It was just at first.'

'Stirling, you're nice to me.'

'Of course I am. My father's your guardian and I'm his deputy.'

We rode in silence for a mile or so. The eucalypts were thick about us; a startled kangaroo, baby in pouch, leaped across our path and then sat on her haunches, looking at us with curiosity. For the first time I saw the beautiful lyre bird, his fantastic tail spread out in all its glory. We pulled up, for he was perched on a tree fern not far off. As we halted he began to imitate the cries of other birds as though giving a performance for our benefit. While we remained stationary I noticed how blackened were the trunks of some of the eucalypts, and I pointed this out to Stirling, who told me they had been so rendered by fire. Then he began to tell me about the terrible forest conflagrations which ravaged the country. I could have no conception of these until I saw one and he hoped I never would, though it seemed hardly likely that I would not if I stayed in Australia.

'Every living thing for miles around is in acute danger,' he told me. 'It is the most fearful tragic thing imaginable. There are dangers in this land, Nora, that you wouldn't dream of.'

'I have thought of the dangers. Remember, my father died here.'

'Robbery with violence can happen anywhere.'

'Where there is greed,' I added. 'And here there is gold, and gold means greed.'

He called my attention to an emu which was running at great speed along the path. I had never seen such a large bird; it was about five feet high.

'You're getting to know the land and its inhabitants,' said Stirling. 'First the family, then the wild life. Look at those trees. I reckon they're all of three hundred feet high.'

'They're magnificent. More beautiful than all the gold in the world.'

'They're not all that benevolent. I've known a falling branch impale a man. Imagine one falling three or two hundred feet. It happens now and then. We call those branches widow-makers out here.'

I looked up at the tall trees and shuddered.

' "In the midst of life we are in death," ' quoted Stirling half serious, half mocking.

I didn't want this morning spoilt by talk of death so I whipped up Tansy and galloped off. Stirling came up behind and passed me. Then it happened. I had been aware all the morning that I was managing Tansy only because she was permitting me to do so. I heard a strange mocking laugh not far off; perhaps Tansy heard it too. I don't quite know what happened but suddenly I was sailing over her head. I had the sense to release the reins when I saw I was falling and luck was with me on that day. I was tossed into a heap of bush, growing up three or four feet from the ground; it was thick and strong enough to hold me. I was scratched and shocked but I was alive. For some moments I was bewildered, staring up at the sky, trying to grasp the bracken which scratched my hands and was breaking under my weight. Then I heard again that mocking laughter and in my somewhat bemused state I half believed that Lynx was somewhere at hand where he could witness and enjoy my plight.

I heard Stirling calling me; and there he was, extricating me from the bush, an expression of great concern on his face.

He said: 'Can you stand?'

'Yes . . . but my ankle hurts.'

'Sit down,' he commanded, and I sat on the grass while he knelt beside me.

He gently pulled off my boot. My ankle was swollen.

'Sprained no doubt,' he said. 'What happened?'

'Where's Tansy?'

'I saw her making off. She'll go home. She knows the way. But what, for heaven's sake . . .?'

'Someone laughed and then I was in the bush.'

'Laughed! Who?'

'I don't know. It was so close. I think it frightened Tansy and so she threw me.'

'We'd better get back,' he said. 'We'll have to see what damage is done. I'll take you on Weston.' He whistled and Weston came obediently. As he helped me to mount I heard the laughter again – one burst followed by another.

'There!'

'Those are birds. The old kookaburras. You'll have to get used to their laughter for you'll hear it often enough.'

So I was carried ignobly home to find that Tansy had already returned. I had been extremely fortunate to have emerged with nothing more than a few bruises and a sprained ankle, but I was sick with shame wondering what Lynx would say when he heard of my adventure.

Adelaide greeted us with relief.

'I heard that Tansy had come home and that you rode her this morning.'

Her voice was faintly reproachful. Hadn't her father said I should ride Blundell?

'She was all right until she was startled,' I explained. 'I managed her all right until then.'

Adelaide was concerned, but I discovered that accidents here were not treated with the same anxiety as they would be at home, because here in the bush they were so frequent. Adelaide applied hot and cold compresses, telling me that she had studied first aid as it was often necessary since there could be a delay of two or three days before a doctor arrived. She made me drink a cup of hot sweet tea and said I must keep my weight off my ankle for the next day or so.

I felt stupid and ashamed of myself but I was relieved that the horse had come home. I lay on a couch in Adelaide's sitting-room. I should be quiet for a while, she said; and when I felt a little recovered from my shock I could read or perhaps do some sewing. There was always a great deal to be done at Whiteladies.

I lay by the open window and thought of how foolish I had been to have ridden a horse which was far too good for me. 'Pride goeth before a fall,' Miss Emily had said often enough; and for once I had to admit that she was right.

Then I heard *his* voice below my window.

'So she rode Tansy after all and came a cropper. Serve her right. At least she shows more spirit than sense.'

I fancied there was a faint note of approval in his voice and I exulted in it.

I lay there idly. What an end to my first day at Whiteladies – *Little* Whiteladies, as I had christened it, for there could only be one true Whiteladies.

Somewhere in the garden I heard the laughter of the kookaburras, mocking me, it seemed.

Adelaide would not allow me to put my foot to the ground for the next three days, so I spent the time in her sitting-room. Stirling carried me to my bedroom every night. Both Adelaide and Stirling were determined to look after me, and show me that they welcomed me as their young sister. I did some sewing for Adelaide. This consisted of making garments for the numerous people who worked in the house. There were several small cottages in the grounds where these people lived and I had already discovered that there were several children.

'My father likes them all to be treated as though they are part of the family,' she said; and she looked at me quickly to see what effect that remark had had on me. I didn't understand then but it gradually dawned on me that many of the children had been fathered by Lynx. Later it became a habit of mine to look for his features. I found them often. It was understandable. Lynx was virile in every sense. He was not the sort of man to lead the existence of a monk. He took these young women according to his whim and no one thought the worse of him for it. I never found those startling blue eyes anywhere else. Even Stirling – the legitimate heir – had not inherited those.

During those days Stirling called in often to see me. I told him I was ashamed of what had happened and hoped Tansy had suffered no harm.

'It's nothing,' he reassured me. 'It's better to be bold than scared out here.' And I was grateful to them for making light of my adventure. I was growing fond of Adelaide, whom I had already begun to regard as my kindly elder sister. She brought me trays with tea and scones served just as they were at home; and there was peach jam and passion fruit jelly which she had made herself.

Those days appeared strange after all that had gone before – so quiet and peaceful. I felt that I had come to a little oasis, but I knew that my stay there would be only temporary. Lynx did not come to see me. I realized that that would be expecting too much. Stirling's visits were mainly in the evenings. He was away most of the day at the mine, making up for lost time, he told me. I heard a lot of talk about the mine and longed to see it, and yet in a way I didn't want to. I felt it would bring back memories of my father too vividly.

Mary, the maid, helped me dress in the mornings; she would bring me a breakfast tray and after that my hot water. She was shy and seemed afraid of something. I tried to discover of what but was not successful. Then Stirling would insist on carrying me to Adelaide's sitting-room, which was unnecessary for I could easily hobble there. All the same, I must admit I liked this attention; I liked the feel of his strong arms supporting me. He carried me so effortlessly, but I told him that this accentuating of my disability only called attention to my folly.

It was on the third day after my accident and I was lying on the sofa in Adelaide's room stitching at a calico shirt, working diligently feeling that this was one way of showing my penitence for being so foolish, when the door opened slightly and Jessica glided in. I felt a sudden shiver run down my back which could have been due to the wild look in her eyes and the noiseless manner in which she had entered the room.

'How are you?' she asked and drawing up a chair sat down near my couch. Imperceptibly I felt myself shrink away from her.

'I'm getting on very well, thanks,' I said. 'In fact I'm a bit of a fraud. I should really be walking about but Adelaide won't hear of it.'

'There are other frauds about.' She smiled. 'And not far away from here either.'

'Is that so?'

She nodded conspiratorially. 'Has *he* been in to see you?'

I knew to whom she referred but I feigned not to do so.

'Who?' I asked.

'Him. The master.'

'No. I didn't expect him.'

'He cares neither for God nor man,' she told me. 'You could have been killed on that horse and he wouldn't have cared.'

'He did warn me not to ride Tansy, so it was entirely my own fault.'

'All he'd care about would be the horse.'

'Well, it's a very fine horse.'

She turned those strangely wild eyes on me. They were brown and I could see the round staring pupils looking full at me.

'Valuable,' she whispered. 'He thinks of goods, property, gold. That's what he cares about.'

'So do many people.'

She came closer to me and I felt trapped on my couch.

'But he cares more than anyone else. He's quite ruthless, as we all find out when we get to know him. I found out. Maybella found out. My uncle found out. He came as nothing . . . nothing . . . a prisoner, a slave. Seven years' transportation and in a year he was ruling us all.'

'He's a very unusual man.'

'Unusual!' She laughed and her laughter reminded me of that of the kookaburras which I insisted had startled my horse. 'There has never been a man like him. I hope there never is another. Beware of the Lynx. He hypnotizes people. My uncle, Maybella . . . and look what happened to Maybella. He killed her.'

'Maybella. She was . . .?'

'He married her, didn't he? Why? Did he want Maybella? Did he care that much for her?' She snapped her fingers. 'And what happened to Maybella, eh? Do you know?'

'I don't, I said, 'but I should like to.'

The door opened and Adelaide came in. She frowned at Jessica. Then she said lightly: 'Oh, there you are, Jessie. Just in time for a cup of coffee. I was making some for myself and Nora.'

She was carrying a tray with a crochet-bordered cloth. The coffee smelt delicious, but I wanted to hear what Jessica had to tell me and I knew she would not go on while Adelaide was there.

Adelaide set down the tray and briskly poured out the coffee. 'Plenty of milk, Nora,' she said. 'That'll do you good. Here, Jessie. Just as you like it.'

Jessica's hands were trembling as she took the cup.

'I think that tomorrow you might walk about a bit, Nora,' went on Adelaide. 'Not too far, of course. In the garden perhaps. Don't go wandering out into the bush yet, will you?'

Jessica had fallen into silence and when she left us Adelaide said. 'Did she talk wildly? She does now and then and I'm afraid this is one of her bad days. It doesn't do to encourage her or to take too much notice of what she says.'

All the same I wanted to hear Jessica's version of what happened to Maybella.

In a week my ankle had completely recovered and I felt as though I had been much longer than that time at Little Whiteladies. I was so anxious to make up for the Tansy incident that I helped Adelaide as much as I could. I began to learn to cook; I did a little gardening; I sewed; and I became like a daughter of the house. Adelaide and Stirling were pleased with me. I began to know the servants and this was when I realized how useful I could be, for the aboriginals were notorious for going 'walk-about' as they called it; and they were constantly disappearing. Even their fear of Lynx didn't prevent them; or perhaps it was one of the reasons for it. And whenever a white servant could not be found, it was always presumed that he or she had gone off to the diggings.

'I wish they'd never found gold in Victoria,' said Adelaide.

It was not long before I was riding again. One could not get along in this country without a horse, so it was no use letting one little mishap deter me. On Stirling's advice I had a strawberry roan named incongruously Queen Anne; she was neither the old hack Blundell was nor was she of the calibre of Tansy.

'When you're used to the country,' said Stirling, 'we'll find a better mount for you. In the meantime be a wise girl and stick to the good old Queen.'

So I did and I knew he was right, for I felt perfectly confident to control my Queen in any circumstances.

When I first saw the mine I looked at it in dismay. We had ridden to it through magnificent country and there it was replacing all that beauty with its ugliness. There was the poppet head supporting the wheels over which the steel ropes passed as the cages were hauled to the surface; the noise was deafening and even while I stood there an explosion rent the air.

'We're using this new substance which Alfred Nobel has invented,' Stirling told me. 'It's called dynamite and it saves endless work because it breaks up the rock and enables us to get at the gold. There are two hundred men working here.'

'Are they content to find gold for your father?'

'They are glad to work here. Most of them have been digging for years. They've known hardship and think it's good to work for a steady wage. They know that those who found fortunes with the simple cradles are few and far between. The chances are too great; the hazards too many. This is a safe job. They eat every day; all they have to do is work for the master.'

He pointed out the stampers, which were a new kind of machine to pound the ore and so extricate the gold from the quartz rock. It was all noise and activity. About the mine were rows of tents in which the miners and their families lived; some even had cottages consisting of two rooms, one back one front; these were the fortunate ones.

I said: 'And your father owns this mine?'

'You have a share in it. Your father put in what money he had. There are other shareholders too, but my father owns the bulk of the shares, so he is the one with the controlling interest.'

'It's nice to know that I am not entirely a pauper. Perhaps I'm even rich.'

'The mine runs at a loss.'

'Then why all this . . . for a loss?'

'Hope is the answer. It goes with gold. There is more hope in this country than there ever was gold.'

'And even your father is affected by this mad gold hunger.'

'Even he. He came from England. He knew people there, rich people, who lived as he said "graciously". They did not concern themselves with money because they had so much that they never gave a thought to it. He told me once that that was how he wanted to live, that was how he was *going* to live one day.'

'But he is secure ... even rich. He commands you all. What more does he want?'

'He wants to bring about the realization of a dream. He wants first to find gold ... such gold as has never before been found. From then he will go on with his plans.'

'What plans?'

'Oh, he has plans. But the first step is his golden fortune. You see how we live. We do not stint ourselves – a large house, many servants, interests in several places. It is costly living thus; and the mine eats up money. You've seen all these workers; they have to be paid. Machinery is expensive. The mine costs a great deal to run. My father wants an easy fortune in gold. Then he might go to England.'

'He could go back now.'

'Not as he wants to go. He would like to go back like a lord.'

I laughed derisively. 'Does he plan to have a title too?'

'Perhaps.'

'So meanwhile he builds a little Whiteladies and has an English garden and throws all his money into a gold mine that doesn't pay.'

'Not at the moment, but later it will. My father will strike gold in a big way. Have no doubt of that. He has always found what he wanted.'

'How long has he been here? Thirty-five years, is it? And all that time he has wanted to go back and never has!'

'He only wants to go back in certain circumstances.'

'He, it seems, suffers as acutely as everyone else from this lust for gold. You talk of him as though he is some sort of god, but he is a worshipper in his turn. He worships gold.'

As we talked an old man passed us. At least, at first I thought he was an old man, until I saw that it was disease which made him seem so. A sudden paroxysm of coughing shook him and he stood doubled up with pain until it was over.

'Poor man,' I said, 'he should be in bed. He should have a doctor.'

I was about to speak to him when Stirling laid a hand on my arm. 'He's one of hundreds,' he said. 'He has the miners' complaint – phthisis. It's caused by dust and grime in the mines; it affects the lungs and in the end kills the victim. There is nothing to be done about it.'

'Nothing!' I cried. 'You mean men go down into the mine and it is known that they can contract this terrible disease?'

'It's a hazard,' said Stirling lightly. 'They know it and they accept it.'

'And when they get it? What then?'

'What then? They die in time. It's a killer.'

I was angry, thinking of that man, their master, who, in his lust for gold, sent those men down into the mine to work for him.

'It's wicked,' I said. 'It should be stopped.'

Stirling laughed at me. 'The trouble with you, Nora, is that you're soft. Life is not. Especially out here. That man has a job. He's fed his family ... if he has any. He came out here looking for gold and failed to find it, as thousands have. So he finds work in the gold mines. It's dangerous work, but there's danger everywhere in life. Even in cosy England there's sudden death. Don't take life so seriously.'

'I take death very seriously. Unnecessary death.' Then I thought of my father who had died for gold just as this man was dying; and I hated gold more fiercely than I ever had before. I saw them loading the dray which would take the gold to the Melbourne bank, and I thought of his setting out on his journey and giving his life to save the gold.

From that moment I personified Gold. I saw it as a cruel woman, greedy, rapacious, sly, capricious. The Gold Goddess – a kind of Circe, a Lorelei, who now and then rewarded those who served her in order to lure more victims from their homes, their families and all that was serene and secure in life that she might destroy them.

'I want to see the spot where my father was shot,' I said.

'Why don't you forget all that?'

'Forget that my father was murdered!'

'There is no good in remembering.'

'Would you forget if *your* father had been killed?'

He flinched. I knew he could not contemplate a world that did not contain the mighty Lynx.

'I loved my father dearly,' I said. 'There was no one like him in the world. And here, in this country, he was wantonly killed by someone who didn't even know him. And you ask me to forget that!'

'Come on, Nora. Let's get away from here.'

He turned and walked his horse to the road. I followed.

'Now,' I said, 'take me to the spot where my father was shot, and after I've seen it I won't speak to you again about him if you don't want me to.'

We rode for some three miles and there he stopped. It was a beautiful spot – quiet and peaceful; and as we stood contemplating that perfect peace, the silence was broken by the notes of a bell bird.

'The dray came along the road from the mine,' said Stirling. 'It was just about here. He was not killed at once, you know. We brought him back to Whiteladies and there he wrote the letter which was sent to you – the last he ever wrote. He had already talked to my father about you. That was how it happened.'

I looked about me at the grove of eucalypts in which the assassin might have hidden. Beyond them was a hill – a small mountain perhaps, down which a stream trickled into the creek below.

It was one of the most beautiful places I had ever seen.

'And here he met his death,' I said bitterly, 'he who was in love with life, who had made such plans and had so many dreams. It need never have happened. He died . . . for gold. I *hate* gold.'

'Come away Nora,' said Stirling. 'He died and you've lost him, but you have us now. Nora, you have me.'

I turned and looked at him; he brought his horse closer to mine and taking my hand pressed it briefly.

'I'll make it up to you, Nora,' he said earnestly. 'You'll see.'

All that day and the next I kept thinking of my father and that poor man who was dying of phthisis; and when I was weeding in Adelaide's garden I suddenly looked up and saw Lynx standing there watching me.

'How long have you been there?' I demanded.

Up went an eyebrow. 'I don't answer questions when they are put so peremptorily.'

'I don't like being watched when I'm unaware of it.'

'I don't like people who are impolite.'

'Nor do I,' I retorted, standing up. The thought of that poor man dying of his lung complaint made me angry and I didn't care whether or not I offended Lynx.

He decided not to be offended. 'I'm glad to see you working,' he said. 'I don't like idleness in this house.'

'If you expect me to work you should say so. Perhaps you would like me to work down in your gold mine.'

He pretended to consider this. 'In what capacity, do you think?'

I decided not to answer that and said: 'I understand that I own some shares in the company.'

'Your father had a few . . . a very few. They are not worth much.'

'Like the mine itself, perhaps.'

'You are an expert on mining?'

'I know nothing of it, and don't want to. I would rather not be connected with such a thing.'

He said: 'I think it is time you and I had a talk. There are certain things we should know about each other.'

'I am eager to know of what concerns me.'

'Come to the library after dinner tonight.'

He left me and I turned to Adelaide's herb garden; the strong smell of sage was in the air. I thought: Tonight I will be bold. I will tell him what I think of this mine in which young men become old men before their time and ruin their lungs.

He did not appear at dinner that night, and I wondered whether when I went to his library he would be there. He was. He was sitting at table sipping a glass of what I presumed to be port wine. I guessed he had eaten dinner alone in this room, which I understood he did on some occasions.

'Ah, he said. 'Come in, Miss Nora. Sit there opposite me where I can see you.' I sat down. The light in the room was dim. Only two of the several oil lamps had been lighted.

'You will have a glass of port wine.'

I declined because he made it sound more like a statement than an invitation.

He lifted the decanter and poured himself another glassful. I noticed his hands then for the first time; the fingers were long and slender and on the little finger of the right hand was a ring with a carved jade stone. There was an elegance about his smallest gesture and I could imagine his living graciously in an old English country mansion.

'You wanted to know about your position here,' he said. 'You are my ward. I am your guardian. This was arranged by your father before his untimely end. He knew the hazards of this country and he often talked, in this room, of his fears and anxieties; and I gave him my promise that in the event of his death before you reached the age of twenty-one, I would take you into my care.'

'He must have had some premonition that he was going to die.'

He shook his head. 'Your father was a man who dreamed wild dreams. He was enthusiastic about them but in his heart he knew they would never come true. Deep in his mind he admitted to himself that he would never make his fortune; but it was only when he considered you that he made practical plans. You can count that as a measure of his affection for you. For you he stepped outside himself and admitted the truth as he knew it to be. So he made this bargain with me and before he died he drew up a document appointing me as your guardian. I agreed to his request – so here we are.'

'Why did he choose you?'

Again that tilt of the eyebrow. 'You say that as though you think me unworthy of his trust?'

'He knew you such a short time.'

'He knew me well enough. We knew each other. Therefore, you have to accept me. You have no alternative.'

'I daresay I could earn my living.'

'In the mine . . . as you suggested? It is not easy for a young woman to earn a living unless it is as a housemaid or something such, which I do assure you would be a very poor one.'

'I have these shares in the mine.'

'They don't amount to much. They wouldn't keep you for long.'

'I would rather not have any money which belonged to me supporting a gold mine.'

'The shares can be sold. They won't realize very much. The mine is known to be a not very profitable concern.'

'Why continue with it?'

'Hope. We always hope.'

'And meanwhile people die while you continue to hope?'

'You are thinking of your father. That is a fate which many people have met in this country. These bushrangers are everywhere. We could all encounter them.'

'I am thinking of a poor man I saw the other day. He was suffering from a lung complaint.'

'Oh . . . phthisis.'

'You speak as though it were about as important as a headache.'

'It's a mining hazard.'

'Like death from bushrangers?'

'Are you suggesting that I close the mine because a man is suffering from phthisis?'

'Yes.'

He laughed. 'You are a reformer, and like most reformers you understand little of what you hope to reform. If I closed my mine what would happen to all my workers? They would be starved to death in a week or so.'

'I want nothing to do with this mine.'

'Your shares shall be sold and the money banked for you. I warn you it will not be much more than a hundred pounds. And if we struck gold . . .'

'I don't want anything to do with gold mining.'

He sighed and looked at me over his port, his eyes glistening. 'You are not very wise. There is a saying at home: "Your heart rules your head." You think with your emotions. That can get you into difficult situations and is not much help at extricating you.'

'You would be different. You think with your head.'

'That's what heads are for.'

'And hearts?'

'To control the circulation of the blood.'

I laughed and so did he.

'Is there anything else you wish to know?' he asked.

'Yes. What am I expected to do here?'

'Do? You will help Adelaide perhaps, as a younger sister would. This is your home now. You must treat it as such.'

I looked round the room seeing for the first time. Books lined one wall, there was an open fireplace in which logs were burning; several pictures hung on the walls and it was exactly as one would expect an English library to be. On a highly polished oak table was a chess set. The pieces were laid out as though someone were about to play, and an exclamation escaped me because I knew that set well. It was beautiful; the pieces were made of white and brownish ivory, and there were brilliants in the crowns of the kings and queens; the squares on the board were of white and deep pink marble. I had played on it with my father.

'That is my father's,' I accused.

'He left it here with me.'

'It would belong to me now.'

'He left it to me.'

I had stood up and went over to look at it closely. I held the white ivory queen in my hand and was reminded so vividly of my father that I wanted to cry.

Lynx stood beside me. 'Your name is on it,' he said, pointing to one of the squares.

'We wrote our names on it when we won for the first time. That's my grandfather. The chess set has been in the family for years.'

'Three generations,' he said. 'And the outsider.' He pointed to his own name written boldly in one of the centre squares.

'So you beat my father.'

'Now and then. And you did, too.'

'He was a fine player. I believe that when I won he allowed me to.'

'When you play with me I shall not allow you to win. I play for myself and you will play for yourself.'

'You are suggesting that we play chess together?'

'Why not? I enjoy the game.'

'On my father's board,' I went on.

'It has become mine. You forgot. And why not play on it? It is a joy to touch such beautiful pieces.'

'I always understood it would be mine.'

'Let me strike a bargain with you. On the day you beat me it shall be yours.'

'Should I be asked to play for what should be mine by right?'

'It is suggested that you play to regain it.'

'Very well. When do we play?'

'Why not now? Would you care to?'

'Yes,' I said. 'I will play now for *my* chess board and men.'

'There is no time like the present. And that is another saying from home.'

We sat down opposite each other. Clearly I could see the golden eyebrows, the white slender hands with the jade ring. Stirling's hands were slightly spatulate and I found myself continually comparing the two men. He reminded me of Stirling, yet the son was like a pale reflection of the father. I hated to admit that I had thought such a thing because it was disloyal to Stirling. Stirling is kind, I thought. This man is cruel. I understand Stirling but who could ever be sure what was behind that glittering blue barrier. He had noticed that I was looking at his hands and held them out for me to see more clearly.

'You see the carving on this ring. It's the head of a lynx. That is what I am called. This ring is my seal. It was given me years ago by my father-in-law.'

'It's a very fine piece of jade.'

'And a fine carving. Suitable, don't you think?'

I nodded and reached for the white king's pawn.

I quickly realized that I was no match for him, but I played with such concentration that again and again I foiled his efforts to checkmate me. It was a defensive game for me and it was three-quarters of an hour before he had cornered me – a climax, I sensed, he had expected to achieve in ten minutes.

'Checkmate,' he said quietly and firmly and I saw that there was no way out.

'But it was a good game, wasn't it?' he went on. 'We must play again some time.'

'If you think me worthy,' I replied. 'I am sure you could find an opponent more in your class.'

'I like playing with you. And don't forget you have to win that set. Don't forget, also, that I am not like your father. I shall give no concessions. When you win you will know that the victory was genuine.'

I was very excited when I left him and I could not sleep for a long time that night; when I did I dreamed that all the pieces on the board came to life and the victorious king had the eyes of the Lynx.

It was October and spring was with us. The garden was beginning to look lovely. I discovered that Stirling had brought over several plants with him and we already had scarlet geraniums and purple lobelias growing on the lawn. I was wishing that I had some definite duties. I went in Adelaide's wake helping where I could, but I felt I was very inadequate. I wanted some task which was my entire responsibility. Adelaide assured me that the help

I gave in the house was invaluable, but I couldn't help feeling that she said this out of kindness.

One day I was in the summer-house where I had often sat while my ankle was strengthening, sitting for a moment because my back ached after weeding, when Jessica seemed to appear from nowhere. What a disconcerting habit this was when people moved so noiselessly and you were suddenly aware of them standing there.

'Why, Jessica!' I cried.

'I saw you coming from the library,' she said. 'You had been with him a long time.'

I felt annoyed to be so spied on. 'Does that matter?' I asked coldly.

'He's taken to you and you're flattered, aren't you? He takes to people and then . . . he's finished with them. He doesn't think of anything, you know, but what use they are to him.'

'Why do you hate him?' I asked.

To my surprise she flushed scarlet and looked as if she were going to burst into tears. 'Hate him? Yes, I do. No . . . I don't know. Everybody's afraid of him.'

'I'm not,' I said uncertainly.

'Are you sure? He's different from other people. You should have seen him when he first came to Rosella Creek.'

'Where's that?'

'It's the property. It's called Herrick's now – after him – but at one time it was Rosella Creek. Uncle Harley ran it then and we had good times. It wasn't so big in those days and there was always something to worry about. That time when the fires encircled us. We just escaped then by the skin of our teeth, Uncle Harley said. Then there was the blight and the floods and the land erosion. But we got through and Maybella would have married well. There was a man who used to come in from Melbourne. His father had a store there and he was comfortably off. He would have spoken for Maybella.'

I had a feeling that I was prying into something I was not meant to know, that Adelaide would have wished me to make some excuse to evade Jessica but the temptation was too strong for me. I wanted to know the strange story of Stirling's father, thoughts of whom were beginning to dominate my life.

So I said: 'Tell me about it.'

She smiled at me slyly. 'You want to know, don't you? You're interested in everything about him. That's what happens to people. It happened to Maybella. She was in a kind of daze from the moment he came. I remember the day he came.'

She paused again and a soft dreamy expression came into her eyes. Her lips softened and she was smiling. I did not prompt her this time. I waited; and then she began to speak quietly but intensely as though she were unaware of me and was recalling the scene for her own pleasure.

'Uncle Harley went to Sydney for the ship that was coming in. He was going to choose a couple of men because we needed help on the station. He said, "I'll bring back two strong rogues. We'll have to be careful of these

convicts but we'll get work out of them. What we need is two strong men."
He rode out with his saddle bags and provisions for the journey; he was
going to pick up a couple of horses for the convicts and they'd be back in two
weeks, he reckoned, that's if they weren't held up by floods and weather. He
was three weeks gone because there'd been rain and some of the creeks were
flooded. Maybella and I were in the kitchen baking in readiness for his
return. He came in and kissed first Maybella and then me. He said: "I've
got two fellows, Maybell." That was what he called her. "One of them
. . . well, you'll see for yourself." And we did. We were standing at the
kitchen window when we first saw him. The size of him amazed us. "What
a big man," said Maybella. "Did *he* come off the ship, then?" Uncle Harley
nodded. "Seven years. Just think of that, my girl. Wrongly accused, he says."
"Don't they all," said Maybella; and we laughed. But he was different.
Those eyes of his burned right through you. You couldn't treat him as a
convict nor even as a servant. Uncle Harley felt it, too. He sort of quailed
before him. He hadn't been there a week before he was talking to him like
an equal. Oh, he was clever. He could do twice the work of an ordinary man
and he was soon telling Uncle Harley how the place could be improved. It
was odd, because Uncle Harley, who had always thought he knew best about
everything, used to listen to him.'

She paused and looked at me. 'You wouldn't believe what a man could
do in such a little time.'

'I could,' I told her.

'Three weeks after his arrival he was taking meals with us. There was
something they had to discuss, Uncle Harley would say. His manners were
different from those of the other men – different from Uncle Harley's. When
he sat at the table with us he made us feel awkward, as though he were the
host and we the servants. He talked a lot to Uncle Harley. He'd take a piece
of paper and make a sketch of this or that bit of the property. He'd tell
Uncle how he could erect some sort of woolshed which would be raised from
the ground so that the wool could be kept dry. He said our wool press was
out of date and that we should have another. Uncle Harley used to listen to
him fascinated and say: "Yes, Herrick," in a sort of hushed reverence as
though he were the master and Uncle the servant. Shearing came and we
had never been so successful. He made everyone come in and work at it –
the gardeners, the servants, anyone with a pair of hands was set to work.
By this time he had become a sort of overseer. They were all afraid of him.
Uncle Harley said: "Nothing escapes you. You've got the eyes of a lynx."
Then they called him Lynx and the aborigines thought he was some sort of
white man's god. They would work when he was there but when he was
absent they would sit with their hands in their laps doing nothing. I
remember how he made us laugh when he drew a picture of himself and it
was so lifelike that you would think he was looking out of the paper. He
coloured the eyes – the same blue as his own and he pinned the picture up
in the woolshed and said: "Even when I'm not here I'm watching you."
They were afraid then; they'd look at the picture and think it really was
Lynx on the wall. That was the sort of man he was. So it was small
wonder . . .'

She stopped again and shook her head as though she wanted to linger over the memory. I waited eagerly for her to continue.

'Maybella was bewitched. The storekeeper's son was nothing to her. Her eyes would light up when Lynx was around and she grew quite pretty. She wasn't really pretty . . . rather plain, in fact. I was prettier than she was – but I was only the master's niece. She would inherit the property because there was no son. There'd be nothing for me. I'd been given a home; that was all. "Don't worry," Maybella used to say. "There'll always be a home here for you, Jessie." And she meant it. She had a kind heart, Maybella had.'

'So she fell in love with him?'

'The place wasn't the same. It had already started to improve. Uncle Harley thought the world of him. "Hi, Lynx," he used to say. "Now this fellow Jim, or Tom – whoever it was – do you think we can trust him to take these bales to Melbourne?" It was always "we". So you see the way things were going. Maybella talked of nothing but him. She was mad about him. I don't think there was anything she wouldn't have done for him – and so it proved. When she was going to have the child she was afraid of telling her father. He was very religious and she thought he might turn her out. I knew there could only be one who was the father and I was horrified. I said, "A convict, Maybella!" And she held up her head and cried: "I don't care. He was wrongly accused and I'm proud. I don't care about anything but that I'm going to have his child." She told her father so, and that was the most astonishing thing of all, because all he said was: "There's only one thing to be done. There'll have to be a wedding." So less than a year since he had come over as a convict to Rosella he had married Maybella. Then Adelaide was born and soon after that he was the master and everyone knew it.'

She turned to me, her eyes blazing with an emotion I could not quite understand. 'If I had been Uncle Harley's daughter *I* should have been the one.'

'Perhaps he loved Maybella.'

She laughed. 'Loved Maybella! He despised Maybella. He showed that clearly. Poor Maybella, she went on adoring him until he killed her.'

'Killed her?'

'As sure as if he'd taken a gun and fired it at her. He was disappointed in Adelaide. He wanted a son. He wanted a son who would look exactly like himself. Poor Maybella nearly died having Adelaide. I thought at the time that it was all the worry beforehand, but it was the same with the others. She wasn't meant to bear children, and she was terrified. She had suffered so much with Adelaide. He called her Adelaide after Adelaide the town. "A tribute to his new country," he said. Perhaps he thought he had done rather well in it. Uncle Harley doted on Adelaide. He would have spoilt her but Maybella didn't take much notice of the child; all her thoughts were for *him*. He had bewitched her all right. He knew it and he seemed to despise her for it.'

'You said he killed her.'

'So he did. Year after year there was a miscarriage. Oh, she was frightened.

She was almost an invalid. But he wanted a son. He had taken over the management of the place – he, a convict. Seven years he had to serve and he served them as the master. Uncle Harley was like Maybella; they were afraid of him; they never did anything without consulting him; and he despised them both. He killed Maybella with her constant pregnancies. We all knew that she was not strong enough to endure them. Uncle Harley died six years after he had gone off to Sydney to bring back the servants. I remember his death-bed. We were there, Maybella, little Adelaide, myself and *him*. Uncle Harley believed in him until the end. "Rosella's yours, Maybella," he said, "yours and Lynx's. He'll look after you and it. I leave you in good hands, daughter. And there'll always be a home for you here, Jessie." Then he died, believing that he had set everything in order. He didn't know that within a year Maybella would be buried beside him.'

'But you said he killed her,' I insisted.

'She died when Stirling was born. I hated him. I said to him: "You'll kill her!" And he looked at me with those contemptuous eyes of his as though he considered me a fool. I loved Maybella. We were like sisters. When she died part of me died. I've heard people say that before. It's a cliché, isn't it? But it can be true, you know. And it was true for me. He killed Maybella because every year he forced her to try to bear the son he wanted, though she was more or less an invalid after Adelaide's birth. But he was cruel and hard. He got his son, though. He got Stirling. And that was what finally killed Maybella. She would have been here today but for his determination to get a son.'

I was silent and she added: 'He always gets what he wants. You'll see.'

I thought of his dream of a golden fortune which he had never found and I said: 'No one gets all they want.'

'He'll ride over everyone to get what *he* wants. He'll have it, in the end.'

'You hate him and yet . . .'

'I hate him for what he did to Maybella.'

'And yet . . .'

She turned on me fiercely. 'Why do you say that?'

'I feel that you don't hate him all the time.'

She drew away from me as though she were afraid of me. Then she rose abruptly and left me.

November had come and it was sheep-shearing time. This was the climax of the year's work. There was a great deal of activity and Stirling and his father were at the property every day. I went over with Adelaide to help with the meals. In the big stone-floored kitchen we worked hard, cooking for the men employed there and the extra hands who had been called in to help at this time. Often in the evenings sundowners would appear at the property and ask to stay the night in return for the help they would give next day. We were never sure how many we should have to cater for.

I found it all of great interest and different from the life we lived at Little Whiteladies.

One day when I was mixing dough and was alone in the kitchen Jacob Jagger came in. He leaned against the table watching me.

'You make a pretty picture, Miss Nora,' he said, his warm little eyes seeming to take in every part of me.

'Thank you,' I replied. 'I hope my bread will be as appreciated as the picture you mention.'

'I like a ready tongue,' he said.

'*I* like the kitchen to myself when I'm working.'

'Pert,' he said, 'very pert. I like that, too.'

'Well, Mr. Jagger,' I returned, 'all I can say is that you are easily pleased.'

'As a rule I'm not all that easy to please where females are concerned.'

'That's unfortunate for you, considering the dearth of them in this part of the world. Now if you would kindly stand aside, I should be grateful. I have to get to the oven.'

He stood aside but would not go. I felt myself flushing as I opened the oven and took out the bread.

'My!' he said. 'That looks good. Almost as good as its maker. I'd like to see you in this kitchen more often, Miss Nora. If you'd like to see round the property at any time when there are not so many people around, you just ask me.'

'I should probably ask Mr. Stirling,' I said, gazing intently at the brown loaves just from the oven. 'Well, good day, Mr. Jagger,' I went on pointedly. 'I am sure Mr. Herrick will be expecting you at the shearing.'

I had implied that I might even mention the fact to Mr. Herrick that he was chatting in the kitchen when I did not wish him to be there; and one mention of Lynx was enough to make him consider his action.

He bowed ironically and left.

When the shearing was over everyone seemed to remember that Christmas would soon be upon us.

'We celebrate it here,' explained Adelaide, 'in very much the same manner as it is celebrated at home. My father likes it to be so.'

She would make Christmas puddings and mincemeat although she would not be able to get all the ingredients which were available in England. They would kill some of the best of the fowls and although it would be high summer everything must be as much like England as possible. I was amused that Adelaide who had never seen England should refer to it as 'home', and that she should know so much about our customs. Even so, she was constantly asking me how this and that was done; and I knew this was to please her father.

She and I took the Cobb's coach into Melbourne and shopped there. That was quite an adventure because we stopped at The Lynx Hotel for two nights and one of the evenings we were taken to the Theatre Royal by Jack Bell, presumably on the instructions of Lynx. We took great pleasure in the shops and I spent some of the money which had been banked for me when my shares in the mine had been sold. I felt quite rich and bought presents – and for myself some strong boots and material to make dresses.

It was about a week after our return when I noticed that Mary, the maid who looked after me, was in distress. When she brought my hot water one morning, she tripped over the rug and went sprawling on the floor, spilling the water.

When it was cleared up, I said to her, 'Something's wrong, isn't it, Mary?'

'Why, Miss Nora,' she said flushing painfully, 'whatever do you mean?'

'You seem distraught. You're constantly dropping things. Come and sit down and tell me what the trouble is.'

At this she did as I bid, and sitting down burst into floods of tears.

Then the story came out. She was going to have a baby and didn't know what to do about it.

'Well,' I said, 'that's bad, But it's not the end of the world. Perhaps you can get married.'

That brought more tears. It wasn't possible, it seemed. She murmured something about going away to bear her shame.

'It's this man's shame as well,' I said firmly. 'He can bear some of it, too.'

There was nothing to be done, she told me. She only hoped she would not be turned away.

'That shan't happen,' I said fiercely, as though I were the mistress of the house and all decisions rested with me. I added that the first thing we must do was tell Adelaide.

Adelaide sighed when I told her.

'It happens far too often,' she said. 'But here we are, away from a town and these people are young and hot-blooded. They don't think of consequences. Who is the man?'

'She won't say.'

I was not surprised when Mary at length revealed that the man was Jacob Jagger.

'Will he marry her?' I asked Adelaide.

'I shouldn't think so for a moment.'

'If your father insists, he will.'

'I don't think he would insist.'

'I should have thought he might very well.'

'You don't know him yet, Nora.'

It seemed I didn't, for he did not take a very serious view of the matter. Mary could have her child in the house and it would be brought up there. As for Jagger, naturally he didn't want to marry a girl like Mary. He managed the property well and it wasn't easy to get men; he had to amuse himself now and then. That was Lynx's view.

I overheard some of the servants discussing it afterwards.

'Master was very mild over the affair,' said one.

'Couldn't be ought else, considering . . .' was the answer.

I knew that meant his own conduct was not exemplary and I wondered why my father had sent me to live in such a household.

Mary was immensely relieved and almost happy. I asked her whether she would have liked to marry the father of her child.

'God forbid, Miss Nora,' she said.

'But you must have liked him . . . once.'

'I never did. He frightened the life out of me.'

'But . . .'

'You're wondering why I did, Miss. Well, he sort of cornered me, and I didn't have much say, come to think of it.'

I said. 'He couldn't have *forced* you!'

'Well, I reckon that's about it,' she replied.

I felt very uneasy.

Chapter Four

It seemed strange to wake up to a hot and sunny Christmas morning. A few days before, Stirling and I had ridden out into the bush and come back with a kind of mistletoe which was a parasite on the gum trees. It wasn't quite like our mistletoe at home, but it served. We hung some over the door and some in the middle of the room. When we had finished Stirling kissed me beneath it.

'May it be the first of many Christmases in Australia,' he said.

'What if your father struck gold?' I demanded. 'Then we should all be transported, lock, stick and barrel, to England.'

He didn't answer that and I knew he didn't want to think of leaving.

We had dinner in the middle of the day and I spent most of the morning in the kitchen with Adelaide. We cooked the chickens while the plum pudding steamed away in a saucepan; the heat was great. I went outside to get a breath of fresh air, but it was as hot outside as in the kitchen. I stood for a moment looking at the flowering gums and reminding myself that this time last year I was at Danesworth House growing more and more anxious because I had not heard from my father. A great deal had happened in a short time.

Adelaide came out and said, 'The passion fruit is ready for picking. Should I pick now?' She answered herself. 'No. It would spoil the illusion and wouldn't be a bit like Christmas at home.'

It was a big party for Christmas. Lynx sat at the head of the table and I retained my seat on his left hand, Stirling opposite as we had sat since the first night. Several men from the property and the mine were there. Jack Bell was busy at the hotel so he did not join us. I had avoided looking at Jacob Jagger since the Mary incident. If he had been in love with her and she with him I should have felt differently. I kept thinking of Mary's description of being 'cornered'. I knew that he constantly looked my way, that he was always endeavouring to make me speak or smile at him. This I refused to do. The man disgusted me. One day I would speak to Stirling about him. Across the table my eyes met those of Stirling, and he smiled at me with such pleasure that I glowed with happiness.

It was a pleasant meal. Lynx was in a benevolent mood; it was clear that he enjoyed presiding over his table, which might have been in an English country house. Mary brought in the Christmas pudding and brandy was poured over it before it was set alight. It tasted good.

We were drowsing over our port when there was a commotion in the kitchen followed by the sound of raised voices and someone crying: 'Let me see him. Or let me see Miss Adelaide.'

Adelaide had turned white; she rose and went out. In a short time she returned. Lynx said: 'What is it?'

'It's the Lambs,' replied Adelaide. 'They've come back.'

'What for?' demanded Lynx.

'They want to come back into the house.'

'They want to come back! I thought they went after gold.'

'They did . . . but they're back.'

'Without the fortune they were going to make?'

'They're in a pitiable state,' said Adelaide.

'I won't have them back,' retorted Lynx coldly.

I tried to catch his eye but he was not looking at me.

'Perhaps . . .' began Adelaide.

'Tell them to go. I don't take people back into this house once they have run away.'

Adelaide turned. I rose in my chair. 'They might be hungry,' I said.

Lynx's steely gaze was on me. 'They went to make a fortune. It's no business of mine if they failed. When they left this house they left it for ever.'

Adelaide went out and I sat down dumbly. The joy of Christmas had gone for me.

When Stirling and I rode out next day I was still thinking of the Lambs.

'It was so cruel,' I said. 'And on Christmas Day.'

Stirling could never bear any criticism of his father. 'The day makes no difference.'

'No,' I agreed. 'It would have been cruel on any day, but on Christmas Day it is worse because it makes nonsense of all Christmas means.'

'We can't allow people to run off when they want to and then come back and expect us to kill the fatted calf.'

'Perhaps not, but they could have been given some food and help.'

'It wouldn't surprise me if Adelaide did.'

'But he wouldn't help them. He's a very hard man.'

'He knows what he's doing. He has to show these people that they can't walk off to look for gold one day and come back the next when they've failed to find it.'

Stirling's jaw was obstinately set. I realized in that moment that I was jealous of his love for his father. It would always be Lynx who came first with him.

We argued the point during our ride and we finally quarrelled when I said he hadn't a mind of his own and readily accepted everything Papa told him. He retorted that I was a self-opinionated schoolmarm who thought

that because I had once taught little girls of five I could teach my elders
... yes, and betters.

I galloped on ahead of him, hurt and angry, because I was beginning to
build up a picture of being with Stirling for ever, marrying him and having
Lynx for a father-in-law. I was not sure whether I wanted the latter or not.
I wished that there were no Lynx and that Stirling's father had been an
ordinary sort of man. And then I thought: No, I wouldn't like that. I could
not imagine the place without Lynx. My growing relationship with him
excited me. I was exultant because he was not indifferent to me. I wanted
him to be interested in me, to listen to me, to respect me and to grow fond
of me. I wanted to be important to him. But I wanted to be more important
to Stirling than anyone else in the world and while Lynx existed I felt that
never would be.

The next day Stirling behaved as though there had been no quarrel
between us. He was treating me as though I were his sister. I did not want
this but I felt happily secure because our relationship was one which would
strengthen as it grew and I was certain that in due course I would be as
necessary to him as he was to me.

The Lambs were never mentioned again. I liked to think that Adelaide
had helped them and I felt sure she had. Mary was happy again and growing
noticeably larger. I saw Jemmy often in the stables; he had developed an
assurance which must always have been not far from the surface. I often
heard him whistling at his work and I felt so happy because we had been
able to help him. Therefore I was surprised when one day in early February
Jemmy was reported missing.

It was the same story. He had confided in one of the stable boys that he
was going off to find gold.

When Lynx heard, he laughed. 'That's another of them,' he said. 'Don't
take him back when he's had enough of the gold fields.'

He asked me that night to have a game of chess with him after dinner.
We did not play immediately, though, and I believed that he wanted to taunt
me about Jemmy, for Stirling had since told him how eager I had been to
help the boy when we had found him on the ship.

'It doesn't do to play the ministering angel, Nora,' he said. 'Come, you
are going to drink a glass of port with me.' He filled the glasses. 'You see
how your Jemmy has turned out.'

'Surely you can understand the desire to find gold?'

'I understand it. I have experienced it.'

'Then why are you so hard on others?'

'I'm not concerned with others – only with myself.'

'You condemn these people because they go off to look for gold.'

'You are mistaken. All I say is that I will not have them back when they
fail. I will not have my servants walking off when the whim takes them.
They are free to walk off, it's true, but not to come back.'

'The Lambs ...'

'Ah, you hated me then, didn't you?'

'I thought you were very hard and on Christmas Day too!'

'My dear, sentimental Nora, the day has nothing to do with it.'

'So Stirling said.'

'You have thrashed the matter out with him?'

'I have discussed it with him.'

'And attacked me furiously.'

'Yes, but he defended you.'

He smiled then. Then he said, 'Nora, life *is* hard, you know, and it is no use being soft in a hard world. You are too sentimental, too emotional. You will be hurt one day.'

'Are you sentimental? Are you emotional? No! But you have been hurt . . . so hurt that you have never forgotten it.'

He raised those bushy eyebrows and regarded me. Then he held out his hands so that his long shirt cuffs were pulled back and I saw the scars on his wrists. 'Manacles,' he said. 'Fetters and chains. The marks are still there.'

'They have no meaning now. You are no longer fettered. You are in command. You rule the lives of all those around you.'

'But the scars remain.'

'In your heart as well as on your wrists.'

He was silent for a moment and his eyes narrowed as he went on. 'You are right, Nora. What happened to me is something which will never be forgotten. Only when a certain action has been taken can the score be settled.'

His eyes blazed and I knew that he was thinking of revenge.

'How long ago did it happen?' I asked.

'It is thirty-five years since I came out here . . . in chains.'

'And you still talk of settling the score!'

'I shall go on thinking of it until the settlement is made.'

'It is a long time to harbour resentment.'

'For such an injury?'

'Times have changed since those days. People are perhaps less cruel. Could it be the times which were to blame?'

'I do not see it that way. But for one man I should never have been obliged to endure those months of degradation and humiliation.'

'But you are here now. You have everything a man could wish for. You are a king in your world. You have a son and daughter, and most people go in fear and trembling of you. Isn't that what you want?'

He looked at me and smiled slowly. 'You are a bold girl, Nora. You don't care in the least that you offend me with your criticism.'

'Men like you hate criticism, I know. All the more reason why some should not be afraid to give it.'

'And you have chosen yourself for that role?'

'I am determined to show you that I am not afraid of you.'

'Suppose I asked you to leave my house?'

'Then I should pack my bag and depart.'

'Where to?'

'I am not without some qualifications. Remember I taught at Danesworth House. I could be a teacher or governess in some family.'

'A sad life for a proud woman.'

'Better than being where she is not wanted.'

His blue eyes were fixed steadily on me. 'And do you think you are not wanted here?'

'I am not sure.'

'The truth, please.'

'I think you have made a promise to my father and that you are a man who likes to keep his promise if . . .'

'Pray go on.'

'If keeping it does not inconvenience you too much.'

'Well, Nora, let me tell you that having you in this house does not inconvenience me one little bit. If there was any sign of this I should cease to think of your existence. You have been truthful with me, so I will be truthful with you. I will say that I did not altogether dislike the addition to my family. I wanted sons, but daughters are very well, and can be useful.'

'Then I am of use?'

'I am not displeased with my family. Come, let us have a game. You still have to win the set, you know.'

We played. I was aware of his growing interest in me. And was elated by it.

Stirling was right. One could not live under his roof and not be affected by him.

The hot summer weather was with us. I would work in the kitchen or in the garden in the mornings and in the afternoons try to find a shady spot under a wattle tree and lie and read, although the flies – and I had never seen so many before – were a pest. It was more comfortable to sit in Adelaide's cool sitting-room and sew with her or read aloud to her as she sewed, which she very much enjoyed. She liked Jane Austen and the Brontës; she was as passionately interested in the English scene as her father was. Sometimes Jessica would creep in and sit and listen while I read. I must confess that I always felt a little uneasy at such times. She would sit very quietly, her hands folded in her lap, and I had the impression that she wanted to be alone with me so that she could talk to me about those days when Lynx had first come to Australia and settled into the place which was then called Rosella Creek.

So passed that summer and when the weather showed signs of becoming a little cooler Adelaide suggested that we take another trip to Melbourne. There were several things she wanted; it was easy to get them brought to the house because one of her father's businesses supplied goods to the small shops and traders on the goldfields; but as Adelaide said, it was a luxury to choose for oneself from a large selection. We could put up at The Lynx and this time, as I was accustomed to the country and was now a very creditable horsewoman, we might ride and I could try camping out, which was often more convenient than waiting on the Cobb coaches. Stirling could accompany us and there should be another man of the party. Someone would certainly have business in Melbourne and wish to join us.

During the summer evenings I had played chess with Lynx several times. He invariably displayed a rather sardonic amusement because he knew how desperately I wanted to beat him. It had become rather an obsession with me and it was typical of our relationship. I had always wanted to show him that I was not in awe of him; perhaps the fact that I continually stressed this showed that I was.

But those evenings in the library with the rose-quartz lamp beside us throwing its rosy glow over the chessmen had become part of my life. I found a certain content in sitting there, watching those long artistic hands with the green jade signet ring. I would grow tense with excitement when I could see him checkmated in a few moves, but he was always ready with some devastating counter movement which turned my attack into defence. I would look up and find those magnetic eyes on me, full of mocking laughter, brilliant with pleasure because he always enjoyed showing me that however I tried to outwit him, he would always win in the end.

'Not this time, Nora,' he would say. 'What a pity. They are such unusual pieces. Look at this castle. So delicately formed. And when you win, you will still play with me, won't you? I should not like the games to cease just because the set has changed hands.'

I began to learn more and more of him; in fact there were times when he seemed to lift that invincible barrier which he had erected round himself. When it was there he was the Lynx, proud, invulnerable, all powerful. But it could be lifted and in some way I had found a means of doing it. It had begun when he had shown me the fetters on his wrists; and then there was the time when he showed me his pictures.

I was a little early going to the library for our game because my watch was ten minutes fast. I knocked but there was no answer so I went in. He was not there, but a curtain on one side of the room had been drawn back to show a door, and this stood ajar. I had not known that there was a door there.

I stood for a while in the room. I had never seen it when he was not there and it was surprising how his absence changed it. It was now an ordinary room – pleasantly furnished, it was true, with its thick rugs and heavy velvet curtains, strong oak chairs and the books lining the wall. A library which one would find in any English country house! On the oak table stood the chess set in readiness for our game.

I crossed the room and looked through the open door. He was there but he did not see me immediately. On a table before him were several canvases and I remembered then what Jessica had told me about the pictures of himself which he had set up to make the aborigines afraid of him.

He glanced up and saw me.

'Why, Nora,' he said, 'is it time?'

'I am a little early. My watch is fast.'

He hesitated – something I had rarely seen him do before. Then he said: 'Come in.'

So I went in. On an easel stood a canvas and on a chair lay a paint-spattered jacket.

'This is my sanctum,' he told me.

'Have I intruded?'

'On the contrary, you are here on my invitation.'

'You are a painter.'

'Is that a question?'

'No. I know it.'

'Are you surprised? You did not expect me to have such talents? Perhaps you consider I have no talent. Judge for yourself.'

He linked his arm through mine; it was the first time there had been any demonstration of affection.

'These pictures on the walls are my work,' he said.

'Then you *are* an artist.'

'You are *not* a connoisseur – that much is evident.'

'But these pictures . . .'

'Lack form, technique, or whatever you like to call it. They are not really very good.'

I had paused before a portrait of a woman. I thought I had seen the face before.

'Well, you like that?'

'Yes. It's soft and gentle and the expression is . . . good.'

'What were you going to say before good?'

'I don't know. Perhaps that she looked helpless, clinging, entirely feminine.'

He nodded and drew me to the next picture. 'Self-portrait.'

There he was. It was a good likeness and I guessed he was an easy subject. The mane of fair hair, the beard, the pride in the expression, and the animal quality – all these would be easy to capture in a facile way. Some of the arrogant power of the man was missing, but that was inevitable.

Then he took me to the table and showed me the canvases there. I saw it. The house. The real Whiteladies. The one Stirling and I had seen when we climbed the oak trees.

I gave an exclamation. 'That's it,' I said.

'You went there with Stirling,' he replied. 'He told me how your scarf blew over the wall and you both went in.'

'I suppose he tells you everything.'

'Whoever tells everything? But I know a great deal of what is in Stirling's mind. After all, he is my son.'

'And you love him as you never loved anyone else.'

'That's not entirely true. I am capable of affection. I don't give it freely, but that may mean that when I do I have the more to give.'

'How could you paint that house when you have never seen it?'

'Who said I have never seen it? I have lived in that house, Nora. I know it well.'

'You lived there! It was yours! So that is why you have built one to look exactly like it.'

'What conclusions you jump to. I lived there, it is true; but I did not say that it was mine. I worked there for a year in the humble position of drawing-master to the young lady of the house.'

'And Stirling happened to discover it . . .'

'You are wrong again. Stirling went there because he knew the house was there. I told him to go.'

'So that was why I had to meet him in Canterbury. Miss Emily Grainger said it was a little odd.'

'It was at my request that he went there.'

'You wanted to know if it had changed since you were last there. Houses don't change much. It's the people living in them . . .'

'Ah, there you have. it. I wanted him to see not so much the house but the people living in it.'

'Because you knew them long ago. He did not say so. He didn't even tell them his name. I don't think they asked. It was all a little odd and unconventional.'

'He would not have told them his name. That might have been unwise.'

'There was some quarrel with this family?'

He laughed bitterly, harshly. Then he said. 'I was hardly in a position to quarrel with them. I was, as I said, the young lady's drawing-master. They were rich then. I don't think they are so happily placed now. Times change. The old man was a gambler . . . and not a clever one. I believe he lost a great deal of money after my departure.'

'A fact which appears to give you some satisfaction, I gather.'

'You gather correctly. Would you not dislike someone who condemned you to exile from your own country, to seven years' servitude in a penal settlement.'

'So it was the owner of Whiteladies!'

'Sir Henry Dorian, no less.'

'For what reasons?'

'Robbery.'

'And you were guiltless.'

'Completely so.'

'And could you not prove your innocence?'

'If I had had justice, yes. But he and his friends saw that I had not. I was in his house unlawfully, he said. I *was* in his house and not at his request, but the object of my visit was not to steal.' He smiled at me. 'You have an enquiring mind, Nora,' he added lightly.

'I admit it. I want to hear more. I remember the place so clearly. I felt when I was there it was important to me in some way. I had no idea at that time that it was connected with my new guardian.'

He shrugged his shoulders. 'A wonderful old place. How I should like to own such a house!' His eyes gleamed with covetousness. 'I have built this place – a poor imitation. No! I want the stones which were used hundreds of years before. There is only one Whiteladies and it is not this one.'

'You have a very comfortable house of the same name.'

'It's a fake, Nora. I hate fakes.'

'It serves well.'

'It serves as a substitute until . . .' He stopped. Then he laughed and added, 'You wheedle, Nora. You lure confidences from me. And the fact that I allow you to, shows you that I already think of you as my daughter. Now isn't that strange? I am not a sentimental man to drool over a daughter – yet I allow you to tempt me to talk.'

'It is always good to talk. I am your ward. I have seen this house and the people there. There was the girl, Minta her name was, and there was Mamma.'

'Tell me about her. Stirling could not describe her. Women are better at that sort of thing than men.'

'Why, Mamma would be the one to whom you taught drawing!'

He nodded.

'She was old . . . well, perhaps not old, but she seemed so.'

'To you she seemed old – as I do.'

'No, not you. One would not think of age in connection with you. But she seemed fretful and concerned about her health. The girl was charming. And there was someone called Lucie.'

'Fretful,' he said and laughed lightly. He indicated the canvas he had already shown me. 'Was she like this? I drew from memory.'

Then I knew of whom the picture reminded me. It was the girl Minta, of course.

'It is a little like the girl,' I said. 'But she is not so helpless-looking. No, the woman in the chair was not like that. Perhaps she might have been years ago.'

'Thirty-five years ago when she was seventeen. She was beautiful then, but she was not very good at drawing. I was going to marry her.'

I was beginning to understand. She was the daughter of the house in which he occupied a minor position. I thought of Jessica's account of his arrival at Rosella Creek.

'So you went to the house to be her drawing-master and you decided to marry her. You admired the house and you would like to have been master of it.'

'I did admire the house and I should have enjoyed owning it, but in those days I was nineteen years old and sentimental. I was even romantic. You may find that hard to believe, but it was so. I fell in love with Arabella and she with me. I was egotistical. You smile. You are thinking, Yes, I can believe that! It was true. I believed myself to be as good as any man and I could not conceive that her father, Sir Henry Dorian, would not welcome me as a son-in-law. I was the drawing-master, it was true. I had nothing but my talents; but on the other hand I could have managed his estate as it had never been managed before. If he had not been such a fool the family might not now be reduced to . . . well, scarcely penury – but it must be trying to have to consider every shilling when you have a position to uphold and have been accustomed to luxury.'

'Tell me what happened.'

'He was outraged by my suggestions. His daughter to marry her drawing-master! No. He had some neighbouring fop in mind for her. Someone of the right family. Very different from the drawing-master. Bella and I decided to elope. There was a maid in the house in whom she confided. Silly Bella! The maid turned traitor. I had been dismissed from the house so I came back one night for her. She had been locked in her room; so I took a ladder from one of the potting-sheds and setting it against the wall climbed into her room. She gave me her jewels and I slipped them into my pockets. At that moment Sir Henry with four of his menservants burst into the room. There, Nora, I have told you the story.'

'But surely she explained to them.'

'She tried to. She wept. She entreated her father to listen. They said she was shocked and did not know what she was saying, that I had threatened her and she was afraid. They were determined to be rid of me. They knew that if I had stayed in England I should in time have persuaded her to come to me. So what an excellent opportunity this was to get me out of the country, to arrange it so that I could not come back.' He lifted his hand and the lynx eyes in the ring glittered.

'It is a terrible story,' I said.

'You would be sure of that if you could picture the filthy prison, the convict ship. I was chained, Nora.' He held out his wrists again. 'The chains made sores; the sores festered. I was battened down in the hold for months on end with all the scum of England. Robbers, prostitutes, murderers . . . all going to Australia. Cargo for the settlers, cheap labour at the best. I remember the day we arrived in Sydney and how we came up on deck; the brilliance of the sunshine, that blue sea around us, and the birds. Yes, what I remember most vividly were the brightly plumaged birds – red-winged parrots, rainbow lorikeets, yellow-crested cockatoos and pink and grey galahs. They swooped and chattered above that sea and the thing that struck me was that they were free. Have you ever felt envious of a bird, Nora? I was then . . . and then I despised myself and started thinking of revenge. One day I would take it, and that made me want to live.'

'Soon after you arrived in Australia you were married.'

'Yes. I married the mother of Adelaide and Stirling.'

'She was the daughter of the man into whose hands you had fallen.'

'Why, you know a great deal of my history. I knew you were inquisitive.'

'It interests me. You quickly forgot your devotion to Arabella.'

'I never forgot my devotion to Arabella. That is one thing you can't accuse me of – fickleness.'

'But you married.'

'Maybella. She was a Bella too.'

'Don't tell me you married her because of her name.'

'No. She could have been Mary, Jane, Grace, Nora . . . any name you can think of. What's in a name?'

'But at least you could call her Bella.'

'Which I did.'

'And did she remind you of that other Bella?'

'Never.' He sounded contemptuous.

'Poor Maybella!' I said.

'It was I admit a marriage of convenience.'

'Convenience for you – perhaps inconvenience for her.'

'She was eager for it.'

'Did she ever regret it?'

'Jessica has been talking to you, I gather. Poor Jessica! She was very jealous of Maybella.'

'She gave me the impression that she was devoted to her.'

'She was that, too. People's motives are so mixed. Yes, certainly she was devoted to Maybella. She nursed her through her many illnesses.'

I forbore to mention that I knew what those illnesses were.

'She wanted to be in Maybella's place,' he added.

'She wished she were the daughter of the house so that she could have been the one to bring you out of bondage.'

'How discerning you are! And how we talk! All that is over and done with.'

'But you said it was not. You said you would never forget.'

'I shan't forget,' he said vehemently and I saw the ring glitter as he clenched his hands. 'But it is past now. Come, let us have our game.'

He drew me into the library and we sat facing each other over the board as we had so many times before.

He was absent-minded that night and I almost beat him. He rallied in time. He did not want me to win – whether it was because he did not want to give up the chess set or because he hated to be beaten by a woman, I was not quite sure. Both probably.

But that night of confidences had drawn us closer together. He might have become a little wary of me and felt that he had betrayed too much – but we were closer for all that.

After that we planned our visit to Melbourne. Stirling, Adelaide and myself were to be accompanied by one of the men from the property; we could do the forty miles or so into the town, taking about three days which would mean camping out for two nights.

'Just a little trip for Nora to try,' was Stirling's description of the jaunt.

We would not take more than we needed, pointed out Adelaide, because it all had to be carried. We had sent on ahead clothes and things we should need for our stay at The Lynx in Melbourne so that they would be waiting for us when we arrived. Then we could be elegantly and fashionably clad; we could do our shopping and have our purchases sent to Whiteladies; then we would journey back, camping on the way.

We were taking a few spare horses and a couple of pack horses; and we should carry a little in our saddle bags. There was a tent which could be used for Adelaide and myself. Stirling and the man who was to accompany us would sleep under the stars. It all sounded exciting and I was looking forward to it.

It was only an hour or so before we were due to start that I discovered that the man who was to accompany us was Jacob Jagger.

'That man!' I protested to Adelaide.

'He has to go into Melbourne on business and he said he would like to take this opportunity.'

'I shouldn't have thought he could have been spared from the property.'

'Really, Nora! What do you know of the property?'

'Well,' I floundered, 'he's supposed to be the manager of it and . . .'

'Even so, he doesn't have to remain there all and every day.'

'I don't like him, Adelaide.'

'Oh, I daresay he's no worse than anyone else.'

'It was that affair of Mary.'

'It happens now and then.'

'But she said that he . . . forced her.'

'Girls tell these tales. We didn't hear anything about the forcing until she was going to have the baby.'

'She seemed to me as though she were absolutely terrified.'

'Of course she was when she knew she was found out. It's always the same story. And you mustn't judge people by the standards you've been used to in England. People out here are . . . isolated. These things happen. My father understands this. He is never hard on these cases. Mary is receiving every consideration, so stop being sorry for her, and don't be hard on Jacob.'

I didn't care what she said. I didn't like the man.

When he arrived he grinned at me.

'I'm happy to be making this trip,' he told me; and I lowered my head coldly and looked away. I was glad Stirling was with us.

Riding along in the early morning, revelling in the aspects of the bush, listening to the birds, now and then catching sight of some wild animal or bright plumage, I refused to be depressed by the presence of Jacob Jagger and my thoughts turned to Stirling.

They were pleasant thoughts. There he rode beside me, now and then turning to smile at me or point out some feature of the countryside which he thought I might have missed. I was contemplating the difference he had made in my life and how important he had become in it. There were times when it seemed that Lynx was more often in my thoughts than his son was, for I thought a great deal of Lynx. I accepted him as the dominant figure on the scene. Stirling reminded me of him in many ways. He was a gentler, kinder version of his father. But one could not help being impressed by Lynx, admiring him, even feeling for him this absurd sort of devotion – which I called idolatory in Stirling – but for Stirling I had a warmer, more human feeling. I could not imagine the house – my little Whiteladies – without Lynx. Even to think of his not being there affected me deeply; and the excitement of the days was intensified by seeing him at the head of the table at dinner, or best of all playing chess with him trying to beat him or, as he said, to wheedle confidences from him. I thought more often of Lynx perhaps than I did of Stirling, but I had no doubt of my feelings for Stirling – I loved him. And I was not sure how to describe my feelings for Lynx. I believed that one day Stirling would ask me to marry him and when he did I would say 'yes' without hesitation. I believed that Lynx would give us his blesssing (for I was sure this would be what he wanted) and that we should be happy ever after. We would be prosperous here – although we would give up the mine. I would urge Stirling to do this. Then my thoughts grew blank because I was thinking as though Lynx were dead . . . dead! That seemed impossible. No one – not even Stirling – had that immense vitality, the reflection of which revitalized one. No, I would persuade *Lynx* and Stirling to abandon the mine. I could not bear to think of men dying of phthisis, nor the look on Lynx's face when he talked of gold.

We rode south and as the day wore on we found a spot where we would pitch our tent. It was near a creek so that we had water, which Stirling went

to get while Jacob Jagger made a fire. Adelaide said she would show me
how to make dampers and we would soon have tea. There was boiled bacon
in the saddle bags and some mutton too.

What an exhilarating experience it would have been but for the fact of
Jacob Jagger's presence. I had to admit that he was very skilful in making
a fire. He insisted on explaining how to make the wood kindle and how
important it was to choose the right spot.

'It's easy to start a forest fire,' he added, 'and that, Miss Nora, is something
I hope you'll never see.'

'The last one was terrible,' put in Adelaide. 'I really thought it was going
to be the end of the property.'

'So did we all,' agreed Jacob Jagger, his plump face more sober than I
had ever seen it. 'There were hours when we were actually ringed by fire.
I was waiting for the gums near the house to explode and that would have
been the end.'

It was difficult for me to imagine the horror of a forest fire. I suppose
nobody can until they have seen one. Now this friendly little fire which
Jagger had made was cooking our dampers and boiling our water for tea.

It was so pleasant lying there, on rugs which Adelaide and I had spread
out on the turf, propped up by our saddles.

'What do you think of camping, Nora?' Stirling was asking me.

'I think it's fun.'

He threw himself down beside me, his elbow resting on the ground, his
arm propping up his head.

'I knew you'd enjoy it.' His eyes were warm with approval. 'I knew you
wouldn't be one of those helpless females who scream at the sight of a
spider.'

'Surely we didn't have to come camping for you to discover that?'

'No. I always knew it.' He was smiling at me in a way which delighted
me. He was fond of me; there was a bond of understanding between us. I
knew that he looked upon me as his protégée. He liked people to admire me,
applaud me; that was why he had been so anxious that I make a good
impression on his father. It showed that he loved me.

This was indeed my home. I should spend the rest of my days here. Little
Whiteladies was the setting for my future happiness. Lynx would be the
master, always, but benign, indulgent and pretending that he was not. He
would accept me as his daughter and love me as such; I believed he was very
close to doing so already. And there would be children – my home would
not be complete without them. Lynx would love them and be proud of them
and love me the more for giving him grandchildren.

It was easy to dream out there in the bush. Perhaps Stirling was dreaming
too and there was a similarity in our thoughts.

When it was dark we sat round the fire talking desultorily and even Jacob
Jagger seemed likeable. Adelaide told us of other journeys she had made
and how on one occasion she had been lost in the bush. She had gone off to
get water and had lost her way back to the camp.

'It's so easy,' she said. 'The contours of the land change so subtly that you
don't realize they've changed. You take what you believe to be the right

track – so many tracks look alike – and then you find you have wandered off in the wrong direction. It's a terrible experience to be lost in the bush.'

'I remember the occasion,' said Stirling. 'We all went off in different directions to look for you. We found you only half a mile away. You'd been going round in circles.'

Adelaide shivered. 'I shall never forget it. Let it be a warning to you, Nora.'

'Oh, we'll take care of Miss Nora,' said Jacob Jagger.

'No fear of that,' added Stirling. 'Still, Nora, take warning. Don't go wandering off on your own.'

I promised not to and we talked some more; then Stirling and Adelaide sang songs which they had sung together as children. They were songs from England. 'Those were the ones our father liked to hear,' said Adelaide. They were 'Cherry Ripe', 'Strawberry Fair', and 'On a Friday Morn When We Set Sail' – all the ballads that English children had been singing for years.

Adelaide and I went into our tent and the fresh air and long ride had made me so tired that I was soon asleep.

I was awakened by the kookaburras laughing overhead. Adelaide and I slipped on our dresses and went down to the creek to wash. She brought back water which she boiled in some quart-sized pots and with this made tea which we drank from tin mugs. Tea had rarely tasted as good before.

We left early after breakfasting from dampers and cold bacon; there was passion fruit jelly, too, which Adelaide had had the foresight to slip into her saddle bag.

How I enjoyed that morning ride through the bush! But there was one incident which spoiled the pleasure of the trip. We stopped at midday and I was putting the water to boil for tea on the fire which Jacob Jagger had made when I was aware of him, standing very close.

'You've certainly taken to the bush, Miss Nora,' he said.

I replied without looking round, 'I find it very interesting.'

'It's a great life,' he said. Then he knelt beside me and the awareness of him made me stand up immediately. I looked over my shoulder. There was no sign of Adelaide or Stirling.

'Where are they?' I asked.

He laughed. 'Not far off. No need to be scared.'

'Scared? I retorted coldly, annoyed because that was exactly what I was, to find myself alone with him. 'Of what?'

'Of me?' he suggested.

'I can see no reason for that.'

He gave an exaggerated sigh of relief.

'I'm glad. There's no need to be. I'm very fond of you, Miss Nora.'

'I'm glad, too, that I need not be scared, as you put it. Your feelings for me don't really concern me either way.'

'Well, we could change that.'

'I think I am the best judge of my feelings.'

Oh, where were Adelaide and Stirling? Why didn't they appear so that there might be an end to this conversation which he was forcing upon me. Well, not really forcing. I supposed I could walk away, but I did not want him to know how abhorrent I found him, for that would be to some extent betraying my fear.

'You are a very haughty young lady. I could change that, too.'

'Since when have you believed that you have the power to mould *my* character?'

'Ever since I saw you. In fact, Miss Nora, I have not ceased to think of you since that moment.'

'How strange!'

'It's not strange at all. You're a very remarkable young lady. The most remarkable I ever saw. I have never felt so interested in a young lady before.'

'What of Mary?' I suggested; and I felt the colour burning in my cheeks.

'Now you wouldn't be jealous of a servant girl!'

'Jealous! You must be mad.' I walked away but he was beside me, walking close. He laid a hand on my arm.

I blazed at him. 'Mr. Jagger, kindly remove your hand. If you ever dare pester me again I shall speak to Mr. Herrick . . . I mean . . . Lynx!'

That name could strike fear into people. Jagger flinched and drew back immediately; and to my immense relief I heard Stirling's voice.

'Nora, is tea ready yet?'

That evening we reached Melbourne. In the excitement of shopping I forgot Jagger. I bought some green silk material from which I planned to make a dress. I saw myself wearing it in the evenings when I played chess with Lynx. Adelaide would help me; she was adept with the needle and she loved having beautiful materials to work with.

She said to me as the material was being measured, 'It's nice to make lovely things. You'll look pretty in that, Nora.' She pressed my arm and said quietly: 'I'm glad you're here with us. I can't imagine what it would be like without you now.'

After four days we left and made the journey back. It was uneventful. I could kindle a fire, make dampers and boil tea in billycans. I had experienced life in the bush.

'You're one of us,' Stirling told me with approval.

I sat at the chess table; the long fingers caressed the ivory queen with her crown of gold and brilliants and he said: 'So you enjoyed your trip?'

'It was wonderful.'

'You liked sleeping rough?'

'Well, for a few nights it was interesting.'

'I like my comforts. I am a sensual man. I'm like a cat. I like to sleep in a warm bed, take a bath frequently, change my linen every day. It's hardly possible to do these things in camp. But you liked it.'

'Perhaps I prefer my comforts too, but it was interesting to see the bush and to get some idea of how people have lived out there.'

'I imagine you are something of a pioneer, Nora. So you found your trip perfect in every way.'

'Well . . .' A vision of Jagger rose before me. I don't know why it was that I had such fear of that man. Perhaps it was due to what had happened to

Mary and the look in her eyes when she said she had been forced. Adelaide
might not believe Mary, but I did.

'Oh . . . a fly in the ointment?'

How insistent he was! I could hide nothing from him.

'Adelaide and Stirling are good at everything,' I said quickly. 'They taught
me how to make fires and dampers and so on . . . and how to live in the
bush.'

'Jagger was with you wasn't he?'

I felt the slow flush creep into my cheeks.

'Oh yes, he was there.'

'He's the best manager we've had,' he said. 'It's not easy to get them.
Most men would rather go after gold. So it's not easy to keep them, and once
they've gone they don't come back. I see to that. Yes, Jagger is a good man
with the property.'

Then the game started. I was quickly beaten on that occasion. I never had
a chance to get into the attack.

'You're not playing well tonight, Nora,' he said. 'Your thoughts are far
away. In the bush perhaps.'

In a few weeks' time Adelaide and I between us had made the green
dress; we had also made up the more serviceable materials. Autumn was
with us and we were preparing for winter. Logs were being brought into
the wood house and Adelaide was stocking up with provisions. We were
sometimes cut off by floods, she explained; and there might even be snow.
Her father did not like to be short of anything so it was her task to make
sure that the house was well provided for. She had made jars of passion fruit
jelly, peach jam and orange marmalade.

After the heat of the summer I found the days delightful for riding and
when Adelaide or Stirling could not accompany me I went alone. I never
forgot Adelaide's warning about being lost in the bush – one of the worst
fates which could befall anyone – so I was always careful to watch for
landmarks. I had my set rides and rarely diverged from them. Only by
promising that I would either ride to Kerry's Creek, Martha's Mound or
Dog Hill could I be given permission to go, and I believe they were always
rather uneasy when I was alone while at the same time they did not wish
to restrict me. Characteristically they had agreed that I should not be coddled;
and I was now a fair horsewoman and could be trusted to manage a horse.

On this morning I decided to ride out to Kerry's Creek – my favourite
spot. Here the creek ran between a grove of ghost gums and when the wattle
was in bloom it was one of the loveliest spots in the neighbourhood. I liked
to tether my horse to one of the gums and sit watching the water. A man
named Kerry had come there twenty years before and found a little gold
along the creek; he had spent ten years trying to find more and had gone
away disappointed. Hence its name. But now it was free of the seekers after
gold for Kerry had proved it to be barren of that much coveted metal.
Perhaps that was why it appealed to me.

I sat there on this lovely late April morning looking into the water and
thinking of everything that had happened over the last months and how

happy I was to have escaped from Danesworth House. Over there now the buds would be appearing on the trees and bushes; the aubrietia and arabis would be in flower; and Mary would be thinking that the cold nights were over and that for a brief spell before the heat of the summer she would be comfortable in her attic bedroom. Poor Miss Graeme would be reminded that spring was here again and another year had passed and she was a year nearer the time when Miss Emily would have no further use for her services.

How sad! Poor Miss Graeme! Poor Mademoiselle, getting less and less able to control her class. And here was I – escaped, as free as those lovely galahs flying overhead. Then I thought of Lynx's coming up from the hold of the convicts' ship and envying the birds.

Dear Stirling! Dear Lynx! I loved them both, and, in a lesser way, Adelaide. In a short while they had become my family and made up in some measure for the loss of my beloved father. I could be happy again. I *was* happy.

I heard a movement somewhere not far distant. How sound carries in the bush! Now I distinctly heard the galloping of horses' hoofs. I stood up and shaded my eyes. I could see no one; so I sat down again and returned to my pleasant ruminating.

Yes, I was happy here. I believed that I was going to marry Stirling. I was young yet, being only eighteen. Perhaps on my nineteenth birthday he would ask me. I pictured us in the library receiving Lynx's congratulations. He would draw me into his arms and kiss me. 'Truly my daughter now,' he would say; and I would feel that happy glow within me. I, who had once been abandoned by my mother and had lost my father, would now be joyfully claimed by the Lynx as his daughter. These were dreams – but one has to be happy to dream pleasant dreams.

There were footsteps behind me. 'Good day, Miss Nora.'

I felt suddenly cold with dread for it was Jacob Jagger who stood behind me. He was almost upon me as I sprang to my feet and faced him. I was immediately aware of the silence all about me – the loneliness of the bush. In a flash I thought of the other occasion when he had stood close to me – but then Stirling and Adelaide were not far off.

'You!' I heard myself stutter.

'You don't look very pleased to see me. And to think I've come here specially to see you!'

'How did you know –'

'I make it my business to know what you're about, Miss Nora. I saw you come this way and I said to myself, "Oh, it's Kerry's Creek this morning." '

'But why should you follow me?'

'You'll know in good time. Don't let's rush this.'

'I don't like your manner, Mr. Jagger.'

'I haven't liked yours for a long time.'

'Then there can be no point in our continuing this conversation.' I turned away, but he had caught my arm and a feeling of terror came to me because I was immediately aware of his strength.

'I have to disagree again, Miss Nora.' He brought his fat, leering face close to mine. 'And this time,' he went on, 'I call the tune.'

'You have forgotten that I may report this when I return.'

'You are not going to return just yet.'

'I fail to understand.'

'You are not as calm as you pretend to be, and I think you do understand a great deal.'

'You are being very offensive, Mr. Jagger. I don't like you. I never have. Now please stand aside. I am ready to go back. Goodbye.'

He laughed most unpleasantly. I couldn't hide the fact that I was terrified. A picture of Mary flashed into my mind. Had it happened so with her?

'You are not going yet, Miss Nora. I've something to say to you. I haven't got a wife. I wouldn't mind having one . . . if she were you.'

'You're talking nonsense.'

'You call an honourable proposal of marriage nonsense?'

'Yes, when it comes from you. So now stand aside. If you attempt to detain me any longer you will regret it.'

He was still laughing at me; there was a tinge of purple in his face now; his mouth was ugly.

'So *you* manage affairs now at Whiteladies, do you? By God, Miss Nora, it's time someone taught you a lesson.'

'I learn my own lessons, thank you.'

'Well, this morning you're going to learn another. I've set my heart on you and nothing on earth is going to stop me having my way.'

I wrenched myself away from him and started to run to the tree where my horse was tethered. I hadn't a chance. He was beside me; then he stood in front of me barring my way.

'Will you leave me, Mr. Jagger?' I panted.

'No, Miss Nora, I will not.'

'Then . . .'

He waited, mocking, his face working with a terrifying passion which I recognized as lust. This was what I had feared since I had first met him. He was a man who could not restrain his desires; he had no doubt found it easy to impose his will on some of the poor serving girls; and Lynx had made it easy for him. But he should realize that I was not as one of those, and that if he dared touch me he would have to answer to Lynx . . . and Stirling.

I tried to push past him but he caught me. His thick horrible lips were on my face. I caught at his hair and pulled it; but I was no match for him. I fought desperately; I kicked him and he gave a yell of pain, and for a moment I was free, running wildly towards my horse, but he was upon me. I fell and he fell with me. I called loudly: 'Lynx! Stirling! Oh, help me.'

I heard two kookaburras laughing as though at my plight. My breath was coming in great sobs; he was angry, hating me, I sensed, but his hatred did not lessen his desire, rather did it increase it.

He muttered that I was a she-devil. I wanted to shout back at him, to tell him I loathed him, that he would have to kill me before I gave in – but I needed my breath for the fight.

I was no weakling but he was a strong man. I heard myself praying: 'Oh God, help me. Oh, Lynx . . . Lynx . . .'

Then I heard a voice, *his* voice, and for a second I thought I had imagined it.

The voice was distinctly: 'Jagger! Get up, Jagger.'

I was lying on the ground, panting, my riding jacket torn, my hair hanging about my face. I pushed it aside with a trembling hand and I saw him, more magnificent than he had ever seemed before, seated on a big white horse. His eyes were like blue ice.

He commanded: 'Stand there, Jagger.'

'Jagger obeyed as if in a trance. Then I saw Lynx raise his hand and I heard a deafening report.

Jagger was lying on the ground and there was blood.

Time appeared to stop. It seemed a very long time, but it could only have been for a few seconds that I lay there where Jagger had thrown me and Lynx remained still on his horse, the smoking pistol in his hand, calm, all-powerful.

'Don't look, Nora,' he said. 'Get up. Get on your horse.'

I obeyed him as Jagger had done. I felt weak and could scarcely breathe, but I went to my horse and mounted. Lynx was beside me and quietly we rode back to Whiteladies.

Adelaide looked after me. I was so shocked that I just lay in my bed and said nothing. She brought me brandy and eggs in milk. I turned away and she insisted, 'my father said you were to have these.' So I took them and felt better.

She gave me something to drink that evening and I did not wake until morning. Then I felt different. I had slept without dreams which I did not think I should ever do again, for I believed that that scene with all its terror and its blood was imprinted on my mind for ever. I kept going over it: the moment when I had turned and seen Jagger and had known I was at his mercy alone in the bush; the mounting horror; and that other moment when Lynx had come as though in answer to my call; I could never forget the sight of him on the white horse and the cold way in which he raised his gun and fired.

'There was blood,' I kept saying to myself. 'On the bushes . . . on the ground . . . blood everywhere. Lynx has killed Jagger.' No I assured myself, he has only wounded him. Even he would not dare kill a man. That would make him a murderer.

But I knew in my heart that Lynx had killed Jagger and it was because of what he had attempted to do to me.

There was a hush over the house. A coffin had been made for Jagger. It was taken into the biggest of the sheds which had been built to store the bales of wool.

Every man in the Lynx Empire – the property, the house, the mine – was summoned to the shed. It was a strange, quiet day, a day of mourning, and yet more than that. It was as though some solemn ritual was about to take place.

Adelaide would say nothing. Stirling came and held me in his arms.

'You're all right, Nora,' he said. 'Don't ever worry again. Don't ever think of it. You're safe now.'

Adelaide came to my room. 'Nora, my father wants you to go to the wool shed. Don't be afraid. You'll feel better. I'm going with you and so is Stirling.'

'I'm not afraid.'

'My father says you are not to be afraid again. He says we should have taken better care of you.'

'You were always warning me that I might get lost in the bush.'

'But I should have thought of this.'

'There was Mary,' I reminded her. 'But you did not believe her.'

'Oh, Nora. My poor Nora. But it is over and it will never happen again. My father is determined on that.'

I shall never forget the scene in the wool shed. This was my first introduction to the law of the land. Justice had been done to Jagger. That was the verdict. Any man finding his daughter in the position I was in had every right to kill her would-be ravisher.

The coffin stood on trestles at one end of the barn; at either end of it burned two candles. Lynx was standing beside it and the candle light caught the blue fire of his eyes.

When he saw me he held out his hand and I went and stood beside him. Adelaide and Stirling remained at the door. The shed was full of men – some of whom I knew, others whom I had never seen.

Lynx took my hand and looking at the coffin said: 'In this box lies what is left of Jacob Jagger. This is my daughter. If any man here lays a hand on her he will receive the same punishment as Jacob Jagger. It will be well for every man among you to remember this. I am, as you will know, a man who keeps his word.'

Then still keeping my hand in his he walked out of the shed with me; and Adelaide and Stirling fell in behind us.

Chapter Five

Nothing could be quite the same afterwards. I had become subdued. I seemed to have grown up suddenly. People looked at me a little furtively – the men of the estate as though they were afraid of me. I suppose every time they saw me they thought of Jacob Jagger.

Stirling managed the property until a new manager could be found in James Madder, who soon learned of the fate of his predecessor and scarcely looked my way. Adelaide tried to make everything normal by behaving as though nothing had happened; but you cannot be involved in sudden death and pretend it is an everyday occurrence.

For some days I had no desire to ride again. I stayed near Adelaide; there was something safe about her. She understood my feelings and was constantly inviting me to help in some task or other. Together we produced new curtains for some of the rooms; we made up materials for ourselves and altered old dresses. There was always some project afoot. Then, of course, there was the garden.

Sometimes I would wake in the night calling for help. I could not always remember the dreams, but they were concerned with that nightmare day.

'Stirling,' I said to him one day when we rode together, 'you never speak of that day. Isn't it better to talk of it?'

'Isn't it best to forget?'

'Do you think that it is something you can ever forget?'

'You have to try. In time it will fade. You'll see.'

'It was like something one dreams of, too bad for reality.'

'I should have been there. I should have guessed. Jagger was a swine. I should have known. Did you have any idea?'

'I was always afraid of him.'

'You didn't say so.'

'I didn't think it was important until that moment when I was alone.'

'Don't speak of it.'

'But we *are* speaking of it. And then your father came. He was there on his white horse and suddenly . . . there was blood. I thought . . .'

'There, I told you not to speak of it. Listen, Nora, it's over. My father was there. He came in time, and that is the end of Jagger. He can never attempt to harm you again.'

'He was killed. Your father *killed* a man because of me.'

'It was the right thing to do. It was the only thing to do.'

'He could have dismissed him. He could have sent him away. Why didn't he do that?'

'My father did what was right. Life is different out here, Nora. Not long ago in England a man could be hanged for stealing a sheep. Out here any man has a right to kill another who attacks his womenfolk.'

'But it was murder.'

'It was justice.'

'But does no one question it?'

'There has been an enquiry. My father would not let you go because he thought it would be too upsetting for you. He would not have you questioned, he said. He told what had happened; he had killed Jagger, he said, and he would do the same to any man who acted as Jagger did towards his daughters. Jagger was notorious. It was well known what kind of man he was. The women of the community would have been in danger if my father's action was not accepted as the right one, and the verdict was that justice had been administered. And that is the truth. You must stop thinking about it.'

They wanted me to live as I had before; to ride when I wished, to stop thinking of that terrible day.

My relationship with Lynx had undergone a subtle change. Even he was ill at ease. I went to him to play my usual game of chess but it was some weeks before I could bring myself to talk of the matter.

I said to him then: 'What brought you to Kerry's Creek on that day.'

He frowned in concentration. 'I'm not entirely sure. I seemed to sense that something was wrong. Do you remember when we talked of that trip you made to Melbourne when you camped on the way? We mentioned Jagger and something in your manner told me that you were afraid of the man. I guessed for what reason ... knowing Jagger. That morning I felt uneasy because I saw him riding in the direction of Kerry's Creek. I wondered where he was going and I asked at the stables which direction you had taken that morning. No one was sure but they said it would either be Martha's Mound, Dog Hill or Kerry's Creek. I decided to ride out after Jagger. That was how it happened.'

'What good fortune for me! And it cost Jagger his life.'

Lynx's eyes glittered. 'You don't think I would have let him live.'

'He forced Mary,' I said. 'She told me so.'

He shrugged his shoulders.

'You can be indifferent to that?' I said.

'That is beside the point. Do you think I could ever be indifferent to anything that happened to you?'

There was silence in the library broken only by the ticking of the clock. It was a beautiful French clock which he had had sent out from London.

He said abruptly: 'Let us have our game of chess.'

So we played the strangest game we had ever played. Hitherto he had always beaten me, but that night I turned the tables. I took his queen and a strange feeling of triumph ran through me as I seized her.

'There,' he said rather mockingly, 'now you have me ... provided you play with care.'

So we played on and an hour passed and every time I was ready to make the winning move he baulked me.

But finally I had him cornered.

'Checkmate!' I cried.

He sat back, his elbows on the table surveying the board as if in dismay, and I knew suddenly that he had allowed me to win, just as my father had.

'You let it happen,' I accused.

'Do you think I would?' he asked.

I looked into those extraordinary eyes and did not know the answer.

Yes, indeed our relationship had changed.

Jessica came into Adelaide's sitting-room where I was sewing. She sat down, looking at me.

'Did you come to hear the book?' I asked. 'Adelaide is busy today so I am not reading.'

'Then we can talk,' said Jessica. 'You affect him deeply,' she went on.

I knew to whom she referred, of course, but I pretended not to.

'He changes when you're there. I've never seen him like that with anyone else ... except perhaps Stirling.'

'Stirling is his son,' I reminded her. 'And he looks upon me as his daughter.'

'Not for Adelaide,' she said with a look of triumph. 'She is his daughter. But he was never like that with Adelaide. He killed a man for you.'

I shivered. 'People don't talk of it.'

'Things are still there even if you don't talk of them.'

'Plants stay green through constant watering,' I said. 'So do memories. If they are pleasant, that's good; if not, it's folly.'

'You're clever with your talk,' she said. 'It may be that. I wonder whether she was clever.'

'Who?'

'That woman in England. Poor Maybella wasn't clever. I was cleverer than she was. If I had been the daughter instead of the niece, I should have been the one. I daresay I would've had sons. I wasn't such a weakling as Maybella. He preferred me.' A cunning look came into her eyes. 'He wasn't faithful to her, you know. There were others besides me.'

Then I understood her feelings for Lynx. He had been her lover. She had loved him and now she hated him; and she had allowed this double-edged emotion to govern her life. She had loved Maybella and been deeply jealous of her; she had alternately loved and hated Maybella's husband. Life had suddenly become very complicated. The present was deeply overshadowed by the past. What had happened in Whiteladies all those years ago haunted the present just as what had happened later at Rosella did.

'Be careful,' warned Jessica. 'It's not good to come too near to him. He's unlucky for women.'

'He's my guardian. He has taken good care of me. Why should I be afraid?'

'Poor Maybella! She was the most unhappy woman I knew. He despised her; he ignored her; if he had quarrelled with her it would have been better for her. But to be nothing to him, nothing but the means of getting a son. That wounded her; if she had not died in childbed, she would've died of a broken heart. I wouldn't die of that. I wasn't so weak. I just let my hatred grow and loved to plague him. For he is plagued by my presence here. I see it in his eyes when he looks at me. He would like me out of the way, but he can't send me away, can he? "Jessie shall always have a home." My uncle said it; Maybella said it. He couldn't flout the dead, could he? But he's a man who would flout the devil. He pretends he doesn't care that I'm here, that it makes no difference one way or the other. I'm just nothing ... nothing in his eyes. But I think he'd like to see the back of me.'

'Whatever took place years ago is best forgotten when no good can be done by remembering.'

She narrowed her eyes and gazed intently at me. 'He didn't kill Jagger for attempted rape. He didn't care about Mary, did he? But this was you. He's killed a man for *you*. That's why I say Beware.'

I put down my sewing. 'Jessica,' I said, 'it is good for you to be concerned for me, but I can look after myself, you know.'

'You couldn't, could you, at Kerry's Creek? So he came to look after you and he killed a man for you.'

I wanted to get away. She was bringing up the memory of that day in all its horror; and superimposed on it was a picture of Lynx arriving at Rosella Creek, with festering sores on his wrists where the manacles had cut into him, and bitter hatred in his heart and a determination that he would one day take his revenge. So he took the short cut to freedom. He married Maybella and Jessica was angry because she had felt that magnetic power and had been his mistress for a time; and had she been the daughter of the house instead of the owner's niece, she would have been Lynx's wife instead of Maybella.

I understood Jessica's bitterness as I never had before. Yes, my experiences had made me grow up.

The winter came and the grazing lands were under water. This was an anxious time for the property, but James Madder proved to be a skilful manager. With the help of Stirling, who was spending more and more time on the property, he worked so hard in these difficult circumstances that the damage proved to be less than had been feared. The winds were bitingly cold and we had snow; it was hard to believe that at Christmas time the heat had been almost unendurable.

There was an explosion in the mine and several men were hurt. Stirling and his father rode over and spent two weeks there. The mine was of greater concern to Lynx than the property. I wondered what disaster would strike next.

I was very sad one morning when the body of a boy was brought in. He had been found by some of the men who worked on the property. Evidently lost in the bush, he had died of exposure and starvation. It was a further blow to discover that the boy was Jemmy, the stowaway. He must have been trying to find the road back to us, though what his reception would have been had he arrived, he must have known. Perhaps he believed that I would have intervened to plead for him and that I should have succeeded again as I had on the ship.

'He was lost in the bush, poor boy,' said Adelaide. 'It can so easily happen, as I told you. One takes the wrong path without knowing and goes on and on through country which looks exactly the same as that a hundred miles back.'

'Poor Jemmy, if only he'd stayed here.'

'If only they would all stay here, but this lust for gold is the irresistible temptation.'

We buried poor Jemmy; and I wondered what he had run away from in London that had been so terrible. Poor Jemmy, who had come to Australia to be buried in the bush.

Lynx talked to me of the boy and there was a return of the old mockery.

'Your efforts were of no avail,' he said.

'How that boy suffered in his short life!'

'He brought on his own suffering. He could have stayed here and lived. But he chose to go after gold . . . and he died.'

'He's not the first one,' I said bitterly.

'Save your sympathy. He was a runner, that boy. He would never have settled anywhere; and if he had ever found gold he would have squandered his fortune and then been in dire straits again.'

'How can you know?'

'I know men and women – and that is Jemmy. So don't grieve for him. You did your best. You brought him here. He left us of his own free will. He chose the way he would go. No one is to blame but himself.'

'Some people have hard decisions to make.'

'We all do. Let's forget him. Come, let us play on your board with your beautiful pieces.'

'I believe you regret letting me win them from you.'

'I do . . . deeply.'

'I don't believe they were ever yours.'

'Then I did right to let you have them back.' He laughed ruefully. 'What matters it, Nora, that they are yours or mine? We still play with them. They are here in this house and this house is your home.' He had brought the board and set it between us. He stood for a moment looking across at me. 'I hope, Nora, that it will always be.'

It was indeed true. Our relationship had changed. There was a new gentleness in his manner.

The winter was over and September had come. I spent a good deal of time out of doors, often in the garden. The bush was lovely in springtime when the wild flowers were in bloom; and I had taken to going out riding alone again. I felt safer than I ever had before. At least that terrible affair had done that for me. Everyone for miles round had heard of it and knew what would happen to any man who dared molest me. They would have to answer to Lynx.

It was a bright and beautiful morning when I rode out. The crows were cawing overhead and the inevitable kookaburras were laughing at the scene; the lovely galahs and rosellas flew back and forth and I feasted my eyes on the wild flowers – reds and blues, pinks and mauves. In a week or so they would be magnificent – so pleasant to the eye after the winter scene, and even in summer there were few blossoms except those of the flowering gums.

I was glad to be here and alive; I had learned to enjoy again the solitude of my rides. During them I could think of the two men who were rarely out of my thoughts. I did not understand my feelings entirely. I loved Stirling, but I was not sure whether I was in love with him. My feelings for Lynx were difficult to define. I admired him; I was to some extent in awe of him. I enjoyed as much as anything else in the world to cross swords with him; I loved to see his eyes flash with appreciation when I said something which amused him.

I said aloud: 'I'm happy.'

And I was. What had gone before did not matter. The future lay bright before me; I only had to move towards it – and it contained both Stirling and Lynx.

I was in a strange mood that morning. I had always avoided the spot where my father had been killed; but I had a sudden desire to go there. I was not going to brood on the past; I would ignore the shadows it cast. I would accept the fact that life was different here, it was cheaper and death could come suddenly, more suddenly than at home. Men lost their way in the bush and died, or they were shot for disobeying the moral code laid down by the people. This was the nature of things and one did not brood.

My father had died. I had lost the one I had loved beyond all others . . . then. But now my life had changed and there was another . . . others, perhaps I should say. I had a father to replace the one I had lost; he was entirely different and I was not sure of my feelings for him, but that he was important to me there was no doubt. And there was Stirling – my dearest Stirling – named after one of the rivers of this country, a tribute to Australia from one of its unwilling sons because here he had found a way of life which was tolerable for a man of his spirit. I did not believe he could live in quite the same way in England. I remembered an occasion when I had mentioned this to him and he had replied: 'Some men can, Nora. It depends. A man can rule his village if he is its squire. He lives in a big house; he controls the lives of all those around him; that is how it was with Sir Henry Dorian.'

I had replied that it was a sad thing when people could not be content with their lot. They might have a great deal but they hankered after what they fancied they had missed. Did he think he could have more power, or whatever it was he craved, in his English village than here in the Lynx Empire?

He had laughed at me; he knew what he wanted; he had fashioned a dream, I told him, and if he ever realized it it might well be that the reality was different from the dream.

How we talked and how reluctant I always was to leave him!

I had come to the clearing – that spot where my father had been shot. The sheer beauty of it was breathtaking. It looked different from when I had last seen it; the multi-coloured wild flowers had transformed it; the ghost gums rose high, majestic and imperious, indifferent to what happened so far below them. Here was the path along which the dray would have come. The bushrangers would have been hiding in the grove of wattles. I must not think of it, or if I did I must remember that it was in the past, and mourning could do no good, and that because it had happened I had a new father. And I had Stirling to love and cherish me – perhaps for ever.

I was thirsty and wondered whether the water in the creek was drinkable. I dismounted, tied up Queen Anne and walked over to the creek. The water was silvery in the sunlight as it trickled down from the high plateau. There were deep gullies on the side of the hills; here and there I saw the granite rock, the slate and what looked like quartz.

I cupped my hands and caught the water as it tumbled down the side of the plateau. It was not drinkable, I decided; it was muddy and as it trickled through my fingers it left a sediment.

I stared. I could not believe it. The sediment was like yellow dust.

I had begun to tremble. I looked up at the plateau. I stared at the trickling water. I held out my hands again and caught it as it fell. There was the same yellow sediment.

Could it be? I had heard such talk of it. Was this possible? Gold! Could it fall into one's hands when one was not searching for it?

I looked up again at the plateau. The sides were steep; the water trickling over could be conveying the message. 'There is gold up here.' But if that was so, why had no one discovered it? The answer to that was: Because someone has to for the first time.

I remembered stories of how shepherds minding their sheep had come across gold in the fields, and a humble shepherd had become a rich man. It had happened more than once.

I stood uncertainly. Then I heard the kookaburras laughing.

It was ironical, if this should be true, that I who hated gold should be the one to find it.

But wait, I cautioned myself. Had I found it? Had I become touched by that madness which gold seemed to bring? I was trembling with excitement. Perhaps it was not gold at all. What did I know of it? It was just some sort of dust which had been coloured by the rocks above me.

I thought of my father's pursuing the back-aching work of cradling and panning for months, the hardships he must have suffered before throwing in his lot with Lynx. I pictured his searching wildly for the precious metal. Could it be possible that I, without thinking, had meant to drink from a stream and had found instead of water, gold!

Then I was certain, for on the bank of the creek lay a small shining piece of metal about the size of a nutmeg. I bent down and picked it up. It was yellow gold.

I don't know how long I stood looking at the nugget. The impulse came to me to throw it away, to ride back and say nothing of what I had found. Something told me that if I took it back it would lead to disaster. I imagined the excitement there would be in the house. Surely if I had discovered it so easily there must be a great deal very near at hand. It had killed my father; it had done something to Lynx. I thought of the Lambs who had gone in search of it, and poor Jemmy. I thought of men dying of phthisis. All for gold.

I looked up at the tall ghost gums as though asking them to decide for me. Their leaves moved slightly in the breeze, aloof, indifferent to the fortunes of men. They had stood there perhaps for hundreds of years. They would have seen the convicts come, the gold rush start and the days before it had all happened when the country was peopled only by the dark men.

There was no answer up there.

Could I find gold and not tell? How could I face Lynx in the library and keep the secret?

I put the nugget into my pocket and rode back to Little Whiteladies.

I went straight to the library. Lynx was there alone. He stood up when he saw me. 'Nora,' he cried. 'What's happened?'

I did not speak. I merely drew the nugget from my pocket and held it out to him in the palm of my hand.

He took it gingerly; he stared at it; I saw the quick colour flame into his face. His eyes were like blue flames. He was on fire with excitement.

'By God,' he exclaimed. 'Where did you get this?'

'At the creek where my father was shot. I held out my hands to get a drink of water from the stream coming from the plateau. It left a deposit in my hands, a yellow dust. I wasn't sure what it was. Then I stopped and found this.'

'You found it! Lying there on the bank of the creek!' He stared at the nugget which he had taken from my hand. 'It'll weigh all of twelve ounces. And you found this dust and this . . . Then it's there somewhere. It's there in quantities . . .' He laughed. 'And Nora found it. My girl, Nora!' He drew me to him and gave me a hug which was almost suffocating. I thought though: He is embracing gold, not me.

He released me; he was still laughing.

'I can't help it,' he said. 'All those years, all that toil and sweat, all that hope. And Nora goes out, thinks she would like a drink of water, and it falls into her hands!'

'It may be nothing much.'

'Nothing much! With the dust coming down in the water so that all you have to do is catch it. And the nugget lying there on the bank! And you say that may be nothing! You don't know gold country.' He was sober suddenly. 'Not a word to anybody . . . nobody at all. We're going out there at once. We'll take Stirling. And no one is to know where we're going. Nobody must guess what's there until I've made it mine.'

I caught his excitement. Gold! And I had found it. I knew how men felt when they had their lucky strike. I was triumphant, exultant, excited as I had never been before – because I had found gold. Then I realized that this sensation did not come from merely finding gold; it was because I had found gold for Lynx.

The weeks slid by in a feverish tension which was all the more intense because the news must be kept secret. No one knew about the find but myself, Stirling and Lynx. No one must know. We lived in terror that anyone should find what I had found.

Lynx and Stirling had examined the terrain and were absolutely certain that it would give the richest yield ever found in Australia. On the top of the plateau, which was difficult to scale – and it must be for this reason that the gold field had never been discovered – was a fortune. It had been there, so close, for all these years. That was what amazed them. They regarded me as though I were some genius to have discovered it.

I myself was elated. *I* had brought them this luck. I had made all this possible. I was to be the maker of their fortunes. I felt proud of myself and refused to listen to the inward warning which demanded to know what good had ever come from gold.

I was caught up in the excitement. I had forgotten all the unhappy events of the past. It was only the urgent need to keep our secret which made me able to hide my exhilaration.

There were conferences in the library in the evenings when I was supposed to be playing chess with Lynx. Stirling would come to join us. Lynx was buying the land and it was not just the ground which held the plateau that he was negotiating for. That would have been to arouse suspicion. He wanted to extend his property, he said; he was thinking of getting more sheep. It was some time before he acquired the land but he and Stirling had already scaled the plateau and found what lay at its summit. There was no doubt that it was gold. They had already discovered rich alluvial deposits as they had expected from the gold dust which was carried down by the stream; but Lynx was certain that the real wealth lay beneath the surface.

'There'll be lodes of gold at various levels,' he explained. 'We'll take the shafts down as deep as need be.'

Stirling was impatient to get to work. So were we all. But for the time, until the golden plateau was Lynx's own, there must be secrecy.

There came the day when he called Stirling and me to the library. He solemnly opened a bottle of champagne and filled three glasses.

He said: 'The land is mine. We have our fortune. We are going to be rich as few people have ever been.'

He handed a glass, first to me then to Stirling before he took the other.

'First,' he said, 'to Nora, the founder of our fortunes.'

'It was sheer luck,' I insisted. 'I shouldn't have known what to do about it without you.'

'You did the right thing. You came straight to me.' His eyes were shining with love and approval; and I thought I had never been so happy in my life.

'Now,' he said, 'to us. The triumphant Triumvirate.'

Then we drank.

I said: 'Are you sure? After all, as yet you have not sunk your shafts.'

Lynx laughed. 'Nora, even now we have found a nugget which weighs two thousand ounces. I'll guarantee it is worth ten thousand pounds. And we have not yet begun. There's gold up there, gold to make any miner's dream come true. Don't fret. We're rich. After all these years you've led us to what we've been looking for.'·

We put down our glasses. I held out my hands. Lynx took one, Stirling the other.

'This is what I wanted more than anything,' I said.

Lynx laughed at me. 'So you felt the gold fever, too, Nora.'

'No, not gold fever. I just want to give you both what you most want.'

Then Lynx held me in his arms again and said softly in a strangely tender voice: 'Nora, my girl Nora.' Then he let me go and handed me as it were to Stirling. Stirling's arms were round me and I clung to him.

'I believe I'm crying,' I said. 'People who don't cry when they're hurt will cry for happiness.'

Now the activity had started. Everyone was talking about the find. Lynx had struck gold – real gold. They had always known he would one day. It was just his luck. The ground yielded its alluvial gold – a fortune in itself. But Lynx was not stopping there. He was sinking deep shafts and he was going to get the gold which he knew lay in the quartz reefs below the ground. He closed the old worthless mine, all workers were transferred to the new one and more were engaged. The scene of my father's murder had changed completely. The birds had deserted the place; the sound of gunpowder explosions had frightened them away; steps had been cut in the earth to enable men to mount the plateau; drays were constantly passing along the road taking the gold to the bank in Melbourne. The place had been renamed. It was: Nora's Hill.

I saw less of Lynx and Stirling. They were always at the mine. A place had been built there so that they could sleep in some sort of comfort when they did not come home. The fortune was being accumulated. I was constantly hearing of nuggets that had been found. I remember the excitement when one over two feet long was discovered. It was mentioned in the Melbourne papers and reckoned to be worth twenty thousand pounds.

There was a kind of breathlessness everywhere, but for me the excitement had worn off. I was not as happy as I had been in the first flush of discovery.

A stranger came to the house and was closeted a long time with Lynx. Adelaide told me that he was her father's lawyer and that he was going to England on Lynx's business.

It was said that Lynx was now a millionaire. This was probably true, but he wasn't satisfied. I wondered if he ever would be.

Once I said to him: 'You are very rich now.'

He admitted it. 'You too, my dear. Don't forget you have your share in our good fortune. Didn't I say it was a triumvirate?'

'How rich?'

'Do you want figures?'

'No. They would mean little to me. But I believe it is rich enough.'

'What do you mean by that?'

'That now you might give up this feverish activity and leave others to work for you.'

'Other people never work for you as you work for yourself.'

'Does it matter? You have enough.'

'I'm going to get all the gold out of that mine, Nora.'

'You are insatiable . . . for gold.'

His eyes gleamed. 'No,' he said. 'I shall know when I have enough. I need to be very rich.'

'And then?'

'And then I shall do what I have always planned to do. I have waited a long time, but now I see the fulfilment in sight.'

He said no more then, but he alarmed me a little because there was a hardening of his lips and I knew that the thought of revenge was in his mind.

Revenge on the man who had had him sent away over thirty-five years ago! Did people harbour feelings of revenge for so long? A man like Lynx did, I knew. It worried me because I knew that there was no happiness to be found in revenge.

The months went by and Christmas had come once more. We had the usual celebrations in the English style: the hot meal in the burning heat of the day; the plum pudding steeped in brandy; the mock mistletoe. I remembered the last Christmas when the Lambs had come and been turned away. I wondered what had happened to them now and remembering the relentlessness of Lynx on that occasion I was apprehensive.

At the beginning of January, the lawyer came to the house and spent a long time with Lynx and Stirling. I was not admitted to these councils, but I noticed that afterwards there was a triumph in Lynx's eyes; and I guessed it had something to do with his dreams of revenge.

One evening he asked me to play a game of chess with him and when I went to him, the door to his studio was open and he called to me to come in.

'Come here, Nora,' he said; and when I went to him he put his hands over my eyes; then he turned me round until I was facing the wall. Then he took his hands away and said: 'Look!'

It was a portrait of me in my riding habit, my top hat slightly to one side, my eyes wide and the colour in my cheeks.

'All my own work,' he said.

'When did you do it?'

'Is that your first question? I show you a portrait of yourself and all you say is "when?"'

'But I did not sit for it.'

'Did you think that was necessary? I know every contour of your face, every fleeting expression.'

'But you have been so busy.'

'I have still had time to think of you. Tell me, do you like it?'

'Isn't it rather flattering?'

'It's as I see you.'

'I'm glad I look like that to you. I don't to myself.'

'That's how you are when you look at me.'

'But why is it hanging there?'

'It's a good place for it . . . the best in the room.'

'But the other picture was there.'

He nodded and I saw it then, with its face to the wall.

'But when you sat at your table you could look straight at it.'

'Now I look straight at this.'

'Is that what you want?'

'My dear Nora, you are not showing your usual good sense. Should I put it there if I didn't?'

I went close and examined it. It did flatter me. Had I ever looked so vital? Were my eyes so large and bright? Did I have that rosy flush? 'It's as I see you,' he had said.

'So now you will look at my picture instead,' I commented.

'Yes.'

'And Arabella . . .'

'She is dead.'

'I see. That's why you have hung me up there. When did you learn that she was dead?'

'Morfell – he's the lawyer who has been to England on business for me – went to Whiteladies. He came back with this news.'

'I see.'

'Do you, Nora?' he said; I believed he was on the verge of confidences, but he changed his mind and suggested we play our game of chess.

The heat was intense – far greater than last summer. The grass was dried up and there was anxiety about the sheep at the station; some of the workers died of the heat; but at Nora's Hill the gold yield continued to be spectacular.

I had seen so little of Stirling since the discovery that when I came face to face with him on the stairs one day I complained of this to him.

'We're busy at the mine, Nora.'

'You always are,' I retorted. 'Sometimes I wish I hadn't found it for you.'

He laughed. 'Where are you going now?'

'To sit in the summer-house.'

'I'll join you in five minutes.'

It was pleasant to be with him, I told him when he came.

'It's a mutual pleasure,' he answered.

'I wish there need not be this mad rush for more and more gold.'

'The mine has to be kept going.'

'Couldn't you sell out now that you have your fortune?'

'I think that's what my father will probably do, in due course.'

'Do you think he ever would? The more he gets the more he wants.'

Stirling rose at once in defence of his father, as I expected him to. I wouldn't have had it otherwise.

'He will know when the moment comes to stop. He's making us all rich, Nora.'

'Yet what have these riches brought us? Things are the same – except that I see less of you.'

'And that's a hardship?'

'The greatest hardship.'

He looked at me with a happy smile. I thought: He loves me. Why does he not say so? Now is the time. They have their gold; they can stop thinking of it. Let us give our minds to more important things.

'It's too much to hope,' I said, 'that you would share this feeling.'

'I told you when you came out here that you would receive frankness and be expected to give it. You know very well it's not too much to hope for.'

'Then I'm gratified. Only I must say you don't make much effort.'

'I'm constantly making efforts which are foiled.'

'Well, don't let's waste the little time we have for talking together in discussing lost causes. How rich is your father now and how rich does he want to be?'

'He has plans. He wants to see them fulfilled. That's how he looks at it.'

'He confides in you.'

'He always has.'

'And you know more than anyone what is in his mind.'

'I think I do. I believe he is going to England.'

'Going to England!' I had a picture of him on the lawns of Whiteladies. 'And we shall stay here?'

'I don't know what his plans are for us.'

'His plans? Should we make our own?'

He was staring ahead of him, a puzzled expression in his eyes. I thought: Lynx has said something to him. There is something I don't know.

I wanted him to tell me that our future was together. I wanted him to ask

me to marry him at once. It was important. I had a feeling that there was
a danger in delay. I loved Stirling. I wanted the future to be as I had so
often imagined it. I knew exactly what I wanted – and I wanted it now.
Now! I thought. We should go to Lynx and tell him. I would say it. 'Stirling
and I are going to be married. I am going to belong here for the rest of my
life.' And the three of us would go to his study and drink a glass of
champagne as we had on that other occasion; and I would make them realize
that this was a far more worthy object of celebration than that other. My
happiness would be shared with Lynx as well as with Stirling. I would say
to him: 'The three of us belong together.' I would make him give up his
ideas of crazy revenge. So even when I was thinking of marriage with
Stirling, it was Lynx who was uppermost in my mind.

Stirling was smiling at me and I was sure that he loved me. 'Now,' I
wanted to say. 'Now is the time.'

But he said nothing. I knew that he wanted to tell me that he loved me
but that something was restraining him.

And that moment passed.

It was a week later before I was alone with Lynx. The heat was more
intense than ever. Even Adelaide felt it and rested in the afternoons. We
longed for the nights but when they came they were so hot that it was
impossible to sleep.

We had played our game and sat over the chess board on which my
defeated king was held by a knight, a bishop and an aggravating pawn.

I said: 'There is something afoot.'

'How would you like to go to England?' asked Lynx.

'Alone?'

'Certainly not. We should all go – you, myself and Stirling.'

'And Adelaide?'

'She would stay behind to hold the fort here – unless she wished to go,
of course.'

'She is allowed free will?'

He laughed at me. 'The asperity of your tone tells me that you do not
altogether relish the idea of visiting your native land.'

'For what purpose?'

'To complete a little business.'

'Revenge?'

'You could call it that.'

'You are very rich now.'

'Rich enough to do everything I have ever dreamed of . . . apart from one
thing.'

'And what puts that out of your reach?'

'Time. Death.'

'Not even you are a match for such adversaries.'

'Not even I,' he admitted.

'Are you in the mood for such confidences?'

'Are you in the mood to receive them?'

'Always . . . from you.'

He laughed with pleasure. 'My dear Nora, my *dearest* Nora, you have done a great deal for me.'

'I know. I discovered gold for you.'

'And perhaps more important . . . I hope more important . . . my youth.'

'That's a little enigmatic.'

'Perhaps one day you will understand.'

'One day? Why not this day?'

He was silent, raising one eyebrow in the familiar gesture which used to intimidate.

'We'll see,' he said. He leaned back in his chair and regarded me seriously. 'You know my lawyer has been to England where he has completed certain business deals for me. There has been a little buying, a little selling of certain shares. But I'll not bore you with the details. This has put me into a position with regard to certain people which gives me a great deal of gratification.'

I said quickly: 'Does it concern Whiteladies?'

'You're a clever girl, Nora. Do you know that the only way in which I was able to live through that most terrible period of my life was by dreaming of myself at Whiteladies . . . not a humble drawing-master but the owner. I saw myself sitting at that table in the hall. You should see that hall, Nora. It's grand. It's noble. The ceiling is carved with the arms of the family; the family motto is engraved there. *Service to Queen and Country.* Elizabeth was the Queen referred to and the decorations are Tudor roses in honour, of course, of the royal house which gave the family its home after turning the pious white ladies out into the countryside to starve or beg. The walls are panelled; the great fireplace is of stone and there are seats carved out of that stone on either side of it. There are suits of armour there in which the men of the family lived up to their motto. There is a dais at one end and a table on it. Kings and queens have dined at that table. *I* wanted to dine at that table. I made a vow, Nora. I was going to be master of Whiteladies. I was going to take my revenge on the man who ruined my life. I knew there was one thing he cared for beyond all else . . . more than his wife or his daughter. Whiteladies! So I said: One day I will take it from him. I will marry his daughter and sit at that table where kings and queens have sat. I will look over that hall and say: "Whiteladies is mine." '

'But he's dead now. So is his daughter. And she was married, you told me. She married the fop whom you so despised.'

'I believed I would wipe away the difficulties.'

'But death and time defeated you, as you say. So what now?'

'I have sworn that Whiteladies shall be mine.'

'And you are going to England to take it.'

He smiled at me. 'You think I can't do it.'

'I can't see how you can if the owners won't let it go.'

'You will, Nora.'

'You are wrong. I know you are wrong. I know that revenge brings no happiness to anyone. You have your home here. You have people who admire you and care for you. Why can't you be content?'

His burning gaze was fixed on me. 'Does that include you, Nora?'

I answered him at once. 'You know it does.'

He leaned forward. 'Why, Nora, I could almost settle for that.'

'If you are wise, you will,' I said. 'You will drop this stupid notion of revenge. It was all very well when it was useful to get you through that unhappy period. Now it is of no use whatsoever and it is folly to continue with it.'

'You dare to scold me, Nora.'

'Yes, I do.'

'No one else does.'

'Then you should be thankful that there is at least one person in your life who is not afraid of you.'

'I am thankful for that.'

'Then why do you not rest here in your contentment?'

'Nora, all these years I have waited. I made a place for myself in this country. I was secure; I had my son; we worked together. I was a man of substance but I had made this solemn vow to myself. If you think I would give up the theme of my life you do not know me.'

'I know you well and I think that you are wrong. We grow up; we change. Because when we are young we set up goals, that does not mean we must continue to follow them when we have learned more wisdom.'

'But Whiteladies is a beautiful house, Nora. Wouldn't you like to live in such a house?'

'I hesitated. 'I like this house.'

'You know this is an imitation – a poor copy. Come, admit it.'

'I do admit that the original Whiteladies is a fine old house.'

'And you would enjoy calling such a place your home?'

'Yes, if it were mine by right.'

'And wouldn't it be, if you had bought and paid for it?'

'I suppose so. But the family who had lived in it for generations would never sell it.'

'They might be forced to. We are only just beginning, Nora. My plans are in their infancy. They could not begin until I had made a vast fortune. Now, thanks to you, that is exactly what I have done. Did I tell you the whole story, Nora? Arabella married the man her father chose for her – a weakling, he was. His name was Hilary Cardew – *Sir* Hilary Cardew he would be when his father died. He could trace his family back to the Conqueror – even farther than the Dorians. He had a certain amount of money. The Cardews' place was some ten miles from Whiteladies. The families had always been friends and young Hilary was meant for Arabella right from the start.'

'And when you went away she married him.'

'I didn't hear of this until years later, not until I was able to send someone over to find out.'

'Why didn't you go yourself?'

'I had vowed to myself that I would not set foot in England until I did so as a millionaire. Besides, I had married Maybella. I had a son and daughter of my own.'

'You might have been satisfied with that.'

'I am a man who always demands the ultimate satisfaction.'

'But doesn't one always have to compromise in life?'

'I don't.'

'But that is exactly what you have had to do.'

'Only with the idea of waiting for complete satisfaction. I always believed that if I had the money I needed I should get what I wanted. I wanted Whiteladies . . . and Arabella at that time.'

'But she had a husband and you had a wife.'

'My wife died with Stirling's birth. I thought I would go back and find Arabella unable to maintain the estate. In fact, had I had the money, that was something I might have arranged. Did I tell you that Sir Henry was a man who did not believe in other people's wasting their time? I gave Arabella a drawing lesson each day, but it was only a matter of two hours at the most. A resident drawing-master was an expense; therefore I acted also as Sir Henry's secretary. I had a flair for business and was soon managing his investments. So I knew exactly how he was placed. He had extravagant tastes; he was a connoisseur of wines; he drank rather to excess; he gambled. His financial status had become a little shaky even while I was there. That was why he wanted the Cardew marriage – to bolster up the family fortunes. But Sir James Cardew was another such as himself. I used to hear them discussing their business affairs. I wrote letters from my employer to Sir James and to his London brokers. I knew a good deal about the financial affairs of both families.'

'And you have found this of use.'

'Recently, yes.'

'Recently?'

'My man in London has been working for me. I have invested a great deal of money in London. I have become richer through this . . . and certain people have become poorer.'

I caught my breath. 'You mean that you have deliberately arranged this?'

He spread his hands. 'Let us say that it has happened. It may be that in order to maintain a certain standard of living it will be necessary for certain people to sell their property.'

'Lynx!' I cried, and indeed he looked like that creature now, the hatred glinting in his eyes, revealing the memory of the humiliation of years. 'You have deliberately impoverished these people?'

'You don't understand these matters, Nora. Never mind.'

'I believe that whatever you do they will never sell the house.'

'If they can't afford to keep it up they will be forced to.'

'I wouldn't,' I declared, 'if I were in their place. I'd think of something to keep it. I'd take paying guests; I'd work myself – particularly if I knew that someone was deliberately trying to take it from me.'

'You would, Nora. But other people are not you. You'll see.'

'They'll never sell. I just know it. I've been there. I've seen that girl.'

'There are more ways of selling than by making a cash bargain and handing over the property.'

'What ways?'

'You will see. One thing I know, Nora. I am going to see my son master of Whiteladies. My grandchildren are going to play on those lawns. They are going to be brought up in gracious surroundings. That is my plan and I am going to see that in this I am not disappointed.'

'And Stirling . . . he wants this?'

'My son knows what's in my mind. It has always been so. He more than anyone knows what I have suffered. I have seen him weep with anger when he looked at the scars on my wrists. I have seen him clench his fists and vow that the score must be settled. And when Whiteladies is mine, I shall be content. I shall be able to tell myself that everything that led to this was worth while.'

I was silent for a moment and he said my name softly. I looked up into his face and his gaze grew gentle. 'I want you to understand this,' he said. 'You belong to us now. We will strengthen that bond. You will grow even closer as the years pass. I had never thought that I could take anyone to my heart as I have taken you.'

'I know,' I told him. 'But I know too that you are wrong. This is revenge. You want to hurt people because long ago *you* were hurt. There is no happiness in revenge. I am certain your attitude is wrong. It can only bring unhappiness.'

'Wait until you see those gardens – those lawns with the grass like green velvet, well tended for hundreds of years. The fountains play over the statue of Hermes and water-lilies float on the water. The walled pond garden is a replica of the one at Hampton Court. On the sunny days in that garden there is perfect peace. The peacocks strut over the lawns. I never saw such beauty, Nora.'

'But you will have to take this away from the people to whom it rightly belongs.'

'The people who took from me my freedom! The people who reduced me to animal status, who all but killed me with their brutality.'

'But you escaped. You married Maybella and escaped.'

'Maybella was a fool.'

'So you used her to escape.'

'It was necessary.'

'You have not been a happy man,' I said. 'You have used people to get what you want. You have spent your life in search of revenge. It should have been spent in search of happiness.'

'You preach, Nora.'

'I say what I feel.'

He laughed suddenly, his eyebrow rising with that odd little quirk.

'Oh, Nora, what should I do without you?'

'I don't know and I suggest you don't put it to the test. Give up your plans. Stay here. Forget about your golden fortune, your cruel plans. Forget revenge and enjoy happiness.'

'I shall be happy. Never fear. And I shall get what I want. I want to talk to you, Nora . . . about the future.'

'Then promise me that future will be here.'

He shook his head. 'Whiteladies,' he said.

'It's wrong. I know it's wrong.'

'I shall have to convince you that it is absolutely right.'

'You wanted to talk to me about the future.'

'You are in too analytical a mood tonight. Tomorrow perhaps.'

We left it at that, but I was uneasy. I kept thinking of the lawn at Whiteladies and the girl and the older woman named Lucie. So the mother in the chair had been Lynx's Arabella and she was now dead. I wondered what had happened to the man she had married and if he were still alive. Then I thought of that awful moment in Kerry's Creek when Lynx's voice had thundered behind me. 'Stand up, Jagger!' And Jagger stood up to be shot dead.

Lynx never hesitated and death meant little to him. He could kill a man and not be haunted by what he had done. I thought of his marrying the poor ineffectual Maybella and insisting on her giving him a son. Was I beginning to understand Lynx? He gave his love to few but for those to whom he gave it he would kill. To be hated by Lynx would be terrifying; and to be loved by him could perhaps be too.

He loved Stirling. He loved me. He was going to have his way and we were all going to bow to his wishes. Every one of us . . . myself, Stirling and the people of Whiteladies. No, not all of us.

I won't be dominated, I told myself, even by Lynx.

The next day there was consternation throughout the district. The bush fires which were burning some thirty miles away were coming in our direction. When I awoke the acrid smell was everywhere and there was no escaping from it. From my window I could see the glow in the sky.

Adelaide was worried. 'It will be on our land,' she said. 'I do hope we're not going to lose anyone. Some of the shepherds' huts are out that way.'

'They'll manage to get away surely. They must be aware of its coming nearer to them.'

'You have no idea what a forest fire can be like, Nora. The trees explode because of the oil in them, and fresh fires break out all round.'

'Aren't precautions taken?'

She smiled again ruefully. 'All I can say is that you have no idea what it's like. I hope you never do.'

The atmosphere of the house had changed. Everywhere was solemn; the servants went about their work not speaking, and when they did it was to talk of the fires.

'They can be seen from Melbourne,' one of them said. 'They say this is one of the worst outbreaks for years.'

'Can't wonder at it – the weather we've been having. Did you hear the thunder last night? The lightning must have struck a grove of gums. That could've started it.'

The wind was fierce – high and hot coming from the north. Rumbles of angry thunder rolled across the sky. I went out into the garden. I couldn't bear the atmosphere indoors; yet outside it seemed worse. The glare of the sky had grown more angry and the hot wind carried on it that unmistakable smell.

The place seemed deserted. I wondered where everyone was. Lynx, I supposed, was at the mine. I doubted whether he would have any fears about that. I presumed the fire could pass over it without disturbing the lodes below although it would ruin the machinery and everything at ground level.

I went indoors and to the top of the house. I looked out. I could see dark clouds of smoke in the distance. I came down again and as I passed Jessica's door she called to me. She was lying on her bed, a cold compress on her forehead.

'That horrid smell!' she said. 'It gives me a headache. It reminds me of once at Rosella. We were ringed by fire. That was before *he* came. Uncle was terrified. He thought we should lose everything. Maybella wanted to run away but Uncle wouldn't let her. He said, Better stay where we were. Maybe we'd run into danger. That's how it is with these fires. You never know where they're going to spring up . . . and in a matter of seconds you're in a ring of fire.'

I didn't want to listen to her, so I left her. I went past Lynx's room knowing he was not there. I felt again the great desire to get out of doors, to ride as far as I could from that smoke cloud on the horizon, to get the smell of smoke and fire out of my nostrils.

I went down to the stables and saddled Queen Anne.

She seemed uneasy as though aware of the danger. I talked to her soothingly. 'We'll go for a ride out into the open air . . . where it's fresh and clean and we can escape from this horrid smell.'

I rode for a mile or so but I could still smell the smoke. I pulled up and looked behind me. If anything the smoke seemed nearer.

I urged the Queen to a gallop and off we went. I forgot the fire and thought about the things Lynx had said to me on the previous night in his study and I wondered whether his plan would ever come to anything.

Stirling and I would marry – in England perhaps. I remembered the old Norman church with its grey stone walls and the graveyard with its crazy-looking tombstones, some of which were propped up against the wall, presumably because no one knew exactly where they belonged. Lynx would give me away in my white wedding-dress and Stirling and I would come down the aisle together while Lynx looked on with pride and gratification. The gates with their white ornamentations would be flung open and our carriage would go through, along the drive to the mansion.

And what of Minta? Poor Minta, she would be living in one of the cottages. Perhaps she would serve teas to the local people with little home-made cakes and scones with jam or honey. Lucie would help her.

How absurdly my mind ran on. I was like my father. I did not believe that Minta and her father – if he was still alive – would ever allow the house to be sold, no matter with what prizes the richest of golden millionaires tempted them.

I pulled up and looked over my shoulder. The smoke was thick now. I couldn't understand it. I was riding away and yet I seemed to be coming nearer.

I realized that I had been foolish to leave the house. But I was not lost. I knew the direction which I had taken. Yet I could not understand why I seemed to be coming nearer to the smoke. The bush was deceptive. So much of it looked alike. But I had been to this spot before and I knew where I was.

Then suddenly I heard an echo. 'Cooee. Nora.'

I called back. It was Stirling.

I curved my hands about my mouth and shouted. 'Stirling . . . here.'

I saw him then. He came galloping towards me. He was white with anger. 'Nora . . . you fool!' he shouted.

'What do you mean?' I retorted sharply.

'Don't you know better than to come out like this? My God, you could be caught. Don't you understand what's happening? Haven't you learned anything?'

'I know there's a fire somewhere.'

'A fire somewhere! Do you know that miles of bushland are ablaze. And you ride blithely out. Come on.'

He turned his horse and meekly I followed.

'You were mad,' he threw over his shoulder.

'I rode away from it. Is that madness?'

'How do you know where it will be next? In seconds you can be surrounded.'

'I should have remembered the warnings. Well, I know now.'

'You don't. You don't understand a thing about it. Can't you imagine? No. You have to risk your life before you understand. If they hadn't seen you leave the stables I wouldn't have known which direction you'd taken.'

'Am I always to be watched?' I remembered with horror that other occasion when I had been seen riding out and followed. I went on irritably: 'Oh, do stop nagging, Stirling. I rode out. That's that. Here I am. All's well and I'll promise not to do it again.'

His mouth was sternly set and he looked remarkably like his father. We rode on in silence for some miles, then I said: 'Stirling, I didn't know you could be so sullen. I'm learning. I must say if there's one thing I dislike –'

I stopped because it was clear that he wasn't listening. I had begun to cough and wherever I turned I saw clouds of smoke.

He pulled up suddenly.

'Which way?' I asked.

'I wish I knew.'

'Well, aren't we going home?'

'I don't know. It looks as though we may be cut off.'

'Cut off by . . .'

'By fire, you idiot!'

'How dare you talk to me like that!'

'Oh God,' he groaned. 'Listen, Nora. We're in danger. We're surrounded. Can't you see that? I just don't know which road to take. Any could be disaster.'

I thought he was exaggerating to teach me a lesson until there was a loud explosion close to us and a grove of gum trees suddenly burst into flame.

'Come on,' said Stirling, and we galloped in the opposite direction. But it was not long before he pulled up again. We were approaching a heavy pall of smoke.

'We're cut off,' said Stirling tersely.

I stood there looking at him fearfully. I felt the smoke in my eyes and nostrils. I was frightened, yet comforted by Stirling's presence. I had a childish notion that if he were there everything would turn out right.

'I wonder,' he was saying to himself. 'There may be time. Come on. Keep close to me. It's worth a try.'

We galloped towards the smoke and suddenly he turned off the bush track and we rode into the bushes.

I heard him mutter: 'It's a chance. The only one. We'll try it.'

A creek containing a very little water lay ahead of us. He dismounted, tore off his coat and asked for mine. I gave it to him. 'We'll have to leave the horses,' he said. 'There's nothing we can do for them. It's just possible they'll find their way.'

'Oh no, Stirling . . .'

'Do as I say. There's just a faint chance of saving ourselves.'

He soaked our coats in the creek and ran to where a grey rock protruded above the creek. In front of this was a small aperture. Stirling thrust the wet coats into my hands and kneeling frantically began to dig out the dirt with his hands. It was loose and soon he had made a hole. He signed me to crawl through it and by this time I knew I must obey unquestioningly.

To my surprise I was in a cave about the size of a small room. Almost immediately Stirling was beside me. He stuffed the wet coats into the aperture. We were in complete darkness.

'Nora.' His voice sounded hoarse with tension.

'I'm here, Stirling.'

Groping he found me and held me against him.

'Better lie down,' he said.

Lying there, we were silent for a second or so, then he said: 'Nora, we'll be lucky if we come out of here alive.'

I was silent, thinking: It's my fault. I was careless. What a lot I have to learn about this country where sudden death seems constantly to be lying in wait for the foolish and unwary.

'Oh Nora,' he said, 'to think you came out here . . . to my country . . . for this.'

'It was my fault, Stirling.'

'No.' His voice was tender. 'It could happen anywhere. Who knows what's happening at the house even now. The fire was getting closer.'

'But Lynx will know . . .' And then I thought of the house being surrounded by fire; I pictured its coming close, so fierce, so all-consuming that not even Lynx could hold it off. The thought of Lynx in danger made me forget that which threatened us. But I told myself he would know what to do. No harm could come to him. I realized then that I had learned to think of him as Stirling did: he was godlike, immortal.

Stirling was whispering: 'I remembered this cave. An aboriginal family lived here. They came to work for my father, and the boy who was my age used to bring me here. It's got to save us, Nora. It's our only chance.'

I knew he was trying to comfort me. Outside, the fire was encircling us; soon the ground above us would be ablaze. How could we possibly survive?

In the darkness he seemed to read my thoughts.

'There is a chance,' he said. 'A slight one; but a chance.'

For the first time in my life I was close to death. I felt lightheaded, as though I were dreaming. Stirling and I would lie forever underground and this would be our grave, though no one would know it. I reached for his hand; it was as though it were on fire. Everything seemed on fire for the heat was becoming unbearable.

His lips were close to my ear. 'The fire will be right above us presently,' he said.

'Soon, Stirling,' I answered. 'Very soon.'

We could hear the roar and crackle, the sudden explosion; and the acrid smell was creeping into the cave.

'If we can keep the smoke out,' said Stirling and paused. 'If not . . .' He didn't go on. There was no need to. I understood. Our chances of survival were very small.

'Stirling,' I said, 'I'm not sorry I came out here.'

He did not answer. We had moved away from each other because the heat was so great but we kept our fingers entwined. There was comfort for me in this; I wondered if he felt it too.

'Nora.' His voice seemed to come to me from a long way off. 'We loved you, Nora. It was different when you came.'

I was loved as I had been when my father was alive. But what did it matter now. He used the past tense as though we were already dead. It can't be long now, I thought. I couldn't die . . . not now that I had found my home and people to love me. I felt angry with fate which had made me suffer and then when I could be happy again to say: This is the end. Now your life is over.

'No,' I said, but so quietly that he did not hear me.

There was nothing we could do but lie still waiting. I had never known there could be heat like this. I was gasping for my breath.

'It's all right, Nora.' I heard a voice – or at least I believed I did. 'Nora, my love, we'll be all right. Lynx would never forgive us if we died.'

It's true, I thought. We have to live . . . for Lynx.

I can't describe the ever-increasing heat. I believe I must have been only half-conscious because there were times during that fearful period when I was not sure where I was. I lay perfectly still, having no strength to move, for in that terrific heat all energy had left me. There was only one thing to do: to lie and wait either for death to come or for life to deliver us.

But all through this terrifying experience I was aware of Stirling close to me; and I knew that he loved me. I was certain that if only I could escape from death the future of which I had dreamed would be mine.

I think I was in a sort of trance, dreaming of a future in which we were all there – the three of us, because I had learned now, if I had not known it before, that Lynx must always have a place in my life – on the lawns of a beautiful old house. My children – mine and Stirling's – were there with their grandfather: a new Lynx, a man who had come to terms with life, who had thrown aside a dream of revenge for one of contentment.

'Nora! Nora!' Stirling's face was close to mine. There was a little light in the cave. The first thing I noticed was the smoke. I started to cough.

'Oh God, Nora, I thought you were dead.'

'What's happened?' I asked.

'The wind's changed. There's a light drizzle falling. The fires will be damped down and they'll stop spreading. We're going to get out of here.' He pulled me to my feet and I staggered, falling against him.

He laughed with relief because I was alive, I knew; he held me against him briefly but with an inexpressible tenderness.

'We're going to get out of here,' he repeated.

My limbs were stiff; I could scarcely move. The temperature in the cave must have been about a hundred and forty degrees, although it was much cooler than it had been.

'You follow me,' he said; and I watched him crawl through the hole. Soon he had dragged me out to stand beside him. It was like walking into an oven; then I held up my face and let the light drizzle fall on it.

A fearful sight met our eyes. The remains of trees were black and smouldering. There was a quietness everywhere and it occurred to me that one subconsciously heard the birds and insects of the bush without being aware of them. Several trees were still burning.

I turned to Stirling who was scarcely recognizable. His face was black; so were his clothes. I knew I presented a similar spectacle.

He put his arms about me and held me close to him. We just stood there, too emotional to speak.

Then I said: 'We're alive, Stirling. We have a future after all.'

He released me and took my hands, looking searchingly into my face. I saw the joy rather than the grime of smoke and dirt, and for a few seconds I was happy.

He said: 'I wonder what's been happening at home.' A terrible fear had taken possession of us both, for although we had just been assuring ourselves that we had a future, neither of us could be happy if it did not contain one other.

'We must get back quickly,' I said. 'We must find out.'

The countryside was devastated and it was difficult to know which scarred and mutilated road to take. I should have been lost without Stirling. He had known this country all his life but even he was bewildered. We were both driven by an urgent desire to know what had happened at Little Whiteladies. Stirling loved me; I was sure of that. I believed that our future lay together, but if we had lost Lynx should we ever be happy again?

I don't know how we made that journey. We were weak from shock; we must have been at least six hours in the cave. Our limbs were cramped, our throats parched; we struggled on and there was only one thought in our minds: Lynx.

Night fell and Stirling said we must rest awhile; we lay down but our minds could not rest.

'How far?' I whispered.

'It can't be more than six or seven miles.'

'Stirling, why don't we go?'

'We must rest for a while.'

'I'd rather go.'

'So would I, but you'd collapse before we got there.'

'Oh Stirling,' I cried. 'You do take care of me.'

'Always, Nora,' he answered.

'For ever,' I murmured; but even then I was thinking of Lynx.

I slept at last and felt it was a measure of Stirling's love for me that he let me sleep. I was apologetic when I awoke. It seemed so wrong to sleep when we did not know what had happened to Lynx.

We trudged on. We did not speak of Lynx but each knew that the other thought of him exclusively, and that our failure to mention him was deliberate.

Never shall I forget the last hour of that walk, and finally discovering the land untouched by fire. There stood the house, impregnable, as though defying destruction to come near.

Stirling gave a shout when we saw it. He started to run pulling me with him.

'Home! he cried. 'We're home.'

Adelaide came running out of the house. She was crying with relief. She took us into her arms and would not let us go. I noticed, as one does on such occasions, how the smoke and grime blackened her gown.

'The master must be told!' she cried. 'Jenny! Mary! They are here. They are home.'

We stumbled into the house.

'*He* . . . is safe,' said Stirling.

'But nearly demented,' replied Adelaide. 'He has been searching for you. He has called in everyone.'

'Look after Nora,' said Stirling.

'He's safe?' I murmured. 'He's truly safe?'

They had put me to bed by the time he came. Only when I was between the cool sheets did I realize how exhausted I was. I lay luxuriating in my bed, having drunk the broth which Adelaide had brought. 'Not too much at first,' she had said. And I lay there thinking of the heat and terror of the dark cave, and Stirling's saying that he would look after me for ever. Lynx was safe. There would be the three of us.

I knew that he was in the house. One sensed his presence. I knew too that he would come to me first . . . even before he went to Stirling. Oh no, surely not. Stirling was his beloved son. I was only the adopted daughter.

He was at the door, his eyes shining with the greatest joy I ever saw in any eyes. Why was everything he did so much more intense than what others did?

'Nora,' he said. 'My Nora.'

Then he came to the bedside and held me in his arms. He put his face close to mine. 'My girl Nora,' he kept saying. I said: 'I'm back, Lynx. Dear, dearest Lynx, we're back together.'

For a few moments he did not speak. He just held me.

Then he said: 'I thought I'd lost you. I was mad with fury. But you're back. My girl Nora.'

'I was terrified of what might be happening to you.'

He laughed loud and confident. As if anything could happen to him!

'All the time,' I told him, 'we thought of you, we talked to you.'

He laughed again and all he said was: 'My girl Nora!'

Later he went to see Stirling.

Chapter Six

We recovered quickly from the shock of our experience. I think the fact that we came back to the house and found it untouched and the family safe made us so happy that we threw off the ill effects of our terrifying adventure with the greatest possible speed.

The damage had been tremendous. The property had suffered most; many sheep had been lost and two of the shepherds had died in their cottages. The mine had escaped.

Adelaide insisted that I stay in bed for two days. I was cosseted and fed with special invalid's food which she said was necessary. Stirling refused to be treated like an invalid; but I enjoyed it.

Jessica came to see me. She sat by my bed looking intently at me. 'I've never seen him so affected as he was,' she said. 'He sent parties out looking for you, risking their lives.'

I smiled happily. I just wanted to lie and think about the future.

When I was up he asked me to come to his library after dinner.

'A game of chess,' I said, remembering that during those hours of semi-consciousness in the cave I had imagined myself in his study, the chessmen between us.

He did not join us for dinner and when I went up he was waiting for me. He looked excited and yet restrained; and different from when I had seen him last.

'You are a little pale, Nora,' he said. 'But you'll recover in a few days' time. You're young and healthy and resilient.'

He poured out two glasses of port wine and brought them over to me. I noticed the eyes of the lynx on his finger glitter as he handed me one.

'To us, Nora. Your safe delivery to me. What should I have done if you had not come back?'

'We have Stirling to thank. Stirling is wonderful.'

'Stirling is wonderful,' he repeated.

I started to talk about the cave, although he had heard it all before. I had suddenly become nervous and felt the need to go on talking.

'My dear,' he said, 'you are back, and you have made me the happiest of men when I should have been the most wretched.'

My hands had started to tremble which, I told myself, was due to the recent shock. But it was not that. A sudden idea had come to me but I would not accept it.

He took my glass from me. 'You're not afraid, Nora. It's not like you to be afraid.'

'Of what should I be afraid?' I demanded.

'There speaks my girl Nora. You have nothing to fear ever . . . because I shall be here to look after you.'

'That's a comforting thought,' I said, with a touch of my old lightness.

'Then be comforted, my dearest. I believe you know what has been in my mind for some time. You have been aware of the change you have wrought in me.'

'I!'

'You have brought my youth back to me. After all, I am not an old man. Do I appear old to you?'

'To me you have always appeared to be immortal. Even before I knew you Stirling spoke of you as though you were Zeus.'

He smiled, but he did not wish to discuss Stirling.

'You are old for your years, my dear,' he said. 'You are no foolish child. Nor were you ever. You had to fend for yourself and I'm glad of it. I never thought this would happen to me. Yes indeed, you have given me back my youth, Nora.'

'How?'

'By being yourself. By coming here among us and showing me that my life lies before me . . . not behind me.'

'I'm glad of that. So you have dropped this stupid notion of revenge.'

He laughed again. He was laughing a good deal tonight.

'You bully me, Nora. You always did. You must go on doing so when we are married. I like it, my darling.'

'When I am married to –' In that second I had told myself I had not heard him correctly. He meant when Stirling and I were married; but in my heart I knew that he was not thinking of Stirling.

'To me,' he said. 'You don't think I'd let you go to anyone else?' There was a fierceness in his eyes which both frightened and delighted me. As ever in his presence I was unsure of my feelings for him.

He gripped me by the shoulders and drew me towards him. 'Never again, my love, will you wander off into a forest fire. I have you back, and I'll keep you with me for as long as we both shall live.'

'Lynx!' I stammered and he gripped me more tightly.

'That ridiculous name!' he said.

'But I always think of you as Lynx,' I said foolishly, as though that mattered when there was so much of importance to think and talk about.

'A predatory animal,' he said. 'It fits. Oh God, Nora, I thought I'd die when you didn't come back. I was fit to throw myself into that raging furnace, and it was only the certain knowledge within me that you'd come back that restrained me. I need you, Nora, as I have never needed anyone. I see that now. What's wrong, my dear?'

'Marriage,' I said. 'I hadn't thought of marriage.'

'What else?'

'You talked of being my father.'

'That was in the beginning. But it changed, didn't it? I'll be everything to you, Nora. You'll lack nothing.'

'I'm bewildered.'

'Not you, Nora. You knew it, really. I was aware of it. You knew it and were glad.'

'But ...'

'There are no buts. I have planned it all.'

'Without consulting me?'

He laughed. 'A touch of the old Nora. Yes, without consulting you in so many words, but it was clear to us both, wasn't it? When we sat there playing our chess, when I let you win the set. You didn't think you could have done that if I hadn't allowed you to, do you?'

I said slowly: 'And Jagger?'

His eyes narrowed. His emotions frightened and yet in some strange way thrilled me. There was a violent hatred on his face.

'Jagger!' he cried. 'Yes, by God, Jagger!'

'You killed him. You killed a man.'

'My love, he had to die. I could never have looked at him again without wanting to murder him. I would have killed him with my own hands some time. At least I let him die quickly.'

'Oh, Lynx,' I said weakly, 'you frighten me.'

'I frighten *you*! When I love you! And I've never loved anyone as I love you. Arabella! What a fantasy! It was my pride that suffered there. I wanted Whiteladies. I wanted to live in that house with my wife and children. And I'm going to, Nora.'

'You go too fast,' I said.

'My imperious Nora!' he retorted with a smile. 'Would you have me go slowly? We are going to Whiteladies, you and I; and you shall sit at the table on the daïs where kings and queens have sat; and the nursery at the top of the house where poor simple Arabella learned her ABC will be for our children.'

'I have not yet said that I agree.'

'My darling, you will not be allowed to do anything else.'

'If I refuse.'

'You won't.'

'What does ... Stirling say? Have you told him?'

'He knows something of my plans.'

'He knows that you are asking me to marry you?'

'He knows. Adelaide knows. They have guessed at my feelings for you for some time past.'

'And Stirling ... he thinks it is a good idea?'

'Of course. He realizes the strength of my feelings for you.'

'And that means that he will wish it too.'

'He has been a good son. He has always been eager for my happiness.'

'I see.'

'So it is only for my imperious Nora to say that she loves me, which I know she does.'

'You are adopting that irritating habit of speaking of me as though I'm not here as you did when you tried to demoralize me on my arrival.'

He laughed delightedly. 'Cruel of me. And foolish really because it never succeeded for a moment, did it? We'll announce to the family that the ceremony is to take place. You know I'm not a man for wasting time.'

'I will not be hurried into anything. I like to make my own decisions.'

'So you shall, for I see that you are as eager for this ceremony to take place as I am.'

'You take too much for granted. I was not prepared for this, I do assure you. I thought of you as my father . . .'

'I will make a better husband than a father, you see.'

I held him off. I said: 'I want time . . . *time*. I shall say nothing until I have thought about this.'

'Tonight I am going to announce to them our imminent marriage.'

'Not yet,' I protested and then wondered why I had put it that way, as though it would come in due course. Marry Lynx! It was a bewildering and exciting project. What had my feelings for him been – something beyond that of an adopted daughter towards a father – and yet there was Stirling.

Stirling! He knew of this and accepted it. I would live under this roof with Stirling and I should be married to Lynx. It was an incongruous situation, but it was what Lynx had been planning.

I turned away but he was at the door before me, barring my way. His eyes were brilliant with a passion which alarmed me as I had been alarmed when I stood face to face with Jagger; and yet at the same time I had no desire to run away from him.

He took my chin in his hands and lifted my face to his. 'You are afraid,' he said, 'afraid of what you have not yet experienced. You have discoveries to make, Nora. We'll make them together. You have nothing to fear, my darling.'

His face was close to me, those gleaming jungle eyes alight with a passion of which I could only guess.

I held him off. 'No,' I said. 'Not yet. I must go away. I must think. I *insist*. If you announce anything I should deny it. I will not be forced.'

He dropped his hands.

'You are afraid of me. Oh God, Nora, is that true?'

'Why will you harp on fear? It is not fear. I object to being told whom I shall marry and when the ceremony will take place before I have been consulted. If this marriage took place it would have to be understood that I am not a puppet to be moved this way and that, nor should I be expected to bow down and worship my husband as though he were one of the gods stepped down from Olympus.'

'Oh Nora, you delight me. So my darling wants time to think. She wants to make her own decisions. My only wish is to give her everything in the world she asks for. This is a small thing compared with the gifts I shall shower on her.'

'The first thing I ask is that you stop that ridiculous habit. It infuriates me.'

We were laughing again – back for a moment to the old relationship.

'Now,' I said, 'I will leave you. I will go to my room and when I have decided I will tell you.'

He dropped the hands which had imprisoned me. As I turned he caught me and I felt his lips on my neck. I wanted both to stay and to escape; and as ever, I did not understand my feelings.

I went to my room and closed the door. I stood against it pressing my cool palms to my burning cheeks.

You knew it, I accused myself, and you refused to see it. You had made up your mind that you would marry Stirling. It had all seemed so right and natural. But I love Stirling, I protested.

Yes, you love Stirling. *And* Lynx.

I could think of no one but Lynx. He filled my mind as he seemed to dominate every room in which he stood. He was exciting; he was magnificent; he was more than human.

I tried to be calm. Marry Lynx! Be with him day and night! I was so inexperienced of life. I had so much to learn of men and marriage; and Lynx would be my instructor. I was aghast at the thought and yet completely obsessed by it. I love *Stirling*, I kept telling myself. It was always Stirling, ever since we stood on the deck of the *Carron Star* together. Yes, but at that time I had not met Lynx.

Yet having met Lynx my feelings towards Stirling had not changed. I remembered that terrible night when we had lain in the cave together and had known that we might never come out alive; and when we had emerged and had known that after all we had a future, it had been like an unspoken declaration of love.

Yet even in the cave Lynx had been constantly in my thoughts – in both our thoughts.

If I married Lynx I should be Stirling's stepmother. Stepmother to the man I had thought of marrying! It was incongruous. Suppose I talked to Stirling? Suppose he told me he loved me? We should have to go away. We could not marry and live under the same roof as Lynx, now that he had declared his passionate need of me.

But when I thought of life without Lynx I was filled with dismay. It would be flat and dull. With Stirling? Yes, perhaps even with him. But Lynx would never allow us to go away. That thought comforted me. I remembered vividly the sight of him on his white horse, the gun in his hands. A murderer! He said he would do the same to any man who laid hands on me. And Stirling?

I was caught up in the whirlwind of my own emotions. I did not know what I should do.

I must see Stirling.

I spent a sleepless night and was up early. I saw Stirling at breakfast and told him I must speak to him soon and alone.

We took our horses and rode out into the bush.

Before we had covered a mile, I said to him, 'Stirling, your father has asked me to marry him.'

'Yes,' he said, his face impassive.

'It surprised me.'

'Did it?'

'He talked to *you* about it?'

'It came out in his plans for going to England.'

So Stirling had indeed known about it for some time. Before the fire. Then I had misunderstood everything. To him I was only a sister. I had made this mistake of believing that our relationship went deeper than that. I had misunderstood everything – Stirling as much as Lynx.

'I see,' I said blankly.

There was silence. His face betrayed nothing. I felt disappointed, deflated. How stupid I had been!

'If I married your father I should be your stepmother,' I said with a foolish little laugh.

'Well?'

'That seems very odd.'

'Why?'

'You're older than I am.'

'It wouldn't be the first time someone had a young stepmother.'

'Stirling, what do you think of it?'

'My father would be happier than he has ever been in his life. And you know how fond of you we have grown. You're already one of us. This will . . .'

I waited breathlessly for him to continue. He shrugged his shoulders.

'It will bring you closer than ever,' he finished.

Again I felt that maze of bewilderment. What did I want? Stirling to break down, to tell me that he could not endure to see me married to another man – even his own father? Did I want him to plan our escape?

I did not know. I think part of me clung to the old dream of myself and Stirling going through the years together, our children climbing on to their grandfather's knee, venerating him, adoring him, as we all did. It was the old conventional dream. But how could Lynx play the background figure in any story?

I started to gallop and immediately heard Stirling's horse thudding behind me. He doesn't care, I thought. He's glad because it's what his father wants. Stirling has no will of his own: his only will is that of his father. He had been fond of me, yes – but as his sister.

So now I knew what I should do. Stirling had made the decision for me. But was that true? Should I ever have been able to tell Lynx that I could not marry him because I loved his son?

I love them both, I thought in desperation. How strange it should be that with the younger man I envisaged the peaceful and conventional life, and with the other – old enough to be my father – the adventure.

When we arrived back at the house Lynx must have seen us for one of the servants came down at once to say that he wished to see me in the library.

It was like a command, I thought with a faint but indulgent exasperation. But while his arrogance irked me I wanted it.

I deliberately delayed and he was impatient.

'How long you took,' he complained.

'I stopped to comb my hair and wash my hands before entering the royal presence.'

'Didn't you know that I expect immediate obedience?'

'I knew you expected it, but things don't always happen as one expects.'

He laughed as he did so readily now. In fact I seemed constantly to amuse him. But perhaps it was the laughter of triumph for he knew that I was going to succumb to his wishes. I think I had known it right from the start . . . in spite of Stirling.

'You are more self-assured this morning than you were last night.'

'I was a little taken by surprise then.'

'And now you have had an opportunity to consider . . .'

'My good fortune?'

'*Our* good fortune,' he amended. 'But you need not go on. I know your answer.'

'You were so sure of it from the beginning that you didn't really think it necessary to ask me.'

'I know what is best for you.'

'Do you also know what is best for yourself?'

'You are best for me and I for you. It's as simple as that. You had a good ride with Stirling?' He looked at me steadily. 'He is delighted. My family knows that my marriage with you is what I desire more than anything in the world. Therefore they are happy that it should take place.'

I held out my hands to him and he grasped them eagerly. 'I am a member of that family,' I said, 'so I suppose I must fall into line.'

I saw the triumph in his eyes as I was caught up in his embrace.

'I shall disappoint you,' I said.

'Impossible.'

'You will find me too young and stupid.'

'And you will be imperious with me.'

'You will be impatient with me.'

'I shall find you as I always have – enchanting.'

'I think it is somehow incongruous.'

'Nonsense. You love me.'

'Is it *lèse-majesté* to love the gods of Olympus as one would an ordinary mortal? Shouldn't one adore merely.'

'That will do for a start,' he said.

There was a ceremonial dinner that evening and every place at the table was filled. I sat beside him. He was benign; his eyes shone rather than glinted. I had never seen him look as he did then and I was elated because I was responsible for it.

He laughed a great deal; he was tolerant with everyone; and at the end of the meal he made the announcement. He and I were shortly to be married – very shortly, he added. This was a great occasion and everyone was to drink the health of his bride-to-be. They stood and lifted their glasses. There were men at the table who had been present at that scene in the wool shed after the shooting of Jacob Jagger. There was Adelaide looking flushed and delighted because at last her father was happy; there was Jessica, her lips pursed, a gloomy Cassandra; and there was Stirling, his face betraying nothing of that which I half hoped to see.

I thought about them as I lay in bed that night – and particularly did I think of Stirling. I tried to look back on everything that had happened between us and ask myself how I could have misconstrued his feelings for me. If he had given me some sign that he loved me . . . but what should I have done? Somehow I knew that I could never have refused Lynx. He would not have allowed it. Nor did I wish him to. He loved me a thousand times more than Stirling ever could. He was capable of deeper, more searing emotions. I should be honoured to have won the love of a man like Lynx. My life would be frightening sometimes perhaps, but exciting.

I could not sleep, and as I lay in the darkness trying to visualize the future, I heard a movement outside my room. My heart started to flutter uncomfortably as the door moved silently open. I thought for a moment: It's the ghost of dead Maybella come to warn me.

I might have known that it would be Jessica. Indeed, she looked like a ghost, with her nightcap tied over her hair which was in steel curlers, her long white flannel nightdress flowing about her and the candle in her hand.

She had come to warn me, I knew.

'Are you asleep?' she asked.

'No. You'll catch cold wandering about the house like that.'

She shook her head. 'I wanted to speak to you.'

'Sit down and wrap the quilt about you.'

She shook her head. She preferred to stand by the bed holding the candle high. It made her look more like a prophetess of doom than she could have done sitting down.

'So it's come to this. You're going to be his wife,' she said. 'There'll be nothing but disaster.'

'Why should there be?'

'I know it. Maybella came to me in a dream last night. She said: "Stop it, Jessie. Save that poor young girl." '

'So Maybella had pre-knowledge of the announcement?'

'The dead know these things. Particularly when they don't rest.'

'Doesn't Maybella?'

Jessica shook her head. 'She comes back to haunt him. After all, he murdered her.'

'I don't think you should say that. She died having her son.'

'It killed her and he knew it would.'

I sighed. 'It's your way of looking at things. I daresay she wanted a son too.'

'And what do you think is going to happen to you?'

'I shall do my best to be a good wife and mistress of the house.'

'He thinks of no one but himself.'

'It's a common enough human failing.'

'Clever talk! It makes him laugh. Maybella had none of that. Then there was that woman in England.'

'You should go back to bed,' I said gently. 'You really are going to catch cold if you don't.'

'Maybella wants me to warn you. He's cruel and selfish. He's lustful and he'll not be faithful to you. He never has been to any woman, so do you think he will be to you?'

'There's always a time to begin.'

'You're making fun of me.'

'I'm not, Jessica. But I don't think you understand. All that has happened is in the past. He and I are going to start a new life together. I will do everything in my power to make it a success and so will he.'

'He'll use you as he uses everyone. What of Stirling, eh?'

'What of Stirling?' I asked.

'Well, there was a time when we thought it would be you two . . . it would have been natural and it was what he wanted.'

'What who wanted?'

'Stirling, of course. We all said it. A match between you two young ones . . . that's what we all wanted . . . that's what we all expected. And what happens? You take his fancy, so he says: "No, Stirling, you stand aside for me and if you don't well, I'll shoot you as I shot that man Jagger." '

'How dare you say such a thing of him!'

'It's what Maybella thinks. He's told Stirling: "Hands off. I want the girl." So Stirling says: "Yes, Papa," as he has been brought up to do. It's always been the same. He must have his way and the devil take the rest.'

'I said: 'I'm tired, Jessica. Nothing you can say will alter my plans. I have promised to marry him and I will keep my promise. We all change. He has changed. He is not the same man who came to Rosella.'

'He *is* the same man. I don't forget. He stood there in the yard and the marks were on his wrists – and nothing was the same afterwards. He comes into your life. He takes you up and when he's finished with you, you are thrown aside. He hasn't altered. It happened to Maybella. It will happen to you.'

'I don't intend to be thrown aside.'

'Nor did she. She thought he was wonderful at first. So will you. He can play the lover all right . . . even when it's all pretence as it was with Maybella. She used to go about in a dream during those first months. She used to say to me: "Ah, Jessie, if only I could explain to you!" I knew . . . even then.'

'It's over, Jessica. There's no point in recalling it.'

'But I want you to know. Maybella wants you to know. Well, I've done my duty.' She came close to the bed; the candle tipped and I thought she would set light to the bedclothes. 'Run away,' she said. 'Run away while there's still time. Run away with Stirling.'

'You're mad,' I said angrily.

She shook her head. Then she said sadly: 'In some ways perhaps, but it's his fault. I see this as clear as daylight. You could persuade Stirling. Try. He'd go. I'm sure of it. Don't let that man win every time. Go away, the two of you.' She gave a hollow chuckle. 'Wouldn't I like to see his face when he was told you'd gone?'

'Your candle grease is dripping on the quilt.'

She straightened the candle and held it under her face. In the dim light it looked like a skull. I thought: So would Maybella have looked if she had indeed come back from the dead to warn me.

'I've done my duty,' she said. 'If you won't listen, that's your look-out.'

'Go back to bed now, Jessica.' I answered. 'And do be careful with that candle.'

She went to the door and looked back at me.

'It's you that should be careful,' she said.

'Thank you for coming,' I replied, for I was sorry for her, she who had loved Lynx – she had betrayed that much to me – she who had no doubt yearned for a return of that old relationship which she believed she had once shared with him.

'I've done what Maybella wanted,' she muttered. 'I can do no more.'

Then she left me to lie there, thinking of what she had said, and wondering afresh about the strange man with whom I was committed to spend the rest of my life, and to ask myself what the future held. And there at the back of my mind was Stirling, who loved me perhaps but who loved Lynx better. And I?

The terrible indecision had come back. I love them both, I thought. My life would be incomplete without either of them. But they had made the decision for me. If Stirling had indeed ever thought of asking me to marry him, he was now handing me over to his father who was waiting with urgent hands and the predatory gleam in his eyes.

Adelaide made my wedding-dress. It was white silk with many frills and flounces and trimmed with rows of lace.

'It will be useful, too, when you go to England,' she said.

To England! I thought. We shall not go to England. I am going to persuade him to stay here, to drop that ridiculous notion of taking Whiteladies away from those pleasant people whom Stirling and I had glimpsed so fleetingly.

'For there,' went on Adelaide, 'you will live in the grand manner. Just think, you will dress for dinner every evening. You will wear velvet. I think green would become you most, Nora. You will sit at one end of the table, and my father, at the other, will be very proud of you.'

'I would rather be here.'

'But there you will live in a befitting style.'

'This style suits me.'

'You forget that your husband will be one of the richest men in England.'

'Who wants to remember that? If one has security that is enough.'

'Not for him, Nora, and his will will be yours when you are married.'

'I don't take that view of marriage. It's a partnership. I shall not change my personality because I'm married.'

'A husband naturally moulds his wife's way of thinking.'

'I shall want to come to my own conclusions.'

Adelaide's indulgent smile irritated me so I burst out: 'I don't think he expects me to change. He became interested in me in the first place because I refused to treat him as though he were some sort of oracle, as the rest of you did.'

Adelaide did not reply but I could see that she clung to her views.

She and I made a trip to Melbourne. How very respectfully I was treated at The Lynx!

I grimaced and said to Adelaide: 'I am the elect. I makes me feel holy in a way.'

We shopped lavishly and bought silks and velvets which Adelaide would make up for me. I bought a sable muff and a sable trimmed mulberry-coloured velvet cloak.

'Don't buy too much here,' advised Adelaide. 'You'll find everything so much more fashionable in England.'

I didn't stress the fact that I was going to make a stand against going back to England.

We arrived back at Little Whiteladies with the goods we had bought.

'I've been in a torment of anxiety,' said Lynx. 'I'll not let you go away without me again.' I was gratified and exultant because I meant so much to him.

Adelaide busied herself at once in her sewing-room. I spent a great deal of time with her – not that I cared much for sewing but at times I wanted to shut myself away from both Stirling and Lynx, so that I might contemplate this step I was taking. There in the sewing-room where the conversation was only desultory and concerned the width of a sleeve or the best way to cut a skirt, I could think of the future and try to come to some decision before I made the final step.

It was nonsense, of course. As if I could draw back! As if I wanted to! But I wished I could understand myself. If it had not been for Stirling ... I might as well say: If it had not been for Lynx ...

No, I told myself a hundred times a day: It is Lynx. It is the strong man I need. And yet I could not get Stirling out of my thoughts.

The time was passing rapidly and I often felt that I wanted to ride out alone into the bush and that there by some miracle I should find the answer which would set my fears at rest. But Lynx had given orders that I was not to ride out alone. I discovered this one morning when I went to the stables and asked the groom to saddle my horse. He told me then that they had all been warned that I should never go riding alone. I was insistent and the groom was alarmed. I was thinking to myself: No, Lynx. I won't be put into a cage. And you will have to know this.

I saddled the horse myself and rode out. I had not gone very far when I heard a horse galloping behind me and I saw the white horse on which he had ridden that day when he had shot Jacob Jagger.

I dug in my spurs but I could not outdistance him. He was soon beside me, his eyes gleaming with excitement. He looked like a satyr, I thought.

'Nora!' he roared.

I pulled up level with him and said: 'Why the excitement?'

'I gave orders that you were not to go riding alone.'

'And if I want to?'

'You won't because you know it is against my wishes.'

'And you won't tell your grooms to do their feeble best to stop me because you know that would be against mine.'

'You know why I don't want you to go out riding alone.'

'Because you think I'm incompetent and fit only for . . . what was that horse's name, Blundell?'

'I suffer torments of fear when you are out of my sight. I visualize all sorts of dangers which you might meet in the bush. It is for this reason that I don't want you to go out alone.'

'Do you mean that for the rest of my life I must always be accompanied wherever I go like some young girl with her duenna?'

'It will be different when we leave here. So it is only for a short while.'

'You know,' I said slowly, 'that I don't want to leave here.'

'That's because you don't realize how much more gracious living can be.'

'I have seen the grand house of which you are thinking.' I turned to him. 'You say you love me.'

'With all my heart.'

'Then you will want to please me.'

'It shall be the object of my life.'

'Then we shall stay here and I shall spent the rest of my days riding with the chosen duenna of the moment whenever I sally forth. But perhaps in due course you will consider that I have grown a little less stupid . . . or perhaps you will not care so much if I did run into some of those dangers you visualize.'

'What nonsense are you talking?'

'It is by no means nonsense. Husbands grow tired of wives. It's not an unusual state of affairs.'

'We shall not be as other husbands and wives.'

'I wonder what it will be like . . . married to a god!'

'You will discover . . . most joyfully.'

He had moved his horse very close to mine. Some galahs were imitating the songs of others. In the distance a brown kangaroo loped over the dry grass. I was very much aware of the sounds and smells of the bush since I had emerged from the cave into the blackened silence.

I said: 'I have grown fond of this country.'

'You will love England more.'

'I want to stay here.'

'It will make no difference to you where we are for we shall be together.'

'Then if it makes no difference why need we go?'

'We have to go. One day you will understand. I will make you see it as I do. Then you will see how inevitable it was. When you are there, where I am going to take you, you will thank me for it, for the rest of your life. Yes, you will.'

'I know what you are thinking. It is that house. It can't be yours. It doesn't belong to you. Your desire to live there is unworthy of you.'

'You have too high an opinion of me, Nora.'

'But you insist on everyone's sharing that high opinion.'

'You're trying to make a saint of me. I'd never be that.'

'Lynx,' I began, 'dear Lynx . . .'

He smiled and said: 'When you speak to me like that I want to lay the earth at your feet.'

'Then, dear Lynx, just give me this. Give me all your plans for revenge and I'll destroy them and it will be as though they never existed.'

'But they do exist, Nora.'

'They can be destroyed.'

'It's too late. They are too strong. They are part of me.'

'You said you loved me.'

'Do you doubt it?'

'If one loves, one wants to give the loved one what he or she most desires.'

'That is why you, who love me, will not ask the impossible. Listen, my love. We are going to England – you, I and Stirling. In time Adelaide will join us. I came to this country unwillingly.'

'It has been good to you.'

He conceded this. 'Yes,' he agreed. 'I served my sentence here. I have my reward . . . gold and Nora.'

'In that order of precedence?'

'You are more important to me than all the gold in Australia.'

'I am glad to hear you confirm this because I was by no means sure. But there is one thing which is more important to you than either of these two contestants for your affections. That is revenge.'

All he would say was: 'One day you will understand.'

As we rode back together he made me promise not to ride out alone again. I reminded him that I had done it often in the past. He then recalled the occasion when I had been thrown from my horse; then there was the affair of Jacob Jagger and the fire.

My riding had improved, I pointed out. I would not take a mount that I couldn't manage. No man would dare molest me now and if there was a fire in the neighbourhood I would be aware of it and certainly would not venture out. What other dangers were there?

'I'm afraid of losing you,' he said. 'That you have come to me is like a miracle. Everything I ever wanted in life is mine, or about to become mine. I don't trust life. I can't help experiencing this fear that just as I am about to grasp complete contentment it may be snatched from me.'

'*You* have such thoughts! You surprise me.'

'I'm serious.'

'Well, I'll make this concession. I won't ride out alone until after the wedding. Then you will have to begin persuading me again.'

'It's a bargain,' he said; and we rode home indulging in that lighthearted banter which seemed to amuse him and which no one had dared exchange with him before.

My wedding-day was almost upon us, and preparations were going on apace. The smell of pies and pastries permeated the house. Adelaide made an enormous wedding-cake of six tiers. But I could not rid myself of the idea that something tremendous was about to happen to prevent the wedding's taking place. There would be some impediment. How absurd! As if anything could prevent happening that on which Lynx had set his heart. Is this a premonition? I asked myself.

Stirling avoided me although I had gone out of my way to seek his company. If only he would say something; that he was as pleased as Adelaide at my approaching marriage hurt me deeply. And yet was he?

We were to be married in the little church about a quarter of a mile from the house; the ceremonial reception would follow in the house itself. In the wardrobe in my room hung my wedding-dress. Adelaide had put it there the previous day; she had only just finished it. It was a work of art, I told her. I was to wear a veil and orange blossom which we had bought in Melbourne.

On the night before my marriage my doubts and fears returned a hundredfold. I suppose, I reassured myself, many brides feel like this on their wedding eves. I kept thinking of Jessica's grim warning. Would he change towards me as he had towards Arabella and Maybella? He had compared his love for me with that he had felt for Arabella as a forest fire compared with a candle flame. A forest fire – an unfortunate comparison! And how absurd to brood on Jessica's grim warnings. She was half mad anyway.

I pictured his eyes tomorrow when he saw me and I wanted to put on my wedding-dress to reassure myself that I looked beautiful. I slipped it on marvelling at the work which had gone into it. What a devoted daughter Adelaide was! And now I should be her stepmother – stepmother to Adelaide and Stirling!

I put the veil over my face and adjusted the orange blossom. The effect was delightful. 'All brides are beautiful,' I said aloud.

'Yes,' I answered myself, 'but you really are, dressed like this.'

'It's only the dress and the veil. It hides your face just enough. Will he think you are beautiful?'

'He already does.'

'As beautiful as Arabella . . . Maybella . . . and the others?'

'What nonsense! They are dead and you are young. You are here and you are not just a desirable young woman. You are more to him than anyone has ever been. You gave him back his youth. He said so. And you gave him gold.'

I started, my cheeks burning. I did wish Jessica would stop that unpleasant habit of creeping about the place and suddenly appearing without warning.

'Jessica,' I said reproachfully, 'I didn't hear you knock.'

'It's because you were talking to yourself. Maybella used to talk to herself. You look just like her with the veil hiding your features. It could be Maybella standing there, more than thirty years ago.'

'I'm sure fashions have changed since then.'

'The veil was different. She didn't have orange blossom. There was just white satin ruching. It was a lovely veil and she looked so beautiful. I've never seen anyone so happy as Maybella was on her wedding morning. But then she didn't know what was waiting for her.'

I tried to be practical. 'Now you're here, Jessica, you can unhook me.'

I took off the veil and orange blossom and laid them in their box. Then I turned my back to her while she fumbled with hooks and eyes.

'It's unlucky to try your dress on the night before your wedding.'

'What nonsense!'

'Maybella tried hers on the night before . . . just as you did. There she was parading in it. "Do I look beautiful, Jessie?" she asked. "I must. He'll expect it." '

'Old wives' tales shouldn't affect us. Now I must get to bed. I have a busy day before me tomorrow. Good night, Jessica.'

She shook her head in resignation. 'Good night.'

I undressed and got into bed but in a short time she was back again.

'I've brought you some hot milk. It will make you sleep.'

'That's kind of you, Jessica.'

She set it down on the table by my bed, and stood there waiting.

'Don't wait,' I said. 'I'll have it in a moment. Good night and thank you.'

She glided out. I had an impulse to lock the door. Then I laughed at myself. Why be afraid of simple Jessica? I took a sip of the milk. I didn't really want it but she would be hurt if I didn't drink it.

I thought of Lynx and all those years ago when he had made love to both of them – Maybella because she was his master's daughter and Jessica presumably because he had wanted to. That was all over. He was changed. He was not the same man who had come into the yard with the marks of manacles on his wrists. But he had never forgotten that nor forgiven it. Oh Lynx, I thought, you are as vulnerable as the rest of us; and I told myself that he needed me to look after him. He, too, had lessons to learn from life; and one was that revenge was futile – a destroyer of peace, and peace was at the very foundations of happiness.

Wise Nora, I commented and smiled to myself. And dear Lynx, to whom on the morrow I should make my vows. It was what I wanted – to be with him, to cherish him, for better for worse, for richer for poorer, in sickness and in health until death did us part. At last I understood. I was the luckiest woman. Lynx loved me. Lynx loved himself, beloved and feared above all other men, Lynx loved *me*.

Now I understood Jessica's hatred; it was due to the fact that she had loved him and lost him. She may have been little or nothing to him but he had been everything to her; and she had seen him marry her cousin, and had lived under the same roof for years. No wonder she had grown a little mad. How mad?

I looked at the milk and a terrible suspicion came to me. On impulse I picked it up and, going to the window, threw it out. Then I laughed at myself.

'Wedding eve dramatics!' I said aloud. 'You imagine that a poor little woman might try to poison you, to take revenge on the man she once loved – perhaps still does – because she cannot bear to see him marry.'

I opened the cupboard door and looked at my dress. Then I opened the box and fingered the veil.

After tomorrow, I thought, all doubts will be gone. We shall be together . . . until death do us part.

I was asleep almost immediately.

I must have dreamed that the ghost of Maybella came to me and stood by my bed. She took the veil and orange blossom from my head – for in the dream I was wearing it – and put there instead a veil with white satin ruching.

Then I heard a voice. It was Jessica's. 'You are ready now, Maybella. But remember it is only for a little while.'

I woke up and was clammy with sweat. In the first few seconds of waking I thought Maybella had indeed returned from the grave to warn me, for there before me was the wedding veil with white satin ruching; and it was a moment or two before I saw that it was draped over the figurine on my dressing table.

I got out of bed and went over to it.

It was the veil of which Jessica had talked. She must have brought it down after I was asleep. I looked at my bedside table. Yes, the glass which had contained the milk had gone.

I took up the veil and looked at it. There was an odour of mothballs surrounding it. I supposed Jessica had treasured it all the intervening years since Maybella had taken the vows which I was about to take tomorrow . . . no, it would be today.

What an old ghoul she was!

I laughed, draped the veil back over the figurine and went back to bed. I slept deeply until Adelaide came in to wake me, bringing with her a cup of tea.

And that day I was married to Lynx.

Everything faded into insignificance but my life with Lynx. I had started on a voyage of discovery and had found new heights and depths of emotion which I had not known existed. Lynx had drawn me away from everyday existence. I was living on another plane.

I said to him: 'You have carried me with you up to Mount Olympus. I feel like a goddess now.'

He loved me, he said, and no one before had ever been loved as I was.

I could believe it. There was no room for anything in my life but the magical presence of Lynx. We rode together; we took meals alone in the library, we even played chess once or twice but he never allowed me to win.

I was gay and lighthearted, and so was he. He was a different man from the one I had first seen in this house; there seemed to be a glow about him – but perhaps that was because I was looking at him through the eyes of love. Once I awoke in the night after a bad dream and for a few moments thought I had lost him. I cried out in fear. And there he was bending over me, his arms about me.

'I thought you'd gone,' I said. 'I thought I'd lost you.'

I heard his laughter in the darkness, exultant, triumphant. I, who had been reluctant to marry him, was now in a cold sweat of terror for a few moments because I had dreamed I had lost him.

The house seemed different. I loved it. I wanted to live in it for ever and make it my home. Adelaide would have made no objections. I could make any changes, have anything I wished, provided it did not clash with Lynx's desires.

'I will refurnish the drawing-room,' I said. 'I would like yellow curtains – but not too bright a yellow.'

'I know,' said Adelaide, 'the colour of gold.'

'Not gold,' I cried. 'The colour of sunshine.'

I wouldn't think about the future. The present offered everything I wanted. *Now* was the important time – not yesterday, not tomorrow.

'Although,' went on Adelaide, 'since you are going away, will you want to refurnish?'

'I don't want to go away, Adelaide.'

'It will be exciting for you.'

'Stirling won't want to leave everything here.'

'Stirling will want to do as his father wishes.' She was looking at me and gently implying: And so must you.

I thought about it: to leave for England with Lynx and Stirling, to leave this wonderful world which I had just discovered to start on a voyage of discovery. Whiteladies . . . that girl on the lawn . . . the older woman. My husband could be a little fanatical with his plotting and planning. I would make him see reason, I promised myself again; but not yet. I was not going to spoil this honeymoon period with the clash of opinions which must inevitably occur.

I said nothing to Lynx of leaving the country. We laughed; we bantered; we were serious; we made love in many moods – light-hearted, tender, abandoned and passionate. I would not have believed there could be so many moods.

I was happy, saying: This is *now*. There has never been such a perfect time. Nothing must spoil it. I must cling to it, make it last for ever.

But nothing lasts for ever.

How tiresome people could be! It seemed that Jessica was deliberately trying to spoil my pleasure in life. When I passed her open door one day she called me into her room and I could not refuse to go although I should have loved to.

She was sitting in front of her mirror trying on my wedding veil.

'Where did you get it?' I asked.

'Ah, you didn't miss it, did you? I just wanted to try it on.'

She looked incongruous with her wild eyes and pale skeleton-like face; and she seemed to read my thoughts for she said: 'I look like the bride in "The Mistletoe Bough". You know the story. She hid in a trunk and was locked in. They found her years later.'

'What a gruesome story!'

'I used to sing that song.'

I thought: Trust you!

'Perhaps it was as well for the bride that she was locked in the trunk.'

'What a thing to say!'

'Slow suffocation, I suppose. But she would soon be overcome by the lack of air. It wouldn't take long. Better than a lifetime of suffering. I can't tell you how Maybella suffered with her miscarriages.'

I turned away. I did not want to think of my husband's first marriage. I knew it had been a marriage of convenience for him. I made excuses for him – a proud man, a captive, wrongly accused; marriage was his only means of escape. I was glad that it had been such a marriage. I wanted no one else to have shared this passion which swept me along as though I were caught in a whirlwind.

Jessica took off the orange blossom and veil and underneath was the one with the satin ruching. She had been wearing the two.

I said accusingly: 'You put that in my room the night before my wedding.'

'Yes, I knew you'd like to have it.'

I thought: She prowls about my room on her own admission. I felt angry with her for prying; and then her helplessness struck me as pitiable and my anger subsided.

She was folding the veils carefully.

'I shall keep them both,' she said. 'I have a lovely sandalwood box. There's plenty of room in it.' She looked at me obliquely. What was she implying? That one day there would be three veils in the box?

But I refused to be affected by a foolish woman whose mind was clearly not well balanced.

I left her and went into the library. Lynx was there, his eyes agleam with pleasure at the sight of me.

Lynx and I went to Melbourne in style. We drove in the special carriage he had had made for himself and we changed horses every ten miles at the coaching inns. He drove part of the way himself, and then how we sped along!

We lived in the grand suite in his hotel, and I was alone some part of the day when he was doing business. I was surprised that he did not take me with him but I realized later that it was because his business concerned his leaving Australia, and knowing my feelings about this, he did not wish to spoil our holiday.

We dined in our private suite and I was so happy that I refused to listen to the voice within which told me that there was another reason for this visit than simple pleasure.

But holiday it was. In the mornings we drove into the nearby country, out to Richmond and beyond along the Yarra Yarra, almost out to the Dandenong country. We went to concerts and to the theatre. Lynx was, of course, well known in Melbourne and there were many invitations, most of which he declined; but he did give an evening's entertainment at the hotel and the big dining-room was turned into a banqueting hall. There was supper and a concert to follow when a new pianist, who was much admired in Europe, was making his début in Australia.

Wearing a white satin dress, my only ornament a diamond brooch and a ring with one enormous diamond, I stood beside him and received our guests. I was proud because I could see the great respect he inspired was not with his family only.

We were congratulated. I knew that eyebrows were raised because I was so much younger than he was. I wanted to explain to them that age was of no importance, particularly where Lynx was concerned. Lynx was ageless; I felt convinced then that he would live for ever – long after I was dead.

I sat listening to the pianist. Those haunting Chopin melodies would always remind me of this evening. There was something sad and wistful about them; I felt that they implied the transience of joy and happiness, the inevitable disillusion. How absurd! It was due to Jessica with her veils and boxes that I should have such thoughts.

Now he had gone into the Military Polonaise. That was stirring and lively and my spirits were lifted.

I heard two women whispering together.

'Lavish! No expense spared.'

'Expense! This is nothing, He's many times a millionaire.'

'What luck! Trust him to get it. And so much.'

'Now he's got this young girl *and* his fortune.'

I shouldn't listen. I wished I hadn't such acute ears. I was sure I heard someone say: 'Do you think it will last?' And I shivered because it seemed as though Jessica was beside me, folding her veils neatly into a box in which there was plenty of room for more.

I was not in the least shy of these people. Since my marriage, I had changed. I had become a woman of the world; I was desired; I was loved by a man who could not enter a room without every eye being turned on him. I could say to myself: 'And he chose me!' And that made me hold my head higher. In my white satin gown I felt perfectly groomed and at ease. Perhaps I looked more than my nineteen years, but that was unimportant since I was the wife of Lynx. I was constantly catching his eye and we exchanged looks of understanding. I wanted him to be proud of me.

I mingled with the guests. We talked of Melbourne and how it had grown since I had arrived in Australia. I discussed the new buildings, the shops and the theatre.

'I hope you will come into Melbourne more often, Mrs. Herrick,' said one woman. 'There is plenty of time before next February.'

I was not quite sure what she meant and I repeated 'February?'

'Isn't that when you are leaving us? Your husband was saying that he thought it would be better to arrive in England during the warm weather.'

'Oh yes,' I said, 'of course.'

'And how excited you must be! I hope you will come back some day. But England was quite recently your home, wasn't it? So it will not be new to you.'

I was not listening. So he had arranged the date of leaving and he had not told me. I felt angry because once more as in the days before our marriage he had shown me that although he would indulge me in unimportant matters of our life, the big issues would be decided by him.

He said: 'What a success you were! I was proud of you. You looked very different from the school teacher who arrived in our midst two years ago.'

I was silently standing before the long mirror and he came and put his arms about me, looking over my head at our reflection.

'I hear you have made arrangements for us to leave for England,' I said stonily.

'Oh, that's it! Did one of those fools tell you? It must have been the Adams woman. Really, Adams should not discuss his client's business with his wife.'

'The fact remains that you have made these arrangements.'

'I like to get everything in hand.'

'That's in five or six months' time, then.'

'I thought you would like to arrive in good weather.'

'That,' I retorted, 'was extremely considerate of you.'

'My darling knows I always consider her comforts.'

I stared at his reflection in the mirror. 'Since we are falling into this irritating habit of discussing her as though she is not present, she will say that she would like her wishes to be considered as assiduously as her comforts.'

'It is my pleasure to give in to those wishes whenever possible.'

'Which means when they don't inconvenience you at all.'

'It's this ridiculous matter of leaving the country. I'm surprised at you, Nora. This town – which I admit is growing and will doubtless be a very fine place in due course – can't be compared with home.'

'I want to stay here,' I said. I turned to him pleadingly. 'Please, I know that it is best for us to stay here.'

'How can you know such things? You talk as though you're a prophetess.'

'I know why you're going to England.'

'I am taking my family there because there they can live in a manner suited to their . . .'

'Fortune,' I said. 'Which was founded by me.'

'My clever Nora! I'll never forget that day you came in and held out the nugget to me. You looked scared as though you had behaved in some reprehensible manner.'

'I wish . . .' I began. But it wasn't true that I wished I hadn't found gold. I was glad now even, as I ever was, that I had been the one to make the miraculous discovery.

He had become tender suddenly as though my discovery of gold gave me the privilege of being stupid about other matters. 'Nora, leave everything to me.'

'I daresay it would please you to have a stupid wife who said, "Yes, yes, you are wonderful. You are always right. Do just as you wish and I will go on saying how right and clever you are." '

He burst out laughing. Then he shook his head at me. 'It's no use, Nora. We're going.'

'And when we get there we are going to acquire Whiteladies by evil hook or wicked crook.'

'How beautifully you express it.'

'So you are determined. Oh, Lynx, why do you want that house? Let's get another house nearby if you like that part of the country. Or we could build our own.'

His face had hardened. He was like the man I had met when I first came. There was a certain coldness in his manner towards me which frightened me and which wounded me more than I had thought possible.

'This is something you don't understand,' he said. 'We are going to England, and when we get there I shall decide what we are going to do.'

'You mean I have no say in it?'

I turned away and walked to the window. I was fighting the impulse to give way, to say: 'I will do as you wish. I only want you to go on loving me.' But that would be false to myself. He had loved me for myself in the beginning. I had not been afraid of him then; I would not be now.

'I mean,' he said, 'that you will be sensible as you usually are and realize that you know nothing of this matter and be happy to leave it to me.'

I turned to him and ran into his arms. 'Then tell me,' I said. 'Tell me everything.'

There was a sofa in the room; he sat down and drew me to him. I lay against him while he began to talk of those long ago days. I had heard it before but I don't think I ever fully realized before the depth of degradation he had plumbed nor how deeply the bitterness had entered his soul. He was going to own that house; the wound festered still; this was the only balm which could heal it.

'Need it be?' I asked. 'It's changed, hasn't it? You have me now.'

'I have you,' he agreed, 'and when I have Whiteladies I shall be completely content.'

'Am I not enough?'

'You give me all I hoped for in human relationships. You are my precious jewel. But I need a setting for you and only one will satisfy me.'

'I would be quite happy in a different setting.'

'But I would not.'

'Because I do not believe this is the right setting for me.'

'How can you know?'

I lifted my head and looked at him fiercely. 'I do know. I am certain of it. Revenge is an evil thing. It hurts people. There is no happiness to be gained by hurting others. Oh, Lynx, you have given me so much. You have changed me. You have taught me how to grow up and I love you with all my heart. I ask this one thing of you. Give up this wild plan.'

'It's the only thing you could ask which I can't give you.'

'But, Lynx, we are together. We have our lives. A house is only bricks and mortar.'

'It can be a symbol.'

'You are rich. You could buy a great house . . . a stately home of your own. There must be some for sale in England.'

'You say you do not wish to go to England.'

'Should I care where we were if we were together?'

'My dearest girl,' he said tenderly.

And because of his softened mood, I went on: 'It is revenge and hatred that I am afraid of. There is no happiness through them. If you acquired this house you would never be happy there.'

'Nonsense!' he said sharply.

'How could you be, knowing you have turned out the rightful owners.'

'For precisely that reason. And they would no longer be the rightful owners. I should. Don't let's speak of it any more. You will see for yourself when you are there.'

'I don't believe in shelving a subject and pretending it doesn't exist just because it is unpleasant.'

He yawned. My common sense told me to drop the subject, to accept what he had planned and perhaps later do my best to heal this terrible wound which he had kept open all these years. But some persistence drove me on.

'There is something petty about it,' I insisted.

'Petty!' he cried. 'What nonsense are you talking?'

'It's like visiting the sins of the fathers on the children.'

'My God, Nora, you've become like some ranting missionary.'

'I only know that it is not only wrong to nurse a grievance, it's also folly.'

'And you call seven years' degrading captivity a grievance?'

'It doesn't matter what suffering there was . . .'

'Certainly not to those who didn't have to endure it.'

'I didn't mean it that way.'

'Do you know what you do mean? Listen, Nora. I'm losing my patience.'

'And I'm in danger of losing mine.'

He laughed, not in the pleasant happy way to which I had become accustomed, but disagreeably. His face hardened and his eyes glinted; he squared his shoulders and looked invincible.

'Perhaps,' he said, 'it is time you and I came to an understanding. You have to realize that I am master in my own house.'

'Does that mean that I am not to speak unless spoken to?'

'I shall always be glad for you to speak when you have something sensible to say. But you must understand without delay that I expect obedience from my wife.'

This was not like the lover I had known. This was the arrogant man of whom I had been aware and resented when I first came to Australia. No, I thought. I shall not be the meek wife he wants. I shall be myself and if I have an opinion I am not going to deny it simply because he doesn't share it. He might have his desires for revenge with which he was not going to allow me to interfere – well, I had my integrity, my determination to preserve myself as an individual, and much as I loved him, much as my being called out for a return to the old tenderness. I was not going to pay the price he was asking for it.

I said: 'If you imagine you will get a meek yes from me to everything you say you have made a mistake. In fact I am beginning to think that our marriage may have been a mistake.'

'You are in a frivolous mood tonight,' he said lightly. 'Your success with the ladies and gentlemen of Melbourne has gone to your head.'

'I am completely serious and this has nothing to do with the ladies and gentlemen of Melbourne. It is a matter between us two. I will not agree with all your views. I cannot regard you as my lord and master whose word must be law and whose opinion is always right because he is a man and I am a woman.'

'Did I ever ask you to be such an insipid fool?'

'It seems you are telling me that is what you expect.'

'Which shows how illogical you are. You know I like to hear your opinions, but I will not have you dictating to me on matters of major importance. I've had enough of this. Let's go to bed.'

But I stood my ground firmly. I knew that we could not dismiss the matter as simply as that. It would be a continual irritation between us. I could see it building up to a great barrier.

'I must discuss this with you.'

'I have said I have nothing to discuss.'

'So you plan to go to England, to acquire Whiteladies and not talk it over with me.'

'If you are going to be sensible . . .'

'That's what I am trying to be. I know this is wrong.'

'Stop talking rubbish.' He caught my arm. 'You look so pretty tonight. The dress is most becoming.'

He started to unhook it but I swung away from him.

'No,' I said. 'I will not be treated in this way.'

I ran into the dressing-room. He was startled and I had locked the door before he reached it. There were tears in my eyes. At least I had prevented his seeing them. I had a feeling that he would despise tears.

It's changed, I thought. The honeymoon is over. My relationship with him was not what I had thought it to be.

I sat down on the small bed and thought about Stirling. Did he really love me? Yes! I answered myself. Remember when we lay in the cave. But his father had said: 'Stand aside. I want her.' So Stirling stood aside. And now Lynx was saying to me: 'You will do as I say. You will take your share in my grand plan for revenge.' And although my brain said: 'It is wrong and no good can come of it,' my heart was crying out: 'What does it matter? You will be with him and he will go on loving you. But if you defy him . . .'

And there was a vision of Jessica holding the sandalwood box in her hands. 'Plenty of room . . .'

Oh yes, the honeymoon was over.

I had spent a sleepless night. I had lain on that uncomfortable bed, having removed my satin dress, hoping that he would knock at the door and beg me to come out. But he did not. It was I who unlocked the door next morning.

He was sitting in a chair reading when I went in. I was in my petticoat, carrying my satin dress.

'Ah,' he said, 'the woman of principles.' His mood had changed. He was no longer angry and the tenderness had come back in spite of the words. 'I trust, madam,' he went on, 'that you had a comfortable night.'

'Hardly that,' I retorted, catching his mood.

'Remorse?'

'A very hard mattress.'

'And you prefer a feather bed.'

'In certain circumstances.'

He laughed. 'My poor child! What a brute I am! I should have insisted that you leave your hard mattress, but you were so full of determination to defend the rights of women and freedom of decision – so what could I do?'

'Nothing. You knew I was determined at all costs.'

'Now you wish to bathe and dress. While you are doing so I will order breakfast to be sent up to us. Are you agreeable to this or would you like to put forward your suggestions?'

'I am perfectly agreeable.'

I was happy. It was not the end. I had been foolish. I must be less blatant. I must persuade him gently, subtly.

We sat at the table which had been wheeled in. I poured out coffee while he served bacon and devilled kidneys from the chafing dishes. There was a cosy intimacy about the scene which made me happy.

'Now,' he said, 'we'll discuss this matter in a civilized manner. We have a difference of opinion. I say that we are going to England and our children will play on the lawns of Whiteladies. My grandchildren will be there with my son and daughter, for Stirling will marry and Adelaide will join us in due course. Whiteladies is not yet in my possession. It maybe a little difficult to arrange, but I always enjoyed surmounting difficulties. Now you, Nora, have your own puritan ideas. To settle old scores seems pagan to you. "An eye for an eye," say I. You say. "Turn the other cheek." But this is my affair. I have to fight for Whiteladies and I shall have an opponent in my own family – my wife. It's a situation which appeals to me.'

'So you are going to England.'

'*We* are going to England.'

'And you are going to acquire this house.'

'By wicked crook or evil hook, remember. And if you are going to stop me – well, Nora, that gives an added fillip to the affair. You are going to show me why I should not acquire Whiteladies. I am going to show you why I should.'

'So you are not going to put from you a wife who does not mildly agree that you are always right?'

'Of what use would such a creature be to me? All things considered, I am reasonably satisfied with my Nora. She can be obstinate at times; she can be arrogant; but what maddens me most is this piety of hers, that missionary spirit . . .'

'And what maddens me,' I said, 'is my husband's irritating habit of talking in my presence as though I am absent.'

'Then we both madden each other, which is as it should be.'

'And you have decided graciously to pardon a wife who doesn't think her husband omnipotent and omniscient?'

'I have come to the conclusion that I love the girl and that means I'll endure a great deal. In fact I am looking forward to some sturdy battles with Nora preaching turn the other cheek; and all the time I shall be showing her how happy she can be in her English mansion.'

'I shall never agree with you.'

'I know,' he said. 'Well, we'll start our journey back today. We have our preparations to make.'

'Preparations . . .'

'For England and the battle between us.'

We left Melbourne that day. There was a compromise between us. I would plunge into my preparations; we were leaving for England in March of the following year, it had been decided – Stirling, Lynx and myself, plus the servants we should need. I would make no objections to these preparations. My task was to persuade Lynx to abandon his plan for taking Whiteladies when the time came.

He never told me what his plans were. I believe he told Stirling. I felt a little shut out; but I stifled that resentment. I was determined that we were not going to take Whiteladies from its owners. Not that I saw how we could. These were not medieval times when castles were taken by force. I would persuade Lynx to buy the house that I wanted. I visualized it – grand and gracious. It would have to satisfy him. But whenever I pictured it it always took the form of Whiteladies.

We were approaching the end of summer and the winds were both cool and fierce. I would hear them whistling across the bush; they rattled our windows and buffeted the house as though they were trying to tear up its foundations.

When I rode out, usually with Lynx, sometimes with Adelaide, never with Stirling whom I now rarely saw, I would shudder at the damage which the fires had done, although many of the trees were not entirely dead and in due course would recover.

Lynx and I had returned to our old relationship, though perhaps we bantered more than we had just after our wedding. He liked to argue with me and enjoyed my having a different point of view. This delighted me. I ceased to fret over his obsession with revenge, for I was certain that I could turn him from it.

We had by no means shelved the matter. We often talked of Whiteladies – but he never explained to me how he hoped to wrest it from its owners.

How suddenly violent life could be in this country! Death was never far away.

That bright sunny morning I was riding out with him to the mine. We were not alone. Stirling was with us, also two or three of the men from the mine. Lynx had recently sold out most of his share and was keeping only a small interest.

'It's the time to sell,' he had explained. 'We've had most of the gilt off the gingerbread though there's still a considerable amount in those quartz reefs. It'll be worked for some years yet.'

He was getting rid of most of his interests in Australia because he was determined never to come back. Adelaide would stay behind for a few months and then would sell up the house and join us. It was all settled.

The sun was warm on that morning but the wind was piercingly fresh and of almost gale force. Lynx rode on ahead of our little party with the men from the mine. Stirling and I were some short distance behind. It was the first time I had been alone with Stirling since my marriage – if one could call this being alone.

'Are you happy about going to England, Stirling?' I asked.

He said he was, and I felt angry with him. He had no will but his father's.

'You are happy about leaving all this?' I persisted.

'And you?'

'At least I have been here a comparatively short time. It is home to you.'

'It'll be all right in England.'

We had come to that spot where Jacob Jagger had lost his life. There seemed to be something eerie about it now. The ghost gums rose high and imperiously indifferent; some of the trees were blackened. So the fire had scorched this spot too. Perhaps, I thought, that is how places become haunted. A man died there . . . suddenly his life was brought to an end in a moment of passion. Could his spirit remain for ever, seeking revenge?

Stirling was glancing at me. Was he, too, thinking of Jagger?

'So the fire got as far as this,' I said; and my words were carried on the wind as it whistled past me.

Then it happened. The great branch fell from the top of the tallest eucalypt. There was a sudden cry as it swooped like an arrow from the sky.

Then I saw Lynx; he had fallen from his horse and was lying on the ground.

I heard someone cry: 'My God, it's a widow-maker.'

They carried him home on an improvised stretcher. How tall he looked – taller in death even than in life! He had died as one of the gods of old might have died – from a falling branch which had descended with such force that it had driven itself through his heart, impaling and pinning him to the ground. And it had happened there, not far from the spot where he had deliberately shot Jacob Jagger.

The widow-maker had caught him as it had caught lesser men before him.

I could not believe it. I went to the library. I touched the chessmen; I took his ring with the lynx engraved on it and I stared at it until it seemed as though it were his eyes which looked at me in place of those glittering stones.

Lynx . . . dead! But he was immortal. I was stunned. I felt as though I myself were dead.

Stirling came to see me and it was then that I was able to shed my pent-up tears. He held me in his arms and we were as close as we had been in the cave when the fire had raged above us.

'We must go to England,' he said. 'It was what he would wish.'

I shuddered and replied: 'He would not wish us to go, Stirling. What good could that do? *He* wanted to go, but that is impossible now. It's over.'

But Stirling shook his head and said: 'He wished us to go. We shall leave as we should have done had he been here.'

I thought then that Lynx was living on to govern our lives. Subconsciously I had always believed that death could not touch him. Perhaps that was so.

MINTA

Chapter One

Tonight as I sat in my room looking down on the lawn I decided that I would write down what had happened. To do so would be to keep the memory of the days with me for ever. One forgets so quickly; impressions become hazy; one's mind distorts, colouring events to make them as one would like them to have been, high-lighting what one wants to preserve, pushing away what one would rather not remember. So I would keep a sort of journal and write down everything truthfully and unvarnished just as it took place.

What prompted me to do this was that afternoon's adventure, the day Stirling came. It was ridiculous really. He had come briefly into my life and there was no reason why he should appear again. It was absurd to feel this urge to write down what had happened. It was an ordinary enough incident. I knew his name was Stirling and the girl's was Nora because they had addressed each other so – perhaps only once, but my mind had been receptive. I was more than usually alert, so I remembered every detail.

Her scarf had blown over the wall and they came to retrieve it. I had a notion that the incident was contrived. A foolish thought really. Why should it have been?

I was on the lawn with Lucie and it was one of Mamma's more fretful days. Poor Mamma, she would never be happy, I knew. She was looking back into a past which could not have been so wonderful as she made it out to be. It seemed that she had missed great happiness. One day she would tell me about it. She had promised to do so.

Lucie and I sat on the lawn. Lucie was working at her tapestry; she was making covers for one of the chairs in the dining-room. My father had dropped his cigar ash on the seat of one of these and burned a hole in the tapestry, which had been worked in 1701. How like Lucie to decide that she would copy the Jacobean design and provide a cover which would be indistinguishable from the rest. In her quiet way Lucie was clever and I was so glad that she was with us. Life would have been very dull without her. She could do most things; she could help my father with his work; she would read the latest novel or from the magazines and newspapers to Mamma; and she was a companion for me. I was marvelling at the similarity of her work to the existing chair seats.

'It's almost exact,' I cried.

'Almost!' she replied in dismay. 'That won't do. It has to be exact in every detail.'

'I'm sure we shall all be satisfied with something slightly less.' I comforted. 'Who is going to peer into it for discrepancies?'

'Some people might . . . in the future.' Lucie's eyes grew dreamy. 'I want people a hundred years hence to look at that chair and say, "Which was the one which was done towards the end of the nineteenth century?" '

'But why?'

Lucie was a little impatient. 'You don't deserve to belong to this house, Minta,' she scolded. 'Think what it means. You can trace your family back to the Tudors' day and beyond. You have this wonderful heritage . . . Whiteladies! And you don't seem to appreciate it.'

'Of course I love Whiteladies, Lucie, and I'd hate to live anywhere else, but it's only a house after all.'

'Only a house!' She raised her eyes to the top of the chestnut tree. 'Whiteladies! Five hundred years ago nuns lived their sheltered lives here. Sometimes I imagine I hear the bells calling them to compline, and at night I fancy I hear their voices as they say their prayers in their cells and the swish of their white robes as they mount the stone staircases.'

I laughed at her. 'Why, Lucie, you care more for the place than any of us.'

'You've just taken it for granted,' she cried vehemently and her mouth was grim. I knew she was thinking of that little house in a grimy town in the Black Country. She had told me about it, and when I thought of that I could understand her love for Whiteladies; and I was so glad that she was with us. In fact she had made me appreciate the home which had been in my family for hundreds of years.

It was I who had brought Lucie into the house. She had taught English literature and history at the boarding-school to which I had been sent, and she had taken rather special care of me during my first months there. She had helped to alleviate the inevitable homesickness; she taught me to adjust myself and be self-reliant; all this she had done in her unobtrusive manner. During my second term we had been told to write an essay on an old house we had visited and naturally I chose Whiteladies. She was interested and asked me where I had seen this house. 'I live in it,' I answered; and after that she often questioned me about it. When the summer holidays came and the rest of us were so excited about going home, I noticed how sad she was and I asked her where she was spending the vacation. She had no family, she told me. She expected she would try to get a post with some old lady. Perhaps she would travel with her. When I said impulsively, 'You should come to Whiteladies!' her delight was touching.

So she came and that was the beginning. In those days the tiresome subject of money was never mentioned. The house was large; there were many unoccupied rooms and we had plenty of servants. Often we had a house full, so Lucie Maryan was just one more. But there was a difference. She made herself so useful. Mamma liked her voice and she did not tire easily; she could listen to Mamma's accounts of her ailments with real sympathy, for she knew a great deal about illnesses and could entertain Mamma with accounts of people who had suffered in various ways. Even my father became interested in her. He was writing a biography of a famous ancestor who had distinguished himself under Marlborough at Oudenarde, Blenheim and Malplaquet. In his study were letters and papers which had been found in a trunk in one of the turrets. He used to say, 'It's a lifetime's work. I often wonder if I shall live long enough to complete it.' I suspected that he dozed most of the afternoon and evening when he was supposed to be working.

On the first visit I remember Lucie's walking with Papa under the trees in the grounds, discussing those battles and Marlborough's relationship with his wife and Queen Anne. My father was delighted with her knowledge and before the end of the visit he had accepted her help in sorting out some of the letters and papers.

That was the beginning. After that it became a matter of course that Lucie should spend her holidays with us. She was so interested in Whiteladies itself that she urged my father to write a study of the house. This appealed to him and he declared that as soon as he had finished with General Sir Harry Dorian he would begin his researches on the history of Whiteladies.

Lucie was passionately fascinated by his work; and I was amused that Papa and Lucie should be so much more interested in the house than Mamma and myself, when my father had merely married into it and Lucie was not connected with it at all.

When I left school my mother suggested that Lucie joined us. We knew what her circumstances were; she was alone in the world, forced to earn her own living; and life at school was not easy. There was so much she could do at Whiteladies.

So Lucie was paid a salary and became a member of our household; we were all fond of her and she was so useful that we could not imagine what we should do without her. She had no specific duties – she was my father's secretary, my mother's nurse and my companion; moreover she was the friend of us all.

I was seventeen on that day when Stirling and Nora came; Lucie was twenty-seven.

One of the servants had brought Mamma's chair into the garden and Lucie put down her work and went over to it. We had chosen a pleasant spot near the Hermes pond under a tree for shade. Mamma could walk quite easily but she liked her invalid's chair and used it frequently. I sat idly watching Lucie wheel Mamma across the lawn, wondering whether it was one of her peevish days. One could often tell by the expression on her face. Oh dear, I thought, I do hope not. It's such a lovely day.

'Do make sure we're not in the sun,' said Mamma. 'It gives me such a headache.'

'This is a very shady spot, Mamma,' I told her.

'The light is so bright today.' Yes, it was one of her bad days.

'I will place your chair so that the light is not on your face, Lady Cardew,' said Lucie.

'Thank you, Lucie.'

Lucie brought the chair to a standstill and Jeffs, the butler, appeared with Jane, the parlourmaid, who carried the tray on which was bread and butter, scones with jam and honey, and fruit cake.

Lucie busied herself with making Mamma comfortable and I sat at the table waiting for one of the servants to bring out the tray with the silver teapot and spirit lamp. When it came I poured out the tea, which Mamma said was too strong. Lucie immediately watered it and Mamma sat sipping in silence. I understood. Her thoughts were in the past.

I glanced at the house. The window on the first floor which belonged to my father's study was open a little. There he would be sitting at his desk, papers spread out round him, dozing I could be certain. He never liked to be disturbed when working; secretly I suspected he was afraid someone would catch him sleeping. Dear Papa, he was never cross with anyone. He was the most easy-going man in the world; he was even patient with Mamma, and it must have required a great deal of forbearance to be constantly reminded that she regretted her marriage.

'Lucie,' she was saying now, 'I want an extra cushion for my back.'

'Yes, Lady Cardew. I think I'll go indoors for one of the larger ones. In any case I'm always afraid the garden ones may be a little damp.'

Mamma nodded and as Lucie went off she murmured: 'She's such a good creature.'

I didn't like Lucie's being referred to as a 'creature'. I was so fond of her. I watched her walking across the grass – rather tall, very straight-backed, her dark hair smoothed down on either side and made into a knot at the nape of her neck. She wore dark colours – mulberry today – and they became her rather olive skin; she had a natural elegance so that not very expensive clothes looked quite modish on her.

'She's a good friend to us all,' I said with slight reproof. I was the only one who occasionally reproved Mamma. My father, hating any sort of fuss, was invariably gentle and placating. I have known him take endless trouble to avoid the smallest unpleasantness. And Lucie, because after all she was employed – a fact which my father and I always strove to make her forget – was quick to respond to my mother's whims, for she was proud and determined that her job should be no sinecure.

'Good heavens, Lucie,' I often said, 'you needn't fear that. You are guide, comforter and friend to us and all for the price of a housekeeper!'

Lucie's reply to that was: 'I shall always be grateful for being allowed to come here. I hope you will never regret taking me in.'

Mamma was saying that the wind was cold and the sun too hot and that the headache she had awakened with had grown worse throughout the day. Lucie came back with the cushion and settled it behind Mamma, who thanked her languidly.

Then they were coming across the lawn. They looked a little defiant as indeed they might, being uninvited and unannounced. He was tall and dark; she was dark, too – not exactly pretty but there was a vitality about her which was obvious as soon as one saw her, and that was very attractive.

'Good afternoon,' said Stirling, 'we have come to get my ward's scarf.'

It seemed an odd announcement. It struck me as strange that he should be her guardian. I thought she was about my age and he perhaps Lucie's. Then I noticed the green scarf lying on the grass. She said something about its blowing from her neck and sailing over the wall.

'By all means . . .' I began. Mamma was looking on in astonishment;

Lucie was unruffled. Then I noticed that the girl's hand was bleeding and I asked if she were hurt. She had grazed it, she told me. It was nothing. Lucie said it should be dressed and she would take her to Mrs. Glee's room where they could bandage it.

There was some protest but eventually Lucie took the girl to Mrs. Glee and I was left alone with Stirling and Mamma.

I asked if they would like tea and he declared his pleasure. He was greatly interested in the house. He was different from any man I knew, but then I knew so few. I was, I suppose, comparing him with Franklyn Wakefield. There could not have been two men less like. I asked him where he lived and was astonished when he said Australia.

'Australia,' said Mamma, leaning forward a little in her chair. 'That's a long way off.'

'Twelve thousand miles or thereabouts.'

There was something very breezy and likeable about him and the intrusion had lifted the afternoon out of its customary monotony.

'Have you come here to stay?' I asked.

'No, I shall be sailing away the day after tomorrow.'

'So soon!' I felt a ridiculous dismay.

'My ward and I leave on the *Carron Star*,' he said. 'I came over to escort her back. Her father has died and we are adopting her.'

'That's very . . . exciting,' I said foolishly.

'Do you think so?' His smile was ironic and I flushed. I feared he was thinking me rather stupid. He was no doubt comparing me with his ward who looked so lively and intelligent.

Mamma asked him about Australia. What was it like. Where did he live? She knew someone who had gone there years ago.

That was interesting, said Stirling. What was the name of the settler she had known?'

'I . . . er can't remember,' said Mamma.

'Well, it's a big place.'

'I often wonder . . .' began Mamma and then stopped.

He said he lived about forty miles north of Melbourne. Was it to Melbourne her friend had gone?

'I couldn't say,' said Mamma. 'I never heard.'

'Was it long ago?' he persisted. There was an odd quirk, about his mouth as though he were very interested and perhaps a little amused about Mamma's friend.

'I find it hard to remember,' said Mamma. Then she added quickly: 'It would be such a long time ago. Thirty years . . . or more.'

'You never kept in touch with your friend?'

'I'm afraid not.'

'What a pity! I might have been able to take him . . . or her . . . news of you.'

'Oh, it was long, long ago,' said Mamma, a little flushed and quite excited. I had never known her like this. Our unexpected visitor seemed to have affected us both strangely.

I gave him tea and noticed his strong brown fingers on the Crown Derby.

He smiled as he took the cup from me; there were wrinkles round his eyes, caused I supposed by the hot sun. I asked him questions about Australia and I was very interested in the property his people owned. There was a hotel, too, in Melbourne, and a gold mine.

'What exciting lives you must lead!' I said.

He admitted it; and for the first time I felt restive. It hadn't occurred to me before how uneventful life was at Whiteladies. Lucie was constantly implying that I should be grateful; he had the opposite effect on me. But it seemed that he, too, was fascinated by Whiteladies. He asked a great many questions about it and we were on this subject when the girl came back with Lucie. Her hand had been bandaged. I poured out tea for her and we continued to talk of the house.

Then Franklyn arrived. There was something very charming about Franklyn. He was so calm. I had known him all my life and never had I seen him ruffled. On the rare occasions when it was necessary for him to reprimand anyone or assert himself in some way, one felt he brought a judicial attitude to the matter and that it was done from a sense of the rightness of things rather than in anger. Some people might have called Franklyn dull. He was far from that.

The contrast between him and Stirling was marked. Stirling might have appeared clumsy if he had been a different kind of man; but Stirling was completely unaware of any disadvantage. He clearly was not impressed by the immaculate cut of Franklyn's suit – if he noticed it at all.

It was difficult to make introductions, so I explained to Franklyn that the scarf had blown over the wall and that they had come to retrieve it.

Then Nora rose and said they must be going and thanked us for our kindness. Stirling was a little put out, and I was pleased because he obviously would have liked to stay; but there was nothing I could do to detain them and Lucie went with them to the gates.

That was all. A trivial incident in a way and yet I could not get them out of my mind; and because I wanted to remember it exactly as it happened, I started this journal.

We sat on the lawn until half past five then my father came down. His hair was ruffled, his face slightly flushed. I thought: He's had a good sleep.

'How did the work go, Sir Hilary?' asked Lucie.

He smiled at her. When he smiled his face lit up and it was as though a light had been turned on behind his eyes. He loved talking about his work.

'It was hard going today,' he said. 'But I tell myself I'm at a difficult stage.'

Mamma looked impatient and Franklyn said quickly: 'There are, I believe, always these stages. If the work went too smoothly there might be a danger of its being facile.'

Trust Franklyn to say the right thing! He sat back in the garden chair looking immaculate, bland and tolerant of us all. I knew that Mamma and my father had decided that Franklyn would make a very good son-in-law. We would join up Wakefield Park and Whiteladies. It would be very convenient, for the two houses were moderately close and the grounds met.

Franklyn's people were not exactly rich but, as it was said, comfortable; and in any case we were not rich either. I believe that something had happened to our finances during the last two years, for whenever money was mentioned Papa would assume a studied vagueness which meant that this was a subject he did not wish to hear of because it bothered him.

However, it would be very convenient if Franklyn and I married. I had even come to regard this as an inevitability. I wondered whether Franklyn did too. He always treated me with a delightful courtesy; but then he extended this to everyone. I had seen the village postmistress flush with pleasure when he exchanged a few words with her. He was tall – all the Wakefields had been tall – and he managed his father's estate with tact and efficiency, being a very good landlord to all the tenants. But behind Franklyn's easy-going charm there was an aloofness. His eyes were slaty grey rather than blue; there was a lack of warmth in them and one felt that if he was never angry, he was never really delighted either. He was equable; and therefore, though a comforting person to be with, hardly an exciting one. Everything about him was conventional: his immaculate dress; his courteous manners; his well-ordered life.

These facts had not occurred to me before. It was because of those two people who had invaded my afternoon that I had begun this assessment. Well, they had gone. I never expected to see them again.

'Exactly,' Papa was saying. 'I always tell myself that I must accept this hard task for the sake of posterity.'

'I am sure,' added Franklyn, 'that you will complete it to the satisfaction of the present generation and those to come.'

My father was pleased, particularly when Lucie added earnestly: 'I am sure you will, too, Sir Hilary.'

Then Lucie and Franklyn began to talk with Papa, and Mamma yawned and said her headache was coming on again, so Lucie took her to her room where she would lie down before dinner.

'Franklyn, you'll dine with us?' said my father; and Franklyn graciously accepted.

Mamma did not appear for dinner. She sent for Lizzie, her maid, to rub eau-de-Cologne on her forehead. Dr. Hunter had been invited to dine with us but he would first spend half an hour or so with Mamma discussing her symptoms before joining us.

Dr. Hunter had come to us only two years ago and seemed young to have the responsibility of our lives and deaths, but perhaps that was because we compared him with old Dr. Hedgling whose practice he had taken over. Dr. Hunter was in his early thirties; he was a bachelor and had a housekeeper who was supposed to look after his material comforts. He was, I fancied, over anxious for our good opinion, while being aware that we considered him a trifle inexperienced. He was an amusing young man and Mamma liked him, which was an important point.

Dinner was quite lively. The young doctor had an amusing way of describing a situation and Franklyn could cap his stories often in a coolly witty manner. I was rather glad that Mamma had decided to have dinner sent up on a tray, for with her constant repetitions of her symptoms she could be a little tiresome and she most certainly would indulge in the recital of them if the doctor were present.

I think my father was pleased, too. He was always different when she was absent; it was almost as though he revelled in his freedom.

The doctor was talking of one or two of his patients, how old Betty Ellery who was bedridden refused to see what she called 'a bit of a boy'. 'While confessing to my youth,' said the doctor, 'I had to insist that my person was intact, and that I was whole and certainly not a bit of myself.'

'Poor Betty!' I said. 'She's been in bed since I was a little girl. I remember going to her with blankets every Christmas, plus a chicken and plum pudding. When the carriage pulled up at her door and we alighted, and she would cry out: "Come in, madam, and you're almost as welcome as the gifts you've brought." I used to sit solemnly in the chair beside her bed and listen to the stories she told of when Grandpapa Dorian was alive and Mamma used to go visiting with her Mamma.'

'The old customs remain,' said Franklyn.

'And a good thing, too, don't you agree, Franklyn?' asked my father.

Franklyn said that in some cases it was good to cling to the old customs; in others better to discard them. And so the conversation continued.

After dinner Lucie and the doctor sat talking earnestly while I chatted with Franklyn. I asked him what he thought of the people who had come that afternoon.

'The young lady of the scarf, you mean.'

'Both of them. They seemed unusual.'

'Did they?' Franklyn clearly did not think so and I could see that he had almost forgotten them. I felt faintly annoyed with him and turned to Lucie and the doctor. The doctor was talking about his housekeeper, Mrs. Devlin, whom he suspected of drinking more than sobriety demanded.

'I hope,' said Lucie, 'that you lock up your spirits.'

'My dear Miss Maryan, if I did I should lose the lady.'

'Would she be such a loss?'

'You clearly have no idea of the trials of a bachelor's existence when he is at the mercy of a couple of maids. Why, I should starve and my house would resemble a pigsty without the supervision of my Mrs. Devlin. I have to forgive her her love of strong drink for the sake of the comfort she brings into my life.'

I smiled at Franklyn. I wondered whether he was thinking the same as I was. Dear Lucie! She must be nearly thirty and if she were ever going to marry she should do it soon and what a good doctor's wife she would make! I could picture her dealing with the patients, helping him along. It was an ideal situation, although we should lose her, and what should we do without her? But we must not, of course, be selfish. This was Lucie's chance, and if she married the doctor, she would be living close to me for the rest of her life.

I turned to Franklyn. I was about to whisper that I thought it would be wonderful if Lucie and Dr. Hunter made a match; but one did not say things like that to Franklyn. He would think it bad taste to whisper of such a matter – or even talk of it openly – when it concerned only the two people involved. Oh dear, how tiresome he could be! And what a lot of fun he was missing in life!

I contrived it so that we talked in one group and Dr. Hunter told us some amusing stories of his life in hospital before he came to the district; and he was very entertaining. But he and Wakefield left soon after ten and we retired for the night.

When I went in to say good-night to my mother she was wide awake. There was a change in her.

She said: 'Sit down, Minta, and talk to me for a while, I shall never sleep tonight.'

'Why is that?' I asked.

'You know, Minta,' she said reproachfully, 'that I never sleep well.'

I thought then that we were going to have an account of her sufferings, but this was not so. She went on quickly: 'I feel I must talk to you. There is so much I have never told you. I hope, my child, that your life will be happier than mine.'

When I thought of her life with an indulgent husband, a beautiful home, servants to attend to every whim, and freedom to do everything she wanted – or almost – I could not agree that she was in need of commiseration. But, as always with Mamma, I made a pretence of listening. I'm afraid that my attention often wandered and I would murmur a sympathetic 'yes' or 'no' or 'how terrible' without really knowing what it was all about.

Then my attention was caught and held because she said: 'It was those people coming this afternoon that brought it all back. The man came from Australia. That was where *he* went all those years ago.'

'Who, Mamma?'

'Charles. I wish you could have known Charles. There was no one quite like him ever.'

'And who was he?'

'How could you say who Charles was? He came here as a drawing-master, my drawing-master. But he was more than that. I remember the day he arrived. I was in the schoolroom then. I was sixteen – younger than you are now. He was a few years older. He came in looking bold and arrogant – not in the least like a drawing-master and said: "Are you Miss Dorian? I've come to teach you." And he taught me so much, Minta, so very much.'

'Mamma,' I said, 'what made those people remind you of him?'

'Because they came from Australia and that was where he went – where they sent him. And that young man reminded me of him in a way. There was an air about him. Do you know what I mean? He didn't care what people thought of him. He knew he was as good – no, better – than anyone. Do you know what I mean?'

'Yes, I do.'

'It was cruel,' she went on. 'I hated your grandfather after that. Charles was innocent. As if he cared about my jewels! He wanted *me* . . . not what I could bring him. I'm sure of that, Minta.'

She had changed. The peevish invalid had disappeared. She even looked beautiful as she must have been years ago. I knew there was something significant about that visit this afternoon and I was enormously interested. 'Tell me about it,' I begged.

'Oh, my dear Minta, it seems like yesterday. I wish I could describe Charles to you.'

'You were in love with him, I suppose.'

'Yes,' she said. 'And I have been all my life.'

I felt this was disloyal to my father and I protested. 'Isn't that because he went out of your life when he was young and handsome and you've always seen him like that? If you could see him now you might have a terrible shock.'

'If I could see him now . . . ' Her eyes were dreamy. 'That young man reminded me so much . . . it brought it all back. Those days when we were in the schoolroom; and then he said we must work out of doors. We would sit under the chestnut tree . . . where we were sitting this afternoon and he would sketch the flowers or a bird and I would have to copy it. Then we went for walks together, studying wild life and trying to put it on paper. He used to talk about Whiteladies as Lucie does. It's strange how people are impressed by the house. He never tired of talking of it. And then we were in love and going to be married, and of course your grandfather would not allow it.'

'You were only about seventeen, Mamma. Perhaps you were carried away.'

'There are some things one can be sure of however young. I was sure of this. Once having known Charles, I was certain that no one else would ever mean to me what he did. He said we must not tell your grandfather, that he would forbid our marriage and something dreadful would happen, for your grandfather was a very powerful man. But he discovered what was going on. Someone must have told him, and Charles was dismissed. We planned to elope. My father was afraid of Charles for he knew he was no ordinary young man. I was guarded all the time but the notes were smuggled in and we made our arrangements. He climbed to my room on the night we were going away together. I gave him my jewellery to put in his pockets and keep for me while we climbed down.' Her lips began to tremble. 'We were betrayed. The jewellery was found on him and he was transported for seven years. Your grandfather was a hard man and my heart was broken.'

'Poor Mamma, what a sad story! But would you have been happy with him?'

'If you had ever known him you would understand. I could be happy with no one else. He thought that if we married, my father would forgive us in time. I was after all his only daughter. Our children would be his grandchildren. Charles used to say: "Our children will play on the lawns of Whiteladies, never fear." But they sent him away and I never saw him again. I shall never, never forget.'

I understood then the reason for all those peevish years. She believed life had cheated her. Her love for this man she had chosen had turned into discontent with the husband who had been chosen for her. I should have been more tolerant towards her. I should try to be now.

'And at the back of my mind,' she went on, in an unusually revelatory manner, 'I always thought there was something I should have done. I was my father's only child. I could have threatened to run away, to kill myself – anything. I believe now that if I had, something would have been done. But I was afraid of your grandfather and I let them take him away without protest and five years later I married your father because that was what my father wished.'

'Well, Mamma,' I reminded her, 'Papa is a very good man. And this drawing-master might not have been all you imagined him to be.'

'Life with him might not always have been easy, but it would have been wonderfully worth while. As it is . . . '

'You have a great deal to be thankful for, Mamma,' I reminded her again; and she smiled at me rather wanly.

'I was a little reconciled when you were born, Minta. But that was a long time after our marriage. I thought we should never have a child. Perhaps if you had arrived earlier . . . and then of course your birth had such an effect on my health.'

She was her wan self again recalling the terrible period of gestation, the fearful ordeal of my arrival. I had heard it before and was not eager to do so again.

'And because those people came this afternoon you were reminded of the past,' I said quickly.

'I wish I knew what happened to him, Minta. To be sent away as a convict. That proud man!'

'I daresay he was ingenious enough to find a niche for himself.'

She smiled. 'That was a thought I consoled myself with.'

There was a knock on the door and Lizzie came in. Lizzie was about a year or so older than my mother. She had been nurse to me and before that my mother's maid. She treated me still as though I were a baby and was more familiar with my mother than any of the servants were. She had thick grey hair which was a riot of curls about her head; it was her only beauty but striking enough even now to make people look twice at her.

'You're keeping your mother from her sleep, Miss Minta,' she said. 'I thought she was tired out.'

'We've been talking,' I said.

Lizzie clicked her tongue. 'I know.' She turned to my mother. 'Shall I settle you for the night?'

My mother nodded so I kissed her good night and went out.

As I shut the door I heard her say eagerly and with the rare excited note in her voice: 'When I saw that young man this afternoon, it took me back years. You remember how he used to sit on the lawn with his sketching pad . . . '

I went to my room. Lizzie would have been here at the time, I thought. She would have seen it all.

Poor Mamma! How dreadful to live one's life in discontent, constantly dreaming of what might have been.

I found it difficult to sleep. The afternoon visitors had affected me as they had my mother.

The memory of that visit stayed with me for days afterwards. I should have liked to discuss it with Lucie but I felt that what my mother had told me had been in confidence. There was a painting of her which had been done about two years after the abortive elopement and she certainly appeared very beautiful. I looked at it differently now and saw the haunting sadness in her eyes. I thought of Grandfather Dorian, whom I vaguely remembered as a great power in the house, whose gruff commands used to send shivers of alarm down my young spine. I could imagine how stern he would have been with his own daughter. He approved of Papa as a husband, of course. Papa had been a titled gentleman of some means and highly suitable; he would have been gentle and submissive and have agreed to take up residence at Whiteladies. He had had a house nearby and an estate in Somerset which had come into his family's possession in 1749 when they had sprung into prominence through their loyalty to the Hanoverian cause. After that they had begun to build their fortune. We used to visit Somerset sometimes twice a year, but Papa had sold the estate two years ago as he had his other house. It was expensive to run them and we needed the money, he said. I wondered how poor Mamma had felt when she knew she was to be married. But she must have known she had lost her Charles for ever. I wondered, too, whether she had made any pretence of loving Papa.

I was in the garden picking flowers for the vases when Dr. Hunter came out of the house. I called to him and he stood smiling at me.

'You have just been to see Mamma?' I asked. He said that he had, and I went on; I'd like to talk to you about her. Don't let her see us though. She may look out from the window. She would immediately imagine that we were discussing some terrible new disease she had contracted.'

'Why not show me the roses?' he suggested.

'A good idea, but better still, come into the pond garden. We'll be really out of sight there.'

The pond garden was surrounded by a pleasant alley which, in summer, made a luxuriantly green arch. I loved the pond garden; it seemed shut away from the rest of the house. I was sure that Mamma and her artist lover had sat there by the water making their plans, feeling shut away from the world. The flowers used to be much more colourful when I was a child. We had more people working in the garden then, and gardeners would change overnight the spring tints for the rich shades of summer. I remember particularly vivid blue delphiniums and the heavy scent of pinks and carnations – and later the bronze and purples of chrysanthemums and the unmistakable odour of the dying year. But now, because it was late summer, the flowers were plentiful. There was a white statue in the pond and waxen-petalled lilies floated on the water. This garden had been copied, Papa told me, two hundred years ago from that one in Hampton Court where it was said Henry VIII had walked with Anne Boleyn.

'How ill is my mother?' I asked the doctor.

'Her illness is within herself,' he answered.

'You mean imaginary?'

'Well, she does have her headaches. She does suffer from lassitude and vague pains.'

'You mean there is nothing really wrong with her.'

'Nothing organically wrong.'

'So her illness is in her mind and she could be better tomorrow if she wanted to.'

'It's not as simple as that. This is a genuine state of sickness.'

'Something happened recently. Some people came and reminded her of the past. She seemed almost young again.'

He nodded. 'She needs an interest in life. She needs to think of something other than herself, past excitements and present boredoms. That's all.'

'What can she be interested in, I wonder?'

'Perhaps when you marry and have grandchildren she will be so enchanted with them that she will find a new interest in life. Interest! That's what she wants.'

'I have no intention of marrying for a long time. Is she to wait for a cure until then?'

He laughed. 'We will do our best. She'll continue with her pills and medicines and find some relief from them.'

'But if she is not physically ill does she need medicine?'

'They are placebos. They help her because she believes in them. I'm sure that is how we have to treat her.'

'What a difficult task – to attempt to cure someone of something that doesn't exist!'

'But you are mistaken. This illness does exist. It is real. This is what I used to attempt to argue out with my predecessor. He believed that an illness was only an illness if it gave an outward and visible sign of being one. Don't worry, Miss Minta. We have your mother's case well in hand. Miss Maryan is very helpful, isn't she?'

'Lucie is wonderful.'

'Yes,' said the doctor, smiling in such a way that he betrayed his feelings for Lucie.

'Have you explained this to her . . . my mother's condition, I mean?'

'She is fully aware of it. In fact she guessed it. We were speaking of it only the other day when she came over for your mother's medicine.'

'The placebo?' I said.

'Yes, the placebo.'

'And how is Mrs. Devlin these days?'

'As usual. She was a little florid of complexion with a slight pinkness at the tip of the nose when I returned home from visiting yesterday.'

'One day she may take a little too much.'

'One day! I suspect it happens most evenings. Well, we should count our blessings, we are told; and apart from one failing she is a treasure. Until I can make other arrangements I must not be too critical.'

'Oh,' I said, 'you are thinking of making other arrangements?'

'Nothing definite . . . as yet.' He looked a little embarrassed and I realized I had been too inquisitive. But I was sure he was referring to Lucie.

We went back to the house and I stood talking to him while he got into his barouche and drove away.

I went to Lucie's room. It was always so neat and tidy; she handled the furniture as though it were sacred, which amused me. This was the room which she had been given on her first visit to Whiteladies and she loved it. Its ceiling was lofty and the family coat of arms was engraved on it; the hanging chandelier was small but beautifully cut; it jingled slightly like temple bells; there was a large window with a window seat padded in mulberry velvet and mulberry-coloured rugs on the floor. The bed had a canopy. It really was charming, I suppose, but we had several similar rooms in Whiteladies and it hadn't struck me that there was anything special about this one until I noticed Lucie's loving care of it.

'I've just been talking to the doctor, Lucie,' I said.

She was sitting at the dressing-table and, looking down, she began moving the toilet articles there. I sat down on the chair with the carved back and the rail on which one could put one's feet. I studied her. She was by no means flamboyantly attractive; it was only that innate elegance which lifted her from the ordinary. Her face was too pale, her features too insignificant for beauty.

'He seems a little . . . unsettled in his domestic arrangements.'

'It's that housekeeper of his.'

'We ought to persuade him to get another. You never know what she might do. She might get to his drug cabinet and help herself to something poisonous.'

'She's not interested in drugs. It's the wine cellar she cares about.'

'But in a mood of drunken exuberance . . . '

'Hers are stupors, I believe.'

'But a doctor's housekeeper should be abstemious.'

'Everyone should be abstemious,' said Lucie gravely.

'I *do* like Dr. Hunter,' I commented. 'I'd like to see him with a wife to help him along. Don't you think that's what he needs?'

'Most professional men need a wife to help them along,' replied Lucie noncommittally.

I laughed. 'There's a lot of the schoolmistress about you still, Lucie,' I said. 'Sometimes I could imagine you in class. Talking of marrying, if you ever decide to, I hope you won't go too far away from us.'

But Lucie was not to be drawn.

It was a sunny afternoon. The house seemed quiet. My mother was resting; my father was, too, I suspected, although he was in his study. Lucie had driven the dog-cart over to the doctor's to collect my mother's medicine; so I brought my embroidery out on to the lawn and sat under the oak tree, thinking as I often did of that day when the scarf had blown over the wall.

Franklyn called. He came over the lawn as he had on that other day and settled into the chair beside me.

'So you're all alone,' he said.

I told him where everyone was.

He made one or two comments about the estate and some of the tenant farmers; this was one of his favourite subjects. He made it his business to know the details of their family life and I had heard that his tenants had nothing to fear from their landlord. He liked to talk to me about these affairs – perhaps because he shared the general view that one day they would be my affairs too, for the wife of a landlord like Franklyn would have her duties to the estate. Franklyn was such a good man, but so predictable. One knew without asking what his views would be on almost any subject one could think of.

I felt a mischievous desire to shock him, so I talked of the matter which was uppermost in my mind – that of Lucie and her relationship with Dr. Hunter.

'Lucie has gone over to Dr. Hunter's to get Mamma's medicine,' I said. 'She enjoys riding over. I daresay she contemplates with pleasure the day when she will be mistress of the house.'

'So they are engaged to be married?' asked Franklyn.

'Nothing has been said, but . . . '

'Then how can you be sure?'

'But isn't it obvious?'

'You mean that there is an attachment? I should say there is the possibility of an engagement, but how can one be sure until it is an actuality?'

Dear Franklyn! He talked like a chairman addressing a board meeting. That was how his mind worked – precise, completely logical. He had a set of conventions and he would adhere to them rigidly.

'But, Franklyn, it will be absolutely ideal.'

'Superficially considered, yes. But one cannot really say that a marriage is ideal until there has been at least a year's trial.'

'Still, I think we should be delighted if Dr. Hunter were to ask Lucie's hand in marriage and she were to accept him. I should like to see Lucie happily settled. After all, Dr. Hunter is so eligible and there is no one else in the district who is suitable to be Lucie's husband, so it will have to be Dr. Hunter. She would have a calming influence on disturbed patients who arrive at the surgery, and she could probably learn to mix medicines. She is very clever.'

'I am sure you are right and it would be an admirable arrangement. There is something I have wanted to say to you for a long time, Araminta.'

He used my full name when he was being solemn so I knew that an important matter was about to be discussed. Is he going to propose? I asked myself. This talk of Lucie's marriage has put ours into his head. I was wrong. Franklyn would never propose marriage on the spur of the moment. If and when he came to ask me, he would come with the appropriate ceremony, having asked Papa's permission first.

'Yes, Franklyn,' I said, with a faint note of alarm in my voice, for I could not rid myself of the thought that he was working towards a proposal which I should be expected to accept – and I didn't want to.

His next words brought relief. 'I have tried to talk to your father but he is not anxious to hear. I could not, of course, talk to your mother. I think that there may well be cause for anxiety concerning your family's financial affairs.'

'You mean we are short of money?'

He hesitated. Then he said: 'I am convinced that your father's affairs are in an uneasy condition. I believe that it is a matter which should not be ignored.'

'Franklyn, will you tell me exactly what you mean?'

'I am a land-owner,' he said, 'not a financier. But one does not have to be that to understand what is going on in the markets. Your father and my father have been friends for years. They had the same man of business, similar investments. The bulk of my possessions are in land, but this is not the case with your father. He has Whiteladies and I am afraid little else. He sold the Somerset property some years ago and the money raised was invested – not wisely, I fear. Your father is not exactly a man of business.'

'Do you mean that we have become poor, Franklyn?'

'Hardly that. But I think you should curb any extravagance in the household. I am warning you because your parents don't seem to understand the necessity not to spend beyond their income. Forgive my candid talk, but I am a little worried. I should not like to see Whiteladies fall into disrepair.'

I felt depressed. So my father was worried about money, or at least he ought to be. He wouldn't be, of course. He would forget what was unpleasant; as for Mamma, she would be completely vague if I broached the subject to her. And Franklyn? What was the motive behind his warning? If he married me he would come to live at Whiteladies as Papa had come. If the house could not be passed down through the male line it would have to be through the female. Mamma had inherited; so would I. The family name might have to change but the blood link was there. So now Franklyn was thinking of Whiteladies; he was concerned because Papa's indigence might make it impossible for him to keep up the house until he, Franklyn, took over.

I remember that when I had told Papa that there was worm in the beams of one of the turret chambers, he had shrugged it aside, and I knew that the matter should have been dealt with. There were several floorboards which were in urgent need of repair and had been neglected for months. My father shut his eyes to these things and now I was picturing ourselves living on at Whiteladies with the place gradually becoming uninhabitable. I could imagine my father shut up in his room refusing to listen while the house slowly crumbled away.

I said: 'What can I do about this?'

'Try to bring in a little economy. If you get a chance talk to your father. Things are not what they were twenty years ago. Taxation has increased; the cost of living has followed; it is a changing world, and we have to adjust ourselves to it.'

'I doubt that I can do very much. If Papa won't listen to you, he won't to me.'

'If you tell him you are a little anxious ... '

'But he won't *do* anything. He just shuts himself into his study and dozes over his manuscript.'

There! I had said it. I had let out the secret of Papa's work. But perhaps it was not really a secret and Franklyn knew as well as I did. What I had done was mention what politeness and convention ruled as unmentionable.

'I'll speak to Lucie,' I said. 'I daresay she would know how to institute economies far better than I.'

'That's an excellent idea,' agreed Franklyn.

Then having done his duty, which I was sure he always would, he changed the subject and we talked of village affairs until I heard Lucie coming back with the dog-cart.

After that night when she had confided in me, Mamma grew more peevish than ever. She spent a great deal of time in her room; trays were sent up at meal-times and I knew that she did justice to the food because I saw Lizzie bringing them away empty several times.

Lizzie was in her confidence and sometimes when I visited her last thing at night, she would seem almost eager to be rid of me and before I was out of the room she would start talking to Lizzie. 'You remember that day when Mr. Herrick and I were in the garden ... ' or 'There was that occasion when Papa asked him to join us for dinner. We were a man short and he was so distinguished. ... ' I imagined she bored poor Lizzie with her reminiscences of the past. But perhaps Lizzie could be more understanding than I since she had seen this superior gentleman who had been transported ignobly to Australia.

Poor Papa! She was so impatient with him. She seemed to have taken a great dislike to him; she was irritable and scarcely took the trouble to answer him civilly. So we were all glad when she decided to stay in her room for meals. It was a situation which I found both distressing and embarrassing. I wished that these people had never come. Once again I was grateful for Lucie's presence for she seemed to know exactly what to do. When Mamma had been very slighting to my father, Lucie would make some comment about his work and he would forget the insult for the compliment. It was such a pity because if ever a man knew how to be happy, that man was my father, with his talent for shrugging aside what was unpleasant. He kept away from my mother as much as possible and Lucie went more frequently to his study, so I daresay the book really was making progress.

Lucie was so devoted to us that our family affairs were hers and while she tried to give my father importance she also sympathized with my mother. I think that, next to Lizzie, she was confided in more than any of us. But it was becoming a somewhat uneasy household.

One day, having been to Dr. Hunter's to get my mother's medicine, Lucie came back looking flushed and disturbed. She took the medicine to my mother's room and when she came out I called her into mine.

'Come in and have a chat,' I said. 'Mamma has been in a terrible mood today.'

Lucie frowned. 'I know. I wish those people hadn't come.'

'It seems so odd. People call like that, strangers, and things change.'

'It had begun before really,' said Lucie. 'But these people reminded your mother of the past.'

'How I wish she could see this superior being now. I daresay he is old and grey and no longer looks so handsome. Poor Papa, I'm sorry for him.'

'Yes,' said Lucie. 'It's so easy to make him happy and such a pity that he can't be.' Then she blurted out: 'Minta, Dr. Hunter has asked me to marry him.'

'Oh, Lucie, congratulations.'

'Thanks, but I haven't decided.'

'But, Lucie, it would be an ideal marriage.'

'How can you know?'

I laughed. 'You sound just like Franklyn. I think you will make a wonderful doctor's wife. He'll be able to get rid of that drunken Devlin and you will look after him perfectly. I do hope he realizes how lucky he is.'

'But I told you I haven't decided yet.'

'You will.'

'You sound as though you'll be glad to be rid of me.'

'How can you say that when you know that one of the reasons why I'm so pleased is that it will keep you near us.'

'But I shan't be at Whiteladies.'

'I believe it's the house you like, Lucie, better than us. It was the same with . . .' No, I was going to forget that insignificant incident. But he *had* been abnormally interested in the house. I could understand it, in a way, because he had lived all his life in Australia and Whiteladies must have been one of the first ancient mansions he had ever seen. But Lucie was as obsessed as he was.

'Well,' I finished, 'you won't be far away.'

'He's very ambitious. I doubt that he will settle to be a country doctor all his life. He plans to go to London to specialize and set up his plate in Harley or Wimpole Street.'

'I hadn't thought of that. Even so, you will make a wonderful doctor's wife, Lucie, and since he is so ambitious you are just the wife for him. I hate the thought of your going, but London is not so far. We could meet often.'

'You make it all sound so simple.'

'Well, I daresay it will be, and in any case he may decide to spend the rest of his life here. What would he specialize in?'

'He's interested in cases like your mothers'.'

'You mean people who are not really ill to begin with but imagine themselves into illness.'

'Diseases of the mind,' said Lucie.

'I shall be desolate if you go, but at the same time I think you should.'

'My dear Minta, you have to let me manage my own affairs, you know. I haven't decided yet.'

I was surprised, realizing there was a great deal about Lucie that I didn't understand. I had imagined her to be calm and precise, choosing the sensible way; but perhaps after all she was romantic. It was clear that she was not passionately in love with Dr. Hunter; but she must realize what a wonderful chance it would be for her to marry him.

It was a misty November day; there was not a breath of wind and everything was depressingly damp. There were countless spiders' webs draped over the bushes, glistening with tiny globules of moisture and everything seemed unusually silent. The mist penetrated the house. It was like a vague presence.

All the morning Lucie had been working about the house; it was wonderful the way she superintended everything. The servants did not mind, except perhaps Mrs. Glee who vaguely suspected that she was taking over some of her duties. Lucie would go down to the kitchen and order the meals after having submitted suggestions to Mamma through Lizzie. Mamma never looked at them but Lucie insisted on their being shown to her. Lucie was a wonderful housekeeper and should have been running a house of her own.

I spent most of the morning in the flower-room. There was not much left in the garden besides chrysanthemums, asters, dahlias and Michaelmas daisies. As I arranged them I was thinking how dull life was here, doing the same things almost at the same time every day. I sniffed the subtle autumnal smell these flowers have and I saw myself through the years ahead arranging the flowers – primroses, daffodils, and the spring sunshine-coloured flowers down to the holly and mistletoe of December – always here in the flower-room which had once been a nun's cell with its stone floor and small high window in the wall with the three bars across it. And I longed for life to change. Afterwards I remembered the fervour of my longing and thought how strange it was that on that day life should change so drastically.

Looking into the starry faces of the daisies, I saw his face, the green eyes, the arrogant features. It was absurd to go on remembering a stranger whom I had met by chance and very likely would never see again.

One of the maids came in to carry the flowers away and put them in the places I had chosen. It was an hour before luncheon would be served, normally I should have taken a walk round the garden but it was such a damp and dismal morning. So I stayed in my room and my thoughts went back and back again to the incident of the girl with the scarf, and I thought of Mamma who in this house had been loved and had loved, and consequently must have been quite unlike the woman she was today. I wondered if I should grow old and peevish, looking back resentfully because life had passed me by.

Dr. Hunter called and was with Mamma for half an hour. Before he left he asked to see me and said he would like to have a little talk with Papa as well so we went up to Papa's study and he and the doctor drank a glass of sherry while Dr. Hunter talked to us of Mamma.

'You must realize,' said Dr. Hunter, 'that there is no reason at all why Lady Cardew should not lead a reasonably normal life. She is breathless, yes – because she is out of condition. She stays in her room nursing a non-existent heart trouble. I am of the opinion that we have all been pandering to her whims, and I think we should now try different tactics.'

As I was listening I was visualizing him in tastefully furnished rooms in Harley Street treating rich patients and going home to Lucie, who would entertain brilliant doctors and learn enough of her husband's profession to join intelligently in the very learned conversation. It pleased me to think of her as the school teacher she had been before I had discovered her. I wondered why she did not give Dr. Hunter his answer.

'We will try a little experiment,' he said. 'Not so much sympathy, please.'

Dr. Hunter went on to expound his theories. He was going to start a new line of healing. He grew very animated talking of the experiments he intended to make. I was sure we should lose him to Harley Street very soon

– and Lucie too to some extent if she married him. If! But of course she would.

'Just a little gentle reproof,' he went on. 'Don't be too harsh at first.'

Papa asked him to stay to luncheon but he was too busy. He finished his sherry and left us.

Mamma came down to luncheon in one of her more difficult moods. 'This weather brings on all my pains,' she grumbled. 'The damp seeps into my bones. You can't imagine the pain.'

Papa, eager to put into practice the doctor's suggestions replied: 'We don't need to employ our imaginations, my dear, because you have described it in such detail so often.'

Mamma was completely taken aback. That my usually tolerant and easy-going father should criticize her in such an unsympathetic manner was a great shock to her.

'So I am a nuisance, am I?' she demanded.

'My dear, you misconstrue.'

'It was what you implied. Oh, I know I am ill, and to those of you who have the great gift of good health, that makes me dull and useless. How unkind you are! If only you knew how I suffer! I could almost wish that you were afflicted with one hundredth part of the pain that I feel – then you might have some understanding. But no, I wouldn't wish that for anyone. What has my life been but one long bed of pain. Ever since you were born, Minta, I have suffered.'

'I'm sorry, Mamma, that I am responsible.'

'Now you are jeering at me. I never thought you would do that openly although I have long known that I was a burden and a nuisance to you. Oh, if only my life had been different. If only I had had the good fortune . . . '

It was an old theme. My father had half risen in his chair, his face pink, his usually mild eyes clouded with distress. I knew that there must have been vague references over the years to what might have been if she had had the good fortune to marry the man of her choice instead of him.

My sympathies were entirely with him and I said: 'Why, Mamma, you have had a very happy life with the best husband in the world.'

She silenced me, looking wildly about the room and staring beyond my father as though she saw something of which we were not aware. I know she was thinking of that man and it was almost as though he were in the room, he who had been taken away and shipped abroad as a thief, as though he were taunting her with what might have been if she had been bolder and insisted on marrying him.

'The best husband in the world!' she cried mockingly. 'What has he done to make him that? He sits in his study working . . . working, he says! *Sleeping* his life away! His book, his famous book! That is like him. He is nothing, nothing. And I might have had a very different life.'

Lucie said: 'Lady Cardew, Dr. Hunter told me that you must not get over-excited. Will you allow me to take you to your room?'

The thought of herself as an invalid soothed her. She turned almost gratefully to Lucie who led her from the room.

Papa and I looked after her. I felt so sorry for him; he looked completely bewildered.

'I don't think Dr. Hunter's treatment worked,' I said. 'Never mind, Papa. We did our best.'

It was an uneasy day. Several of the servants must have heard my mother's outburst. My father seemed to have drunk a little, there was something shame faced about him. We had all suspected that he dozed at his desk and that most of the work had been done by Lucie; but it had never been said to his face before – and now that it had been, the fact had a significance it had never had before.

My mother spent the day in her room declaring that she did not want to see anybody. I saw Lizzie, who told me she had slept for some part of the afternoon having worn herself out crying.

'She'll be better tomorrow, Miss Minta,' comforted Lizzie.

I talked it over with Lucie, who was very distressed.

'It's quite clear that criticism doesn't help Mamma,' I said.

'Your father is too gentle by nature. Perhaps he should have continued as he began.'

'He is too kind to take up a new role. It's like changing his character.'

'It was natural that Lucie would not admit that Dr. Hunter's diagnosis was wrong. She repeated Lizzie's words: 'She'll be better tomorrow.'.

Before I retired that night I went up to my mother's room, but hesitated before entering. As I stood at the door I heard my mother's voice: 'You're wicked! Oh, how I wish I could go back all those years. I'd know what to do because you're wicked . . . wicked.'

I pictured my father's mild bewildered eyes and I decided that I would not go into that room. So I went to my own and lay awake for a long time thinking of the sadness of my parents' lives and all the lost years when they might have been happy.

Neither of them was to blame. I wished that I had been able to go in and tell them this, to implore them to forget the past and start afresh from now.

How I wished that I *had* gone in that night! I never saw my mother alive again.

Next morning when Lizzie went in to awaken her she found her dead.

Chapter Two

Lizzie said afterwards that she had a strange premonition; she was waiting for the bell to ring for the early morning tea and when it didn't come she went in.

'She was lying there,' said Lizzie, and there was something different about her. And when I went close . . . oh, my God!'

Lizzie had been hysterical and incoherent but she did run for Lucie and Lucie came to me. I awoke with a start to find them both standing by my bed.

Lucie said: 'Minta, you have to prepare yourself for a shock.'

I scrambled up and stared at them.

'It's your mother,' said Lucie. 'Something dreadful . . .'

'Is she . . . dead?'

Lucie nodded slowly. She was unlike herself – her eyes were wide, her pupils seemed dilated and her mouth quivered; I felt she was fighting hard to control herself. Lizzie started to sob.

'After all these years. . . . It's not true. There's a mistake. She's fainted, that's what it is.'   .

'I have sent for Dr. Hunter,' said Lucie.

'And my father?' I asked.

'I haven't sent word to him yet. I thought we'd wait until the doctor came. There's nothing he can do.'

'But he should know.'

'I went into her room,' murmured Lizzie. 'You see, she hadn't rung. . . .' Then she covered her face with her hands and continued to sob.

I snatched up my dressing-gown and said: 'I'll go to her.'

Lucie shook her head. 'Don't,' she said.

'But I must. I don't believe she's dead. Only yesterday Dr. Hunter was saying . . .'

I had moved past Lucie to the door, she was beside me and walked with me to my mother's room.

'Don't, Minta,' whispered Lucie. 'Wait . . . wait until the doctor's been.'

She held my hand tightly and drew me gently along the corridor to her room.

By the time Dr. Hunter arrived my father was up. Lucie had talked to him as she had talked to me, soothing us, really taking matters in hand. My father was quite willing for her to do this; so was I.

It was Lucie who went with the doctor into my mother's room.

'Take your father to the library and stay there till we come,' she said. 'Look after your father. This is a terrible shock for him.'

It seemed a long time before the doctor and Lucie came to us. It was in fact fifteen minutes.

Dr. Hunter was shaken; a good deal of his jaunty assurance had deserted him. No wonder! Since yesterday he had said my mother's ailments were more or less imaginary, and now she was dead.

'So it's true?' my father said blankly.

'She died of a heart failure during the night,' said Dr. Hunter.

'So she had a bad heart after all, Doctor?'

'No.' He spoke defiantly. 'It could happen to any of us at any time. There was nothing organically wrong with her heart. Of course the invalid life she led was not conducive to good health. This was a case of the heart's suddenly failing to function.'

'Poor Mamma!' I said.

I was sorry for Dr. Hunter. He seemed so distressed; he kept his eyes on my father's face as though he expected sympathy. Sympathy for what? Making a wrong diagnosis? Suspecting his patient was a malingerer and treating her as such when she was seriously ill?

Lucie's eyes were fixed on him but he avoided looking at her. Once or twice he turned his gaze on me and then hastily back to my father.

'This is a great shock,' I said. 'Yesterday she was her normal self . . . '

'It happens like this now and then,' said the doctor.

'Minta and her father are very upset, naturally,' said Lucie. 'If they'll allow me I'll make the necessary arrangements.'

My father looked at her with gratitude and the doctor said: 'That would be very satisfactory, I think.'

Lucie signed to him and they went out together, leaving me with my father in the library. He raised his eyes to my face and I could not help being aware that it was shock not grief I saw there. Nor could I fail to notice his relief.

Later we went to see Mamma; she was lying in bed, her eyes closed; the frills of her white nightdress were up to her chin. She looked more peaceful in death than she ever had in life.

Something strange had happened to the house. It was no longer the same. Mamma lay in the churchyard where our family had been buried for the last five hundred years. The family vault had been ceremoniously opened; and we had gone through the mournful burial service. The shutters had been opened, the blinds drawn up. Lizzie had been ill for a week or so after the funeral and had emerged among us, gaunt and subdued.

Lucie had changed too; there was a certain aloofness about her. My father was different; it was as though a burden had been removed from his shoulders, and although he had tried to, he could not altogether hide his relief.

But perhaps the most changed of us all was Dr. Hunter. Before my mother's death he had been a sociable young man; ambitious in the extreme, he had been the friend of local families as well as their doctor. He had endeavoured to make people forget his youth by his excessive confidence; he had clearly been eager to climb to the top of his profession. The change in him was subtle, but nevertheless marked – certainly to me.

I thought I understood. My mother had been ill. The pain she had complained of had been real; he had seen her, though, as a fractious, discontented woman – which she was – and had allowed his assessment of her character to cloud his judgment. It seemed clear to me that he had made a faulty diagnosis and that this had so upset his confidence in himself that it was having a marked effect on him. It would throw doubt on his advanced theories on which he was basing his career. I was sorry for him.

He called rarely at the house. None of us needed him professionally until I called him in to see Lizzie because I became worried about her. This was a week or so after the funeral and then I had a conversation with him.

'You're not looking well yourself, Doctor,' I said.

'Are you saying "Physician, heal thyself"?'

'I believe you are worrying about my mother's death.'

I was immediately sorry that I had introduced the subject so abruptly, for a nervous twitch started in his cheek, and his head jerked sharply like a puppet's.

'No, no,' he said quickly. 'It is not such an unusual case as as you appear to think. It can happen to completely healthy people. A clot of blood to the brain or heart and death can be the result. There is in some cases no warning. And your mother was scarcely a healthy woman, although there was nothing organically wrong. I have read of many such cases. I have encountered several when I was in hospital. No, no. It was not so very unusual.'

He was talking too fast and too persuasively. If what he said was true, why should he blame himself? It was unfortunate that the very day before she died he had told me that she had imagined her illness and we must ignore it.

'All the same,' I said, 'you seem to reproach yourself.'

'Not in the least. It is something one cannot foresee.'

'I'm so glad I'm mistaken. We know that you took the utmost care of my mother.'

He seemed a little reconciled, but I was sure he was avoiding us for he never called socially at Whiteladies.

My father shut himself in his study for long periods. Lucie told me that he was great deal more upset than he appeared to be, and the fact that for the first time he had spoken to his wife unsympathetically, filled him with remorse.

'I am trying to get him working really hard on the book,' said Lucie. 'I think it best for him.'

Lucie was wonderful during that time. She asked if Lizzie might be her personal maid. 'Not,' she said deprecatingly, 'that I need one, nor in my position should have one. I think, though, that for a time it would do Lizzie good. She has had a terrible shock.'

I said she must do as she liked for I was sure she knew best.

'Dear Minta,' she said, '*you* are the mistress of Whiteladies now.'

It was a thought which hadn't occurred to me before.

Franklyn was with us constantly from the day of my mother's death. He helped my father in all the ways which Lucie couldn't. I often wondered what we should have done at that time without Lucie or Franklyn.

He rode over to Whiteladies every day and I could be sure of seeing him some time. We talked about my mother and how unhappy she had been and I said how sad it was that she had gone through life never enjoying it, apart from one little episode when her magnificent drawing-master had come to the house and she had fallen in love with him. I rather enjoyed talking about such things with Franklyn because his prosaic views and his terse way of expressing them amused me.

'I suppose,' I said, 'that it's better to have had one exciting experience in your life than go along at a smooth and comfortable level all the time . . . even though you do spend the rest of your life repining.'

'That seems to me a very unreasonable deduction,' said Franklyn.

'You would say that! I am sure your life will be comfortable and easy for ever and ever, unruffled by any incident, disturbing or ecstatic.'

'Another unreasonable deduction.'

'But you would never make any mistake; therefore the element of excitement is removed.'

'Why do you think it is only interesting to make mistakes?'

'If you know how everything is going to work out . . . '

'But nobody knows how everything is going to work out. You are being quite illogical, Minta.'

And I laughed for the first time since my mother had died.

I tried to explain to him the change in the household. 'It's as though the ghost of Mamma cannot rest.'

'That's pure imagination on your part.'

'Indeed it's not. Everybody has changed. Haven't you noticed it? But of course you haven't. You never notice things like that.'

'I appear to be completely unobservant to you?'

'Only psychologically. For all practical purposes your powers of observation would be very keen.'

'How kind of you to say so.'

'Sarcasm does not become you, Franklyn. Nor is it natural to you. You are much too kind. But there *is* a change in the household. My father is relieved . . . '

'Minta!'

'Now you are shocked. But the truth should not shock anyone.'

'I think you should be more restrained in your conversation.'

'I am only talking to you, Franklyn. There is no one else in the world to whom I would say this. And how can we blame him? I know one is not supposed to speak ill of the dead and therefore you never would. But Mamma was beastly to him, so it is only natural that he should feel relieved. Lizzie goes round looking lost and yet she and Mamma were always quarrelling and Lizzie was always on the point of being dismissed or leaving voluntarily.'

'That is not unusual in attachments such as theirs, and it is quite natural that she should be "lost", as you say. She has been deprived of a mistress.'

'But poor Dr. Hunter is worse than any of them. I am sure he blames himself. He seems to avoid calling at the house.'

'It is natural that he should since the invalid is no longer there.'

'And Lucie has changed.'

'I'm sorry to hear that. She appears to be the most sensible member of the household.'

'She seems shut in, aloof, not so easy to talk to. I suppose she's worried about Dr. Hunter. I wonder she didn't announce their engagement when it happened.'

'Why?'

'Well, as Dr. Hunter is depressed and thinks he made the wrong diagnosis. . . . '

'Who said he did?'

'Well, I think he did.'

'You should not say such a thing, even to me. It's slander when discussing a professional man.'

'But, Franklyn, you are not a court of law.'

'You must not be frivolous, Minta. You must stop this romanticising, this attempt to build up a dramatic situation.'

'It's because you're such a close friend that I can say anything to you. Besides, I like to shock you. But I wanted to tell you something. Yesterday Lucie came to me and suggested we get rid of Mrs. Glee. She's not really needed, she says. Lucie can do all that she does, for now that Mamma is dead Lucie is relieved of a lot of her duties.'

'It seems a reasonable and logical suggestion. I have tried to tell you many times that you are living beyond your means. Mrs. Glee is the most expensive of your retainers. Yes, it's an excellent idea.'

'You would see the practical side of it. The point is, if Lucie is going to take on Mrs. Glee's duties and run Whiteladies, what of her marriage to Dr. Hunter?'

'There was nothing arranged.'

'He had asked her. She was considering. It was just before Mamma's death. Poor Dr. Hunter!'

'Has it occurred to you that his depression may be due to the fact that his proposal has not been accepted?'

'I still think it has something to do with Mamma's death.'

'Minta, it's time you grew up. I wish you would. That would be desirable in many ways.'

I guessed then that he was thinking that when I showed more maturity he would ask me to marry him; and into my mind there flashed a picture of that scene on the lawn with Stirling lolling, somewhat ungracefully, in the chair, talking about Australia and Whiteladies.

And I thought: No, I'll not grow up yet. My immaturity is a kind of protection.

A few mornings later a rather disturbing incident occurred. I was in the flower-room splitting the stalks of some bronze-coloured chrysanthemums when Mrs. Glee burst in.

'I'd like a word with you, Miss Minta,' she said.

Her face was red and her little eyes like pieces of black jet. She didn't have to tell me she was angry.

'Certainly, Mrs. Glee. Come into the library.'

'There's no need for that. I'll tell you here and now. I've had orders to go and I'd like to know why, because these orders have come from a certain quarter and I've yet to learn that I take orders from that direction.'

'From Miss Maryan?' I said. 'As a matter of fact, Mrs. Glee, we have become much poorer in the last few years and we have to cut our expenses in some ways.'

'And I'm chosen as the victim, eh?'

'Not a victim, Mrs. Glee. It's simply a matter of necessity.'

'Now, miss,' she said, 'I've nothing against you. You're innocent of all this. A blind man could see that. But if people ought to leave this house – and I'd be the first to admit it mightn't be a bad thing if they did – there's some you could do better without than me.'

'It's very sad to have to do without anyone, and only a matter of finance.'

'You've had the words put into your mouth, Miss Minta. There's some funny things going on in this house. I could tell you . . . '

'What things?'

Mrs. Glee pressed her lips together with an air of martyrdom. 'Things it's not my place to mention. You're the mistress of the house now your poor mother's gone, and it's not for you to take a step back and let others help themselves to what's yours by rights.'

'I shan't do that, Mrs. Glee.'

'You might be forced into it. I don't like the way things are going in this house and it's not all that sorry I'll be to pack my bags and be off. But I'm sorry for *you*, Miss Minta.'

'How kind of you. I'm sure I don't deserve your sympathy.'

It was evidently the right line for her anger calmed considerably; she was changing rapidly from virago to prophet of doom.

She took a step closer to me and said: 'Your poor Mamma going off like that, and that Lizzie. What of her, eh? If anyone should go, she should. The way she talked to that poor dead soul. Shouting and screaming they were, the night before. I heard your poor mother say that Lizzie was to go. It was her last wish, you might say. And now Lizzie's to be kept on and I'm told to go. I, who never had a cross word with the dear dead lady. You see, Miss Minta, it's a funny state of affairs, wouldn't you say?'

'Hardly funny,' I said. 'Lizzie was very fond of my mother and my mother of her. Their quarrels meant nothing.'

'The last one did. But it's not so much Lizzie. She's nothing. It's Other People.'

'Which people?'

'Well, Miss Minta, have you ever thought you might soon be having a new Mamma?'

'No.'

'You see!' She folded her arms across her ample chest. 'I'm telling you, Miss Minta. It's not that I care for myself. I've had enough of service anyway. I'm going to my cousin once removed down Dover way. Very comfortably off she is and her rheumatics are crippling her. She wants someone to look after her, be a companion to her, and she'll leave me the cottage and a little bit to keep me going. So I'm not concerned for myself. But I says: There's that innocent young lady. And there's some funny things going on in Whiteladies. And that's why I'm warning you.'

'I'm so pleased, Mrs. Glee, about your cousin.'

'You're a sweet young lady, Miss Minta, and I've often said so. But I'll repeat this: There's something peculiar going on and you should know of it. There's someone who wants to run this household. There's someone who has the trap set and there's innocent people who will walk right into it. And I'm to go. Why? Because I see a bit farther than my nose.'

I sighed and picking up the pot carried it out of the flower-room. I looked over my shoulder and said: 'I'm sure your cousin will be pleased to have you, Mrs. Glee.'

She stood shaking her head prophetically and I went through into the library. I put the pot down as soon as I comfortably could because my hands were shaking. I was quite upset, and relieved too, when, a few days later, declaring that she would not stay a minute longer than was necessary where she was not wanted, Mrs. Glee accepted a month's wages and departed.

Her absence made no difference to the running of the house. Lucie was busy, but then she always had been. My mother had never been interested in household affairs, and Mrs. Glee had been mainly occupied in keeping the maids in order and preserving a certain dignity in the servants' quarters. Lucie did this and much more besides. The maids were glad to be rid of the formidable Mrs. Glee and readily accepted Lucie in her place. I saw less of Lucie, but my father saw more of her.

I was always waiting for Lucie to confide in me about Dr. Hunter, but she didn't. She was in my father's study for an hour in the morning and again after tea.

'I'm urging him to get on seriously with the book,' she told me. 'It's the best thing for him. It keeps his mind off the tragedy.'

Lizzie took her tea in the morning just as she had taken Mamma's, and Lucie kept her busy doing her room and Papa's, and all sorts of sewing for the household at which Lizzie was very good.

Two months passed in this way. Christmas came and went. We celebrated it very quietly. Franklyn and his parents came to dine with us on Christmas Day and they stayed to supper. We played a quiet game of whist – Papa and Lady Wakefield, Franklyn and I; and Lucie was there sitting quietly by the fire chatting with Sir Everard and at appropriate times making sure that the servants brought in refreshments and performed those duties necessary to our comforts.

I recalled the Christmas before when we had dined in the great hall under bunches of holly and mistletoe, and how one of the most merry members of the party had been Dr. Hunter. Mamma had been at one end of the table enjoying talking to the doctor of her ailments. Lucie, of course, had been present, unobtrusive and competent. I remember she had worn a dress the colour of mauve orchids and how elegant she had looked in spite of the fact that she had made the dress herself. Now Lizzie made clothes on Lucie's instructions – Lucie designing, Lizzie stitching. It was an excellent combination.

After the guests had gone and everyone had retired for the night I slipped on my dressing-gown and went along to Lucie's room.

'Do you mind?' I said. 'I couldn't sleep.'

She offered me the chair with the mulberry cushions and she sat on the bed.

'I kept thinking of last Christmas,' I said.

'Poor Minta, you miss your mother.'

I frowned. I didn't want to be hypocritical. I had loved Mamma, but she had made life uncomfortable from time to time and I couldn't forget the last scene in the dining-room and the look of abject misery I had seen on my father's face.

I said quickly: 'What about you and Dr. Hunter, Lucie? You were considering marrying him.'

'Who said I was? Do you want me to go?'

'How can you ask such a thing! We should be lost without you. But I think poor Dr. Hunter is in greater need of comfort and as you love him . . .'

'You jump to conclusions, Minta. I'm fond of the doctor. I'm fond of you all here, and when your mother died I seemed to be needed.'

'But you mustn't make such a sacrifice.'

'It's willingly made . . . if such it is.'

'But I'm so sorry for the doctor. I think he's very unhappy and you could help him. He feels he didn't do the right thing . . . for Mamma.'

'How can you be sure of that?'

'It's obvious. He thought she was pretending and it turned out she wasn't. Perhaps if he had believed she was really ill he would have treated her case differently. Perhaps that was what she needed.'

'But you are accusing him of incompetence!'

'I'm not. I know he's competent. But people make mistakes.'

'Doctors can't afford to. For heaven's sake, don't talk of this to anyone.'

'I wouldn't to anyone but you . . . and Franklyn, who doesn't count.'

'Not to anyone,' she said fervently. 'Promise me.'

I thought: She does love him then? I promised readily.

'And forget it, Minta,' she went on. 'Put it right out of your mind. It's . . . unhealthy. Your mother died of a stroke. It could happen to anybody. I have heard of people, healthy people, being struck down suddenly, and your mother had impaired her constitution by her invalidism.'

'I know, Lucie, I know.'

'Your mother is dead and buried. We must try to go on from there.'

I nodded.

'Don't forget,' she added gently, 'that I am here to help and comfort you. Wasn't it always like that, from the time of our schooldays?'

I agreed that it was. 'But you shouldn't make sacrifices, Lucie. We can look after ourselves. And you wouldn't be far away at the doctor's house.'

Lucie shook her head. 'I don't think I shall ever be at the doctor's house,' she said. 'I believe my place is here ... in Whiteladies.'

'I repeat, Lucie, you must not sacrifice yourself.'

'Martyrs are tiresome people,' she said with a smile. 'I have no intention of being one. This is where I want to be, Minta. This is where I want to stay.'

I should have seen it coming but it was a shock when it did.

It was May – six months after my mother's death – a lovely day, almost summer, with the birds singing their delighted chorus and the buds sprouting everywhere, the chestnuts in blossom and the orchard a mass of pink and white and in the air was that unmistakable feeling that life is wonderful and happiness is just round the corner. This is the miracle of the English spring.

I had been for a ride after luncheon as far out as the Wakefield estates and had come in thinking how pleasant a cup of tea would be. It wanted another quarter of an hour to four o'clock, so I went and sat under the chestnut tree.

And there Lucie joined me. I watched her walking across the lawn. She was very different from the school teacher she had been when I first met her. There had been an air of defiance about her then. Now she walked with a springy step and the new gown which Lizzie had made to her instructions became her well. She was what the French call *une jolie laide*. Taken feature by feature she was decidedly plain, but there was an unusual charm in the complete picture which almost amounted to beauty.

'I want to talk to you rather specially,' she said.

'Come and sit down, Lucie.'

She did. I looked at her profile – the too long nose, the jutting chin.

'I have something very important to say to you and I am unsure how you will take it.'

'You look sure that I am going to like it.'

'I wish I were.'

'Why do you keep me in suspense? Tell me quickly. I'm impatient to hear.'

She took a deep breath and said: 'Minta, I am going to marry your father.'

'Lucie!'

'There! You are shocked.'

'But ... Lucie!'

'Does it seem so incongruous?'

'Well, it's so unexpected.'

'We have been fond of each other for a long time.'

'But he's years older than you, Lucie.'

'You are finding excuses to oppose us.'

'I'm not. It's true that you are half his age.'

'What of it? I'm serious for my years. Don't you agree?'

'But you and the doctor ... '

'You imagined a great deal about that affair.'

'But he did ask you to marry him.'

'And I didn't accept him.'

'And now you and Papa . . . '

'Does it worry you that I shall be your stepmother?'

'Of course not. And how could I not want you to be a member of the family? You are in any case. It's just that . . . '

'It seems unsuitable?'

'It's just that it hadn't occurred to me.' I thought then: This is what Mrs. Glee *was* referring to. So it must have been obvious to others if not to me.

She went on: 'We have grown very close during the last months when I have tried to comfort him. He reproached himself a little – unnecessarily, I have constantly to assure him. I think we shall be very happy, Minta. But I feel I want your approval. I couldn't be happy without it.'

'But what I say is of no importance, surely?'

'It's of the utmost importance to me. Oh Minta, please say you will welcome me as your stepmother.'

For my answer I stood up and put my arms about her.

'Dearest Lucie,' I said, 'it's a wonderful thing for Papa and for me. I was thinking of you.'

She stroked my hair. 'You are so romantic. You decided that the doctor was for me and you built up a pretty picture of my launching him to success. Well, it's not to be. What appears to be romantic does not always bring happiness. I am happy now, Minta. I want to be here. You and your father are my dear ones. This is my home. Go to your father now. Tell him I have told you the news and impress on him how happy it has made you.'

So Lucie and I went to Papa and I told him that it was wonderful news; and he was happy as I had never seen him before.

'We shall have to wait for the full year to pass,' said Lucie, 'or people will talk.'

'Let them talk,' said my father.

But Lucie thought it best to wait; and already he was relying on her judgment.

She was right, of course; and they waited.

It was a misty November day, very much like the one when Mamma had died that Lucie became Lady Cardew, my stepmother.

How different was our household now! The servants knew they must obey Lucie. She never lost her temper; she was always gracious. I doubt White-ladies had ever had a more respected chatelaine.

She loved the house and the house seemed to respond to her love. I have seen her stand on the lawn looking at it with a sort of wonder, as though she couldn't really believe that she was the mistress of it.

I used to tease her about it. 'I believe you are the reincarnation of a nun. You knew this place was your home from the moment you set eyes on it.'

'Minta's romantic nonsense,' she said teasingly.

Very little was done about my father's book. She had so much to occupy her now, and since he was not continually told what an unsatisfactory husband he was he did not feel the need to justify himself. He took an interest in the gardens and the house. Lucie quickly discovered that repairs were necessary.

It was soon after that that I saw her really shaken out of her usual calm. She told me about it because it was not easy to discuss such matters with Papa.

'Your father's financial affairs are in a wretched state,' she said. 'Those lawyers of his are no good whatsoever. He has lost a great deal of money on the stock exchange lately and has been misguided enough to jeopardize the house by borrowing money on it.'

'Franklyn hinted at this some time ago.'

'You didn't tell me.'

'I didn't think you'd be interested.'

'Not interested in Whiteladies!'

'Well, now you are of course. What does it mean, Lucie?'

'I'm not sure. I must find out. Whiteladies must not be in danger.'

'I think that now you're in command we shall be all right.'

She was pleased with that remark, but a little impatient. We were reckless. We didn't deserve Whiteladies because we had jeopardized it.

She would sit in Papa's study with a pile of bills and papers before her.

'We must cut down here,' she would say. 'We could economize there. We must make Whiteladies safe now and for the future.'

My father admired her greatly. He had a childish belief that now Lucie was mistress of Whiteladies everything would be all right. I shared that view. There had always been a quality about Lucie that inspired confidence.

I told her often how glad I was that she was now definitely a member of the family. I had only wanted her to marry the doctor, I pointed out, so that she could stay near us.

She was pleased. 'Stepmother is not an ugly word in this house,' she commented.

'Darling Lucie, it was a lucky day for us when you came to Whiteladies,' I told her; I knew my father told her the same.

Neither of us could openly say this, but Whiteladies was a happier and more peaceful place since my mother had died.

Then Lucie surprised us again. She told me first. I thought she had been a little subdued for a few weeks, and one day when I was sitting in my favourite spot in the pond garden, she came out there to me.

'I have something to tell you,' she said, 'and I want you to be the first to know. Even your father doesn't know yet.'

I turned to her, not understanding the ecstatic expression in her smoky eyes.

'I hope you'll be pleased, but I'm not sure.'

'Please tell me . . . quickly.'

She laughed in a rather embarrassed way. 'I'm going to have a baby.'

'Lucie! When?'

'A long time yet . . . in seven months' time, I should say.'

'It's . . . wonderful.'

'You think so?'

'Don't you?'

She gripped her hands together. 'It's what I've always longed for.'

I threw my arms about her neck.

'Oh, Lucie, how happy I am! Just imagine – a baby in the house! It'll be lovely. I wonder whether it will be a girl or a boy. Which do you want?'

'I don't know. A boy, I suppose. Most people like the first born to be a boy.'

'So you anticipate having a family!'

'I didn't say that. But I'm so excited. But I wanted to be absolutely sure before telling your father.'

'Let's tell him now. No, you should tell him on your own. You wouldn't want an intruder at a time like this.'

'You are the sweetest stepdaughter anyone ever had.'

She left me sitting here, watching a dragonfly hover over the pond and settle momentarily on the statue.

This, I thought, will compensate Lucie for everything. That horrid little house in the Midlands, all the hardships of her youth. What a happy day for Lucie!

My father was bewildered at first, then delighted. I am sure he had never thought he would have other children. But Lucie, it seemed, could provide everything. There was no talk in the house now of anything but the coming baby. Lucie softened considerably; as her body grew more shapeless and she lost her elegance she gained a new beauty. She loved to sit with me and talk about the baby. She planned the layette and Lizzie sewed it. Those were the lovely peaceful months of waiting.

We tried to coddle Lucie but she wouldn't let us. Her baby was going to be strong and healthy, she said. He wasn't going to have an invalid for a mother. I noticed she referred to the baby as 'he', which showed she wanted a boy, although I guessed that when the child came she wouldn't care what its sex was.

Dr. Hunter was calling frequently at Whiteladies now. He told me that there was nothing to worry about whatsoever. Lucie was strong and healthy; she would produce a lusty child.

It was Franklyn who pointed out to me what a difference the birth of a child might make to me personally.

'If the child is a boy,' he said, 'he will be your father's heir, for when your mother married him her property passed into his possession. Has this occurred to you?'

'I hadn't thought of it.'

'What an impractical girl you are! Whiteladies would go to your father's son. You would have no claim to it unless some moral duty made him leave it to you.'

'Whiteladies would always be my home, Franklyn. What would it matter if it belonged to my stepbrother . . . or would he be half-brother?'

Franklyn said it could make a great deal of difference to me and implied that I was most unworldly.

I laughed at him, but he was very serious.

Such pleasant days they were. During summer afternoons on the lawn and winter evenings by the fire, we eagerly awaited the birth of Lucie's child. My father seemed younger; he was so proud of Lucie and could scarcely bear her out of his sight.

And then in November – the same month in which my mother had died but two years later – the child was born.

It was a girl and was christened Druscilla.

I think Lucie was a little disappointed that she had not borne a son and so was my father, but the delight at finding themselves parents of a charming little girl soon dispersed that.

Druscilla quickly became the most important person in the household; we all vied for her favours; we were all delighted when she chose to crow at us.

I often marvelled at the way in which everything had changed since my mother had died.

That was the state of affairs when Stirling and Nora came back to England.

NORA

Chapter One

I was going to England and it was much against my will. I had argued persistently with Stirling.

'What good will it do?' I kept asking; and he set his lips stubbornly together and said: 'I'm going. It was his wish.'

'It was different when he was alive,' I insisted. 'I never agreed with his ideas but they had some meaning then.'

It was no use trying to reason with Stirling; and in a way I was glad of this controversy because it took our minds from the terrible searing sorrow which we were both experiencing. When I was arguing with Stirling I was not thinking of Lynx lying on the brown earth, of their carrying his body home on the improvised stretcher; and I had to stop myself thinking of that. I knew it was the same with Stirling. There was something else we both knew. There was no comfort for either of us but in each other.

We should have turned to Adelaide. Her sound good sense would have served us well. She said she would not leave home; she was going to stay and keep things going for when we came back.

I wanted to stay, yet I wanted to go. I wanted to get right away from the house I had called Little Whiteladies. There were too many memories there; and yet I took a fierce and morbid delight in remembering every interview with Lynx, every game of chess we had played. But perhaps what decided me was that Stirling was going, and I had to be with Stirling. My relationship with Stirling was something I could not quite understand. I saw it as through a misted glass. How often in the past had I thought of marrying Stirling and yet when Lynx had married me that had seemed inevitable; and Stirling had made no protest. I believed that he felt towards me as I did towards him; but for the mighty personality of Lynx we should have married and been content. So now I had to be with Stirling. He and I could only have lived through those desolate weeks which followed the death of Lynx because of the knowledge that it was a desolation shared, and we belonged together.

'I am going to England,' he said firmly. 'He would want me to.'

So I knew I must go too.

Jessica came gliding into my bedroom one late afternoon when I was busy with preparations.

'So you're going,' she said. 'I knew you would. You kept saying you'd stay but I knew you'd go.'

I didn't answer and she sat on the bed watching me.

'So he's gone,' she went on. 'He died, just like any other mortal being. Who would have thought it could have happened to him? But has he gone,

Nora? He'd break free of death, wouldn't he, just as he broke free of captivity? Out he came on the convict ship, like all the others, a prisoner. Then within a few weeks he breaks the fetters. Could he break the fetters of death?'

'What do you mean, Jessica?'

'Will he come back? Do you think he'll come back, Nora?'

'He's dead,' I said.

'You were lucky. You lost him before you knew him.'

'I knew him well,' I retorted. 'I was closer to him than anyone.'

She narrowed her eyes. 'You didn't get to know the bad man in him. He was bad, Nora. Bad! You'd have found out in time just as the others did. All bad men see themselves as greater than other people. They see the rest of us as counters to be moved about to please them. You were a counter, Nora – a pretty counter, a favourite one . . . for the time being. He cherished you, but you were a counter all the same.'

I said: 'Look here, Jessica, I have a lot to do. Don't think you can change my feelings towards him. I knew him as you never could.'

'I'll leave you with your pleasant dreams. Nobody can prove them false now, can they? But he'll come back. He'll find some way to cheat death as he cheated others. He's not gone. You can sense him here now. He's watching us now, Nora. He's laughing at me, because I'm trying to make you see the truth.'

'I wish you were right,' I said vehemently. 'I wish he would come back.'

'Don't say that!' she cried fearfully, looking over her shoulder. 'If you wish too fiercely he might come.'

'Then I'll wish it with all my heart.'

'He wouldn't come back as you knew him. He's no longer flesh and blood. But he'll come back . . . just the same.'

I turned away from her and, shaking her head sadly, she went out. I buried my face in the clothes which I had laid out on the bed and I kept seeing hundreds of pictures of him: Lynx the master, a law unto himself; a man different from all others. And lifting my face I said: 'Lynx, are you there? Come back. I want to talk to you. I want to tell you that I hate your plans for revenge now as I always did. Come back, Lynx.'

But there was no sign – no sound in the quiet room.

Adelaide drove with us to Melbourne and we stayed a night at The Lynx; the next day she came aboard to say goodbye to us. I am sure Stirling was as thankful as I was for precise Adelaide, who kissed us affectionately and repeated that she would keep the home going until we returned. So calm, so prosaic, I wondered then whether she was like her mother for she bore no resemblance to Lynx. As our ship slipped away she stood on the quay waving to us. There were no tears. She might have been seeing us off for a trip to Sydney.

I remembered sailing from England on the *Carron Star*. How different I was from that girl! Since then I had known Lynx. The inexperienced young girl had become a rich widow – outwardly poised, a woman of the world.

Stirling stood beside me as he had on that other occasion; and I felt comforted.

Turning, I smiled at him and I knew he felt the same.

We went first to the Falcon Inn. How strange it was to sit in that lounge where I had first met Stirling and pour the tea, which had been brought to us, and hand him the plate of scones. He was aware of it too. I knew by the way he smiled at me.

'It seems years ago,' he said; and indeed it did. So much had happened. We ourselves had changed.

We had talked a great deal in the ship coming over. He was going to buy Whiteladies because, he said, the owners would be willing to sell. They would, in fact, have no alternative. He would offer a big price for it – a price such as they could not possibly get elsewhere. What did it matter? He was the golden millionaire.

'You can't be certain they'll sell,' I insisted.

'They've *got* to sell, Nora,' was his answer. 'They're bankrupt.'

I knew who had helped to make them so and I was ashamed. The triumvirate, he had called us when I had discovered the mine. I wished I were not part of this.

There were things they could do, I pointed out. They could take paying guests, for instance.

'They wouldn't know how!' Stirling laughed and in that moment he was amazingly like Lynx.

My feelings were in a turmoil. I set myself against them. I felt there was something in what Jessica had said. Lynx was still with us. And I didn't want those people to sell the house. I was on their side.

Stirling's eyes looked like pieces of green glass glinting through his sun-made wrinkles. He was so like Lynx that my spirits rose and I was almost happy. Whatever I said, he would acquire Whiteladies. It would be as Lynx wanted it. The Herrick children would play on the lawns and in time be the proud owners; and those children would be mine and Stirling's. I could almost hear Lynx's voice: 'That's my girl Nora.' And I thought of the lawn on which I had once sat uneasily and the house with its grey towers – ancient and imposing – and understood the desire to possess it.

'The first thing to do is to let it be known that we are looking for a house,' said Stirling. 'We have taken a fancy to the district and want to settle here for a while. We are particularly interested in antiquity and have a great fancy for a house such as Whiteladies. I have already mentioned this to the innkeeper.'

'You lose no time,' I said.

'Did you expect me to? I had quite a conversation with the fellow. He remembered our staying here before, or so he said. He tells me that Lady Cardew died and that Sir Hilary married the companion or whatever she was.'

'Her name was Lucie, I believe.'

He nodded at me, smiling.

'I thought she was very humble,' I went on. 'Not quite one of the family. That will be changed now, I daresay.'

'You're very interested in them, Nora.'

'Aren't you?'

'Considering we have come across the world to buy their house, I certainly am.'

'You are too sure,' I told him. 'How can you know what price will be asked?'

He looked at me in astonishment. What did it matter? He was the golden millionaire. But sometimes a price is not asked in gold.

That very day we paid a visit to the local house agent, and learned that a temporary refuge could be found which seemed the ideal place while we were looking round. By a stroke of great good luck the Wakefields were letting the Mercer's House – a pleasant place and ideal for our purpose while we searched. Only, he warned us, there was no house in the neighbourhood to be compared with Whiteladies except perhaps Wakefield Park itself – and even that was no Whiteladies. We said we were very interested in renting the Mercer's House and made an appointment to see it the next day.

The house agent drove us over in his brougham where Mr. Franklyn Wakefield was waiting to receive us. I remembered him at once and a glance at Stirling showed that he did too.

He bowed to me first, then to Stirling. His manners seemed very formal but his smile was friendly.

'I hope you will like the Mercer's House,' he said, 'though you may find it a little old-fashioned. I have heard it called inconvenient.'

'I'm sure it won't be,' I told him, secretly amused because the agent's reports had been so glowing while it seemed that its owner was doing his best to denigrate it. 'In fact we are enchanted by it ... from the outside, aren't we, Stirling?'

Stirling said characteristicaly that it was in fact the *inside* of the house with which we must concern ourselves if we were going to live in it.

'Therefore,' said Mr. Wakefield, 'I am sure you will wish to inspect it thoroughly.'

'We shall,' said Stirling, rather grimly, I thought; and I remembered that he had taken a dislike to Franklyn Wakefield from the first moment he had seen him.

I said quickly: 'You understand we should only be taking the house temporarily?'

'I was cognizant of the fact,' said Mr. Wakefield with a smile. 'But I daresay that however short the time you will wish for the maximum of comfort.'

I looked at the house with its elegant architecture – Queen Anne, I guessed. Over the walls hung festoons of Virginia creeper and I imagined what a glorious sight it would be in the autumn. There were two lawns in front of the house – one on either side of the path – trim and well kept. I felt the need to make up for Stirling's boorishness by being as charming as possible to Mr. Wakefield.

'If the inside is half as delightful as the outside, I shall be enchanted,' I said. He looked pleased and I went on. 'Am I right in thinking it is Queen Anne or early Georgian?'

'It was built in 1717 by an ancestor of mine and has been in the family ever since. We've used it as a sort of Dower House for members of the family. At this time there is no one who could occupy it. That is why we thought it advisable to seek a tenant.'

'Houses need to be lived in,' I said. 'They're a little sad when empty.'

Stirling gave an explosive laugh. 'Really, Nora! You're giving bricks and mortars credit for feelings they don't possess.'

'I think Mrs. . . . .'

'Herrick,' I supplied.

'I think Mrs. Herrick has a good point,' said Mr. Wakefield. 'Houses soon become unfit for human habitation if they remain unoccupied too long.'

'Well, we'd better look round,' said Stirling.

The house was elegantly furnished. I exclaimed with pleasure at the carved ceiling in the hall. 'That,' explained Mr. Wakefield, 'is the Mercer's coat of arms you see engraved on the ceiling. You will see it in many of the rooms.'

'Of course, it's the Mercer's House, isn't it?'

We went into the drawing-room with its french windows opening on to a lawn.

'We should need at least two gardeners,' said Stirling as though determined to find fault with the place. 'Would they be easy to get?'

'There is no problem about that,' Mr. Wakefield assured him. 'The gardens are taken care of by our own gardeners at the Park. The cost of this has been included in the details the agent will have given you.'

'We are not concerned with the price,' said Stirling and I felt myself blush at what seemed to be his ostentation.

'Nor, I might add, are we,' went on Mr. Wakefield. He smiled directly at me. 'The important point is to find the right tenant. I am sure, Mrs. Herrick, that you and your husband would like to be alone to look over the house.'

I said quickly: 'We are not husband and wife. I am a widow and Mr. Herrick's stepmother.'

If he was surprised he didn't show it. Mr. Wakefield's manners were impeccable. He would have been brought up to believe that to show his feelings was the gravest social error. He, of course, added tact to his many social graces, and it was true that I wanted to be free to discuss the house with Stirling.

'If you would let us take our time . . .'

'But certainly, and if you would care to call at the Park when you have finished . . . that is, if you are interested . . . I should be delighted to see you there. I could send a carriage for you, or if you cared for the walk it is just across the park – about half a mile.'

I said we would walk and he left us.

As the door shut on him Stirling threw himself on to a sofa and began to laugh.

'If you would care to inspect this domicile, madam, and then take a short peregrination across the park . . .'

'Shut up, Stirling, he wasn't as prim as that.'

'Our landlord! My God!'

'It's not the landlord with which we have to concern ourselves but with the house.'

'We should have to see him sometimes, I suppose. He'd call . . . or perhaps his wife would. Do you imagine he has a wife? I wonder what she's like. She will alight from her carriage and leave three cards. Is that the correct number? And we should be invited to call and be bored to death.'

'How do you know we should be bored? How do you know he has a wife?'

'Of course we'd be bored and of course he has a wife. Mr. Wakefield's life would run according to a pattern and you can be sure that pattern includes a wife.'

'I wonder what Wakefield Park is like.'

'Great old ancestral mansion.'

'Like Whiteladies.'

'There is no place in the world like Whiteladies.'

'Well, are we going to take this house?'

'Let's stay at the inn. If we're his tenants that might involve social obligations.'

'Which I am sure you would have no hesitation in ignoring.'

'You are right for once, Nora.'

'For once! What do you mean? I'm going to look all over this house, and I can tell you this: I like it. I've a great desire to know who the Mercer was and what connection a mere tradesman could possibly have with the elegant Mr. Wakefield.'

We inspected the dining-room and descended to the enormous stone-flagged kitchen. I liked it. I liked the large pantries, and stillroom, the buttery and the laundry. It was a fascinating house.

'It's big,' said Stirling.

'Too big for a millionaire!' I demanded ironically. 'You practically told him you were.'

'I felt you were on his side.'

'What nonsense! As if it were a matter of taking sides. Let's go up the staircase.'

There were three floors and some twelve rooms. The rooms were big and airy; I loved the long windows which reached to the floor.

'We're going to take it, Stirling,' I said; and he did not contradict. He was really as fascinated with the house as I was; and being tenants of the Wakefields, we could almost certainly meet the owners of Whiteladies. I was not sure what plans Stirling had and how quickly he hoped to acquire the place, but I guessed it would take a long time, and it would certainly be more satisfactory having the Mercer's House than an inn as our temporary home while we waited.

'Well?' he asked, when we had been through the house.

'We're going to tell Mr. Wakefield that we're taking it.'

We walked across the park and to the house which was called Wakefield Park. It was a big house – early Victorian, I judged, with its heavy ornate architecture. It looked strong and solid. On the front lawn was a pond in which a fountain played. White stone steps led to a terrace on which were seats. The flowers grew neatly, even primly. 'It's just the sort of house he would have,' I commented.

'You can be sure everything is in its proper place,' added Stirling. Then he mimicked: 'It is fitting that each and every appurtenance of this house is lodged in the place assigned to it.'

'I don't believe you like him.'

'Do you?'

'I like the Mercer's House. That's good enough.'

Along one wall of the house was a vinery. I could see the vine trained along the glass to catch the sun. There were pots of exotic-looking flowers in there too.

'You must admit,' I said, 'that there is something imposing about his house.'

We mounted the steps of the terrace to the porch, on one side of which hung a bell. When pulled this gave a hollow clanging and almost immediately a manservant appeared.

'You would be Mr. and Mrs. Herrick,' he said. 'Mr. Wakefield is in the library with Sir Everard and her ladyship. I'm requested to conduct you there.'

I threw Stirling a glance as much to say: 'You see how well ordered everything is.' 'What did you expect from Mr. Wakefield?' he flashed back.

The hall was enormous and somewhat oppressive. The heads of two stags adorned the wall on either side of that of a tiger. There were various portraits which we had no time then to study. A staircase with elaborately carved banisters curved upwards. We mounted this in the wake of the butler.

'Mr. and Mrs. Herrick!' he announced after knocking and opening a door.

Mr. Wakefield was there with a youngish man and an elderly man and woman.

'So good of you to come,' said Mr. Wakefield. 'May I present you to my parents – Sir Everard and Lady Wakefield and Dr. Hunter.

Lady Wakefield was a frail old lady who gave me a pleasant smile; then I turned to Sir Everard.

'You will forgive my not rising,' he said; and I noticed he was in a wheelchair with a tartan rug about his knees.

The doctor shook hands.

'Dr. Hunter has just been making one of his calls,' said Lady Wakefield. 'If you are going to live here, and need a good doctor – which I hope you won't – you will find him excellent. Franklyn, do ring for fresh tea.'

'I have already told them to bring it if and when Mr. and Mrs. Herrick called.'

'So thoughtful,' said Lady Wakefield with an adoring look at her son, who said in his dignified manner: 'Pray be seated.'

'We have come to tell you that we are delighted with the Mercer's House,' I told him, 'and we want to take it.'

'Splendid,' said Mr. Wakefield.

'It's time it was lived in,' added Sir Everard. 'It doesn't do the place any good to be left standing empty.'

'It's a charming old place,' put in the doctor.

There was a knock at the door and a trolley was wheeled in accompanied by a footman and a parlourmaid. Life was clearly lived in an elegant fashion at Wakefield Park.

'Mr. and Mrs. Herrick are looking for a house in the neighbourhood, I gathered,' said Franklyn. 'That's why they are taking the Mercer's House temporarily.'

'They are not easy to find,' the doctor warned us. 'That is, if you want a house of character.'

'We do,' I replied.

'We have noticed a charming old place,' began Stirling.

'Whiteladies!' Lady Wakefield smiled. 'A most unusual place. It's actually built on the site of an old convent. In fact some of the old convent still remains.'

'The Cardews are great friends of ours,' said Sir Everard. 'If you come here to live you will be meeting them.'

'That will be very interesting.' Stirling gave me a look which was almost a grimace and I said quickly: 'We are very intrigued by the Mercer's House and are wondering how it came to have such a name.'

'My great-great-grandfather built it,' explained Mr. Wakefield. 'He was a mercer of London where he made enough money to retire to the country and build himself a house. This he did. But he never forgot his trade so he called his house the Mercer's House.'

'The family prospered,' Sir Everard carried on the story, 'and my father built this house which was better suited to his needs and Mercer's was occupied by aunts and cousins and any members of the family who needed it . . . until two years ago. A sister of mine occupied it; and since she died it has been empty. It was my son's idea that we should let it and you will be the first outside the family to live in it.'

'That's very interesting,' I said. 'I am sure we are going to enjoy it.'

Stirling said to me: 'I fancy it was this Whiteladies that we visited briefly when we were here last. We have recently arrived from Australia,' he explained to the company.

'I had a brother who went there,' began Sir Everard. I could see he was a garrulous old gentleman, for his wife, smiling indulgently at him, said quickly: 'So you were at Whiteladies . . . briefly?'

I explained the incident of the scarf and Mr. Wakefield looked delighted. 'I remember the occasion,' he said.

'What an excellent memory you must have!' I told him. 'There was a lady in a chair . . .'

'Lady Cardew. She has since died. There is now another Lady Cardew.'

'And a very pretty young girl.'

'That would be Minta,' said Lady Wakefield. 'Such a dear girl!' Her indulgent smile was turned on her son. Oh yes, I thought, there will be a match between Minta and Mr. Wakefield. 'She has a little half-sister now – Druscilla – daughter of the second Lady Cardew.'

'And Minta, is she married?'

Again that roguish look for Mr. Wakefield. 'Not yet.'

The doctor, who had said very little, took out his watch and looked at it. 'I should be on my way,' he said.

'So many people needing your services,' commented Lady Wakefield.

'You will be going back to the Falcon Inn, I daresay,' said the doctor to us. 'Could I give you a lift?'

'It's an excellent idea,' said Mr. Wakefield. 'But if you are not going that way, Doctor, I will arrange . . .'

The doctor said that he was in fact going that way, so we thanked the Wakefields and I assured them that we would be ready to move into the Mercer's House the following week when all that was necessary to be settled would have been completed.

That would be admirable, said Mr. Wakefield; and soon we were rolling along in the doctor's brougham.

'Charming people,' he said of the Wakefields.

'I hope our neighbours at this Whiteladies are as charming,' murmured Stirling.

I noticed then a tightening of the doctor's lips and I wondered what that meant. He seemed to realize that I was studying him and said quickly: 'I daresay you will be able to judge for yourself in due course.'

He dropped us at the inn and when he had gone I said to Stirling: 'He was a bit odd about the people at Whiteladies. Did you notice his face when I mentioned them?'

But Stirling had noticed nothing.

I felt better than I had since the death of Lynx. I was interested in life again. I disapproved of this crazy scheme to rob its owners of Whiteladies – and indeed the more I thought of it the more crazy it seemed – but at the same time I was fascinated by these people and it was almost as though, as Jessica had said, Lynx had come back and was urging me to act against my will.

I was eager to live in the Mercer's House. I liked the Wakefield family. I had heard from the innkeeper who was a gossip that Sir Everard and Lady Wakefield had despaired of having children and that they were well into middle age when their son was born. They doted on him; and he would say this for Mr. Franklyn, he was a good son if ever there was one, and it wouldn't be many more months he was sure before there was a match between the Park and Whiteladies.

'That would be Miss Minta,' I said.

'You'd be right there. A sweet young lady, and highly thought of hereabouts.'

'Then Mr. Franklyn will be lucky.'

'They'll be a lucky pair.'

'And Whiteladies? I suppose that will one day be Miss Minta's – but she'll be at Wakefield Park.'

'Don't you believe it. She'll be at Whiteladies. It'll go to her – the eldest – and who'd have thought there'd be another. Sir Hilary at his time of life too! But a new young wife, you know how it is.'

I nodded sagely. He was a good source of information. I should miss our talks when we moved to Mercer's.

There were two servants attached to the place – a parlourmaid and a housemaid.

'We can't say they haven't thought of our comfort,' I said to Stirling, who agreed reluctantly. He could think of little but Whiteladies and was all impatience to approach the family.

'How?' I demanded. 'For heaven's sake be tactful. You can't exactly call and say, "I'd like your house and insist you sell it to me," you have to feel your way.'

'Don't be afraid. I'll know how to deal with it. But everything takes so much time.'

Two days before we were due to move into the Mercer's House, the landlord's wife came to my room and told me that 'a person' was downstairs asking to see me. She had been 'put' into the inn-parlour. I went down and found a middle-aged woman waiting there.

'You would be Mrs. Herrick?' she asked.

I said I was.

'My name's Glee – Mrs. Amy Glee. I was housekeeper up at Whiteladies until Madam decided she had no need of my services.'

She could not have said anything more inclined to arouse my interest.

'Madam?'

'The new Lady Cardew,' she said with a significant sniff.

'Oh, and why have you come to see me?'

'I hear you're taking Mercer's, and I thought you might be needing a housekeeper. I *know* you'll be needing one because I've had experience of Ellen and Mabel. They were both at Whiteladies at one time . . . and when they started getting rid of servants those two went to the Park.'

'I see,' I said.

'They'll work, but only if watched. I know their type and there's many like them. Now, madam, if you don't want to spend all your time watching lazy maids . . .'

'Were you at Whiteladies long?'

'Fifteen years, and good service I gave.'

I recognized her now. She was the woman to whom Lucie had taken me when my hand was bandaged.

'I am sure you did,' I said.

'Fifteen years and then told to go. Mind you, I was all right. I had my cousin once removed . . . down Dover way. She died six months back and left me the cottage and something besides. It's not for the need that I've come. But I'm a woman who likes to be on the go. And told to leave I was – after fifteen years. I was all right, but I might not have been.'

There was something about the pursed lips, the jerk of the head which aroused my curiosity. I decided that we needed a housekeeper at the Mercer's House.

Chapter Two

I enjoyed settling into the house. I felt that I could be happy there in a placid way and that was what I wanted. I had had enough adventure. I had seen a man killed; I had experienced strange and not altogether understood emotions; I had been the wife of a man who had dominated me and of whom I had never known the like. That was enough. I could never know those wild joys and fears again, and perhaps I did not want to. Lynx could never come back; and I wondered whether I could ever have known real peace with him. But here in this elegant country house, built by the rich London mercer nearly two hundred years ago, I could perhaps find a new way of life. He had come to live here in peace; I sensed that. The Mercer's House would be my refuge as it had been that of the mercer. Here I would be in charge of my own destiny; I could mould my life to my own inclination. Sometimes I wondered whether I had always known that my life with Lynx would be brief. He had been so much older than I. True, I had believed him to be immortal. Often now I could not believe that he was really dead.

One thing was certain: I was fortunate to have known him and to have been loved by him; but I had to convince myself it was over; and since I must rebuild my life, the Mercer's House was the best place in which to do it. Sometimes I felt Jessica was right and he was beside me, guiding me, urging me in that direction where he wanted me to go. I had believed that he wanted me to marry Stirling and that had he not desired me himself would have arranged our marriage before he died. So I dreamed of marrying Stirling. We would abandon the crazy idea of acquiring Whiteladies. Perhaps we would buy the Mercer's House and our children would be born there. Minta should marry Franklyn Wakefield and our children and theirs should play in the lawns of Whiteladies. So after all Lynx's grandchild should play on those smooth and velvety lawns. But would Lynx ever be satisfied with a compromise?

So I dreamed.

We had not been a week in the Mercer's House when Minta came to call. She had changed little. She was very pretty and much as I remembered her. There was a certain innocence about her which I found appealing.

'Franklyn Wakefield told me you were here,' she said. 'How very interesting. Of course I remember the time you came. Your scarf blew over the wall.'

As it was mid-morning I asked if she would care for coffee or perhaps a glass of wine. She said she would like the coffee so I rang the bell.

Ellen appeared, neat and trim, and Minta smiled at her and said: 'Good

morning, Ellen.' Of course the girl had worked at Whiteladies before going
to Wakefield Park.

When she had left us, Minta said: 'I hope you are well looked after. Mr.
Wakefield was very anxious that you should be. Ellen and Mabel are such
good girls.'

Mrs. Glee had other opinions but Minta would believe the best of
everybody.

'Our housekeeper keeps them in good order.'

'Oh yes, you have Mrs. Glee.'

'I see that our actions have been well observed.'

She laughed. 'This is country life, you know. Everyone is always interested
in newcomers and wonders whether they are going to enter into local affairs.'

'Is that expected of us?'

'Shall we say it might be hoped. You won't be pestered if you show you
wish to remain aloof, but somehow I don't think *you* will.'

'There is my stepson,' I said.

'Oh yes.' She smiled. 'It seems so strange. You are so young to have a
grown-up stepson. But I have a stepmother who is not much older than I.
When we met previously I thought you were brother and sister until . . .'

'It is rather a complicated relationship. I married Stirling's father and
now he's dead and I am a widow . . .'

My voice trembled. I was seeing him carried home on that stretcher. I
was thinking of that immense vitality; that excitement which he had brought
into my life and which was gone for ever.

'I'm sorry,' said Minta. I realized she was very sensitive to the feelings
of others. I liked her, and thought what an admirable wife she would make
for Franklyn Wakefield. I liked him, too. There was something worthy
about them both. Nice people, I thought. Yes, that was the word. *Nice!*
Unexciting but good. There would be few surprises. They were different
from people like Lynx, Stirling and myself. They were lacking in our egoism,
perhaps. They seemed colourless. But perhaps that was unfair when applied
to such a charming girl as Minta.

I said quickly: 'It's over. One has to learn to forget.' She nodded and I
went on: 'I remember so clearly the first day I saw Whiteladies. It impressed
us both so much. The lawn and the kind way in which you received us. And
then of course the way my hand was bandaged.'

'That was Lucie. She is my stepmother now. You will meet her. My
mother died . . .' A look of sorrow touched her face. She was easy to read
and one of her charms was the changing expressions of her face.

'I gathered she was an invalid,' I said.

'Yes, but . . .' I waited but she did not finish the sentence. 'Lucie has been
wonderful. She has been so good to Papa. She helps with his work and
manages the house perfectly.'

'I am so glad.'

'And we have an addition to the family. My little half-sister Druscilla.
She's a darling. She is nearly a year old.'

'It's not really so long ago that we met for the first time,' I commented,
'and so much has happened since then.'

I was thinking: I became Lynx's wife and his widow. I must have betrayed my thoughts for she changed the subject quickly; 'You will enjoy it here, I'm sure. It's rather a pleasant community.'

Ellen brought in the coffee with Mrs. Glee close behind. Mrs. Glee gave Minta a triumphant: 'Good morning, Miss Cardew!' to which Minta replied how glad she was to see Mrs. Glee again and then assured me that Mrs. Glee would take admirable care of the household. Mrs. Glee's head shook with pleasure and righteousness as she supervised Ellen serving coffee.

When she had gone Minta said: 'She really is a wonderful housekeeper. I'm glad you have her. We should never have let her go if we could have afforded to keep her.'

So it was true that they were not well off. Perhaps Stirling would succeed after all. But it was a different matter selling a house from ridding themselves of an expensive servant.

'I daresay Maud Mathers will be calling on you soon. She's the rector's daughter. His wife is dead but Maud is indefatigable in parish affairs. She's a good, sensible girl and I'm sure you'll like her. But, please, I want your first visit to be to Whiteladies. I shall ask Mr. Wakefield to join us for dinner. Sir Everard and Lady Wakefield rarely leave the Park. They are not fit for it. Now will you promise me?'

I readily gave the promise.

I was sure, I told her, that Stirling would be delighted to accept the invitation; and at that moment Stirling came in.

I said: 'Stirling, Miss Cardew has called. Do you remember?'

'But of course!' exclaimed Stirling; and I saw the excitement leap into his eyes. She noticed it, too, and she flushed prettily. 'This is a great pleasure,' he added with feeling.

I knew he was thinking he was making progress.

'Have some coffee,' I said and went over to the table to pour it for him.

'We are invited to Whiteladies,' I told him.

'I am delighted,' he replied.

She was smiling. She had become more animated since Stirling had arrived. Naturally, I thought, he seems exciting because she is accustomed to Franklyn Wakefield.

It was rather gratifying to discover what a stir we had made in the neighbourhood. We did seem rather incongruous, I supposed – a young man close to thirty with a stepmother just entering her twenties, living together in the Mercer's House. It was the most respectable of relationships; besides we had the servants as chaperons plus the presence of Mrs. Glee. Stirling's rooms were on the first floor, mine on the second; his at the front, mine at the back. Mrs. Glee, in black bombazine, dispelled any gossip for it was inconceivable that she would be found in any house where the slightest impropriety was practised.

She came to me every morning to discuss the menu for the day; she behaved as though we were a large household; and I realized that this ceremony was necessary to her dignity. It was only when she discussed

Whiteladies that she forgot her decorum. I confess that I lured her to talk of that household which was of the utmost interest to me.

'I don't like it, madam,' she reiterated on an old theme one morning after we had decided what should be prepared for luncheon. 'For years I served Lady Cardew – the *first* Lady Cardew, that is – and I venture to say that *she* never had cause for complaint. And then suddenly I'm told my services are to be dispensed with. They could do without me. As though, Madam, what I did was of such little importance that I could go and no difference be noticed.'

'I gathered from Miss Cardew that economies were necessary,' I said.

'Economies! There was money wasted in that house. Oh no, the second Lady Cardew wanted me out of the way. She wanted to run the place. She didn't want anyone there who might see what she was up to. And that's the long and the short of it, madam.'

'I daresay it had to be, you know. The expense of keeping up a place like Whiteladies must be great.'

Mrs. Glee sniffed. 'I always thought there was something going on in that house.'

'Oh?' Of course I shouldn't be discussing my neighbours with my housekeeper, but the temptation to do so was irresistible.

'Oh yes,' went on Mrs. Glee. 'She'd make up her mind what she wanted and she didn't want anyone there who might see through her. After all, what was she in those days? A sort of companion, neither one thing nor the other.'

'Miss Cardew seems very fond of her stepmother.'

'Miss Cardew's one of the blessed innocents. Wouldn't see what was going on right under her nose if you was to ask me.'

'She seems a very charming young lady.'

'She and her father . . . a pair of babes in the wood. Oh, you can smile, Mrs. Herrick, but she was after the doctor at one time. We all thought there'd be a match there, and then her ladyship dies and "No thank you," said madam to the doctor, "I'm after her ladyship's shoes." ' Mrs. Glee's language became more colourful as she warmed to her subject, and I felt I must put an end to these observations which I believed were decidedly prejudiced.

'Well, I hope, Mrs. Glee, you don't regret the change too much. Miss Cardew was saying how lucky we were to get you.'

'Miss Cardew was always the lady.'

'I'm sure of that. And I think we'll have the apple pie. Mr. Herrick is very partial to that.'

Confidences were over; we were back to business.

Franklyn Wakefield picked us up in his carriage. Our own had not yet been delivered but Stirling already had four fine horses in the stables.

I liked the courtly manner in which I was handed into the carriage. He asked if I liked riding with my back to the horses or otherwise. I told him I had no preference.

'I daresay you rode a great deal in Australia.'

'Everywhere,' I told him. 'It was necessary. We even camped out. Do you remember, Stirling, that occasion when we rode some forty miles or so to Melbourne . . . and then back?'

I could smell the perfume of the eucalypts; I remembered Adelaide boiling the kettle and Jagger coming close to me while I knelt by the fire. Would there always be these memories?

'You will be an expert horsewoman.'

I shrugged my shoulders, and he went on: 'I would like to show you my estate one day. Perhaps we could ride out together and I could introduce you to the countryside.'

Stirling started to talk about the vastness of the property in Australia in a rather brash, patronizing way which made me frown; and the more I frowned the more bombastic he became. Franklyn listened politely and made no effort to cap Stirling's stories which I should have been tempted to had I been in his place. It was a pity Stirling could not hide his contempt for Franklyn who, of course, completely disguised his reaction. A lesson in good manners, I would remind Stirling when we were alone.

To arrive at Whiteladies after dusk was an experience. The place looked mysteriously romantic and – in odd contrast – almost sinister. There was a lantern hanging in the porch which creaked slightly as it swung and as we mounted the steep stone steps an excitement possessed me. I glanced at Stirling. His eyes gleamed; I was aware of his tension.

Franklyn pulled the bell rope and we heard the clanging echoing through the hall. The door was iron-studded and looked impregnable; there was a grille through which we saw the eyes of the manservant before he opened the door.

Then we were in the hall; the floor was stone-flagged, the panelling intricate; candles guttered in the sconces. So it must have looked nearly forty years ago when Lynx came here to give his Arabella drawing lessons. How could I ever forget him when there were a thousand things everywhere I went to remind me of him!

Minta appeared at the staircase on one end of the hall. 'I heard the bell,' she said, descending. She looked radiant and as dainty as a fairy princess in the candle light. 'I'm so pleased that you've come.'

'We're pleased that you invited us,' said Stirling. 'It's a great occasion, I can tell you, to be guests in this house.'

Minta said she wasn't sure whether it was the house or its inhabitants that pleased him.

'Both!' replied Stirling.

'If you're interested in architecture,' put in Franklyn, 'you couldn't have a better example of the Tudor than you have here. Some of it is a little later but the house is fundamentally Tudor.'

'Living in Australia, I have had no opportunity of visiting these ancient houses,' said Stirling. 'So it's a great novelty to me. Not so Nora. She was a tenderfoot, you know. She was only out there a mere two years or so.'

'I'm fascinated by Whiteladies all the same.'

'We must show you over the house,' promised Minta. 'Perhaps after dinner. First you must meet my father and stepmother.'

Stirling started up the stairs after her, and as Franklyn and I followed he poined out the carving which was the work of a sixteenth-century artist. He was sure of this because that particular artist always left his special mark – a nun's head. There were examples of his work in other houses in this part of the country. It might have been that his first big commission was the carving in Whiteladies and ever after he had used the nun's head as his symbol.

'As soon as one begins to delve into the past one makes all sorts of interesting discoveries,' he said.

'Do you delve into the past?' I asked.

'In a dilettantish manner. I am interested in this part of the world. We've had several discoveries. We've found old coins and jewellery belonging to the Stone and Bronze Ages. But I'm interested in the more recent past. The history of old houses, for instance; and this one is one of the most fascinating I've ever known.'

'I find it fascinating too,' I said; and by this time we had reached the top of a staircase and Minta had thrown open the door of a room.

It was delightful with its tall mullioned windows and lofty ceiling; the cupola had been so designed to make this appear even higher than it was. I imagined that in daylight the wood carving was magnificent. There were portraits on the walls, and the furniture I judged to be early eighteenth century. It was extremely elegant; in daylight I was to discover that it was somewhat shabby, but that was not noticeable at this time.

I recognized Lucie immediately though she had changed. She had a new dignity and was striking in an unobtrusive way. She appeared to be very modestly dressed in puce-coloured velvet but the dress was beautifully cut and elegant in its simplicity. She was reserved, yet completely mistress of the occasion. Her dark hair was simply dressed but becomingly. She came forward and took my hand.

'This is a pleasure,' she said. She spoke gently but without warmth. 'I remember you well. Minta has been telling me.'

Then she turned to Stirling. 'Oh yes, indeed. I do remember. After all it is not so long ago. Come and meet my husband.'

Sir Hilary – Minta's father – came towards us and shook hands. He looked frail and had the same guileless expression I had noticed in Minta. Innocent, I thought, and quite unworldly; and then immediately I was thinking of his marrying the woman whom Lynx had loved, and it seemed incongruous that I should be here taking up the threads of Lynx's past. Here I should remember him as vividly as I had done in Australia.

'We are so pleased to have neighbours,' he said. 'Franklyn has told me all about your taking the Mercer's House. You're lucky to get it. It's a gem of a house.'

Franklyn was near. 'We're lucky to have such tenants at Mercer's,' he said.

'Ah, Franklyn, and how are your parents today?'

Franklyn said they were very lively and well; and Sir Hilary went on to ask questions about them. He was obviously interested in their ailments and comparing them with his own.

Two other guests arrived. I had already met the doctor who looked, I thought, quite ill at ease; and with him was Miss Maud Mathers, the vicar's daughter, a rather tall young woman with an outdoor complexion and a breezy manner. I was immediately convinced that she was a great asset to her father in the parish.

Dinner was served in a dining-room the same size and similar in many ways – the same type of ceiling, the same panelling – to the drawing-room. Minta mentioned that they used this dining-room most of the time although for occasions when there were many guests, such as Christmas time, they used the hall.

'In the old days we used it more than we do today,' she explained. 'We used to have a houseful of guests. I'm sure my parents didn't know half the people they entertained. Now of course we have to be careful.'

'One day perhaps it will be different,' said Stirling.

I was uneasy. He was showing his obsession with the place too clearly. There was something so honest about Stirling. I loved him for it, but I felt it would be better to hide his intentions as yet. He had no subtlety. Now Franklyn. . . . I was continually comparing the two, and everything about Stirling I loved, although I did not necessarily applaud or admire it. Now he was being almost naïve as his covetous eyes roamed about the house.

I noticed there was only one parlourmaid and the butler was the man who had opened the door. They evidently had few servants. The meal was well cooked and well served, which I imagined was due to Lucie's supervision. She had her eyes on everything and I was quickly aware that the servants were in awe of her.

Conversation at the dinner-table ranged over a number of subjects. Sir Hilary and Franklyn discussed the Wakefield estate; Stirling was asking Minta questions about the house; Lucie from one end of the table was looking after her guests and joining in here and there; I was seated next to the doctor and opposite me was Maud Mathers, who talked in an animated way about parish affairs.

'You'll love the church, Mrs. Herrick. It's the same period as this house. The tower is quite impressive, isn't it, Dr. Hunter?'

The doctor agreed that it was a fine old church.

'I hope you'll come along to some of our social affairs,' said Miss Mathers.

'Do you intend staying long in the neighbourhood?' the doctor wanted to know.

'It's difficult to say,' I answered. 'My stepson is enamoured of this part of the world and he has fallen in love with Whiteladies.'

'It's the sort of house about which people get obsessions,' said Maud. 'I believe one or two people have wanted to buy it.'

'I understand it's been in the family for centuries.'

'Yes, handed down from generation to generation. Not like our house, which goes with the living.'

'Miss Cardew has promised to show us round after dinner.'

Lucie joined in the conversation. 'Most people want to see over the house.'

'You must get tired of showing them.'

'I never get tired. I'm as fascinated with the place as everyone else, except of course those who are born in it, like Minta. I always tell her she doesn't appreciate it. It will be the same with Druscilla.' She smiled. 'My daughters,' she added.

'And how is Druscilla?' asked the doctor.

Lucie's smile gave luminosity to her face. Mother love, I thought, plus candle light. 'She is quite well now.' She turned to me. 'I'm like all mothers with a first child. I fuss. I call the doctor in for nothing.'

'It's called "first baby nerves",' said the doctor.

'It shows a mother's tender care,' Maud put in. 'And I'm sure Dr. Hunter understands and doesn't blame any of the mothers in the parish for their over-anxiety.'

'Oh, I'm very tolerant,' said the doctor lightly.

'A necessary qualification,' added Lucie almost sarcastically.

I seemed to be sensitive that night. I was aware of a certain tension between the doctor and Lucie Cardew. Or was I imagining it? I fancied that he was very interested in her, that he admired her and she did not return his esteem. Then once again I was thinking of Lynx. There would have been dinner-parties such as this one to which the drawing-master would not have been invited. I could imagine his anger at slights, his determination that one day he would sit at the head of this table.

I came out of my reverie to hear Lucie say: 'Oh, Maud, you know you spoil her. She's getting quite arrogant.'

'She's such a darling,' Maud insisted, 'and so bright.'

'I can hear you are talking about my little sister,' said Minta. Then she told a story illustrating the intelligence of the absent Druscilla; and soon afterwards the ladies were conducted to the drawing-room and the men left at the table with their port. There Maud dominated the conversation, which seemed to be mainly about the proceeds of the coming sale of work which would help in the repair of the inevitably beetle-ridden church roof. It would be held in the grounds of Wakefield Park, which Sir Everard and Lady Wakefield had kindly placed at their disposal.

'It used to be Whiteladies,' Minta explained to me, 'but the Park is so much more suitable.'

'Is it?' I asked. 'I should have thought . . .'

'Oh, we're ancient, but the Park gardens are so much better than ours nowadays. We only have two gardeners. In my grandfather's day there were six. It means that quite a lot of the place has gone wild, and the flowers at the Park are superb.'

Another indication of poverty, but she seemed quite unperturbed by it. I wondered how Stirling was getting on at the table.

Later the men joined us and after coffee Minta said she knew that Stirling and I wanted to see the house, so she would show us now.

'Be careful of the bartizan if you go up there,' warned Lucie.

'I will,' promised Minta. She explained to us as we went out of the room. 'The stonework is beginning to crumble in some parts of the house.'

'What is this bartizan?' asked Stirling.

'It's a sort of battlemented overhanging turret on the top of the tower. Lucie's afraid it's going to collapse.'

'Shouldn't it be put right?'

'It will be one day when we can afford it.'

'But if it's dangerous . . .'

'Oh, there's so much that needs to be done. You've no idea.'

'Yes, I have,' said Stirling.

She smiled at him as though she thought he was clever. 'Most people never think that a house like this needs constant expenditure if it's to be kept in order. And if this is neglected for some years . . .' She raised her eyebrows.

'But surely it shouldn't be neglected,' insisted Stirling.

'If the money isn't available it has to be.'

'I'm sorry . . .' began Stirling.

She shrugged her shoulders. 'All my life people have been saying that Whiteladies would fall about our ears if necessary repairs weren't done. I get used to it.'

'But a house like this is a sort of trust.'

'Yes,' she agreed. 'A sort of trust. This is the entrance into the old part. These were really the convent walls. You'll be able to see how thick they are in a minute. Mind these stairs. They're rather dangerous.'

We mounted the spiral stone staircase, holding the rope banister. The steps were steep and worn in the middle.

'I've never seen anything like it,' said Stirling, and there was a lilt of excitement in his voice.

'I'm glad you find it exciting,' said Minta, who hadn't noticed the acquisitive gleam in Stirling's eyes.

Through the old part of the house we went. Minta had picked up a lantern from the walls and Stirling carried it. We followed her up winding flights of steps into alcoves that were like cells. It was very cold.

'We sometimes use this for storing things,' said Minta. 'When I was young I can remember venison and great hams being kept here. That was when we entertained a good deal and there were more servants.'

She took us back to the inhabited part of the house.

'This section was built a little later than the main part. It was in the time of Elizabeth Tudor so it is built in the shape of an E. This is the main block; there are two projecting wings on either side and this short section in between.'

'One could get lost in such a house,' I said.

'I was lost once,' Minta told us. 'They searched and searched for me. I was in what we called the studio. There's an enormous cupboard there and for some reason no one thought of looking in it. The studio was given the name when my mother had drawing lessons there.'

'I'd like to see it,' I said.

'You shall, though there's nothing special about it except that it has a good north light.'

Nothing special! When he had sat there with her, instructing her, falling in love with her!

'My mother, you know, was the daughter of the house – the only child. When my father married her he came to live here.'

'So there weren't always Cardews at Whiteladies.'

'No. We haven't been able to keep the family name going. There have been several family names. They're inscribed on the wall in the library. There have been six changes of name in three hundred years. It seems to be a feature of the family that every now and then a woman inherits. She marries and the family name is changed. That's what happened to my mother.'

'And it will to you.'

'Well . . .' She laughed with an insouciance which implied that she was completely unconcerned as to whether Whiteladies came into her possession or not. 'Before Druscilla was born we thought she might be a boy. In which case . . .'

'But she would not have been in the direct line,' insisted Stirling. 'Your father married into the family and his present wife is nothing to do with it, so . . .'

'Oh no,' said Minta quickly. 'When people marry they become the family. It has always been like that. Whiteladies is my father's now . . .'

'You could have lost Whiteladies!' cried Stirling, 'and you don't seem to care.'

'I should like to have a little brother. My father would love to have a son. He was so proud when Druscilla was born.'

'But if there was a son it seems you could lose Whiteladies.'

'I don't think of Whiteladies as a possession exactly. It's the family home. Whoever owned it, it would be home, always.'

'Unless,' suggested Stirling, 'it passed out of the family.'

I flashed him a warning glance. He was going too far too fast.

'That couldn't happen,' she said with a look of surprise. 'It's always been the family's house.'

'But if it were a burden . . .'

'A burden! Oh, I see what you mean . . . financially.' She laughed almost merrily. 'It's always been a financial burden.'

'If it became too heavy a one . . .'

'It's always been too heavy a one. Now this is the way to the studio I was telling you about. We have to get up the narrow flight. It's at the top of the wing . . . to get the light, you see.' She threw open a door. 'There! Look at the dust. It's not used nowadays and I suppose the servants don't often come up here. There's far too much for them to do. My mother used to come up here a lot. Oh, there's the cupboard. It's enormous . . . one of those you can walk about in. I think I must have come up here to look for her; then I wandered into the cupboard and shut myself in.'

The room was plainly furnished. There was a big table, some chairs and an easel.

'I was never any good at drawing,' went on Minta. 'Perhaps Druscilla will be. Then we can use the studio again.'

She opened the cupboard door. It was the size of a small room and down one side were shelves on which were a few pencils, crayons and two drawing-boards. Minta picked up one; on it were several sketches of a horse. That was Lynx's work. I would know it anywhere. Oh Lynx, I thought, how could I ever have imagined that I would be able to forget!

'Not much to see here,' said Minta and I felt angry with her, which was stupid. How could she guess at the turmoil in my heart?

She took us to the library after that and showed us the crest and the coat of arms and the names of the family very artistically inscribed on the branches of a fig tree – Merrivale, Charton, Delmer, Berrington, Dorian and Cardew. Stirling was staring as though fascinated. I knew he was adding a new name: Herrick.

We climbed more stairs. 'This is the east wing of that E. We don't use this part now, but my mother was fond of it. When Lucie married my father she decided it would be economical to close this part of the house. Lucie is wonderful at managing things. I am sure our affairs are in better shape since she started looking after them.'

I could well believe that.

'This was my mother's room. Lucie had the furniture covered in dust sheets. The servants don't like to come up here.'

'Why?' asked Stirling.

'You know how it is when there has been a recent death ... or perhaps you don't. Servants get superstitious. My mother died rather suddenly.'

'I thought she had been an invalid for some time,' I said.

'Well, a sort of invalid. We all thought she rather imagined her illness and then she died of a heart attack. We felt we'd misjudged her – and Lizzie, who had been her maid, started imagining things.'

'Things?'

'Oh, that my mother wouldn't rest and she believed she was still in the house ... her ghost, she meant. Poor Lizzie, she had been with Mamma since she was a girl. She was so sensible and practical, but Mamma's death seemed to unnerve her. Lucie is taking her in hand, though, and she's getting better.'

I looked round the room. Her room! Here she would come after the drawing lesson to dream about him. It was in this room that they had found him with jewels in his pockets. I believed I could sense the great drama which had taken place there.

Minta was ushering us out and leading the way along the corridor. 'There's a staircase at the end of this landing,' she was saying. I was still thinking of that room. It happened forty years ago, I reminded myself. And I could feel the frustration and agony of Lynx when he was caught, trapped; and he knew he could not hope for justice. And because of this Stirling and I were here now. Poor innocent Minta! She did not know that the apparently courteous guests whom she was graciously showing round were two harpies planning to take Whiteladies from her.

I wanted to see that room again. I wanted to be in it alone. I wanted to sense the atmosphere of that tragic night when Lynx's pride was humbled. Minta and Stirling had turned a corner. I hastily slipped back into the room. It was different now. Without the lamp I could just make out the humps of furniture under the dust sheets because light from a half moon shone through the windows.

Oh Lynx, I thought, I understand your misery, but it's all over. It must be forgotten. We'll have the Mercer's House, Stirling and I – and Minta and Franklyn will be our friends. Your grandchildren shall play on the lawns of Whiteladies. That's how your dream will come true.

No! I could almost hear his scorn. He wanted revenge. I could hear his voice in my mind thundering: No!

Then my heart began to beat fast because there was something in the room. I sensed a presence. Someone was watching me.

'Lynx!' I breathed. 'Oh, Lynx, come back.'

A shape materialized in the doorway and moved towards me.

'You're Mrs. Herrick.' A human voice. Not that of Lynx.

'You startled me,' I said.

'I'm sorry, madam, I'm sure. I wasn't expecting anyone in Miss Arabella's room.'

'Miss Cardew is showing us the house.' Understandably she looked round for Miss Cardew. 'They went on without me and I wandered back in here.'

She peered at me as though I were of rather special interest to her. 'You're Mrs. Herrick,' she said. 'There was someone here long ago . . . of that name.'

'You must have been here a long time.'

'I was two years older than Miss Arabella. I was under-nurse when I was fourteen. Because there wasn't much difference in our ages we were together . . . a lot.'

'You're Lizzie,' I said.

She nodded. 'I was there . . . all the way through. And now she's dead and there's another Lady Cardew.'

It was eerie in this room with nothing to light it but the moon, and the odd shapes of furniture seemed as though at any moment they might take on life. I knew instinctively that this woman had known and loved him. It was impossible for anyone to be unaffected by him. She reminded me of Jessica.

'You come from Australia and that was where he went . . . this man who was here once. I know you were his wife but he had another before you. That's his son. There's a likeness, though he's not the man his father was. There's something in the air. I can feel it. It's as though he's come back.'

'He's dead,' I said sharply, 'so he can't come back.'

'He could if he wanted to. He could do anything. Don't make any mistake about that. Something's going to happen. It always does where he is . . . and he's here. I'm sure of it. I knew him well.'

I shivered. She was so like Jessica and I felt that I was caught up in some intricate pattern which kept repeating itself.

'The others will be wondering what has happened to me,' I said.

She ignored that. 'Lady Cardew died suddenly,' she said. 'We weren't expecting it. It was very strange. Sometimes I think . . .'

Fortunately I heard Minta's voice calling me.

'I'm here,' I called.

She stood in the doorway, Stirling holding the lamp behind her.

'Oh, Lizzie!' she said rather reproachfully.

'I've been talking to Mrs. Herrick,' said Lizzie almost defiantly.

'Well, now we've found you we'd better continue with the tour,' said

Minta. She added gently: 'Lizzie, I should get back to your room if I were you. It's rather chilly to hang about here.'

'Yes, Miss Minta,' said Lizzie meekly.

Minta turned and we all followed her. On the next landing Lizzie disappeared and Minta took us to show us the carved banisters which led up to the minstrels' gallery.

'I hope Lizzie didn't scare you,' said Minta. 'She's been rather odd since my mother died.'

'Like Jessica,' said Stirling. And to Minta: 'She's a cousin of my mother's and she went a bit queer when my mother died. *They* were always together.'

'Very like Jessica,' I agreed. 'They are two devoted people.'

'I must speak to her,' went on Minta. 'She mustn't go wandering round these closed-up rooms. This minstrels' gallery was put in in the sixteenth century when this wing was built. You didn't notice it from the hall because the curtains were drawn.'

We examined it and I pretended to show interest but my encounter with Lizzie had started up so many memories that my thoughts were far away. I kept imagining Lynx in this house attracting the young lady whom he was teaching – and the maid at the same time.

When we rejoined the others the doctor was about to take his leave. He had one or two patients he wanted to look in on and he said he would take Maud home at the same time. I suggested that we ought to go too and Franklyn immediately offered to drive us home. So we said goodbye and soon were driving the short distance to the Mercer's House.

'What a place!' Stirling was saying. 'I have never been in such a house.'

'I should think not,' I retorted. 'It's unique.'

'There are other houses which have been built on the site of old monasteries ... and with some of the original stones,' said Franklyn. 'Fountains Abbey in Yorkshire springs to mind.'

'It's a pity,' said Stirling, 'that they can't afford the necessary repairs.'

'A great pity,' agreed Franklyn.

'Perhaps they'd be wise to sell it to someone who could put it to rights.'

'Oh never!' cried Franklyn. 'It's an institution. It's a tradition.'

'That sort of house belongs to posterity,' said Stirling rather pompously. 'If people can't afford to run it they should let it go.'

'If it were mine, I never would,' I said.

'And you can be sure,' added Franklyn, 'that the Cardews never will either.'

The lights of Mercer's were visible and we drove the rest of the way in silence.

We were too excited for bed. We went into the drawing-room and Stirling threw himself on to the sofa. I sat down in the armchair looking at him.

'The first move,' he said.

'Well, if you think you've made a move, I don't.'

'We've been there. We've inspected the house. My goodness, it needs some money spent on it, and they haven't two brass farthings to rub together.'

'Exaggeration! And who wants to rub brass farthings together, which I'm sure they could easily do if they had a mind to.'

'You're becoming infected by Mr. Franklyn Wakefield. That's just the sort of thing he would have said.'

'Then he'd be talking sense.'

'But, seriously, Nora, what a satisfactory evening!'

'Was it? I came away with the impression that they would never for one moment consider selling Whiteladies.'

'What will they do? Let it fall about their ears?'

'It's in no danger of imminent collapse.'

'It'll be worthless if they let it go much farther.'

'It'll always be their home. Let them enjoy it. I happen to like this Mercer's House. It's really far more comfortable.'

'It'll do until we move into Whiteladies.'

'And when will that be?'

'In the not far distant future. I feel it in my bones.'

'I wouldn't rely on them.'

'You're determined to be pessimistic.'

'I think I see this more clearly than you do.'

'Let's be practical.'

'Yes, let's. But they are not what you would call practical people. They'll never sell Whiteladies. That's been made clear. Franklyn implied it. He would know.'

'He would know nothing. He's quite obtuse. He knows how to bow and make the sort of remark people want to hear. That's the sum total of his accomplishments. And since when have you been on Christian name terms?'

'We aren't. I only call him Franklyn privately. I think you underestimate him.'

'Listen, Nora. These people are not like us. They've been brought up to luxury. They haven't the same stamina and vitality. We're different. Think of our fathers. They had ambition, the ability to go out and get what they wanted. We have inherited that. They haven't. They were brought up in their mansions; they think they'll inherit from Papa and that's that. But if there's nothing for them to inherit, what then? I'll make a bet with you, Nora. We'll be in Whiteladies this time next year.'

'I don't think so.'

'It's the wrong attitude. You invite failure when you're certain of it.'

'Perhaps I don't think it would be such a failure.'

'It was what my father wanted,' he said. 'It's what he would expect.' And it was as though Lynx looked at me through his eyes, so that I felt I was a traitor and was silent.

Stirling smiled at me tenderly. 'You'll see,' he said.

We were invited not only to Whiteladies and Wakefield Park but to the vicarage and several other houses. We had become part of the life of the neighbourhood, Maud Mathers saw to that. I was glad to be of use, for I had taken a great liking to her. She seemed to have such good sound sense. I had a great respect for her, too. My feelings for Minta and Franklyn were to some extent affected by Stirling's attitude towards them. He seemed to despise them faintly. He was continually stressing that they weren't like us; they had been brought up in a different school. Whenever he discussed them a faintly pitying note would creep into his voice. I laughed at him for it, but it had its effect on me.

Lucie exasperated him a little. I knew why. She was more like ourselves. She had not been brought up to accept a life of luxury; she was practical and obviously doing everything she could to live within the means at their disposal. Stirling was aware of this. It hurt me in a way to see how he rejoiced in the ill fortunes of the Cardews. He had an obsession. Yet I could not entirely disapprove, for everything he did was due to his devotion to his father's memory.

On the Saturday before harvest festival I went to the church to help Maud decorate. We worked hard arranging chrysanthemums, asters, dahlias and Michaelmas daisies round the altar. There were enormous vegetable marrows, too, and tomatoes and cabbages all on display. Bunches of corn were tied up with red ribbon and set side by side with loaves of delicious crusty bread which would later be distributed to the needy.

'It's been a good year for the harvest,' said Maud, looking down at me from the ladder, on the top rung of which she was standing draping russet-coloured leaves over a brass rail.

'Be careful you don't fall,' I warned.

'I've decorated this spot in the same way for the last five years. I'm sure-footed.'

I came over to steady the ladder and hold it for her.

'What on earth would happen if you were out of action?' I asked.

'Father would have lots of helpers who would do just as well.'

'I don't believe it. And just think of the work you'd give poor Dr. Hunter. He's over-worked already.'

'Yes,' she said soberly, 'he is.'

She came down the ladder then and I noticed how rosy her cheeks were. 'I've often told him he should have help,' she went on. 'Sometimes I feel anxious for him.' She bit her lip. She was embarrassed. 'He seems . . . worried. It's having so much to do.'

I was sure she was right, I told her. I'd noticed it too.

'Do you think these bronze chrysanthemums would look well with the leaves?' I asked her.

'Perfect. I do wish something could be done about Dr. Hunter.' Then she started to talk about him, his selfless devotion to his cases; the good he had done to this one and that.

As I arranged the flowers and leaves I thought: She's in love with him.

I rode a good deal that autumn. Life in Australia had made a competent horsewoman of me and riding seemed the easiest and most convenient method of getting around. Stirling sometimes accompanied me. He was getting restive and making all sort of plans. He was going to acquire land and saw himself as a local squire, which I told him, would be usurping Franklyn Wakefield's place.

'There's no reason why there shouldn't be two of us,' he would say. But the first task was to get possession of Whiteladies and he was no nearer doing that than when we had arrived.

He wanted to go to see Sir Hilary and make an offer. I dissuaded him because I was certain he would be disappointed; and he accepted my advice when I reminded him that he might set the Cardews against him if they guessed at his motive for cultivating their friendship.

I often rode with Franklyn Wakefield. He made a habit of calling at Mercer's and suggesting he show me some part of the country which I hadn't seen before. I enjoyed those rides. We would often tether our horses outside some old inn – he always seemed to be well known in these places – and lunch off bread and cheese and cider. The food always tasted exceptionally good and I enjoyed meeting the people to whom he introduced me. I was aware of the great respect in which he and his family were held and this pleased me.

I loved the odours of autumn – the mist which was often in the air; the smell of burning leaves as we passed some garden; the nip in the air which made my skin tingle. I watched the trees gradually denuded of their leaves to make a lacy pattern against the grey-blue sky. And I learned much about the responsibilities of a country squire, for he took them seriously; I became accustomed to his rather pedantic style of speaking and grew to like it. When I was with him I forgot that slightly patronizing attitude of Stirling's which had rubbed off on me. There was something dependable about this man which I respected. I realized, too, how great was his affection for his parents. He was devoted to them. So he was to his tenants and I was astonished by how much he knew – and cared – about their affairs.

One rather warm November day when the red sun was veiled by mist, and spiders' webs were draped across the hedgerows, we rode out together. He was rather subdued that day and I asked him if anything had happened to upset him.

'It's not unexpected,' he answered. 'Dr. Hunter thinks my father can only have another six months to live.'

'Oh, I am sorry.'

'He is old and his condition is worsening. I am more particularly worried about my mother.'

'She is ill, too?

'No, but they have been so close all their lives. They were neighbours and knew each other from childhood. I can't imagine what would happen to her if my father died.'

'She will have you.'

'I don't think that would be enough. She will be so heartbroken it will kill her.

'Do you think people die of broken hearts?'

'This would be a broken life.'

I thought of myself and Lynx. He had meant so much to me and yet here I was, as alive as I had ever been.

We rode in silence and he sensed my sympathy, I knew.

It was that day that we found the kittens. When we called at one of the farms on his estate, the farmer's wife came out from the kitchen wiping her floury arms and Franklyn introduced me as the new tenant at Mercer's.

'A fine old house,' commented the farmer's wife, 'and you couldn't have a better landlord.'

She insisted on our drinking a glass of her very own elderberry wine and eating one of the buns which she had just taken from the oven. We sat on chairs in the kitchen and she told Franklyn about the farmer's intention to let gravel-three-acres lie fallow next year. A big tabby cat came in and, purring, rubbed itself against my legs.

'That's old Tibbles looking for a saucer of milk again,' said the farmer's wife. 'She's lost interest in her last litter.'

'How many cats have you now?' asked Franklyn.

'Well, to tell the truth, Mr. Wakefield, I've lost count. I can't bring myself to destroy the little things and in next to no time they're no longer kitties and have little ones of their own. They scratch around in the barns so they don't trouble us and they keep the mice away.'

When the farmer came in he took us out to show us the new barn he was putting up and that was when I saw the kitten. There were ten or twelve cats – most of them just passing out of the kitten stage – and I noticed one in particular because she was not so pretty as the rest and was, in fact, rather thin and cowed. When I called her she came readily and I wished I had something to give her to eat.

'This one seems a little outsider,' I said.

'You get them now and then,' said the farmer. 'They're not so strong as the rest and can't fend for themselves.'

I said on impulse: 'We haven't a cat. May I have her?'

'We'd be glad for you to take any that you want,' was the farmer's answer; and I knew I was going to enjoy taking this little one and feeding her and cosseting her to make up for the hard time I was sure she had had on the farm.

We were about to leave the barn when another small cat came running up. She was tawny – much the same colouring as the one I had chosen, but much prettier though she had the same undcrfed look. She mewed piteously and I thought: She wants to come too. I said: 'I'll have the two. They'll be company for each other.'

The farmer's wife found a basket and the two little cats were put in it. Franklyn carried them and we rode off. On our way we called at Whiteladies as Franklyn wanted to see Sir Hilary. Minta came out and was most interested in the cats. While Franklyn was with her father we took them out of the basket and gave them a saucer of milk apiece.

'They're darlings,' cried Minta. 'And never had a look-in at meal times. These will be quite different from those cats who started life as pampered pets.'

I saw that she would like to have one so I suggested she should. She was delighted.

'You choose,' I said, 'and we'll name them.'

When they had licked their saucers clean they sat licking themselves.

'That one is more beautiful,' said Minta.

'The other has more dignity.'

We tried several names and at length I suggested Bella and Donna – Bella for the beauty and Donna for the dignified one.

Minta chose Bella; so I left her behind at Whiteladies.

It was only a few weeks later that we heard about the copse. Stirling came in in a mood of great excitement. The Cardews were putting up for sale the copse which was on the edge of their grounds.

'They're obviously being forced to raise money,' he said.

I heard about it from Franklyn. When he said he would buy the copse I asked if he planned to cut down the timber and build on it. He shook his head. 'No. I'll leave it as it is.' I guessed he was thinking that when he married Minta it would be as though the land had not changed hands.

I was astonished when I saw him next to learn that he had *not* bought the copse. Someone had made a very big offer for it. I began to feel uneasy when I heard this. I couldn't wait to see Stirling.

I knew before I said anything. It was what he would call making a move.

'So you've bought the Whiteladies copse,' I said.

'How did you know?'

'And,' I went on, 'you've paid about twice as much as it's worth.'

'What does that matter?'

'Not at all to our golden millionaire. Why didn't you tell me?'

'You've become very odd lately, Nora. You're getting more like Them and less like Us.'

'If you mean I try to act tactfully . . .'

'Oh, come now. What's tactless about paying a high price for something to help people out.'

'When they know it's you they'll be embarrassed.'

'They weren't embarrassed to take my cheque and get twice as much as the land's worth.'

'Sir Hilary . . .'

'Knows nothing about business.'

'Well, Minta . . .'

'She knows even less. It's Lady Cardew who has the business head in that house.'

'So you arranged it with her.'

'I arranged it with my man of business.'

'I don't think you should have done it, Stirling.'

'Why not?'

'Because Franklyn Wakefield was going to buy that land and if he had it would have remained in the family.'

'I don't follow your reasoning.'

'Then you must be blind. Franklyn is going to marry Minta, and when he does he'll be able to deal with Whiteladies.'

'It's going to take more than he's got to put that place to rights.'

'How do you know?'

'I make it my business to know. It needs thousands spent on it. Wakefield's comfortably off but he's no . . .'

'Millionaire,' I added.

He nodded, smiling. He was certainly a man with an obsession.

Minta spoke to me about the copse. 'I know now that it was Mr. Herrick who bought it. He paid far more than it was worth.'

'He can afford it,' I said rather tersely.

Her eyes shone warmly. 'It was very kind of him.'

'I think he wanted it rather badly.'

'He couldn't have wanted it. There is plenty of land about which is far more valuable.'

But not Whiteladies, I thought. And I could see by Stirling's manner that he believed he already had a foot in the door.

You're wrong, Stirling, I thought. It isn't going to work out your way. You'll settle in at Mercer's or we'll go back to Australia. I knew then that it wouldn't have mattered to me either way – as long as I was with Stirling.

Christmas was almost upon us. During the week before, Stirling and I with Maud, Minta and Franklyn accompanied a party of carol singers round the village to collect money for the church. We went to Wakefield Park afterwards where hot soup was served to us. I gathered it was a custom and that long ago Whiteladies had been the setting for it. Franklyn appeared to be taking over Whiteladies' duties, and when he marries, I thought, he'll go and live there and old customs will revert to what they once were.

Seeing his father seated in his chair with the tartan rug over his knees and his mother hovering close, it occurred to me that he had delayed asking Minta to marry him because of his parents. When he was married he would be expected to live at Whiteladies and he wished to remain with his father for what time was left to him.

We all met again on Christmas morning at church and in the late afternoon went to Wakefield Park where we were to dine. The place looked festive hung with holly and mistletoe and I was reminded of Adelaide's attempts to bring an English atmosphere into our home on the other side of the world.

It was the traditional Christmas – turkey and plum pudding blazing with brandy, and gifts for everyone from a Christmas tree in the centre of the drawing-room. Toasts were drunk to our hosts, to their guests and particularly to newcomers. There were several guests besides ourselves and after dinner more called in. In a large ballroom we danced, to the music of two violins, the old country dances – Jenny Pluck Pears and Sir Roger de Coverley – and afterwards we waltzed and some of us tried the minuet. I enjoyed it all and tried not to think of Christmases spent in Australia. Franklyn's parents stayed up until the end and I noticed the old man nodding and beating time to the music, and how his eyes and those of his wife followed Franklyn all the time.

'It was a lovely Christmas,' I told Franklyn; and he replied in his stilted way how pleased he was that I had not been bored by their old customs.

On the way home Stirling admitted it had been an enjoyable day and told me he had invited them all to the Mercer's House for the New Year.

'We must put our heads together,' he said, 'and plan something equal to Mr. Franklyn Wakefield's entertainment.'

I was a little ashamed of that New Year's party. Stirling had sent for a firm of London caterers to come down and manage the whole thing. He scattered invitations throughout the place. Special plate was brought down; expert chefs came to do the cooking; and he even decided that we should have footmen in blue velvet livery wearing powdered wigs.

I laughed aloud. 'It's ridiculous,' I said, 'for a small country house like this – and appalling bad taste.'

'I wish we could have it in Whiteladies,' he said wistfully. 'Imagine that hall . . .'

'This is not Whiteladies, and what are these people going to think when they see your hired flunkeys.'

But I could not dissuade him.

Mrs. Glee was inclined to be indignant. 'I could have managed very well, Mrs. Herrick, with an extra maid or two and I would have known where to get them,' she scolded reproachfully. 'I hope Mr. Herrick is not dissatisfied with my cooking.'

I assured her that this was not the case and that Mr. Herrick had acted without consulting me. I should have planned a very different sort of party – with Mrs. Glee's help, of course.

She was mollified and when she saw the decorated dining-room and drawing-rooms and all the preparations, she began to take an immense pride in them. We were going to outshine Whiteladies and that meant something to her. She became quite excited, especially as she would take an authoritative part in the proceedings.

I don't know whether I could call that evening a success. At least it was memorable. Fancy lamp-posts had been fixed outside the house and red carpet laid down on the steps of the portico. Stirling had hired a band which was set up in a little room between the dining- and drawing-rooms and the players wore red breeches with white Hungarian blouses. The table decorations were a masterpiece of roses which were very expensive at that time of the year. The guests were duly impressed and faintly embarrassed in the midst of such grandeur; consequently it was not such a merry party as we had had at Wakefield Park. Stirling had arranged for a pianist to entertain us and afterwards we danced in the drawing-room which had been made ready for this purpose. It was not a ballroom such as they had at Wakefield Park, but it was when the dancing started that the party became enjoyable. We danced folk dances which Maud led because she ran a class for them, and then everyone became more natural. At a quarter to twelve we sat down waiting for midnight to strike; and when it did we joined hands and sang 'Auld Lang Syne'. I had Franklyn on one side of me, Minta on the other; and I felt happy because I knew them.

When the last of the guests had gone Stirling and I sat down in the drawing-room and talked about the evening.

'You have made your point admirably,' I told him. 'Your friends and neighbours will no longer doubt that they have a millionaire in their midst.'

'It's rather a pleasant thing to be.'

'When it gets you what you want; but do remember money won't buy everything.'

'Name a few things it won't.'

'Those things which are not for sale.'

'You'll see. I've made up my mind I'm going along to have a talk with Sir Hilary.'

'When?'

'In a few days' time.'

'So you're waiting a few days! Tactful of you but I marvel at your sloth. Why not go along tomorrow and say: "Sir Hilary, I've made it clear to you that I am a millionaire, an ostentatious fellow who likes to stress the point. I'm ready to pay what you ask." '

'You've changed, Nora. Sometimes I wonder whether you're on my side.'

'I'm always on your side,' I said.

He smiled, understanding. That was love between us, unshakeable, inevitable. I could criticize him; he could mock me; it didn't matter. We were meant for each other and it would always be like that. True, I married Lynx; but then Lynx had decided that. And I was so close to Stirling that I shared his adoration of the strange man who had been his father. Stirling had had no choice but to stand aside for Lynx; and I had no choice but to stand aside for Whiteladies . . . which after all was for Lynx. But we were one – Stirling and I. After a year of widowhood I would become his wife.

As he smiled at me that night I was as certain of this as I had been during that time in the cave when we had lain close together while a forest fire raged over our heads and we thought never to come out alive. There was the same understanding between us now.

By the end of January Stirling's patience gave out and he went to see Sir Hilary. I was in the library when he came in, his face white, his lips tight and a look of blank despair in his eyes.

'What's happened?' I cried.

'I've just come from Whiteladies.'

'Is something terribly wrong there?'

He nodded. 'I've made an offer to Sir Hilary.'

'And he refused. Is that all? I could have told you it would happen.'

He sat down heavily and stared at the tip of his boot. 'He says he can't sell . . . ever. No matter what offer he had, he couldn't. "I'm saddled with the house and so is the family," he said. Those were his words. Saddled with it! There's some clause that won't allow them to sell. It was made by some ancestor who had a gambling son. The house remains in the family . . . whatever happens.'

I felt as though a burden had been lifted from my shoulders. 'That's settled it. You've done all you can and there's an end to the matter.'

'Yes,' he said, 'it would seem so.'

'You tried. No one, not even Lynx, could have done more.'

'I didn't expect this.'

'I know. But I told you there are some things which are not for sale. Now you can put it out of your mind and start planning for the future.'

'You're glad, I believe.'

'I think it's wrong to try to take from people something which belongs to them.'

'He used to talk so much about it. He was determined that we should be there.'

'But he didn't know of this clause, did he? And I never agreed with him. He could be wrong . . . sometimes. His firm intention was to be revenged and revenge is wrong. There is no happiness in it.'

He was silent and I knew he wasn't listening to me. He was thinking of all his wasted efforts.

I went to him and laid a hand on his shoulder. 'What shall we do now?' I asked. 'Shall we go back to Australia?'

He didn't answer, but he stood up and put his arms round me.

'Nora,' he said. He repeated my name and kissed me as he never had before. It was a lover's kiss – and I was happy.

I thought we would talk freely after that because we had made a tacit admission of our feelings; but this was not the case. Stirling was more withdrawn than he had been before. He was silent – almost morose; he went out riding alone. Once I saw him coming back, his horse sweating.

'You've been overworking that poor animal,' I accused, hoping he would tell me what was on his mind.

I thought I knew. He loved me, but Lynx was between us. Lynx, his father, had been my husband; and that made a strange relationship between us.

It will pass, I assured myself. What Lynx would want more than anything would be for Stirling and me to marry. We were the two he had loved best in the world; he would want us to be together. We shall call our first son Charles after him. We will never forget him.

So I was unprepared for what happened next.

Stirling came in one late afternoon just at dusk. Ellen had brought in the lamps and drawn the curtains and I was alone in the drawing-room. There was a strange expression on his face as though he were sleep-walking.

'I'd better tell you right away,' he said. 'I'm engaged to be married.'

I could not believe I had heard him correctly.

'I've just asked Minta to marry me,' he went on.

I heard my voice then, cold, terse, indifferent almost. 'Oh . . . I see.'

'You *do* see, don't you?' he said almost imploringly.

'Of course. It's the only way to buy Whiteladies.'

'It *was* the only way . . . in view of the fact that it can't go out of the family.'

'Congratulations,' I said harshly.

I had to get out of the room or I should rage and storm at him. I should lay bare my hopes and longings. I couldn't stay in that room trying to speak to him calmly. So I pushed past him to the door. I sped up to my room and locked myself in.

Then I lay on my bed and stared at the Mercer's coat of arms on the ceiling and I wished that I were dead.

How I lived through the weeks which followed I am not sure. I had to look on at Minta's bliss. How she loved him! I could understand that. Once she had been contented enough at the prospect of marrying Franklyn Wakefield, no doubt; and then he had come – this strong, vital Stirling who, when he wanted something, would allow no obstacle to stand in his way. Poor Minta; Did she guess why he was marrying her? Often I wanted to tell her. I had to keep a tight control on my tongue to prevent myself shouting at her; and all the time I could feel nothing but pity for her. Poor innocent little dupe! The victim of one strange man's desire for revenge and of another's tenacious need to fulfil a duty. Poor innocent Minta, who believed herself loved! She was not marrying for the sake of Whiteladies even though it would now be completely restored to its old perfection. It would be a cherished house. I could imagine Stirling's thorough assessment of the necessary repairs. No expense spared. Here comes the golden millionaire.

And what happiness would come from such a marriage, I asked myself bitterly. I was jealous, angry and humiliated. *I* loved Stirling and I had believed he had loved me. And so he did. But his duty towards Lynx came before his love for me. A voice within me said: As your infatuation for Lynx came before your love for Stirling, remember?

Lynx was still with us, ruling our lives.

If I was deeply unhappy I was determined not to show it. I think I managed very well. Stirling made sure that we were rarely alone together. He spent a lot of time at Whiteladies. He was, as I guessed, making that assessment of necessary repairs and he threw himself into the task with all the ardour a normal man might have showered on his bride.

Minta came to see me and sat in the drawing-room nursing Donna. She was so happy, she said. She would tell me a secret. She had been in love with Stirling ever since we came to the Mercer's House. No, before that really. Did I remember the occasion when we had all met for the first time? And when he came back . . . it seemed like fate.

Not fate, I thought, but Lynx.

'Stirling *adores* Whiteladies. He'll love living there.'

It's the only reason for his marriage, I thought grimly.

'He makes me see it differently. More as Lucie does.'

'And Lucie? Is Lucie pleased?'

She wrinkled her brows and I warmed towards Lucie, who, with her practical good sense, saw farther than Minta and her father.

'Lucie's worried about me. I think she has the idea that I'm a child still. She taught me at school long ago and I don't think she ever sees me as anything but one of her less bright pupils.'

So Lucie didn't altogether approve.

'And what I wanted to say, Nora, is this: If you would like to come and live at Whiteladies there will always be a home for you there.'

'Me! At Whiteladies. Oh, but you don't want your step-mother-in-law . . .' I heard myself giggle a little wildly.

'That absurd title. I know Stirling wants you to come.'

'Has he said so?'

'Well, of course.'

No, I thought. Never! How could I live under the same roof and see them together and think of all that should have been mine? And Stirling loved me. He knew it. Poor innocent little Minta, who did not understand the devious people who surrounded her.

'Well, I've grown very attached to the Mercer's House.'

'What, that big house all to yourself! Don't imagine we should live in each other's pockets. Whiteladies is vast. You could have your own wing. There are the apartments which used to be my mother's.'

'It's good of you, Minta, but I think I'll be better here for a while. I may go back to Australia.'

'Please don't say that. We should hate it . . . Stirling and I.'

And how I hated the proprietary way in which she spoke of him. My feelings were tempestuous and I was wretchedly unhappy. But I could only feel pity for Minta.

They were married that April – just as the buds were showing on the trees and the dawn chorus was at its most joyful.

Maud had decorated the church and I had helped her, which was bitter irony. How she had chattered! She was so happy for Minta.

'If ever a girl was in love that girl is Minta,' she said. And I knew Maud was imagining herself walking down the aisle on the arm of Dr. Hunter, a bride. I could feel a great sympathy for Maud, but at least she did not have to see the man she loved married to someone else.

Right up the wedding-day I kept assuring myself that something would happen to prevent this marriage; but the day arrived and Sir Hilary gave his daughter away and the Reverend John Mathers performed the service.

I sat and watched Stirling at the altar taking his vows to Minta. On one side of me was Lucie, on the other Franklyn. Lucie looked rather stern as though she feared for the marriage. And Franklyn? What were his feelings? He gave no indication that he suffered from seeing the girl who was surely intended for him marrying someone else. But that was characteristic of him.

The responses were over; they were signing the register; soon the wedding march would peal forth and they would come down the aisle together. It was like an evil dream.

And there they were – Minta, a radiant bride, Stirling inscrutable; and the organ playing the Wedding March from *Lohengrin*. It was over.

We left the church and with Franklyn beside me, I came out into the uncertain April sunshine.

MINTA

Chapter One

I am not sure when I first began to suspect that someone was trying to kill me. At first it was a hazy notion, one which I dismissed as ridiculous – and then it became a certainty. I had become a frightened and unhappy woman.

Yet on the day when I married Stirling I was, I was sure, the happiest bride in the world. I couldn't believe that this wonderful thing had happened to me. In fact, on the day he proposed to me I was taken completely by surprise. Stirling was different from anyone I had ever known. There was a special quality about him. Nora had it too. They were the sort of people whose lives seemed so much more exciting than mine; and that made them stimulating to be with. Nora was by no means beautiful but she had more charm than anyone I knew; she was poised and had a rare dignity; I felt one only had to look at Nora to be attracted by her. Her life had been so unusual. There was the marriage to Stirling's father of which she spoke very little, but I had noticed that whenever her husband's name was mentioned there was a sort of breathless pause – with Stirling as well as Nora – as though they were talking of some deity. The fact that she had been his wife elevated her in some way, made her different from other people. Stirling had the same quality. They were not easy to know; they were unpredictable; they were unlike people I had known all my life – people like Maud Mathers and Franklyn – and even Lucie whom I understood and knew so well.

I had never hoped that Stirling would care for me. I used to think that he and Nora would be well matched, and had she not been his stepmother they might have married. And then that day came and he said without warning: 'Minta, I want to marry you.' I blinked and stammered: 'What did you say?' because I was certain I had misheard.

He took my hands and kissed them and said he wanted to marry me. I told him that I loved him and had ever since I had first seen him; but I didn't dream he felt the same about me.

We told Father right away. He was delighted because he knew Stirling was rich and that when we were married I shouldn't be haunted by poverty as he had always been. He summoned the household – including our few servants – and told them the news; and he sent down to the wine cellars for the last of the champagne so that everyone could drink our health. The servants did this readily. They were doubtless thinking that their wages would now be paid regularly.

But there were two people in the house who weren't pleased.

The first was Lucie. Dear Lucie, she always behaved as though I had just emerged from the schoolroom and needed looking after. She came to my room after Stirling had gone and sat on the bed as she used to in those days when she came to Whiteladies for holidays.

'Minta,' she said, 'are you absolutely sure?'

'I was never more sure of anything. It's wonderful, because I never thought he could possibly care for me.'

'Why not?' she demanded. 'You happen to be a beautiful young woman and I always thought you'd make a good marriage.'

'Yet you're looking worried.'

'I am . . . a little.'

'But why?'

'I don't know. It's a feeling I have.'

'Oh, Lucie, everybody's delighted. And even if I wasn't in love with him, it's good from every point of view, isn't it? He'll stop all our worries about money; and you know how you're always fretting about the house falling into ruin.'

'I know. I love this house and it is in urgent need of repair, but that doesn't mean I think you should marry because of it.'

'You're being a fussy old hen, Lucie.'

'Since I married your father I've looked upon you as my daughter. And before that, as you know, I was very fond of you. I want you to be happy, Minta.'

'But I am. Never so as now.'

'I wish you would wait . . . not rush into things.'

'You've become a gloomy old prophetess. What's wrong with Stirling?'

'Nothing, I hope, but it's all too quick. I had no idea that he was in love with you. He's never given me that impression.'

'Nor me either.' I giggled like a foolish schoolgirl. 'But he's different, Lucie. He's lived a different life from ours. You shouldn't expect him to behave like ordinary people. He wouldn't show his feelings.'

'That's the trouble. He doesn't. He certainly didn't show he was in love with you.'

'Why else should he want to marry me? I can't bring him a fortune.'

'He's very interested in the house. He might be seeking the background marriage into a family like ours could give him. After all, who is he? That rather vulgar display at the New Year shows a certain lack of breeding.'

'Lucie, how dare you say such things!'

'I'm sorry.' She was immediately contrite. 'I'm letting my anxieties run away with me. Forgive me, Minta.'

'Dearest Lucie. I'm the one who should ask forgiveness. I know you're worried solely on my account. But really there's nothing to worry about. I'm perfectly happy.'

'Well, you won't rush things too much, will you?'

'Not too much,' I promised. But I knew Stirling wanted an early marriage and everything now would be what Stirling wanted.

The other dissenter was Lizzie. How dramatic – and rather tiresome – she had become since Mamma died. Lizzie had to wait until I was in bed before she came in, glided was the word, with her candle held high like some ghost. She was in a long white flannelette nightdress which added to the ghostly illusion. I was aware of being too excited for sleep, and was going over the wonderful moment when Stirling asked me to marry him.

She pushed open the door and I said: 'What are you doing roaming about the house, Lizzie? You might set your nightdress alight with that candle.'

'I have to come and see you, Miss Minta.'

'At this time of night!'

'Time doesn't matter.'

'Well, I think it does, Lizzie, because I'm tired and you ought to be in bed.'

She took no notice but sat on the edge of my bed.

'So you're going to get married . . . to him.'

'I'm going to marry Mr. Stirling Herrick, if that's to whom you refer.'

'That's him, all right. And the likeness is there. You'd know who he is at once.'

'Please don't speak of my future husband disrespectfully, Lizzie.'

'There's something unnatural about it. It seems a funny thing to me. His father wanting to marry your mother and now he's here and going to marry you.'

'What are you talking about, Lizzie.'

'It was his father who was here all those years ago.'

'His father! That was Mrs. Herrick's husband.'

'A real mix-up,' said Lizzie. 'That's what I think's so funny about it. Your mother was mad about him and she wasn't the only one.'

'Go to bed, Lizzie. You're rambling.'

'No I'm not. What I say is true. It's as though he's come back. In a way I always thought he would.'

Events started to fall into shape in my mind. I said: 'Lizzie, do you mean that my mother's artist was . . .'

'That's right. Mr. Charles Herrick. You can see his name on some of the drawings in the studio cupboard. He came here to teach her drawing, then he went away . . . sent away to Australia for theft and your mother never saw him again. She was never the same after, and now he's dead they say, but there's this other one and you're planning to marry him. Doesn't that seem like some sort of fate?'

'I don't understand it. I think you could be mistaken.'

'I'm not mistaken. There's some who don't lie down when they're dead and he's one of them.'

'You're making a dramatic situation out of a perfectly normal one.'

'I hope so, Miss Minta. I certainly hope so. But how did he come here, out of the blue? He's bewitched you just as his father did your mother . . . and others.'

'I'll ask Mr. Herrick about this when he comes back.'

'You ask him and listen carefully to the answers.'

'Now, Lizzie, I'm sleepy.'

'I take the hint, but I've warned you. I can't do more than that.'

Then she picked up the candle and went out.

But I did not sleep. I was too excited. Could it be true that Stirling's father was my mother's artist? And what a strange coincidence that Nora's scarf should have blown over *our* wall. What did it mean? But did it matter? What was important was that Stirling had asked me to marry him. Was it the house he wanted, as Lucie seemed to suggest? Was it some sort of pattern as Lizzie thought it to be? And finally, what did it matter? I was going to marry Stirling.

Stirling said there was no need for delay. He was eager to become my husband.

I mentioned what Lizzie had told me.

'It's true,' he admitted, 'that my father was a drawing-master at White-ladies, wrongly accused of theft and sent to Australia. There he quickly made good. It was a grossly unfair charge to make against a great man. When I came to England to take Nora back I naturally wanted to look at the house where my father had worked, Nora's scarf blew over the wall and we came in to get it.'

There seemed nothing extraordinary about that. It was all so logical – except of course for the fact that Stirling had never mentioned his father's connection with the house before this.

'I'm sorry about your father,' I said.

'He wouldn't need pity.'

'But to be wrongly accused.'

'It happened often in those days.'

'You were so fond of him, Stirling.'

'He was my father.'

'You have a certain reverence of him. It's the same with Nora.'

'If you had known him you would have understood.'

'Poor Nora! How she must have suffered when he died!'

He didn't speak but turned his face away. I feared I had been tactless. He never liked to speak of Nora. I thought it was because he was worried about her future so I said that if ever she wanted to come to Whiteladies she would be very welcome.

'After all, she is like your sister. I know she is, in fact, your stepmother, but that seems ridiculous. She's so attractive. I always feel unworldly beside her. I wish I were more like her.'

Stirling didn't say anything; he just stared ahead as though I weren't there. He's thinking of his father, I told myself; and I was glad that he was capable of such deep devotion.

There were so many preparations for the marriage. Maud Mathers was excited by it and envious in the nicest possible way. She immediately began working out how she would decorate the church. 'I wish it were May instead of April,' she said. 'It would give us more opportunity with the flowers.'

Lucie supervised the making of my wedding-dress. We had Jenny Callow and her daughter Flora to come in and work on it and make some other clothes for me. It was like old times because when I was a little girl before we became so poor, Jenny used to work full time at Whiteladies. Flora was a little girl then, learning her trade from her mother. I remember her standing by holding the pins. Then Jenny had to go and people used to get her to do dressmaking for them so that she could make a living.

The only person I could chatter with was Maud. Lucie would have been ideal but I couldn't bear her silent disapproval. I would have liked to talk to Nora but she kept out of the way. I was disappointed; I thought she was going to be like a sister. Maud wanted to know where we were going for the honeymoon and when I told her that we hadn't discussed this she was faintly disappointed.

'Venice!' she said. 'Sailing down the Grand Canal in a gondola. Or perhaps Florence. Strolling to the bridge where Dante and Beatrice met. Rome and the Forum and standing on the spot where Julius Caesar was struck down. I always think Italy is the place for honeymoons.'

I was surprised. I had not thought Maud so romantic.

When I mentioned a honeymoon to Stirling he said: 'Why should we go away? What could be more fascinating than Whiteladies?'

'You mean stay at home!'

'It's only just become my home,' said Stirling. 'There's nothing I'd like so much as to explore it. Of course if you would like to go away . . .'

But I wanted to do exactly what he wanted. 'There won't be a honeymoon yet,' I told Maud. 'That will come later.'

So the dresses were made and the cake baked; and Father said there was no need to consider the expense of the wedding. I was getting a handsome settlement and because of my marriage Whiteladies would be gradually restored to its old magnificence.

A week before the wedding Lucie came to my room one night for a talk.

'There's just one thing I want to say, Minta,' she told me. 'If you want to change your mind you shouldn't hesitate.'

'Change my mind! Whatever for?'

'It's all been rather hurried and there's been so much talk about how good this is for Whiteladies. But if you decided not to marry, we'd manage. We've managed so far. I don't want you to feel you have to marry for the sake of the house.'

'I never felt that for one moment, Lucie. I love the house and hate to see it crumbling away, but I wouldn't marry for it. It's just the greatest good fortune that Stirling happens to be rich and loves the house. He's going to put it all to rights. You'll be glad. I know you will. You've worried a lot about the house.'

'I'll be glad, of course, but nothing would compensate for your making the wrong marriage.'

'Set your mind at rest. The reason I am marrying Stirling is because I love him.'

That satisfied her. She started to talk about the wedding and hoped Maud would look well in the cerise-coloured silk she had chosen. Maud was to be Maid of Honour. I had hoped Nora would be but she had said it would be absurd for a married woman to take the part and had shown so clearly that she did not wish for it that I hadn't tried to persuade her. Lucie said it was a pity Druscilla wasn't old enough to be a bridesmaid and I agreed. We had asked Dr. Hunter to be best man. There again Franklyn would have been the obvious choice but somehow it seemed wrong to ask him because I knew so many people had expected him to be the bridegroom at my wedding. But, as I said, what did all this matter? The important thing was that I married Stirling.

And so at last came our wedding-day – the happiest day of my life. After Mr. Mathers had performed the ceremony we went back to Whiteladies and the reception was held in the great hall where the brides of our family had celebrated their marriages through the centuries. On that day Stirling seemed as though he were enraptured. He loves me, I thought. He couldn't look like that if he did not.

He stood in the hall with me by the great cake and guided my hand as I cut it, and there was something about him which I can only describe as triumph.

There were the usual speeches – Father's rather rambling and sentimental; Dr. Hunter's short and rather witty; Franklyn's conventional – the sort of speeches that had been made at weddings for the last hundred years. Stirling answered. He was direct. It was a happy day for him, he said. He felt he had come home.

Some of the guests stayed on to a dinner-party and afterwards we danced in the hall which made a wonderful ballroom. Stirling and I waltzed round together. He was not a good dancer but I loved him the more because of that.

'You'll find me lacking in fancy manners,' he told me.

'I know I shall love what I find,' I replied.

Then the guests left and we were alone. I was a little afraid of my inadequacy, but Stirling was kind. It was almost as though he were sorry for me and I was enchanted by his unexpected tenderness.

Yes, that was the happiest day of my life.

Chapter Two

It was a strange honeymoon. On the first day Stirling wanted me to take him on a tour of the house. 'Just the two of us,' he said.

I was delighted and we went round together. He was horrified by the state of things and made a lot of notes. I remember how he probed the oak beams in some of the rooms. 'Worm!' he commented. 'They could collapse at any moment. We'll have to get to work on them right away.'

'You're more like an assessor than a husband,' I told him.

'This is your house,' he retorted. 'It's in trust for our children. We have to see that it is kept in order.'

I hadn't realized how thoroughly neglected the house had been. 'It will need a fortune spent on it, Stirling,' I said. 'There's no need to do everything at once.'

'*I* have a fortune,' he said. I laughed because what Lucie called his ostentatiousness amused me. He was rich and proud of being so because his father had made that fortune and everything his father had done was wonderful in his opinion. 'And,' he went on, 'nothing is going to be left. I'm going to see that your house is in perfect order.'

'I wish you wouldn't say *your* house in that way, Stirling. What I have is yours. You know that.'

Then he smiled in a way which touched me deeply. He kissed me gently and said: 'You're a sweet girl, Minta, I'm sorry that I am as I am.'

I laughed at him and said, 'But that's why I love you.' He put his arms round me and held me against him. 'We're going to be very happy,' I told him, for it was as though he was the one who needed assurance then.

'Our children will play on the lawns of Whiteladies,' he said solemnly.

'A restored and beautiful Whiteladies which has lost its woodworm and whose bartizans will stand for another thousand years.'

What energy Stirling had and he spent it on the house! Within three months the rot had been arrested and Whiteladies was beginning to be a fine old house again. But he wasn't satisfied. There was still a good deal to be done. That time was what I called the Whiteladies Summer.

At the beginning of September tragedy struck Wakefield Park. Sir Everard had another stroke and died. It had been expected for we all knew that he couldn't live long, but it was a shock nevertheless. Especially for Lady Wakefield. She was lost without her husband; Franklyn was with her all the time but she fretted and a week after the funeral she took to her bed and for some weeks lay there without any will to leave it. In the middle of October she died and everyone said it was a 'happy release'.

Poor Franklyn was distressed, but he was not the man to show it. Dr. Hunter told us that he had warned Franklyn of the inevitability of his father's death and the fact that Lady Wakefield had died so soon afterwards was as she would have wanted it. Dr. Hunter had come to Whiteladies to see Druscilla. Lucie was always calling him. She worried ridiculously about that child. In fact where Druscilla was concerned she was by no means her usual practical self.

'She had no will to live,' said Dr. Hunter. 'I've known it happen like that many times. People have been together all their lives. One goes and the other follows immediately.'

Father was upset about losing his dear friends. He insisted on going to the funeral. Lucie was quite cross about it because there was a keen east wind blowing; she declared she would not allow him to go out. Yes, she did fuss us. It was because she had never had a family before and that made us rather precious to her. Father usually gave in but he was adamant on this occasion. He said he was determined to 'see the last of his old friend'. So he drove to the church and followed the cortège to the graveside and stood there in the wind, his hat in his hand.

I was sad for Franklyn, knowing how devoted he was to his parents, and was glad Nora was there because I felt that her presence comforted Franklyn. I had known for some time that he admired her. Towards him she showed a certain aloofness but she was friendly in a way. I remarked to Stirling that it would be rather a pleasant solution for Nora if she married Franklyn, for she constantly talked as though she intended to return to Australia.

'They're completely unsuited to each other,' said Stirling coldly. 'Franklyn!' he added quite contemptuously as though Franklyn wouldn't make a good husband.

'You don't know Franklyn,' I defended my old friend. 'He's one of the kindest people in the world.'

He turned away quite angrily. Nora had married his father, of course, and I supposed the thought of anyone's supplanting him was distasteful.

Still, I continued to think how pleasant it would be if Franklyn and Nora could marry, I wondered whether the idea was in Franklyn's mind. I was sure it was not in Nora's.

A few days after Lady Wakefield's funeral Father developed a cold. Lucie fussed terribly as she always did when he was ill and made him stay in bed. He should never have gone to the funeral, she grumbled.

She sent for Dr. Hunter and kept him with her a long time. When the doctor left the sick room I asked him to come into the library and asked him if my father was really ill or was it just Lucie's worrying.

'It's a chill,' he said, 'but he's near to bronchitis. I hope we've caught it in time. Perhaps a few days in bed.'

Poor Dr. Hunter! He looked very tired himself; and I thought of his going home to that rather dismal little house where his housekeeper might or might not be in a drunken stupor. Why didn't he marry Maud? She would look after him.

I insisted on his drinking a glass of sherry before he went out to his brougham; that brought a little colour into his cheeks and he seemed more cheerful.

'I'll look in this evening,' he promised, 'just to make sure your father is going along as he should.'

But when he came that evening, Father had bronchitis. In a few days this had turned to pneumonia. I had rarely seen Lucie so upset and I thought how lucky Father was to have such a devoted wife, for I had believed that for Lucie hers had been a marriage of convenience. I knew she had wanted Whiteladies to be her home for ever and no doubt she had enjoyed being Lady Cardew; but when I saw how upset she was I realized how deeply she cared for my father. She wouldn't leave the sick room; she was with him day and night, only snatching an hour or so's sleep in the next room if I sat with him.

'I don't trust those servants,' she said. 'He might want something.'

'If you don't rest you'll be ill yourself,' I scolded.

I sat with him but as soon as he started to cough she was up.

We waited for the crisis; but I knew Dr. Hunter didn't think there was much hope. Father was old and had been failing in health for some time. Pneumonia was a serious illness, even for the young.

Father wanted Lucie at his bedside all the time and was uneasy if she wasn't there. I thought how wonderful it was to see their love for each other and I remembered how peevish my mother had always been. I was glad my father had found happiness in the end with a woman like Lucie.

We were both with him when he died but his hand was in Lucie's. I shall never forget the look on her face when she lifted it to me. It was as though she had lost everything she cared for.

'Lucie darling,' I said, 'you still have Cilla.'

I led her to Druscilla's room. It was nine o'clock and the child was asleep. Nevertheless I picked her up and put her into Lucie's arms.

'Mamma,' said Druscilla sleepily and a little crossly.

And Lucie stood there tragically straining the child to her till I took Druscilla away and put her back in her bed. It was perhaps a rather sentimental and dramatic gesture but it did some good. Lucie braced herself and I knew she was realizing that she had Druscilla to live for.

Christmas came. Last year we had gone to Wakefield Park; this year the festivities should be held at Whiteladies. They could not be as lavish as they would be next year, said Stirling, because of my father's death, but they should be worthy of the house. It must be understood that Whiteladies, not Wakefield Park, was the focal point of the neighbourhood.

Lucie had gone about like a ghost in her widow's weeds. In fact they rather became her. Druscilla was nearly two; she had become imperious and demanding, the pet of the household. Lucie loved her passionately but refused to spoil her as I fear the rest of us did. I adored her and constantly longed to have a child of my own. Stirling wanted it too. He was always talking about our children's playing on the lawns of Whiteladies.

Once I had thought I was pregnant and it had turned out not to be so. I was very upset about that and determined that I wouldn't say anything to anyone next time until I was sure. Lucie was always asking pointed questions. 'When you have a child of your own . . .' she would say. Once she said: 'Perhaps you want a child too passionately. I've heard it said that sometimes when people do they can't conceive. It's a sort of perversity of nature.'

When I told her about Stirling's ideas for taking up the old Christmas ceremonies as we used to in the past she thought it a good idea.

'Whiteladies is the great house,' she said. 'Wakefield Park is an upstart. I think your husband has the right idea.'

I was glad that she was beginning to like Stirling and change her suspicions about the reason why he had married me.

'When you have your family you will probably want me to leave,' she said one day.

'What nonsense!' I cried. 'This is your home. Besides, what should we do without you?'

'It won't always be like that. I am just the stepmother – not really needed.'

'When have I ever not needed you?' I demanded.

'I shall know when the times comes for me to go,' she said.

'I wish you wouldn't say such a thing.'

'All right. We'll forget. But I'd never stay if I weren't wanted.'

That was good enough, I told her. She always would be.

How Stirling enjoyed planning for Christmas! A great deal of the essential work had been done on the house and he took a personal pride in it; but there was much still to be done. He had already increased the staff. Now we had six gardeners and the grounds were beginning to look beautiful. There were always workmen in the house and some rooms were out of bounds because the floor was up or the panelling being repaired.

Two weeks before Christmas I was almost sure that I was pregnant. I longed to tell someone but decided not to. I didn't want to raise Stirling's hopes. Oddly enough, Lizzie guessed. She was dusting Druscilla's room, which was one of her duties, and I had gone in to see the child, who was sitting on the floor playing with her bricks, so I knelt down and we built a house together. I couldn't take my eyes from that small face with the delicate baby nose and the tiny tendrils of hair at the brow. I was thinking of my own baby when Lizzie said in that forthright way of hers: 'So it's like that, is it?'

'Like what?' I demanded.

Lizzie cradled an imaginary baby in her arms. I flushed and Druscilla cried: 'What have you got there, Lizzie?'

Lizzie said: 'You'd be surprised, miss, wouldn't you, if I told you another baby. That would put Miss Cilla's little nose out of joint, wouldn't it?'

Druscilla touched her little nose and said: 'What's that?'

I kissed her and said: 'Lizzie's playing.'

'You couldn't fool me,' said Lizzie. 'There's always a way of telling.'

Druscilla impatiently called my attention to the bricks and I thought: Is it true? Is there a way of telling?

Christmas had come and gone. The Christmas bazaar had been held in the newly restored hall of Whiteladies; Stirling had provided lavish entertainment free of charge, something which had never been done before. It was a great success and everyone enjoyed our new affluence. We entertained the carol singers at Whiteladies and soup and wine and rich plum cake were served to them. I heard one of the elder members say that it was like old times and even then they hadn't been treated to such good wine.

We had only a small dinner-party on Christmas Day because of our recent bereavement – just the family, with Nora and Franklyn; and on Boxing Day we all went to Wakefield Park.

The new year came and then I experienced the first of those alarming incidents.

That morning at breakfast Stirling was talking – as was often the case – about the work which was being done in the house.

'They've started on the bartizan,' he said. 'There's more to be done up there than we thought at first.'

'Won't it be wonderful when it's all finished,' I cried. 'Then we can enjoy living in a house that is not constantly overrun by workmen.'

'Everything that has been done has been very necessary,' Stirling reminded me.

'If my ancestors can look down on what's happening at Whiteladies, they'll call you blessed.'

He was silent for a while and then he said: 'A big house should be the home of a lot of people.' He turned to Lucie and said: 'Don't you agree?'

'I do,' she answered.

'And you were talking of leaving us,' I accused. 'We shan't allow it. Shall we, Stirling?'

'Minta could never manage without you,' said Stirling, and Lucie looked pleased, which made me happy.

'Then there's Nora,' I went on. 'How I wish she would come here. It's absurd . . . one person in the big Mercer's House.'

'She's considering leaving us,' said Stirling.

'We must certainly not allow that to happen.'

'How can we prevent it if she wants to go?' he asked quite coldly.

'She's been saying she's going for a long time, but still she stays. I think she has a reason for staying.'

'What reason?' He looked at me as though he disliked me, but I believed it was the thought of Nora's going that he disliked. I shrugged my shoulders and he went on: 'Go and have a look at what they've done to the bartizan some time. We mustn't let the antiquity be destroyed. They'll have to go very carefully with the restoration.'

He liked me to take an interest in the work that was being done so I said I would go that afternoon before dark (it was dark just after four at this time of the year). I shouldn't have a chance in the morning as I'd promised to go and have morning coffee with Maud who was having a twelfth-night bazaar and was worried about refreshments. That would take the whole of the morning, and Maud had asked me to stay for luncheon. Stirling didn't seem to be listening. I looked at him wistfully; he was by no means a demonstrative husband. Sometimes I thought he made love in a perfunctory manner – as though it were a duty which had to be performed.

Of course I had always known that he was unusual. He had always stressed the fact that he had no fancy manners, for he had not been brought up in an English mansion like *some* people. He was referring to Franklyn. Sometimes I think he positively disliked Franklyn and I wondered whether it was because he knew that Franklyn admired Nora and he didn't think any man could replace his father.

He needn't have worried, I was sure. If Franklyn was in love with Nora, Nora was as coldly aloof from him as I sometimes thought Stirling was from me. But I loved Stirling deeply and no matter how he felt about me I should go on loving him. There were occasions in the night when I would wake up depressed and say to myself: He married you for Whiteladies. And indeed his obsession with the house could have meant that that was true. But I didn't believe it in my heart. It was just that he was not a man to show his feelings.

I came back from the vicarage at half past three. It was a cloudy day so that dusk seemed to be almost upon us. I remembered the bartizan, and as Stirling would very likely ask me that evening if I had been up to look at it, I decided I had better do so right away, for any lack of interest in the repairs on my part seemed to exasperate him.

The tower from which the bartizan projected was in the oldest part of the house. This was the original convent. It wasn't used as living quarters but Stirling had all sorts of ideas for it. There was a spiral staircase which led up to the tower and a rope banister. In the old days we had rarely come here and when I had made my tour of inspection with Stirling it had been almost as unfamiliar to me as to him. Now there were splashes of whitewash on the stairs and signs that workmen had been there.

It was a long climb and half-way up I paused for breath. There was silence about me. What a gloomy part of the house this was! The staircase was broken by a landing and this led to a wide passage on either side of which were cells like alcoves.

As I stood on this landing I remembered an old legend I had heard as a child. A nun had thrown herself from the bartizan, so the story went. She had sinned by breaking her vows and had taken her life as a way out of the world. Like all old houses, Whiteladies must have its ghost and what more apt than one of the white ladies? Now and then a white figure was supposed to be seen on the tower or in the bartizan. After dark none of the servants would go to the tower or even pass it on their way to the road. We had never thought much about the story, but being alone in the tower brought it back to my mind. It was the sort of afternoon to inspire such thoughts – sombre, cloudy, with a hint of mist in the air. Perhaps I heard the light sound of a step on the stairs below me. Perhaps I sensed as one does a presence nearby. I wasn't sure, but as I stood there, I felt suddenly cold as though some unknown terror was creeping up on me.

I turned away from the landing and started up the stairs. I would have a quick look and come down again. I must not let Stirling think I was not interested. I was breathless, for the stairs were very steep and I had started to hurry. Why hurry? There was no need to . . . except that I wanted to be on my way down; I wanted to get away from this haunted tower.

I paused. Then I heard it. A footstep – slow and stealthy on the stair. I listened. Silence. Imagination, I told myself. Or perhaps it was a workman. Or Stirling come to show me how they were getting on.

'Is anyone there?' I called.

Silence. A frightening silence. I thought to myself: I'm not alone in this tower. I am sure of it. Someone is close . . . not far behind me. Someone who doesn't answer when I call.

Sometimes I think there is a guardian angel who dogs our footsteps and warns us of danger. I felt then that I was being urged to watch, that danger was not far behind me.

I ran to the top of the tower. I stood there, leaning over the parapet, gripping the stone with my hands. I looked down below, far below and I thought: Someone is coming up the stairs. I shall be alone here with that person . . . alone on this tower.

Yes. It was coming. Stealthy footsteps. The creak of the door which led to the last steps. Three more of those steps and then . . . I stood stood there clinging to the stones, my heart thundering while I prayed for a miracle.

Then the miracle was there below me. Maud Mathers came into sight with her quick, rather ungainly stride.

I called: 'Maud! Maud!'

She stopped and looked about her.

Oh God help me, I prayed. It's coming close. Maud was looking up. 'Minta! What are you doing up there?' Hers was the sort of voice which could be heard at the back of the hall when the village put on its miracle play.

'Just looking at the work that's being done.'

'I've brought your gloves. You left them at the vicarage. I thought you might want them.'

I was laughing with relief. I turned and looked over my shoulder. Nothing. Just nothing! I had experienced a moment of panic and Maud with her common sense had dispelled it.

'I'll come right down,' I said. 'Wait for me, Maud, I'm coming now.'

I ran down those stairs and there was no sign of anyone. It was fancy, I told myself. The sort of thing that happens to women when they're pregnant.

I didn't think of that incident again until some time afterwards.

By the end of January I was certain that I was going to have a child. Stirling was delighted – perhaps triumphant was the word – and that made me very happy. I realized then that he had become more withdrawn than ever. I began to see less of him. He was constantly with the workmen; he was also buying up land in the neighbourhood. I had the feeling that he wanted to outdo Franklyn in some way, which was ridiculous really because the Wakefields had been at the Park for about a hundred years and however much land Stirling acquired there couldn't be a question of rivalry.

Lucie cosseted me and was excited about the baby. She wanted to talk about it all the time. 'It will be Druscilla's niece or nephew. What a complicated household we are!'

I was very amused when I discovered that Bella, the little cat which Nora had given me, was going to have kittens. I had grown very fond of Bella. She was a most unusual cat and Nora assured me that Donna was the same. They followed us as dogs do; they were affectionate and liked nothing so much as to sit in our laps and be stroked. They would purr away and I always smiled when I was at Mercer's to see Donna behave in exactly the same way as Bella did. And when I knew Bella was going to have kittens I couldn't resist going over to tell Nora.

I was a little uneasy with Nora nowadays. I hadn't felt like that before my marriage, but now there seemed a certain barrier between us which might have been of her erecting because it certainly wasn't of mine.

She was in the greenhouse where she was trying to grow orchids and Donna was sitting on the bench watching her at her work.

'Nora, what do you think?' I cried. 'Bella's going to have kittens.'

She turned to look at me and laughed and she was how I liked her to be – amused and friendly.

'What a coincidence!' she said.

'You mean . . . both of us.'

Nora nodded. 'Poor Donna will be piqued when she knows.'

At the mention of her name Donna mewed appreciatively and rubbed herself against Nora's arm. 'So she's stolen a march on you, eh?' said Nora to the cat. And to me. 'What will you do with them?'

'Keep one and find a home for the others. I think they'd like one at the vicarage.'

So we went in and Mrs. Glee served coffee in that rather truculent way of hers which amused Nora and was meant to show how much better things were done at Mercer's than at Whiteladies.

'I'm giving a dinner-party next week,' said Nora. 'You must come, Minta.'

'I'm sure we should love to.'

'It's going to be a rather special occasion.' She didn't say what and I didn't probe. I was sure it was no use in any case. Nora was the sort of person who could not be coaxed into saying what she did not want to.

While we were drinking coffee we heard the sounds of a horse's hoofs on the stable cobbles.

'It's Franklyn,' said Nora, looking out of the window. 'He calls in frequently. We enjoy a game of chess together. I think he's rather lonely since his parents died.'

Franklyn came in looking very distinguished, I thought. I wondered whether there would be an announcement of their engagement and this was what the party was going to be for. One couldn't tell from either of them. But Franklyn's frequent visits to Mercer's seemed significant. After all, I knew him very well and I was sure he was in love with Nora.

I really looked forward to the dinner-party. It seemed to me that it would be such a pleasant rounding off if Nora married Franklyn and we all lived happily ever after.

But on the night of the dinner-party I had a shock. There was no mention of an engagement. Instead Nora told us that this would be one of the last dinner-parties she would give because she had definitely decided to go back to Australia.

Bella was missing. We guessed of course that she had hidden herself away in order to have her kittens, but we had no idea where. Lucie said it was a habit cats had. I was rather worried because I thought she would need food, but, as Lucie said, we shouldn't worry about her for she would know where to come when she wanted it.

She appeared after a day and night and it was clear that she had had her kittens.

'We'll have to follow her,' said Lucie, 'and find out where they are.'

We did, and, to our amazement, Bella led us to the tower. Work had had to stop up there because some special wood was needed and it was hard to obtain. Stirling had said that there could be no makeshift so that part of the work had had to be postponed. The door leading to the tower must have been left open, so Bella had found her way up there. She had gone right to the top where workmen had left a piece of sacking and on this were four of the loveliest little kittens 1 had ever seen. They were tawny like Bella and I was enchanted by the little blind things and touched by Bella's devotion to them. She purred while I admired them but showed her disapproval when I touched them and she was very uneasy if anyone else approached.

'We'd better leave them up there,' said Lucie. 'She won't like it if they're moved. She might try to hide them. Cats have been known to do that.'

'I'll look after them,' I said. 'I shall bring Bella's food up here myself.'

I went over at once to tell Nora about the kittens and where they'd been found and she said she would be over in a day or so to see them.

I went up the spiral staircase every day and I often thought of that occasion when I had taken fright. The feeling of fear had completely vanished now. The fact that Bella had used the tower for her kittens had made it marvellously normal. I made a habit of going up every morning at about eleven o'clock with a jug of cream for Bella and her food. She expected me and would be delighted each morning when I would inspect the kittens to see how they had progressed.

I was going up one morning when Nora arrived. 'To see the kittens?' I asked.

'You too,' she told me. She had become more friendly since the day I had ridden over and told her about the kittens.

'I was just going to feed them,' I said. 'Come up with me.'

It really seemed as though I had a guardian angel, for I believe that might very well have been the end of me if Nora hadn't come with me. I put the saucer on the stone ledge as I always did while I poured out the milk. It saved stooping. Nora was standing slightly behind me and as I put the saucer in its place and started to pour out the milk there was a sudden rumble. Nora had caught at my skirts and was clinging to them. The stone ledge on which I had placed the saucer seemed suddenly to crumble. I heard the crash of falling masonry. I didn't know what had happened because Nora had pulled me backwards with such force that we both fell.

Nora was on her feet first, her face ashen. 'Minta! Are you all right?'

I wasn't sure. I was too dazed. I could think of nothing but that sudden collapse and myself being hurled forward, Nora with me . . . down from the topmost point of Whiteladies as the nun had gone long ago.

'The fools!' cried Nora. 'They should have warned us. That balustrade was unsafe.' Then she was kneeling beside me. 'Minta . . .?' I knew she was thinking of my baby. I could feel the movements of the child and I was filled with relief because it was still alive. 'I'll get help quickly,' went on Nora. 'Stay there. Don't move.'

I half raised myself when she had gone. Bella was licking her kittens, unaware of the near-tragedy which had just been enacted. I shivered and waited again for my child to let me know that it continued to live. I was afraid to get up lest I did some harm to it and it seemed a long time before Nora came back. Lucie was with her, her face strained and anxious.

'Minta!' She was kneeling beside me. 'This is terrible. Those men should be shot.'

'How are we going to get her down the stairs?' asked Nora.

'We won't,' said Lucie, 'until Dr. Hunter's seen her.'

'There's something about this tower that I don't like,' I said.

'What?' asked Lucie.

'Something . . . evil.'

'You're talking like the servants,' said Lucie sharply. She hated what she called 'silly fancies'. Practical as ever, she had brought a cushion and blankets and she and Nora stayed with me until Dr. Hunter came.

He made me stand up. 'No bones broken,' he said. He frowned at the balustrade. 'How could such a thing be allowed!' he demanded.

'They've been hammering away for weeks,' said Lucie. 'We ought to have thought something like this might have happened. When you think of an old place like this suddenly being knocked about . . . In any case the kittens shall be brought down. The cat may not like it but she'll have to put up with it. I'm sending Evans up to bring them down and put them somewhere in the stables.'

'You can walk down to your room,' said Dr. Hunter to me. 'But I think a few days' rest would be good . . . just so that we can make sure. Feet up, eh?'

'I'll see that she does that,' said Lucie firmly.

So no harm was done but Lucie insisted that I rest. She needn't have worried. I was determined to carry out the doctor's orders, thinking of the safety of my child. But two nights later I had a dream. I was in the tower and suddenly the terror I had experienced there came upon me. I peered about me but could see nothing. Yet there was something there – some faceless thing which was trying to force me over the parapet.

I awoke with a start and for a few moments thought I was actually in the tower. Then I was aware of my warm and comfortable bed. I was alone in it. Stirling slept in another room now. He had said something about its being better for the baby.

I lay thinking and remembered that time when I had mounted the stairs to the tower and had thought that someone was following me and the fear that I had felt then was like that which I had experienced in the dream. Maud had been below. But suppose she had not been down below. I thought of myself clutching that stone balustrade, the evil presence coming close behind me . . . and no one below! This was an example of the nonsensical imaginings of a pregnant woman who so feels the need to protect her unborn child that she imagines people are trying to kill her. Why? For what purpose?

I shook myself fully awake and laughed at myself. The first incident had been pure imagination; the second an accident which could have happened to anybody. There was no reason why anyone should want to harm me.

But soon I was to discover that there could be a reason.

Stirling wanted to give a dinner-party – a rather elaborate one. He reckoned that we were no longer a house of mourning; we had been unable to entertain as he had wished at Christmas and he wanted to do something now.

I know that he was upset by Nora's intention to leave us and I particularly wanted to please him. He planned to use the minstrels' gallery and as it was years since we had players up there I went up with two of the maids to make sure everything was in order. Later I discovered that I had lost a stone from a garnet and pearl brooch which had been my mother's and it occurred to me that I might have lost it in the gallery. I went along to search and that was how I came to be there and overheard the scene between Nora and Stirling. There were red velvet ruchings over the lower woodwork of the gallery and heavy curtains of the same material which could be drawn back when the musicians were playing. I was on my hands and knees looking for the stone, completely hidden from anyone in the hall below by the red velvet ruchings, when someone came into the hall and I was about to stand up when I heard Stirling say in a voice which I had never heard him use before: 'Nora!'

Nora said: 'I came to see Minta.'

I stood up but they didn't see me and before I could call to them Stirling said: 'I've got to talk to you, Nora. I can't go on like this.'

She answered angrily: 'Shouldn't you have thought of that before you married Whiteladies?'

I should have called to them but I knew that only if they were unaware of me could I discover something of what could well be of the utmost importance to me. On impulse I shamelessly played the eavesdropper. I knelt to conceal myself from them.

'Oh God,' he said, and I hardly recognized his voice, so different was it from the way in which he ever spoke to me, 'if only I could go back.'

She taunted him. 'And then? You would listen to me? You would have seen the folly of marrying for the sake of settling old scores?'

I put my hand over my heart. It was making such a noise. I was going to learn something terrifying unless I stood up at once and announced the fact that I was here. I couldn't. I had to know.

'Nora,' he said. 'Oh Nora, I can't go on like this. And you're threatening to go away. How could you! It would be heartless.'

'Heartless!' She laughed cruelly. 'Heartless ... as you were when you married. How did you think *I* felt about that?'

'You knew it had to be.'

'Had to be!' There was great scorn in her voice. 'You talk as though you were under some compulsion.'

'You know why ...'

'Lynx is dead,' she said. '*That* died with him. I shall go back to Australia. It's the only way. You chose this marriage. Now you have to meet your obligations.'

'Nora, don't go. I can't bear it if you go.'

'And if I stay?'

'There'll be a way. I swear I'll find some way.'

'Don't forget you have to see your children playing on the lawns of

Whiteladies. How will you do that? You thought it was going to be so easy. All the golden millionaire had to do was make the family bankrupt.'

'That was done before.'

'And we suspect how. It's nothing to be proud of. But it didn't work out as you thought it would. Only the family could inherit this place . . . so you had to marry into the family.' She laughed bitterly. 'All this for these stones, these walls. If they could laugh they'd be laughing at us. No. I'm going to Australia. I've written to Adelaide. You've made your bed, as they say. Now you have to lie in it.'

'I love you, Nora. Are you going to deny that you love me?' She was silent and he cried out. 'You can't deny it. You've always known it. That night of the fire . . .'

'You let me marry Lynx,' she said.

'But that was . . . Lynx.'

'Oh yes,' she said, almost viciously, 'your god.'

'Yours too, Nora.'

'If you had loved me . . .'

'You two were the most important things on earth. Of course I loved you then, and if you had loved me enough . . .'

'I know,' she said impatiently. 'But it was Lynx then, and it's Lynx now. We can't escape from him. He's dead but he lives on. You had a choice, though. When you found out you couldn't buy this place you could have come back with me to Australia. Or we could have stayed here. It wouldn't have mattered to me if . . .'

'If we were together,' he said triumphantly.

'But it's too late. You've married. You'll stay married.' Her voice was cruel again. 'You've got to see those children playing on the lawn. Remember?'

She spoke as though she hated him and I knew how deeply he had wounded her. I knew so much now. In the last few minutes everything had fallen into shape. Dominating all our lives was his father who had once lived here and who had been deeply wronged – a great, powerful man, whose influence lived on after he was dead.

'Too late,' she said. 'And you've no one to blame but yourself. When you told me . . . I wanted to die. I hated you, Stirling, because . . .'

'Because you love me.'

'It's too late. You chose. Now you must live with your choice.'

'It can't be too late,' Stirling said. 'There's always a way and I'll find it, Nora. I swear it. Promise to be patient.'

'Patient! What are you talking about? You're married. You're married to Whiteladies. This wonderful, marvellous unique old house is your bride. You can't just walk out, you know.'

'Nora!'

'I shall go on with my plans. The sooner I leave the better.'

'And you think you'll be happy back there . . . without him . . . without me?'

'I have not thought of happiness. Only the need to go.'

'I won't allow it. There's a way out. I promise you I'll find a way. Only Nora, don't go . . . don't go.'

Again she laughed at him. How cruel Nora could be! 'You're shouting. You'll tell the whole household what you have done.'

Then the door was noisily shut. I peered through the ruching and saw Stirling was alone. He covered his face and his hands as though to shut out the sight of the hall with its dais and tapestries and vaulted ceiling – everything that had made it the wonderful old house worth the greatest sacrifice to attain – even worth marrying me in order to take possession of it.

I remained in the gallery after Stirling had gone. My knees were cramped. I had forgotten the lost garnet. I understood everything now. I should have seen it before, his sudden proposal when he had seen that there was no other means of acquiring the house; his perfunctory love-making; his moroseness when Nora announced that she was leaving. Everything fell into place.

I wished that I were worldly like Nora. Then I should know what to do. I wanted to confide in someone. If Nora had not been involved I should have chosen her. There was Lucie. I hesitated. Lucie had been suspicious of the match right from the first. Lucie was wise and Lucie loved me.

I went to my room still feeling dazed. I shouldn't have listened. Listeners rarely hear any good of themselves. How many times had I heard that?

Bella came and rubbed herself against my legs. The kitten I had kept was playing with the blind cord. I thought of that day on the tower and how the balustrade had crumbled . . . and then I thought of the occasion when I believed I had been followed up there; and I heard a voice ringing in my ears, Stirling's voice: 'I'll find a way.'

'No,' I said, 'that's stupid. He didn't mean that.' But how did I know what he meant? What did I know of him – or rather what had I known before a short while ago? At least now I knew that he had married me because of some vow to own Whiteladies. I knew that he was capable of deceit, that he had pretended to love me when what he wanted was the house. I knew that he loved another woman and that he was planning in some way to end his marriage with me in order to marry her.

How? I asked myself; and some horrible voice within me said: 'It almost happened in the tower. There was the balustrade . . . and that other occasion.' I tried not to think of his creeping stealthily up the stairs, seizing me from behind and throwing me over the tower. That was fancy. Fancy! Hadn't I heard a movement? Hadn't I sensed evil? Nora had saved me once. At least *she* was not in the plot . . . if plot there was. But I couldn't believe that of Stirling.

My head was throbbing and I could not think clearly. I don't know why I went to Lizzie's room, but I did.

'Are you all right, Miss Minta?' she asked.

'I have a headache.'

'Sometimes women get them in your condition.'

'Tell me about that artist who came to teach my mother drawing.'

'Mr. Charles Herrick,' she said slowly. 'And now you're Mrs. Herrick and there's another Mrs. Herrick at Mercer's. And soon another little Herrick will come into the world.'

'What was he like?'

'Like your Mr. Herrick but different. I never saw anyone quite like him. He stood out and above everyone else. You'd have thought he owned the place. Your mother worshipped him.'

'And you too, Lizzie.'

'Yes,' she admitted. 'And he wasn't averse, I might tell you.'

'He loved my mother.'

'He loved her for what she stood for. He was proud and poor and he saw himself as lord of the house.'

'And then?'

'There were ructions. "Get out," he was told and he went, but he came back for your mother. They were going to elope.' Lizzie started to laugh. 'He came up by the ladder. She was ready to go with him. She gave him her jewels. She had some valuable pieces. He put them into his pocket and then ... they burst into the room and caught him ... and that was the last we saw of him.'

'Somebody warned them.'

'Yes,' she said slyly.

'It was you, Lizzie, wasn't it?'

Her face puckered. 'You know!' She cried. 'Your mother knew. I told her on the night she died. The shock killed her. She would never have forgiven me if she'd lived. She raged at me. She said that but for me her whole life would have been different. She'd have gone away with him; he'd never have gone to Australia.'

'But he went and he made a vow and because of that, Lizzie, because of you ...'

I walked out of the room, leaving her staring blankly before her.

I was bewildered, still not knowing how to act.

I couldn't go down to luncheon because I couldn't face anyone. Lucie came up to my room.

'Minta, what's wrong?'

'I feel ill, Lucie.'

'My dear, you're trembling. I'll get a hot-water bottle.'

'No, Lucie. Just sit by the bed and talk to me.'

She sat down and I started to talk. In whom could I confide who would be more sympathetic than Lucie, who for so many years had been closer than my own mother? I told her what I had overheard in the minstrels' gallery.

'You see, Lucie, he loves Nora. He married me for Whiteladies.'

Lucie was thoughtful for some moments; then she said: 'Nora is going back to Australia. You and Stirling will make a life for yourselves. It will be a compromise, but marriage often is.'

'No,' I said. 'He loves her and won't be able to forget her. There's a great bond between them – it's part hate and part love, or so it seemed, for Nora sounded as though she hated him and loved him at the same time. She hated him because he'd hurt her by marrying me. I've been lying here trying to think of something I can do.'

'Minta, my dearest child, the best thing you can do is nothing. This sort of thing has happened before. Stirling is married to you. You are going to have his child. Nora will go to Australia. You'll be surprised. In a few years' time he will have forgotten her and so will you.'

'He won't let her go,' I insisted. 'He said so.'

'Impulsive talk. He has no say and Nora is a wise woman of the world. She knows that nothing can be done. You are his wife. When she goes away he may fret for a while but time heals everything. He'll be reconciled. You have a great deal to offer him, Minta.'

'No, no. I've been trying to think of what I should do. I even thought of going away.'

'Where to?'

'I can't think where.'

'You are not being practical. You'll stay here and I'll be at hand to look after you.'

'But I did think of going . . . somewhere. I even started to write a letter to him.'

She went over to my desk and picked up a sheet of paper. On it I had written:

'Dear Stirling, I was in the minstrels' gallery when you and Nora were talking so I know that you love her and there seems only one thing to do. I must stand aside . . .'

I had got no farther, having paused there to wonder what I could do. Angrily, Lucie threw it into the waste-paper basket. Then she came back to the bed.

'You are overwrought,' she said. 'I am going to take care of you and I promise you that in time all this will seem nothing to you. He couldn't have been so much in love with Nora or he would never have married you.'

'You're a great comfort, Lucie, but . . .'

'You trust me. Now you're to stay in bed for the rest of the day, then you won't have to face anybody. I'll go along to Dr. Hunter and tell him to come and have a look at you, shall I?'

'Dr. Hunter can't help over this.'

'Yes, he can. He can give you something to make you sleep and that's what you need really. I'll tell everyone you're resting today. You haven't been yourself since that fall in the tower.'

I shivered. I couldn't tell even Lucie of the horrible suspicion that had come to me. But merely talking to Lucie had made me feel better. She went out and left me, and I lay still, trying to believe what she had told me and failing wretchedly.

I stayed in bed for the rest of the day. Lucie brought supper for me on a tray, but I couldn't touch the roast chicken nor the cheese and fruit. She had been to Dr. Hunter's, but he was out on a case and that stupid Mrs. Devlin had seemed as though she had been drinking. However, she had left a message for him to come and see me in the morning. I could have one of the pills he had given me at the time of my fall. Lucie would have some milk sent up for me to take with it.

'Won't you try and eat something?' she asked.

'I couldn't, Lucie.'

About nine o'clock she sent Lizzie up with some hot milk and biscuits. Lizzie looked subdued and this clearly had something to do with her outburst earlier that day. I couldn't feel the same about Lizzie any more. Her action had had such a tremendous impact on all our lives. I looked distastefully at the milk and turned away, so Lizzie put it on my bedside table.

I closed my eyes and I must have dozed, for when I awoke my heart started to pound furiously for someone was standing by my bed. It was Stirling. I couldn't face him then so I pretended to be still asleep. He stood there looking at me and I wondered what was in his mind. Was he thinking of putting a pillow over my face and smothering me? I didn't care if he did. Who would have believed it was possible to love a man whom one suspected of murdering one. Nora loved and hated him at the same time and I loved him while I suspected him of wanting to kill me. How complex were human emotions!

He went out after a while. I lay still and the same thoughts went round and round in my mind and suddenly I was startled by a movement near the window. I sat up in bed and doing so knocked over the tray. The kitten followed by Bella came running over from the window. I realized that it was their playing with the blind cord that had awakened me. The kitten discovered the milk and started to lap noisily, so I put the tray on the floor and they finished it between them. Bella jumped on to the bed, purring, and I stroked her. After a while she jumped down and I tried to sleep. I couldn't, of course. I just lay there going over everything and finally I was so exhausted that I did sleep.

Lizzie came in. It was eight-thirty. I was usually up by this time.

'Her ladyship sent me to ask how you were this morning.'

'I'm tired,' I said. 'Just leave me. Don't pull up the blind.'

'So you're staying in bed for a while?'

I said I was. She went out and a little later Lucie came in. 'Just to see how you feel,' she said.

I was half asleep, so she went on: 'I won't disturb you. A little rest will do you good.'

It was about half past ten when there was a light tap on my door. It was Mary, one of the housemaids. She said: 'Mrs. Herrick's called. She wants to see you.'

Nora! My heart was leaping about uncomfortably. I wanted to see Nora, to talk to her. I was turning over in my mind whether I might tell her what I had heard. I had always felt an urge to confide in Nora. But how could I in this case?

I heard myself say uncertainly: 'Ask her to come up.'

'Shall I draw the blinds, Miss Minta.'

I hesitated. 'N . . . no. Not just yet.' I wanted to know whether I could face Nora first. My hair was unkempt; I should have washed, tidied myself before seeing her. But it was too late now. The maid was gone and when she came back Nora was with her.

Nora was wearing a grey riding habit and she looked elegant and worldly. There was a gentleness in her face. I knew that she was sorry because I was married to Stirling – not only because that meant he wasn't free for her. She was sorry because she thought I was going to be unhappy.

'Oh, you are resting,' she said. 'I heard that you weren't feeling well.'

'I didn't feel very well yesterday and since the fall Dr. Hunter likes me to rest a lot.'

'I'm sure he's right.' A faint light came through the slats of the blind and she drew a chair up to the bed. 'I thought I must come and see you,' she went on. 'I shan't have much more opportunity.'

'You are determined to leave us, then?'

'I've definitely made up my mind.'

'I shall miss you. As for Stirling . . .' My voice trembled.

She said quickly: 'I always thought I should go back some time.'

'You must have been very happy there.'

She drew her brows together and said: 'Yes. I daresay you are longing for the child to be born.'

'Yes, I am.'

'And Stirling, too.'

Children playing on the lawns of Whiteladies! I thought.

'The waiting period can be irksome,' I said. 'Franklyn will miss you.'

'In a year or so you will have forgotten me . . . all of you.'

I shook my head. I had a great desire to see her face more clearly. She hid her feelings well but I thought: She must be as unhappy as I am. I said: 'It's dark in here.'

'Shall I pull up the blinds?' She rose and went over to the window. I heard her give a little gasp. She was staring at the floor. Then hastily she pulled up the blind and looked down again.

'What is it?' I cried, starting up.

'Bella and the kitten . . .'

I leaped out of bed. I caught my breath in horror. Their bodies looked oddly contorted. They were both dead. I knelt down beside them. I could not bring myself to touch those once lively little bodies which I had loved.

'They're dead,' said Nora. 'Minta, what can it be?'

I knew. I remembered the milk dripping on to the floor and Stirling standing by my bed.

'There was poison in my milk,' I said quite calmly. 'Of course it was meant for me.' Then I began to laugh and I couldn't stop myself. 'I've a charmed life. First Maud . . . then you, and now the cats.'

She took me by the shoulders and shook me. 'What do you mean?' she demanded. 'What *do* you mean? Control yourself, for God's sake. Don't touch the cats. You don't know what's wrong. Let me help you back to bed. Remember the child.'

She drew me back to the bed. I was saying: 'It's all very simple, Nora. Someone is trying to kill me. There have been other attempts. But I have a charmed life . . .'

She was very pale. 'I don't believe it,' she said. 'I don't believe it.' And said it as though she were trying to convince herself. And I knew what was in her mind. She had heard him say it. He had said to her: 'I'll find a way.' I heard her whispering to herself. 'No . . . no . . . It's not true.'

'Nora,' I said, 'it can't always miss, can it . . . not every time?'

'You've got to get away from . . . from here. We have to think about it. I can't leave you here. You must come back with me to Mercer's. We can talk there . . . we can plan . . .'

I thought: Go with *her*! *She* is the reason why he wants to be rid of me. He wants Nora *and* Whiteladies. How can I go with her? But she had saved me once before.

'What will they say if I go with you?' I said. 'What will Stirling say?'

'We must save him . . . and you,' she answered. It was as though she were speaking to herself. It was an admission that the thoughts which were in my mind were shared by her.

There was a knock on the door. Nora looked at me in dismay. It was the maid again.

'The doctor is here, Miss Minta. I've brought him up.'

Dr. Hunter was immediately behind her and he came into the room.

'Lady Cardew suggested I pop in and have a look at you,' he said. He gazed at us both in astonishment. 'Is anything wrong?'

I left it to Nora to explain. I heard her say: 'We're very alarmed, Dr. Hunter. Come and look at the cats.'

She took him over to the window and he knelt down to look at Bella and her kitten. When he rose his face was ashen.

'What happened?' he asked.

'They drank the milk which was intended for Minta,' said Nora. 'Were they poisoned?'

'It could be so.'

'What should we do?'

'I will take the cats away.'

'I was suggesting that I take Minta with me to the Mercer's House.'

'That's an excellent idea,' said the doctor. He turned to me and said. 'Get up and dress quickly. Go out of the house as though nothing extraordinary has happened. Go to the Mercer's House with Mrs. Herrick right away and stay there until I come.'

So he left us, taking the cats with him; and I dressed hastily and, wrapping myself in my cloak, went out of the house with Nora.

NORA

Chapter One

I shall never forget that journey back to the Mercer's House and the thoughts which crowded into my mind. Stirling was trying to murder his wife. That was what he had meant when he had said he would find a way. Why had I not gone back to Australia months before? I should have gone as soon as he had married her.

Half my mind rejected the thought and then I kept thinking of that terrible day which was engraved indelibly on my memory when Jagger had caught me and fought with me and Lynx had come and shot him dead. He had killed a man because he had dared touch what he thought of as his; it was not because of attempted rape. I would never forget the poor little maid Mary who had suffered through Jagger. That had been shrugged aside as of little importance. Stirling was the son of Lynx. They were ruthless, both of them. They held life cheaply – that was, other people's lives. Stirling had been determined to get Whiteladies and now that he regretted the great sacrifice he wanted to start again. He could only do this by ridding himself of Minta. No, Stirling, I thought. And Lynx, this is where your revenge has led us!

I had made Minta mount my horse and I walked beside it, leading it. The poor girl looked as though she would collapse at any moment. No wonder! She had miraculously escaped death – and not only once, for I was sure that the crumbling parapet had been a trap for her.

I called one of the stable boys to look after the horse and took her into the house. We went into the drawing-room with its rosewood furniture and Regency striped wallpaper and sat looking at each other helplessly.

'Nora,' she asked me, 'what do you think of it?'

I couldn't bear to talk of my suspicions, so I said that the cats might have died of some strange disease. There were mysterious illnesses among animals of which we knew very little. She started to talk about animals she had had when a child and some of the things which had happened to them. But we were not thinking of what we were saying. I said I would make some tea and she said she would help. It gave us something to do and all the time we were trying to work out some plan. She must stay with me, I said. I couldn't bear her to be out of my sight. I was terrified of what might happen to her.

There was about her a surprising indifference. She had been greatly shocked by what had happened so perhaps that was why she gave that impression of not caring. I was desperately sorry for her. She was going to bear Stirling's child and I had been envious of that, but I was overcome by a desire to protect her.

We drank the tea. It was now past midday. At Whiteladies they would be wondering where she was, although one of the maids had seen us leave and I had murmured something about Mrs. Herrick's coming over to the Mercer's House with me.

It was one o'clock when Lucie arrived. Her hair was disordered by the wind; she had evidently come out hastily when she had discovered that Minta was not in her room and she had learned where she was.

As she came into the drawing-room and saw Minta her expression was one of relief. 'Oh Minta, my dear, I wondered what had happened.'

They embraced and Lucie said: 'Why didn't you say you were going out? I thought you were in your room.'

'Nora came to see me and I came over with her.'

'But you've had no breakfast. You've . . .'

'We were rather disturbed,' I said. 'We found the cats dead.'

'The cats . . . what cats?'

'Bella and the kitten,' said Minta. 'They were lying on the floor near the window . . . their bodies stiff and odd-looking.' Her lips trembled. 'It was horrible.'

'Cats!' repeated Lucie, bewildered.

'Dr. Hunter took them away,' I explained.

'Do please tell me what all this is about.'

I didn't want her to know. I thought: There'll be an enquiry and they'll find out. Oh Stirling, how could you! As if I could love you after that!

Minta said simply: 'I don't think the doctor wanted us to talk about it yet.' She turned to me. 'But it will be all right to tell Lucie. Lucie, the milk which was in my room . . . I didn't drink it.'

'What milk?' said Lucie.

'There was some milk sent up. You told Lizzie to bring it, didn't you?'

'Oh yes. I remember.'

'I didn't drink it. I knocked it over and the cats drank it. Now they're dead.'

'But what has this to do with the milk?'

She spoke in such a matter-of-fact tone that my fears abated a little and relief came to me. I thought: We're imagining things . . . both of us. Of course the cats' death had nothing to do with the milk!

'So the cats are dead,' went on Lucie, 'and that has upset you. I did hear that some of the farmers were putting down poison for a fox that's raiding the fowl houses. Bella's constantly roaming about.'

I looked at Minta and saw the relief in her face too.

Lucie went on to stress the point: 'What did you think the *milk* had to do with it?'

'We thought there was something wrong with the milk,' I said, 'and that because they had drunk it . . .'

Lucie looked puzzled. 'You thought the milk was *poisoned*! But who on earth . . . Really, what's happened to both of you?'

'Of course that's the answer,' I said. 'The cats were poisoned by something on the farms. It stands to reason.'

'Is that tea you have in that pot?' said Lucie. 'I could do with a cup.'

'It's cold, but I'll send for some more.'

'Thanks. Then I think we should go back, Minta. You want to take greater care of yourself. What odd fancies you get!'

I rang for tea and when it came and I was pouring out we heard the sound of carriage wheels and Mabel came in to announce that Dr. Hunter had called.

'Dr. Hunter!' said Lucie. 'What's he doing here?'

I told Mabel to show him in. To my astonishment, Stirling was with him. Lucie rose in her chair and said: 'What *is* this?'

The doctor said: 'I've come to talk to you and what I have to say should be heard by all. I should have witnesses. I should have said it all before this happened.'

'Is it about the cats?' demanded Lucie.

I looked at Stirling but I couldn't read his expression.

'The cats were poisoned,' said the doctor.

'Something they picked up at a farm?' I asked, and there was a terrible fear in my heart.

The doctor said: 'I think I'd better begin at the beginning. This goes back a long way.' He drew a deep breath. 'I am to blame for a good deal.'

'Don't you think you ought to consider very carefully what you are saying?' asked Lucie gently.

'I have considered for a long time. This makes it necessary. I am going to tell the truth. I am going to tell what I should have told long ago. It was when Lady Cardew died that it started.'

'I don't think you should say this, doctor,' said Lucie in a very quiet voice. 'I think you may regret it.'

'I can only regret not having confessed before.' He did not look at Lucie. 'Lady Cardew was not really ill. She had had a disappointment in her life and brooded on it. She came to terms with life by practising a kind of invalidism. It is not unusual with some people. I gave her placebos from time to time. She would take her doses and believe herself to be helped by them. They were in fact nothing but coloured water. Then she died. I should have told the truth then. She died of taking an overdose of a strong sleeping draught. This particular drug was missing from my dispensary, and I believed I had given it to her in mistake for her placebo. I should have admitted this, but instead I wrote on her death certificate that she had died of a heart attack. She had always thought that she had a diseased heart. Her heart was in fact strong. What I did was unpardonable. I was ambitious. In those days I dreamed of specializing. To have admitted that I had mistakenly given a dangerous drug in mistake for a placebo would have ruined my career. I might never have been able to practise again.'

'You are a fool,' said Lucie sadly.

'You are right.' He looked at her mournfully.

'I would advise you to stop this silly tirade which will only bring you to disaster,' she went on.

'At least it will bring me peace of mind. Because *I* did not give her the wrong drug. It was someone else who gave it to her ... someone who came to my house when I was absent, bringing wine for my housekeeper and drinking with her until she was insensible and then going to my dispensary and taking the drugs.'

'I think the doctor has lost his senses,' said Lucie.

'I had,' he replied, 'but I've regained them now.'

'Can't you see that he is mad?' she demanded of Stirling.

'It doesn't seem so to me,' said Stirling.

'I refuse to listen to any more,' said Lucie. 'That's if you're going on, Dr. Hunter.'

'I am going on to tell everything, right to the end, right till today when I discovered that two cats died of the same drug which killed Lady Cardew.'

Lucie stood up. 'You *are* mad, you know,' she said.

'I know how the drug was obtained,' said the doctor. 'It was in exactly the same way. Mrs. Devlin has admitted that you came with whisky this time. A little gift for her? Should we try a little tot? And she sat there drinking until she dozed and then you took the keys and went to the dispensary, just exactly as you did on another occasion. She has told me that she remembers it happening before.'

'I won't stay to listen to such nonsense,' said Lucie. 'I shall call another doctor. I shall tell him to get a strait-jacket and bring it here right away.'

She stood at the door looking at us. Minta stared at her incredulously. The doctor's expression was unfathomable. I fancied there was a certain tenderness in it.

'Lucie,' he said, 'you need care.'

She had gone. We heard her running down the stairs and the slamming of the door.

The doctor went on: 'It's not a pleasant story, but I have to tell it. It's the end of everything for us both ... but at least another murder must be prevented.' He was looking at Minta. 'Thank God it didn't happen this time. You see, I was strongly attracted by Lucie and asked her to marry me. If she had ... I believe all would have been well. But she had an obsession. It was the great house, the title. She had known great poverty as a child. She feared poverty and longed for security. She was educated by an aunt who was stern and showed her no affection, and she became a teacher. It was a precarious living; she was always in danger of losing her post and being thrown on to an overcrowded market. She was overawed and impressed by the grandeur of Whiteladies.'

I looked at Stirling and I knew he was thinking of Lynx.

'I think she was fond of me in the beginning. I believe she would have married me, but she was helping Sir Hilary a good deal and she realized how much he had come to depend on her. She saw the possibilities and was excited by them, and so this obsession was born. Lucie is a woman of great determination but the desire to possess Whiteladies unbalanced her mind – and she was tempted. Once she had taken one fatal step she was set on her path. In murdering Lady Cardew she had become a criminal and there was no limit to what she was prepared to do.'

'She murdered my mother,' said Minta. 'And she would have murdered me. Why?'

'She was Lady Cardew but that was not enough. Minta would inherit the house. When Sir Hilary died she would be merely a dependant having no control. She could not endure that. If she could have a son it would be different. But Sir Hilary was old. I was fascinated by Lucie and I did not know that she had committed murder. Druscilla is my daughter.'

There was a short silence before he went on: 'She longed for a son. Her rage when Druscilla was born was great. But she would not give up. She was determined to have a son who would inherit Whiteladies and prevent its passing to Minta. But Minta married and Sir Hilary died. There was no hope then except through Druscilla, who was believed to be Sir Hilary's daughter. If Minta were out of the way . . .' He lifted his hands helplessly. 'You see it all now. The whole sordid story. I swear I did not realize all that had happened until I saw those cats today. I knew that she had wanted a son so that she could rule the house through him. I did not know that she had committed murder and planned another. Only today did I see the complete picture. Mrs. Devlin admitted that Lucie came yesterday and brought whisky and that she, Mrs. Devlin, drank too much. She was asleep the whole afternoon and when I went into my dispensary I found the drug missing . . . as it had been on that other occasion. That is the story.'

I was conscious of a great relief. Stirling was looking at Minta with fear and horror and I thought: He is fond of her after all. Who could help being fond of Minta?

I said: 'What are we going to do?'

Nobody answered, but the matter was decided for us.

Minta's face creased in sudden agony, and she said: 'I think my pains are starting.'

It seemed then that reality was forcing fantasy aside, for this story of what had happened was like a fantasy to us all. It is disconcerting to discover that someone whom one has regarded as a friend, a normal human being, is a murderer. Yet I could believe this of Stirling! I excused myself. I had after all seen his father shoot a man.

There was not time to do anything then but think of Minta and we all became practical. Fortunately Dr. Hunter was with us. I said: 'I don't think Minta should go back to Whiteladies. She should stay here. I can look after her.'

Dr. Hunter, no longer a man with a terrible secret on his conscience, became the efficient doctor. I ordered servants to put a warming-pan and hot-water bottles in the bed in the spare bedroom next to my own; and we took Minta to it. We were all very anxious because the baby was not due for another four weeks.

The child was born late that day – a perfect child, though premature. It would need very special care and the doctor had summoned a nurse who would come to the Mercer's House solely to care for it. He himself would be in constant attendance. Minta herself was very weak. The shocks of the last weeks culminating in the so recent one were responsible, said Dr. Hunter. We must take special care of Minta.

I promised I would do this and I was determined to. I believed that if I could help bring Minta back to health I should in some way expiate my guilt in loving her husband.

I shall never forget Stirling's face when he heard that he had a son. I knew he would be called Charles after his grandfather and that he must live so that Lynx's dream could be realized – a child of his own name to play on the lawns of Whiteladies.

What a strange, unreal kind of day! Looking back on it, it seems like a dream, too fantastic for reality; but there had been other days like that in my life and perhaps there would be more.

Lucie could not be found anywhere. We thought she had run away. She was in the tower and in the morning they found her body on the flagstones below the bartizan. The wall above, which had been boarded up since that occasion when Minta and I had been up there together, was broken away.

The servants said: 'It was a terrible accident. The wall gave way and Lady Cardew was thrown to the ground.'

Chapter Two

I was proud of Stirling. He took on the role of country squire as though it had always been his. Lady Cardew was dead – it was an accident, was the verdict. It was explained by all the work that was being done in Whiteladies which had shaken the old house to its foundations. That, said Stirling, was the best explanation.

He asked me to talk to the doctor to make him see reason. Stirling's idea was that the entire matter should be forgotten. There was no need for anyone – who did not already know it – to know the truth. The danger was removed. Lucie was dead; she could do no more harm. Dr. Hunter insisted that he had been guilty of grave indiscretion and was a disgrace to his profession. He didn't think he could allow matters to stand as they were. So the day after little Charles was born Stirling and I talked to him together.

I said: 'You have your skill. You have brought this child into the world and you know how difficult that was. If you hadn't been here Minta would have died and the child with her. Are you going to throw away that skill?'

'There are other doctors,' he said.

'But you belong here.'

'Another doctor would come and there would be no need of me.'

'And what of Maud?' I asked. 'You're fond of her. She's fond of you.'

'It's impossible,' said the doctor.

'It's not!' I cried indignantly. 'You must stop dramatizing yourself and think of Maud. Are you going to make her unhappy?'

He protested but I saw that I had made my point.

The days passed; the baby was two weeks old, still fragile, still in the care of his nurse, still needing the doctor's constant attention. They were two strange weeks. I looked after Minta. Motherhood had changed her. She seemed older and more beautiful – her features finely drawn, but there was a brooding sadness in her eyes.

Franklyn often called at Mercer's. He would sit and talk to Minta about the estate and the old days and ask questions about the baby. I thought how much more suitable than Stirling he would have been as a husband for Minta. They were of a kind, just as Stirling and I were.

Stirling came too. He would sit in Minta's room but there was an embarrassment between them. I wondered whether he knew that she had suspected him of attempting to kill her.

Once he and Franklyn came to the house at the same time so I left Stirling with Minta and Franklyn and I went to the drawing-room to play a game of chess.

As I sat there I thought of Lynx's hand stretched out to move the pieces, the ring on his finger. I treasured that ring. It brought back so many poignant memories.

And then before the game was over Franklyn said suddenly: 'Nora, will you marry me?'

I drew away from the table. 'No, Franklyn,' I said firmly.

'I wish you would,' he said quietly.

I smiled and he asked me why.

'It seems a strange way to offer marriage – almost as though you were inviting me to take a glass of sherry.'

'I'm sorry,' he said.

'I shouldn't have said that.'

'You should always say what's in your mind to me. I know I'm rather inadequate at expressing my feelings.'

'I like that.'

'I'm glad. I'm very fond of you and I hoped you might like me . . . a little.'

'Much more than a little but . . .'

'Not enough to marry me?'

'We are different kinds of people, Franklyn.'

'Does that make marriage impossible?'

'We shouldn't be compatible. You are good, precise, your life is well ordered . . .'

'My dear Nora, you overrate me.'

'I believe you would never do anything that wasn't reasonable and conventional. You are in control of your life.'

'Shouldn't one be?'

'Oh yes. It's very admirable. But hard to live up to. I can only say that we are different and I can't marry you.'

I looked into his face, but I was not really seeing him. I saw another face – a strong face that could be cruel and passionate, the face of a man who could dominate me as Franklyn never could. Even now it was impossible to analyse my feelings for Lynx. To marry him had been a compulsion. Yet I knew that now I yearned for Stirling because I had known ever since we met that we belonged together. Yet how could I reconcile this with my marriage to Lynx?

And Franklyn and myself! Minta and Stirling! We were star-crossed. Lynx like a mischievous god had made us dance to his tune and we had ended up with the wrong partners.

'No, Franklyn,' I said firmly. 'I can't marry you.'

The child was flourishing but Minta was not. Each day she seemed more wan, a little more fragile.

'She's not picking up,' said the doctor. 'She's listless.'

None of Mrs. Glee's special dishes could tempt her. Mrs. Glee was almost in tears when they came back untouched to the kitchen. Maud came to visit Minta bringing some of her own honey and blackcurrant jelly. A radiant Maud, this; she told me that the doctor had proposed.

'And been accepted, of course,' I said.

She nodded. 'He has told me everything and we're going to adopt Druscilla. Isn't that wonderful? And it's only right. Mr. Herrick agrees.'

I told Minta about it.

'Everything is working out well,' I said. 'Now you must eat what's brought to you and try to show some interest in life. What about your son, eh?'

'You can take him.'

'I! When you are well I shall be off to Australia.'

'Are you still determined to go?'

I assured her I was. She looked very sad and I told her that I should come back in a few years and then there would perhaps be a brother or sister for our little Charles. She shook her head.

I was really worried about her and it dawned on me that there was something on her mind.

My guilty conscience set me brooding. I thought constantly of Minta. One night I was so disturbed about her that I couldn't sleep. I rose and went to her room. The lamp there was kept burning all night and as I went in I was horrified to find how cold it was; then I saw that the window was wide open letting in the chilly night air. Minta had thrown off all the bedclothes and lay there in her nightdress only.

I went quickly to the bedside. I touched the sheets and found they were damp. I noticed the empty water jug on the bedside table.

First I shut the window; then I went back to the bed.

'Who did this?' I demanded. I lifted her from the bed and seizing a blanket wrapped it round her. I made her sit in a chair, while I took off the sheets and put on fresh ones. I boiled water on the spirit lamp and filled the hot-water bottles; when I got her into bed she was still shivering. She seemed dazed and she was certainly delirious; I am sure I should never have discovered what was in her mind if she had not been.

I sat by her bed listening to her rambling. It was about Stirling, herself, *myself*. So she knew. She talked of the child who would play on the lawns of Whiteladies. That phrase which had haunted me! I would be there for she herself would be dead. It was the only way to make Stirling happy.

'It's so hard to die,' she said. 'I have to die, though, because that's the only way.'

Piece by piece I fitted it together. And during that hour of delirium she showed me what was in her mind as she never would had her mind been clear. I was appalled and ashamed by the extent of her love for Stirling since she was ready to die for him.

A great determination came to me. I was going to nurse her back to health; I was going to make her live. Stirling must love her in time . . . if I were not there. If we could grow away from this absurd obsession that we were meant for each other (for if it were true would we ever have allowed anything to stand in our way?) he would learn to be happy with Minta. Perhaps it wouldn't be the intoxicating passion which for a while I had known with Lynx, but it could be a good life; and Stirling would have the gratification of knowing that he had fulfilled his father's wishes.

Within a week Minta began to improve. I spoke to her severely. I knew what she had done, I told her; and it must not occur again. It was cowardly to take one's life.

'For others?' she asked.

'For any reason,' I replied firmly. 'Life is meant to be lived.'

She told me then how she had discovered that Stirling and I loved each other, for she had been secreted in the minstrels' gallery. I tried to remember what we had said and I knew it must be damning.

'And you love Stirling,' she said. 'You were meant for each other. You are alike in so many ways. You are strong, adventurous people.'

'Who knows what love is?' I asked. 'It takes a lifetime to discover. I believe that love at its best is not the passion of a moment. It is something that one builds over the years. You can build it with Stirling.'

'But Stirling loves you. I heard him speak to you as he never did to me.'

'One day he will. Then he will have forgotten what I looked like.'

'It's not true, Nora.'

'It is something you can prove to be true in time.'

I half convinced her. Her health was improving rapidly and the baby was getting stronger. I'll never forget the first day she was able to hold him in her arms. I knew then that she had something to live for and so did she.

I knew, too, that it was time for me to leave.

I was going within the next three weeks. I had told Stirling that nothing would induce me to stay. He had his son; he had his wife; it was his duty to make up to Minta for all the anxiety he had caused her.

He realized this. He knew that Minta had suspected him of trying to kill her. That had shaken him considerably and made him feel tender and protective towards her. It was a beginning and I told him that in time he might become worthy of her.

Franklyn came to play a game of chess.

He said: 'I've decided to go to Australia.'

'You! You'd hate it.'

'Why should I?'

'Because it's not . . . England. It's a new country. It's vigorous, perhaps rough, and things are done differently over there from the way they are here.'

'Why shouldn't I be different for a change?'

'Why are you going?'

He looked at me intently and said: 'You know why.'

'Oh no,' I protested. 'You couldn't. Not because of . . . me!'

'You are determined to go. It seems the only thing I can do is to come too. I can't lose you, you know.'

'There is your estate. What about Wakefield Park?'

'I can put a manager in. That's simple. In fact I've already settled that little detail.'

'But you *love* Wakefield Park.'

'There is something I love more.'

I could not meet his eyes. I felt ashamed.

'Me, for instance?' I asked.

'But of course.'

I stood on the deck of the *Brandon Star* and watched the shores of England recede. I was going back. Once I had stood on the deck of a ship bound for the same destination and Stirling had stood beside me.

Now Stirling was in England and I had said goodbye to him, to Minta, to the baby, to Whiteladies; and another man stood beside me.

Stirling and I were two of a kind. We had often said it. But Franklyn was with me now and Minta was with Stirling. We had despised them, mocked them because they were not like us.

No, I thought. They had a power to love which we lacked. Minta had been ready to die for Stirling; Franklyn had given up his beloved lands to come to me. What was love? Had Stirling and I understood love such as that?

'Very soon you'll see the last of England,' said Franklyn. 'Does that make you sad?'

I turned to look at him, seeing him afresh.

'Not as I thought it would,' I admitted. 'We're going to a great country, a land of endless opportunities.'

We smiled at each other; and the love I saw in his eyes was a glow that warmed me. I knew then that I wanted to learn more of his sort of love – and Minta's – that love which does not look for sensation or continual excitement, the love that is built not on the shifting sands of violent passion but on the steady rock of deep and abiding affection.

As the land slid away below the horizon, I believed that I might find it.

KING OF THE CASTLE

King of the Castle

For
Monique Madeleine Paule Régnier

Chapter One

Even as the branch-line train came into the station halt I was saying to myself: 'It's not too late. You could go straight back even now.'

During the journey – I had crossed the Channel the night before and had been travelling all day – I had been mustering my courage, assuring myself that I was no foolish girl but a sensible woman who had decided to take a certain action and was going to carry it through. What happened to me when I reached the castle depended on others; but I promised myself I should act with dignity, and behave as though I were not desperately anxious, hiding from them the fact that when I thought of what my future could be if they rejected me, I faced panic. I should let no one know how much this commission meant to me.

My appearance I felt – for the first time in my life – was in my favour. I was twenty-eight and, in my dun-coloured travelling cloak and felt hat of the same colour, calculated to be useful rather than decorative, and after having travelled all night, I certainly looked my age. I was unmarried and had frequently intercepted pitying glances on that account and had heard myself referred to as 'an old maid' and 'on the shelf.' This had irritated me with its implication that the main reason for a woman's existing was dedication to the service of some man – a masculine assumption which, since my twenty-third birthday, I had determined to prove false; and I believed I was doing so. There could be other interests in life; and I consoled myself that I had found one.

The train slowed down. The only other person who alighted was a peasant woman carrying a basket of eggs under one arm and a live fowl under the other.

I took out my bags – there were several of them, for they contained all I possessed – my small wardrobe and the tools I should need for my work.

The only porter was at the barrier.

'Good day, madame,' he was saying. 'If you don't hurry the baby will be born before you get there. I heard your Marie had started her pains three hours back. The midwife's gone to her.'

'Pray it'll be a boy this time. All those girls. What the good Lord is thinking of . . .'

The porter was more interested in me than in the sex of the expected baby. I was aware that while he was talking he was watching me.

My bags were now beside me and as he stepped forward about to blow his whistle and send the train on its journey, an old man came hurrying on to the little platform.

'Hé, Joseph!' the porter greeted him and nodded towards me.

Joseph looked at me and shook his head. 'Gentleman,' he said.

'Are you from the Château Gaillard?' I asked in French, which I had spoken fluently from childhood. My mother had been French and when we had been alone we had conversed in that language although in my father's presence English was always spoken.

Joseph came towards me, his mouth slightly open, his eyes incredulous. 'Yes, mademoiselle but . . .'

'You have come to pick me up.'

'Mademoiselle, I have come for a Monsieur Lawson.' He spoke the English name with difficulty.

I smiled and tried to force a nonchalance into my manner, reminding myself that this was the smallest of the hurdles over which I should have to jump. I pointed to the labels on my baggage: D. Lawson.

Then realizing that Joseph probably couldn't read I explained: 'I am *Mademoiselle* Lawson.'

'From England?' he asked.

I assured him this was so.

'I was told an English gentleman.'

'There has been some mistake. It is an English lady instead.'

He scratched his head.

'Shouldn't we be going?' I asked. I looked down at my baggage. The porter came slowly over, and as he and Joseph exchanged glances I said with authority: 'Please put my baggage into the er . . . conveyance and we will leave for the château.'

I had practised self-control for years and there was no trace of the apprehension I was feeling. My manner was as effective here as it was at home. Joseph and the porter carried my bags to the waiting trap; I followed, and in a few moments we were on our way.

'The château is far from here?' I asked.

'Two kilometres or so, mademoiselle. You will see it soon.'

I looked about me at the rich wine-growing land. It was the end of October and the harvest was over; I supposed they would now be preparing for the next year's crop. We skirted the little town with its square dominated by the church and *hôtel de ville*, with its branching narrow streets, its shops and houses; and then I had my first glimpse of the château.

I shall never forget that moment. My common sense – of which in the last year I had consoled myself I had plenty as a compensation for having little else – disappeared; and I forgot the difficulties in which I had recklessly placed myself. In spite of all the alarming possibilities which logical reasoning suggested were inevitable, I laughed quite audibly and said equally audibly: 'I don't care what happens. I'm glad I came.'

Fortunately I had spoken in English and Joseph could not understand. I said quickly: 'So that is Château Gaillard!'

'That's the château, mademoiselle.'

'Not the only Gaillard in France. I know the other in Normandy, of course. The one where Richard Coeur de Lion was kept a prisoner.' Joseph grunted and I hurried on: 'Ruins are fascinating, but old castles which have been preserved through the centuries are far more so.'

'The old château has had some narrow escapes. Why, in the days of the Terror it was almost destroyed.'

'How fortunate that it wasn't!' I heard the emotion in my voice and hoped Joseph hadn't. I was enchanted by the château; I longed to live in it, to explore it, to become familiar with it. I felt it was where I was meant to be, and that if I were sent away I should be desperately unhappy – and not only because I did not know what I should do if I went back to England.

Briefly I allowed that alarming possibility to come between me and my contemplation of the château. There was a distant cousin somewhere in the north of England – actually a cousin of my father's of whom he had spoken now and then. 'If anything happened to me you could always go to my cousin Jane. She's a difficult woman; you'd have a wretched time; but at least she would do her duty.' What a prospect for a woman who, having been denied those personal attractions which are the key to marriage, had developed a defensive shell, largely made up of pride. Cousin Jane . . . never! I had told myself. I would rather become one of those poor governesses depending on the whims of indifferent employers or mischievous children who could be even more diabolically cruel. I would rather place myself in the service of some querulous old woman as a lady's companion. No, I should be desolate, not because the dark pit of loneliness and humiliation gaped before me, but because I should be denied the infinite joy of doing the work I loved the best in the world in a setting which merely by its existence could make my life interesting.

It was not quite as I had imagined it; it surpassed expectations. There are occasions in life when reality is more exciting, more enchanting than the picture the imagination has supplied – but they are rare; and when they come they should be savoured to the full.

Perhaps I had better enjoy these moments because they might be the last I would enjoy for a long time.

So I gave myself up to the contemplation of that magnificent piece of fifteenth-century architecture standing there in the midst of the vine country. My practised eyes could place it within a decade or two. There had been extensive building in the sixteenth and seventeenth centuries, but the additions had not detracted from the symmetry; rather they gave it its character. I could see the cylindrical towers which flanked the main building. The chief staircase would, I knew, be in the polygonal tower. I was fairly knowledgeable about old houses and although often in the past I had resented my father's attitude towards me, I was grateful for all he had taught me. The aspect was purely medieval; and the solid buttresses and towers gave an air of having been built for defence. I calculated the thickness of those walls with their narrow slits of windows. A fortress surely. As my eyes went from the keep overlooking the drawbridge to the moat – dry, of course – I caught a glimpse of rich green grass growing there. Excitement gripped me, as I gazed up at the corbelled parapet supported by numerous machicolations about the outer façade.

Old Joseph was saying something. I guessed he had decided that the arrival having turned out to be a woman instead of a man was no concern of his.

'Yes,' he was saying, 'things don't change at the château. Monsieur le Comte sees to that.'

Monsieur le Comte. He was the man I should have to face. I pictured him, the aloof aristocrat, the sort who would have driven through the streets of Paris in his tumbrel to the guillotine with haughty indifference. So he would banish me.

'Ridiculous,' he would say. 'My summons was clearly meant for your father. You will leave immediately.'

It would be useless to say: 'I am as competent as my father was. I worked with my father. In fact I know more about old paintings than he did. That was the side of the business he always left to me.'

The side of the business! How explain to a haughty French count that a woman could be as efficient, as clever at the specialised work of restoring old paintings as a man.

'Monsieur le Comte, I am an artist myself . . .'

I could picture his scornful looks. 'Mademoiselle, I am not interested in your qualifications. I sent for Monsieur Lawson. I did not send for you. Therefore oblige me by leaving my house' (. . . my residence? . . . my castle?) 'without delay.'

Joseph was looking at me shrewdly. I could see that he was thinking that it was very odd that Monsieur le Comte had sent for a woman.

I longed to ask questions about the Comte, but naturally I could not. It would have been useful if I could have learned a little about the household, but it was out of the question to inquire. No. I must put myself into the right mood; I must feel that there was nothing unusual in taking my father's place, so that I could convey this to others.

In my pocket was the request. That was the wrong word. Monsieur le Comte would rarely request; he would command as a king to a subject.

The king in his castle! I thought. Monsieur le Comte de la Talle summons D. Lawson to the Château Gaillard to carry out the work on his pictures as arranged. Well, I was Dallas Lawson, and if that summons was meant for Daniel Lawson, then my answer was that Daniel Lawson had been dead for ten months and that I, his daughter, who in the past had helped him in his work, was now carrying on in his place.

It was about three years earlier that my father had been in correspondence with the Comte, who had heard of his work, for Father had been well known as an authority on old buildings and paintings. Perhaps in the circumstances it was natural that I should grow up with a reverence for these things, which had turned into a passion. Father encouraged me in this and we spent many weeks in Florence, Rome and Paris doing nothing but looking at art treasures; and every moment I could spare in London was spent in the galleries.

With a mother who was not very strong and a father who was almost always absorbed in his work, I was thrown a great deal on my own resources. We saw few people and I had never formed the habit of making friends easily. Not being a pretty girl I felt at a disadvantage and there seemed to be a constant need to hide this which made me develop a far from attractive, over-dignified manner. Yet I longed to share experiences with others; I longed for friends. I was passionately interested in the affairs of others, which always seemed more exciting than anything that could happen to me. I would listen enraptured to conversations which were not intended for my ears; I would sit quietly in the kitchen while our two servants, one elderly, one young, discussed their ailments and love affairs respectively, and stand quietly listening to people in shops when I was shopping with my mother; or if anyone came to the house I was often discovered in what my father called eavesdropping. It was a habit of which he did not approve.

But when I went to my art school, for a while I began to live my life first-hand as it were, rather than through my ears. Yet that did not satisfy Father either, for there I fell in love with a young student. In romantic moments I still wistfully remembered those spring days when we wandered through St. James's and Green Parks and listened to the orators at Marble Arch, and strolled along the Serpentine into Kensington Gardens. I could never be there without remembering; that was why I never went if I could help it. Father had objected because Charles had no money. Moreover Mother, who by that time had become an invalid, needed me.

There was no great renunciation scene. That romance had just grown out of spring-time and youth; and with the coming of autumn it was over.

Perhaps Father had thought it would be better if I had not the opportunity to become involved with anyone else, for he suggested I leave the art school and work more closely with him. He said he would teach me far more than I could ever learn at school. He was right, of course; but although I learned so much from him, my opportunity to meet people of my own age and live my individual life was lost. My time was divided between working with Father and looking after Mother. When she died I was stunned by my grief for a long time and when I recovered a little I felt that I was no longer young; and as, long ago, I had convinced myself that I was not attractive to men, I turned my desire for love and marriage into a passion for paintings.

'The work suits you,' my father once said. 'You want to restore everything.'

I understood what he meant. I had wanted to make Charles into a great painter when he wanted to be a carefree student. Perhaps that was why I lost him. I wanted to restore Mother to her old vigour and interest in life. I tried to chivvy her out of her lassitude. I never tried to change Father. That would have been quite impossible. I realized that I had inherited my forcefulness from him, and at the time he was stronger than I.

I remember the day the first letter came from Château Gaillard. The Comte de la Talle had a gallery of pictures which were in need of attention; and he would like to consult my father about certain restoration of the château. Could Monsieur Lawson come to Château Gaillard, estimate what work was necessary, and if a satisfactory arrangement could be reached, stay until it was completed?

Father had been delighted. 'I will send for you if possible,' he had told me. 'I shall need your help with the pictures. You will enjoy the place. It's fifteenth-century and I believe a great deal of the original is there. It'll be quite fascinating.'

I was excited. First because I longed to spend a few months in a French château; secondly because Father was beginning to accept my superior knowledge where pictures were concerned.

However, a letter had arrived from the Comte postponing the appointment. Circumstances made the visit impossible at present, he wrote, giving no detailed explanation. He would probably be in touch later.

About two years after receiving that letter Father had died quite suddenly of a stroke. It had been a terrible shock to realize I was on my own. I felt bereft, lonely and bewildered – moreover I had very little money. I had become accustomed to helping Father in his work and I wondered what would happen, for although people had accepted the fact that I was his assistant and no doubt very useful in that capacity, how would they feel about my standing on my own?

I talked this over with Annie, our elderly servant, who had remained with us for years and was going off to share a home with a married sister. She thought there were only two things I could do. I could be a governess, as many ladies had to be, or a companion.

'I'd hate either,' I told her.

'Beggars can't be choosers, Miss Dallas. There's many a young lady, educated like yourself, who's found herself left – and been forced to.'

'There's the work I've done with Father.'

She nodded, but I knew she was thinking that no one would want to employ a young woman to do the things my father had done. That I could do them, was not the point. I was a woman, and therefore no one would believe my work could possibly be any good.

Annie was still with me when the summons came. The Comte de la Talle was now ready for Monsieur D. Lawson to begin the work.

'After all, I *am* D. Lawson,' I pointed out to Annie. 'I can restore pictures as well as my father could, and I can see no reason why I should not.'

'I can,' replied Annie grimly.

'It's a challenge. It's either this or spending my days teaching. Father's lawyers have assured me of the urgent need to earn a living. Fancy teaching children to draw when they have no talent and don't want to learn! Or perhaps spending my time with a fretful old lady who finds fault with everything I do!'

'You have to take what comes, Miss Dallas.'

'*This* has come to me – so it's exactly what I am doing.'

'It's not right. People won't like it. It was all very well going with your father and working with him. You can't go on your own.'

'I did finish the work after he died ... at Mornington Towers, you remember.'

'Well, that was what he started. But to go to France ... a foreign country ... a young lady ... *alone!*'

'You mustn't think of me as a young lady, Annie. I'm a restorer of pictures. That's quite different.'

'Well, I hope you'll not forget that you're a young lady all the same. And you can't go, Miss Dallas. It wouldn't be right. I know it. It would be bad for you.'

'Bad? In what way?'

'Not . . . quite nice. What man would want to marry a young lady who'd been off abroad all by herself?'

'I'm not looking for a husband, Annie. I'm looking for work. And I'll tell you this: my mother was exactly the same age when she and her sister came to England to stay with their aunt. The two girls actually went to the theatre alone. Fancy that! Mother told me she did something even more daring. She went to a political meeting once – in a cellar in Chancery Lane . . . and, as a matter of fact, that was where she met Father. So, if she hadn't been bold and adventurous she wouldn't have had a husband – at least not that one.'

'You were always one for making what you wanted sound right. I know you of old. But I say this: It's not right. And I stick to that.'

But it had to be right. And so, after a great deal of consideration and trepidation, I had decided to accept the challenge and come to Château Gaillard.

We crossed the drawbridge and as I looked at those ancient walls with their moss and ivy, supported by the great buttresses, as I gazed at the cylindrical towers, at the rounded roofs rising to conical points, I was praying that I might not be sent away. We passed under the archway and entered a courtyard with grass growing between the cobbles, and I was struck by the silence. In the centre of the courtyard was a well about which was a parapet and stone pillars supporting a dome. There were a few steps leading to a loggia in front of one side of the building, and I saw the words 'de la Talle' entwined in the fleurs-de-lis cut into the wall above a door.

Joseph took out my bags, set them by this door and shouted: 'Jeanne.'

A maid appeared and I noticed the startled look in her eyes when she saw me. Joseph told her that I was Mademoiselle Lawson, I was to be taken to the library and my arrival was to be made known. The bags would be taken to my room later.

I was so excited at the prospect of entering the castle that I felt quite reckless. I followed Jeanne through the heavy studded door into a great hall on the stone walls of which hung magnificent tapestries and weapons. I quickly noticed one or two pieces of furniture in the *régence* style – one of these a magnificent table of carved gilt wood, with the delicate lattice work which became so popular in France during the early eighteenth century. The tapestries, which were exquisite and of the same period as the furniture, were in the Beauvais style with Boucher-like figures. It was wonderful; and my desire to pause and examine almost overcame my fear, but already we had turned off the hall and were mounting a flight of stone steps.

Jeanne held aside a heavy curtain and I was stepping on a thick carpet in great contrast to the stone steps. I stood in a short dark corridor at the end of which was a door. When this was thrown open the library was disclosed.

'If Mademoiselle will wait . . .'

I inclined my head. The door was shut and I was alone.

The room was lofty, the ceiling beautifully painted. There would be great treasure in this place, I knew; and I could not bear to be sent away. The walls were lined with leather-bound books and there were several stuffed heads of animals which seemed to guard them ferociously.

The Comte is a mighty hunter, I thought, and imagined him relentlessly pursuing his prey.

A clock with a carved cupid poised above its face stood on the mantelpiece and on either side of it were two delicately coloured Sèvres vases. The chairs were upholstered in tapestry and their framework was decorated with flowers and scrolls.

But impressed as I was by these treasures, I was too apprehensive to give them my full attention. I was thinking of my coming interview with the formidable Comte and rehearsing what I would say to him. There must be no loss of dignity on my part. I must remain calm, yet I must not appear too eager. I must disguise the fact that I longed to be allowed to work here, that I might succeed and so move on to win further commissions. I believed that my future hung on the next few minutes. And how right I was.

I heard Joseph's voice. 'In the library, monsieur . . .'

Footsteps. Any moment now I should face him. I went to the fireplace. Logs were laid there but there was no fire; I looked at the painting above the Louis XV clock, not seeing it; my heart was beating fast and I was gripping my hands in an effort to stop them trembling, when the door opened. I pretended not to be aware of it so that I might gain a few seconds' respite in which to compose myself.

There was a brief silence, then a cool voice said: 'This is most extraordinary.'

He was about an inch taller than I, but I was tall. The dark eyes were at the moment puzzled, but they looked as though they could be warm; the long aquiline nose suggested arrogance; but the full lips were not unkind. He was dressed in riding clothes which were very elegant – a trifle too elegant. His cravat was ornate and there was a gold ring on the little finger of each hand. He was fastidious in the extreme and not as formidable as I had imagined him. This should have pleased me, but I felt faintly disappointed. Yet this man was more likely to be sympathetic towards me than the Comte of my imagination.

'Good day,' I said.

He took a few steps forward. He was younger than I had thought he would be, for he could not have been more than a year or so older than I . . . perhaps my own age.

'No doubt,' he said, 'you will be good enough to explain.'

'Certainly. I have come to work on the paintings which are in need of attention.'

'We understood that *Monsieur* Lawson was to arrive to-day.'

'That would have been quite impossible.'

'You mean he will come later?'

'He died some months ago. I am his daughter, and am continuing with his commitments.'

He looked rather alarmed. 'Mademoiselle Lawson, these paintings are very valuable . . .'

'It would scarcely be necessary to restore them if they were not.'

'We could only allow an expert to handle them,' he said.

'*I* am an expert. My father was recommended to you. I worked with him. In fact the restoration of buildings was his forte . . . pictures were mine.'

This is the end, I thought. He is annoyed to have been placed in a distasteful situation. He will never let me stay. I made a desperate effort. 'You had heard of my father. Then that means you had heard of me. We worked together.'

'You did not explain . . .'

'I believed the matter was urgent. I thought it wiser to obey the summons without delay. If my father had accepted the commission I should have come with him. We always worked together.'

'Pray be seated,' he said.

I sat down in a chair with a carved wooden back which forced me to sit up straight while he threw himself on to a settee, his legs stretched out before him.

'Did you think, Mademoiselle Lawson,' he said slowly, 'that had you explained that your father was dead we should have declined your services?'

'I believed that your object was to have the pictures restored and was under the impression that it was the work which was important, not the sex of the restorer.' Again that arrogance, which was really the outward sign of my anxiety! I was certain that he was going to tell me to go. But I *had* to fight for a chance, because I knew that if only I could get it I could show them what I could do.

His brow was wrinkled as though he were trying to come to a decision; he was watching me covertly. He gave a little laugh which was quite mirthless and said: 'It seems strange that you did not write and tell us.'

I rose to my feet. Dignity demanded it.

He stood up. I had rarely felt as wretchedly miserable as I did when I haughtily walked to the door.

'One moment, mademoiselle.'

He had spoken first. It seemed a small victory.

I looked over my shoulder without turning.

'Only one train leaves our station each day. This is at nine o'clock in the morning. It would be necessary for you to drive some ten kilometres to catch a main-line train for Paris.'

'Oh!' I allowed dismay to show on my face.

'You see,' he went on, 'you have placed yourself in a very awkward situation.'

'I did not think that my credentials would be slighted without scrutiny. I have never worked before in France and was quite unprepared for such a reception.'

It was a good thrust. He rose to it. 'Mademoiselle, I assure you, you will be treated as courteously in France as you would be anywhere else.'

I raised my shoulders. 'I suppose there is an inn – a hotel – where I could stay the night?'

'We could not allow that. We can offer you hospitality.'

'It is good of you,' I said coldly, 'but in the circumstances . . .'

'You spoke of credentials.'

'I have recommendations from people who were very pleased with my work – in England. I have worked in some of our great houses and have been entrusted with masterpieces. But you are not interested.'

'That is not true, mademoiselle. I *am* interested. Anything connected with the château is of the utmost concern to me.' His face had changed as he spoke. It was illumined by a great passion – the love for this old house. I warmed towards him. I should have felt as he did if such a place were my home. He went on hurriedly: 'You must admit that I am justified in my surprise. I expected a man of experience and am confronted by a young lady . . .'

'I am no longer young, I assure you.'

He made no effort to refute this, still seeming preoccupied with his own thoughts – his emotions where the château was concerned, his indecision as to whether to allow me, whose skill he doubted, near his wonderful paintings.

'Perhaps you would show me your credentials.'

I walked back to the table and from an inner pocket of my cloak took a bundle of letters and handed them to him. He signed for me to be seated. Then he too sat and began to read the letters. I folded my hands in my lap and clasped them firmly. A moment before, I thought I had lost; now I was not so sure.

I watched him while pretending to study the room. He was trying to make up his mind what he should do. This surprised me. I had imagined the Comte to be a man who was rarely in doubt, who made quick decisions, having no difficulty as to the wisdom of them since he would believe himself always to be right.

'They are very impressive,' he said as he handed them back to me. He looked full at me for some seconds, then went on rather hesitantly: 'I expect you would like to see the pictures.'

'There seems little point if I am not to work on them.'

'Perhaps you will, Mademoiselle Lawson.'

'You mean . . .'

'I mean that I think you should stay here at least for a night. You have had a long journey. You are tired, I am sure. And as you are such an expert' – he glanced at the letters in my hand – 'and have been so highly congratulated by such eminent people, I am sure you would at least wish to see the pictures. We have some excellent examples of painting in the château. I do assure you that it is a collection worthy of your attention.'

'I am sure it is. But I think I should be getting to my hotel.'

'I don't recommend it.'

'Oh?'

'It is very small and the food is not of the best. You would be more comfortable in the château, I am sure.'

'I should not care to make a nuisance of myself.'

'But of course you would not. I am going to insist that you stay here, and that you now allow me to call the maid to take you to your room. It has been prepared, you know, although of course we did not know it was to be for a lady. Still, that need not concern you. The maid will bring some food to your room. Then I suggest you rest awhile and later you must see the paintings.'

'Then you mean that you want me to do the work I came to do?'

'You could give us your advice first, could you not?'

I felt so relieved I changed my feelings towards him. The dislike of a moment ago turned to liking.

'I would do my best, Monsieur le Comte.'

'You are under a delusion, mademoiselle. I am not the Comte de la Talle.'

I was unable to control my amazement. 'Then who . . .'

'Philippe de la Talle, the Comte's cousin. So you see it is not I whom you have to please. It is the Comte de la Talle. He is the one who will decide whether or not he will entrust you with the restoration of his paintings. I assure you that if the decision rested with me I should ask you to begin without delay.'

'When can I see the Comte?'

'He is not at the château and will doubtless be absent for some days. I suggest that you remain with us until his return. In the meantime you can examine the paintings and then be ready to estimate what is needed by the time of his return.'

'Some days!' I said in dismay.

'I fear so.'

As he moved to the bell rope and pulled it, I was thinking: This is a respite. At least I shall have a few days in the château.

I guessed my room was close to the keep. The window aperture was large enough to contain two stone benches on either side although it narrowed to a slit. I could only look out by standing on tiptoe; below me was the moat and beyond that the trees and vineyards. I was amused that even as I reviewed the uncertainty of my position I could not stop myself assessing the house and its treasures. Father had been the same. The most important thing in his life had been ancient monuments; and paintings a good second. With me it was paintings first, but I had inherited something of his passion for buildings.

The lofty room was full of shadows even though it was early in the day, for, picturesque as the window embrasure was, it excluded the light. The thickness of the walls astonished me, although I had been prepared for it; the huge tapestry which covered almost the entire surface of one was in muted shades of peacock blue, in fact, peacocks figured in it – peacocks in a garden of fountains, colonnades, reclining women and gallants, clearly sixteenth-century. The bed was canopied and behind it was a curtain, and when I drew this aside I recognized what was beyond as a *ruelle* – an alcove found in French châteaux. This one was large enough to be like a small room and contained a cupboard, a hip-bath, and a dressing-table on which stood a mirror. I caught a glimpse of myself and laughed suddenly.

Yes, I did look capable. Almost formidable. I was travel-stained, my hat was pushed too far back on my head so that it was even less becoming than usual; my hair – long, thick and straight, my only good point – was completely hidden.

The maid had brought the hot water and asked if I would care for cold chicken and a carafe of the *vin du pays*. I replied that it would suit me admirably; and I was glad when she went, for her obvious curiosity and excitement at my presence was a reminder of what a reckless thing I had done.

I took off my cloak and the unbecoming hat. Then I took out the pins and let my hair fall about my shoulders. How different I looked now – not only younger, but vulnerable. Now I could be that frightened girl behind the confident woman I pretended to be. Appearances were important, I must remember. I was proud of my hair. It was dark brown but the touches of chestnut in it were so marked that they shone almost red in sunlight.

I washed from head to foot in the hip-bath and felt refreshed. Then I put on clean linen and a grey merino skirt with a light cashmere blouse of a matching colour. The blouse buttoned high at the neck and I assured myself that in it I could be mistaken for a woman of thirty – when I put up my hair, of course. I disliked the grey for I took a great pleasure in colours. I knew instinctively that a certain shade of blue, green or red or lavender would have given character to the grey skirt; but much as I loved combining colours to produce beauty I had never wanted to experiment with my clothes. The light coats I wore for my work were in dull brown, as plain and severe as those my father had worn – in fact I wore his, which were a little too broad but fitted otherwise.

There was a knock on the door as I was buttoning my blouse. I caught a glimpse of myself in the mirror on the dressing-table. My cheeks had flushed a little; and with my hair which fell to my waist and spread itself about my shoulders like a cloak, I certainly looked different from the undaunted woman who had been shown into the room.

I called: 'Who is there?'

'Mademoiselle, your tray.' The maid had come into the room. I held back my hair with one hand and drew aside the curtain very slightly with the other.

'Please leave it there.'

She put it down and went out. I realized then how hungry I was, so I came out to inspect the tray. A leg of chicken, a twist of crusty bread still warm from the oven, butter, cheese and a carafe of wine. I sat down there and then and ate. It was delicious. The wine of the country, made from grapes grown within sight of the castle! The food and wine made me sleepy. Perhaps the latter was very potent; in any case I was tired. I had travelled through the previous day and night; I had slept little the night before that and I had scarcely eaten either.

I felt a dreamy contentment creeping over me. I was here in the château for a while at any rate. I was going to see the treasures of the place. I remembered other occasions when I had stayed with Father in great houses. I recalled the excitement of coming upon some rare work of art, that glow of understanding and appreciation which was like sharing in the joy of the Creator. Surely similar experiences were waiting for me in this château ... if only I could stay to enjoy them.

I closed my eyes and felt the rocking of the train; I thought of the life of the castle and the life outside it. The peasants tending the grape-vines, exulting in the *vendange*. I wondered whether the peasant-woman's child was born and whether it was a boy; I wondered what the Comte's cousin was thinking of me, or whether he had dismissed me from his mind. I slept and dreamed I was in a picture gallery, that I was cleaning a picture and that the colours which were emerging were more brilliant than any I had ever seen before – emeralds against grey . . . scarlet and gold.

'Mademoiselle . . .'

I started out of my chair, and for a moment couldn't remember where I was. A woman was standing before me – small, thin, her brows brought together in a frown which suggested anxiety rather than annoyance. Her dusty-looking hair was arranged in curls and bangs, puffed up and frizzed in a vain attempt to hide how scanty it was. Anxious grey eyes studied me from under the frown. She wore a white blouse adorned with little pink satin bows and a dark blue skirt. Her hands nervously plucked at the pink bow at her throat.

'I fell asleep,' I said.

'You must be very tired. Monsieur de la Talle has suggested that I should take you to the gallery, but perhaps you would rather rest a little longer.'

'Oh, no, no. What is the time?' I consulted the gold watch – it had belonged to my mother – which was pinned to my blouse. As I did so I saw the hair falling over my shoulders and I felt myself flush slightly. Hastily I pushed it back. 'I must have been so tired that I slept. I've been travelling through the night.'

'Of course. I will come back.'

'That is good of you. Will you please tell me who you are? You know I am Miss Lawson come from England to er . . .'

'Yes, I know. We were expecting a gentleman. I am Mademoiselle Dubois, the governess.'

'Oh – I had no idea . . .' I stopped. Why should I have any idea as to who was who in this household? The thought of my hair flowing down my back was disconcerting. It was making me stammer in a way I never should if I could have presented my usual severe demeanour.

'Perhaps you would prefer me to come back in say . . . half an hour?'

'Give me ten minutes in which to make myself presentable and then I shall be very happy to accept your kind offer, Mademoiselle Dubois.'

She ceased to frown and smiled rather uncertainly. As soon as she had left me I went back to the *ruelle* and looked at myself. What a sight! I thought. My face flushed, my eyes bright, and my hair in such confusion! I seized my hair and drew it tightly back from my forehead; I plaited it and wound the plaits into a bulky mound which I pinned up on the top of my head. I looked taller that way. The flush was dying from my cheeks and my eyes were now dull grey. They were the shade of water and reflected the colours I wore as the sky will change the colour of the sea. For that reason I should have worn greens and blues; but having assured myself that my assets did not lie in personal attractions and that if I were going to win the confidence of my employers I must present myself as a sensible woman, I cultivated dull colours as I did my somewhat prickly exterior. I believed they were the necessary weapons for a woman alone in the world with her own battles to fight. Now my mouth was set in the firm no-nonsense lines which I tried to adopt; and by the time Mademoiselle Dubois returned I was ready to play my familiar role.

She looked startled when she saw me, so I knew what a bad impression I had made in the first place. Her eyes went to my head and I felt a grim satisfaction, for now there was not a hair out of place – it was neat and severe as I liked it to be.

'I am so sorry I disturbed you.' The woman was too apologetic. That little matter was over and it was my fault for falling asleep and not hearing her knock. I told her this and added: 'So Monsieur de la Talle has asked you to show me the gallery. I am most eager to see the pictures.'

'I know little about pictures, but . . .'

'You say you are the governess. So there are children in the château.'

'There is only Geneviève. Monsieur le Comte has only one child.'

My curiosity was strong, but one could not ask questions. She hesitated as though she wanted to talk; and how I wanted to know! But I was in command of myself and growing more and more optimistic as the moments passed. It was wonderful what the brief rest and the food, the wash and change of clothes had done for me.

She sighed. 'Geneviève is very difficult.'

'Children often are. How old is she?'

'Fourteen.'

'Then I am sure you can easily control her.'

She gave me an incredulous look; then her mouth twisted slightly. 'It is evident, Mademoiselle Lawson, that you do not know Geneviève.'

'Spoilt, I imagine, being the only one?'

'Spoilt!' Her voice had an odd note. Fear? Apprehension? I couldn't quite place it. 'Oh, that . . . as well.'

She was ineffectual. That much was obvious. The last person I should have chosen as a governess. If they would choose a woman like this for such a post surely my chances of getting the restoration commission were good. Although I was a woman I must look far more capable than this poor creature. And wouldn't the Comte consider the education of his only child as important as the restoration of his pictures? That remained to be seen, of course. I was impatient for my encounter with this man.

'I can tell you, Mademoiselle Lawson, that to control that girl is impossible.'

'Perhaps you are not stern enough,' I said lightly, then changed the subject. 'This is a vast place. Are we near the gallery?'

'I will show you. You will get lost here at first. I did. In fact even now I often find myself in difficulties.'

You would always find yourself in difficulties, I thought.

'I suppose you have been here for some time,' I asked, merely to make conversation as we passed out of the room and went along a corridor to a flight of stairs.

'Quite a long time . . . eight months.'

I laughed. 'You call that long?'

'The others didn't stay as long. No one else stayed longer than six.'

My mind switched from the carving on the banister to the daughter of the house. So this was why Mademoiselle Dubois remained. Geneviève was so spoilt that it was difficult to keep a governess. One would have thought that the stern King in his Castle could have controlled his daughter. But perhaps he did not care enough. And the Comtesse? Strangely enough before Mademoiselle Dubois had mentioned the daughter I had not thought of a Comtesse. Naturally there must be one, since there was a child. She was probably with the Comte now and that was why I had been received by the cousin.

'In fact,' she went on, 'I am constantly telling myself that I shall go. The trouble is . . .'

She did not finish, nor did she need to because I understood very well. Where could she go? I pictured her in some dreary lodging . . . or perhaps she had a family. . . . But in any case she would have to earn a living. There were many like her – desperately exchanging pride and dignity for food and shelter. Oh yes, I understood absolutely. None better, for it was a fate I could envisage for myself. The gentle-woman without means. What could be more difficult to bear than genteel poverty! Brought up to consider oneself a lady, educated as well as – perhaps better than – the people one must serve. Continually aware of being kept in one's place. Living with neither the vulgar gusto of the servants below stairs nor with the comfort of the family. To exist in a sort of limbo. Oh, it was intolerable, and yet how often inevitable. Poor Mademoiselle Dubois! She did not know what pity she aroused in me . . . and what fears.

'There are always disadvantages in every post,' I comforted.

'Oh, yes, indeed yes. And here there is so much . . .'

'The château seems to be a storehouse of treasures.'

'I believe the pictures are worth a fortune.'

'So I have heard.' My voice was warm. I put out a hand to touch the linenfold panelling of the room through which we were passing. A beautiful place, I thought; but these ancient edifices were in constant need of attention. We had passed into a large room, the kind which in England we called a solarium, because it was so planned to catch the sun, and I paused to examine the coat of arms on the wall. It was fairly recent and I wondered whether there might be murals under the limewash. I thought it very possible. I remembered the excitement when my father had once discovered some valuable wall-painting which had been hidden for a couple of centuries. What a triumph if I could make such a discovery! The personal triumph would of course be secondary and I had thought of that only because of my reception. It would be a triumph for art as all such discoveries are.

'And the Comte is doubtless very proud of them.'

'I . . . I don't know.'

'He must be. In any case he is concerned enough to want them examined and if necessary restored. Art treasures are a heritage. It is a privilege to own them and one has to remember that art – great art – doesn't belong to one person.'

I stopped. I was on my favourite hobby-horse, as Father would say. He had warned me. 'Those who are interested probably share your knowledge; those who are not are bored.'

He was right, and Mademoiselle Dubois fitted into the second category.

She laughed, a small tinkly laugh without any mirth or pleasure in it. 'I should hardly expect the Comte to express his feelings to *me*.'

No, I thought. Nor should I.

'Oh, dear,' she murmured. 'I hope I haven't lost my way. Oh, no . . . this is it.'

'We are now almost in the centre of the château,' I said. 'This is the original structure. I should say we are immediately beneath the round tower.'

She looked at me incredulously.

'My father's profession was the restoration of old houses,' I explained. 'I learned a great deal from him. In fact we worked together.'

She seemed momentarily to resent that in me which was the exact reverse to her own character. She said almost severely: 'I know that a man was expected.'

'My father was expected. He was coming about three years ago and then for some reason the appointment was cancelled.'

'About three years ago,' she said blankly. 'That would be when . . .'

I waited, and as she did not continue I said: 'That would be before you were here, wouldn't it? My father was coming and somewhat peremptorily he was told it was not convenient. He died almost a year ago and as I have continued with work that was outstanding, naturally I came in his place.'

She looked as though such a precedure was far from natural and I secretly agreed with her. But I had no intention of betraying myself to her as she had betrayed herself to me.

'You speak very good French for an Englishwoman.'

'I am bilingual. My mother was French, my father English.'

'That is fortunate . . . in the circumstances.'

'In any circumstances it is fortunate to be in command of languages.'

My mother had said I was too tutorial. It was a trait I should curb. I fancy it had increased since Father had died. *He* once said I was like a ship firing all guns to show I was equipped to defend myself just in case another should be preparing to open fire on me.

'You are right, of course,' said Mademoiselle Dubois meekly. 'This is the gallery where the pictures are.'

I forgot her then. I was in a long room lightened by several windows, and on the walls . . . the pictures! Even in their neglect they were splendid, and a quick look was enough to show me that they were very valuable. They were chiefly of the French school. I recognized a Poussin and Lorrain side by side and was struck as never before by the cold discipline of one and the intense drama of the other. I revelled in the pure golden light of the Lorrain landscape and wanted to point out to the woman beside me that light and feathery brushwork which might have been learned from Titian, and how the dark pigments had been used over rich colour to give that wondrous effect of light and shade. And there was a Watteau . . . so delicate, arabesque and pastel . . . and yet somehow conveying by a mood the storm about to break. I walked as if in a trance from an early Boucher painted before his decline set in and a perfect example of the rococo style, to a gay erotic Fragonard.

Then I was angry because they were all in need of urgent attention. How was it they had been allowed to get into this state! Some I could see had darkened badly; there was a dull foggy film on others which we called 'bloom.' A few were scratched and streaked with water. The brown acid left by flies was visible; and in some places the paint had flaked off. There were isolated burns as though someone had held a candle too closely.

I moved silently from picture to picture forgetful of everything else. I calculated that there was almost a year's work in what I had seen so far and there was probably a great deal more than that – as there always was when one began to examine these things more closely.

'You find them interesting,' said Mademoiselle Dubois vapidly.

'I find them of immense interest, and certainly in need of attention.'

'Then I suppose you will get down to work right away.'

I turned to look at her. 'It is by no means certain that I shall do the work. I am a woman, you see, and therefore not considered capable.'

'It is unusual work for a woman.'

'Indeed it is not. If one has a talent for this kind of work, one's sex is of no importance whatever.'

She laughed that foolish laugh. 'But there is men's work and women's work.'

'There are governesses and tutors, aren't there?' I hoped I made it clear that I had no intention of continuing this aimless conversation, by changing the subject. 'It depends of course on the Comte. If he is the man of prejudice . . .'

A voice not far off cried: 'I want to see her. I tell you, Nounou, I *will* see her. Esquilles has been ordered to take her to the gallery.'

I looked at Mademoiselle Dubois. *Esquilles!* Splinters! I saw the allusion; she must have heard herself called that often enough.

A low soothing voice and then: 'Let go, Nounou. You silly old woman. Do *you* think you can stop *me*.'

The door of the gallery was flung open and the girl whom I at once recognized as Geneviève de la Talle stood there. Her dark hair was worn loose – and was almost deliberately untidy; her beautiful dark eyes danced with enjoyment; she was dressed in a gown of mid-blue which was becoming to her dark looks. I would have known immediately, even if I had not been warned, that she was unmanageable.

She stared at me and I returned the gaze. Then she said in English: 'Good afternoon, miss.'

'Good afternoon, mademoiselle,' I answered in the same tongue. She seemed amused and advanced into the room. I was aware of a grey-haired woman behind her. This was obviously the nurse, Nounou. I guessed she had been with the girl from babyhood and helped with the spoiling.

'So you've come from England,' said the girl. 'They were expecting a man.'

'They were expecting my father. We worked together, and as he, being dead, is unable to come, I am continuing with his commitments.'

'I don't understand,' she said.

'Shall we speak in French?' I asked in that language.

'No,' she replied imperiously. 'I can speak English well.' She said, 'I am Mademoiselle de la Talle.'

'I did assume that.' I turned to the old woman, smiled and said good day.

'I find these pictures most interesting,' I said to her and Mademoiselle Dubois, 'but it is obvious that they have been neglected.'

Neither of them answered, but the girl, evidently annoyed to be ignored, said rudely: 'That will be no concern of yours since you won't be allowed to stay.'

'Hush, my dear,' whispered Nounou.

'I will not hush unless I want to. Wait until my father comes home.'

'Now, Geneviève . . .' The nurse's anxious eyes were on me, apologizing for the bad manners of her charge.

'You'll see,' said the girl to me. 'You may think you are going to stay, but my father . . .'

'If,' I said, 'your father's manners resemble yours, nothing on earth would induce me to stay.'

'Please speak English when you address me, miss.'

'But you appear to have forgotten that language as you have your manners.'

She began to laugh suddenly and twisted herself free of the nurse's grasp and came up to me.

'I suppose you are thinking I'm very unkind,' she said.

'I am not thinking of you.'

'What are you thinking of then?'

'At the moment of these pictures.'

'You mean they are more interesting than I am?'

'Infinitely,' I answered.

She did not know what to reply. She shrugged and turning away from me said pettishly in a lowered voice: 'Well, I've seen her. She's not pretty and she's old.'

With that she tossed her head and flounced out of the room.

'You must forgive her, mademoiselle,' murmured the old nurse. 'She's in one of her moods. I tried to keep her away. I'm afraid she's upset you.'

'Not in the least,' I answered. 'She is no concern of mine . . . fortunately.'

'Nounou,' called the girl, imperious as ever. 'Come here at once.'

The nurse went out, and raising my eyebrows I looked at Mademoiselle Dubois.

'She's in one of her moods. There's no controlling them. I'm sorry.'

'I'm sorry for you and the nurse.'

She brightened. 'Pupils can be difficult but I have never found one quite so . . .' She looked furtively at the door and I wondered whether Geneviève added eavesdropping to her other charming characteristics. Poor woman, I thought, I didn't want to add to her difficulties by telling her I thought she was foolish to suffer such treatment. I said: 'If you care to leave me here I'll make an examination of the pictures.'

'Can you find your way back to your room do you think?'

'I'm sure I can. I took careful note as we came along. Remember, I'm used to old houses.'

'Well, then, I'll leave you. You can always ring if you want anything.'

'Thank you for your help.'

She went out noiselessly, and I turned to the pictures, but I was too disturbed to work seriously. This was a strange household. The girl was impossible. What next? The Comte and the Comtesse? What should I find them like? And the girl was ill-mannered, selfish and cruel. And to have discovered this in five minutes of her company was disconcerting. What sort of environment, what sort of upbringing had produced such a creature?

I looked at those walls with their priceless neglected pictures and in those few moments I thought: Perhaps the wisest thing would be to leave first thing in the morning. I might apologize to Monsieur de la Talle, agree that I had been wrong to come, and leave.

I had wanted to escape from a fate which I knew, since my encounter with Mademoiselle Dubois (Splinters, poor thing), could be quite terrible. I had so desperately wanted to continue with work I loved; and because of that I had come here under false pretences and laid myself open to insult.

I was so firmly convinced that I must go that I almost believed some instinct was warning me to do so. In that case I would not tempt myself by studying these pictures further. I would go to the room they had given me, and try to rest in preparation for the long journey back to-morrow.

I walked towards the door and as I turned the handle it refused to move. Oddly enough in those seconds I felt a real panic. I could have imagined that I was a prisoner, that I could not escape if I wanted to; and then it seemed as though the very walls were closing in on me.

My hand was limp on the handle and the door opened. Philippe de la Talle was standing outside. Now I understood that the reason I couldn't open it was that he had been on the point of coming in.

Perhaps, I thought, they don't trust me here. Perhaps someone always has to be with me in case I attempt to steal something. That was absurd, I knew, and it was unlike me to think illogically. But I had had scarcely any sleep for two nights and was deeply concerned about my future. It was understandable that I was not quite myself.

'You were on the point of leaving, mademoiselle?'

'I was going to my room. There seems no point in remaining. I have decided to leave to-morrow. I must thank you for your hospitality and I am sorry to have troubled you. I should not have come.'

He raised his eyebrows. 'You have changed your mind? It is because you think the repairs beyond your capacity?'

I flushed angrily. 'By no means,' I said. 'These pictures have been badly neglected – criminally neglected . . . from an artist's point of view, that is – but I have restored far worse. I merely feel that my presence is resented in this place and that it would be better for you to find someone . . . of your own sex since that seems to be important to you.'

'My dear Mademoiselle Lawson,' he said almost gently, 'everything rests with my cousin to whom the pictures belong . . . to whom everything in the château belongs. He will be back within a few days.'

'Nevertheless I think I should leave in the morning. I can repay you for your hospitality by giving you an estimate for restoring one of the pictures in the gallery which you will find useful when engaging someone else.'

'I fear,' he said, 'that my niece has been rude to you. My cousin will be annoyed with me if he does not see you. You should not take any notice of the girl. She's quite ungovernable, when her father is away. He is the only one who can put fear into her.'

I thought to myself then: I believe you are afraid of him too. And I was filled with almost as great a desire to see the Comte as I was to work on his pictures.

'Mademoiselle, will you stay for a few days and at least hear what my cousin has to say?'

I hesitated, then I said: 'Very well, I will stay.'

He seemed relieved.

'I shall go to my room now. I realize I am too tired to work satisfactorily to-day. To-morrow I will make a thorough study of the pictures in this gallery and when your cousin returns I shall have a clear estimate to give him.'

'Excellent,' he said, and stood aside for me to pass.

As soon as it was light next morning, refreshed after a good night's sleep, I arose exhilarated. I intended to have a look at the château grounds and perhaps explore the neighbourhood. I wanted to see the little town, for the old church had struck me as being about the same period as the château; and no doubt the *hôtel de ville* was as ancient.

I had had dinner in my room yesterday evening and it had been excellent. Soon afterwards I had gone to bed and slept immediately. Now the morning brought optimism with it.

I washed and dressed and rang for breakfast. The hot coffee, home-made crusty bread and butter which arrived almost immediately were delicious.

As I ate I thought of the events of yesterday and they no longer seemed as strange as they had the previous night. I had yet to discover what sort of household this was; all I knew at present was that it was an unusual one. There was Cousin Philippe, in charge during the absence of the master and mistress; a spoilt girl who behaved badly when her father was absent no doubt because when he was there she was in such awe of him; there was the weak and ineffectual governess and poor grey old Nounou, the nurse who had no more control over her than the governess had. Apart from that there was Joseph the groom and numerous servants, male and female, necessary to care for such a vast establishment. There was nothing unusual in such a household; and yet I had sensed mystery. Was it the manner in which everyone who had mentioned him had spoken of the Comte: He was the only one whom the girl feared. Everyone was in awe of him. Everything depended on him. Certainly whether or not *I* stayed did.

I made my way to the gallery, where I enjoyed a peaceful morning examining the pictures and making detailed notes of the damage to each one. It was a fascinating task and I was astonished how quickly the morning passed. I forgot about the household in my absorption, and was astonished when a maid knocked at the door and announced that it was twelve o'clock and that she would bring *déjeuner* to my room if I wished.

I found that I was hungry and said that would be very agreeable. I packed up my papers and went back to my room, where the maid served me with a delicious soup, followed by meat and salad, in its turn followed by cheese and fruit. I wondered if I should eat alone in my room all the time I was here – that was if I met with the approval of Monsieur le Comte. I was beginning to think of him as Monsieur le Comte and to say his name to myself with a kind of mockery. 'Others may be afraid of you, Monsieur le Comte, but you will find I am not.'

The afternoon was not a good time for working, I had always found; besides, I needed a little exercise. I could not, of course, explore the castle itself without permission, but I could look at the grounds and the countryside.

I had no difficulty in finding my way down to the courtyard to which Joseph had brought me, but instead of going out to the draw-bridge I crossed the loggia connecting the main building with a part of the château which had been built at a later date and passing through another courtyard I found my way to the south side of the castle. Here were the gardens, and, I thought grimly, if Monsieur le Comte neglects his pictures he does not his gardens, for obviously great care was bestowed on them.

Before me lay three terraces. On the first of these were lawns and fountains, and I imagined that during the spring the flowers were exquisite; even now, in autumn, they were colourful. I walked along a stone path to the second terrace; here, laid out with parterres, were ornamental gardens, each separated from the next by box hedges and yews neatly clipped into various shapes, predominant among them the fleur-de-lis. Typical, I thought, of Monsieur le Comte! On the lowest of the terraces was the kitchen-garden, but even this was ornamental, neatly divided into squares and rectangles, some separated from each other by trellises about which vines climbed; and the whole was bordered by fruit trees.

The place was deserted. I guessed that the workers were taking a siesta, for even at this time of the year the sun was hot. At three o'clock they would be back at work and continue until dark. There must be many of them to keep the place in such good order.

I was standing under the fruit trees when I heard a voice calling: 'Miss! Miss!' and turning saw Geneviève running towards me.

'I saw you from my window,' she said. She laid her hand on my arm and pointed to the château. 'You see that window right at the top there . . . that's mine. It's part of the nurseries.' She grimaced. She had spoken in English. 'I learned that off by heart,' she explained, 'just to show you I could. Now let's talk in French.'

She looked different now, calm, serene, a little mischievous perhaps, but more as one would expect a well-brought-up, fourteen-year-old girl to look, and I realized that I was seeing Geneviève without one of her moods.

'If you wish,' I replied in that language.

'Well, I should like to speak to you in English, but as you pointed out, mine is not very good, is it?'

'Your accent and intonation made it almost unintelligible. I suspect you have a fair vocabulary.'

'Are you a governess?'

'I am certainly not.'

'Then you ought to be. You'd make a good one.' She laughed aloud. 'Then you wouldn't have to go round under false pretences, would you?'

I said coolly: 'I am going for a walk. I will say good-bye to you.'

'Oh, no, don't. I came down to talk to you. First I have to say I'm sorry. I was rude, wasn't I? And you were very cool . . . but then you have to be, don't you. It's what one expects of the English.'

'I am half-French,' I said.

'That accounts for the spirit in you. I saw you were really angry. It was only your voice that was cold. Inside you were angry, now weren't you?'

'I was naturally surprised that a girl of your obvious education could be so impolite to a guest in your father's house.'

'But you weren't a guest, remember. You were there under . . .'

'There is no point in continuing this conversation. I accept your apology and now I will leave you.'

'But I came down specially to talk to you.'

'But I came down to walk.'

'Why shouldn't we walk together?'

'I did not invite you to accompany me.'

'Well, my father didn't invite you to Gaillard, did he, but you came.' She added hastily: 'And I'm glad you came . . . so perhaps you'll be glad if I come with you.'

She was trying to make amends, and it was not for me to be churlish, so I smiled.

'You're prettier when you smile,' she said. 'Well,' she put her head on one side, 'not exactly pretty. But you look younger.'

'We all look more pleasant when we smile. It is something you might remember.'

Her laughter was high and quite spontaneous. I found myself joining in and laughing at myself. She was pleased and so was I to have her company; for I was almost as interested in people as I was in pictures. Father had tried to curb that interest. He called it idle curiosity – but it was strong in me and perhaps I had been wrong to suppress it.

Now I was eager for Geneviève's company. I had seen her once in a mood and now as a lively but extremely curious girl; but who was I to criticize curiosity, who had more than my fair share of it?

'So,' she said, 'we'll go for a walk together and I will show you what you want to see.'

'Thank you. That will be very pleasant.'

She laughed again. 'I hope you will enjoy being here, miss. Suppose I talk to you in English, will you speak slowly so that I can understand?'

'Certainly.'

'And not laugh if I say something silly?'

'Certainly I shall not laugh. I admire your desire to improve your English.'

She was smiling again and I knew that she was thinking how like a governess I was.

'I am not very good,' she said. 'They are all afraid of me.'

'I don't think they are afraid of you. They are perhaps distressed – and disgusted – by the unbecoming way in which you sometimes behave.'

This amused her but she was serious almost immediately.

'Were you afraid of your father?' she asked, lapsing into French. I sensed that because she was interested in the subject she must speak in the language easier to her.

'No,' I replied. 'I was in awe of him, perhaps.'

'What's the difference?'

'One can respect people, admire them, look up to them, fear to offend them. It is not the same as being afraid of them.'

'Let's go on talking in French. This conversation is too interesting for English.'

She is afraid of her father, I thought. What sort of man is he to inspire fear in her? She was an odd child – wayward, perhaps violent; and he was to blame, of course. But what of the mother – what part had she played in this strange child's upbringing?

'So you weren't really afraid of your father?'

'No. Are you afraid of yours?'

She didn't answer, but I noticed that a haunted expression had come into her eyes.

I said quickly: 'And . . . your mother?'

She turned to me then. 'I will take you to my mother.'

'What?'

'I said I would take you to her.'

'She is in the château?'

'I know where she is. I'll take you to her. Will you come?'

'Why, yes. Certainly. I shall be delighted to meet her.'

'Very well. Come on.'

She went ahead of me. Her dark hair was neatly tied back with a blue ribbon and perhaps it was the way of dressing it which so changed her appearance. Her head was set arrogantly on sloping shoulders; her neck was long and graceful. I thought: She will be a beautiful woman.

I wondered whether the Comtesse was like her; then I began rehearsing what I would say to her. I must put my case clearly to her. Perhaps she as a woman would feel less prejudiced against my work.

Geneviève halted and came to walk beside me. 'I'm two different people, am I not?'

'What do you mean?'

'There are two sides to my character.'

'We all have many sides to our character.'

'But mine is different. Other people's characters are all of a piece. I am two distinct people.'

'Who told you this?'

'Nounou. She says I'm a Gemini – that means I have two different faces. My birthday is in June.'

'This is a fantasy. Everyone who is born in June is not like you.'

'It is not fantasy. You saw how horrid I was yesterday. That was the bad me. To-day I'm different. I'm good. I said I was sorry, didn't I?'

'I hope you *were* sorry.'

'I said I was, and I shouldn't have said it if I wasn't.'

'Then when you are being foolish, remember that you'll be sorry afterwards and don't be foolish.'

'Yes,' she said, 'you should be a governess. They always make everything sound so easy. I can't help being horrid. I just am.'

'Everyone can help the way he or she behaves.'

'It's in the stars. It's fate. You can't go against fate.'

Now I saw where the trouble lay. This temperamental girl was in the hands of a silly old woman and another who was half scared out of her wits; in addition there was the father who terrified her. But there was the mother, of course. It would be interesting to meet her.

Perhaps she too was in awe of the Comte. Most assuredly this was so since everyone else was. I pictured her a gentle creature, afraid to go against him. He was becoming more and more of a monster with every fresh piece of information.

'You can be exactly as you wish to be,' I said. 'It is absurd to tell yourself you have two characters and then try to live up to the unpleasant one.'

'I don't try. It just happens.'

Even as I spoke I despised myself. It was always so easy to solve other people's troubles. She was young and at times seemed childish for her age. If we could become friends I might be able to help her.

'I am eager to meet your mother,' I said; she did not answer but ran on ahead of me.

I followed her through the trees but she was more fleet than I and not so encumbered by her skirts. I lifted mine and ran but I lost sight of her.

I stood still. The trees were thicker here and I was in a small copse. I was not sure which way I had entered it and as I had no idea in which direction Geneviève had gone I felt suddenly lost. It was one of those moments such as I had experienced in the gallery when I had been unable to open the door. A strange feeling as though panic were knocking, gently as yet, on my mind.

How absurd to feel so in broad daylight! The girl was tricking me. She had not changed. She had deluded me into thinking that she was sorry; her conversation had almost amounted to a cry for help – and it was all a game, a pretence.

Then I heard her calling: 'Miss! Miss, where are you? This way.'

'I'm coming,' I said and went in the direction of her voice.

She appeared among the trees. 'I thought I'd lost you.' She took my hand as though she feared I would escape from her and we went on until after a short time the trees were less thick and then stopped abruptly. Before us was an open space in which the grasses grew long. I saw at once that the monuments erected there were to the dead and guessed we were in the graveyard of the de la Talles.

I understood. Her mother was dead. She was going to show me where she was buried. And she called this introducing me to her mother.

I felt shocked and a little alarmed. She was indeed a strange girl.

'All the de la Talles come here when they die,' she said solemnly. 'But I often come here too.'

'Your mother is dead?'

'Come, I'll show you where she is.'

She drew me through the long grass to an ornate monument. It was like a small house and on top of it was a beautifully sculptured group of angels holding a large marble book, on which was engraved the name of the person who was buried there.

'Look,' she said, 'there's her name.'

I looked. The name on the book was Françoise, Comtesse de la Talle, aged thirty years. I looked at the date. It was three years ago.

So the girl had been eleven years old when her mother died.

'I come down often,' she said, 'to be with her. I talk to her. I like it. It's so quiet.'

'You shouldn't come,' I said gently. 'Not alone.'

'I like to come alone. But I wanted you to meet her.'

I don't know what prompted me to say it but I blurted out: 'Does your father come?'

'He never does. He wouldn't want to be with her. He didn't want to before. So why should he now?'

'How can you know what he would like?'

'Oh, I do know. Besides, it's because he wanted her to be here that she's here now. He always gets what he wants, you know. He didn't want her.'

'I don't think you understand.'

'Oh, yes, I do.' Her eyes flashed. 'It's you who don't understand. How could you? You've only just come. I know he didn't want her. That was why he murdered her.'

I could find nothing to say. I could only look at the girl in horror. But she seemed unaware of me as now she laid her hands lovingly on those marble slabs.

The stillness all around me; the warmth of the sun; the sight of those mausoleums which housed the bones of long-dead de la Talles. It was macabre; it was fantastic. My instincts warned me to get away from the house; but even as I stood there I knew that I would stay if I could and that there was more to fascinate me in Château Gaillard than the paintings I loved.

Chapter Two

It was my second day at the Château Gaillard. I had not been able to sleep during the night, mainly because the scene in the graveyard had so startled me that I could not get it out of my mind.

We had walked slowly back to the château and I had told her that she must not say such things of her father; she had listened to me quietly and made no comment; but I would never forget the quiet certainty in her voice when she had said: 'He murdered her.'

It was gossip, of course. Where had she heard it? It must be from someone in the house. Could it be the nurse? Poor child! How terrible for her! All my animosity towards her had disappeared. I felt I wanted to know more of her life, what her mother had been like, how those terrible suspicions had been planted in her mind.

But the matter made me very uneasy.

I had eaten a lonely dinner in my room and had gone through the notes I had made; then I tried to read a novel. The evening seemed long; and I wondered whether this was the life I should be expected to lead if I was allowed to stay on. In other great houses we had had our meals with the managers of the estates and sometimes with the families themselves. I had never before felt so lonely when working. But of course I must remember that I was not yet accepted; this was necessarily a period of waiting.

I went to the gallery and spent all the morning examining the pictures, assessing darkening of pigment, failing of paint which we called 'chalking' and other deteriorations such as cracks in the paint which had caught the dust and grime. I tried to work out what materials I should need beyond those which I had brought with me, and I planned to ask Philippe de la Talle if I could look at some of the other pictures in the château, particularly some of the murals I had noticed.

I returned to my room for lunch and afterwards went out. I had made up my mind that to-day I should have a look at the surrounding country and perhaps the town.

All about me lay the vineyards and I took the road through them although it led away from the town. I would look at the town to-morrow. I imagined what activity there must be during the harvest and wished that I had been here earlier to see it. Next year . . . I thought, and then laughed at myself. Did I really think I should be here next year?

I had come to several buildings and beyond them I saw a house of red brick and there were the inevitable shutters at all the windows – green in this case. They added a charm to the house which I realized must be about one hundred and fifty years old – built, I guessed, some fifty years or so before the Revolution. I could not resist the temptation of going a little nearer to examine it.

There was a lime tree in front of the house and as I came near a high shrill voice called: 'Hallo, miss.' Not 'mademoiselle,' as might have been expected, but 'miss,' pronounced 'mees,' which told me of course that whoever was calling was aware of my identity.

'Hallo,' I answered, but looking over the iron gates I could see no one.

I heard a chuckle and, looking up, saw a boy swinging in the tree like a monkey. He took a sudden leap and was beside me. 'Hallo, miss. I'm Yves Bastide.'

'How do you do?'

'This is Margot. Margot, come down and don't be silly.'

'I am not silly.'

The girl wriggled out of the branches and slid perilously down the trunk to the ground. She was slightly smaller than the boy.

'We live there,' he told me.

The girl nodded, her eyes bright and inquisitive.

'It's a very pleasant house.'

'We all live in it . . . *all* of us.'

'That must be very nice for all of you.'

'Yves! Margot!' called a voice from the house.

'We've got miss, Gran'mère.'

'Then invite her to come in, and remember your manners.'

'Miss,' said Yves with a little bow, 'will you come in to see Gran'mère.'

'I should be pleased to.' I smiled at the girl, who gave me a pretty curtsy. How different, I thought, from Geneviève.

The boy ran forward to open the wrought-iron gates and gravely bowed as he held them for me to pass through. The girl walked beside me up the path between the bushes calling: 'We're here, Gran'mère.'

I stepped into a large hall and from an open door a voice called: 'Bring the English lady in here, my children.'

In a rocking-chair sat an old woman; her face was brown and wrinkled, her plentiful white hair piled high on her head; her eyes were bright and very dark; her heavy lids fell like hoods over them; her thin veined hands, smudged with brown patches which at home were called 'the flowers of death,' gripped the arms of her rocking-chair.

She smiled at me almost eagerly as though she had been expecting my coming and welcomed it.

'You will forgive my not rising, mademoiselle,' she said. 'My limbs are so stiff some days it takes me all of the morning to get out of my chair and all of the afternoon to get back into it.'

'Please stay where you are.' I took the extended hand and shook it. 'It is kind of you to invite me in.'

The children had taken a stand on either side of her chair and were regarding me intently and proudly as though I was something rather rare which they had discovered.

I smiled. 'You seem to know me. I'm afraid you have the advantage.'

'Yves, a chair for Mademoiselle.'

He sprang to get one for me and carefully set it down facing the old lady.

'You will soon hear of us, mademoiselle. Everyone knows the Bastides.'

I settled in the chair. 'How did you know *me*?' I asked.

'Mademoiselle, news travels quickly round the neighbourhood. We heard that you had arrived and hoped that you would call on us. You see we are so much a part of the château. This house was built for a Bastide, mademoiselle. There have been Bastides in it ever since. Before that the family lived on the estates because Bastides were always the wine growers. It is said there would have been no Gaillard wine if there had never been Bastides.'

'I see. The vines belong to you.'

The lids came down over her eyes and she laughed aloud. 'Like everything else in this place the vines belong to Monsieur le Comte. This is his land.

This house is his. Everything is his. We are his work-people, and although we say that without the Bastides there could be no Gaillard wine, we mean that the wine produced here would not be worthy of the name.'

'I have always thought how interesting it must be to watch the wine-growing process . . . I mean, to see the grapes appear and ripen and be made into wine.'

'Ah, mademoiselle, it is the most interesting thing in the world . . . to us Bastides.'

'I should like to see it.'

'I hope you will stay with us long enough to.' She turned to the children: 'Go and find your brother, my children. And your sister and your father, too. Tell them we have a visitor.'

'Please – you mustn't disturb them on my account.'

'They would be very disappointed if they knew you had called and they had missed you.'

The children ran away. I said how charming they were and that their manners were delightful. She nodded, well pleased; and I knew that she understood why I had made such a comment. I could only be comparing them with Geneviève.

'At this time of day,' she explained, 'there is not so much activity out of doors. My grandson, who is in charge now, will be in the cellars; his father, who cannot work out of doors since his accident, will be helping him, and my granddaughter Gabrielle will be working in the office.'

'You have a large family, and all engaged in the wine-growing business.'

She nodded. 'It is the family tradition. When they are old enough Yves and Margot will join the rest of the family.'

'How pleasant that must be, and the whole family live together in this lovely house! Please tell me about them.'

'There is my son Armand, the father of the children. Jean Pierre is the eldest of them and he is twenty-eight – he'll be twenty-nine soon. He manages everything now. Then there is Gabrielle, who is nineteen – a gap of ten years, you see, between the two. I thought Jean Pierre would be the only one all those years, and then suddenly Gabrielle was born. Then another gap and Yves came, and after that, Margot. There's only a year between those two. It was too soon and their mother was too old for childbearing.'

'She is . . .?'

She nodded. 'That was a bad time. Armand and Jacques, one of the workers, were in the cart when the horses bolted. They were both injured. Armand's wife, poor girl, thought he would die, and I suppose it all seemed too much for her. She caught the fever and died leaving little Margot . . . only ten days old.'

'How very sad.'

'The bad times pass, mademoiselle. It is eight years ago. My son is well enough to work; my grandson is a good boy and really head of the family now. He became a man when it was necessary to shoulder responsibilities. But that is life, is it not?' She smiled at me. 'I talk too much of the Bastides. I will weary you.'

'Indeed you do not. It is all very interesting.'

'But your work must be so much more so. How do you find it at the château?'

'I have only been there a very short time.'

'You are going to find the work interesting?'

'I don't know if I am going to do the work. Everything depends on . . .'

'On Monsieur le Comte. Naturally.' She looked at me and shook her head. 'He is not an easy man.'

'He is unpredictable?'

She lifted her shoulders. 'He was expecting a man. We were all expecting a man. The servants talked of the Englishman who was coming. You cannot keep secrets in Gaillard, mademoiselle. At least most of us can't. My son says I talk too much. He, poor boy, talks little. The death of his wife changed him, mademoiselle, changed him sadly.'

She was alert, listening, and I heard the sound of horse's hoofs. A proud smile touched her face, changed it subtly. 'That,' she said, 'will be Jean Pierre.'

In a few moments he stood in the doorway. He was of medium height, with hair of a lightish brown – bleached, I imagined, by the sun; his dark eyes narrowed to slits as he smiled, and his skin was tanned almost to copper colour. There was about him an air of immense vitality.

'Jean Pierre!' said the old woman. 'This is Mademoiselle from the château.'

He came towards me, smiling as though, like the rest of the family, he was delighted to see me. He bowed ceremoniously.

'Welcome to Gaillard, mademoiselle. It is kind of you to call on us.'

'It was not exactly a call. Your young brother and sister saw me passing and invited me in.'

'Good for them! I hope this will be the first of many visits.' He drew up a chair and sat down. 'What do you think of the château?'

'It's a fine example of fifteenth-century architecture. I have not had much opportunity so far of studying it but I think it has characteristics similar to those of Langeais and Loches.'

He laughed. 'You know more of our country's treasures than we do, mademoiselle, I'll swear.'

'I don't suppose that is so, but the more one learns the more one realizes how much more there is to learn. For me it is pictures and houses, for you . . . the grape.'

Jean Pierre laughed. He had spontaneous laughter, which was attractive. 'What a difference! The spiritual and the material!'

'I think it must be exciting – as I was saying to Madame Bastide – to plant the vines, to tend the grapes, to watch over them and then to make them into wine.'

'It's a matter of hazards,' said Jean Pierre.

'So is everything.'

'You have no idea, mademoiselle, the torments we suffer. Will there be a frost to kill the shoots? Will the grapes be sour because the weather has been too cool? Each day the vines must be examined for mildew, black rot and all the pests. So many pests have one ambition and that is to spoil the grape-harvest. Not until the harvest is gathered in are we safe – and then you should see how happy we are.'

'I hope I shall.'

He looked startled. 'You have started work at the château, mademoiselle?'

'Scarcely. I am not yet accepted. I have to await . . .'

'The decision of Monsieur le Comte,' put in Madame Bastide.

'It is natural, I suppose,' I said, moved rather unaccountably by a desire to defend him. 'One could say I had come under false pretences. They were expecting my father and I did not tell them that he was dead and that I proposed to take over his commitments. Everything depends on Monsieur le Comte.'

'Everything always depends on Monsieur le Comte,' said Madame Bastide resignedly.

'Which,' added Jean Pierre with his sunny smile, 'mademoiselle will say is natural since the château belongs to him, the pictures on which she plans to work belong to him, the grapes belong to him . . . in a sense we all belong to him.'

'The way you talk it would seem we were back before the Revolution,' murmured Madame Bastide.

Jean Pierre was looking at me. 'Here, mademoiselle, little has changed through the years. The château stands guarding the town and the surrounding country as it did through the centuries. It retains its old character and we whose forefathers depended on its bounty still depend on it. There has been little change in Gaillard. That is how Monsieur le Comte de la Talle would have it, so that is how it is.'

'I have a feeling that he is not greatly loved by those who depend on him.'

'Perhaps only those who love to depend, love those they depend on. The independent ones always rebel.'

I was a little mystified by this conversation. There was clearly strong feeling concerning the Comte in this household, but I was becoming more and more anxious to learn everything I could about this man on whom *my* fate depended, so I said: 'Well, at the moment, I'm on sufferance awaiting his return.'

'Monsieur Philippe would not dare give a decision for fear of offending the Comte,' said Jean Pierre.

'He is much in awe of his cousin?'

'More than most. If the Comte does not marry, Philippe could be the heir, for the de la Talles follow the old royalty of France, and the Salic law which applied to the Valois and the Bourbons is for the de la Talles as well. But, like everything else, it rests with the Comte. As long as some male heir inherits he could pass over his cousin for some other relative. Sometimes I think Gaillard is mistaken for the Versailles of Louis the Fourteenth.'

'I imagine the Comte to be young . . . at least not old. Why should he not marry again?'

'It is said that the idea is distasteful to him.'

'I should have thought a man of his family pride would have wanted a son – for he is undoubtedly proud.'

'He is the proudest man in France.'

At that moment the children returned with Gabrielle and their father, Armand. Gabrielle Bastide was strikingly lovely. She was dark like the rest of the family, but her eyes were not brown but a deep shade of blue and those eyes almost made of her a beauty. She had a sweet expression and was more subdued than her brother.

I was explaining to them that I had had a French mother, which accounted for my fluency in their language, when a bell began to ring so suddenly that I was startled.

'It is the maid summoning the children for *goûter*,' said Madame Bastide.

'I will go now,' I said. 'It has been so pleasant. I hope we shall meet again.'

But Madame Bastide would not hear of my going. I must, she said, stay to try some of the wine.

Bread with layers of chocolate between it for the children, and for us little cakes and wine, were brought in. We talked of the vines, pictures, and life in the neighbourhood. I was told I must visit the church and the old *hôtel de ville*: and most of all I must come back and visit the Bastides. I must look in whenever I was passing. Both Jean Pierre and his father – who said very little – would be delighted to show me anything I wished to see.

The children were sent out to play when they had finished their bread and chocolate and the conversation turned once more to the château. Perhaps it was the wine – to which I, certainly, was unaccustomed, particularly at that hour of the day – but I grew more indiscreet than I would normally have been.

I was saying: 'Geneviève is a strange girl. Not in the least like Yves and Margot. They are so spontaneous, so natural – normal, happy children. Perhaps the château is not a good environment for a child to grow up in.' I was speaking recklessly and I didn't care. I had to find out more about the château and most of all the Comte.

'Poor child!' said Madame Bastide.

'Yes,' I went on, 'but I believe it is three years since her mother died, and that is time for one so young to have recovered.'

There was silence, then Jean Pierre said: 'If Mademoiselle Lawson is long at the château she will soon learn.' He turned to me. 'The Comtesse died of an overdose of laudanum.' I thought of the girl in the graveyard and I blurted out: 'Not . . . murder!'

'They called it suicide,' said Jean Pierre.

'Ah,' put in Madame Bastide, 'the Comtesse was a beautiful woman.' And with that she returned to the subject of the vineyards . We talked of the great calamity which had hit most of the vineyards in France a few years ago when the vine-louse had attacked the vines, and because Jean Pierre loved the vineyards so devotedly when he spoke of them he made everyone share his enthusiasm. I could picture the horror when the vine-louse was discovered to be attached to the roots of the vine; I could feel the intense tragedy to all those concerned when they had to face the problem of whether or not to flood the vineyards.

'There was disaster throughout France at that time,' he said. 'That was less than ten years ago. Is that not so, Father?'

His father nodded.

'It has been a slow climb back to prosperity, but it's coming. Gaillard suffered less than most.'

When I rose to go, Jean Pierre said he would walk back with me. Although there was no danger of my losing my way, I was glad of his company for I found the Bastides warm and friendly – a quality I had come to treasure. It occurred to me that when I was with them I myself became a different person from the cool and authoritative woman I showed to the people of the château. I was like a chameleon changing my colour to fit in with the landscape. But it was done without thought, so it was absolutely natural. I had never before realized how automatically I put on my defensive armour, but it was very pleasant to be in company where I did not need it.

As we came out of the gate and took the road to the château I asked: 'The Comte . . . is he really so terrifying?'

'He is an autocrat . . . one of the old aristocrats. His word is law.'

'He has had tragedy in his life.'

'I believe you are sorry for him. When you meet him you'll see that pity is the last thing he would need.'

'You said that they called his wife's death suicide . . .' I began.

He interrupted me swiftly. 'We do not even speak of such things.'

'But . . .'

'But,' he added, 'we keep them in our minds.'

The château loomed before us; it looked immense, impregnable. I thought of all the dark secrets it could be keeping and felt a shiver run down my spine.

'Please don't bother to come any farther,' I said. 'I am sure I am keeping you from your work.'

He stood a few paces from me and bowed. I smiled and turned towards the castle.

I went to bed early that night to make up for the previous night's lack of sleep. I dozed and my dreams were hazy. It was strange, because at home I rarely dreamed. This was muddled dreaming of the Bastides, of cellars containing bottles of wine, and through these dreams flitted a vague faceless shape whom I knew to be the dead Comtesse. Sometimes I felt her presence without seeing her; it was as though she were behind me whispering a warning, 'Go away. Don't you become involved in this strange household.' Then again she would be jeering at me. Yet I was not afraid of her. There was another shady shape to strike terror into me. Monsieur le Comte. I heard the words as though from a long way; then growing so loud that it was like someone shouting in my ears.

I awoke startled. Someone *was* shouting. There were voices below and scurrying footsteps along the corridor. The château was waking up although it was not morning. In fact the candle I hastily lighted showed me my watch lying on the table and this told me it was only just after eleven.

I knew what was happening. It was what everyone was waiting for and dreading.

The Comte had come home.

I lay sleepless, wondering what the morning would bring.

The château was quiet when I awoke at my usual time. Briskly I rose and rang for my hot water. It came promptly. The maid looked different, I told myself. She was uneasy. So the Comte had his effect even on the humblest servants.

'You would like your *petit déjeuner* as usual, mademoiselle?'

I looked surprised and said: 'But of course, please.'

I guessed they were all talking about me, asking themselves what my fate would be. I looked round the room. Perhaps I shall never sleep here again, I thought. Then I was unhappy thinking of leaving the château, never really knowing these people who had taken such a hold on my imagination. I wanted to know more of Geneviève, to try to understand her. I wanted to see what effect on Philippe de la Talle his cousin's return would have. I wanted to know how far Nounou was responsible for the waywardness of her charge. I should have liked to hear what had happened to Mademoiselle Dubois before she had come to the château. Then of course there were the Bastides. I wanted to sit in that cosy room and talk about the vines and the château. But most of all I wanted to meet the Comte – not just once and briefly to receive my dismissal, but to learn more of a man who, it seemed generally believed, had been responsible for the death of his wife, even if he had not actually administered the poison dose.

My breakfast came and I felt too excited for food, but I was determined none of them should say that I was so frightened that I had been unable to eat, so I drank two cups of coffee as usual and ate my twist of hot bread. Then I went along to the gallery.

It was not easy to work. I had already prepared an estimate which Philippe de la Talle had said would be given to the Comte on his return. He had smiled at me when I gave it to him and glancing through it had remarked that it looked like the work of an expert. I was sure he was hoping it would please the Comte – partly, I imagined, to justify his having allowed me to stay, but there was an element of kindness in him, I was sure, which made him want me to have the job because I had betrayed how badly I needed it. I summed him up as a man who would be kind, unless being so made too many demands upon him.

I imagined the Comte's receiving my estimate, hearing that a woman had come instead of a man. But I could not picture him clearly. All I could imagine was a haughty man in white wig and crown. It was a picture I had seen either of Louis XIV or XV. The King . . . the King of the Castle.

I had a note-pad with me and tried to jot down a few points which I had passed over on my previous examination. If he will let me stay, I told myself, I shall become so absorbed in the work that he can have · murdered twenty wives for all I care.

There was one painting in the gallery which had particularly caught my attention. It was a portrait of a woman. The costume placed it in the eighteenth century – mid or perhaps a little later. It interested me not because of the excellence of the work – there were better pictures in the gallery – but because although it was of a later date than most of them it was in a greater state of deterioration. The varnish was very dark and the whole surface was mottled as though it suffered from a skin disease. It looked to me as though it had been exposed to the weather.

I was contemplating this picture when I heard a movement behind me. I swung round to find that a man had entered the gallery and was standing there watching me. I felt my heart pound and my legs tremble. I knew at once that I was at last face to face with the Comte de la Talle.

'It is Mademoiselle Lawson, of course,' he said. Even his voice was unusual – deep, cold.

'You are the Comte de la Talle?'

He bowed. He did not come towards me. His eyes surveyed me across the gallery, and his manner was as cool as his voice. I noticed that he was tallish, and I was struck by his leanness. There was a slight resemblance to Philippe; but there was none of Philippe's femininity in this man. He was darker than his cousin; his cheekbones were high and this gave his face the pointed look which seemed almost satanic. His eyes were very dark – sometimes they could seem almost black, I discovered later, depending on his mood; they were deeply set and his lids were heavy; his aquiline nose gave to his face the look of haughtiness; his mouth was mobile; it changed according to the man he was. But at this time I knew only one man – the arrogant King of the Castle on whom my fate depended.

He wore a black riding-coat with a velvet collar and above his white cravat his face was pale, even cruel.

'My cousin has told me of your coming.' He advanced towards me now. He walked as a king might have walked through the hall of mirrors.

I had regained my poise very quickly. There was nothing like haughtiness to bring out my bristling armour.

'I am glad you have returned, Monsieur le Comte,' I said, 'for I have been waiting several days to know whether you wish me to stay and do the work.'

'It must have been tiresome for you to be uncertain whether or not you were wasting your time.'

'I have found the gallery very interesting, I assure you, so it will not have been an unpleasant way of wasting time.'

'It is a pity,' he said, 'that you did not tell us of your father's death. It would have saved so much trouble.'

So I was to go. I felt angry because I was so miserable. Back to London, I thought. I should have to find a lodging. And how could I afford to live until I discovered a post? I looked down the years and saw myself becoming more and more like Mademoiselle Dubois. What nonsense! As if I ever should! I could go to Cousin Jane. Never, never!

I hated him in that moment because I believed he guessed the thoughts which were passing through my mind. He would know that a woman as independent as I, must have been desperate to have come in the first place, and he was enjoying tormenting me. How she must have hated him, that wife of his! Perhaps she killed herself to get away from him. I should not be surprised if that were the answer.

'I did not realize that you were so old-fashioned in France,' I said with a touch of venom. 'At home I have done this work with my father. No one minded because I was a woman. But as you have different notions here there is nothing more to be said.'

'I disagree. There is a great deal to be said.'

'Then,' I said, lifting my eyes to his face, 'perhaps you will begin to say it.'

'Mademoiselle Lawson, you would like to restore these pictures, would you not?'

'It is my profession to restore paintings and the more in need of repair they are, the more interesting the task becomes.'

'And you find mine in that need?'

'You must know that some of these pictures are in poor condition. I was examining this one when I realized you had come in. What kind of treatment could it have had to be in that state?'

'Pray, Mademoiselle Lawson, do not look at me so sternly. I am not responsible for the state of the picture.'

'Oh? I presumed it had been some time in your possession. You see, there is a failing in the paint. It is chalky. Obviously it has been ill-treated.'

A smile twisted his mouth and his face changed. There might have been a glimmer of amusement there now.

'How vehement you are! You might be fighting for the rights of man rather than for the preservation of paint on canvas.'

'When would you wish me to leave?'

'Not until we have talked, at least.'

'Since you find you cannot employ a woman I do not think we should have anything to talk about.'

'You are very impulsive, Mademoiselle Lawson. Now I should have thought that was a characteristic a restorer of old paintings could well do without. *I* have not said I would not employ a woman. That was your suggestion.'

'I can see that you disapprove of my being here. That is enough.'

'Did you expect approval of your . . . deception?'

'Monsieur le Comte,' I said, 'I worked with my father. I took over his commissions. You had previously approached him to come here. I thought the arrangement still stood. I see no deception in that.'

'Then you must have been surprised by the astonishment you caused.'

I replied shortly: 'It would be difficult to do delicate work of this nature in an atmosphere of disapproval.'

'That I can well understand.'

'Therefore . . .'

'Therefore?' he repeated.

'I could leave to-day if I could be taken to the main-line station. I understand there is only one morning train from the Gaillard halt.'

'How thoughtful of you to look into such arrangements. But I must repeat, Mademoiselle Lawson, you are too impulsive. You must understand my uneasiness. And if you will forgive my saying so, you do not look old enough to have had a great deal of experience in skilled work of this nature.'

'I have worked with my father for years. There are some who grow old and never acquire the skill. It is a feeling in oneself for the work, an understanding, a love of painting that is born in one.'

'You are poetical as well as an artist, I see. But at ... er ... thirty or so ... one would necessarily not have had a lifetime's experience.'

'I am twenty-eight,' I retorted hotly; and I saw at once that I had fallen into the trap. He had determined to bring me off the pedestal on which I was trying to take a firm stand and show me that I was after all an ordinary woman who couldn't bear to be thought older than she was.

He raised his eyebrows; he was finding the interview amusing. I saw that I had betrayed my desperate situation and the streak of cruelty in him made him want to prolong the indecision, to torment me for as long as possible.

For the first time since I had set out on this adventure I lost my control. I said: 'There is no point in continuing. I realize that you have decided I cannot do this work because I am a woman. Well, monsieur, I leave you with your prejudices. So I will go either to-day or to-morrow.'

For a few seconds he looked at me in mock bewilderment, but as I moved towards the door, he was swiftly beside me.

'Mademoiselle, you have not understood. Perhaps your knowledge of French is not as expert as your knowledge of painting.'

Once more I rose to the bait. 'My mother was French. I have understood perfectly every word you have said.'

'Then I am to blame for lack of lucidity. I have no wish that you shall go ... just yet.'

'Your manner suggests that you are not prepared to trust me.'

'Your own assumption, mademoiselle, I do assure you.'

'Then you mean you wish me to stay?'

He pretended to hesitate. 'If I may say so without offence, I should like you to undergo a little ... test. Oh please, mademoiselle, do not accuse me of prejudice against your sex. I am prepared to believe that there may be brilliant women in the world. I am impressed by what you tell me of your understanding and love of painting. I am also interested in the estimates of damage and the cost of repairing the pictures you have examined. It is all very clear and reasonable.'

I was afraid that my eyes had begun to shine with hope and so would betray my excitement. If, I told myself, he realized how very eagerly I desired this commission he might continue baiting me.

He *had* seen. 'I was going to suggest ... but then you may have decided that you would prefer to leave to-day or to-morrow.'

'I have come a long way, Monsieur le Comte. Naturally I should prefer to stay and carry out the work – providing it could be done in a congenial atmosphere. What were you going to suggest?'

'That you restore one of the pictures and if that is satisfactorily accomplished you continue with the rest.'

I was happy in that moment. I should have been relieved, of course, for I was certain of my capabilities. The immediate future was taken care of.

No ignoble return to London! No Cousin Jane! But it was more than that. An inexplicable feeling of joy, anticipation, excitement. I could not explain. I was certain that I could pass this test, and that meant a long stay at the castle. This wonderful old place would be my home for months to come. I could explore it, as well as its treasures. I could continue my friendship with the Bastides. I could indulge my curiosity concerning the inhabitants of the château.

I was insatiably curious. I had known this since my father had pointed it out to me – and deplored this trait; but I could not stop myself wanting to know what went on behind the façade people showed the world. To discover this was like removing the film of decay from an old painting; and to learn what the Comte was like would be revealing a living picture.

'This proposition seems to appeal to you.'

So once more I had betrayed my feelings, something I prided myself on rarely doing. But perhaps he was particularly perceptive.

'It seems a very fair one,' I said.

'Then, it's agreed.' He held out his hands. 'We will shake on it. An old English custom, I believe. You, mademoiselle, have been kind enough to discuss the problem in French; we will seal the bargain in English.'

As he held my hand his dark eyes looked into mine and I felt decidedly uncomfortable. I felt suddenly innocent, unworldly, and that was, I was sure, how he intended I should feel.

I withdrew my hand with a hauteur which I trusted hid my embarrassment. 'Which picture would you select for the . . . test?' I asked.

'What of the one you were examining when I came in?'

'That would be excellent. It is more in need of restoration than anything in the gallery.'

We walked over to it and stood side by side examining it.

'It has been very badly treated,' I said severely. I was now on firm ground. 'It is not very old – a hundred and fifty years at most – and yet . . .'

'An ancestress of mine.'

'It is a pity she was subjected to such treatment.'

'A great pity. But there was a time in France when people like her were submitted to even greater indignity.'

'I should say that this picture has probably been exposed to the weather. Even the colour of her gown is faded, though alizarin is usually stable. I can't see in this light the true colour of the stones about her neck. You see how darkened they have become. The same with the bracelet and the earrings.'

'Green,' he said. 'I can tell you that. They are emeralds.'

'It would be a wonderful picture when restored. That dress as it must have been when it was painted, and the emeralds.'

'It will be interesting to see what it looks like when you have finished with it.'

'I shall start at once.'

'You have all you require?'

'For a beginning. I will go to my room for what I need and get down to work immediately.'

'I can see you are all eagerness and I am delaying you.'

I did not deny this and he stood aside for me as I passed triumphantly from the gallery. I felt I had come satisfactorily through my first encounter with the Comte.

What a happy morning I spent working in the gallery! No one disturbed me. I had returned with my tools to find that two of the menservants had taken the picture from the wall. They asked if there was anything I needed. I told them I would ring if there was. They looked at me with some respect. They would go back to the servants' quarters, I knew, and spread the news that the Comte had given his permission for me to stay.

I had put on a brown linen coat over my dress and I looked very businesslike. Oddly enough as soon as I put on that coat I felt competent. I wished I had been wearing it during my meeting with the Comte.

I settled down to study the condition of the paint. Before I attempted to remove the varnish I must assess the tightness of the paint to the ground. It was clear that there was more discoloration here than from the ordinary accumulation of dust and grime. I had often found that before using a resin on varnish it was wise to wash carefully with soap and water. It took me a long time to decide on this course but eventually I did.

I was surprised when a maid knocked on the door to remind me that it was time for *déjeuner*. This I took in my room and as it was a practice never to work after lunch, I slipped out of the château and walked to the Maison Bastide. It seemed only courteous to tell them what had happened since they had shown such interest in whether or not I stayed.

The old lady was in her rocking chair and delighted to see me. The children, she told me, were having lessons with Monsieur le Curé; Armand, Jean Pierre and Gabrielle were working; but it was a great pleasure to see me.

I seated myself beside her and said: 'I have seen the Comte.'

'I heard he was back at the château.'

'I am to restore a picture and if it is a success I am to complete the work. I have already started; it is a portrait of one of his ancestors. A lady in a red dress and stones which at the moment are the colour of mud. The Comte says they are emeralds.'

'Emeralds,' she said. 'They could be the Gaillard emeralds.'

'Family heirlooms?'

'They were . . . once upon a time.'

'And no longer so?'

'Lost. I think during the Revolution.'

'I suppose the château passed out of the hands of the family then?'

'Not exactly. We are far from Paris, and there was less trouble here. But the château was overrun.'

'It seems to have survived fairly well.'

'Yes. It's a story that's been handed down to us. They were forcing their way in. Perhaps you have seen the chapel? It is in the oldest part of the castle. You will notice that over the door on the outer wall there is broken masonry. Once a statue of St. Geneviève stood there high over the door. The revolutionaries were bent on desecrating the chapel. Fortunately for Château Gaillard they tried to pull down St. Geneviève first; they were drunk on château wine when they attached ropes about the figure, but it was heavier than they thought and it collapsed on them and killed three of them. They took it for an omen. It was said afterwards that St. Geneviève saved Gaillard.'

'So that is why Geneviève is so called?'

'There have always been Genevièves in the family; and although the Comte of the day went to the guillotine, his son, who was a baby then, was cared for and in time went back to the château. This is a story we Bastides like to tell. We were for the People – for liberty, fraternity and equality, against the aristocrats – but we kept the baby Comte here in this house and we looked after him till it was all over. My husband's father used to tell me about it. He was a year or so older than the young Comte.'

'So your family history is close to theirs.'

'Very close.'

'And the present Comte . . . he is your friend?'

'The de la Talles were never friends of the Bastides,' she said proudly. 'Only patrons. They don't alter . . . and nor do we.'

She changed the subject and after a while I left and went back to the château. I was eager to continue with my work.

During the afternoon one of the servants came to the gallery to tell me that Monsieur le Comte would be pleased if I joined the family for dinner that night. They dined at eight o'clock, and as it would be such a small party it would be in one of the smaller dining-rooms. The maid said that she would take me there if I would be ready at five minutes to eight.

I felt too bewildered to work after that. The maid had spoken to me with respect, and this could only mean one thing: not only was I considered worthy to restore his pictures, but of even greater honour, I was to dine in his company.

I wondered what I should wear. I had only three dresses suitable for evening, none of them new. One was brown silk with coffee-coloured lace, the second very severe black velvet with a ruffle of white lace at the throat, and the third grey cotton with a lavender silk stripe. I decided at once on the black velvet.

I could not work by artificial light, so as soon as the daylight faded I went to my room. I took out the dress and looked at it. Velvet fortunately did not age, but the cut was by no means fashionable. I held it up to myself and looked at my reflection. My cheeks were faintly pink, my eyes reflecting the black velvet looked dark and a strand of hair had escaped from the coil. Disgusted with my silliness I put down the dress and was adjusting my hair when there was a knock at the door.

Mademoiselle Dubois entered. She looked at me disbelievingly and then stammered: 'Mademoiselle Lawson, is it true that you have been invited to dine with the family?'

'Yes. Does it surprise you?'

'*I* have never been asked to dine with the family.'

I looked at her and was not surprised. 'I dare say they want to discuss the paintings with me. It's easier to talk over the dinner table.'

'The Comte and his cousin, you mean?'

'Yes. I suppose so.'

'I think you should be warned that the Comte has not a good reputation where a woman is concerned.'

I stared at her. 'He doesn't regard me as a woman!' I retorted. 'I'm here to restore his paintings.'

'They say that he is callous, and in spite of that some find him irresistible.'

'My dear Mademoiselle Dubois, I have never yet found any man irresistible and don't intend to start at my time of life.'

'Well, you are not all that old.'

Not all that old! Did she too think I was thirty?

She saw that I was annoyed and hurried on deprecatingly: 'There was that poor unfortunate lady – his wife. The rumours one hears are . . . quite shocking. It's terrifying, isn't it, to think that we are under the same roof with a man like that.'

'I don't think either of us need be afraid,' I said.

She came close to me. 'I lock my door at nights . . . while he is in the house. You should do the same. And I should be very careful . . . to-night. It might be that he wants to amuse himself while he's here with someone in the house. You can never be sure.'

'I will be careful,' I said to placate and get rid of her.

As I dressed I wondered about her. Did she in the quiet of her room dream erotic dreams of an enamoured Comte's attempts to seduce her? I was certain that she was in as little danger of such a fate as I was.

I washed and put on the velvet gown. I coiled my hair high on my head using many pins to make sure no strands escaped. I put on a brooch of my mother's – simple but charming, consisting of a number of small turquoises set in seed pearls. I was ready a full ten minutes before the maid knocked on the door to take me to the dining-room.

We went into the seventeenth-century wing of the château – the latest addition – to a large vaulted chamber, a dining-hall in which, I imagined, guests were entertained. It would have been absurd for a small party to sit at such a table and I was not surprised when I was led on to a small room – small, that is, by Gaillard standards – leading off this dining-hall. It was a pleasant room; there were midnight-blue velvet curtains at the windows – mullioned, I imagined, and different from the embrasures in the thick walls which narrowed to slits and while providing the utmost protection from outside, excluded the light. At each end of the marble mantelpiece stood a candelabrum in which candles burned. There was a similar one in the centre of a table which was laid for dinner.

Philippe and Geneviève were already there. They were both subdued. Geneviève wore a dress of grey silk with a lace collar; her hair was tied behind her back with a pink silk bow, and she looked almost demure and quite unlike the girl I had met previously. Philippe in evening clothes, was even more elegant than on our first meeting; and he seemed genuinely pleased to see me there.

He smiled pleasantly. 'Good evening, Mademoiselle Lawson.' I returned

the greeting and it was almost as though there was a friendly conspiracy
between us.

Geneviève was bobbing an uneasy curtsy.

'I dare say you have had a busy day in the gallery,' said Philippe.

I replied that I had and was making preparations. It was necessary to test
so many things before one attempted the delicate work of restoration.

'It must be quite fascinating,' he said. 'I am sure you will be successful.'

I was sure he meant it, but all the time he was talking to me I was aware
that he was listening for the arrival of the Comte.

He came precisely at eight and we took our places at the table – the Comte
at its head, I on his right, Geneviève on his left, and Philippe opposite him.
The soup was served without delay while the Comte asked me how I was
progressing in the gallery.

I repeated what I had said to Philippe about my start on the pictures, but
he expressed more interest, whether because he was concerned for his
pictures or whether he was making an attempt to be polite, I was not sure.

I told him that I had decided that the picture should first be washed with
soap and water so that any surface grime should be removed.

He regarded me with an amused glint in his eyes and said: 'I have heard
of that. The water has to stand in a special pot and the soap made during
the dark of moon.'

'We are no longer ruled by such superstitions,' I replied.

'You are not superstitious then, mademoiselle?'

'Not more than most people of to-day.'

'That could be a good deal. But I am sure you are too practical for such
fancies; and that is as well while you stay in this place. We have had people
here . . .' His eyes turned to Geneviève, who seemed to shrink into her chair.
'. . . governesses who have refused to stay. Some of them declared the château
was haunted; some gave no reason but silently departed. Something here
was intolerable . . . either my château or my daughter.'

There was a cool distaste in his eyes as they rested on Geneviève and I
felt resentment rising. He was the sort of man who must have a victim. He
had baited me in the gallery; now it was Geneviève's turn. In my case it was
different. I had come under false pretences and I was able to take care of
myself. But a child – for Geneviève was little more – and a nervous, highly
strung one at that! And yet what had he said? Very little. The venom was
in his manner. It was not unexpected, either. Geneviève was afraid of him.
So was Philippe. So was everyone in the place.

'If one were superstitious,' I said, feeling I had to come to Geneviève's
rescue, 'it would be very easy for one's fancies to grow in a place like this.
I have stayed in some very ancient houses with my father yet I have never
encountered a single ghost.'

'English ghosts would perhaps be more restrained than French ones. They
would not appear without an invitation, which means they would only visit
the fearful. But then perhaps I am wrong.'

I flushed. 'They would surely take their code of manners from the days
in which they lived, and etiquette in France was always more rigid than in
England.'

'You are right, of course, Mademoiselle Lawson. The English would be far more likely to come uninvited. Therefore you are safe in this château . . . provided you do not invite strange company.'

Philippe was listening intently; Geneviève with some awe. For me, I think because I dared engage in conversation with her father.

Fish had replaced the soup and the Comte lifted his glass to me. 'I trust you will like the wine, Mademoiselle Lawson. It is our own vintage. Are you a connoisseur of wines as well as of pictures?'

'It is a subject about which I know very little.'

'You will hear a great deal about it while you are here. Often it is the main topic of conversation. I trust you will not find it tiresome.'

'I am sure I shall find it most interesting. It is always pleasant to learn.'

I saw the smile at the corner of his mouth. Governess! I thought. Certainly if I ever had to take up that profession I should have the right demeanour for it.

Philippe spoke rather hesitantly: 'What picture are you starting on, Mademoiselle Lawson?'

'A portrait, painted last century – in the middle, I should think. I place it about seventeen-forty.'

'You see, Cousin,' said the Comte, 'Mademoiselle Lawson is an expert. She loves pictures. She chided me for neglecting them as though I were a parent who had failed in his duty.'

Geneviève looked down at her place in embarrassment. The Comte turned to her. 'You should take advantage of Mademoiselle Lawson's presence here. She could teach you enthusiasm.'

'Yes, Papa,' said Geneviève.

'And,' he went on, 'if you can persuade her to talk to you in English, you might be able to speak that language intelligibly. You should try to persuade Mademoiselle Lawson when she is not engaged with her pictures, to tell you about England and the English. You could learn from their less rigid etiquette. It might give you confidence, and er . . . aplomb.'

'We have already spoken together in English,' I said. 'Geneviève has a good vocabulary. Pronunciation is always a problem until one has conversed freely with natives. But it comes in time.'

Again spoken like a governess! I thought; and I knew he was thinking the same. But I had done my best to support Geneviève and defy him. My dislike was growing with every moment.

'It is an excellent opportunity for you, Geneviève. Do you ride, Mademoiselle Lawson?'

'Yes. I am fond of riding.'

'There are horses in the stables. One of the grooms would advise you which was your most suitable mount. Geneviève rides too . . . a little. You might ride together. The present governess is too timid. Geneviève, you could show Mademoiselle Lawson the countryside.'

'Yes, Papa.'

'Our country is not very attractive, I fear. The wine-growing land rarely is. But if you ride out a little way I am sure you will find something to please you.'

'You are very kind. I should like to ride.'

He waved a hand, and Philippe, no doubt feeling that it was time he made an effort in the conversation, took the subject back to pictures.

I talked about the portrait I was working on. I explained one or two details and made them rather technical in the hope of confusing the Comte. He listened gravely with a faint smile lurking at the corners of his mouth. It was disconcerting to suspect that he knew what was going on in my mind. If this were so, he would know that I disliked him, and oddly enough this seemed to add to his interest in me.

'I am certain,' I was saying, 'that although this is far from a masterpiece, the artist had a mastery of colour. I can see this already. I am sure the colour of the gown will be startling, and the emeralds, restored to the colour the artist intended will be magnificent.'

'Emeralds . . .' said Philippe.

The Comte looked at him. 'Oh, yes, this is the picture in which they are seen in all their glory. It will be interesting to see them . . . if only on canvas.'

'That,' murmured Philippe, 'is the only chance we shall have of seeing them.'

'Who knows?' said the Comte. He turned to me. 'Philippe is very interested in our emeralds.'

'Aren't we all?' retorted Philippe with unusual boldness.

'We should be if we could lay our hands on them.'

Geneviève said in a high, excited voice: 'They must be somewhere, Nounou says they are in the château. If we could find them . . . oh, wouldn't it be exciting!'

'That old nurse of yours is sure to be right,' said the Comte with sarcasm. 'And I do agree that it would be *exciting* to find them . . . apart from the fact that the discovery would add considerably to the family's fortunes.'

'Indeed!' said Philippe, his eyes glowing.

'Do you think they are in the château?' I asked.

Philippe said eagerly: 'They have never been discovered elsewhere and stones like that would be recognized. They could not be disposed of easily.'

'My dear Philippe,' said the Comte. 'You forget the time when they were lost. A hundred years ago, Mademoiselle Lawson, such stones could have been broken up, sold separately and forgotten. The markets must have been flooded with stones which had been stolen from the mansions of France by those who had little understanding of their value. It is almost certain that this was the fate of the Gaillard emeralds. The *canaille* who ransacked our houses and stole our treasures had no appreciation of what they took.' The momentary anger which had shown in his eyes faded and he turned to me. 'Ah, Mademoiselle Lawson, how fortunate that you did not live in those days. How would you have endured to see great paintings desecrated, thrown out of windows to lie neglected and exposed to the weather . . . to collect – what is it – bloom?'

'It was tragic that so much that was beautiful was lost.' I turned to Philippe: 'You were telling me about the emeralds.'

'They were in the family for years,' he said. 'They were worth . . . it is difficult to say, for values have changed so much. They were priceless. They were kept in our strongroom at the château. Yet they were lost at the time of the Revolution. No one knew what had become of them. But the belief has always been that they are somewhere in the château.'

'Periodically there are treasure hunts,' said the Comte. 'Someone has a theory and there is a great deal of excitement. We look. We dig. We attempt to discover hidden places in the château that have not been opened for years. This produces a great deal of activity but never any emeralds.'

'Papa,' cried Geneviève, 'couldn't we have a treasure hunt now?'

The pheasant had been brought in. It was excellent but I scarcely tasted it. I found the conversation all-absorbing. I had been in a state of exaltation all day because I was going to stay here.

'You have so impressed my daughter, Mademoiselle Lawson,' said the Comte, 'that she thinks you will succeed where others have failed. You want a renewed search, Geneviève, because you feel that now Mademoiselle Lawson is here she cannot fail.'

'No,' said Geneviève, 'I didn't think that. I just want to look for the emeralds.'

'How ungracious you are! Forgive her, Mademoiselle Lawson. And Geneviève, I suggest that you show Mademoiselle Lawson the château.' He turned to me: 'You have not yet explored it I am sure, and with your lively and most intelligent curiosity you will want to. I believe your father understood architecture as you do pictures and that you worked with him. Why, who knows, you might discover the hiding place which has baffled us for a hundred years.'

'I should be interested to see the château,' I admitted, 'and if Geneviève will show me I shall be delighted.'

Geneviève did not look at me and the Comte frowned at her. I said quickly: 'We will make an appointment if that is agreeable to you, Geneviève?'

She looked at her father and then at me. 'To-morrow morning?' she said.

'I am working in the morning, but to-morrow afternoon I should be most happy to come.'

'Very well,' she mumbled.

'I am sure it will be a profitable excursion for you, Geneviève,' said the Comte.

Through the soufflé we talked of the neighbourhood – mostly of the vineyards. I felt I had made great progress. I had dined with the family, something poor Mademoiselle Dubois had never achieved; I had been given permission to ride – I had brought my old riding-habit with me hopefully; I was to be shown over the château the next day; and I had achieved some sort of relationship with the Comte, although I was not sure what sort.

I was rather pleased when I could retire to my room, but before I left, the Comte said that there was a book in the library which I might like to see.

'My father had a man down here to write it,' he explained. 'He was extremely interested in the history of our family. The book was written and printed. It is years since I read it, but I do believe it would interest you.'

I said that I was sure it would and I should be delighted to see it.

'I will have it sent to you,' he told me.

I took my leave of the company when Geneviève did and we left the men together. She conducted me to my room and bade me a cool good night.

I had not been long in my room when there was a knock on the door and a maid entered with the book.

'Monsieur le Comte said you wanted this,' she told me.

She went out leaving me standing with the book in my hand. It was a slim volume and there were some line drawings of the castle. I was sure I should find it absorbing, but at the moment my mind was full of the evening's events.

I did not want to go to bed for my mind was too stimulated for sleep, and my thoughts were dominated by the Comte. I had expected him to be unusual. After all he was a man surrounded by mystery. His daughter was afraid of him; I was not sure about his cousin, but I suspected he was too. The Comte was a man who liked those about him to fear him, and yet despised them for doing it. That was the conclusion I had come to. I had noted the exasperation those two had aroused in him and yet by his manner he had added to their fear. I wondered what his life had been like with the woman who had been unfortunate enough to marry him. Had she cowered from his contempt? How had he ill-treated her? It was not easy to think of him indulging in physical violence . . . and yet how could I be sure of anything where he was concerned? I scarcely knew him . . . yet.

The last word excited me. I had to admit it. For how did he think of me? Scarcely at all. He had looked me over, had decided to give me the job, and that could well be the end of his interest. Why had I been invited to dine with the family? So that he could look more intently at a human specimen who interested him vaguely? Because there was nothing else of interest at the castle? Dining alone with Philippe and Geneviève would be somewhat boring. I had defied him – not altogether successfully for he was too clever not to see through my defence – and because I was bold it had amused him to submit me to further examination, to attempt to deflate me.

He was a sadist. That was my conclusion. He was responsible for his wife's death, for even if he had not administered the dose he had driven her to take it. Poor woman! What must her life have been? How wretched could a woman be to be driven to take her life. Poor Geneviève, who was her daughter! I must try to understand that girl, somehow make a friend of her. I felt she was a lost child wandering through a maze, growing increasingly more afraid that she would never find a way out.

And I, who prided myself on being a practical woman, could grow quite fanciful in this place, where strange events must have happened over centuries, where a woman so recently had died unhappily.

To drive this man out of my thoughts I tried to think of another. How different was the open face of Jean Pierre Bastide!

Then suddenly I began to smile. It was strange that I who had never been interested in a man since I had loved Charles years ago had now found two who were constantly in my thoughts.

How foolish! I admonished myself. What have either of them to do with you?

I picked up the book the Comte had given me and began to read.

The castle had been built in the year 1405 and there was still much of the original structure standing. The two wings which flanked the old building had been added later, they were well over a hundred feet tall and the cylindrical forts gave them added solidity. Comparisons were drawn to the royal château of Loches and it seemed that life in Château Gaillard was conducted in much the same manner as it was in Loches; for in Gaillard the de la Talles ruled as kings. Here they had their dungeons in which they imprisoned their enemies. In the most ancient part of the building there was one of the most perfect examples of the *oubliette.*

When these dungeons had been examined by the writer of the book, cages had been discovered similar to those in Loches, small hollows cut out of stone in which there was not room for a man to stand up; in these, human beings had been chained and left to die by fifteenth-, sixteenth- and seventeenth-century de la Talles in the same way as Louis XI had dealt with his enemies. One man, left to die in the *oubliette*, had attempted to cut his way to freedom and had succeeded in boring a passage which had brought him out to one of the cages in the dungeons where he had died in frustrated despair.

I read on, fascinated not only by the descriptions of the château but by the history of the family.

Often during the centuries the family had been in conflict with the kings; more often they had stood beside them. One of the women of the house had been a mistress of Louis XV before she married into the family and it was this king who had presented her with an emerald necklace of great value. It was considered no dishonour to be a mistress of the king, and the de la Talle who had married her when she left the royal service had sought to vie with the king's generosity and had presented his wife with an emerald bracelet made up of priceless stones to match those of the necklace. But a bracelet was less valuable than a necklace; so there had been a tiara of emeralds and two emerald rings, a brooch and a girdle all set with emeralds, as proof that de la Talles could stand equal with royalty. Thus the famous de la Talle emeralds had come into being.

The book confirmed what I alread knew, that the emeralds had been lost during the Revolution. Until then they had been kept with other treasures in the strong-room in the gun-gallery to which no one but the master of the house had the key or even knew where the key was hidden. So it had been until the Terror broke out all over France.

It was late but I could not stop reading and I had come to the chapter headed 'The de la Talles and the Revolution.'

Lothair de la Talle, the Comte at that time, was a man of thirty; he had married a few years before that fatal year and was called to Paris for the meeting of the States General. He never returned to the castle; he was one of the first whose blood was spilt on the guillotine. His wife Mary Louise, twenty-two years old and pregnant, remained in the château with the old Comtesse, Lothair's mother. I pictured it clearly; the hot days of July; the news being brought to that young woman of her husband's death; her grief for her husband, her fears for the child soon to be born. I imagined her at the highest window of the highest tower, straining her eyes over the countryside; wondering if the revolutionaries would come marching her way; asking herself how long the people of the district would allow her to live in peace.

All through the sultry days she must have waited, afraid to go into the little town, watchful of the work-people who toiled in the vineyards, of the servants who doubtless grew a little less subservient with the passing of each day. I pictured the proud old Comtesse, desperately trying to preserve the old ways, and what those two brave women must have suffered during those terrible days.

Few escaped the Terror – and eventually it reached the Château Gaillard. A band of revolutionaries were marching on the château, waving their banners, singing the new song from the south. The workers left the vineyard; from the little cottages of the town ran the women and children. The stall-holders and the shopkeepers spilled into the square. The aristocrats had had their day. They were the masters now.

I shivered as I read how the young countess had left the castle and sheltered in a nearby house. I knew what house it was; I knew which family have taken her in. Had I not heard that the family histories were entwined? The de la Talles were never friends though, only patrons. I could clearly remember Madame Bastide's proud looks when she had said that.

So Madame Bastide, who must have been Jean Pierre's great-grand-mother, had sheltered the Comtesse. She had ruled her household so that even the men had not dared to disobey her. They were with the reolutionaries preparing to pillage the castle while she hid the Comtesse in her house and forbade them all to whisper outside the house a word of what was happening.

The old Comtesse refused to leave the château. She had lived there; she would die there. And she went into the chapel there to await death at the hands of the rebels. Her name was Geneviève and she prayed to St. Geneviève for help. She heard the rough shouting and coarse laughter as the mob broke into the castle; she knew they were tearing down the paintings and the tapestries, throwing them from the windows to their comrades.

And there were those who came to the chapel. But before they entered they sought to tear down the statue of St. Geneviève which had been set up over the door. They climbed up to it but they could not move it. Inflamed with wine they called to their comrades. Before they continued to pillage the château they must break down the statue.

At the altar the old Comtesse continued to pray to St. Geneviève while the shouting grew louder and every moment she expected the rabble to break into the chapel and kill her.

Ropes were brought; to the drunken strains of the 'Marseillaise' and 'Ca Ira' they worked. She heard the great shout that went up. 'Heave, comrades . . . all together!' And then the crash, the screams . . . and the terrible silence.

The château was out of danger; St. Geneviève lay broken at the door of the chapel, but beneath her lay the bodies of three dead men; she had saved the château, for superstitious, fearful in spite of their professed ungodliness, the revolutionaries slunk away. A few bold ones had tried to rally the mob but it was useless. Many of them came from the surrounding district and they had lived their lives under the shadow of the de la Talles. They feared them now as they had in the past. They had one wish and that was to turn their backs on Château Gaillard.

The old Comtesse came out of the chapel when all was silent. She looked at the broken statue and kneeling beside it gave thanks to her patron saint. Then she went into the château and with the help of one servant attempted to set it to rights. There she lived alone for some years, caring for the young Comte who was stealthily brought back to his home. His mother had died in giving birth to him, which was not surprising considering all that she had suffered before his birth, and the fact that Madame Bastide had been afraid to call the midwife to her. There they lived for years in the château – the old Comtesse, the young child and one servant; until the times changed and the Revolution passed and life at the château began to slip back into the old ways. Servants came back; repairs were made; the vineyards became prosperous. But although the strong-room in which they had been kept was untouched, the emeralds had disappeared and were lost to the family from that time.

I closed the book. I was so tired that I was soon asleep.

Chapter Three

I spent the next morning in the gallery. I was half-expecting a visit from the Comte after the interest he had shown the night before, but he did not come.

I had lunch in my room as usual, and when I had finished there was a knock on my door and Geneviève came in.

Her hair was neatly tied behind her back and she looked subdued as she had last night at dinner. It occurred to me that her father's being in the house had a marked effect upon her.

First we mounted the staircase in the polygonal tower and reached the summit of the building. In the tower she pointed out to me the surrounding country speaking in slow, rather painful English, as the Comte had suggested. I believed that although at times she hated and feared him, she had a desire to win his respect.

'Mademoiselle, can you see a tower right away to the south? That is where my grandfather lives.'

'It is not very far.'

'It is nearly twelve kilometres. You can see it to-day only because the air is so clear.'

'Do you visit him often?'

She was silent, looking at me suspiciously. I said: 'It is not so very far.'

'I go sometimes,' she said. 'Papa does not go. Please do not tell him.'

'He would not wish you to go?'

'He has not said so.' Her voice was faintly bitter. 'He doesn't say much to me, you know. Please promise not to tell him.'

'Why should I tell him?'

'Because he talks to you.'

'My dear Geneviève, I have met him only twice. Naturally he talks about his paintings to me. He is concerned for them. He is not likely to speak to me of other things.'

'He doesn't usually talk to people . . . who come to work here.'

'They probably don't come to restore his paintings.'

'I think he was interested in *you*, mademoiselle.'

'He was concerned as to what I should do to his works of art. Now, look at this vaulted ceiling. Notice the shape of the arched door. That enables you to place it within a hundred years or so.' Actually I wanted to talk about her father, to ask how he usually behaved to people in the house; I wanted to know why he would not wish her to visit her grandfather.

'You speak too fast, mademoiselle, I cannot follow.'

We descended the staircase, and when we had reached the bottom she said in French: 'Now you have been to the top you must see the lower part. Did you know that we had dungeons in the château, mademoiselle?'

'Yes, your father sent me a book which had been written for an ancestor of yours. It gave a very good idea of what the château contained.'

'We used to keep our prisoners here, mademoiselle. If anyone offended a Comte de la Talle he was put into the dungeons. My mother told me. She took me there once and showed me. She said that you didn't have to be in a dungeon, though, to be imprisoned. She said stone walls and chains were one way of keeping prisoners; there were others.'

I looked at her sharply, but her eyes were wide and innocent and the demure look was still on her face.

'In the royal château there were dungeons . . . *oubliettes* they called them because people were sent into them and forgotten. They are the prisons of the forgotten. Did you know, mademoiselle, that the only way into these prisons was through trap doors which could not easily be seen from above?'

'Yes. I have read of these places. The victim was made to stand unsuspectingly on the trap door, which was opened by pressing a lever in another part of the room; suddenly the floor opened beneath him and he would fall down.'

'Down into the *oubliette*. It is a long drop. I've seen it. Perhaps his leg would be broken and there would be no one to help him; he would lie there forgotten with the bones of others who had gone before him. Mademoiselle, are you afraid of ghosts?'

'Of course not.'

'Most of the servants are. They won't go into the room above the *oubliette* . . . at least they won't go alone. They say at night there are noises in the *oubliette* . . . queer groaning noises. Are you sure you want to see it?'

'My dear Geneviève, I have stayed in some of the most haunted houses in England.'

'Then you are safe. Papa said, didn't he, that French ghosts would be more polite than English ones and only come when expected. If you aren't frightened and don't believe in them you wouldn't be expecting them, would you? That was what he meant.'

How she remembered his words! I thought then: The child needs more than discipline. She needs affection. It was three years since her mother had died. How she must have missed it since then with such a father!

'Mademoiselle, you are sure you are not afraid of the *oubliette*?'

'Quite sure.'

'It is not as it was,' she said almost regretfully. 'They cleared out a lot of bones and horrid things a long time ago when there was a search for the emeralds. It was my grandfather who did that, and of course the first place you would look for them would be in the *oubliette*, wouldn't it? They didn't find them though, so they weren't there. They say they were taken away but I think they're here. I wish Papa would have a treasure hunt again. Wouldn't that be fun?'

'I expect thorough searches have been made. From what I have read it seems certain that they were stolen by the revolutionaries who broke into the château.'

'But they didn't break into the strong-room, did they? And yet the emeralds were gone.'

'Perhaps the emeralds were sold before the Revolution. Perhaps they hadn't been in the château for years. I'm merely guessing. But suppose one of your ancestors needed money and sold them. He – or she – might not have told anyone of this. Who can say?'

She looked at me with surprise. Then she said triumphantly: 'Have you told my father that?'

'I'm sure the idea has occurred to him. It's one obvious solution.'

'But the woman in the picture you are working on is wearing them. They must have been in the family then.'

'They could have been imitation.'

'Mademoiselle, no de la Talle would wear imitation jewels.'

I smiled and then gave a little exclamation of pleasure for we had come to a narrow and uneven staircase. 'This leads underground, mademoiselle. There are eighty steps. I've counted them. Can you manage? Hold the rope banister.'

I did so and followed her down; the staircase became spiral and narrow so there was only room for us to go in single file.

'Can't you feel the cold, mademoiselle?' There was a note of excitement in her voice. 'Oh, imagine being brought down here knowing that you might never come up again. We are now down below the level of the moat. This is where we used to keep people who had offended us.'

Having passed down the eighty steps we were confronted by a heavy oak door studded with iron; words had been carved on it and they stood out clearly and ironically.

> *'Entrez, Messieurs, Mesdames,*
> *chez votre maître le Comte de la Talle.'*

'You were thinking it a pleasant welcome, mademoiselle?' She was smiling at me slyly and it was as though another girl peeped out from behind that demure expression.

I shuddered.

She came close to me and whispered: 'But it is all over now, mademoiselle. This is no longer *chez nous*. We never entertain here now. Come along in. Look at these holes in the walls. They are called *cages*. Look at the chains. We used to chain them here and give them bread and water now and then. They never lived long, though. You see, it is dark even now, but with the door shut there is no light at all . . . no light . . . no air. Next time we come we must bring candles . . . or a lantern would be better. The air is so close. If I had brought a light I could have shown you the writing on the walls. Some of them scratched prayers to the saints and the Holy Mother. Some of them scratched what revenge they would take on the de la Talles.'

'It's unhealthy down here,' I said, looking at the fungoid growth on the slimy walls. 'And as you say, we can see little without a light.'

'The *oubliette* is on the other side of the wall. Come on. I will show you. The *oubliette* is even more haunted than this place, mademoiselle, because there were the truly forgotten ones.'

She smiled secretly and led the way up the stairs. Throwing open a door she announced: 'This is now the gun-gallery.'

I stepped inside and saw the guns of all shapes and sizes ranged about the walls. The ceiling was vaulted and supported by stone pillars; the floor appeared to be of flagged stone and was covered in places by rugs. There were the same stone window seats which were in my bedroom and the alcoves narrowing to a slit letting in a little light. I had to admit to myself, although I would not to Geneviève, that there was something chillingly forbidding about this chamber. It had not been altered for hundreds of years and I could imagine the unsuspecting victim coming into the room. There was one chair, so ornately carved that it was almost like a throne. I wondered that such a piece of furniture was left in a room like this. It was a large wooden chair, and the carving on the back was of the fleurs-de-lis and arms of the de la Talle family. I pictured the man who would sit there – and naturally I pictured the present Comte – talking to his victim, and then suddenly the pressing of the lever which would release the spring of the trap door; the agonizing scream, or the moment of silent terror as the victim realized what was happening to him as the floor opened and he fell down to join those who had gone before him, never again to see the light of day, to join the forgotten.

'Help me with the chair, mademoiselle,' said Geneviève. 'The spring is under it.'

Together we pushed aside the throne-like chair and Geneviève rolled up the rug. 'There,' she went on. 'I press here . . . and look . . . see . . . it's happening.'

There was a groaning, squeaking sound and it was as though a large square hole had appeared in the floor.

'In the old days it happened quickly and noiselessly. Look down there, mademoiselle. You can't see much, can you. But there is a rope ladder. It's kept in the cupboard here. Twice a year some of the men servants go down there, to clean it I suppose. Of course it's all right now. No bones, mademoiselle, no mouldering bodies. There are only ghosts ... and you don't believe in them.'

She had brought out the rope ladder, hung it on two hooks, which had evidently been fixed for it beneath the floorboards, and let it fall.

'There, mademoiselle, are you coming down with me?' She started to descend, laughing up at me. 'I know you're not afraid.'

She reached the floor and I followed her.

We were in a small chamber; a little light penetrated from the open trap door and there was just enough to show me the piteous engravings on the walls.

'Look at those openings in the walls. They were for a purpose. The prisoners thought there was a way out through them. There's a sort of maze in which you can lose yourself; you see they would think that if they could find the way through these passages they would be free. They only lead back to the *oubliette*. It's called exquisite torture.'

'That's interesting,' I said. 'I have never heard of that. This must be unique.'

'Do you want to examine it, mademoiselle? I knew you would because you are not afraid, are you? You are so brave, and you don't believe in ghosts.'

I went to the opening in the wall and took a few steps into the darkness. I touched the cold wall and it took me some seconds to realize that this did not lead anywhere. It was merely an alcove cut into the thickness of the wall.

I turned and heard a low chuckle. Geneviève had ascended the ladder and was pulling it up.

'You love the past, mademoiselle,' she said. 'Well, this is like it. The de la Talles do still leave their victims to perish in their *oubliettes*.'

'Geneviève!' I cried shrilly.

She laughed. 'You're a liar,' she retorted shrilly. 'But perhaps you don't know it. Now is the time to find out whether you're afraid of ghosts!'

The trap door shut with a bang. For the moment the darkness seemed intense and then my eyes grew accustomed to the dimness. It was some more seconds before the horror of my position began to dawn on me.

The girl had planned this last night when her father had suggested she should show me the château. After a while she would release me. All I had to do was keep a hold on my dignity, to refuse to admit even to myself the rising panic and wait until I was free.

'Geneviève!' I called. 'Open that trap door immediately.'

I knew that my voice could not be heard. The walls were thick, so were the slabs over my head. What would be the point of an *oubliette* where the screams of the victims could be heard. The very description implied what happened to those who were incarcerated here. Forgotten!

I had been foolish to trust her. I had had a glimpse of her nature when I had first seen her; yet I had allowed myself to be deceived by her apparent docility. Suppose she was more than mischievous? Suppose she was wicked?

With sudden horror I asked myself what would happen when I was

missed. But when should I be missed? Not until dinner time when either
a tray would be brought to my room or I should be summoned to dine at the
family table. And then . . . Should I have to wait in this gruesome place all
those hours?

Another thought occurred to me. What if she went to my room, hid my
things, making it seem that I had left? She might even forge a note explaining
that I had gone because I was not pleased with my reception . . because I
no longer cared to do the work.

Was she capable of that?

She could be – the daughter of a murderer!

Was that fair? I know scarcely anything of the mystery surrounding the
Comte's wife – all I knew was there there was a mystery. But this girl was
strange; she was wild; I now believed she was capable of anything.

In those first moments of near-panic I understood a little of what those
victims must have felt when the found themselves in this terrible place. But
I could not compare myself with them. They would have fallen damaging
their limbs; I had at least descended by the ladder. I was the victim of a joke;
they of revenge. It was quite different. Soon the trap door would open, the
girl's head would appear. I must be very stern with her, at the same time
showing no sign of panic and above all retaining my dignity.

I sat on the floor leaning against the cold stone wall and looked up at the
trap door. I tried to see the time by the watch pinned to my blouse. I could
not do so, but the minutes were ticking away. It was useless to pretend I was
not frightened. A sense of terrible doom impregnated the place; the air was
close; I felt stifled; and I knew that I, who had always prided myself on my
calmness, was near to panic.

Why had I come to the château? How much better to have tried to find
a respectable post as a governess to which I should have been so well fitted!
How much better to have gone to Cousin Jane, to have nursed her, waited
on her, read to her, listened to her a hundred times a day reminding me that
I was a poor relation!

I wanted a chance to live quietly, without excitement, I should not mind
as long as I could live. How often had I said I would rather be dead than
live a life of servitude – and I had thought I meant it. Now I was ready to
barter independence, a life of interest – anything – for the chance of
remaining alive. I would never have thought it possible until this moment.
How much did I know of myself? Could it be that the armour I put on to
face the world deceived me as much as it did others?

I was trying to think of anything which would turn my thoughts from this
terrible place in which it seemed to me tortured minds and bodies of those
who had suffered had left something behind them.

'Do you believe in ghosts, mademoiselle?'

Not in the broad sceptical daylight when I am within easy reach of my
fellow human beings. In a dark *oubliette* into which I had been tricked and
left . . . I did not know.

'Geneviève!' I called. And the note of panic in my voice frightened me.

I stood up and paced up and down. I called again and again until my
voice was hoarse. I sat down and tried to be calm; then I paced up and down

again. I found myself looking furtively over my shoulder. I began to tell myself that I was watched. I kept my eyes on the opening in the wall which I could just make out and which Geneviève had said was a maze and I knew to be a dark alcove . . . but I was expecting someone . . . something to emerge.

I was afraid that I was going to sob or scream. I tried to take a grip on myself by saying aloud that I would find a way out, although I knew there was no way. I sat down again and tried to shut out the gloom by covering my face with my hands.

I started up in dismay. There was a sound. I put my hand to my mouth automatically to suppress the scream. I fixed my eyes on that dark aperture.

A voice said: 'Mademoiselle!' And the place had lightened. I gave a great sob of relief. The trap door was open, and the grey frightened face of Nounou was looking down at me.

'Mademoiselle, are you all right?'

'Yes . . . Yes . . .' I had run to look up at her.

'I will get the ladder,' she said.

It seemed a long time before she came back, but she had the ladder. I grasped it and stumbled up, so eager to reach the top that I almost fell.

Her frightened eyes searched my face. 'That naughty girl! Oh, dear, I don't know what will become of us all. You look so pale . . . so distrait.'

'Who would not, shut in that place! I'm forgetting to thank you for coming. I can't tell you how . . .'

'Mademoiselle, will you come to my room. I will give you some good strong coffee. I would like to talk to you, too, if you will allow me.'

'It is good of you. But where is Geneviève?'

'You are angry, naturally. But I can explain.'

'Explain! What is there to explain? Did she tell you what she had done?'

The nurse shook her head. 'Please come to my room. It is easy to talk there. Please, I must speak to you. I want you to understand. Besides, it was a terrible ordeal. You are shocked. Who would not be?' She slipped her arm through mine. 'Come, mademoiselle, it is best for you.'

Still feeling dazed I allowed myself to be led away from that dreadful room which I was sure I should never willingly enter again. She had the soothing manner of one who has spent a lifetime looking after the helpless, and in my present mood her gentle authority was what I needed.

I did not notice where she was leading me but when she threw open a door to show a small and cosy room I realized that we were in one of the newer wings.

'Now, you must lie down. Here on the sofa. So much more restful than sitting.'

'This isn't necessary.'

'Forgive me, mademoiselle, it is very necessary. I am going to make you some coffee.' There was an open fire in her grate and on a hob a kettle was singing. 'Good hot strong coffee. It will help you to feel better. My poor mademoiselle, it has been terrible for you!'

'How did you know what happened?'

She turned to the fire and busied herself with the coffee.

'Geneviève came back by herself. I saw by her face . . .'

'You guessed?'

'It happened before. There was one of the governesses. Not like you at all
. . . A pretty young lady – a little brazen perhaps . . . Geneviève did the
same thing to her. It was soon after her mother died . . . not long afterwards.'

'So she shut her governess in the *oubliette* as she did me. How long did
she stay there?'

'Longer than you did. You see, as she was the first, I didn't find out until
some time. Poor young lady, she was fainting with fear. She refused to stay
in the château after that . . . and that was the end of her as far as we were
concerned.'

'You mean that girl makes a habit of this!'

'Only twice. Please, mademoiselle, do not excite yourself. It is bad for you
after what happened.'

'I want to see her. I shall make her understand . . .'

I realized that the reason I was so angry was because I had been near to
panic and was ashamed of myself, disappointed and surprised. I had always
believed myself to be so self-reliant and it was as though I had removed a
film from a painting and found something unsuspected beneath. And here
was another discovery, I was doing that which I had so often condemned in
others – turning my anger on someone else because I was angry with myself.
Of course Geneviève had behaved abominably – but it was my own conduct
that was upsetting me now.

Nounou came and stood beside the sofa, clasping her hands together and
looking down at me.

'It is not easy for her, mademoiselle. A girl like her to lose her mother.
I have tried to do my best.'

'She was devoted to her mother?'

'Passionately. Poor child, it was a terrible shock to her. She has never
recovered from it. I trust you will remember that.'

'She is undisciplined,' I said. 'Her behaviour on the first occasion we met
was intolerable, and now this . . . I suppose I should have been left there
indefinitely if you had not discovered what she had done.'

'No. She only wanted to frighten you, perhaps because you seemed so
well able to take care of yourself and she, poor child, is so definitely not.'

'Tell me,' I said, 'why is she so strange?'

She smiled with relief. 'That is what I want to do, mademoiselle, to tell
you.'

'I should like to understand what makes her act as she does.'

'And when you do, mademoiselle, you will forgive her. You will not tell
her father what has happened this afternoon? You will not mention it to
anyone?'

I was unsure. I said promptly: 'I certainly intend to speak to Geneviève
about it.'

'But to no one else, I beg of you. Her father would be very angry and she
dreads his anger.'

'Wouldn't it be good for her to realize the wickedness of what she did?
We shouldn't pat her on the back and tell her nothing matters because you
came and rescued me.'

'No, speak to her if you wish, but I must talk to you first. There are things I want to tell you.'

She turned away and busied herself at the table.

'About,' she said slowly, 'her mother's death.'

I waited for her to go on. She could not have been more eager to tell me than I was to hear. But she would not speak until she had made the coffee. She left the brown jug to stand and came back to the couch.

'It was terrible . . . *that* to happen to a young girl of eleven. She was the one who found her dead.'

'Yes,' I agreed, 'that would be terrible.'

'She used to go in and see her mother first thing in the morning. Imagine a young girl going in and finding that!'

I nodded. 'But it was three years ago and terrible as it was it does not excuse her for locking me in that place.'

'She has never been the same since. She changed afterwards. There were these fits of naughtiness in which she seemed to delight. It is because she misses her mother's love; because she is afraid . . .'

'Of her father?'

'So you have seen that. At the same time there were the questions and inquiries. It was so bad for her. The whole household believed that he had done it. He had his mistress . . .'

'I see. The marriage was unhappy. Did he love his wife when they were first married?'

'Mademoiselle, he could only love himself.'

'And did she love him?'

'You have seen how he frightens Geneviève. Françoise was afraid too.'

'Was *she* in love with him when she married him?'

'You know how marriages are arranged between such families. But perhaps it is not so in England. In France among our noble families marriages are always arranged by the parents. Isn't it so in England?'

'Not to the same extent. Families are apt to disapprove of a choice but I do not think the rules are so rigid.'

She shrugged her shoulders. 'Here it is so, mademoiselle. And Françoise was betrothed to Lothair de la Talle when they were in their teens.'

'Lothair . . .' I repeated.

'Monsieur le Comte. It is a family name, mademoiselle. There have always been Lothairs in the family.'

'It is a king's name,' I said. 'That is why.' She looked puzzled and I said quickly: 'I'm sorry. Pray go on.'

'The Comte had his mistress as Frenchmen do. No doubt he was more fond of her than of his affianced bride, but she was not suitable to be his wife, and so my Françoise married him.'

'You were her nurse too?'

'I came to her when she was three days old, and was with her till the end.'

'And now Geneviève has taken her place in your affections?'

'I trust to be with her always as I was with her mother. When it happened

I couldn't believe it. Why should it have happened to my Françoise? Why should she have taken her own life? It was unlike her.'

'Perhaps she was unhappy.'

'She did not hope for the impossible.'

'Did she know of his mistress?'

'Mademoiselle, in France these things are accepted. She was resigned. She feared him; and I fancied she was glad of those visits to Paris. When he was there . . . he was not in the château.'

'It does not sound to me like a happy marriage.'

'She accepted it.'

'And yet . . . she died.'

'She did not kill herself.' The old woman put her hand hands over her eyes and whispered as though to herself: 'No, she did *not* kill herself.'

'But wasn't that the verdict?'

She turned on me almost fiercely. 'What other verdict could there be . . . except murder?'

'I heard it was an overdose of laudanum. How did she get it?'

'She often had toothache. I had the laudanum in my little cupboard and I used to give it to her. It soothed the toothache and sent her to sleep.'

'Perhaps she accidentally took too much.'

'She did not mean to kill herself. I am sure of it. But that was what they said. They had to . . . hadn't they . . . for the sake of Monsieur le Comte?'

'Nounou,' I said, 'are you trying to tell me that the Comte murdered his wife?'

She stared at me as though startled. 'You cannot say I said that, mademoiselle. I said no such thing. You are putting words into my mouth.'

'But if she did not kill herself . . . then someone must have.'

She turned to the table and poured out two cups of coffee.

'Drink this, mademoiselle, and you will feel better. You are overwrought.'

I could have told her that in spite of my recent unpleasant experience I was less overwrought than she, but I wanted to glean as much as I could, and I realized that I was more likely to do so from her than from anyone else.

She gave me the cup and then drew a chair up to the sofa and sat down beside me.

'Mademoiselle, I want you to understand what a cruel thing this was which happened to my little Geneviève. I want you to forgive her . . . to help her.'

'Help her? *I*?'

'Yes, you can. If you will forgive her. If you will please not tell her father.'

'She is afraid of him. I sensed that.'

Nounou nodded. 'He paid attention to you at dinner. She told me. And in a different way he paid attention to the pretty young governess. Do please understand. It is something to do with her mother's death. It brings it back to her. You see, there is gossip and she knew that there was another woman.'

'Does she hate her father?'

'It is a strange relationship, mademoiselle. He is so aloof. Sometimes she might not be there, for all the notice he takes of her. At others he seems to take a delight in taunting her. It's as though he dislikes her, as though he's disappointed in her. If he would show her a little affection . . .' She lifted her shoulders. 'He is a strange, hard man, mademoiselle, and since the scandals he has become more so.'

'Perhaps he does not know what is said of him. Who would dare tell him of these rumours?'

'No one. But he is aware. He has been different since her death. He is no monk, mademoiselle, but he seems to have a contempt for women. Sometimes I think he is a most unhappy man.'

Perhaps, I thought, it is not very good taste to discuss the master of the house with one of his servants; but I was avidly curious and could not have stopped myself had I wanted to. This was something else I was discovering about myself. I refused to listen to my conscience.

'I wonder he has not married again,' I said. 'Surely a man in his position would want a son.'

'I do not think he will marry again, mademoiselle. It is for that reason that he sent for Monsieur Philippe.'

'So he *sent* for Philippe?'

'Not long ago. I dare say Monsieur Philippe will be expected to marry and his son will have everything.'

'I find that very hard to understand.'

'Monsieur le Comte *is* hard to understand, mademoiselle. I have heard that he lives very gaily in Paris. Here he is much alone. He is melancholy and seems to take pleasure only in the discomfort of everyone else.'

'What a charming man!' I said scornfully.

'Ah, life is not easy at the château. And most difficult of all for Geneviève.' She laid her hand on mine; it was cold. I knew in that moment how dearly she loved her charge and how anxious she was. 'There is nothing wrong with her,' she insisted. 'These tantrums of hers . . . she will grow out of them. There was nothing wrong with her mother. A gentler, sweeter girl it would be difficult to find.'

'Don't worry,' I said, 'I shall not mention what happened to her father nor to anyone. But I think I should speak to her.'

Nounou's face cleared. 'Yes, you speak to her . . . and if you should be in conversation with Monsieur le Comte . . . and could tell him . . . say how clever she is at speaking English . . . how gentle she is . . . how calm . . .'

'Her English would quickly improve, I'm sure. But I could scarcely call her calm.'

'Because it is said her mother took her own life, people are inclined to say she is highly strung.'

I thought she certainly was but did not say so. Oddly enough Nounou had brought me here to soothe me and I was ending by soothing her.

'Françoise was the most natural, normal little girl you could have met.' She set down her cup and going to the other side of the room returned with a wooden box inlaid with mother-of-pearl.

'I keep some of her things in here. I look at them sometimes to remind me. She was such a good child. Her governesses were delighted with her. I often tell Geneviève how good she was.'

She opened the box and took out a book bound in red leather. 'She pressed her flowers in this. She was fond of flowers. She'd roam through the fields gathering them. And she would pick some from the gardens. There, look at that forget-me-not. You see this handkerchief? She did that for me. Such pretty embroidery. She would embroider for me for Christmas and fête days and she'd always hide it when I came near to keep it a surprise. Such a good, quiet girl. Girls like that don't take their lives. She was good, and she was religious too. She had a way of saying her prayers that would make your heart ache; she used to decorate the chapel here herself. She would have thought it a sin to take her life.'

'Did she have brothers and sisters?'

'No, she was an only child. Her mother was . . . not strong. I nursed her too. She died when Françoise was nine years old, and Françoise was eighteen when she herself married.'

'And she was quite happy to marry?'

'I do not think she knew what marriage meant. I remember the night of the *dîner contrat*. You understand, mademoiselle? Perhaps you do not have this in England? But here in France when two people are to marry, there are the contracts to be talked of and agreed on; and when this is done there is the *dîner contrat* – the dinner at the bride's house, and there she dines with her family and the bridegroom and some members of his family, and afterwards the contracts are signed. She is very happy then, I think. She would be the Comtesse de la Talle and the de la Talles are the most important family – and the richest – for miles. It was a good match, an achievement. Then there was the civil marriage and after that the marriage in church.'

'And after that she was less happy?'

'Ah, life cannot be all that a young girl dreams, mademoiselle.'

'Particularly married to the Comte de la Talle.'

'As you have said, mademoiselle.' She held out the box to me. 'But you see what a sweet girl she was, her pleasures so simple. It was a shock to her to marry a man like the Comte.'

'The sort of shock many young girls have to face.'

'You speak truth, mademoiselle. She used to write in her little books, she called them. She like to keep an account of the things that happened. I keep the little books.' She went to a cupboard, unlocked it with a key which dangled from a bunch at her waist, and took out a small note-book. 'This is the first. See how good her handwriting is.'

I opened the book and read: 'May 1st. Prayers with Papa and the servants. I repeated the collect to him and he said I had made progress. I went to the kitchen and watched Marie baking the bread. She gave me a piece of sugar cake and said not to tell because she was not supposed to be baking sugar cake.'

'A sort of diary,' I commented.

'She was so young. Not more than seven. How many of seven can write as well? Let me get you more coffee, mademoiselle. Look at the book. I often read it. It brings her back to me.'

I turned the pages, glancing at the large childish handwriting. 'I think I will make a tray-cloth for Nounou. It will take a long time but if it is not finished in time for her birthday she can have it for Christmas.' 'Papa talked to me to-day after prayers. He said I must always be good and try to forget myself.' 'I saw Mama to-day. She did not know who I was. Papa talked to me afterwards and said that she might not be with us much longer.' 'I have blue silks for the tray-cloth. I will find some pink as well. Nounou nearly saw it to-day. That was very exciting.' 'I heard Papa praying in his room yesterday. He called me in and made me pray with him. Kneeling hurts my knees, but Papa is so good he does not notice.' 'Papa said he will show me his greatest treasure on my next birthday. I shall be eight. I do wonder what it is.' 'I wish there were children to play with. Marie said that in the house where she used to work there were nine. All those brothers and sisters would be nice. There would be one who was my special one.' 'Marie made a cake for my birthday. I went to the kitchen to watch her make it.' 'I thought Papa's treasure would be pearls and rubies but it is only an old robe with a hood. It's black and smells fusty after being shut up. Papa said I must not mistake the shadow for the substance.'

Nounou was standing over me. 'It's rather sad,' I said. 'She was a lonely child.'

'But good. You can learn that. That brings her to life. She had a sweet temper. And it comes through, doesn't it? She accepts things as they are – do you know what I mean?'

'Yes, I think I know.'

'Not the sort, you see, to take her own life. There was nothing hysterical about her. And really Geneviève is the same . . . at heart.'

I was silent, sipping the coffee she had brought me. I felt drawn towards her because of the deep devotion she had felt to the mother and daughter. I sensed in a way that she was trying to win me to her point of view.

In that case I should be frank with her.

'I think I ought to tell you,' I said, 'that on the first day I was here Geneviève took me to see her mother's grave.'

'She often goes there,' said Nounou quickly, lights of fear darting to her eyes.

'She did it in a peculiar way. She said she was taking me to see her mother . . . and I thought that I was going to be taken to a living woman.'

Nounou nodded, her eyes averted.

'Then she said that her father had murdered her mother.'

Nounou's face wrinkled in fear.

She laid her hand on my arm. 'But you understand, don't you? The shock of finding her . . . her own mother. And then the gossip. It was *natural*, wasn't it?'

'I shouldn't like to think it was natural for a child to accuse her father of murdering her mother.'

'The shock . . .' she repeated. 'She needs *help*, mademoiselle. Think of this household. The death . . . the whispers in the château . . . the gossip outside. I know that you are a *sensible* woman. I know that you will want to do all you can.'

The hands were clutching at my arm; the lips moved as though mouthing words that she dared not say.

She was a frightened woman and because of my recent experience at the hands of her charge she was asking my help.

I said cautiously: 'It would certainly have been a great shock. She must be treated with care. Her father does not seem to realize this.'

Nounou's face twisted in lines of bitterness. She hates him, I thought. She hates him for what he is doing to her daughter . . . and what he did to his wife.

'But *we* realize it,' said Nounou. I was touched and I put out my hand and pressed hers.

It was as though we made a pact then. Her face brightened and she said: 'We've let our coffee get cold. I'll make some more.'

And there in that little room I knew that I was being caught up in the life of the château.

Chapter Four

I told myself it was not my affair to assess whether or not the master of the house was a murderer, but to discover how much restoration the paintings needed and what methods should be used to produce the best results; and during the weeks that followed I became absorbed in my work.

Guests came to the château, which meant that I was not invited to dinner. I was not really displeased about this, as the Comte's attitude towards me disturbed me. I felt that he was almost hoping that I would fail. I feared that he might undermine my confidence, and while I was occupied in my delicate task I had to believe it would be a complete success.

But after leaving me alone for a few days he came to the gallery one morning when I was at work.

'Oh, dear, Mademoiselle Lawson,' he exclaimed as he looked at the picture before me. 'What *are* you doing?'

I was startled, for the picture had been reacting perfectly to my treatment and I felt the colour rush to my cheeks. I was about to protest angrily when he went on: 'You are going to restore such colour to this painting that you will remind us all over again of those tiresome emeralds.'

He was amused to see my relief that he had not implied criticism of my work.

I said sharply to hide my embarrassment: 'Then you are becoming convinced that a woman might have some ability?'

'I always suspected you had great ability. Who but a woman of character and determination would have come to us in the first place, eager to defend what is – I am sure misguidedly – called the weaker sex?'

'My only wish is to do a good job.'

'If all the militant females in the past had had your good sense, what a lot of trouble might have been saved!'

'I hope I shall be able to save you trouble, for I can assure you that had these paintings been neglected much longer . . .'

'I am aware of it. That was why I decided to ask your father here. Alas, he could not come. But in his place we have his daughter. How fortunate we are!'

I turned to the painting, but I was afraid to touch it. I dared not make a false move. Work such as this needed complete absorption.

He came and stood close to me, and although he pretended to be studying the picture, I believe he was watching me.

'It seems so interesting,' he said. 'You must explain to me.'

'I have carried out one or two tests, and naturally before beginning I have made sure that I am using what, in my opinion, is the best treatment.'

'And what is the best treatment?' His eyes were fixed on my face, and again I felt the uncomfortable colour in my cheeks.

'I'm using a mild alcohol solvent. It wouldn't be active on a hardened layer of oil paint, but this paint has been mixed with a soft resin.'

'How clever of you!'

'It is part of my work.'

'At which you are such an expert.'

'Are you convinced of that then?' My voice sounded a little too eager and I felt my lips harden to counteract the effect my remarks might have had.

'You are in the process of convincing me. You like this picture, Mademoiselle Lawson?'

'It's interesting. It's not one of your best. It doesn't compare, of course, with the Fragonards or Bouchers. But I think the artist was a master of colour. The alizarin is beautiful. He is daring in his use of colour. His brush strokes are a little harsh, but . . .' I broke off because I sensed he was laughing at me. 'I'm afraid I become rather boring when I talk about paintings.'

'You are too self-critical, Mademoiselle Lawson.'

I! Self-critical! It was the first time anyone had ever told me that. And yet I knew it was true. I knew that I was like a hedgehog, putting out my prickles in self-defence. So I had betrayed myself.

'You will soon have restored this picture,' he went on.

'And then I shall know whether you have decided if I am worthy to be given this commission.'

'I'm sure you have no doubt what the verdict will be,' he answered, and smiling, left me.

A few days later the picture was finished and he came to pass judgment. He stood for some seconds frowning at it, and I felt my spirits sinking although before he had come in I had felt pleased with my work, knowing I had done a good job. The colours were startling and the fabric of the gown and the artist's facility in handling his paint reminded me of Gainsborough. All this had been hidden when I had started the work; now it was revealed.

And he stood there looking dismayed.

'So,' I said, 'you are not pleased?'

He shook his head.

'Monsieur le Comte, I don't know what you expect, but I assure you that anyone who *understands* painting . . .'

He turned his attention from the picture to me; he had raised those proud eyebrows very slightly; his mouth was curved in a smile which belied the astonishment his eyes were trying to convey.

'. . . as you do,' he finished for me. 'Ah, yes, if I possessed that talent, I should cry: "This is a miracle. That which was hidden has now been shown to us in all its glory!" It's true. It's magnificent. But I'm still thinking of those emeralds. You have no idea what trouble they have caused us. Now, due to you, Mademoiselle Lawson, there will be new treasure hunts. There will be new speculations.'

I knew that he was teasing me and I told myself fiercely that he had been hoping I should fail. Now he was reluctant to admit that I had succeeded admirably, and as he couldn't deny it, was talking about his emeralds.

It was typical of the man, I told myself; and then quickly added a reminder that whatever he was, was no concern of mine. *He* was of no importance to me; I was only interested in his paintings.

'And as far as the picture is concerned you have no complaints?' I asked coolly.

'You live up to your credentials.'

'Then you will wish me to continue with the rest of the paintings?'

An expression I did not understand flickered across his face. 'I should be very disappointed if you did not.'

I felt radiant. I had won.

But my triumph was not complete, for as he stood there smiling at me, I knew he was reminding me how well aware he was of my doubts and fears and everything I had sought to hide.

Neither of us had noticed that Geneviève had come into the gallery, and as she did not make her presence known she could have been there for some seconds watching us.

The Comte saw her first. 'What do you want, Geneviève?' he asked.

'I . . . I came to see how Mademoiselle Lawson was getting on with the picture.'

'Then come and see.'

She came, looking sullen as she so often did in company.

'There!' he said. 'Is it not a revelation?'

She did not answer.

'Mademoiselle Lawson expects to be complimented on her work. You remember what the picture was like before.'

'No, I don't.'

'Such lack of artistic appreciation! You must try to persuade Mademoiselle Lawson to teach you to understand pictures while she is with us.'

'So . . . she is going to stay?'

His voice changed suddenly. It was almost caressing. 'I hope,' he said, 'for a long time. Because you see there are so many in the château who need her attentions.'

Geneviève gave me a swift glance; her eyes were hard; they looked like black stones. She turned to the picture and said: 'Perhaps if she is so clever she will find the emeralds for us.'

'You see Mademoiselle Lawson, it is exactly as I said.'

'They certainly look magnificent,' I replied.

'No doubt due to the artist's ... er ... facility with paint?'

I cared nothing for his mockery, nor for the brooding resentment of his daughter. It was these beautiful paintings which were my concern, and the fact that they were now shrouded in the fog of neglect only made my project the more exciting.

Even in that moment he knew what I was thinking, for he bowed and said: 'I will leave you, Mademoiselle Lawson. I can see you are eager to be alone ... with the pictures.' He signed to Geneviève to go with him; and when they had gone I stood there in the gallery and let my eyes revel first in one and then in another.

I had rarely been so excited in my life.

Now that I was staying at the château to complete the work I decided to take advantage of the Comte's offer and make use of the stables, which would enable me to see more of the country. I had already explored the little town; had drunk coffee in the *pâtisserie*, chatting with the genial but inquisitive proprietress, who was pleased to welcome anyone from the château. She had talked with reverence but sly knowingness of Monsieur le Comte, with respectful contempt of Monsieur Philippe, and with pity for Mademoiselle Geneviève. And mademoiselle was there to clean the pictures! Well, well, that was very interesting, that was, and she hoped mademoiselle would come again and next time perhaps take a little of the *gâteau de la Maison* which was highly thought of in Gaillard.

I had wandered through the market and had seen the glances in my direction; I had visited the ancient *hôtel de ville* and the church.

So the prospect of going farther afield was pleasant and I was particularly pleased that I was expected at the stables.

A suitable mount was found for me named Bonhomme and we approved of each other from the beginning.

I was surprised and pleased when Geneviève asked me if she could accompany me one morning. She was in one of her demure moods and as we rode I asked her why she had been so foolish as to shut me in the *oubliette*.

'Well, you weren't afraid, so you said, and I didn't think it would hurt you.'

'It was a stupid thing to do. Suppose Nounou hadn't found out!'

'I should have rescued you after a while.'

'After a while! Do you know some people might have died of fright?'

'Died!' she said fearfully. 'No one dies of being shut up.'

'Some nervous people might have died of fright.'

'But *you* never would.' She regarded me intently. 'You didn't tell my father. I thought you might . . . as you and he are so friendly.'

She rode on a little way in advance, and when we returned to the stables she said casually: 'I'm not allowed to ride alone. I always have to take one of the grooms with me. There was no one to ride with me this morning, so I shouldn't have had a ride if you hadn't come with me.'

'I'm glad to have been of service,' I replied coolly.

I met Philippe when I was in the gardens and I fancied he knew I was there and had come out purposely to talk to me.

'Congratulations,' he said. 'I've been looking at the picture. The difference is remarkable. It's hardly recognizable.'

I glowed with pleasure. How different, I thought, from the Comte. He is genuinely pleased.

'I'm so glad you think so.'

'Who could help thinking so! It's miraculous. I'm delighted – not only that the picture is a success but that you've proved you could do it.'

'How kind of you!'

'I'm afraid I was rather ungracious when you arrived. I was so taken by surprise and not sure what would be expected of me.'

'You were not ungracious, and I can well understand your surprise.'

'You see, this was my cousin's affair, and naturally I wanted to do what he would wish.'

'Naturally. And it is good of you to take such an interest.'

He wrinkled his brow. 'I feel a kind of responsibility . . .' he began. 'I hope that you will not regret coming here.'

'Indeed no. The work is proving to be most interesting.'

'Oh, yes . . . yes . . . the work.'

He began to speak rather hurriedly of the gardens and insisted on showing me the sculptured decorations which had been done by Le Brun soon after he had completed the frescoes in the Hall of Mirrors at Versailles.

'Fortunately they escaped at the time of the Revolution,' he explained; and I sensed his reverence for everything connected with the château. I liked him for it – also for his gracious apology for anything he might have said to hurt me during our first interview and his obvious pleasure in the fact that I had succeeded.

My days had formed themselves into a pattern. I was in the gallery early and worked steadily all through the morning. After lunch I usually went out, returning before dusk, which at this time of the year was soon after four o'clock. Then I would occupy myself with mixing solutions or reading notes of past experiments which filled my time until after dinner. Sometimes I took this alone in my room, but on several occasions Mademoiselle Dubois had asked me to dine in her room. I could not refuse these invitations although I wanted to; I listened to her life history: how she was the daughter of a lawyer, brought up not to work, how her father had been let down through a partner, how he had died of a broken heart and how she, being penniless, had been obliged to become a governess. Told in her self-pitying

way the story seemed incredibly dull and I made up my mind not to inflict
boredom on her by telling her my own.

After dinner I would read one of the books I had found in the library, for
Philippe had told me that the Comte would be pleased if I made use of
anything I wanted there.

As the days passed through that November, I was on the periphery of the
château life, aware of it yet not aware of it, just as I heard the music in my
room – conscious of it, yet only now and then did I know what was being
played.

One day when I had left the château on Bonhomme I met Jean Pierre on
horseback. He greeted me with customary gaiety and asked whether I was
going to call on his family. I told him I was.

'Ride with me first over to the St. Vallient vineyards and then we will go
back together.'

I had never been St. Vallient way and agreed. I always enjoyed his
company and the Bastide household never seemed the same without him.
He had a vitality and gaiety which appealed to me.

We talked of Christmas, which would soon be with us.

'You will spend the day with us, mademoiselle?' he asked.

'Is that a formal invitation?'

'You know that I am never formal. It is just a heartfelt wish on behalf of
the family that you will honour us.'

I remarked that I should be delighted and it was good of them to want
me.

'The motives are entirely selfish, mademoiselle.' With one of those quick
gestures which were characteristic of him he leaned towards me and touched
my arm. I met his warm glance unwaveringly, telling myself that his manner
of making me feel I was important to him was merely the natural courtesy
Frenchmen showed automatically towards all women.

'I shall tell you nothing of our Christmas celebrations now,' he said. 'It
must all be a surprise to you.'

When we reached the St. Vallient vineyards I was introduced to Monsieur
Durand, who was in charge of them. His wife brought out wine and little
cakes, which were delicious, and Jean Pierre and Monsieur Durand discussed
the quality of the wine. Then Monsieur Durand took Jean Pierre off to talk
business while his wife was left to look after me.

She knew a great deal about me, for clearly the affairs of the château
were the pivot round which gossip revolved. What did I think of the château,
the Comte? I gave guarded answers and she evidently thought she would
glean little from me so she talked of her own affairs, how anxious she was
on Monsieur Durand's behalf because he was too old to continue with his
work.

'The anxieties! Each year it is the same, and since the big trouble ten
years ago, it has not been good here at St. Vallient. Monsieur Jean Pierre
is a wizard. The château wine is becoming as good as it ever was. I trust
soon that Monsieur le Comte will allow my husband to retire.'

'Must he await permission from Monsieur le Comte?'

'Indeed yes, mademoiselle. Monsieur le Comte will give him his cottage.

How I long for that day! I will keep a few chickens and a cow . . . perhaps two; and that will be the best for my husband. It is too much for an old man. How can he, when he is no longer young, fight all the hazards? Who but the good God can say when the frost is coming to destroy the vines? And when the summers are too humid there are always the pests. The spring frosts are the worst, though. The day will be fine and then the frost comes like a thief in the night to rob us of our grapes. And if there is not enough sun then the grapes are sour. It is a life for a young man . . . such as Monsieur Jean Pierre.'

'I hope then that you will soon be allowed to retire.'

'It is all in the hands of God, mademoiselle.'

'Or, perhaps,' I suggested, 'Monsieur le Comte.'

She lifted her hands as though to say that was the same thing.

After a while Jean Pierre returned and we left St. Vallient. We talked of the Durands and he said that the poor old man had had his day and it was time he retired.

'I was hearing how he had to wait for the Comte's decision.'

'Oh yes,' replied Jean Pierre. 'Everything here depends on him.'

'You resent it?'

'The days of despotic rulers are supposed to have ended.'

'You could always break away. He could not prevent you.'

'Leave our home?'

'If you hate him so much . . .'

'Did I give that impression?'

'When you speak of him, your voice hardens and there is a look in your eyes . . .'

'It is nothing. I am a proud man, perhaps too proud. This place is my home as much as his. My family has been here through centuries just as his has. The only difference is that his lived in the château. But we were all brought up in the shadows of the château, and this is our home . . . just as it is his.'

'I understand that.'

'If I do not like the Comte I am merely in the fashion. What does he care for this place? He is hardly ever here. He prefers his mansion in Paris. He does not deign to notice us. We are not worthy of his attention. But I would never let him drive me from my home. I work for him because I must and I try not to see him or think of him. You will feel the same. I expect you already do.'

He began to sing suddenly; he had a pleasant tenor voice which vibrated with emotion.

> *'Qui sont-ils, les gens qui sont riches?*
> *Sont-ils plus que moi qui n'ai rien?*
> *Je cours, je vas, je vir, je viens;*
> *Je n'ai pas peur de perd' ma fortune.*
> *Je cours, je vas, je vir, je viens,*
> *Pas peur de perdre mon bien.'*

He finished and smiled at me, waiting for my comments.

'I like that,' I said.

'I am so pleased; so do I.'

He was looking at me so intently that I lightly touched my horse's flank. Bonhomme broke into a gallop. Jean Pierre was close behind me; and so we returned to Gaillard.

As we passed the vineyard I saw the Comte. He could only have come from the vineyard buildings. He inclined his head in greeting when he saw us. 'You wished to see me, Monsieur le Comte?' asked Jean Pierre.

'Another time will do,' answered the Comte, and rode on.

'Should you have been there when he called?' I asked.

'No. He knew I was going to St. Vallient. It was on his instructions that I went.'

He was puzzled, but as we passed the buildings on the way to the Bastide house Gabrielle came out. Her cheeks were flushed and she looked very pretty.

'Gabrielle,' called Jean Pierre. 'Here is Mademoiselle Lawson.'

She smiled at me rather absently, I thought.

'The Comte called, I see,' said Jean Pierre. His manner had changed also. 'What did he want?'

'To look at some figures . . . that was all. He will call another time to see you.'

Jean Pierre wrinkled his brows and he kept looking at his sister.

Madame Bastide welcomed me as warmly as ever, but I noticed all the time I was there how absentminded Gabrielle was and that even Jean Pierre was subdued.

While I was working in the gallery next morning the Comte looked in.

'And how is the work progressing?' he asked.

'Satisfactorily, I think,' I answered.

He looked quizzically at the picture on which I was working. I pointed out the surface coating, which was brittle and discoloured, and said that I had come to the conclusion that the varnish was responsible for the buckling of the paint.

'I'm sure you're right,' he said lightly. 'I am glad too that you don't spend all your time working.'

I thought he was referring to the fact that he had seen me riding on the previous day when I might have been working in the gallery and I retorted hotly: 'My father always said that it was not wise to work after luncheon. The work demands great concentration, and after having worked all the morning one is possibly not as alert as one should be.'

'You looked surprisingly alert when we met yesterday.'

'Alert?' I repeated the word foolishly.

'At least,' he went on, 'as though the amenities we have to offer are as interesting outside the château as in.'

'You mean the horse? You did say I might ride if I had the opportunity.'

'I am delighted that you are able to find opportunities . . . and friends with whom to share them.'

I was startled. Surely he could not object to my being friendly with Jean Pierre.

'It is kind of you to take an interest in how I spend my leisure time.'

'Well, you know I happen to have a great regard for . . . my pictures.'

We walked round the gallery studying them, but I fancied he was not doing so with real attention; and I believed he was critical of my riding – not with Jean Pierre, but riding when I might have been working. The idea made me indignant. I had quoted an estimate for the work, but of course if I completed it quickly I would cease to live at the château and so cease to be a burden on the household.

I blurted out: 'If you are not satisfied with the speed at which I am working . . .'

He spun round as though delighted and smiled at me across the distance which separated us. 'What gave you such an idea, Mademoiselle Lawson?'

'I thought . . I imagined . . .'

His head was slightly on one side. He was discovering traits in my character of which I myself had not been aware. He was saying: See how quickly you take offence! Why? Because you feel yourself to be vulnerable . . . very vulnerable?

'Then,' I went on lamely, 'you are satisfied with what I am doing?'

'Immensely so, Mademoiselle Lawson.'

I turned back to my work and he continued to walk round the gallery. I was not looking when he went out and shut the door quietly behind him.

I could not work comfortably for the rest of that morning.

Geneviève came running after me when I was on my way to the stables.

'Mademoiselle, will you ride over to Carrefour with me?'

'Carrefour?'

'My grandfather's house. If you won't come I shall have to take one of the grooms. I'm going to see my grandfather. I'm sure he'd like to meet you.'

If I had been inclined to refuse such an ungracious invitation the mention of her grandfather decided me.

Through Nounou's conversation and the little note-books which Françoise had written I had a clear picture of a neat little girl with her innocent secrets and her charming ways. Now the opportunity to meet the little girl's father and to see the house which formed a background to the life portrayed in those note-books was irresistible.

Geneviève sat her horse with the ease of one who had been in the saddle from early childhood. Occasionally she pointed out landmarks to me and at one spot pulled up so that we could look back at the château.

It was an impressive sight seen from the distance; here one could get a better conception of the symmetry of those ancient embattled walls, the massive buttresses, the cylindrical towers and the sharp conical points which rose from the roofs. There it stood in the midst of the vineyards; I could see the church spire and the *hôtel de ville* standing guard over the houses of the little town.

'You like it?' asked Geneviève.

'I think it's a lovely sight.'

'It all belongs to Papa but it never will to me. I should have been a son. Then Papa would have been pleased with me.'

'If you are good and well-mannered he will be pleased with you,' I replied sententiously.

She looked at me with the scorn I felt I deserved. 'Really, mademoiselle, you do talk just like a governess. They always say things they don't mean. They tell you you should do this . . . but they don't always do it themselves.' She looked at me sideways, laughing to herself. 'Oh, I don't mean Esquilles. She should never do anything. But there are some . . .'

I remembered suddenly the governess whom she had shut in the *oubliette* and I did not pursue the conversation.

She touched her horse's flanks and galloped ahead of me, a charming picture with her hair flying out from under her riding hat. I came up beside her.

'If Papa had had a son we need not have Cousin Philippe here. That would have been pleasant.'

'I am sure he is always kind to you.'

She gave me a sidelong glance.

'At one time I was going to marry him.'

'Oh . . . I see. And not now?'

She shook her head. 'I don't care. You don't imagine I should want to marry Philippe, do you?'

'He is considerably older than you.'

'Fourteen years . . . just double.'

'But I suppose as you grew older the disparity would not seem so great.'

'Well, Papa decided against it. Tell me, why do you think he did that, mademoiselle? You know so much.'

'I assure you I know nothing of your father's intentions. I know nothing of your father . . .' I was surprised at the heat in which I had spoken, for it was quite uncalled for.

'So you don't know everything! I'll tell you something. Philippe was very angry when he knew Papa wouldn't let him marry me.'

She tossed her head and smiled complacently so I retorted: 'Perhaps he does not know *you* very well.'

That made her laugh. 'It's nothing to do with me really,' she admitted. 'It's being Papa's daughter. No, when my mother was . . . when my mother died, Papa changed his mind. He changed a great deal then. I think he wanted to insult Philippe.'

'Why should he want to insult Philippe?'

'Oh . . . just because it amuses him. He hates people.'

'I am sure that is not the truth. People don't hate – indiscriminately – without reason.'

'My father is not like ordinary people.' She spoke almost proudly – her voice unconsciously vibrating with hatred, a queer inverted hatred which was touched with respect.

'We are all different,' I said quickly.

Her laughter was high-pitched and I noticed that it took on this quality when she talked of her father.

'He hates me,' she went on. 'I am like my mother, you see. Nounou says I grow more like her every day. I remind him of her.'

'You have listened to too much gossip.'

'Perhaps *you* haven't listened to enough.'

'Listening to gossip is not a very admirable way of spending the time.'

That made her laugh again. 'All I can say, miss, is that you don't always spend your time admirably.'

I felt myself flush with that annoyance which a home truth inspires.

She pointed at me. 'You love to gossip, miss. Never mind. I like you for it. I couldn't *bear* you if you were as good and proper as you make out to be.'

'Why don't you speak to your father naturally – not as though you're afraid of him,' I said.

'But everybody's afraid of him.'

'I am not.'

'Really, miss?'

'Why should I be? If he doesn't like my work he can say so and I should go away and never see him again.'

'Yes, it might be easy for you. My mother was afraid of him . . . terribly afraid of him.'

'Did she tell you so?'

'Not in words, but I knew. And you know what happened to her.'

I said: 'Isn't it time we went on? We shan't be back before dark if we dally like this.'

She looked at me pleadingly for a moment and then said: 'Yes, but do you think when people die . . . not like ordinary die but when they are . . . Do you think that some people don't rest in their graves? Do you think they come back looking for . . .'

I said sharply: 'Geneviève, what are you saying?'

'Miss,' she said, and it was like a cry for help, 'sometimes at night I wake up startled and I think I hear noises in the château.'

'My dear Geneviève, everyone awakes startled now and then. It's usually a bad dream.'

'Footsteps . . . tapping . . . I hear it. I do. I *do*. And I lie there shivering . . . expecting to see . . .'

'Your mother?'

This girl was frightened; she was stretching out to me for help. It was no use telling her she was speaking nonsense, that there were no ghosts. That would not help her at all because she would think it was merely grown-up talk to soothe the children.

I said: 'Listen, Geneviève, suppose there are ghosts, suppose your mother did come back?'

She nodded, her eyes enormous with interest.

'She loved you, didn't she?'

I saw her hands tighten on the reins. 'Oh, yes, she loved me . . . no one loved me like she did.'

'She would never have hurt you, would she? Do you think that now she is dead she would have changed towards you?'

I saw the relaxed expression; I was pleased with myself. I had found the comfort she so desperately needed.

I went on: 'When you were a child she looked after you: if she saw you about to fall she would rush to pick you up, wouldn't she?' She nodded. 'Why should she change towards you because she is dead? I think what you hear is creaking boards in a very old house, the rattling of doors, windows ... anything like that. There could be mice ... But just suppose there are ghosts. Don't you think your mother would be there to *protect* you from harm?'

'Yes,' she said, her eyes shining. 'Yes, she would. She loved me.'

'Remember that if you awake startled in the night.'

'Oh, yes,' she said. 'I will.'

I was pleased, and felt that to continue the conversation might spoil the effect I had made so I moved on and in a short while we were cantering side by side.

We did not speak again until we reached Maison Carrefour.

It was an old house standing back from the crossroads. A thick stone wall surrounded it, but the elaborately-wrought iron gates were open. We went through these gates and under a wide archway and were in an inner courtyard. There were green shutters at the windows, and I was immediately conscious of a deep silence. I had imagined the home of the bright little girl who had recorded her daily life in her note-books to be different from this.

Geneviève glanced at me quickly to guess my reactions, but I hoped I betrayed nothing.

We left our horses in the stables and Geneviève led me to a door.

She lifted the heavy knocker and I heard the sound reverberating through the lower part of the house. There was silence; then came the shuffle of footsteps, and a manservant appeared.

'Good day, Maurice,' said Geneviève. 'Mademoiselle Lawson has come with me to-day.'

The courtesies exchanged, we were in the hall, the floor of which was covered with mosaic tiles.

'How is my grandfather to-day, Maurice?' asked Geneviève.

'Much the same, mademoiselle. I will see if he is ready.'

The manservant disappeared for a few moments before he came back to the hall and said that his master would see us now.

There was no fire in the room and the chill struck me as I entered. At one time it must have been beautiful, for it was perfectly proportioned. The ceiling was carved and there was an inscription on it which I couldn't see clearly except that it was in medieval French; the closed shutters kept out all but the minimum of light and the room was austerely furnished. In a wheelchair sat an old man. He startled me for he was more like a corpse than a living human being; his eyes were sunken in his cadaverous face and were too brilliant. In his hands he held a book which he had closed as we entered. He was wearing a brown dressing-gown tied with a brown cord.

'Grandfather,' said Geneviève, 'I have come to see you.'

'My child,' he answered in a surprisingly firm voice, and held out a thin white hand on which blue veins stood out.

'And,' went on Geneviève,' I have brought Mademoiselle Lawson who has come from England and is cleaning my father's pictures.'

The eyes which were all that seemed alive about him were trying to probe my mind.

'Mademoiselle Lawson, you will forgive me not rising. I can do so only with great difficulty and the help of my servants. I am pleased you have come with my granddaughter. Geneviève, bring a chair for Mademoiselle Lawson . . . and for yourself.'

'Yes, Grandfather.'

We sat before him. He was charmingly courteous; he asked me about my work, expressed great interest and said that Geneviève must show me his collection. Some of it might be in need of restoration. The thought of living, even temporarily, in such a house as this, depressed me. For all its mystery the château was alive. Alive! That was it. This was like a house of the dead.

Now and then he addressed Geneviève and I noticed how his eyes rested on her. He had given me his polite attention but the intentness of his scrutiny of her surprised me. He cares deeply for her, I thought. Why should she think herself unloved – for I had come to the conclusion that this was one of the main reasons for her bad behaviour – when she had such a doting grandparent.

He wanted to hear what she was doing, how she was progressing with her lessons. I was surprised that he spoke of Mademoiselle Dubois as though he knew her intimately while I had gathered from Geneviève that he had never actually met her. Nounou he knew well, of course, for she had once been part of his household, and he spoke of her as though she were an old friend.

'How is Nounou, Geneviève? I trust you are kind to her. Remember she is a good soul. Simple, perhaps, but she does her best. She always did. And she is good to you. Always remember that and treat her kindly, Geneviève.'

'Yes, Grandfather.'

'I hope you don't grow impatient with her.'

'Not often, Grandfather.'

'Sometimes?' He was alert, uneasy.

'Well, only a little. I just say: "You are a silly old woman".'

'That's unkind. Did you pray afterwards to the saints for forgiveness?'

'Yes, Grandfather.'

'It is no use asking for forgiveness if you commit the same sin immediately afterwards. Guard your temper, Geneviève. And if you are ever tempted to do foolish things remember the pain that causes.'

I wondered how much he knew of the wildness of his grand-daughter and whether Nounou paid him visits and told him. Did he know that she had shut me in the *oubliette*?

He sent for wine and the biscuits which were usually served with it. These were brought by an old woman whom I guessed to be one of the Labisses. She wore a white cap on her grey hair, and somewhat morosely set down the wine without a word. Geneviève murmured a greeting and the woman bobbed a curtsy and went out.

While we were drinking the wine the old man said: 'I had heard that the pictures were to be restored but I did not expect a lady to do them.'

I explained about my father's death and that I was completing his commitments.

'There was a little consternation at first,' I said, 'but the Comte seems pleased with my work.'

I saw his lips tighten and his hand clench on the rug.

'So ... he is pleased with you.' His voice and his whole expression changed. I saw that Geneviève was sitting on the edge of her chair nervously watching her grandfather.

'At least he implies that he is, by allowing me to continue with the pictures,' I said.

'I hope,' he began and his voice sank and I did not catch the rest of the sentence.

'I beg your pardon.'

He shook his head. The mention of the Comte's name had evidently upset him. So here was another who hated that man. What was it in him that inspired such fear and such hatred? Conversation became uneasy after that and Geneviève, seeking to escape, asked if she might show me the grounds.

We left the main hall and went through several passages until we came to a stone-floored kitchen; she took me through this to a garden.

'Your grandfather is pleased to see you,' I commented. 'I believe he would like you to come often to see him.'

'He doesn't notice. He forgets. He is very old and hasn't been the same since ... his stroke. His mind isn't clear.'

'Does your father know you come?'

'He doesn't ask.'

'You mean he never comes here?'

'He hasn't been since my mother died. Grandfather wouldn't want him, would he? Can you imagine my father here?'

'No,' I answered truthfully.

I looked back at the house and saw the curtains in an upper room move. We were being watched. Geneviève followed my gaze. 'That's Madame Labisse. She's wondering who you are. She doesn't like it the way it is now; she would like to go back to the old days. Then she was parlourmaid and Labisse was footman. I don't know what they are now. They wouldn't stay except for the fact that Grandfather has left them a legacy provided they're in his service when he dies.'

'It's a strange household,' I said.

'That's because Grandfather is only half-alive. He has been like it for three years. The doctor says he cannot live for many more years – so I suppose the Labisses think it worth while.'

Three years, I thought. That was the time of Françoise's death. Was he so affected that he had had a stroke? If he loved her as he obviously did his granddaughter, I could understand it.

'I know what you're thinking,' cried Geneviève. 'You're thinking that that was the time my mother died. Grandfather had his stroke a week before she died. Wasn't it strange . . . everyone was expecting him to die, but she was the one.'

How strange! She had died of an overdose of laudanum a week after her father had a stroke. Had it affected her so much that she had taken her life?

Geneviève had turned back to the house and I walked silently beside her. There was a door in the wall and she quickly passed through it holding it for me to do the same. We were in a small cobbled courtyard; it was very quiet here. Geneviève walked across the cobbles and I followed, feeling as though I were joining in a conspiracy.

We were standing in a dark lobby.

'Where is this?' I asked, but she put a hand to her lips.

'I want to show you something.'

She crossed the lobby and led the way to a door which she pushed open. It was a room bare of everything but a pallet bed and a prie-dieu and a wooden chest. The floor was of stone flags and there were no rugs or carpets.

'Grandfather's favourite room,' she said.

'It's like a monk's cell,' I said.

She nodded delightedly. She looked about her furtively and opened the chest.

'Geneviève,' I said, 'you have no right . . .'

But curiosity would not let me resist looking at what lay there. I thought in astonishment, it's a hair shirt. There was something else that made me shudder. A whip!

Geneviève let the lid of the chest fall.

'What do you think of this house, mademoiselle?' she asked. 'It is as interesting as the château, don't you think?'

'It is time we left,' I said. 'We must say good-bye to your grandfather.'

She was silent all the way home. As for myself I could not get that strange house out of my thoughts. It was like something that clings to the memory after a nightmare.

The guests who had been staying at the castle left and I was immediately aware of the change. I became less aloof from the life of the place. For instance when I was leaving the gallery one morning I came face to face with the Comte.

He said: 'Now that all the visitors have gone, you should dine with us now and then, Mademoiselle Lawson. *En famille*, you understand? I am sure you could enlighten us all on your favourite subject. Would you care to do so?'

I replied that it would be a pleasure.

'Well, join us to-night,' he said.

I felt elated as I went to my room. My encounters with him were always stimulating although often they left me tingling with rage. I took my black velvet dress and laid it on my bed, and while I was doing this there was a knock on my door and Geneviève came in.

'Are you going out to dinner to-night?' she asked.

'No, I'm dining with you.'

'You look pleased. Did Papa ask you?'

'It is a pleasure to receive an invitation when they are rather rare.'

She stroked the velvet thoughtfully. 'I like velvet,' she said.

'I was just going to the gallery,' I told her. 'Did you want to see me about something?'

'No, I only wanted to see you.'

'You can come to the gallery with me.'

'No, I don't want to.'

I went alone to the gallery and was there until it was time to change for dinner. I sent for hot water and washed in the *ruelle* in an absurd but happy state of expectation. But when I came to put on my dress I stared at it in horror. I could not believe what I saw. When I had laid it out it had been ready to slip on; now the skirt hung in jagged and uneven strips. Someone had ripped it from waist to hem; the bodice, too, had been slashed across.

I picked it up and stared at it in bewilderment and dismay.

'It's not possible,' I said aloud. Then I went to the bell-rope and pulled. Josette came hurrying to me. 'Why, mademoiselle ...'

As I held out the dress to her she clapped her hands over her mouth to stop the exclamation.

'What does it mean?' I demanded.

'Oh ... but it's wicked. Oh, but *why?*'

'I can't understand it,' I began.

'I didn't do it, mademoiselle. I swear I didn't do it. I only came to bring the hot water. It must have been done then.'

'I didn't think for a moment you did it, Josette. But I'm going to find out who did.'

She ran out crying almost hysterically: 'I didn't do it. I didn't do it. I won't be blamed.'

And I stood in my room staring at the ruined dress. Then I went to my wardrobe and took out the grey with the lavender stripe. I had only just hooked it up when Josette appeared dramatically waving a pair of scissors.

'I knew who'd done it,' she announced. 'I went to the schoolroom and found these ... just where she'd laid them down. Look, mademoiselle, pieces of velvet are still in them. See these little bits. They're velvet.'

I knew, as I had known almost as soon as I had seen the ruined dress. Geneviève. But why had she done this? Did she hate me so much?

I went along to Geneviève's room. She was sitting on her bed staring blankly before her while Nounou was pacing up and down crying.

'Why did you do it?' I asked.

'Because I wanted to.'

Nounou stood still staring at us.

'You behave like a baby. You don't think before you act, do you?'

'Yes, I do. I thought I'd like to do it, so when you went to the gallery, I went for my scissors.'

'And now you're sorry?'

'I'm not.'

'I am. I haven't many dresses.'

'You might wear it all cut up. It might be becoming. I'm sure some people would think so.' She began to laugh helplessly and I could see that she was near to tears.

'Stop it,' I commanded. 'It's a foolish way to behave.'

'It's the way to cut up a dress. Whish! You should have heard the scissors. It was lovely.' She went on laughing and Nounou put a hand to her shoulder only to have it shaken off.

I left them; it was useless to try to reason with her while she was in that mood.

The dinner to which I had looked forward was an uncomfortable meal. I was conscious all the time of Geneviève, who had appeared, sullen and silent. She was watching me furtively all through the meal, waiting, I knew, for me to betray her to her father.

I talked a little, mostly about the pictures and the château, but I felt I was being rather dull and disappointing to the Comte, who had wanted perhaps to provoke spirited answers to his teasing manner.

I was glad to escape to my room, which I did immediately the meal was over. I was turning over in my mind what I should do. I should have to reason with Geneviève; I should have to explain to her that she could not find lasting pleasure in behaving as she did.

It was while I was meditating about this that Mademoiselle Dubois came to my room.

'I must talk to you,' she said. 'What a commotion!'

'You've heard about my dress?'

'The whole household knows of it. Josette went to the *sommelier* and he went to the Comte. Mademoiselle Geneviève has played too many tricks.'

'And so . . . he knows.'

She regarded me slyly. 'Yes . . . he knows.'

'And Geneviève?'

'She's in her room cowering behind the skirts of Nounou. She'll be punished and she deserves it.'

'I can't think why she takes a delight in doing such things.'

'Mischief! Malice! She's jealous of your being asked to dine with the family and the Comte taking such an interest.'

'Naturally he would be interested in his pictures.'

She tittered. 'I've always been careful. Of course when I came here I had no idea what sort of place it was. A Comte . . . a château . . . it sounds wonderful. But when I heard those terrible stories, I was quite terrified. I was ready to pack my bags and go. But I decided to give it a chance, though I saw how dangerous it was. A man like the Comte, for instance . . .'

'I should not think you would be in any danger from him.'

'A man whose wife died like that! You are rather innocent, Mademoiselle Lawson. As a matter of fact I had to leave my last post because of the unwelcome attentions of the master of the house.'

She had grown quite pink with, I told myself cynically, the exertion of imagining herself desirable. I am sure all the near-seductions she talked of had only taken place in her imagination.

'How awkward for you,' I said.

'When I came here I knew I had to take special care in view of the Comte's reputation. There will always be scandal surrounding him.'

'There will always be scandal when there are those to make it,' I put in.

I disliked her for so many things; for her enjoyment of others' discomfort, for her stupid simpering suggestions that she was a *femme fatale*; and irrationally, for her long nose, which made her look like a shrew-mouse. Poor woman, as if she could help her appearance! But the meanness of her soul was in her face that night and I disliked her. I told myself I hated those who stood in judgment on others.

I was glad when she had gone. My thoughts were occupied by Geneviève. Our relationship had suffered a big setback and I was disappointed. The loss of my dress troubled me little compared with the absence of the confidence I had felt I was beginning to inspire. And oddly enough, in spite of what she had done, I felt a new tenderness towards her. Poor child! She was in need of care; and she was groping blindly, trying to call attention to herself, I was sure. I wanted to understand her; I wanted to help her. It occurred to me that she received very little help and understanding in this house – despised and rejected by her father, spoiled by her nurse. Something should be done, I was sure. It was not often that I acted on impulse but I did then.

I went to the library and knocked at the door. There was no answer so I went in and pulled the bell-rope. When one of the men-servants appeared, I asked if he would take a message to the Comte as I wished to speak to him.

Only when I saw the surprise in the man's face was I aware of the greatness of my temerity, but I still felt that the need to act was so urgent that I didn't care. On reflection I expected him to return and say that the Comte was too busy to see me and perhaps a meeting could be arranged the next day, but to my surprise when the door opened it was to admit the Comte.

'Mademoiselle Lawson, you sent for me?'

I flushed at the irony. 'I wished to speak to you, Monsieur le Comte.'

He frowned. 'This disgraceful affair of the dress. I must apologise for my daughter's behaviour.'

'I had not come for an apology.'

'You are very forgiving.'

'Oh, I was angry when I saw the dress.'

'Naturally. You will be recompensed and Geneviève shall make you an apology.'

'That is not what I want.'

The puzzled expression on his face might have been feigned. He gave the impression, as he so often did, of knowing exactly what was going on in my mind.

'Then perhaps you will tell me why you . . . summoned me here?'

'I did not summon you. I asked if you would see me here.'

'Well, I am here. You were very quiet during dinner. It was no doubt due to this foolish affair, and you were being discreet, displaying national sang-froid and hiding the indignation you felt towards my daughter. But now the secret is out and you no longer have any need to fear you are telling tales. And so . . . you have something to say to me.'

'I wanted to talk about Geneviève. Perhaps it is presumptuous of me . . .' I paused for a reassurance that this was not so, but it did not come.

'Please go on,' was all he said.

'I am concerned about her.'

He signed for me to be seated and sat opposite me. As he opened his eyes wider and sat back in his chair folding his hands with the carved jade signet ring on his little finger, I could believe all the rumours I had heard of him. The aquiline nose, the proud set of the head on the shoulders, the enigmatic mouth, and the eyes whose expression was unfathomable, belonged to a man who was born to rule; a man who believed in his divine right to have his own way and found it natural to remove anything or anyone who stood in his path.

'Yes, Monsieur le Comte,' I went on, 'I am concerned for your daughter. Why do you think she did this?'

'She will no doubt explain.'

'How can she? She doesn't even know herself. She has suffered a terrible ordeal.'

Was it my imagination or did he seem to grow a little more alert?

'What ordeal was this?' he asked.

'I mean . . . the death of her mother.'

His gaze met mine, steady, implacable, arrogant.

'That was several years ago.'

'But she found her mother dead.'

'I see that you have been well informed of the family's history.'

I stood up suddenly. I took a step towards him. He immediately rose – although I was tall he was considerably taller than I – and looked down at me. I tried to read the expression in those deeply set eyes.

'She is lonely,' I said. 'Don't you see? Please don't be harsh with her. If you would only be kind to her . . . if only . . .'

He was no longer looking at me; a faintly bored expression had come into his face.

'Why, Mademoiselle Lawson,' he said, 'I thought you had come here to restore our pictures, not ourselves.'

I felt defeated.

I said: 'I'm sorry. I shouldn't have come. I should have known it was useless.'

He led the way to the door; he opened it and bowed his head slightly as I went through.

I went back to my room wondering what I had done.

The next morning I went to the gallery to work as usual, expecting a summons from the Comte because I was certain that he would not allow such interference to pass. I had wakened often during the night to recall that scene, exaggerating it to such an extent that it was as though the devil himself had sat opposite me in that chair watching me through heavy-lidded eyes.

Lunch was brought up as usual. While I was eating it, Nounou came up. She looked very old and tired and I guessed she had scarcely slept all night.

'Monsieur le Comte has been in the schoolroom all the morning,' she burst out. 'I can't think what it means. He has been looking at all the exercise books and asking questions. Poor Geneviève is almost hysterical with fright.' She looked at me fearfully and added: 'It's so unlike him. But he has asked this, that and the other and says he thinks she is quite ignorant. Poor Mademoiselle Dubois is almost in a state of collapse.'

'No doubt he feels it is time he took some notice of his daughter.'

'I don't know what it means, miss. I wish I did.'

I went for a walk, taking a road which neither passed the Bastides' house nor led into the town. I did not want to meet anyone; I merely wanted to be alone to think about Geneviève and her father.

When I returned to the château it was to find Nounou in my room waiting for me.

'Mademoiselle Dubois has gone,' she announced.

'What?' I cried.

'Monsieur le Comte just gave her her salary in lieu of notice.'

I was shaken. 'Oh . . . poor woman! Where will she go? It seems so . . . ruthless.'

'The Comte makes up his mind quickly,' said Nounou, 'and then he acts.'

'I suppose there will be a new governess, now.'

'I do not know what will happen, miss.'

'And Geneviève, how is she?'

'She never had any respect for Mademoiselle Dubois . . . and to tell the truth nor did I. She is afraid, though.'

After Nounou had gone I sat in my room wondering what would happen next. And what of myself? He could not call me inefficient. The work on the pictures was progressing very satisfactorily; but people were dismissed for other failings. Insolence, for one thing. And I had dared summon him to his own library, to criticize his treatment of his daughter. Now that I came to consider it calmly I had to admit that it would be understandable if I received my orders to go. As for the pictures, he could find someone to continue with the work. I was by no means indispensable.

Then, of course, there was the affair of the dress. I had been the loser, but every time he saw me he would remember what his daughter had done – and remember, moreover, that I had had too close a glimpse into his family's secrets.

Geneviève came to my room and uttered a sullen apology which I knew she did not mean. I was too depressed to say much to her.

When I was hanging up my things for the night I looked for the dress, which I had thrown into the wardrobe. It was no longer there. I was surprised and wondered whether Geneviève had removed it, but I decided to say nothing about its disappearance.

I was working in the gallery when the summons came.

'Monsieur le Comte would like to see you in the library Mademoiselle Lawson.'

'Very well,' I said. 'I will be there in a few moments.' I picked up the sable brush I had been using and studied it thoughtfully. It is my turn now, I thought.

The door shut and I gave myself a few seconds in which to compose myself. Whatever happened I should pretend indifference. At least he would not be able to say I was incompetent.

I braced myself to go to the library. I thrust my hands into the pockets of the brown linen coat I was wearing, for fear they might tremble and betray my agitation. I wished my heart would not beat so fast; it might be obvious. I was glad my thick matt skin did not flush easily; but I guessed my eyes would be brighter than usual.

Without any outward show of haste I went to the library. As I approached the door I touched my hair and was reminded that it was probably untidy as it often became when I was working. All to the good. I did not want him to think I had prepared myself for the interview.

I knocked at the door.

'Please come in.' His voice was soft, inviting, but I did not trust his gentleness.

'Ah, Mademoiselle Lawson.'

He was smiling at me, intently, mischievously. What sort of mood was this?

'Please sit down.'

He took me to a chair which faced the window, so that the light was full on my face, and seated himself in shadow. I felt it was an unfair advantage.

'When we last met you were kind enough to express an interest in my daughter,' he said.

'I am very interested in her.'

'So good of you, particularly as you came here to restore the pictures. One would imagine you had little time to spare for that which did not concern your work.'

Now it was coming. I was not progressing fast enough. I was not giving satisfaction. This afternoon I would be speeding on my way from the château just as yesterday poor Mademoiselle Dubois had gone.

A horrible depression came over me. I could not bear to go. I should be more wretched than I had ever been in my life. I should never forget the château. I should be tormented by memories all my life. I wanted so much to know the truth about the château . . . about the Comte himself – whether he was such a monster as most people seemed to think him. Had he always been as he was now? If not, what had made him so?

Did he know what I was thinking? He had paused and was watching me intently.

'I don't know what you will think of my proposition, Mademoiselle Lawson, but one thing I do know is that you will be absolutely frank.'

'I shall try to be.'

'My dear Mademoiselle Lawson, you do not have to *try*. You are so naturally. It is an admirable characteristic and may I say one which I greatly admire.'

'You are very kind. Please tell me of this . . . proposition.'

'I feel my daughter's education has been neglected. Governesses are a problem. How many of them take the posts because they have a vocation? Very few. Most take them because, having been brought up to do nothing, they suddenly find themselves in a position where they have to do something. It is not a good motive for undertaking this most important occupation. In your profession it is necessary to have a gift. You are an artist . . .'

'Oh, no . . . I would not claim . . .'

'An artist *manquée*,' he finished and I sensed his mockery.

'Perhaps,' I said coolly.

'You see how different from these poor dejected ladies who come to teach our children! I have decided to send my daughter to school. You were gracious enough to offer an opinion as to her well-being. Please give me that candid opinion on this.'

'I think it could be an excellent idea, but it would depend on the school.'

He waved his hand. 'This is no place for a highly-strung child. Do you agree? It is for antiquarians, those whose passion is architecture, paintings . . . and those who are imbued with the old traditions – antiquated too, you might say.'

He had read my thoughts. He knew that I saw him as the autocrat, the upholder of the divine right of the nobility. He was telling me so.

I said: 'I suppose you are right.'

'I know I am. I have chosen a school in England for Geneviève.'

'Oh!'

'You seem surprised. Surely you believe that the best schools are in England?'

Here was mockery again and I said rather too warmly: 'That could be possible.'

'Exactly. There she would not only learn to speak the language but to acquire that excellent sang-froid with which you, mademoiselle, are so lavishly endowed.'

'Thank you. But she would be far from her home.'

'A home in which, as you pointed out to me, she is not particularly happy.'

'But she could be. She is capable of great affection.'

He changed the subject. 'You work during the mornings in the gallery, but not in the afternoons. I'm glad that you are making use of the stables.'

I thought: He has been watching me. He knows how I spend my time. I believed I knew what was coming. He was going to send me away as he had Mademoiselle Dubois. My impertinence was as distasteful to him as her incompetence.

I wondered whether he had submitted her to an interview like this. He was a man who liked to hunt his prey before the kill. I remembered that thought occurring to me once before in this library.

'Monsieur le Comte,' I said, 'if you are not satisfied with the work I have done, please tell me. I will prepare to leave at once.'

'Mademoiselle Lawson, you are very hasty. I am pleased to discover at least this flaw in you, because it prevents you from being perfect. Perfection is so dull. I did not say I was displeased with your work. In fact I find your work excellent. Some time I shall come to you in the gallery and ask you to show me how you get such excellent results. Let me tell you what I have in mind. If my daughter is to go to England she must have a good knowledge of the language. I do not propose that she shall go immediately. Perhaps not for another year. In the meantime she will take lessons from the curé. He will be at least as good as the governess who has just left us. Indeed he must be, for he couldn't be worse. But it is her English about which I am most concerned. Until the spring you will be in the gallery only during the mornings. That leaves you some free time. I was wondering whether you would undertake to teach Geneviève English when you are not engaged on the pictures. I am sure she would profit greatly from such an arrangement.'

I was so overcome by my emotion that I could not speak.

He went on quickly: 'I do not mean that you would confine yourself to a schoolroom, but that you and she should ride together . . . walk together. . . . She knows the fundamentals of grammar. At least I hope so. It is practice in conversation that she needs, and of course to acquire a reasonably good accent. You understand what I mean?'

'Yes, I understand.'

'You would of course be reimbursed. That is a matter which you could discuss with my steward. Now what do you say?'

'I . . . I accept with pleasure.'

'That is excellent.' He stood up and was holding out his hand. I put mine in his. He gripped it firmly and shook it.

I was so happy. The thought occurred to me that I had rarely been as happy in my life.

It was a week later when, entering my bedroom, I found a large,cardboard box on my bed. I thought there had been a mistake until I saw my name on it; and at the foot of the label was an address in Paris.

I opened the box.

Green velvet in a rich jewel colour. Emerald green velvet! I took it out of the box. It was an evening gown, simply cut, but exquisite.

Certainly there must be some mistake. All the same I held it against me and went to the mirror. My shining eyes reflected the colour so that they seemed to match the velvet. It was beautiful. Why had it come to me?

I laid it reverently on my bed and examined the box. There I found a parcel wrapped in tissue paper and when I unrolled this, there was my old black velvet. I understood, before I read the card which fell out. I saw the crest which I had begun to know well and on the card was written: 'I trust this will replace the one which was spoilt. If it is not what you need, we must try again. Lothair de la Talle.'

I went to the bed; I picked up the dress; I had it against me; I hugged it. In fact I behaved like a foolish girl. And all the time my other self, the one I was always trying to be, was saying: Ridiculous! You can't accept it. And the real Me, the one who only appeared now and then but was there all the time lying in wait to betray me, was saying: It's the most beautiful dress. Every time you put it on you will feel excited. Why, in such a dress you could be an attractive woman.

Then I laid the dress on the bed and said: 'I shall go to him at once and tell him that I cannot dream of accepting it.'

I tried to compose my features into a severe mould, but I kept thinking of his coming into my room – or sending someone – to find the ruined black velvet, sending it to Paris with the order: 'Make a gown to these measurements. Make the finest gown you have ever made.'

How stupid I was! What was happening to me?

I had better see him so that the dress could be sent back to Paris without delay.

I went down to the library. Perhaps he was expecting me, for he might be aware that the dress had arrived. As if he would care *when* the dress arrived. He had merely decided it should be given to me as recompense and then forgotten all about it.

He was there.

'I must speak to you,' I said, and as always, because I was embarrassed, I sounded arrogant. He noticed it, for a smile briefly touched his lips and the amused glint leaped into his eyes.

'Please sit down, Mademoiselle Lawson. You are agitated.'

I was immediately at a disadvantage because the last thing I wanted was to betray my feelings, which I did not entirely understand myself. It was unlike me to be so excited about clothes.

'By no means,' I said. 'I have merely come to thank you for sending me the dress to replace mine and to tell you that I cannot accept it.'

'So it has arrived. Does it not fit, then?'

'I . . . cannot say. I have not tried it. There was no need for you to send for it.'

'Forgive my disagreement, but in my opinion there was every need.'

'But no. It was a very old dress. I had had it for years, and this one is er . . .'

'I see that you do not like it.'

'That is not the point at issue.' Again the severity in my voice made him smile.

'Really? What *is* the point at issue?'

'That I cannot dream of accepting the dress.'

'Why not?'

'Because it is not necessary.'

'Now come, Mademoiselle Lawson, be frank and say that you consider accepting a . . . garment from me is improper – if that is what you mean.'

'I think no such thing. Why should I?'

Again he made that entirely French gesture which implied anything one wished it to. 'I do not know. I do not imagine for one moment that I could understand what goes on in *your* mind. I was merely trying to find some reason why having had an article ruined in this house you could not accept a replacement.'

'This is a *dress*.'

'Why should a dress be different from any other object?'

'This is a purely personal thing.'

'Ah! Purely personal! If I had destroyed one of your solutions would you not have allowed me to replace it? Or is it really because this is a dress . . . something you would wear . . . something intimate, shall we say?'

I could not look at him; there was a warmth in his expression which disturbed me.

I turned away from his gaze and said: 'There was no need for the gown to be replaced. In any case the green velvet is far more valuable than the one for which it was meant to compensate me.'

'Value is difficult to assess. The black dress was clearly more valuable to *you*, since you were distressed to have lost it and are reluctant to accept this one.'

'I think you wilfully misunderstand.'

He came to me swiftly and laid a hand on my shoulder. 'Mademoiselle Lawson,' he said gently, 'it will displease me if you refuse to accept this dress. Your own was destroyed by a member of my family and I wish to replace it. Will you please accept it?'

'Since you put it that way . . .'

His hand fell from my shoulder but he was still standing close. I felt uneasy yet indescribably happy.

'Then you will. You are very generous, Mademoiselle Lawson.'

'It is you who are generous. There was no need . . .'

'I repeat there was every need.'

'. . . to replace it so extravagantly,' I finished.

He laughed suddenly and I realized I had never heard him laugh like that before. There was no bitterness, no mockery.

'I hope,' he said, 'that one day I shall be allowed to see you wearing it.'

'I have very few occasions for wearing such a dress.'

'But since it is such an *extravagant* dress perhaps those occasions should be created.'

'I do not see how that can be,' I replied, my voice growing colder as my hidden emotions grew greater. 'I can only say it was unnecessary, but good of you. I will accept the dress and thank you for your generosity.'

I moved to the door but he was there before me, opening it, inclining his head so that I could not see his expression.

As I went up to my room my emotions were overwhelming. If I had been wise I should have analysed them. I should have been wise, but of course I wasn't.

Chapter Five

My interest in the Comte and his affairs added such a zest to my life that each morning I would awaken with a feeling of expectation, telling myself that this very day might be the one when I would learn something new, begin to understand him more, and perhaps find the clue which would tell me whether he was a murderer or a much-maligned man.

Then, without warning, he went to Paris, and I heard that he would return just before Christmas when there would be guests at the château. I shall find myself on the edge of affairs, I thought, looking in from outside.

I took on my new duties with enthusiasm and I was rather pleased to find that Geneviève by no means resented me but was in fact eager to learn English. The prospect of going to school was a terrifying one, but it was too far in the future to be a real menace. She would ask me questions about England when we went for our rides and we even found some amusement in our English conversations. She was taking lessons with the curé, and although none shared her lessons, she often saw the Bastide children on their way to the curé's house and I believed it was good for her to mix with the other children.

One morning while I was in the gallery Philippe came in. When the Comte was not at the castle he seemed to take on a new stature. Now he looked like a pale shadow of his cousin, but having been made more and more aware of the Comte's virility, I was struck afresh by the weakness – almost effeminacy – of Philippe.

But his smile was very friendly as he asked how the work was progressing.

'You are skilful,' he commented when I showed him.

'It is care that is needed as much as skill.'

'And expert knowledge.' He was standing before the picture I had restored. 'One has the feeling that one could put out a hand and touch those emeralds,' he said.

'The skill of the painter, not the restorer.'

He continued to gaze wistfully at the picture and once more I sensed his deep love for the château and everything connected with it. That was how I should feel were I a member of such a family.

Turning suddenly and catching my eyes on him, he looked faintly embarrassed as though he were wondering whether he should say what was in his mind. Then he said quickly: 'Mademoiselle Lawson, are you happy here?'

'Happy? I find the work very satisfying.'

'The work, yes. I know how you feel about that. I was thinking of . . .' He made a gesture with his hand.

'. . . the atmosphere here . . . the family.' I looked surprised and he went on: 'There was that unfortunate affair of the dress.'

'It is all forgotten now.' I wondered whether my face betrayed my pleasure as I thought of the green dress.

'In a household like this one . . .' He stopped as though he did not know how to go on. 'If you found it intolerable here . . .' he went on hurriedly, 'if you wished to leave . . .'

'To leave!'

'I meant if it became difficult. My cousin might . . . er . . .' He abandoned what he had been going to say, but I knew he was thinking, as I was, of the green velvet dress and the fact that the Comte had given it to me. He saw something significant in that. But it was evidently too dangerous to discuss. How he feared his cousin! He smiled brightly. 'A friend of mine has a fine collection of pictures and some are in need of restoration. They could keep you busy for a long time, I have no doubt.'

'It will be a long time before I finish here.'

'My friend, Monsieur de la Monelle, needs his pictures restored immediately. I thought that if you were unhappy here . . . or you felt you would like to get away . . .'

'I have no wish to leave this work.'

He looked alarmed, fearful that he had said too much. 'It was only a suggestion.'

'You are very kind to be so concerned.'

His smile was very charming. 'I feel responsible. On that first occasion I could have sent you away.'

'But you didn't. I appreciate that.'

'Perhaps it would have been better.'

'Oh, no! I find the work here absorbing.'

'It's a wonderful old place.' He spoke almost eagerly. 'But it is not the happiest of households, and in view of what happened in the past . . . My cousin's wife died, you know, in rather mysterious circumstances.'

'I have heard that.'

'And my cousin can be rather ruthless in getting what he wants. I shouldn't have said that. He has been good to me. I am here . . . it is now my home . . . thanks to him. It is only that I have this feeling of responsibility towards you and I would like you to know that if you did need my help . . . Mademoiselle Lawson, I hope you will say nothing of this to my cousin.'

'I understand. I shan't mention it.'

'But please bear in mind: if my cousin . . . if you should feel you ought to get away, please come to me.'

He went to one of the paintings and asked questions about it, but I did not think he was paying attention to the answers.

When his eyes met mine they were rather shy, diffident, but very warm. He was certainly anxious on my behalf and I understood that he was warning me about the Comte.

I felt I had a good friend in the château.

Christmas was almost upon us. Geneviève and I were riding every day and there was a marked improvement in her English. I told her of our Christmases in England and how we brought in the holly and mistletoe; how we kissed under the mistletoe; how everyone had to have a stir at the Christmas puddings and what a great day it was when they were boiling and we hauled out the tiny basin, with the 'taster' in it. What an important moment that was when we each had our spoonful, for the taster was an indication of what the whole boiling of puddings would be.

'My grandmother was alive then,' I said. 'That was my mother's mother. She was French and had to learn all our customs, but she took to them very quickly and she would never have dreamt of giving up any of them.'

'Tell me some more, miss,' begged Geneviève.

So I told her how I used to sit on a high stool beside my mother and help stone the raisins and peel the almonds.

'I used to eat them whenever I could.'

That amused Geneviève. 'Oh, miss, fancy *your* being a little girl once.'

I told her about waking on Christmas morning to find my stocking filled.

'*We* put our *shoes* by the fireplace . . . at least some people do. I don't.'

'Why don't you?'

'Nounou would be the only one to remember. And you can't have one pair of shoes; you want a lot, otherwise it's no fun.'

'You tell me.'

'Well, you put your shoes round the fireplace on Christmas Eve when you come in from Midnight Mass and then you go to bed. In the morning, the little presents are inside your shoes and the big ones round it. We did it when my mother was alive.'

'And then you stopped?'

She nodded.

'It's a nice custom.'

'*Your* mother died,' she said. 'How did she die?'

'She was ill for a long time. I nursed her.'

'You were grown up then?'

'Yes, I suppose you would call it that.'

'Oh, miss. I believe you were *always* grown up.'

We called in at the Bastides' on our way back to the château. I had encouraged this because I felt that she should meet people outside the château, particularly children, and although Yves and Margot were younger than she was and Gabrielle older, at least they were nearer her age than anyone else she knew.

There was excitement in that household because of the nearness of Christmas – whispering in corners and hinting at secrets.

Yves and Margot were busy making the crèche. Geneviève watched them with interest and, while I talked to Madame Bastide, went over to join them.

'The children are so excited,' said Madame Bastide. 'It is always so. Margot tells us every morning how many hours it is until Christmas Day.'

We watched them arrange the brown paper to look like rocks. Yves took out his painting set and painted moss on it and Margot started to colour the stable brown. On the floor lay the little sheep which they had made themselves and which they would set up on the rocks. I watched Geneviève. She was quite fascinated.

She looked into the cradle. 'It's empty,' she said, rather scornfully.

'Of course it's empty! Jesus isn't born yet,' retorted Yves.

'It is a miracle,' Margot told her. 'We go to bed on Christmas Eve . . .'

'After we put our shoes round the fire . . .' added Yves.

'Yes, we do that . . . and the cradle is empty and then . . . on Christmas morning when we get up to look, the little Jesus is lying in it.'

Geneviève was silent.

After a while she said: 'Can I do something?'

'Yes,' replied Yves. 'We want more shepherds' crooks. Do you know how to make them?'

'No,' she said humbly.

'Margot will show you.'

I watched the two girls, their heads close together, and I said to myself: This is what she needs.

Madame Bastide followed my gaze. She said: 'And you think Monsieur le Comte will allow this? You think he will agree to this friendship between our children and his daughter?'

I said: 'I have never seen her so . . . relaxed, so unconscious of herself.'

'Ah, but Monsieur le Comte will not wish his daughter to be carefree. He wants her to be the grand lady of the château.'

'This companionship is what she needs. You have invited me to join you on Christmas Day. May I bring her with me? She has talked about Christmas so wistfully.'

'You think it will be permitted?'

'We can try,' I said.

'But Monsieur le Comte . . .?'

'I will answer to him,' I replied boldly.

A few days before Christmas the Comte returned to the château. I had expected that he would seek me out to discover either how his daughter or his paintings were progressing, but he did no such thing. This was probably because he was thinking of the guests who would soon be arriving.

There would be fifteen people, I heard from Nounou. Not so many as usually came, but entertaining was rather a delicate matter when there was no lady of the house.

I was out riding with Geneviève the day before Christmas Eve when we met a party of riders from the château. The Comte rode at the head of them and beside him was a beautiful young woman. She wore a high black riding-hat swathed with grey and there was a grey cravat at her throat. The masculinity of her riding-habit served to accentuate her femininity, and I noticed at once how bright was her hair, how delicate her features. She was like a piece of china from the collection in the blue drawing-room which I had seen once or twice. Such women always made me feel even taller than I was, even more plain.

'Here is my daughter,' said the Comte, greeting us almost affectionately.

We pulled up, the four of us, for the rest of the party were some way behind.

'With her governess?' added the beautiful creature.

'Certainly not. This is Miss Lawson from England who is restoring our pictures.'

I saw the blue eyes take on a coolly appraising expression.

'Geneviève, you will have met Mademoiselle de la Monelle.'

Mademoiselle de la Monelle! I had heard the name before.

'Yes, Papa,' said Geneviève. 'Good day, mademoiselle.'

'Mademoiselle Lawson, Mademoiselle de la Monelle.'

We greeted each other.

'Pictures must be quite fascinating,' she said.

I knew then. This was the name of the people whom Philippe had mentioned as having pictures to be restored.

'Miss Lawson thinks so.' And to us, so cutting short the encounter: 'Were you returning?'

We said we were and rode on.

'Would you say she was beautiful?' asked Geneviève.

'What was that?'

'You're not listening,' accused Geneviève and repeated the question.

'I should think most people would.'

'I said you, miss. Do you think so?'

'She has a type of looks which most people admire.'

'Well, *I* don't like her.'

'I hope you won't take your scissors to *her* room, because if you did anything like that there would be trouble . . . not only for you but for others. Have you thought of what has happened to poor Mademoiselle Dubois?'

'She was a silly old woman.'

'That's no reason for being unkind to her.'

She laughed rather slyly. 'Well, you came out of that affair well, didn't you? It's a lovely dress my father gave you. I don't suppose you ever had a dress like that in your life before. So you see I really did you a good turn.'

'I don't agree. It was an embarrassing situation for us all.'

'Poor old Esquilles! It wasn't fair really. She didn't want to go. You wouldn't want to go either.'

'No, I shouldn't. I'm very interested in my work.'

'And in us?'

'Certainly I hope to see you more fluent in your English than you are.' Then I relented and said: 'No, I should not want to leave you, Geneviève.'

She smiled, but almost immediately the malicious look came into her face. 'Nor my father,' she said. 'But I don't think he will be taking much notice of you now, miss. Did you see the way he looked at *her*?'

'At her?'

'You know who I mean. Mademoiselle de la Monelle. And she *is* beautiful.'

She rode on and looked over her shoulder at me, laughing.

I touched Bonhomme's flanks and broke into a gallop. Geneviève was beside me.

I could not get Mademoiselle de la Monelle's beautiful face out of my mind, and both Geneviève and I were silent as we rode back to the château.

The next day I came face to face with the Comte on my way to the gallery. I thought as he was no doubt preoccupied with his guests he would merely greet me and pass on, but he paused.

'And how is my daughter progressing with her English?'

'Very well. I think you will be pleased.'

'I knew you would be an excellent teacher.'

Did I look so much like a governess? I wondered.

'She is interested, and that is a great help. She is happier now.'

'Happier?'

'Yes, haven't you noticed?'

He shook his head. 'But I accept your word.'

'There is always a reason why young people want to destroy things . . . without reason. Do you agree with me?'

'I am sure you are right.'

'I think she feels the loss of her mother deeply, and misses the fun that most children have.'

He did not flinch at the mention of his dead wife.

'Fun, Mademoiselle Lawson?' he repeated.

'She has been telling me how they used to put their shoes in front of the fire on Christmas Eve . . . rather wistfully I thought.'

'Isn't she rather old for that sort of thing?'

'I don't think one is ever too old.'

'You surprise me.'

'It's a pleasant custom,' I insisted. 'We have decided that we will follow it this Christmas and . . . perhaps you will be surprised by my presumption but . . .'

'You have ceased to surprise me.'

'I thought that you might put your present with the others. That would delight her.'

'You think that by finding a gift in a shoe instead of shall we say at the dinner-table, my daughter is less likely to play childish tricks?'

I sighed. 'Monsieur le Comte, I see I *have* been presumptuous. I'm sorry.'

I passed quickly on and he did not attempt to stop me.

I went to the gallery, but I could not work. I felt too disturbed. I had two images in my mind: the proud innocent man showing a defiant face to the world and . . . the callous murderer.

Which was the true one? I wished I knew! But then what concern was it of mine? I was concerned with the pictures, not the man.

On Christmas Eve we all went to the midnight service in the old Gaillard church. The Comte sat in the first of the pews reserved for the château family with Geneviève beside him and the guests in the pews immediately behind. Farther back I sat with Nounou; and as the servants were all there the château pews were full.

I saw the Bastide family in their best clothes. Madame all in black and

Gabrielle looking very pretty in grey. There was the young man with her whom I had seen now and then about the vineyard; he was Jacques, who had been with Armand Bastide at the time of the accident; I knew him by the scar on his left cheek.

Yves and Margot could scarcely keep still; Margot was no doubt counting the minutes now instead of the hours.

I saw that Geneviève was watching them and I guessed that she was wishing that instead of going back to the château she was going to the Bastides' house that she might join in the fun which only children can give to Christmas.

I was glad I had announced that I was going to put my shoes by the schoolroom fire and suggested that she did the same. It could not but be a quiet little party when compared with the frivolity which would take place on Christmas morning round the Bastide fireplace, but still, it would be better than nothing; and I had been surprised by Geneviève's enthusiasm. After all, she had never been used to a large family; and when her mother had been alive it must have been the three of them – Geneviève, Françoise, Nounou and perhaps the governess of the time. And what of the Comte? Surely when his wife was alive and his daughter young, he would have joined the Christmas customs.

The nursery quarters were not far from my own and consisted of four rooms adjoining one another. There was first the schoolroom, lofty with a vaulted ceiling and embrasures with the stone window-seat benches which were a feature of the château. In this was a huge fireplace large enough, as Nounou had said, to roast an ox. To one side of it was an enormous pewter couldron which was always full of logs. There were three doors which led from this room – one was Geneviève's bedroom; one Nounou's; and the other was reserved for the governess.

Into the schoolroom we solemnly went after we returned from church and there we laid our shoes before the dying fire.

Geneviève went to bed and when we guessed she was asleep Nounou and I laid out gifts in the shoes. I had a scarf of scarlet silk for Geneviève which I thought could be used as a cravat and would be most becoming to her dark colouring and useful for riding. For Nounou I had what Madame Latière at the *pâtisserie* had assured me were her favourite sweets, a kind of cushion made of rum and butter in a very charming box. Nounou and I pretended not to see our own gifts, said good night and went back to our rooms.

I was awakened early next morning by Geneviève.

'Look, miss. Look!' she cried.

I sat up startled and then remembered that it was Christmas morning.

'The scarf is lovely. Thank you, miss.' She was wearing it over her dressing-gown. 'And Nounou has given me handkerchiefs . . . all beautifully embroidered. And there is too . . . Oh, miss, I haven't opened it. It's from Papa. It says so. Read it.'

I was sitting up in bed as excited as she was.

'It was by my shoe with the others, miss.'

'Oh,' I cried. 'That's wonderful!'

'He hasn't done it for years. I wonder why this year . . .'

'Never mind. Let's see what it is.'

It was a pearl pendant on a slender gold chain. 'Oh, it's lovely,' I cried.

'Fancy!' she said. 'He put it there.'

'You're pleased with it?'

She could not speak; she nodded.

'Put it on,' I said, and helped her fasten it.

She went to the looking-glass and studied herself. Then she came back to the bed and, picking up my scarf which she had taken off to put the pendant on, she laid it across her shoulders.

'Happy Christmas, miss,' she said gaily.

I thought it was going to be one.

She insisted that I go into the schoolroom. 'Nounou's not up yet. She can have hers later. Now, miss, do look at yours.' I picked up Geneviève's parcel. It was a book about the castle and the neighbourhood. She watched me delightedly while I opened it.

'How I shall enjoy that!' I cried. 'So you knew how fascinated I was.'

'Yes, you show it, miss. And you do like old houses so much, don't you? But you mustn't start reading it now.'

'Oh, Geneviève, thank you. It was good of you to think of me.'

She said: 'Look. You've got a tray-cloth from Nounou. I know who did that. My mother. Nounou's got a whole boxful of them.'

The handkerchiefs; the tray-cloth . . . they were all the work of Françoise! I wondered that Nounou had parted with them.

'And there's something else for you, miss.' I had seen the parcel and a wild thought had come into my head which, while quite crazy, was so exciting, that I was afraid to pick up the parcel for fear of almost certain disappointment.

'Open it! Open it!' commanded Geneviève. I did and found an exquisite miniature set with pearls. It portrayed a woman holding a spaniel in her arms. The head of the dog was just visible and I knew by the hair style of the woman that this had been painted some hundred and fifty years ago.

'Do you like it?' cried Geneviève. 'Who gave it?'

'It's beautiful but too valuable. I . . .'

Geneviève picked up a note which had fallen from the parcel. On it was written: 'You will recognize the lady whom you have so expertly cleaned. She would probably be as grateful to you as I am, so it seems fitting that you should have this. I had intended to give it to you when I came across it the other day, but since you like our old customs it is here in your shoe. Lothair de la Talle.'

'It's Papa!' cried Geneviève excitedly.

'Yes. He's pleased with my work on the pictures and this is his appreciation.'

'Oh . . . but in your shoe! Who would have thought . . .'

'Well, he must have thought that while he was putting your pendant in your shoe he could put this in mine.'

Geneviève was laughing uncontrollably.

I said: 'This is the lady in the portrait with the emeralds. That is why he has given it to me.'

'You like it, miss? You *do* like it?'

'Well, it is a very beautiful miniature.'

I handled it lovingly, noting the exquisite colouring and the lovely setting of pearls. I had never possessed anything so beautiful.

Nounou appeared. 'Such a noise!' she said. 'It woke me. Happy Christmas.'

'Happy Christmas, Nounou.'

'Just look what Papa has given me, Nounou. And in my shoe.'

'In your shoe?'

'Oh, wake up, Nounou. You're half asleep. It's Christmas morning. Look at your presents. If you don't open them I will. Open mine first.'

Geneviève had bought her a primrose-coloured apron which Nounou declared was just what she wanted; then she expressed her pleasure over my bonbons. The Comte had not forgotten her either; there was a large fleecy woollen shawl in a shade of dark blue.

Nounou was puzzled. 'From Monsieur le Comte . . . but why?'

'Doesn't he usually remember Christmas?' I asked.

'Oh, yes, he remembers. The vineyard workers all have their turkeys, and the indoor servants have gifts of money. The steward gives them out. It has always been the custom.'

'Show her what you've got, miss.'

I held out the miniature.

'Oh!' said Nounou, and for a moment she looked at me blankly; then I saw the speculation in her eyes.

I was responsible for this giving of presents, Nounou was thinking. I knew it; and I was glad. But Nounou was disturbed.

Chapter Six

In the morning Geneviève and I walked to the Bastides. Madame Bastide, hot from the kitchen, came out to greet us waving a ladle; Gabrielle looked over her shoulder, for her services were also needed in the kitchen, from which a delicious smell was coming. Yves and Margot dashed at Geneviève and told her what they had found in their shoes; I was glad she could tell them what she had found in hers; I noticed with what pleasure she displayed her gifts. She went to the crèche and called out in delight as she peered into the cradle.

'He's here!' she cried.

'Of course,' retorted Yves. 'What did you expect? It's Christmas morning.'

Jean Pierre came in with a load of logs and his face lit up with pleasure.

'This is a great day when château people sit down at our table.'

'Geneviève could scarcely wait for this,' I told him.

'And you?'

'I too have looked forward to it.'

'Then, we must see that you are not disappointed.'

Nor were we. It was a gay occasion; the table which Gabrielle had decorated so charmingly with feathery evergreens was overcrowded that day, for Jacques and his mother had joined the party. She was an invalid and it was touching to see how tender Jacques was to her; and with Madame Bastide, her son and four grandchildren besides Geneviève and myself we made a sizeable party, kept merry by the excitement of the children.

Madame Bastide sat at the head of the table and her son opposite her. I was on Madame Bastide's right hand, Geneviève on that of her son. We were the guests of honour and here as in the château etiquette was observed.

The children chattered all the time and I was glad to see that Geneviève was listening intently and occasionally joining in. Yves would not allow her to be shy. I was certain that it was company such as this that she needed, for she seemed happier than I had ever seen her before. About her neck was her pendant. I guessed she would never want to take it off and would perhaps sleep in it.

Madame Bastide carved the turkey, which was stuffed with chestnuts and served with a purée of mushrooms. It was quite delicious, but the great moment was when a large cake was brought in to the delighted shrieks of the children.

'Who will get it? Who will get it?' chanted Yves. 'Who'll be King for the day?'

'It might be a Queen,' Margot reminded him.

'It'll be a King. What's the good of a Queen?'

'If a Queen has the crown she can rule.'

'Be silent, children,' scolded Madame Bastide. 'Does Mademoiselle Lawson know of this old custom?'

Jean Pierre was smiling at me across the table. 'You see that cake,' he said.

'Of course she sees it,' cried Yves.

'It's big enough,' added Gabrielle.

'Well,' went on Jean Pierre, 'inside it is a crown – a tiny crown. Now the cake is going to be cut into ten pieces – one for each and all the cake must be eaten . . . and with care . . .'

'You might have the crown,' shrieked Yves.

'With care,' went on Jean Pierre, 'for someone round this table is going to find the crown in the cake.'

'And when it is found?'

'King for the day,' shouted Yves.

'Or Queen for the day,' added Margot.

'They wear the crown?' I asked.

'It's too little,' Gabrielle told me. 'But . . .'

'Better than that. The one who gets the crown is King – or as Margot says Queen – for the day,' explained Jean Pierre. 'It means that he . . . or

she . . . rules the household. What he . . .' he smiled at Margot – 'or she
. . . says is law.'

'For the whole of the day!' cried Margot.

'If I get it,' said Yves, 'you can't think what I'll do!'

'What?' demanded Margot.

But he was too overcome by mirth to tell, and everyone was impatient for
the cutting of the cake.

There was a tense silence while Madame Bastide plunged in the knife;
the cake was cut and Gabrielle stood up to take the plate and hand it round.
I was watching Geneviève, delighted to see how she could join in the simple
fun.

There was no sound as we started to eat – only the ticking of the clock
and the crackle of logs in the fireplace.

Then suddenly there was a shout and Jean Pierre was holding up the
little gold-coloured crown.

'Jean Pierre has it! Jean Pierre has it!' sang out the children.

'Call me Your Majesty when you address me,' retorted Jean Pierre with
mock dignity. 'I order my coronation to take place without delay.'

Gabrielle went out of the room and returned carrying, on a cushion, a
metal crown, decorated with tinsel. The children wriggled on the seats with
delight, and Geneviève watched round-eyed.

'Who does Your Majesty command should crown you?' asked Gabrielle.

Jean Pierre pretended to survey us all regally; then his eyes fell on me.
I glanced towards Geneviève and he took the message at once.

'Mademoiselle Geneviève de la Talle step forward,' he said.

Geneviève leapt to her feet, her cheeks pink, her eyes shining.

'You have to put the crown on his head,' Yves told her.

So Geneviève walked solemnly to the cushion which Gabrielle held and,
taking the crown, put it on Jean Pierre's head.

'Now you kneel and kiss his hand,' commanded Yves, 'and swear to serve
the King.'

I was watching Jean Pierre sitting back in his chair, the crown on his
head, while Geneviève kneeled at his feet on the cushion òn which Gabrielle
had carried the crown. His expression was one of complete triumph. He
certainly played the part well.

Yves broke up the solemn proceedings by demanding what was His
Majesty's first command. Jean Pierre thought for a while and then he looked
at Geneviève and me and said: 'That we dispense with formality. Everyone
here is commanded to call everyone else by their Christian names.'

I saw Gabrielle look at me apprehensively so I smiled and said: 'Mine is
Dallas. I hope you can all say it.'

They all repeated it with the accent on the last syllable and there was
laughter from the children as I corrected each one in turn.

'Is it a well-known English name?' asked Jacques.

'Like Jean Pierre and Yves in France?' added Yves.

'By no means. It's entirely my own and there's a reason for it. My father
was Daniel, my mother Alice. Before I was born he wanted a girl; she

wanted a boy; he wanted it named after my mother, she after him. Then I appeared . . . and they merged their names and made Dallas.'

This delighted the children, who started a game of linking names to see who could get the most amusing.

And immediately we were on Christian-name terms and it was extraordinary how that broke down all formality.

Jean Pierre sat back, his crown on his head like a benevolent monarch, and yet now and then I thought I could see a trace of arrogance which reminded me of the Comte.

He caught me watching him and laughed.

He said to me: 'It is good of you, Dallas, to join in our games.'

And for some absurd reason I was relieved to find he referred to this as a game.

When the Bastides' maid came to put up the shutters I was reminded how time was flying. It had been such a pleasant afternoon; we had played games, miming and guessing all under the command of Jean Pierre; we had danced, for Armand Bastide's contribution to the jollity had been to play the violin.

There was only one time as good as Christmas, Margot confided in me as she taught me how to dance the *Sautière Charentaise*, and that was grape harvest . . . but she didn't think even that was quite as good for there weren't the presents and the tree and King-for-a-day.

'Grape harvest is really for the grown-ups,' added Yves sagely. 'Christmas is ours.'

I was delighted to see Geneviève throw herself so wholeheartedly into the playing of games. I could see that she wanted the afternoon to go on and on; but I knew that we should return to the château. Even now our absence would have been noticed and I did not know what reaction there would be.

I told Madame Bastide that we must most regretfully be leaving and she signed to Jean Pierre.

'My subjects wish to speak with me?' he said, his warm brown eyes twinkling first at me, then at Geneviève.

'We have to go,' I explained. 'We'll slip away . . . quietly. Then they won't notice that we've gone.'

'Impossible! They'll all be desolate. I don't know whether I shan't have to exercise my royal prerogative . . .'

'We'll go now. I hate taking Geneviève away. She has had such a wonderful time.'

'I will accompany you to the château.'

'Oh, there is no need . . .'

'No need . . . when it's growing dark! I shall insist. You know I can.' His eyes were a little wistful. 'Only for to-day, it is true, but I must make the most of my hour of power.'

We were all rather silent during the walk back to the château, and when we reached the drawbridge Jean Pierre halted and said: 'There! You are safely home.'

He took my hand in one of his and Geneviève's in the other. He kissed them both; and still held them. Then to my surprise he drew me towards him and kissed my cheek; and immediately did the same to Geneviève.

We were startled, both of us, but he was smiling.

'The King can do no wrong,' he reminded us. 'Tomorrow I shall be plain Jean Pierre Bastide, but to-day I am King of my little castle.'

I laughed, and taking Geneviève's arm said: 'Well, thank you, and good day.'

He bowed and we went across the drawbridge into the castle.

Nounou was waiting for us, a little anxious.

'Monsieur le Comte came to the schoolroom. He asked where you were, and I had to tell him.'

'Of course,' I said, my heart beginning to beat fast.

'You see you were not here for *déjeuner.*'

'There is no need to keep anything secret,' I replied.

'He wishes to see you when you return.'

'Both of us?' said Geneviève and I thought how she had changed from the excited girl who had joined in the Bastides' games.

'No, only Mademoiselle Lawson. He will be in the library until six o'clock. You would just catch him, miss.'

'I will go to him at once,' I said; and I went out leaving Nounou and Geneviève together.

He was there reading, and when I entered he languidly, almost reluctantly, laid aside his book.

'You wished to see me?' I asked.

'Please sit down, Mademoiselle Lawson.'

'I must thank you for the miniature. It is quite lovely.'

He bowed his head. 'I thought you would appreciate it. You recognized her, of course.'

'Yes. The likeness is there. I feel you have been too generous.'

'Can one be too generous?'

'It was kind of you to put the gifts in the shoes.'

'You had made my duty plain to me.' He smiled and looked down at his hands. 'You have had a pleasant visit?'

'We have been at the Maison Bastide. I think it excellent for Geneviève to be with young people.' I spoke defiantly.

'I am sure you are right.'

'She enjoyed the games . . . the Christmas festivities . . . the simplicity of it all. I hope you do not disapprove.'

He lifted his shoulders and spread his hands in a gesture which might have meant anything.

'Geneviève should join us for dinner to-night,' he said.

'I am sure she will enjoy that.'

'I don't suppose we can vie with the bonhomie, the camaraderie, you enjoyed earlier in the day, but you too must join us . . . if you wish, Mademoiselle Lawson.'

'Thank you.'

He inclined his head to indicate that the interview was over; I rose and he followed me to the door, which he held open for me.

'Geneviève was delighted with your gift,' I told him. 'I wish you could have seen her face when she took off the wrappings.'

He smiled and I was very happy. I had expected a reprimand and instead had been given an invitation.

This was a wonderful Christmas.

It was my first opportunity to wear the new dress. As I put it on I felt excited – strangely expectant as though the fact that I was wearing a dress he had chosen for me made a different woman of me.

But of course he hadn't chosen it. He had merely asked the Paris house to send a dress to fit a woman who had worn the black velvet. Yet the colour was the most becoming I could have worn. Was that chance? Or had he suggested it? My eyes looked brilliantly green and my hair was the colour of polished chestnuts. I believed I was almost attractive in that dress.

It was in a mood of exhilaration that I started down the stairs, and as I did so I came face to face with Mademoiselle de la Monelle. She looked enchanting in a gown of lavender chiffon trimmed with green satin bows; her fair hair was worn in curls held high with a clip of pearls and some glistening coils falling over her long slender neck. She looked at me in some bewilderment as though she were trying to remember where we had met before. I imagined I looked very different in this gown from how I looked in my shabby riding-habit.

'I'm Dallas Lawson,' I said. 'I'm restoring the pictures.'

'You are joining us?' There was a cold surprise in her voice which I found offensive.

'On the Comte's invitation,' I replied as coolly.

'Is that so?'

'Indeed, yes.'

Her eyes were taking in the details of my dress, assessing its cost; it seemed to surprise her as much as the Comte's invitation.

She turned and went on ahead of me. The gesture seemed to imply that even if the Comte was so eccentric as to invite someone who was working for him to mingle with his friends, *she* did not wish to know me.

The guests were gathered in one of the smaller rooms near the banqueting hall. The Comte had already become deep in conversation with Mademoiselle de la Monelle and was unaware of my entrance, but Philippe made his way towards me. I fancied he knew that I might be feeling a little uneasy and had been waiting for me. Another example of his kindness.

'May I say how elegant you look.'

'Thank you. I wanted to ask you whether the Mademoiselle de la Monelle who is here is a member of the family whose collection of paintings you mentioned.'

'Why . . . er . . . yes. Her father is here too. But I hope you won't mention this to my cousin.'

'Of course not. In any case I think it would be very unlikely that I should leave the château to go to her home.'

'You may think that now, but . . . if at any time . . .'

'Yes, I will remember it.'

Geneviève came over to us. She was wearing a dress of pink silk and looked rather sullen – scarcely a hint of the girl who had crowned the King for the day a short while ago.

At that moment dinner was announced and we went into the banqueting hall, where the glittering table was lit by candelabra placed at intervals.

I was seated next to an elderly gentleman who was interested in pictures and we talked together. I supposed I had been put there to entertain him. Turkey was served with chestnuts and truffles, but I did not enjoy it as I had that at the Bastides' – perhaps because I was so conscious of Mademoiselle de la Monelle seated next to the Comte, who seemed absorbed in her animated conversation.

How foolish I was to think I was attractive because I was wearing a beautiful dress! How much more foolish to imagine that he who had known many charming women would be aware of me when he was in the company of this one. Then I heard him mention my name –

'Mademoiselle Lawson has to answer for this.'

I looked up and met his eyes, and I did not know whether he was displeased with me or merely amused.

I fancied he had disapproved of my taking his daughter to eat Christmas dinner with his work-people, that he knew I was aware of this, and that he wanted me to be in doubt of what form his disapproval would take.

Mademoiselle de la Monelle was looking at me too. Her eyes, I thought, are ice-blue, cold and calculating. She was irritated because I, for the second time this evening, had been brought to her notice.

'Yes, Mademoiselle Lawson,' went on the Comte. 'Last night we were looking at the picture and your work on my ancestress was greatly admired. She has lived under a cloud for so many years. Now she has emerged, so have her emeralds. It's those emeralds . . .'

'Every so often interest in them is revived,' said Philippe.

'And, Mademoiselle Lawson, *you* have started the new revival.' He was looking at me in mock exasperation.

'And you don't wish for one?' I asked.

'Who knows? One of these new outbursts of interest may result in their discovery. Last night when the pictures were examined someone suggested a treasure hunt and the cry went up. So a treasure hunt there has to be. You must join in, of course.'

Mademoiselle de la Monelle laid a hand on his arm. 'I shall be terrified to wander about this place . . . alone.'

Someone replied that he very much doubted she would be allowed to do that; and there was laughter in which the Comte joined.

Then he was looking at me again, the laughter still in his eyes. 'A mock treasure hunt. You'll hear about it later. We're going to start soon because we don't know how long it will last. Gautier has been preparing the clues all morning.'

It was an hour or so later when the treasure hunt started. Clues had been written on pieces of paper and hidden at certain places all over the château.

Everyone was presented with the first clue from which they had to work out from the cryptic message where to go for the second; if they found the right place they would discover a little pile of papers there from which they would take one on which the next clue would be written; obviously the one who solved the final clue first would be the winner.

There was a great deal of chatter and exclamations of horror while they read their clues. Several of the guests went off in pairs. I could see neither the Comte, Philippe nor Geneviève and I felt as though I were in a household of strangers. No one approached me. Perhaps they wondered why a woman who was merely in the château to work for the Comte should have been asked to join the party. I supposed that had I lived in France I should have gone home for Christmas; did the fact that I was here, brand me as someone with nowhere to go?

I saw a young man and woman slip out hand in hand and it occurred to me that the object of a game like this was not so much to solve the clues but to give opportunities for flirtation.

I turned my attention to the clue and read:

'Go to do homage and drink if you are thirsty.'

After a few seconds' reflection that seemed simple. To do homage was to court and in the courtyard was a well.

I made my way through the loggia to the courtyard and sure enough there on the parapet round the well was a large stone under which the clues had been put. I took one out and hurried back into the castle. I looked at the next clue, which took me to the top of the tower. The castle had been especially lighted for this occasion and on the walls candles glowed in branches of three.

By the time I had discovered three of the clues I became excited by the game, and I found myself playing it with a great determination, for there is something fascinating about a treasure hunt – even a game – especially when it is played in an ancient château. And although this was a game there had been other more serious hunts. How they must have searched for those emeralds!

The sixth clue took me down to dungeons where I had only once been before, with Geneviève. The stairs were lighted so I did not think I had been mistaken in imagining I should find the clue somewhere down there.

Down the narrow stairs I went, clinging to the rope. I was in the dungeons. No, it couldn't be there – there were no lights. Gautier would not have set a clue in this gruesome place.

I was about to mount the stairs when I heard voices just above.

'But Lothair . . . my dear.'

I stepped back into the darkness, although there was no need to for they were not coming down the stairs.

I heard the Comte's voice, warm as I had never heard it before. 'I shall have to be content to have you here . . . always.'

'Have you thought what it will be like for me . . . living under the same roof?'

I should not have stood there, but I could not decide what I should do. To mount the stairs and confront them would embarrass us all. Perhaps they would go away and never know that I had overheard them. The woman was Mademoiselle de la Monelle and she was speaking to the Comte as though he were her lover.

'My dear Claude, you will be happier this way.'

'If it could be you . . . instead of Philippe.'

'You wouldn't be happy. You would never feel safe.'

'Do you imagine I should think you were going to murder me!'

'You don't understand. The scandal would be revived. You can't imagine how unpleasant it would be. It would be a canker to destroy everything. I have vowed never to marry again.'

'So you would have me go through this farce with Philippe.'

'It will be better for you. Now we must go back. But not together.'

'Lothair . . . just one moment.'

There was a short silence during which I imagined their embrace. Then I heard the footfalls growing fainter and I felt most desolately alone in the darkness.

I remounted the steps, no longer thinking of the clues. I knew that the Comte and Mademoiselle de la Monelle were lovers – or in love – and that he would not marry her. A man who had been suspected of murdering his first wife would be watched with suspicion if he took a second. It would be a delicate situation which only a strong-minded woman who loved him devotedly could handle. I did not think Mademoiselle de la Monelle fitted into that category. Perhaps he knew it too, for he was shrewd and I imagined that his head would always command his heart. So, if my inference was right, he had devised a scheme for marrying her to Philippe and keeping her in the house. It was cynical; but then so was he. It was, I told myself bitterly, typical of the man. Through the ages kings had found complaisant husbands for their mistresses because they could not – or would not – marry them themselves.

I was disgusted. I wished that I had never come to the château. If I could escape . . . Take the way out Philippe had offered and go to the home of Mademoiselle de la Monelle . . . As if I should escape that way! And how strange that it should have been to *her* home he had suggested sending me! There was only one retreat – home to England. I played with the idea, knowing very well I would not leave the château until I was forced to.

And what concern of yours are the murky love affairs of a dissolute French Comte? I asked myself. None whatever.

And to prove it I took a fresh look at the clue. It led me, instead of to the dungeons, to the gun gallery in which was the *oubliette*. I hoped I should not have to descend the ladder; surely Gautier would not have laid a clue there. I was right. I found what I wanted on the window seat; and when I read what was written on the paper I was told to report to the banqueting hall with all the clues, for that would take me to the end of the treasure hunt.

When I arrived there it was to find Gautier seated at a table drinking a glass of wine.

When he saw me he stood up and cried: 'Don't tell me you've found them all, Mademoiselle Lawson!'

I said I had and gave them to him.

'Well,' he said, 'you're the first in.'

'Perhaps,' I said, thinking of the Comte and Mademoiselle de la Monelle, 'the others didn't try very hard.'

'Well now, all you have to do is to go to the cabinet there for the treasure.'

I went to it, opened the drawer he indicated and found a cardboard box about two inches square.

'That's it,' he said. 'There'll be a ceremonial presentation.'

He picked up a brass bell and began to ring it.

It was the signal that the hunt was over and everyone should return to the hall.

It took some time for them all to assemble; I noticed that some were flushed and a little ruffled. The Comte, however, arrived looking as cool as ever; he came in alone and I noticed that Mademoiselle de la Monelle was with Philippe.

The Comte smiled when he knew that I was the winner and I fancied he was amused.

'Of course,' commented Philippe with a friendly smile, 'Mademoiselle Lawson had an unfair advantage. She's an expert on old houses.'

'Here is the treasure,' said the Comte, opening the box to disclose a brooch – a green stone on a slender gold bar.

One of the women cried: 'It looks like an emerald.'

'All the treasure hunts in this château are for emeralds. Didn't I tell you?' replied the Comte.

He took it from the box and said: 'Allow me, Mademoiselle Lawson.' And he pinned it on my dress.

'Thank you . . .' I murmured.

'Rather thank your skill, I don't think anyone else found more than three of Gautier's clues.'

Someone said: 'Had we known the prize was an emerald we might have tried harder. Why didn't you warn us, Lothair?'

Several of them came up to admire the brooch, among them Claude de la Monelle. I could sense her indignation. Her white fingers touched the brooch quickly.

'It really is an emerald!' she murmured. And as she turned away she added: 'Mademoiselle Lawson is a very clever woman, I am sure.'

'Oh, no,' I replied quickly. 'It was merely because *I* played the game.'

She turned back and for a moment our eyes met. Then she laughed and went to stand close to the Comte.

Musicians appeared and took their places on a dais. I watched Philippe and Mademoiselle de la Monelle lead the dance. Others fell in but no one approached me, and I felt suddenly so desolate that I wanted nothing so much as to slip away. This I did as quickly as possible and made my way to my room.

I unpinned the brooch and looked at it. Then I took out the miniature and thought of that moment when I had unwrapped it and seen who had sent it. How much happier I had been then than when he had pinned the emerald brooch on my dress! As my eyes fell on those white hands with the jade signet ring I had imagined them caressing Mademoiselle de la Monelle while they planned that she should marry Philippe because he, Lothair, the Comte de la Talle, had no wish to marry again.

There was no doubt that he saw himself as a king in his own world. He commanded and others obeyed; and no matter how cynical the proposal he put to those whom he considered to be his subjects, they were expected to obey.

How could I possibly make excuses for such a man?

Yet it had been such a happy Christmas until I had overheard that conversation.

I undressed thoughtfully and lay in bed listening to the far-off music. Down there they would be dancing and no one would miss me. How foolish I had been to indulge in day-dreams in which I had deceived myself into believing that I was of some importance to the Comte. This night had shown me how preposterous that was. I didn't belong here. I had not understood there were such men in the world as the Comte de la Talle. But I was beginning to. To-night I had learned a great deal.

Now I must be reasonable, sensible. I tried not to think of the Comte and his mistress, and another picture came into my mind. Jean Pierre with the crown on his head – King for a day.

I thought of his complacent expression, the pleasure he had taken in his temporary power.

All men, I thought, would be kings in their own castles.

And with that I fell into a sleep, but in my dreams I was disturbed and I was aware of a great shadow hanging over me which I knew was the hopeless future, but I covered up my eyes and refused to see it.

Chapter Seven

On the first day of the New Year Geneviève told me that she was going to ride over to Maison Carrefour to see her grandfather and wanted me to accompany her.

I thought it would be interesting to see the old house again so I readily agreed.

'When my mother was alive,' Geneviève told me, 'we always went to see Grandfather on New Year's Day. All children in France do the same.'

'It's a nice custom.'

'Cake and chocolate are brought for the children while the grown-ups drink wine and eat wine cakes. Then the children play the piano or the violin to show how they are getting on. Sometimes they have to recite.'

'Are you going to do this?'

'No, I shall have to say my catechism, though. My grandfather likes prayers better than the piano or the violin.'

I wondered how she felt about the visits to that strange house, and couldn't resist asking: 'You like going?'

She frowned and looked puzzled. 'I don't know. I want to go, and then . . . when I'm there, sometimes I feel as though I can't bear it any more. I want to run out . . . right away and never go there again. My mother used to talk of it so much that I sometimes feel I've lived there myself. I don't know whether I want to go or not, miss.'

When we reached the house Maurice let us in and took us to the old man, who looked more feeble than when I had last seen him.

'You know what day it is, Grandfather?' asked Geneviève.

And when he did not answer, she put her lips to his ear and said: 'New Year's Day! So I've come to see you. Mademoiselle Lawson is here, too.'

He caught my name and nodded. 'Good of you to come. You will excuse my not rising.'

We sat down near him. Yes, he had changed. There was a complete lack of serenity in his eyes; they looked like those of a lost man who is trying hard to find his way through a jungle. I guessed what he was searching for was memory.

'Shall I ring the bell?' asked Geneviève. 'We are rather hungry. I should like my cakes and chocolate, and I'm sure Mademoiselle Lawson is thirsty.'

He did not answer so she rang the bell. Maurice appeared and she ordered what she wanted.

'Grandfather is not so well to-day,' she said to Maurice.

'He has his bad days, Mademoiselle Geneviève.'

'I don't think he knows what to-day is,' Geneviève sighed and sat down. 'Grandfather,' she went on, 'we had a treasure hunt on Christmas night at the château and Mademoiselle Lawson won.'

'The only treasure is in Heaven,' he said.

'Oh, yes, Grandfather, but while you're waiting for that it's nice to find some on earth.'

He looked puzzled. 'You say your prayers?'

'Night and morning,' she answered.

'It is not enough. You, my child, must pray more earnestly than most. You have need of help. You were born in sin.'

'Yes, Grandfather, I know we all are but I do say my prayers. Nounou makes me.'

'Ah, the good Nounou! Always be kind to Nounou; she is a good soul.'

'She wouldn't let me forget my prayers, Grandfather.'

Maurice returned with wine, cakes and chocolate.

'Thank you, Maurice,' said Geneviève. 'I will serve them. Grandfather,' she continued, 'on Christmas Day Mademoiselle Lawson and I went to a party and they had a crèche and a cake with a crown in it. I wish you had had lots of sons and daughters, then their children would have been my cousins. They would all be here to-day and we could have had a cake with a crown in it.'

He didn't follow what she was saying; and had turned his gaze on me.

I tried to make some sort of conversation but I could only think of that cell-like room and the chest which contained the whip and hair shirt.

He was a fanatic – that much was obvious. But why had he become so? And what sort of life had Françoise led here? Why had she died when he had had a stroke? Was it because she could not endure to live without him? Without this man – this wild-eyed cadaverous fanatic in this gloomy house with its cell and chest ... when she was married to the Comte and the château was her home!

Everyone may not think that such a glorious fate as you do. . . .

I checked my thoughts. What had made me think such a thing? A glorious fate . . . when one who had suffered it – yes, suffered was the word . . . had killed herself.

But why ... why? What had started as idle curiosity was becoming a burning desire to know. Yet, I quickly told myself, there is nothing unusual in this. This passionate interest in the affairs of others was inherent. I had this curiosity to know how people's minds worked just as I cared deeply why a painter had used such a subject, why he had portrayed it in such a way, what had been behind his interpretation, his use of colour and mood.

The old man could not take his eyes from me. 'I can't see you very well,' he said. 'Could you come closer?'

I drew my chair close to him.

'It was wrong,' he whispered, 'quite wrong.'

He was talking to himself and I glanced at Geneviève, who was busily selecting a piece of chocolate from the dish Maurice had brought.

'Françoise must not know,' he said.

I knew his mind was wandering then and that I had been right when I had thought he was not so well as when we had last seen him.

He peered at me. 'Yes, you do look well to-day. Quiet.'

'Thank you, I feel well.'

'It was a mistake ... It was my cross and I was not strong enough to carry it.'

I was silent, wondering whether we ought to call Maurice.

He did not take his eyes from my face, and drew himself back in his chair as though he were afraid of me; as he moved, the rug about him slipped and I caught it and wrapped it about him. He recoiled and shouted: 'Go away. Leave me. You know my burden, Honorine.'

I said: 'Call Maurice.' And Geneviève ran from the room.

The old man had gripped my wrist; I felt his nails in my skin. 'You are not to blame,' he said. 'The sin is mine. It is my burden. I carry it to my grave ... Why are you not ...? Why did I ...? Oh, the tragedy ... Françoise ... little Francoise. Go away. Keep away from me. Honorine, why do you tempt me?'

Maurice came hurrying into the room. He took the rug and wrapped it round the old man and said over his shoulder: 'Slip outside. It would be better.'

So Geneviève and I went out of the room while Maurice took the crucifix which was hanging about the old man's neck and put it into his hands.

'That was frightening,' I said.

'Were you very frightened, miss?' asked Geneviève, almost pleased.

'He was wandering in his mind.'

'He often does. After all he's very old.'

'We shouldn't have come.'

'That's what Papa says.'

'You mean he forbids it?'

'Not exactly, because he isn't told when I'm coming. But if he knew, he would have.'

'Then . . .'

'Grandfather was my mother's father. Papa doesn't like him for that reason. After all he didn't like my mother, did he?'

As we rode back to the château, I said to Geneviève: 'He thought I was someone else. Once or twice he called me Honorine.'

'She was my mother's mother.'

'He seemed . . . afraid of her.'

Geneviève was thoughtful. 'It's odd that my grandfather should be afraid of anyone.'

I couldn't resist talking to Nounou about our visit to Carrefour.

She shook her head. 'Geneviève shouldn't,' she said. 'It's better not.'

'She wanted to go because of the New Year custom of visiting grandparents.'

'Customs are good in some families – not in others.'

'They are not observed much in this family,' I suggested.

'Oh, customs are for the poor. They make something to live for.'

'I think rich and poor enjoy them. But I wish we hadn't gone. Geneviève's grandfather was wandering in his mind and it was not pleasant.'

'Mademoiselle Geneviève should wait until he sends for her. She shouldn't pay these surprise calls.'

'He must have been very different when you were there . . . when Françoise was a child, I mean.'

'He was always a strict man. With himself and others. He should have been a monk.'

'Perhaps he thought so. I have seen that cell-like place where I imagined he slept at one time.'

Nounou nodded again. 'Such a man should never have married,' she said. 'But Françoise didn't know what was going on. I tried to make it all natural for her.'

'What was going on?' I asked.

She shot a sharp look at me. 'He wasn't cut out to be a father. He wanted the house run like a . . . monastery.'

'And her mother . . . Honorine.'

Nounou turned away. 'She was an invalid.'

'No,' I said, 'not a happy childhood for poor Françoise . . . a father a fanatic, a mother an invalid.'

'*I* saw that she was happy.'

'Yes, she sounds happy with her embroidery and piano lessons. She writes about them as though she enjoys them. When her mother died . . .'

'Yes?' said Nounou sharply.

'Was she very unhappy?'

Nounou rose and from a drawer took another of those little notebooks. 'Read it,' she said.

I opened it. She had been for a walk. She had had her music lesson. She had embroidered the altar cloth she was working on; she had had lessons with her governess. The orderly life of an ordinary little girl.

And then came the entry: 'Papa came to the schoolroom this morning when we were doing history. He looked very sad and said: "I have news for you, Françoise. You have no mother now!" I felt I ought to cry but I couldn't. And Papa looked at me so sadly and sternly. "Your mother has been ill for a long time and could never have been well. This is God's answer to our prayers." I had not prayed that she should *die*, I said; and he replied that God worked in a mysterious way. We had prayed for my mother and this was a happy release. "Her troubles are over now," he said. And he went out of the schoolroom.'

'Papa has been sitting in the death chamber for two days and nights. He has not left it and I have been there too to pay my respects to the dead. I knelt by the bed for a long time and I cried bitterly. I thought it was because Maman was dead but it was really because my knees hurt and I didn't like being there. Papa prays all the time; and it is all about forgiveness for his sins. I was frightened for if *he* is so sinful what about the rest of us who don't pray half as much as he does?'

'Maman wears a nightdress in her coffin. Papa says she is now at peace. All the servants have been in to pay their last respects. Papa stays there and prays all the time for forgiveness.'

'To-day was the funeral. It was a magnificent sight. The horses wore plumes and sable trappings. I walked with Papa at the head of the procession with a black veil all over my face and the new black frock which Nounou sat up all night to finish. I cried when we came out of the church and stood beside the hearse while the orator told everyone that Maman had been a saint. It seemed dreadful that such a *good* person should die.'

'It is quiet in the house. Papa is in his cell. I know he is praying because when I stood outside the door I could hear him. He prays for forgiveness, that his great sin may die with him, that he alone shall suffer. I think he is asking God not to be too hard on Maman when she gets to heaven and that whatever the Great Sin was, it was his fault not hers.'

I finished reading and looked up at Nounou.

'What is this Great Sin? Did you ever discover?'

'He was a man who saw sin in laughter.'

'I wonder he married. I wonder he didn't go into a monastery and live his life there.'

Nounou would only lift her shoulders.

The Comte went to Paris in the New Year and Philippe accompanied him. I was progressing with my work and now had several pictures to show for it. It was tremendously exhilarating to see their original beauty. It gave me great pleasure merely to look at them and to remember how little by little those glowing colours had emerged when they had been released from the grime of years. But this was more than a return to beauty; it was my own vindication. I had never enjoyed work as I did this; and I had never found a house which intrigued me as Château Gaillard did.

January was exceptionally cold and there was a great deal of activity in the vineyards, where it was feared the frosts would kill the vines. Geneviève and I often stopped during our rides or walks to watch the workers. Sometimes we called in at the Bastides' and on one occasion Jean Pierre took us down to the cellars and showed us the casks of wine which were maturing and explained to us the processes through which the wine had to pass.

Geneviève said that the deep cellars reminded her of the *oubliette* in the château to which Jean Pierre remarked that nothing was forgotten here. He showed us how the light was admitted through small apertures in order to regulate the temperature; he warned us that no plants or flowers must be brought down here as they give something to the wine which would spoil the taste.

'How old are these cellars?' Geneviève wanted to know.

'They've been here as long as there was wine here . . . and that's hundreds of years ago.'

'And while they looked after their wine and made sure the temperature was all right,' commented Geneviève, 'they were putting people into the dungeons and leaving them to freeze and starve to death.'

'Wine being more important to your noble ancestors than their enemies, naturally.'

'And all those years ago it was the Bastides who made the wine.'

'And there was one Bastide who earned the honour of becoming an enemy of your noble ancestors. His bones lie in the château.'

'Oh, Jean Pierre! Where?'

'In the *oubliette*. He was insolent to the Comte de la Talle, was called before him, and never seen again. He went to the château, but he never came out. Imagine him. Called before the Comte. "Come in, Bastide. Now what is this trouble you are making?" The bold Bastide tries to explain, falsely believing that he is as good as his masters; and then Monsieur le Comte moves his foot and the ground opens . . . down goes the insolent Bastide where others have gone before him. To freeze to death, to starve to death . . . to die of the wounds he receives in the fall. What does it matter? He is no longer a nuisance to Monsieur le Comte.'

'You still sound resentful,' I said in surprise.

'Oh, no. There was the Revolution. Then it was the turn of the Bastides.'

He was not talking seriously, for almost immediately he was laughing.

The weather changed suddenly and the vines were no longer in acute danger, although, Jean Pierre told us, the spring frost could be the most dangerous enemy of all to the grape because it could strike unexpectedly.

Those days stand out as the peaceful days. There were happy little incidents which I remember vividly. Geneviève and I were often together; our friendship was growing slowly but steadily. I made no attempt to force it, for although I was growing closer to her there were times when she seemed a stranger to me. She had been right when she had said she had two personalities. Sometimes I found her watching me almost slyly: at others she was naïvely affectionate.

I thought constantly of the Comte and when he was absent once again I started to build up a picture of him which common sense warned me was not true. I remembered his tolerance in giving me a chance to prove my ability, and his generosity, when he found he had been wrong to doubt me, in admitting it by giving me the miniature. Then he had put the presents in the shoes, which showed a desire to make his daughter happy. I was sure he had been pleased that I had won the emerald brooch. Why? Simply because he wanted me to have something of value that would be a little nest-egg for the future.

I shivered, contemplating that future. I could not stay indefinitely at the château. I had restored a number of the pictures in the gallery and those were the ones I had been employed to deal with. The work would not last for ever. Yet in this pleasant dream-world in which I lived during those weeks, it was firmly fixed in my mind that I should be at the château for a long time to come.

Some people find it easy to believe things are what they want them to be. I had never been like that . . . until now, preferring always to face the truth, priding myself on my good sense. I had changed since I had come here; and oddly enough I would not look deep enough into my mind to discover why.

Mardi Gras was the time for carnival, and Geneviève was as excited as Yves and Margot, who showed her how to make paper flowers and masks; and because I thought it was good for her to join in these activities we rode into the little town on one of the Bastides' carts and behind our grotesque masks we pelted each other with paper flowers.

We were present in the square when they hung the Carnival Man from the mock gibbet and we actually danced in the crowd.

Geneviève was ecstatic when we returned to the castle.

'I've often heard of Mardi Gras,' she declared, 'but I never knew it was such fun.'

'I hope,' I said, 'that your father would not have objected to your being there.'

'We shall never know,' she answered mischievously, 'because we're not going to tell him, are we, miss?'

'If he asked we should certainly tell him,' I retorted.

'He never would. He's not interested in us, miss.'

Was she a little resentful? Perhaps, but she cared less about his neglect than she had once. And Nounou raised no objections as long as wherever Geneviève went I was with her. She seemed to have a faith in me which I found flattering.

And when I took her into the town Jean Pierre had been with us. It was he who suggested these jaunts; he delighted in them; and Geneviève enjoyed his company. No harm could come to Geneviève while she was with the Bastides, I assured myself.

It was during the first week of Lent that the Comte and Philippe returned to the château.

The news spread rapidly throughout the household and in the town.

Philippe was betrothed. He was going to marry Mademoiselle Claude de la Monelle.

The Comte came to me in the gallery where I was working. It was a lovely sunny morning, and now that the days were longer I was spending more time in the gallery. The brightness made more obvious my work of restoration, and he studied the pictures with pleasure.

'Excellent, Mademoiselle Lawson,' he murmured; and his eyes were on me, dark with the expression which always set me wondering.

'And what's this operation?' he asked.

I explained to him that the painting on which I was working had been badly damaged and that layers of paint were missing. I was filling them with gesso putty and afterwards I should retouch with paint.

'You are an artist, Mademoiselle Lawson.'

'As you once remarked . . . an artist *manquée.*'

'And you have forgiven though not forgotten that unkind observation?'

'One does not have to forgive others for speaking the truth.'

How strong-minded you are. We as well as our pictures have need of you.'

He had taken a step nearer to me and his eyes were still fixed on my face. It could not be with admiration? I knew what I looked like. My brown coat had never been becoming: my hair had a habit of escaping from its pins and I was always unaware of it until something happened to make me; my hands were stained with the materials I used. It was certainly not my appearance which interested him.

It was the way in which philanderers behaved to all women, of course. The thought spoilt my pleasure in the moment and I tried to push it away.

I said: 'You need have no fear. I shall use a paint which is easily soluble in case it should have to be removed. Colours ground in synthetic resin are, you know.'

'I did not know,' he replied.

'It is so. You see, when these pictures were painted, artists mixed their own paints. They and they alone knew the secrets . . . and each painter had his own method. That is what makes the old masters unique. It's so difficult to copy them.'

He bowed his head.

'Retouching is a delicate operation,' I went on. 'Naturally a restorer should not attempt to add his ideas to an original.'

He was amused, realizing perhaps that I was talking to hide my embarrassment. Then he said suddenly: 'I can see that could be disastrous. It would be like trying to make a person what you thought he should be. Instead of which you should help to bring out the good . . . subdue the evil.'

'I was thinking only of painting. It is the only subject on which I could speak with some knowledge.'

'And your enthusiasm when you speak of it proclaims you an expert. Tell me, how is my daughter progressing with her English?'

'She is making excellent progress.'

'And you do not find teaching her and the care of the pictures too much for you?'

I smiled. 'I enjoy them both so much.'

'I'm glad that we can provide you with so much pleasure. I thought you might find our country life dull.'

'By no means. I have to thank you for allowing me the use of your stables.'

'Something else you enjoy?'

'Very much.'

'Life here at the château has been much quieter than in the past.' He looked over my head and added coldly: 'After my wife's death we did not entertain as we used to and we have never gone back to the old ways. It will probably be different now that my cousin is to be married and his wife will be mistress of the château.'

'Until,' I said impulsively, 'you yourself marry.'

I was sure I detected bitterness in his voice as he said: 'What makes you imagine I should do so?'

I felt I had been guilty of tactlessness and I said in self-defence: 'It seems perhaps natural that you should . . . in time.'

'I thought that you knew the circumstances of my wife's death, Mademoiselle Lawson?'

'I have heard . . . talk,' I replied, feeling like a woman who has put one foot in a quagmire and must withdraw quickly before she is completely submerged.

'Ah,' he said, 'talk! There are people who believe I murdered my wife.'

'I am sure you would not be affected by such nonsense.'

'You are embarrassed?' He was smiling, taunting me now. 'That shows me that you do not think it is necessarily nonsense. You think me capable of the darkest deeds. Admit it.'

My heart had begun to beat uncomfortably fast. 'You are joking, of course,' I said.

'This is what we expect of the English, Mademoiselle Lawson. This is unpleasant, so we will not discuss it.' His eyes were angry suddenly. 'No, we will not discuss it; better to continue to believe in the victim's guilt.'

I was startled. 'You are quite wrong,' I said quietly.

He had recovered his calm as quickly as he had lost it. 'And you, Mademoiselle Lawson, are admirable. You understand, though, that in the circumstances I should never marry again. But you are surprised that I should discuss my views on marriage with you?'

'I'll admit I am.'

'But then you are such a sympathetic listener. I do not mean sympathetic in the usual sentimental sense. I mean that you betray such calm good sense, such frankness, and these qualities have lured me to the indiscretion of discussing my private affairs with you.'

'I am not sure whether I should thank you for your compliments or apologize for luring you to indiscretion.'

'You mean that as you do everything – or almost everything – you say. That is why I am going to ask you a question, Miss Lawson. Will you give me a frank answer?'

'I will try to.'

'Well, here it is: Do you think I murdered my wife?'

I was startled; his heavy lids half hid his eyes but I knew he was watching me intently, and for a few significant seconds I did not answer.

'Thank you,' he said.

'I have not answered yet.'

'But you have. You wanted time to find a tactful answer. I did not ask for tact. I wanted truth.'

'You must allow me to speak, having asked my opinion.'

'Well?'

'I do not believe for one moment that you gave your wife a dose of poison, but . . .'

'But . . .'

'Perhaps you . . . disappointed her . . . perhaps you did not make her happy. I mean perhaps she was unhappy being married to you and rather than continue so she took her life.'

He was looking at me with the twisted smile on his lips. I sensed in him then a deep unhappiness and there came to me an overwhelming desire to make him happy. It was absurd, but it was there, and I could not deny it. I believed that I had seen a little of the man beneath that exterior of arrogance and indifference to others.

It was almost as though he read my thoughts, for his expression hardened as he replied: 'Now you see, Mademoiselle Lawson, why I have no desire to marry; you think I am obliquely guilty, and you being such a wise young woman are no doubt right.'

'You are thinking me foolish, tactless, gauche . . . everything that you most dislike.'

'I find you . . . refreshing, Mademoiselle Lawson. You know that. But I believe you have a saying in your country. "Give a dog a bad name and hang him." Is that so?' I nodded. 'Well, here you see that dog with his bad name. A bad name is one of the easiest things to live up to. There! In exchange for the lesson you gave me on restoring pictures I have given you one on family history. What I set out to tell you was that, as soon as Easter is over, my cousin and I will leave for Paris. There is no reason why Philippe's marriage should be delayed. He and I will attend the *diner-contrat* at the bride's house and after that there will be ceremonies. The honeymoon will follow and when they return to the château we shall do a little more entertaining.'

How could he talk so calmly of this matter? When I considered his part in it, I felt angry with him for behaving so and with myself for so easily forgetting his faults and being ready to accept him on his own terms, one might say, every time he presented himself to me in a new light.

He went on: 'We shall give a ball as soon as they return. The new Madame de la Talle will expect it. Then two nights later we shall have a ball for everyone connected with the château . . . the vine-workers, the

servants, everyone. It is an old custom when the heir to the château marries.
I hope you will attend both these ceremonies.'

'I shall be delighted to join in with the workers, but I am not sure that
Madame de la Talle would wish me to be a guest at her ball.'

'I wish it and if I invite you she will welcome you. You are not sure of
that? My dear Miss Lawson, I am the master of the house. Only my death
can alter that.'

'I am sure of it,' I answered, 'but I came here to work and am not
prepared for grand functions.'

'But I am sure you will adjust yourself to the unexpected. I must not
detain you further. I see you are waiting to return to your work.'

With that he left me – bewildered, excited, and with the faint warning
that I was sinking lower into a quicksand from which every day it was
becoming more difficult to escape. Did he know this? Was his conversation
meant to convey a warning?

The Comte and Philippe left for Paris the day after Good Friday; and on
Monday I went to call on the Bastides, where I found Yves and Margot
playing in the garden. They called out to me to come and see the Easter eggs
which they had found on Sunday – some in the house, some in the out-
houses; there were as many as they found last year.

'Perhaps you don't know, miss,' said Margot, 'that the bells all go to Rome
for the benediction and on the way they drop eggs for the children to find.'

I admitted that I had never heard that before.

'Then don't you have Easter eggs in England?' asked Yves.

'Yes . . . but just as presents.'

'These are presents, too,' he told me. 'The bells don't really drop them.
But we find them, you see. Would you like one?'

I said I would like to take one for Geneviève, who would be pleased to
hear that they had found it.

The egg was carefully wrapped up and solemnly presented to me, and I
told them I had come to see their mother.

Glances were exchanged and Yves said: 'She's gone out . . .'

'With Gabrielle,' added Margot.

'Then I'll see her some other day. Is anything wrong?'

They lifted their shoulders to indicate ignorance, so I said good-bye and
continued my walk.

This took me to the river and there I saw their maid-servant Jeanne with
a *brouette* of clothes. She was beating them with a piece of wood as she
washed them in the river.

'Good afternoon, Jeanne,' I said.

'Good afternoon, miss.'

'I've been to the house. But I've missed Madame Bastide.'

'She has gone into the town.'

'It's so rarely that she is out at this time of day.'

Jeanne nodded and grimaced at her stick.

'I hope all is well, miss.'

'Have you reason to think is isn't?'

'I have a daughter of my own.'

I was puzzled and wondered whether I had been mistaken in the patois. 'You mean Mademoiselle Gabrielle . . .'

'Madame is most distressed and I know that she has taken Mademoiselle Gabrielle to the doctor.' She spread her hands. 'I pray to the saints that there is nothing wrong, but when the blood is hot, mademoiselle, these things will happen.'

I could not believe what she was hinting, so I said: 'I hope Mademoiselle Gabrielle has nothing contagious.'

I left her smiling to herself at what she thought was my innocence. I felt very anxious, though, on behalf of the Bastides, and on my way back I called at the house.

Madame Bastide was at home; she received me, her face stony with bewilderment and grief.

'Perhaps I've called at the wrong time,' I said. 'I'll go, unless there is anything I can do.'

'No,' she said. 'Don't go. This is not a matter which can be kept secret for long . . . and I know you are discreet. Sit down, Dallas.'

She herself sat heavily and leaning her arm on the table covered her face with one hand.

I waited in embarrassment, and after a few minutes when I believed she was contemplating how much to tell me she lowered her hand and said, 'That this should have happened in our family!'

'Is it Gabrielle?' I asked.

She nodded.

'Where is she?'

She jerked her head to the ceiling. 'In her room. She's stubborn. She won't say a word.'

'She's ill?'

'Ill. I'd rather she were. I'd rather anything . . . but this.'

'Can nothing be done?'

'She won't tell us. She won't say who it is. I never believed this could be. She was never a girl to go gadding about. She's always been so quiet.'

'Perhaps it can all be worked out.'

'I hope so. I dread what Jean Pierre will say when he hears. He's so proud. He'll be so angry with her.'

'Poor Gabrielle!' I murmured.

'Poor Gabrielle! I wouldn't have believed it. And not a word until I found out, and then . . . I saw how frightened she was, so I guessed I was right. I thought she'd been looking peaky lately; worried . . . never joining in with the family; and then we were getting the washing ready this morning, and she fainted. I was pretty certain then, so down to the doctor we went and he confirmed what I feared.'

'And she refused to tell you the name of her lover?'

Madame Bastide nodded. 'That's what worries me. If it was one of the young men . . . well, we'd not like it but we could put it to rights. But as she won't say, I'm afraid . . . Why should she be afraid to tell us if it could all be put right? That's what I want to know. It looks as if it's someone who can't do the right thing.'

I asked if I could make some coffee, and to my surprise she allowed me to. She sat at the table staring blankly before her and when I had made it I said could I take a cup up to Gabrielle.

Permission given I carried the cup upstairs and when I knocked at the door Gabrielle said: 'It's no use, Grand'mère.' So I opened the door and went in holding the cup of steaming coffee.

'You . . . Dallas!'

'I've brought you this. I thought you might like it.'

She lay and looked at me with leaden eyes.

I pressed her hand. Poor Gabrielle, her position was that of thousands of girls and to each it is a new and personal tragedy.

'Is there anything we can do?' I asked.

She shook her head.

'You can't marry and . . .'

She shook her head more violently and turned it away so that I could not see her face.

'Is he . . . married already?'

She closed her lips tightly and refused to answer.

'Well, in that case, he can't marry you and you'll just have to try and be as brave as possible.'

'They're going to hate me,' she said. 'All of them . . . It won't be the same again.'

'That's not true,' I said. 'They're shocked . . . they're hurt . . . but they'll grow away from that, and when the child comes they'll love it.'

She smiled at me wanly. 'You always want to make things right, Dallas, people as well as pictures. There's nothing you can do, though. I've made my bed, as they say, and I'm the one that's got to lie on it.'

'Someone else should be with you in this trouble.'

But she was stubborn and would not tell anything.

I went sadly back to the château remembering that happy table on Christmas Day and thinking how suddenly, how alarmingly, life could change. There was no security in happiness.

The Comte did not return to the château immediately after the wedding. Philippe and his bride had gone to Italy for their honeymoon and I wondered whether the Comte had found someone with whom to amuse himself now that he had so cynically handed Claude to Philippe.

That, I told myself angrily, was the most reasonable explanation of his absence.

He did not return until it was almost time for Claude and Philippe to come home and even then he made no attempt to see me alone. I asked myself whether he sensed my disapproval. As if he would care for that! Still, he might decide that I was being even more presumptuous than usual.

I was very disappointed, for I had been hoping to talk to him again and I was dreading the time when Philippe and his wife returned. I was certain that Claude already disliked me and I imagined she was the sort of woman who would make no secret of her dislike. Perhaps it would be necessary to take up Philippe's offer to find me other employment. In spite of my growing apprehension, the thought of leaving the château was distinctly depressing.

After the three weeks' honeymoon they returned, and on the very day following her arrival I had an encounter with Claude and discovered how deeply she disliked me.

I was coming from the gallery when we met.

'I should have thought you would have finished the work by now,' she said. 'I remember how well advanced you were at Christmas time.'

'Restoring pictures is a very exacting task. And the collection in the gallery has been sadly neglected.'

'But I thought it would present little difficulty to *such* an expert.'

'There are always difficulties and a great deal of patience is required.'

'Which is why you need such concentration and cannot work all day?'

So she had noticed my method! And was she hinting that I was wasting time in order to prolong my stay at the castle?

I said warmly: 'You can be assured, Madame de la Talle, that I shall finish the pictures as quickly as possible.'

She bowed her head. 'It is a pity that they could not have been completed in time for the ball which we are giving to our friends. I expect you, like the rest of the household, are looking forward to the *second* ball.'

She swept past me before I had time to answer. She was clearly indicating that she would not expect to see me at the first. I wanted to cry out: 'But the Comte has already invited me. And he is still the master of the house!'

I went to my room and looked at the green velvet dress. Why shouldn't I go? *He* had asked me and he would expect me. What a triumph to be welcomed by him under the haughty nose of the new Madame de la Talle.

But by the night of the ball I had changed my mind. He had not found an opportunity of being with me. Did I really think that he would take my side against hers?

I went to bed early on the night of the ball. I could hear the music now and then from the ballroom as I lay trying to read but actually picturing the brilliant scene. On the dais the musicians would be playing behind the banks of carnations which I had seen the gardeners arranging during the day. I pictured the Comte opening the ball with his cousin's wife. I imagined myself in my green dress with the emerald brooch I had won at the treasure hunt pinned to it. Then I began thinking of the emeralds in the portrait and myself wearing them. I should look like a comtesse.

I gave a snort of laughter and picked up my book. But I found it difficult to concentrate. I thought of the voices I had heard from the top of the staircase which led to the dungeons and I wondered whether those two were together now. Were they congratulating each other on their cleverness in arranging this marriage which brought her under his roof?

What an explosive situation! What would come out of it? It was small wonder that scandal surrounded the Comte. Had he been as reckless in his treatment of his wife?

I heard footsteps in the corridor outside my room. I listened. They had stopped outside my door. Someone was standing there. I could distinctly hear the sound of breathing.

I sat up in bed, my eyes fixed on the door; then suddenly the handle turned.

'Geneviève!' I cried. 'You startled me.'

'I'm sorry. I've been standing outside wondering whether you were asleep.'

She came and sat on the bed. Her blue silk ball dress was charming but her expression sullen.

'It's a hateful ball,' she said.

'Why?'

'*Aunt* Claude!' she said. 'She's not my aunt. She's the wife of Cousin Philippe.'

'Speak English,' I said.

'I can't when I'm angry. I have to think too much and I can't be angry and think at the same time.'

'Then perhaps it would be an even better idea if you spoke English.'

'Oh miss, you sound just like old Esquilles. To think that woman is going to live here . . .'

'Why do you dislike her so?'

'I don't dislike her. I hate her.'

'What has she done to you?'

'She's come here to live. If she would stay in one place all the time I wouldn't mind because then I shouldn't have to go where she was.'

'Please, please, Geneviève, don't plan to shut her in the *oubliette*.'

'Nounou would get her out so that wouldn't be any good.'

'Why have you turned against her? She's very pretty.'

'I don't like pretty people. I like them plain like you, miss.'

'What a charming compliment.'

'They spoil things.'

'She's hardly been here long enough to spoil anything.'

'She will, though. You see. My mother didn't like pretty women either. They spoilt it for her.'

'You can't know anything about that.'

'I do, I tell you. She used to cry. And then they'd quarrel. They quarrelled quietly. I always think quiet quarrels are worse than noisy ones. Papa just says cruel things quietly and that makes them more cruel. He says them as though they amuse him . . . as though people amuse him because they're so stupid. He thought she was stupid. It made her very unhappy.'

'Geneviève, I don't think you should go on brooding on what happened so long ago, and you don't really know very much about it.'

'I know that he killed her, don't I?'

'You know no such thing.'

'They say she killed herself. But she didn't. She wouldn't have left me all alone.'

I laid my hand over hers. 'Don't think about it,' I begged.

'But you have to think about what's happening in your own home! It's because of what happened that Papa hasn't got a wife. That's why Philippe's had to get married. If I had been a son it would have been different. Papa doesn't like me because I'm not a son.'

'I'm sure you imagine your father doesn't like you.'

'I don't like you much when you pretend. You're like all grown-up people. When they don't want to answer they pretend they don't know what you're talking about. I think my father killed my mother and she comes back from the grave to have her revenge on him.'

'What nonsense!'

'She walks about the château at night with the other ghosts from the *oubliette*. I've heard them, so it's no use your saying they're not there.'

'Next time you hear them, come and tell me.'

'Shall I, miss? I haven't heard them for a long time. I'm not frightened, because my mother wouldn't let them hurt me. Remember you told me that?'

'Let me know when you hear them next.'

'Do you think we could go and look for them, miss?'

'I don't know. We would listen first.'

She leaned towards me and cried: 'It's a promise.'

At the château there was talk of little else but the ball for the servants and the vine-workers, and preparations went on with more feverish activity than for those given by the Comte for his friends. There was chattering in courtyards and corridors and the servants were obviously humoured during that day.

I wore my green dress for the occasion. I felt the need for confidence. I dressed my hair high on my head and the effect was pleasing.

I was thinking a great deal about Gabrielle Bastide and wondering whether she had come to any decision.

Boulanger, the *sommelier*, was the master of ceremonies, and he received everyone in the banqueting hall of the castle. There was to be a buffet supper during the evening and the newly married pair, together with the Comte and Geneviève, would appear when the ball was in progress. They would slip in, so I was told, unceremoniously and dance with a few of the company; and then Boulanger would – as if by chance – discover their presence and propose the health of the newly married couple which would be drunk by all in the best château wine.

The Bastide family had already arrived by the time I joined the ball. Gabrielle was with them, looking very pretty, although melancholy, in a dress of pale blue which I guessed she had made herself, for I had heard that she was very good with her needle.

Madame Bastide had come on the arm of her son Armand; and she took an early opportunity of whispering to me that Jean Pierre did not yet know; they hoped to have discovered the name of the man and have arranged a marriage by the time he did.

Jean Pierre sought me out and we danced together to the tune of the *Sautière Charentaise* which I had heard before in the Bastide house and to which the words Jean Pierre had once sung to me were set.

He sang them softly as we danced:

'*Qui sont-ils les gens qui sont riches . . .*'

'You see,' he said, 'even here, in all this splendour, I can still sing those words. This is a great occasion for us humble folk. It is not often that we have an opportunity of dancing in the château ballroom.'

'Is it any better than dancing in your own home? I did enjoy Christmas Day so much – and so did Geneviève. In fact I am sure she preferred your celebrations to those of the château.'

'She is a strange girl, that one.'

'I loved to see her so happy.'

He smiled at me warmly and I kept thinking of Gabrielle coming in with the crown on the cushion and later when he had kissed us as a privilege due to the King for the day.

'She has been happier since you came here, perhaps,' he added. 'She is not the only one.'

'You flatter me.'

'Truth is not flattery, Dallas.'

'In that case I am pleased to know I am so popular.'

He pressed my hand lightly. 'Inevitably so,' he assured me. 'Ah, look . . . the great ones are with us. I do declare Monsieur le Comte has his eyes on us. Perhaps he is looking for you, as the one who not being as humble as his servants or those who work in his vineyards, as a most suitable partner.'

'I am sure he thinks no such thing.'

'You are hot in his defence.'

'I am quite cool and he has no need of my defence.'

'We shall see. Shall we have a little bet – you and I? I will say that the first one he dances with will be you.'

'I never gamble.'

The music had stopped. 'As if by chance,' murmured Jean Pierre, 'Monsieur Boulanger has given the discreet sign. Stop dancing! The great are among us.' He led me to a chair and I sat down. Philippe and Claude had separated from the Comte, who was coming in my direction. The music struck up again. I turned my head towards the musicians, expecting every moment to see him standing there, for I, like Jean Pierre, had thought he would choose to dance with me.

I was astonished to see him dance past with Gabrielle.

I turned to Jean Pierre with a laugh.

'I rather regret I do not gamble.'

Jean Pierre was looking after the Comte and his sister with a puzzled look.

'And I regret,' he said, turning to me, 'that you will have to be content with the master of the vineyard instead of the master of the castle.'

'I am delighted to do so,' I replied lightly.

As we danced I saw Claude with Boulanger and Philippe with Madame Duval, who was the head of the female staff. I supposed the Comte had chosen Gabrielle as the member of the Bastide family, who were the head of the vineyards.

When the dance was over Boulanger made his speech, and the health of Philippe and Claude was drunk by everyone present. After that the musicians played what I learned was the *Marche pour Noce* and this was led by Philippe and Claude.

It was then that the Comte approached me.

In spite of my determination to remain aloof I felt my cheeks flush slightly as he took my hand lightly and asked for the pleasure of the dance.

I said: 'I am not sure that I know the dance. This seems to be something indigenous to France.'

'No more than the *noce* itself, and you cannot pretend, Mademoiselle Lawson, that we are the only nation who marry.'

'I had no intention of doing so. But this dance is unknown to me.'

'Did you dance much in England?'

'Not often. I rarely had the opportunity.'

'A pity. I was never much of a dancer myself but I suspect you would dance well as you do everything else, if you had the will to. You should seize every opportunity . . . even if you are not eager to mingle with the company. You did not accept my invitation to the ball. I wondered why.'

'I thought I explained that I had not come prepared to attend grand functions.'

'But I had hoped that as I expressed my special desire that you would be there, you would have come.'

'I did not think that my absence would have been noticed.'

'It was . . . and regretted.'

'Then I am sorry.'

'You do not appear to be.'

'I meant that I am sorry to have caused regret – not to have missed the ball.'

'That is good of you, Mademoiselle Lawson. It shows a pleasant concern for the feelings of others which is always so comforting.'

Geneviève danced past with Jean Pierre. She was laughing up at him; I saw that the Comte had noticed this.

'My daughter is like you, Mademoiselle Lawson; she prefers certain entertainments to others.'

'No doubt this seems a trifle gayer than the more grand occasion.'

'How can you know that when you weren't there?'

'It was a suggestion – not a statement of fact.'

'I might have known. You are also so meticulous. You must give me another lesson in restoration. I was fascinated by the last. You will find me visiting you in the gallery one morning.'

'That will be a pleasure.'

'Will it?'

I looked into those strange hooded eyes and said: 'Yes, it will be.'

The dance was over and he could not dance with me again; that would be to invite comment. Not more than once with each member of the household; and after six dances he would be free to go, so Jean Pierre told me. It was the custom. He, Philippe, Claude and Geneviève would perform their duty and one by one slip away – not all together; that would appear too formal and informality was the order of the day; but the Comte would go first and the others choose their time.

It was as he said. I noticed the Comte slip away quietly. After that I had no great wish to stay.

I was dancing with Monsieur Boulanger when I saw Gabrielle leave the ballroom. She gave a quick look round, pretended to examine the tapestry on the wall and then another quick look and she was out of the door.

For one second I had glimpsed her desperate expression and I was afraid of what she might be going to do.

I had to make sure; so as soon as the music stopped and I could escape from my partner I took an opportunity of slipping out too.

I had no idea where she had gone. I wondered what a desperate girl would do. Throw herself down from the top of the castle? Drown herself in the old well in the courtyard?

As I stood outside the ballroom I realized the unlikelihood of either. If Gabrielle was going to commit suicide why should she choose the castle, unless of course there was some reason . . .

I knew of one which I would not accept. But while my mind rejected it my footsteps by some instinct led me towards the library where I had had my interviews with the Comte.

I wanted very much to be able to laugh at the notion which had come into my head.

I reached the library. I could hear the sound of voices and I knew whose they were. Gabrielle's breathless . . . rising to hysteria. The Comte's low yet resonant.

I turned and went to my room. I had no desire to go back to the ballroom. No desire for anything but to be alone.

A few days later I went to call at Maison Bastide, where Madame Bastide received me with pleasure, and I could see that she was feeling much better than she had when I had last been in the house.

'The news is good. Gabrielle is going to be married.'

'Oh, I am so pleased.'

Madame Bastide smiled at me. 'I knew you would be,' she said. 'You have made our trouble yours.'

My relief was obvious. I was laughing at myself. (You fool, you suspicious fool, why do you always believe the worst of him!)

'Please tell me,' I begged. 'I am so happy about this and I can see you are.'

'Well,' said Madame Bastide, 'in time people will know it was a hasty marriage . . . but these things happen. They have forestalled their marriage vows as so many young people do, but they will confess and be shriven. And they will not bring a bastard into the world. It is the children who suffer.'

'Yes, of course. And when will Gabrielle be married?'

'In three weeks. It is wonderful, for Jacques is now able to marry. That was the trouble. He could not support a wife and a mother, and knowing this Gabrielle had not told him of her condition. But Monsieur le Comte will make everything right.'

'Monsieur le Comte!'

'Yes. He has given Jacques charge of the St. Vallient vineyard. For a long time Monsieur Durand has been too old. He is now to have his cottage on the estate and Jacques will take over St. Vallient. But for Monsieur le Comte, it would have been difficult for them to marry.'

'I see,' I said slowly.

Gabrielle was married, and although there was a good deal of gossip which I heard on my expeditions to the little town and in the château and vineyard district, these comments were always whispered with a shrug of the shoulders. Such affairs provided the excitement of a week or two and none could be sure when their own families would be plunged into a similar situation. Gabrielle would marry and if the baby arrived a little early, well, babies had a habit of doing that the whole world over.

The wedding was celebrated at the Maison Bastide with all that Madame Bastide considered essential in spite of the fact that there had been little time to prepare. The Comte, so I heard, had been good to his workers and had given the couple a handsome wedding present which would buy the furniture they needed; and as they were taking over some of the Durands' pieces, because naturally the old couple couldn't fit them into a small cottage, they could settle in at once.

The change in Gabrielle was astonishing. Serenity replaced fear and she looked prettier than ever. When I went over to St. Vallient to see her and Jacques's old mother she made me very welcome. There was so much I should have liked to ask her but I could not, of course; I wanted to tell her that I did not want to know merely to satisfy an idle curiosity.

When I left she asked me to look in again when I was riding that way and I promised to do so.

It was four or five weeks after the wedding. We were now well into spring and the climbing stems of the vines were beginning to grow fast. There was continual activity out of doors which would continue until harvest.

Geneviève was with me but our relationship was no longer as harmonious as it had been. The presence of Claude in the château affected her adversely and I was continually on tenterhooks wondering what turn it would take. I had felt I was making some progress with her; and now it was as though I had achieved a false brightness on a picture by using a solution which could only give a temporary effect and might even be injurious to the paint.

I said: 'Shall we call on Gabrielle?'

'I don't mind.'

'Oh, well, if you are not eager, I'll go alone.'

She shrugged her shoulders but continued to ride beside me.

'She's going to have a baby,' she said.

'That,' I replied, 'will make her and her husband very happy.'

'It will arrive a little too soon, though, and everyone is talking about it.'

'Everyone! I know many who are not. You really shouldn't exaggerate. And why are you not speaking in English?'

'I'm tired of speaking in English. It's such a tiresome language.' She laughed. 'It was a marriage of convenience. I've heard that said.'

'All marriages should be convenient.'

That made her laugh again. Then she said: 'Good-bye, miss. I'm not coming. I might embarrass you by talking indelicately . . . or even looking. You never know.'

She spurred her horse and turned away. I was about to follow her because she was not supposed to be riding about the countryside alone. But she had the start of me and had disappeared into a small copse.

It was less than a minute later when I heard the shot.

'Geneviève!' I called. As I galloped towards the copse, I heard her scream. The branches of the trees caught at me as though to impede me – and I called again: 'Geneviève, where are you? What's happened?'

She was sobbing: 'Oh, miss . . . miss . . .'

I went in the direction of her voice. I found her; she had dismounted and her horse was standing patiently by.

'What's happening . . .' I began; and then I saw the Comte lying on the grass, his horse beside him. There was blood all over his riding-jacket.

'He's . . . he's been . . . killed,' stammered Geneviève.

I leaped to the ground and knelt beside him. A terrible fear came to me then.

'Geneviève,' I said, 'go quickly for help. St. Vallient is nearest. Send someone for a doctor.'

Those next minutes are hazy in my mind. I listened to the thudding of hoofbeats as Geneviève reached the road and galloped off.

'Lothair . . .' I murmured, saying his unusual name for the first time and saying it aloud. 'It can't be. I couldn't bear it. I could bear anything but that you should die.'

I noticed the short thick lashes; the hoodlike lids drawn like shutters taking away the light from his life . . . from mine for evermore.

Such thoughts come and go while one's hands are more practical. As I lifted his hands a wild exultation came to me for I felt the pulse although it was feeble.

'Not . . . dead,' I whispered. 'Oh, thank God . . . thank God.' I heard the sob in my voice and was aware of a wild happiness surging through me.

I unbuttoned the jacket. If he had been shot through the heart as I had imagined, there should have been a bullet hole. I could find none. He was not bleeding.

Quite suddenly the truth dawned on me. He had not been shot. The blood came from the horse lying beside him.

I took off my jacket and rolled it into a pillow to support his head, and I fancied I saw the colour warm in his face; his eyelids flickered.

I heard myself saying: 'You're alive . . . *alive* . . . Thank God.'

I was praying silently that help would come soon. I knelt there, my eyes upon his face, my lips silently moving.

Then the heavy lids flickered; they lifted and his eyes were on me. I saw the faint lift of his lips as I bent towards him.

I felt my own lips tremble; the emotion of the last minutes was unbearable – the fear replaced by sudden hope which in itself must be tinged with fear.

'You will be all right,' I said.

He closed his eyes, and I knelt there waiting.

Chapter Eight

The Comte was suffering from nothing more than concussion and bruises. It was his horse that had been shot. The accident was discussed for days in the château, the vineyards and the town. There was an inquiry but the identity of the one who had fired the shot was not brought to light, for the bullet was one which could have come from a hundred guns in the neighbourhood. The Comte could remember little of the incident. He could only say that he had been riding in the copse, had ducked to pass under a tree and the next thing he knew was that he was being put on a stretcher. It was believed that ducking had probably saved his life for the bullet had ricocheted, hit the branch of a tree and then struck the horse's head. It had all happened in less than a second; the horse had fallen and the Comte had been thrown into unconsciousness.

I was happy during the days that followed. I knew it was an uneasy situation, but only one thing mattered: he was alive.

Because I had always been sensible, even during those days of exquisite relief I asked myself what the future held. What had happened to me that I had allowed a man to become so important to me? He could hardly have a similar interest in me; and if he did his reputation was such that any sensible woman would avoid him. And had I not prided myself on being a sensible woman?

But there was nothing in my life in those days but blissful relief.

I walked down to the *pâtisserie* in the market square. I often went there during my afternoon walks and had a cup of coffee.

Madame Latière, the proprietress, welcomed me, and plunged quickly into the topic of the day.

'A mercy, mademoiselle. I hear Monsieur le Comte is unharmed. His saint was watching over him that day.'

'Yes, he was fortunate.'

'A terrible thing, mademoiselle. Our woods aren't safe, it seems. And they haven't caught the one who did it.'

I shook my head.

'I've told Latière not to ride through *those* woods. I shouldn't like to see him on a stretcher. Though Latière's a good man, mademoiselle. He hasn't an enemy in the place.'

I stirred my coffee uneasily.

She flicked a serviette over the table absently. 'Ah, Monsieur le Comte. He is *galant – fort galant*. My grandfather often talked of the Comte of his day. No girl in the neighbourhood safe . . . but he always found a husband if there was trouble, and believe me, they didn't suffer for it. We've a saying here that in Gaillard you often come across château features. Handed down through the generations. Oh, well, there's human nature for you.'

'What a change in the vineyards in these last weeks,' I said, 'I'm told that if the weather stays warm and sunny this will be a good year.'

'A good harvest.' She laughed. 'That will make up to Monsieur le Comte for what has happened in the woods, eh?'

'I hope so.'

'Well, it's a warning, would you not say so, mademoiselle? He'll not ride in those woods for a while, I'll swear.'

'Perhaps not,' I said uneasily, and finishing my coffee, rose to go.

'*Au revoir*, mademoiselle,' said Madame Latière rather wistfully. I think she had hoped for more gossip.

I couldn't resist going over to see Gabrielle the very next day. She had changed since I had last seen her; her manner was nervous, but when I complimented her on her new house, which was looking charming, she was pleased.

'It is more than I dared hope,' she said.

'And you are feeling well?'

'Yes, I have seen Mademoiselle Carré; she is the midwife, you know. She is satisfied and now it is only a matter of waiting. *Maman*, Jacques's mother, is always at hand and so good to me.'

'Do you want a girl or a boy?'

'A boy, I think. Everyone likes the first to be a boy.'

I pictured him playing in the garden – a small sturdy little fellow. Would he have château features?

'And Jacques?'

She blushed.

'Oh, he is happy, very happy.'

'How fortunate that . . . it all worked out so well.'

'Monsieur le Comte is very kind.'

'Everybody doesn't think so. At least the one who took a shot at him didn't.'

She clenched her hands together. 'You think it was deliberate. You don't think . . .'

'He had a lucky escape. It must have been a shock to you when it happened . . . so near here.'

As soon as I had said that I was ashamed of myself, for I knew that if there could be any foundation for my suspicion about the Comte and Gabrielle I must be hurting her deeply; yet I had to know whether the Comte was the father of her child.

But she did not resent what I had said and that made me happy, for she did not seem to grasp the implication which, I was sure, had she been guilty she would immediately have done.

She said: 'Yes, it was a great shock. Fortunately Jacques wasn't far away and he got the man with the stretcher.'

Still, I had to pursue my investigation. 'Do you think the Comte has enemies about here?'

'Oh, it was an accident,' she said quickly.

'Well,' I added, 'he wasn't hurt much.'

'I'm so thankful.' There were tears in her eyes. I wondered whether they were tears of gratitude or something that went deeper.

A few days later I was walking in the gardens when I came face to face with the Comte. I was in the middle terrace with its ornamental gardens and parterres separated from each other by boxwood hedges, and wandering into one of these I found him sitting on a stone bench overlooking a small lily pond in which the goldfish were visible.

The sun was hot in the enclosed garden and at first I thought he was asleep. I stood looking at the scene for a few seconds and then was about to go away when he called to me: 'Mademoiselle Lawson.'

'I hope I am not disturbing you.'

'It's the pleasantest of disturbances. Do come and sit down for a while.'

I went to the seat and sat beside him.

'I've never really thanked you for your prompt action in the woods.'

'I'm afraid I did nothing praiseworthy.'

'You acted with commendable promptitude.'

'I only did what anyone would in the circumstances. Are you feeling recovered now?'

'Absolutely. Apart from certain strained muscles. I am told that in a week or so all that will pass. In the meantime I hobble round with my stick.'

I looked at his hands with the jade signet ring on the little finger which curled about the ivory-topped walking stick. He wore no wedding ring as was the custom for men in France. I wondered whether he was just naturally flouting conventions or whether that was significant.

He glanced at me and said: 'You look . . . so contented, Mademoiselle Lawson.'

I was startled. I wondered how much of my feelings I had divulged.

'This setting,' I said quickly. 'The warm sun . . . the flowers, the fountain . . . it's all so beautiful. Who wouldn't be contented in such a garden? What is the statue in the middle of the pond?'

'It's Perseus rescuing Andromeda. Rather a pleasant piece of work. You must take a close look at it. It was done about two hundred years ago by a sculptor whom one of my ancestors brought to the château. It would appeal to you particularly.'

'Why particularly?'

'I think of you as a female Perseus rescuing art from the dragon of decay, age, vandalism and so on.'

'That's a very poetic fancy. You surprise me.'

'I'm not such a Philistine as you imagine. When you have given me a few more lessons in the gallery I shall become quite knowledgeable. You will see.'

'I am sure you will have no wish to acquire knowledge which would be no use to you.'

'I always understood that all knowledge was useful.'

'Some more than others, and as one can't acquire it all it might be a waste of time to clutter the mind with that which is of no practical use . . . at the expense of so much that is.' He lifted his shoulders and smiled. And I went on: 'It could be useful to know who caused the accident in the woods.'

'You think so?'

'Of course. What if it were repeated?'

'Well, then there might be a more unfortunate outcome . . . or fortunate, of course. It depends on which way you look at it.'

'I find your attitude extraordinary. You don't seem to care that someone who intended to murder you is not discovered.'

'How? My dear Mademoiselle Lawson, there have been numerous inquiries. It is not so easy to identify a bullet as you imagine. There is a gun in almost every cottage. Hares abound in the neighbourhood. They are good in the pot and they do some damage. The shooting of them has never been discouraged.'

'Then if someone was shooting a hare why shouldn't they come forward and say so?'

'What! When they shot my horse instead?'

'So someone was shooting in the woods and the bullet hit the tree and then killed the horse. Wouldn't that person with the gun have been aware of you in the woods?'

'Let us say he . . . or she . . . was not.'

'So you accept the theory that it was an accident?'

'Why not, since it's a reasonable theory.'

'It's a comfortable theory, but I should not have thought you were a man to accept a theory because it was comfortable.'

'Perhaps when you know me better you will change your mind.' He was smiling at me. 'It is so pleasant here. I hope you had no other plans. If not, will you stay and talk awhile? Then I will take you to the pond and you can have a closer look at Perseus. It's really a little masterpiece. The look of determination on his face is quite extraordinary. He is determined of course to slay his monster. Now talk to me about the pictures. How are they progressing? You are such a worker. In a short time you will have finished work in the gallery and we shall have our pictures looking as they did when they were first painted. It's fascinating, Mademoiselle Lawson.'

I talked of the pictures and after a while we looked at the statues. Then we returned to the château together.

Our progress through the terraces was necessarily slow; and as we went into the château I fancied that I saw a movement at the schoolroom window. I wondered who was watching us – Nounou or Geneviève?

Suddenly interest in the Comte's accident waned because the vines were in danger. They were now growing rapidly towards the peak at which they would arrive in early summer when the black-measles scare arose.

The news spread through the town and the château.

I went to see Madame Bastide to hear what was happening. As we sat drinking coffee together she told me what damage black measles could do.

If it wasn't kept down the whole crop could be contaminated – perhaps not only this year but for years to come.

Jean Pierre and his father were working half the night. The vines had to be sprayed with a sodium arsenite spray and too much of such a solution could be harmful, too little could fail to destroy the pest.

'That is life,' said Madame Bastide with a philosophical shrug and proceeded to tell me once more of the great calamity when the vinelouse had destroyed vines all over the country.

'Years it took us to bring prosperity back to the vines,' she declared. 'And every year there are these troubles . . . if it is not the black measles it is the grape-leaf-hopper or the root-worm. Ah, Dallas, who would be a vine grower?'

'Yet when the harvest is safely gathered in what a joy it must be.'

'You are right.' Her eyes shone at the thought. 'You should see us then. That is a time when we go wild with joy.'

'And if there hadn't been continual danger you couldn't feel quite so gay.'

'It is true. There is no time in Gaillard like the harvest . . . and to enjoy we must first suffer.'

I asked how Gabrielle was getting on.

'She is very happy. And to think it was Jacques all the time.'

'Were you surprised?'

'Oh, I don't know. They were children together . . . always good friends. Perhaps one does not see the change coming. The girl is suddenly the woman, the boy the man; and there is nature waiting for them. Yes, I was surprised that it should be Jacques, though I should have known she was in love. She has been so absentminded lately. Ah, well, there it is. Everything is settled happily now. Jacques will do well at St. Vallient. Now of course he will be working as we are here for these pests spread fast. It would be bad luck if one struck St. Vallient just as Jacques has taken over.'

'It was good of the Comte to offer Jacques St. Vallient at this time,' I said. 'It was just at the right moment.'

'Sometimes the good God gives us evidence of his loving care.'

I walked thoughtfully back to the château. Of course, I assured myself, Gabrielle had spoken to the Comte of her predicament, and because she was pregnant by Jacques, who was unable to support both a wife and his mother, the Comte had given Jacques St. Vallient. The Durands were too old to manage it now in any case. Naturally that was what had happened.

I was changing. I was becoming adept at believing what I wanted to.

Nounou was pleased when I called in at her private room which I did fairly frequently; she would always have the coffee waiting for me and we would sit and talk together – almost always of Geneviève, and Françoise.

At this time when the whole district was worrying about black measles, Nounou's one concern was the fretfulness of Geneviève; her room seemed to be the one place where the vines were not discussed.

'I'm afraid she does not like Monsieur Philippe's wife,' said Nounou, peering at me anxiously from under her heavy brows. 'She never liked a woman in the house since . . .'

I would not meet her eye; I did not want Nounou to tell me what I already knew about the Comte and Claude.

I said briskly: 'It is a long time since her mother died. She must grow away from it.'

'If she had had a brother it would have been different. But now the Comte has brought Monsieur Philippe here and has married him to that woman ...' I knew she had seen me chatting with the Comte in the gardens and was warning me.

'I dare say Philippe was eager to marry,' I said. 'Otherwise why should he? You talk as though ...'

'I talk of what I know. The Comte will never marry. He dislikes women.'

'I have heard rumours that he is rather fond of them.'

'Fond! Oh, no, miss.' She spoke bitterly. 'He was never fond of anyone. A man can amuse himself with what he despises, and if he has a certain nature the more contemptuous he is, the more amusement he gets, if you follow me. Oh, well, it's no concern of ours, you're thinking, and you're right. But I expect you'll soon be leaving us and forgetting all about us.'

'I haven't looked so far ahead as that.'

'I thought you hadn't.' She smiled dreamily. 'The château is a little kingdom of its own. I can't imagine living anywhere else ... yet I only came here when Françoise did.'

'It must be very different from Carrefour.'

'Everything's different here.'

Remembering the gloomy mansion which had been Françoise's home I said: 'Françoise must have been very happy when she first came.'

'Françoise wasn't ever happy here. He didn't care for her, you see.' She looked at me earnestly. 'It's not in him to care for anyone ... only to use people. He uses everyone – his workers, who produce the wine ... and us here in the château.'

I said indignantly: 'But isn't it always so? One can't expect one man to work a vineyard himself. Everyone has servants.'

'You did not understand me, miss. How could you? I say he did not love Françoise. It was an arranged marriage. Well, so are most in their station, but good comes from these marriages. Some are the better for being arranged, but not this one. Françoise was there because his family thought her a suitable wife; she was there to provide the family. As long as she did that he cared nothing for her. But she ... she was young and sensitive ... she did not understand. So ... she died. The Comte is a strange man, miss. Do not mistake that.'

'He is ... unusual.'

She looked at me sadly and she said: 'I wish I could show you how she was before ... and after. I wish you could have known her.'

'I wish it too.'

'There are the little books she used to write in.'

'Yes, they give me an idea of what she was like.'

'She was always writing in them and when she was unhappy they were a great pleasure to her. Sometimes she would read them aloud to me. "Do you remember this, Nounou?" she would say; and we'd laugh together. At

Carrefour she was an innocent young girl. But when she married the Comte, she had to learn so much and learn quickly. How to be the mistress of a château . . . but that was not all.'

'How did she feel when she first came here?' My eyes strayed to the cupboard in which Nounou kept her treasures. There was the box containing the pieces of embroidery which Françoise had given her for her birthdays and there were those revealing note-books which contained the story of Françoise's life. I wanted to read about the Comte's wooing; I wanted to know Françoise, not as a young girl living her secluded life in Carrefour with her strict father and her doting Nounou, but as the wife of the man who had begun to dominate my life.

'When she was happy she did not write in her little books,' said Nounou. 'And when she first came here there were so many excitements . . . so much to do. Even I saw little of her.'

'So she *was* happy at first.'

'She was a child. She believed in life . . . in people. She had been told she was fortunate, and she believed it. She was told that she would be happy . . . and she believed that too.'

'And when did she start to be unhappy?'

Nounou spread her hands and looked down at them as though she expected to find the answer there.

'She soon began to understand life was not as she had imagined it would be. And then she was going to have Geneviève and she had something to dream of. That was a disappointment, for everyone hoped for a son.'

'Did she confide in you, Nounou?'

'Before her marriage she would tell me everything.'

'And not afterwards?'

Nounou shook her head. 'It was only when I read . . .' she nodded to the cupboard, 'that I understood. She was not such a child. She understood much . . . and she suffered.'

'Do you mean he was unkind to her?'

Nounou's mouth hardened. 'She needed to be loved,' she said.

'And she loved him?'

'She was terrified of him.'

I was startled by her vehemence. 'Why?' I asked. Her mouth trembled and she turned away. I saw from her expression that she was looking into the past. Then suddenly her mood changed and she said slowly: 'She was fascinated by him . . . at first. It's a way he has with some women.'

She seemed to come to a decision, for she stood up suddenly and went to the cupboard and taking the key which was always kept dangling at her waist she opened it.

I saw the note-books all neatly stacked together. She selected one.

'Read about it,' she said. 'Take it away and read about it. But don't let anyone else see it . . . and bring it back safely to me.'

I knew I should refuse; I felt I was prying not only into her private life but into his. But I couldn't; I had to know.

Nounou was worried on my account. She believed that the Comte was to some extent interested in me. She was telling me in this oblique way that the man who had brought his mistress into the house and married her to his cousin was also a murderer. She was telling me that if I allowed myself to become involved with such a man I too could be in danger. In what way, she could not say. But she was warning me all the same.

I took the book back to my room. I could scarcely wait to read it; and as I read it I was disappointed. I had expected dramatic revelations.

There were the entries not unlike those I had read before. She had her own little plot in the garden where she grew her own flowers. It was such a pleasure to grow flowers. 'I want Geneviève to love them as I do.' 'My first roses. I cut them and kept them in a vase in my bedroom. Nounou says flowers should not be kept in your bedroom at night because they take all the air which you need. I told her it was nonsense but to please her I let her take them out.' Reading through those pages I searched in vain for his name. It was not until almost at the end of the book that he was mentioned.

'Lothair returned from Paris to-day. Sometimes I think he despises me. I know I am not clever like the people he meets in Paris. I must try really harder to learn something about the things he is interested in. Politics and history, literature and pictures. I wish I did not find them so dull.'

'We all went riding to-day – Lothair, Geneviève and myself. He was watching Geneviève. I was terrified that she would take a toss. She was so nervous.'

'Lothair has gone away. I am not sure where but I expect to Paris. He did not tell me.'

'Geneviève and I had the young children at the château to-day. We are teaching them their catechism. I want Geneviève to understand what her duty is as daughter of the château. We talked about it afterwards and it was so peaceful. I love the evenings when they begin to darken and Nounou comes to draw the curtains and light the lamps. I reminded her how I had always liked that part of the day at Carrefour when she would come and close the shutters . . . just before it was dark, so that we never really saw the darkness. I told her this. And she said "You are full of fancies, cabbage." She has not called me "cabbage" since before my marriage.'

'I went to Carrefour to-day. Papa was pleased to see me. He says that Lothair should build a church for the poor and I must persuade him to do this.'

'I spoke to Lothair about the church. He asked me why they wanted another church when they had one in the town. I told him that Papa thought that if they had a church close to the vineyard they could go in and worship at any hour of the day. It was for the good of their souls. Lothair said they had to concern themselves during working hours with the good of the grape. I don't know what Papa will say when I see him again. He will dislike Lothair more than ever.'

'Papa says Lothair should dismiss Jean Lapin because he is an atheist. He says that by continuing to employ him Lothair is condoning his sin and Lapin should be sent away and his family with him. When I told Lothair he laughed and said he would decide who should work for him and Lapin's opinions were no concern of his, still less of my father's. Sometimes I think

Lothair dislikes Papa so much that he wishes he had never married me. And I know Papa wishes I had never married Lothair.'

'I went to Carrefour to-day. Papa took me to his bedroom and made me kneel and pray with him. I dream about Papa's bedroom. It is like a prison. It is so cold kneeling on the stone flags that I feel cramped long afterwards. How can he sleep on such a hard pallet made of nothing but straw? The crucifix on the wall is the only brightness there; there is nothing else but the pallet and prie-dieu in the room. Papa talked after we had prayed. I felt wicked . . . sinful.'

'Lothair came back to-day, and I am afraid. I felt I should scream if he came near me. He said: "What is the matter with you?" And I could not tell him how frightened I was of him. He went out of the room. I believe he was very angry. I think Lothair is beginning to hate me. I am so different from the women he likes . . . the women I believe he is with in Paris. I picture them in diaphanous gowns, laughing and drinking wine . . . abandoned women . . . gay and amorous. It is horrible.'

'I was frightened last night. I thought he was coming to my room. I heard his footsteps outside. He stopped at the door and waited. I thought I should scream aloud in terror . . . but then he went away.'

I had come to the last entry in the book.

What did it mean? Why had Françoise been so frightened of her husband? And why had Nounou shown me that book? If she wanted me to know the story of Françoise's life why did she not give them all to me? I knew there were others there. Could it be that Nounou, through those books which revealed the secrets of Françoise's life, knew the secret of her death? And was it for this reason that she was warning me to leave the château?

I took the book back to Nounou the next day.

'Why did you give me this one to read?' I asked.

'You said you wanted to know her.'

'I feel I know her less than ever. Have you other books? Did she go on writing right until the time of her death?'

'She did not write so much after she wrote that one. I used to say to her: "Françoise *chérie*, why don't you write in your little notebooks?" And she would say: "There is nothing to write now, Nounou." And when I said "Nonsense!" she scolded me, and said I wanted to pry. It was the first time she'd said that. I knew she was afraid to write down what she felt.'

'But why was she afraid?'

'Don't we all have thoughts which we would not wish to be known?'

'You mean she did not want her husband to know that she was afraid of him?' She was silent and I went on: 'Why was she afraid of him? You know, Nounou?'

She pursed her lips tightly together as though nothing on earth would make her speak.

But I knew that there was some dark secret; and I believed that had she not thought that I was of some use to Geneviève she would have told me to leave the château because she feared for me. But I knew that she would sacrifice me willingly for the sake of Geneviève.

She knew something about the Comte which she was trying to tell me. Did she know that he had murdered his wife?

The desire to know was becoming an obsession. But it was more than a desire to know; it was a desperate need to prove him innocent.

We were riding when Geneviève, speaking in her rather slow English, told me that she had heard from Esquilles.

'Such an important person she seems to have become, miss. I will show you her letter.'

'I am so pleased that she is happily settled.'

'Yes, she is companion to Madame de la Condère and Madame de la Condère is very appreciative. They live in a fine mansion, not as ancient as ours but much more *comme il faut*. Madame de la Condère gives card parties and old Esquilles often joins them to make up the number. It gives her an opportunity of mixing in the society to which by rights she should belong.'

'Well, all's well that ends well.'

'And, miss, you will be glad to hear that Madame de la Condère has a nephew who is a very charming man and he is always very agreeable to Esquilles. I must show you her letter. She is so coy when she writes of him. I do believe she has hopes of becoming Madame Nephew before long.'

'Well, I'm very pleased. I have thought about her now and then. She was so suddenly dismissed, and it was all due to your naughtiness.'

'She mentions Papa. She says how grateful she is to him for finding her such a congenial situation.'

'He . . . found it?'

'Of course. He arranged for her to go to Madame de la Condère. He wouldn't just have turned her out. Or would he?'

'No,' I said firmly. 'He wouldn't turn her out.'

That was a very happy morning.

The atmosphere lightened considerably during the next weeks. The black measles had been defeated and there was rejoicing throughout the vineyards and the towns which depended on their prosperity.

Invitations came to the château for the family to a wedding of a distant connection. The Comte said he was too bruised to go – he continued to walk with a stick – and that Philippe and his wife must represent their branch of the family.

I knew that Claude was resentful and hated the idea of going and leaving the Comte at the château. I was in one of the small walled gardens when she walked past with the Comte. We did not see each other but I heard their voices – hers quite distinctly for it was high-pitched and very audible when she was angry.

'They'll expect *you*!'

'They'll understand. You and Philippe will explain about my accident.'

'Accident! A few bruises!' He said something which I did not hear and she went on: 'Lothair . . . *please*!'

'My dear, I shall stay here.'

'You don't listen to me now. You seem as if . . .'

His voice was low, almost soothing, and by the time he had finished speaking they were out of earshot. There was no doubt of the relationship which existed between them, I thought sadly.

But to Paris went Claude and Philippe, and I thrust aside my doubts and fears and prepared to enjoy Claude's absence.

The days were long and full of sunshine. The vines were in bloom. Each day I rose with a feeling of anticipation. I had never been so happy in my life; yet I knew that my happiness was about as dependable as an April day. I could make some alarming discovery; I could be sent away. In a moment the skies could darken and the sun be completely blotted out. All the more reason to bask in it while it was there.

As soon as Philippe and Claude had left, the Comte's visits to the gallery had become more frequent. Sometimes I fancied he was escaping from something, searching and longing to discover. There were times when I caught a glimpse of a different man behind his teasing smiles. I even had the idea that he enjoyed our interviews as much as I did.

When he left me I would come to my senses and laugh at myself asking: How far are you prepared to delude yourself?

There was a simple explanation of what was happening: There was no one at the château to amuse him; therefore he found me and my earnestness for my work diverting. I must remember that.

But he *was* interested in painting, and knowledgeable too. I recalled that pathetic entry in Françoise's diary. She must try to learn something of the things which interested him. Poor frightened little Françoise! Why had she been afraid?

There were times when his face would darken with a cynicism which I imagined could be alarming to a meek and simple woman. There might even be a touch of sadism, as though he delighted in mockery and the discomfort it brought to others. But to me those expressions of his were like a film which something in his life had laid over his true nature – just as lack of care will spoil a picture.

I was arrogant. Governessy, as Geneviève would say. Did I really think that because I could bring its old glory back to a painting I could change a man?

But I was obsessed by my desire to know him, to probe beneath that often sardonic mask, to change the expression of the mouth from a certain bitter disillusion. But before I could attempt this . . . I must know my subject.

How had he felt towards the woman whom he had married? He had ruined her life. Had she ruined his? How could one know when the past was engulfed in secrecy?

The days when I did not see him were empty; and those encounters which seemed so short left me elated and exhilarated by a happiness I had never in my life known before.

We talked of pictures; of the château; of the history of the place and the days of the château's glory during the reigns of the fourteenth and fifteenth Louis. 'Then there was the change. Nothing was ever the same again, Mademoiselle Lawson. Some saw it coming years before. "*Après moi le déluge*," said Louis XV. And *déluge* there was, with his successor going to the guillotine and taking so many of our people with him. My own great-great-grandfather was one of them. We were fortunate not to lose our estates. Had we been nearer Paris we should have done so. But you read about the miracle of St. Geneviève and how she saved us from disaster.' His tone lightened. 'You are thinking that perhaps we were not worth saving.'

'I was thinking no such thing. As a matter of fact I think it's a pity when estates have to pass out of families. How interesting to trace one's family back hundreds of years.'

'Perhaps the Revolution did some good. If they had not stormed the château and damaged these pictures, we should not have needed your services.'

I shrugged my shoulders. 'If the pictures had not been damaged, they would not have needed restoration certainly. They might have needed cleaning.'

'But you might not have come here, Miss Lawson. Think of that.'

'I am sure the Revolution was a greater catastrophe than that would have been.'

He laughed; and he was different then. I caught a glimpse of the light-hearted person through the mask. It was a wonderful moment.

I joined him and Geneviève for dinner each night during the absence of Philippe and Claude. The conversation was animated between us, and Geneviève would look on in a kind of bewilderment; but attempts to draw her in were not very successful. She, like her mother, seemed to be afraid of him.

Then one evening when we went down to dinner he was not there. He had left no message that he would not be in, but after waiting for twenty minutes, dinner was served and we ate alone.

I felt very uneasy. I kept picturing him lying hurt – or worse – in the woods. If someone had tried to kill him and failed wasn't it plausible that they should have another attempt?

I tried to eat, tried to disguise my anxiety, which Geneviève did not share, and I was glad when I could go to my room to be alone.

I walked up and down; I sat at my window; I could not rest. There was a mad moment when I thought of going to the stables and taking a horse to look for him. How could I do so at night and what right had I to concern myself in his affairs?

Of course, I reminded myself, the Comte who had been such a gracious companion to me had been the invalid. He had been recuperating from his accident and while he was confined to the château found me a substitute for his friends.

Why hadn't I seen it?

It was daylight before I slept – and when the maid brought my breakfast to my room I looked at her in surreptitious anxiety to see if she had heard any terrible news. But she was as placid as ever.

I went down to the gallery feeling tired and strained and in no mood to work; but I had told myself that if anything had happened I should have heard by now.

I had not been there very long when he came into the gallery. I started when I saw him and he looked at me strangely.

I said without thinking: 'Oh . . . you are all right then?'

His face was expressionless, but he regarded me intently.

'I'm sorry I missed seeing you at dinner last night,' he said.

'Oh . . . yes. I . . . wondered . . .'

What was the matter with me? I was stammering like the foolish girls I so despised.

He continued to look at me and I was certain he had detected the signs of sleeplessness. What a fool I had been! Did I expect him to explain to me when he went out visiting his friends? Of course he would go out. He had only confined himself to the château because of his accident.

'I believe,' he said, 'you were concerned for my safety.' Did he know the state of my feelings as well as – or perhaps better than – I knew them myself? 'Tell me, did you imagine me shot through the heart . . . no, the head, because I believe you secretly think, Mademoiselle Lawson, that I have a stone where my heart should be. An advantage in a way. A bullet can't pierce a stone.'

I knew it was no use denying my concern so I tacitly admitted it in my reply. 'If you had been shot once it seemed plausible to imagine that it might happen again.'

'It would be too coincidental, don't you think? A man shooting a hare happens to shoot my horse. It's the sort of thing that could only happen once in a lifetime. And you are expecting it twice in a few weeks.'

'The hare theory might not be the true one.'

He sat down on the sofa beneath the picture of his ancestress in emeralds and regarded me on my stool. 'Are you comfortable there, Mademoiselle Lawson?'

'Thank you.' I could feel animation coming back into my body; everything was gay again. I had only one fear now. Was I betraying myself?

'We've talked about pictures, old castles, old families, revolutions, yet never about ourselves,' he said almost gently.

'I am sure those subjects are more interesting than I personally could be.'

'Do you really think that?'

I shrugged my shoulders – a habit I had learned from those about me. It was a good substitute for the answer expected to a difficult question.

'All I know is that your father died and you took his place.'

'There is little else to know. Mine has been a life like many others of my class and circumstances.'

'You never married. I wonder why.'

'I might reply as the English milkmaid, "Nobody asked me, sir, she said".'

'That I find extraordinary. I am sure you would make an excellent wife for some fortunate man. Just imagine how useful you would be. His pictures would always be in perfect condition.'

'What if he had none?'

'I am sure you would very quickly remedy that omission.'

I did not like the light turn of the conversation. I fancied he was making fun of me; and it was a subject about which, in view of my new emotions, I did not care to be mocked.

'I am surprised that you should be an advocate for marriage.' As soon as I had spoken I wished I hadn't. I flushed and stammered: 'I'm sorry . . .'

He smiled, the mockery gone.

'And I'm not surprised that you are surprised. Tell me, what does D stand for? Miss D. Lawson. I should like to know. It is such an unusual name.'

I explained that my father had been Daniel and my mother Alice.

'Dallas,' he repeated my name. 'You smile?'

'It's the way in which you say it . . . with the accent on the last syllable. We put it on the first.'

He tried it out again, smiling at me. '*Dal*las *Dal*las.' He made me feel that he liked saying it.

'You yourself have an unusual name.'

'It's been used by my family for years . . . since the first King of the Franks. We have to be royal, you see. We throw in an occasional Louis, a Charles, a Henri. But we must have our Lothairs. Now let me tell you how wrongly *you* pronounce *my* name.'

I said it and he laughed and made me say it again.

'Very good, *Dal*las,' he said. 'But then everything you do you do well.'

I told him about my parents and how I had helped Father in his work. Somehow it came through that they had dominated my life and kept me from marriage. He mentioned this.

'Perhaps it was better so,' he said. 'Those who don't marry, often regret the omission; but those who do so, often regret far more bitterly. They long to go back in time and not do what they did. Well, that's life, isn't it?'

'That may be so.'

'Take myself. I was married when I was twenty to a young woman who was chosen for me. It is so in our families, you know.'

'Yes.'

'These marriages are often successful.'

'And yours was?' My voice was almost a whisper.

He did not answer and I said quickly: 'I'm sorry. I am being impertinent.'

'No. You should know.'

I wondered why, and my heart began to beat uncomfortably.

'No, the marriage was not a success. I think I am incapable of being a good husband.'

'Surely a man could be . . . if he wanted to.'

'Mademoiselle Lawson, how could a man who is selfish, intolerant, impatient and promiscuous be a good husband?'

'Simply by ceasing to be selfish, intolerant and so on.'

'And you believe that one can turn off these unpleasant qualities like a tap?'

'I think one can try to subdue them.'

He laughed suddenly and I felt foolish.

'I amuse you?' I said coolly. 'You asked an opinion and I gave it.'

'It's absolutely true, of course. I could imagine you subduing such unpleasant characteristics if only I could so far stretch my imagination as to picture you possessing them. You know how disastrously my marriage ended.'

I nodded.

'My experiences as a husband have convinced me that I should abandon that role for ever.'

'Perhaps you are wise to make such a decision.'

'I was sure you would agree.'

I knew what he meant. If what he suspected was true and I had allowed my feelings for him to become too deep, I should be warned.

I felt humiliated and wounded and I said briskly: 'I am very interested in some of the wall surfaces I have noticed about the château. It has occurred to me that there might be some murals hidden beneath the lime wash.'

'Oh?' he said; and I thought he was not paying attention to what I said.

'I remember my father's making a miraculous discovery on the walls of an ancient mansion in Northumberland. It was a wonderful painting which had been hidden for centuries. I feel certain that there must be similar discoveries here.'

'Discoveries?' he repeated. 'Yes?'

What was he thinking of? That stormy married life with Françoise? But had it been stormy? Deeply unhappy, entirely unsatisfactory since he had determined never to run the risk of such an experience again.

I was aware of an intense passion engulfing me. I thought: What could I do? How could I leave this and go back . . . to England . . . back to a new life where there was no château full of secrets, no Comte whom I longed to restore to happiness?

'I should like to have a closer look at those walls,' I went on.

He said almost fiercely, as though denying everything that had gone before: '*Dal*las, my château and myself are at your disposal.'

Chapter Nine

A few days later Philippe and Claude returned from Paris, and the intimacy which had grown between the Comte and myself seemed as though it had never been.

Claude and he often rode together. Philippe was not so fond of being in the saddle. Sometimes I watched them from the window of my room, laughing and talking together; and I remembered that conversation I had heard between them on the night of the ball.

Well, now she was married to Philippe and her home was in the château. She was mistress of it – although not the Comte's wife.

I soon became aware of her rule. It was the day after her return and about fifteen minutes before dinner when there was a knock on my door. I was surprised to see the maid with my tray, for during the absence of Philippe and Claude I had taken this meal in the dining-room and had already changed into my brown silk in preparation for doing so.

When the maid set the food out on the little table I asked who had told her to bring it.

'Madame ordered it. Boulanger sent Jeanne to change the table because she had laid a place for you. Madame said that you would be taking your meals in your own room. Boulanger said in the kitchens how was he to know? You had been dining with Monsieur le Comte and Mademoiselle Geneviève. Well, those were Madame's orders.'

I felt my eyes blazing with anger, which I managed to hide from the maid.

I pictured their going in to dinner. I imagined his looking round for me and his consternation when I was not there.

'And where is Mademoiselle Lawson?'

'I have told them to take up her tray. She cannot expect to eat at table with us. After all, she is not a guest; she is employed to work here.'

I saw his face darken with contempt for her and . . . regard for me.

'What nonsense. Boulanger, another place please. And go at once to Mademoiselle Lawson's room and tell her that I am looking forward to her presence at dinner.'

I waited. The food on the tray was getting cold.

It did not happen as I had hoped. There was no message.

Now if ever I should see what a fool I was. This woman was his mistress. He had married her to Philippe so that she could be at the château without arousing scandal, because he was wise enough to see that he could afford no more scandal since even kings in their castles had to be a little careful.

Af for me – I was the odd Englishwoman, who was so intense about her work and to whom it was amusing to talk for a time when one was indisposed and confined to the château.

Naturally her presence was not needed when Claude was at hand. Moreover Claude was the mistress of the château.

Startled out of my sleep, I awoke in terror, for someone was in my room, standing there at the bottom of my bed.

'Miss.' Geneviève glided towards me, a lighted candle in her hand.

'I heard the tapping, miss. Only a few minutes ago. You said to come and tell you.'

'Geneviève . . .' I sat up in bed, my teeth chattering. I must have had a nightmare in those seconds before waking.

'What's the time?'

'One o'clock. It woke me up. Tap . . . tap . . . and I was frightened and you said we'd go and see . . . together.'

I put my feet into slippers and hastily put on my dressing-gown.

'I expect you imagined it, Geneviève.'

She shook her head. 'It's like it was before. Tap . . . tap . . . as though someone is trying to let you know where they are.'

'Where?'

'Come to my room. I can hear it there.'

I followed her through the château to the nursery which was in the oldest part of the house.

I said: 'Have you awakened Nounou?'

She shook her head. 'Nounou never wakes once she's asleep. She says once she gets off she sleeps the sleep of the dead.'

We went into Geneviève's room and listened. There was silence.

'Wait a minute, miss,' she pleaded. 'It stops and goes on.'

'From what direction?'

'I don't know. . . . Down below, I think.'

The dungeons were immediately below this part of the château. Geneviève would know that, and to a girl of her imagination this fact might have given her ideas.

'It'll come again soon, I know it will,' said Geneviève. 'There! I thought I heard . . .'

We sat tense, listening; a bird gave its call from the lime trees.

'It's an owl,' I said.

'Of course it is. Do you think I don't know that! There!'

Then I heard it. Tap tap. Softly then louder.

'It's below,' I said.

'Miss . . . you said you wouldn't be afraid.'

'We'll go and see if we can find out what's happening.'

I took the candle from her and led the way down the staircase to the lower floors.

Geneviève's belief in my courage gave me that quality. I should have been very uneasy walking about the château alone like this at night.

We reached the door of the gun gallery and paused there listening. Distinctly we heard a sound. I was not sure what it was, but I felt the goose pimples rising on my flesh. Geneviève gripped my arm and in the candle-light I saw her startled eyes. She was about to speak but I shook my head.

Then came the sound again.

It was from the dungeons below.

There was nothing I wanted so much as to turn and go back to my room; I was sure Geneviève felt the same; but because she did not expect such behaviour from me I could not tell her that I, too, was afraid, that it was all very well to be bold by daylight and quite another matter in the dungeons of an old château at dead of night.

She pointed down the stone spiral staircase and holding up my long skirts with the same hand as that which grasped the candle, for I needed the other to grip the rope banister, I led the way down the stairs.

Geneviève behind me, suddenly lurched forward. It was fortunate that she fell against me, thus preventing herself from tripping down the stairs. She gave a little scream and immediately clapped her hands to her mouth.

'It's all right,' she whispered. 'I tripped over my dressing-gown.'

'For heaven's sake hold it up.'

She nodded and for a few seconds we stood there on that spiral staircase trying to steady ourselves; my heart was leaping about uncomfortably and

I knew Geneviève's was doing the same. I believed that in a moment she would be saying: 'Let's go back. There's nothing here.' And I would be willing enough.

But some persistent faith in my invincibility prevented her from speaking.

Now there was absolute silence everywhere. I leaned against the stone wall and could feel the coldness through my clothes in contrast to Geneviève's hot hand which was gripping my arm. She did not look at me.

This was absurd, I thought. What was I doing wandering about the château at night? Suppose the Comte should discover me? What a fool I should look! I should go straight back to my room now and in the morning report the sounds I had heard during the night. But Geneviève would think I was afraid if I did that. She would not be wrong either. If I did not go on now she would lose that respect for me which I believe was what gave me some authority over her; and if I was to help her overcome the demons in her which forced her to strange acts, I must retain that authority.

I gathered my skirts higher, descended the staircase, and when I reached the bottom pushed open the iron-studded door to the dungeons. The dark cavern yawned ahead of us, and the sight of it made me more reluctant than ever to go on.

'This is where the sound comes from,' I whispered.

'Oh . . . miss . . . I can't go in there.'

'It's only the old cages.'

Geneviève was tugging on my arm. 'Let's go back, miss.'

It would be folly to go walking down there with only the light of the candle to guide us. The floor was uneven and Geneviève's near-fall on the stairs was a warning. How much more dangerous it would be down here! This was what I told myself. But the truth was that the cold eeriness of the place was so repellent that all my instincts called out to me to go back.

I lifted the candle high. I saw the damp walls, the fungoid growth, the darkness going on unendingly it seemed. I could see one or two of the cages with the great chains which had held men and women prisoners of the de la Talles.

'I said: 'Is anyone there?'

My voice echoed uncannily. Geneviève pressed her body against me, and I could feel her shaking.

I said: 'There's no one here, Geneviève.'

She was only too ready to admit it. 'Let's go miss.'

I said: 'We'll come and have a look in daylight.'

'Oh yes . . . yes. . . .'

She had seized my hand and was pulling me. I wanted to turn and hurry from the place, but in those seconds I was conscious of a horrible fascination. I could easily believe that somewhere in the darkness, someone was watching me . . . luring me onwards . . . farther into the darkness to some sort of doom.

'Miss . . . come on.'

The feeling had passed, and I turned. As Geneviève went before me up the staircase, I felt as though my feet were made of lead and I could scarcely lift them; I almost fancied I heard a footstep behind me. It was as though icy hands were laid on me pulling me back into the gloom. It was all imagination; my throat was constricted so that I could scarcely breathe, my heart a great weight in my chest. The candle dipped erratically and for one second of horror I was afraid it was going out. I felt we should never reach the top of that stairway. The ascent could not have taken more than a minute or so, but it seemed like ten. I stood breathless at the top of the stairs . . . outside the room in which was the *oubliette*.

'Come on, miss,' said Geneviève, her teeth chattering. 'I'm cold.'

We climbed the stairs.

'Miss,' said Geneviève, 'can I stay in your room for to-night?'

'Of course.'

'I . . . I might disturb Nounou if I went back.'

I did not point out that Nounou was never disturbed; I knew that she had shared my fear and was afraid to sleep alone.

I lay awake for a long time, going over every minute of that nocturnal adventure.

Fear of the unknown, I told myself, was an inheritance from our savage forebears. What had I feared in the dungeons? Ghosts of the past? Something that did not exist outside a childish imagination?

Yet when I did sleep my dreams were haunted by the sound of tapping. I dreamed of a young woman who could not rest because she had died violently. She wanted to return to explain to me exactly how she had died.

Tap! Tap!

I started up in bed. It was the maid with my breakfast.

Geneviève must have awakened early, for she was no longer in my room.

The next afternoon I went down to the dungeons alone. I had intended to ask Geneviève to accompany me, but she was nowhere to be found and as I was a little ashamed of my terror of the night before, I wanted to show myself that there was nothing to fear.

Nevertheless I had heard Geneviève's tapping sound and I should like to discover what that was.

It was a sunny day – and how different everything looked in sunshine! Even the old staircase, in the light which came through one of the long narrow slits in the wall, was not in complete darkness. It looked gloomy, of course, but different from the light of one small candle.

I reached the entrance to the dungeons and stood staring into the gloom. Even on one of the lightest days of the year it was not easy to see, but after I had stood peering there for a short while my eyes grew accustomed to the dimness. I could make out the outline of several of those horrible little openings which were called the cages, and as I stepped farther into the dungeon, the heavy door closed behind me and I could not suppress a little scream for a dark shadow loomed up behind me and a hand caught my arm.

'Mademoiselle Lawson!'

I gasped. The Comte was standing behind me.

'I . . .' I began. 'You startled me.'

'It was foolish of me. How dark it is with the door shut.' Still he did not open it. I was conscious of him very close to me.

'I wondered who was here,' he said. 'I might have known it would be you. You are so interested in the château. So naturally you love to explore . . . and a gruesome place like this would be particularly attractive.'

He had laid a hand on my shoulder. If I had wanted to protest at that moment I should have been unable to; I was filled with fear – the more frightening because I did not know what I feared.

His voice sounded close to my ear. 'What did you hope to discover, Mademoiselle Lawson?'

'I hardly know. Geneviève heard noises and last night we came down to investigate. I said we would come back by daylight.'

'So she is coming too?'

'She may.'

He laughed.

'Noises?' he said. 'What noises?'

'A tapping sound. Geneviève has mentioned it before. She came to my room because I was interested and I had said that if she heard it again we would investigate.'

'You can guess what it is,' he said. 'Some death-watch beetle settling down to a banquet off the old château. We've had them before.'

'Oh . . . I see.'

'It would have occurred to you, of course. You must have encountered him in some of your stately homes of England.'

'Of course. But these stone walls . . .'

'There's plenty of wood in the place.' He drew away from me, and going to the door threw it open. Now I could see more clearly, the miserable caves, the dreadful rings and chains . . . and the Comte, looking pale, I thought, and his expression more veiled even than usual. 'If we have some beetle in the place it means trouble.' He grimaced and lifted his shoulders.

'You will have this investigated?'

'In time,' he said. 'After the grape harvest perhaps. It takes those wretches a long time to tap this place away. It was only ten years ago that it was overhauled. There shouldn't be much trouble.'

'You suspected it?' I asked. 'Is that why you were investigating?'

'No,' he said. 'I saw you turn down the staircase and followed. I thought perhaps you had made a discovery.'

'A discovery? What sort of discovery?'

'Uncovered some work of art. You remember you were telling me?'

'Down here?'

'One would never be sure where the treasure lay, would one?'

'No, I suppose not.'

'At the moment,' he said, 'we will say nothing of the tapping. I don't want Gautier to hear. He'll be all for getting the experts in right away. We must wait until after the harvest. You've no idea, Mademoiselle Lawson, although you will when you see for yourself, what feverish excitement there is when the grapes ripen. We could not have workmen in the château at such a time.'

'May I tell Geneviève what your answer to her tapping is?'

'Yes, do tell her. Tell her to go to sleep and not listen for it.'

'I will,' I said.

We mounted the stairs together and as usual in his company my feelings were mixed. I felt as though I had been caught prying and on the other hand I was elated to be talking to him again.

I explained to Geneviève when we went riding together the next day.

'Beetles!' she cried. 'Why, they're almost as bad as ghosts.'

'Nonsense,' I laughed. 'They're tangible creatures and they can be destroyed.'

'If not, they destroy houses. Ugh! I don't like the thought of our having beetles. And what are they tapping for?'

'They tap on the wood with their heads to attract their mates.'

That made Geneviève laugh and we became rather gay. I saw that she was relieved.

It was a lovely day. There had been heavy intermittent showers all the morning and the grass and trees smelt wonderfully fresh.

The grapes, which had been severely pruned so that about ninety per cent of the growth had been cut away, were looking fine and healthy. Only the best remained, and they would have plenty of room to absorb the sunshine to make them sweet and give a real château wine.

Geneviève said suddenly, 'I wish you came to dinner, miss.'

'Thank you, Geneviève,' I said, 'but I cannot come uninvited and in any case I am perfectly content with a tray in my room.'

'Papa and you used to talk together.'

'Naturally.'

She laughed.

'I wish *she* hadn't come here. I don't like her. I don't think she likes me either.'

'You are referring to your Aunt Claude?'

'You know to whom I'm referring and she's not my aunt.'

'It's easier to call her so.'

'Why? She's not much older than I am. They seem to forget I'm grown up. Let's go to the Maison Bastide and see what they're doing.'

Her face, which had been set in discontented lines when she had talked of Claude, changed at the prospect of going to the Bastides', and as I was afraid of these sudden moods of hers, I was very willing to turn Bonhomme in the direction of their house.

We found Yves and Margot in the garden. They carried baskets on their arms and were bent double examining the front path as they sang in their thin childish voices and now and then shouting to each other.

We tied our horses to the post and Geneviève ran to them asking what they were doing.

'Don't you know?' demanded Margot, who was at this stage of her young life inclined to think those who did not know what she knew were excessively ignorant.

'Snails!' cried Geneviève.

Yves looked up at her grinning and held out his basket to show her. In it lay several snails.

'We're going to have a feast!' he told her.

He stood up and began to dance, singing:

> *'C'était un petit bonhomme luron*
> *C'était un petit bonhomme*
> *Qui allait a Montbron . . .'*

He squealed: 'Look at this one. He'll never go to Montbron. Come on *mon petit bonhomme.*' He grinned at Geneviève. 'We're going to have a feast of snails. The rain has brought them out. Get a basket and come and help.'

'Where?' asked Geneviève.

'Oh, Jeanne will give you one.'

Geneviève ran off to the back of the house and round to the kitchen where Jeanne was busy preparing some *pot-au-feu*; and I thought how she changed when she came to this house.

Yves rocked on his haunches.

'You must come and join in the feast, Miss Dallas,' he said.

'Not for two weeks,' shrilled Margot.

'We keep them for two weeks and then they're served with garlic and parsley.' Yves smoothed his hands over his stomach reminiscently. 'Delicious!'

Then he began to hum his *escargot* song to himself while Geneviève came back with a basket and I went into the house to talk to Madame Bastide.

Two weeks later when the snails the children had collected were ready to be eaten, Geneviève and I were invited to the Maison Bastide. Their habit of making a celebration out of simple occasions was an endearing one and was for the benefit of the children. I thought what an excellent idea it was because Geneviève was always happier at such times and when she was happier her conduct improved. She really seemed as if she wanted to please.

But as we rode over we met Claude, who appeared to be coming from the vineyards. I saw her before she saw us; her face was flushed and there was an air of absorption about her; I was struck afresh by her beauty. However, when she saw us her expression changed.

She asked where we were going and I told her we had been invited to the Bastides'.

When she rode on Geneviève said: 'I believe she would have liked to forbid us to go. She thinks she is mistress here but she's only Philippe's wife. She behaves as though . . .'

Her eyes narrowed, and I thought: She is less innocent than we have believed. She *knows* of the relationship between this woman and her father.

I said nothing and we rode on until we came to the Maison Bastide. Yves and Margot were waiting for us and greeted us vociferously.

It was the first time I had tasted snails, and they all laughed at my reluctance. I am sure they were delicious, but I could not eat them with the same enthusiasm as the rest of the party.

The children talked of snails and how they asked their saints to send the rain to bring them out, while Geneviève listened eagerly to all they said. She was shouting as loudly as the others and joining in when they sang the *escargot* song.

Jean Pierre came in the middle of it. I had seen less of him lately for he had been so busy in the vineyards. He greeted me with his usual gallantry, and I noticed with some alarm the change in Geneviève when he entered. She seemed to throw off her childishness, and it was apparent to me that she listened eagerly to everything he said.

'Come and sit next to me, Jean Pierre,' she cried, and without hesitation he drew a chair to the table and wedged it in between her and Margot.

They talked of snails, and Jean Pierre sang to them in his rich tenor voice while Geneviève watched him, a dreamy expression in her eyes.

Jean Pierre caught my glance and immediately turned his attention to me. Geneviève burst out: 'We've got beetles in the Château. I wouldn't mind if they were snails. Do snails ever come indoors? Do they ever tap with their shells?'

She was making a desperate bid for his attention and she had it.

'Beetles in the château?' he asked.

'Yes, they tap. Miss and I went down to see in the night, didn't we, miss? Right down into the dungeons we went. I was scared. Miss wasn't. Nothing would scare you, miss, would it?'

'Certainly not beetles,' I said.

'But we didn't know it was beetles till Papa told you.'

'Beetles in the château,' repeated Jean Pierre. 'Death watch? That's set Monsieur le Comte in a panic, I'll swear.'

'I have never yet seen him in a panic and he certainly was not over this.'

'Oh, miss,' cried Geneviève, 'wasn't it awful . . . down there in the dungeon and we only had the candle. I was certain someone was there . . . watching us. I felt it, miss. I did really.' The children were listening with round-eyed attention, and Geneviève could not resist the temptation to focus the interest on herself. 'I heard a noise . . .' she went on. 'I knew there was a ghost down there. Someone who had been kept a prisoner and had died and whose soul couldn't rest . . .'

I could see that she was getting too excited. There was a rising hysteria in her. I caught Jean Pierre's eyes, and he nodded.

'Well,' he cried, 'who is going to dance the "March of the Escargots"? It is only fitting that having feasted off them we should dance in their honour. Come, Mademoiselle Geneviève. We will lead the dance.'

Geneviève sprang up with alacrity, her face flushed, her eyes shining, and putting her hand in that of Jean Pierre she danced round the room.

We left the Maison Bastide about four o'clock. As we entered the château one of the maids came running to me and told me that Madame de la Talle wished to see me in her boudoir as soon as possible.

I did not wait to change but went to her in my riding-habit.

I knocked on her bedroom door and heard her voice rather muffled bidding me enter. I did so. There was no sign of her in the elaborately-furnished room with its four-poster bed hung with peacock-blue silk hangings.

I noticed an open door, and through it she called to me: 'In here, Mademoiselle Lawson.'

Her boudoir was a room about half the size of her bedroom. It was fitted with a large mirror, hip-bath, dressing-table, chairs and sofa, and contained an overpowering smell of scent. She herself was reclining on the sofa wrapped in a pale blue silk robe, her yellow hair falling about her shoulders. I hated admitting it to myself but she looked very beautiful and seductive.

She regarded one bare foot which was thrust out from the blue robe.

'Oh, Mademoiselle Lawson, you've just come in. You've been to the Bastides'?'

'Yes,' I said.

'Of course,' she went on, 'we have no objection to your friendship with the Bastides.'

I looked puzzled and she added with a smile: 'Certainly not. *They* make our wine; *you* clean our pictures.'

'I don't see the connection.'

'I am sure you will, Mademoiselle Lawson, if you consider it. I am thinking of Geneviève. I am sure Monsieur le Comte would not wish her to be on terms of such . . . intimate friendship with . . . his servants.' I was about to protest when she went on quickly, and there was almost a gentle note in her voice as though she were trying to make this as easy as possible for me: 'Perhaps we protect our young girls more here than you do in England. We feel it unwise to allow them to mix too freely with those not in their social class. It could in some circumstances lead to . . . complications. I am sure you understand.'

'Are you suggesting that I should prevent Geneviève's calling at the Bastides' house?'

'You do agree that it is unwise?'

'I think you give me credit for carrying more weight than I do. I am sure I could not prevent her doing what she wished. I can only ask her to come to you so that you can make your wishes known to her.'

'But you accompany her to these people. It is due to your influence . . .'

'I am sure I could not stop her. I will tell her you wish to speak to her.'

And with that, I left her.

I had retired to my room that night and was in bed but not asleep when the disturbance started.

I had heard shrill screams of fear and anger, and putting on my dressing-gown went into the corridor. I could hear someone calling out in protest. Then I heard Philippe's voice.

As I stood at the door of my room hesitating what to do, one of the maids came running by.

'What's wrong?' I cried.

'Snails in Madame's bed.'

I went back to my room and sat down thoughtfully. So this was Geneviève's answer. She had taken the reprimand demurely enough, or so it had seemed – while she planned her revenge. There would be trouble about this.

I went along to her room and knocked lightly on the door. There was no answer so I went in to find her lying on her back pretending to be asleep.

'It's no use,' I said.

So she opened one eye and laughed at me.

'Did you hear the shouting, miss?'

'Everyone must have heard it.'

'Imagine her face when she saw them!'

'It's not really very funny, Geneviève.'

'Poor miss. I'm always sorry for people who have no sense of humour.'

'And I'm sorry for people who play senseless pranks for which they alone will have to suffer. What do you think is going to be the outcome of this?'

'She is going to learn to mind her own affairs and not pry into mine.'

'It might not turn out as you think.'

'Oh, stop it! You're as bad as she is. She is trying to stop my going to see Jean Pierre and the rest of them. She won't, I tell you.'

'If your father forbids it . . .'

She stuck out her lower lip. 'Nobody is going to forbid me to see Jean Pierre . . . and the rest of them.'

'The way to deal with this is not to play schoolgirl tricks with snails.'

'Oh, isn't it? Didn't you hear her shout? I'll bet she was terrified. Just serve her right.'

'You don't imagine that she will let this pass?'

'She can do what she likes. I'm going to do what I like.'

I could see that it was no use talking to her, so I left her. But I was growing alarmed; not only by her foolish behaviour, which I was sure would only result in her disadvantage, but by the fact of her growing obsession with Jean Pierre.

I was in the gallery next morning when Claude came in. She was dressed in a dark blue riding-habit and wore a blue bowler riding-hat. Beneath it her eyes were deep blue; I knew she was very angry and trying to hide this.

'There was a disgraceful scene last night,' she said. 'Perhaps you heard.'

'I heard something.'

'Geneviève's manners are deplorable. It is not to be wondered at, considering the company she keeps.'

I raised my eyebrows.

'And I think, Mademoiselle Lawson, that you are in some ways to blame. You will agree that it is since you came here that she has become so friendly with the wine-growers.'

'That friendship has nothing to do with her bad manners. They were deplorable when I arrived.'

'I am convinced that your influence is not a good one, Mademoiselle Lawson, and for that reason I am asking you to leave.'

'To leave!'

'Yes, it's by far the best way. I shall see that you are paid what is due to you and my husband may help you to find other work. But I don't want any arguments. I should like you to be out of the château within two hours.'

'But this is absurd. I haven't finished my work.'

'We will get someone to take it over.'

'You don't understand. I use my own methods. I can't leave this picture until it's finished.'

'I am mistress here, Mademoiselle Lawson, and I am asking you to leave.'

How sure she was of herself! Had she reason to be? Had she so much influence with him? Had she but to ask favours for them to be granted? She was clearly of that opinion. She had complete confidence that the Comte would deny her nothing.

Her lips curled. 'Very well. You shall receive your orders from him.'

I was conscious of a cold fear. There must be a strong reason for that absolute assurance. Perhaps she had already discussed me with the Comte. Perhaps she had already asked for my dismissal and he, being eager to indulge her, had granted this wish. I tried to hide my apprehension as I followed her to the library.

She threw open the door and cried: 'Lothair!'

'Claude,' he said, 'my dear?'

He had risen from his chair and was coming towards us when he saw me. For half a second he was taken aback. Then he bowed his head in acknowledgment of my presence.

'Lothair,' she said. 'I have told Mademoiselle Lawson that she cannot remain. She refused to take her dismissal from me, so I have brought her to you so that you can tell her.'

'Tell her?' he asked, looking from her angry face to my scornful one. I was conscious in that moment how beautiful she was. Anger had put a deep flush in her cheeks which accentuated the blue of her eyes, the whiteness of her perfectly-shaped teeth.

'Geneviève put snails in my bed. It was horrible.'

'My God!' he murmured under his breath. 'What pleasure does she get from playing these foolish tricks?'

'She thinks it is very amusing. Her manners are appalling. What can be expected . . . did you know that her dearest friends are the Bastides?'

'I did not know,' said the Comte.

'Well, I can assure you it is so. She is constantly there. She tells me that she does not care for any of us here. We are not so pleasant, so amusing, so clever as her dear friend Jean Pierre Bastide. Yes, he is her dearest friend although she adores the whole family. The Bastides! You know what they are.'

'The best wine-growers in the district,' said the Comte.

'The girl scuttled into a hasty marriage only a short while ago.'

'Such scuttling is not such a rare occurrence in our district, Claude, I do assure you.'

'And this wonderful Jean Pierre. He's a gay fellow – so I've heard. Are you going to allow your daughter to behave like a village girl who in a very short time will have to learn to er . . . scuttle out of an unfortunate position?'

'You are becoming too excited, Claude. Geneviève shall not be allowed to do anything unbecoming. But how does this concern Mademoiselle Lawson?'

'She has fostered this friendship; she accompanies Geneviève to the

Bastides'. She is their great friend. That is all very well. It is because she has introduced Geneviève into their circle that I say she must go.'

'Go?' said the Comte. 'But she hasn't finished the pictures. Moreover she has been talking to me about wall panels.'

She went close to him, lifting those wonderful blue eyes to his face.

'Lothair,' she said, 'please listen to me. I am thinking of Geneviève.'

He looked beyond her at me. 'You do not say anything, Mademoiselle Lawson.'

'I shall be sorry to leave the pictures unfinished.'

'That is unthinkable.'

'You mean . . . you are on her side?' demanded Claude.

'I mean that I can't see what good Mademoiselle Lawson's going could bring to Geneviève, and I *can* see what harm it would bring to my pictures.'

She stood back from him. For a moment I thought she was going to strike him; instead she looked as though she were about to burst into tears, and turning walked out of the room.

'She is very angry with you,' I said.

'With me? I thought it was with you.'

'With both of us.'

'Geneviève has behaved badly again.'

'Yes, I fear so. It was because she was forbidden to go to the Bastides'.'

'And you have taken her there?'

'Yes.'

'You thought it wise?'

'At one time I thought it very wise. She misses the society of young people. A girl of her age should have friends. It is because she had none that she is so unpredictable . . . given to moods and tantrums, playing these tricks.'

'I see. And it was an idea of yours to give her this companionship?'

'Yes. I have seen her very happy at the Bastides'.'

'And you also?'

'Yes. I have enjoyed their company very much.'

'Jean Pierre has a reputation for being . . . gallant.'

'Who has not? Gallantry is as common in this part of your country as the grape.' To be in his company made me reckless. I felt I had to discover what his feelings were towards me . . . and how they compared with what he felt for Claude. I said: 'I've been thinking that perhaps it would be as well if I left. I could go in say . . . two weeks. I think I could finish the pictures I have started on by that time. That would satisfy Madame de la Talle, and as Geneviève could scarcely go riding alone to the Bastides', this matter would be nearly settled.'

'One cannot run one's life for the sake of neatness, Mademoiselle Lawson.'

I laughed and he laughed with me.

'Now please,' he said, 'no more talk of leaving us.'

'But Madame de la Talle . . .'

'Leave me to deal with her.'

He looked at me, and for one glorious moment it seemed as though the mask slipped from his face. He might have been telling me that he could no more bear to lose me than I could bear to go.

When next I saw Geneviève I noticed the sullen set of her lips.

She told me she hated everyone . . . the whole world. Chiefly she hated the woman who called herself Aunt Claude.

'She has forbidden me again to go to the Maison Bastide, miss. And this time Papa was with her. He said I must not go there without permission from him. That means never . . . because he'll never give it.'

'He might. If . . .'

'No. She has told him not to and he does what she tells him. It's strange to think of him doing what anyone tells him . . . but he does what she says.'

'I'm sure he doesn't always.'

'You don't know, miss. Sometimes I think you don't know much about anything but speaking English and being a governess.'

'Governesses at least have to know a good deal before they can teach.'

'Don't try to change the subject miss. I hate everybody in this house, I tell you. One day I'll run away.'

A few days later I met Jean Pierre. I was riding alone, for Geneviève had avoided me since her outburst.

He came galloping up to me, his expression one of extreme pleasure as it always was when he saw me.

'Look at those grapes!' he cried. 'Did you ever see the like? We shall have wine this year worthy of bottling with the château label. If nothing goes wrong,' he added hastily as though placating some god who might be listening and punish him for arrogance. 'There's only one other season I remember when they were as good.' His expression changed suddenly. 'But I might not be here to see this harvest.'

'What!'

'Hints, so far. But Monsieur le Comte is looking for a good man to send to the Mermoz vineyard, and I am a very good man, so I'm told.'

'Leave Gaillard! But how could you do that?'

'Simply by moving myself to Mermoz.'

'It's impossible.'

'With God and the Comte all things are possible.' He was passionately angry suddenly. 'Oh, don't you see, Dallas, we are of no importance to Monsieur le Comte. We are pawns to be moved this way and that all for the benefit of the games he plays. He does not want me here, shall we say . . . well, then, I am moved across the chequer board to another place. I am a danger here . . . to Monsieur le Comte.'

'A danger? How could you be?'

'How can a humble pawn threaten to put the king in check? That is the subtlety of the game. We do not see how we disturb or threaten the peace of mind of the great. But if we do for a moment we are whisked far away. Do you understand?'

'He is very kind to Gabrielle. He settled her in St. Vallient with Jacques.'

'Oh, very kind . . .' murmured Jean Pierre.

'And why should he want *you* out of the way?'

'There could be several reasons. It may be because you and Geneviève had visited us.'

'Madam de la Talle wanted to dismiss me because of it. In fact she appealed to the Comte.'

'And he wouldn't hear of it?'

'He wants his pictures restored.'

'Is that all, do you think? Dallas, be careful. He's a dangerous man.'

'What do you mean?'

'Women are fascinated by danger, so they tell me. His wife, poor lady, was most unhappy. She was unwanted so she departed.'

'What are you trying to tell me, Jean Pierre?'

'To take care,' he said. 'To take great care.' He leaned towards me and taking my hand, kissed it. 'It is important to me.'

Chapter Ten

The atmosphere of the château had grown heavy with tension. Geneviève was sullen and I wondered what was going on in her mind. As for Claude, she was angry and humiliated because the Comte had refused to comply with her wishes and I sensed her brooding resentment against me. She read a significance in his championing of me – and so did I.

Philippe was uneasy. He came to me when I was in the gallery almost shyly as though he did not want to be discovered there. I imagined that he was afraid of his wife as well as the Comte.

'I hear that you have had a disagreement with ... my wife. I'm sorry about it. It's not that I wish you to go, Mademoiselle Lawson. But here in this house ...' He lifted his shoulders.

'I feel I should finish what I have begun.'

'And you will do so ... soon?'

'Well, there is more to do yet.'

'And when it is finished you can rely on me to help if I can ... but if you should decide to go before, I could probably find you other similar work.'

'I will remember.'

He went away rather sadly and I thought: He is a man who is all for peace. He has no spirit. Perhaps that is why he is here.

Yet strangely enough there was a similarity between him and the Comte; his voice was like the Comte's, his features too. Yet one was so positive, the other negative. Philippe must always have lived in the shadow of his rich and powerful relations. Perhaps that had made him the man he was – timidly seeking peace. But he had been kind to me from the first and I believed now that he wanted me to go because of the conflict between myself and his wife.

Perhaps he was right. Perhaps I should leave as soon as I had finished the picture on which I was working. No good could come of my staying here. The emotions the Comte aroused in me could only become more involved; the scars which separation must necessarily inflict would only be deeper.

I will go, I promised myself. And then because in my heart I was determined not to leave, I began to look for the wall-painting which I suspected might be hidden under the limewash that covered the walls. I could become absorbed again in this work and forget the conflicts which swirled about me; and at the same time give myself an excuse for staying at the château.

The room I was particularly interested in was a small one leading from the gallery. There was a window facing north which gave an excellent light and from it I could look across the gentle slopes of vineyards in the direction of Paris.

I remembered how excited my father had been on the occasion when he had seen a wall rather similar to this. He had told me then how in many English mansions wall-paintings had been hidden under coats of lime-wash. They had been covered, he said, perhaps because they had been damaged or because the pictures had become no longer pleasing.

The removal of coats of lime-wash – and there could be several – was a delicate operation. I had watched my father perform it and had even helped him; I had a natural flair for this type of work. It is difficult to say but perhaps it is an instinct – my father had it and I seemed to have inherited it – but from the moment I had seen that wall I had been excited by it and I was ready to swear that the lime-wash was hiding something.

I set to work with a palette knife, but I could not loosen the outer coat and I could naturally use only the lightest touch; one careless move could ruin what might prove a very valuable painting.

I worked at this for an hour and a half. I knew that it was unwise to work longer since the utmost concentration was needed, and during that time I had discovered nothing to substantiate my suspicion.

But the next day I was fortunate. I was able to flake away a small piece of lime-wash – no more than about one sixteenth of an inch it was true, but I was certain on that second day that there was a picture on the wall.

This was indeed the wisest thing I could do, for it took my mind from the rising emotional tension of the château.

I was working on the wall when Geneviève came into the gallery.

'Miss!' she called. 'Miss, where are you?'

'Here,' I answered.

As she ran in I saw that she was distraught.

'It's a message from Carrefour, miss. My grandfather is worse. He's asking for me. Come with me.'

'Your father . . .'

'He is out . . . riding with her. Please, miss, do come. Otherwise I'll have to go with the groom.'

I stood up and said I would change quickly and see her in the stables in ten minutes' time.

'Don't be longer,' she begged.

As we rode to Carrefour together she was silent; I knew that she dreaded these visits and yet was fascinated by them.

When we reached the house Madame Labisse was in the hall waiting for us.

'Ah, mademoiselle,' she said, 'I am glad you have come.'

'He is very ill?' I asked.

'Another stroke. Maurice found him when he took his *petit déjeuner*. The doctor has been and it was then that I sent for mademoiselle.'

'Do you mean he's . . . dying?' asked Geneviève in a hollow voice.

'We cannot say, Mademoiselle Geneviève. He still lives, but he is very ill.'

'May we go to him now?'

'Please come.'

'You stay,' said Geneviève to me.

We went into that room which I had seen before. The old man was lying on the pallet and Madame Labisse had made some attempt at comfort. She had put a coverlet over him and had placed a small table and chairs in the room. There was even a rug on the floor. But the bare walls decorated only by the crucifix and the prie-dieu in the corner preserved the appearance of a monk's cell.

He was lying back on the pillows – a pathetic sight, his eyes set in dark caverns and the flesh falling away from each side of his long nose. He looked like a bird of prey.

'It is Mademoiselle Geneviève, monsieur,' murmured Madame Labisse.

An expression flickered over his face so that I guessed he recognized her. His lips moved and his speech was slurred and muffled.

'Granddaughter . . .'

'Yes, Grandfather. I am here.'

He nodded, and his eyes were on me. I did not believe he could see with the left one; it seemed dead, but the right was alive.

'Come closer,' he said, and Geneviève moved nearer to the bed. But he was looking at me.

'He means you, miss,' whispered Geneviève. So we changed chairs and I took the one nearest him, which seemed to satisfy him.

'Françoise,' he said. Then I understood, he was under the impression that I was Geneviève's mother.

'It's all right. Please don't worry,' I said.

'Don't . . .' he muttered. 'Careful. Watch . . .'

'Yes, yes,' I said soothingly.

'Should never have married . . . that man. Knew it was . . . wrong. . . .'

'It's all right,' I assured him soothingly.

But his face was contorted.

'You must . . . He must . . .'

'Oh, miss,' said Geneviève, 'I can't bear it. I'll come back in a minute. He's rambling. He doesn't know I'm here. Must I stay?'

I shook my head and she went away leaving me in that strange room alone with the dying man. I sensed that he had noticed her disappearance and was relieved. He seemed to make a great effort.

'Françoise . . . Keep away from him. Do not let him . . .'

'Why?' I said. 'Why keep away from him.'

'Such sin . . . such sin,' he moaned.

'You must not distress yourself,' I said.

'Come back here. . . . Leave the château. There is only doom and disaster there . . . for you.'

The effort required for such a long speech seemed to have exhausted him. He closed his eyes, and I felt afraid and frustrated for I knew he could have told me so much.

He opened his eyes suddenly.

'Honorine, you're so beautiful. Our child . . . What will become of her? Oh, sin . . . sin.'

Exhaustion overcame him. I thought he was dying. I went to the door to call Maurice.

'The end cannot be far off,' said Maurice.

Labisse looked at me and nodded.

'Mademoiselle Geneviève should be here.'

'I will go and bring her,' I said, glad to escape from the room of death.

As I walked along the corridor I was conscious of the gloom. Death was close. I sensed it. But it was more than that. It was like a house from which all light had been excluded, a house in which it had been considered sinful to laugh and be happy. How could poor Françoise have been happy in such a house? How glad she must have been to escape to the castle!

I had reached a staircase and stood at the foot looking up.

'Geneviève,' I called softly.

There was no answer. On a landing was a window the light from which was almost shut out because the heavy curtains were half-drawn across it. I imagined this was how they always were kept. I went to them and looked out at the overgrown garden. I tried to open the window, but could not do so. It must have been years since anyone had opened it.

I was hoping to see Geneviève in the garden and sign to her; but she was not there.

I called her name again; there was still no reply, so I started up the stairs.

The stillness of the house closed in on me. I wondered whether Geneviève was hiding in one of those rooms, keeping away from the sick-room because she hated the thought of death. It was like her to run away from what she found intolerable. Perhaps that was at the root of her trouble. I must make her see that if she was afraid of something it was better to look it straight in the face.

'Geneviève!' I called. 'Where are you?'

I opened a door. It was a dark bedroom, the curtains half-drawn as they were on the landing. I shut the door and opened another. This part of the house could not have been used for years.

There was another flight of stairs, and this I guessed would lead to the nurseries, for these were usually at the top of the house.

In spite of what was happening in the room below I was thinking also of the childhood of Françoise, of which I had read in those note-books which Nounou doled out one by one. It occurred to me then that Geneviève had probably listened to stories of her mother's childhood in this house, and if she wanted to hide, where would she be more likely to come than to the nurseries?

I was certain that I should find her up here.

'Geneviève,' I called more loudly than as yet. 'Are you up here?'

No answer. Only a faint return of my own voice like a ghostly echo to mock me. If she were there she was not going to let me know.

I opened the door. Before me was a room which though lofty was not large. There was a pallet on the floor, a table, a chair, a prie-dieu at one end and a crucifix on the wall. It was furnished as that room in which the old man now lay. But there was a difference about this room. Across the only window, which was high in the wall, were bars. The room was like a prison cell. I knew instinctively that it *was* a prison cell.

I felt an impulse to shut the door and hurry away; but curiosity was too strong. I entered the room. What was this house? I asked myself. Was it conducted like a monastery, a convent? I knew that Geneviève's grandfather regretted he had not become a monk. The 'treasure' in the chest explained that – a monk's robe was his dearest possession. I had learned that from the first of Françoise's note-books. And the whip? Had he scourged himself . . . or his wife and daughter?

And who had lived here? In this room someone had awakened every morning to that barred window; those bleak walls, to this austerity. Had he . . . or she . . . desired it? Or . . .

I noticed the scratching on the distempered walls. I looked closer. 'Honorine,' I read, 'the prisoner.'

So I was right. It was a prison. Here she had been detained against her will. She was like those people who had lived in the dungeons at the château.

I heard the sound of slow padding steps on the stairs. I stood very still waiting. Those were not Geneviève's steps.

Someone was on the other side of the door. I heard distinctly the sound of breathing, and I went swiftly to the door and pulled it open.

The woman looked at me with wide incredulous eyes.

'Mademoiselle!' she cried.

'I was looking for Geneviève, Madame Labisse,' I told her.

'I heard someone up here. I wondered. . . You are wanted downstairs. The end is very near.'

'And Geneviève?'

'I believe she is hiding in the garden.'

'It is understandable,' I said. 'The young do not wish to look on death. I thought I might find her in the nurseries, which I guessed would be up here.'

'The nurseries are on the lower floor.'

'And this . . .?' I began.

'This was Mademoiselle Geneviève's grandmother's room.'

I looked up at the barred window.

'I looked after her until she died,' said Madame Labisse.

'She was very ill?'

Madame Labisse nodded coldly. I was too inquisitive, she seemed to be telling me. In the past she had not given secrets away for she was paid well to keep them; and she was not going to jeopardize her future by betraying them now.

She was right; Geneviève was hiding in the garden. It was only after her grandfather was dead that she returned to the house.

The family went over to Carrefour for the funeral, which was, I heard, carried out with the pomp usual on such occasions. I stayed behind. Nounou did not go either; she had one of her headaches, she said, and when she had one of them she was fit for nothing but her own bed. I guessed the occasion would have aroused too many painful memories for her.

Geneviève went over in the carriage with her father, Philippe and Claude; and when they had left I went along to see Nounou.

I found her, as I expected, not in bed; and I asked if I could stay and talk with her awhile.

She replied that she would be glad of my company, so I made coffee and we sat together.

The subject of Carrefour and the past was one which both fascinated and frightened her, and she was half-evasive, half eager.

'I don't think Geneviève wanted to go to the funeral,' I said.

She shook her head. 'I wish she need not have gone.'

'But it was expected of her. She is growing up – scarcely a child any more. How do you think she is? Less inclined to tantrums? More calm?'

'She was always calm enough . . .' lied Nounou.

I looked at her sadly and she looked sadly back. I wanted to tell her that we should get nowhere by pretence.

'When I was last at the house I saw her grandmother's room. It was very strange. It was like a prison. And she felt it too.'

'How can you know?' she demanded.

'Because she said so.'

Her eyes were round with horror. 'She . . . told you . . . How . . .'

I shook my head. 'She did not return from the dead, if that's what you're thinking. She wrote on the wall that she was a prisoner. I saw it. "Honorine, the prisoner." Was she a prisoner? You would know. You were there.'

'She was ill. She had to stay in her room.'

'What a strange room for an invalid . . . right at the top of the house. It must have made a lot of work for the servants . . . carrying to her up there.'

'You are very practical, miss. You think of such things.'

'I should think the servants thought of it, too. But why should she think of herself as a prisoner? Wasn't she allowed to go out?'

'She was ill.'

'Invalids are not prisoners. Nounou, tell me about it. I feel it's important . . . to Geneviève, perhaps.'

'How could it be? What are you driving at, miss?'

'To understand would enable me to help. I want to help Geneviève. I want to make her happy. She's had an unusual upbringing. That place where her mother lived and then this castle . . . and everything that happened.

You must see that all that could affect a child . . . an impressionable, highly-strung child. I want you to help me to help her.'

'I would do anything in the world to help her.'

'Please tell me all you know, Nounou.'

'But I know nothing . . . nothing . . .'

'But Françoise wrote in her note-books, didn't she? You haven't shown them all to me.'

'She didn't intend anyone to see them.'

'Nounou . . . there are others, aren't there . . . more revealing . . .?'

She sighed, and taking the key from the chain at her waist she unlocked her cupboard.

She selected a note-book and gave it to me. I noticed from where she took it. There was another there – the last in the line – and I hoped that she would give me that too. But she didn't.

'Take it away and read it,' she said. 'And bring it straight back to me. Promise you'll show no one else and bring it straight back.'

I promised.

This was different. This was the woman in great fear. She was afraid of her husband. As I read I could not rid myself of the feeling that I was spying into the mind and heart of a dead woman. But he was concerned in this. What would he think of me if he knew what I was doing?

Yet I must read on. With every day I spent in the château it was becoming more and more important for me to know the truth.

'I lay in bed last night praying that he would not come to me. Once I thought I heard his steps, but it was only Nounou. She knows how I feel. She hovers . . . praying with me, I know. I am afraid of him. He knows it. He cannot understand why. Other women are so fond of him. Only I am afraid.'

'I saw Papa to-day. He looked at me as he often does, as though he would look deep into my mind, as though he is trying to discover every moment of my life . . . but mostly that. "How is your husband?" he says to me. And I stammer and blush for I know what he is thinking. He said: "There are other women, I have heard." And I did not answer. He seemed pleased that there were. "The devil will take care of him for God will not," he said. Yet he seems pleased that there are other women and I know why. Anything is preferable to my being sullied.'

'Nounou prowls about. She is very frightened. I am so afraid of the nights. I find it so hard to get to sleep. Then I awake startled and fancy someone has come into the room. It's an unnatural marriage. I wish I were a little girl again playing in the nursery. The best time was before Papa showed me the treasure in the trunk . . . before *Maman* died. I wish I didn't have to grow up. But then of course I should never have had Geneviève.'

'Geneviève flew into a passion to-day. It was because Nounou said she must stay indoors. She has a slight cold and Nounou was worried. She locked Nounou in her room and the poor creature waited patiently there until I went to find her. She didn't want to betray Geneviève. We were both frightened afterwards when we scolded Geneviève. She was so . . . wild and naughty. I said she reminded me of her grandmother and Nounou was so upset by her naughtiness.'

'Nounou said, "Never say that again, Françoise dear. Never, never." I realized she meant what I had said of Geneviève's being like her grandmother.'

'Last night I awoke in a fright. I thought Lothair had come into the room. I saw Papa during the day. He made me more frightened than usual perhaps. It was a dream. It was not Lothair. Why should he come? He knows I hate his coming. He no longer tries to make me see life from his way. I know that is because he does not care for me. He is glad to escape. I am sure of it. But I dreamed he was there and it was a horrible nightmare for I believed he would be cruel to me. But it was only a dream. Nounou came in. She had been lying awake listening, she said. I said, "I can't sleep, Nounou. I'm frightened," so she gave me some laudanum. She uses it for her headaches. She says it takes the pain away and makes her sleep. So I took it and I slept, and in the morning it all seemed like a nightmare . . . nothing more. He would never force himself on me now. He doesn't care enough. There are others.'

'I told Nounou I had a raging toothache, and she gave me laudanum. It is such a comfort to know that when I can't sleep there it is in the bottle waiting to help me.'

'A sudden thought came to me to-day. It can't be true. But it could be. I wonder if it is. I am frightened that it might be . . . and yet in a way I'm not. I shan't tell anyone yet . . . certainly not Papa; he would be horrified. He loathes anything to do with it, although he is my father, which is strange, so it could not always have been so. I shan't tell Lothair . . . not until it is necessary. I shan't even tell Nounou. Not yet in any case. But she'll find out sooner or later. Well, I'll wait and see. I may be imagining it.'

'Geneviève came in this morning a little late. She had overslept. I was quite frightened that something might have happened to her. When she came she just ran to me; she sobbed when we hugged each other and I couldn't calm her down. Dear Geneviève. I should love to tell her but not yet . . . oh no, not yet.'

That was the end and I had not discovered what I wanted to know; but there was one thing I had discovered – that the important note-book was the last one, the one I had seen in Nounou's cupboard. Why had she not given me that one?

I went back to her room. She was lying on the couch, her eyes closed.

'Nounou,' I said, 'what was it . . . the secret? What did it mean? What was she afraid of?'

She said: 'I'm in such pain. You've no idea how these headaches affect me.'

'I'm sorry. Is there anything I can do?'

'Nothing . . . There is nothing to be done but to keep quiet.'

'There is the last book,' I said. 'The one she wrote in before she died. Perhaps the answer is in that book. . . .'

'There is nothing,' she said. 'Will you draw the curtains. The light hurts me.'

I laid the note-book on the table near her couch, drew the curtains and went out.

But I had to see that last note-book. I was sure it would give me some clue as to what had really happened in the days before Françoise's death.

During the next day I made such a discovery that I almost forgot my desire to see the note-book. I had been working patiently on the suspected wall-painting, very cautiously flaking pieces of lime-wash with a fine ivory paper-knife, when I uncovered . . . paint! My heart began to hammer with excitement, my fingers to tremble. I had to restrain the impulse to work on fervently. This I dared not do. I was far too excited and I could not trust myself. If it were true that I was on the point of discovering a wall-painting – and I believed this could well be – my hands must be absolutely steady; I should have to curb this wild excitement.

I stood a few paces back, my eyes fixed on that magic fraction of what I believed to be paint. There was a film over it which might be difficult to remove, so it was not easy to assess the colour. But it was there . . . I was sure of it.

I did not want to say anything until I was sure what I was about to discover would be worthwhile.

During the next days I worked almost furtively, but as I revealed little by little I became more and more certain that I was about to expose a painting of some value.

I was determined that the first to hear of this should be the Comte; and in the middle of the morning I left my tools in the gallery and went along to the library in the hope of finding him. He was not there, and, as I had done on a previous occasion, I rang the bell and when the servant appeared I asked that Monsieur le Comte should be told that I wished to speak to him urgently in the library.

I was told that he had left for the stables a few moments before.

'Please go and tell him that I want to see him at once. It is most important.'

When I was alone I wondered if I had been too impulsive. After all, perhaps he would think such an item of news could wait until a more propitious moment. It might be that he would not share my excitement. But he must, I told myself. After all, the picture had been found in his house.

I heard his voice in the hall; and the door of the library was flung open and he stood there looking at me in some surprise. He was dressed for riding and had clearly come straight from the stables.

'What is it?' he asked; and in that moment I realized he was expecting to hear something had happened to Geneviève.

'A most important discovery! Can you come and look at it now? There is a picture under the lime-wash after all . . . and I think there is no doubt that it is a valuable one.'

'Oh,' he said; and then his lips betrayed some amusement. 'Of course I must come.'

'I have interrupted something . . .'

'My dear Mademoiselle Lawson, such an important discovery must come before all else, I'm sure.'

'Please come and see.'

I led the way to that small room which led from the gallery and there it was – just a small part exposed, but there was no doubt that it was a hand lying on velvet and on the fingers and at the wrist were jewels.

'It is a little sombre at the moment but you can see it is in need of cleaning. It's a portrait, and you can tell by the way the paint has been put on . . . and the fold of that velvet . . . that a master has been at work.'

'You mean, my dear Mademoiselle Lawson, that *you* can.'

'Isn't it wonderful?' I said to him.

He looked into my face and smiling said: 'Wonderful.'

I felt vindicated. I was certain there had been something there under the lime-wash and all those hours of work were not in vain.

'There is very little so far . . .' he went on.

'Oh, but it's there. Now I have to make sure that I mustn't get too excited, which could mean impatience. I am longing to expose the rest, but I must go to work very carefully. I have to be sure not to damage it in any way.'

He laid his hand on my shoulder. 'I am very grateful to you.'

'Perhaps now you are not sorry you decided to trust your pictures to a woman.'

'I quickly learned that you are a woman to whom I would trust a great deal.'

The pressure of his hand on my shoulder; the brilliance of those hooded eyes, the joy of discovery, were intoxicating. I thought recklessly: This is the happiest moment of my life.

'Lothair!' It was Claude standing there frowning at us. 'What on earth has happened? You were there . . . and then you suddenly disappeared.'

He dropped his hand and turned to her. 'I had a message,' he said. 'An urgent message. Mademoiselle Lawson has made a miraculous discovery.'

'What?' She came towards us and looked from him to me.

'A most miraculous discovery!' he repeated, looking at me.

'What is this all about?'

'Look!' said the Comte. 'She has exposed a painting . . . a valuable one, apparently.'

'That! It looks like a smudge of paint.'

'You say that, Claude, because you do not see it with the artist's eye. Now Mademoiselle Lawson tells me that it is part of a portrait by an artist of great talent because of the way the paint is put on.'

'You have forgotten that we are riding this morning.'

'Such a discovery makes my forgetfulness excusable, don't you agree, Mademoiselle Lawson?'

'It is very rarely that such discoveries are made,' I replied.

'We are late already,' said Claude, without looking at me.

'You must tell me more some other time, Mademoiselle Lawson,' said the Comte, as he followed her to the door; but as he reached it, he turned to smile at me. Claude saw the look which passed between us and I was aware of the intensity of her dislike.

That thought was almost more intoxicating than anything else that had happened.

I worked with an intensity during the next few days which I knew to be dangerous; but by the end of three days I had uncovered more of the figure and as each inch was exposed I grew more and more certain that I was right in thinking that the painting was valuable.

One morning, however, I had a shock, for when I was working on one part of the lime-wash I uncovered something I could not understand. A letter emerged. There was writing on the wall. Something which might confirm the date of the painting? My hand was trembling. Perhaps I should have stopped work until I felt more calm, but that would be asking too much. I had uncovered the letters BLI. I worked carefully round them and I had '*oubliez.*' I could not give up. Before the morning was over, by working with great care I had the words '*Ne m'oubliez pas.*' 'Forget me not.' I was certain too that they had been painted at a much later date than the portrait which was now half-exposed.

It was something to show the Comte. He came to the room and we examined it together. He shared my excitement, or made a good pretence of doing so.

The door opened behind me. I was smiling as I carefully pressed the edge of the knife to the border of the lime-wash. He is growing as excited by this discovery as I am and finding it difficult to keep away, I thought.

There was a deep silence in the room and as I turned the smile must have faded quickly from my face for it was not the Comte who stood there but Claude.

She gave me a half-smile which seemed to cover a certain embarrassment. I could not understand this new mood.

'I heard you had uncovered some words,' she said. 'May I see?' She came close to the wall and peered at it murmuring: ' "*Ne m'oubliez pas*".' Then she turned to me, her eyes puzzled. 'How did you know it was there?'

'It's an instinct perhaps.'

'Mademoiselle Lawson . . .' She hesitated as though she found it difficult to say what was in her mind. 'I'm afraid I've been rather hasty. The other day . . . You see, I was alarmed for Geneviève.'

'Yes, I understand.'

'And I thought . . . I thought that the best thing . . .'

'Would be for me to go?'

'It wasn't only Geneviève.'

I was taken aback. Was she going to confide in me? Was she going to tell me that she was jealous of the Comte's regard for me? Impossible!

'You may not believe me, but I was thinking of you, too. My husband has spoken to me of you. We both feel that . . .' She frowned and looked at me helplessly. 'We feel you might want to get away.'

'Why?'

'There could be reasons. I just wanted you to know that I've heard of a possibility . . . a really exciting one. Between us, my husband and I could probably arrange a brilliant opportunity for you. I know how interested you are in old buildings and I dare say you would welcome the chance to examine in detail some of our old churches and abbeys. And of course the picture galleries.'

'I should, of course, but . . .'

'Well, we have heard of a little project. A party of ladies are planning a tour to inspect the treasures of France. They want a guide – someone who has a deep knowledge of what they will see. Naturally they would not want a man to accompany them, and so they thought that if there were such a lady who could conduct them and explain to them . . . It's a unique chance. It would be well paid and I can assure you it would lead to excellent opportunities. It would enhance your reputation and I know give you an entry into many of our oldest families. You would be in great demand, for the ladies who wish to make this tour are all art-fanciers and have collections of their own. It seems such an excellent opportunity.'

I was amazed. She was certainly eager to be rid of me. Yes, indeed, she must be jealous!

'It sounds a fascinating project,' I said. 'But this work . . .' I waved my hand towards the wall.

'You will finish it shortly. Consider this project. I really think you should.'

She was like a different person. There was a new gentleness about her. I could almost believe that she was genuinely concerned for me. I thought of making a minute examination of the treasures of France; I thought of discussing these with people who were as interested in them as I was. She could not have offered a more dazzling bait.

'I can get more details for you,' she said eagerly. 'You will think about it, Mademoiselle Lawson?'

She hesitated again as though she would say more, and, deciding against it, left me.

I was puzzled. She was either a jealous woman who was ready to go to great lengths to be rid of me, or she was warning me against the Comte. She might be implying: Be careful. See how he uses women. Myself . . . married to Philippe for *his* convenience; Gabrielle married to Jacques. What will happen to *you* if you stay here and let him govern your life for that little while it pleases him to do so?

But in my heart I believed she suspected the Comte had some regard for me, and wanted me out of the way. It was an exhilarating thought. But . . . for how long? Then I thought of the proposition she had laid before me. It was one which an ambitious woman eager to advance in her profession would be foolish to reject. It was a chance which came once in a lifetime.

When I thought of that – and the possibilities the future held for me here in the château, I was tormented with doubts and fears and the hopes of wild, and what my good sense told me were hopeless, impossibilities.

I called on Gabrielle. She was noticeably pregnant but she seemed very happy. We talked about the coming baby and she showed me the layette she was preparing.

I asked after Jacques and then she talked to me more frankly than she had before.

'Having a baby changes you. The things that seem important before no longer seem anything but trivial. The child is all-important. I can't understand now why I was so frightened. If I had told Jacques we could have arranged something. But I was so scared . . . and now it all seems so foolish.'

'What does Jacques feel?'

'He scolds me for being so foolish. But I was afraid because we'd wanted to marry for so long and we knew we couldn't because we had his mother to support. We just could not have managed to live . . . the three of us.'

How stupid I had been to suspect the Comte was the father of her child. How could she have been so radiantly happy if this had been the case?

'But for the Comte . . .' I said.

'Ah, but for the Comte!' She was smiling placidly.

'It seems strange to me that you could not tell Jacques but you could tell *him*.'

Again that smile. 'Oh, no. He would understand. I knew it. Besides he was the one who could help . . . and he did. Jacques and I will always be grateful to him.'

This meeting with Gabrielle did something to lift the indecision which Claude's offer had brought to me. I would not leave the château until it was absolutely necessary, no matter how dazzling the prospect laid before me.

Now I had two overwhelming interests: to uncover what lay beneath the lime-wash and to reveal the true character of the man who was beginning to mean so much – far too much – in my life.

The words 'Forget me not' had been intriguing, and I was hoping to uncover more, but I did not. What I did uncover was the face of a dog which appeared to be crouching at the feet of the woman of whom the painting was going to prove a portrait. It was while I was working in this section that I discovered paint which I thought might be part of a later work. I suffered moments of horror because I knew it was a practice to cover old paintings with a layer of lime-wash and repaint on the new layer; in which case I might have destroyed a picture which had been painted over the one on which I was working.

I could only go on with what I had begun, and to my amazement, in an hour I had revealed that what seemed like a painting was something which had been added to the original picture – although at a later date.

It was extraordinary and it grew more so, for the dog was revealed to be in a case which was the shape of a coffin; and beneath this were those words 'Forget me not.'

I laid down my knife and looked at it. The dog was a spaniel like the one in the miniature which the Comte had given me at Christmas. I was certain that this was a portrait of the same woman – the subject of the first picture I had cleaned, of my miniature and now the wall-painting.

I wanted to show this to the Comte, so I went to the library. Claude was there alone. She looked up hopefully when she saw me and I realised immediately that she thought I had come to accept her offer.

'I was looking for the Comte,' I said.

Her face hardened and the old dislike was visible. 'Did you propose to *send* for him?'

'I thought he would be interested to look at the wall.'

'When I see him I will tell him you sent for him.'

I pretended not to see the mockery.

'Thank you,' I said, and went back to my work.

But the Comte did not come.

Geneviève had a birthday in June which was celebrated by a dinner-party at the château. I did not attend this although Geneviève had invited me. I made excuses knowing full well that Claude, who was after all the hostess, had no desire for my presence.

Geneviève herself did not mind whether I went or not; nor, it seemed, to my chagrin, did the Comte. It was a very lukewarm affair and Geneviève was almost sullen about it.

I had bought her a pair of grey gloves which she had admired in one of the town's shop windows and she did say she was pleased with these, but she was in one of her gloomy moods and I felt that it would have been better not to have celebrated a birthday in such circumstances.

The day after, we went riding together, and I asked how she had enjoyed the party.

'I didn't,' she declared. 'It was hateful. What's the good of having a party· when you don't invite the guests? I would have liked a real party . . . perhaps with a cake and a crown in it . . .'

'That's not a birthday custom.'

'What does it matter? In any case there must be birthday customs. I expect Jean Pierre would know. I'll ask him.'

'You know what your Aunt Claude feels about your friendship with the Bastides.'

Fury broke out all over her face. 'I tell you I shall choose my own friends. I'm grown up now. They'll have to realize it. I'm fifteen.'

'It's not really such a great age.'

'You're just as bad as the rest of them.'

For a few moments I saw her stormy profile before she broke into a gallop and was away. I tried to follow her but she was determined I shouldn't.

After a while I rode back to the château alone; I was very uneasy about Geneviève.

The hot days of July passed like a dream to me; August had come, and the grapes were just ripening in the sun. As I passed the vineyards one of the workers would usually comment on them. 'A good harvest this year, mademoiselle.'

In the *pâtisserie* where now and then I took coffee and a slice of the *gâteau de la maison*, Madame Latière talked to me of the size of the grapes. They would be sweetened by all the sunshine they had had this year.

The harvest was almost upon us, and it seemed that the thoughts of all were on it. It was a kind of climax. I still had work to do on the wall-painting; and there were pictures still to be cleaned; but I could not stay indefinitely at the château. Was I being foolish to reject Claude's offer?

But I refused to think of leaving the château; I had lived in it for about ten months but I felt that I had never truly been alive before I had come; and a life away from it seemed impossible, vague, no life at all. Nothing, however interesting, could compensate me if I went away.

Often I recalled the conversations which had taken place between us and asked myself if I had read something into them which did not exist; I was not sure whether the Comte had been mocking me, in truth telling me to mind my own business, or whether he had been telling me obliquely of his regard for me.

I threw myself into the life of the château, and when I heard of the annual *kermesse* I wanted to play my part.

It was Geneviève who told me.

'You ought to have a stall, miss. What will you sell? You've never been to a *kermesse* before, have you?'

I told her that they occurred regularly in our villages and towns. I had made all sorts of things for our church bazaars and I imagined that a *kermesse* was not very different from these.

She wanted to hear about this and when I told her she was delighted, agreeing that I was very well acquainted with what went on at a *kermesse*.

I had a notion for painting flowers on cups and saucers and ashtrays. And when I had completed a few and shown them to Geneviève, she laughed with pleasure. 'But, miss, that's wonderful. They've never had anything like it at our *kermesse* before.' I painted enthusiastically – not only flowers but animals on mugs – little elephants, rabbits and cats. Then I had the idea of painting names on the mugs. Geneviève would sit beside me telling me what names I should do. I did Yves and Margot, of course; and she named other children who would most certainly be at the *kermesse*.

'That's a certain sale,' she cried. 'They won't be able to resist buying mugs with their own names on. May I be at your stall? Trade will be so brisk you'll need an assistant.'

I was very happy to see her so enthusiastic.

'Papa will be here for this *kermesse*,' she told me. 'I don't remember his being here for one before.'

'Why was he not here?'

'Oh, he was always in Paris . . . or somewhere. He had been here more than ever before. I heard the servants talking about it. It is since his accident.'

'Oh?' I said, attempting to appear unconcerned.

Perhaps, I reminded myself caustically, it is because Claude is here.

I talked of the *kermesse*; I thought of the *kermesse*; and I was delighted because Geneviève shared my excitement and recalled previous ones.

'This,' I said, 'must be the most successful of all.'

'It will ·be, miss. We have never had mugs with children's names on before. The money we make goes to the convent. I shall tell the Holy Mother that she has to be grateful to you, miss.'

'*Il ne faut pas vendre le peau de l'ours avant de l'avoir tuer,*' I reminded her. And added in English: 'We mustn't count our chickens before they're hatched.'

She was smiling at me, thinking, I knew, that whatever the occasion I would always play the governess.

One afternoon when we were returning from our ride I had the idea of using the moat. I had never explored it before so we went down there together. The grass was green and lush; and I suggested that it would be original to have the stalls there.

Geneviève thought it an excellent idea. 'Everything should be different this time, miss. We've never used the old moat before, but of course it's ideal. How warm it is down here!'

'It's sheltered from all the breezes,' I said. 'Can you imagine the stalls against the grey walls?'

'I'm sure it'll be fun. We will have it here. Do you feel shut in down here, miss?'

I saw what she meant. It was so silent and the tall grey walls of the château so close were overpowering.

We had walked all round the château and I was wondering whether my suggestion to have the stalls here on the uneven ground of the dried-up moat had not been rather hastily made, considering how much more comfortable one of the well-kept lawns would be, when I saw the cross. It was stuck in the earth close to the granite wall of the château, and I pointed it out to Geneviève.

She was on her hands and knees examining it and I joined her.

'There's some writing on it,' she said.

We bent over to examine it.

I read out 'Fidèle, 1747. It's a grave,' I added. 'A dog's grave.'

Geneviève raised her eyes to me. 'All those years ago! Fancy.'

'I believe he's the dog on my miniature.'

'Oh, yes, the one Papa gave you for Christmas. Fidèle! What a nice name.'

'His mistress must have loved him to bury him like that . . . with a cross and his name and the date.'

Geneviève nodded.

'Somehow,' she said, 'it makes a difference. It makes the moat a sort of graveyard.'

I nodded.

'I don't think we would want to have the *kermesse* down there where poor Fidèle is buried.'

I agreed. 'And we should all be badly bitten too. There are lots of unpleasant insects in this long grass.'

We entered a door of the château and as the cool of those thick walls closed in on us, she said: 'I'm glad we found poor Fidèle's grave, though, miss.'

'Yes,' I said, 'so am I.'

The day of the *kermesse* was hot and sunny. Marquees had been set up on one of the lawns, and early in the morning the stall-holders arrived to set out their wares. Geneviève worked with me to make ours gay; she had spread a white cloth over the counter and had decorated it most tastefully with leaves, and on this we set out our painted crockery. It looked very charming, and I secretly agreed with Geneviève that ours was the most outstanding of all the stalls. Madame Latière from the *pâtisserie* was supplying refreshments in a tent; needlework figured largely in the goods for sale; there were flowers from the château gardens; cakes, vegetables, ornaments and pieces of jewellery. Claude would rival us, Geneviève told me, because she would sell some of her clothes, and she had wardrobes full of them; of course everyone would want to wear her clothes, which they knew came from Paris.

The local musicians, led by Armand Bastide and his violin, would play intermittently all the afternoon and when it was dusk the dancing would begin.

I was certainly proud of my mugs and the first buyers were the Bastide children who shrieked delightedly when they found their own names as though they were there by a coincidence; and as I provided plain mugs to be painted with any names which were not already on display, I was kept busy.

The *kermesse* was opened by the Comte – and this in itself made it a special occasion – for as I was told several times in the first half-hour, it was the first *kermesse* he had attended for years. 'Not since the death of the Comtesse.' This was significant, said some. It meant that the Comte had decided that life should be more normal at the château.

Nounou came by and insisted that I paint a mug with her name on it. I worked under a blue sunshade which spread itself over our stall; I was conscious of the hot sun, the smell of flowers, the jumble of voices and constant laughter, and I was very happy under that blue sunshade.

The Comte came by and stood watching me at work.

Geneviève said: 'Oh, Papa, isn't she good at it? The quick way she does it. You must have one with your name on it.'

'Yes, certainly I must,' he agreed.

'Your name isn't here, Papa. You didn't do a Lothair, miss?'

'No, I didn't think we should need one.'

'You were wrong there, Mademoiselle Lawson.'

'Yes,' agreed Geneviève gleefully as though she, as much as her father, enjoyed seeing that I could make a mistake. 'You were wrong there.'

'It's a wrong which can quickly be remedied if the commission is serious,' I retorted.

'It's very serious.'

He leaned against the counter while I selected one of the plain mugs. 'Have you any preference for colour?'

'Please choose for me. I am sure your taste is excellent.'

I looked at him steadily. 'Purple, I think, purple and gold.'

'Royal colours?' he asked.

'Most appropriate,' I retaliated.

A little crowd had collected to watch me paint a mug for the Comte. There was a little whispering among the watchers.

I felt as though the blue umbrella sheltered me from all that was unpleasant. Yes, I was certainly happy on that afternoon.

There was his name in royal purple – the 'i' dotted with a touch of gold paint, and a full stop after the name also in gold.

There was an exclamation of admiration from those who looked on and somewhat deliriously I painted a gold fleur-de-lis below the name.

'There,' I said, 'Isn't that fitting?'

'You must pay for it, Papa.'

'If Mademoiselle Lawson will name the price.'

'A little more, I think, don't you, miss, because after all it *is* a special one.'

'A great deal more, I think.'

'I am in your hands.'

There was an exclamation of amazement as the Comte dropped his payment into the bowl Geneviève had placed on the counter. I was sure it meant that we should have the largest donation to the convent.

Geneviève was pink with pleasure. I believe she was almost as happy as I was.

As the Comte moved on I saw Jean Pierre at my side. 'I would like a mug,' he said, 'and a fleur-de-lis also.'

'Please do one for him, miss,' pleaded Geneviève, smiling up at him.

So I did.

Then everyone was asking for fleur-de-lis, and mugs already sold were brought back.

'It will cost more for the fleur-de-lis,' cried Geneviève in triumph.

And I painted and Geneviève grew pinker with pleasure, while Jean Pierre stood by smiling at us.

It had been a triumph. My mugs had earned more than any other stall. Everyone was talking about it.

And with the dusk the musicians began to play and there was dancing on the lawn and in the hall for those who preferred it.

This was the way it always was, Geneviève told me, yet there had never been a *kermesse* like this one.

The Comte had disappeared. His duties did not extend beyond being present at the *kermesse*; Claude and Philippe had left too; I found myself wistfully looking for the Comte, hoping that he would return and seek me out.

Jean Pierre was at my side. 'Well, what do you think of our rural pleasures?'

'That they are very much like the rural pleasures I have known all my life.'

'I'm glad of that. Will you dance with me?'

'I shall be pleased to.'

'Shall we go on to the lawn? It is so hot in here. It's much more pleasant to dance under the stars.'

He took my hand and led me in the dreamy waltz which the musicians had started to play.

'Life here interests you,' he asked, and his lips were so close to my ear that he seemed to whisper. 'But you cannot stay here for ever. You have your own home.'

'I have no home. Only Cousin Jane is left.'

'I do not think I like Cousin Jane.'

'But why not?'

'Because you do not. I hear it in your voice.'

'Do I betray my feelings so easily?'

'I understand you a little. I hope to understand you more, for we are good friends, aren't we?'

'I hope so.'

'We have been very happy . . . my family and I . . . that you should treat us as friends. Please tell me, what shall you do when the work at the château is finished?'

'I shall leave here, of course. But it is not yet finished.'

'And they are pleased with you . . . up at the château. That is obvious. Monsieur le Comte looked this afternoon as though he approved of . . . of you.'

'Yes, I think he is pleased. I flatter myself that I have done good work on his pictures.'

He nodded. 'You must not leave us, Dallas,' he said. 'You must stay with us. We could not be happy if you went away . . . none of us. Myself especially.'

'You are so kind. . . .'

'I will always be kind to you . . . for the rest of our lives. I could never be happy again if you went away. I am asking you to stay here always . . . with me.'

'Jean Pierre!'

'I want you to marry me. I want you to assure me that you will never leave me . . . never leave us. This is where you belong. Don't you know it, Dallas?'

I had stopped short and he had slipped his arm through mine and drew me into the shelter of one of the trees.

'This could not be,' I said.

'Why not? Tell me why not?'

'I am fond of you . . . I shall never forget your kindness to me when I first came here . . .'

'But, you are telling me, you do not love me?'

'I'm telling you that although I am fond of you I don't think I should make you a good wife.'

'But you do like me, Dallas?'

'Of course.'

'I knew it. And I will not ask you to say yes or no now. Because it may be that you are not ready.'

'Jean Pierre, you must understand that I . . .'

'I understand, my dearest.'

'I don't think you do.'

'I shall not press the matter but you will not leave us. And you will stay as my wife . . . because you could not bear to leave us . . . and in time . . . in time, my Dallas . . . you will see.'

He took my hand and kissed it quickly.

'Do not protest,' he said. 'You belong with us. And there can be no one else for you but me.'

Geneviève's voice broke in on my disturbed thoughts.

'Oh, there you are, miss. I was looking for you. Oh, Jean Pierre, you must dance with me. You promised you would.'

He smiled at me; I saw the lift of the eyebrows – as expressive as that of the shoulders.

As I watched him dance away with Geneviève, I was vaguely apprehensive. For the first time in my life I had received a proposal of marriage. I was bewildered. I could never marry Jean Pierre. How could I when . . . Was it because I had betrayed my feelings? Could it be that as he stood at my stall that afternoon the Comte had betrayed his?

The joy had gone out of the day. I was glad when the dancing was over, when the 'Marseillaise' had been played and the revellers went home and I to my room in the château to think of the past and grope blindly towards the future.

I found it difficult to work the next day and I was afraid that I should damage the wall-painting if I continued in this absentminded mood. So I accomplished little that morning, but my thoughts were busy. It seemed incredible that I who since my abortive affair with Charles had never had a lover should now be attractive to two men, one of whom had actually asked me to marry him. But it was the Comte's intentions that occupied my thoughts. He had looked younger, almost gay, when he had stood by the stall yesterday. I was certain in that moment that he could be happy; and I believed that I was the one to make him so. What presumption! The most he could be thinking of was one of those light love affairs in which it seemed he indulged from time to time. No, I was sure that was not true.

After I had taken breakfast in my room Geneviève burst in on me. She looked at least four years older because she had pinned up her long hair into a coil on the top of her head which made her taller and more graceful.

'Geneviève, what *have* you done?' I cried.

She burst into loud laughter. 'Do you like it?'

'You look . . . older.'

'That's what I want. I'm tired of being treated like a child.'

'Who does treat you so?'

'Everybody. You, Nounou, Papa . . . Uncle Philippe and his hateful Claude . . . Just everybody. You haven't said whether you like it.'

'I don't think it . . . suitable.'

That made her laugh. 'Well, I think it is, miss, and that is how I shall wear it in future. I'm not a child any more. My grandmother married when she was only a year older.'

I looked at her in astonishment. Her eyes were gleaming with excitement. She looked wild; and I felt very uneasy, but I could see it would be useless to talk to her.

I went along to see Nounou, and asked after her headaches. She said they had troubled her less during the last few days.

'I'm a little anxious about Geneviève,' I told her. The startled look came into her eyes. 'She's put her hair up. And she no longer looks like the child she is.'

'She is growing up. Her mother was so different . . . always so gentle. She seemed a child even after Geneviève's birth.'

'She said that her grandmother was married when she was sixteen . . . almost as though she was planning to do the same.'

'It's her way,' said Nounou.

But two days later Nounou came to me in some distress and told me that Geneviève who had gone out riding alone that afternoon had not come home. It was then about five o'clock.

I said: 'But surely one of the grooms was with her. She never goes riding alone.'

'She did to-day.'

'You saw her?'

'Yes, from my window. I could see she was in one of her moods so I watched. She was galloping across the meadow and there was no one with her.'

'But she knows she's not allowed . . . '

I looked at Nounou helplessly.

'She has been in this mood since the *kermesse*,' sighed Nounou, 'And I was so happy to see how interested she was. Then . . . she seemed to change.'

'Oh, I expect she'll be back soon. I believe she just wants to prove to us that she's grown up.'

I left her then and in our separate rooms we waited for Geneviève's return. I guessed that Nounou, like myself, was wondering what steps we should have to take if the girl had not returned within the next hour.

We were spared that, for half an hour or so after I had left Nounou, from my window I saw Geneviève coming into the castle.

I went to the schoolroom through which she would have to pass to her own bedroom, and as I entered Nounou came out of her room.

'She's back,' I said.

Nounou nodded. 'I saw her.'

Shortly afterwards Geneviève came up.

She looked flushed and almost beautiful with her dark eyes brilliant. When she saw us waiting there she smiled mischievously at us and taking off her hard riding-hat threw it on the schoolroom table.

Nounou was trembling and I said: 'We were anxious. You know you are not supposed to go riding alone.'

'Really, miss, that was long ago. I'm past that now.'

'I didn't know it.'

'You don't know everything – although you think you do.'

I was deeply depressed, because the girl who stood before us defying us, jeering at us, was no different from the one who had been so rude to me on my arrival. I had thought that we had made some progress but I realized there had been no miracle. Although occasionally she could be interested and pleasant, she was wild as ever when the desire to be so took possession of her.

'I am sure your father would be most displeased.'

She turned on me angrily. 'Then tell him. Tell him. You and he are such friends.'

I said angrily: 'You are being absurd. It is very unwise for you to ride alone.'

She stood still smiling secretly and I wondered in that moment whether she had been alone. The thought was even more alarming.

Suddenly she swung round and faced us. 'Listen,' she said, 'both of you. I shall do as I like. Nobody . . . just nobody . . . is going to stop me.'

Then she picked up her hat from the table and went into her room slamming the door behind her.

Those were uneasy days. I had no wish to go to the Bastides', for I feared to meet Jean Pierre and I felt that the pleasant friendly relationship which I had always enjoyed would be spoilt. The Comte had gone up to Paris for a few days after the *kermesse*. Geneviève avoided me. I tried to throw myself even more wholeheartedly into work and now that more of the wall-painting was emerging this helped my troubled mind.

I was working one morning when I looked up suddenly and found that I was not alone. This was an unpleasant habit of Claude's. She would come into a room noiselessly and one would be startled to find her there.

She looked very pretty that morning in a blue morning gown, piped with burgundy-coloured ribbon. I smelt the faint musk-rose scent she used.

'I hope I didn't startle you, Mademoiselle Lawson?' she said pleasantly.

'Of course not.'

'I thought I would speak to you. I am growing more and more uneasy about Geneviève. She is becoming impossible. She was very rude to me and to my husband this morning. Her manners seem to have deteriorated lately.'

'She is a child of moods but she can be charming.'

'I find her extremely ill-mannered and gauche. I hardly think any school would want her if she behaved like this. I noticed her behaviour with the wine-grower at the *kermesse*. In her present mood there could be trouble if she became too headstrong. She can no longer be called a child and I fear she might form associations which could be . . . dangerous.'

I nodded, for I understood clearly what she meant. She was referring to Geneviève's obsession with Jean Pierre.

She moved closer to me. 'If you could use your influence with her . . . If she knew we were concerned she would be all the more reckless. But I can see you realize the dangers.'

She was looking at me quizzically. I guessed she was thinking that if there should be trouble of the nature she was hinting at, I should in a way be to blame. Wasn't I the one who had fostered this friendship? Geneviève had scarcely been aware of Jean Pierre before my friendship with the family.

I felt uneasy and a little guilty.

She went on: 'Have you thought any more of that proposition I put to you the other day?'

'I feel I must finish my work here before I consider anything else.'

'Don't leave it too long. I heard a little more about it yesterday. One of the party is thinking of starting an exclusive art school in Paris. I think there would be a very good opening there.'

'It sounds almost too good to be true.'

'It's a chance in a lifetime, I should imagine. But, of course, the decision will have to be made fairly soon.'

She smiled at me almost apologetically and left.

I tried to work but I could not put my mind to it. She wanted me to go. That much was evident. Was she piqued because some of that attention which she felt should be hers was given to me by the Comte? It might be. But was she also genuinely concerned for Geneviève? This could be, I was ready to admit, a very real problem. Had I misjudged her?

I soon became convinced that Claude was really concerned about Geneviève. That was when I heard her in deep conversation with Jean Pierre in the copse in which the Comte had had his accident. I had been to see Gabrielle and was on my way back to the château and had taken the short cut through the copse, when I heard their voices. I did not know what was said and I wondered why they had chosen such a rendezvous. Then it occurred to me that the meeting might not have been arranged. They had met by chance and Claude had decided to take the opportunity of telling Jean Pierre that she did not approve of Geneviève's friendship with him.

It was, after all, no concern of mine and I turned hastily away. Skirting the copse, I rode back to the château. But the incident confirmed me in my opinion that Claude really was worried about Geneviève. And in my pride I had thought her main feeling was jealousy of the Comte's interest in me!

I tried to put all these disturbing matters out of my mind by concentrating on my work. The picture was growing – and there she was before me – the lady with the emeralds, for discoloured as they were I could see by the shape of the ornaments that they were identical to those which I had seen on the first picture I had cleaned. The same face. This was the woman who had been the mistress of Louis XV and had started the emerald collection. In fact the picture was very like that other except that in this her dress was of blue velvet and in the other red and in this one, of course, nestling against the blue velvet of her skirt was the spaniel. It was the inscription that puzzled me. 'Forget me not.' And now I had uncovered the dog in his glass coffin and saw there was something lying beside him. It had been a moment of excitement so great when I had uncovered that object that I almost forgot my personal dilemma.

Beside the dog in the glass coffin was something which looked like a key, at one end of which was an ornamental fleur-de-lis.

I was sure it was meant to convey something, for the lettering, the case in which the dog was enclosed, and the key, if key it was, were not part of a later painting; they had been put on to the original portrait of the woman and dog – and by a hand which could be called nothing more than that of an unskilled amateur.

As soon as the Comte returned to the château I should show him this.

The more I thought about the addition to the wall-painting the more significant it seemed. I tried to think of it exclusively; other thoughts were too painful. Geneviève avoided me. She went riding alone every afternoon and no one prevented her. Nounou shut herself in her room and I believe re-read the earlier diaries in a vain endeavour I suppose to relive the peaceful days with a more amenable charge.

I was worried about Geneviève and wondered if Claude was right and I was partly to blame.

I thought of our first meeting, how she had shut me in the *oubliette* and how even before that she had promised to introduce me to her mother and had taken me to her grave and there informed me that she had been murdered . . . by her father.

I suppose it was this memory which led me one afternoon to the graveyard of the de la Talles.

I went to that of Françoise and read her name once more on the open marble book and then I looked for the grave of the lady in the portrait. She must be there.

I did not know her name, only that she was one of the Comtesses de la Talle, but since she had been a mistress of Louis XV in her youth I guessed that the date of her death must be somewhere in the second half of the eighteenth century, and eventually I discovered a Marie Louise de la Talle who had died in the year 1761. This would doubtless be the lady of the pictures, and as I approached the vault with its statues and decorations my foot touched something. I stared down incredulously, for what I saw was a cross similar to that which I had discovered in the moat. I bent down to look and I discovered that a date had been scratched on it. There were letters too. I knelt down. I could just read it. 'Fidèle 1790.'

The same name! Only the date was different. The dog had been buried in the moat in 1749. This dog had the same name and a different date. This Fidèle had died when the revolutionaries were marching on the château, when the young Comtesse had had to flee, not only for her own life but for that of the unborn child.

Surely there was something significant about this? I was deeply conscious of it as I stood there. Whoever had painted the coffin-like case about the dog and had written the words 'Forget me not' on the picture was trying to convey something. What?

And here I had stumbled on this second grave of Fidèle and the date was important. I knelt down and looked at the cross. Beneath the name Fidèle and the date, some words had been scratched.

'*N'oubliez pas* . . . ' I made out, and my heart beat wild with excitement then, for the inscription was like that on the picture. '*N'oubliez pas ceux qui furent oubliés.*'

What did it indicate?

Of only one thing was I certain; and that was that I was going to find out, for it had occurred to me that this was not the grave a beloved mistress had made for a dog. There was one dog's grave and that was in the moat. Someone who had lived in the year 1790 – that most fateful and eventful year for the French people – was trying to send a message over the years.

It was a challenge and one I must accept.

I rose to my feet and left the graveyard making my way through the small copse to the gardens. I remembered passing a shed in which I knew gardening tools were kept, and there I found a spade and went back to the graveyard.

As I made my way through the copse I had a sudden uneasy feeling that I was being watched. I stood still. There was silence except for the sudden flutter of a bird in the leaves above me.

'Is anyone there?' I called.

But there was no answer. You're being foolish, I told myself. You're nervous. You're reaching out for the past and it's making you uneasy. You're changed since you came to the château. You used to be a sensible young woman. Now you do all manner of foolish things. . . .

What would anyone think if they found me with a spade, intent on digging in the graveyard?

Then I would explain. But I didn't want to explain. I wanted to take my discovery complete and exciting to the Comte. Reaching the cross I looked over my shoulder. I could see no one, but it would not be difficult for someone to have followed me through the copse, to be hiding now behind one of those houselike tombs which the French erect to their dead.

I began to dig.

The small box was very near the surface and I saw at once that it was not big enough to contain the remains of a dog. I picked it up and brushed off the dirt. It was made of metal and there were words scratched on this, similar to those on the cross. '1790. *N'oubliez pas ceux qui furent oubliés.*'

It was difficult to open the box for it had become wedged with rust. But eventually I managed it; and I think I must have been expecting what was inside.

I knew as soon as I picked it up that when I had uncovered the wall-painting I had uncovered a message which had been intentionally left. For there in the box was the key which was lying beside the dog in the picture. I knew it because at one end was the fleur-de-lis.

Now I had to find the lock which fitted the key and then I should know what the one who had drawn that message had wanted to say. It was a link with the past. It was the most thrilling discovery I or my father had ever made. I wanted to tell someone . . . not anyone . . . the Comte, of course.

I looked down at the key in my hand. Somewhere in the château there would be the lock to fit it.

I must find it.

I put the key carefully into the pocket of my dress. I closed the box and put it back in the earth. Then I covered it. In a few days no one would know that the ground had been disturbed.

I went to the toolshed and carefully replaced the spade. Then I went into the château and up to my room. But it was not until I was there and the door was shut that I could rid myself of the notion that I had been overlooked.

Those were days of burning heat. The Comte stayed in Paris and I had now exposed the whole of the wall-painting and was cleaning it. A process which would not take me very long; and when I had done that and the few pictures in the gallery I should really have no excuse for staying. If I were wise I should tell Claude that I wanted to take up her suggestion.

The harvest was almost upon us.

I had a feeling that we were moving towards a climax and when the harvest was over this episode in my life would be over too.

Wherever I went I carried the key with me in the pocket of one of my petticoats. It was a very secure pocket, in which I carried anything I was afraid of losing, for it buttoned tightly and there was no way in which articles hidden there could be lost.

I had thought a great deal about the key and I had come to the conclusion that if I could find the lock to it I should discover the emeralds. Everything pointed to this. The coffin had been painted over the dog in the picture in the year 1790 – that very year when the revolutionaries had marched on the château. I was certain the emeralds had been taken from the strong-room and hidden somewhere in the château and this was the key to open the receptacle in which they lay. This key was the property of the Comte and I had no right to keep it; but I should give it to no one else, and together he and I should seek to find the lock which fitted it.

I had a great desire to find that lock myself. To await him on his return and say to him: 'Here are your emeralds.'

They could not be in a casket. That would have been discovered long ago. It must be a cupboard, a safe, somewhere which had gone undetected for a hundred years.

I began by examining every inch of my own room, tapping the panelling where I thought there might possibly be a cavity.

And as I did this I stopped short suddenly, remembering the tapping Geneviève and I had heard in the night. Someone else was searching as I was. Who? The Comte? That was understandable, but why should he, who owned the château and had every right to look for hidden treasure which belonged to him, seek to find it by stealth?

I thought of the treasure hunt when I had found the clues and I knew that the words scratched on the box were a clue of a similar sort.

Could those who had been forgotten be those prisoners of the past who had been chained to their cages or dropped into the *oubliette*? The servants believed those dungeons to be haunted and refused to go there. That might have applied to the revolutionaries storming the château. Somewhere down there was the lock which would fit the key I carried in my petticoat pocket.

It must be in the *oubliette* of course. The word forgotten was the clue to that.

I remembered the trap door, the rope ladder and 'the occasion when Geneviève had shut me there. I longed to explore the *oubliette*, and yet remembering how I had once been shut down there I was reluctant to go alone.

Should I tell Geneviève of my discovery? I decided against it. No, I must go alone but I must make sure that it was known I was there so that if by some chance that trap door should be shut down I should be rescued.

I went along to Nounou.

'Nounou,' I said, 'I am going to explore the *oubliette* this afternoon. I think there may be something interesting under the lime-wash.'

'Like that picture you've been finding?'

'Something like that. There's only the rope ladder for getting in and out, so if I should not be back in my room by four o'clock, you would know where to find me.'

Nounou nodded. 'Though she wouldn't do it again,' she said. 'You need have no fear of that, miss.'

'No; but that's where I shall be.'

'I'll remember.'

I also took the precaution of mentioning where I should be to the maid who brought my lunch.

'Oh, will you, miss,' she said. 'Rather you than me.'

'You don't like the place?'

'Well, miss. When you think of what's gone on there. They say it's haunted. You know that, don't you?'

'That's often said about such places.'

'Well, all those people . . . shut down there to pine away . . . Ugh, rather you than me.'

I touched the key beneath my skirts and thought of the pleasure I should have when I took the Comte to his *oubliette* and said to him: 'I have found your treasure.'

I was not going to let the fear of ghosts scare me.

As I stood in that room with its trap door which was the only entry to the *oubliette*, watching the play of sunlight on the weapons decorating the walls, it occurred to me that the lock which would fit the key might be in this room, for those who were about to be forgotten had first passed this way.

Guns of various shapes and kinds! Were they ever used now? I knew it was the duty of one of the servants to come to this room periodically and make sure everything was well kept. I had heard it said that the servants came in twos.

If there was anything here surely it would have been discovered long ago.

As I stood there my eyes caught something gleaming on the floor and I went swiftly to it.

It was a pair of scissors – the kind which I had seen used for snipping off grapes which were not up to the required standard. There had been occasions when, as I had stood talking to him, I had seen Jean Pierre take such a pair of scissors from his pockets and use them on the vines.

I stopped and picked up the scissors. They were of an unusual shape. Could there be two pairs so much alike? And if not, how had Jean Pierre's scissors come to be here?

I slipped them into my pocket thoughtfully. Then deciding that what I sought was more likely to be in the *oubliette*, I took out the rope ladder, opened the trap door and descended to that place of doom where the forgotten had perished. I shivered as I relived those dreadful moments when Geneviève had pulled up the ladder and shut the trap door leaving me to experience a little of what hundreds must have felt before within these walls.

It was an eerie place, close, confined, dark, except for the light which came through the trap door.

But I had not come to let my fancies rule my common sense. Here was where the forgotten had ended their days and this was where the clue had led me. I believed that somewhere in this enclosed space was the lock which the key would open.

I examined the walls. Here was the familiar lime-wash which must have been done about eighty years ago. I tapped the wall gently to test it for cavities but I could find nothing of interest. I looked about me, at the ceiling, at the flagged stone floors. I went into the aperture which Geneviève had told me was a maze. Could it be in there somewhere? The light was too poor for me to examine it well, but as I put out my hand to touch the stone pillar I could not imagine how anything could be secreted there.

I decided to make a thorough examination of the walls, and while I was doing this what little light there was disappeared.

I gave a little cry of horror and turned to the trap door.

Claude was looking down at me.

'Making discoveries?' she asked.

I stood looking up at her and moved towards the rope ladder. She pulled it a few inches from the ground rather playfully.

'I'm wondering whether there are any to make,' I answered.

'You know so much about ancient castles. I saw you come here and guessed what you were up to.'

I thought: She is watching me, all the time, hoping that I will make the decision to go.

I reached out to touch the ladder but laughingly she jerked it upwards.

'Don't you feel a little alarmed down there, Mademoiselle Lawson?'

'Why should I?'

'Think of all the ghosts of dead men who have died horrible deaths cursing those who left them there to die.'

'They would have no grudge against me.'

I kept my eyes on the rope ladder which she held just out of my reach.

'You might slip and fall down there. Anything could happen. You might be a prisoner there . . . like those others.'

'Not for long,' I answered. 'They would come to look for me. I have told Nounou and others that I'll be here so I shouldn't be left long.'

'You're very practical as well as clever. Do you think you are going to find wall. paintings down there?'

'In castles like this one never knows what one will find. That's where the excitement comes in.'

'I should like to join you.' She let the ladder fall and I felt a relief as I was able to touch it. 'But I don't think I will,' she went on. 'If you discover something you will let us know fast enough, I'm sure.'

'I shall let it be known. I'm coming up now, in any case.'

'And you'll be investigating again?'

'Very probably, although the examination I have made to-day makes me think I shan't find anything down here.'

Firmly I grasped the ladder and climbed up to the room.

Claude had made me forget my discovery in the gun-room, but no sooner had I returned to my room than I remembered the scissors in my pocket.

It was early so I decided I would take a walk to the Maison Bastide to ask if they belonged to Jean Pierre.

I found Madame Bastide alone. I showed her the scissors and asked if they were her grandson's.

'Why, yes,' she said, 'He's been looking for those.'

'You're sure they are his?'

'Undoubtedly.'

I laid them on the table.

'Where did you find them?'

'In the château.'

I saw the fear leap into her eyes, and in that moment the incident seemed to take on a greater significance.

'Yes, in the gun-room. I thought it was an odd place to find them.'

There was a silence while I was deeply aware of the clock on the mantelpiece ticking away the seconds.

'He lost them some weeks ago – when he went to see Monsieur le Comte,' said Madame Bastide, but I felt she was trying to excuse Jean Pierre's being in the château and to suggest that he had lost the scissors before the Comte's departure.

We avoided looking at each other. I knew Madame Bastide was alarmed.

I couldn't sleep very well that night. It had been a disturbing day. I wondered what Claude's motives had been when she had followed me to the *oubliette*. What would have happened if I had not taken the precaution of telling Nounou and the maid that I should be there? I shivered. Did Claude want me out of the way and was she growing impatient because I was still hesitating to take the solution she had offered me?

And then finding Jean Pierre's scissors in the gun-room had been disturbing – particularly in view of Madame Bastide's reaction when I returned them.

It was small wonder that I felt restless.

I was half-dozing when the door of my room opened and I awoke with a start, my heart beating so fast that I felt it would burst. I sensed that there was something evil in my room.

Starting up in bed I saw a figure swathed in blue at the foot of my bed. I was half-dreaming, I suppose, because for a few seconds I thought I really was face to face with one of the château ghosts. Then I saw it was Claude.

'I'm afraid I frightened you. I didn't think you would be asleep yet. I knocked at your door but you didn't answer.'

'I was dozing,' I said.

'I wanted to talk to you.'

I looked surprised and she went on: 'You're thinking I've had better

opportunities . . . but it's not easy to tell you. I had to wait until I could
. . . and I kept putting it off.'

'What have you to tell me?'

'I'm going to have a child,' she said..

'Congratulations!' But why, I thought, wake me to tell me that?

'I want you to understand what this means.'

'That you are going to have a child? I think this is good news and I
suppose not wholly unexpected.'

'You are a woman of the world.'

I was a little surprised to hear myself referred to as such, and I did not
protest although I felt she was attempting to flatter me, which was strange.

'If he is a boy he will be the future Comte.'

'You are presuming that the Comte will have no sons of his own.'

'But surely you know enough of the family history to understand that
Philippe is here because the Comte has no wish to marry. If he does not,
then my son will inherit.'

'That may be so,' I said. 'But what is it you are trying to tell me?'

'I'm telling you that you should accept the proposition I have put to you
before it is too late. The offer won't remain open indefinitely. I was going
to talk to you this afternoon but I found it too difficult.'

'What do you want to say to me?'

'I want to be quite frank. Whose child do you think I am going to have?'

'Your husband's, of course.'

'My husband has no interest in women. In any case he is impotent. You
see how this simplifies the plan. The Comte does not want to marry but he
would like his son to inherit. Do you understand?'

'It is no concern of mine.'

'No, that's true. But I'm trying to help you. I know you think that strange,
but it's true. I haven't always been very pleasant to you, I know. So you
wonder why I should bother to help you. I don't know why . . . except that
people like you can get hurt even worse than most. The Comte is a man who
will have his own way. His family have always been like that. They care
for nothing but getting their own way. You should leave here. You should
let me help you. I can do it now, but unless you make up your mind, you
will lose this chance. You admit it's an excellent chance?'

I did not answer. I could only think of her implication that the child she
carried was the Comte's. I didn't want to believe it but it fitted in with what
I knew. This would ensure his child's inheriting the titles and estates. And
Philippe, the complaisant, would pose as the child's father to the outside
world. It was the price he must pay to be called Comte, should the real
Comte die before him; it was the price he must pay to call the château his
home.

She is right, I thought. I must get away.

She was watching me intently and she said gently, almost tenderly: 'I
know how you feel. He has been . . . attentive, hasn't he? He has never met
anyone quite like you before. You are different from the rest of us, and he
always was attracted by novelty. That is why nothing can last with him.
You should go to prevent yourself being hurt . . . badly.'

She was like a ghost at the foot of my bed, warning me to avert the tragedy which loomed over me.

She went on: 'Shall I arrange for you to go on that tour?'

I answered quietly: 'I will think about it.'

She shrugged, and turning, glided to the door. There she paused to look back at me.

'Good night,' she said softly, and she was gone.

I lay awake for a long time.

I should be deeply hurt if I stayed. I had not realized until now how deeply, how bitterly.

Chapter Eleven

When the Comte returned to the château a few days later, he seemed preoccupied and did not seek me out. As for myself I was so horrified by what Claude had told me that I was anxious to avoid him. I told myself that had I truly loved him I should not have believed Claude, but the fact was that I felt there was a possibility of her story being true; and oddly enough it made no difference to my feelings for the Comte. I did not love him for his virtues. I had seen him for the man he was – in fact I had believed ill of him which had proved to be wrong as in the case of Gabrielle and Mademoiselle Dubois – and knowing all this I had blindly allowed myself to be fascinated.

The fact was, I could not understand my feelings. All I knew was that he dominated my life, that without him life would be flat, dull, meaningless. I could not even ask him now if Claude's story was true. There was too big a barrier between us. The man was an enigma to me – and yet it seemed to me that my whole world would be devoid of hope for happiness if he went out of it.

It was not sensible; it was not what I should have expected of myself; and yet I had done it.

I could only call that being recklessly and hopelessly involved. Involved! How typical of me to try to find another word for being in love because, I admonished myself scornfully, I was afraid to face up to the fact that I loved a man irrevocably.

There was a rising tension during those days. There was only one thing I was certain of. This situation could not remain static. It was explosive; we were working towards some crisis and when it came my future would be decided.

There was always, I imagined, this atmosphere of excitement as the harvest approached. But this was my personal crisis. I was coming to the end of the work; I could not stay on indefinitely at the château. I should have to talk of my future and I experienced complete desolation when I considered that I might tell the Comte that I was going and he would let me go.

I had strayed into this feudal life and I with my strict English upbringing had tried to become a part of it. How wrong I might have been! I clung to that word 'might.' It was the only hope I had.

Into this strange period of waiting there came suddenly the sense of danger ... danger of a different sort from that in which a foolish woman allows herself to dream of an impossible romance. Imminent danger. It was because of an uneasy feeling that I was being watched. Little sounds – unmistakable yet unidentifiable – as I walked through the corridors to my room. The extra sense that comes unexpectedly and which sets one turning sharply to look over the shoulder. This had suddenly crept upon me and it persisted.

I was very conscious of the key which I carried about with me in my petticoat pocket. I had promised myself that I would show it to the Comte and that together we should search for the lock which it would fit. But since Claude had talked to me I felt unable to face him.

I had promised myself a few more days of exploration; secretly I pictured myself going to him and telling him I had discovered his emeralds, for I was growing more and more certain that that was what I should find. Perhaps, I thought in my heart, he would be so overwhelmed, so delighted, that even if he had not thought seriously of me before, he would do so then.

What stupid ideas women in love will get! I reminded myself. They live in a world of romance which has little connection with reality. They make charming pictures and then convince themselves that they are true.

Surely I was beyond that sort of behaviour.

He had not been to see how the wall-painting was progressing, which surprised me. At times I wondered whether Claude talked of me to him and they smiled together at my innocence. If it were true that she was to have his child then they would be very intimate. I couldn't believe it – but that was the romantic woman in me. Looking at the situation from a practical point of view it seemed logical enough – and weren't the French noted for their logic? What to my English reasoning would seem an immoral situation, to their French logic would seem satisfactory. The Comte, having no desire for marriage yet wishing to see his son inherit the name, fortune, estates and everything that was important to him; Philippe as his reward would inherit before the boy if the Comte should die, and the château was his home; Claude could enjoy her relationship with her lover without suffering any loss of dignity. Of course it was reasonable; of course it was logical.

But to me it was horrible and I hated it, and I did not try to see him for I feared I should betray my feelings. In the meantime I was watchful.

One afternoon I walked over to see Gabrielle, now very obviously pregnant and contented. I enjoyed my visit, for we talked of the Comte and Gabrielle was one of the people who had a high regard for him.

When I left her I took the short cut through the woods and it was while I was there that the feeling of being followed came upon me more strongly than before. On this occasion I was truly alarmed. Here was I alone in the woods – those very woods in which the Comte had received his injury. The fear had come suddenly upon me, with the crackle of undergrowth, the snapping of a twig.

I stopped and listened. All was silent; and yet I was conscious of danger.

An impulse came to me to run and I did so. Such panic possessed me that I almost screamed aloud when my skirt was caught by a bramble. I snatched it away leaving a little of the stuff behind, but I did not stop.

I was certain I heard the sound of hurrying steps behind me, and when the trees thinned out I looked behind me, but there was no one.

I came out of the copse. There was no sign of anyone emerging from the woods, but I did not pause long. I started the long walk back to the château.

Near the vineyards I met Philippe on horseback.

He rode up to me and as soon as he saw me exclaimed: 'Why Mademoiselle Lawson, is anything wrong?'

I guessed I still looked a little distraught so there was no point in hiding it.

'I had rather an unpleasant experience in the woods. I thought I was being followed.'

'You shouldn't go into the woods alone, you know.'

'No, I suppose not. But I didn't think of it.'

'Fancy, I dare say, but I can understand it. Perhaps you were remembering how you found my cousin there when he was shot, and that made you imagine someone was following you. It might have been someone after a hare.'

'Probably.'

He dismounted and stood still to look at the vineyards.

'We're going to have a record harvest,' he said. 'Have you ever seen the gathering of the grapes?'

'No.'

'You'll enjoy it. It won't be long now. They're almost ready. Would you care to take a look into the sheds? You'll see them preparing the baskets. The excitement is growing.'

'Should we disturb them?'

'Indeed not. They like to think that everyone is as excited as they are.'

He led me along a path towards the sheds and talked to me about the grapes. He admitted that he had not attended a harvest for years. I felt embarrassed in his company. I saw him now as the weak third party in a distasteful compact. But I could not gracefully make my escape.

'In the past,' he was saying, 'I used to stay at the château for long periods in the summer, and I always remembered the grape harvest. It seemed to go on far into the night and I would get out of bed and listen to them singing as they trod the grapes. It was a most fascinating sight.'

'It must have been.'

'Oh, yes, Mademoiselle Lawson. I never forgot the sight of men and women stepping into the trough and dancing on the grapes. And there were musicians who played the songs they knew and they danced and sang. I remember watching them sink lower and lower into the purple juice.'

'So you are looking forward to this harvest.'

'Yes, but perhaps everything seems more colourful when we are young. But I think it was the grape harvest which decided me that I'd rather live at Château Gaillard than anywhere else on earth.'

'Well, now you have that wish.'

He was silent and I noticed the grim lines about his mouth. I wondered what he felt about the relationship between the Comte and his wife. There was an air of effeminacy about him which made more plausible Claude's account, and the fact that his features did in some way resemble those of his cousin made this complete difference in their characters the more apparent. I could believe that he wanted more than anything to live at the château, to own the château, to be known as the Comte de la Talle, and for all this he had bartered his honour, and married the Comte's mistress and would accept the Comte's illegitimate son as his ... all for the sake of one day, if the Comte should die, being King of the Castle, for I was sure that if he had refused to accept the terms laid down by the Comte, he would not have been allowed to inherit.

We talked of the grapes and the harvests he remembered from his childhood and when we came to the sheds I was shown the baskets which were being prepared and I listened while Philippe talked to the workers.

He walked his horse back to the château and I thought him friendly, reserved, a little deprecating and found myself making excuses for him.

I went up to my room and as soon as I entered it I was aware that someone had been there during my absence.

I looked about me; then I saw what it was. The book I had left on my bedside table was on the dressing-table. I knew I had not left it there.

I hurried to it and picked it up. I opened the drawer. Everything appeared to be in order. I opened another and another. Everything was tidy.

But I was sure that the book had been moved.

Perhaps, I thought, one of the servants had been in. Why? No one usually came in during that time of day.

And then on the air I caught the faint smell of scent. A musk-rose scent which I had smelt before. It was feminine and pleasant. I had smelt it when Claude was near.

I was certain then that while I was out Claude had been in my room. Why? Could it be that she knew I had the key and had she come to see if I had hidden it somewhere in my room?

I stood still and my hands touched the pocket of my petticoat through my skirt. There was the key safe on my person. The scent had gone. Then again there it was – faint, elusive, but significant.

It was the next day when the maid brought a letter to my room from Jean Pierre, who said he must see me without delay. He wanted to speak to me alone so would I come to the vineyards as soon as possible where we could talk without being interrupted. He begged me to come.

I went out into the hot sunshine, across the drawbridge and towards the vineyards. The whole countryside seemed to be sleeping in the hot afternoon;

and as I walked along the path through the vines now laden with their rich ripe fruit Jean Pierre came to meet me.

'It's difficult to talk here,' he said. 'Let's go inside.' He took me into the building and to the first of the cellars.

It was cool there and seemed dark after the glare of the sun; here the light came through small apertures and I remembered hearing how it was necessary to regulate the temperature by the shutters.

And there among the casks Jean Pierre said: 'I am to go away.'

'Go away,' I repeated stupidly. And then: 'But when?'

'Immediately after the harvest.'

He took me by the shoulders. 'You know why, Dallas.'

I shook my head.

'Because Monsieur le Comte wants me out of the way.'

'Why?'

He laughed bitterly. 'He does not give his reasons. He merely gives his orders. It no longer pleases him that I should be here – so, although I have been here all my life, I am now to move on.'

'But surely if you explain ... '

'Explain what? That this is my home ... as the château is his? We, my dear Dallas, are not supposed to have such absurd sentiments. We are serfs ... born to obey. Did you not know that?'

'This is absurd, Jean Pierre.'

'But no. I have my orders.'

'Go to him ... tell him ... I am sure he will listen.'

He smiled at me. 'Do you know why he wants me to go away? Can you guess? It is because he knows of my friendship with you. He does not like that.'

'What should it mean to him?' I hoped Jean Pierre did not notice the excited note in my voice.

'It means that he is interested in you ... in his way.'

'But this is ridiculous.'

'You know it is not. There have always been women ... and you are different from any he has ever known. He wants your undivided attention ... for a time.'

'How can you know?'

'How can I know? Because I know *him*. I have lived here all my life and although he is frequently away, this is his home too. Here he lives as he can't live in Paris. Here he is lord of us all. Here we have stood still in time and he wants to keep it like that.'

'You hate him, Jean Pierre.'

'Once the people of France rose against such as he is.'

'You've forgotten how he helped Gabrielle and Jacques.'

He laughed bitterly. 'Gabrielle like all women has a fondness for him.'

'What are you suggesting?'

'That I don't believe in this goodness of his. There's always a motive behind it. To him we are not people with lives of our own. We are his slaves, I tell you. If he wants a woman then anyone who stands in his way is removed and when she is no longer required, well . . . You know what happened to the Comtesse.'

'Don't dare say such things.'

'Dallas! What's happened to you?'

'I want to know what you were doing in the gun-room at the château.'

'I?'

'Yes, I found your grape scissors there. Your mother said you had missed them and that they were yours.'

He was taken aback a little. Then he said: 'I had to go to the château to see the Comte on business . . . that was just before he went away.'

'And it took you to the gun-room?'

'No.'

'But that's where I found them.'

'The Comte wasn't at home so I thought I'd have a look round the château. You're surprised. It's a very interesting place. I couldn't resist looking round. That was the room, you know, where an ancestor of mine last saw the light of day.'

'Jean Pierre,' I said, 'you shouldn't hate anyone so much.'

'Why should it all be his? Do you know that he and I are blood relations? A great-great-grandfather of mine was half-brother to a Comte – the only difference was that his mother was not a Comtesse.'

'Please don't talk like this.' A terrible thought struck me and I said: 'I believe you would kill him.'

Jean Pierre did not answer and I went on: 'That day in the woods . . . '

'I didn't fire that shot. Do you imagine I'm the only one who hates him?'

'You have no reason to hate him. He has never harmed you. You hate him because he is what he is and you want what he has.'

'It's a good reason for hating.' He laughed suddenly. 'It's just that I'm furious with him now because he wants to send me away. Wouldn't you hate anyone who wanted to send you away from your home and the one you loved? I did not come here to talk of hating the Comte but of loving you. I shall go to Mermoz when the harvest is over and I want you to come with me, Dallas. You belong here among us. After all we are your mother's people. Let us be married and we will laugh at him then. He has no power over you.'

No power over me! I thought; but you are wrong, Jean Pierre. No one has ever before had this power to regulate my happiness, to excite and depress me.

Jean Pierre had seized my hands; he drew me towards him, his eyes shining.

'Dallas, marry me. Think how happy that you will make us all – you, me, my family. You are fond of us, aren't you?'

'Yes,' I said, 'I am fond of you all.'

'And do you want to go away . . . back to England? What will you do there, Dallas, my darling? Have you friends there? Then why have you been content to leave them so long? You want to be here, don't you? You feel that you belong here?'

I was silent. I thought of it. The life Jean Pierre was offering me. I imagined myself being caught up in the excitement of the vineyards, taking my easel out and developing that little talent I had for painting. Visiting the family at the Maison Bastide . . . But no, then I should see the château; I should never be able to look at it without a pain in my heart; and there would be times when I should see the Comte perhaps. He would look at me and bow courteously. And perhaps he would say to himself: Who is that woman? I have seen her somewhere. Oh, she is that Mademoiselle Lawson who came to do the pictures and married Jean Pierre Bastide over at Mermoz.

Better to go right away than that – better to take the opportunity which Claude had offered and which was still open – although it would probably not remain so much longer.

'You hesitate,' said Jean Pierre.

'No. It can't be.'

'You do not love me?'

'I don't really know you, Jean Pierre.' The words had escaped me, and I had not meant to say them.

'But we are old friends, I thought.'

'There is so much that we don't know about each other.'

'All I have to know of you is that I love you.'

Love? I thought. Yet you do not speak of it as vehemently as you do of hate.

His hatred of the Comte was stronger than his love for me; and it occurred to me then that one had grown out of the other. Was Jean Pierre eager to marry me because he thought that the Comte was attracted by me? As that thought came to me I was conscious of a great revulsion against him and he no longer seemed like the old friend in whose home I had spent so many hours. He was a sinister stranger.

'Come, Dallas,' he said, 'say we'll be married. And I'll go to the Comte and tell him that I shall be taking a bride with me to Mermoz.'

There it was! He would go to the Comte in triumph.

'I'm sorry, Jean Pierre,' I said, 'but this is not the way.'

'You mean you will not marry me?'

'No, Jean Pierre, I can't marry you.'

He dropped my hands and a look of baffled rage crossed his features. Then he lifted his shoulders.

'But,' he said, 'I shall continue to hope.'

I had a great desire to escape from the cellar. Such hatred of one man towards another was terrifying; and I, who had felt so self-sufficient in the past, so able to take care of myself, had now begun to learn the meaning of fear.

I was glad to come out into the hot light of day.

I went straight to my room and thought about Jean Pierre's proposal. He had not the manner of a man in love. He had shown me how deeply he could feel when he talked of the Comte. To spite the Comte he would marry me. This horrifying thought brought with it its elation. He had noticed, then, the Comte's interest in me. Yet since his return from Paris he had scarcely seemed aware of me.

The next morning I was working on the wall-painting to which I was putting the finishing touches when Nounou came to me in great distress.

'It's Geneviève,' she said. 'She's come in and gone straight to her room. She's half crying, half laughing and I can't get out of her what's wrong. I wish you'd come and help me.'

I went with her to Geneviève's room. The girl was certainly in a wild mood. She had thrown her riding-hat and crop into a corner of the room and when I entered was sitting on her bed glowering into space.

'What's wrong, Geneviève?' I asked. 'I might be able to help.'

'Help! How can you help? Unless you go and ask my father ... ' She looked at me speculatively.

I said coldly: 'Ask what?'

She didn't answer; she clenched her fists and beat them on the bed. 'I'm not a baby!' she cried. 'I'm grown up. I won't stay here if I don't want to. I'll run away.'

Nounou caught her breath in fear but asked: 'Where to?'

'Anywhere I like and you won't find me.'

'I don't think I should be eager to if you remain in your present mood.'

She burst out laughing but was sober almost at once. 'I tell you, miss, I won't be treated like a child.'

'What has happened to upset you? How have you been treated like a child?'

She stared at the tips of her riding-boots. 'If I want friends, I shall have them.'

'Who said you shouldn't?'

'I don't think people should be sent away just because ... ' She stopped and glared at me. 'It's no business of yours. Nor yours, Nounou. Go away. Don't stand staring at me as though I'm a baby.'

Nounou looked ready to burst into tears and I thought I could handle this better if she were not there, continually to remind Geneviève that she was her nurse. So I signed to her to leave us. She went readily.

I sat on the bed and waited. Geneviève said sullenly, 'My father is sending Jean Pierre away because he's my friend.'

'Who said so?'

'No one has to say so. I know.'

'But why should he be sent away for that reason?'

'Because I'm Papa's daughter and Jean Pierre is one of the wine-growers.'

'I don't see the point.'

'Because I'm growing up, that's why. Because ... ' She looked at me and her lips quivered. Then she threw herself on to the bed and burst into loud sobs which shook her body.

I leaned over her. 'Geneviève,' I said gently, 'do you mean that they're afraid you'll fall in love with him?'

'Now you laugh!' she cried, turning a hot face to glare at me. 'I tell you I'm old enough. I'm not a child.'

'I didn't say you were. Geneviève, are you in love with Jean Pierre?'

She didn't answer, so I went on: 'And Jean Pierre?'

She nodded. 'He told me that was why Papa is sending him away.'

'I see,' I said slowly.

She laughed bitterly. 'It's only to Mermoz. I shall run away with him. I shan't stay here if he goes.'

'Did Jean Pierre suggest this?'

'Don't keep questioning me. You're not on my side.'

'I am, Geneviève. I am on your side.'

She raised herself and looked at me. 'Are you?'

I nodded.

'I thought you weren't because . . . because I thought you liked him too. I was jealous of you,' she admitted naïvely.

'There's no need to be jealous of me, Geneviève. But you have to be reasonable, you know. When I was young I fell in love.'

The thought made her smile. 'Oh, no, miss, *you*!'

'Yes,' I said tartly, 'even I.'

'That must have been funny.'

'It seemed tragic rather.'

'Why? Did your father send him away?'

'He couldn't do that. But he made me see how impossible it would have been.'

'And would it have been?'

'It usually is when one is very young.'

'Now you're trying to influence me. I tell you I won't listen. I'll tell you this, though, that when Jean Pierre goes to Mermoz *I* am going with him.'

'He'll go after the harvest.'

'And so shall I,' she said with determination.

I could see that it was no use talking to her when she was in this mood.

I was worried, asking myself what this meant. Had she imagined that Jean Pierre was in love with her, or had he told her so? Could he have done this at the same time that he was asking me to marry him?

I thought of Jean Pierre in the cellar, his eyes brilliant with hatred.

It seemed to me that the ruling passion of his life was hatred of the Comte, and because he thought that the Comte was interested in me he had asked me to marry him. Because Geneviève was the Comte's daughter . . . could it be that he was attempting to seduce her?

I was very uneasy.

The following day had been fixed for the gathering of the grapes. All day long the sky overhead had been a cloudless blue; the sun was hot and the abundant grapes were ripe for picking.

I was not thinking of the next day. I was thinking of Jean Pierre and his desire for revenge on the Comte. I was watching Geneviève, for in her present mood I could not guess what she would do next. Nor could I rid myself of that sinister feeling that I myself was being watched.

I longed for a *tête-à-tête* with the Comte but he seemed to ignore me and I thought perhaps it was as well since my own feelings were in such a turmoil. Claude made several significant references to my work's growing near its termination. How she wanted to be rid of me! On the few occasions when I encountered him Philippe was as remote yet friendly as he had ever been.

After Geneviève's outburst I had been wondering how to act and I suddenly thought that the one person who might help me was Jean Pierre's grandmother.

The afternoon was almost turning into evening when I went to see her. I guessed she would be alone in the house for there was a great deal of activity in the vineyards, preparing for the next day, and even Yves and Margot were not near the house.

She welcomed me as always, and without preamble I told her how worried I was.

'Jean Pierre has asked me to marry him,' I said.

'And you do not love him?'

I shook my head.

'He does not love me, either,' I went on. 'But he hates the Comte.'

I saw how the veins in her hands stood out as she clenched them together.

'There is Geneviève,' I went on. 'He has led her to believe ... '

'Oh, no!'

'She is excitable and vulnerable and I'm afraid for her. She's in a state of hysteria because he is being sent away. We must do something ... I'm not sure what. But I'm afraid something dreadful will happen. This hatred of his ... it's unnatural.'

'It's born in him. Try to understand it. Every day he looks at the château there and he thinks: "Why should it be the Comte's ... that and the power that goes with it! Why not ... ?" '

'But this is absurd. Why should he feel this? Everyone in the neighbourhood sees the château but they don't think it should be theirs.'

'It's different. We Bastides have château blood in us. Bastide! Here in the south a *bastide* is a country house ... but might it not once have been *Bâtard*? That is how names come about.'

'There must be plenty of people hereabouts who, as they say, have château blood.'

'That's so, but with the Bastides it was different. We were closer to the château. We belonged to it, and it is not so many years that we can forget. My husband's father was the son of a Comte de la Talle. Jean Pierre knows this; and when he looks at the château, when he sees the Comte, he thinks: So might I have ridden about the land. These vineyards might have been mine ... and the château too.'

'It's ... unhealthy to think so.'

'He has always been proud. He has always listened to the stories of the château which were handed down in our family. He knows how the Comtesse sheltered here in this house ... how her son was born here, how he lived here until he went back to join his grandmother in the château. You see, the Madame Bastide who sheltered him had a son of her own; he was a year older than the little Comte – but they had the same father.'

'It makes a strong link, I see, but it doesn't explain this envy and hatred going on over years.'

Madame Bastide shook her head and I burst out: 'You must make him see reason. There'll be a tragedy if he goes on in this way. I sense it. In the woods when the Comte was shot . . . '

'That was not Jean Pierre.'.

'But if he hates him so much . . . '

'He is not a murderer.'

'Then who . . . ?'

'A man such as the Comte has his enemies.'

'None could hate him more than your grandson. I don't like it. It must be stopped.'

'You must always restore people to what you think they should be, Dallas. Human beings are not pictures, you know. Nor . . . '

'Nor am I so perfect that I should seek to reform others. I know. But I find this alarming.'

'If you could know the secret thoughts which go on in our minds there might often be cause for alarm. But, Dallas, what of yourself? You are in love with the Comte, are you not?'

I drew away from her in dismay.

'It is as clear to me as Jean Pierre's hatred is to you. You are alarmed not because Jean Pierre hates, but because he hates the Comte. You fear he will do him some harm. This hatred has been going on for years. It is necessary to Jean Pierre. It soothes his pride. You are in greater danger through your love, Dallas, than he is through his hate.'

I was silent.

'My dear, you should go home. I, an old woman, who sees far more than you think, tell you that. Could you be happy here? Would the Comte marry you? Would you live here as his mistress? I don't think so. That would suit neither him nor you. Go home while there is still time. In your own country you will learn to forget, for you are still young and will meet someone whom you will learn to love. You will have children and they will teach you to forget.'

'Madame Bastide,' I said. 'You are worried.'

She was silent.

'You are afraid of what Jean Pierre will do.'

'He has been different lately.'

'He has asked me to marry him; he has convinced Geneviève that she is in love with him . . . What else?'

She hesitated. 'Perhaps I should not tell you. It has been on my mind since I knew. When the Comtesse fled from the revolutionaries and took refuge here she was grateful to the Bastides and she left with them a small gold casket. Inside this casket was a key.'

'A key!' I echoed.

'Yes, a small key. I have never before seen one like it. At one end was a fleur-de-lis.'

'Yes?' I prompted impatiently.

'The casket was for us. It is worth a great deal. It is kept locked away in case we should ever be in great need. The key was to be kept until it was asked for. It was not to be given up until then.'

'And was it never asked for?'

'No, it never was. According to the story which had been handed down we were to tell no one we had it for fear the wrong people should ask. So we never mentioned the key . . . nor the casket. It was said that the Comtesse had talked of two keys . . . the one in our casket and the one hidden in the château.'

'Where is the key? May I see it?'

'It disappeared . . . a short time ago. I believe someone has taken it.'

'Jean Pierre!' I whispered. 'He is trying to find the lock in the château which fits the key.'

'That could be so.'

'And when he does?'

She gripped my hand. 'If he finds what he seeks that will be the end of his hatred.'

'You mean . . . the emeralds.'

'If he had the emeralds he would think he had his share. I am afraid that that is what is in his mind. I am afraid that this . . . obsession is like a canker in his mind. Dallas, I am afraid of where it will lead him.'

'Could you talk to him?'

She shook her head.

'It's no use. I have tried in the past. I'm fond of you. You must not be hurt too. Everything here seems peaceful on the surface . . . but nothing is what it seems. We none of us show our true face to the world. You should go away. You should not be involved in this years-old strife. Go home and start again. In time this will seem like a dream to you and we will all be like puppets in a shadow show.'

'It could never be so.'

'Yes, my dear, it could be . . . for that is life.'

I left her and went back to the château.

I knew I could stand aside no longer. I had to act. How – I was not sure.

Half past six in the morning – and this was the call of *vendange*. From all over the neighbourhood men, women and children were making their ways to the vineyards where Jean Pierre and his father would give them instructions. At least, I told myself, for to-day there could be no concern for anything but the gathering of the grape.

In the château kitchens according to ancient custom food was being prepared to provide meals for all the workers, and as soon as the dew was off the grapes the gathering began.

The harvesters were working in pairs, one carefully cutting the grapes, making sure that those which were not perfect were discarded, while the other held the osier to receive them, keeping it steady so as not to bruise the grapes.

From the vineyards came the sound of singing as the workers joined together in the songs of the district. This again was an old custom Madame Bastide had once told me and there was a saying that '*Bouche qui mord à la chanson ne mord pas à la grappe.*'

I did not work on that morning. I went to the vineyards to watch. I did not see Jean Pierre. He would have been too busy to pay much attention to me, too busy to pay attention to Geneviève, too busy to hate.

I felt that I was not part of all that. I had no job to do. I didn't belong, and that was symbolic.

I went to the gallery and looked at my work which in so very short a time would be finished.

Madame Bastide, who was my good friend, advised me to go. I wondered whether by avoiding me the Comte was telling me the same. He had some regard for me, I was sure, and that thought would sustain me a little when I went away. However sad I was I should remind myself: But he had some regard for me. Love? Perhaps I was not one to inspire a *grande passion*. The thought almost made me laugh. If I could see this clearly I should see how absurd the whole thing was. Here was this man: worldly, experienced, fastidious . . . and there was I: the unattractive woman intense about one thing only, her work, all that he was not! – priding herself on her common sense, in which she had shown, by her behaviour, she was sadly lacking. But I should remind myself: He had some regard for me.

His aloofness was the measure of that regard and he, like Madame Bastide, was saying to me: Go away. It is better so.

I took the key from my pocket. I must give it to the Comte and tell him how I had found it. Then I would say to him: 'The work is almost finished. I shall be leaving shortly.'

I looked at the key. Jean Pierre had one exactly like it. And he was searching for that lock even as I had.

I thought of those occasions when I had felt myself observed. Could it have been Jean Pierre? Had he seen me that day in the graveyard? Was he afraid that I should find what he was so desperately seeking?

He must not steal the emeralds, for whatever he told himself, it would be stealing, and if he were caught . . .

It would be unbearable. I thought of the misery that would come to those people of whom I had grown so fond.

It would be no use remonstrating with him. There was only one thing to do: find the emeralds before he did. If they were here at all they must be in the dungeons because they were certainly not in the *oubliette*.

Here was an opportunity, for there was scarcely anyone in the château to-day. I remembered seeing a lantern near the door of the dungeon and I promised myself that this time I would light it, so that I could explore properly. I made my way to the centre of the château and descended the stone staircase. I reached the dungeons and as I opened the iron-studded door it creaked dismally.

I felt the chill of the place but I was determined to go on, so I lighted the lantern and held it up. It showed me the damp walls, the fungoid growth on them, the caves cut out of the wall, and here and there rings to which the chains were attached.

A gloomy place, dark, uninviting, still after all these years haunted by the sufferings of the forgotten men and women of a cruel age.

Where could there possibly be a lock here to fit the key?

I advanced into the gloom and as I did so was aware of that sense of creeping horror. I knew exactly how men and women had felt in the past when they had been brought to this place. I sensed the terror, the hopelessness.

It seemed to me then that every nerve in my body was warning me: Get away. There's danger here. And I seemed to develop an extra sense of awareness as perhaps one does in moments of acute danger. I knew I was not alone, that I was being watched.

I remember thinking: Then if someone is lurking in wait for me why doesn't that someone attack me now . . .

But I knew that whoever was there was waiting . . . waiting for me to do something, and when I did, the danger would be upon me. Oh, Jean Pierre, I thought, you wouldn't hurt me – even for the Gaillard emeralds.

My fingers were trembling. I despised myself. I was no better than the servants who would not come here. I was afraid, even as they were, of the ghosts of the past.

'Who's there?' I cried, in a voice which sounded bold.

It echoed in a ghostly eerie way.

I knew that I must get out at once. It was that instinct warning me. Now! And don't come back here alone.

'Is anyone there?' I said. Then again speaking aloud: 'There's nothing there. . . . '

I didn't know why I had spoken aloud. It was some answer to the fear which possessed me. It was not a ghost who was lurking there in the shadows. But I had more to fear from the living than the dead.

I backed – trying to do so slowly and deliberately – to the door. I blew out the lantern and put it down. I was through that iron-studded door; I mounted the stone staircase and once at the top of it hurriedly went to my room.

I must never go there alone again, I told myself. I pictured that door shutting on me. I pictured the peril overtaking me. I was not sure in what form, but I believed that I might then have had my wish to remain at the château for evermore.

I had come to a decision. I was going to talk to the Comte without delay.

It was characteristic that at Gaillard the grapes were trodden in the traditional way. In other parts of the country there might be presses, but at Gaillard the old methods were retained.

'There are no ways like the old ways,' Armand Bastide had said once. 'No wine tastes quite like ours.'

The warm air was filled with the sounds of revelry. The grapes were gathered and were three feet deep in the great trough.

The treaders, ready for the treading, had scrubbed their legs and feet until they shone; the musicians were tuning up. The excitement was high.

The scene touched by moonlight was fantastic to me, who had never seen anything like it before. I watched with the rest while the treaders, naked to the thighs, wearing short white breeches, stepped into the trough and began to dance.

I recognized the old song which Jean Pierre had first sung to me, and it had a special significance now:

'Qui sont-ils les gens qui sont riches?
Sont-ils plus que moi qui n'ai rien . . .'

I watched the dancers sink deeper and deeper into the purple morass; their faces gleaming, their voices raised in song. The music seemed to grow wilder; and the musicians closed in on the trough. Armand Bastide led the players with his violin; there was an accordion, a triangle and a drum, and some of the treaders used castanets as they went methodically round and round the trough.

Brandy was passed round to the dancers and they roared their appreciation as the singing grew louder, the dance more fervent.

I caught a glimpse of Yves and Margot; they with other children were wild with excitement, dancing together, shrieking with laughter as they pretended they were treading grapes.

Geneviève was there, her hair high on her head. She looked excited and secretive and I knew that her restless glances meant that she was looking for Jean Pierre.

And suddenly the Comte was beside me. He was smiling, as though he was pleased, and I felt absurdly happy because I believed that he had been looking for me.

'Dallas,' he said, and the use of my Christian name on his lips filled me with pleasure. Then: 'Well, what do you think of it?'

'I have never seen anything like it.'

'I'm glad we have been able to show you something you haven't seen before.'

He had taken my elbow in the palm of his hand.

'I must speak to you,' I said.

'And I to you. But not here. There is too much noise.'

He drew me away from the crowd. Outside, the air was fresh; I looked at the moon, gibbous, almost drunken-looking, the markings on its surface clear, so that it really did look like a face up there, laughing at us.

'It seems a long time since we have talked together,' he said. 'I could not make up my mind what to say to you. I wanted to think . . . about us. I did not want you to think me rash . . . impetuous. I did not think you would care for that.'

'No,' I replied.

We had started to walk towards the château.

'Tell me first what you wished to say,' he said.

'In a few weeks I shall have finished my work. The time will have come for me to go.'

'You must not go.'

'But there will be no reason for me to stay.'

'We must find a reason . . . Dallas.'

I turned to him. It was no time for banter. I must know the truth. Even if I betrayed my feelings I must know it.

'What reason could there be?'

'That I asked you to stay because I should be unhappy if you left.'

'I think you should tell me exactly what you mean.'

'I mean that I could not let you go away. That I want you to stay here always . . . to make this place your home. I'm telling you that I love you.'

'Are you asking me to marry you?'

'Not yet. There are things we must talk over first.'

'But you have decided not to marry again.'

'There was one woman in the world who could make me change my mind. I didn't even know she existed, and how was I to guess that chance should send her to me?'

'You are certain?' I asked and I heard the joy in my voice.

He stood still and took my hands in his; he looked solemnly into my face. 'Never more certain in my life.'

'And yet you do not ask me to marry you?'

'My dearest,' he said, 'I would not have you waste your life.'

'Should I waste it . . . if I loved you?'

'Do not say if. Say you do. Let us be completely truthful with each other. Do you love me, Dallas?'

'I know so little of love. I know that if I left here, if I never saw you again, I should be more unhappy than I had ever been in my life.'

He leaned towards me and kissed me gently on the cheek. 'That will do for a start. But how can you feel so . . . for me?'

'I don't know.'

'You know me for what I am . . . I want you to. I could not let you marry me unless you really knew me. Have you thought of that, Dallas?'

'I have tried not to think of what seemed to me quite impossible, but secretly I have thought of it.'

'And you thought it impossible?'

'I did not see myself in the role of *femme fatale*.'

'God forbid.'

'I saw myself as a woman – scarcely young, without any personal charm, but able to take care of herself, one who had put all foolish romantic notions behind her.'

'And you did not know yourself.'

'If I had never come here I should have become that person.'

'If you had never met me . . . And if I had never met you . . .? But we met and what did we do? We began to wipe off the bloom . . . the mildew . . . you know the terms. And now here we are. Dallas, I'll never let you leave me . . . but you must be sure . . .'

'I am sure.'

'Remember you have become a little foolish . . . a little romantic. Why do you love me?'

'I don't know.'

'You don't admire my character. You have heard rumours. What if I tell you that a great many of those rumours are true?'

'I did not expect you to be a saint.'

'I have been ruthless . . . often cruel . . . I have been unfaithful . . . promiscuous . . . selfish . . . arrogant. What if I should be so again?'

'That I am prepared for. I am, as you know self-opinionated . . . governessy as Geneviève will tell you . . .'

'Geneviève . . .' he murmured, and then with a laugh: 'I am also prepared.'

His hands were on my shoulders; I felt a rising passion in him and I was responding with all my being. But he was seeking for control; it was as though he was holding off that moment when he would take me in his arms and we should forget all else but the joy of being together at last in reality.

'Dallas,' he said, 'you must be *sure*.'

'I am . . . I am . . . never more sure. . . .'

'You would take me then?'

'Most willingly.'

'Knowing . . . what you know.'

'We will start again,' I said. 'The past is done with. What you were or what I was before we met is of no importance. It is what we shall be together.'

'I am not a good man.'

'Who shall say what is goodness?'

'But I have improved since you came.'

'Then I must stay to see that you go on improving.'

'My love,' he said softly, and held me against him, but I did not see his face.

He released me and turned me towards the château.

It rose before us, like a fairy castle in the moonlight, the towers seeming to pierce that midnight-blue backcloth of the sky.

I felt like the Princess in a fairy story. I told him so.

'Who lived happy ever after,' I said.

'Do you believe in happy endings?' he asked.

'Not perpetual ecstasy. But I believe it is for us to make our own happiness and I am determined that we shall do that.'

'You will make sure of it for both of us. I'm content. You will always achieve what you set out to do. I think you determined to marry me months ago. Dallas, when our plans are known there will be gossip. Are you prepared for that?'

'I shall not care for gossip.'

'But I do not want you to have illusions.'

'I believe I know the worst. You brought Philippe here because you had decided not to marry. How will he feel?'

'He will go back to his estates in Burgundy and forget he was once going to inherit when I died. After all, he might have had a long time to wait, and who knows, when it came to him he might have been too old to care.'

'But his son would have inherited. He might have cared for him.'

'Philippe will never have a son.'

'And his wife? What of her? I have heard that she was your mistress. It's true, isn't it?'

'At one time.'

'And you married her to Philippe who you did not think would have a son so that she could bear yours?'

'I am capable of such a plan. I told you that I am a scoundrel, didn't I? But I need you to help me overcome my vices. You must never leave me, Dallas.'

'And the child?' I asked.

'What child?'

'Her child . . . Claude's child.'

'There is no child.'

'But she has told me that she is to have a child . . . your child.'

'It is not possible,' he said.

'But if she is your mistress?'

'Was, I said, not is. You began to use your influence on me as soon as we met. Since she married Philippe there has been nothing between us. You look dubious. Does that mean you don't believe me?'

'I believe you,' I said. 'And . . . I'm glad. I can see that she wanted me to go. But it doesn't matter. Nothing matters now.'

'You will probably hear of other misdeeds now and then.'

'They will all be in the past. It will be the present and future which will be my affair.'

'How I long for the time when my affairs are entirely yours.'

'Could we say that they are from now on . . .?'

'You delight me; you enchant me. Who would have believed I could hear such sweetness from your lips?'

'I should not have believed it myself. You have put a spell on me.'

'My darling! But we must settle this. Please . . . please ask me more questions. You must know the worst now. What else have you heard of me?'

'I thought you were the father of Gabrielle's child.'

'That was Jacques.'

'I know now. I know too that you were kind to Mademoiselle Dubois. I know that you are good at heart. . . .'

He put an arm round me and as we walked across the drawbridge he said: 'There is one thing you have not mentioned. You do not ask about my marriage.'

'What do you expect me to ask?'

'You must have heard rumours.'

'Yes, I have heard them.'

'Little else was talked of in these parts at the time. I believe half the countryside believed I murdered her. They will think you are a brave woman to marry a man who, so many believed, murdered his wife.'

'Tell me how she died.'

He was silent.

'Please . . .' I said, 'please tell me.'

'I can't tell you.'

'You mean . . .'

'This is what you must understand, Dallas.'

'You know how she died?'

'It was an overdose of laudanum.'

'How, tell me how?'

'You must never ask me.'

'But I thought we were to be truthful with each other . . . always.'

'That is why I can't tell you.'

'Is the answer so bad, then?'

'The answer is bad,' he said.

'I don't believe you killed her. I won't believe it.'

'Thank you . . . thank you, my dear. We must not talk of it again. Promise me not to.'

'But I must know.'

'It is what I feared. Now you look at me differently. You are uncertain. That is why I did not ask you to marry me. I could not until you had asked that question . . . and until you had heard my reply.'

'But you have not replied.'

'You have heard all I have to say. Will you marry me?'

'Yes . . . it is no use anyone's trying to tell me you're a murderer. I don't believe it. I'll never believe it.'

He picked me up in his arms then.

'You've given your promise. May you never regret it.'

'You are afraid to tell me. . . .'

He put his lips to mine and the passion burst forth. I was limp clinging to him, bewildered, ecstatic, in my romantic dream.

When he released me he looked sombre.

'There will be gossip to face. There will be those who whisper behind our backs. They will warn you . . .'

'Let them.'

'It will not be an easy life.'

'It is the life I want.'

'You will have a stepdaughter.'

'Of whom I am already fond.'

'A difficult girl who may become more so.'

'I shall try to be a mother to her.'

'You have done much for her already, but . . .'

'You seem determined to tell me why I should not marry you. Do you want me to say no?'

'I should never allow you to say no.'

'And what if I did?'

'I should carry you to one of the dungeons and keep you there.'

Then I remembered the key and I told him how I had discovered it.

'I was hoping to present you with your long lost emeralds,' I said.

'If this is the key to them I'll present them to you,' he told me.

'Do you think this key really does open wherever they are?'

'We can find out.'

'When?'

'Now. The two of us. Yes, we'll go exploring together.'

'Where do you think?'

'I think in the dungeons. There are fleurs-de-lis in one of the caves exactly like this. It may well be that one of them will give us the clue. You would like to go now?'

I was suddenly aware of others besides ourselves. Jean Pierre searching in the château for the emeralds . . . we must find them before he did, for if he found them, he would steal them and bring disgrace on his family.

'Yes, please,' I said. 'Now.'

He led the way to the stables, where he found a lantern; he lighted this and we made our way to the dungeons.

'I think I know where we will find the lock,' he told me. 'It's coming back now. I remember years ago when I was a boy there was an examination of the dungeons and this cave with the fleur-de-lis decorations was discovered. It was noticed because it was so unusual. A dado of fleurs-de-lis around the cave. It seemed such a strange idea to decorate such a place. Evidently there was a purpose.'

'Didn't they look to see if there was a locked hiding-place?'

'Evidently there was no sign of that. The theory was that some poor prisoner had somehow managed to make them – no one knew how – and fit them on the wall of his cage. How he worked in the gloom was a mystery.'

We reached the dungeons and he swung open the iron-studded door. How different it was entering that dark and gloomy place with him; all fear was gone. I felt in a way it was symbolic. Whatever happens, if we're together, I can face it, I thought.

With one hand he held the lantern high; with the other he took my hand.

'The cave is somewhere here,' he said.

The smell of decay and dampness was in the close atmosphere; my foot touched one of those iron rings to which a rusting chain was attached.

Horrible! And yet I was not afraid.

He gave a sudden exclamation.

'Come and look here.'

I was beside him and there I saw the fleurs-de-lis. There were twelve of them placed at intervals round the cave about six inches from the ground.

He gave me the lantern and crouched down. He tried to push aside the first of the flowers but it would not move because it was so firmly attached to the wall. I watched him touch them in turn. At the sixth he paused.

'Just a minute,' he said. 'This one seems loose.'

He gave an exclamation; I lifted the lantern higher and saw him push the flower aside. Beneath it was the lock.

The key fitted, and actually turned in the lock. 'Can you see a door here?' he asked.

'There must be something,' I answered. 'The lock is there.' I tapped the wall.

'There is a cavity behind this wall,' I cried.

He threw his weight against the side of the cave and to our excitement there was a groaning sound and slowly a part of the wall appeared to move.

'It is a door,' I said.

He tried again. A small door swung back suddenly and I heard him exclaim in triumph.

I went to stand beside him, the lantern bobbing in my hand.

I saw what was like a cupboard – a small space about two feet by two and inside it a casket which might have been silver.

He lifted it out and looked at me.

'It looks,' he said, 'as though we've found the emeralds.'

'Open it,' I cried.

Like the door, it offered some resistance; but there they were – the rings, bracelets, girdle, necklaces and tiara which I had restored to colour on the portrait.

And as we stood there looking at each other over that casket I realized that he was looking at me not the stones.

'So you have restored the treasure to the château,' he said.

And I knew he wasn't thinking of the emeralds.

That was the happiest moment I was to know for a long time. It was like reaching the top of a mountain and having done so suddenly being flung down into despair.

Was it a creak of that iron-studded door? Was it a movement in the gloom?

The thought of danger came to us both simultaneously. We knew that we were not alone.

The Comte drew me quickly to his side and put an arm about me.

'Who is there?' he shouted.

A figure loomed out of the darkness.

'So you found them?' said Philippe.

I looked into his face and was terrified, for the dim light of the lantern which I still held showed me a man I had never seen before. Philippe's features, yes, but gone was the lassitude, the air of delicate effeminacy. Here was a desperate man, a man with one grim purpose.

'You were looking for them too?' asked the Comte.

'You got there before me. So it was you, Mademoiselle Lawson . . . I was afraid you would.'

The Comte pressed my shoulder. 'Go now,' he began.

But Philippe interrupted. 'Stay where you are, Mademoiselle Lawson.'

'Have you gone mad?' demanded the Comte.

'By no means. Neither of you will leave here.'

The Comte, still gripping me, took a step forward, but stopped short when Philippe raised his hand. He was holding a gun.

'Don't be a fool, Philippe,' said the Comte.

'You won't escape this time, Cousin, though you did in the woods.'

'Give me the gun.'

'I need it to kill you.'

With a swift movement the Comte thrust me behind him. Philippe's short grim laugh echoed oddly in that place.

'You won't save her. I'm going to kill you both.'

'Listen to me, Philippe.'

'I've had to listen to you too often. Now it's your turn to listen to me.'

'You propose to kill me because you want what is mine, is that it?'

'You're right. If you'd wanted to live you shouldn't have planned to marry Mademoiselle Lawson; you shouldn't have found those emeralds. You should have left something for me. Thank you, Mademoiselle Lawson, for leading me to them, but they're mine now. Everything is mine.'

'And you think you're going to get away with . . . murder?'

'Yes, I've thought it out. I meant to catch you together . . . like this. I didn't know Mademoiselle Lawson would be so obliging as to find the emeralds for me first. So it couldn't be better. Murder and suicide. Oh, not mine, Cousin. I want to live . . . live in my own right . . . not under your shadow, for once. Mademoiselle Lawson will have taken a gun from the gun-room, killed you and then herself. You played into my hands so beautifully – your reputation being what it is.'

'Philippe, you *fool.*'

'I've done with talking. Now's the time for action. You first, Cousin . . . we must have it in the right order. . . .'

I saw the gun raised. I tried to move to protect him but he held me firmly behind him. Involuntarily I shut my eyes. I heard the ear-splitting sound. Then after the explosion . . . silence. Faint with terror I opened my eyes.

Two men were struggling on the floor – Philippe and Jean Pierre.

I was past surprise. I was scarcely aware of them. I just knew that I was not going to lose my life in the dungeons, but I was losing everything that would make that life worth living, for on the floor bleeding from his wounds, lay the man I loved.

Chapter Twelve

Outside the sounds of revelry went on. They did not know, those who celebrated the grape harvest, that the Comte lay on his bed near to death; that Philippe lay in his under the influence of the sleeping draught the doctor had given him; that Jean Pierre and I sat in the library waiting.

Two doctors were with the Comte. They had sent us down here to wait and the waiting seemed endless.

It was not yet eleven o'clock and I seemed to have lived through a lifetime since I had stood in the dungeons with the Comte and suddenly come face to face with death.

And so strangely, there sat Jean Pierre, his face pale, his eyes bewildered as though he too did not understand what he was doing there.

'How long they are,' I said.

'Don't fret. He won't die.'

I shook my head.

'No,' said Jean Pierre, almost bitterly. 'He won't die until he wants to. Doesn't he always . . .' A smile twisted his lips. 'Sit down,' he said with a new authority. 'You can do no good by walking up and down. A second earlier and I'd have saved him. I left it that second too long.'

He had taken on a new authority. Sitting there he might have been the Comte. For the first time I noticed the château features – an irrelevant detail with which to concern myself at such a time!

It was Jean Pierre who had dominated that grisly scene. He it was who had sent me to call the doctors, who had planned what we should do.

'We should as yet say little of what has happened in the dungeons,' he cautioned, 'for you can be sure that the Comte will want the story told his way. I expect the gun will have gone off accidentally. He wouldn't want Monsieur Philippe to be accused of attempted murder. We'd better be discreet until we know what he wants.'

I clung to that. Until we know. Then we should know. He would open his eyes and live again.

'If he lives . . .' I began.

'He'll live,' said Jean Pierre.

'If only I could be sure . . .'

'He wants to live.' He paused for a moment, then went on: 'I saw you leave. How could I help it? Monsieur Philippe saw you . . . why, everyone must have seen, and guessed how things were. I watched you. I followed you to the dungeons . . . as Philippe did. But the Comte will want to live . . . and if he wants to, he will.'

'Then Jean Pierre, *you* will have saved his life.'

He wrinkled his brow. 'I don't know why I did it,' he said. 'I could have let Philippe shoot him. He's a first-class shot. The bullet would have gone through his heart. That's what he was aiming for. I knew it . . . and I said to myself: "This is the end of you, Monsieur le Comte." And then . . . I did it . . . I sprang on Philippe; I caught his arm. . . . Just that second too late. Half a second, shall we say. . . . If I'd been that half a second earlier the bullet would have hit the ceiling . . . half a second later and it would have pierced his head. I couldn't have got their earlier, though. I wasn't near enough. I don't know why I did it. I just didn't think.'

'Jean Pierre,' I repeated, 'if he lives you will have saved his life.'

'It's queer,' he admitted.

And there was silence.

I had to talk of something else. I could not bear to think of him lying there unconscious . . . while his life slowly ebbed away, taking with it all my hopes of happiness.

'You were looking for the emeralds,' I said.

'Yes. I meant to find them and go away. It would not have been stealing. I had a right to something. . . . Now, of course, I shall have nothing. I shall go to Mermoz and be his slave all my life . . . if he lives, and he will live because of what I did.'

'We shall never forget it, Jean Pierre.'

'You will marry him?'

'Yes.'

'So I lose you too.'

'You never wanted *me*, Jean Pierre. You wanted only what you thought he did.'

'It's strange . . . how he's always been there . . . all my life, I hate him, you know. There have been times when I could have taken a gun to him . . . and to think . . . if he lives it will be because I saved his life. I wouldn't have believed it of myself.'

'None of us knows how we'll act in certain circumstances . . . not until we come right face to face with them. It was a wonderful thing you did to-night, Jean Pierre.'

'It was a crazy thing. I wouldn't have believed it. I hated him, I tell you. All my life I've hated him. He has all that I want. He *is* all that I want to be.'

'All that Philippe wanted, too. He hated him as you did. It was envy. That's one of the seven deadly sins, Jean Pierre, and I believe, the deadliest. But you triumphed over it. I'm so glad, Jean Pierre, so glad.'

'But I tell you it wasn't meant. Or perhaps it was. Perhaps I never meant it when I thought I'd like to kill him. But I would have stolen the emeralds if I'd had a chance.'

'But you would never have taken his life. You know that now. You would even have married me, perhaps. You might have tried to marry Geneviève. . . .'

His face softened momentarily. 'I might yet,' he said. 'That would upset the noble Comte.'

'And Geneviève? You would use her for your revenge?'

'She's a charming girl. Young . . . and wild. . . . Like myself perhaps, unaccountable. And she's the Comte's daughter. Don't think I'm a reformed character because I've done this crazy thing to-night. I won't make promises about Geneviève.'

'She's a young and impressionable girl.'

'She's fond of me.'

'She must not be hurt. Life has not been easy for her.'

'Do you think I'd hurt her?'

'No, Jean Pierre. I don't think you're half as wicked as you like to think you are.'

'You don't know much about me, Dallas.'

'I think I know a great deal.'

'You'd be surprised if you did. I had my plans . . . I was going to see that my son was master of the château if I could never be.'

'But how?'

'He had plans, you know, before he was going to marry you. He wasn't marrying again, so he decided he'd bring his mistress here and marry her to Philippe. His son and hers would inherit the château. Well, it wasn't going to be his son but mine.'

'You . . . and Claude?'

He nodded triumphantly. 'Why not? She was angry because he didn't notice her. Philippe's no man, and so . . . Well, what do you think.'

I was listening for the approach of the doctors. I was only thinking of what was going on in that room above.

The doctors came into the room. There were two of them from the town, and they would know a great deal about us all. It was one of these who had attended the Comte when Philippe had shot him in the woods.

I had stood up and both doctors looked straight at me.

'He's . . .' I began.

'He's sleeping now.'

I looked at them mutely imploring them to give me some hope.

'It was a near thing,' said one of them almost tenderly. 'A few inches more and . . . He was fortunate.'

'He'll recover?' My voice sounded loud and vibrant with emotion.

'He's by no means out of danger. If he gets through the night . . .'

I sank back into my chair.

'I propose to stay here until morning,' said one of the doctors.

'Yes, please do.'

'How did it happen?' asked the elder of the two.

'The gun Monsieur Philippe was carrying went off,' said Jean Pierre. 'Monsieur le Comte will be able to give an account of what happened . . . when he recovers.'

The doctors nodded. And I wondered if they had both been here on the day Françoise died; and if then they waited for the Comte's account of that tragedy.

I didn't care what had happened then. All I asked was that he would recover.

'You're Mademoiselle Lawson, aren't you?' asked the younger doctor.

I said I was.

'Is your name Dallas – or something like that?'

'Yes.'

'I thought he was trying to say it. Perhaps you would care to sit by his bed. He won't speak to you, but just in case he's aware he might like to have you there.'

I went to his bedroom and sat there through the night watching him, praying that he would live. In the early morning he opened his eyes and looked at me and I was sure he was content to find me there.

I said: 'You must live. . . . You cannot die and leave me now.'

He said later that he heard me and for that reason he refused to die.

In a week we knew it was only a matter of time before he recovered. He had a miraculous constitution, said the doctors, and had had a miraculous escape; now it was for him to make a miraculous recovery.

He gave his account of what had happened. It was as we had thought. He had no wish for it to be known that his cousin had attempted to murder him. Philippe and Claude left for Burgundy, and in an interview between the two cousins was told that he should never come back to the château.

I was glad not to have to see Claude again now that I knew that she had hoped to find the emeralds, that she had become interested in the wall-painting when the words had been disclosed and she probably guessed that I had stumbled on some clue. She and Philippe would have worked together, watching me; she had searched my room while he detained me in the vineyards. It must have been Philippe who had followed me in the copse that day. Had he intended to shoot me as he had attempted to shoot the

Comte? They had wanted to be rid of me and had tried their hardest to make me leave by offering me work elsewhere; that was when they had believed the Comte was becoming too interested in me, for if he married their schemes would have been ruined.

Claude was a strangely complex woman. I was sure she had been sorry for me at one time and had, partly for my own good, wanted to save me from the Comte. She could not believe that a woman such as I could possibly arouse any lasting affection in such a man – for even an attractive woman like herself had been unable to. I pictured her working with her husband and with Jean Pierre – ready to go away with Jean Pierre if he found the emeralds, ready to stay with Philippe if he did.

I was glad, too, that Jean Pierre was free of her, for I would always have a fondness for him.

The Comte had said that the Mermoz vineyards should be his. 'It is a small reward,' he said, 'for saving my life.'

I did not tell him then what I knew; in fact I think he may have known already, for he did not ask what Jean Pierre had been doing in the dungeons.

Those were days of hopes and fears. It was with me that the doctors discussed his progress and I found I had an aptitude for nursing. But perhaps my special interest in this patient brought out this quality.

We would sit in the garden and talk of our future. We talked of Philippe and Jean Pierre. Philippe, I guessed, had first wanted me to stay at the château because he thought I should never attract the Comte, and when he found he was wrong sought to get rid of me. He must have planned with Claude that I should be offered the task of restoring her father's pictures so that I could be removed from Gaillard. And she had tried to lure me with a very tempting offer. Then of course he had planned my removal in a more sinister fashion.

We came to the conclusion that the secret cupboard had been constructed in that spot where a wretched prisoner had long ago tunnelled his way from the *oubliette* to the dungeons. The Comte thought he remembered his grandfather's mentioning that this had happened.

The emeralds had been put away in the strong-room. Perhaps one day I should wear them. The thought still seemed incongruous to me.

I wished that there could have been a neat ending to everything. I had a passion for neatness which I longed to satisfy. Sometimes I sat in the sunny garden and looked up at the machicolated towers of the château and felt that I was living in a fairy tale. I was a princess in disguise who had rescued a prince on whom a spell had been laid. I had lifted the spell and he would be happy again, happy ever after. That was what I wanted to be sure of .now . . . in the Indian summer of the pond garden, with the man I was soon to marry beside me, growing stronger every day.

But life is not a fairy tale.

Jean Pierre had left for Mermoz; Geneviève was sullen because he had left. Her head was full of wild plans; and one noble action had not changed Jean Pierre's character overnight.

And across my happiness there hung a dark shadow. I wondered if I should ever forget the first Comtesse.

They knew I was to marry the Comte. I had seen their glances . . . Madame Latière, Madame Bastide . . . all the servants.

It was a fairy tale. The humble young woman who came to the castle and married the Comte.

Geneviève, who was smarting under the loss of Jean Pierre, did not mince her words.

'You're brave, aren't you?'

'Brave? What do you mean?'

'If he murdered one wife why not another?'

No, there could be no neat happy ending.

I began to be haunted by Françoise. How strange it was. I had said I did not believe in the rumours I had heard; nor did I; but they haunted me.

He didn't kill her, I would say to myself a dozen times a day.

Yet why did he refuse to tell me the truth?

'There must be no lies between us,' he had said.

And for this reason he could not tell me.

There came the opportunity and I found myself unable to resist it.

It happened like this. It was afternoon and the château was quiet. I was anxious about Geneviève and went along to Nounou's room. I wanted to talk to her about the girl. I wanted to try to understand how deep this feeling for Jean Pierre had gone.

I knocked at the door of Nounou's sitting-room. There was no answer so I went in. Nounou was lying on a couch; there was a dark handkerchief over her eyes and I guessed she was suffering from one of her headaches.

'Nounou,' I said gently, but there was no answer.

My eyes went from the sleeping woman to the cupboard in which those little note-books were kept and I saw that Nounou's key was in the cupboard door. It was usually kept on the chain she wore about her waist and it was unusual for her not to return it there immediately after using it.

I bent over her. She was breathing deeply; she was fast asleep. I looked again at the cupboard, and the temptation was irresistible. I had to know. I reasoned with myself: She showed you the others so why should you not see that one? After all, Françoise is dead; and if the books could be read by Nounou why not by you?

It's important, I assured myself. It's of the utmost importance. I *must* know what is in that last book.

I went quietly to the cupboard; I looked over my shoulder at the sleeping woman and opened the cupboard door. I saw the bottle, the small glass. I lifted it up and smelt it. It had contained laudanum which she kept for her headaches, the same opiate which had killed Françoise.

Nounou had taken a dose because her headache was unbearable. I had to know. It was no use considering my scruples.

I picked the note-book at the end of the row; I knew that they would be in absolute order. I glanced inside. Yes. This was the one I wanted.

I went to the door.

Nounou had still not stirred. I sped to my own room and with wildly beating heart began to read.

'So I am going to have a child. This time it may be a boy. That will please him. I shall tell no one yet. Lothair must be the first to know. I shall say to him: "Lothair, we are going to have a child. Are you pleased?" Of course I am frightened. I am frightened of so much. But when it is over it will be worthwhile. What will Papa say? He will be hurt ... disgusted. How much happier he would be if I went to him and told him I was going into a convent. Away from the wickedness of the world, away from lust, away from vanity. That is what he would like. And I shall go to him and say "Papa, I am going to have a child." But not yet. I shall choose the right time. That is why I must say nothing yet. In case Papa should get to know.'

'They say a woman changes when she is going to have a child. I have changed. I could have been so happy. I almost am. I dream of the child. He will be a boy for that is what we want. It is right that the Comtes de la Talle should have sons. That is why they marry. If it were not necessary they could be content with their mistresses. They are the ones they really care for. But now it will be different. He will look at me in a different light. I shall not be only the one he was obliged to marry for the sake of the family; I shall be the mother of his son.'

'It is wonderful. I should have known this before. I should not have listened to Papa. Yesterday when I went to Carrefour I did not tell him. I could not bring myself to do so. And the reason is that I am so happy because it is so, and he will besmirch it. He will look at me with those stern cold eyes of his and he will be seeing it all ... everything that led up to my having the child ... not as it was ... but as he believed it to be ... horrible ... sinful ... I wanted to cry to him: "No, Papa it is not like that. You are wrong. I should never have listened to you." Oh, that room where we knelt together and you prayed that I should be protected from the lusts of the flesh! It was because of that that I shrank from him. I keep thinking now of the night before my marriage. Why did he agree? He regretted it almost immediately afterwards. I remember after the night of the *contrat de mariage* dinner how we prayed together and he said: "My child, I wish this need never take place." And I said: "Why, Papa, everyone is congratulating me!" And he answered: "That's because a match with the de la Talles is considered a good one, but I would be happy if I thought you would be living a life of purity." I did not understand then. I said I would try to be a pure woman; and he kept murmuring about the lusts of the flesh. And then the night before the church wedding we prayed together and I was ignorant and knew nothing of what was expected of me, except that it was shameful and that my father regretted he could not spare me such shame. And thus it was I came to my husband. . . .'

'But it is different now. I have come to understand that Papa is wrong. He should never have married. He wanted to be a monk. He was on the point of becoming one and then he found that he wanted to marry and he changed his mind and married my mother. But he hated himself for his weakness and his monk's robe was his greatest treasure. He is mistaken. I know that now. I might have been happy. I might have learned how to make Lothair love me if Papa had not frightened me, if he had not taught me that the marriage bed was shameful. I try not to blame him. All these years when my husband turned from me, when he has spent his nights with other women – perhaps they need not have been. I begin to see that I have turned him from me with my shivering shrinking sense of sin. I shall go to Carrefour to-morrow and I shall tell Papa that I am going to have a child. I shall say: "Papa, I feel no shame . . . only pride. Everything is going to be different from now on." '

'I did not go to Carrefour as I promised myself. My wisdom tooth started to ache again. Nounou said to me: "Sometimes when a woman has a baby she loses a tooth. You're not *so*, are you?" I flushed and she knew. How could I keep a secret from Nounou? I said: "Don't tell anyone yet, Nounou. I haven't told him. He should know first, shouldn't he? And I want to tell Papa too." Nounou understood. She knows me so well. She knows how Papa makes me pray when I go there. She knows that Papa would like to see me in a convent. She knows what he thinks of marriage. She rubbed a clove on my gum and said that should make it better; and I sat on the foot-stool leaning against her as I used to when I was little. And I talked to Nounou. I told her how I felt, I said: "Papa was wrong, Nounou. He made me feel that marriage was shameful. It was because of this . . . because *I* made my marriage intolerable that my husband turned to others." "You're not to blame," she said. "*You* have broken none of the commandments." "Papa made me feel unclean," I said. "From the beginning it was so. So my husband turned from me. I could never explain to him. He thought me cold, and you know, Nounou, he is not a cold man. He needed a warm, affectionate, clever woman. He has not been treated fairly." Nounou wouldn't have it. She said *I* had done no wrong. I accused her of agreeing with Papa. I said: "I believe you too would rather have seen me in a convent than married . . ." And she did not deny it. I said: "You too think marriage is shameful, Nounou." And she did not deny that, either. My tooth was no better so she gave me a few drops of laudanum in water and made me lie on the couch in her room. Then she locked the bottle in her cupboard and sat down beside me. "That'll make you drowsy," she said. "That'll send you into a nice sleep." And it did.'

'This is too terrible. I do not believe I shall ever forget it as long as I live. It keeps coming in and out of my mind. Perhaps if I write it down I can stop going over and over it. Papa is very ill. It began like this: I went to see him to-day. I had made up my mind I would tell him about the child. He was in his room when I arrived and I went straight to him. He was sitting at the table reading the Bible when I went in. He looked up and then laid the red silk book-marker in the place and closed the book. "Well, my child," he said. I went to him and kissed him. He seemed to notice the change in me at once, for he looked startled and a little alarmed. He asked me about Geneviève, and if I had brought her. I told him I had not. Poor child, it is too much to expect her to pray for so long. She grows restive and that agitates him more than ever. I assured him that she was a good child. He said that he thought that she had a tendency to waywardness. It must be watched. Perhaps it was because I am about to become a mother again that I felt rebellious. I did not want Geneviève to go to her husband – when her time came – as I had gone to mine. I said rather sharply that I thought she was normal, as a child should be. One did not expect children to behave as the holy saints. He stood up and he looked terrible. "Normal," he said, "Why do you say that?" And I answered: "Because it is natural for a child to be a little wayward, as you call it, now and then. Geneviève is. I shall not punish her for it." "To spare the rod is to spoil the child," he replied. "If she is wicked she should be beaten." I was horrified. "You are wrong, Papa," I said. "I do not agree with you. Geneviève shall not be beaten. Nor shall any of my children." He looked at me in astonishment and I blurted out: "Yes, Papa, I am going to have a child. This time a boy, I hope. I shall pray for a boy . . . and you must pray too." His mouth twitched. He said: "You are to have a child. . . ." I answered joyfully: "Yes, Papa. And I'm happy . . . happy . . . happy. . . ." "You are hysterical," he said. "I feel hysterical. I feel I want to dance with joy." Then he gripped the table and seemed to slide down to the floor. I caught at him and broke his fall. I could not understand what had happened to him. I knew that he was very ill. I called the Labisses and Maurice. They came and got him to his bed. I was faint myself. They sent for my husband and then I learned that my father was very ill. I believed he was dying.'

'That was two days ago. He was asking for me. All day he asks for me. He likes me to sit with him. The doctor thinks it is good for him that I should. I am still at Carrefour. My husband is here too. I have told him. I said to him: "It was when I told Papa that I was going to have a child that he became so ill. It was the shock, I believe." And my husband comforted me. He said: "He had been ill for a long time. This was a stroke and it could have happened at any time." "But," I said, "he did not *want* me to have children. He thinks it is sinful." And my husband said I must not worry. It would be bad for the child. And he is pleased. I know he is pleased for I believe above all things he wants a son.'

'I sat with Papa to-day. We were alone. He opened his eyes and saw me there. He said: "Honorine . . . is that you, Honorine?" And I said "No. It is Françoise." But he kept saying "Honorine" so I knew that he was mistaking me for my mother. I sat there by the bed thinking of the old days when she had been alive. I did not see her every day. Sometimes she was dressed in an afternoon gown with ribbons and laces and Madame Labisse brought her down to the drawing-room. She would sit in her chair and say little and I always thought what a strange mother she was. But she was very beautiful. Even as a child I knew that. She looked like a doll I once had; her face was smooth and pink and there were no wrinkles on it. She had a tiny waist yet she was plump and curved like pictures I had seen of beautiful women. I sat by his bed thinking of her and how one day I had come in and found her laughing, and laughing in such an odd way as though she couldn't stop and Madame Labisse's taking her off to her room where she seemed to stay for a long time. I knew her room because I had been there once. I had climbed the stairs to be with her. And I found her there sitting on her chair with her feet in little velvet slippers on her footstool. It was warm in the room and it was snowing outside I remember. There was a lamp very high on the wall and a guard round the fire such as I had in my nursery. And I noticed too the window, for there was only a small one and there were no curtains at it, but bars across. I went to her and sat at her feet and she said nothing to me but she liked having me there for she fondled my hair and ruffled it and pulled it, and made it very untidy and suddenly she started to laugh in that odd way I had heard. Madame Labisse came in and found me there and told me to go away at once. And she told Nounou, for I was scolded and told I was never to go up those stairs again. So I only saw Mamma when she came to the drawing-room. But when he kept talking of Honorine I sat there remembering. He said suddenly: "I must go, Honorine. I *must* go. No, I cannot stay." Then he was praying: "Oh God, I am a weak and sinful man. This woman tempted me and for her I became the sinner I am. And my punishment has come. You are testing me, O Lord, and Thy miserable servant has betrayed Thee . . . seventy times seven he has betrayed Thee." I said: "Papa, it is all right, this is not Honorine. It is I, Françoise, your daughter. And you are not sinful. You have been a good man." And he answered: "Eh? What's that?" And I went on talking to him, trying to soothe him.'

'That night I understood a great deal about my father. As I lay in bed the picture became clear to me. He had yearned for sanctity; he had wanted to be a monk, but there was a sensual streak in him which fought with his piety. Being the man he was he would have suffered torture . . . knowing of this streak, seeking to suppress it. Then he met my mother and he desired her; he turned from the thought of a monastery and married instead. But even though he married he had sought to suppress his desire and when he failed he despised himself. My mother was beautiful; as a child I had realized that; and to him she was irresistible. I pictured him, pacing up and down, steeling himself to stay away from her. He thought physical love sinful but he had been unable to resist it. I could imagine those days and nights when he shut himself in his austere room, when he lay on his pallet, when he scourged himself. He would be awaiting vengeance, for he was a man who believed in vengeance. Every small fault of mine or the servants had to be punished. At morning prayers that was the theme of his daily sermon. "Vengeance is mine, said the Lord." Poor Papa! How unhappy he must have been! Poor *Maman*! What sort of marriage had she had? Then I saw what he had done to me and mine and I wept for the tragedy of it. Then I said to myself: "But there is time yet. I am going to bear a child. So perhaps it is not too late." And I wondered how I could help Papa. But I could see no way.'

'This morning Nounou came in to draw the blinds and she looked at me anxiously. She said I looked drawn. I had had a sleepless night. It was true. I had lain awake for hours thinking of Papa and what he had done to my life. Was it the tooth? she asked. She thinks of me still as a child and does not seem to believe that I could be concerned with important problems. I let her think it was the tooth for I knew it would be impossible to talk to her – nor did I want to. "You must have some laudanum to-night, my child," she said. I answered: "Thank you, Nounou." '

'When I went over to Carrefour Maurice told me that Papa had been waiting for me. He kept watching the door and every time anyone went in he would say my name. They were all relieved that I had come. So I went in and sat by his bedside, although when I went in his eyes were closed and even when he opened them, after a while, he did not take much notice of me. Then I noticed that he was mumbling to himself. He kept saying: "The Vengeance of the Lord . . ." over and over again. He was very anxious, I could see that. I bent over him and whispered: "Papa, you have nothing to fear. You have done what you thought right. What more can anyone do?" "I am a sinner," he said. "I was tempted into sin. 'Twas not her fault. She was beautiful . . . she loved the pleasures of the flesh and she lured me to follow her. Even after I knew I could not resist her. That is the sin, child. That is the greatest sin of all." I said: "Papa, you are distressing yourself. Lie still." "Is that Françoise?" he asked. "Is that my daughter?" I answered that it was. He said: "And is there a child?" "Yes, Papa. Your little granddaughter, Geneviève." His face puckered and I was frightened. He began to whisper: "I have seen the signs. The sins of the fathers . . . Oh my God, the sins of the fathers . . ." I felt I had to comfort him. I said: "Papa, I think I understand. You loved your wife. That was no sin. It is natural to love, natural for me and women to have children. That is the way the world goes on." He kept murmuring to himself and I wondered whether to call Maurice. Occasionally a coherent sentence emerged. "I knew it. There was the hysteria. . . . There was the time when we found her playing with fire. There was the time when we found her building a fire in the bedroom, laying the sticks across each other. . . . We were always finding sticks laid as though for a fire . . . in cupboards . . . under beds. . . . She would run out to gather sticks. . . . Then the doctors came." "Papa," I said, "do you mean that my mother was mad?" He did not answer, but went on as though I had not spoken: "I could have sent her away. I should have sent her away . . . but I could not do without her . . . and I still went to her . . . even though I knew. And in time there was fruit of her madness. That is my sin and there will be vengeance. . . . I watch for it . . . wait for it." I was frightened, I forgot he was a sick man. I knew that what he was telling me was the truth as he saw it. I knew now why my mother had been kept in the room with the barred windows; I knew the reason for our strange household. My mother *had* been mad. It was for this reason that my father had not wanted me to marry. "Françoise," he mumbled. "Françoise . . . my daughter." "I am here, Papa." "I watched over Françoise," he said. "She was a good child . . . quiet, shy, retiring . . . not like her mother. Not brazen, bold . . . in love with the sins of the flesh. No, my daughter has escaped . . . But it is written 'unto the third and fourth generation . . .' She was sought in marriage by the de la Talles . . . and I gave my consent. That was my sin of pride. I could not say to the Comte when he asked for my daughter for his son: 'Her mother is mad.' So I said my daughter should marry and then I scourged myself for my pride and my lust for I was guilty of two of the deadliest sins. But I did not stop the marriage and so my daughter went to the château." I tried to soothe him. "All is well, Papa. There is nothing to fear. The past is done with. All is well now." "Unto the third and fourth generation . . ." he whispered. "The sins of the fathers . . ." I have seen it in the child. She is wild and she has the look of her grandmother. I know the signs. She will be like her grandmother . . . unable to resist the pleasures of the flesh . . . and the evil seed will pass on and on through the generations to come." "You can't mean Geneviève . . . my little girl." He whispered: "The seed is there in Geneviève . . . I have seen it. It will grow and grow until it destroys her. I should have warned my daughter. She has escaped but her children will not!" I was frightened. I began to see so much more than I ever had before. I knew now why he had been overcome with horror when I had told him I was to have another child. I sat by my bed numb with horror.'

'There is no one I can talk to. When I returned from Carrefour I went into one of the flower gardens and sat alone for a long time thinking of it. Geneviève! My daughter! Incidents from the past rose in my mind. It was like watching a play in a series of scenes, all significant leading to a climax. I remembered violent rages; her way of laughing immoderately and I heard her laughter mingling with echoes from the past. My mother . . . my daughter. They even looked alike . . . The more I tried to recall my mother's face the more she looked like Geneviève. I knew now that I should watch my daughter as my father had watched me. Every little misdemeanour of her childhood which I had once thought of as a prank took on a new significance. The evil seed had passed on through me to the coming generation. My father, who had wanted to be a monk, had been unable to suppress his passion for his wife even though he knew her to be mad, and as a result I had been born – and I in my turn had borne a child. Then the horror of my situation made me tremble with fear for not only was there my poor Geneviève. There was the unborn child.'

'I did not go to Carrefour yesterday. I could not. I made the excuse that my tooth was bad. Nounou fussed over me. She gave me a few drops of her laudanum and that sent me to sleep. I felt refreshed when I awoke but my anxieties were soon nagging at my mind. The child I longed for . . . what would it be like? What of my poor Geneviève? She came in this morning, as she always does first thing. I heard her with Nounou outside the door. Nounou said: "Your mother is not well. She has a toothache and wants to rest." "But I always go in," replied my daughter. "Not to-day, my dear. Let your *Maman* rest." But Geneviève flew into a rage. She stamped her feet and when Nounou tried to hold her off she bit poor Nounou's hand. I lay there shivering. He is right. These sudden passions are more than childish temper. Nounou can't control them . . . nor can I. I called that she was to come in and she came, her eyes bright with angry tears, her lips sullen. She threw herself at me; she hugged me far too wildly, far too passionately. "Nounou is trying to keep us apart. I won't let her. I'll kill her." That was how she talked, wildly, extravagantly. She doesn't mean it, I always said. It is just her way. Just her way! Honorine's way. My father had noticed the seed in her. I believed it was there . . . and I was seized with terror.'

'Papa was asking for me. So I went over to Carrefour. "He waits for you to come all the time," they told me. "He watches the door. He asks for your mother," they say. "He thinks you are your mother perhaps." So I sat by his bed and he looked at me with those wild glazed eyes and he said my name and sometimes that of my mother. He murmured of sin and vengeance but he was not as coherent as he had been. I thought he was dying. I could see that he was working himself up to an excitement and I bent over him to hear what he was saying. "A child?" he said. "There is going to be a child?" I thought he was thinking of what I had told him until I realized he was farther back in time. "A child . . . Honorine is going to have a child. How could this have happened? Oh, but it is God's vengeance. I knew . . . and in spite of my knowledge . . . I went to her and this is the vengeance of the Lord . . . 'unto the third and fourth generation . . . and the seed . . . the evil seed . . . will live for ever.' " "Papa," I said, "it is all long ago. Honorine is dead and I am well. There is nothing wrong with me." His wild uncomprehending eyes were on me. He murmured: "They told me she was with child. I remember the day well. 'You are to be a father,' they said. And they smiled at me . . . not knowing the horror that was in my heart. It had come. Vengeance had come. My sin would not die with me. It would live to the third and fourth generation. I went to her room that night . . . I stood over her. She was sleeping. I held the pillow in my hands. I could press it over her face . . . that would be the end . . . the end of her and the child. But she was beautiful . . . her black hair . . . the round childishness of her face . . . and I was a coward, so I fell upon her, embracing her and I knew I could never kill her." "You distress yourself, Papa." I said. "It is over. Nothing can change what is done. I am here now . . . and I am well, I assure you." He was not listening to me and I was thinking of Geneviève and the child who was not yet born.'

'I couldn't sleep last night. I kept thinking of Papa's grief. And I could not forget Geneviève. I thought of the wildness in her, which frightened Nounou. I knew why. Nounou had known my mother. Nounou's fears were a reflection of my father's. I had seen Nounou watching my daughter. I dozed and suffered a nightmare. There was someone in a room with a barred window. I had to kill her; I stood there with a pillow in my hand. It was my mother . . . but she had Geneviève's face and in her arms she carried a child . . . a child who was not yet born. I made her lie down and I stood over her with the pillow. I woke up crying: "No! No!" I was shivering. I couldn't rest after that. I was afraid to sleep for fear of more nightmares so I took some of Nounou's laudanum and then I fell into a long dreamless sleep.'

'When I awoke this morning my mind was very clear. If my child is a boy, I thought, he will carry on the line of the de la Talles. And I thought of that evil seed of madness entering the château like a ghost that would haunt it for the centuries to come. I should have brought that to them. Geneviève? She had Nounou to care for her. And Nounou *knows*. Nounou will watch over her. She will see that she never marries. Perhaps Nounou will persuade her to go into a convent as Papa wanted to persuade me. But the child . . . if it is a boy . . . Papa lacked the courage. It needs courage. Had Papa killed my mother I should never have been born. I should have known no pain . . . nothing. And that is how it would be with the child.'

'Last night a strange thing happened. I awoke from a nightmare and I remembered the peaceful sleep which comes from the little green bottle with the crinkly sides. Crinkly, Nounou told me, because if you should pick it up in the dark you would know it for a poison bottle. Poison! But it gives such sweet sleep, such relief! I thought how easy it would be to take twice . . . three times . . . the dose Nounou gave me for my toothache . . . and then no more fears . . . no more worries. The child would know nothing. The child would be saved from coming into the world, to be continually watched for the first sign of the evil seed. I reached for the bottle and I thought: "I will not be a coward as Papa was." I thought of myself old as he is now . . . lying on my deathbed, reproaching myself for all the unhappiness I had brought to my children. I looked at the bottle and I was afraid. I took a few drops and slept and in the morning I told myself "That is not the way." '

'It is night and the fears are with me again. I can't sleep. I keep thinking of Papa and my mother in the room with the bars, and I am very conscious of the child I am carrying. Nounou, please take care of Geneviève. I leave her to your care. I am wondering now whether I have the courage which Papa lacked. I believe that had he succeeded it would have been better for so many of us. My little Geneviève would never have been born . . . Nounou would have been saved her fears . . . *I* should never have been born. I believe my father was right. I can see the bottle. Green with the crinkly sides. I will put my note-book with the others in the cupboard and Nounou will find them. She loves reading about the days when I was little and says my books bring them back. She will explain to them why . . . I wonder if I can. I wonder if it is right . . . Now I shall try to sleep . . . but if I can't . . . In the morning I shall write that this is how one feels at night . . . By daylight it seems different. But Papa lacked the courage . . . I wonder if I shall have enough. I wonder. . . .'

The writing stopped there. But I knew what had happened. She had found what she would call the courage and because of it she and her unborn child died that night.

The pictures conjured up by Françoise's writing filled my mind. I saw it all so clearly; the house with the grim secret; the room with the barred window, the guarded fire; the lamp high in the wall; the wild and passionate woman; the austere husband who yet found her irresistible; his battle with his senses; his abandonment to passion and the result which to his fanatical mind seemed like vengeance. The birth of Françoise, the watchful eyes, the secluded upbringing . . . and then marriage to the Comte. I saw why that marriage had been a failure from the beginning. The girl, innocent and ignorant, had been taught to regard marriage with horror; the disillusion of them both; she in finding a virile young husband, he a frigid wife.

And everyone in the château had been aware of the unsatisfactory nature of the marriage and when Françoise died through an overdose of laudanum they would have asked themselves: Did her husband have a hand in it?

It was so cruelly unfair and Nounou was to blame. She had read what I had read; she knew what I had just discovered and yet she had allowed the Comte to be suspected of murdering his wife. Why had she not produced this book which explained so clearly?

Well, the truth should be known now.

I looked at the watch pinned to my blouse. The Comte would be in the garden. He would be wondering why I had not joined him as I always did when he was there. We would sit looking at the pond making plans for our marriage which would take place as soon as he was sufficiently recovered.

I went down to join him and found him alone impatiently awaiting me. He saw immediately that something had happened.

'Dallas!' He said my name with that note of tenderness which never failed to move me; now it filled me with anger that he, an innocent man, should have been so unjustly accused.

'I know the truth about Françoise's death,' I blurted out. 'Everyone shall know now. It is all here. . . . She wrote it herself. It is a clear explanation. She killed herself.'

I saw the effect those words had on him and I went on triumphantly. 'She kept note-books . . . little diaries. Nounou has had them all this time. Nounou *knew* . . . and she said nothing. She allowed you to be blamed. It's monstrous. But now everyone shall know.'

'Dallas, my dear, you are excited.'

'Excited! I have discovered this secret. I can now show this . . . admission . . . to the world. No one else will dare say that you killed Françoise.'

He laid his hand over mine. 'Tell me what you have discovered,' he said.

'I was determined to find out. I knew of the note-books. Nounou had shown me some. So I went to her room. She was asleep, her cupboard was open . . . so I took the last one. I had guessed that there might be some clue there but I had not thought I should find the answer so clear . . . so indisputable.'

'What did you find?'

'She killed herself because of the fear of madness. Her mother was mad and her father told her this when he was rambling after his stroke. He told her how he tried to kill her mother . . . how he had failed . . . how much better it would have been if he had. Don't you see? She was so . . . unworldly. That comes through in her diaries. She would accept . . . fatalistically what was put into her mind. . . . But it's here . . . as clear as we could wish. Never again shall anyone accuse you of murder.'

'I am glad you found this. Now there need be no secrets between us. Perhaps I should have told you. I think I should have done in time. But I was afraid that even you might have betrayed by some look . . . by some gesture . . .'

I looked at him searchingly. 'Of course I knew that you had not killed her. You don't think for a moment I believed that absurd gossip. . . .'

He took my face in his hands and kissed me. 'I like to think,' he said, 'that you doubted me and loved me just the same.'

'Perhaps it's true,' I admitted. 'I can't understand Nounou. How could she have known and kept quiet?'

'For the same reason that I did.'

'As . . . you did?'

'I knew what happened. She left a note for me, explaining.'

'You knew she took her own life, and why, and yet you let them . . .'

'Yes, I knew and I let them.'

'But why . . . *why*? It's so unfair . . . so cruel . . .'

'I was used to being gossiped about . . . slandered, I deserved most of it. You know I warned you you would not marry a saint.'

'But . . . murder.'

'It's your secret now, Dallas.'

'Mine. But I'm going to make this known . . .'

'No. There's something you've forgotten.'

'What?'

'Geneviève.'

I stared at him in understanding.

'Yes, Geneviève,' he went on. 'You know her nature. It is wild, excitable. How easy it would be to send her the way her grandmother went. Since you have been here she has changed a little. Oh, not a great deal. We can't expect it . . . but I think that one of the easiest ways to send a highly-strung person toppling into madness would be the continual watching, the suggestion that there is some seed in her which could develop. I don't want her watched in that way. I want her to have every chance to grow up normally. Françoise took her life for the sake of the child she was to have; I at least can face a little gossip for the sake of our daughter. You understand now, Dallas?'

'Yes, I understand.'

'I'm glad, for now there are no secrets between us.'

I looked across the grass to the pond. It was hot now but the afternoon was already late and the evenings were drawing in. It was only a year ago that I had come here. So much, I thought, to happen in one short year.

'You are silent,' he said. 'Tell me what you are thinking.'

'I was thinking of all that has happened since I first came here. Nothing is as it seemed when I came to the château . . . when I saw you all for the first time. I saw you so differently from what you are . . . and now I find you capable of this . . . great sacrifice.'

'My darling, you are too dramatic. This . . . sacrifice has cost me little. What do I care for what is said of me? You know I am arrogant enough to snap my fingers at the world and say: think what you will. But although I snap my fingers at the world there is one whose good opinion is of the greatest importance to me. . . . That is why I sit here basking in her approval, allowing her to set the halo on my head. I know of course that she will soon discover it was an illusion . . . but it's pleasant to wear it for a while.'

'Why do you always want to denigrate yourself?'

'Because I'm afraid beneath my arrogance.'

'Afraid. You. Of what?'

'That you will stop loving me.'

'And what of me? Don't you think I have a similar fear?'

'It is comforting to know you can be capable of folly now and then.'

'I think,' I said, 'that this is the happiest moment of my life.'

He put an arm about me and we sat close together for some minutes looking over the peaceful garden.

'Let's make it last,' he said.

He took the note-book from me and tore off the cover. Then he struck a match and applied it to the leaves.

I watched the blue and yellow flame creep over the childish handwriting. Soon there was nothing left of Françoise's confession.

He said: 'It was unwise to keep it. Will you explain to Nounou?'

I nodded. I picked up the cover of the note-book and slipped it into my pocket.

Together we watched a piece of blackened paper tossed across the lawn. I thought of the future – of whispers that would now and then reach me, of the wildness of Geneviève, of the complex nature of the man I had chosen to love. The future was a challenge. But then I had always been one to accept a challenge.

MISTRESS OF MELLYN

Chapter One

'There are two courses open to a gentlewoman when she finds herself in penurious circumstances,' my Aunt Adelaide had said. 'One is to marry, and the other to find a post in keeping with her gentility.'

As the train carried me through wooded hills and past green meadows, I was taking this second course; partly, I suppose, because I had never had an opportunity of trying the former.

I pictured myself as I must appear to my fellow travellers if they bothered to glance my way, which was not very likely: A young woman of medium height, already past her first youth, being twenty-four years old, in a brown merino dress with cream lace collar and little tufts of lace at the cuffs. (Cream being so much more serviceable than white, as Aunt Adelaide told me.) My black cape was unbuttoned at the throat because it was hot in the carriage, and my brown velvet bonnet, tied with brown velvet ribbons under my chin, was of the sort which was so becoming to feminine people like my sister Phillida but, I always felt, sat a little incongruously on heads like mine. My hair was thick with a coppery tinge, parted in the centre, brought down at the sides of my too-long face, and made into a cumbersome knot to project behind the bonnet. My eyes were large, in some lights the colour of amber, and were my best feature; but they were too bold – so said Aunt Adelaide; which meant that they had learned none of the feminine graces which were so becoming to a woman. My nose was too short, my mouth too wide. In fact, I thought, nothing seemed to fit; and I must resign myself to journeys such as this when I travel to and from the various posts which I shall occupy for the rest of my life, since it is necessary for me to earn a living, and I shall never achieve the first of those alternatives: a husband.

We had passed through the green meadows of Somerset and were now deep in the moorland and wooded hills of Devon. I had been told to take good note of that masterpiece of bridge-building, Mr. Brunel's bridge, which spanned the Tamar at Saltash and, after crossing which, I should have left England behind me and have passed into the Duchy of Cornwall.

I was becoming rather ridiculously excited about crossing the bridge. I was not a fanciful woman at this time – perhaps I changed later, but then a stay in a house like Mount Mellyn was enough to make the most practical of people fanciful – so I could not understand why I should feel this extraordinary excitement.

It was absurd, I told myself. Mount Mellyn may be a magnificent mansion; Connan TreMellyn may be as romantic as his name sounds; but that will be no concern of yours. You will be confined to below stairs, or perhaps to the attics above stairs, concerned only with the care of little Alvean.

What strange names these people had! I thought, staring out of the window. There was sun on the moorland but the grey tors in the distance looked oddly menacing. They were like petrified people.

This family to which I was going was Cornish, and the Cornish had a language of their own. Perhaps my own name, Martha Leigh, would sound odd to them. Martha! It always gave me a shock when I heard it. Aunt Adelaide always used it, but at home when my father had been alive he and Phillida never thought of calling me Martha. I was always Marty. I could not help feeling that Marty was a more lovable person than Martha could ever be, and I was sad and a little frightened because I felt that the River Tamar would cut me off completely from Marty for a long time. In my new post I should be Miss Leigh, I supposed; perhaps Miss, or more undignified still – Leigh.

One of Aunt Adelaide's numerous friends had heard of 'Connan Tre-Mellyn's predicament.' He needed the right person to help him out of his difficulties. She must be patient enough to care for his daughter, sufficiently educated to teach her, and genteel enough for the child not to suffer through the proximity of someone who was not quite of her own class. Obviously what Connan TreMellyn needed was an impoverished gentlewoman. Aunt Adelaide decided that I fitted the bill.

When our father, who had been vicar of a country parsonage, had died, Aunt Adelaide had swooped on us and taken us to London. There should be a season, she told us, for twenty-year-old Martha and eighteen-year-old Phillida. Phillida had married at the end of that season; but after four years of living with Aunt Adelaide, I had not. So there came a day when she pointed out the two courses to me.

I glanced out of the window. We were drawing into Plymouth. My fellow passengers had alighted and I sat back in my seat watching the activities on the platform.

As the guard was blowing his whistle and we were about to move on, the door of the carriage opened and a man came in. He looked at me with an apologetic smile as though he were hinting that he hoped I did not mind sharing the compartment with him, but I averted my eyes.

When we had left Plymouth and were approaching the bridge, he said: 'You like our bridge, eh?'

I turned and looked at him.

I saw a man, a little under thirty, well dressed, but in the manner of the country gentleman. His tail coat was dark blue, his trousers grey; and his hat was what in London we called a 'pot hat' because of its resemblance to that vessel. This hat he laid on the seat beside him. I thought him somewhat dissipated, with brown eyes that twinkled ironically as though he were fully aware of the warnings I must have received about the inadvisability of entering into conversation with strange men.

I answered: 'Yes, indeed. I think it is a very fine piece of workmanship.'

He smiled. We had crossed the bridge and entered Cornwall.

His brown eyes surveyed me and I was immediately conscious of my somewhat drab appearance. I thought: He is only interested in me because there is no one else to claim his attention. I remembered then that Phillida had once said that I put people off by presuming, when they showed interest, that I believed it was because no one else was available. 'See yourself as a makeshift,' was Phillida's maxim, 'and you'll be one.'

'Travelling far?' he asked.

'I believe I have now only a short distance to go. I leave the train at Liskeard.'

'Ah, Liskeard.' He stretched his legs and turned his gaze from me to the tips of his boots. 'You have come from London?' he went on.

'Yes,' I answered.

'You'll miss the gaiety of the big city.'

'I once lived in the country so I know what to expect.'

'Are you staying in Liskeard?'

I was not sure that I liked this catechism, but I remembered Phillida again: 'You're far too gruff, Marty, with the opposite sex. You scare them off.'

I decided I could at least be civil, so I answered: 'No, not in Liskeard. I'm going to a little village on the coast called Mellyn.'

'I see.' He was silent for a few moments and once more turned his attention to the tips of his boots.

His next words startled me. 'I suppose a sensible young lady like you would not believe in second sight . . . and that sort of thing?'

'Why . . .' I stammered. 'What an extraordinary question!'

'May I look at your palm?'

I hesitated and regarded him suspiciously. Could I offer my hand to a stranger in this way? Aunt Adelaide would suspect that some nefarious advances were about to be made. I thought in this case she might be right. After all I was a woman, and the only available one.

He smiled. 'I assure you that my only desire is to look into the future.'

'But I don't believe in such things.'

'Let me look anyway.' He leaned forward and with a swift movement secured my hand.

He held it lightly, scarcely touching it, contemplating it with his head on one side.

'I see,' he said, 'that you have come to a turning point in your life . . . You are moving into a strange new world which is entirely different from anything you have known before. You will have to exercise caution . . . the utmost caution.'

I smiled cynically. 'You see me taking a journey. What would you say if I told you I was visiting relatives and could not possibly be moving into your strange new world?'

'I should say you were not a very truthful young lady.' His smile was puckish. I could not help feeling a little liking for him. I thought he was a somewhat irresponsible person, but he was very lighthearted and, being in his company, to some extent made me share that lightheartedness. 'No,' he went on, 'you are travelling to a new life, a new post. There's no mistake about that. Before, you lived a secluded life in the country, then you went to the town.'

'I believe I implied that.'

'You did not need to imply it. But it is not the past which concerns us on occasions like this, is it? It is the future.'

'Well, what of the future?'

'You are going to a strange house, a house full of shadows. You will have to walk warily in that house, Miss er—'

He waited, but I did not supply what he was asking for, and he went on: 'You have to earn your living. I see a child there and a man. . . . Perhaps it is the child's father. They are wrapped in shadows. There is someone else there . . . but perhaps she is already dead.'

It was the deep sepulchral note in his voice rather than the words he said which momentarily unnerved me.

I snatched my hand away. 'What nonsense!' I said.

He ignored me and half closed his eyes. Then he went on: 'You will need to watch little Alice, and your duties will extend beyond the care of her. You must most certainly beware of Alice.'

I felt a faint tingling which began at the base of my spine and seemed to creep up to my neck. This, I supposed, was what is known as making one's flesh creep.

Little Alice! But her name was not Alice. It was Alvean. It had unnerved me for the moment because it had sounded similar.

Then I felt irritated and a little angry. Did I look the part then? Was it possible that I already carried the mark of the penurious gentlewoman forced to take the only course open to her? A governess!

Was he laughing at me? He lay back against the upholstery of the carriage, his eyes still closed. I looked out of the window as though he and his ridiculous fortune-telling were of not the slightest interest to me.

He opened his eyes then and took out his watch. He studied it gravely, for all the world as though this extraordinary conversation had not taken place between us.

'In four minutes' time,' he said briskly, 'we shall pull into Liskeard. Allow me to assist you with your bags.'

He took them down from the rack. 'Miss Martha Leigh,' was clearly written on the labels, 'Mount Mellyn, Mellyn, Cornwall.'

He did not appear to glance at these labels and I felt that he had lost interest in me.

When we came into the station, he alighted and set my bags on the platform. Then he took off the hat which he had set upon his head when he picked up the bags, and with a deep bow he left me.

While I was murmuring my thanks I saw an elderly man coming towards me, calling: 'Miss Leigh! Miss Leigh! Be you Miss Leigh then?' And for the moment I forgot about my travelling companion.

I was facing a merry little man with a brown, wrinkled skin and eyes of reddish brown; he wore a corduroy jacket and a sugar-loaf hat which he had pushed to the back of his head and seemed to have forgotten. Ginger hair sprouted from under this, and his brows and moustaches were of the same gingery colour.

'Well, Miss,' he said, 'so I picked you out then. Be these your bags? Give them to me. You and me and old Cherry Pie 'ull soon be home.'

He took my bags and I walked behind him, but he soon fell into step beside me.

'Is the house far from here?' I asked.

'Old Cherry Pie'll carry us there all in good time,' he answered, as he loaded my bags into the trap and I climbed in beside him.

He seemed to be a garrulous man and I could not resist the temptation of trying to discover, before I arrived, something about the people among whom I was going to live.

I said: 'This house, Mount Mellyn, sounds as though it's on a hill.'

'Well, 'tis built on a cliff top, facing the sea, and the gardens run down to the sea. Mount Mellyn and Mount Widden are like twins. Two houses, standing defiant like, daring the sea to come and take 'em. But they'm built on firm rock.'

'So there are two houses,' I said. 'We have near neighbours.'

'In a manner of speaking. Nansellocks, they who are at Mount Widden, have been there these last two hundred years. They be separated from us by more than a mile, and there's Mellyn Cove in between. The families have always been good neighbours until—'

He stopped and I prompted: 'Until—?'

'You'll hear fast enough,' he answered.

I thought it was beneath my dignity to probe into such matters so I changed the subject. 'Do you keep many servants?' I asked.

'There be me and Mrs. Tapperty and my girls, Daisy and Kitty. We live in the rooms over the stables. In the house there's Mrs. Polgrey and Tom Polgrey and young Gilly. Not that you'd call her a servant. But they have her there and she passes for such.'

'Gilly!' I said. 'That's an unusual name.'

'Gillyflower. Reckon Jennifer Polgrey was a bit daft to give her a name like that. No wonder the child's what she is.'

'Jennifer? Is that Mrs. Polgrey?'

'Nay! Jennifer was Mrs. Polgrey's girl. Great dark eyes and the littlest waist you ever saw. Kept herself to herself until one day she goes lying in the hay – or maybe the gillyflowers – with someone. Then, before we know where we are, little Gilly's arrived; as for Jennifer – her just walked into the sea one morning. We reckoned there wasn't much doubt who Gilly's father was.'

I said nothing and, disappointed by my lack of interest, he went on: 'She wasn't the first. We knowed her wouldn't be the last. Geoffry Nansellock left a trail of bastards wherever he went.' He laughed and looked sideways at me. 'No need for you to look so prim, Miss. He can't hurt you. Ghosts can't hurt a young lady, and that's all Master Geoffry Nansellock is now . . . nothing more than a ghost.'

'So he's dead too. He didn't . . . walk into the sea after Jennifer?'

That made Tapperty chuckle. 'Not him. He was killed in a train accident.

You must have heard of that accident. It was just as the train was running out of Plymouth. It ran off the lines and over a bank. The slaughter was terrible. Mr. Geoff, he were on that train, and up to no good on it either. But that was the end of him.'

'Well, I shall not meet him, but I shall meet Gillyflower, I suppose. And is that all the servants?'

'There are odd boys and girls – some for the gardens, some for the stables, some in the house. But it ain't what it was. Things have changed since the mistress died.'

'Mr. TreMellyn is a very sad man, I suppose.'

Tapperty lifted his shoulders.

'How long is it since she died?' I asked.

'It would be little more than a year, I reckon.'

'And he has only just decided that he needs a governess for little Miss Alvean?'

'There have been three governesses so far. You be the fourth. They don't stay, none of them. Miss Bray and Miss Garrett, they said the place was too quiet for them. There was Miss Jansen – a real pretty creature. But she was sent away. She took what didn't belong to her. 'Twas a pity. We all liked her. She seemed to look on it as a privilege to live in Mount Mellyn. Old houses were her hobby, she used to tell us. Well, it seemed she had other hobbies besides, so out she went.'

I turned my attention to the countryside. It was late August and, as we passed through lanes with banks on either side, I caught occasional glimpses of fields of corn among which poppies and pimpernels grew; now and then we passed a cottage of grey Cornish stone which looked grim, I thought, and lonely.

I had my first glimpse of the sea through a fold in the hills, and I felt my spirits lifted. It seemed that the nature of the landscape changed. Flowers seemed to grow more plentifully on the banks; I could smell the scent of pine trees; and fuchsias grew by the roadside, their blossoms bigger than any we had ever been able to cultivate in our vicarage garden.

We turned off the road from a steep hill and went down and down nearer the sea. I saw that we were on a cliff road. Before us stretched a scene of breath-taking beauty. The cliff rose steep and straight from the sea on that indented coast; grasses and flowers grew there, and I saw sea pinks and red and white valerian mingling with the heather – rich, deep, purple heather.

At length we came to the house. It was like a castle, I thought, standing there on the cliff plateau – built of granite like many houses I had seen in these parts, but grand and noble – a house which had stood for several hundred years, and would stand for several hundred more.

'All this land belongs to the Master,' said Tapperty with pride. 'And if you look across the cove, you'll see Mount Widden.'

I did look and saw the house. Like Mount Mellyn it was built of grey stone. It was smaller in every way and of a later period. I did not give it much attention because now we were approaching Mount Mellyn, and that was obviously the house which was more interesting to me.

We had climbed to the plateau and a pair of intricately wrought-iron gates confronted us.

'Open up there!' shouted Tapperty.

There was a small lodge beside the gates and at the door sat a woman knitting.

'Now, Gilly girl,' she said, 'you go and open the gates and save me poor legs.'

Then I saw the child who had been sitting at the old woman's feet. She rose obediently and came to the gate. She was an extraordinary looking girl with long straight hair almost white in colour and wide blue eyes.

'Thanks, Gilly girl,' said Tapperty as Cherry Pie went happily through the gates. 'This be Miss, who's come to live here and take care of Miss Alvean.'

I looked into a pair of blank blue eyes which stared at me with an expression impossible to fathom. The old woman came up to the gate and Tapperty said: 'This be Mrs. Soady.'

'Good day to you,' said Mrs. Soady. 'I hope you'll be happy here along of us.'

'Thank you,' I answered, forcing my gaze away from the child to the woman. 'I hope so.'

'Well, I do hope so,' added Mrs. Soady. Then she shook her head as though she feared her hopes were somewhat futile.

I turned to look at the child but she had disappeared. I wondered where she had gone, and the only place I could imagine was behind the bushes of hydrangeas which were bigger than any hydrangeas I had ever seen, and of deep blue, almost the colour of the sea on this day.

'The child didn't speak,' I observed as we went on up the drive.

'No. Her don't talk much. Sing, her do. Wander about on her own. But talk . . . not much.'

The drive was about half a mile in length and on either side of it the hydrangeas bloomed. Fuchsias mingled with them, and I caught glimpses of the sea between the pine trees. Then I saw the house. Before it was a wide lawn and on this two peacocks strutted before a peahen, their almost incredibly lovely tails fanned out behind them. Another sat perched on a stone wall; and there were two palm trees, tall and straight, one on either side of the porch.

The house was larger than I had thought when I had seen it from the cliff path. It was of three stories, but long and built in an L shape. The sun caught the glass of the mullioned windows and I immediately had the impression that I was being watched.

Tapperty took the gravel approach to the front porch and, when we reached it, the door opened and I saw a woman standing there. She wore a white cap on her grey hair; she was tall, with a hooked nose and, as she had an obviously dominating manner, I did not need to be told that she was Mrs. Polgrey.

'I trust you've had a good journey, Miss Leigh,' she said.

'Very good, thank you,' I told her.

'And worn out and needing a rest, I'll be bound. Come along in. You shall have a nice cup of tea in my room. Leave your bags. I'll have them taken up.'

I felt relieved. This woman dispelled the eerie feeling which had begun, I realized, since my encounter with the man in the train. Joe Tapperty had done little to disperse it, with his tales of death and suicide. But Mrs. Polgrey was a woman who would stand no nonsense, I was sure of that. She seemed to emit common sense, and perhaps because I was fatigued by the long journey I was pleased about this.

I thanked her and said I would greatly enjoy the tea, and she led the way into the house.

We were in an enormous hall which in the past must have been used as a banqueting room. The floor was of flagged stone, and the timbered roof was so lofty that I felt it must extend to the top of the house. The beams were beautifully carved and the effect decorative. At one end of the hall was a dais and at the back of this a great open fireplace. On the dais stood a refectory table on which were vessels and plates of pewter.

'It's magnificent,' I said involuntarily; and Mrs. Polgrey was pleased.

'I superintend all the polishing of the furniture myself,' she told me. 'You have to watch girls nowadays. Those Tapperty wenches are a pair of flibbertigibbets, I can tell 'ee. You'd need eyes that could see from here to Land's End to see all they'm up to. Beeswax and turpentine, that's the mixture, and nothing like it. All made by myself.'

'It certainly does you credit,' I complimented her.

I followed her to the end of the hall where there was a door. She opened this and a short flight of some half a dozen steps confronted us. To the left was a door which she indicated and after a moment's hesitation, opened.

'The chapel,' she said, and I caught a glimpse of blue slate flagstones, an altar and a few pews. There was a smell of dampness about the place.

She shut the door quickly.

'We don't use it nowadays,' she said. 'We go to the Mellyn church. It's down in the village, the other side of the cove . . . just beyond Mount Widden.'

We went up the stairs and into a room which I saw was a dining room. It was vast and the walls were hung with tapestry. The table was highly polished and there were several cabinets in the room within which I saw beautiful glass and china. The floor was covered with blue carpet and through the enormous windows I saw a walled courtyard.

'This is not *your* part of the house,' Mrs. Polgrey told me, 'but I thought I would take you round the front of the house to my room. It's as well you know the lay of the land, as they say.'

I thanked her, understanding that this was a tactful way of telling me that as a governess I would not be expected to mingle with the family.

We passed through the dining room to yet another flight of stairs and mounting these we came to what seemed like a more intimate sitting room. The walls were covered with exquisite tapestry and the chair backs and seats were beautifully wrought in the same manner. I could see that the furniture was mostly antique and that it all gleamed with beeswax and turpentine and Mrs. Polgrey's loving care.

'This is the punch room,' she said. 'It has always been called so because it is here that the family retires to take punch. We follow the old custom still in this house.'

At the end of this room was another flight of stairs; there was no door leading to them, merely a heavy brocade curtain which Mrs. Polgrey drew aside, and when we had mounted these stairs we were in a gallery, the walls of which were lined with portraits. I gave each of them a quick glance, wondering if Connan TreMellyn were among them; but I could see no one depicted in modern dress, so I presumed his portrait had not yet taken its place among those of his ancestors.

There were several doors leading from the gallery, but we went quickly along it, to one of those at the far end. As we passed through it I saw that we were in a different wing of the house, the servants' quarters I imagined, because the spaciousness was missing.

'This,' said Mrs. Polgrey, 'will be *your* part of the house. You will find a staircase at the end of this corridor which leads to the nurseries. Your room is up there. But first come to my sitting room and we'll have that tea. I told Daisy to see to it as soon as I heard Joe Tapperty was here. So there shouldn't be long to wait.'

'I fear it will take some time to learn my way about the house,' I said.

'You'll know it in next to no time. But when you go out you won't go the way I brought you up. You'll use one of the other doors; when you've unpacked and rested awhile, I'll show you.'

'You're very kind.'

'Well, I do want to make you happy here with us. Miss Alvean needs discipline, I always say. And what can I do about giving in to her, with all I have to do! A nice mess this place would be in if I let Miss Alvean take up *my* time. No, what she wants is a sensible governess, and 'twould seem they'm not all that easy to come by. Why, Miss, if you show us that you can look after the child, you'll be more than welcome here.'

'I gather I have had several predecessors.' She looked a trifle blank and I went on quickly. 'There have been other governesses.'

'Oh yes. Not much good, any of them. Miss Jansen was the best, but it seemed she had habits. You could have knocked me down with a feather. She quite took *me* in!' Mrs. Polgrey looked as though she thought that anyone who could do that must be smart. 'Well, I suppose appearances are deceptive, as they say. Miss Celestine was real upset when it came out.'

'Miss Celestine?'

'The young lady at Widden. Miss Celestine Nansellock. She's often here. A quiet young lady and she loves the place. If I as much as move a piece of furniture she knows it. That's why she and Miss Jansen seemed to get on. Both interested in old houses, you see. It was such a pity and such a shock. You'll meet her sometime. As I say, scarcely a day passes when she's not here. There's some of us that think. . . . Oh, my dear life! 'twould seem as though I'm letting my tongue run away with me, and you longing for that cup of tea.'

She threw open the door of the room and it was like stepping into another world. Gone was the atmosphere of brooding antiquity. This was a room which could not have fitted into any other time than the present, and I realized that it confirmed my impression of Mrs. Polgrey. There were antimacassars on the chair; there was a 'what-not' in the corner of the room filled with china ornaments including a glass slipper, a gold pig and a cup with 'A present from Weston' inscribed on it. It seemed almost impossible to move in a room so crammed with furniture. Even on the mantelpiece Dresden shepherdesses seemed to jostle with marble angels for a place. There was an ormolu clock which ticked sedately; there were chairs and little tables everywhere, it seemed. It showed Mrs. Polgrey to me as a woman of strong conventions, a woman who would have a great respect for the right thing – which would, of course, be the thing she believed in.

Still, I felt something comfortingly normal about this room as I did about the woman.

She looked at the main table and tutted in exasperation; then she went to the bell rope and pulled it. It was only a few minutes later when a black-haired girl with saucy eyes appeared carrying a tray on which was a silver teapot, a spirit lamp, cups and saucers, milk and sugar.

'And about time too,' said Mrs. Polgrey. 'Put it here, Daisy.'

Daisy gave me a look which almost amounted to a wink. I did not wish to offend Mrs. Polgrey so I pretended not to notice.

Then Mrs. Polgrey said: 'This is Daisy, Miss. You can tell her if you find anything is not to your liking.'

'Thank you Mrs. Polgrey, and thank you, Daisy.'

They both looked somewhat startled and Daisy dropped a little curtsy, of which she seemed half ashamed, and went out.

'Nowadays . . .' murmured Mrs. Polgrey, and lighted the spirit lamp.

I watched her unlock the cabinet and take out the tea canister which she set on the tray.

'Dinner,' she went on, 'is served at eight. Yours will be brought to your room. But I thought you would be needing a little reviver. So when you've had this and seen your room, I'll introduce you to Miss Alvean.'

'What would she be doing at this time of day?'

Mrs Polgrey frowned. 'She'll be off somewhere by herself. She goes off by herself. Master don't like it. That's why 'e be anxious for her to have a governess, you see.'

I began to see. I was sure now that Alvean was going to be a difficult child.

Mrs. Polgrey measured the tea into the pot as though it were gold dust, and poured the hot water on it.

'So much depends on whether she takes a fancy to you or not,' went on Mrs. Polgrey. 'She's unaccountable. There's some she'll take to and some she won't. Her was very fond of Miss Jansen.' Mrs. Polgrey shook her head sadly. 'A pity she had habits.'

She stirred the tea in the pot, put on the tea cosy and asked me: 'Cream? Sugar?'

'Yes, please,' I said.

'I always do say,' she remarked, as though she thought I needed some consolation, 'there ain't nothing like a good cup of tea.'

We ate tea biscuits with the tea, and these Mrs. Polgrey took from a tin which she kept in her cabinet. I gathered, as we sat together, that Connan TreMellyn, the Master, was away.

'He has an estate farther west,' Mrs. Polgrey told me. 'Penzance way.' Her dialect was more noticeable when she was relaxed as she was now. 'He do go to it now and then to see to it like. Left him by his wife, it were. Now *she* was one of the Pendletons. They'm from Penzance way.'

'When does he return?' I asked.

She looked faintly shocked, and I knew that I had offended because she said in a somewhat haughty way: 'He will come back in his own time.'

I saw that if I was going to keep in her good books, I must be strictly conventional; and presumably it was not good form for a governess to ask questions about the master of the house. It was all very well for Mrs. Polgrey to speak of him; she was a privileged person. I could see that I must hastily adjust myself to my own position.

Very soon after that she took me up to my room. It was large with big windows equipped with window seats from which there was a good view of the front lawn, the palm trees and the approach. My bed was a four-poster and seemed in keeping with the rest of the furniture; and although it was a big bed it looked dwarfed in a room of this size. There were rugs on the floor, the boards of which were so highly polished that the rugs looked somewhat dangerous. I could see that I might have little cause to bless Mrs. Polgrey's love of polishing everything within sight. There was a tallboy and a chest of drawers; and I noticed that there was a door in addition to the one by which I had entered.

Mrs. Polgrey followed my gaze. 'The schoolroom,' she said. 'And beyond that is Miss Alvean's room.'

'I see. So the schoolroom separates us.'

Mrs. Polgrey nodded.

Looking round the room I saw that there was a screen in one corner and as I approached this I noticed that it shielded a hip bath.

'If you want hot water at any time,' she said, 'ring the bell and Daisy or Kitty will bring it to you.'

'Thank you.' I looked at the open fireplace and pictured a roaring fire there on winter days. 'I can see I'm going to be very comfortable here.'

'It's a pleasant room. You'll be the first governess to have it. The other governesses used to sleep in a room on the other side of Miss Alvean's room. It was Miss Celestine who thought this would be better. It's a more pleasant room, I must say.'

'Then I owe thanks to Miss Celestine.'

'A very pleasant lady. She thinks the world of Miss Alvean.' Mrs. Polgrey shook her head significantly and I wondered whether she was thinking that it was only a year since the master's wife had died, and that perhaps one day he would marry again. Who more suitable to be his wife than his neighbour who was so fond of Miss Alvean? Perhaps they were only waiting for a reasonable lapse of time.

'Would you like to wash your hands and unpack? Dinner will be in two hours' time. But perhaps first you would like to take a look at the schoolroom.'

'Thank you, Mrs. Polgrey,' I said, 'but I think I'll wash and unpack first.'

'Very well. And perhaps you'd like a little rest. Travelling is so fatiguing, I do know. I'll send Daisy up with hot water. Meals could be taken in the schoolroom. Perhaps you'd prefer that?'

'With Miss Alvean?'

'She takes her meals nowadays with her father, except her milk and biscuits last thing. All the children have taken meals with the family from the time they were eight years old. Miss Alvean's birthday was in May.'

'There are other children?'

'Oh, my dear life, no! I was talking of the children of the past. It's one of the family rules, you see.'

'I see.'

'Well, I'll be leaving you. If you cared for a stroll in the grounds before dinner, you could take it. Ring for Daisy or Kitty and whoever is free will show you the stairs you will use in future. It will take you down to the kitchen garden, but you can easily get from there to wherever you want to go. Don't 'ee forget though – dinner at eight.'

'In the schoolroom.'

'Or in your own room if you prefer it.'

'But,' I added, 'in the governess's quarters.'

She did not know what to make of this remark, and when Mrs. Polgrey did not understand, she ignored. In a few minutes I was alone.

As soon as she had gone the strangeness of the house seemed to envelop me. I was aware of silence – the eerie silence of an ancient house.

I went to the window and looked out. It seemed a long time ago that I had driven up to the house with Tapperty. I heard the august notes of a bird which might have been a linnet.

I looked at the watch pinned to my blouse and saw that it was just past six o'clock. Two hours to dinner. I wondered whether to ring for Daisy or Kitty and ask for hot water; but I found my eyes turning to the other door in my room, the one which led to the schoolroom.

The schoolroom was, after all, my domain, and I had a right to inspect it, so I opened the door. The room was larger than my bedroom but it had the same type of windows and they were all fitted with window seats on which were red plush fitted cushions. There was a table in the centre of the room. I went over to it and saw that there were scratches on it and splashes of ink, so I guessed that this was the table where generations of TreMellyns had learned their lessons. I tried to imagine Connan TreMellyn as a little boy, sitting at this table. I imagined him a studious boy, quite different from his erring daughter, the difficult child who was going to be my problem.

A few books lay on the table. I examined them. They were children's readers, containing the sort of stories and articles which looked as if they were of an uplifting nature. There was an exercise book on which was scrawled 'Alvean TreMellyn. Arithemetic.' I opened it and saw several sums, to most of which had been given the wrong answers. Idly turning the pages I came to a sketch of a girl, and immediately I recognized Gilly, the child whom I had seen at the lodge gates.

'Not bad,' I muttered. 'So our Alvean is an artist. That's something.'

I closed the book. I had the strange feeling, which I had had as soon as I entered the house, that I was being watched.

'Alvean!' I called on impulse. 'Are you there, Alvean? Alvean, where are you hiding?'

There was no answer and I flushed with embarrassment, feeling rather absurd in the silence.

Abruptly I turned and went back to my room. I rang the bell and when Daisy appeared I asked her for hot water.

By the time I had unpacked my bags and hung up my things it was nearly eight o'clock, and precisely as the stable clock was striking eight Kitty appeared with my tray. On it was a leg of roast chicken with vegetables and, under a pewter cover, an egg custard.

Daisy said: 'Are you having it in here, Miss, or in the schoolroom?'

I decided against sitting in that room where I felt I was overlooked.

'Here, please, Daisy,' I answered. Then, because Daisy looked the sort of person who wanted to talk, I added: 'Where is Miss Alvean? It seems strange that I have not seen her yet.'

'She's a bad 'un,' cried Daisy. 'Do 'ee know what would have happened to Kit and me if we'd got up to such tricks? A good tanning – that's what we'd have had – and in a place where 'tweren't comfortable to sit down on after. Her heard new Miss was coming, and so off her goes. Master be away and we don't know where her be until the house boy comes over from Mount Widden to tell we that she be over there – calling on Miss Celestine and Master Peter, if you do please.'

'I see. A sort of protest at having a new governess.'

Daisy came near and nudged me. 'Miss Celestine do spoil the child. Dotes on her so's you'd think she was her own daughter. Listen! That do sound like the carriage.' Daisy was at the window beckoning me. I felt I ought not to stand at the window with a servant spying on what was happening below, but the temptation to do so was too strong for me.

So I stood beside Daisy and saw them getting out of the carriage . . . a young woman, whom I judged to be of my own age or perhaps a year or so older, and a child. I scarcely looked at the woman; my attention was all on the child. This was Alvean on whom my success depended, so naturally enough in those first seconds I had eyes for no one but her.

From what I could see she looked ordinary enough. She was somewhat tall for her eight years; her light brown hair had been plaited, and I presumed it was very long, for it was wound round her head; this gave her an appearance of maturity and I imagined her to be terrifyingly precocious. She was wearing a dress of brown gingham with white stockings and black shoes with ankle straps. She looked like a miniature woman and, for some vague reason, my spirits fell.

Oddly enough she seemed to be conscious that she was being watched, and glanced upwards. Involuntarily I stepped back, but I was sure she had seen the movement. I felt at a disadvantage before we had met.

'Up to tricks,' murmured Daisy at my side.

'Perhaps,' I said as I walked into the centre of the room, 'she is a little alarmed at the prospect of having a new governess.'

Daisy let out a burst of explosive laughter. 'What, her! Sorry, Miss, but that do make me laugh, that do.'

I went to the table and, sitting down, began to eat my dinner. Daisy was about to go when there was a knock on the door and Kitty entered.

She grimaced at her sister and grinned rather familiarly at me. 'Oh, Miss,' she said, 'Mrs. Polgrey says that when you'm finished will you go down to the punch room. Miss Nansellock be there and her would like to see you. Miss Alvean have come home. They'd like 'ee to come down as soon as you can. 'Tis time Miss Alvean were in her own room.'

'I will come when I have finished my dinner,' I said.

'Then would you pull the bell when you'm ready, Miss, and me or Daisy'll show you the way.'

'Thank you.' I sat down and, in a leisurely fashion, finished my meal.

I rose and went to the mirror which stood on my dressing table. I saw that I was unusually flushed and that this suited me; it made my eyes look decidedly the colour of amber. It was fifteen minutes since Daisy and Kitty had left me and I imagined that Mrs. Polgrey, Alvean and Miss Nansellock would be impatiently awaiting my coming. But I had no intention of becoming the poor little drudge that so many governesses were. If Alvean was what I believed her to be, she needed to be shown, right at the start, that I was in charge and must be treated with respect.

I rang the bell and Daisy appeared.

'They'm waiting for you in the punch room,' she said. 'It's well past Miss Alvean's supper time.'

'Then it is a pity that she did not return before,' I replied serenely.

When Daisy giggled, her plump breasts, which seemed to be bursting out of her cotton bodice, shook. Daisy enjoyed laughing, I could see. I judged her to be as lighthearted as her sister.

She led the way to the punch room through which I had passed with Mrs. Polgrey on my way to my own quarters. She drew aside the curtains and with a dramatic gesture cried: 'Here be Miss!'

Mrs. Polgrey was seated in one of the tapestry-backed chairs, and Celestine Nansellock was in another. Alvean was standing, her hands clasped behind her back. She looked, I thought, dangerously demure.

'Ah,' said Mrs. Polgrey, rising, 'here is Miss Leigh. Miss Nensellock have been waiting to see you.' There was a faint reproach in her voice. I knew what it meant. I, a mere governess, had kept a *lady* waiting while I finished my dinner.

'How do you do?' I asked.

They looked surprised. I suppose I should have curtsied or made some gesture to show that I was conscious of my menial position. I was aware of the blue eyes of the child fixed upon me; indeed I was aware of little but Alvean in those first few seconds. Her eyes were startlingly blue. I thought, she will be a beauty when she grows up. And I wondered whether she was like her father or mother.

Celestine Nansellock was standing by Alvean, and she laid a hand on her shoulder.

'Miss Alvean came over to see us,' she said. 'We're great friends. I'm Miss Nansellock of Mount Widden. You may have seen the house.'

'I did so on my journey from the station.'

'I trust you will not be cross with Alvean.'

I answered, looking straight into those defiant blue eyes: 'I could hardly scold for what happened before my arrival, could I?'

'She looks on me . . . on us . . . as part of her own family,' went on Celestine Nansellock. 'We've always lived so close to each other.'

'I am sure it is a great comfort to her,' I replied; and for the first time I gave my attention solely to Celestine Nansellock.

She was taller than I, but by no standards a beauty. Her hair was of a nondescript brown and her eyes were hazel. There was little colour in her face and an air of intense quietness about her. I decided she had little personality, but perhaps she was overshadowed by the defiance of Alvean and the conventional dignity of Mrs. Polgrey.

'I do hope,' she said, 'that if you need my advice about anything, Miss Leigh, you won't hesitate to call on me. You see, I am quite a near neighbour, and I think I am looked on here as one of the family.'

'You are very kind.'

Her mild eyes looked into mine. 'We want you to be happy here, Miss Leigh. We all want that.'

'Thank you. I suppose,' I went on, 'the first thing to do is to get Alvean to bed. It must be past her bedtime.'

Celestine smiled. 'You are right. Indeed it is. She usually has her milk and biscuits in the schoolroom at half past seven. It is now well past eight. But to-night I will look after her. I suggest that you return to your room, Miss Leigh. You must be weary after your journey.'

Before I could speak Alvean cried out: 'No, Celestine. I want *her* to. She's my governess. She should, shouldn't she?'

A hurt look immediately appeared in Celestine's face, and Alvean could not repress the triumph in hers. I felt I understood. The child wanted to feel her own power; she wanted to prevent Celestine from superintending her retirement simply because Celestine wished so much to do it.

'Oh, very well,' said Celestine. 'Then there's no further need for me to stay.'

She stood looking at Alvean as though she wanted her to beg her to stay, but Alvean's curious gaze was all for me.

'Good night,' she said flippantly. And to me: 'Come on. I'm hungry.'

'You've forgotten to thank Miss Nansellock for bringing you back,' I told her.

'I didn't forget,' she retorted. 'I never forget anything.'

'Then your memory is a great deal better than your manners,' I said.

They were astonished – all of them. Perhaps I was a little astonished myself. But I knew that if I were going to assume control of this child I should have to be firm.

Her face flushed and her eyes grew hard. She was about to retort, but, not knowing how to do so, she ran out of the room.

'There!' said Mrs. Polgrey. 'Why, Miss Nansellock, it was good of you—'

'Nonsense, Mrs. Polgrey,' said Celestine. 'Of course I brought her back.'

'She will thank you later,' I assured her.

'Miss Leigh,' said Celestine earnestly, 'it will be necessary for you to go carefully with that child. She has lost her mother ... quite recently.' Celestine's lips trembled. She smiled at me. 'It is such a short time ago and the tragedy seems near. She was a dear friend of mine.'

'I understand,' I replied. 'I shall not be harsh with the child, but I can see she needs discipline.'

'Be careful, Miss Leigh.' Celestine had taken a step closer and laid a hand on my arm. 'Children are delicate creatures.'

'I shall do my best for Alvean,' I answered.

'I wish you good luck.' She smiled and then turned to Mrs. Polgrey. 'I'll be going back now. I want to get back before dark.'

Mrs. Polgrey rang the bell and Daisy appeared.

'Take Miss to her room, Daisy,' she commanded. 'And has Miss Alvean got her milk and biscuits?'

'Yes, M'am,' was the answer.

I said good night to Celestine Nansellock, who inclined her head. Then I left with Daisy.

I went into the schoolroom where Alvean sat at a table drinking milk and eating biscuits. She deliberately ignored me as I went to the table and sat beside her.

'Alvean,' I said, 'if we're going to get along together, we'd better come to an understanding. Don't you think that would be advisable?'

'Why should I care?' she replied curtly.

'But of course you'll care. We shall all be happier if we do.'

Alvean shrugged her shoulders. 'If we don't,' she told me brusquely, 'you'll have to go. I'll have another governess. It's of no account to me.'

She looked at me triumphantly and I knew that she was telling me I was merely a paid servant and that it was for her to call the tune. I felt myself shiver involuntarily. For the first time I understood the feelings of those who depended on the goodwill of others for their bread and butter.

Her eyes were malicious and I wanted to slap her.

'It should be of the greatest account,' I answered, 'because it is far more pleasant to live in harmony than in discord with those about us.'

'What does it matter, if they're *not* about us ... if we can have them sent away?'

'Kindness matters more than anything in the world.'

She smiled into her milk and finished it.

'Now,' I said, 'to bed.'

I rose with her and she said: 'I go to bed by myself. I am not a baby, you know.'

'Perhaps I thought you were younger than you are because you have so much to learn.'

She considered that. Then she gave that shrug of her shoulders which I was to discover was characteristic.

'Good night,' she said, dismissing me.

'I'll come and say good night when you are in bed.'

'There's no need.'

'Nevertheless, I'll come.'

She opened the door which led to her room from the schoolroom. I turned and went into mine.

I felt very depressed because I was realizing the size of the problem before me. I had no experience of handling children, and in the past when I thought of them I had visualized docile and affectionate little creatures whom it would be a joy to care for. Here I was with a difficult child on my hands. And what would happen to me if it were decided that I was unfit to undertake her care? What did happen to penurious gentlewomen who failed to please their employers?

I could go to Phillida. I could be one of those old aunts who were at the beck and call of all and lived out their miserable lives dependent on others. I was not the sort of person to take dependence lightly. I should have to find other posts.

I accepted the fact that I was a little frightened. Not until I had come face to face with Alvean had I realized that I might not succeed with this job. I tried not to look down the years ahead when I might slip from one post to another, never giving satisfaction. What happened to women like myself, women who, without those attractions which were so important, were forced to battle against the world for a chance to live?

I felt that I could have thrown myself on my bed and wept, wept with anger against the cruelty of life, which had robbed me of two loving parents and sent me out ill-equipped into the world.

I imagined myself appearing at Alvean's bedside, my face stained with tears. What triumph for her! That was no way to begin the battle which I was sure must rage between us.

I walked up and down my room, trying to control my emotions. I went to the window and looked out across the lawns to the hilly country beyond. I could not see the sea because the house was so built that the back faced the coast and I was at the front. Instead I looked beyond the plateau on which the house stood, to the hills.

Such beauty! Such peace without, I thought. Such conflict within. When I leaned out of the window I could see Mount Widden across the cove. Two houses standing there over many years; generations of Nansellocks, generations of TreMellyns had lived here and their lives had intermingled so that it could well be that the story of one house was the story of the other.

I turned from the window and went through the schoolroom to Alvean's room.

'Alvean,' I whispered. There was no answer. But she lay there in the bed, her eyes tightly shut, too tightly.

I bent over her.

'Good night, Alvean. We're going to be friends, you know,' I murmured. There was no answer. She was pretending to be asleep.

Exhausted as I was, my rest was broken that night. I would fall into sleep and then awake startled. I repeated this several times until I was fully awake.

I lay in bed and looked about my room in which the furniture showed up in intermittent moonlight like dim figures. I had a feeling that I was not alone; that there were whispering voices about me. I had an impression that there had been tragedy in this house which still hung over it.

I wondered if it was due to the death of Alvean's mother. She had been dead only a year; I wondered in what circumstances she had died.

I thought of Alvean who showed a somewhat aggressive face to the world. There must be some reason for this. I was sure that no child would be eager to proclaim herself the enemy of strangers without some cause.

I determined to discover the reason for Alvean's demeanour. I determined to make her a happy, normal child.

It was light before sleep came; the coming of day comforted me because I was afraid of the darkness in this house. It was childish, but it was true.

I had breakfast in the schoolroom with Alvean, who told me, with pride, that when her father was at home she had breakfast with him.

Later we settled to work, and I discovered that she was an intelligent child; she had read more than most children of her age and her eyes would light up with interest in her lessons almost in spite of her determination to preserve a lack of harmony between us. My spirits began to rise and I felt that I would in time make a success of this job.

Luncheon consisted of boiled fish and rice pudding, and afterwards when Alvean volunteered to take me for a walk, I felt I was getting on better with her.

There were woods on the estate, and she said she wished to show them to me. I was delighted that she should do so and gladly I followed her through the trees.

'Look,' she cried, picking a crimson flower and holding it out to me. 'Do you know what this is?'

'It's betony, I believe.'

She nodded. 'You should pick some and keep it in your room, Miss. It keeps evil away.'

I laughed. 'That's an old superstition. Why should I want to keep evil away?'

'Everybody should. They grow this in graveyards. It's because people are buried there. It's grown there because people are afraid of the dead.'

'It's foolish to be afraid. Dead people can hurt no one.'

She was placing the flower in the buttonhole of my coat. I was rather touched. Her face looked gentle as she fixed it and I had a notion that she felt a sudden protective feeling towards me.

'Thank you, Alvean,' I said gently.

She looked at me and all the softness vanished from her face. It was defiant and full of mischief.

'You can't catch me,' she cried; and off she ran.

I did not attempt to do so. I called: 'Alvean, come here.' But she disappeared through the trees and I heard her mocking laughter in the distance.

I decided to return to the house, but the wood was thick, and I was not sure of my direction. I walked back a little way but it seemed to me that it was not the direction from which we had come. A panic seized me, but I told myself this was absurd. It was a sunny afternoon and I could not be half an hour's walk from the house. Moreover, I did not believe that the wood could be very extensive.

I was not going to give Alvean the satisfaction of having brought me to the wood to lose me. So I walked purposefully through the trees; but as I walked they grew thicker and I knew that we had not come this way. My anger against Alvean was rising when I heard the crackle of leaves as though I were being followed. I was sure the child was somewhere near, mocking me.

Then I heard singing; it was a strange voice, slightly off key, and the fact that the song was one of those which were being sung in drawing rooms all over the country did nothing to reassure me.

> *'Alice, where art thou?*
> *One year back this even*
> *And thou wert by my side,*
> *Vowing to love me,*
> *Alice, what e'er may betide—'*

'Who is there?' I called.

There was no answer, but in the distance I caught a glimpse of a child with lint-white hair, and I knew that it was only little Gilly who had stared at me from the hydrangea bushes by the lodge gates.

I walked swiftly on and after a while the trees grew less dense and through them I saw the road. I came out into this and realized that I was on the slope which led up to the plateau and the lodge gates.

Mrs. Soady was sitting at the door of the lodge as she had been when I arrived, her knitting in her hands.

'Why, Miss,' she called. 'So you've been out walking then?'

'I went for a walk with Miss Alvean. We lost each other in the woods.'

'Ah yes. So her run away, did her.' Mrs. Soady shook her head, as she came to the gate trailing her ball of wool behind her.

'I expect she'll find her way home,' I said.

'My dear life, yes. There ain't an inch of them woods Miss Alvean don't know. Oh, I see you've got yourself a piece of betony. Like as not 'tis as well.'

'Miss Alvean picked it and insisted on putting it in my buttonhole.'

'There now! You be friends already.'

'I heard the little girl, Gilly, singing in the woods,' I said.

'I don't doubt 'ee. Her's always singing in the woods.'

'I called to her but she didn't come.'

'Timid as a doe, she be.'

'Well, I think I'll be getting along. Goodbye, Mrs. Soady.'

'Good day to 'ee, Miss.'

I went up the drive, past the hydrangeas and the fuchsias. I realized I was straining my ears for the sound of singing, but there was no sound but that of an occasional small animal in the undergrowth.

I was hot and tired when I reached the house. I went straight up to my room and rang for water and, when I had washed and brushed my hair, went into the schoolroom where tea was waiting for me.

Alvean was at the table; she looked demure and made no reference to our afternoon's adventure; nor did I.

After tea I said to her: 'I don't know what rules your other governesses made, but I propose we do our lessons in the morning, have a break between luncheon and tea, and then start again from five o'clock until six, when we will read together.'

Alvean did not answer; she was studying me intently.

Then suddenly she said: 'Miss, do you like my name? Have you ever known anyone else called Alvean?'

I said I liked the name and had never heard it before.

'It's Cornish. Do you know what it means?'

'I have no idea.'

'Then I will tell you. My father can speak and write Cornish.' She looked wistful when she spoke of her father, and I thought: He at least is one person she admires and for whose approval she is eager. She went on: 'In Cornish, Alvean means Little Alice.'

'Oh!' I said, and my voice shook a little.

She came to me and placed her hands on my knees; she looked up into my face and said solemnly: 'You see, Miss, my mother was Alice. She isn't here any more. But I was called after her. That's why I am little Alice.'

I stood up because I could no longer bear the scrutiny of the child. I went to the window.

'Look,' I said, 'two of the peacocks are on the lawn.'

She was standing at my elbow. 'They've come to be fed. Greedy things! Daisy will soon be coming with their peas. They know it.'

I was not seeing the peacocks on the lawn. I was remembering the mocking eyes of the man on the train, the man who had warned me that I should have to beware of Alice.

Chapter Two

Three days after my arrival at Mount Mellyn, the Master of the house returned.

I had slipped into a routine as far as my duties were concerned. Alvean and I did lessons each morning after breakfast, and apart from an ever present desire to disconcert me by asking questions which, I knew, she hoped

I should not be able to answer, I found her a good pupil. It was not that she meant to please me; it was merely that her desire for knowledge was so acute that she could not deny it. I believe that there was some plot in her head that if she could learn all I knew she could then confront her father with a question: Since there is no more Miss can teach me, is there any point in her remaining here?

I often thought of tales I had heard of governesses whose declining years were made happy by those whom they had taught as children. No such happy fate would be mine – at least as far as Alvean was concerned.

I had been shocked when I first heard the name of Alice mentioned, and after the daylight had passed I would consequently feel that the house was full of eerie shadows. That was pure fancy of course. It had been a bad beginning, meeting that man in the train and his talk of second sight.

I did wonder, when I was alone in my room and the house was quiet, of what Alice had died. She must have been quite a young woman. It was, I told myself, because she was so recently dead – for after all a year was not a very long time – that her presence seemed to haunt the place.

I would wake in the night to hear what I thought were voices, and they seemed to be moaning: 'Alice. Alice. Where is Alice?'

I went to my window and listened, and the whispering voices seemed to be carried on the air.

Daisy who, like her sister, was by no means a fanciful person, explained away my fancies the very next morning when she brought my hot water.

'Did 'ee hear the sea last night, Miss, in old Mellyn Cove? Sis . . . sis . . . sis . . . woa . . . woa . . . woa . . . all night long. Just like two old biddies having a good gossip down there.'

'Why, yes, I heard it.'

''Tis like that on certain nights when the sea be high and the wind in a certain direction.'

I laughed at myself. There was an explanation to everything.

I had grown to know the people of the household. Mrs. Tapperty called me in one day for a glass of her parsnip wine. She hoped I was comfortable at the house; then she told me of the trial Tapperty was to her because he couldn't keep his eyes nor his hands from the maidens – and the younger the better. She feared Kitty and Daisy took after their father. It was a pity for their mother was, according to herself, a Godfearing body who would be seen in Mellyn Church every Sunday, night and morning. Now the girls were grown up she had not only to wonder whether Joe Tapperty was after Mrs. Tully from the cottages, but what Daisy was doing in the stables with Billy Trehay or Kitty with that house boy from Mount Widden. It was a hard life for a Godfearing woman who only wanted to do right and see right done.

I went to see Mrs. Soady at the lodge gates and heard about her three sons and their children. 'Never did I see such people for putting their toes through their stockings. It's one body's work to keep them in stockings.'

I was very eager to learn about the house in which I lived, and the intricacies of heel-turning did not greatly excite me; therefore I did not often call on Mrs. Soady.

I tried on occasions to catch Gilly and talk to her; but although I saw her now and then, I did not succeed. I called her, but that only made her run away more swiftly. I could never hear her soft crooning voice without being deeply disturbed.

I felt that something should be done for her. I was angry with these country folk who, because she was unlike they were, believed her to be mad. I wanted to talk to Gilly if that were possible. I wanted to find out what went on behind that blank blue stare.

I knew she was interested in me, and I believed that in some way she had sensed my interest in her. But she was afraid of me. Something must have happened to frighten her at some time, because she was so unnaturally timid. If I could only discover what, if I could teach her that in me at least she had nothing to fear, I believed I could help her to become a normal child.

During those days I believe I thought more of Gilly than I did of Alvean. The latter seemed to me to be merely a naughty spoilt child; there were thousands such. I felt that the gentle creature called Gillyflower was unique.

It was impossible to talk to Mrs. Polgrey about her granddaughter, for she was such a conventional woman. In her mind a person was either mad or sane, and the degree of sanity depended on the conformity with Mrs. Polgrey's own character. As Gilly was as different from her grandmother as anyone could be, Gilly was therefore irremediably crazy.

So although I did broach the subject with Mrs. Polgrey she was grimly uncommunicative and told me by her looks alone to remember that I was here to take charge of Miss Alvean, and that Gilly was no concern of mine.

This was the state of affairs when Connan TreMellyn returned to Mount Mellyn.

As soon as I set eyes on Connan TreMellyn he aroused deep feelings within me. I was aware of his presence, indeed, before I saw him.

It was afternoon when he arrived. Alvean had gone off by herself and I had sent for hot water to wash before I went for a stroll. Kitty brought it and I noticed the difference in her from the moment she entered the room. Her black eyes gleamed and her mouth seemed a little slack.

'Master be home,' she said.

I tried not to show that I was faintly disturbed; and at that moment Daisy put her head round the door. The sisters looked very much alike just then. There was about them both a certain expectancy which sickened me. I thought I understood the expression in the faces of these lusty girls. I suspected that neither of them was virgin. There was suggestion in their very gestures and I had seen them in scuffling intimacy with Billy Trehay in the stables and with the boys who came in from the village to work about the place. They changed subtly when they were in the presence of the opposite sex and I understood what that meant. Their excitement over the return of the Master, of whom I gathered everyone was in awe, led me to one conclusion, and I felt faintly disgusted, not only with them but with myself for entertaining such thoughts.

Is he *that* sort of man then? I was asking myself.

'He came in half an hour ago,' said Kitty.

They were studying me speculatively and once more I thought I read their thoughts. They were telling themselves that there would be little competition from me.

My disgust increased and I turned away.

I said coolly: 'Well, I'll wash my hands and you can take the water away. I am going for a walk.'

I put on my hat and, even as I went out quickly by way of the back stairs, I sensed the change. Mr. Polgrey was busy in the gardens, and the two boys who came in from the village were working as though their lives depended on it. Tapperty was cleaning out the stables; he was so intent on his work that he did not notice me.

There was no doubt that the whole household was in awe of the Master.

As I wandered through the woods I told myself that if he did not like me I could leave at any time. I supposed I could stay with Phillida while I looked round. At least I had some relations to whom I could go. I was not entirely alone in the world.

I called on Alvean, but my voice was lost in the thickness of the trees and there was no response. Then I called: 'Gilly! Are you there, Gillyflower? Do come and talk to me if you are. I won't hurt you.'

There was no answer.

At half past three I went back to the house and, as I was mounting the back stairs to my quarters, Daisy came running after me.

'Master have been asking for you, Miss. He do wish to see you. He be waiting in the punch room.'

I inclined my head and said: 'I will take off my things and then go to the punch room.'

'He have seen you come in, Miss, and have said for you to go right away.'

'I will take off my hat first,' I answered. My heart was beating fast and my colour was heightened. I did not know why I felt antagonistic. I believed that I should soon be packing my bags and going back to Phillida; and I decided that if it had to be done it should be done with the utmost dignity.

In my room I took off my hat and smoothed my hair. My eyes were certainly amber to-day. They were resentful, which seemed ridiculous before I had met the man. I told myself as I went down to the punch room that I had built up a picture of him because of certain looks I had seen in the faces of those two flighty girls. I had already assured myself that poor Alice had died of a broken heart because she had found herself married to a philanderer.

I knocked at the door.

'Come in.' His voice was strong – arrogant, I called it even before I set eyes on him.

He was standing with his back to the fireplace and I was immediately conscious of his great height; he was well over six feet tall, and the fact that he was so thin – one could almost say gaunt – accentuated this. His hair was black but his eyes were light. His hands were thrust into the pockets of his riding breeches and he wore a dark blue coat with a white cravat. There was an air of careless elegance about him as though he cared nothing for his clothes but could not help looking well in them.

He gave an impression of both strength and cruelty. There was sensuality in that face, I decided – that came through; but there was much else which was hidden. Even in that moment when I first saw him I knew that there were two men in that body – two distinct personalities – the Connan TreMellyn who faced the world, and the one who remained hidden.

'So, Miss Leigh, at last we meet.'

He did not advance to greet me, and his manner seemed insolent as though he were reminding me that I was only a governess.

'It does not seem a long time,' I answered, 'for I have only been in your house a few days.'

'Well, let us not dwell on the time it has taken us to get together. Now you are here, let that suffice.'

His light eyes surveyed me mockingly, so that I felt awkward and unattractive, and that I stood before a connoisseur of women when even to the uninitiated I was not a very desirable specimen.

'Miss Polgrey gives me good reports of you.'

'That is kind of her.'

'Why should it be kind of her to tell me the truth? I expect that from my employees.'

'I meant that she has been kind to me and that has helped to make this good report possible.'

'I see that you are a woman who does not use the ordinary clichés of conversation but means what she says.'

'I hope so.'

'Good. I have a feeling that we shall get on well together.'

His eyes were taking in each detail of my appearance, I knew. He probably was aware that I had been given a London season and what Aunt Adelaide would call 'every opportunity", and had failed to acquire a husband. As a connoisseur of women he would know why.

I thought, at least I shall be safe from the attentions which I feel sure he tries to bestow on all attractive women with whom he comes into contact.

'Tell me,' he said, 'how do you find my daughter? Backward for her age?'

'By no means. She is extremely intelligent, but I find her in need of discipline.'

'I am sure you will be able to supply that lack.'

'I intend to try.'

'Of course. That is why you are here.'

'Please tell me how far I may carry that discipline.'

'You are thinking of corporal punishment?'

'Nothing was farther from my thoughts. I mean, have I your permission to apply my own code? To restrict her liberty, shall we say, if I feel she needs such punishment.'

'Short of murder, Miss Leigh, you have my permission to do what you will. If your methods do not meet with my approval, you will hear.'

'Very well, I understand.'

'If you wish to make any alterations in the . . . curriculum, I think is the word . . . you must do so.'

'Thank you.'

'I believe in experiments. If your methods have not made an improvement in say . . . six months . . . well, then we could review the situation, could we not?'

His eyes were insolent. I thought: He intends to get rid of me soon. He was hoping I was a silly, pretty creature not averse to carrying on an intrigue with him while pretending to look after his daughter. Very well, the best thing I can do is to get out of this house.

'I suppose,' he went on, 'we should make excuses for Alvean's lack of good manners. She lost her mother a year ago.'

I looked into his face for a trace of sorrow. I could find none.

'I had heard that,' I answered.

'Of course you had heard. I'll swear there were many ready to tell you. It was doubtless a great shock to the child.'

'It must have been a great shock,' I agreed.

'It was sudden.' He was silent for a few seconds and then he continued: 'Poor child, she has no mother. And her father . . .?' He lifted his shoulders and did not complete his sentence.

'Even so,' I said, 'there are many more unfortunate than she is. All she needs is a firm hand.'

He leaned forward suddenly and surveyed me ironically.

'I am sure,' he said, 'that you possess that necessary firm hand.'

I was conscious in that brief moment of the magnetism of the man. The clear-cut features, the cool, light eyes, the mockery behind them – all these I felt were but a mask hiding something which he was determined to keep hidden.

At that moment there was a knock on the door and Celestine Nansellock came in.

'I heard you were here, Connan,' she said, and I thought she seemed nervous. So he had that effect even on those of his own station.

'How news travels!' he murmured. 'My dear Celestine, it was good of you to come over. I was just making the acquaintance of our new governess. She tells me that Alvean is intelligent and needs discipline.'

'Of course she is intelligent!' Celestine spoke indignantly. 'I hope Miss Leigh is not planning to be too harsh with her. Alvean is a *good* child.'

Connan TreMellyn threw an amused glance in my direction. 'I don't think Miss Leigh entirely agrees with that,' he said. 'You see our little goose as a beautiful swan, Celeste my dear.'

'Perhaps I am over fond—'

'Would you like me to leave now?' I suggested, for I had a great desire to get away from them.

'But I am interrupting,' cried Celestine.

'No,' I assured her. 'We had finished our talk, I believe.'

Connan TreMellyn looked in some amusement from her to me. It occurred to me that he probably found us equally unattractive. I was sure that neither of us was the least like the woman he would admire.

'Let us say it is to be continued,' he said lightly. 'I fancy, Miss Leigh, that you and I will have a great deal more to discuss, regarding my daughter.'

I bowed my head and left them together.

In the schoolroom tea was laid, ready for me. I felt too excited to eat, and when Alvean did not appear I guessed she was with her father.

At five o'clock she still had not put in an appearance, so I summoned Daisy and sent her to find the child and to remind her that from five to six we had work to do.

I waited. I was not surprised because I had expected Alvean to rebel. Her father had arrived and she preferred to be with him rather than come to me for an hour of our reading.

I wondered what would happen when the child refused to come to the schoolroom. Could I go down to the punch room or the drawing room or wherever they were and demand that she return with me? Celestine was with them and she would take her stand on Alvean's side against me.

I heard footsteps on the stairs. The door of Alvean's room which led into the schoolroom was opened, and there stood Connan TreMellyn holding Alvean by the arm.

Alvean's expression astonished me. She looked so unhappy that I found myself feeling sorry for her. Her father was smiling and I thought he looked like a satyr, as though the situation which caused pain to Alvean and embarrassment to me amused him – and perhaps for these reasons. In the background was Celestine.

'Here she is,' announced Connan TreMellyn. 'Duty is duty, my daughter,' he said to Alvean. 'And when your governess summons you to your lessons, you must obey.'

Alvean muttered and I could see that she was hard put to it to restrain her sobs: 'But it is your first day, Papa.'

'But Miss Leigh says there are lessons to be done, and she is in command.'

'Thank you, Mr. TreMellyn,' I said. 'Come and sit down, Alvean.'

Alvean's expression changed as she looked at me. All the wistfulness was replaced by anger and a fierce hatred.

'Connan,' Celestine said quietly, 'it *is* your first day back, you know, and Aleavn so looked forward to your coming.'

He smiled but I thought how grim his mouth was.

'Discipline,' he murmured. 'That, Celeste, is of the utmost importance. Come, we will leave Alvean with her governess.'

He inclined his head in my direction, while Alvean threw a pleading glance at him which he quite obviously ignored.

The door shut leaving me alone with my pupil.

That incident had taught me a great deal. Alvean adored her father and he was indifferent to her. My anger against him increased as my pity for the child grew. Small wonder that she was a difficult child. What could one expect when she was such an unhappy one? I saw her ... ignored by the father whom she loved, spoiled by Celestine Nansellock. Between them they were doing their best to ruin the girl.

I would have liked Connan TreMellyn better, I told myself, if he had decided to forget discipline on his first day back, and devote a little time to his daughter's company.

Alvean was rebellious all that evening, but I insisted on her going to bed at her usual time. She told me she hated me, though there was no need for her to have mentioned a fact which was apparent.

I felt so disturbed when she was in her bed that I slipped out of the house and went into the woods, where I sat on a fallen tree trunk, brooding.

It had been a hot day and there was a deep stillness in the woods.

I wondered whether I was going to keep this job. It was not easy to say at this stage, and I was not sure whether I wanted to go or stay.

There were so many things to keep me. There was, for one thing, my interest in Gillyflower; there was my desire to wipe the rebellion from Alvean's heart. But I felt less eagerness for these tasks now that I had seen the Master.

I was a little afraid of the man although I could not say why. I was certain that he would leave *me* alone, but there was something magnetic about him, some quality which made it difficult for me to put him out of my mind. I thought more of dead Alice than I had before, because I could not stop myself wondering what sort of person she could have been.

I amused him in some way. Perhaps because I was so unattractive in his eyes; perhaps because he knews that I belonged to that army of women who are obliged to earn their living and are so dependent on the whim of people like himself. Was there a streak of sadism in his nature? I believed so. Perhaps poor Alice had found it intolerable. Perhaps she, like poor Gilly-flower's mother, had walked into the sea.

As I sat there I heard the sound of footsteps coming through the wood and I hesitated, wondering whether to wait there or go back to the house.

A man was coming towards me, and there was something familiar about him which made my heart beat faster.

He started when he saw me; then he began to smile and I recognized him as the man I had met on the train.

'So we meet,' he said. 'I knew our reunion would not be long delayed. Why, you look as though you have seen a ghost. Has your stay at Mount Mellyn made you look for ghosts? I've heard some say that there *is* a ghostly atmosphere about the place.'

'Who are you?' I asked.

'My name is Peter Nansellock. I have to confess to a little deception.'

'You're Miss Celestine's brother?'

He nodded. 'I knew who you were when we met in the train. I deliberately bearded you in your carriage. I saw you sitting there, looking the part, and I guessed. Your name on the labels of your baggage confirmed my guess for I knew that they were expecting Miss Martha Leigh at Mount Mellyn.'

'I am comforted to learn that my looks conform with the part I have been called upon to play in life.'

'You really are a most untruthful young lady. I remember I had reason to reprimand you for the same sort of thing at our first meeting. You are in fact quite discomfited to learn that you were taken for a governess.'

I felt myself grow pink with indignation. 'Because I am a governess that is no reason why I should be forced to accept insults from strangers.'

I rose from the tree trunk, but he laid a hand on my arm and said pleadingly: 'Please let us talk awhile. There is much I have to say to you. There are things you should know.'

My curiosity overcame my dignity and I saw down.

'That's better, Miss Leigh. You see I remember your name.'

'Most courteous of you! And how extraordinary that you should first notice a mere governess's name and then keep it in your memory.'

'You are like a hedgehog,' he retorted. 'One only has to mention the word "governess" and up come your spines. You will have to learn resignation. Aren't we taught that we must be content in that station of life to which we have been called?'

'Since I resemble a hedgehog, at least I am not spineless.'

He laughed and then was immediately sober. 'I do not possess second sight, Miss Leigh,' he said quietly. 'I know nothing of palmistry. I deceived you, Miss Leigh.'

'Do you think I was deceived for a moment?'

'For many moments. Until this one, in fact, you have thought of me with wonder.'

'Indeed, I have not thought of you at all.'

'More untruths! I wonder if a young lady with such little regard for veracity is worthy to teach our little Alvean.'

'Since you are a friend of the family your best policy would be to warn them at once.'

'But if Connan dismissed his daughter's governess, how sad that would be! I should wander through these woods without hope of meeting her.'

'I see you are a frivolous person.'

'It's true.' He looked grave. 'My brother was frivolous. My sister is the only commendable member of the family.'

'I have already met her.'

'Naturally. She is a constant visitor to Mount Mellyn. She dotes on Alvean.'

'Well, she is a very near neighbour.'

'And we, Miss Leigh, shall in future be very near neighbours. How does that strike you?'

'Without any great force.'

'Miss Leigh, you are cruel as well as untruthful. I hoped you would be grateful for my interest. I was going to say, if ever things should become intolerable at Mount Mellyn you need only walk over to Mount Widden. There you would find me most willing to help. I feel sure that among my wide circle of acquaintances I could find someone who is in urgent need of a governess.'

'Why should I find life intolerable at Mount Mellyn?'

'It's a tomb of a place, Connan is overbearing, Alvean is a menace to anyone's peace, and the atmosphere since Alice's death is not congenial.'

I turned to him abruptly and said: 'You told me to beware of Alice. What did you mean by that?'

'So you remember?'

'It seemed a strange thing to say.'

'Alice is dead,' he said, 'but somehow she remains. That's what I always feel at Mount Mellyn. Nothing was the same after the day she . . . went.'

'How did she die?'

'You have not heard the story yet?'

'No.'

'I should have thought Mrs. Polgrey or one of those girls would have told you. But they haven't, eh? They're probably somewhat in awe of the governess.'

'I should like to hear the story.'

'It's a very simple one. The sort of thing which must happen in many a home. A wife finds life with her husband intolerable. She walks out . . . with another man. It's ordinary enough, you see. Only Alice's story had a different ending.'

He looked at the tips of his boots as he had when we were travelling in the train to Liskeard together. 'The man in the case was my brother,' he went on.

'Geoffry Nansellock!' I cried.

'So you have heard of him!'

I thought of Gillyflower, whose birth had so distressed her mother that she had walked into the sea.

'Yes,' I said, 'I've heard of Geoffry Nansellock. He was evidently a philanderer.'

'It sounds a harsh word to apply to poor old Geoff. He had charm . . . all the charm of the family, some say.' He smiled at me. 'Others may think he did not get it all. He was not a bad sort. I was fond of old Geoff. His great weakness was women. He loved women; he found them irresistible. And women love men who love them. How can they help it? I mean, it is such a compliment, is it not? One by one they fell victim to his charm.'

'He did not hesitate to include other men's wives among his victims.'

'Spoken like a true governess! Alas, my dear Miss Leigh, it appeared he did not . . . since Alice was among them. It is true that all was not well at Mount Mellyn. Do you think Connan would be an easy man to live with?'

'It is surely not becoming for a governess to discuss her employer in such a manner.'

'What a contrary young lady you are, Miss Leigh. You make the most of your situation. You use the governess when you wish to, and then expect others to ignore her when you do not wish her to be recognized. I believe that anyone who is obliged to live in a house should know something of its secrets.'

'What secrets?'

He bent a little closer to me. 'Alice was afraid of Connan. Before she married him she had known my brother. She and Geoffry were on the train . . . running away together.'

'I see.' I drew myself away from him because I felt it was undignified to be talking of past scandals in this way, particularly as these scandals had nothing whatever to do with me.

'They identified Geoffry although he was badly smashed up. There was a woman close to him. She was so badly burned that it was impossible to recognize her as Alice. But a locket she was wearing was recognized as one she was known to possess. That was how she was identified . . . and of course there was the fact that Alice had disappeared.'

'How dreadful to die in such a way!'

'The prim governess is shocked because poor Alice died in the act of forming a guilty partnership with my charming but erring brother.'

'Was she so unhappy at Mount Mellyn?'

'You have met Connan. Remember he knew that she had once been in love with Geoffry, and Geoffry was still in the offing. I can imagine life was hell for Alice.'

'Well, it was very tragic,' I said briskly. 'But it is over. Why did you say, "Beware of Alice," as though she were still there?'

'Are you fey, Miss Leigh? No, of course you are not. You are a governess with more than your fair share of commonsense. You would not be influenced by fantastic tales.'

'What fantastic tales?'

He grinned at me, coming even closer, and I realized that in a very short time it would be dark. I was anxious to get back to the house, and my expression became a little impatient.

'They recognized her locket, not her. There are some who think that it was not Alice who was killed on the train with Geoffry.'

'Then if it was not, where is she?'

'That is what some people ask themselves. That is why there are long shadows at Mount Mellyn.'

I stood up. 'I must get back. It will soon be dark.'

He was standing beside me – a little taller than I – and our eyes met.

'I thought you should know these things,' he said almost gently. 'It seems only fair that you should know.'

I began walking back in the direction from which I had come.

'My duties are with the child,' I answered somewhat brusquely. 'I am not here for any other purpose.'

'But how can even a governess, overburdened with common sense though she may be, know to what purposes fate will put her?'

'I think I know what is expected of me.' I was alarmed because he walked beside me; I wanted to escape from him that I might be alone with my thoughts. I felt this man impaired my precious dignity to which I was clinging with that determination only possible to those who are in constant fear of losing what little they possess. He had mocked me in the train. I felt he was waiting for an opportunity to do so again.

'I am sure you do.'

'There is no need for you to escort me back to the house.'

'I am forced to contradict you. There is every reason.'

'Do you think I am incapable of looking after myself?'

'I think none more capable of doing that than yourself. But as it happens I was on my way to call, and this is the most direct way to the house.'

I was silent until we came to Mount Mellyn.

Connan TreMellyn was coming from the stable.

'Hallo there, Con!' cried Peter Nansellock.

Connan TreMellyn looked at us in mild surprise, which I supposed was due to the fact that we were together.

I hurried round to the back of the house.

It was not easy to sleep that night. The events of the day crowded into my mind and I saw pictures of myself and Connan TreMellyn, pictures of Alvean, of Celestine, and of myself in the woods with Peter Nansellock.

The wind was in a certain direction that night, and I could hear the waves thundering into Mellyn Cove.

In my present mood it certainly seemed that there were whispering voices down there, and that the words they said to each other were: 'Alice! Alice! Where is Alice? Alice, where are you?'

Chapter Three

In the morning the fancies of the previous night seemed foolish. I asked myself why so many people – including myself – wanted to make a mystery of what had happened in this house. It was an ordinary enough story.

I know what it is, I told myself. When people consider an ancient house like this, they make themselves believe it could tell some fantastic stories if it could only speak. They think of the generations who have lived and suffered within these walls, and they grow fanciful. So that when the mistress of the house is tragically killed they imagine her ghost still walks and that, although she is dead, she is still here. Well, I am a sensible woman, I hope. Alice was killed on a train, and that was the end of Alice.

I laughed at my folly in allowing myself to be caught up in such notions. Had not Daisy or Kitty explained that the whispering voices, which I heard in the night, were merely the sound of waves thundering in the cove below?

From now on I was entertaining no more such fantastic thoughts.

My room was filled with sunshine and I felt differently from the way I had felt on any other morning. I was exhilarated. I knew why. It was due to that man, Connan TreMellyn. Not that I liked him – quite the reverse; but it was as though he had issued a challenge. I was going to make a success of this job. I was going to make of Alvean not only a model pupil but a charming, unaffected, uninhibited little girl.

I felt so pleased that I began to hum softly under my breath.

Come into the Garden, Maud . . . That was a song Father used to like to play while Phillida sang, for in addition to her other qualities Phillida possessed a charming voice. Then I passed to *Sweet and Low*, and I for a moment forgot the house I was in and saw Father at the piano, his glasses slipping down his nose, his slippered feet making the most of the pedals.

I was almost astonished to find that I had unconsciously slipped into the song I had heard Gilly singing in the woods: *Alice, where are thou—*

Oh no, not that, I said sharply to myself.

I heard the sound of horses' hoofs and I went to the window to look out. No one was visible. The lawns looked fresh and lovely with the early morning dew on them. What a beautiful sight, I thought; the palm trees gave the scene a tropical look and it was one of those mornings when there was every promise of a beautiful day.

'One of the last we can expect this summer, I daresay,' I said aloud; and I threw open my window and leaned out, my thick coppery plaits, the ends tied with pieces of blue ribbon for bedtime, swinging out with me.

I went back to *Sweet and Low* and was humming this when Connan TreMellyn emerged from the stables. He saw me before I was able to draw back, and I felt myself grow scarlet with embarrassment to be seen with my hair down and in my nightgown thus.

He called jauntily: 'Good morning, Miss Leigh.'

In that moment I said to myself: So it was his horse I heard. And has he been riding in the early morning, or out all night? I imagined his visiting one of the gay ladies of the neighbourhood if such existed. That was my opinion of him. I was angry that he should be the one to show no embarrassment whatsoever while I was blushing – certainly in every part that was visible.

'Good morning,' I said, and my voice sounded curt.

He was coming swiftly across the lawn, hoping, I was sure, to embarrass me further by a closer look at me in my night attire.

'A beautiful morning,' he cried.

'Extremely so,' I answered.

I withdrew into my room as I heard him shout: 'Hallo, Alvean! So you're up too.'

I was standing well back from the window now and I heard Alvean cry: 'Hallo, Papa!' and her voice was soft and gentle with that wistful note which I had detected when she spoke of him on the previous day. I knew that she was delighted to have seen him, that she had been awake in her room when she had heard his voice, and had dashed to her window, and that it would make her extremely happy if he stopped awhile and chatted with her.

He did no such thing. He went into the house. Standing before my mirror, I looked at myself. Most unbecoming, I thought. And quite undignified. Myself in a pink flannelette nightdress buttoned high at the throat, with my hair down and my face even now the colour of the flannelette!

I put on my dressing gown and on impulse crossed the schoolroom to Alvean's room. I opened the door and went in. She was sitting astride a chair and talking to herself.

'There's nothing to be afraid of really. All you have to do is hold tight and not be afraid . . . and you won't fall off.'

She was so intent on what she was doing that she had not heard the door open, and I stood for a few seconds watching her, for she had her back to the schoolroom door.

I learnt a great deal in that moment. He was a great horseman, this father of hers; he wanted his daughter to be a good horsewoman, but Alvean, who desperately wanted to win his approval, was afraid of horses.

I started forward, my first impulse to talk to her, to tell her that I would teach her to ride. It was the one thing I could do really well because we had always had horses in the country, and at five Phillida and I were competing in local shows.

But I hesitated because I was beginning to understand Alvean. She was an unhappy child. Tragedy had hit her in more ways than one. She had lost her mother, and that was the biggest tragedy which could befall any child; but when her father did not seem anything but indifferent to her, and she adored him, that was a double tragedy.

I quietly shut the door and went back to my room. I looked at the sunshine on the carpet and my elation returned. I *was* going to make a success of this job. I was going to fight Connan TreMellyn, if he wanted it that way. I was going to make him proud of his daughter; I was going to force him to give her that attention which was her right and which none but a brute would deny her.

Lessons were trying that morning. Alvean was late for them, having breakfasted with her father in accordance with the custom of the family. I pictured them at the big table in the room which I had discovered was used as a dining room when there were no guests. They called it the small dining room, but it was only small by Mount Mellyn standards.

He would be reading the paper, or looking through his letters, I imagined; Alvean would be at the other end of the table hoping for a word, which of course he would be too selfish to bestow.

I had to send for her to come to lessons; and that she deeply resented.

I tried to make lessons as interesting as I could, and I must have succeeded, for in spite of her resentment towards me she could not hide her interest in the history and geography lessons which I set for that morning.

She took luncheon with her father while I ate alone in the schoolroom, and after that I decided to approach Connan TreMellyn.

While I was wondering where I could find him I saw him leave the house and go across to the stables. I immediately followed him and, when I arrived at the stables, I heard him giving orders to Billy Trehay to saddle Royal Russet for him.

He looked surprised to see me; and then he smiled and I was sure that he was remembering the last time he had seen me – in dishabille.

'Why,' he said, 'it is Miss Leigh.'

'I had hoped to have a few words with you,' I said primly. 'Perhaps this is an inconvenient time.'

'That depends,' he said, 'on how many words you wish us to exchange.' He took out his watch and looked at it. 'I can give you five minutes, Miss Leigh.'

I was aware of Billy Trehay, and if Connan TreMellyn was going to snub me I was eager that no servant should overhear.

Connan TreMellyn said: 'Let us walk across the lawn. Ready in five minutes, Billy?'

'Very good, Master,' answered Billy.

With that Connan TreMellyn began to walk away from the stables, and I fell into step beside him.

'In my youth,' I said, 'I was constantly in the saddle. I believe Alvean wishes to learn to ride. I am asking your permission to teach her.'

'You have my permission to try, Miss Leigh,' he said.

'You sound as though you doubt my ability to succeed.'

'I fear I do.'

'I don't understand why you should doubt my ability to teach when you have not tested my skill.'

'Oh, Miss Leigh,' he said almost mockingly, 'you wrong me. It is not your ability to teach that I doubt; it is Alvean's to learn.'

'You mean others have failed to teach her?'

'I have failed.'

'But surely—'

He lifted a hand. 'It is strange,' he said, 'to find such fear in a child. Most children take to it like breathing.'

His tone was clipped, his expression hard; I wanted to shout at him: What sort of father are you! I pictured the lessons, the lack of understanding, the expectation of miracles. No wonder the child had been scared.

He went on: 'There are some people who can never learn to ride.'

Before I could stop myself I had burst out: 'There are some people who cannot teach.'

He stopped to stare at me in astonishment, and I knew that nobody in this house had ever dared to talk to him in such a way.

I thought: This is it. I shall now be told that my services are no longer required, and at the end of the month I may pack my bags and depart.

There was a violent temper there, and I could see that he was fighting to control it. He still looked at me and I could not read the expression in those light eyes. I believed it was contemptuous. Then he glanced back at the stables.

'You must excuse me, Miss Leigh,' he said; and he left me.

I went straight back to Alvean. I found her in the schoolroom. There was the sullen defiant look in her eyes, and I believed she had seen me talking to her father.

I came straight to the point. 'Your father has said I may give you riding lessons, Alvean. Would you like that?'

I saw the muscles of her face tighten, and my heat sank. Would it be possible to teach a child who was as scared as that?

I went on quickly, before she had time to answer: 'When we were your age my sister and I were keen riders. She was two years younger than I and we used to compete together in the local shows. The exciting days in our lives were those when there was a horse show in our village.'

'They have them here,' she said.

'It's great fun. And once you've really mastered the trick you feel quite at home in the saddle.'

She was silent for a moment, then she said: 'I can't do it. I don't like horses.'

'You don't like horses!' My voice was shocked. 'Why, they're the gentlest creatures in the world.'

'They're not. They don't like me. I rode Grey Mare and she ran fast and wouldn't stop, and if Tapperty hadn't caught her rein she would have killed me.'

'Grey Mare wasn't the mount for you. You should have a pony to start with.'

'Then I had Buttercup. She was as bad in a different way. She wouldn't go when I tried to make her. She took a mouthful of the bushes on the bank and I tugged and tugged and she wouldn't move for me. When Billy Trehay said "Come on, Buttercup," she just let go and started walking away as though it were all my fault.'

I laughed and she threw me a look of hatred. I hastened to assure her that was the way horses behaved until they understood you. When they did understand you they loved you as though you were their very dear friend.

I saw the wistful look in her eyes then and I exulted because I knew that the reason for aggressiveness was to be found in her intense loneliness and desire for affection.

I said: 'Look here, Alvean, come out with me now. Let's see what we can do together.'

She shook her head and looked at me suspiciously. I knew she felt that I might be trying to punish her for her ungraciousness towards me by making her look foolish. I wanted to put my arm about her, but I knew that was no way to approach Alvean.

'There's one thing to learn before you can begin to ride,' I said as though I had not noticed her gesture, 'and that is to love your horse. Then you won't be afraid. As soon as you're not afraid, your horse will begin to love you. He'll know you're his master, and he wants a master; but it must be a tender, loving master.'

She was giving me her attention now.

'When a horse runs away as Grey Mare did, that means that she is frightened. She's as frightened as you are, and her way of showing it is to run. Now when you're frightened you should never let her know it. You just whisper to her, "it's all right, Grey Mare . . . I'm here." As for Buttercup – she's a mischievous old nag. She's lazy and she knows that you can't handle her, so she won't do as she's told. But once you let her know you're the master she'll obey. Look how she did with Billy Trehay!'

'I didn't know Grey Mare was frightened of me,' she said.

'Your father wants you to ride,' I told her.

It was the wrong thing to have said; it reminded her of past fears, past humiliations; I saw the stubborn fear return to her eyes, and felt a new burst of resentment towards that arrogant man who could be so careless of the feelings of a child.

'Wouldn't it be fun,' I said, 'to surprise him. I mean ... suppose you learned and you could jump and gallop, and he didn't know about it ... until he saw you do it.'

It hurt me to see the joy in her face and I wondered how any man could be so callous as to deny a child the affection she asked.

'Alvean,' I said. 'Let's try.'

'Yes,' she said, 'let's try. I'll go and change into my things.'

I gave a little cry of disappointment, remembering that I had no riding habit with me. During my years with Aunt Adelaide I had had little opportunity for wearing it. Aunt Adelaide was no horsewoman herself and consequently was never invited to the country to hunt. Thus I had no opportunity for riding. To ride in Rotten Row would have been far beyond my means. When I had last looked at my riding clothes I had seen that the moth had got at them. I had felt resigned. I believed that I should never need them again.

Alvean was looking at me and I told her: 'I have no riding clothes.'

Her face fell and then lit up. 'Come with me,' she said. She was almost conspiratorial and I enjoyed this new relationship between us which I felt to be a great advance towards friendship.

We went along the gallery until we were in that part of the house which Mrs. Polgrey had told me was not for me. Alvean paused before a door and I had the impression that she was steeling herself to go in. She at length threw open the door and stood aside for me to enter, and I could not help feeling that she wanted me to go in first.

It was a small room which I judged to be a dressing room. In it was a long mirror, a tallboy, a chest of drawers and an oak chest. Like most of the rooms in the house this room had two doors. These rooms in the gallery appeared to lead from one to another, and this other door was slightly opened and, as Alvean went to it and looked round the room beyond, I followed her.

It was a bedroom in there. A large room beautifully furnished, the floor carpeted in blue, the curtains of blue velvet; the bed was a four-poster and, although I knew it to be large, it was dwarfed by the size of the room.

Alvean seemed distressed to see my interest in the bedroom. She went to the communicating door and shut it.

'There are lots of clothes here,' she said. 'In the chests and the tallboy. There's bound to be riding clothes. There'll be something you can have.'

She had thrown up the lid of the chest and it was something new for me to see her so excited. I was delighted to have discovered a way to her affections that I allowed myself to be carried along.

In the chest were dresses, petticoats, hats and boots.

Alvean said quickly: 'There are a lot of clothes in the attics. Great trunks of them. They were grandmamma's and great grandmamma's. When there were parties they used to dress up in them and play charades—'

I held up a lady's black beaver hat – obviously meant to be worn for riding. I put it on my head and Alvean laughed with a little catch in her voice. That laughter moved me more than anything had done since I had entered this house. It was the laughter of a child who is unaccustomed to laughter and laughs in a manner which is almost guilty. I determined to have her laughing often and without the slightest feeling of guilt.

She suddenly controlled herself as though she remembered where she was. 'You look so funny in it, Miss,' she said.

I got up and stood before the long mirror. I certainly looked unlike myself. My eyes were brilliant, my hair looked quite copper against the black. I decided that I looked slightly less unattractive than usual, and that was what Alvean meant by 'funny'.

'Not in the least like a governess,' she explained. She was pulling out a dress, and I saw that it was a riding habit made of black woollen cloth and trimmed with braid and ball fringe. It had a blue collar and blue cuffs and it was elegantly cut.

I held it up against myself. 'I think,' I said, 'that this would fit.'

'Try it on,' said Alvean. Then . . . 'No, not here. You take it to your room and put it on.' She suddenly seemed obsessed by the desire to get out of this room. She picked up the hat and ran to the door. I thought that she was eager for us to get started on our lesson, and there was not a great deal of time if we were to be back for tea at four.

I picked up the dress, took the hat from her and went back to my room. She hurried through to hers, and I immediately put on the riding habit.

It was not a perfect fit, but I had never been used to expensive clothes and was prepared to forget it was a little tight at the waist, and that the sleeves were on the short side, for a new woman looked back at me from my mirror, and when I set the beaver hat on my head I was delighted with myself.

I ran along to Alvean's room; she was in her habit, and when she saw me her eyes lit up and she seemed to look at me with greater interest than ever before.

We went down to the stables and I told Billy Trehay to saddle Buttercup for Alvean and another horse for myself as we were going to have a riding lesson.

He looked at me with some astonishment, but I told him that we had little time and were impatient to begin.

When we were ready I put Buttercup on a leading rein and took her with Alvean on her back into the paddock.

For nearly an hour we were there and when we left it I knew that Alvean and I had entered into a new relationship. She had not accepted me completely – that would have been asking too much – but I did believe that from that afternoon she knew that I was not an enemy.

I concentrated on giving her confidence. I made her grow accustomed to sitting her horse, to talking to her horse. I made her lean back full length on Buttercup's back and look up at the sky; then I made her shut her eyes. I gave her lessons in mounting and dismounting. Buttercup did no more than walk round that field, but I do believe that at the end of the hour I had done a great deal towards making Alvean lose her fear; and that was what I had determined should be the first lesson.

I was astonished to find that it was half past three, and I think Alvean was too.

'We must return to the house at once,' I said, 'if we are to change in time for tea.'

As we came out of the field a figure rose from the grass and I saw to my surprise that it was Peter Nansellock.

He clapped his hands as we came along.

'Here endeth the first lesson,' he cried, 'and an excellent one. I did not know,' he went on, turning to me, 'that equestrian skill was included in your many accomplishments.'

'Were you watching us, Uncle Peter?' demanded Alvean.

'For the last half hour. My admiration for you both is beyond expression.'

Alvean smiled slowly. 'Did you really admire us?'

'Much as I could be tempted to compliment two beautiful ladies,' he said placing his hand on his heart and bowing elegantly, 'I could never tell a lie.'

'Until this moment,' I said tartly.

Alvean's face fell and I added: 'There is nothing very admirable in learning to ride. Thousands are doing it every day.'

'But the art was never so gracefully taught, never so patiently learned.'

'Your uncle is a joker, Alvean,' I put in.

'Yes,' said Alvean almost sadly, 'I know.'

'And,' I added, 'it is time that we returned for tea.'

'I wonder if I might be invited to schoolroom tea?'

'You are calling to see Mr. TreMellyn?' I asked.

'I am calling to take tea with you two ladies.'

Alvean laughed suddenly; I could see that she was not unaffected by what I supposed was the charm of this man.

'Mr. TreMellyn left Mount Mellyn early this afternoon,' I said. 'I have no idea whether or not he has returned.'

'And while the cat's away . . .' he murmured, and his eyes swept over my costume in a manner which I could only describe as insolent.

I said coolly: 'Come along, Alvean, we must go at once if we are to be in time for tea.'

I let the horse break into a trot, and holding Buttercup's leading rein, started towards the house.

Peter Nansellock walked behind us, and when we reached the stables I saw him making for the house.

Alvean and I dismounted, handed our horses to two of the stable boys, and hurried up to our rooms.

I got out of the riding habit and into my dress and, glancing at myself, I thought how drab I looked in my grey cotton. I made a gesture of impatience at my folly and picked up the riding habit to hang in my cupboard, deciding that I would take the first opportunity of asking Mrs. Polgrey if it was in order for me to use it. I was afraid I had acted on impulse by doing so this afternoon, but I had been stung into prompt action, I realized, by the attitude of Connan TreMellyn.

As I lifted the habit I saw the name on the waist band. It gave me a little start, as I suppose everything in that connection would do for some time. 'Alice TreMellyn' was embossed in neat and tiny letters on the black satin facings.

Then I understood. That room had been her dressing room; the bedroom I had glimpsed, her bedroom. I wondered that Alvean had taken me there and given me her mother's clothes.

My heart felt as though it were leaping into my throat. This, I said to myself, is absurd. Where else could we have found a modern riding habit? Not in those chests in the attics she had spoken of; the clothes in those were used for charades.

I was being ridiculous. Why should I not wear Alice's riding habit? She had no need for it now. And was I not accustomed to wearing cast-off clothes?

Boldly I picked up the riding dress and hung it in my cupboard.

I was impelled to go to my window and looked along the line of windows, trying to place that one which would have been that of her bedroom. I thought I placed it.

In spite of myself I shivered. Then I shook myself. She would be glad I used her habit, I told myself. Of course she would be glad. Am I not trying to help her daughter?

I realized that I was reassuring myself – which was ridiculous.

What had happened to my commonsense? Whatever I told myself I could not hide the fact that I wished the dress had belonged to anyone but Alice.

When I had changed there was a knock on my door and I was relieved to see Mrs. Polgrey standing there.

'Do come in,' I said. 'You are just the lady I wished to see.'

She came into my room, and I was very fond of her in that moment. There was an air of normality about her such as must inevitably put fancy to flight.

'I have been giving Miss Alvean a riding lesson,' I said quickly, for I was anxious to have this matter of the dress settled before she could tell me why she had come. 'And as I had no riding habit with me she found one for me. I believe it to have been her mother's.' I went to my wardrobe and produced it.

Mrs. Polgrey nodded.

'I wore it this once. Perhaps it was wrong of me.'

'Did you have the Master's permission to give her this riding lesson?'

'Oh yes, indeed. I made sure of that.'

'Then there is nothing to worry about. He would have no objection to your wearing the dress. I can see no reason why you should not keep it in your room, providing of course you only wear it when giving Miss Alvean her riding lesson.'

'Thank you,' I said. 'You have set my mind at rest.'

Mrs. Polgrey bowed her head in approval. I could see that she was rather pleased that I had brought my little problem to her.

'Mr. Peter Nansellock is downstairs,' she said.

'Yes, we saw him as we came in.'

'The Master is not at home. And Mr. Peter has asked that you entertain him for tea – you and Miss Alvean.'

'Oh, but should we . . . I mean should I?'

'Well, yes, Miss, I think it would be in order. I think that is what the Master would wish, particularly as Mr. Peter suggests it. Miss Jansen, during the time she was here, often helped to entertain. Why, there was an occasion I remember, when she was invited to the dinner table.'

'Oh!' I said, hoping I sounded duly impressed.

'You see, Miss, having no mistress in the house, makes it a little difficult at times; and when a gentleman expressly asks for your company – well, I really don't see what harm there could be in it. I have told Mr. Nansellock that tea will be served in the punch room and that I am sure you will be ready to join him and Miss Alvean. You have no objection?'

'No, no. I have no objection.'

Mrs. Polgrey smiled graciously. 'Then will you come down?'

'Yes, I will.'

She sailed out as majestically as she had arrived; and I found myself smiling not without a little complacence. It was turning out to be a most enjoyable day.

When I reached the punch room, Alvean was not there but Peter Nansellock was sprawling in one of the tapestry-covered chairs.

He leaped to his feet on my entrance.

'But this is delightful.'

'Mrs. Polgrey has told me that I am to do the honours in the absence of Mr. TreMellyn.'

'How like you, to remind me that you are merely the governess!'

'I felt,' I replied, 'that it was necessary to do so, since you may have forgotten.'

'You are such a charming hostess! And indeed I never saw you look less like a governess than when you were giving Alvean her lesson.'

'It was my riding habit. Borrowed plumes. A pheasant would look like a peacock, if it could acquire the tail.'

'My dear Miss Pheasant, I do not agree. "Manners makyth the man" – or woman – not fine feathers. But let me ask you this before our little Alvean appears. What do you think of this place? You are going to stay with us?'

'It is really more a question of how this place likes me, and whether the powers that be decide to keep me.'

'Ah – the powers that be in this case are a little unaccountable, are they not? What do you think of old Connan?'

'The adjective you use is inaccurate, and it is not my place to give an opinion.'

He laughed aloud showing white and perfect teeth. 'Dear Governess,' he said, 'you'll be the death of me.'

'I'm sorry to hear it.'

'Though,' he went on, 'I have often thought that to die of laughing must be a very pleasant way to do so.'

This banter was interrupted by the appearance of Alvean.

'Ah, the little lady herself!' cried Peter. 'Dear Alvean, how good it is of you and Miss Leigh to allow me to take tea with you.'

'I wonder why you want to,' replied Alvean. 'You never have before . . . except when Miss Jansen was here.'

'Hush, hush! You betray me,' he murmured.

Mrs. Polgrey came in with Kitty. The latter set the tray on a table, while Mrs. Polgrey lighted the spirit lamp. I saw that a canister of tea was on the tray. Kitty laid a cloth on a small table and brought in cakes and cucumber sandwiches.

'Miss, would you care to make the tea yourself?' asked Mrs. Polgrey. I said I would do so with pleasure, and Mrs. Polgrey signed to Kitty, who was staring at Peter Nansellock with an expression close to idolatry.

Kitty seemed reluctant to leave the room and I felt it was unkind to have dismissed her. I believed that Mrs. Polgrey was also to some extent under the spell of the man. It must be, I told myself, because he is such a contrast to the master. Peter managed to flatter with a look, and I had noticed that he was ready to lavish this flattery on all females; Kitty, Mrs. Polgrey and Alvean, no less than on myself.

So much for its worth! I told myself and I felt a little piqued, for the man had that comforting quality of making any woman in his company feel that she was an attractive one.

I made tea and Alvean handed him bread and butter.

'What luxury!' he cried. 'I feel like a sultan with two beautiful ladies to wait on me.'

'You're telling lies again,' cried Alvean. 'We're neither of us ladies, because I'm not grown up and Miss is a governess.'

'What sacrilege!' he murmured, and his warm eyes were on me, almost caressingly. I felt uncomfortably embarrassed under his scrutiny.

I changed the conversation briskly. 'I think Alvean will make a good horsewoman in time,' I said. 'What was your opinion?'

I saw how eagerly the girl waited on his words.

'She'll be the champion of Cornwall; you see!'

She could not hide her pleasure.

'And,' he lifted a finger and wagged it at her – 'don't forget whom you have to thank for it.'

The glance Alvean threw at me was almost shy, and I felt suddenly happy, and glad that I was here. My resentment against life had never been so far away; I had ceased to envy my charming sister. At that moment there was only one person I wanted to be: That person was Martha Leigh, sitting in the punch room taking tea with Peter Nansellock and Alvean TreMellyn.

Alvean said: 'It's to be a secret for a while.'

'Yes, we're going to surprise her father.'

'I'll be as silent as the grave.'

'Why do people say "silent as the grave"?' asked Alvean.

'Because,' put in Peter, 'dead men don't talk.'

'Sometimes they have ghosts perhaps,' said Alvean looking over her shoulder.

'What Mr. Nansellock meant,' I said quickly, 'was that he will keep our little secret. Alvean, I believe Mr. Nansellock would like some more cucumber sandwiches.'

She leapt up to offer them to him; it was very pleasant to have her so docile and friendly.

'You have not paid a visit to Mount Widden yet, Miss Leigh,' he said.

'It had not occurred to me to do so.'

'That is a little unneighbourly. Oh, I know what you're going to say. You did not come here to pay calls; you came to be a governess.'

'It is true,' I retorted.

'The house is not as ancient nor as large as this one. It has no history, but it's a pleasant place and I'm sure my sister would be delighted if you and Alvean paid us a visit one day. Why not come over and take tea with us?'

'I am not sure . . .' I began.

'That it lies within your duties? I'll tell you how we'll arrange it. You shall bring Miss Alvean to take tea at Mount Widden. Bringing her to us and taking her home again, I am sure, would come well within the duties of the most meticulous governess.'

'When shall we come?' asked Alvean.

'This is an open invitation.'

I smiled. I knew what that meant. He was again talking for the sake of talking; he had no intention of asking me to tea. I pictured him, coming over to the house, attempting a flirtation with Miss Jansen who, by all accounts, was an attractive young woman. I knew his sort, I told myself.

The door opened suddenly and, to my embarrassment – which I hoped I managed to hide – Connan TreMellyn came in.

I felt as though I had been caught playing the part of mistress of the house in his absence.

I rose to my feet, and he gave me a quick smile. 'Miss Leigh,' he said, 'is there a cup of tea for me?'

'Alvean,' I said, 'ring for another cup, please.'

She got up to do so immediately but she had changed. Now she was alert, eager to do the right thing and please her father. It made her somewhat clumsy, and as she rose from her chair she knocked over her cup of tea. She flushed scarlet with mortification.

I said: 'Never mind. Ring the bell. Kitty will clear it up when she comes.'

I knew that Connan TreMellyn was watching with some amusement. If I had known he would return I should have been very reluctant to entertain Peter Nansellock to tea in the punch room, which I was sure my employer felt was definitely not my part of the house.

Peter said: 'It was most kind of Miss Leigh to act as hostess. I begged her to do so, and she graciously consented.'

'It was certainly kind,' said Connan TreMellyn lightly.

Kitty came and I indicated the mess of tea and broken china on the carpet. 'And please bring another cup for Mr. TreMellyn,' I added.

Kitty was smirking a little as she went out. The situation evidently amused her. As for myself, I felt it ill became me. I was not the type to make charming play with the teacups and, now that the Master of the house had appeared, I felt awkward, even as I knew Alvean had. *I* must be careful to avoid disaster.

'Had a busy day, Connan?' asked Peter.

Connan TreMellyn then began to talk of complicated estate business, which I felt might have been to remind me that my duties consisted of dispensing tea and nothing else. I was not to imagine that I was in truth a hostess. I was there as an upper servant, nothing more.

I felt angry with him for coming in and spoiling my little triumph. I wondered how he would react when I presented him with the good little horsewoman I was determined Alvean was to become. He would probably make some slighting remark and show us such indifference that we should feel our trouble was wasted.

You poor child, I thought, you are trying to win the affections of a man who doesn't know the meaning of affection. Poor Alvean! Poor Alice!

Then it seemed to me that Alice had intruded into the punch room. In that moment I pictured her more clearly than I had ever done before. She was a woman of about my height, a little more slender at the waist – but then I had never gone in wholeheartedly for tight lacing – a trifle shorter. I could fit this figure into a black riding habit with blue collar and cuffs and black beaver hat. All that was vague and shadowy was the face.

The cup and saucer was brought to me and I poured out his tea. He was watching me, expecting me to rise and take it to him.

'Alvean,' I said, 'please pass this to your father.'

And she was very eager to do so.

He said a brief 'thanks,' and Peter took advantage of the pause to draw me into the conversation.

'Miss Leigh and I met on the train on the day she arrived.'

'Really?'

'Indeed, yes. Although of course she was not aware of my identity. How could she be? She had never heard then of the famous Nansellocks. She did not even know of the existence of Mount Widden. I knew her of course. By some strange irony of chance I shared her compartment.'

'That,' said Connan, 'is very interesting.' And he looked as though nothing could be less so.

'So,' went on Peter, 'it was a great surprise to her when she found that we were near neighbours.'

'I trust,' said Connan, 'that it was not an unpleasant one.'

'By no means,' I said.

'Thank you, Miss Leigh, for those kind words,' said Peter.

I looked at my watch, and said: 'I am going to ask you to excuse Alvean and me. It is nearly five o'clock and we have our studies between five and six.'

'And we must,' said Connan, 'on no account interfere with those.'

'But surely,' cried Peter, 'on such an occasion there could be a little relaxation of the rules.'

Alvean was looking eager. She was unhappy in her father's presence but she could not bear to leave it.

'I think it would be most unwise,' I said, rising. 'Come along, Alvean.'

She threw me a look of dislike and I believed that I had forfeited the advance I had made that afternoon.

'Please, Papa . . .' she began.

He looked at her sternly. 'My dear child, you heard what your governess said.'

Alvean blushed and looked uncomfortable, but I was already saying 'Good afternoon' to Peter Nansellock and making my way to the door.

In the schoolroom Alvean glared at me.

'Why do you have to spoil everything?' she demanded.

'Spoil?' I repeated. 'Everything?'

'We could have done our reading any time . . . any time—'

'But we do our reading between five and six, not any time,' I retorted, and my voice sounded the colder because I was afraid of the emotion which was rising in me. I wanted to explain to her: You love your father. You long for his approval. But, my dear child, you do not know the way to make it yours. Let me help you. But of course I said no such thing. I had never been demonstrative and could not begin to be so now.

'Come,' I went on, 'we have only an hour, so let us not waste a minute of that time.'

She sat at the table sullenly glaring at the book which we were reading. It was Mr. Dickens's *Pickwick Papers* which I had thought would bring light relief into my pupil's rather serious existence.

She had lost her habitual enthusiasm; she was not even attending, for she looked up suddenly and said: 'I believe you hate him. I believe you cannot bear to be in his company.'

I replied: 'I do not know to whom you refer, Alvean.'

'You do,' she accused. 'You know I mean my father.'

'What nonsense,' I murmured; but I was afraid my colour would deepen. 'Come,' I said, 'we are wasting time.'

And so I concentrated on the book and told myself that we could not read together the nightly adventure concerning the elderly lady in curlpapers. That would be most unsuitable for a child of Alvean's age.

That night when Alvean had retired to her room I went for a stroll in the woods. I was beginning to look upon these woods as a place of refuge, a place in which to be quiet and think about my life while I wondered what shape it would take.

The day had been eventful, a pleasant day until Connan TreMellyn had come into it and disturbed the peace. I wondered if his business ever took him away for long periods – really long periods, not merely a matter of a few days. If this were so, I thought, I might have a chance of making Alvean into a happier little girl.

Forget the man, I admonished myself. Avoid him when possible. You can do no more than that.

It was all very well but, even when he was not present, he intruded into my thoughts.

I stayed in the woods until it was almost dusk. Then I made for the house, and I had not been in my room more than a few minutes when Kitty knocked.

'I thought I 'eard 'ee come in, Miss,' she said. 'Master be asking for 'ee. He be in his library.'

'Then you had better take me there,' I said, 'for it is a room I have never visited.'

I should have liked to comb my hair and tidy myself a little, but I had a notion that Kitty was constantly looking for one aspect of the relationship between any man or woman and I was not going to have her thinking that I was preening myself before appearing before the master.

She led me to a wing of the house which I had as yet not visited, and the vastness of Mount Mellyn was brought home to me afresh. These, I gathered, were the apartments which were set aside for his especial use, for they seemed more luxurious than any other part of the house which I had so far seen.

Kitty opened a door, and with that vacuous smile on her face announced: 'Miss be here, Master.'

'Thank you, Kitty,' he said. And then, 'Oh, come along in, Miss Leigh.'

He was sitting at a table on which were leather-bound books and papers. The only light came from a rose quartz lamp on the table.

He said: 'Do sit down, Miss Leigh.'

I thought: He has discovered that I wore Alice's riding habit. He is shocked. He is going to tell me that my services are no longer required.

I held my head high, even haughtily, waiting.

'I was interested to learn this afternoon,' he began, 'that you had already made the acquaintance of Mr. Nansellock.'

'Really?' The surprise in my voice was not assumed.

'Of course,' he went on, 'it was inevitable that you would meet him sooner or later. He and his sister are constant visitors at the house, but—'

'But you feel that it is unnecessary that he should make the acquaintance of your daughter's governess,' I said quickly.

'That necessity, Miss Leigh,' he replied reprovingly, 'is surely for you or him to decide.'

I felt embarrassed and I stumbled on: 'I imagine that you feel that, as a governess, it is unbecoming of me to be ... on terms of apparently equal footing with a friend of your family.'

'I beg you, Miss Leigh, do not put words into my mouth which I had no intention of uttering. What friends you make, I do assure you, must be entirely your own concern. But your aunt, in a manner of speaking, put you under my care when she put you under my roof, and I have asked you to come here that I may offer you a word of advice on a subject which, I fear, you may think a little indelicate.'

I was flushing scarlet and my embarrassment was not helped by the fact that this, I was sure, secretly amused him.

'Mr. Nansellock has a reputation for being ... how shall I put it ... susceptible to young ladies.'

'Oh!' I cried, unable to suppress the exclamation, so great was my discomfort.

'Miss Leigh.' He smiled, and for a moment his face looked almost tender. 'This is in the nature of a warning.'

'Mr. TreMellyn,' I cried, recovering myself with an effort, 'I do not think I am in need of such a warning.'

'He is very handsome,' he went on, and the mocking note had come back to his voice. 'He has a reputation for being a charming fellow. There was a young lady here before you, a Miss Jansen. He often called to see her. Miss Leigh, I do beg of you not to misunderstand me. And there is another thing I would also ask: Please do not take all that Mr. Nansellock says too seriously.'

I heard myself say in a high-pitched voice unlike my habitual tone: 'It is extremely kind of you, Mr. TreMellyn, to concern yourself with my welfare.'

'But of course I concern myself with your welfare. You are here to look after my daughter. Therefore it is of the utmost importance to me.'

He rose and I did the same. I saw that this was dismissal.

He came swiftly to my side and placed his hand on my shoulder.

'Forgive me,' he said. 'I am a blunt man, lacking in those graces which are so evident in Mr. Nansellock. I merely wish to offer you a friendly warning.'

For a few seconds I looked into those cool light eyes and I thought I had a fleeting glimpse of the man behind the mask. I was sobered suddenly and, in a moment of bewildering emotions, I was deeply conscious of my loneliness, of the tragedy of those who are alone in the world with no one who really cares for them. Perhaps it was self-pity. I do not know. My feelings in that moment were so mixed that I cannot even at this day define them.

'Thank you,' I said; and I escaped from the library back to my room.

Each day Alvean and I went to the field and had an hour's riding. As I watched the little girl on Buttercup I knew that her father must have been extremely impatient with her, for the child, though not a born rider perhaps, would soon be giving a good account of herself.

I had discovered that every November a horse show was held in Mellyn village, and I had told Alvean that she should certainly enter for one of the events.

It was enjoyable planning this, because Connan TreMellyn would be one of the judges and we both imagined his astonishment when a certain rider, who came romping home with first prize, was his daughter who he had sworn would never learn to ride.

The triumph in that dream was something Alvean and I could both share. Hers was of course the more admirable emotion. She wanted to succeed for the sake of the love she bore her father; for myself I wanted to imply: See, you arrogant man, I have succeeded where you failed!

So every afternoon, I would put on Alice's riding habit (I had ceased to care to whom it had previously belonged, for it had become mine now) and we would go to the field and there I would put Alvean through her paces.

On the day we tried her first gallop we were elated.

Afterwards she returned to the stables with me and I watched her run on ahead after we had left the horses there. Every now and then she would jump into the air – a gesture, I thought, of complete joyousness. I knew she was seeing herself at the show anticipating that glorious moment when her father stared at her in astonishment and cried: 'You . . . Alvean! My dear child, I am proud of you.'

I was smiling to myself as I crossed the lawn in her wake. When I entered the house she was nowhere to be seen, and I pictured her taking the stairs several at a time.

This was more like the normal, happy child I intended her to become.

I mounted the first flight of stairs and came to a dark landing, when there was a step on the next flight, and I heard a quick gasp and voice which said: 'Alice!'

For a second my whole body seemed to freeze. Then I saw that Celestine Nansellock was standing on the stairs; she was gripping the banisters and was so white that I thought she was going to faint.

I understood. It was she who had spoken. She had seen me in Alice's riding habit and she believed in that second that I *was* Alice . . . or her ghost.

'Miss Nansellock,' I said quickly to reassure her, 'Alvean and I have been having a riding lesson.'

She swayed a little; her face had turned a greyish colour.

'I'm sorry I startled you,' I went on.

She murmured: 'For the moment I thought—'

'I think you should sit down, Miss Nansellock. You've had a shock.' I bounded up the stairs and took her arm. 'Would you care to come into my bedroom and sit down awhile?'

She nodded, and I noted that she was trembling.

'I am so sorry to have upset you,' I said as I threw open the door of my room. We went in, and I put her gently into a chair.

'Shall I ring for brandy?' I asked.

She shook her head. 'I'm all right now. You did startle me, Miss Leigh. I see now it is the clothes.'

'It is a little dark on that landing,' I said.

She repeated: 'For the moment, I thought. . . .' Then she looked at me again, fearfully, perhaps hopefully. I believed she was thinking that I was an apparition which had assumed the face of Martha Leigh, the governess, and would change at any moment.

I hastened to reassure her. 'It's only these clothes,' I said.

'Mrs. TreMellyn had a habit exactly like that. I remember the collar and cuffs so well. We went riding together . . . only a day or so before . . . You see, we were great friends, always together, and then. . . .' She turned away and wiped her eyes.

'You thought I was Mrs. TreMellyn returned from the dead.' I said. 'I understand.'

'It was so foolish of me. It seems so odd that you should have a riding habit . . . so exactly like hers.'

'This was hers,' I said.

She was startled. She put out a hand and touched the skirt. She held it between thumb and forefinger and her eyes had a hazy look as though she were staring into the past.

I went on quickly: 'I have to give Alvean riding lessons, and I lacked the suitable clothes. The child took me to what I now know to have been her mother's apartments, and found this for me. I asked Mrs. Polgrey if it were in order for me to wear it and she assured me that it was.'

'I see,' said Celestine. 'That explains everything. Please don't mention my folly, Miss Leigh. I'm glad no one else saw it.'

'But anyone might have been startled, particularly as—'

'As what?'

'As there seems to be this feeling about Alice . . . about Mrs. TreMellyn.'

'What feeling?'

'Perhaps there isn't a feeling. Perhaps it is my imagination only, but I did imagine that there was a belief in the house that she was not . . . at rest.'

'What an extraordinary thing to say! Why should she not be at rest? Who told you this?'

'I . . . I'm not sure,' I floundered. 'Perhaps it is merely my imagination. Perhaps no one suggested anything, and the idea just came to me. I'm sorry that I upset you.'

'You must not be sorry, Miss Leigh. You have been kind to me. I feel better now. She stood up. 'Don't tell anyone I was so silly. So you are giving Alvean riding lessons. I am glad. Tell me, are you getting along with her better now? I fancied, when you arrived, that there was a little antagonism . . . on her part.'

'She is the kind of child who would automatically be antagonistic to authority. Yes, I think we are becoming friends. These riding lessons have helped considerably. By the way, they are secret from her father.'

Celestine Nansellock looked a little shocked, and I hurried on: 'Oh, it is only her good progress which is a secret. He knows about the lessons. Naturally I asked his permission first. But he does not realize how well she is coming along. It is to be a surprise.'

'I see,' said Celestine. 'Miss Leigh, I do hope she is not over-strained by these lessons.'

'Strained? But why? She is a normal healthy child.'

'She is highly strung. I wonder whether she has the temperament to make a rider.'

'She is so young that we have a chance of forming her character, which will have its effect on her temperament. She is enjoying her lessons and is very eager to surprise her father.'

'So she is becoming your friend, Miss Leigh. I am glad of that. Now I must go. Thank you again for your kindness. And do remember . . . not a word to anyone.'

'Certainly not, if it is your wish.'

She smiled and went out.

I went to the mirror and looked at myself – I'm afraid this was becoming a habit since I had come here – and murmured: 'That might be Alice . . . apart from the face.' Then I half closed my eyes and let the face become blurred while I imagined a different face there.

Oh yes, it must have been a shock for Celestine.

And I was not to say anything. I was very willing to agree to this. I wondered what Connan TreMellyn would say if he knew that I was going about in his wife's clothes and frightened practical people like Celestine Nansellock when they saw me in dim places.

I felt he would not wish me to continue to look so like Alice.

So, since I needed Alice's clothes for my riding lessons with Alvean, and since I was determined they should continue, that I might have the pleasure of saying, I told you so! to Alvean's father, I was as anxious as Celestine Nansellock that nothing should be said about our encounter on the landing.

A week passed and I felt I was slipping into a routine. Lessons in the schoolroom and the riding field progressed favourably. Peter Nansellock came over to the house on two occasions, but I managed to elude him. I was deeply conscious of Connan TreMellyn's warning and I knew it to be reasonable. I faced the fact that I was stimulated by Peter Nansellock and that I could very easily find myself in a state of mind when I was looking forward to his visits. I had no intention of placing myself in that position for I did not need Connan TreMellyn to tell me that Peter Nansellock was a philanderer.

I thought now and then of his brother Geoffry, and I concluded that Peter must be very like him; and when I thought of Geoffry I thought also of Mrs. Polgrey's daughter of whom she had never spoken; Jennifer with the 'littlest waist you ever saw,' and a way of keeping herself to herself until she had lain in the hay or the gillyflowers with the fascinating Geoffry – the outcome of which had been that one day she walked into the sea.

I shivered to contemplate the terrible pitfalls which lay in wait for unwary women. There were unattractive ones like myself who depended on the whims of others for a living; but there were those even more unfortunate creatures, those who attracted the roving eyes of philanderers and found one day that the only bearable prospect life had to offer was its end.

My interest in Alvean's riding lessons and her father's personality had made me forget little Gillyflower temporarily. The child was so quiet that she was easily forgotten. Occasionally I heard her thin reedy voice, in that peculiar off-key singing out of doors or in the house. The Polgreys' room was immediately below my own, and Gillyflower's was next to theirs, so that when she sang in her own room her voice would float up to me.

I used to say to myself when I heard it: If she can learn songs she can learn other things.

I must have been given to day-dreams, for side by side with that picture of Connan TreMellyn, handing his daughter the first prize for horse-jumping at the November horse show and giving me an apologetic and immensely admiring and appreciative glance at the same time, there was another picture. This was of Gilly sitting at the schoolroom table side by side with Alvean, while I listened to whispering in the background: 'This could never have happened but for Miss Martha Leigh. You see she is a wonder with the children. Look what she had done for Alvean . . . and now for Gilly.'

But at this time Alvean was still a stubborn child and Gillyflower elusive and, as the Tapperty girls said: 'With a tile loose in the upper story.'

Then into those more or less peaceful days came two events to disturb me.

The first was of small moment, but it haunted me and I could not get it out of my mind.

I was going through one of Alvean's exercise books, marking her sums, while she was sitting at the table writing an essay; and as I turned the pages of the exercise book a piece of paper fell out.

It was covered with drawings. I had already discovered that Alvean had a distinct talent for drawing, and one day, when the opportunity offered itself, I intended to approach Connan TreMellyn about this, for I felt she should be encouraged. I myself could teach her only the rudiments of the art, but I believed she was worthy of a qualified drawing teacher.

The drawings were of faces. I recognized one of myself. It was not bad. Did I really look as prim as that? Not always, I hoped. But perhaps that was how she saw me. There was her father . . . several of him. He was quite recognizable too. I turned the page and this was covered with girls' faces. I was not sure who they were meant to be. Herself? No . . . that was Gilly, surely. And yet it had a look of herself.

I stared at the page. I was so intent that I did not realize she had leaned across the table until she snatched it away.

'That's mine,' she said.

'And that,' I retaliated, 'is extremely bad manners.'

'You have no right to pry.'

'My dear child, that paper was in your arithmetic book.'

'Then it had no right to be there.'

'You must take your revenge on the paper,' I said lightly. And then more seriously: 'I do beg of you not to snatch things in that ill-mannered way.'

'I'm sorry,' she murmured still defiantly.

I turned back to the sums, to most of which she had given inaccurate answers. Arithmetic was not one of her best subjects. Perhaps that was why she spent so much of her time drawing faces instead of getting on with her work. Why had she been so annoyed? Why had she drawn those faces which were part Gilly's, part her own?'

I said: 'Alvean, you will have to work harder at your sums.'

She grunted sullenly.

'You don't seem to have mastered the rules of practice nor even simple multiplication. Now if your arithmetic were half as good as your drawing I should be very pleased.'

Still she did not answer.

'Why did you not wish me to see the faces you had drawn? I thought some of them quite good.'

Still no answer.

'Particularly,' I went on, 'that one of your father.'

Even at such a time the mention of his name could bring that tender, wistful curve to her lips.

'And those girl's faces. Do tell me who they were supposed to be – you or Gilly?'

The smile froze on her lips. Then she said almost breathlessly: 'Who did you take them for, Miss?'

'Whom,' I corrected gently.

'*Whom* did you take them for then?'

'Well, let me look at them again.'

She hesitated, then she brought out the paper, and handed it to me; her eyes were eager.

I studied the faces. I said: 'This one could be either you or Gilly.'

'You think we're alike then?'

'N . . . no. I hadn't thought so until this moment.

'And now you do,' she said.

'You are of an age, and there often seems to be a resemblance between young people.'

'I'm not like her!' she cried passionately. 'I'm not like that . . . idiot.'

'Alvean, you must not use such a word. Don't you realize that it is extremely unkind?'

'It's true. But I'm not like her. I won't have you say it. If you say it again I'll ask my father to send you away. He will . . . if I ask him. I only have to ask and you'll go.'

She was shouting, trying to convince herself of two things, I realized. One that there was not the slightest resemblance between herself and Gilly, and the other that she only had to ask her father for something, and her wishes would be granted.

Why? I asked myself. What was the reason for this vehemence?

There was a shut-in expression on her face.

I said, calmly looking at the watch pinned to my grey cotton bodice: 'You have exactly ten minutes in which to finish your essay.'

I drew the arithmetic book towards me and pretended to give it my attention.

The second incident was even more upsetting.

It had been a moderately peaceful day, which meant that lessons had gone well. I had taken my late evening stroll in the woods and when I returned I saw two carriages drawn up in front of the house. One I recognized as from Mount Widden so I guessed that either Peter or Celestine was visiting. The other carriage I did not know, but I noticed a crest on it, and it was a very fine carriage. I wondered to whom it belonged before I told myself that it was no concern of mine.

I went swiftly up the back stairs to my apartment.

It was a warm night and as I sat at my window I heard music coming from another of the open windows. I realized that Connan TreMellyn was entertaining guests.

I pictured them in one of the rooms which I had not even seen. Why should you, I asked myself. You are only a governess. Connan TreMellyn, his gaunt body clothed elegantly, would be presiding at the card table or perhaps sitting with his guests listening to music.

I recognized the music as from Mendelssohn's *Midsummer Night's Dream* and I felt a sudden longing to be down there among them; but I was astonished that this desire should be greater than any I had ever had to be present at Aunt Adelaide's *soirées* or the dinner parties Phillida gave. I was overcome with curiosity and could not resist the temptation to ring the bell and summon Kitty or Daisy who always knew what was going on and were only too happy to impart that knowledge to anyone who was interested to hear it.

It was Daisy who came. She looked excited.

I said: 'I want some hot water, Daisy. Could you please bring it for me?'

'Why yes, Miss,' she said.

'There are guests here to-night, I understand.'

'Oh yes, Miss. Though it's nothing to the parties we used to have. I reckon now the year's up, the Master will be entertaining more. That's what Mrs. Polgrey says.'

'It must have been very quiet during the last year.'

'But only right and proper . . . after a death in the family.'

'Of course. Who are the guests to-night?'

'Oh, there's Miss Celestine and Mr. Peter of course.'

'I saw their carriage.' My voice sounded eager and I was ashamed. I was no better than any gossiping servant.

'Yes, and I'll tell you who else is here.'

'Who?'

'Sir Thomas and Lady Treslyn.'

She looked conspiratorial as though there was something very important about these two.

'Oh?' I said encouragingly.

'Though,' went on Daisy, 'Mrs. Polgrey says that Sir Thomas bain't fit to go gallivanting at parties, and should be abed.'

'Why, is he ill?'

'Well, he'll never see seventy again and he's got one of those bad hearts. Mrs. Polgrey says you can go off sudden with a heart like that, and don't need no pushing either. Not that—'

She stopped and twinkled at me. I longed to ask her to continue, but I felt it was beneath my dignity to do so. Disappointingly she seemed to pull herself up sharply.

'*She's* another kettle of fish.'

'Who?'

'Why, Lady Treslyn of course. You ought to see her. She's got a gown cut right down to here and the loveliest flowers on her shoulder. She's a real beauty, and you can see she's only waiting—'

'I gather she is not the same age as her husband.'

Daisy giggled. 'They say there's nearly forty years' difference in their ages, and she'd like to pretend it was fifty.'

'You don't seem to like her.'

'Me? Well, if I don't, some do!' That sent Daisy into hysterical laughter again, and as I looked at her ungainly form in her tight clothes and listened to her wheezy laughter, I was ashamed of myself for sharing the gossip of a servant, so I said: 'I *would* like that hot water, Daisy.'

Daisy subsided and went off to get it, leaving me with a clearer picture of what was happening in that drawing room.

I was still thinking of them when I had washed my hands and unpinned my hair preparatory to retiring for the night.

The musicians had been playing a Chopin waltz and it had seemed to spirit me away from my governess's bedroom and tantalize me with pleasures outside my reach – a dainty beauty, a place of salons such as that somewhere in this house, wit, charm, the power to make the chosen man love me.

I was startled by such thoughts. What had they to do with a governess such as myself.

I went to the window. The weather had been fine and warm for so long that I did not believe it could continue. The autumn mists would soon be with us and I heard that they and the gales which blew from the south-west were, as Tapperty would say, 'something special in these parts.'

I could smell the sea and hear the gentle rhythm of the waves. The 'voices' were starting up in Mellyn Cove.

And then suddenly I saw a light in a dark part of the house and I felt the goose-pimples rise on my flesh. I knew that window belonged to the room to which Alvean had taken me to choose my riding habit. It was Alice's dressing room.

The blind had been down. I had not noticed that before. Indeed I was sure it had not been like that earlier in the evening because, since I had known that that was Alice's room, I had made a habit – which I regretted and of which I had tried to cure myself – of glancing at the window whenever I looked out of my own.

The blind was of thin material, for behind it I distinctly saw the light. It was a faint light but there was no mistaking it. It moved before my astonished eyes.

I stood at my window staring out and, as I did so, I saw a shadow on the blind. It was that of a woman.

I heard a voice close to me saying: 'It is Alice!' and I realized that I had spoken aloud.

I'm dreaming, I told myself. I'm imagining this.

Then again I saw the figure silhouetted against the blind.

My hands which gripped the window sill were trembling as I watched that flickering light. I had an impulse to summon Daisy or Kitty, or go to Mrs. Polgrey.

I restrained myself, imagining how foolish it should look. So I remained staring at the window.

And after a while all was darkness.

I stood at my window for a long time watching, but I saw nothing more.

They were playing another Chopin waltz in the drawing room, and I stood until I was cold even on that warm September night.

Then I went to bed but I could not sleep for a long time.

And at last, when I did sleep, I dreamed that a woman came into my room; she was wearing a riding habit with blue collar and cuffs, trimmed with braid and ball fringe. She said to me: 'I was not on that train, Miss Leigh. You wonder where I was. It is for you to find me.'

Through my dreams I heard the whispering of the waves in the caves below; and the first thing I did on rising next morning – which I did as soon as dawn appeared in the sky – was to go to my window and look across at the room which – little more than a year ago – had belonged to Alice.

The blinds were drawn up. I could clearly see the rich blue velvet curtains.

Chapter Four

It was about a week later when I first saw Linda Treslyn.

It was a few minutes past six o'clock. Alvean and I had put away our books and had gone down to the stables to look at Buttercup who we thought had strained a tendon that afternoon.

The farrier had seen her and given her a poultice. Alvean was really upset, and this pleased me because I was always delighted to discover her softer feelings.

'Don't 'ee fret, Miss Alvean,' Joe Tapperty told her. 'Buttercup 'll be right as two dogs on a bright and frosty morning afore the week's out; you see! Jim Bond, he be the best horse-doctor between here and Land's End, I do tell 'ee.'

She was cheered and I told her that she should take Black Prince in Buttercup's place to-morrow.

She was excited about this for she knew Black Prince would test her mettle, and I was glad to see that her pleasure was only faintly tinged with apprehension.

As we came out of the stables I looked at my watch.

'Would you care for half an hour's stroll through the gardens?' I asked. 'We have half an hour to spare.'

To my surprise she said she would, and we set off.

The plateau on which Mount Mellyn stood was a piece of land a mile or so wide. The slope to the sea was steep but there were several zigzag paths which made the going easier. The gardeners spent a great deal of time on this garden which was indeed beautiful with the flowering shrubs which grew so profusely in this part. At various points arbours had been set up, constructed of trellis work around which roses climbed. They were beautiful even as late as this and their perfume hung on the air.

One could sit in these arbours and gaze out to sea; and from these gardens the south side of the house was a vision of grandeur, rising nobly, a pile of grey granite there on the top of the cliff like a mighty fortress. It was inevitable that the house should have a defiant air, as though it represented a challenge, not only to the sea but to the world.

We made our way down those sweet-smelling paths and were level with the arbour before we noticed that two people were there.

Alvean gave a little gasp and, following her gaze, I saw them. They were sitting side by side and close. She was very dark and one of the most beautiful women I had ever seen; her features were strongly marked and she wore a gauzy scarf over her hair, and in this gauze sequins glistened. I thought that she looked like someone out of *A Midsummer Night's Dream* – Titania perhaps, although I had always imagined her fair. She had that quality of beauty which attracts the eyes as a needle is attracted by a magnet. You have to look whether you want to or not; you have to admire. Her dress was pale mauve of some clinging material such as chiffon and it was caught at the throat with a big diamond brooch.

Connan spoke first. 'Why,' he said, 'it is my daughter with her governess. So, Miss Leigh, you and Alvean are taking the air.'

'It is such a pleasant evening,' I said, and I made to take Alvean's hand, but she eluded me in her most ungracious manner.

'May I sit with you and Lady Treslyn, Papa?' she asked.

'You are taking a walk with Miss Leigh,' he said. 'Do you not think that you should continue to do so?'

'Yes,' I answered for her. 'Come along, Alvean.'

Connan had turned to his companion. 'We are very fortunate to have found Miss Leigh. She is . . . admirable!'

'The perfect governess this time, I hope for your sake, Connan,' said Lady Treslyn.

I felt awkward, as though I were in the position of a horse standing there while they discussed my points. I was sure he was aware of my discomfiture and rather amused by it. There were times when I believed he was a very unpleasant person.

I said, and my voice sounded very chilly: 'I think it is time we turned back. We were merely taking an airing before Alvean retires for the night. Come, Alvean,' I added. And I seized her arm so firmly that I drew her away.

'But,' protested Alvean, 'I want to stay. I want to talk to you, Papa.'

'But you can see I am engaged. Some other time, my child.'

'No,' she said. 'It is important . . . now.'

'It cannot be all that important. Let us discuss it tomorrow.'

'No . . . no . . . Now!' Alvean's voice had a hysterical note in it; I had never before known her defy him so utterly.

Lady Treslyn murmured: 'I see Alvean is a very determined person.'

Connan TreMellyn said coolly: 'Miss Leigh will deal with this matter.'

'Of course. The perfect governess. . . .' There was a note of mockery in Lady Treslyn's voice, and it goaded me to such an extent that I seized Alvean's arm roughly and almost dragged her back the way we had come.

She was half sobbing, but she did not speak until we were in the house.

Then she said: 'I hate her. You know, don't you, Miss Leigh, that she wants to be my new mamma.'

I said nothing then. I thought it dangerous to do so because I always felt that it was so easy to be overheard. It was only when we reached her room and I had followed her in and shut the door that I said: 'That was an extraordinary remark to make. How could she wish to be your mamma when she has a husband of her own?'

'He will soon die.'

'How can you know that?'

'Everybody says they are only waiting.'

I was shocked that she should have heard such gossip and I thought: I will speak to Mrs. Polgrey about this. They must be careful what they say in front of Alvean. Is it those girls, Daisy and Kitty ... or perhaps Joe Tapperty or his wife?

'She's always here,' went on Alvean. 'I won't let her take my mother's place. I won't let anybody.'

'You are becoming quite hysterical about improbabilities, and I must insist that you never allow me to hear you say such things again. It is degrading to your papa.'

That made her thoughtful. How she loves him! I thought. Poor little Alvean, poor lonely child!

A little while before, I had been sorry for myself as I stood in that beautiful garden and was forced to be quizzed by the beautiful woman in the arbour. I had said to myself: 'It is not fair. Why should one person have so much, and others nothing? Should I be beautiful in chiffon and diamonds? Perhaps not as Lady Treslyn was, but I am sure they would be more becoming than cotton and merino and a turquoise brooch which had belonged to my grandmother.'

Now I forgot to be sorry for myself, and my pity was all for Alvean.

I had seen Alvean to bed and had returned to my room, conscious of a certain depression. I kept thinking of Connan TreMellyn out there in the arbour with Lady Treslyn, asking myself if he were still there and what they talked about. Each other! I supposed. Of course Alvean and I had interrupted a flirtation. I felt shocked that he should indulge in such an undignified intrigue, for it seemed wholly undignified to me, since the lady had a husband to whom she owed her allegiance.

I went to the window and I was glad that it did not give me a view of the south gardens and the sea. I leaned my elbows on the sill and looked out at the scented evening. It was not quite dark yet but the sun had disappeared and the twilight was on us. My eyes turned to the window where I had seen the shadow on the blind.

The blinds were drawn up and I could see the blue curtains clearly. I stared at them, fixedly. I don't know what I expected. Was it to see a face appear at the window, a beckoning hand? There were times when I could laugh at myself for my fancies, but the twilight hour was not one of them.

Then I saw the curtains move, and I knew that someone was in that room.

I was in an extraordinary mood that evening. It had something to do with meeting Connan TreMellyn and Lady Treslyn together in the arbour, but I had not sufficiently analysed my feelings at this date to understand it. I felt our recent encounter to have been humiliating but I was ready to risk another which might be more so. Alice's room was not in my part of the house but I was completely at liberty to walk in the gardens if I wished to. If I were caught I should look rather foolish. But I was reckless. I did not care. Thoughts of Alice obsessed me. There were times when I felt such a burning desire to discover what mystery lay behind her death that I was prepared to go to any lengths.

So I slipped out of my room. I left my wing of the house and went along the gallery to Alice's dressing room. I knocked lightly on the door and, with my heart beating like a sledge hammer, I swiftly opened it.

For a second I saw no one. Then I detected a movement by the curtains. Someone was hiding behind them.

'Who is it?' I asked, and my voice successfully hid the trepidation I was feeling.

There was no answer, but whoever was behind those curtains was very eager not to be discovered.

I strode across the room, drew aside the curtains and saw Gilly cowering there.

The lids of her blank blue eyes fluttered in a terrified way. I put out a hand to seize her and she shrank from me towards the window.

'It's all right, Gilly,' I said gently. 'I won't hurt you.'

She continued to stare at me, and I went on: 'Tell me, what are you doing here?'

Still she said nothing. She had begun to stare about the room as though she were asking someone for help and for a moment I had the uncanny feeling that she *saw* something – or someone – I could not see.

'Gilly,' I said, 'you know you should not be in this room, do you not?' She drew away from me, and I repeated what I had said.

Then she nodded and immediately afterwards shook her head.

'I am going to take you back to my room, Gilly. Then we'll have a little talk.'

I put my arm about her; she was trembling. I drew her to the door but she came very reluctantly, and at the threshold of the room she looked back over her shoulder; then she cried out suddenly: 'Madam ... come back, Madam. Come ... *now*!'

I led her firmly from the room and shut the door behind us, then almost had to drag her along to my bedroom.

Once there I firmly shut my door and stood with my back against it. Her lips were trembling.

'Gilly,' I said, 'I do want you to understand that I won't hurt you. I want to be your friend.' The blank look persisted and taking a shot in the dark I went on: 'I want to be your friend as Mrs. TreMellyn was.'

That startled her and the blank look disappeared for a moment. I had stumbled on another discovery. Alice had been kind to this poor child.

'You went there to look for Mrs. TreMellyn, did you not?'

She nodded.

She looked so pathetic that I was moved to a demonstration of feeling unusual with me. I knelt down and put my arms about her; now our faces were level.

'You can't find her, Gilly. She is dead. It is no use looking for her in this house.'

Gilly nodded and I was not sure what she implied – whether she agreed with me that it was no use, or whether she believed that she could find Mrs. TreMellyn in the house.

'So,' I went on, 'we must try to forget her, mustn't we Gilly?'

The pale lids fell over the eyes to hide them from me.

'We'll be friends,' I said. 'I want us to be. If we were friends, you wouldn't be lonely, would you?'

She shook her head, and I fancied that the eyes which surveyed me had lost something of their blankness; she was not trembling now, and I was sure that she was no longer afraid of me.

Then suddenly she slipped out of my grasp and ran to the door. I did not pursue her and, as she opened the door and turned to look back at me, there was a faint smile on her lips. Then she was gone.

I believed that I had established a little friendliness between us. I believed that she had lost her fear of me.

Then I thought of Alice, who had been kind to this child. I was beginning to build up the picture of Alice more clearly in my mind.

I went to the window and looked across the L-shaped building to the window of the room, and I thought of that night when I had seen the shadow on the blind.

My discovery of Gilly did not explain that. It was no child I had seen silhouetted there. It had been a woman.

Gilly might hide herself in Alice's room, but the shadow I had seen on the blind that night did not belong to her.

It was the next day when I went to Mrs. Polgrey's room for a cup of tea. She was delighted to invite me. 'Mrs. Polgrey,' I had said, 'I have a matter which I feel to be of some importance, and I should very much like to discuss this with you.

She was bridled with pride. I could see that the governess who sought her advice must be, in her eyes, the ideal governess.

'I shall be delighted to give you an hour of my company and a cup of my best Earl Grey,' she told me.

Over the teacups she surveyed me with an expression bordering on the affectionate.

'Now, Miss Leigh, pray tell me what it is you would ask of me.'

'I am a little disturbed,' I told her, stirring my tea thoughtfully. 'It is due to a remark of Alvean's. I am sure that she listens to gossip, and I think it most undesirable in a child of her age.'

'Or in any of us as I am sure a young lady of your good sense would feel,' replied Mrs. Polgrey with what I could not help feeling was a certain amount of hypocrisy.

I told her how we had walked in the cliff gardens and met the master with Lady Treslyn. 'And then,' I went on, 'Alvean made this offensive remark. She said that Lady Treslyn hoped to become her mamma.'

Mrs. Polgrey shook her head. She said: 'What about a spoonful of whisky in your tea, Miss? There's nothing like it for keeping up the spirits.'

I had no desire for the whisky but I could see that Mrs. Polgrey had, and she would have been disappointed if I had refused to join her in her tea tippling, so I said: 'A small teaspoonful, please, Mrs. Polgrey.'

She unlocked the cupboard, took out the bottle and measured out the whisky even more meticulously than she measured her tea. I found myself wondering what other stores she kept in that cupboard of hers.

Now we were like a pair of conspirators and Mrs. Polgrey was clearly enjoying herself.

'I fear you will find it somewhat shocking, Miss,' she began.

'I am prepared,' I assured her.

'Well, Sir Thomas Treslyn is a very old man and only a few years ago he married this young lady, a play-actress, some say, from London. Sir Thomas went there on a visit and returned with her. He set the neighbourhood agog, I can tell you, Miss.'

'I can well believe that.'

'There's some that say she's one of the handsomest women in the country.'

'I can believe that too.'

'Handsome is as handsome does.'

'But it remains handsome outwardly,' I added.

'And men can be foolish. The Master has his weakness,' admitted Mrs. Polgrey.

'If there is gossip I am most anxious that it shall not reach Alvean's ears.'

'Of course you are, Miss. But gossip there is, and that child's got ears like a hare's.'

'Do you think Daisy and Kitty chatter?'

Mrs. Polgrey came closer and I smelt the whisky on her breath. I was startled, wondering whether she could smell it on mine. 'Everybody chatters, Miss.'

'I see.'

'There's some as say that they'm not the sort to wait for blessing of clergy.'

'Well, perhaps they are not.'

I felt wretched. I hate this, I told myself. It's so sordid. So horrible for a sensitive girl like Alvean.

'The Master is impulsive by nature and in his way he is fond of the women.'

'So you think—'

She nodded gravely. 'When Sir Thomas dies there'll be a new mistress in this house. All they have to wait for now is for him to go. Mrs. TreMellyn, her . . . her's already gone.'

I did not want to ask the question which came to my lips but it seemed as though there were some force within me which would not let me avoid it. 'And was it so . . . when Mrs. TreMellyn was alive?'

Mrs. Polgrey nodded slowly. 'He visited her often. It started almost as soon as she came. Sometimes he rides out at night and we don't see him till morning. Well, he'm Master and 'tis for him to make his own rules. 'Tis for us to cook and dust and housekeep, or teach the child . . . whatsoever we'm here for. And there's an end of it.'

'So you think that Alvean is only repeating what everyone knows? When Sir Thomas dies Lady Treslyn *will* be her new mamma.'

'There's some on us that thinks it's more than likely, and some that wouldn't be sorry to see it. Her ladyship's not the kind to interfere much with our side of the house; and 'tis better to have these things regularized, so I do say.' She went on piously: 'I'd sooner see the Master of the house I serve living in wedlock than in sin, I do assure you. And so would we all.'

'Could we warn the girls not to chatter, before Alvean, of these matters?'

'As well try to keep a cuckoo from singing in the spring. I could wallop them two till I dropped with exhaustion and still they'd gossip. They can't help it. It be in their blood. And there's nothing much to choose between one girl and the other. Nowadays—'

I nodded sympathetically. I was thinking of Alice, who had watched the relationship between her husband and Lady Treslyn. No wonder she had been prepared to run away with Geoffry Nansellock.

Poor Alice! I thought. What you must have suffered, married to such a man.

Mrs. Polgrey was in such an expansive mood that I felt I might extend the conversation to other matters in which I happened to be interested.

I said: 'Have you ever thought of teaching Gilly her letters?'

'Gilly! Why that would be a senseless thing to do. You must know, Miss, that Gilly is not quite as she should be.' Mrs. Polgrey tapped her forehead.

'She sings a great deal. She must have learned the songs. If she could learn songs, could she not learn other things?'

'She's a queer little thing. Reckon it was the way she come. I don't often talk about such things, but I'll swear you've been hearing about my Jennifer.' Mrs. Polgrey's voice changed a little, became touched with sentiment. I wondered if it had anything to do with the whisky and how many spoonfuls she had taken that day. 'Sometimes I think that Gillyflower is a cursed child. Us didn't want her; why, she was only a little thing in a cradle ... two months old ... when Jennifer went. The tide brought her body in two days after. 'Twas found there in Mellyn Cove.'

'I'm sorry,' I said gently.

Mrs. Polgrey shook herself free of sentiment. 'Her'd gone, but there was still Gilly. And right from the first her didn't seem quite like other children.'

'Perhaps she sensed the tragedy,' I ventured.

Mrs. Polgrey looked at me with hauteur. 'We did all we could for her – me and Mr. Polgrey. He thought the world of her.'

'When did you notice that she was not like other children?'

'Come to think of it it would be when she was about four years old.'

'That would be how many years ago?'

'About four.'

'She must be the same age as Alvean. She looks so much younger.'

'Born a few months after Miss Alvean. They'd play together now and then ... being in the house, you do see, and being of an age. There was an accident when she was, let me see ... she'd be approaching her fourth birthday.'

'What sort of accident?'

'She was playing in the drive there, not far from the lodge gates. The Mistress were riding along the drive to the house. She was a great horsewoman, the Mistress. Gilly, her darted out from the bushes and caught a blow from the horse. She fell on her head. It was a mercy she weren't killed.'

'Poor Gilly,' I said.

'The Mistress were distressed. Blamed herself although 'twas no blame to her. Gilly should have known better. She'd been told to watch the roads often enough. Darted out after a butterfly, like as not. Gilly has always been taken with birds and flowers and insects and such like. The Mistress made much of her after that. Gilly used to follow her about and fret when she was away.'

'I see,' I said.

Mrs. Polgrey poured herself another cup of tea and asked me if I would have another. I declined. I saw her tilt the teaspoonful of whisky into the cup. 'Gilly,' she went on, 'were born in sin. Her had no right to come into the world. It looks like God be taking vengeance on her, for it do say that the sins of the fathers be visited on the children.'

I felt a sudden wave of anger sweep over me. I was in revolt against such distortions. I felt I wanted to slap the face of the woman who could sit there calmly drinking her whisky and accepting the plight of her little grand-daughter as God's will.

I marvelled too at the ignorance of these people, who did not connect Gilly's strangeness with the accident she had had but believed it was due punishment for her parents' sins meted out to her by a vengeful God.

But I said nothing, because I believed that I was battling against strange forces in this house and, if I were going to succeed, I needed all the allies I could command.

I wanted to understand Gilly. I wanted to soothe Alvean. I was discovering a fondness for children in myself which I had not known I possessed before I came into this house. Indeed since I had come here I had begun to discover quite a lot about myself.

There was one other reason why I wanted to concentrate on the affairs of these two children; doing so prevented my thinking of Connan TreMellyn and Lady Treslyn. Thoughts of them made me feel quite angry; at this time I called my anger 'disgust.'

So I sat in Mrs. Polgrey's room, listening to her talk, and I did not tell her what was in my mind.

There was excitement throughout the house because there was to be a ball – the first since Alice's death – and for a week there was little talk of anything else. I found it difficult to keep Alvean's attention on her lessons; Kitty and Daisy were almost hysterical with delight, and I was constantly coming upon them clasped in each other's arms in attempts to waltz.

The gardeners were busy. They were going to bring in flowers from the greenhouses to decorate the ballroom and were eager that the blooms should do them credit; and invitations were being sent out all over the countryside.

'I fail to see,' I said to Alvean, 'why you should feel this excitement. Neither you nor I will take part in the ball.'

Alvean said dreamily: 'When my mother was alive there were lots of balls. She loved them. She danced beautifully. She used to come in and show me

how she looked. She was beautiful. Then she would take me into the
solarium and I would sit in a recess behind the curtains and look down on
the hall through the peep.'

'The peep?' I asked.

'Ah, you don't know.' She regarded me triumphantly. I suppose it was
rather pleasing to her to discover that her governess, who was constantly
shocked by her ignorance, should herself be discovered in that state.

'There is a great deal about this house that I do not know,' I said sharply.
'I have not seen a third of it.'

'You haven't seen the solarium,' she agreed. 'There are several peeps in
this house. Oh, Miss, you don't know what peeps are, but a lot of big houses
have them. There's even one in Mount Widden. My mother told me that
it is where the ladies used to sit when the men were feasting and it was
considered no place for them among the men. They could look down and
watch, but they must not *be* there. There's one in the chapel . . . a sort of
one. We call it the lepers' squint there. They couldn't come in because they
were lepers, so they could only look through the squint. But I shall go to the
solarium and look down on the hall through the peep up there. Why Miss,
you ought to come with me. Please do.'

'We'll see,' I said.

On the day of the ball Alvean and I took our riding lesson as usual, only
instead of riding Buttercup Alvean was mounted on Black Prince.

When I had first seen the child on that horse I had felt a faint twinge of
uneasiness, but I stifled this, for I told myself that if she were going to
become a rider she must get beyond the Buttercup stage. Once she had
ridden Prince she would gain more confidence, and very likely never wish
to go back to Buttercup.

We had done rather well for the first few lessons. Prince behaved admirably
and Alvean's confidence was growing. We had no doubt, either of us, that
she would be able to enter for at least one of the events at the November
horse show.

But this day we were not so fortunate. I suspect that Alvean's thoughts
were on the ball rather than on her riding. She was still diffident with me,
except perhaps during our riding lessons, when oddly enough we were the
best of friends; but as soon as we had divested ourselves of our riding kit we
seemed automatically to slip back to the old relationship. I had tried to
change this without success.

We were about half-way through the lesson when Prince broke into a
gallop. I had not allowed her to gallop unless she was on the leading rein;
and in any case there was little room for that sort of thing in the field; and
I wanted to be absolutely sure of Alvean's confidence before I allowed her
more licence.

All would have been well if Alvean had kept her head and remembered
what I had taught her, but as Prince started to gallop she gave a little cry
of fear and her terror seemed immediately to communicate itself to the
frightened animal.

Prince was off; the thud of his hoofs on the turf struck terror into me. I saw Alvean, forgetting what I had taught her, swaying to one side.

It was all over in a flash because as soon as it happened I was on the spot. I was after her immediately. I had to grasp Prince's bridle before he reached the hedge for I believed that he might attempt to jump and that would mean a nasty fall for my pupil. Fear gave me new strength and I had his rein in my hands and had pulled him up just as he was coming up to the hedge. I brought him to a standstill while a white-faced trembling Alvean slid unharmed to the ground.

'It's all right,' I said. 'Your mind was wandering. You haven't reached the stage when you can afford to forget for a moment what you're doing.'

I knew that was the only way to deal with her. Shaken as she was, I made her remount Prince; I knew that she had become terrified of horses through some such incident as this. I had overcome that fear and I was not going to allow it to return.

She obeyed me, although reluctantly. But by the time our lesson was finished she was well over her fright, and I knew that she would want to ride next day. So I was more satisfied that day that I would eventually make a rider of Alvean than I had been before.

It was when we were leaving the field that she suddenly burst out laughing.

'What is it?' I asked, turning my head, for I was riding ahead of her.

'Oh, Miss,' she cried. 'You've split!'

'What *do* you mean?'

'Your dress has split under the armhole. Oh . . . it's getting worse and worse.'

I put my hand behind my back and realized what had happened. The riding habit had always been a little too tight for me and during my efforts to save Alvean from a nasty fall the sleeve seam had been unable to stand the extra strain.

I must have shown my dismay, for Alvean said: 'Never mind, Miss. I'll find you another. There *are* more, I know.'

Alvean was secretly amused as we went back to the house. Odd that I had never seen her in such good spirits. It was however somewhat disconcerting to discover that the sight of my discomfiture could give her so much pleasure that she could forget the danger through which she had so recently passed.

The guests had begun to arrive. I had been unable to resist taking peeps at them from my window. The approach was filled with carriages, and the dresses I had glimpsed made me gasp with envy.

The ball was being held in the great hall which I had seen earlier that day. Before that I had not been in it since my arrival, for I always used the back staircase. It was Kitty who had urged me to take a peep. 'It looks so lovely, Miss. Mr. Polgrey's going round like a dog with two tails. He'll murder one of us if anything happens to his plants.'

I thought I had rarely seen a setting so beautiful. The beams had been decorated with leaves. 'An old Cornish custom,' Kitty told me, 'specially at Maytime. But what's it matter, Miss, if this be September. Reckon there'll be other balls now the period of mourning be up. Well, so it should be.

Can't go on mourning for ever, can 'ee. You might say this is a sort of
Maytime, don't 'ee see? 'Tis the end of one old year and the beginning of
another like.'

I said, as I looked at the pots of hothouse blooms which had been brought
in from the greenhouses and the great wax candles in their sconces, that the
hall did Mr. Polgrey and his gardeners great credit. I pictured how it would
look when those candles were lighted and the guests danced in their colourful
gowns, their pearls and their diamonds.

I wanted to be one of the guests. How I wanted it! Kitty had begun to
dance in the hall, smiling and bowing to an imaginary partner. I smiled. She
looked so abandoned, so full of joy.

Then I thought that I ought not to be here like this. It was quite
unbecoming. I was as bad as Kitty.

I turned away and there was a foolish lump in my throat.

Alvean and I had supper together that evening. She obviously could not
dine with her father in the small dining room, as he would be busy with his
guests.

'Miss,' she said, 'I've put a new riding habit for you in your cupboard.'

'Thank you,' I said; 'that was thoughtful of you.'

'Well, you couldn't go riding in that!' cried Alvean, pointing derisively at
my lavender gown.

So it was only that I might not miss a riding lesson for want of the clothes,
that she had taken such trouble on my behalf! I should have known that.

I asked myself in that moment whether I was not being rather foolish.
Did I expect more than people were prepared to give? I was nothing to
Alvean except when I could help her to attain what she wanted. It was as
well to remember that.

I looked down distastefully at my lavender cotton gown. It was the
favourite of the two which had been specially made for me by Aunt Adelaide's
dressmaker when I had obtained this post. One was of grey – a most
unbecoming colour to me – but I fancied I looked a little less prim, a little
less of a governess in the lavender. But how becoming it seemed, with its
bodice buttoned high at the neck and the cream lace collar and the cream
lace cuffs to match. I realized I was comparing it with the dresses of Connan
TreMellyn's guests.

Alvean said: 'Hurry and finish, Miss. Don't forget we're going to the
solarium.'

'I suppose you have your father's permission . . .' I began.

'Miss, I always peep from the solarium. Everybody knows I do. My
mother used to look up and wave to me.' Her face puckered a little. 'To-
night,' she went on, as though she were speaking to herself, 'I'm going to
imagine that she's down there after all . . . dancing there. Miss, do you think
people come back after they're dead?'

'What an extraordinary question! Of course not.'

'You don't believe in ghosts then. Some people do. They say they've seen
them. Do you think they lie when they say they see ghosts, Miss?'

'I think that people who say such things are the victims of their own
imaginations.'

'Still,' she went on dreamily, 'I shall imagine she is there . . . dancing there. Perhaps if I imagine hard enough I shall see her. Perhaps I shall be the victim of my imagination.'

I said nothing because I felt uneasy.

'If she *were* coming back,' she mused, 'she would come to the ball, because dancing was one of the things she liked doing best.' She seemed to remember me suddenly. 'Miss,' she went on, 'if you'd rather not come to the solarium with me, I don't mind going alone.'

'I'll come,' I said.

'Let's go now.'

'We will first finish our meal,' I told her.

The vastness of the house continued to astonish me, as I followed Alvean along the gallery, up stone staircases through several bedrooms, to what she told me was the solarium. The roof was of glass and I understood why it had received its name. I thought it must be unbearably warm in the heat of the summer.

The walls were covered with exquisite tapestries depicting the story of the Great Rebellion and the Restoration. There was the execution of the first Charles, and the second shown in the oak tree, his dark face peering down at the Roundhead soldiers; there were pictures of his arrival in England, of his coronation and a visit to his shipyards.

'Never mind those now,' said Alvean. 'My mother used to love being here. She said you could see what was going on. There are two peeps up here. Oh, Miss, don't you want to see them?'

I was looking at the escritoire, at the sofa and the gilt-backed chairs; and I saw her sitting here, talking to her daughter here – dead Alice who seemed to become more and more alive as the days passed.

There were windows at each end of this long room, high windows curtained with heavy brocade. The same brocade curtains hung before what I presumed to be doors of which there appeared to be four in this room – the one by which we had entered, another at the extreme end of the room and one other on either side. But I was wrong about the last two.

Alvean had disappeared behind one of these curtains and called to me in a muffled voice, and when I went to her I found we were in an alcove. In the wall was a star-shaped opening, quite large but decorated so that one would not have noticed it unless one had been looking for it.

I gazed through it and saw that I was looking down into the chapel. I could see clearly all but one side of the chapel – the small altar with the triptych and the pews.

'They used to sit up here and watch the service if they were too ill to go down, my mother told me. They had a priest in the house in the old days. My mother didn't tell me that. She didn't know about the history of the house. Miss Jansen told me. She knew a lot about the house. She loved to come up here and look through the peep. She used to like the chapel too.'

'You were sorry when she went, Alvean, I believe.'

'Yes, I was. The other peep's on the other side. Through that you can see into the hall.'

She went to the other side of the room and drew back the hangings there. In the wall was a similar star-shaped opening.

I looked down on the hall and caught my breath for it was a magnificent sight. Musicians were on the dais and the guests, who had not yet begun to dance, stood about talking.

There were a great many people down there and the sound of the chatter rose clearly up to us. Alvean was breathless beside me, her eyes searching ... in a manner which made me shiver slightly. Did she really believe that Alice would come from the tomb because she loved to dance?

I felt an impulse to put my arm about her and draw her to me. Poor motherless child, I thought. Poor bewildered little creature!

But of course I overcame that impulse. Alvean had no desire for my sympathy, I well knew.

I saw Connan TreMellyn in conversation with Celestine Nansellock, and Peter was there too. If Peter was one of the most handsome men I had ever seen, Connan, I told myself, was the most elegant. There were few in that brilliant assembly whose faces were known to me, but I did see Lady Treslyn there. Even among the magnificently brilliant gathering she stood out. She was wearing a gown which seemed to be composed of yards and yards of chiffon, which was the colour of flame, and I guessed that she was one of the few who would have dared to wear such a colour. Yet had she wanted to attract attention to herself she could not have chosen anything more calculated to bring this result. Her dark hair looked almost black against the flame; her magnificent bust and shoulders were the whitest I had ever seen. She wore a band of diamonds in her hair, which was like a tiara, and diamonds sparkled about her person.

Alvean's attention was caught by her even as mine was and her brows were drawn together in a frown.

'*She* is there then,' she murmured.

I said: 'Is her husband present?'

'Yes, the little old man over there talking to Colonel Penlands.'

'And which is Colonel Penlands?' She pointed the colonel out to me, and I saw with him a bent old man, white-haired and wrinkled. It seemed incredible that he should be the husband of that flamboyant creature.

'Look!' whispered Alvean. 'My father is going to open the ball. He used to do it with Aunt Celestine, and at the same time my mother used to do it with Uncle Geoffry. I wonder who he will do it with this time.'

'With whom he will do it,' I murmured absentmindedly, but my attention, like Alvean's was entirely on the scene below.

'The musicians are going to start now,' she said. 'They always start with the same tune. Do you know what it is? It's the *Furry* Dance. Some of our ancestors came from Helston way and it was played then and it always has been since. You watch! Papa and Mamma used to dance the first bar or so with their partners, and all the others fell in behind.'

The musicians had begun, and I saw Connan take Celestine by the hand and lead her into the centre of the hall; Peter Nansellock followed, and he had chosen Lady Treslyn to be his partner.

I watched the four of them dance the first steps of the traditional dance, and I thought, Poor Celestine! Even gowned as she was in blue satin she looked ill at ease in that quartette. She lacked the elegance and nonchalance of Connan, the beauty of Lady Treslyn and the dash of her brother.

I thought it was a pity that he had to choose Celestine to open the ball, but that was tradition. The house was filled with tradition. Such and such was done because it always had been done, and often for no other reason. Well, that was the way in great houses.

Neither Alvean nor I seemed to tire of watching the dancers. An hour passed and we were still there. I fancied that Connan glanced up once or twice. Did he know of his daughter's habit of watching? I thought that it must be Alvean's bedtime, but that perhaps on such an occasion a little leniency would be permissible.

I was fascinated by the way she watched the dancers tirelessly, fervently, as though she were certain that if she looked long enough she would see that face there which she longed to see.

It was now dark, but the moon had risen. I turned my eyes from the dance floor to look through the glass roof at that great gibbous moon which seemed to be smiling down on us. No candles for you, it seemed to say; you are banished from the gaiety and the glitter, but I will give you my soft and tender light instead.

The room, touched by moonlight, had a supernatural character all its own. I felt in such a room anything might happen.

I turned my attention back to the dancers. They were waltzing down there and I felt myself swaying to the rhythm. No one had been more astonished than myself when I had proved to be a good dancer. It had brought me partners at the dances to which Aunt Adelaide had taken me in those days when she had thought it possible to find a husband for me; alas for Aunt Adelaide, those invitations to the dances had not been extended to other pursuits.

And as I listened entranced I felt a hand touch mine and I was so startled that I gave an audible gasp.

I looked down. Standing beside me was a small figure, and I was relieved to see that it was only Gillyflower.

'You have come to see the dancers?' I said.

She nodded.

She was not quite so tall as Alvean and could not reach the star-shaped peep, so I lifted her in my arms and held her up. I could not see very clearly in the moonlight but I was sure the blankness had left her eyes.

I said to Alvean: 'Bring a stool and Gillyflower can stand on it; then she will be able to see quite easily.'

Alvean said: 'Let her get it herself.'

Gilly nodded and I put her on the floor; she ran to the stool and brought it with her. I thought, since she understands, why can she not talk with the rest of us?

Alvean did not seem to want to look now that Gilly had come. She moved away from the peep and as the musicians below began the opening bars of that waltz which always enchanted me – I refer to Mr. Strauss's *Blue Danube Waltz* – Alvean began to dance across the floor of the solarium.

The music seemed to have affected my feet. I don't know what came over me that night. It was as though some spirit of daring had entered into my body, but I could not resist the strains of the *Blue Danube Waltz*. I danced towards Alvean. I waltzed as I used to in those ballrooms to which I went accompanied by Aunt Adelaide, but I was sure that I never danced as I did that night in the solarium.

Alvean cried out with pleasure; I heard Gilly laugh too.

Alvean cried: 'Go on, Miss. Don't stop, Miss. You do it well.'

So I went on dancing with an imaginary partner, dancing down the moonlit solarium with the lopsided moon smiling in at me. And when I reached the end of the room a figure moved towards me and I was no longer dancing alone.

'You're exquisite,' said a voice, and there was Peter Nansellock in his elegant evening dress, and he was holding me as it was the custom to hold a partner in the waltz.

My feet faltered. He said: 'No . . . no. Listen, the children are protesting. You must dance with me, Miss Leigh, as you were meant to dance with me.'

We went on dancing. It was as though my feet, having begun would not stop.

But I said: 'This is most unorthodox.'

'It is most delightful,' he answered.

'You should be with the guests.'

'It is more fun to be with you.'

'You forget—'

'That you are a governess? I could, if you would allow me to.'

'There is no earthly reason why you should forget.'

'Only that I think you would be happier if we could all forget it. How exquisitely you dance!'

'It is my only drawing room accomplishment.'

'I am sure it is one of many that you are forced to squander on this empty room.'

'Mr. Nansellock, do you not think this little jest has been played out?'

'It is no jest.'

'I shall now rejoin the children.' We had come close to them and I saw little Gilly's face enrapt, and I saw the admiration in Alvean's. If I stopped dancing I should revert to my old position; while I went on dancing I was an exalted being.

I thought how ridiculous were the thoughts I was entertaining; but tonight I wanted to be ridiculous, I wanted to be frivolous.

'So here he is.'

To my horror I saw that several people had come into the solarium, and my apprehension did not lessen when I saw the flame-coloured gown of Lady Treslyn among them, for I was sure that wherever that flame-coloured dress was there Connan TreMellyn would be.

Somebody started to clap; others took it up. Then *The Blue Danube* ended.

I put my hand to my hair in my acute embarrassment. I knew that dancing had loosened the pins.

I thought: I shall be dismissed to-morrow for my irresponsibility, and perhaps I deserve it.

'What an excellent idea,' said someone. 'Dancing in moonlight. What could be more agreeable? And one can hear the music up here almost as well as down there.'

Someone else said: 'This is a beautiful ballroom, Connan.'

'Then let us use it for that purpose,' he answered.

He went to the peep and shouted through it: 'Once more – *The Beautiful Blue Danube*.'

Then the music started.

I turned to Alvean and I gripped Gilly by the hand. People were already beginning to dance. They were talking together and they did not bother to lower their voices. Why should they? I was only the governess.

I heard a voice: 'The governess. Alvean's, you know.'

'Forward creature! I suppose another of Peter's light ladies.'

'I'm sorry for the poor things. Life must be dull for them.'

'But in broad moonlight! What could be more depraved?'

'The last one had to be dismissed, I believe.'

'This one's turn will come.'

I was blushing hotly. I wanted to face them all, to tell them that my conduct was very likely less depraved than that of some of them.

I was furiously angry and a little frightened. I was aware of Connan's face in the moonlight for he was standing near to me, looking at me, I feared, in a manner signifying the utmost disapproval, which I was sure he was feeling.

'Alvean,' he said, 'go to your room and take Gillyflower with you.'

She dared not disobey when he spoke in those tones.

I said as coolly as I could: 'Yes, let us go.'

But as I was about to follow the children I found my arm gripped and Connan had come a little closer to me.

He said: 'You dance extremely well, Miss Leigh. I could never resist a good dancer. Perhaps it is because I scarcely excel in the art myself.'

'Thank you,' I said. But he still held my arm.

'I am sure,' he went on, 'that *The Blue Danube* is a favourite of yours. You looked . . . enraptured.' And with that he swung me into his arms and I found that I was dancing with him among his guests . . . I in my lavender cotton and my turquoise brooch, they in their chiffons and velvets, their emeralds and diamonds.

I was glad of the moonlight. I was so overcome with shame, for I believed that he was angry and that his intention was to shame me further.

My feet caught the rhythm and I thought to myself: Always in future *The Blue Danube* will mean to me a fantastic dance in the solarium with Connan TreMellyn as my partner.

'I apologize, Miss Leigh,' he said, 'for my guests' bad manners.'

'It is what I must expect and no doubt what I deserve.'

'What nonsense,' he said, and I told myself that I was dreaming, for his voice which was close to my ear sounded tender.

We had come to the end of the room and, to my complete astonishment, he had whirled me through the curtains and out of the door. We were on a small landing between two flights of stone stairs in a part of the house which I had not seen before.

We stopped dancing, but he still kept his arms about me. On the wall a paraffin lamp of green jade burned; its light was only enough to show me his face. It looked a little brutal I thought.

'Miss Leigh,' he said, 'you are very charming when you abandon your severity.'

I caught my breath with dismay for he was forcing me against the wall and kissing me.

I was horrified as much by my own emotions as by what was happening. I knew what that kiss meant: You are not averse to a mild flirtation with Peter Nansellock; therefore why not with me?

My anger was so great that it was beyond my control. With all my might I pushed him from me and he was so taken by surprise that he reeled backwards. I lifted my skirts and began to run as fast as I could down the stairs.

I did not know where I was but I went on running blindly and eventually found the gallery and so made my way back to my own room.

There I threw myself on to my bed and lay there until I recovered my breath.

There is only one thing I can do, I told myself, and that is get away from this house with all speed. He has now made his intentions clear to me. I have no doubt at all that Miss Jansen was dismissed because she refused to accept his invitations. The man is a monster. He appeared to think that anyone whom he employed belonged to him completely. Did he imagine he was an eastern pasha? How dared he treat me in such a way!

There was a constricted feeling in my throat which made me feel as though I were going to choke. I was more desperately unhappy than I had ever been in my life. It was due to him. I would not face the truth, but I really cared more deeply than I had about anything else that he should regard me with such contempt.

These were the danger signals.

I had need now of my common sense.

I rose from my bed and locked my door. I must make sure that my door was locked during the last night I would spend in this house. The only other way to my room would be through Alvean's room and the schoolroom, and I knew he would not attempt to come that way.

Nevertheless I felt unsafe.

Nonsense, I said to myself, you can protect yourself. If he should dare enter your room you could pull the bell rope immediately.

The first thing I would do would be to write to Phillida. I sat down and tried to do this but my hands were trembling and my handwriting was so shaky that the note looked ridiculous.

I could start packing.

I did this.

I went to the cupboard and pulled open the door. For a moment I thought someone was standing there, and I cried out in alarm; which showed the nervous state to which I had been reduced. I saw what it was almost immediately: The riding habit which Alvean had procured for me. She must have hung it in my wardrobe herself. I had forgotten all about this afternoon's little adventure for what had happened in the solarium and after had temporarily obliterated everything else.

I packed my trunk in a very short time, for my possessions were not many. Then, as I was more composed, I sat down and wrote the letter to Phillida.

When I had finished writing I heard the sound of voices below and I went to my window. Some of the guests had come out on to the lawn, and I saw them dancing down there. More came out.

I heard someone say: 'It's such a heavenly night. That moon is too good to miss.'

I stood back in the shadows watching, and eventually I saw what I had been waiting for. There was Connan. He was dancing with Lady Treslyn; his head was close to hers. I imagined the sort of things he was saying to her.

Then I turned angrily from the window and tried to tell myself that the pain I felt within me was disgust.

I undressed and went to bed. I lay sleepless for a long time and when I did sleep I had jumbled dreams that were of Connan, myself and Lady Treslyn. And always in the background of these dreams was that shadowy figure who had haunted my thoughts since the day I had come here.

I awoke with a start. The moon was still visible and in the room in my half awakened state I seemed to see the dark shape of a woman.

I knew it was Alice. She did not speak yet she was telling me something. 'You must not go from here. You must stay. I cannot rest. You can help me. You must help us all.'

I was trembling all over. I sat up in bed. Now I saw what had startled me. When I had packed I had left the door of the cupboard open, and what appeared to be the ghost of Alice was only her riding habit.

I was late up next morning because when I had slept I had done so deeply, and it was Kitty banging on the door with my hot water who awakened me. She could not get in and clearly she wondered what was wrong.

I leaped out of bed and unlocked the door.

'Anything wrong, Miss?' she said.

'No,' I answered sharply, and she waited a few seconds for my explanation of the locked door.

I was certainly not going to give it to her, and she was so full of last night's ball that she was not as interested as she would have been had there been nothing else to absorb her.

'Wasn't it lovely, Miss? I watched from my room. They danced on the lawn in the moonlight. My dear life, I never saw such a sight. It was like it used to be when the mistress was here. You look tired, Miss. Did they keep you awake?'

'Yes,' I said, 'they did.'

'Oh, well, it's all over now. Mr. Polgrey's already having the plants taken back. Fussing over them like a hen with her chicks, he be. The hall do look a sorry mess this morning, I can tell 'ee. It's going to take Daisy and me all day to get it cleared up, you see.'

I yawned and she put my hot water by the hip bath and went out. In five minutes' time she was back again.

I was half clothed, and wrapped a towel about me to shield myself from her too inquisitive eyes.

'It's Master,' she said. 'He's asking for you. Wants to see you right away. In the punch room. He said, "Tell Miss Leigh it is most urgent."'

'Oh,' I said.

'Most urgent, Miss,' Kitty repeated, and I nodded.

I finished washing and dressed quickly. I guessed what this meant. Very likely there would be some complaint. I would be given my notice because I was inefficient in some way. I began to think of Miss Jansen, and I wondered whether something of this nature had happened in her case. 'Here one day and gone the next.' Some trumped-up case against her. What if he should trump up a case against me?

That man is quite unscrupulous! I thought.

Well, I would be first. I would tell of my decision to leave, before he had a chance to dismiss me.

I went down to the punch room prepared for battle.

He was wearing a blue riding jacket and he did not look as though he had been up half the night.

'Good morning, Miss Leigh,' he said, and to my astonishment he smiled.

I did not return the smile. 'Good morning,' I said. 'I have already packed my bags and would like to leave as soon as possible.'

'Miss Leigh!' His voice was reproachful, and I felt an absurd joy rising within me. I was saying to myself: He doesn't want you to go. He's not asking you to go. He's actually going to apologize.

I heard myself say in a high, prim voice, which I should have hated in anyone else as selfrighteous and priggish: 'I consider it the only course open to me after—'

He cut in: 'After my outrageous conduct of last night. Miss Leigh, I am going to ask you to forget that. I fear the excitement of the moment overcame me. I forgot with whom I was dancing. I have asked you to overlook my depravity on this occasion, and to say generously – I am sure you are generous, Miss Leigh – we will draw a veil over that unpleasant little incident and go on as we were before.'

I had a notion that he was mocking me but I was suddenly so happy that I did not care.

I was not going. The letter to Phillida need not be posted. I was not to leave in disgrace.

I inclined my head and I said: 'I accept your apology, Mr. TreMellyn. We will forget this unpleasant and unfortunate incident.'

Then I turned and went out of the room.

I found that I was taking the stairs three at a time; my feet were almost dancing as they had been unable to resist dancing last night in the solarium.

The incident was over. I was going to stay. The whole house seemed to warm to me. I knew in that moment that if I had to leave this place I should be quite desolate.

I had always been given to self-analysis and I said to myself, Why this elation? Why would you be so wretched if you had to leave Mount Mellyn?

I had the answer ready: Because there is some secret here. Because I want to solve it. Because I want to help those two bewildered children; for Alvean is as bewildered as poor little Gillyflower.

But perhaps that was not the only reason. Perhaps I was a little more than interested in the Master of the house.

Perhaps had I been wise I should have recognized the danger signals. But I was not wise. Women in my position rarely are.

That day Alvean and I took our riding lesson as usual. It went off well and the only remarkable thing about it was that I wore the new riding habit. It was different from the other, for it consisted of the tightly fitting dress of light-weight material and with it was a jacket, tailored almost like a man's.

I was delighted that Alvean showed no sign of fear after her small mishap of the day before, and I said that in a few days' time we might attempt a little jumping.

We arrived back at the house and I went to my room to change before tea.

I took off the jacket, thinking of the shock these things had given me in the night, and I laughed at my fears, for I was in very high spirits that day. I slipped out of the dress with some difficulty (Alice had been just that little bit more slender than I), put on my grey cotton – Aunt Adelaide had warned me that it was advisable not to wear the same dress two days running – and was about to hang up the riding habit in the cupboard when I felt something in the pocket of the coat.

I thrust in my hand in surprise, for I was sure I had had my hands in the pockets before this and nothing had been there.

There was nothing actually in the pocket now but there was something beneath the silk lining. I laid the jacket on the bed and examining it soon discovered the concealed pocket. I merely had to unhook it and there it was; in it was a book, a small diary.

My heart beat very fast as I took it out because I knew that this belonged to Alice.

I hesitated for a moment but I could not resist the impulse to look inside. Indeed I felt in that moment that it was my duty to look inside.

On the fly leaf was written in a rather childish hand 'Alice TreMellyn.' I looked at the date. It was the previous year so I knew that she had written in that diary during the last year of her life.

I turned the leaves. If I had expected a revelation of character I was soon disappointed. Alice had merely used this as a record for her appointments. There was nothing in this book to make me understand her more.

I looked at the entries. 'Mount Widden to tea.' 'The Trelanders to dine.' 'C to Penzance.' 'C due back.'

Still it was written in Alice's handwriting and that made it exciting to me.

I turned to the last entry in the book. It was under the twentieth of August. I looked back to July. Under the fourteenth was written: 'Treslyns and Trelanders to dine at M.M.' 'See dressmaker about blue satin.' 'Do not forget to see Polgrey about flowers.' 'Send Gilly to dressmaker.' 'Take Alvean for fitting.' 'If jeweller has not sent brooch by sixteenth go to see him.' And on the sixteenth: 'Brooch not returned must go along to-morrow morning. Must have it for dinner party at Trelanders on eighteenth.'

It all sounded very trivial. What I had believed might be a great discovery was nothing very much. I put the book back into the pocket and went along to have tea in the schoolroom.

While Alvean and I were reading together a sudden thought struck me. I didn't know the exact date of Alice's death but it must have been soon after she was writing those trivial things in her diary. How odd that she should have thought it worth while to make those entries when she was planning to leave her husband and daughter for another man.

It suddenly became imperative to know the exact date of her death.

Alvean had had tea with her father because several people had come to pay duty calls and compliment Connan on last night's ball.

Thus I was free to go out alone. So I made my way down to Mellyn village and to the churchyard where I presumed Alice's remains would have been buried.

I had not seen much of the village before as I had had little opportunity of going so far except when we went to church on Sunday, so it was an interesting tour of exploration.

I ran almost all the way downhill and was very soon in the village. I reminded myself that it would be a different matter toiling uphill on my way back.

The village in the valley nestled about the old church, the grey tower of which was half covered in ivy. There was a pleasant little village green and a few grey stone houses clustered round it among which was a row of very ancient cottages which I guessed were of the same age as the church. I promised myself that I would make a closer examination of the village later. In the meantime I was most eager to find Alice's grave.

I went through the lych gate and into the churchyard. It was very quiet there at this time of the day. I felt I was surrounded by the stillness of death and I almost wished that I had brought Alvean with me. She could have pointed out her mother's grave.

How could I find it among these rows of grey crosses and headstones, I wondered as I looked about me helplessly. Then I thought, the TreMellyns would no doubt have some grand memorial to their dead; I must look for the most splendid vault, and I am sure I shall quickly find it that way.

I saw a huge vault of black marble and gilt not far off. I made for this and quickly discovered it to be that of the Nansellock family.

A sudden thought occurred to me. Geoffry Nansellock would lie here, and he died on the same night as Alice. Were they not found dead together?

I discovered the inscription engraved on the marble. This tomb contained the bones of defunct Nansellocks as far back as the middle seventeen hundreds. I remembered that the family had not been in Mount Widden as early as there had been TreMellyns at Mount Mellyn.

It was not difficult to find Geoffry's name for his was naturally the last entry on the list of the dead.

He died last year, I saw, on the 17th of July.

I was all eagerness to go back and look at the diary and check up that date.

I turned from the tomb and as I did so I saw Celestine Nansellock coming towards me.

'Miss Leigh,' she cried. 'I thought it was you.'

I felt myself flush because I remembered seeing her last night among the guests in the solarium, and I wondered what she was thinking of me now.

'I took a stroll down to the village,' I answered, 'and found myself here.'

'I see you're looking at my family tomb.'

'Yes. It's a beautiful thing.'

'If such a thing can be beautiful. I come here often,' she volunteered. 'I like to bring a few flowers for Alice.'

'Oh, yes,' I stammered.

'You saw the TreMellyn vault, I suppose?'

'No.'

'It's over here. Come and look.'

I stumbled across the long grass to the vault which rivalled that of the Nansellocks in its magnificence.

On the black slab was a vase of Michaelmas daisies – large perfect blooms that looked like mauve stars.

'I've just put them there,' she said. 'They were her favourite flowers.'

Her lips trembled, and I thought she was going to burst into tears.

I looked at the date and I saw it was that on which Geoffry Nansellock had died.

I said: 'I shall have to go back now.'

She nodded. She seemed too moved to be able to speak. I thought then: She loved Alice. She seems to have loved her more than anyone else.

It was on the tip of my tongue to tell her about the diary I had discovered, but I hesitated. The memory of last night's shame was too near to me. I might be reminded that I was, after all, only the governess. And what right had I, in any case, to meddle in their affairs.

I left her there and as I went away I saw her sink to her knees. I turned again later and saw that her face was buried in her hands and her shoulders were heaving.

I hurried back to the house and took out the diary. So on the 16th of July last year, on the day before Alice was supposed to have eloped with Geoffry Nansellock, she had written in her diary that if her brooch was not returned on the next day she must go along to the jeweller as she needed it for a dinner party to be held on the 18th.

That entry had not been made by a woman who was planning to elope.

I felt that I had almost certain proof in my hands that the body which had been found with Geoffry Nansellock's on the wrecked train was not Alice's.

I was back at the old question. What had happened to Alice? If she was not lying inside the black marble vault, where was she?

Chapter Five

I felt I had discovered a vital clue but it took me no further. Each day I woke up expectant, but of the days which passed one was very like another. Sometimes I pondered on several courses of action. I wondered whether I would go to Connan TreMellyn and tell him that I had seen his wife's diary and that it clearly showed she had not been planning to leave.

Then I told myself I did not quite trust Connan TreMellyn, and there was one thought concerning him which I did not want to explore too thoroughly. I had already begun to ask myself the question: Suppose Alice was not on the train, and something else happened to her; who would be most likely to know what that was? Could it be Connan TreMellyn?

There was Peter Nansellock. I might discuss this matter with him, but he was too frivolous; he turned every line of conversation towards the flirtatious.

There was his sister. She was the most likely person. I knew that she had been fond of Alice; they must have been the greatest friends. Celestine was clearly the one in whom I could best confide. And yet I hesitated. Celestine belonged to that other world into which I had been clearly shown on more than one occasion, I had no right to intrude. It was not for me, a mere governess, to set myself up as investigator.

The person in whom I might confide was Mrs. Polgrey, but again I shrank from doing this. I could not forget her spoonfuls of whisky and her attitude towards Gilly.

So I decided that for the time being I would keep my suspicions to myself. October was upon us. I found the changing seasons delightful in this part of the world. The blustering south-west wind was warm and damp, and it seemed to carry with it the scent of spices from Spain. I had never seen so many spiders' webs as I did that October. They draped themselves over the hedges like gossamer cloth sewn with brilliants. When the sun came out it was almost as warm as June. 'Summer do go on a long time in Cornwall,' Tapperty told me.

The sea mist would come drifting in, wrapping itself about the grey stone of the house so that from the arbour in the south gardens it would sometimes be completely hidden. The gulls seemed to screech on a melancholy note on such days as though they were warning us that life was a sorrowful affair. And in the humid climate the hydrangeas continued to flower – blue, pink and yellow – in enormous masses of bloom such as I should not have expected to find outside a hot-house. The roses went on flowering, and with them the fuchsias.

When I went down to the village one day I saw a notice outside the church to the effect that the date of the horse show was fixed for the 1st of November.

I went back and told Alvean. I was delighted that she had lost none of her enthusiasm for the event. I had been afraid that, as the time grew near, her fear might have returned.

I said to her: 'There's only three weeks. We really ought to get in a little more practice.'

She was quite agreeable.

We could, I suggested, rearrange our schedule. Perhaps we could ride for an hour both in the mornings and the afternoons.

She was eager. 'I'll see what can be done,' I promised.

Connan TreMellyn had gone down to Penzance. I discovered this quite by accident. Kitty told me, when she brought in my water, one evening.

'Master have gone off this afternoon,' she said ''Tis thought he'll be away for a week or more.'

'I hope he's back in time for the show,' I said.

'Oh, he'll be back for that. He be one of the judges. He'm always here for that.'

I was annoyed with the man. Not that I expected him to tell me he was going; but I did feel he might have had the grace to say good-bye to his daughter.

I thought a good deal about him and I found myself wondering whether he had really gone to Penzance. I wondered whether Lady Treslyn was at home, or whether she had found it necessary to pay a visit to some relative.

Really! I admonished myself. 'Whatever has come over you? How can you entertain such thoughts? It's not as though you have any proof!

I promised myself that while Connan TreMellyn was away there was no need to think of him, and that would be a relief.

I was not entirely lying about that. I did feel relaxed by the thought that he was out of the house. I no longer felt it necessary to lock my door; but I continued to do so, purely on account of the Tapperty girls. I did not want them to know that I locked it for fear of the Master – and although they were quite without education, they were sharp enough where such matters were concerned.

'Now,' I said to Alvean, 'we will concentrate on practising for the show.'

I procured a list of the events. There were two jumping contests for Alvean's age group, and I decided that she should take the elementary one, for I felt that she had a good chance of winning a prize in that; and of course the whole point of this was that she *should* win a prize and astonish her father.

'Look, Miss,' said Alvean, 'there's this one. Why don't *you* go in for this?'

'Of course I shall do no such thing.'

'But why not?'

'My dear child, I am here to teach you, not to enter for competitions.'

A mischievous look came into her eyes. 'Miss,' she said, 'I'm going to enter you for that. You'd win. There's nobody here can ride as well as you do. Oh, Miss, you must!'

She was looking at me with what I construed as shy pride, and I felt a thrill of pleasure. I enjoyed her pride in me. She wanted me to win.

Well, why not? There was no rule about social standing in these contests, was there?

I fell back on my stock phrase for ending an embarrassing discussion: 'We'll see,' I said.

One afternoon we were riding close to Mount Widden and met Peter Nansellock.

He was mounted on a beautiful bay mare, the sight of which made my eyes glisten with envy.

He came galloping towards us and pulled up, dramatically removing his hat and bowing from the waist.

Alvean laughed delightedly.

'Well met, dear ladies,' he cried. 'Were you coming to call on us?'

'We were not,' I answered.

'How unkind! But now you are here you must come in for a little refreshment.'

I was about to protest when Alvean cried: 'Oh, do let's, Miss. Yes, please, Uncle Peter, we'll come in.'

'I had hoped you would call before this,' he said reproachfully.

'We had received no definite invitation,' I reminded him.

'For you there is always welcome at Mount Widden. Did I not make that clear?'

He had turned his mare and we all three walked our horses side by side. He followed my gaze, which was fixed on the mare.

'You like her?' he said.

'Indeed I do. She's a beauty.'

'She's a real beauty, are you not, Jacinth my pet?'

'Jacinth. So that's her name.'

'Pretty, you're thinking. Pretty name for a pretty creature. She'll go like the wind. She's worth four of that lumbering old cart horse you're riding, Miss Leigh.'

'Lumbering old cart horse? How absurd! Dion is a very fine horse.'

'Was, Miss Leigh. *Was!* Do you not think that the creature has seen better days? Really, I should have thought Connan could have given you something better from his stables than poor old Dion.'

'It was not a matter of his giving her any horse to ride,' said Alvean in hot defence of her father. 'He does not know what horses we ride, does he, Miss. These are the horses which Tapperty said we could have.'

'Poor Miss Leigh! She should have a mount worthy of her. Miss Leigh, before you go, I would like you to take a turn on Jacinth. She'll quickly show you what it feels like to be on a good mount again.'

'Oh,' I said lightly, 'we're satisfied with what we have. They serve my purpose – which is to teach Alvean to ride.'

'We're practising for the show,' Alvean told him. 'I'm going in for one of the events, but don't tell Papa; it's to be a surprise.'

Peter put his finger to his lips. 'Trust me. I'll keep your secret.'

'And Miss is entering for one of the events too. I've made her!'

'She'll be victorious,' he cried. 'I'll make a bet on it.'

I said curtly: 'I'm not at all sure about this. It is only an idea of Alvean's.'

'But you must, Miss!' cried Alvean. 'I insist.'

'We'll both insist,' added Peter.

We had reached the gates of Mount Widden which were wide open. There was no lodge here as at Mount Mellyn. We went up the drive – where the same types of flowers grew in profusion – the hydrangeas, fuchsias and fir trees which were indigenous to this part of the country.

I saw the house, grey stone as Mount Mellyn was, but much smaller and with fewer outbuildings. I noticed immediately that it was not so well cared for as what in that moment I presumptuously called 'our' house and I felt an absurd thrill of pleasure because Mount Mellyn compared so favourably with Mount Widden.

There was a groom in the stables and Peter told him to take charge of our horses. He did so and we went into the house.

Peter clapped his hands and shouted: 'Dick! Where are you, Dick?'

The houseboy, whom I had seen when he had been sent over to Mount Mellyn with messages, appeared; and Peter said to him: 'Tea, Dick. At once, in the library. We have guests.'

'Yes, Master,' said Dick and hurried away.

We were in a hall which seemed quite modern when compared with our own hall. The floor was tessellated and there was a wide staircase at one end of it which led to a gallery containing oil paintings, presumably of the Nansellock family.

I laughed at myself for scorning the place, which was very much larger and much grander than the vicarage in which I had spent my childhood. But it had a neglected air – one might almost say one of decay.

Peter took us into the library, a huge room, the walls of which were lined with books on three sides. I noticed that the furniture was dusty and that dirt was visible in the heavy curtains. What they need, I thought, is a Mrs. Polgrey with her beeswax and turpentine.

'I pray you sit down, dear ladies,' said Peter. 'It is to be hoped that tea will not long be delayed, although I must warn you that meals are not served with the precision which prevails in our rival across the cove.'

'Rival?' I said in surprise.

'Well, how could there fail to be a little rivalry? Here we stand, side by side. But the advantages are all with them. They have the grander house, and the servants to deal with it. Your father, dear Alvean, is a man of property. We Nansellocks are his poor relations.'

'You are not our relations,' Alvean reminded him.

'Now is that not strange? One would have thought that, living side by side for generations, the two families would have mingled and become one. There must have been charming TreMellyn girls and charming Nansellock men. How odd that they did not join up and become relations! I suppose the mighty TreMellyns always looked down their arrogant noses at the poor Nansellocks and went farther afield to make their marriages. But now there is the fair Alvean. How maddening that we have no boy of your age to marry you, Alvean. *I* shall have to wait for you. There is nothing for it but that.'

Alvean laughed delightedly. I could see that she was quite fascinated by him; and I thought, Perhaps he is more serious than he pretends. Perhaps he has already begun courting Alvean in a subtle way.

Alvean began to talk about the show and he listened attentively. I occasionally joined in, and so the time passed until tea was brought to us.

'Miss Leigh, will you honour us by pouring out?' Peter asked me.

I said I should be happy to do so, and I placed myself at the head of the tea table.

Peter watched me with attention which I found faintly embarrassing because, not only was it admiring, but contented.

'How glad I am that we met,' he murmured as Alvean handed him his cup of tea 'To think that, if I had been five minutes earlier or five minutes later, our paths might not have crossed. What a great part chance plays in our lives.'

'Possibly we should have met at some other time.'

'There may not be much more time left to us.'

'You sound morbid. Do you think that something is going to happen to one of us?'

He looked at me very seriously. 'Miss Leigh,' he said 'I am going away.'

'Where, Uncle Peter?' demanded Alvean.

'Far away, my child, to the other side of the world.'

'Soon?' I asked.

'Possibly with the New Year.'

'But where are you going?' cried Alvean in dismay.

'My dearest child, I believe you are a little hurt at the thought of my departure.'

'Uncle, where?' she demanded imperiously.

'To seek my fortune.'

'You're teasing. You're always teasing.'

'Not this time. I have heard from a friend who was at Cambridge with me. He is in Australia, and there he has made a fortune. Gold! Think of it, Alvean. You too, Miss Leigh. Lovely gold . . . gold which can make a man . . . or woman . . . rich. And all one has to do is pluck it out of the ground.'

'Many go in the hope of making fortunes,' I said, 'but are they all successful?'

'There speaks the practical woman. No, Miss Leigh, they are not all successful; but there is something named hope which, I believe, springs eternal in the human breast. All may not have gold but they can all have hope.'

'Of what use is hope if it is proved to be false?'

'Until she is proved false she can give so much pleasure, Miss Leigh.'

'Then I wish that your hopes may not prove false.'

'Thank you.'

'But I don't want you to go, Uncle Peter.'

'Thank *you*, my dear. But I shall come back a rich man. Imagine it. Then I shall build a new wing on Mount Widden. I will make the house as grand as – no, grander than – Mount Mellyn. And in the years to come people will say it was Peter Nansellock who saved the family fortunes. For, my dear young ladies, someone has to save them . . . soon.'

He then began to talk of his friend who had gone to Australia a penniless young man and who, he was sure, was now a millionaire, or almost.

He began planning how he would rebuild the house, and we both joined in. It was a pleasant game – building a house in the mind, to one's own desires.

I felt exhilarated by his company. He at least, I thought, has never made me feel my position. The very fact of his poverty – or what to him seemed poverty – endeared him to me.

It was an enjoyable tea time.

Afterwards he took us out to the stables and both he and Alvean insisted on my mounting Jacinth, and showing them what I could do with her. My saddle was put on her, and I galloped her and jumped with her, and she responded to my lightest touch. She was a delicious creature and I envied him his possession of her.

'Why,' he said, 'she has taken to you, Miss Leigh. Not a single protest at finding a new rider on her back.'

I patted her fondly and said: 'She's a beauty.'

And the sensitive creature seemed to understand.

We then mounted our horses, and Peter came to the gates of Mount Mellyn with us, riding Jacinth.

As we went up to our rooms I decided that it had indeed been a very enjoyable afternoon.

Alvean came to my room and stood for a while, her head on one side. She said: 'He likes you, I think, Miss.'

'He is merely polite towards me,' I replied.

'No, I think he likes you rather specially . . . in the way he liked Miss Jansen.'

'Did Miss Jansen go to tea at Mount Widden?'

'Oh yes. I didn't have riding lessons with her, but we used to walk over there. And one day we had tea just as we did this afternoon. He'd just bought Jacinth then and he showed her to us. He said he was going to change her name to make her entirely his. Then he said her name was to be Jacinth. That was Miss Jansen's name.'

I felt foolishly deflated. Then I said: 'He must have been very sorry when she left so suddenly.'

Alvean was thoughtful. 'Yes, I think he was. But he soon forgot all about her. After all—'

I finished the sentence for her: 'She was only the governess, of course.'

It was later that day when Kitty came up to my room to tell me that there was a message for me from Mount Widden.

'And something more too, Miss,' she said; it was clearly something which excited her, but I refrained from questioning her since I should soon discover what this was.

'Well,' I said, 'where is the message?'

'In the stables, Miss.' She giggled. 'Come and see.'

I went to the stables, and Kitty followed at a distance.

When I arrived there I saw Dick, the Mount Widden houseboy; and, to my astonishment, he had the mare, Jacinth, with him.

He handed me a note.

I saw that Daisy, her father, and Billy Trehay were all watching me with amused and knowing eyes.

I opened the note and read it. It said:

Dear Miss Leigh,

You could not hide from me your admiration for Jacinth. I believe she reciprocates your feelings. That is why I am making you a present of her. I could not bear to see such a fine and graceful rider as yourself on poor old Dion. So pray accept this gift.

> Your admiring neighbour,
> *Peter Nansellock*

In spite of efforts to control myself I felt the hot colour rising from my neck to my forehead. I knew that Tapperty found it hard to repress a snigger.

How could Peter be so foolish! Was he laughing at me? How could I possibly accept such a gift, even if I wanted to? Horses have to be fed and stabled. It was almost as though he had forgotten this was not my home.

'Is there an answer, Miss?' asked Dick.

'Indeed there is,' I said. 'I will go to my room at once, and you may take it back with you.'

I went with as much dignity as I could muster in front of such an array of spectators back to the house, and in my room I wrote briefly:-

Dear Mr. Nansellock,

Thank you for your magnificent gift which I am, of course, quite unable to accept. I have no means of keeping a horse here. It may have escaped you that I am employed in this house as a governess. I could not possibly afford the upkeep of Jacinth. Thank you for the kind thought.

> Yours truly,
> *Martha Leigh*

I went straight back to the stables. I could hear them all laughing and talking excitedly as I approached.

'Here you are, Dick,' I said. 'Please take this note to your master with Jacinth.'

'But . . .' stammered Dick. 'I was to leave her here.'

I looked straight into Tapperty's lewd old face. 'Mr. Nansellock,' I said, 'is fond of playing jokes.'

Then I went back to the house.

The next day was Saturday and Alvean said that, as it was a half holiday, could we not take the morning off and go to the moors. Her Great-Aunt Clara had a house there, and she would be pleased to see us.

I considered this. I thought it would be rather pleasant to get away from the house for a few hours. I knew that they must all be talking about me and Peter Nansellock.

I guessed that he had behaved with Miss Jansen as he was behaving with me, and it amused them all to see the story of one governess turning out so much like another.

I wondered about Miss Jansen. Had she perhaps been a little frivolous? I pictured her stealing, whatever she was supposed to have stolen, that she might buy herself fine clothes to appear beautiful in the sight of her admirer.

And he had not cared when she was dismissed. A fine friend he would be!

We set out after breakfast. It was a beautiful day for riding for the October sun was not fierce and there was a soft south-west wind. Alvean was in high spirits, and I thought this would be a good exercise in staying power. If she could manage the long ride to her great aunt's house and back without fatigue I should be delighted.

I felt it was pleasant to get away from the watchful eyes of the servants, and it was delightful to be in the moorland country.

I found the great tracts of moor fitted my mood. I was enchanted by the low stone walls, the grey boulders and the gay little streams which trickled over them.

I warned Alvean to be watchful of boulders, but she was sure-seated and alert now, so I did not feel greatly concerned.

We studied the map which would guide us to Great-Aunt Clara's house – a few miles south of Bodmin. Alvean had travelled there   a carriage once or twice and she thought she would know the road; but the moor was the easiest place in the world in which to lose oneself, and I thought that we could profit by the occasion to learn a little map-reading.

But I had left a great deal of my severity behind and I found myself laughing with Alvean when we took the wrong road and had to retrace our steps.

But at length we reached The House on the Moors which was the picturesque name of Great-Aunt Clara's home.

And a charming house it was, set there on the outskirts of a moorland village. There was the church, the little inn, the few houses and The House on the Moors which was like a small manor house.

Great-Aunt Clara lived here with three servants to minister to her wants, and when we arrived there was great excitement as we were quite unexpected.

'Why, bless my soul if it b'aint Miss Alvean!' cried an elderly housekeeper. 'And who be this you have brought with 'ee, my dear?'

'It is Miss Leigh, my governess,' said Alvean.

'Well now! And be there just the two on you? And b'aint your papa here?'

'No. Papa has gone to Penzance.'

I wondered then whether I had been wrong in acceding to Alvean's wishes, and had forgotten my position by imposing myself on Great-Aunt Clara without first asking permission.

I wondered if I should be banished to the kitchen to eat with the servants. Such a procedure did not greatly disturb me and I would rather have done that than sit down with a haughty, disapproving old woman.

But I was soon reassured. We were taken into a drawing room and there was Great-Aunt Clara, a charming old lady seated in an armchair, white-haired, pink-cheeked with bright friendly eyes. There was an ebony stick beside her, so I guessed she had difficulty in walking.

Alvean ran to her and she was warmly embraced.

Then the lively blue eyes were on me.

'So you are Alvean's governess, my dear,' she said. 'Well, that is nice. And how thoughtful of you to bring her to see me. It is particularly fortunate, for I have my grandson staying with me and I fear he grows a little weary of having no playmates of his own age. When he hears Alvean has arrived he'll be quite excited.'

I did not believe that the grandson could be any more excited than Great-Aunt Clara herself. She was certainly charming to me, so much so that I forgot my diffidence and I really did feel like a friend calling on a friend, rather than a governess bringing her charge to see a relative.

Dandelion wine was brought out and we were pressed to take a glass. There were wine cakes with it and I must say I found the wine delicious. I allowed Alvean to take a very small glass of it but when I had taken mine I wondered whether I had been wise, for it was certainly potent.

Great-Aunt Clara wished to hear all the news of Mount Mellyn; she was indeed a garrulous lady, and I guessed it was due to the fact that she lived a somewhat lonely life in her house on the moors.

The grandson appeared – a handsome boy a little younger than Alvean – and the pair of them went off to play, although I warned Alvean not to go too far away as we must be home before dark.

As soon as Alvean had left us I saw that Great-Aunt Clara was eager for a real gossip; and whether it was due to the fact that I had taken her potent dandelion wine or whether I believed her to be a link with Alice, I am not sure; but I found her conversation fascinating.

She spoke of Alice as I had not until now heard her spoken of – with complete candour; and I quickly realized that from this gossipy lady I was going to discover a great deal more than I could from anyone else.

As soon as we were alone she said: 'And now tell me how things really are at Mount Mellyn.'

I raised my eyebrows as though I did not fully comprehend her meaning.

She went on: 'It was such a shock when poor Alice died. It was so sudden. Such a tragic thing to happen to such a young girl – for she was little more than a girl.'

'Is that so?'

'Don't tell me you haven't heard what happened.'

'I know very little about it.'

'Alice and Geoffry Nansellock, you know. They went off together ... eloped. And then this terrible accident.'

'I have heard that there was an accident.'

'I think of them – those two young people – quite often, in the dead of the night. And then I blame myself.'

I was astonished. I did not understand how this gentle talkative old lady could blame herself for Alice's infidelity to her husband.

'One should never interfere in other people's lives. Or should one? What do you think, my dear? If one can be helpful—'

'Yes,' I said firmly, 'if one can be helpful I think one should be forgiven for interference.'

'But how is one to know whether one is being helpful or the reverse?'

'One can only do what one thinks is right.'

'But one might be doing right and yet be quite unhelpful?'

'Yes, I suppose so.'

'I think of her so much . . . my poor little niece. She was a sweet creature. But, shall I say, not equipped to face the cruelties of fate.'

'Oh, was she like that?'

'I can see that you, Miss Leigh, are so good for that poor child. Alice would be so happy if she could see what you've done for her. The last time I saw her she was with her . . . with Connan. She was not nearly so happy . . . so relaxed as she is to-day.'

'I'm so glad of that. I am encouraging her to ride. I think that has done her a world of good.' I was loath to interrupt that flow of talk from which I might extract some fresh evidence about Alice. I was afraid that at any moment Alvean and the grandson would return, and I knew that in their presence there would be no confidences. 'You are telling me about Alvean's mother. I am sure you have nothing with which to reproach yourself.'

'I wish I could believe that. It worries me sometimes. Perhaps I shouldn't weary you. But you seem so sympathetic, and you are there, living in the house. You are looking after little Alvean like . . . like a mother. It makes me feel very grateful to you, my dear.'

'I am paid for doing it, you know.' I could not resist that remark, and I thought of the smile it would have brought to Peter Nansellock's lips.

'There are some things in this world which cannot be bought. Love . . . devotion . . . they are some of them. Alice stayed with me before her marriage. Here . . . in this house. It was so convenient, you see. It was only a few hours' ride from Mount Mellyn. It gave the young people a chance to know each other.'

'The young people?'

'The engaged pair.'

'Did they not know each other then?'

'The marriage had been arranged when they were in their cradles. She brought him a lot of property. They were well matched. Both rich, both of good families. Connan's father was alive then and, you know, Connan was a wild boy with a will of his own. The feeling was that they should be married as soon as possible.'

'So he allowed this marriage to be arranged for him?'

'They both took it as a matter of course. Well, she stayed with me several months before the wedding. I loved her dearly.'

I thought of little Gilly and I said: 'I think a great many people loved her dearly.'

Great-Aunt Clara nodded; and at that moment Alvean and the grandson came in.

'I want to show Alvean my drawings,' he announced.

'Well, go and get them,' said his grandmother. 'Bring them down and show her here.'

I believed that she realized she had talked a little too much and was afraid of her own garrulity. It was clear to me that she was the sort of woman who could never keep a secret; how could she when she was ready to confide secret family history to me, a stranger?

The grandson returned with his portfolio, and the children sat at the table. I went over to them and I was so proud of Alvean's attempts at drawing that I determined to speak to her father about that at the first opportunity.

Yet as I watched, I felt frustrated. I was sure that Great-Aunt Clara had been on the point of confiding something to me which was of the utmost importance.

Aunt Clara gave us luncheon and we left immediately after.

We found our way back with the utmost care, but I was determined to ride out again, and that before long, to the house on the moors.

When I was strolling through the village one day I passed the little jeweller's shop there. But perhaps that was scarcely the term to use when describing it. There were no valuable gems in the window; but a few silver brooches and plain gold rings, some engraved with the word Mizpah, or studded with semi-precious stones such as turquoises, topaz, and garnets. I guessed that the villagers bought their engagement and wedding rings here and that the jeweller made a living by doing repairs.

I saw in the window a brooch in the form of a whip. It was of silver, and quite tasteful, I decided, although it was by no means expensive.

I wanted to buy that whip for Alvean and give it to her the night before the horse show, telling her that it was to bring her luck.

I opened the door and went down the three steps into the shop.

Seated behind the counter was an old man wearing steel-rimmed spectacles. He let his glasses fall to the tip of his nose as he peered at me.

'I want to see the brooch in the window,' I said. 'The silver one in the form of a whip.'

'Oh yes, Miss,' he said, 'I'll show it to you with pleasure.'

He brought it from the window and handed it to me.

'Here,' he said, 'pin it on and have a look at it.' He indicated the little mirror on the counter. I obeyed him and decided that the brooch was neat, not gaudy, and in the best of taste.

As I was looking at it I noticed a tray of ornaments with little tickets attached to them. They were clearly jewellery which he had received for repair. Then I wondered whether this was the jeweller to whom Alice had brought her brooch last July.

The jeweller said to me: 'You're from Mount Mellyn, Miss?'

'Yes,' I said; and I smiled encouragingly. I was becoming very ready to talk to anyone who I thought might have any information to offer me on this subject which appeared to obsess me. 'As a matter of fact I want to give the brooch to my pupil.'

Like most people in small villages he was very interested in those living around him.

'Ah,' he said, 'poor motherless little girl. It's heartening to think she has a kind lady like yourself to look after her now.'

'I'll take the brooch,' I told him.

'I'll find a little box for it. A nice little box makes all the difference when it be a matter of a present, don't you agree, Miss?'

'Most certainly.'

He bent down and from under the counter brought a small cardboard-box which he began to stuff with cotton-wool.

'Make a little nest for it, Miss,' he said with a smile.

I fancied that he was loth to let me go.

'Don't see much of them from the Mount these days. Mrs. TreMellyn, her was often in.'

'Yes, I suppose so.'

'See a little trinket in the window and she'd buy it . . . sometimes for herself, sometimes for others. Why, she was in here the day she died.'

His voice had sunk to a whisper and I felt excitement grip me. I thought of Alice's diary which was still in the concealed pocket of her habit.

'Really?' I said encouragingly.

He laid the brooch in the cotton-wool and looked at me. 'I thought 'twas a little odd at the time. I remember it very clearly. She came in here and said to me: "Have you got the brooch done, Mr. Pastern? It's very important that I should have it. I'm anxious to wear it to-morrow. I'm going to a dinner party at Mr. and Mrs. Trelanders', and Mrs. Trelander gave me that brooch as a Christmas present so you see it's most important I should wear it to show her I appreciate it." ' His eyes were puzzled as they looked into mine. 'She were a lady who talked like that. She'd tell you where she was going, why she wanted a thing. I couldn't believe my ears when I heard she'd left home that very evening. Didn't seem possible that she could have been telling me about the dinner party she was going to the next day, you see.'

'No,' I said, 'it was certainly very strange.'

'You see, Miss, there was no need for her to say anything to me like. If she'd said it to some it might seem as though she was trying to pull the wool over their eyes. But why should she say such a thing to me, Miss? That's what I've been wondering. Sometimes I think of it . . . and still wonder.'

'I expect there's an answer,' I said. 'Perhaps you misunderstood her.'

He shook his head. He did not believe that he had misunderstood. Nor did I. I had seen the entry in her diary and what I had read there confirmed what the jeweller had said.

Celestine Nansellock rode over next day to see Alvean. We were about to go for our riding lesson, and she insisted on coming with us.

'Now, Alvean,' I said, 'is the time to have a little rehearsal. See if you can surprise Miss Nansellock as you hope to surprise your father.'

We were going to practise jumping, and we rode down through the Mellyn village and beyond.

Celestine was clearly astonished by Alvean's progress.

'But you've done wonders with her, Miss Leigh.'

We watched Alvean canter round the field. 'I hope her father is going to be pleased. She has entered for one of the events in the show.'

'He'll be delighted, I'm sure.'

'Please don't say anything to him beforehand. We do want it to be a surprise.'

Celestine smiled at me. 'He'll be very grateful to you, Miss Leigh. I'm sure of that.'

'I'm counting on his being rather pleased.'

I was conscious of her eyes upon me as she smiled at me benignly. She said suddenly: 'Oh, Miss Leigh, about my brother Peter. I did want to speak to you confidentially about that matter of Jacinth.'

I flushed faintly, and I was annoyed with myself for doing so.

'I know he gave you the horse and you returned it as too valuable a gift.'

'Too valuable a gift to accept,' I answered, 'and too expensive for me to be able to maintain.'

'Of course. I'm afraid he is very thoughtless. But he is the most generous man alive. He's rather afraid he has offended you.'

'Please tell him I'm not offended, and if he thinks awhile he will understand why I can't accept such a gift.'

'I explained to him. He admires you very much, Miss Leigh, but there was an ulterior motive behind the gift. He wanted a good home for Jacinth. You know that he plans to leave England.'

'He did mention it.'

'I expect he will sell some of the horses. I shall keep a couple for myself, but there is no point in keeping an expensive stable with only myself at the house.'

'No, I suppose not.'

'He saw you on Jacinth and thinks you'd be a worthy mistress for her. That was why he wanted you to have her. He's very fond of that mare.'

'I see.'

'Miss Leigh, you would like to possess a horse like that?'

'Who wouldn't?'

'Suppose I asked Connan if it could be taken into his stables and kept there for you to ride. How would that be?'

I replied emphatically: 'It is most kind of you, Miss Nansellock, and I do appreciate your desire – and that of your brother – to please me. But I do not wish for any special favours here. Mr. TreMellyn has a full and adequate stable for the needs of us all. I should be very much against asking for special favours for myself.'

'I see,' she said, 'that you are very determined and very proud.'

She leaned forward and touched my hand in a very friendly manner. There was a faint mist of tears in her eyes. She was touched by my position, and understood how desperately I clung to my pride because it was my only possession.

I thought her kind and considerate, and I could understand why Alice had made a friend of her. I felt that I too could easily become her friend, for she had never made me in the least conscious of my social position in the house.

One day, I thought, I'll tell her what I've discovered about Alice.

But not yet. I was, as her brother had said, as spiky as a hedgehog. I did not think for a moment that I should be rebuffed by Celestine Nansellock, but just at this time I was not going to run any risk.

Alvean joined us, and Celestine complimented her on her riding. Then we went back to the house, and tea, over which I presided, was served in the punch room.

I thought what a happy afternoon that was.

Connan TreMellyn came back the day before the show. I was glad he had not returned before, because I was afraid that Alvean might betray her excitement.

I was entered for one of the early events in which points were scored, particularly for jumping. It was what they called a mixed event which meant that men and women competed together.

Tapperty, who knew I was going to enter, wouldn't hear of my riding on Dion.

'Why, Miss,' he said, the day before the show, 'if you'd have took Jacinth when she was offered you, you would have got first prize. That mare be a winner and so would you be, Miss, on her back. Old Dion, he's a good fellow, but he ain't no prize winner. How'd you say to taking Royal Rover?'

'What if Mr. TreMellyn objected?'

Tapperty winked. 'Nay, he'd not object. He'll be riding out to the show on May Morning, so old Royal 'ull be free. I'll tell 'ee what, just suppose master was to say to me "Saddle up Royal Rover for me, Tapperty." Right, then I'd saddle the Rover for him and it would be May Morning for you, Miss. Nothing 'ud please master more than for to see his horse win a prize.'

I was anxious to show off before Connan TreMellyn and I agreed to Tapperty's suggestion. After all, I was teaching his daughter to ride and that meant that I could, with the approval of his head stable man, make my selection from the stables.

The night before the show I presented Alvean with the brooch.

She was extremely delighted.

'It's a whip!' she cried.

'It will pin your cravat,' I said, 'and I hope bring you luck.'

'It will, Miss. I know it will.'

'Well, don't rely on it too much. Remember luck only comes to those who deserve it.' I quoted the beginning of an old rhyme which Father used to say to us.

'Your head and your heart keep boldly up,

Your chin and your heels keep down.' I went on: 'And when you take your jump together . . . go with Prince.'

'I'll remember.'

'Excited?'

'It seems so long in coming.'

'It'll come fast enough.'

That night when I went in to say good night to her I sat on her bed and we talked about the show.

I was a little anxious about her, because she was too excited, and I tried to calm her down. I told her she must go to sleep for if she did not she would not be fresh for the morning.

'But how does one sleep, Miss,' she asked, 'when sleep won't come?'

I realized then the magnitude of what I had done. A few months before, when I had come to this house, this girl had been afraid to mount a horse; now she was looking forward to competing at the horse show.

That was all well and good. I would have preferred her interest not to have been centred so wholeheartedly on her father. It was his approval which meant so much to her.

She was not only eager; she was apprehensive, so desperately did she long for his admiration.

I went to my room and came back with a book of Mr. Longfellow's poems.

I sat down by her bed and began to read to her, for I knew of nothing to turn the mind to peace than his narrative poem, 'Hiawatha.'

I often quoted it when I was trying to sleep and then I would feel myself torn from the events of this world in which I lived and in my imagination I would wander along through the primeval forests with the 'rushings of great rivers' . . . and their wild reverberations.'

The words flowed from my lips. I knew I was conjuring up visions for Alvean. She had forgotten the show . . . her fears and her hopes. She was with the little Hiawatha sitting at the feet of the good Nokomis and – she slept.

I woke up on the day of the horse show to find the mist had penetrated my room. I got out of bed and went to the window. Little wisps of it encircled the palm trees and the feathery leaves of the evergreen pines were decorated with little drops of moisture.

'I hope the mist lifts before the afternoon,' I said to myself.

But all through the morning it persisted, and there were anxious looks and whispers throughout the house where everyone was thinking of the show. Most of the servants were going. They always did, Kitty told me, because the master had special interest in it as one of the judges, and Billy Trehay and some of the stable boys were entrants.

'It do put master in a good mood to see his horses win,' said Kitty: 'but they say he's always harder on his own than on others.'

Immediately after luncheon Alvean and I set out; she was riding Black Prince and I was on Royal Rover. It was exhilarating to be on a good horse, and I felt as excited as Alvean; I fear I was just as eager to shine in the eyes of Connan TreMellyn as she was.

The show was being held in a big field close to the village church, and when we arrived the crowds were already gathering.

Alvean and I parted company when we reached the field and I discovered that the event in which I was competing was one of the first.

The show was intended to start at two-fifteen, but there was the usual delay, and at twenty past we were still waiting to begin.

The mist had lifted slightly, but it was a leaden day; the sky was like a grey blanket and everything seemed to have accumulated a layer of moisture.

The sea smell was strong but the waves were silent to-day and the cry of the gulls was more melancholy than ever.

Connan arrived with the other judges; there were three of them, all local worthies. Connan, I saw, had come on May Morning, as I expected, since I had been given Royal Rover.

The village band struck up a traditional air and everyone stood still and sang.

It was very impressive, I thought, to hear those words sung with such fervour in that misty field:

> '*And shall they scorn Tre Pol and Pen,*
> *And shall Trelawney die?*
> *Then twenty thousand Cornish men*
> *Will know the reason why.*'

A proud song, I thought, for an insular people; and they stood at attention as they sang. I noticed little Gillyflower standing there, singing with the rest, and I was surprised to see her; she was with Daisy and I hoped the girl would look after her.

She saw me and I waved to her, but she lowered her eyes at once, yet I could see that she was smiling to herself and I was quite pleased.

A rider came close to me and a voice said: 'Well, if it is not Miss Leigh, herself!'

I turned and saw Peter Nansellock; he was mounted on Jacinth.

'Good afternoon,' I said, and my eyes lingered on the perfection of Jacinth.

I was wearing a placard with a number on my back which had been put there by one of the organizers.

'Don't tell me,' said Peter Nansellock, 'that you and I are competitors in this first event.'

'Are you in it then?'

He turned, and I saw the placard on his back.

'I haven't a hope,' I said.

'Against me?'

'Against Jacinth,' I answered.

'Miss Leigh, you could have been riding her.'

'You must have been mad to do what you did. You set the stables talking.'

'Who cares for stable boys?'

'I do.'

'Then you are not being your usual sensible self.'

'A governess has to care for the opinions of all and sundry.'

'You are not an ordinary governess.'

'Do you know, Mr. Nansellock,' I said lightly, 'I believe all the governesses in your life were no ordinary governesses. If they had been, perhaps they would have had no place in your life.'

I gave Royal Rover a gentle touch on the flank and he responded immediately.

I did not see Peter again until he was competing. He went before I did. I watched him ride round the field. He and Jacinth seemed like one animal.

Like a centaur, I thought. Were they the creatures with the head and shoulders of a man and the body of a horse?

'Oh, perfect,' I exclaimed aloud as I watched him take the jumps and canter gracefully round the field. And who couldn't, I said to myself maliciously, on a mare like that!

A round of applause followed him as he finished his turn.

Mine did not come until some time later.

I saw Connan TreMellyn in the judges' stand. And I whispered: 'Royal Rover, help me. I want you to beat Jacinth. I want you to win this prize. I want to show Connan TreMellyn that there is one thing I can do. Help me, Royal Rover.'

The sensitive ears seemed to prick up as Royal Rover moved daintily forward and I knew that he heard me, and would respond to the appeal in my voice.

'Come on, Rover,' I whispered. 'We can do it.'

And we went round as faultlessly, I hoped, as Jacinth had. I heard the applause burst out as I finished, and walked my horse away.

We waited until the rest of the competitors were finished and the results were called. I was glad that they were announced at the end of each event. People were more interested immediately after they had seen a performance. The practice of announcing all winners at the end of the meeting I had always thought to be a sort of anti-climax.

'This one is a tie,' Connan was saying. 'Two competitors scored full marks in this one. It's most unusual, but I am happy to say that the winners are a lady and a gentleman: Miss Martha Leigh on Royal Rover, and Mr. Peter Nansellock on Jacinth.'

We trotted up to take our prizes.

Connan said: 'The prize is a silver rose bowl. How can we split it? Obviously we cannot do that so the lady gets the bowl.'

'Of course,' said Peter.

'But you get a silver spoon,' Connan told him. 'Consolation for having tied with a lady.'

We accepted our prizes, and as Connan gave me mine he was smiling, very well pleased.

'Good show, Miss Leigh. I did not know anyone could get so much out of Royal Rover.'

I patted Royal Rover and said, more for his hearing than anyone else's: 'I couldn't have had a better partner.'

Then Peter and I trotted off; I with my rose bowl, he with his spoon.

Peter said: 'If you had been on Jacinth you would have been the undisputed winner.'

'I should still have had to compete against you on something else.'

'Jacinth would win any race . . . just look at her. Isn't she perfection? Never mind, you got the rose bowl.'

'I shall always feel that it is not entirely mine.'

'When you arrange your roses you will always think, Part of this belonged to that man . . . what was his name? He was always charming to me, but I was a little acid with him. I'm sorry now.'

'I rarely forget people's names, and I feel I have nothing to regret in my conduct towards you.'

'There is a way out of this rose bowl situation. Suppose we set up house together. It could have a place of honour there. "Ours," we could say, and both feel happy about it.'

I was angry at this flippancy, and I said: 'We should, I am sure, feel far from happy about everything else.'

And I rode away.

I wanted to be near the judges' stand when Alvean appeared. I wanted to watch Connan's face as his daughter performed. I wanted to be close when she took her prize – which I was sure she would, for she was eager to win and she had worked hard. The jumps should offer no difficulty to her.

The elementary jumping contest for eight-year-olds began and I was feverishly impatient, waiting for Alvean's turn as I watched those little girls and boys go through their performances. But there was no Alvean. The contest was over and the results announced.

I felt sick with disappointment. So she had panicked at the last moment. My work had been in vain. When the great moment came her fears had returned.

When the prizes were being given I went in search of Alvean, but I could not find her, and as the more advanced jumping contest for the eight-year-old group was about to begin, it occurred to me that she must have gone back to the house. I pictured her abject misery because after all our talk, all our practice, her courage had failed her at the critical moment.

I wanted to get away, for now my own petty triumph meant nothing to me, and I wanted to find Alvean quickly, to comfort her if need be, and I felt sure she would need my comfort.

I rode back to Mount Mellyn, hung up my saddle and bridle, gave Royal Rover a quick rub-down and a drink, and left him munching an armful of hay in his stall while I went into the house.

The back door was unlatched and I went in. The house seemed very quiet. I guessed that all but Mrs. Polgrey were at the horse show. Mrs. Polgrey would probably be in her room having her afternoon doze.

I went up to my room and called Alvean as I went.

There was no answer so I hurried through the schoolroom to her room which was deserted. Perhaps she had not come back to the house. I then remembered that I had not seen Prince in the stables. But then I had forgotten to look in his stall.

I came back to my room and stood uncertainly at the window. I thought, I'll go back to the show. She's probably still there.

And as I stood at the window I knew that someone was in Alice's apartments. I was not sure how I knew. It may only have been a shadow across the window-pane. But I was certain that someone was there.

Without thinking very much of what I would do when I discovered who was there I ran from my room, through the gallery to Alice's rooms. My riding-boots must have made a clatter along the gallery. I threw open the door of the room and shouted: 'Who is here? Who is it?'

No one was in the room, but I saw in that fleeting second, the communicating door between the two rooms close.

I had a feeling that it might be Alvean who was there, and I was sure that Alvean needed me at this moment. I had to find her, and any fear I might have had, disappeared. I ran across the dressing room and opened the door of the bedroom. I looked round the room. I ran to the curtains and felt them. There was no one there. Then I ran to the other door and opened it. I was in another dressing room and the communicating door – similar to that in Alice's – was open. I went through and immediately I knew that I was in Connan's bedroom for I saw a cravat, which he had been wearing that morning, flung on the dressing table. I saw his dressing gown and slippers.

The sight of these made me blush and realize that I was trespassing in a part of the house where I had no right to be.

But someone other than Connan had been there before me. Who was it?

I went swiftly across the bedroom, opened the door and found myself in the gallery.

There was no sign of anyone there so I went slowly back to my room.

Who had been in Alice's room? Who was it who haunted the place?

'Alice,' I said aloud. 'Is it you, Alice?'

Then I went down to the stables. I wanted to get back to the show and find Alvean.

I had saddled Royal Rover and was riding out of the stable yard when I saw Billy Trehay hurrying towards the house.

He said: 'Oh Miss, there's been an accident. A terrible accident.'

'What?' I stammered.

'It's Miss Alvean. She took a toss in the jumping.'

'But she wasn't in the jumping!' I cried.

'Yes she were. In the eight-year-olds. Advanced class. It was the high jump. Prince stumbled and fell. They went rolling over and over ...'

For a moment I lost control of myself; I covered my face with my hands and cried out in protest.

'They were looking for you, Miss,' he said.

'Where is she then?'

'She were down there in the field. They'm afraid to move her. They wrapped her up and now they'm waiting for Dr. Pengelly to come. They think she may have broken some bones. Her father's with her. He kept saying, "Where's Miss Leigh?" And I saw you leave so I came after you. I think perhaps you'd better be getting down there, Miss ... since he was asking for you like.'

I turned away and rode as fast as I dared down the hill into the village, and as I rode I prayed, and scolded:

'Oh God, let her be all right. Oh Alvean, you little fool! It would have been enough to take the simple jumps. That would have pleased him enough. You could have done the high jumps next year. Alvean, my poor, poor child.'

And then: 'It's his fault. It's all his fault. If he had been a human parent this wouldn't have happened.'

And so I came to the field. I shall never forget what I saw there: Alvean lying unconscious on the grass, and the group round her and others standing about. There would be no more competitions that day.

For a moment I was terrified that she had been killed.

Connan's face was stern as he looked at me.

'Miss Leigh,' he said, 'I'm glad you've come. There's been an accident. Alvean . . .'

I ignored him and knelt down beside her.

'Alvean . . . my dear . . .' I murmured.

She opened her eyes then. She did not look like my arrogant little pupil. She was just a lost and bewildered child.

But she smiled.

'Don't go away . . .' she said.

'No, I'll stay here.'

'You did go . . . before . . .' she murmured, and I had to bend low to catch her words.

And then I knew. She was not speaking to Martha Leigh, the governess. She was speaking to Alice.

Chapter Six

Dr. Pengelly had arrived on the field and had diagnosed a broken tibia; but he could not say if any further damage had been done. He set the fractured bone and drove Alvean back to Mount Mellyn in his carriage while Connan and I rode back together in silence.

Alvean was taken to her room and given a sedative by the doctor.

'Now,' he said, 'there is nothing we can do but wait. I'll come back again in a few hours' time. It may be that the child is suffering acute shock. In the meantime we will keep her warm and let her sleep. She should sleep for several hours, and at the end of that time we shall know how deeply she has suffered from this shock.'

When the doctor had left, Connan said to me: 'Miss Leigh, I want to have a talk with you. Come to the punch room . . . now, will you please.'

I followed him there and he went on:

'There is nothing we can do but wait, Miss Leigh. We must try to be calm.'

I realized that he could never have seen me agitated as I was now, and he had probably considered me incapable of such deep feeling.

Impulsively I said: 'I find it hard to be as calm about my charge as you are about your daughter, Mr. TreMellyn.'

I was so frightened and worried that I wanted to blame someone for what had happened so I blamed him.

'Whatever made the child attempt such a thing?' he demanded.

'You made her,' I retorted. 'You!'

'I! But I had no idea that she was so advanced in her riding.'

I realized later that I was on the verge of hysteria. I believed that Alvean might have done herself some terrible injury and I felt almost certain that a child of her temperament would never want to ride again. I believed I had been wrong in my methods. I should not have tried to overcome her fear of horses; I had tried to win my way into her affections by showing her the way to win those of her father.

I could not rid myself of a terrible sense of guilt, and I was desperately trying to. I was saying to myself, This is a house of tragedy. Who are you to meddle in the lives of these people? What are you trying to do? To change Alvean? To change her father? To discover the truth about Alice? What do you think you are? God?

But I wouldn't blame myself entirely. I was looking for a scapegoat. I was saying to myself, He is to blame. If he had been different, none of this would have happened. I'm sure of that.

I had lost control of my feelings and on the rare occasions when people like myself do that, they usually do it more completely than those who are prone to hysterical outbursts.

'No,' I cried out, 'of course you had no idea that she was so advanced. How could you when you had never shown the slightest interest in the child? She was breaking her heart through your neglect. It was for that reason that she attempted this thing of which she was not capable.'

'My dear Miss Leigh,' he murmured. 'My dear Miss Leigh.' And he was looking at me in complete bewilderment.

I thought to myself, What do I care! I shall be dismissed, but in any case I have failed. I had hoped to do the impossible – to bring this man out of his own selfishness to care a little for his lonely daughter. And what have I done – made a complete mess of it and perhaps maimed the child for life. A fine one I was to complain of the conduct of others.

But I continued to blame him, and I no longer cared what I said.

'When I came here,' I went on, 'it did not take me long to understand the state of affairs. That poor motherless child was starved . . . Oh, I know she had her broth and her bread and butter at regular intervals. But there is another starvation besides that of the body. She was starved of the affection which she might expect from a parent and, as you see, she was ready to risk her life to win it.'

'Miss Leigh, please, I beg of you, do be calm, do be reasonable. Are you telling me that Alvean did that . . .'

But I would not let him speak. 'She did that for you. She thought it would please you. She has been practising for weeks.'

'I see,' he said. Then he took his handkerchief from his pocket and wiped my eyes. 'You do not realize it, Miss Leigh,' he went on almost tenderly, 'but there are tears on your cheeks.'

I took the handkerchief from him and angrily wiped my tears away. 'They are tears of anger,' I said.

'And of sorrow. Dear Miss Leigh, I think you care very much for Alvean.'

'She is a child,' I said, 'and it was my job to care for her. God knows, there are few others to do it.'

'I see,' he answered, 'that I have been behaving in a very reprehensible manner.'

'How could you . . . if you had any feeling? Your own daughter! She lost her mother. Don't you see that because of that she needed special care?'

Then he said a surprising thing: 'Miss Leigh, you came here to teach Alvean, but I think you have taught me a great deal too.'

I looked at him in amazement; I was holding his handkerchief a few inches from my tear-stained face; and at that moment Celestine Nansellock came in.

She looked at me in some astonishment, but only for a second. Then she burst out: 'What is this terrible thing I've heard?'

'There's been an accident, Celeste,' said Connan. 'Alvean was thrown.'

'Oh . . . no!' Celestine uttered a piteous cry. 'And what . . . and where . . . ?'

'She's in her room now,' Connan explained. 'Pengelly's set the leg. Poor child. At the moment she is asleep. He gave her something to make her sleep. He's coming again in a few hours' time.'

'But how badly . . . ?'

'He's not sure. But I've seen accidents like this before. I think she'll be all right.'

I was not sure whether he meant that or whether he was trying to soothe Celestine who was so upset. I felt drawn towards her; she was the only person, I believed, who really cared about Alvean.

'Poor Miss Leigh is very distressed,' said Connan. 'I think she fancies it is her fault. I do want to assure her that I don't think that at all.'

My fault! But how could I be blamed for teaching the child to ride? And having taught her, what harm was there in her entering for a competition? No, it was his fault, I wanted to shout. She would have been content to do what she was capable of, but for him.

I said with defiance in my voice: 'Alvean was so anxious to impress her father that she undertook more than she could do. I am sure that had she believed her father would be content to see her victorious in the elementary event she would not have attempted the advanced.

Celestine had sat down and covered her face with her hands. I thought fleetingly of the occasion when I had seen her in the churchyard, kneeling by Alice's grave. I thought, Poor Celestine, she loves Alvean as her own child, because she has none of her own and perhaps believes she never will have.

'We can only wait and see,' said Connan.

I rose and said: 'There is no point in my remaining here. I will go to my room.'

But Connan put out a hand and said almost authoritatively: 'No, stay here, Miss Leigh. Stay with us. You care for her deeply, I know.'

I looked down at my riding habit – Alice's riding habit – and I said: 'I think I should change.'

It seemed that in that moment he looked at me in a new light – and perhaps so did Celestine. If they did not look at my face I must have appeared to be remarkably like Alice.

I knew it was important that I change my clothes, for in my grey cotton dress with its severe bodice I should be the governess once more and that would help me to control my feelings.

Connan nodded. He said: 'But come back when you've changed, Miss Leigh. We have to comfort each other, and I want you to be here when the doctor returns.'

So I went to my room and I took off Alice's riding habit and put on my own grey cotton.

I was right. The cotton did help to restore my equilibrium. I began to wonder, as I buttoned the bodice, what I had said, in my outburst, to Connan TreMellyn.

The mirror showed me a face that was ravaged by grief and anxiety, eyes which burned with anger and resentment, and a mouth that was tremulous with fear.

I sent for hot water. Daisy wanted to talk, but she saw that I was too upset to do so and she went quickly away.

I bathed my face and when I had done so I went down to the punch-room and rejoined Connan and Celestine, there to await the coming of Dr. Pengelly.

It seemed a long time before the doctor returned. Mrs. Polgrey made a pot of strong tea and Connan, Celestine and I sat together drinking it. I did not feel astonished then, but I did later, because the accident seemed to have made them both forget that I was merely the governess. But perhaps I mean it made Connan forget; Celestine had always treated me without that condescension which I thought I had discerned in others.

Connan seemed to have forgotten my outburst and treated me with a courtly consideration and a new gentleness. I believed he was anxious that I should not blame myself in any way, and he knew that the reason I had turned on him so vehemently was because I wondered whether I had been at fault.

'She'll get over this,' he said. 'And she'll want to ride again. Why, when I was a little older than herself I had an accident which I'm sure was worse than this one. I got it in the collar-bone and was unable to ride for weeks. I could scarcely wait to get back on a horse.'

Celestine shivered. 'I shall never have a moment's peace if she rides again after this.'

'Oh Celeste, you would wrap her in cotton wool. And then what would happen? She would go out and catch her death of cold. You must not coddle children too much. After all, they've got to face the world. They must be prepared for it in some way. What does the expert have to say to that?'

He was looking at me anxiously. I knew he was trying to keep up our spirits. He knew how deeply Celestine and I felt about this, and he was trying to be kind.

I said: 'I believe one shouldn't coddle. But if children are really set against something I don't think they should be forced to do it.'

'But she was not forced to ride.'

'She did it most willingly,' I answered. 'But I cannot be sure whether she did it from a love of riding or from an intense desire to please you.'

'Well,' he said almost lightly, 'is it not an excellent thing that a child should seek to please a parent?'

'But it should not be necessary to risk a life for the sake of a smile.'

My anger was rising again and my fingers gripped the cotton of my skirt as though to remind me that I was not in Alice's riding habit now. I was the governess in my cotton gown, and it was not for me to press forward my opinions.

Both Celestine and Connan were surprised at my remark, and I went on quickly: 'For instance, Alvean's talents may lie in another direction. I think she has artistic ability. She has done some good drawings. Mr. TreMellyn, I have been going to ask you for some time whether you would consider letting her have drawing lessons.'

There was a tense silence in the room and I wondered why they both looked so startled.

I blundered on: 'I am sure there is great talent there, and I do not feel that it should be ignored.'

Connan said slowly: 'But Miss Leigh, you are here to teach my daughter. Why should it be necessary to engage other teachers?'

'Because,' I replied boldly, 'I believe she has a special talent. I believe it would be an added interest in her life if she were to be given drawing lessons. These should be given by a specialist in the art. She is good enough for that. I'm merely a governess, Mr. TreMellyn, I am not an artist as well.'

He said rather gruffly: 'Well, we shall have to go into this at some time.'

He changed the subject, and shortly afterwards the doctor arrived.

I waited outside in the corridor while Connan and Celestine were with Alvean and the doctor.

A hundred images of disaster crowded into my mind. I imagined that she died of her injuries. I saw myself leaving the place, never to return. If I did that I should feel that my life had been incomplete in some way. I realized that if I had to go away I should be a very unhappy woman. Then I thought of her, maimed for life, more difficult than she had been previously, a wretched and unhappy little girl; and myself devoting my life to her. It was a gloomy picture.

Celestine joined me.

'This suspense is terrible,' she said. 'I wonder whether we ought to get another doctor. Dr. Pengelly is sixty. I am afraid . . .'

'He seemed efficient,' I said.

'I want the best for her. If anything happens to her . . .'

She was biting her lips in anguish, and I thought how strange it was that she, who always seemed so calm about everything else, should be so emotional over Alice and her daughter.

I wanted to put my arm about her and comfort her, but of course, remembering my position, I did no such thing.

Doctor Pengelly came out with Connan, and the doctor was smiling.

'Injuries,' he said, 'a fractured tibia. Beyond that . . . there's very little wrong.'

'Oh, thank God!' cried Celestine, and I echoed her words.

'A day or so and she'll be feeling better. It'll just be a matter of mending that fracture. Children's bones mend easily. There's nothing for you two ladies to worry about.'

'Can we see her?' asked Celestine eagerly.

'Yes, of course you can. She's awake now, and she asked for Miss Leigh. I'm going to give her another dose in half an hour, and that will ensure a good night's sleep. You'll see a difference in her in the morning.'

We went into the room. Alvean was lying on her back looking very ill, poor child; but she gave us a wan smile when she saw us.

'Hallo, Miss,' she said. 'Hallo, Aunt Celestine.'

Celestine knelt by the bed, took her hand and covered it with kisses. I stood on the other side of the bed and the child's eyes were on me.

'I didn't do it,' she said.

'Well, it was a good try.'

Connan was standing at the foot of the bed.

I went on: 'Your father was proud of you.'

'He'll think I was silly,' she said.

'No he doesn't,' I cried vehemently. 'He is here to tell you so.'

Connan came round to the side of the bed and stood beside me.

'He's proud of you,' I said. 'He told me so. He said it didn't matter that you fell. He said all that mattered was that you tried; and you'd do it next time.'

'Did he? Did he?'

'Yes, he did,' I cried; and there was an angry note in my voice because he still said nothing and the child was waiting for him to confirm my words.

Then he spoke. 'You did splendidly, Alvean. I *was* proud of you.'

A faint smile touched those pale lips. Then she murmured: 'Miss . . . oh Miss . . .' And then: 'Don't go away, will you. Don't *you* go away.'

I sank down on my knees then. I took her hand and kissed it. The tears were on my cheeks again.

I cried: 'I'll stay, Alvean. I'll stay with you always . . .'

I looked up and saw Celestine watching me from the other side of the bed. I was aware of Connan, standing beside me. Then I amended those words, and the governess in me spoke. 'I'll stay as long as I'm wanted,' I said firmly.

Alvean was satisfied.

When she was sleeping we left her and, as I was about to go to my room, Connan said: 'Come into my library a moment with us, Miss Leigh. The doctor wants to discuss the case with you.'

So I went into his library with him, Celestine and the doctor, and we talked of the nursing of Alvean.

Celestine said: 'I shall come over every day. In fact I wonder, Connan, whether I won't come over and stay while she's ill. It might make things easier.'

'You ladies must settle that,' answered Dr. Pengelly. 'Keep the child amused. We don't want her getting depressed while those bones are knitting together.'

'We'll keep her amused,' I said. 'Any special diet, Doctor?'

'For a day or so, light invalid foods. Steamed fish, milk puddings, custards and so on. But after a few days let her have what she wants.'

I was almost gay, and this swift reversal of feelings made me slightly light-headed.

I listened to the doctor's instructions and Connan's assurance that there was no need for Celestine to stay at the house; he was sure Miss Leigh would manage and it would be wonderfully comforting for Miss Leigh to know that in any emergency she could always ask for Celestine's help.

'Well Connan,' said Celestine, 'perhaps it's as well. People talk. And if I stayed here ... Oh, people are so ridiculous. But they are always ready to gossip.'

I saw the point. If Celestine lived at Mount Mellyn, people would begin to couple her name with Connan's; whereas the fact that I, an employee of the same age, lived in the house aroused no comment. I was not of the same social standing.

Connan laughed and said: 'How did you come over, Celeste?'

'I rode over on Speller.'

'Right. I'll ride back with you.'

'Oh, thank you, Connan. It's nice of you. But I can go alone if you'd rather ...'

'Nonsense! I'm coming.' He turned to me. 'As for you, Miss Leigh, you look exhausted. I should advise you to go to bed and have a good night's sleep.'

I was sure I could not rest, and my expression must have implied this for the doctor said: 'I'll give you a draught, Miss Leigh. Take it five minutes before retiring for the night. I think I can promise you a good night's sleep.'

'Thank you,' I said appreciatively, for I suddenly realized how exhausted I was.

I believed that to-morrow I should wake up my usual calm self, able to cope with whatever new situation should be the result of all that had happened to-day.

I went to my room, where I found a supper tray waiting for me. It contained a wing of cold chicken, appetising enough on most occasions, but to-night I had no appetite.

I toyed with it for a while and ate a few mouthfuls, but I was too upset to eat.

I thought it would be an excellent idea to take Dr. Pengelly's sleeping draught and retire for the night.

I was about to do so when there was a knock on my door.

'Come in,' I called; and Mrs. Polgrey came. She looked distraught. No wonder, I thought. Who in this household isn't?

'It's terrible,' she began.

But I cut in quickly: 'She'll be all right, Mrs. Polgrey. The doctor said so.'

'Oh yes, I heard the news. It's Gilly, Miss. I'm worried about her.'

'Gilly!'

'She didn't come back from the show, Miss. I haven't seen her since this afternoon.'

'Oh, she's wandering about somewhere, I expect. I wonder if she saw . . .'

'I can't understand it, Miss. I can't understand her being at the show. She'm afeared of going near the horses. You could have knocked me down with a feather when I heard she was there. And now . . . she's not come in.'

'But she does wander off alone, doesn't she?'

'Yes, but she'll always be in for her tea. I don't know what can have become of her.'

'Has the house been searched?'

'Yes, Miss. I've looked everywhere. Kitty and Daisy have helped me. So's Polgrey. The child's not in the house.'

I said: 'I'll come and help look for her.'

So instead of going to bed I joined in the search for Gillyflower.

I was very worried because on this day of tragedy I was prepared for anything to happen. What could have happened to little Gilly? I visualized a thousand things. I thought she might have wandered on to the beach and been caught by the tide, and I pictured her little body thrown up by the waves in Mellyn Cove as her mother's had been eight years ago.

That was morbid. No, Gilly had gone wandering and had fallen asleep somewhere. I remembered that I had seen her often in the woods. But she would not be lost if she were in the woods. She knew every inch of them.

I nevertheless made my way to the woods, calling 'Gilly! Gilly!' as I went; and the mist, which was rising again with the coming of evening, seemed to catch my voice and muffle it as though it were cotton wool.

I searched those woods thoroughly because my intuition told me that she was there, and that she was not lost but hiding.

I was right. I came across her lying in a clearing surrounded by small conifers.

I had seen her in this spot once or twice and I guessed it was a haven to her.

'Gilly!' I called. 'Gilly!' And as soon as she heard my voice she sprang to her feet. She was poised to run but she hesitated when I called to her: 'Gilly, it's all right. I'm here all alone and I won't hurt you.'

She looked like a wild fairy child, her extraordinary white hair hanging damply about her shoulders.

'Why, Gilly,' I said, 'You'll catch cold, lying on that damp grass. Why are you hiding, Gilly?'

Her big eyes watched my face, and I knew that it was fear of something which had driven her to this refuge in the woods.

If only she would talk to me! I thought. If only she would explain.

'Gilly,' I said, 'we're friends, aren't we? You know that. I'm your friend – as Madam was.'

She nodded and the fear slipped from her face. I thought, she has seen me in Alice's well-cut riding clothes and, I believe, in her confused little mind she had bracketed us together in some way.

I put my arm about her; her dress was damp and I could see the mist on her pale brows and lashes.

'Why, Gilly, you are cold.'

She allowed me to cuddle her. I said: 'Come on, Gilly, we're going back. Your grandmamma is very anxious. She is wondering what has become of you.'

She allowed me to lead her from the clearing, but I was aware of the reluctant drag of her feet.

I kept my arm firmly about her, and I said: 'You were at the horse show this afternoon.'

She turned to me and as she buried her face against me, her little hands gripped the cloth of my dress. I was conscious of her trembling.

Then in a flash of understanding I began to see what had happened. This child, like Alvean, was terrified of horses. Of course she was. Had she not been almost trampled to death by one?

I believed that, as Alvean had been suffering from temporary shock, so was this child; but the shock which had come to her was of longer duration, and she had never known anyone who had been able to help her fight the darkness which had descended upon her.

In that misty wood I felt like a woman who has a mission. I was not going to turn my face from a poor child who needed help.

She was suffering from a return of that earlier shock. This afternoon she had seen Alvean beneath a horse's hoofs as she herself had been – after all it happened only four years ago.

At that moment I heard the sound of horse's hoofs in the wood, and I shouted: 'Hallo, I've found her.'

'Hallo! Coming, Miss Leigh.' And I was exhilarated – almost unbearably so – because that was Connan's voice.

I guessed that he had returned from Mount Widden to discover that Gilly was lost, and that he had joined the search party. Perhaps he knew that I had come to the woods and decided to join me.

He came into sight and Gilly shrank closer to me, keeping her face hidden.

'She's here,' I called. He came close to us and I went on: 'She is exhausted, poor child. Take her up with you.'

He leaned forward to take her, but she cried out: 'No! No!'

He was astonished to hear her speak, but I was not. I had already discovered that in moments of stress she did so.

I said: 'Gilly. Go up there with the master. I'll walk beside you and hold your hand.'

She shook her head.

I went on: 'Look! This is May Morning. She wants to carry you, because she knows you're tired.'

Gilly's eyes turned to look at May Morning, and, in the fear I saw there, was the clue.

'Take her,' I said to Connan, and he stooped and swung her up in his arms and set her in front of him.

She tried to fight, but I kept on talking to her soothingly. 'You're safe up there. And we'll get back more quickly. You'll find a nice bowl of bread and milk waiting for you, and then there'll be your warm cosy bed. I'll hold your hand all the time and walk beside you.'

She no longer struggled but kept her hand in mine.

And so ended that strange day, with myself and Connan bringing in the lost child.

When she was lifted from the horse and handed to her grandmother, Connan gave me a smile which I thought was infinitely charming. That was because it held none of the mockery which I had seen hitherto.

I went up to my room, exultation wrapped about me as the mist wrapped itself about the house. It was tinged with melancholy but the joy was so strong that the mingling of my feelings was difficult to understand.

I knew of course what had happened to me. To-day had made it very clear. I had done a foolish thing – perhaps the most foolish thing I had ever done in my life.

I had fallen in love for the first time, and with someone who was quite out of my world. I was in love with the master of Mount Mellyn, and I had an uneasy feeling that he might be aware of it.

On the table by my bed was the draught which Dr. Pengelly had given me.

I locked the door, undressed, drank the draught and went to bed.

But before I got into bed I looked at myself in my pink flannelette nightdress, primly buttoned up to the throat. Then I laughed at the incongruity of my thoughts and said aloud in my best governess's tones: 'In the morning, after the good night's rest Dr. Pengelly's potion will give you, you'll come to your senses.'

The next few weeks were the happiest I had so far spent in Mount Mellyn. It soon became clear that Alvean had suffered no great harm. I was delighted to find that she had lost none of her keenness for riding and asked eager questions about Black Prince's slight injuries, taking it for granted that she would soon ride him again.

We resumed school after the first week; she was pleased to do so. I also taught her to play chess, and she picked up the game with astonishing speed; and if I handicapped myself by playing without my queen she was even able to checkmate me.

But it was not only Alvean's progress which made me so happy. It was the fact that Connan was in the house; and what astonished me was that, although he made no reference to my outburst on the day of the accident, he had clearly noted it and would appear in Alvean's room with books and puzzles which he thought would be of interest to her.

In the first days I said to him: 'There is one thing that pleases her more than all the presents you bring; that is your own company.'

He had answered: 'What an odd child she must be to prefer me to a book or a game.'

I smiled at him and he returned my smile; and again I was aware of that change in his expression.

Sometimes he would sit down and watch our game of chess. Then he would range himself on Alvean's side against me. I would protest and demand I be allowed to have my queen back.

Alvean would sit smiling, and he would say: 'Look, Alvean. We'll put our bishop there, and that'll make our dear Miss Leigh look to her defences.'

Alvean would giggle and throw me a triumphant glance, and I would be so happy to be with the two of them that I grew almost careless and nearly lost the game. But not quite. I never forgot that between Connan and me there was a certain battle in progress and I always wanted to prove my mettle. Though it was only a game of chess I wanted to show him I was his match.

He said one day: 'When Alvean's movable we'll drive over to Fowey and have a picnic.'

'Why go to Fowey,' I asked, 'when you have a perfect picnic beach here?'

'My dear Miss Leigh' – he had acquired a habit of calling me his dear Miss Leigh – 'do you not know that other people's beaches are more exciting than one's own?'

'Oh yes, Papa,' cried Alvean. 'Do let's have a picnic.'

She was so eager to get well for the picnic that she ate all the food which was brought to her and talked of the expedition continually. Dr. Pengelly was delighted with her; so were we all.

I said to Connan one day: 'But you are the real cure. You have made her so happy, because at last you let her see that you are aware of her existence.'

Then he did a surprising thing. He took my hand and lightly kissed my cheek. It was very different from that kiss which he had given me on the night of the ball. This was swift, friendly, passionless yet affectionate.

'No,' he said, 'it is you who are the real cure, my dear Miss Leigh.'

I thought he was going to say something more. But he did not do so. Instead he left me abruptly.

I did not forget Gilly. I determined to fight for her as I had for Alvean, and I thought the best way of doing so was to speak to Connan about it. He was in that mood, I believed, to grant me what I asked. I should not have been surprised if, when Alvean was about again, he changed to his old self – forgetful of her, full of mockery for me. So I decided to strike my blow for Gilly while I had a chance of success.

I boldly went down to the punch room, when I knew he was there one morning, and asked if I might speak to him.

'But of course, Miss Leigh,' he replied. 'It is always a pleasure to speak to you.'

I came straight to the point. 'I want to do something for Gilly.'

'Yes?'

'I do not believe she is half-witted. I think that no one has made any attempt to help her. I have heard about her accident. Before that, I understand, she was quite a normal little girl. Don't you see that it might be possible to make her normal once again?'

I saw a return of that mockery to his eyes as he said lightly: 'I believe that as with God, so with Miss Leigh, all things are possible.'

I ignored the flippancy. 'I am asking your permission to give her lessons.'

'My dear Miss Leigh, does not the pupil you came here to teach take up all your time?'

'I have a little spare time, Mr. TreMellyn. Even governesses have that. I would be ready to teach Gilly in my own time, providing of course you do not expressly forbid it.'

'If I forbade you I am sure you would find some way of doing it, so I think it would be simpler if I say: "Go ahead with your plans for Gilly. I wish you all success." '

'Thank you,' I said; and turned to go.

'Miss Leigh,' he called. I stood waiting.

'Let us go on that picnic soon. I could carry Alvean if necessary to and from the carriage.'

'That would be excellent, Mr. TreMellyn. I'll tell her at once. I know it will delight her.'

'And you, Miss Leigh, does it delight you?'

For a moment I thought he was coming towards me and I started back. I was suddenly afraid that he would place his hands on my shoulders and that at his touch I might betray myself.

I said coolly: 'Anything which is going to be so good for Alvean delights me, Mr. TreMellyn.'

And I hurried back to Alvean to tell her the good news.

So the weeks passed – pleasurable, wonderful weeks which I sometimes felt could never be repeated.

I had taken Gilly to the schoolroom and I had even managed to teach her a few letters. She delighted in pictures and quickly became absorbed in them. I really believed she enjoyed our lessons for she would present herself at the schoolroom each day at the appointed time.

She had been heard to speak a few words now and then and I knew that the whole household was watching the experiment with amusement and interest.

When Alvean was well enough to take lessons in the schoolroom I should have to be prepared for opposition. Alvean's aversion to Gilly was apparent. I had brought the child into the sick-room on one occasion and Alvean had immediately become sulky. I thought, when she is quite well I shall have to reconcile her to Gilly. But that was one of the problems of the future. I knew very well that when life returned to normal I could not expect these days of pleasure to continue.

There were plenty of visitors for Alvean. Celestine was there every day. She brought fruit and other presents for her. Peter came and she was always pleased to see him.

Once he said to her: 'Do you not think I am a devoted uncle to call and see you so often, Alvean?'

She had retorted: 'Oh, but you don't come to see me only, do you, Uncle Peter. You come mainly for Miss.'

He had replied in characteristic style: 'I come to see you both. How fortunate I am to have two such charming ladies on whom to call.'

Lady Treslyn called with expensive books and flowers for Alvean, but Alvean received her sullenly and would scarcely speak to her.

'She is an invalid still, Lady Treslyn,' I explained; and the smile which was flashed upon me almost took my breath away, so beautiful was it.

'Of course I understand,' Lady Treslyn told me. 'Poor child! Mr. TreMellyn tells me that she has been brave and you have been wonderful. I tell him how lucky he is to have found such a treasure. "They are not easy to come by," I said. I reminded him of how my last cook walked out in the middle of a dinner party. She was another such treasure.'

I bowed my head and hated her – not because she had linked me in her mind with her cook, but because she was so beautiful, and I knew that rumours persisted about her and Connan and I feared that there was truth in them.

Connan seemed different when this woman was in the house. I felt he scarcely saw me. I heard the sounds of their laughter and I wondered sadly what they said to each other. I saw them in the gardens and I told myself there was an unmistakable intimacy in the very way they walked together.

Then I realized what a fool I had been, for I had been harbouring thoughts which I would not dare express, even to myself. I tried to pretend they did not exist. But they did – and in spite of my better sense they kept intruding.

I dared not look into the future.

Celestine one day suggested that she should take Alvean over to Mount Widden for the day and look after her there.

'It would be a change,' she said.

'Connan,' she added, 'you shall come to dinner, and you can bring her back afterwards.'

He agreed to do so. I was disappointed not to be included in the invitation; which showed what a false picture I had allowed myself to make of the situation during these incredible weeks. Imagine myself – the governess – invited to dine at Mount Widden!

I laughed at my own foolishness, but there was a note of bitterness and sadness. It was like waking up to a chilly morning after weeks of sunshine so brilliant that you thought it was going to last for ever; it was like the gathering of storm clouds in a summer sky.

Connan drove Alvean over in the carriage and I was left alone, for the first time since I arrived here without any definite duties.

I gave Gilly her lesson but I did not believe in taxing the child too much and when I had returned her to her grandmother I wondered what I was going to do.

Then an idea struck me. Why should I not go for a ride, a long ride? Perhaps on the moors.

I immediately remembered that day when Alvean and I had ridden to her Great-Aunt Clara. I began to feel rather excited. I was remembering the mystery of Alice again, which I had forgotten during those halcyon weeks of Alvean's convalescence. I began to wonder whether I had been so interested in Alice's story because I needed some interest to prevent me from brooding on my own.

I thought to myself, Great-Aunt Clara will want to hear how Alvean is getting on. In any case she had made it clear that I should be welcomed any time I called. Of course it would be different, calling without Alvean; but then I believed that she had been more interested to talk to me than to the child.

So I made up my mind.

I went to Mrs. Polgrey and said: 'Alvean will be away all day. I propose to take a day's holiday.'

Mrs. Polgrey had become very fond of me since I had taken such an interest in Gilly. She really did love the child, I believed. It was merely because she had assumed that Gilly's strangeness had been the price which had to be paid for her parents' sins that she had accepted her as *non compos mentis*.

'And none deserves a holiday more, Miss,' she said to me. 'Where are you going?'

'I think I'll go on to the moors. I'll take luncheon at an inn.'

'Do you think you should, Miss, by yourself?'

I smiled at her. 'I am very well able to take care of myself, Mrs. Polgrey.'

'Well, there be bogs on the moor and mists and the Little People, some say.'

'Little People indeed!'

'Ah, don't 'ee laugh at 'em, Miss. They don't like people to laugh at 'em. There's some as say they've seen 'em. Little gnome-like men in sugarloaf hats. If they don't like 'ee they'll lead 'ee astray with their fairy lanterns, and afore you knows where you be you'm in the middle of a bog that sucks 'ee down and won't let 'ee go however much you do struggle.'

I gave a shiver. 'I'll be careful, and I wouldn't dream of offending the Little People. If I meet any I'll be very polite.'

'You'm mocking, Miss, I do believe.'

'I'll be all right, Mrs. Polgrey. Don't have any fears about me.'

I went to the stables and asked Tapperty which horse I could have to-day.

'There's May Morning if you'd like her. She be free.'

I told him I was going to the moors. 'A good chance to see the country,' I added.

'Trust you, Miss. Bain't much you miss.' And he laughed to himself as though enjoying some private joke.

'You be going with a companion, Miss?' he asked slyly.

I said that I was going alone, but I could see that he did not believe me.

I felt rather angry with him because I guessed that his thoughts were on Peter Nansellock. I believed that my name had been coupled with his since he had been so foolish as to send Jacinth over for me.

I wondered too if my growing friendship with Connan had been noted. I was horrified at the possibility. Oddly enough I could bear to contemplate their sly remarks which I was sure were exchanged out of my hearing, about

Peter and me; it would be a different matter if they talked in that way of me and Connan.

How ridiculous! I told myself as I walked May Morning out of the stables and down to the village.

There is nothing to talk about between you and Connan. But there is, I answered myself; and I fell to thinking of those two occasions when he had kissed me.

I looked across the cove at Mount Widden. Wistfully I hoped that I should meet Connan coming back. But I didn't of course; he would stay there with Alvean and his friends. Why should I imagine that he would want to come back to be with me? I was letting this foolish habit of day dreaming get the better of my common sense.

But I continued to hope until I had left the village well behind me and I came to the first grey wall and boulders of the moor.

It was a sparkling December morning and there were great golden patches of gorse dotted over the moor.

I could smell the peaty soil, and the wind which had veered a little to the north was fresh and exhilarating.

I wanted to gallop across the moor with that wind in my face. I gave way to my desire and while I did so I imagined that Connan was riding beside me and that he called me to stop that he might tell me what a difference I had made to his life as well as Alvean's, and that, incongruous as it seemed, he was in love with me.

In this moorland country it was possible to believe in fantastic dreams; as some told themselves that these tracts of land were inhabited by the Little People, so I told myself that it was not impossible that Connan TreMellyn would fall in love with me.

At midday I arrived at The House on the Moor. It was very like that other occasion; the elderly housekeeper came out to welcome me and I was taken into Great-Aunt Clara's sitting room.

'Good day to you, Miss Leigh! And all alone to-day?'

So no one had told her of Alvean's accident. I was astonished. I should have thought Connan would have sent someone over to explain, since the old lady was obviously interested in her great-niece.

I told her about the accident and she looked very concerned. I hastily added that Alvean was getting on well and would soon be about again.

'But you must be in need of some refreshment, Miss Leigh,' she said. 'Let us have a glass of my elderberry wine; and will you stay to luncheon?'

I said it was most kind of her to invite me and if it were not causing too much inconvenience I should be delighted to do so.

We sipped our elderberry wine, and once more I was conscious of that heady feeling which I had experienced after her dandelion wine on the previous occasion. Luncheon consisted of mutton with caper sauce exceedingly well cooked and served; and afterwards we retired to the drawing room for what she called a little chat.

This was what I had been hoping for, and I was not to be disappointed.

'Tell me,' she said, 'how is dear little Alvean? Is she happier now?'

'Why ... yes, I think she is very much happier. In fact I think she has been more so since her accident. Her father has been so attentive, and she is so fond of him.'

'Ah,' said Great-Aunt Clara, 'her father.' She looked at me, and her bright blue eyes showed her excitement. I knew she was one of those women who cannot resist talking; and since she spent so much of her time with only her own household, the coming of a visitor such as myself was an irresistible temptation.

I was determined to make the temptation even more irresistible. I said tentatively: 'There is not the usual relationship between them, I fancy.'

There was a slight pause, and then she said quickly: 'No. I suppose it is inevitable.'

I did not speak. I waited breathlessly, afraid that she might change her mind. She was hovering on the edge of confidences and I felt that she could give me some vital clue to the situation at Mount Mellyn, to the story of the TreMellyns which I was beginning reluctantly to admit might very well become my story.

'I sometimes blame myself,' she said, as though she were talking to herself; and indeed her blue eyes looked beyond me as though she were looking back over the years and was quite unconscious of my presence.

'The question is,' she went on, 'how much should one interfere in the lives of others.'

It was a question which had often interested me. I had certainly tried to interfere in the lives of people I had met since I entered Mount Mellyn.

'Alice was with me after the engagement,' she went on. 'Everything could have changed then. But I persuaded her. You see, I thought *he* was the better man.'

She was being a little incoherent, and I was afraid to ask her to elucidate lest I broke the spell. She might remember that she was betraying confidences to a young woman who was more curious than she should be.

'I wonder what would have happened if she had acted differently then. Do you ever play that game with yourself, Miss Leigh? Do you ever say, now if at a certain point I ... or someone else ... had done such and such ... the whole tenor of life for that person would have changed?'

'Yes,' I said. 'Everybody does. You think that things would have been different for your niece and for Alvean.'

'Oh yes ... for her – Alice – more than most. She had come to a real turning-point. A cross-roads, one might say. Go this way and you have such and such a life. Go that way and everything will be quite different. It frightens me sometimes because if she had turned to the right instead of the left ... as it were ... she might be here to-day. After all, if she had married Geoffry there would not have been any need to run away with him, would there?'

'I see you were in her confidence.'

'Indeed yes. I'm afraid I had quite a big part in shaping what happened. That's what alarmed me. Did I do right?'

'I am sure you did what you thought was right, and that is all any of us can do. You loved your niece very much, did you not?'

'Very much. My children were boys, you see, and I'd always wanted a girl. Alice used to come and play with my family . . . three boys and no girl. I used to hope that she might marry one of them. Cousins though. Perhaps that would not have been so good. I didn't live in this house then. We were in Penzance. Alice's parents had a big estate some few miles inland. That's her husband's now of course. She had a good fortune to bring to a husband. All the same, perhaps it would not have been good for cousins to marry. In any case they were set on the marriage with the TreMellyns.'

'So that was arranged.'

'Yes. Alice's father was dead, and her mother – she was my sister – had always been very fond of Connan TreMellyn . . . the elder I mean. There have been Connans in that family for centuries. The eldest son was always given the name. I think my sister would have liked to marry the present Connan's father, but other marriages were arranged for them, and so they wanted their children to marry. They were betrothed when Connan was twenty and Alice eighteen. The marriage was to take place a year later.'

'So it was indeed a marriage of convenience.'

'How odd it is! Marriages of convenience often turn out to be marriages of inconvenience, do they not? They thought it would be a good idea if she came to stay with me. You see, I was within a few hours' riding distance from Mount Mellyn, and the young people could meet often like that . . . without her staying at the house. Of course you might say, why did not her mother take her to stay at Mount Mellyn? My sister was very ill at that time and not able to travel. In any case it was arranged that she should stay with me.'

'And I suppose Mr. TreMellyn rode over to see her often.'

'Yes. But not as often as I should have expected. I began to suspect that they were not as well matched as their fortunes were.'

'Tell me about Alice,' I said earnestly. 'What sort of girl was she?'

'How can I explain her to you. The word light comes to my mind. She was light-hearted, light-minded. I do not mean she was light in her morals – which is a sense in which some people use the word. Although of course, after what happened . . . But who shall judge? You see, he came over here to paint. He did some beautiful pictures of the moors.'

'Who? Connan TreMellyn?'

'Oh, dear me, no! Geoffry. Geoffry Nansellock. He was an artist of some reputation. Did you not know that?'

'No,' I said. 'I know nothing of him except that he was killed with Alice last July twelvemonth.'

'He came over here often while she was with me. In fact he came more often than Connan did. I began to wonder how matters stood. There was something between them. They would go off together and he'd have his painting things with him. She used to say she was going to watch him at work. She would be a painter herself one day. But of course it was not painting they did together.'

'They were . . . in love?' I asked.

'I was rather frightened when she told me. You see, there was going to be a child.'

I caught my breath in surprise. Alvean, I thought. No wonder he could not bring himself to love her. No wonder my statement that she possessed artistic talent upset him and Celestine.

'She told me two weeks before the day fixed for her wedding. She was almost certain, she said. She did not think she could be mistaken. She said, "What shall I do, Aunt Clara? Shall I marry Geoffry?"

'I said: "Does Geoffry want to marry you, my dear?" And she answered: "He would have to, would he not, if I told him."

'I know now that she should have told him. It was only right that she should. But her marriage was already arranged, Alice was an heiress and I wondered whether Geoffry had hoped for this. You see the Nansellocks had very little and Alice's fortune would have been a blessing to them. I wondered . . . as one does wonder. He had a certain reputation too. There had been others who found themselves in Alice's condition, and it was due to him. I did not think she would be very happy with him for long.'

There was silence, and I felt as though vital parts of a puzzle were being fitted together to give my picture meaning.

'I remember her . . . that day,' the old lady continued. 'It was in this very room. I often go over it. She talked to me about it . . . unburdening herself as I'm unburdening myself to you. It's been on my conscience for the last year . . . ever since she died. You see, she said to me: "What shall I do, Aunt Clara? Help me. . . . Tell me what I should do."

'And I answered her. I said: "There's only one thing you can do, my dear; and that is go on with your marriage to Connan TreMellyn. You're betrothed to him. You must forget what happened with Geoffry Nansellock." And she said to me: "Aunt Clara, how can I forget? There'll be a living reminder, won't there?" Then I did this terrible thing. I said to her: "You must marry. Your child will be born prematurely." Then she threw back her head and laughed and laughed. It was hysterical laughter. Poor Alice, she was near breaking-point.'

Great-Aunt Clara sat back in her chair; she looked as though she had just come out of a trance. I really believe she had been seeing, not me sitting opposite her, but Alice.

She was now a little frightened because she was wondering whether she had told me too much.

I said nothing. I was picturing it all; the wedding which would have been a ceremonial occasion; the death of Alice's mother almost immediately afterwards; and Connan's father had died the following year. The marriage had been to please them and they had not lived long to enjoy it. And Alice was left with Connan – my Connan – and Alvean, the child of another man, whom she had tried to pass off as his. She had not succeeded – that much I knew.

He had kept up the pretence that Alvean was his daughter, but he had never accepted her as such in his mind. Alvean knew it; she admired him so much; but she suspected something was wrong and she was uncertain; she longed to be accepted as his daughter. Perhaps he had never really discovered whether she was or not.

The situation was fraught with drama. And yet, I thought, what good can come of brooding on it? Alice is dead; Alvean and Connan are alive. Let them forget what happened in the past. If they were wise they would try to make happiness for each other in the future.

'Oh, my dear,' sighed Great-Aunt Clara, 'how I talk! It is like living it all again. I have wearied you.' A little fear crept into her voice. 'I have talked too much and you, Miss Leigh, have played no part in all this. I trust you will keep what I have said, to yourself.'

'You may trust me to do so,' I assured her.

'I knew it. I would not have told you otherwise. But in any case, it is all so long ago. It has been a comfort to talk to you. I think about it all sometimes during the night. You see, it might have been right for her to marry Geoffry. Perhaps she thought so, and that was why she tried to run away with him. To think of them on that train! It seems like the judgment of God, doesn't it?'

'No,' I said sharply. 'There were many other people on that train who were killed. They weren't all on the point of leaving their husbands with other men.'

She laughed on a high note. 'How right you are! I knew you had lots of common sense. And you don't think I did wrong? You see, I sometimes tell myself that, if I had persuaded her not to marry Connan, she wouldn't. That is what frightens me. I pointed the way to her destiny.'

'You must not blame yourself,' I said. 'Whatever you did you did because you thought it was best for her. And we after all make our own destinies. I am sure of that.'

'You do comfort me, Miss Leigh. You will stay and have tea with me, won't you?'

'It is kind of you, but I think I should be back before dark.'

'Oh yes, you must be back before dark.'

'It grows dark so early at this time of year.'

'Then I must not be selfish and keep you. Miss Leigh, when Alvean is well enough, you will bring her over to see me?'

'I promise I shall.'

'And if you yourself feel like coming over before that. . . .'

'Depend upon it, I shall come. You have given me a very pleasant and interesting time.'

The fear came back into her eyes. 'You will remember it was in confidence?'

I reassured her. I knew that this charming old lady's greatest pleasure in life must have been sharing confidences, telling a little more than was discreet. Well, I thought, we all have our little vices.

She came to the door to wave me on when I left.

'It's been so pleasant,' she reiterated. 'And don't forget.' She put her finger to her lips and her eyes sparkled.

I imitated the gesture and, waving, rode off.

I was very thoughtful on the way home. This day I had learned so much.

I was nearly at Mellyn village when the thought struck me that Gilly was Alvean's half-sister. I remembered then the drawings I had seen of Alvean and Gilly combined.

So Alvean knew. Or did she merely fear? Was she trying to convince herself that her father was not Geoffry Nansellock – which would make her Gilly's half-sister? Or did her great desire for Connan's approval really mean that she was longing for him to accept her as his daughter?

I felt a great desire to help them all out of this morass of tragedy into which Alice's indiscretion had plunged them.

I can do it, I told myself. I will do it.

Then I thought of Connan with Lady Treslyn, and I was filled with disquiet. What absurd and impossible dreams I was indulging in. What chance had I – a governess – of showing Connan the way to happiness?

Christmas was rapidly approaching, and it brought with it all that excitement which I remembered so well from the old days in my father's vicarage.

Kitty and Daisy were constantly whispering together, and Mrs. Polgrey said that they nearly drove her crazy, and that their work was more skimped than usual, though that had to be seen to be believed. She went about the house sighing 'Nowadays. . . .' and shaking her head in sorrow. But even she was excited.

The weather was warm, more like the approach of spring than of winter. On my walks in the woods I noticed that the primroses had begun to bloom.

'My dear life,' said Tapperty, 'primroses in December be nothing new to we. Spring do come early to Cornwall.'

I began to think about Christmas presents and I made a little list. There must be something for Phillida and her family, and Aunt Adelaide; but I was mainly concerned with the people at Mount Mellyn. I had a little money to spend, as I used very little and had saved most of what I had earned since I had taken my post at Mount Mellyn.

One day I went into Plymouth and did my Christmas shopping. I bought books for Phillida and her family and had them sent direct to her; I bought a scarf for Aunt Adelaide and that was sent direct too. I spent a long time choosing what I would give the Mellyn household. Finally, I decided on scarves for Kitty and Daisy, red and green which would suit them; and a blue one for Gilly to match her eyes. For Mrs. Polgrey I bought a bottle of whisky which I was sure would delight her more than anything else, and for Alvean some handkerchiefs in many colours, with A embroidered on them.

I was pleased with my purchases. I was beginning to grow as excited about Christmas as Daisy and Kitty were.

The weather continued very mild, and on Christmas Eve I helped Mrs. Polgrey and the girls to decorate the great hall and some of the other rooms.

The men had been out the previous day and brought in ivy, holly, box and bay. I was shown how the pillars in the great hall were entwined with these leaves and Daisy and Kitty taught me how to make Christmas bushes; they were delightedly shocked by an ignorance like mine. I had never before heard of a Christmas bush! We took two wooden hoops – one inserted into the other – and this ball-like framework we decorated with evergreen leaves and furze; then we hung oranges and apples on it; and I must say this made a pretty show. These we hung in some of the windows.

The biggest logs were carried in for the fireplaces, and the house was filled with laughter, while the servants' hall was decorated in exactly the same manner as the great hall.

'We do have our ball here while the family be having theirs,' Daisy told me; and I wondered to which ball I should go. Perhaps to neither. A governess's position was somewhere in between, I supposed.

'My life!' cried Daisy, 'I can scarcely wait for the day. Last Christmas was a quiet one ... had to be on account of the house being in mourning. But we in the servants' hall managed pretty well. There was dash-an-darras and metheglin to drink, and Mrs. Polgrey's sloe gin had to be tasted to be believed. There was mutton and beef, I remember, and hog's pudding. No feast in these parts ain't complete without hog's pudding. You ask Father!'

All through Christmas Eve the smell of baking filled the kitchen and its neighbourhood. Tapperty, with Billy Trehay and some of the boys from the stables, came to the door just to smell it. Mrs. Tapperty was up at the house all day working in the kitchen. I scarcely recognized the usually calm and dignified Mrs. Polgrey. She was bustling about, her face flushed, purring, stirring and talking ecstatically of pies which bore the odd names of squab and lammy, giblet, muggety and herby.

I was called in to help. 'Do 'ee keep your eye on that saucepan, Miss, and should it come to the boil tell I quickly.' Mrs. Polgrey's dialect became more and more broad as the excitement grew, and I could scarcely understand the language which was being bandied about in the kitchen that Christmas.

I was smiling fatuously at a whole batch of pasties which had just come out of the oven, golden-brown pastry with the smell of savoury meats and onions, when Kitty came in shouting: 'Ma'am, the curl singers be here.'

'Well, bring 'em, bring 'em in, ye daftie,' cried Mrs. Polgrey, forgetting dignity in the excitement and wiping her hand across her sweating brow. 'What be 'ee waiting for? Don't 'ee know, me dear, that it be bad luck to keep curl singers waiting?'

I followed her into the hall, where a company of village youths and girls had gathered. They were already singing when we arrived, and I understood that the curl singers were what were known in other parts of the country as carol singers.

They rendered 'The Seven Joys of Mary,' 'The Holly and the Ivy,' 'The Twelve Days of Christmas' and 'The First Noël.' We all joined in.

Then the leader of the group began to sing:

> 'Come let me taste your Christmas beer
> That is so very strong,
> And I do wish that Christmas time,
> With all its mirth and song,
> Was twenty times as long.'

Then Mrs. Polgrey signed to Daisy and Kitty, who were already on their way, I guessed, to bring refreshment to the party after this gentle reminder.

Metheglin was served to the singers with blackberry and elderberry wine, and into their hands were thrust great pasties, some containing meat, some fish. The satisfaction was evident.

And when they had finished eating and drinking, a bowl – which was tied with red ribbons and decorated with furze – was handed to Mrs. Polgrey who very majestically placed some coins in it.

When they had gone Daisy said: 'Well, now that lot have come a-gooding, what's to be next?'

She delighted in my ignorance of course when I had to ask what a-gooding meant.

'My dear life, you don't know all, Miss, do 'ee now. To go a-gooding means to go collecting for Christmas wine or a Christmas cake. What else?'

I realized that I had a great deal to learn concerning the habits of the Cornish, but I did feel that I was enjoying their way of celebrating Christmas.

'Oh, Miss, I forgot to tell 'ee,' cried Daisy. 'There be a parcel in your room. I took it up just afore them come a-gooding, and forgot to tell 'ee till now.' She was surprised because I lingered. 'A parcel, Miss! Don't 'ee want to see what it is? 'Twas so size, and 'twas a box like as not.'

I realized that I had been in a dream. I felt that I wanted to stay here for ever, and learn all the customs of this part of the world. I wanted to make it my part of the world.

I shook myself out of that dream. What you really want, I told myself, is some fairy-tale ending to your story. You want to be the mistress of Mount Mellyn. Why not admit it?

I went up to my room, and there I found Phillida's parcel.

I took out a shawl of black silk on which was embroidered a pattern in green and amber. There was also am amber comb of the Spanish type. I stuck the comb in my hair and wrapped the shawl about me. I was startled by my reflection. I looked exotic, more like a Spanish dancer than an English governess.

There was something else in the parcel. I undid it quickly and saw that it was a dress – one of Phillida's which I had greatly admired. It was of green silk, the same shade of green as in the shawl. A letter fell out.

'Dear Marty,

How is the governessing? Your last letter sounded as though you found it intriguing. I believe your Alvean is a little horror. Spoilt child, I'll swear. Are they treating you well? It sounded as if that side of it was not too bad. What is the matter with you, by the way? You used to write such amusing letters. Since you've been in that place you've become uncommunicative. I suspect you either love it or hate it. Do tell.

The shawl and comb are my Christmas gift. I hope you like them because I spent a lot of time choosing. Are they too frivolous? Would you rather have had a set of woollen underwear or some improving book? But I heard from Aunt Adelaide that she was sending you the former. There is a distinctly governessy flavour in your letters. All sound and fury, Marty, my dear, signifying nothing. I am wondering whether you'll be sitting down to dine with the family this Christmas or presiding in the servants' hall. I'm sure it will be the former. They couldn't help but ask you. After all it is Christmas. You'll dine with the family even if there's one of those dinner parties where a guest doesn't turn up and they say, "Send for the governess. We cannot be thirteen." So our Marty goes to dine in my old green and her new scarf and comb, and there she attracts a millionaire and lives happily ever after.

Seriously, Marty, I did think you might need something for the festivities. So the green gown is a gift. Don't think of it as a cast-off. I love the thing and I'm giving it to you, not because I'm tired of it, but because it always suited you better than me.

I shall want to hear all about the Christmas festivities. And, dear sister, when you're the fourteenth at the dinner table don't freeze likely suitors with a look or give them one of your clever retorts. Be a nice gentle girl and, kind lady, I see romance and fortune in the cards for you.

Happy Christmas, dear Marty, and do write soon sending the real news. The children and William send their love. Mine to you also.

Phillida.'

I felt rather emotional. It was a link with home. Dear Phillida, she did think of me often then. Her shawl and comb were beautiful, even if a little incongruous for someone in my humble position; and it was good of her to send the dress.

I was startled by a sudden cry. I spun round and saw Alvean at the door which led to the schoolroom.

'Miss!' she cried. 'So it's you!'

'Of course. Who did you think it was?'

She did not answer, but I knew.

'I've never seen you look like that, Miss.'

'You've never seen me in a shawl and comb.'

'You look . . . pretty.'

'Thank you, Alvean.'

She was a little shaken. I knew who she had thought it was standing in my room.

I was the same height as Alice, and if I were less slender that would not be obvious with the silk shawl round me.

Christmas Day was a day to remember all my life.

I awoke in the morning to the sounds of excitement. The servants were laughing and talking together below my window.

I opened my eyes and thought: Christmas Day. And then: My first Christmas at Mount Mellyn.

Perhaps, I said to myself trying to throw a cold douche over my exuberance which somehow made me apprehensive because it was so great, it will be not only your first but your last.

A whole year lay between this Christmas and the next. Who could say what would happen in that time?

I was out of bed when my water was brought up. Daisy scarcely stopped a moment, she was so full of excitement.

'I be late, Miss, but there be so much to do. You'd better hurry now or you'll not be in time to see the wassail. They'll be coming early, you can depend on that. They know the family 'ull be off to church, so they mustn't be late.'

There was no time to ask questions so I washed and dressed and took out my parcels. Alvean's had already been put by her bed the previous night.

I went to the window. The air was balmy and it had that strong tang of spices in it. I drew deep breaths and listened to the gentle rhythm of the waves. They said nothing this morning; they merely swished contentedly. This was Christmas morning when for a day all troubles, all differences might be shelved.

Alvean came to my room. She was carrying her embroidered handkerchiefs rather shyly. She said: 'Thank you, Miss. A happy Christmas!'

I put my arms about her and kissed her, and although she seemed a little embarrassed by this demonstration she returned my kiss.

She had brought a brooch so like the silver whip I had given her that I thought for a moment that she was returning my gift.

'I got it from Mr. Pastern,' she said. 'I wanted one as near mine as possible, but not too near, so that we shouldn't get them mixed up. Yours has got a little engraving on the handle. Now we'll each have one when we go riding.'

I was delighted. She had not ridden since her accident, and she could not have shown me more clearly that she was ready to start again.

I said: 'You could not have given me anything I should have liked better, Alvean.'

She was very pleased, although she murmured in an offhand way: 'I'm glad you like it, Miss.' Then she left me abruptly.

This, I told myself, is going to be a wonderful day. It's Christmas.

My presents proved to be a great success. Mrs. Polgrey's eyes glistened at the sight of the whisky; as for Gilly, she was delighted with her scarf. I suppose the poor child had never had anything so pretty before; she kept stroking it and staring at it in wonder. Daisy and Kitty were pleased with their scarves too; and I felt I had been clever in my choice.

Mrs. Polgrey gave me a set of doilies with a coy whisper: 'For your bottom drawer, me dear.' I replied that I would start one immediately, and we were very gay. She said that she would make a cup of tea and we'd sample my whisky, but there wasn't the time.

'My dear life, when I think of all there has to be done to-day!'

The wassail singers arrived in the morning and I heard their voices at the door of the great hall.

> 'The Master and Mistress our wassail begin
> Pray open your door and let us come in
> With our wassail, wassail, wassail.
> And joy come to our jolly wassail.'

They came into the hall, and they also carried a bowl into which coins were dropped; and all the servants crowded in and, as Connan entered, the singing grew louder and the verse was repeated.

'The Master and the Mistress . . .'

I thought, Two years ago, Alice would have stood there with him. Does he remember? He showed no sign. He sang with them and ordered that the

stirrup cup, the dash-an-darras, be brought out with the saffron cake and
pasties and gingerbread, which had been made for the occasion.

He moved nearer to me.

'Well, Miss Leigh,' he said under cover of singing, 'what do you think of
a Cornish Christmas?'

'Very interesting.'

'You haven't seen half yet.'

'I should hope not. The day has scarcely begun.'

'You should rest this afternoon.'

'But why?'

'For the feasting this evening.'

'But I . . .'

'Of course you will join us. Where else would you spend your Christmas
Day? With the Polgreys? With the Tappertys?'

'I did not know. I wondered whether I was expected to hover between the
great hall and the servants' hall.'

'You look disapproving.'

'I am not sure.'

'Oh, come, this is Christmas. Do not wonder whether you should be sure
or not. Just come. By the way, I have not wished you a merry Christmas
yet. I have something here . . . a little gift. A token of my gratitude, if you
like. You have been so good to Alvean since her accident. Oh, and *before* of
course, I have no doubt. But it has been brought to my notice so forcibly
since . . .'

'But I have only done my duty as a governess. . . .'

'And that is something you would always do. I know it. Well, let's say
this is merely to wish you a merry Christmas.'

He had pressed a small object into my hand, and I was so overcome with
pleasure that I felt it must show in my eyes and betray my feelings to him.

'You are very good to me,' I said. 'I had not thought . . .'

He smiled and moved away to the singers. I had noticed Tapperty's eyes
on us. I wondered whether he had seen the gift handed to me.

I wanted to be alone, for I felt so emotionally disturbed. The small case
he had pressed into my hand was demanding to be opened. I could not do
so here.

I slipped out of the hall and ran up to my room.

It was a small, blue plush case, the sort which usually contained jewellery.

I opened it. Inside, on oyster-coloured satin, lay a brooch. It was in the
form of a horseshoe, and it was studded with what could only be diamonds.

I stared at it in dismay. I could not accept such a valuable object. I must
return it of course.

I held it up to the light and saw the flash of red and green in the stones.
It must be worth a great deal of money. I possessed no diamonds, but I could
see that these were fine ones.

Why did he do it? If it had been some small token I should have been so
happy. I wanted to throw myself on to my bed and weep.

I could hear Alvean calling me. 'Miss, it's time for church. Come on,
Miss. The carriage is waiting to take us to church.'

I hastily put the brooch into its box and put on my cape and bonnet as Alvean came into the room.

I saw him after church. He was going across to the stables and I called after him.

He hesitated, looked over his shoulder and smiled at me.

'Mr. TreMellyn. It is very kind of you,' I said as I ran up to him, 'but this gift is far too valuable for me to accept.'

He put his head on one side and regarded me in the old mocking manner.

'My dear Miss Leigh,' he said lightly. 'I am a very ignorant man, I fear. I have no notion how valuable a gift must be before it is acceptable.'

I flushed hotly and stammered: 'This is a very valuable ornament.'

'I thought it so suitable. A horseshoe means luck, you know. And you have a way with horses, have you not?'

'I . . . I have no occasion to wear such a valuable piece of jewellery.'

'I thought you might wear it to the ball to-night.'

For a moment I had a picture of myself dancing with him. I should be wearing Phillida's green silk dress, which would compare favourably with those of his guests because Phillida had a way with clothes. I would wear my shawl, and my diamond brooch would be proudly flaunted on the green silk, because I treasured it so much, and I treasured it because he had given it to me.

'I feel I have no right.'

'Oh,' he murmured, 'I begin to understand. You feel that I give the brooch in the same spirit as Mr. Nansellock offered Jacinth.'

'So . . .' I stammered, 'you knew of that?'

'Oh, I know most things that go on here, Miss Leigh. You returned the horse. Very proper and what I would expect of you. Now the brooch is given in a very different spirit. I give it to you for a reason. You have been good to Alvean. Not only as a governess but as a woman. Do you know what I mean? There is more to the care of a child, is there not, than arithmetic and grammar. You gave her that little extra. The brooch belonged to Alvean's mother. Look upon it like this, Miss Leigh: It is a gift of appreciation from us both. Does that make it all right?'

I was silent for a few moments. Then I said: 'Yes . . . that is different, of course. I accept the brooch. Thank you very much, Mr. TreMellyn.'

He smiled at me – it was a smile I did not fully understand, because it seemed to hold in it many meanings.

I was afraid to try to understand.

'Thank you,' I murmured again; and I hurried back to the house.

I went up to my room and took out the brooch. I pinned it on my dress, and immediately my lavender cotton took on a new look.

I would wear the diamonds to-night. I would go in Phillida's dress and my comb and shawl, and on my breast I would wear Alice's diamonds.

So on this strange Christmas Day I had a gift from Alice.

I had dined in the middle of the day in the small dining room with Connan and Alvean, the first meal I had taken with them in this intimacy. We had eaten turkey and plum pudding and had been waited on by Kitty and Daisy. I could feel that certain significant looks were being directed towards us.

'On Christmas Day,' Connan had said, 'you could not be expected to dine alone. Do you know, Miss Leigh, I fear we have treated you rather badly. I should have suggested that you should go home to your family for Christmas. You should have reminded me.'

'I felt I had been here too short a time to ask for a holiday,' I answered. 'Besides . . .'

'In view of Alvean's accident, you felt you should stay,' he murmured. 'It is good of you to be so thoughtful.'

Conversation in the small dining room was animated. The three of us discussed the Christmas customs, and Connan told us stories of what had happened in previous years, how on one occasion the wassailers had arrived late so that the family had gone to church and they had to wait outside and serenade them all the way home.

I imagined Alice with him now. I imagined her sitting in the chair I now occupied. I wondered what the conversation was like then. I wondered if now, seeing me there, he was thinking of Alice.

I kept reminding myself that it was merely because it was Christmas that I was sitting here. That after the festivities were over I should revert to my old place.

But I was not going to think of that now. To-night I was going to the ball. Miraculously I had a dress worthy of the occasion. I had a comb of amber and a brooch of diamonds. I felt, To-night I shall mingle with these people on my own terms. It will be quite unlike that occasion when I danced in the solarium.

I took Connan's advice that afternoon and tried to rest so that I might stay fresh until the early morning. Much to my surprise I did manage to sleep. I must have slept lightly for I dreamed, and as so often in this house, my dreams were of Alice. I thought that she came to the ball, a shadowy wraith of a figure whom no one but I could see, and she whispered to me as I danced with Connan: 'This is what I want, Marty. I like to see this. I like to see you sitting in my chair at luncheon. I like to see your hand in that of Connan. You . . . Marty . . . you . . . not another. . . .'

I awoke with reluctance. That was a pleasant dream. I tried to sleep again, tried to get back to that half-world where ghosts came back from the tomb and told you that they longed for you to have all that you most wanted in life.

Daisy brought me a cup of tea at five o'clock. On Mrs. Polgrey's instructions, she told me.

'I've brought 'ee a piece of Mrs. Polgrey's fuggan to take with it,' she said, indicating a slice of raisin cake. 'If there's more you do want, 'tis only for you to say.'

I said: 'This will be ample.'

'Then you'll be wanting to get ready for the ball, will 'ee not, Miss?'

'There's plenty of time,' I told her.

'I'll bring 'ee hot water at six, Miss. That'll give 'ee plenty of time to dress. The Master 'ull be receiving the guests at eight. That's how it always was. And don't forget – 'tis but buffet supper at nine, so there's a long time to go afore you get more to eat. Are you sure you wouldn't like something more than that there piece of fuggan?'

I was sure I was going to find it difficult to eat what she had brought so I said: 'This is quite enough, Daisy.'

'Well, 'tis for you to say, Miss.'

She stood at the door a moment, her head on one side, watching me. Speculatively? Was she regarding me with a new interest?

I pictured them in the servants' hall, Tapperty leading the conversation.

Were they always wondering what new relationship had begun – or was about to begin – between the Master of the house and the governess?

I was at the ball in Phillida's green dress with the tight, low-cut bodice and the billowing skirt. I had dressed my hair differently, piling it high on my head; it was necessary to do so in order to do justice to the comb. On my dress sparkled the diamond brooch.

I was happy. I could mingle with the guests as one of them. No one would know, unless told, that I was only the governess.

I had waited until the ballroom was full before I went down. Then I could best mingle with the guests. I had only been there a few minutes when Peter was at my elbow.

'You look dazzling,' he said.

'Thank you. I am glad to surprise you.'

'I'm not in the least surprised. I always knew how you could look, given the chance.'

'You always know how to pay the compliment.'

'To you I always say what I mean. One thing I have not yet said to you, and that is "A happy Christmas." '

'Thank you. I wish you the same.'

'Let us make it so for each other. I have brought no gift for you.'

'But why should you?'

'Because it is Christmas, and a pleasant custom for friends to exchange gifts.'

'But not for . . .'

'Please . . . please . . . no reminders of governessing to-night. One day I am going to give you Jacinth, you know. She is meant for you. I see Connan is about to open the ball. Will you partner me?'

'Thank you, yes.'

'It's the traditional dance, you know.'

'I don't know it.'

'It's easy. You only have to follow me.' He began humming the tune to me. 'Haven't you seen it done before?'

'Yes, through the peep in the solarium at the last ball.'

'Ah, that last ball! We danced together. But Connan cut in, didn't he?'

'It was somewhat unconventional.'

'Very, for our governess. I'm really surprised at her.'

The music had begun, and Connan was walking into the centre of the hall holding Celestine by the hand. To my horror I realized that Peter and I would have to join them and dance those first few bars with them.

I tried to hold back, but Peter had me firmly by the hand.

Celestine was surprised to see me there; but if Connan was he gave no sign. I imagined that Celestine reasoned: It is all very well to ask the governess as it is Christmas. But should she immediately thrust herself into such a prominent position?

However, I believed her to be of too sweet a nature to show her astonishment after that first start of surprise. She gave me a warm smile.

I said: 'I shouldn't be here. I don't really know the dance. I didn't realize . . .'

'Follow us,' said Connan.

'We'll look after you,' echoed Peter.

And in a few seconds the others were falling in behind us.

Round the hall we went to the tune of *The Furry Dance*.

'You're doing excellently,' said Connan with a smile as our hands touched.

'You will soon be a Cornishwoman,' added Celestine.

'And why not?' demanded Peter. 'Are we not the salt of the earth?'

'I am not sure that Miss Leigh thinks so,' replied Connan.

'I am becoming very interested in all the customs of the country,' I added.

'And in the inhabitants, I hope,' whispered Peter.

We danced on. It was simple enough to learn, and when it was over I knew all the movements.

As the last bars were played I heard someone to say: 'Who is the striking-looking young woman who danced with Peter Nansellock?'

I wanted for the answer to be: 'Oh, that's the governess.'

But it was different: 'I've no idea. She certainly is . . . unusual.'

I was exultant. I doubt that I had ever been so happy in my life.

I knew that in the time to come I should treasure every minute of that wonderful evening, for I was not only at the ball, I was a success at the ball.

I did not lack partners; and even when I was forced to admit that I was the governess, I continued to receive the homage due to an attractive woman. What had happened to change me, I wondered. Why couldn't I have been like this at Aunt Adelaide's parties? But if I had, I should never have come to Mount Mellyn.

Then I knew why I had not been like this. It was not only the green dress, the amber comb and the diamond brooch; I was in love, and love was the greatest beautifier of all.

Never mind if I was ridiculously, hopelessly in love. I was like Cinderella at the ball, determined to enjoy myself until the stroke of twelve.

A strange thing happened while I was dancing. I was with Sir Thomas Treslyn, who turned out to be a courteous old gentleman, a little wheezy during the dance so I suggested that he might prefer to sit out the rest of it. He was very grateful to me and I felt quite fond of him. I was ready to be fond of anyone on that night.

He said: 'I'm getting a little too old for the dance, Miss er . . .'

'Leigh,' I said. 'Miss Leigh. I'm the governess here, Sir Thomas.'

'Oh indeed,' he said. 'I was going to say, Miss Leigh, it is extremely kind of you to think of my comfort when you must be longing to dance.'

'I'm quite happy to sit for a while.'

'I see that you are kind as well as very attractive.'

I remembered Phillida's instructions and accepted the compliments nonchalantly as though I had been accustomed to them all my life.

He was relaxed and confidential. 'It's my wife who likes to come to these affairs. She has so much vitality.'

'Ah yes,' I said, 'she is very beautiful.'

I had noticed her, of course, the very moment I entered the ballroom; she was in pale mauve chiffon over an underskirt of green; she evidently had a passion for chiffon and such clinging materials, and it was understandable considering her figure; she wore quantities of diamonds. The mauve toning down the green was exquisite and I wondered whether my own vivid emerald was not a little blatant compared with hers. She looked outstandingly beautiful, as she would in any assembly.

He nodded, a little sadly I thought.

And as I sat talking, my eyes, wandering round the hall, went suddenly to the peep high in the wall, that star-shaped opening which merged so perfectly into the murals that none would have guessed it was there.

Someone was watching the ball through the peep, but it was impossible to see who it was.

I thought: Of course it is Alvean. Did she not always watch the ball through the peep? Then I was suddenly startled for, as I was sitting there, watching the dancers, I saw Alvean. I had forgotten that this was a special occasion – Christmas Day – and just as, on such a day, the governess might come to the ball, so might Alvean.

She was dressed in a white muslin dress with a wide blue sash and I saw that she wore the silver whip pinned to the bodice of her dress. All these things I noticed with half my attention. I looked swiftly up to the peep. The face, unrecognizable, indefinable, was still there.

Supper was served in the dining room and the punch room. There was a buffet in both these rooms and guests helped themselves, for according to custom the servants on this day of days were having their own ball in their own hall.

I saw that these people who so rarely waited on themselves now found it quite good fun to do so. Piled on dishes were the results of all that kitchen activity; small pies of various kinds, called here pasties – not the enormous ones which were eaten frequently in the kitchen, but dainty ones. There were slices of beef, and chicken and fish of various descriptions. There was a great bowl of hot punch; another of mulled wine; there was mead, whisky and sloe gin.

Peter Nansellock, with whom I had had the supper dance, led me into the punch room. Sir Thomas Treslyn was already there with Celestine, and Peter led me to the table at which they were sitting.

'Leave it to me,' he said. 'I'll feed you all.'

I said: 'Allow me to help you.'

'Nonsense,' he replied. 'You remain with Celeste.' He whispered banter-
ingly: 'You're not the governess to-night, Miss Leigh; you're a lady like the
rest of them. Don't forget it; then no one else will.'

But I was determined that I would not be waited on and I insisted on
going to the buffet with him.

'Pride,' he murmured, slipping his hand through my arm. 'Wasn't that
the sin by which fell the angels?'

'It may have been ambition; I am not sure.'

'Well, I'll warrant you're not without a dash of that either. Never mind.
What will you eat? Perhaps it is as well you came. Our Cornish food often
seems odd to you foreigners from the other side of the Tamar.'

He began loading one of the trays which had been put there in readiness.

'Which sort of pie will you have? Giblet, squab, nattling or muggety?
Ha, here's taddage too. I can recommend the squab: layers of apple and
bacon, onions and mutton and young pigeon. The most delicious Cornish
fare.'

'I'm ready to try it,' I said.

'Miss Leigh,' he went on, 'Martha . . . has anyone ever told you that your
eyes are like amber?'

'Yes,' I answered.

'Has anyone ever told you you're beautiful?'

'No.'

'Then that oversight should be and is rectified immediately.'

I laughed and at that moment Connan came into the room with Lady
Treslyn.

She sat down with Celestine, and Connan came over to the buffet.

'I am enlightening Miss Leigh about our Cornish food. She doesn't know
what a "fair maid" is. Is that not odd, Con, seeing that she is one herself?'

Connan looked excited; his eyes smiling into mine were warm. He said:
'Fair maids, Miss Leigh, is another name for pilchards served like this with
oil and lemon.' He took a fork and put some on two plates. 'It is a contraction
of the old Spanish fumado, and we always say here that it is food fit for a
Spanish don.'

'A relic, Miss Leigh,' interrupted Peter, 'of those days when the Spaniards
raided our shores and took too great an interest in another kind of fair maid.'

Alvean had come in and was standing beside me. I thought she looked
tired.

'You should be in bed,' I said.

'I'm hungry,' she told me.

'After supper we'll go up.'

She nodded and with sleepy pleasure she piled food on a plate.

We sat round the table, Alvean, Peter, Celestine, Sir Thomas, Connan
and Lady Treslyn.

It seemed like a dream that I should be there with them. Alice's brooch
glittered on my dress, and I thought: Thus, two years ago, she would have
sat . . . as I am sitting now. Alvean would not have been here then; she
would have been too young to have been allowed to come, but apart from

that and the fact that I was in Alice's place, it must have been very like other occasions. I wondered if any of the others thought this.

I remembered the face I had seen at the peep, and what Alvean had said on the night of that other ball. I could not remember the exact words but I knew that it had been something about her mother's love of dancing and how, if she came back, she would come to a ball. Then Alvean had half-hoped to see her among the dancers ... What if she watched from another place? I thought of that ghostly solarium in moonlight and I said to myself: 'Whose face did I see at the peep?'

Then I thought: Gilly! What if it were Gilly? It must have been Gilly. Who else could it have been?

My attention was brought back to the group at the table when Connan said: 'I'll get you some more whisky, Tom.' He rose and went to the buffet. Lady Treslyn got up quickly and went to him. I found it difficult to take my eyes from them. I thought how distinguished they looked – she in green shaded mauve draperies, the most beautiful woman at the ball and he, surely the most distinguished of the men.

'I'll help you, Connan', she said, and I heard them laughing together.

'Look out,' said Connan, 'we're spilling it.'

They had their backs to us, and as I watched them I thought that with the slightest provocation I could have burst into tears because now I clearly saw the ridiculousness of my hopes.

She had slipped her arm through his as they came back to the table. The intimate gesture wounded me deeply. I suppose I had drunk too much of the mead, or metheglin as they called it. Mead. It was such a soft and gentle name. But the mead which was made at Mount Mellyn was very potent.

I said to myself coldly: It is time you retired.

As he gave the glass to Sir Thomas – who emptied it with a speed which surprised me – I noticed that there were smudges of shadow under Alvean's eyes, and I said: 'Alvean, you look tired. You should be in bed.'

'Poor child!' cried Celestine at once. 'And she only just recovering. . . .'

I rose. 'I will take Alvean to bed now,' I said. 'Come along, Alvean.'

She was half-asleep already and made no protest but rose meekly to her feet.

'I will say good night to you all,' I said.

Peter rose to his feet. 'We'll see you later,' he said.

I did not answer. I was desperately trying not to look at Connan, for I felt he was not aware of me; that he would never be aware of anyone when Lady Treslyn was near.

'*Au revoir*,' said Peter, and as the others echoed the words absentmindedly I went out of the punch room, holding Alvean by the hand.

I felt as Cinderella must have felt with the striking of the midnight hour.

My brief glory was over. Lady Treslyn had made me realize how foolish I had been to dream.

Alvean was asleep before I left her room. I tried not to think of Connan and Lady Treslyn while I went to my room and lighted the candles on my dressing table. I looked attractive; there was no doubt of it. Then I said to myself, Anyone looks attractive by candlelight.

The diamonds winked back at me, and I was immediately reminded of the face I had seen at the peep.

I thought afterwards that I must have drunk too freely of the metheglin, because on impulse I went down to the landing below my own. I could hear the shouts coming from the servants' hall. So they were still merry-making down there. The door to Gilly's room was ajar, and I went in. There was enough moonlight for me to see that the child was in her bed, but sitting up, awake.

'Gilly,' I said.

'Madam!' she cried and her voice was joyful. 'I knew you'd come to-night.'

'Gilly, you know who this is.' What had made me say such a foolish thing?

She nodded.

'I'm going to light your candle,' I said, and I did so.

Her eyes regarded my face with that blank blue stare, and came to rest on the brooch. I sat on the edge of the bed. I knew that when I had first come in she had thought I was someone else.

She was contented though, which showed the confidence she was beginning to feel in me.

I touched the brooch and said: 'Once it was Mrs. TreMellyn's.'

She smiled and nodded.

I said: 'You spoke when I came in. Why do you not speak to me now?'

She merely smiled.

'Gilly,' I said, 'were you at the peep in the solarium tonight? Were you watching the dancers?'

She nodded.

'Gilly, say "Yes." '

'Yes,' said Gilly.

'You were up there all alone? You weren't afraid?'

She shook her head and smiled.

'You mean no, don't you, Gilly? Say "no." '

'No.'

'Why weren't you afraid?'

She opened her mouth and smiled. Then she said: 'Not afraid because . . .'

'Because?' I said eagerly.

'Because,' she repeated.

'Gilly,' I said. 'Were you alone up there?'

She smiled and I could get her to say no more.

After a while I kissed her and she returned my kiss. She was fond of me, I knew. I believed that in her mind she confused me with someone else, and I knew who that person was.

Back in my room I did not want to take off my dress. I felt that as long as I wore it, I could still hope for what I knew to be impossible.

So I sat by my window for an hour or so. It was a warm night and I was comfortable with my silk shawl about me.

I heard some of the guests coming out to their carriages. I heard the
exchange of good-byes.

And while I was there I heard Lady Treslyn's voice. Her voice was low
and vibrant, but she spoke with such intensity that I caught every syllable
and I knew to whom she was speaking.

She said: 'Connan, it can't be long now. It won't be long.'

Next morning when Kitty brought my water, she did not come alone.
Daisy was with her. I heard their raucous voices mingling and, in my half-
waking state, thought they sounded like the gulls.

'Morning, Miss.'

They wanted me to wake up quickly; they had exciting news. I saw that
in their faces.

'Miss . . .' they were both speaking together, both determined to be the
one to impart the startling information, 'last night . . . or rather this
morning . . .'

Then Kitty rushed on ahead of her sister: 'Sir Thomas Treslyn was taken
bad on the way home. He was dead when they got to Treslyn Hall.'

I sat up in bed, looking from one excited face to the other.

One of the guests . . . dead! I was shocked. But this was no ordinary death,
no ordinary death.

I realized, no less than Kitty and Daisy, what such news could mean to
Mount Mellyn.

Chapter Seven

Sir Thomas Treslyn was buried on New Year's Day.

During the preceding week gloom had settled on the house, and it was all
the more noticeable because it followed on the heels of the Christmas
festivities. All the decorations had been left about the house, and there was
divided opinion as to which was the more unlucky – to remove them before
Twelfth Night or to leave them up and thereby show lack of respect.

They all appeared to consider that the death touched us closely. He had
died between our house and his own; our table was the last at which he had
sat. I realized that the Cornish were a very superstitious people, constantly
on the alert for omens, eager to placate supernatural and malignant powers.

Connan was absentminded. I saw little of him, but when I did he seemed
scarcely aware of my presence. I imagined he was considering all that this
meant to him. If he and Lady Treslyn had been lovers there was no obstacle
now to their regularizing their union. I knew that this thought was in the
minds of many, but no one spoke of it. I guessed that Mrs. Polgrey would

consider it unlucky to do so until Sir Thomas had been buried for some weeks.

Mrs. Polgrey called me to her room and we had a cup of Earl Grey laced with a spoonful of the whisky I had given her.

'This is a shocking thing,' she said. 'Sir Thomas to die on Christmas Day as he did. Although 'tweren't Christmas Day but Boxing Day morning,' she added in a slightly relieved tone, as though this made the situation a little less shocking. 'And to think,' she went on, reverting to her original gloom, 'that ours was the last house he rested in, my food was the last that passed his lips! The funeral is a bit soon, do you not think, Miss?'

I began to count the days on my fingers. 'Seven days,' I said.

'They could have kept him longer, seeing it's winter.'

'I suppose they feel that the sooner it's over the sooner they'll recover from the shock.'

She herself looked shocked indeed. I think she thought it was disrespectful or unlucky to suggest that anyone would want to recover quickly from their grief.

'I don't know,' she said, 'you hear tales of people being buried alive. I remember years ago, when I was a child, there was a smallpox epidemic. People panicked and buried quick. It was said that some was buried alive.'

'There is surely no doubt that Sir Thomas is *dead*.'

'Some seem dead and are not dead, after all. Still seven days should be long enough to tell. You'll come to the funeral with me, Miss?'

'I?'

'But why not? I think we should show proper respect to the dead.'

'I have no mourning clothes.'

'My dear life, I'll find a bonnet for 'ee. I'll give 'ee a black band to sew on your cloak. Reckon that 'ud be all right if we were just at the grave. 'Twouldn't do for 'ee to go into the church like, but then 'twouldn't be right either ... you being the governess here, and them having so many friends as will attend to fill Mellyn Church to the full.'

So it was agreed that I should accompany Mrs. Polgrey to the churchyard.

I was present when Sir Thomas's body was lowered into the tomb.

It was an impressive ceremony, for the funeral had been a magnificent one in accordance with the Treslyn's rank in the duchy. Crowds attended, but Mrs. Polgrey and I hovered only in the distance. I was glad of this; she deplored it.

It was enough for me to see the widow in flowing black draperies yet looking as beautiful as she ever had. Her lovely face was just visible among the flowing black, which seemed to become her even as green and mauve had on the night of the Christmas ball. She moved with grace and she looked even more slender in her black than in the brilliant colours I had seen her wear, intensely feminine and appealing.

Connan was there, and I thought how elegant and distinguished he looked; I tried to fathom the expression on his face that I might discover his feelings. But he was determined to hide those feelings from the world; and I thought, in the circumstances, that was just as well.

I watched the hearse with the large waving black plumes and I saw the coffin, carried by six bearers and covered with velvet palls of deep purple and black, taken into the church. I saw the banks of flowers and the mourners in their deathly black, the only colour being the white handkerchiefs which the women held to their eyes – and they had wide black borders.

A cold wind had swept the mists away and the winter sun shone brightly on the gilt of the coffin as it was lowered into the grave.

There was a deep silence in the churchyard, broken only by the sudden cry of gulls.

It was over and the mourners, Connan, Celestine and Peter among them, went back to their carriages which wound their way to Treslyn Hall.

Mrs. Polgrey and I returned to Mount Mellyn, where she insisted on the usual cup of tea and its accompaniment.

We sat drinking, and her eyes glittered. I knew she was finding it difficult to restrain her tongue. But she said nothing of the effect this death might have on us all at Mount Mellyn. So great was her respect for the dead.

Sir Thomas was not forgotten. I heard his name mentioned often during the next few weeks. Mrs. Polgrey shook her head significantly when the Treslyns were mentioned, but her eyes were sharp and full of warning.

Daisy and Kitty were less discreet. When they brought my water in the mornings they would linger. I was a little cunning, I think. I longed to know what people were saying but I did not want to ask, yet I managed to draw them out without, I hoped, seeming to do so.

It was true they did not need a lot of encouragement.

'I saw Lady Treslyn yesterday,' Daisy told me, one morning. 'Her didn't look like a widow, in spite of the weeds.'

'Oh? In what way?'

'Don't 'ee ask me, Miss. She was quite pale and not smiling, but I could see something in her face . . . if you do get my meaning.'

'I'm afraid I don't.'

'Kit were with me. She said the same. Like as though she were waiting and content because she wouldn't have to wait long. A year though. Seems a long time to *me*.'

'A year? What for?' I asked, although I knew very well what for.

Daisy looked at me and giggled.

''Twon't do for them to be seeing too much of each other for a bit, will it, Miss. After all, him dying here . . . almost on our doorstep. 'Twould seem as though they'd almost willed him to it.'

'Oh, Daisy, that's absurd. How could anybody?'

'Well, that's what you can't say till you know, 'twould seem.'

The conversation was getting dangerous. I dismissed her with 'I must hurry. I see I'm rather late.'

When she had gone, I thought: So there is talk about them. They are saying he was willed to die.

As long as that's all they say, that won't do much harm.

I wondered how careful they were being. I remembered hearing Phillida say that people in love behaved like ostriches. They buried their heads in the sand and thought, because they saw no one, no one saw them.

But they were not two inexperienced lovers.

No, I thought bitterly, it is clear that both are very experienced. They knew the people among whom they lived. They would be careful.

It was later that day, when I was in the woods, that I heard the sounds of horses' hoofs walking nearby and then I heard Lady Treslyn say: 'Connan. Oh, Connan!'

They had met then . . . and to meet as near the house as this was surely foolish.

In the woods their voices carried. The trees hid me, but snatches of their conversation came to me.

'Linda! You shouldn't have come.'

'I know . . . I know. . . .' Her voice fell and I could not hear the rest.

'To send that message . . .' That was Connan. I could hear him more clearly than her, perhaps because I knew his voice so well. 'Your messenger will have been seen by some of the servants. You know how they gossip.'

'I know, but . . .'

'When did this come . . .?'

'This morning. I had to show it to you right away.'

'It's the first?'

'No, there was one two days ago. That's why I had to see you, Connan. No matter what . . . I'm frightened. . . .'

'It's mischief,' he said. 'Ignore it. Forget it.'

'Read it,' she cried. 'Read it.'

There was a short silence. Then Connan spoke. 'I see. There's only one thing to be done. . . .'

The horses had begun to move. In a few seconds they might come past the spot where I was. I hurried away through the trees.

I was very uneasy.

That day Connan left Mount Mellyn.

'Called away to Penzance,' Mrs. Polgrey told me. 'He said he was unsure how long he would be away.'

I wondered if his sudden departure had anything to do with the disquieting news which Lady Treslyn had brought to him that morning in the woods.

Several days passed. Alvean and I resumed our lessons and Gilly too came to the schoolroom.

I would give Gilly some small task while I worked with Alvean, such as trying to make letters in a tray of sand, or on a slate, or counting beads on an abacus. She was contented to do this and I believed that she was happy in my company, that from me she drew a certain comfort which had its roots in security. She had trusted Alice and she was transferring that trust to me.

Alvean had rebelled at first but I had pointed out the need to be kind to those less fortunate than ourselves, and at length I had worked on her sympathy so that she accepted Gilly's presence, although a little sullenly. But I had noticed that now and then she would throw a glance at the child, and I was sure that at least she was very interested in her.

Connan had been away a week and it was a cold February morning when Mrs. Polgrey came into the schoolroom. I was very surprised to see her, for she rarely interrupted lessons; she was holding two letters in her hand and I could see that she was excited.

She made no excuses for her intrusion and said: 'I have heard from the Master. He wants you to take Miss Alvean down to Penzance at once. Here is a letter for you. No doubt he explains more fully in that.'

She handed me the letter and I was afraid that she would see that my hand shook a little as I opened it.

> *My dear Miss Leigh,* I read,
> I will be here for a few weeks, I think, and I am sure you will agree that it would be very desirable for Alvean to join me here. I do not think she should miss her lessons, so I am asking you to bring her and be prepared to stay for a week or so.
> Perhaps you could be ready to leave to-morrow. Get Billy Trehay to drive you to the station for the 2.30 train.
>
> *Connan TreMellyn*

I knew that the colour had rushed to my face. I hoped I had not betrayed the extreme joy which took possession of me.

I said: 'Alvean, we are to join your father to-morrow.'

Alvean leapt up and threw herself into my arms, a most unusual display, but it moved me deeply to realize how much she cared for him.

This helped me to regain my own composure. I said: 'That is for to-morrow. To-day we will continue with our lessons.'

'But, Miss, there's our packing to do.'

'We have this afternoon for that,' I said primly. 'Now, let us return to our work.'

'I turned to Mrs. Polgrey. 'Yes,' I said, 'Mr. TreMellyn wishes me to take Alvean to him.'

She nodded. I could see that she thought it very strange, and this was because he had never before shown such interest in the child.

'And you're leaving to-morrow.'

'Yes. Billy Trehay is to be given instructions to drive us to the station in time for the 2.30 train.'

She nodded.

When she had gone I sat down in a daze. I could not concentrate more than Alvean could. It was some time before I remembered Gilly. She was looking at me with that blank expression in her eyes which I had dreamed of banishing.

Gilly understood more than one realised.

She knew that we were going away and that she would be left behind.

I could scarcely wait to begin my packing. Alvean and I had luncheon together in the schoolroom but neither of us was interested in food, and immediately after the meal we went to our rooms to do the packing.

I had very little to pack. My grey and mauve dresses were clean, for which

I was thankful, and I would wear my grey merino. It was not very becoming but it would be too difficult to pack.

I took out the green silk dress which I had worn at the Christmas ball. Should I take it? Why not? I had rarely possessed anything so becoming, and who knew, there might be an occasion when I could wear it.

I took out my comb and shawl, stuck the comb in my hair and let the shawl fall negligently about my shoulders.

I thought of the Christmas ball – that moment when Peter had taken my hand and had drawn me into the *Furry Dance*. I heard the tune in my head and began to dance, for the moment really feeling I was in the ballroom and that it was Christmas night again.

I had not heard Gilly come in, and I was startled to see her standing watching me. Really, the child did move too silently about the house.

'I stopped dancing, flushing with embarrassment to have been caught in such silly behaviour. Gilly was regarding me solemnly.

She looked at the bag on my bed and the folded clothes beside it, and imediately my pleasure left me for I understood that Gilly was going to be very unhappy if we went away.

I stooped down and put my arms about her. 'It'll only be for a little while, Gilly.'

She screwed her eyes up tightly and would not look at me.

'Gilly,' I said, 'listen. We'll soon be back, you know.'

She shook her head and I saw tears squeeze themselves out of her eyes.

'Then,' I went on, 'we'll have our lessons. You shall draw me more letters in the sand, and soon you will be writing your name.'

But I could see that she refused to be comforted.

She tore herself from me and ran to the bed and began pulling the things out of my trunk.

'No, Gilly, no,' I said. I lifted her up in my arms and went to a chair. I sat for a while rocking her. I went on: 'I'm coming back, you know, Gilly. In less than no time I'll be here. It will seem as though I've never been away.'

She spoke then: 'You won't come back. She . . . She . . .'

'Yes, Gilly, yes?'

'She . . . went.'

For the moment I forgot even the fact that I was going to Connan, because I was certain now that Gilly knew something, and what she knew might throw some light on the mystery of Alice.

'Gilly,' I said, 'did she say good-bye to you before she went?'

Gilly shook her head vehemently, and I thought she was going to burst into tears.

'Gilly,' I pleaded, 'try to talk to me, try to tell me. . . . Did you see her go?'

Gilly threw herself at me and buried her face against my bodice. I held her tenderly for a moment, then withdraw myself and looked into her face; but her eyes were tightly shut.

She ran back to the bed and again started to pull the things out of my trunk.

'No. . . .' she cried. 'No . . . no. . . .'

Swiftly I went to her. 'Look, Gilly,' I said, 'I'm coming back. I'll only be away a short time.'

'She stayed away!'

We were back at that point where we started. I did not believe I could discover anything more from her at this stage.

She lifted her little face to mine and all the blankness had gone from the eyes; they were tragic.

I saw in that moment how much my care of her had meant to her, and that it was impossible to make her understand that if I went away it was not for ever. Alice had been kind to her and Alice had gone. Her experiences had taught her that that was the way of life.

A few days . . . a week in the life of Gilly . . . would be like a year to most of us. I knew then that I could not leave Gilly behind.

Then I asked myself what Connan would say if I arrived with both children.

I believed that I could adequately explain my reasons. However, I was not going to leave Gilly behind. I could let Mrs. Polgrey know that the master expected the two children; she would be pleased; she trusted Gilly with me, and she had been the first to admit that the child had improved since I had tried to help her.

'Gilly,' I said. 'I'm going away for a few days. Alvean and you are coming with me.' I kissed her upturned face. And I repeated because she looked so bewildered: 'You are coming with me. You'll like that, won't you.'

It was still some seconds before she understood, and then she shut her eyes tightly and lowered her head; I saw she smiled. That moved me more than any words could have done.

I felt I was ready to brave Connan's displeasure to bring such happiness to this poor child.

The next morning we set out early, and the whole household turned out to see us go. I sat in the carriage with a child on either side of me, and Billy Trehay in TreMellyn's livery sat jauntily in the driver's seat talking to the horses.

Mrs. Polgrey stood, her arms folded across her bosom, and her eyes were on Gilly. It was clear that she was delighted to see her little granddaughter riding with myself and Alvean.

Tapperty stood with his daughters on either side of him; and their twinkling eyes, all so much alike, were full of speculation.

I did not care. I felt so light-headed as we drove off that it was all I could do to prevent myself breaking into song.

It was a bright sunny morning and there was a slight frost in the air which sparkled on the grass, and the thin layer of ice on the ponds and streams.

We rattled along at a good speed over the rough roads. The children were in high spirits; Alvean chattered a good deal, and Gilly sat contentedly beside me. I noticed that she clutched my skirt with one hand, and the gesture filled me with tenderness for her. I was deeply aware of my responsibility towards this child.

Billy was talkative, and when we passed a grave at a crossroads, he uttered a prayer for the poor lost soul who was buried there.

'Not that the soul will rest, me dears. A person who meets death that way never rests. 'Tis the same if they meet death any way violent like. They can't stay buried underground. They *walks*.'

'What nonsense!' I said sharply.

'Them that knows no better call wisdom nonsense,' retorted Billy, piqued.

'It seems to me that many people have too lively imaginations.'

The children's eyes I noticed were fixed on my face.

'Why,' I said quickly as we passed a cob cottage with beehives in the garden, 'look at those hives! What's that over them?'

''Tis black crêpe,' said Billy. 'It means death in the family. Bees would take it terrible hard if they weren't told of the death and helped to share in the mourning.'

I was glad when we arrived in the station.

We were met at Penzance by a carriage and then began the journey to Penlandstow. It was growing dark when we turned into a drive and I saw a house loom up before us. There was a man in the porch with a lantern who called out: 'They be here. Run and tell master. He did say to let him know the minute they did come.'

We were a little stiff and both children were half-asleep. I helped them down and as I turned, I saw Connan standing beside me. I could not see him very clearly in the dim light but I did know that he was pleased to see me. He took my hand and pressed it warmly.

Then he said an astonishing thing. 'I've been anxious. I visualized all sorts of mishaps. I wished I'd come and brought you here myself.'

I thought: He means Alvean, of course. He is not really talking to me.

But he was facing me, and smiling; and I felt I had never been quite so happy in the whole of my life.

I began: 'The children . . .'

He smiled down at Alvean.

'Hallo, Papa,' she said. 'It's lovely to be here with you.'

He laid a hand on her shoulder, and she looked up at him almost pleadingly, as though she were asking him to kiss her. That, it seemed, was asking too much.

He merely said: 'I'm glad you've come, Alvean. You'll have some fun here.'

Then I brought Gilly forward.

'What . . .' he began.

'We couldn't leave Gilly behind,' I said. 'You know you gave me your permission to teach her.'

He hesitated for a moment. Then he looked at me and laughed. I knew in that moment that he was so pleased to see me – me, not the others – that he would not have cared whom I brought with me as long as I came myself.

It was no wonder that as I walked into Alice's old home I felt as though I were entering an enchanted place.

During the next two weeks it seemed that I had left behind me the cold hard world of reality and stepped into one of my own making, and that everything I desired was to be mine.

From the moment I arrived at Penlandstow Manor I was treated, not as a governess, but as a guest. In a few days I had lost my sensitivity on this point and, when I had cast that off, I was like the high-spirited girl who had enjoyed life in the country vicarage with her father and Phillida.

I was given a pleasant room next to Alvean's and when I asked that Gilly should be put near me this was done.

Penlandstow was a house of great charm which had been built in the Elizabethan era. It was almost as large as Mount Mellyn and as easy to lose oneself in.

My room was large and there were padded window seats upholstered in red velvet, and dark red curtains. My bed was a fourposter hung with silk embroidered curtains. The carpet was of the same deep red, and this would have given warmth to the room even if there had not been a log fire burning in the open grate.

My bag was brought up to this room and one of the maids proceeded to unpack while I stood by the fire watching the blue flames dart among the logs.

The maid curtsied when she had laid my things on the bed, and asked if she might put them away. This was not the manner in which to treat a governess, I thought. Kind and friendly as Daisy and Kitty had been, they had not been ready to wait on me like this.

I said I would put my things away myself but would like hot water to wash.

'There be a little bathroom at the end of the landing, Miss,' I was told. 'Shall I show it to 'ee and bring 'ee hot water up there?'

I was taken along to the room in which there was a big bath; there was also a hip bath.

'Miss Alice had the room afore her married and went away,' I was told; and with a little shock I remembered that I was in Alice's old home.

When I had washed and changed my dress – I put on the lavender cotton – I went along to see Alvean. She had fallen asleep on her bed so I left her. Gilly was also asleep in her room. And when I returned to my own the maid who had shown me the bathroom came in and said that Mr. TreMellyn had asked that, when I was ready, I would join him in the library.

I said I was ready then and she took me to him.

'It is indeed pleasant to see you here, Miss Leigh,' he said.

'It will be very agreeable for you to have your own daughter here . . .' I began.

And he interrupted me with a smile. 'I said it was pleasant to see you here, Miss Leigh. I meant exactly that.'

I flushed. 'That is kind of you. I have brought certain of the children's lesson books along. . . .'

'Let us give them a little holiday, shall we? Lessons I suppose there must be, if you say so, but need they sit at their desks all the time?'

'I think their lessons might be curtailed on an occasion like this.'

He came and stood close to me. 'Miss Leigh,' he said, 'you are delightful.'

I drew back startled, and he went on: 'I'm glad you came so promptly.'

'Those were your orders.'

'I did not mean to order, Miss Leigh. Merely to request.'

'But . . .' I began; and I was apprehensive because he seemed different from the man I had known. He was almost like a stranger – a stranger who fascinated me no less than that other Connan TreMellyn, a stranger who frightened me a little, for I was unsure of myself, unsure of my own emotions.

'I was so glad to escape,' he said. 'I thought you would be too.'

'Escape . . . from what?'

'From the gloom of death. I hate death. It depresses me.'

'You mean Sir Thomas. But . . .'

'Oh, I know. A neighbour merely. But still it did depress me. I wanted to get right away. I am so glad you have joined me . . . with Alvean and the other child.'

I said on impulse: 'I hope you did not think it was presumptuous of me to bring Gillyflower. She would have been heartbroken if I had not brought her.'

Then he said a thing which set my senses swimming: 'I can understand her being heartbroken if she had to part from you.'

I said quickly: 'I suppose the children should have a meal of some sort. They are exhausted and sleeping now. But I do feel they need some refreshment before they go to bed. It has been a tiring day for them.'

He waved a hand. 'Order what you wish for them, Miss Leigh. And when you have seen to them, you and I will dine together.'

I said: 'Alvean dines with you . . . does she not?'

'She will be too tired to-night. We will have it alone.'

So I ordered what I wanted for the children, and I dined with Connan in the winter parlour. It was a strange and exhilarating experience to dine with that man in candlelight. I kept telling myself that it could not be real. If ever anything was the stuff that dreams were made of, this was.

He talked a great deal; there was no sign of the taciturn Connan that evening.

He told me about the house, how it had been built in the shape of an E as a compliment to the queen who had been reigning when it was built. He drew the shape to show me. 'Two three-sided courtyards,' he said, 'and a projecting centre block, if you see what I mean. We are in the central block now. The main feature of it is the hall, the staircase and the gallery, and these smaller rooms such as the winter parlour which, I think you will agree, is ideally suited for a small company.'

I said I thought it was a delightful house, and how fortunate he was to possess two such magnificent places.

'Stone walls do not bring satisfaction, Miss Leigh. It is the life one lives within these walls which is of the greatest importance.'

'Yet,' I retaliated, 'it is some comfort to have charming surroundings in which to live one's life.'

'I agree. And I cannot tell you how glad I am that you find my homes so charming.'

When we had eaten he took me to the library and asked me if I would play a game of chess with him. I said I would be delighted.

And we sat there in that beautiful room with its carved ceiling and thick piled carpet, lighted by lamps the bowls of which were made of artistically painted china of oriental origin. I was happier than I had ever dreamed I could be.

He had set out the ivory pieces on the board, and we played in silence.

It was a deep, contented silence, or so it seemed to me. I knew I should never forget the flickering firelight, the ticking of the gilded clock which looked as though it might have belonged to Louis XIV, as I watched Connan's strong lean fingers on the ivory pieces.

Once, as I frowned in concentration, I was conscious of his eyes fixed on me and, lifting them suddenly, I met his gaze. It was of amusement, and yet of speculation. In that moment I thought: He has asked me here for a purpose. What is it?

I felt a shiver of alarm, but I was too happy to entertain such feelings.

I moved my piece and he said: 'Ah!' And then: 'Miss Leigh, oh my dear Miss Leigh, you have, I think, walked straight into the trap I have set for you.'

'Oh . . . no!' I cried.

He moved a knight which immediately menaced my king. I had forgotten that knight.

'I believe it is . . .' he said. 'Oh no, not entirely. Check, Miss Leigh. But not checkmate.'

I saw that I had allowed my attention to wander from the game. I sought hurriedly to save myself, but I could not. With every move the inevitable end was more obvious.

I heard his voice, gentle, full of laughter. 'Checkmate, Miss Leigh.'

I sat for a few seconds staring at the board. He said: 'I took an unfair advantage. You were tired after the journey.'

'Oh no,' I said quickly. 'I suspect you are a better player than I am.'

'I suspect,' he replied, 'that we are very well matched.'

I retired to my room soon after that game.

I went to bed and tried to sleep, but couldn't. I was too happy. I kept going over in my mind his reception of me, our meal together, his words: 'We are very well matched.'

I even forgot that the house in which I now lay had been Alice's home – a fact which at one time would have seemed of utmost interest to me – I forgot everything but that Connan had sent for me and, now that I was here, seemed so delighted to have me.

The next day was as pleasant and unpredictable as the first. I did a few lessons with the children in the morning and in the afternoon Connan took us for a drive. How different it was, riding in his carriage than jogging along behind Tapperty or Billy Trehay.

He drove us to the coast and we saw St. Michael's Mount rising out of the water.

'One day,' he said, 'when the spring comes, I'll take you out there and you can see St. Michael's chair.'

'Can we sit in it, Papa?' asked Alvean.

'You can if you are prepared to risk a fall. You'll find your feet dangling over a drop of seventy feet or so. Nevertheless, many of your sex think it worth while.'

'But why, Papa, why?' demanded Alvean, who was always delighted when she had his undivided attention.

'Because,' he went on, 'there is an old saying that if a woman can sit in St. Michael's chair before her husband, she will be the master of the house.

Alvean laughed with pleasure and Gilly, who I had insisted on bringing with us, stood there smiling.

Connan looked at me. 'And you, Miss Leigh,' he said, 'would you think it worth while to try?'

I hesitated for a second, and then met his gaze boldly. 'No, Mr. TreMellyn, I don't think I should.'

'Then you would not desire to be the master in the house?'

'I do not think that either a husband or his wife should be master in that sense. I think they should work together and, if one has an opinion which he or she feels to be the only right one, he or she should adhere to it.'

I flushed a little; I imagined how Phillida would smile if she heard that.

'Miss Leigh,' said Connan, 'your wisdom puts our foolish folklore to shame.'

We drove back in winter sunshine and I was happy.

I did not dine with him that evening because I had asked that I might have my meals in the schoolroom with Gilly. Alvean dined with her father. And afterwards I sat in the room reading. He did not ask me to join him that evening.

I went to bed early and lay for a long time thinking of the strange turn life had taken, and I knew that when I awoke next morning I should do so with a feeling of expectation, because I believed that something wonderful was about to happen to me.

I awoke with a start. Someone was in my room. There was a movement by my bed. I started up. It was early morning. I knew this because I could see that the sky was streaked with pale pink light.

'Who is there?' I cried.

Then I saw Gilly.

She was wearing one of Alvean's old dressing gowns which I had altered to fit her, and her feet were in a pair of slippers which I had brought for her.

I said: 'What are you doing here, Gilly?'

She opened her mouth as though to speak. I waited, but she smiled at me and nodded.

'I said: 'What has happened, Gilly? It is something, I know. You must
tell me.'

She pointed to the door and stared at it.

I felt a shiver run down my spine because Gilly often made me think that
she could see things which I could not.

'There's nothing there,' I said.

She nodded again and then she spoke: 'She's here. She's here.'

I felt my heart beat fast. I thought: She means that Alice is here. This was
Alice's home. She has found Alice here.

'Mrs. TreMellyn . . .' I whispered.

She smiled rapturously and continued to nod.

'You . . . you've seen her?'

Gilly nodded again.

'In this house?'

Again the nod.

'I'll take you to her.' The words tumbled out. 'She wants me to.'

I got out of bed and with trembling fingers wrapped my dressing gown
about me and put my feet into my slippers.

Gilly took my hand.

We went through a gallery and down a short staircase. Gilly rapped with
her fingers on the door and appeared to listen.

She looked up at me and nodded as though she had heard someone tell
her to enter. I had heard nothing. It was very uncanny.

Then she opened the door. We were in a room which was shadowy, for
the day was young yet.

Gilly pointed, and for a few seconds I thought I saw a woman standing
there. She was dressed in a ball dress and her fair hair fell about her
shoulders in long silken curls.

I stared, and then I saw that I was looking at a life-size oil painting.

I knew I was face to face with Alice.

I went close to the painting and looked up at it. The blue eyes looked
straight out of the picture at me and it seemed as though words were forming
themselves on those red lips.

I forced myself to say: 'What a good artist must have painted that picture!'

But perhaps because it was not yet quite light, because this grey house
was sleeping, because Gilly had brought me here in her own strange way,
I felt that this was more than a picture.

'Alice,' I whispered. And I stared at that painted face, and, practical
woman that I was, I half expected her to step out of the frame and talk to
me.

I wondered when that had been painted . . . before or after the disastrous
marriage, before she 'had known she was to have Geoffry's child or after.

'Alice,' I said to myself, 'where are you now, Alice? You are haunting me,
Alice. Since I have known you I have known what haunting means.'

Gilly was holding my hand.

I said: 'It's only a picture, Gilly.'

She reached out a small finger and touched the white ball-dress.

Gilly had loved her. I looked into that soft young face and thought I understood why.

Poor Alice, who had been caught up in too many emotions, what had become of her?

I suddenly realized that it was a winter's morning and I was lightly clad.

'We'll catch our deaths,' I said practically; and taking Gilly's hand in mine I firmly shut the door on Alice.

I had been at Penlandstow a week, and I was wondering how much longer this idyllic interlude could last, when Connan spoke to me of what was in his mind.

The children were in bed and Connan asked me if I would join him in a game of chess in the library.

There I found him, the pieces set out on the board, sitting looking at them.

The curtains had been drawn and the fire burned cheerfully in the great fireplace. He rose as I entered and I quickly slipped into my place opposite him.

He smiled at me and I thought his eyes took in every detail of my appearance, in a manner which I might have found offensive in anyone else.

I was about to move king's pawn when he said: 'Miss Leigh, I did not ask you down here to play. There is something I have to say to you.'

'Yes, Mr. TreMellyn?'

'I feel I have known you a very long time. You have made such a difference to us both – Alvean and myself. If you went away, we should miss you very much. I am certain that we should both want to ensure that you do not leave us.'

I tried to look at him and failed because I was afraid he would read the hopes and fears in my eyes.

'Miss Leigh,' he went on, 'Will you stay with us . . . always?'

'I . . . I don't understand. I . . . can't believe . . .'

'I am asking you to marry me.'

'But . . . but that is impossible.'

'Why so, Miss Leigh?'

'Because . . . because it is so incongruous.'

'Do you find me incongruous . . . repulsive? Do please be frank.'

'I . . . No indeed not! But I am the governess here. . . .'

'Precisely. That is what alarms me. Governesses sometimes leave their employment. It would be intolerable for me if you went away.'

I felt I was choking with my emotions. I could not believe this was really happening to me. I remained silent. I dared not try to speak.

'I see that you hesitate, Miss Leigh.'

'I am so surprised.'

'Should I have prepared you for the shock?' His lips twitched slightly at the corner. 'I am sorry, Miss Leigh. I thought I had managed to convey to you something of my feelings in this matter.'

I tried to picture it all in those few seconds – myself going back to Mount Mellyn as the wife of the Master, slipping from the role of governess to that of Mistress of the house. Of course I would do it and in a few months they would forget that I had once been the governess. Whatever else I lacked I had my dignity – perhaps a little too much of it, according to Phillida. But I should have thought that a proposal would have been made in a different way. He did not take my hand; he did not touch me; he merely sat at the table watching me in an almost cool and calculating manner.

He went on: 'Think of how much good this could bring to us all, my dear Miss Leigh. I have been so impressed by the manner in which you have helped Alvean. The child needs a mother. You would supply that need . . . admirably.'

'Should two people marry for the sake of a child, do you think?'

'I am a most selfish man. I never would.' He leaned forward across the table and his eyes were alight with something I did not understand. 'I would marry for my own satisfaction.'

'Then . . .' I began.

'I confess I was not considering Alvean alone. We are three people, my dear Miss Leigh, who could profit from this marriage. Alvean needs you. And I. . . . I need you. Do you need us? Perhaps you are more self-sufficient than we are, but what will you do if you do not marry? You will go from post to post, and that is not a very pleasant life. When one is young, handsome and full of spirit it is tolerable . . . but sprightly governesses become ageing governesses.'

I said icily: 'Do you suggest that I should enter into this marriage as an insurance against old age?'

'I suggest only that you do what your desires dictate, my dear Miss Leigh.'

There was a short silence during which I felt an absurd desire to burst into tears. This was something I had longed for, but a proposal of marriage should have been an impassioned declaration, and I could not rid myself of the suspicion that there was something other than Connan's love for me which had inspired it. It seemed to me as though he were offering me a list of reasons why we should marry, for fear I should discover the real one.

'You put it on such a practical basis,' I stammered. 'I had not thought of marriage in that way.'

His eyebrows lifted and he laughed, looking suddenly very gay. 'How glad I am. I thought of you always as such a practical person, so I was trying to put it to you in the manner in which I felt it would appeal to you most.'

'Are you seriously asking me to marry you?'

'I doubt if I have ever been so serious in my life as I am at this moment. What is your answer? Please do not keep me in suspense any longer.'

I said I must have time to consider this.

'That is fair enough. You will tell me to-morrow?'

'Yes,' I said. 'I will tell you to-morrow.'

I rose and went to the door. He was there before me. He laid his fingers on the door handle and I waited for him to open it, but he did no such thing. He stood with his back to the door and caught me up in his arms.

He kissed me as I had never been kissed, never dreamed of being kissed; so that I knew that there was a life of the emotions of which I was totally ignorant. He kissed my eyelids, my nose, my cheeks, my mouth and my throat until he was breathless, and I was too.

Then he laughed.

'Wait until the morning!' he mocked. 'Do I look the sort of man who would wait until the morning? Do you think I am the sort of man who would marry for the sake of his daughter? No, Miss Leigh . . .' he mocked again, 'my dear, *dear* Miss Leigh . . . I want to marry you because I want to keep you a prisoner in my house. I don't want you to run away from me, because, since you came, I have thought of little else but you, and I know I am going on thinking of you all my life.'

'Is this true?' I whispered. 'Can this be true?'

'Martha!' he said. 'What a stern name for such an adorable creature! And yet, how it fits!'

I said: 'My sister calls me Marty. My father did too.'

'Marty,' he said. 'That sounds helpless, clinging . . . feminine. . . . You can be a Marty sometimes. For me you will be all three. Marty, Martha and Miss Leigh, my very dear Miss Leigh. You see you *are* all three, and my dearest Marty would always betray Miss Leigh. I knew from her that you were interested in me. Far more interested than Miss Leigh would think proper. How enchanting! I shall marry not one woman but three!'

'Have I been so blatant?'

'Tremendously so . . . adorably so.'

I knew that it was foolish to pretend. I gave myself up to his embrace, and it was wonderful beyond my imaginings.

At length I said: 'I have a terrible feeling that I shall wake up in bed at Mount Mellyn and find I have dreamed all this.'

'Do you know,' he said seriously, 'I feel exactly the same.'

'But it is so different for you. You can do as you will . . . go where you will . . . dependent on no one.'

'I am dependent no longer. I depend on Marty, Martha, my dear Miss Leigh.'

He spoke so seriously that I could have wept with tenderness. The changing emotions were almost too much for me to bear.

This is love! I thought. The emotion which carries one to the very heights of human experience and, because it can carry one so high, one is in continual danger of falling; and one must never forget, the higher the delight, the more tragic the fall.

But this was not the moment to think of tragedy. I loved, and miraculously I was loved. I had no doubt in that library of Penlandstow that I was loved.

For love such as this, one would be prepared to risk everything.

He put his hands on my shoulders and looked long into my face.

He said: 'We'll be happy, my darling. We'll be happier than either you or I ever dreamed possible.'

I knew that we should be. All that had gone before would give us a finer appreciation of this joy we could bring each other.

'We should be practical,' he said. 'We should make our plans. When shall we marry? I do not like delay. I am the most impatient man alive, where my own pleasures are concerned. We will go home to-morrow, and there we

will announce our engagement. No, not to-morrow . . . the day after. I have
one or two little commitments here to-morrow. And as soon as we are home
we will give a ball to announce our engagement. I think that in a month
after that we should be setting out on our honeymoon. I suggest Italy, unless
you have any other ideas?'

I sat with my hands clasped. I must have looked like an ecstatic schoolgirl.

'I wonder what they will think at Mount Mellyn.'

'Who, the servants? You may be sure they have a pretty shrewd idea of
the way things are; servants have, you know. Servants are like detectives in
the house. They pick up every little clue. You shiver. Are you cold?'

'No, only excited. I still believe I'm going to wake up in a moment.'

'And you like the idea of Italy?'

'I would like the idea of the North Pole in some company.'

'By which, my darling, I hope you mean mine.'

'That was my intention.'

'My dear Miss Leigh,' he said, 'how I love your astringent moods. They
are going to make conversation throughout our lives so invigorating.' I had
an idea then that he was making comparisons between Alice and myself,
and I shivered again as I had when he had made that remark about the
detectives.

'You are a little worried about the reception of the news,' he went on.
'The servants . . . the countryside . . . Who cares? Do you? Of course you
do not. Miss Leigh has too much good sense for that. I am longing to tell
Peter Nansellock that you are to be my wife. To tell the truth I have been
somewhat jealous of that young man.'

'There was no need to be.'

'Still I was anxious. I had visions of his persuading you to go to Australia
with him. That was something I should have gone to great lengths to
prevent.'

'Even so far as asking me to marry *you*?'

'Farther than that if the need had arisen. I should have abducted you and
locked you up in a dungeon until he was far away.'

'There was no need for the slightest apprehension.'

'Are you quite sure? He is very handsome, I believe.'

'Perhaps he is. I did not notice.'

'I could have killed him when he had the effrontery to offer you Jacinth.'

'I think he merely enjoys being outrageous. He probably knew I should
not accept it.'

'And I need not fear him?'

'You need never fear anyone,' I told him.

Then once more I was in that embrace, and I was oblivious of all but the
fact that I had discovered love, and believed, as doubtless hosts of lovers have
before, that there was never love such as that between us two.

At length he said: 'We'll go back the day after to-morrow. We'll start
making arrangements immediately. In a month from now we'll be married.
We'll put up the banns as soon as we return. We will have a ball to announce
our engagement and invite all our neighbours to the wedding.'

'I suppose it must be done in this way?'

'Tradition, my darling. It is one of the things we have to bow down to. You'll be magnificent, I know. You're not nervous?'

'Of your country neighbours, no.'

'You and I will open the ball this time together, dearest Miss Leigh.'

'Yes,' I said; and I pictured myself in the green dress wearing the amber comb in my hair with the diamond horseshoe glittering on the green background.

I had no qualms about taking my place in his circle.

Then he began to talk of Alice. 'I have never told you,' he said, 'of my first marriage.'

'No,' I answered.

'It was not a happy one.'

'I'm sorry.'

'A marriage which was arranged. This time I shall marry my own choice. Only one who has suffered the first can realize the joy of the second. Dearest, I have not lived the life of a monk, I fear.'

'I guessed it.'

'I am a most sinful man, as you will discover.'

'I am prepared for the worst.'

'Alice . . . my wife . . . and I were most unsuited, I suppose.'

'Tell me about her.'

'There is little to tell. She was a gentle creature, quiet, anxious to please. She seemed to have little spirit. I understood why. She was in love with someone else when she married me.'

'The man she ran away with?' I asked.

He nodded. 'Poor Alice! She was unfortunate. She chose not only the wrong husband but the wrong lover. There is little to choose between us . . . myself and Geoffry Nansellock. We were of a kind. In the old days there was a tradition of the *droit de seigneurs* in these parts. Geoffry and I did our best to maintain that.'

'You are telling me that you have enjoyed many love affairs.'

'I am a dissolute, degenerate philanderer. I am going to say *was*. Because from this moment I am going to be faithful to one woman for the rest of my life. You do not look scornful or sceptical. Bless you for that. I mean it, dearest Marty. I swear I mean it. It is because of those experiences of the past that I know the difference between them and this. This is love.'

'Yes,' I said slowly, 'you and I will be faithful together because that is the only way we can prove to each other the depth and breadth of our love.'

He took my hands and kissed them, and I had never known him so serious. 'I love you,' he said. 'Remember that . . . always remember it.'

'I intend to.'

'You may hear gossip.'

'One does hear gossip,' I admitted.

'You have heard of Alice and that Alvean is not my daughter? Oh, darling, someone told you and you do not want to betray the teller. Never mind. You know. It is true. I could never love the child. In fact I avoided the sight of her. She was an unpleasant reminder of much that I wished to forget. But when you came I felt differently. You made me see her as a lonely child, suffering from the sins of grown-up people. You see, you changed me, Marty dear. Your coming changed the whole household. That is what confirms me in my belief that with us it is going to be different from anything that has ever happened to me before.'

'Connan, I want to make that child happy. I want to make her forget that there is a doubt as to her parentage. Let her be able to accept you as her father. It is what she needs.'

'You will be a mother to her. Then I must be her father.'

'We are going to be so happy, Connan.'

'Can you see into the future?'

'I can see into ours, for our future is what we make it, and I intend that it shall be one of complete happiness.'

'And what Miss Leigh decides shall be, will be. And you will promise me not to be hurt if you hear gossip about me?'

'You are thinking of Lady Treslyn, I know. She has been your mistress.'

He nodded.

Then I said: 'She will never be again. That is all over.'

He kissed my hand. 'Have you not sworn eternal fidelity?'

'But, Connan,' I said, 'she is so beautiful and she will still be there.'

'But I am in love,' he answered, 'for the first time in my life.'

'And you were not in love with her?'

'Lust, passion,' he answered, 'they sometimes wear the guise of love; but when one meets true love one recognizes them for what they are. Dearest, let us bury all that is past. Let us start afresh from this day forth . . . you and I . . . for better for worse. . . .'

I was in his arms again. 'Connan,' I said, 'I am not dreaming, am I? Please say I am not dreaming.'

It was late when I left him. I went to my room in a haze of happiness. I was afraid to sleep for fear I should wake up and find it had all been a dream.

In the morning I went to Alvean's room and told her the news.

For a few seconds a satisfied smile appeared at the corners of her mouth; then she assumed indifference, but it was too late. I knew that she was pleased.

'You'll stay with us all the time now, Miss,' she said.

'Yes,' I assured her.

'I wonder if I shall ever ride as well as you.'

'Probably better. You'll be able to have more practice than I ever could.'

Again that smile touched her lips. Then she was serious.

'Miss,' she said, 'what shall I call you? You'll be my stepmother, won't you?'

'Yes, but you can call me what you like.'

'Not Miss!'

'Well, hardly. I shan't expect Miss any more.'

'I expect I shall have to call you Mamma.' Her mouth hardened a little.

'If you do not like that you could call me Martha in private. Or Marty. That's what my father and sister always called me.'

'Marty,' she repeated. 'I like that. It sounds like a horse.'

'What could be better praise,' I cried, and she regarded my amusement with continued seriousness.

I went to Gilly's room.

'Gilly,' I said, 'I'm going to be Mrs. TreMellyn.'

The blankness left the blue eyes and her smile was dazzling. Then she ran to me and buried her head in my bodice. I could feel her body shaking with laughter.

I could never be quite sure what was going on among all the shadowy vagueness of Gilly's mind, but I knew she was contented. She had bracketed me with Alice in her mind and I felt that she was less surprised than I or Alvean, or anyone else, would be.

To Gilly it was the most natural thing in the world that I should take Alice's place.

I believe that, from that moment, for Gilly I became Alice.

It was a merry journey home. We sang Cornish songs all the way to the station. I had never seen Connan so happy. I thought, this is how it will be all the rest of our lives.

Alvean joined in the singing, so did Gilly; and it was astonishing to hear that child, who scarcely ever spoke, singing quietly as though to herself.

We sang the 'Twelve Days of Christmas.' Connan had a rich baritone voice which was very pleasant to hear and I felt I had reached the very peak of happiness as he sang the first lines.

> 'The first day of Christmas my true love sent to me
> A partridge in a pear tree.'

We went through the song and I.had difficulty in remembering all the gifts after the five golden rings; and we laughed together hilariously while we argued as to how many maids there were a-milking, and how many geese a-laying were sent.

'But they were not very sensible things,' said Alvean, 'except of course the five gold rings. I think he was pretending he loved her more than he really did.'

'But he was her true love,' I protested.

'How could she be sure?' asked Alvean.

'Because he told her so,' answered Connan.

'Then he ought to have given her something better than a partridge in a pear tree. I expect the partridge flew away and the pears were those hard ones which are used for stewing.'

'You must not be hard on lovers,' Connan cried. 'All the world loves them, and you have to keep in step.'

And so we laughed and bantered until we boarded the train.

Billy Trehay met us with the carriage and I was astonished when we reached the house, for I then realized that Connan must have sent a message to arrive before we did. He wanted me to be received with honours. Even so I was unprepared for the reception which was waiting for us in the hall.

The servants were all there – the Polgrey and Tapperty families and others from the gardens and stables, and even the village boys and girls who came to help and whom I scarcely knew.

They were lined up ceremoniously, and Connan took my arm as we entered the hall.

'As you know,' he said, 'Miss Leigh has promised to marry me. In a few weeks' time she will be your Mistress.'

The men bowed and the women curtsied, but I was conscious, as I smiled at them and walked along the line with Connan, that there was a certain wariness in their eyes.

As I had guessed, they were not ready to accept me as mistress of the house . . . yet.

There was a big fire in my room and everything looked cosy and welcoming. Daisy brought my hot water. She was a little remote, I thought. She did not stop and chat with me as she had hitherto.

I thought: I will regain their confidence, but of course I had to remember that, as the future Mistress of the house, I must not gossip as I once had.

I dined with Connan and Alvean and afterwards I went up with Alvean; and when I had said good night to her I joined Connan in the library.

There were so many plans to make, and I gave myself up to the complete joy of contemplating the future.

He asked me if I had written to my family, and I told him that I had not yet done so. I still could not quite believe this was really happening to me.

'Perhaps this token will help you to remember,' he said. Then he took a jewel case from a drawer in the bureau and showed me a beautiful square-cut emerald set in diamonds.

'It's . . . quite beautiful, far too beautiful for me.'

'Nothing is too beautiful for Martha TreMellyn,' he said, and he took my left hand and put the ring on the third finger.

I held it out and stared at it.

'I never thought to possess anything so lovely.'

'It's the beginning of all the beautiful things I shall bring to you. It's the partridge in the pear tree, my darling.'

Then he kissed my hand and I told myself that, whenever I doubted the truth of all that was happening to me I could look at my emerald and know I was not dreaming.

Next morning when I went down Connan had gone out on business, and after I had given Alvean and Gilly their lessons – for I was eager that everything should go on as before – I went to my room, and I had not been there for more than a few minutes when there was a discreet knock.

'Come in,' I said; and Mrs. Polgrey entered.

She looked a little furtive, and I knew that something significant had happened.

'Miss Leigh,' she said, 'there will be things which we have to discuss. I was wondering if you would come to my room. I have the kettle on. Could you drink a cup of tea?'

I said I would like that. I was very anxious that there should be no difference in our relationship which, from my point of view, had always been a very pleasant and dignified one.

In her room we drank tea. There was no suggestion of whisky this time, and this secretly amused me although I made no reference to it. I should be the mistress of the house, and it was very different for *her* to know of the tea-tippling than the mere governess.

She again congratulated me on my engagement and told me how delighted she was. 'In fact,' she said, 'the whole household is delighted.' She asked me then if I intended to make changes, and I answered that, while the household was so efficiently run by herself, I should make none at all.

This was a relief to her, I could see, and she settled down to come to the point.

'While you've been away, Miss Leigh, there's been a bit of excitement in these parts.'

'Oh?' I said, feeling that we were now coming to the reason for my visit.

'It's all along of the sudden death of Sir Thomas Treslyn.'

My heart had begun to leap in a disconcerting manner.

'But,' I said, 'he is buried now. We went to his funeral.'

'Yes, yes. But that need not be the end, Miss Leigh.'

'I don't understand, Mrs. Polgrey.'

'Well, there's been rumours . . . nasty rumours, and letters have been sent.'

'To . . . to whom?'

'To her, Miss Leigh . . . to the widow. And, it seems, to others . . . and as a result they're going to dig him up. There's going to be an examination.'

'You mean . . . they suspect someone poisoned him?'

'Well, there's been these letters, you see. And him dying so sudden. What I don't like is that he was here last . . . It's not the sort of thing one likes to have connected with the house. . . .'

She was looking at me oddly. I thought I saw speculation in her eyes.

I wanted to shut from my mind all the unpleasant thoughts which kept coming to me.

I saw again Connan and Lady Treslyn in the punch room together, their backs towards me . . . laughing together. Had Connan loved me then? One would not have thought so. I thought of the words they had spoken in my hearing when the party was over. 'It will not be long . . . now.' She had said that . . . and to him. And then there was the conversation I had partly overheard in the woods.

What did this mean?

There was a question that hammered in my brain. But I would not let my mind dwell on it.

I dared not. I could not bear to see all my hopes of happiness shattered. I had to go on believing, so I would not ask myself questions.

I looked expressionlessly into Mrs. Polgrey's face.

'I thought you'd want to know,' she said.

Chapter Eight

I was afraid, more afraid than I had ever been since I came to this house.

The body of Sir Thomas Treslyn, who had died after supping at Mount Mellyn, was to be exhumed. People were suspicious of the manner in which he died and, as a result, there had been anonymous letters. Why should they be suspicious? Because his wife wanted him out of the way; and it was known that Connan and Linda Treslyn had been lovers. There had been two obstacles to their union – Alice and Sir Thomas. Both had died suddenly.

But Connan had no wish to marry Lady Treslyn. He was in love with me.

A terrible thought had struck me. Did Connan know that there was to be this exhumation? Had I been living in a fool's paradise? Was my wonderful dream-come-true nothing but a living nightmare?

Was I being used by a cynic? Why did I not use the harsher word? Was I being used by a *murderer*?

I would not believe it. I loved Connan. I had sworn to be faithful to him all my life. How could I make such a vow when I believed the worst of him at the first crisis?

I tried to reason with myself. You're crazy, Martha Leigh. Do you really think that a man such as Connan TreMellyn could suddenly fall in love with *you*!

Yes, I do. I do, I retorted hotly.

But I was a frightened woman.

I could see that the household was divided between two topics of conversation: the exhumation of Sir Thomas and the proposed marriage of the master and the governess.

I was afraid to meet the stern eyes of Mrs. Polgrey, the lewd ones of Tapperty and the excited ones of his daughters.

Did they, as I had begun to do, connect these two events?

I asked Connan what he thought of the Treslyn affair.

'Mischief-makers,' he said. 'They'll have an autopsy and find he died a natural death. Why, his doctor had been attending him for years and has always told him that he must expect to go off like that.'

'It must be very worrying for Lady Treslyn.'

'She will not worry unduly. Indeed, since she has been pestered by letter-writers she may well be relieved to have the matter brought to a head.'

I pictured the medical experts. They would no doubt be men who knew the Treslyns and Connan. As Connan was going to marry me – and he was very eager to spread the news – was it possible that they would approach the matter in a different spirit from that in which they would if they believed Lady Treslyn was eager to marry again? Who could say?

I must drive away these terrible thoughts. I would believe in Connan, I had to; if I did not I must face the fact that I had fallen in love with a murderer.

The invitations for the ball had gone out hastily – too hastily, I thought. Lady Treslyn, being in mourning and with the autopsy pending, was of course not invited. It was to take place only four days after our return from Penlandstow.

Celestine and Peter Nansellock rode over the day before the ball.

Celestine put her arms about me and kissed me.

'My dear,' she said, 'how happy I am. I have watched you with Alvean and I know what this is going to mean to her.' There were tears in her eyes. 'Alice would be so happy.'

I thanked her and said: 'You have always been such a good friend to me.'

'I was so grateful that at last the child had found a governess who really understood her.'

I said: 'I thought Miss Jansen did that.'

'Miss Jansen, yes. We all thought so. It was a pity she was not honest. Perhaps though it was the temptation of a moment. I did all I could to help her.'

'I'm so glad somebody did.'

Peter had come up. He took my hand and kissed it lightly. Connan's look of displeasure made my heart beat fast with happiness, and I was ashamed of my suspicions.

'Fortunate Connan,' cried Peter exuberantly. 'No need to tell you how much I envy you, is there! I think I've made it clear. I've brought over Jacinth. I told you I'd make you a present of her, didn't I? Well, she's my wedding present. You can't object to that, can you?'

I looked at Connan. 'A present for us both,' I said.

'Oh no,' said Peter. 'She's for you. I'll think of something else for Con.'

'Thank you, Peter,' I said. 'It's most generous of you.'

He shook his head. 'Couldn't bear the thought of her going to anyone else. I feel sentimental about that mare. I want a good home for her. You know I'm going at the end of next week.'

'So soon?'

'Everything has been speeded up. There's no point in delaying further.' He looked at me significantly; 'Now,' he added.

I saw that Kitty, who was serving us with wine, was listening with all attention.

Celestine was talking earnestly to Connan, and Peter went on: 'So it's you and Con after all. Well, you'll keep him in order, Miss Leigh. I'm sure of that.'

'I'm not going to be his governess, you know.'

'I'm not sure. Once a governess, always a governess. I thought Alvean seemed not displeased by the new arrangement.'

'I think she's going to accept me.'

'I think you're an even greater favourite than Miss Jansen was.'

'Poor Miss Jansen! I wonder what became of her.'

'Celeste did something for her. She was rather worried about the poor girl, I think.'

'Oh, I'm so glad.'

'Helped her to find another place . . . with some friends of ours actually. The Merrivales who have a place on the edge of Dartmoor. I wonder how our gay Miss Jansen likes Hoodfield Manor. Finds it a bit dull, I should imagine, with Tavistock, the nearest town, quite six miles away.'

'It was very kind of Celestine to help her.'

'Well, that's Celestine all over.' He lifted his glass. 'To your happiness, Miss Leigh. And whenever you ride Jacinth, think of me.'

'I shall . . . and of Jacinth's namesake, Miss Jansen.'

He laughed. 'And if,' he went on, 'you should change your mind . . .'

I raised my eyebrows.

'About marrying Connan, I mean. There'll be a little homestead for you on the other side of the world. You'll find me ever faithful, Miss Leigh.'

I laughed and sipped my wine.

The next day Alvean and I went riding together, and I was mounted on Jacinth. She was a wonderful creature and I enjoyed every moment of the ride. I felt that this was another of the glorious things which were happening to me. I even had my own mount now.

The ball was a great success and I was surprised how ready the neighbourhood was to accept me. The fact that I had been Alvean's governess was forgotten. I felt that Connan's neighbours were reminding each other that I was an educated young woman and that my family background was passibly good. Perhaps those who were fond of him were relieved because he was engaged to be married, for they would not wish him to be involved in the Treslyn scandal.

The day after the ball Connan had to go away again on business.

'I neglected a great deal during our stay in Penlandstow,' he said. 'There were things I simply forgot to do. It is understandable. My mind was on other matters. I shall be away a week, I think, and when I come back it'll be but a fortnight before our wedding. You'll be getting on with your preparations, and darling, if there's anything you want to do in the house . . . if there's anything you want to change, do say so. It mightn't be a bad idea to ask Celestine's advice; she's an expert on old houses.'

I said I would, because it would please her, and I wanted to please her.

'She was kind to me right from the first,' I said. 'I shall always have a soft feeling for her.'

He said good-bye and drove off while I stood at my window, waving. I did not care to do so from the porch because I was still a little shy of the servants.

When I went out of my room I found Gilly standing outside the door. Since I had told her that I was to be Mrs. TreMellyn she had taken to following me around. I was beginning to understand the way her mind worked. She was fond of me in exactly the same way that she had been fond of Alice and, with the passing of each day, the two of us became in her mind merged into one. Alice had disappeared from her life; she was going to make sure that I did not.

'Hallo, Gilly,' I said.

She dropped her head in that characteristic way of hers and laughed to herself.

Then she put her hand in mind and I led her back to my room.

'Well, Gilly,' I said, 'in three weeks' time I am going to be married, and I am the happiest woman in the world.'

I was really trying to reassure myself, for sometimes talking to Gilly was like talking to oneself.

I thought of what Connan had said about altering anything I wished to in the house, and I remembered that there were some parts of it which I had not even seen yet.

I suddenly thought of Miss Jansen and what I had been told about her having a different room from the one I occupied. I had never seen Miss Jansen's room and I decided that I would now go along and inspect it. I need have no qualms now about going to any part of the house I wished, for in a very short time I should be mistress of it.

'Come along, Gilly,' I said. 'We'll go and see Miss Jansen's room.'

She trotted along contentedly by my side, and I thought how much more intelligent she was than people realized, for it was she who led me to Miss Jansen's room.

There was nothing very unusual about it. It was smaller than mine. But there was a rather striking mural. I was looking at this when Gilly tugged my arm and drew me close to it. She pulled up a chair and stood on it. Then I understood. There, in this wall, was a peep like that in the solarium. I looked through it and saw the chapel. It was of course a different view from that to be seen in the solarium, as it was from the opposite side.

Gilly looked at me, delighted to have shown me the peep. We went back to my room, and clearly she did not want to leave me.

I could see that she was apprehensive. I understood of course. Her somewhat confused mind had so clearly associated me with Alice that she expected me to disappear as Alice had done.

She was determined to keep an eye on me so that this should not happen.

All through the night a south-west gale was blowing in from the sea. The rain which came with it was driven horizontally against our windows, and even the solid foundations of Mount Mellyn seemed to shake. It was one of the wettest nights I had known since my arrival in Cornwall.

The next day the rain continued; everything in my room – mirrors, the furniture – was misty and damp. It was what happened often enough, Mrs. Polgrey told me, when the south-west wind came bringing rain with it, which it invariably did.

Alvean and I could not go out riding that day.

By the following morning the skies had cleared a little, and the heavy rain gave way to a light drizzle. Lady Treslyn called, but I did not see her. She did not ask for me; it was Mrs. Polgrey who told me she had called and that she had wished to see Connan.

'She seemed very distressed,' said Mrs. Polgrey. 'She'll not rest until this terrible business is over.'

I felt sure that Lady Treslyn had come over to talk to Connan about his engagement to me and that she was probably distressed because he was not at home.

Celestine Nansellock also called. We had a chat about the house. She said she was so pleased because I was becoming very interested in Mount Mellyn.

'Not only as a home,' she said, 'but as a house.' She went on: 'I have some old documents about Mount Mellyn and Mount Widden. I'll show them to you one day.'

'You must help me,' I told her. 'It'll be fun discussing things together.'

'You'll make some changes?' she asked.

'If I do,' I assured her, 'I shall ask your advice.'

She left before luncheon, and in the afternoon Alvean and I went down to the stables for the horses.

We stood by while Billy Trehay saddled them for us.

'Jacinth be frisky, to-day, Miss,' he told me.

'It's because she had no exercise yesterday.' I stroked her muzzle and she rubbed against my hand to show she shared my affection.

We took our usual ride down the slope, past the cove and Mount Widden; then we went along the cliff path. The view here was particularly beautiful with the jagged coast stretched out before us and Rame Head lying in the water, hiding Plymouth and its Sound from view.

Some of the paths were narrow, cut into the cliffs at spots where it had been convenient to do so. Up and down we went; sometimes we were almost down to the sea; at others we climbed high.

It was not very easy going, for the rain had whipped up the mud and I began to feel a little anxious about Alvean. She sat firmly in her saddle – no novice now – but I was conscious of Jacinth's mood and I expected Black Prince's was not much different, although, of course, he hadn't Jacinth's fiery temperament. At times I had to rein her in firmly; a gallop would have been more to her taste than this necessarily slow careful walk along paths which were a good deal more dangerous than when we had come this way on our last ride.

There was one spot on this cliff path which was particularly narrow; above the path loomed the cliff face, dotted with bushes of gorse and brambles; below it, the cliff fell almost sheer to the sea. The path was safe enough ordinarily; but I felt a little nervous about Alvean's using it on a day like this.

I noticed that some of the cliff had fallen in places. This was continually happening. Tapperty had often said that the sea was gradually claiming the land, and that in his grandfather's day there had been a road which had now completely disappeared.

I thought of turning back, but if we did I would have to explain my fears to Alvean; I did not want to do this while she was mounted.

No, I thought, we'll continue on this path until we can climb to the top road. Then we'll go home a roundabout way, but on firm land.

We had come to that danger spot and I noticed that the ground was even more slippery here, and that there had been a bigger fall of cliff than I had seen on other portions of the path.

I held Jacinth in and walked her slowly in front of Alvean and Black Prince, for we naturally had to go in single file.

I pulled up and looked over my shoulder, saying: 'We're going very slowly here. You just follow.'

Then I heard it. I turned quickly as the boulder came tumbling down bringing in its wake shale, turf and vegetation. It passed within a few inches of Jacinth. I stared, in fascinated horror, as it went hurtling down to the sea.

Jacinth reared. She was terrified and ready to plunge anywhere . . . over the cliff . . . down to the sea . . . to escape what had startled her.

It was fortunate for me that I was an experienced rider, and that Jacinth and I knew each other so well. Thus it was all over in a matter of seconds. I had her under control. She grew calm as I began to talk to her in a voice which was meant to be soothing but which shook a little.

'Miss! What happened?' It was Alvean.

'It's all over,' I answered, trying to speak lightly. 'You managed perfectly.'

'Why, Miss, I thought Black Prince was going to start a gallop.'

He would, I thought, if Jacinth had.

I was terribly shaken and afraid to show it, either to Alvean or Jacinth.

I suddenly felt the need to get off that dangerous path immediately. I glanced nervously up and said: 'It's not safe to be on these paths . . . after the weather we've been having.'

I don't know what I expected to see up there, but I was staring at the thickest of the bushes. Did I see a movement there, or did I imagine it? It would be easy for someone to hide up there. What if a boulder had become dislodged by the recent rains. What an excellent opportunity if someone wanted to be rid of me. It merely had to be rolled down at that moment when I was on the path – a perfect target. Alvean and I had made a habit of coming along this path at a certain time.

I shivered and said: 'Let's go on. We'll get on to the top road and won't go back along the cliff path.'

Alvean was silent; and when in a few minutes we were on the road she looked at me oddly. I saw that she was not unaware of the danger through which we had passed.

It was not until we were back in the house that I realized how alarmed I was. I was telling myself that a terrifying pattern was being formed. Alice had died; Sir Thomas Treslyn had died; and now I, who was to be Connan's wife, might easily have met my death on the cliff path this day.

I longed to tell Connan of my fears.

But I was a sensible, practical woman. Was I going to refuse to look facts in the face because I was afraid of what I might see there if I did so?

Suppose Connan had not really gone away. Suppose he had wanted an accident to happen to me while he was believed to be away from home. I thought of Lady Treslyn at the Christmas ball. I thought of her beauty, her sensuous, voluptuous beauty. Connan had admitted that she had been his mistress. Had been? Was it possible that anyone, knowing her, could want me?

The proposal had been so sudden. It had come at a time when his mistress's husband was about to be exhumed.

It was small wonder that the practical governess had become a frightened woman.

To whom could I go for help?

There was Peter or Celestine . . . only those two, I thought. No, I could not betray these terrible suspicions of Connan to them. It was bad enough that I entertained them myself.

'Don't panic,' I cautioned myself. 'Be calm. Think of something you can do.'

I thought of the house, vast and full of secrets, a house in which it was possible to peep from certain rooms into others. There might be peeps as yet undiscovered. Who could say? Perhaps someone was watching me now.

I thought of the peep in Miss Jansen's room and that set me thinking of her sudden dismissal. Then I was saying to myself: 'Hoodfield Manor near Tavistock.'

I wondered if Miss Jansen was still there. There was a good chance that she might be for she must have gone there about the same time as I came to Mount Mellyn.

Why should I not try to meet her? She might have some light to throw on the secrets of this house.

I was desperately afraid, and at such times it is always conforting to take action.

I felt better when I had written the letter.

> *Dear Miss Jansen.*
>
> I am the governess at Mount Mellyn and I have heard of you. I should like to meet you. I wonder if that would be possible. If so, I should like our meeting to be as soon as you can manage it.
>
> Yours sincerely,
> *Martha Leigh.*

I went out quickly to post the letter before I could change my mind. Then I tried to forget it.

I longed for a message from Connan. There was none. Each day I looked for his return. I thought: When he comes home I am going to tell him of my fears, because I must do so. I am going to tell him of what happened on the cliff path. I am going to ask him to tell me the truth. I am going to say to him: Connan, why did you ask me to marry you? Was it because you love me and want me to be your wife, or was it because you wished to divert suspicion from yourself and Lady Treslyn?

The devilish scheme which I had invented seemed to gain credibility with every passing moment.

I said to myself: Perhaps Alice died by accident, and that gave them the idea of ridding themselves of Sir Thomas, who was the only obstacle to their marriage. Did they slip something into his whisky? Why not? It could not have been merely by chance that the boulder came hurtling down at the precise moment. Now there was to be an exhumation of Sir Thomas and the countryside knew of the relationship between Connan and Lady Treslyn. So Connan became engaged to the governess in order to divert suspicion. The governess is now an obstacle even as Alice was, even as Sir Thomas was. So the governess could have an accident on her newly acquired mare to which it might be said that she had not yet grown accustomed.

The road is clear for the guilty lovers and all they need do is wait until scandal has blown over.

How could I imagine such things of the man I loved? Could one love a man and think such thoughts of him?

I do love him, I told myself passionately. So much that I would rather meet death at his hands than leave him and be forced to endure an empty life without him.

Three days later there was a letter from Miss Jansen, who said she was eager to meet me. She would be in Plymouth the following day and if I would meet her at the White Hart, which was not far from the Hoe, we might have luncheon together.

I told Mrs. Polgrey that I was going into Plymouth to shop. That seemed plausible enough since my wedding was due to take place in three weeks' time.

I made straight for the White Hart.

Miss Jansen was already there – an extremely pretty fair-haired girl. She greeted me with pleasure and told me that Mrs. Plint, the innkeeper's wife, had said that we might have luncheon together in a small room of our own.

We were conducted to this private room and there took stock of each other.

The innkeeper's wife talked with enthusiasm of duck and green peas and roast beef, but we were, neither of us, very interested in food.

We ordered roast beef, I think it was, and as soon as we were alone, Miss Jansen said to me: 'What do you think of Mount Mellyn?'

'It's a wonderful old place.'

'One of the most interesting houses I ever saw,' she replied.

'I did hear, from Mrs. Polgrey I think, that old houses specially interested you.'

'They do. I was brought up in one. However, the family fortunes declined. That's what happens to so many of us who become governesses. I was sorry to leave Mount Mellyn. You have heard why I went?'

'Y . . . yes,' I said hesitantly.

'It was a very distressing affair. I was furiously angry to be unjustly accused.'

She was so frank and sincere that I believed her, and I made that clear.

She looked pleased; and then the food was brought in.

As we sat eating it in a somewhat desultory way she told me of the affair.

'The Treslyns and the Nansellocks had been having tea at the house. You know the Treslyn's and the Nansellocks of course?'

'Oh yes.'

'I mean, I expect you know quite a lot about them. They are such friends of the family, are they not?'

'Indeed yes.'

'I had been treated rather specially.' She flushed slightly, and I thought, Yes, you are so pretty. Connan would have thought so. I was aware of a flash not so much of jealousy as uneasiness as I wondered whether in the years to come I was going to be continually jealous of Connan's appreciation of the attractive members of my sex.

She went on: 'They had called me in to tea, because Miss Nansellock wanted to ask some questions about Alvean. She did dote on that child. Does she still?'

'Indeed yes.'

'She is such a kind person. I don't know what I should have done without her.'

'I am so glad somebody was kind to you.'

'I think that she looks upon Alvean as her child. There was a rumour that Miss Nansellock's brother was the father of Alvean, which would make her Miss Nansellock's niece. Perhaps that is why . . .'

'She certainly does feel strongly about Alvean.'

'So I was called down to talk to her, and I was given tea and chatted with them – as though I were a guest as they were. I think that Treslyn woman resented it . . . she resented my presence there altogether. Perhaps they were a little too attentive to me – I mean Mr. Peter Nansellock and Mr. TreMellyn. Lady Treslyn has a hot temper, I am sure. In any case I believe she arranged the whole thing.'

'She couldn't be so vile!'

'Oh, but I am sure she could, and she was. You see, she was wearing a diamond bracelet and the safety chain had broken. It had caught in the upholstery of the chair, I think. She said, "I won't wear it. I'll take it down to old Pastern to get it repaired as soon as we leave." She took it off and put it on the table. I left them at tea and went to the schoolroom to do some work with Alvean. It was while we were there that the door was thrown open and they all stood there looking at me accusingly.

'Lady Treslyn said something about having a search made because her diamond bracelet was missing. She was truculent. One would have thought she was already the mistress of the house. Mr. TreMellyn said very kindly that Lady Treslyn was asking that my room be searched, and he hoped I would not object. I was very angry and I said: "Come on, search my room. Nothing will satisfy me, but that you should."

'So we all went into my room, and there in a drawer, hidden under some of my things was the diamond bracelet.

'Lady Treslyn said I was caught red-handed, and she was going to have me sent to prison. The others all pleaded with her not to make a scandal. Finally they agreed that if I went at once the matter would be forgotten. I was furious. I wanted an inquiry. But what could I do? They had found the thing there, and whatever I had to say after that they wouldn't believe me.'

'It must have been terrible for you,' I began to shiver.

She leaned across the table and smiled in a kindly way at me. 'You are afraid that they may do something similar to you. Lady Treslyn is determined to marry Connan TreMellyn.'

'Do you think so?'

'I do. I am sure there was something between them. He was, after all, a widower and not the sort of man, I think, to live without women. One knows his sort.'

I said: 'I suppose he made advances to you?'

She shrugged her shoulders. 'At least Lady Treslyn imagined that I might be a menace, and I am sure she chose that way to get rid of me.'

'What a foul creature she is! But Miss Nansellock was kind.'

'Very kind. She was with them, of course, when they found the bracelet; and when I was packing she came to my room. She said: "I'm very distressed, Miss Jansen, that this should have happened. I know they found the bracelet in your drawer, but you didn't put it there, did you?" I said: "Miss Nansellock, I swear I didn't." I can tell you, I was hysterical. It had all happened so suddenly. I didn't know what was to become of me. I had very little money and I would have to go to some hostel to look for work, and I knew I could not expect a testimonial. I shall never forget her kindness to me. She asked me where I was going and I gave her this address in Plymouth. She said: "I know the Merrivales are going to want a governess for a month or so. I am going to see that you get that job." She lent me some money, which I have now paid back, although she did not want me to do so; and that's how I lived until I went to the Merrivales. I have written, thanking Miss Nansellock, but how can one thank people adequately who do so much for one when one is in such dire need?'

'Thank goodness there was someone to help.'

'Heaven knows what would have become of me if she had not been there. Ours is a precarious profession, Miss Leigh. We are at the mercy of our employers. No wonder so many of us become meek and down-trodden.' She brightened. 'I try to forget all that. I'm going to be married. He is a doctor who looks after the family. In six months' time my governessing days will be over.'

'Congratulations! As a matter of fact I, too, am engaged to be married.'

'How wonderful!'

'To Connan TreMellyn,' I added.

She stared at me in astonishment. 'Why . . .' she stammered, 'I wish you the best of luck.'

I could see that she was a little embarrassed and trying to remember what she had said about Connan. I felt too that she thought I should need that good luck.

I could not explain to her that I would rather have one stormy year with Connan than a lifetime of peace with anyone else.

'I wonder,' she said after a pause, 'why you wanted to see me.'

'It is because I had heard of you. They talk of you often. Alvean was fond of you and there are things I want to know.'

'But you, who are soon to be a member of the family, will know so much more than I can tell you.'

'What do you think of Gilly – Gillyflower?'

'Oh, poor little Gilly. A strange, mad Ophelia-like creature. I always felt that one day we should find her floating on the stream with rosemary in her hands.'

'The child had a shock.'

'Yes, the first Mrs. TreMellyn's horse nearly trampled her to death.'

'You must have gone there soon after the death of Mrs. TreMellyn.'

'There were two others before me. I heard they left because the house was too spooky. A house couldn't be too spooky for me.'

'Oh yes, you're an expert on old houses?'

'Expert! Indeed I'm not. I just love them. I've seen a great many and I've read a great deal about them.'

'There was a peep in your room. Gilly showed it to me the other day.'

'Do you know, I lived in that room three weeks without knowing it was there.'

'I'm not surprised. The peeps are so cleverly concealed in the murals.'

'That's an excellent way of doing it. Do you know those in the solarium?'

'Oh yes.'

'One overlooking the hall, the other, the chapel. I think there's a reason for that. You see, the hall and the chapel would be the most important parts of the house at the time that was built.'

'You know a great deal about period and so on. At what period was Mount Mellyn built?'

'Late Elizabethan. At the time when people had to keep the presence of priests in their houses secret. I think that's why they had all these peeps and things.'

'How interesting.'

'Miss Nansellock is an expert on houses. That was something we had in common. Does she know we're meeting?'

'No one knows.'

'You mean, you came here without telling even your future husband?'

Confidences trembled on my lips. I wondered if I dared share them with this stranger. I wished it were Phillida sitting opposite me. Then I could have poured out my heart to her; I could have listened to her advice, which I was sure would be good.

But, although I had heard Miss Jansen's name mentioned so much since I had come to Mount Mellyn, she was still a stranger to me. How could I say to a stranger: I suspect the man I am engaged to marry of being involved in a plot to murder me.

No! It was impossible.

But, I reasoned, she had suffered accusation and dismissal. There was a kind of bond between us.

How far, I asked myself, are hot-blooded people prepared to go for the satisfaction of their lust?

I could not tell her.

'He is away on business,' I said. 'We are to be married in three weeks' time.'

'I wish you the best of luck. It must have happened very suddenly.'

'It was August when I went to the house.'

'And you had never met before?'

'Living in the same house one quickly gets to know people.'

'Yes, I suppose that is so.'

'And you yourself must have become engaged in almost as short a time.'

'Oh yes, but . . .'

I knew what she was thinking. Her pleasant country doctor was a very different person from the Master of Mount Mellyn.

I went on quickly: 'I wanted to meet you because I believed you had been falsely accused. I am sure that many people at the house think that.'

'I'm glad.'

'When Mr. TreMellyn returns I shall tell him that I have seen you, and I shall ask if something can be done.'

'It is of little consequence now. Dr. Luscombe knows what happened. He is very indignant. But I have made him see that no good purpose could be served by bringing up the matter again. If Lady Treslyn ever tried to make more mischief, then something could be done. But she won't; her only desire was to get rid of me, and that she did . . . quite effectively.'

'What a wicked woman she is! She did not consider the effect on you. But for the kindness of Miss Nansellock. . . .

'I know. But don't let's talk of it. You will tell Miss Nansellock that you have seen me?"

'Yes, I will.'

'Then tell her that I am engaged now to Dr. Luscombe. She will be so pleased. And there's something else I would like her to know. Perhaps you'll be interested too. It's about the house. The house will soon be your home, won't it? I envy you the house. It's one of the most interesting places I've ever seen.'

'What were you going to tell me to pass on to Miss Nansellock?'

'I've been doing a little research on architecture, and so on, of the Elizabethan period, and my fiancé arranged for me to see Cotehele, the Mount Edgcumbes' place. They were delighted to let me see it because they are understandably proud of it. It's more like Mount Mellyn than any house I've ever seen. The chapel is almost identical, even to the lepers' squint. But the squint at Mount Mellyn is much bigger, and the construction of the walls is slightly different. As a matter of fact I've never seen a squint quite like that at Mount Mellyn before. Do tell Miss Nansellock. She would be most interested, I'm sure.'

'I'll tell her. I expect she'll be more interested to hear that you are so happy and that you are going to marry.'

'Don't forget to tell her too that I remember I owe it all to her. Give her my kindest regards and my best thanks.'

'I will,' I said.

We parted, and on my journey home I felt I had obtained from Miss Jansen some fresh light on my problem.

There was no doubt that Lady Treslyn arranged for Miss Jansen's dismissal. Miss Jansen was very pretty indeed. Connan admired her and Alvean was fond of her. Connan would consider marriage because he would want sons; and Lady Treslyn, possessive as a tigress, was not going to allow him to marry anyone but herself.

I believed now that Lady Treslyn was planning to remove me as she had removed Miss Jansen; but because I was already engaged to Connan she would have to use more drastic methods in my case.

But Connan did not know of this attempt on my life.

I refused to believe that of him and, refusing, I felt a great deal happier.

Moreover, I had made up my mind. When Connan came back I was going to tell him everything – all I had discovered, all I had feared.

The decision brought me great comfort.

Two days passed, and still Connan had not returned.

Peter Nansellock came over to say good-bye. He was leaving late that night for London on his way to join the ship which would carry him to Australia.

Celestine was with him when he came to say good-bye. They thought Connan would have returned by now. As a matter of fact while they were there a letter arrived from Connan. He was coming back if possible late that night; if not, as early as possible next day.

I felt tremendously happy.

I gave them tea and, as we talked, I mentioned Miss Jansen.

I saw no reason why I should not do so in front of Peter, because it was he who had told me that Celestine had found her a job with the Merrivales.

'I met Miss Jansen the other day,' I began.

They were both startled.

'But how?' asked Peter.

'I wrote and asked her to meet me.'

'What made you do that?' asked Celestine.

'Well, she had lived here, and there was a mystery about her, and I thought it would be rather interesting, so, as I was going to Plymouth. . . .'

'A charming creature,' mused Peter.

'Yes. You'll be pleased to hear that she's engaged to be married.'

'How interesting,' cried Celestine, her face growing pink. 'I'm delighted.'

'To the local doctor,' I added.

'She'll make an excellent doctor's wife,' said Celestine.

'Her husband's male patients will all be in love with her,' put in Peter.

'That could be disconcerting,' I replied.

'But good for business,' murmured Peter. 'Did she send us greetings?'

'Particularly to your sister,' I smiled at Celestine. 'She is so grateful to you; you were wonderful to her. She says she'll never forget.'

'It was nothing. I could not let that woman do what she did and stand by doing nothing.'

'You think Lady Treslyn deliberately planted that theft on her? I know Miss Jansen does.'

'There is no doubt of it,' said Celestine firmly.

'What an unscrupulous woman she must be!'

'I believe that to be so.'

'Well, Miss Jansen is happy now, so good came out of evil. By the way, I have a special message for you. It's about the house.'

'What house?' asked Celestine with great interest.

'This one. Miss Jansen has been to Cotehele and has been comparing their squint, in the chapel, with ours. She says ours is quite unique.'

'Oh really! That's very interesting.'

'It's bigger, she says – I mean ours is. And there's something about the construction of the walls.'

'Celestine is aching to go down and have a look at it,' said Peter.

She smiled at me: 'We'll look at it together sometime. You're going to be the Mistress of the house, so you ought to take an interest in it.'

'I'm becoming more and more interested. I'm going to ask you to teach me lots about it.'

She smiled at me warmly. 'I'll be glad.'

I asked Peter what train he was catching, and he answered that it would be the ten o'clock from St. Germans.

'I'll ride to the station,' he said, 'and stable the horse there. The baggage has gone on ahead of me. I shall go alone. I don't want any fond farewells at the station. After all, I shall no doubt be home this time next year ... with a fortune. *Au revoir*, Miss Leigh,' he went on. 'I'll come back one day. And if you do feel like coming with me ... it's not too late even now.'

He spoke flippantly, and his eyes were full of mischief. I wondered what he would say if I suddenly agreed to his proposal, if I suddenly told him that I was filled with terrible doubts about the man I had promised to marry.

I went down to the porch to say my last farewells. The servants were there for he was a great favourite. I guessed that he had bestowed many a sly kiss on Daisy and Kitty, and they were sad to see him go.

He looked very handsome in the saddle and beside him Celestine seemed insignificant.

We stood waving to them.

His last words were: 'Don't forget, Miss Leigh ... if you should change your mind!'

Everybody laughed and I joined in with them. I think we all felt a little sad that he was going.

As we were going back into the house, Mrs. Polgrey said to me: 'Miss Leigh, could I have a word with you?'

'But certainly. Shall I come to your room?'

She led the way there.

'I've just had word,' she said. 'The result of the autopsy. Death through natural causes.'

I felt floods of relief sweeping over me.

'Oh, I'm so pleased about that.'

'So are we all. I can tell you, I didn't like the things that were being said ... and him dying after he'd had supper here.'

'It seems as though it was all a storm in a teacup,' I said.

'Something like that, Miss Leigh. But there you are – people talk and something has to be done.'

'Well, it must be a great relief to Lady Treslyn.'

She looked a little embarrassed and I guessed she was wondering what she had said to me in the past about Connan and Lady Treslyn. It must have been disconcerting to discover that I was going to be Connan's wife. I decided to sweep aside her embarrassment for ever, and said: 'I hoped you were going to offer me a cup of your special Earl Grey.'

She was pleased and rang for Kitty.

We talked of household affairs while the kettle boiled, and when tea was made she tentatively brought out the whisky and when I nodded a tea-spoonful was put into each cup. I felt then that we had indeed resumed the old friendly relationship.

I was glad, because I could see this made her happy, and I wanted everyone about me to be as happy as I was.

I kept on telling myself: If Lady Treslyn really did attempt to kill me by sending that boulder crashing down in front of me when I was mounted on Jacinth, Connan knew nothing about it. Sir Thomas died a natural death, so there was nothing to hide; he had no reason to ask me to marry him except the one which he gave me; he loves me.

It was nine o'clock and the children were in bed. It had been a warm and sunny day and there were signs of spring everywhere.

Connan was coming home either to-night or to-morrow and I was happy.

I wondered what time he would arrive. Perhaps at midnight. I went to the porch to look for him because I had imagined I heard horses' hoofs in the distance.

I waited. The night was still. The house always seemed very quiet at times like this for all the servants would be in their own quarters.

I guessed that Peter would be on his way to the station by now. It was strange to think that I might never see him again. I thought of our first meeting in the train; he had begun by playing his mischievous tricks on me even then.

Then I saw someone coming towards me. It was Celestine, and she had come by way of the woods, not along the drive as usual.

She was rather breathless.

'Why, hallo,' she said. 'I came to see you. I felt so lonely. Peter's gone. It's rather sad to think that I shan't see him for a long time.'

'It does make one sad.'

'He played the fool a great deal, of course, but I am very fond of him. Now I've lost both my brothers.'

'Come in,' I said.

'Connan's not back, I suppose?'

'No. I don't think he can possibly be here before midnight. He wrote that he had business to attend to this morning. I expect he'll arrive to-morrow. Won't you come in?'

'Do you know, I rather hoped you'd be alone.'

'Did you?'

'I wanted to have a look at the chapel . . . that squint, you know. Ever since you gave me Miss Jansen's message I've been eager to see it. I didn't say so in front of Peter. He's apt to laugh at my enthusiasm.'

'Do you want to have a look at it now?'

'Yes, please. I've a theory about it. There may be a door in the panelling which leads to another part of the house. Wouldn't it be fun if we could discover it and tell Connan about it when he arrives?'

'Yes,' I agreed, 'it would.'

'Let's go now then.'

We went through the hall and, as we did so, I glanced up at the peep, because I had an uncanny feeling that we were being watched. I thought I saw a movement up there, but I was not sure, and said nothing.

We went along to the end of the hall, through the door, down the stone steps, and were in the chapel.

The place smelt damp. I said: 'It smells as though it hasn't been used for years.' And my voice echoed weirdly through the place.

Celestine did not answer. She had lighted one of the candles which stood on the altar. I watched the long shadow which the flickering light threw against the wall.

'Let's get into the squint,' she said. 'Through this door. There is another door in the squint itself which opens on to the walled garden. That was the way the lepers used to come in.'

She carried the candle high and I found that we were in a small chamber.

'This is the place,' I said, 'which is bigger than most of its kind.'

She did not answer. She was pressing different parts of the wall.

I watched her long fingers at work.

Suddenly she turned and smiled at me. 'I've always had a theory that somewhere in this house there is a priest's hole . . . you know, the hidy hole of the resident priest into which he scuttled when the queen's men arrived. As a matter of fact I know that one TreMellyn did toy with the idea of becoming a Catholic. I'll swear there is a priest's hole somewhere. Connan would be delighted if we found it. He loves this place as much as I do . . . as much as you're going to. If I found it . . . it would be the best wedding present I could give him, wouldn't it? After all, what can you give people who have all they want?'

She hesitated, and her voice was high with excitement. 'Just a minute. There's something here.' I came close to her, and caught my breath with amazement, for the panel had moved inward and shown itself as a long narrow door.

She turned to look at me and she looked unlike herself. Her eyes were brilliant with excitement. She put her head inside the aperture and was about to go forward when she said: 'No, you first. It's going to be your house. You should be the first to enter it.'

I had caught her excitement. I knew how pleased Connan would be.

I stepped ahead of her and was aware of an unrecognizable pungent odour.

She said: 'Have a quick look. It's probably a bit foul in there. Careful. There are probably steps.' She held the candle high, and I saw there were two of them. I went down those steps and, as I did so, the door shut behind me.

'Celestine!' I cried in terror. But there was no answer. 'Open that door,' I screamed. But my voice was caught and imprisoned in the darkness, and I knew that I was a prisoner too – Celestine's prisoner.

The darkness shut me in. It was cold and eerie – foul, evil. Panic seized me. How can I explain such terror? There are no words to describe it. Only those who have suffered it could understand.

Thoughts – hideous thoughts – seemed to be battering on my brain. I had been a fool. I had been trapped. I had accepted what seemed obvious, I had walked the way she who wished to be rid of me had directed; and like a fool I had asked no questions.

My fear numbed my brain as it did my body.

I was terrified.

I mounted the two steps. I beat my fists against what now seemed to be a wall. 'Let me out. Let me out . . .' I cried.

But I knew that my voice would not be heard beyond the lepers' squint. And how often did people go to the chapel?

She would slip away . . . no one would know she had even been in the house.

I was so frightened I did not know what to do. I heard my own voice sobbing out my terror, and it frightened me afresh because, for the moment, I did not recognize it as my own.

I felt exhausted and limp. I knew that one could not live for long in this dark, damp place. I pulled at the wall until I tore my nails and I felt the blood on my hands.

I began to look about me because my eyes were becoming familiar to the gloom. Then I saw that I was not alone.

Someone had come here before me. What was left of Alice lay there. At last I had found her.

'Alice,' I screamed. 'Alice. It is you then? So you were here in the house all the time?'

There was no answer from Alice. Her lips had been silent for more than a year.

I covered my face with my hands. I could not bear to look. There was the smell of death and decay everywhere.

I wondered: How long did Alice live after the door had closed on *her*? I wanted to know because so long I might expect to live.

I think I must have fainted for a long time and I was delirious when I came to. I heard a voice babbling; it must have been my own because it could not have belonged to Alice.

I was mercifully only half-conscious. But it was as though a part of me understood so much.

During that time I spent in the dark and gruesome place I was not sure who I was. Was I Martha? Was I Alice?

Our stories were so much alike. I believed the pattern was similar. They had said she ran away with Geoffry. They would say I had run away with Peter. Our departure had been cleverly timed. 'But why . . .' I said, 'but why. . . .'

I knew whose shadow I had seen on the blind. It was hers . . . that diabolical woman. She had known of the existence of that little diary which I had discovered in Alice's coat pocket and she was searching for it because she knew it could provide one of those small clues which might lead to discovery.

I knew that she did not love Alvean, that she had tricked us all with her gentle demeanour. I knew that she was incapable of loving anyone. She had used Alvean as she had used others, as she was going to use Connan.

It was the house that she loved.

I pictured her during those delirious moments looking from her window at Mount Widden across the cove – coveting a house as fiercely as man ever coveted woman or woman man.

'Alice,' I said. 'Alice, we were her victims . . . you and I.'

And I fancied Alice talked to me . . . and told me of the day Geoffry had caught the London train and how Celestine had come to the house and told her of the great discovery in the chapel.

I saw Alice . . . pale, pretty, fragile Alice crying out in pleasure at the discovery, taking those fatal steps forward to death.

But it was not Alice's voice I heard. It was my own.

Yet I thought she was with me. I thought that at last I had found her, and that we had comfort to offer each other as I waited to go with her into the shadowy world which had been hers since she was led by Celestine Nansellock into the lepers' squint.

There was a blinding light in my eyes. I was being carried.

I said: 'Am I dead then, Alice?'

And a voice answered: 'My darling . . . my darling . . . you are safe.'

It was Connan's voice, and it was his arms which held me.

'Are there dreams in death then, Alice?' I asked.

I was conscious of a voice which whispered: 'My dearest . . . oh, my dearest. . . .' And I was laid upon a bed, and many people stood about me.

Then I saw the light glinting on hair which looked almost white.

'Alice, there is an angel.'

Then the angel answered and said: 'It's Gilly. Gilly brought them to you. Gilly watched and Gilly saw. . . .'

And oddly enough it was Gilly who brought me back to the world of reality. I knew that I was not dead, that some miracle had happened; that it was in truth Connan's arms which I had felt about me, Connan's voice I heard.

I was in my own bedroom from the window of which I could see the lawns and the palm trees and the room which had once been Alice's, on the blind of which I had seen the shadow of Alice's murderer who had sought to kill me too.

I called out in terror. But Connan was beside me.

I heard his voice, tender, soothing, loving. 'It's all right, my love . . . my only love. I'm here . . . I'm with you for evermore.'

Afterwards

This is the story I tell my great-grandchildren. They have heard it many times, but there is always a first time for some.

They ask for it again and again. They play in the park and in the woods; they bring me flowers from the south gardens, a tribute to the old lady who can always charm them with the story of how she married their great-grandfather.

To me it is as clear as though it happened yesterday. Vividly I remember my arrival at the house and all that preceded those terrifying hours I spent in the dark with dead Alice.

The years which followed with Connan have often been stormy ones. Connan and I were both too strong-willed, I suppose, to live in perpetual peace; but they were years in which I felt I had lived life richly, and what more could one ask than that?

Now he is old, as I am, and three more Connans have been born since that day we married – our son, grandson and great-grandson. I was glad I was able to give Connan children. We have five sons and five daughters, and they in their turn were fruitful.

When the children hear the story they like to check up all the details. They want every incident explained.

Why was it believed that the woman who died in the train was Alice? Because of the locket she wore. But it was Celestine who identified the locket as one which, she said, she had given Alice, but which, of course, she had never seen before in her life.

She had been eager that I should accept Jacinth when Peter had first offered the mare to me – I suppose because she feared it was just possible that Connan might be interested in me and therefore she was ready to encourage the friendship between myself and Peter; and it was she who later, discovering the loosened boulder on the cliff, had lain in wait for me and attempted to kill or maim me.

She was the sender of the anonymous letters to Lady Treslyn and the public prosecutor, commenting on the suspicious circumstances of Sir Thomas's death. She had believed that if there was a big enough scandal, marriage between Connan and Lady Treslyn would have been impossible for years. She had reckoned without Connan's feelings for me; thus when she knew that I was engaged to marry him, she immediately planned to remove me. She failed to do this on the cliff path; therefore I was to join Alice; the fact that Peter was leaving for Australia on that day must have made her decide on this method. The whole household knew that Peter's attitude to me had been a flirtatious one, and it would appear that I had run away with him.

It was Celestine who had put the diamond bracelet in Miss Jansen's room because the governess was learning too much about the house and the knowledge would inevitably lead her to the lepers' squint and Alice. She had worked on Lady Treslyn's jealousy of the pretty young governess for she had known Lady Treslyn to be a vindictive woman who, given the opportunity, would bring all her malice to bear on Miss Jansen.

She was in love – passionately in love with Mount Mellyn and she wanted to marry Connan only because thus she would be Mistress of the house. So in the first place, discovering the secret of the squint she had kept it to herself, and had chosen her opportunity to murder Alice. She knew of the love affair between Alice and her brother Geoffry; she knew that Alvean was his child. It worked out so easily because she had waited for her opportunity. If it had not been possible to make Alice's death appear to have occurred in the train accident she would have found some other way of disposing of her as she had intended to dispose of me through Jacinth.

But she had reckoned without Gilly. Who would have thought that a poor simple child should play such a big part in this diabolical plan? But Gilly had loved Alice as later she was to love me. Gilly had known Alice was in the house for Alice had made a habit of coming to say good night to her when she did the same to Alvean; she had always done it before she went out to a dinner party. Because she had never forgotten, Gilly did not believe she had forgotten this time. Gilly therefore continued to believe that Alice had never left the house, and had gone on looking for her. It was Gilly's face which I had seen at the peep. Gilly knew all the peeps in the house and used them frequently, because she was always watching for Alice.

Thus she had seen Celestine and myself enter the hall from the solarium. I imagined her crossing the room and looking through the peep on the other side of the room so that she saw us enter the chapel. We crossed to the squint, but that side of the chapel could not easily be seen from the solarium peep, and so Gilly sped along to Miss Jansen's room, where from that peep she could have a good view of the squint. She was just in time to see us disappearing through the door, and waited for us to come out. She waited and waited, for Celestine naturally left by the door to the courtyard and slipped away so that, since she believed that no one had seen her come into the house except myself, she could let it appear that she had not been there at all.

Thus, while I lived through that period of horror in Alice's death-chamber, Gilly was standing on her stool in Miss Jansen's room, watching the door to the lepers' squint.

Connan returned at eleven and expected the household to give him a welcome.

Mrs. Polgrey received him. 'Go and tell Miss Leigh that I am here,' he said. He must have been a little piqued because he was – and still is – the sort of man who demands the utmost affection and attention, and the fact that I could be sleeping when he came home was inconceivable to him.

I pictured the scene: Mrs. Polgrey reporting that I was not in my room,

the search for me, that terrible moment when Connan believed what Celestine
had intended he should believe.

'Mr. Nansellock came over this afternoon to say good-bye. He caught the
ten o'clock from St. Germans. . . .'

I have wondered often how long it would have been before they discovered
that I had not run away with Peter. I could imagine what might have
happened. Connan's losing that belief in life which I believed I was beginning
to bring back to him, perhaps continuing his *affaire* with Linda Treslyn.
But it would not have led to marriage, Celestine would have seen to that.
And in time she would have found some way of making herself mistress of
Mount Mellyn; insidiously she would have made herself necessary to Alvean
and to him.

How strange, I thought, that all this might have come to pass and the
only two who could have told the truth would have been two skeletons
behind the walls of the lepers' squint. Who would have believed that even
at this day the story of Alice and Martha would never have been known,
had not a simple child, born in sorrow, living in shadow, led the way to the
truth.

Connan told me often of the uproar in the house when I was missing. He
told me of the child, who came and stood patiently beside him, waiting to
be heard; how she tugged at his coat and sought for the words to explain.

'God forgive us,' he says, 'it was some time before we would listen to her,
and so we delayed bringing you out of that hellish place.'

But she had led them there . . . through the door into the lepers' squint.
She had seen us, she said.

And for a moment Connan had thought that Peter and I had left the
house together, slipping out that way so that we should not be noticed.

It was dusty in the squint – for no one had entered it since Alice had gone
there with her murderer; but in the dust on the wall was the mark of a
hand, and when Connan saw it he began to take Gilly seriously.

It was not easy to find the secret spring in the door even if it had been
known that it was there. There was an agonizing search of ten minutes
while Connan was ready to tear the walls down.

But they found it and they found me. They found Alice too.

They took Celestine to Bodmin where she was eventually to be tried for
the murder of Alice. But before the trial could take place she was a raving
lunatic. At first I believed that this was yet another scheme of hers. It may
have started that way, but she did not die until twenty years after, and all
that time she spent locked away from the world.

Alice's remains were buried in the vault where those of an unknown
woman lay. Connan and I were married three months after he had brought
me out of the darkness. That experience had affected me even more than I
realized at the time, and I suffered from nightmares for a year or more. It
was a great shock to have been buried alive even though one's tomb was
opened before life was extinguished.

Phillida came to my wedding with William and the children. She was
delighted. So was Aunt Adelaide, who insisted that the wedding take place

from her town house. Thus Connan and I had a smart London wedding. Not that we cared, but it pleased Aunt Adelaide who, for some reason, seemed to have the idea in her head that it was all her doing.

And so we honeymooned, as we had originally intended, in Italy and then we came home to Mount Mellyn.

I dream over the past when I have told the story to the children. I think of Alvean happily married to a Devonshire squire. As for Gilly, she never left me. She is with me now. At any moment she will appear on the lawn with the eleven o'clock coffee which on warm days we take in that arbour in the south gardens where I first saw Lady Treslyn and Connan together.

I must confess that Lady Treslyn continued to plague me during the first years of my married life. I discovered that I could be a jealous woman – and a passionate one. Sometimes I think Connan liked to tease me, in repayment, he said, for the jealousy he had felt of Peter Nansellock.

But she went to London after a few years, and we heard she married there.

Peter came back some fifteen years after he left. He had acquired a wife and two children but no fortune; he was, however, as gay and full of vitality as ever. In the meantime Mount Widden had been sold; and later one of my daughters married the owner, so the place has become almost as much home to me as Mount Mellyn.

Connan said he was glad when Peter came back, and I laughed at the thought of his ever feeling he needed to be jealous. When I told him this, he replied: 'You're even more foolish about Linda Treslyn.'

That was one of those moments when we both knew that there was no one for us but each other.

And so the years passed and now, as I sit here thinking of it all, Connan is coming down the path from the gardens. In a moment I shall hear his voice.

Because we are alone he will say: 'Ah, my dear Miss Leigh . . .' as he often does in his most tender moments. That is to remind me that he does not forget those early days; and there will be a smile on his lips which tells me that he is seeing me, not as I am now, but as I was then, the governess somewhat resentful of her fate, desperately clinging to her pride and her dignity – falling in love in spite of herself – his dear Miss Leigh.

Then we shall sit in the warm sunshine, thankful for all the good things which life has brought us.

Here he comes and Gilly is behind him . . . still a little different from other people, still speaking rarely, singing as she works, in the off-key voice that makes us think she is a little out of this world.

As I watch her I can see so clearly the child she once was, and I think of the story of Jennifer, the mother who one day walked into the sea, and how that story was part of my story, and how delicately and intricately our lives were woven together.

Nothing remains, I thought, but the earth and the sea which are here just as they were on the day Gilly was conceived, on the day Alice walked unheeding into her tomb, on the day I felt Connan's arms about me and I knew he had brought me back to life.

We are born, we suffer, we live, we die, but the waves continue to beat upon the rocks; the seed time and the harvest come and go, but the earth remains.